Short Stories

1888 – 1895

Anton Chekhov

ISBN: 978-1492709244

First Edition, 2013

CONTENTS

A STORY WITHOUT A TITLE

In the fifth century, just as now, the sun rose every morning and every evening retired to rest. In the morning, when the first rays kissed the dew, the earth revived, the air was filled with the sounds of rapture and hope; while in the evening the same earth subsided into silence and plunged into gloomy darkness. One day was like another, one night like another. From time to time a storm-cloud raced up and there was the angry rumble of thunder, or a negligent star fell out of the sky, or a pale monk ran to tell the brotherhood that not far from the monastery he had seen a tiger -- and that was all, and then each day was like the next.

The monks worked and prayed, and their Father Superior played on the organ, made Latin verses, and wrote music. The wonderful old man possessed an extraordinary gift. He played on the organ with such art that even the oldest monks, whose hearing had grown somewhat dull towards the end of their lives, could not restrain their tears when the sounds of the organ floated from his cell. When he spoke of anything, even of the most ordinary things -- for instance of the trees, of the wild beasts, or of the sea -- they could not listen to him without a smile or tears, and it seemed that the same chords vibrated in his soul as in the organ. If he were moved to anger or abandoned himself to intense joy, or began speaking of something terrible or grand, then a passionate inspiration took possession of him, tears came into his flashing eyes, his face flushed, and his voice thundered, and as the monks listened to him they felt that their souls were spell-bound by his inspiration; at such marvellous, splendid moments his power over them was boundless, and if he had bidden his elders fling themselves into the sea, they would all, everyone of them, have hastened to carry out his wishes.

His music, his voice, his poetry in which he glorified God, the heavens and the earth, were a continual source of joy to the monks. It sometimes happened that through the monotony of their lives they grew weary of the trees, the flowers, the spring, the autumn, their ears were tired of the sound of the sea, and the song of the birds seemed tedious to them, but the talents of their Father Superior were as necessary to them as their daily bread.

Dozens of years passed by, and every day was like every other day, every night was like every other night. Except the birds and the wild beasts, not one soul appeared near the monastery. The nearest human habitation was far away, and to reach it from the monastery, or to reach the monastery from it, meant a journey of over seventy miles across the desert. Only men who despised life, who had renounced it, and who came to the monastery as to the grave, ventured to cross the desert.

What was the amazement of the monks, therefore, when one night there knocked at their gate a man who turned out to be from the town, and the most ordinary sinner who loved life. Before saying his prayers and asking for the Father Superior's blessing, this man asked for wine and food. To the question how he had come from the town into the desert, he answered by a long story of hunting; he had gone out hunting, had drunk too much, and lost his way. To the suggestion that he should enter the monastery and save his soul, he replied with a smile: "I am not a fit companion for you!"

When he had eaten and drunk he looked at the monks who were serving him, shook his head reproachfully, and said:

"You don't do anything, you monks. You are good for nothing but eating and drinking. Is that the way to save one's soul? Only think, while you sit here in peace, eat and drink and dream of beatitude, your neighbours are perishing and going to hell. You should see what is going on in the town! Some are dying of hunger, others, not knowing what to do with their gold, sink into profligacy and perish like flies stuck in honey. There is no faith, no truth in men. Whose task is it to save them? Whose work is it to preach to them? It is not for me, drunk from morning till night as I am. Can a meek spirit, a loving heart, and faith in God have been given you for you to sit here within four walls doing nothing?"

The townsman's drunken words were insolent and unseemly, but they had a strange effect upon the Father Superior. The old man exchanged glances with his monks, turned pale, and said:

"My brothers, he speaks the truth, you know. Indeed, poor people in their weakness and lack of understanding are perishing in vice and infidelity, while we do not move, as though it did not concern us. Why should I not go and remind them of the Christ whom they have forgotten?"

The townsman's words had carried the old man away. The next day he took his staff, said farewell to the brotherhood, and set off for the town. And the monks were left without music, and without his speeches and verses. They spent a month drearily, then a second, but the old man did not come back. At last after three months had passed the familiar tap of his staff was heard. The monks flew to meet him and showered questions upon him, but instead of being delighted to see them he wept bitterly and did not utter a word. The monks noticed that he looked greatly aged and had grown thinner; his face looked exhausted and wore an expression of profound sadness, and when he wept he had the air of a man who has been outraged.

The monks fell to weeping too, and began with sympathy asking him why he was weeping, why his face was so gloomy, but he locked himself in his cell without uttering a word. For seven days he sat in his cell, eating and drinking nothing, weeping and not playing on his organ. To knocking at his door and to the entreaties of the monks to come out and share his grief with them he replied with unbroken silence.

At last he came out. Gathering all the monks around him, with a tear-stained face and with an expression of grief and indignation, he began telling them of what had befallen him during those three months. His voice was calm and his eyes were smiling while he described his journey from the monastery to the town. On the road, he told them, the birds sang to him, the brooks gurgled, and sweet youthful hopes agitated his soul; he marched on and felt like a soldier going to battle and confident of victory; he walked on dreaming, and composed poems and hymns, and reached the end of his journey without noticing it.

But his voice quivered, his eyes flashed, and he was full of wrath when he came to speak of the town and of the men in it. Never in his life had he seen or even dared to imagine what he met with when he went into the town. Only then for the first time in his life, in his old age, he saw and understood how powerful was the devil, how fair was evil and how weak and faint-hearted and worthless were men. By an unhappy chance the first dwelling he entered was the abode of vice. Some fifty men in possession of much money were eating and drinking wine beyond measure. Intoxicated by the wine, they sang songs and boldly uttered terrible, revolting words such as a God-fearing man could not bring himself to pronounce; boundlessly free, self-confident, and happy, they feared neither God nor the devil, nor death, but said and did what they liked, and went whither their lust led them. And the wine, clear as amber, flecked with sparks of gold, must have been irresistibly sweet and fragrant, for each man who drank it smiled blissfully and wanted to drink more. To the smile of man it responded with a smile and sparkled joyfully when they drank it, as though it knew the devilish charm it kept hidden in its sweetness.

The old man, growing more and more incensed and weeping with wrath, went on to describe what he had seen. On a table in the midst of the revellers, he said, stood a sinful, half-naked woman. It was hard to imagine or to find in nature anything more lovely and fascinating. This reptile, young, longhaired, dark-skinned, with black eyes and full lips, shameless and insolent, showed her snow-white teeth and smiled as though to say: "Look how shameless, how beautiful I am." Silk and brocade fell in lovely folds from her shoulders, but her beauty would not hide itself under her clothes, but eagerly thrust itself through the folds, like the young grass through the ground in spring. The shameless woman drank wine, sang songs, and abandoned herself to anyone who wanted her.

Then the old man, wrathfully brandishing his arms, described the horse-races, the bull-fights, the theatres, the artists' studios where they painted naked women or moulded them of clay. He spoke with inspiration, with sonorous beauty, as though he were playing on unseen chords, while the monks, petrified, greedily drank in his words and gasped with rapture. . . .

After describing all the charms of the devil, the beauty of evil, and the fascinating grace of the dreadful female form, the old man cursed the devil, turned and shut himself up in his cell. . . .

When he came out of his cell in the morning there was not a monk left in the monastery; they had all fled to the town.

SLEEPY

Night. Varka, the little nurse, a girl of thirteen, is rocking the cradle in which the baby is lying, and humming hardly audibly:

"Hush-a-bye, my baby wee,
While I sing a song for thee."

A little green lamp is burning before the ikon; there is a string stretched from one end of the room to the other, on which baby-clothes and a pair of big black trousers are hanging. There is a big patch of green on the ceiling from the ikon lamp, and the baby-clothes and the trousers throw long shadows on the stove, on the cradle, and on Varka. . . . When the lamp begins to flicker, the green patch and the shadows come to life, and are set in motion, as though by the wind. It is stuffy. There is a smell of cabbage soup, and of the inside of a boot-shop.

The baby's crying. For a long while he has been hoarse and exhausted with crying; but he still goes on screaming, and there is no knowing when he will stop. And Varka is sleepy. Her eyes are glued together, her head droops, her neck aches. She cannot move her eyelids or her lips, and she feels as though her face is dried and wooden, as though her head has become as small as the head of a pin.

"Hush-a-bye, my baby wee," she hums, "while I cook the groats for thee. . . ."

A cricket is churring in the stove. Through the door in the next room the master and the apprentice Afanasy are snoring. . . . The cradle creaks plaintively, Varka murmurs -- and it all blends into that soothing music of the night to which it is so sweet to listen, when one is lying in bed. Now that music is merely irritating and oppressive, because it goads her to sleep, and she must not sleep; if Varka -- God forbid! -- should fall asleep, her master and mistress would beat her.

The lamp flickers. The patch of green and the shadows are set in motion, forcing themselves on Varka's fixed, half-open eyes, and in her half slumbering brain are fashioned into misty visions. She sees dark clouds chasing one another over the sky, and screaming like the baby. But then the wind blows, the clouds are gone, and Varka sees a broad high road covered with liquid mud; along the high road stretch files of wagons, while people with wallets on their backs are trudging along and shadows flit backwards and forwards; on both sides she can see forests through the cold harsh mist. All at once the people with their wallets and their shadows fall on the ground in the liquid mud. "What is that for?" Varka asks. "To sleep, to sleep!" they answer her. And they fall sound asleep, and sleep sweetly, while crows and magpies sit on the telegraph wires, scream like the baby, and try to wake them.

"Hush-a-bye, my baby wee, and I will sing a song to thee," murmurs Varka, and now she sees herself in a dark stuffy hut.

Her dead father, Yefim Stepanov, is tossing from side to side on the floor. She does not see him, but she hears him moaning and rolling on the floor from pain. "His guts have burst," as he says; the pain is so violent that he cannot utter a single word, and can only draw in his breath and clack his teeth like the rattling of a drum:

"Boo--boo--boo--boo. . . ."

Her mother, Pelageya, has run to the master's house to say that Yefim is dying. She has been gone a long time, and ought to be back. Varka lies awake on the stove, and hears her father's "boo--boo--boo." And then she hears someone has driven up to the hut. It is a young doctor from the town, who has been sent from the big house where he is staying on a visit. The doctor comes into the hut; he cannot be seen in the darkness, but he can be heard coughing and rattling the door.

"Light a candle," he says.

"Boo--boo--boo," answers Yefim.

Pelageya rushes to the stove and begins looking for the broken pot with the matches. A minute passes in silence. The doctor, feeling in his pocket, lights a match.

"In a minute, sir, in a minute," says Pelageya. She rushes out of the hut, and soon afterwards comes back with a bit of candle.

Yefim's cheeks are rosy and his eyes are shining, and there is a peculiar keenness in his glance, as though he were seeing right through the hut and the doctor.

"Come, what is it? What are you thinking about?" says the doctor, bending down to him. "Aha! have you had this long?"

"What? Dying, your honour, my hour has come. . . . I am not to stay among the living."

"Don't talk nonsense! We will cure you!"

"That's as you please, your honour, we humbly thank you, only we understand. . . . Since death has come, there it is."

The doctor spends a quarter of an hour over Yefim, then he gets up and says:

"I can do nothing. You must go into the hospital, there they will operate on you. Go at once . . . You must go! It's rather late, they will all be asleep in the hospital, but that doesn't matter, I will give you a note. Do you hear?"

"Kind sir, but what can he go in?" says Pelageya. "We have no horse."

"Never mind. I'll ask your master, he'll let you have a horse."

The doctor goes away, the candle goes out, and again there is the sound of "boo--boo--boo." Half an hour later someone drives up to the hut. A cart has been sent to take Yefim to the hospital. He gets ready and goes. . . .

But now it is a clear bright morning. Pelageya is not at home; she has gone to the hospital to find what is being done to Yefim. Somewhere there is a baby crying, and Varka hears someone singing with her own voice:

"Hush-a-bye, my baby wee, I will sing a song to thee."

Pelageya comes back; she crosses herself and whispers:

"They put him to rights in the night, but towards morning he gave up his soul to God. . . . The Kingdom of Heaven be his and peace everlasting. . . . They say he was taken too late. . . . He ought to have gone sooner. . . ."

Varka goes out into the road and cries there, but all at once someone hits her on the back of her head so hard that her forehead knocks against a birch tree. She raises her eyes, and sees facing her, her master, the shoemaker.

"What are you about, you scabby slut?" he says. "The child is crying, and you are asleep!"

He gives her a sharp slap behind the ear, and she shakes her head, rocks the cradle, and murmurs her song. The green patch and the shadows from the trousers and the baby-clothes move up and down, nod to her, and soon take possession of her brain again. Again she sees the high road covered with liquid mud. The people with wallets on their backs and the shadows have lain down and are fast asleep. Looking at them, Varka has a passionate longing for sleep; she would lie down with enjoyment, but her mother Pelageya is walking beside her, hurrying her on. They are hastening together to the town to find situations.

"Give alms, for Christ's sake!" her mother begs of the people they meet. "Show us the Divine Mercy, kind-hearted gentlefolk!"

"Give the baby here!" a familiar voice answers. "Give the baby here!" the same voice repeats, this time harshly and angrily. "Are you asleep, you wretched girl?"

Varka jumps up, and looking round grasps what is the matter: there is no high road, no Pelageya, no people meeting them, there is only her mistress, who has come to feed the baby, and is standing in the middle of the room. While the stout, broad-shouldered woman nurses the child and soothes it, Varka stands looking at her and waiting till she has done. And outside the windows the air is already turning blue, the shadows and the green patch on the ceiling are visibly growing pale, it will soon be morning.

"Take him," says her mistress, buttoning up her chemise over her bosom; "he is crying. He must be bewitched."

Varka takes the baby, puts him in the cradle and begins rocking it again. The green patch and the shadows gradually disappear, and now there is nothing to force itself on her eyes and cloud her brain. But she is as sleepy as before, fearfully sleepy! Varka lays her head on the edge of the cradle, and rocks her whole body to overcome her sleepiness, but yet her eyes are glued together, and her head is heavy.

"Varka, heat the stove!" she hears the master's voice through the door.

So it is time to get up and set to work. Varka leaves the cradle, and runs to the shed for firewood. She is glad. When one moves and runs about, one is not so sleepy as when one is sitting down. She brings the wood, heats the stove, and feels that her wooden face is getting supple again, and that her thoughts are growing clearer.

"Varka, set the samovar!" shouts her mistress.

Varka splits a piece of wood, but has scarcely time to light the splinters and put them in the samovar, when she hears a fresh order:

"Varka, clean the master's goloshes!"

She sits down on the floor, cleans the goloshes, and thinks how nice it would be to put her head into a big deep golosh, and have a little nap in it. . . . And all at once the golosh grows, swells, fills up the whole room.

Varka drops the brush, but at once shakes her head, opens her eyes wide, and tries to look at things so that they may not grow big and move before her eyes.

"Varka, wash the steps outside; I am ashamed for the customers to see them!"

Varka washes the steps, sweeps and dusts the rooms, then heats another stove and runs to the shop. There is a great deal of work: she hasn't one minute free.

But nothing is so hard as standing in the same place at the kitchen table peeling potatoes. Her head droops over the table, the potatoes dance before her eyes, the knife tumbles out of her hand while her fat, angry mistress is moving about near her with her sleeves tucked up, talking so loud that it makes a ringing in Varka's ears. It is agonising, too, to wait at dinner, to wash, to sew, there are minutes when she longs to flop on to the floor regardless of everything, and to sleep.

The day passes. Seeing the windows getting dark, Varka presses her temples that feel as though they were made of wood, and smiles, though she does not know why. The dusk of evening caresses her eyes that will hardly keep open, and promises her sound sleep soon. In the evening visitors come.

"Varka, set the samovar!" shouts her mistress. The samovar is a little one, and before the visitors have drunk all the tea they want, she has to heat it five times. After tea Varka stands for a whole hour on the same spot, looking at the visitors, and waiting for orders.

"Varka, run and buy three bottles of beer!"

She starts off, and tries to run as quickly as she can, to drive away sleep.

"Varka, fetch some vodka! Varka, where's the corkscrew? Varka, clean a herring!"

But now, at last, the visitors have gone; the lights are put out, the master and mistress go to bed.

"Varka, rock the baby!" she hears the last order.

The cricket churrs in the stove; the green patch on the ceiling and the shadows from the trousers and the baby-clothes force themselves on Varka's half-opened eyes again, wink at her and cloud her mind.

"Hush-a-bye, my baby wee," she murmurs, "and I will sing a song to thee."

And the baby screams, and is worn out with screaming. Again Varka sees the muddy high road, the people with wallets, her mother Pelageya, her father Yefim. She understands everything, she recognises everyone, but through her half sleep she cannot understand the force which binds her, hand and foot, weighs upon her, and prevents her from living. She looks round, searches for that force that she may escape from it, but she cannot find it. At last, tired to death, she does her very utmost, strains her eyes, looks up at the flickering green patch, and listening to the screaming, finds the foe who will not let her live.

That foe is the baby.

She laughs. It seems strange to her that she has failed to grasp such a simple thing before. The green patch, the shadows, and the cricket seem to laugh and wonder too.

The hallucination takes possession of Varka. She gets up from her stool, and with a broad smile on her face and wide unblinking eyes, she walks up and down the room. She feels pleased and tickled at the thought that she will be rid directly of the baby that binds her hand and foot. . . . Kill the baby and then sleep, sleep, sleep. . . .

Laughing and winking and shaking her fingers at the green patch, Varka steals up to the cradle and bends over the baby. When she has strangled him, she quickly lies down on the floor, laughs with delight that she can sleep, and in a minute is sleeping as sound as the dead.

THE STEPPE

I

Early one morning in July a shabby covered chaise, one of those antediluvian chaises without springs in which no one travels in Russia nowadays, except merchant's clerks, dealers and the less well-to-do among priests, drove out of N., the principal town of the province of Z., and rumbled noisily along the posting-track. It rattled and creaked at every movement; the pail, hanging on behind, chimed in gruffly, and from these sounds alone and from the wretched rags of leather hanging loose about its peeling body one could judge of its decrepit age and readiness to drop to pieces.

Two of the inhabitants of N. were sitting in the chaise; they were a merchant of N. called Ivan Ivanitch Kuzmitchov, a man with a shaven face wearing glasses and a straw hat, more like a government clerk than a merchant, and Father Christopher Sireysky, the priest of the Church of St. Nikolay at N., a little old man with long hair, in a grey canvas cassock, a wide-brimmed top-hat and a coloured embroidered girdle. The former was absorbed in thought, and kept tossing his head to shake off drowsiness; in his countenance an habitual business-like reserve was struggling with the genial expression of a man who has just said good-bye to his relatives and has had a good drink at parting. The latter gazed with moist eyes wonderingly at God's world, and his smile was so broad that it seemed to embrace even the brim of his hat; his face was red and looked frozen. Both of them, Father Christopher as well as Kuzmitchov, were going to sell wool. At parting with their families they had just eaten heartily of pastry puffs and cream, and although it was so early in the morning had had a glass or two. . . . Both were in the best of humours.

Apart from the two persons described above and the coachman Deniska, who lashed the pair of frisky bay horses, there was another figure in the chaise -- a boy of nine with a sunburnt face, wet with tears. This was Yegorushka, Kuzmitchov's nephew. With the sanction of his uncle and the blessing of Father Christopher, he was now on his way to go to school. His mother, Olga Ivanovna, the widow of a collegiate secretary, and Kuzmitchov's sister, who was fond of educated people and refined society, had entreated her brother to take Yegorushka with him when he went to sell wool and to put him to school; and now the boy was sitting on the box beside the coachman Deniska, holding on to his elbow to keep from falling off, and dancing up and down like a kettle on the hob, with no notion where he was going or what he was going for. The rapid motion through the air blew out his red shirt like a balloon on his back and made his new hat with a peacock's feather in it, like a coachman's, keep slipping on to the back of his head. He felt himself an intensely unfortunate person, and had an inclination to cry.

When the chaise drove past the prison, Yegorushka glanced at the sentinels pacing slowly by the high white walls, at the little barred windows, at the cross shining on the roof, and remembered how the week before, on the day of the Holy Mother of Kazan, he had been with his mother to the prison church for the Dedication Feast, and how before that, at Easter, he had gone to the prison with Deniska and Ludmila the cook, and had taken the prisoners Easter bread, eggs, cakes and roast beef. The prisoners had thanked them and made the sign of the cross, and one of them had given Yegorushka a pewter buckle of his own making.

The boy gazed at the familiar places, while the hateful chaise flew by and left them all behind. After the prison he caught glimpses of black grimy foundries, followed by the snug green cemetery surrounded by a wall of cobblestones; white crosses and tombstones, nestling among green cherry-trees and looking in the distance like patches of white, peeped out gaily from behind the wall. Yegorushka remembered that when the cherries were in blossom those white patches melted with the flowers into a sea of white; and that when the cherries were ripe the white tombstones and crosses were dotted with splashes of red like bloodstains. Under the cherry trees in the cemetery Yegorushka's father and granny, Zinaida Danilovna, lay sleeping day and night. When Granny had died she had been put in a long narrow coffin and two pennies had been put upon her eyes, which would not keep shut. Up to the time of her death she had been brisk, and used to bring soft rolls covered with poppy seeds from the market. Now she did nothing but sleep and sleep. . . .

Beyond the cemetery came the smoking brickyards. From under the long roofs of reeds that looked as though pressed flat to the ground, a thick black smoke rose in great clouds and floated lazily upwards. The sky was murky above the brickyards and the cemetery, and great shadows from the clouds of smoke crept over the fields and across the roads. Men and horses covered with red dust were moving about in the smoke near the roofs.

The town ended with the brickyards and the open country began. Yegorushka looked at the town for the last time, pressed his face against Deniska's elbow, and wept bitterly.

"Come, not done howling yet, cry-baby!" cried Kuzmitchov. "You are blubbering again, little milksop! If you don't want to go, stay behind; no one is taking you by force!

"Never mind, never mind, Yegor boy, never mind," Father Christopher muttered rapidly -- "never mind, my boy. . . . Call upon God. . . . You are not going for your harm, but for your good. Learning is light, as the saying is, and ignorance is darkness. . . . That is so, truly."

"Do you want to go back?" asked Kuzmitchov.

"Yes, . . . yes, . . ." answered Yegorushka, sobbing.

"Well, you'd better go back then. Anyway, you are going for nothing; it's a day's journey for a spoonful of porridge."

"Never mind, never mind, my boy," Father Christopher went on. "Call upon God. . . . Lomonosov set off with the fishermen in the same way, and he became a man famous all over Europe. Learning in conjunction with faith brings forth fruit pleasing to God. What are the words of the prayer? For the glory of our Maker, for the comfort of our parents, for the benefit of our Church and our country. . . . Yes, indeed!"

"The benefit is not the same in all cases," said Kuzmitchov, lighting a cheap cigar; "some will study twenty years and get no sense from it."

"That does happen."

"Learning is a benefit to some, but others only muddle their brains. My sister is a woman who does not understand; she is set upon refinement, and wants to turn Yegorka into a learned man, and she does not understand that with my business I could settle Yegorka happily for the rest of his life. I tell you this, that if everyone were to go in for being learned and refined there would be no one to sow the corn and do the trading; they would all die of hunger."

"And if all go in for trading and sowing corn there will be no one to acquire learning."

And considering that each of them had said something weighty and convincing, Kuzmitchov and Father Christopher both looked serious and cleared their throats simultaneously.

Deniska, who had been listening to their conversation without understanding a word of it, shook his head and, rising in his seat, lashed at both the bays. A silence followed.

Meanwhile a wide boundless plain encircled by a chain of low hills lay stretched before the travellers' eyes. Huddling together and peeping out from behind one another, these hills melted together into rising ground, which stretched right to the very horizon and disappeared into the lilac distance; one drives on and on and cannot discern where it begins or where it ends. . . . The sun had already peeped out from beyond the town behind them, and quietly, without fuss, set to its accustomed task. At first in the distance before them a broad, bright, yellow streak of light crept over the ground where the earth met the sky, near the little barrows and the windmills, which in the distance looked like tiny men waving their arms. A minute later a similar streak gleamed a little nearer, crept to the right and embraced the hills. Something warm touched Yegorushka's spine; the streak of light, stealing up from behind, darted between the chaise and the horses, moved to meet the other streak, and soon the whole wide steppe flung off the twilight of early morning, and was smiling and sparkling with dew.

The cut rye, the coarse steppe grass, the milkwort, the wild hemp, all withered from the sultry heat, turned brown and half dead, now washed by the dew and caressed by the sun, revived, to fade again. Arctic petrels flew across the road with joyful cries; marmots called to one another in the grass. Somewhere, far away to the left, lapwings uttered their plaintive notes. A covey of partridges, scared by the chaise, fluttered up and with their soft "trrrr!" flew off to the hills. In the grass crickets, locusts and grasshoppers kept up their churring, monotonous music.

But a little time passed, the dew evaporated, the air grew stagnant, and the disillusioned steppe began to wear its jaded July aspect. The grass drooped, everything living was hushed. The sun-baked hills, brownish-green and lilac in the distance, with their quiet shadowy tones, the plain with the misty distance and, arched above them, the sky, which seems terribly deep and transparent in the steppes, where there are no woods or high hills, seemed now endless, petrified with dreariness. . . .

How stifling and oppressive it was! The chaise raced along, while Yegorushka saw always the same -- the sky, the plain, the low hills. . . . The music in the grass was hushed, the petrels had flown away, the partridges were out of sight, rooks hovered idly over the withered grass; they were all alike and made the steppe even more monotonous.

A hawk flew just above the ground, with an even sweep of its wings, suddenly halted in the air as though pondering on the dreariness of life, then fluttered its wings and flew like an arrow over the steppe, and there was no telling why it flew off and what it wanted. In the distance a windmill waved its sails. . . .

Now and then a glimpse of a white potsherd or a heap of stones broke the monotony; a grey stone stood out for an instant or a parched willow with a blue crow on its top branch; a marmot would run across the road and -- again there flitted before the eyes only the high grass, the low hills, the rooks. . . .

But at last, thank God, a waggon loaded with sheaves came to meet them; a peasant wench was lying on the very top. Sleepy, exhausted by the heat, she lifted her head and looked at the travellers. Deniska gaped, looking at her; the horses stretched out their noses towards the sheaves; the chaise, squeaking, kissed the waggon, and the pointed ears passed over Father Christopher's hat like a brush.

"You are driving over folks, fatty!" cried Deniska. "What a swollen lump of a face, as though a bumble-bee had stung it!"

The girl smiled drowsily, and moving her lips lay down again; then a solitary poplar came into sight on the low hill. Someone had planted it, and God only knows why it was there. It was hard to tear the eyes away from its graceful figure and green drapery. Was that lovely creature happy? Sultry heat in summer, in winter frost and snowstorms, terrible nights in autumn when nothing is to be seen but darkness and nothing is to be heard but the senseless angry howling wind, and, worst of all, alone, alone for the whole of life. . . . Beyond the poplar stretches of wheat extended like a bright yellow carpet from the road to the top of the hills. On the hills the corn was already cut and laid up in sheaves, while at the bottom they were still cutting. . . . Six mowers were standing in a row swinging their scythes, and the scythes gleamed gaily and uttered in unison together "Vzhee, vzhee!" From the movements of the peasant women binding the sheaves, from the faces of the mowers, from the glitter of the scythes, it could be seen that the sultry heat was baking and stifling. A black dog with its tongue hanging out ran from the mowers to meet the chaise, probably with the intention of barking, but stopped halfway and stared indifferently at Deniska, who shook his whip at him; it was too hot to bark! One peasant woman got up and, putting both hands to her aching back, followed Yegorushka's red shirt with her eyes. Whether it was that the colour pleased her or that he reminded her of her children, she stood a long time motionless staring after him.

But now the wheat, too, had flashed by; again the parched plain, the sunburnt hills, the sultry sky stretched before them; again a hawk hovered over the earth. In the distance, as before, a windmill whirled its sails, and still it looked like a little man waving his arms. It was wearisome to watch, and it seemed as though one would never reach it, as though it were running away from the chaise.

Father Christopher and Kuzmitchov were silent. Deniska lashed the horses and kept shouting to them, while Yegorushka had left off crying, and gazed about him listlessly. The heat and the tedium of the steppes overpowered him. He felt as though he had been travelling and jolting up and down for a very long time, that the sun had been baking his back a long time. Before they had gone eight miles he began to feel "It must be time to rest." The geniality gradually faded out of his uncle's face and nothing else was left but the air of business reserve; and to a gaunt shaven face, especially when it is adorned with spectacles and the nose and temples are covered with dust, this reserve gives a relentless, inquisitorial appearance. Father Christopher never left off gazing with wonder at God's world, and smiling. Without speaking, he brooded over something pleasant and nice, and a kindly, genial smile remained imprinted on his face. It seemed as though some nice and pleasant thought were imprinted on his brain by the heat.

"Well, Deniska, shall we overtake the waggons to-day?" asked Kuzmitchov.

Deniska looked at the sky, rose in his seat, lashed at his horses and then answered:

"By nightfall, please God, we shall overtake them."

There was a sound of dogs barking. Half a dozen steppe sheep-dogs, suddenly leaping out as though from ambush, with ferocious howling barks, flew to meet the chaise. All of them, extraordinarily furious, surrounded the chaise, with their shaggy spider-like muzzles and their eyes red with anger, and jostling against one another in their anger, raised a hoarse howl. They were filled with passionate hatred of the horses, of the chaise, and of the human beings, and seemed ready to tear them into pieces. Deniska, who was fond of teasing and beating, was delighted at the chance of it, and with a malignant expression bent over and lashed at the sheep-dogs with his whip. The brutes growled more than ever, the horses flew on; and Yegorushka, who had difficulty in keeping his seat on the box, realized, looking at the dogs' eyes and teeth, that if he fell down they would instantly tear him to bits; but he felt no fear and looked at them as malignantly as Deniska, and regretted that he had no whip in his hand.

The chaise came upon a flock of sheep.

"Stop!" cried Kuzmitchov. "Pull up! Woa!"

Deniska threw his whole body backwards and pulled up the horses.

"Come here!" Kuzmitchov shouted to the shepherd. "Call off the dogs, curse them!"

The old shepherd, tattered and barefoot, wearing a fur cap, with a dirty sack round his loins and a long crook in his hand -- a regular figure from the Old Testament -- called off the dogs, and taking off his cap, went up to the chaise. Another similar Old Testament figure was standing motionless at the other end of the flock, staring without interest at the travellers.

"Whose sheep are these?" asked Kuzmitchov.

"Varlamov's," the old man answered in a loud voice.

"Varlamov's," repeated the shepherd standing at the other end of the flock.

"Did Varlamov come this way yesterday or not?"

"He did not; his clerk came. . . ."

"Drive on!"

The chaise rolled on and the shepherds, with their angry dogs, were left behind. Yegorushka gazed listlessly at the lilac distance in front, and it began to seem as though the windmill, waving its sails, were getting nearer. It became bigger and bigger, grew quite large, and now he could distinguish clearly its two sails. One sail was old and patched, the other had only lately been made of new wood and glistened in the sun. The chaise drove straight on, while the windmill, for some reason, began retreating to the left. They drove on and on, and the windmill kept moving away to the left, and still did not disappear.

"A fine windmill Boltva has put up for his son," observed Deniska.

"And how is it we don't see his farm?"

"It is that way, beyond the creek."

Boltva's farm, too, soon came into sight, but yet the windmill did not retreat, did not drop behind; it still watched Yegorushka with its shining sail and waved. What a sorcerer!

II

Towards midday the chaise turned off the road to the right; it went on a little way at walking pace and then stopped. Yegorushka heard a soft, very caressing gurgle, and felt a different air breathe on his face with a cool velvety touch. Through a little pipe of hemlock stuck there by some unknown benefactor, water was running in a thin trickle from a low hill, put together by nature of huge monstrous stones. It fell to the ground, and limpid, sparkling gaily in the sun, and softly murmuring as though fancying itself a great tempestuous torrent, flowed swiftly away to the left. Not far from its source the little stream spread itself out into a pool; the burning sunbeams and the parched soil greedily drank it up and sucked away its strength; but a little further on it must have mingled with another rivulet, for a hundred paces away thick reeds showed green and luxuriant along its course, and three snipe flew up from them with a loud cry as the chaise drove by.

The travellers got out to rest by the stream and feed the horses. Kuzmitchov, Father Christopher and Yegorushka sat down on a mat in the narrow strip of shade cast by the chaise and the unharnessed horses. The nice pleasant thought that the heat had imprinted in Father Christopher's brain craved expression after he had had a drink of water and eaten a hard-boiled egg. He bent a friendly look upon Yegorushka, munched, and began:

"I studied too, my boy; from the earliest age God instilled into me good sense and understanding, so that while I was just such a lad as you I was beyond others, a comfort to my parents and preceptors by my good sense. Before I was fifteen I could speak and make verses in Latin, just as in Russian. I was the crosier-bearer to his Holiness Bishop Christopher. After mass one day, as I remember it was the patron saint's day of His Majesty Tsar Alexandr Pavlovitch of blessed memory, he unrobed at the altar, looked kindly at me and asked, 'Puer bone, quam appelaris?' And I answered, 'Christopherus sum;' and he said, 'Ergo connominati sumus' -- that is, that we were namesakes. . . Then he asked in Latin, 'Whose son are you?' To which I answered, also in Latin, that I was the son of deacon Sireysky of the village of Lebedinskoe. Seeing my readiness and the clearness of my answers, his Holiness blessed me and said, 'Write to your father that I will not forget him, and that I will keep you in view.' The holy priests and fathers who were standing round the altar, hearing our discussion in Latin, were not a little surprised, and everyone expressed his pleasure in praise of me. Before I had moustaches, my boy, I could read Latin, Greek, and French; I knew philosophy, mathematics, secular history, and all the sciences. The Lord gave me a marvellous memory. Sometimes, if I read a thing once or twice, I knew it by heart. My preceptors and patrons were amazed, and so they expected I should make a learned man, a luminary of the Church. I did think of going to Kiev to continue my studies, but my parents did not approve. 'You'll be studying all your life,' said my father; 'when shall we see you finished?' Hearing such words, I gave up study and took a post. . . . Of course, I did not become a learned man, but then I did not disobey my parents; I was a comfort to them in their old age and gave them a creditable funeral. Obedience is more than fasting and prayer.

"I suppose you have forgotten all your learning?" observed Kuzmitchov.

"I should think so! Thank God, I have reached my eightieth year! Something of philosophy and rhetoric I do remember, but languages and mathematics I have quite forgotten."

Father Christopher screwed up his eyes, thought a minute and said in an undertone:

"What is a substance? A creature is a self-existing object, not requiring anything else for its completion."

He shook his head and laughed with feeling.

"Spiritual nourishment! "he said. "Of a truth matter nourishes the flesh and spiritual nourishment the soul!

"Learning is all very well," sighed Kuzmitchov, "but if we don't overtake Varlamov, learning won't do much for us."

"A man isn't a needle -- we shall find him. He must be going his rounds in these parts."

Among the sedge were flying the three snipe they had seen before, and in their plaintive cries there was a note of alarm and vexation at having been driven away from the stream. The horses were steadily munching and snorting. Deniska walked about by them and, trying to appear indifferent to the cucumbers, pies, and eggs that the gentry were eating, he concentrated himself on the gadflies and horseflies that were fastening upon the horses' backs and bellies; he squashed his victims apathetically, emitting a peculiar, fiendishly triumphant, guttural sound, and when he missed them cleared his throat with an air of vexation and looked after every lucky one that escaped death.

"Deniska, where are you? Come and eat," said Kuzmitchov, heaving a deep sigh, a sign that he had had enough.

Deniska diffidently approached the mat and picked out five thick and yellow cucumbers (he did not venture to take the smaller and fresher ones), took two hard-boiled eggs that looked dark and were cracked, then irresolutely, as though afraid he might get a blow on his outstretched hand, touched a pie with his finger.

"Take them, take them," Kuzmitchov urged him on.

Deniska took the pies resolutely, and, moving some distance away, sat down on the grass with his back to the chaise. At once there was such a sound of loud munching that even the horses turned round to look suspiciously at Deniska.

After his meal Kuzmitchov took a sack containing something out of the chaise and said to Yegorushka:

"I am going to sleep, and you mind that no one takes the sack from under my head."

Father Christopher took off his cassock, his girdle, and his full coat, and Yegorushka, looking at him, was dumb with astonishment. He had never imagined that priests wore trousers, and Father Christopher had on real canvas trousers thrust into high boots, and a short striped jacket. Looking at him, Yegorushka thought that in this costume, so unsuitable to his dignified position, he looked with his long hair and beard very much likeRobinson Crusoe. After taking off their outer garments Kuzmitchov and Father Christopher lay down in the shade under the chaise, facing one another, and closed their eyes. Deniska, who had finished munching, stretched himself out on his back and also closed his eyes.

"You look out that no one takes away the horses!" he said to Yegorushka, and at once fell asleep.

Stillness reigned. There was no sound except the munching and snorting of the horses and the snoring of the sleepers; somewhere far away a lapwing wailed, and from time to time there sounded the shrill cries of the three snipe who had flown up to see whether their uninvited visitors had gone away; the rivulet babbled, lisping softly, but all these sounds did not break the stillness, did not stir the stagnation, but, on the contrary, lulled all nature to slumber.

Yegorushka, gasping with the heat, which was particularly oppressive after a meal, ran to the sedge and from there surveyed the country. He saw exactly the same as he had in the morning: the plain, the low hills, the sky, the lilac distance; only the hills stood nearer; and he could not see the windmill, which had been left far behind. From behind the rocky hill from which the stream flowed rose another, smoother and broader; a little hamlet of five or six homesteads clung to it. No people, no trees, no shade were to be seen about the huts; it looked as though the hamlet had expired in the burning air and was dried up. To while away the time Yegorushka caught a grasshopper in the grass, held it in his closed hand to his ear, and spent a long time listening to the creature playing on its instrument. When he was weary of its music he ran after a flock of yellow butterflies who were flying towards the sedge on the watercourse, and found himself again beside the chaise, without noticing how he came there. His uncle and Father Christopher were sound asleep; their sleep would be sure to last two or three hours till the horses had rested. . . . How was he to get through that long time, and where was he to get away from the heat? A hard problem. . . . Mechanically Yegorushka put his lips to the trickle that ran from the waterpipe; there was a chilliness in his mouth and there was the smell of hemlock. He drank at first eagerly, then went on with effort till the sharp cold had run from his mouth all over his body and the water was spilt on his shirt. Then he went up to the chaise and began looking at the sleeping figures. His uncle's face wore, as before, an expression of business-like reserve. Fanatically devoted to his work, Kuzmitchov always, even in his sleep and at church when they were singing, "Like the cherubim," thought about his business and could never forget it for a moment; and now he was probably dreaming about bales of wool, waggons, prices, Varlamov. . . . Father Christopher, now, a soft, frivolous and absurd person, had never all his life been conscious of anything which could, like a boa-constrictor, coil about his soul and hold it tight. In all the numerous enterprises he had undertaken in his day what attracted him was not so much the business itself, but the bustle and the contact with other people involved in every undertaking. Thus, in the present expedition, he was not so much interested in wool, in Varlamov, and in prices, as in the long journey, the conversations on the way, the sleeping under a chaise, and the meals at odd times. . . . And now, judging from his face, he must have been dreaming of Bishop Christopher, of the Latin discussion, of his wife, of puffs and cream and all sorts of things that Kuzmitchov could not possibly dream of.

While Yegorushka was watching their sleeping faces he suddenly heard a soft singing; somewhere at a distance a woman was singing, and it was difficult to tell where and in what direction. The song was subdued, dreary and melancholy, like a dirge, and hardly audible, and seemed to come first from the right, then from the left, then from above, and then from underground, as though an unseen spirit were hovering over the steppe and singing. Yegorushka looked about him, and could not make out where the strange song came from. Then as he listened he began to fancy that the grass was singing; in its song, withered and half-dead, it was without words, but plaintively and passionately, urging that it was not to blame, that the sun was burning it for no fault of its own; it urged that it ardently longed to live, that it was young and might have been beautiful but for the heat and the drought; it was guiltless, but yet it prayed forgiveness and protested that it was in anguish, sad and sorry for itself. . . .

Yegorushka listened for a little, and it began to seem as though this dreary, mournful song made the air hotter, more suffocating and more stagnant. . . . To drown the singing he ran to the sedge, humming to himself and trying to make a noise with his feet. From there he looked about in all directions and found out who was singing. Near the furthest hut in the hamlet stood a peasant woman in a short petticoat, with long thin legs like a heron. She was sowing something. A white dust floated languidly from her sieve down the hillock. Now it was evident that she was singing. A couple of yards from her a little bare-headed boy in nothing but a smock was standing motionless. As though fascinated by the song, he stood stock-still, staring away into the distance, probably at Yegorushka's crimson shirt.

The song ceased. Yegorushka sauntered back to the chaise, and to while away the time went again to the trickle of water.

And again there was the sound of the dreary song. It was the same long-legged peasant woman in the hamlet over the hill. Yegorushka's boredom came back again. He left the pipe and looked upwards. What he saw was so unexpected that he was a little frightened. Just above his head on one of the big clumsy stones stood a chubby little boy, wearing nothing but a shirt, with a prominent stomach and thin legs, the same boy who had been standing before by the peasant woman. He was gazing with open mouth and unblinking eyes at Yegorushka's crimson shirt and at the chaise, with a look of blank astonishment and even fear, as though he saw before him creatures of another world. The red colour of the shirt charmed and allured him. But the chaise and the men sleeping under it excited his curiosity; perhaps he had not noticed how the agreeable red colour and curiosity had attracted him down from the hamlet, and now probably he was surprised at his own boldness. For a long while Yegorushka stared at him, and he at Yegorushka. Both were silent and conscious of some awkwardness. After a long silence Yegorushka asked:

"What's your name?"

The stranger's cheeks puffed out more than ever; he pressed his back against the rock, opened his eyes wide, moved his lips, and answered in a husky bass: "Tit!"

The boys said not another word to each other; after a brief silence, still keeping his eyes fixed on Yegorushka, the mysterious Tit kicked up one leg, felt with his heel for a niche and clambered up the rock; from that point he ascended to the next rock, staggering backwards and looking intently at Yegorushka, as though afraid he might hit him from behind, and so made his way upwards till he disappeared altogether behind the crest of the hill.

After watching him out of sight, Yegorushka put his arms round his knees and leaned his head on them. . . . The burning sun scorched the back of his head, his neck, and his spine. The melancholy song died away, then floated again on the stagnant stifling air. The rivulet gurgled monotonously, the horses munched, and time dragged on endlessly, as though it, too, were stagnant and had come to a standstill. It seemed as though a hundred years had passed since the morning. Could it be that God's world, the chaise and the horses would come to a standstill in that air, and, like the hills, turn to stone and remain forever in one spot? Yegorushka raised his head, and with smarting eyes looked before him; the lilac distance, which till then had been motionless, began heaving, and with the sky floated away into the distance. . . . It drew after it the brown grass, the sedge, and with extraordinary swiftness Yegorushka floated after the flying distance. Some force noiselessly drew him onwards, and the heat and the wearisome song flew after in pursuit. Yegorushka bent his head and shut his eyes. . . .

Deniska was the first to wake up. Something must have bitten him, for he jumped up, quickly scratched his shoulder and said:

"Plague take you, cursed idolater!"

Then he went to the brook, had a drink and slowly washed. His splashing and puffing roused Yegorushka from his lethargy. The boy looked at his wet face with drops of water and big freckles which made it look like marble, and asked:

"Shall we soon be going?"

Deniska looked at the height of the sun and answered:

"I expect so."

He dried himself with the tail of his shirt and, making a very serious face, hopped on one leg.

"I say, which of us will get to the sedge first?" he said.

Yegorushka was exhausted by the heat and drowsiness, but he raced off after him all the same. Deniska was in his twentieth year, was a coachman and going to be married, but he had not left off being a boy. He was very fond of flying kites, chasing pigeons, playing knuckle-bones, running races, and always took part in children's games and disputes. No sooner had his master turned his back or gone to sleep than Deniska would begin doing something such as hopping on one leg or throwing stones. It was hard for any grown-up person, seeing the genuine enthusiasm with which he frolicked about in the society of children, to resist saying, "What a baby!" Children, on the other hand, saw nothing strange in the invasion of their domain by the big coachman. "Let him play," they thought, "as long as he doesn't fight!" In the same way little dogs see nothing strange in it when a simple-hearted big dog joins their company uninvited and begins playing with them.

Deniska outstripped Yegorushka, and was evidently very much pleased at having done so. He winked at him, and to show that he could hop on one leg any distance, suggested to Yegorushka that he should hop with him along the road and from there, without resting, back to the chaise. Yegorushka declined this suggestion, for he was very much out of breath and exhausted.

All at once Deniska looked very grave, as he did not look even when Kuzmitchov gave him a scolding or threatened him with a stick; listening intently, he dropped quietly on one knee and an expression of sternness and alarm came into his face, such as one sees in people who hear heretical talk. He fixed his eyes on one spot, raised his hand curved into a hollow, and suddenly fell on his stomach on the ground and slapped the hollow of his hand down upon the grass.

"Caught!" he wheezed triumphantly, and, getting up, lifted a big grasshopper to Yegorushka's eyes.

The two boys stroked the grasshopper's broad green back with their fingers and touched his antenna, supposing that this would please the creature. Then Deniska caught a fat fly that had been sucking blood and offered it to the grasshopper. The latter moved his huge jaws, that were like the visor of a helmet, with the utmost unconcern, as though he had been long acquainted with Deniska, and bit off the fly's stomach. They let him go. With a flash of the pink lining of his wings, he flew down into the grass and at once began his churring notes again. They let the fly go, too. It preened its wings, and without its stomach flew off to the horses.

A loud sigh was heard from under the chaise. It was Kuzmitchov waking up. He quickly raised his head, looked uneasily into the distance, and from that look, which passed by Yegorushka and Deniska without sympathy or interest, it could be seen that his thought on awaking was of the wool and of Varlamov.

"Father Christopher, get up; it is time to start," he said anxiously. "Wake up; we've slept too long as it is! Deniska, put the horses in."

Father Christopher woke up with the same smile with which he had fallen asleep; his face looked creased and wrinkled from sleep, and seemed only half the size. After washing and dressing, he proceeded without haste to take out of his pocket a little greasy psalter; and standing with his face towards the east, began in a whisper repeating the psalms of the day and crossing himself.

"Father Christopher," said Kuzmitchov reproachfully, "it's time to start; the horses are ready, and here are you, . . . upon my word."

"In a minute, in a minute," muttered Father Christopher. "I must read the psalms. . . . I haven't read them to-day."

"The psalms can wait."

"Ivan Ivanitch, that is my rule every day. . . . I can't . . ."

"God will overlook it."

For a full quarter of an hour Father Christopher stood facing the east and moving his lips, while Kuzmitchov looked at him almost with hatred and impatiently shrugged his shoulders. He was particularly irritated when, after every "Hallelujah," Father Christopher drew a long breath, rapidly crossed himself and repeated three times, intentionally raising his voice so that the others might cross themselves, "Hallelujah, hallelujah, hallelujah! Glory be to Thee, O Lord!" At last he smiled, looked upwards at the sky, and, putting the psalter in his pocket, said:

"Finis!"

A minute later the chaise had started on the road. As though it were going backwards and not forwards, the travellers saw the same scene as they had before midday.

The low hills were still plunged in the lilac distance, and no end could be seen to them. There were glimpses of high grass and heaps of stones; strips of stubble land passed by them and still the same rooks, the same hawk, moving its wings with slow dignity, moved over the steppe. The air was more sultry than ever; from the sultry heat and the stillness submissive nature was spellbound into silence. . . . No wind, no fresh cheering sound, no cloud.

But at last, when the sun was beginning to sink into the west, the steppe, the hills and the air could bear the oppression no longer, and, driven out of all patience, exhausted, tried to fling off the yoke. A fleecy ashen-grey cloud unexpectedly appeared behind the hills. It exchanged glances with the steppe, as though to say, "Here I am," and frowned. Suddenly something burst in the stagnant air; there was a violent squall of wind which whirled round and round, roaring and whistling over the steppe. At once a murmur rose from the grass and last year's dry herbage, the dust curled in spiral eddies over the road, raced over the steppe, and carrying with it straws, dragon flies and feathers, rose up in a whirling black column towards the sky and darkened the sun. Prickly uprooted plants ran stumbling and leaping in all directions over the steppe, and one of them got caught in the whirlwind, turned round and round like a bird, flew towards the sky, and turning into a little black speck, vanished from sight. After it flew another, and then a third, and Yegorushka saw two of them meet in the blue height and clutch at one another as though they were wrestling.

A bustard flew up by the very road. Fluttering his wings and his tail, he looked, bathed in the sunshine, like an angler's glittering tin fish or a waterfly flashing so swiftly over the water that its wings cannot be told from its antenna, which seem to be growing before, behind and on all sides. . . . Quivering in the air like an insect with a shimmer of bright colours, the bustard flew high up in a straight line, then, probably frightened by a cloud of dust, swerved to one side, and for a long time the gleam of his wings could be seen. . . .

Then a corncrake flew up from the grass, alarmed by the hurricane and not knowing what was the matter. It flew with the wind and not against it, like all the other birds, so that all its feathers were ruffled up and it was puffed out to the size of a hen and looked very angry and impressive. Only the rooks who had grown old on the steppe and were accustomed to its vagaries hovered calmly over the grass, or taking no notice of anything, went on unconcernedly pecking with their stout beaks at the hard earth.

There was a dull roll of thunder beyond the hills; there came a whiff of fresh air. Deniska gave a cheerful whistle and lashed his horses. Father Christopher and Kuzmitchov held their hats and looked intently towards the hills. . . . How pleasant a shower of rain would have been!

One effort, one struggle more, and it seemed the steppe would have got the upper hand. But the unseen oppressive force gradually riveted its fetters on the wind and the air, laid the dust, and the stillness came back again as though nothing had happened, the cloud hid, the sun-baked hills frowned submissively, the air grew calm, and only somewhere the troubled lapwings wailed and lamented their destiny. . . .

Soon after that the evening came on.

III

In the dusk of evening a big house of one storey, with a rusty iron roof and with dark windows, came into sight. This house was called a posting-inn, though it had nothing like a stableyard, and it stood in the middle of the steppe, with no kind of enclosure round it. A little to one side of it a wretched little cherry orchard shut in by a hurdle fence made a dark patch, and under the windows stood sleepy sunflowers drooping their heavy heads. From the orchard came the clatter of a little toy windmill, set there to frighten away hares by the rattle. Nothing more could be seen near the house, and nothing could be heard but the steppe. The chaise had scarcely stopped at the porch with an awning over it, when from the house there came the sound of cheerful voices, one a man's, another a woman's; there was the creak of a swing-door, and in a flash a tall gaunt figure, swinging its arms and fluttering its coat, was standing by the chaise. This was the innkeeper, Moisey Moisevitch, a man no longer young, with a very pale face and a handsome beard as black as charcoal. He was wearing a threadbare black coat, which hung flapping on his narrow shoulders as though on a hatstand, and fluttered its skirts like wings every time Moisey Moisevitch flung up his hands in delight or horror. Besides his coat the innkeeper was wearing full white trousers, not stuck into his boots, and a velvet waistcoat with brown flowers on it that looked like gigantic bugs.

Moisey Moisevitch was at first dumb with excess of feeling on recognizing the travellers, then he clasped his hands and uttered a moan. His coat swung its skirts, his back bent into a bow, and his pale face twisted into a smile that suggested that to see the chaise was not merely a pleasure to him, but actually a joy so sweet as to be painful.

"Oh dear! oh dear!" he began in a thin sing-song voice, breathless, fussing about and preventing the travellers from getting out of the chaise by his antics. "What a happy day for me! Oh, what am I to do now? Ivan Ivanitch! Father Christopher! What a pretty little gentleman sitting on the box, God strike me dead! Oh, my goodness! why am I standing here instead of asking the visitors indoors? Please walk in, I humbly beg you. . . . You are kindly welcome! Give me all your things. . . . Oh, my goodness me!"

Moisey Moisevitch, who was rummaging in the chaise and assisting the travellers to alight, suddenly turned back and shouted in a voice as frantic and choking as though he were drowning and calling for help:

"Solomon! Solomon!"

"Solomon! Solomon!" a woman's voice repeated indoors.

The swing-door creaked, and in the doorway appeared a rather short young Jew with a big beak-like nose, with a bald patch surrounded by rough red curly hair; he was dressed in a short and very shabby reefer jacket, with rounded lappets and short sleeves, and in short serge trousers, so that he looked skimpy and short-tailed like an unfledged bird. This was Solomon, the brother of Moisey Moisevitch. He went up to the chaise, smiling rather queerly, and did not speak or greet the travellers.

"Ivan Ivanitch and Father Christopher have come," said Moisey Moisevitch in a tone as though he were afraid his brother would not believe him. "Dear, dear! What a surprise! Such honoured guests to have come us so suddenly! Come, take their things, Solomon. Walk in, honoured guests."

A little later Kuzmitchov, Father Christopher, and Yegorushka were sitting in a big gloomy empty room at an old oak table. The table was almost in solitude, for, except a wide sofa covered with torn American leather and three chairs, there was no other furniture in the room. And, indeed, not everybody would have given the chairs that name. They were a pitiful semblance of furniture, covered with American leather that had seen its best days, and with backs bent backwards at an unnaturally acute angle, so that they looked like children's sledges. It was hard to imagine what had been the unknown carpenter's object in bending the chairbacks so mercilessly, and one was tempted to imagine that it was not the carpenter's fault, but that some athletic visitor had bent the chairs like this as a feat, then had tried to bend them back again and had made them worse. The room looked gloomy, the walls were grey, the ceilings and the cornices were grimy; on the floor were chinks and yawning holes that were hard to account for (one might have fancied they were made by the heel of the same athlete), and it seemed as though the room would still have been dark if a dozen lamps had hung in it. There was nothing approaching an ornament on the walls or the windows. On one wall, however, there hung a list of regulations of some sort under a two-headed eagle in a grey wooden frame, and on another wall in the same sort of frame an engraving with the inscription, "The Indifference of Man." What it was to which men were indifferent it was impossible to make out, as the engraving was very dingy with age and was extensively flyblown. There was a smell of something decayed and sour in the room.

As he led the visitors into the room, Moisey Moisevitch went on wriggling, gesticulating, shrugging and uttering joyful exclamations; he considered these antics necessary in order to seem polite and agreeable.

"When did our waggons go by?" Kuzmitchov asked.

"One party went by early this morning, and the other, Ivan Ivanitch, put up here for dinner and went on towards evening."

"Ah!. . . Has Varlamov been by or not?"

"No, Ivan Ivanitch. His clerk, Grigory Yegoritch, went by yesterday morning and said that he had to be to-day at the Molokans' farm."

"Good! so we will go after the waggons directly and then on to the Molokans'."

"Mercy on us, Ivan Ivanitch!" Moisey Moisevitch cried in horror, flinging up his hands. "Where are you going for the night? You will have a nice little supper and stay the night, and to-morrow morning, please God, you can go on and overtake anyone you like."

"There is no time for that. . . . Excuse me, Moisey Moisevitch, another time; but now I must make haste. We'll stay a quarter of an hour and then go on; we can stay the night at the Molokans'."

"A quarter of an hour!"squealed Moisey Moisevitch. "Have you no fear of God, Ivan Ivanitch? You will compel me to hide your caps and lock the door! You must have a cup of tea and a snack of something, anyway."

"We have no time for tea," said Kuzmitchov.

Moisey Moisevitch bent his head on one side, crooked his knees, and put his open hands before him as though warding off a blow, while with a smile of agonized sweetness he began imploring:

"Ivan Ivanitch! Father Christopher! Do be so good as to take a cup of tea with me. Surely I am not such a bad man that you can't even drink tea in my house? Ivan Ivanitch!"

"Well, we may just as well have a cup of tea," said Father Christopher, with a sympathetic smile; "that won't keep us long."

"Very well," Kuzmitchov assented.

Moisey Moisevitch, in a fluster uttered an exclamation of joy, and shrugging as though he had just stepped out of cold weather into warm, ran to the door and cried in the same frantic voice in which he had called Solomon:

"Rosa! Rosa! Bring the samovar!"

A minute later the door opened, and Solomon came into the room carrying a large tray in his hands. Setting the tray on the table, he looked away sarcastically with the same queer smile as before. Now, by the light of the lamp, it was possible to see his smile distinctly; it was very complex, and expressed a variety of emotions, but the predominant element in it was undisguised contempt. He seemed to be thinking of something ludicrous and silly, to be feeling contempt and dislike, to be pleased at something and waiting for the favourable moment to turn something into ridicule and to burst into laughter. His long nose, his thick lips, and his sly prominent eyes seemed tense with the desire to laugh. Looking at his face, Kuzmitchov smiled ironically and asked:

"Solomon, why did you not come to our fair at N. this summer, and act some Jewish scenes?"

Two years before, as Yegorushka remembered very well, at one of the booths at the fair at N., Solomon had performed some scenes of Jewish life, and his acting had been a great success. The allusion to this made no impression whatever upon Solomon. Making no answer, he went out and returned a little later with the samovar.

When he had done what he had to do at the table he moved a little aside, and, folding his arms over his chest and thrusting out one leg, fixed his sarcastic eyes on Father Christopher. There was something defiant, haughty, and contemptuous in his attitude, and at the same time it was comic and pitiful in the extreme, because the more impressive his attitude the more vividly it showed up his short trousers, his bobtail coat, his caricature of a nose, and his bird-like plucked-looking little figure.

Moisey Moisevitch brought a footstool from the other room and sat down a little way from the table.

"I wish you a good appetite! Tea and sugar!" he began, trying to entertain his visitors. " I hope you will enjoy it. Such rare guests, such rare ones; it is years since I last saw Father Christopher. And will no one tell me who is this nice little gentleman?" he asked, looking tenderly at Yegorushka.

"He is the son of my sister, Olga Ivanovna," answered Kuzmitchov.

"And where is he going?"

"To school. We are taking him to a high school."

In his politeness, Moisey Moisevitch put on a look of wonder and wagged his head expressively.

"Ah, that is a fine thing," he said, shaking his finger at the samovar. "That's a fine thing. You will come back from the high school such a gentleman that we shall all take off our hats to you. You will be wealthy and wise and so grand that your mamma will be delighted. Oh, that's a fine thing!"

He paused a little, stroked his knees, and began again in a jocose and deferential tone.

"You must excuse me, Father Christopher, but I am thinking of writing to the bishop to tell him you are robbing the merchants of their living. I shall take a sheet of stamped paper and write that I suppose Father Christopher is short of pence, as he has taken up with trade and begun selling wool."

"H'm, yes . . . it's a queer notion in my old age," said Father Christopher, and he laughed. "I have turned from priest to merchant, brother. I ought to be at home now saying my prayers, instead of galloping about the country like a Pharaoh in his chariot. . . . Vanity!"

"But it will mean a lot of pence!"

"Oh, I dare say! More kicks than halfpence, and serve me right. The wool's not mine, but my son-in-law MikhailÕs!"

"Why doesn't he go himself?"

"Why, because . . . His mother's milk is scarcely dry upon his lips. He can buy wool all right, but when it comes to selling, he has no sense; he is young yet. He has wasted all his money; he wanted to grow rich and cut a dash, but he tried here and there, and no one would give him his price. And so the lad went on like that for a year, and then he came to me and said, 'Daddy, you sell the wool for me; be kind and do it! I am no good at the business!' And that is true enough. As soon as there is anything wrong then it's 'Daddy,' but till then they could get on without their dad. When he was buying he did not consult me, but now when he is in difficulties it's Daddy's turn. And what does his dad know about it? If it were not for Ivan Ivanitch, his dad could do nothing. I have a lot of worry with them."

"Yes; one has a lot of worry with one's children, I can tell you that," sighed Moisey Moisevitch. "I have six of my own. One needs schooling, another needs doctoring, and a third needs nursing, and when they grow up they are more trouble still. It is not only nowadays, it was the same in Holy Scripture. When Jacob had little children he wept, and when they grew up he wept still more bitterly."

"H'm, yes . . ." Father Christopher assented pensively, looking at his glass. "I have no cause myself to rail against the Lord. I have lived to the end of my days as any man might be thankful to live. . . . I have married my daughters to good men, my sons I have set up in life, and now I am free; I have done my work and can go where I like. I live in peace with my wife. I eat and drink and sleep and rejoice in my grandchildren, and say my prayers and want nothing more. I live on the fat of the land, and don't need to curry favour with anyone. I have never had any trouble from childhood, and now suppose the Tsar were to ask me, 'What do you need? What would you like?' why, I don't need anything. I have everything I want and everything to be thankful for. In the whole town there is no happier man than I am. My only trouble is I have so many sins, but there -- only God is without sin. That's right, isn't it?"

"No doubt it is."

"I have no teeth, of course; my poor old back aches; there is one thing and another, . . . asthma and that sort of thing. . . . I ache. . . . The flesh is weak, but then think of my age! I am in the eighties! One can't go on forever; one mustn't outstay one's welcome."

Father Christopher suddenly thought of something, spluttered into his glass and choked with laughter. Moisey Moisevitch laughed, too, from politeness, and he, too, cleared his throat.

"So funny!" said Father Christopher, and he waved his hand. "My eldest son Gavrila came to pay me a visit. He is in the medical line, and is a district doctor in the province of Tchernigov. . . . 'Very well . . .' I said to him, 'here I have asthma and one thing and another. . . . You are a doctor; cure your father!' He undressed me on the spot, tapped me, listened, and all sorts of tricks, . . . kneaded my stomach, and then he said, 'Dad, you ought to be treated with compressed air.' " Father Christopher laughed convulsively, till the tears came into his eyes, and got up.

"And I said to him, 'God bless your compressed air!' " he brought out through his laughter, waving both hands. "God bless your compressed air!"

Moisey Moisevitch got up, too, and with his hands on his stomach, went off into shrill laughter like the yap of a lap-dog.

"God bless the compressed air!" repeated Father Christopher, laughing.

Moisey Moisevitch laughed two notes higher and so violently that he could hardly stand on his feet.

"Oh dear!" he moaned through his laughter. "Let me get my breath. . . . You'll be the death of me."

He laughed and talked, though at the same time he was casting timorous and suspicious looks at Solomon. The latter was standing in the same attitude and still smiling. To judge from his eyes and his smile, his contempt and hatred were genuine, but that was so out of keeping with his plucked-looking figure that it seemed to Yegorushka as though he were putting on his defiant attitude and biting sarcastic smile to play the fool for the entertainment of their honoured guests.

After drinking six glasses of tea in silence, Kuzmitchov cleared a space before him on the table, took his bag, the one which he kept under his head when he slept under the chaise, untied the string and shook it. Rolls of paper notes were scattered out of the bag on the table.

"While we have the time, Father Christopher, let us reckon up," said Kuzmitchov.

Moisey Moisevitch was embarrassed at the sight of the money. He got up, and, as a man of delicate feeling unwilling to pry into other people's secrets, he went out of the room on tiptoe, swaying his arms. Solomon remained where he was.

"How many are there in the rolls of roubles?" Father Christopher began.

"The rouble notes are done up in fifties, . . . the three-rouble notes in nineties, the twenty-five and hundred roubles in thousands. You count out seven thousand eight hundred for Varlamov, and I will count out for Gusevitch. And mind you don't make a mistake. . ."

Yegorushka had never in his life seen so much money as was lying on the table before him. There must have been a great deal of money, for the roll of seven thousand eight hundred, which Father Christopher put aside for Varlamov, seemed very small compared with the whole heap. At any other time such a mass of money would have impressed Yegorushka, and would have moved him to reflect how many cracknels, buns and poppy-cakes could be bought for that money. Now he looked at it listlessly, only conscious of the disgusting smell of kerosene and rotten apples that came from the heap of notes. He was exhausted by the jolting ride in the chaise, tired out and sleepy. His head was heavy, his eyes would hardly keep open and his thoughts were tangled like threads. If it had been possible he would have been relieved to lay his head on the table, so as not to see the lamp and the fingers moving over the heaps of notes, and to have let his tired sleepy thoughts go still more at random. When he tried to keep awake, the light of the lamp, the cups and the fingers grew double, the samovar heaved and the smell of rotten apples seemed even more acrid and disgusting.

"Ah, money, money!" sighed Father Christopher, smiling. "You bring trouble! Now I expect my Mihailo is asleep and dreaming that I am going to bring him a heap of money like this."

"Your Mihailo Timofevitch is a man who doesn't understand business," said Kuzmitchov in an undertone; "he undertakes what isn't his work, but you understand and can judge. You had better hand over your wool to me, as I have said already, and I would give you half a rouble above my own price -- yes, I would, simply out of regard for you. . . ."

"No, Ivan Ivanitch." Father Christopher sighed. "I thank you for your kindness. . . . Of course, if it were for me to decide, I shouldn't think twice about it; but as it is, the wool is not mine, as you know. . . ."

Moisey Moisevitch came in on tiptoe. Trying from delicacy not to look at the heaps of money, he stole up to Yegorushka and pulled at his shirt from behind.

"Come along, little gentleman," he said in an undertone, "come and see the little bear I can show you! Such a queer, cross little bear. Oo-oo!"

The sleepy boy got up and listlessly dragged himself after Moisey Moisevitch to see the bear. He went into a little room, where, before he saw anything, he felt he could not breathe from the smell of something sour and decaying, which was much stronger here than in the big room and probably spread from this room all over the house. One part of the room was occupied by a big bed, covered with a greasy quilt and another by a chest of drawers and heaps of rags of all kinds from a woman's stiff petticoat to children's little breeches and braces. A tallow candle stood on the chest of drawers.

Instead of the promised bear, Yegorushka saw a big fat Jewess with her hair hanging loose, in a red flannel skirt with black sprigs on it; she turned with difficulty in the narrow space between the bed and the chest of drawers and uttered drawn-out moaning as though she had toothache. On seeing Yegorushka, she made a doleful, woe-begone face, heaved a long drawn-out sigh, and before he had time to look round, put to his lips a slice of bread smeared with honey.

"Eat it, dearie, eat it!" she said. "You are here without your mamma, and no one to look after you. Eat it up."

Yegorushka did eat it, though after the goodies and poppy-cakes he had every day at home, he did not think very much of the honey, which was mixed with wax and bees' wings. He ate while Moisey Moisevitch and the Jewess looked at him and sighed.

"Where are you going, dearie?" asked the Jewess.

"To school," answered Yegorushka.

"And how many brothers and sisters have you got?"

"I am the only one; there are no others."

"O-oh!" sighed the Jewess, and turned her eyes upward. "Poor mamma, poor mamma! How she will weep and miss you! We are going to send our Nahum to school in a year. O-oh!"

"Ah, Nahum, Nahum!" sighed Moisey Moisevitch, and the skin of his pale face twitched nervously. "And he is so delicate."

The greasy quilt quivered, and from beneath it appeared a child's curly head on a very thin neck; two black eyes gleamed and stared with curiosity at Yegorushka. Still sighing, Moisey Moisevitch and the Jewess went to the chest of drawers and began talking in Yiddish. Moisey Moisevitch spoke in a low bass undertone, and altogether his talk in Yiddish was like a continual "ghaal-ghaal-ghaal-ghaal, . . ." while his wife answered him in a shrill voice like a turkeycock's, and the whole effect of her talk was something like "Too-too-too-too!" While they were consulting, another little curly head on a thin neck peeped out of the greasy quilt, then a third, then a fourth. . . . If Yegorushka had had a fertile imagination he might have imagined that the hundred-headed hydra was hiding under the quilt.

"Ghaal-ghaal-ghaal-ghaal!" said Moisey Moisevitch.

"Too-too-too-too!" answered the Jewess.

The consultation ended in the Jewess's diving with a deep sigh into the chest of drawers, and, unwrapping some sort of green rag there, she took out a big rye cake made in the shape of a heart.

"Take it, dearie," she said, giving Yegorushka the cake; "you have no mamma now -- no one to give you nice things."

Yegorushka stuck the cake in his pocket and staggered to the door, as he could not go on breathing the foul, sour air in which the innkeeper and his wife lived. Going back to the big room, he settled himself more comfortably on the sofa and gave up trying to check his straying thoughts.

As soon as Kuzmitchov had finished counting out the notes he put them back into the bag. He did not treat them very respectfully and stuffed them into the dirty sack without ceremony, as indifferently as though they had not been money but waste paper.

Father Christopher was talking to Solomon.

"Well, Solomon the Wise!" he said, yawning and making the sign of the cross over his mouth. "How is business?"

"What sort of business are you talking about?" asked Solomon, and he looked as fiendish, as though it were a hint of some crime on his part.

"Oh, things in general. What are you doing?"

"What am I doing?" Solomon repeated, and he shrugged his shoulders. "The same as everyone else. . . . You see, I am a menial, I am my brother's servant; my brother's the servant of the visitors; the visitors are Varlamov's servants; and if I had ten millions, Varlamov would be my servant."

"Why would he be your servant?"

"Why, because there isn't a gentleman or millionaire who isn't ready to lick the hand of a scabby Jew for the sake of making a kopeck. Now, I am a scabby Jew and a beggar. Everybody looks at me as though I were a dog, but if I had money Varlamov would play the fool before me just as Moisey does before you."

Father Christopher and Kuzmitchov looked at each other. Neither of them understood Solomon. Kuzmitchov looked at him sternly and dryly, and asked:

"How can you compare yourself with Varlamov, you blockhead?"

"I am not such a fool as to put myself on a level with Varlamov," answered Solomon, looking sarcastically at the speaker. "Though Varlamov is a Russian, he is at heart a scabby Jew; money and gain are all he lives for, but I threw my money in the stove! I don't want money, or land, or sheep, and there is no need for people to be afraid of me and to take off their hats when I pass. So I am wiser than your Varlamov and more like a man!"

A little later Yegorushka, half asleep, heard Solomon in a hoarse hollow voice choked with hatred, in hurried stuttering phrases, talking about the Jews. At first he talked correctly in Russian, then he fell into the tone of a Jewish recitation, and began speaking as he had done at the fair with an exaggerated Jewish accent.

"Stop! . . ." Father Christopher said to him. "If you don't like your religion you had better change it, but to laugh at it is a sin; it is only the lowest of the low who will make fun of his religion."

"You don't understand," Solomon cut him short rudely. "I am talking of one thing and you are talking of something else. . . ."

"One can see you are a foolish fellow," sighed Father Christopher. "I admonish you to the best of my ability, and you are angry. I speak to you like an old man quietly, and you answer like a turkeycock: 'Bla---bla---bla!' You really are a queer fellow. . . ."

Moisey Moisevitch came in. He looked anxiously at Solomon and at his visitors, and again the skin on his face quivered nervously. Yegorushka shook his head and looked about him; he caught a passing glimpse of Solomon's face at the very moment when it was turned three-quarters towards him and when the shadow of his long nose divided his left cheek in half; the contemptuous smile mingled with that shadow; the gleaming sarcastic eyes, the haughty expression, and the whole plucked-looking little figure, dancing and doubling itself before Yegorushka's eyes, made him now not like a buffoon, but like something one sometimes dreams of, like an evil spirit.

"What a ferocious fellow you've got here, Moisey Moisevitch! God bless him!" said Father Christopher with a smile. "You ought to find him a place or a wife or something. . . . There's no knowing what to make of him. . . ."

Kuzmitchov frowned angrily. Moisey Moisevitch looked uneasily and inquiringly at his brother and the visitors again.

"Solomon, go away!" he said shortly. "Go away!" and he added something in Yiddish. Solomon gave an abrupt laugh and went out.

"What was it?" Moisey Moisevitch asked Father Christopher anxiously.

"He forgets himself," answered Kuzmitchov. "He's rude and thinks too much of himself."

"I knew it!" Moisey Moisevitch cried in horror, clasping his hands. "Oh dear, oh dear!" he muttered in a low voice. "Be so kind as to excuse it, and don't be angry. He is such a queer fellow, such a queer fellow! Oh dear, oh dear! He is my own brother, but I have never had anything but trouble from him. You know he's. . ."

Moisey Moisevitch crooked his finger by his forehead and went on:

"He is not in his right mind; . . . he's hopeless. And I don't know what I am to do with him! He cares for nobody, he respects nobody, and is afraid of nobody. . . . You know he laughs at everybody, he says silly things, speaks familiarly to anyone. You wouldn't believe it, Varlamov came here one day and Solomon said such things to him that he gave us both a taste of his whip. . . . But why whip me? Was it my fault? God has robbed him of his wits, so it is God's will, and how am I to blame?"

Ten minutes passed and Moisey Moisevitch was still muttering in an undertone and sighing:

"He does not sleep at night, and is always thinking and thinking and thinking, and what he is thinking about God only knows. If you go to him at night he is angry and laughs. He doesn't like me either. . . . And there is nothing he wants! When our father died he left us each six thousand roubles. I bought myself an inn, married, and now I have children; and he burnt all his money in the stove. Such a pity, such a pity! Why burn it? If he didn't want it he could give it to me, but why burn it?"

Suddenly the swing-door creaked and the floor shook under footsteps. Yegorushka felt a draught of cold air, and it seemed to him as though some big black bird had passed by him and had fluttered its wings close in his face. He opened his eyes. . . . His uncle was standing by the sofa with his sack in his hands ready for departure; Father Christopher, holding his broad-brimmed top-hat, was bowing to someone and smiling -- not his usual soft kindly smile, but a respectful forced smile which did not suit his face at all -- while Moisey Moisevitch looked as though his body had been broken into three parts, and he were balancing and doing his utmost not to drop to pieces. Only Solomon stood in the corner with his arms folded, as though nothing had happened, and smiled contemptuously as before.

"Your Excellency must excuse us for not being tidy," moaned Moisey Moisevitch with the agonizingly sweet smile, taking no more notice of Kuzmitchov or Father Christopher, but swaying his whole person so as to avoid dropping to pieces. "We are plain folks, your Excellency."

Yegorushka rubbed his eyes. In the middle of the room there really was standing an Excellency, in the form of a young plump and very beautiful woman in a black dress and a straw hat. Before Yegorushka had time to examine her features the image of the solitary graceful poplar he had seen that day on the hill for some reason came into his mind.

"Has Varlamov been here to-day?" a woman's voice inquired.

"No, your Excellency," said Moisey Moisevitch.

"If you see him to-morrow, ask him to come and see me for a minute."

All at once, quite unexpectedly, Yegorushka saw half an inch from his eyes velvety black eyebrows, big brown eyes, delicate feminine cheeks with dimples, from which smiles seemed radiating all over the face like sunbeams. There was a glorious scent.

"What a pretty boy!" said the lady. "Whose boy is it? Kazimir Mihalovitch, look what a charming fellow! Good heavens, he is asleep!"

And the lady kissed Yegorushka warmly on both cheeks, and he smiled and, thinking he was asleep, shut his eyes. The swing-door squeaked, and there was the sound of hurried footsteps, coming in and going out.

"Yegorushka, Yegorushka!" he heard two bass voices whisper. "Get up; it is time to start."

Somebody, it seemed to be Deniska, set him on his feet and led him by the arm. On the way he half-opened his eyes and once more saw the beautiful lady in the black dress who had kissed him. She was standing in the middle of the room and watched him go out, smiling at him and nodding her head in a friendly way. As he got near the door he saw a handsome, stoutly built, dark man in a bowler hat and in leather gaiters. This must have been the lady's escort.

"Woa!" he heard from the yard.

At the front door Yegorushka saw a splendid new carriage and a pair of black horses. On the box sat a groom in livery, with a long whip in his hands. No one but Solomon came to see the travellers off. His face was tense with a desire to laugh; he looked as though he were waiting impatiently for the visitors to be gone, so that he might laugh at them without restraint.

"The Countess Dranitsky," whispered Father Christopher, clambering into the chaise.

"Yes, Countess Dranitsky," repeated Kuzmitchov, also in a whisper.

The impression made by the arrival of the countess was probably very great, for even Deniska spoke in a whisper, and only ventured to lash his bays and shout when the chaise had driven a quarter of a mile away and nothing could be seen of the inn but a dim light.

IV

Who was this elusive, mysterious Varlamov of whom people talked so much, whom Solomon despised, and whom even the beautiful countess needed? Sitting on the box beside Deniska, Yegorushka, half asleep, thought about this person. He had never seen him. But he had often heard of him and pictured him in his imagination. He knew that Varlamov possessed several tens of thousands of acres of land, about a hundred thousand sheep, and a great deal of money. Of his manner of life and occupation Yegorushka knew nothing, except that he was always "going his rounds in these parts," and he was always being looked for.

At home Yegorushka had heard a great deal of the Countess Dranitsky, too. She, too, had some tens of thousands of acres, a great many sheep, a stud farm and a great deal of money, but she did not "go rounds," but lived at home in a splendid house and grounds, about which Ivan Ivanitch, who had been more than once at the countess's on business, and other acquaintances told many marvellous tales; thus, for instance, they said that in the countess's drawing-room, where the portraits of all the kings of Poland hung on the walls, there was a big table-clock in the form of a rock, on the rock a gold horse with diamond eyes, rearing, and on the horse the figure of a rider also of gold, who brandished his sword to right and to left whenever the clock struck. They said, too, that twice a year the countess used to give a ball, to which the gentry and officials of the whole province were invited, and to which even Varlamov used to come; all the visitors drank tea from silver samovars, ate all sorts of extraordinary things (they had strawberries and raspberries, for instance, in winter at Christmas), and danced to a band which played day and night. . . .

"And how beautiful she is," thought Yegorushka, remembering her face and smile.

Kuzmitchov, too, was probably thinking about the countess. For when the chaise had driven a mile and a half he said:

"But doesn't that Kazimir Mihalovitch plunder her right and left! The year before last when, do you remember, I bought some wool from her, he made over three thousand from my purchase alone."

"That is just what you would expect from a Pole," said Father Christopher.

"And little does it trouble her. Young and foolish, as they say, her head is full of nonsense."

Yegorushka, for some reason, longed to think of nothing but Varlamov and the countess, particularly the latter. His drowsy brain utterly refused ordinary thoughts, was in a cloud and retained only fantastic fairy-tale images, which have the advantage of springing into the brain of themselves without any effort on the part of the thinker, and completely vanishing of themselves at a mere shake of the head; and, indeed, nothing that was around him disposed to ordinary thoughts. On the right there were the dark hills which seemed to be screening something unseen and terrible; on the left the whole sky about the horizon was covered with a crimson glow, and it was hard to tell whether there was a fire somewhere, or whether it was the moon about to rise. As by day the distance could be seen, but its tender lilac tint had gone, quenched by the evening darkness, in which the whole steppe was hidden like Moisey Moisevitch's children under the quilt.

Corncrakes and quails do not call in the July nights, the nightingale does not sing in the woodland marsh, and there is no scent of flowers, but still the steppe is lovely and full of life. As soon as the sun goes down and the darkness enfolds the earth, the day's weariness is forgotten, everything is forgiven, and the steppe breathes a light sigh from its broad bosom. As though because the grass cannot see in the dark that it has grown old, a gay youthful twitter rises up from it, such as is not heard by day; chirruping, twittering, whistling, scratching, the basses, tenors and sopranos of the steppe all mingle in an incessant, monotonous roar of sound in which it is sweet to brood on memories and sorrows. The monotonous twitter soothes to sleep like a lullaby; you drive and feel you are falling asleep, but suddenly there comes the abrupt agitated cry of a wakeful bird, or a vague sound like a voice crying out in wonder "A-ah, a-ah!" and slumber closes one's eyelids again. Or you drive by a little creek where there are bushes and hear the bird, called by the steppe dwellers "the sleeper," call "Asleep, asleep, asleep!" while another laughs or breaks into trills of hysterical weeping -- that is the owl. For whom do they call and who hears them on that plain, God only knows, but there is deep sadness and lamentation in their cry. . . . There is a scent of hay and dry grass and belated flowers, but the scent is heavy, sweetly mawkish and soft.

Everything can be seen through the mist, but it is hard to make out the colours and the outlines of objects. Everything looks different from what it is. You drive on and suddenly see standing before you right in the roadway a dark figure like a monk; it stands motionless, waiting, holding something in its hands. . . . Can it be a robber? The figure comes closer, grows bigger; now it is on a level with the chaise, and you see it is not a man, but a solitary bush or a great stone. Such motionless expectant figures stand on the low hills, hide behind the old barrows, peep out from the high grass, and they all look like human beings and arouse suspicion.

And when the moon rises the night becomes pale and dim. The mist seems to have passed away. The air is transparent, fresh and warm; one can see well in all directions and even distinguish the separate stalks of grass by the wayside. Stones and bits of pots can be seen at a long distance. The suspicious figures like monks look blacker against the light background of the night, and seem more sinister. More and more often in the midst of the monotonous chirruping there comes the sound of the "A-ah, a-ah!" of astonishment troubling the motionless air, and the cry of a sleepless or delirious bird. Broad shadows move across the plain like clouds across the sky, and in the inconceivable distance, if you look long and intently at it, misty monstrous shapes rise up and huddle one against another. . . . It is rather uncanny. One glances at the pale green, star-spangled sky on which there is no cloudlet, no spot, and understands why the warm air is motionless, why nature is on her guard, afraid to stir: she is afraid and reluctant to lose one instant of life. Of the unfathomable depth and infinity of the sky one can only form a conception at sea and on the steppe by night when the moon is shining. It is terribly lonely and caressing; it looks down languid and alluring, and its caressing sweetness makes one giddy.

You drive on for one hour, for a second. . . . You meet upon the way a silent old barrow or a stone figure put up God knows when and by whom; a nightbird floats noiselessly over the earth, and little by little those legends of the steppes, the tales of men you have met, the stories of some old nurse from the steppe, and all the things you have managed to see and treasure in your soul, come back to your mind. And then in the churring of insects, in the sinister figures, in the ancient barrows, in the blue sky, in the moonlight, in the flight of the nightbird, in everything you see and hear, triumphant beauty, youth, the fulness of power, and the passionate thirst for life begin to be apparent; the soul responds to the call of her lovely austere fatherland, and longs to fly over the steppes with the nightbird. And in the triumph of beauty, in the exuberance of happiness you are conscious of yearning and grief, as though the steppe knew she was solitary, knew that her wealth and her inspiration were wasted for the world, not glorified in song, not wanted by anyone; and through the joyful clamour one hears her mournful, hopeless call for singers, singers!

"Woa! Good-evening, Panteley! Is everything all right?"

"First-rate, Ivan Ivanitch!

"Haven't you seen Varlamov, lads?"

"No, we haven't."

Yegorushka woke up and opened his eyes. The chaise had stopped. On the right the train of waggons stretched for a long way ahead on the road, and men were moving to and fro near them. All the waggons being loaded up with great bales of wool looked very high and fat, while the horses looked short-legged and little.

"Well, then, we shall go on to the Molokans'!" Kuzmitchov said aloud. "The Jew told us that Varlamov was putting up for the night at the Molokans'. So good-bye, lads! Good luck to you!"

"Good-bye, Ivan Ivanitch," several voices replied.

"I say, lads," Kuzmitchov cried briskly, "you take my little lad along with you! Why should he go jolting off with us for nothing? You put him on the bales, Panteley, and let him come on slowly, and we shall overtake you. Get down, Yegor! Go on; it's all right. . . ."

Yegorushka got down from the box-seat. Several hands caught him, lifted him high into the air, and he found himself on something big, soft, and rather wet with dew. It seemed to him now as though the sky were quite close and the earth far away.

"Hey, take his little coat!" Deniska shouted from somewhere far below.

His coat and bundle flung up from far below fell close to Yegorushka. Anxious not to think of anything, he quickly put his bundle under his head and covered himself with his coat, and stretching his legs out and shrinking a little from the dew, he laughed with content.

"Sleep, sleep, sleep, . . ." he thought.

"Don't be unkind to him, you devils!" he heard Deniska's voice below.

"Good-bye, lads; good luck to you," shouted Kuzmitchov. "I rely upon you!"

"Don't you be uneasy, Ivan Ivanitch!"

Deniska shouted to the horses, the chaise creaked and started, not along the road, but somewhere off to the side. For two minutes there was silence, as though the waggons were asleep and there was no sound except the clanking of the pails tied on at the back of the chaise as it slowly died away in the distance. Then someone at the head of the waggons shouted:

"Kiruha! Sta-art!"

The foremost of the waggons creaked, then the second, then the third. . . . Yegorushka felt the waggon he was on sway and creak also. The waggons were moving. Yegorushka took a tighter hold of the cord with which the bales were tied on, laughed again with content, shifted the cake in his pocket, and fell asleep just as he did in his bed at home. . . .

When he woke up the sun had risen, it was screened by an ancient barrow, and, trying to shed its light upon the earth, it scattered its beams in all directions and flooded the horizon with gold. It seemed to Yegorushka that it was not in its proper place, as the day before it had risen behind his back, and now it was much more to his left. . . . And the whole landscape was different. There were no hills now, but on all sides, wherever one looked, there stretched the brown cheerless plain; here and there upon it small barrows rose up and rooks flew as they had done the day before. The belfries and huts of some village showed white in the distance ahead; as it was Sunday the Little Russians were at home baking and cooking -- that could be seen by the smoke which rose from every chimney and hung, a dark blue transparent veil, over the village. In between the huts and beyond the church there were blue glimpses of a river, and beyond the river a misty distance. But nothing was so different from yesterday as the road. Something extraordinarily broad, spread out and titanic, stretched over the steppe by way of a road. It was a grey streak well trodden down and covered with dust, like all roads. Its width puzzled Yegorushka and brought thoughts of fairy tales to his mind. Who travelled along that road? Who needed so much space? It was strange and unintelligible. It might have been supposed that giants with immense strides, such as Ilya Muromets and Solovy the Brigand, were still surviving in Russia, and that their gigantic steeds were still alive. Yegorushka, looking at the road, imagined some half a dozen high chariots racing along side by side, like some he used to see in pictures in his Scripture history; these chariots were each drawn by six wild furious horses, and their great wheels raised a cloud of dust to the sky, while the horses were driven by men such as one may see in one's dreams or in imagination brooding over fairy tales. And if those figures had existed, how perfectly in keeping with the steppe and the road they would have been!

Telegraph-poles with two wires on them stretched along the right side of the road to its furthermost limit. Growing smaller and smaller they disappeared near the village behind the huts and green trees, and then again came into sight in the lilac distance in the form of very small thin sticks that looked like pencils stuck into the ground. Hawks, falcons, and crows sat on the wires and looked indifferently at the moving waggons.

Yegorushka was lying in the last of the waggons, and so could see the whole string. There were about twenty waggons, and there was a driver to every three waggons. By the last waggon, the one in which Yegorushka was, there walked an old man with a grey beard, as short and lean as Father Christopher, but with a sunburnt, stern and brooding face. It is very possible that the old man was not stern and not brooding, but his red eyelids and his sharp long nose gave his face a stern frigid expression such as is common with people in the habit of continually thinking of serious things in solitude. Like Father Christopher he was wearing a wide-brimmed top-hat, not like a gentleman's, but made of brown felt, and in shape more like a cone with the top cut off than a real top-hat. Probably from a habit acquired in cold winters, when he must more than once have been nearly frozen as he trudged beside the waggons, he kept slapping his thighs and stamping with his feet as he walked. Noticing that Yegorushka was awake, he looked at him and said, shrugging his shoulders as though from the cold:

"Ah, you are awake, youngster! So you are the son of Ivan Ivanitch?"

"No; his nephew. . . ."

"Nephew of Ivan Ivanitch? Here I have taken off my boots and am hopping along barefoot. My feet are bad; they are swollen, and it's easier without my boots . . . easier, youngster . . . without boots, I mean. . . . So you are his nephew? He is a good man; no harm in him. . . . God give him health. . . . No harm in him . . . I mean Ivan Ivanitch. . . . He has gone to the Molokans'. . . . O Lord, have mercy upon us!"

The old man talked, too, as though it were very cold, pausing and not opening his mouth properly; and he mispronounced the labial consonants, stuttering over them as though his lips were frozen. As he talked to Yegorushka he did not once smile, and he seemed stern.

Two waggons ahead of them there walked a man wearing a long reddish-brown coat, a cap and high boots with sagging bootlegs and carrying a whip in his hand. This was not an old man, only about forty. When he looked round Yegorushka saw a long red face with a scanty goat-beard and a spongy looking swelling under his right eye. Apart from this very ugly swelling, there was another peculiar thing about him which caught the eye at once: in his left hand he carried a whip, while he waved the right as though he were conducting an unseen choir; from time to time he put the whip under his arm, and then he conducted with both hands and hummed something to himself.

The next driver was a long rectilinear figure with extremely sloping shoulders and a back as flat as a board. He held himself as stiffly erect as though he were marching or had swallowed a yard measure. His hands did not swing as he walked, but hung down as if they were straight sticks, and he strode along in a wooden way, after the manner of toy soldiers, almost without bending his knees, and trying to take as long steps as possible. While the old man or the owner of the spongy swelling were taking two steps he succeeded in taking only one, and so it seemed as though he were walking more slowly than any of them, and would drop behind. His face was tied up in a rag, and on his head something stuck up that looked like a monk's peaked cap; he was dressed in a short Little Russian coat, with full dark blue trousers and bark shoes.

Yegorushka did not even distinguish those that were farther on. He lay on his stomach, picked a little hole in the bale, and, having nothing better to do, began twisting the wool into a thread. The old man trudging along below him turned out not to be so stern as one might have supposed from his face. Having begun a conversation, he did not let it drop.

"Where are you going?" he asked, stamping with his feet.

"To school," answered Yegorushka.

"To school? Aha! . . . Well, may the Queen of Heaven help you. Yes. One brain is good, but two are better. To one man God gives one brain, to another two brains, and to another three. . . . To another three, that is true. . . . One brain you are born with, one you get from learning, and a third with a good life. So you see, my lad, it is a good thing if a man has three brains. Living is easier for him, and, what's more, dying is, too. Dying is, too. . . . And we shall all die for sure."

The old man scratched his forehead, glanced upwards at Yegorushka with his red eyes, and went on:

"Maxim Nikolaitch, the gentleman from Slavyanoserbsk, brought a little lad to school, too, last year. I don't know how he is getting on there in studying the sciences, but he was a nice good little lad. . . . God give them help, they are nice gentlemen. Yes, he, too, brought his boy to school. . . . In Slavyanoserbsk there is no establishment, I suppose, for study. No. . . . But it is a nice town. . . . There's an ordinary school for simple folks, but for the higher studies there is nothing. No, that's true. What's your name? . . ."

"Yegorushka."

"Yegory, then. . . . The holy martyr Yegory, the Bearer of Victory, whose day is the twenty-third of April. And my christian name is Panteley, . . . Panteley Zaharov Holodov. . . . We are Holodovs. . . . I am a native of -- maybe you've heard of it -- Tim in the province of Kursk. My brothers are artisans and work at trades in the town, but I am a peasant. . . . I have remained a peasant. Seven years ago I went there -- home, I mean. I went to the village and to the town. . . . To Tim, I mean. Then, thank God, they were all alive and well; . . . but now I don't know. . . . Maybe some of them are dead. . . . And it's time they did die, for some of them are older than I am. Death is all right; it is good so long, of course, as one does not die without repentance. There is no worse evil than an impenitent death; an impenitent death is a joy to the devil. And if you want to die penitent, so that you may not be forbidden to enter the mansions of the Lord, pray to the holy martyr Varvara. She is the intercessor. She is, that's the truth. . . . For God has given her such a place in the heavens that everyone has the right to pray to her for penitence."

Panteley went on muttering, and apparently did not trouble whether Yegorushka heard him or not. He talked listlessly, mumbling to himself, without raising or dropping his voice, but succeeded in telling him a great deal in a short time. All he said was made up of fragments that had very little connection with one another, and quite uninteresting for Yegorushka. Possibly he talked only in order to reckon over his thoughts aloud after the night spent in silence, in order to see if they were all there. After talking of repentance, he spoke about a certain Maxim Nikolaitch from Slavyanoserbsk.

"Yes, he took his little lad; . . . he took him, that's true . . ."

One of the waggoners walking in front darted from his place, ran to one side and began lashing on the ground with his whip. He was a stalwart, broad-shouldered man of thirty, with curly flaxen hair and a look of great health and vigour. Judging from the movements of his shoulders and the whip, and the eagerness expressed in his attitude, he was beating something alive. Another waggoner, a short stubby little man with a bushy black beard, wearing a waistcoat and. a shirt outside his trousers, ran up to him. The latter broke into a deep guffaw of laughter and coughing and said: "I say, lads, Dymov has killed a snake!"

There are people whose intelligence can be gauged at once by their voice and laughter. The man with the black beard belonged to that class of fortunate individuals; impenetrable stupidity could be felt in his voice and laugh. The flaxen-headed Dymov had finished, and lifting from the ground with his whip something like a cord, flung it with a laugh into the cart.

"That's not a viper; it's a grass snake!" shouted someone.

The man with the wooden gait and the bandage round his face strode up quickly to the dead snake, glanced at it and flung up his stick-like arms.

"You jail-bird!" he cried in a hollow wailing voice. "What have you killed a grass snake for? What had he done to you, you damned brute? Look, he has killed a grass snake; how would you like to be treated so?"

"Grass snakes ought not to be killed, that's true," Panteley muttered placidly, "they ought not. . . They are not vipers; though it looks like a snake, it is a gentle, innocent creature. . . . It's friendly to man, the grass snake is."

Dymov and the man with the black beard were probably ashamed, for they laughed loudly, and not answering, slouched lazily back to their waggons. When the hindmost waggon was level with the spot where the dead snake lay, the man with his face tied up standing over it turned to Panteley and asked in a tearful voice:

"Grandfather, what did he want to kill the grass snake for?"

His eyes, as Yegorushka saw now, were small and dingy looking; his face was grey, sickly and looked somehow dingy too while his chin was red and seemed very much swollen.

"Grandfather, what did he kill it for?" he repeated, striding along beside Panteley.

"A stupid fellow. His hands itch to kill, and that is why he does it," answered the old man; "but he oughtn't to kill a grass snake, that's true. . . . Dymov is a ruffian, we all know, he kills everything he comes across, and Kiruha did not interfere. He ought to have taken its part, but instead of that, he goes off into 'Ha-ha-ha!' and 'Ho-ho-ho!' . . . But don't be angry, Vassya. . . . Why be angry? They've killed it -- well, never mind them. Dymov is a ruffian and Kiruha acted from foolishness -- never mind. . . . They are foolish people without understanding -- but there, don't mind them. Emelyan here never touches what he shouldn't; he never does;. . . that is true, . . . because he is a man of education, while they are stupid. . . . Emelyan, he doesn't touch things."

The waggoner in the reddish-brown coat and the spongy swelling on his face, who was conducting an unseen choir, stopped. Hearing his name, and waiting till Panteley and Vassya came up to him, he walked beside them.

"What are you talking about?" he asked in a husky muffled voice.

"Why, Vassya here is angry," said Panteley. "So I have been saying things to him to stop his being angry. . . . Oh, how my swollen feet hurt! Oh, oh! They are more inflamed than ever for Sunday, God's holy day!"

"It's from walking," observed Vassya.

"No, lad, no. It's not from walking. When I walk it seems easier; when I lie down and get warm, . . . it's deadly. Walking is easier for me."

Emelyan, in his reddish-brown coat, walked between Panteley and Vassya and waved his arms, as though they were going to sing. After waving them a little while he dropped them, and croaked out hopelessly:

"I have no voice. It's a real misfortune. All last night and this morning I have been haunted by the trio 'Lord, have Mercy' that we sang at the wedding at Marionovsky's. It's in my head and in my throat. It seems as though I could sing it, but I can't; I have no voice."

He paused for a minute, thinking, then went on:

"For fifteen years I was in the choir. In all the Lugansky works there was, maybe, no one with a voice like mine. But, confound it, I bathed two years ago in the Donets, and I can't get a single note true ever since. I took cold in my throat. And without a voice I am like a workman without hands."

"That's true," Panteley agreed.

"I think of myself as a ruined man and nothing more."

At that moment Vassya chanced to catch sight of Yegorushka. His eyes grew moist and smaller than ever.

"There's a little gentleman driving with us," and he covered his nose with his sleeve as though he were bashful. "What a grand driver! Stay with us and you shall drive the waggons and sell wool."

The incongruity of one person being at once a little gentleman and a waggon driver seemed to strike him as very queer and funny, for he burst into a loud guffaw, and went on enlarging upon the idea. Emelyan glanced upwards at Yegorushka, too, but coldly and cursorily. He was absorbed in his own thoughts, and had it not been for Vassya, would not have noticed Yegorushka's presence. Before five minutes had passed he was waving his arms again, then describing to his companions the beauties of the wedding anthem, "Lord, have Mercy," which he had remembered in the night. He put the whip under his arm and waved both hands.

A mile from the village the waggons stopped by a well with a crane. Letting his pail down into the well, black-bearded Kiruha lay on his stomach on the framework and thrust his shaggy head, his shoulders, and part of his chest into the black hole, so that Yegorushka could see nothing but his short legs, which scarcely touched the ground. Seeing the reflection of his head far down at the bottom of the well, he was delighted and went off into his deep bass stupid laugh, and the echo from the well answered him. When he got up his neck and face were as red as beetroot. The first to run up and drink was Dymov. He drank laughing, often turning from the pail to tell Kiruha something funny, then he turned round, and uttered aloud, to be heard all over the steppe, five very bad words. Yegorushka did not understand the meaning of such words, but he knew very well they were bad words. He knew the repulsion his friends and relations silently felt for such words. He himself, without knowing why, shared that feeling and was accustomed to think that only drunk and disorderly people enjoy the privilege of uttering such words aloud. He remembered the murder of the grass snake, listened to Dymov's laughter, and felt something like hatred for the man. And as ill-luck would have it, Dymov at that moment caught sight of Yegorushka, who had climbed down from the waggon and gone up to the well. He laughed aloud and shouted:

"I say, lads, the old man has been brought to bed of a boy in the night!"

Kiruha laughed his bass laugh till he coughed. Someone else laughed too, while Yegorushka crimsoned and made up his mind finally that Dymov was a very wicked man.

With his curly flaxen head, with his shirt opened on his chest and no hat on, Dymov looked handsome and exceptionally strong; in every movement he made one could see the reckless dare-devil and athlete, knowing his value. He shrugged his shoulders, put his arms akimbo, talked and laughed louder than any of the rest, and looked as though he were going to lift up something very heavy with one hand and astonish the whole world by doing so. His mischievous mocking eyes glided over the road, the waggons, and the sky without resting on anything, and seemed looking for someone to kill, just as a pastime, and something to laugh at. Evidently he was afraid of no one, would stick at nothing, and most likely was not in the least interested in Yegorushka's opinion of him. . . . Yegorushka meanwhile hated his flaxen head, his clear face, and his strength with his whole heart, listened with fear and loathing to his laughter, and kept thinking what word of abuse he could pay him out with.

Panteley, too, went up to the pail. He took out of his pocket a little green glass of an ikon lamp, wiped it with a rag, filled it from the pail and drank from it, then filled it again, wrapped the little glass in the rag, and then put it back into his pocket.

"Grandfather, why do you drink out of a lamp?" Yegorushka asked him, surprised.

"One man drinks out of a pail and another out of a lamp," the old man answered evasively. "Every man to his own taste. . . . You drink out of the pail -- well, drink, and may it do you good. . . ."

"You darling, you beauty!" Vassya said suddenly, in a caressing, plaintive voice. "You darling!"

His eyes were fixed on the distance; they were moist and smiling, and his face wore the same expression as when he had looked at Yegorushka.

"Who is it you are talking to?" asked Kiruha.

"A darling fox, . . . lying on her back, playing like a dog."

Everyone began staring into the distance, looking for the fox, but no one could see it, only Vassya with his grey muddy-looking eyes, and he was enchanted by it. His sight was extraordinarily keen, as Yegorushka learnt afterwards. He was so long-sighted that the brown steppe was for him always full of life and interest. He had only to look into the distance to see a fox, a hare, a bustard, or some other animal keeping at a distance from men. There was nothing strange in seeing a hare running away or a flying bustard -- everyone crossing the steppes could see them; but it was not vouchsafed to everyone to see wild animals in their own haunts when they were not running nor hiding, nor looking about them in alarm. Yet Vassya saw foxes playing, hares washing themselves with their paws, bustards preening their wings and hammering out their hollow nests. Thanks to this keenness of sight, Vassya had, besides the world seen by everyone, another world of his own, accessible to no one else, and probably a very beautiful one, for when he saw something and was in raptures over it it was impossible not to envy him.

When the waggons set off again, the church bells were ringing for service.

V

The train of waggons drew up on the bank of a river on one side of a village. The sun was blazing, as it had been the day before; the air was stagnant and depressing. There were a few willows on the bank, but the shade from them did not fall on the earth, but on the water, where it was wasted; even in the shade under the waggon it was stifling and wearisome. The water, blue from the reflection of the sky in it, was alluring.

Styopka, a waggoner whom Yegorushka noticed now for the first time, a Little Russian lad of eighteen, in a long shirt without a belt, and full trousers that flapped like flags as he walked, undressed quickly, ran along the steep bank and plunged into the water. He dived three times, then swam on his back and shut his eyes in his delight. His face was smiling and wrinkled up as though he were being tickled, hurt and amused.

On a hot day when there is nowhere to escape from the sultry, stifling heat, the splash of water and the loud breathing of a man bathing sounds like good music to the ear. Dymov and Kiruha, looking at Styopka, undressed quickly and one after the other, laughing loudly in eager anticipation of their enjoyment, dropped into the water, and the quiet, modest little river resounded with snorting and splashing and shouting. Kiruha coughed, laughed and shouted as though they were trying to drown him, while Dymov chased him and tried to catch him by the leg.

"Ha-ha-ha!" he shouted. "Catch him! Hold him!"

Kiruha laughed and enjoyed himself, but his expression was the same as it had been on dry land, stupid, with a look of astonishment on it as though someone had, unnoticed, stolen up behind him and hit him on the head with the butt-end of an axe. Yegorushka undressed, too, but did not let himself down by the bank, but took a run and a flying leap from the height of about ten feet. Describing an arc in the air, he fell into the water, sank deep, but did not reach the bottom; some force, cold and pleasant to the touch, seemed to hold him up and bring him back to the surface. He popped out and, snorting and blowing bubbles, opened his eyes; but the sun was reflected in the water quite close to his face. At first blinding spots of light, then rainbow colours and dark patches, flitted before his eyes. He made haste to dive again, opened his eyes in the water and saw something cloudy-green like a sky on a moonlight night. Again the same force would not let him touch the bottom and stay in the coolness, but lifted him to the surface. He popped out and heaved a sigh so deep that he had a feeling of space and freshness, not only in his chest, but in his stomach. Then, to get from the water everything he possibly could get, he allowed himself every luxury; he lay on his back and basked, splashed, frolicked, swam on his face, on his side, on his back and standing up -- just as he pleased till he was exhausted. The other bank was thickly overgrown with reeds; it was golden in the sun, and the flowers of the reeds hung drooping to the water in lovely tassels. In one place the reeds were shaking and nodding, with their flowers rustling -- Styopka and Kiruha were hunting crayfish.

"A crayfish, look, lads! A crayfish!" Kiruha cried triumphantly and actually showed a crayfish.

Yegorushka swam up to the reeds, dived, and began fumbling among their roots. Burrowing in the slimy, liquid mud, he felt something sharp and unpleasant -- perhaps it really was a crayfish. But at that minute someone seized him by the leg and pulled him to the surface. Spluttering and coughing, Yegorushka opened his eyes and saw before him the wet grinning face of the dare-devil Dymov. The impudent fellow was breathing hard, and from a look in his eyes he seemed inclined for further mischief. He held Yegorushka tight by the leg, and was lifting his hand to take hold of his neck. But Yegorushka tore himself away with repulsion and terror, as though disgusted at being touched and afraid that the bully would drown him, and said:

"Fool! I'll punch you in the face."

Feeling that this was not sufficient to express his hatred, he thought a minute and added:

"You blackguard! You son of a bitch!"

But Dymov, as though nothing were the matter, took no further notice of Yegorushka, but swam off to Kiruha, shouting:

"Ha-ha-ha! Let us catch fish! Mates, let us catch fish."

"To be sure," Kiruha agreed; "there must be a lot of fish here."

"Styopka, run to the village and ask the peasants for a net!

"They won't give it to me."

"They will, you ask them. Tell them that they should give it to us for Christ's sake, because we are just the same as pilgrims."

"That's true."

Styopka clambered out of the water, dressed quickly, and without a cap on he ran, his full trousers flapping, to the village. The water lost all its charm for Yegorushka after his encounter with Dymov. He got out and began dressing. Panteley and Vassya were sitting on the steep bank, with their legs hanging down, looking at the bathers. Emelyan was standing naked, up to his knees in the water, holding on to the grass with one hand to prevent himself from falling while the other stroked his body. With his bony shoulder-blades, with the swelling under his eye, bending down and evidently afraid of the water, he made a ludicrous figure. His face was grave and severe. He looked angrily at the water, as though he were just going to upbraid it for having given him cold in the Donets and robbed him of his voice.

"And why don't you bathe?" Yegorushka asked Vassya.

"Oh, I don't care for it, . . ." answered Vassya.

"How is it your chin is swollen?"

"It's bad. . . . I used to work at the match factory, little sir. . . . The doctor used to say that it would make my jaw rot. The air is not healthy there. There were three chaps beside me who had their jaws swollen, and with one of them it rotted away altogether."

Styopka soon came back with the net. Dymov and Kiruha were already turning blue and getting hoarse by being so long in the water, but they set about fishing eagerly. First they went to a deep place beside the reeds; there Dymov was up to his neck, while the water went over squat Kiruha's head. The latter spluttered and blew bubbles, while Dymov stumbling on the prickly roots, fell over and got caught in the net; both flopped about in the water, and made a noise, and nothing but mischief came of their fishing.

"It's deep," croaked Kiruha. "You won't catch anything."

"Don't tug, you devil!" shouted Dymov trying to put the net in the proper position. "Hold it up."

"You won't catch anything here," Panteley shouted from the bank. "You are only frightening the fish, you stupids! Go more to the left! It's shallower there!"

Once a big fish gleamed above the net; they all drew a breath, and Dymov struck the place where it had vanished with his fist, and his face expressed vexation.

"Ugh!" cried Panteley, and he stamped his foot. "You've let the perch slip! It's gone!"

Moving more to the left, Dymov and Kiruha picked out a shallower place, and then fishing began in earnest. They had wandered off some hundred paces from the waggons; they could be seen silently trying to go as deep as they could and as near the reeds, moving their legs a little at a time, drawing out the nets, beating the water with their fists to drive them towards the nets. From the reeds they got to the further bank; they drew the net out, then, with a disappointed air, lifting their knees high as they walked, went back into the reeds. They were talking about something, but what it was no one could hear. The sun was scorching their backs, the flies were stinging them, and their bodies had turned from purple to crimson. Styopka was walking after them with a pail in his hands; he had tucked his shirt right up under his armpits, and was holding it up by the hem with his teeth. After every successful catch he lifted up some fish, and letting it shine in the sun, shouted:

"Look at this perch! We've five like that!"

Every time Dymov, Kiruha and Styopka pulled out the net they could be seen fumbling about in the mud in it, putting some things into the pail and throwing other things away; sometimes they passed something that was in the net from hand to hand, examined it inquisitively, then threw that, too, away.

"What is it?" they shouted to them from the bank.

Styopka made some answer, but it was hard to make out his words. Then he climbed out of the water and, holding the pail in both hands, forgetting to let his shirt drop, ran to the waggons.

"It's full! " he shouted, breathing hard. "Give us another!"

Yegorushka looked into the pail: it was full. A young pike poked its ugly nose out of the water, and there were swarms of crayfish and little fish round about it. Yegorushka put his hand down to the bottom and stirred up the water; the pike vanished under the crayfish and a perch and a tench swam to the surface instead of it. Vassya, too, looked into the pail. His eyes grew moist and his face looked as caressing as before when he saw the fox. He took something out of the pail, put it to his mouth and began chewing it.

"Mates," said Styopka in amazement, "Vassya is eating a live gudgeon! Phoo!"

"It's not a gudgeon, but a minnow," Vassya answered calmly, still munching.

He took a fish's tail out of his mouth, looked at it caressingly, and put it back again. While he was chewing and crunching with his teeth it seemed to Yegorushka that he saw before him something not human. Vassya's swollen chin, his lustreless eyes, his extraordinary sharp sight, the fish's tail in his mouth, and the caressing friendliness with which he crunched the gudgeon made him like an animal.

Yegorushka felt dreary beside him. And the fishing was over, too. He walked about beside the waggons, thought a little, and, feeling bored, strolled off to the village.

Not long afterwards he was standing in the church, and with his forehead leaning on somebody's back, listened to the singing of the choir. The service was drawing to a close. Yegorushka did not understand church singing and did not care for it. He listened a little, yawned, and began looking at the backs and heads before him. In one head, red and wet from his recent bathe, he recognized Emelyan. The back of his head had been cropped in a straight line higher than is usual; the hair in front had been cut unbecomingly high, and Emelyan's ears stood out like two dock leaves, and seemed to feel themselves out of place. Looking at the back of his head and his ears, Yegorushka, for some reason, thought that Emelyan was probably very unhappy. He remembered the way he conducted with his hands, his husky voice, his timid air when he was bathing, and felt intense pity for him. He longed to say something friendly to him.

"I am here, too," he said, putting out his hand.

People who sing tenor or bass in the choir, especially those who have at any time in their lives conducted, are accustomed to look with a stern and unfriendly air at boys. They do not give up this habit, even when they leave off being in a choir. Turning to Yegorushka, Emelyan looked at him from under his brows and said:

"Don't play in church!"

Then Yegorushka moved forwards nearer to the ikon-stand. Here he saw interesting people. On the right side, in front of everyone, a lady and a gentleman were standing on a carpet. There were chairs behind them. The gentleman was wearing newly ironed shantung trousers; he stood as motionless as a soldier saluting, and held high his bluish shaven chin. There was a very great air of dignity in his stand-up collar, in his blue chin, in his small bald patch and his cane. His neck was so strained from excess of dignity, and his chin was drawn up so tensely, that it looked as though his head were ready to fly off and soar upwards any minute. The lady, who was stout and elderly and wore a white silk shawl, held her head on one side and looked as though she had done someone a favour, and wanted to say: "Oh, don't trouble yourself to thank me; I don't like it. . . ." A thick wall of Little Russian heads stood all round the carpet.

Yegorushka went up to the ikon-stand and began kissing the local ikons. Before each image he slowly bowed down to the ground, without getting up, looked round at the congregation, then got up and kissed the ikon. The contact of his forehead with the cold floor afforded him great satisfaction. When the beadle came from the altar with a pair of long snuffers to put out the candles, Yegorushka jumped up quickly from the floor and ran up to him.

"Have they given out the holy bread?" he asked.

"There is none; there is none," the beadle muttered gruffly. "It is no use your. . ."

The service was over; Yegorushka walked out of the church in a leisurely way, and began strolling about the market-place. He had seen a good many villages, market-places, and peasants in his time, and everything that met his eyes was entirely without interest for him. At a loss for something to do, he went into a shop over the door of which hung a wide strip of red cotton. The shop consisted of two roomy, badly lighted parts; in one half they sold drapery and groceries, in the other there were tubs of tar, and there were horse-collars hanging from the ceiling; from both came the savoury smell of leather and tar. The floor of the shop had been watered; the man who watered it must have been a very whimsical and original person, for it was sprinkled in patterns and mysterious symbols. The shopkeeper, an overfed-looking man with a broad face and round beard, apparently a Great Russian, was standing, leaning his person over the counter. He was nibbling a piece of sugar as he drank his tea, and heaved a deep sigh at every sip. His face expressed complete indifference, but each sigh seemed to be saying:

"Just wait a minute; I will give it you."

"Give me a farthing's worth of sunflower seeds," Yegorushka said, addressing him.

The shopkeeper raised his eyebrows, came out from behind the counter, and poured a farthing's worth of sunflower seeds into Yegorushka's pocket, using an empty pomatum pot as a measure. Yegorushka did not want to go away. He spent a long time in examining the box of cakes, thought a little and asked, pointing to some little cakes covered with the mildew of age:

"How much are these cakes?"

"Two for a farthing."

Yegorushka took out of his pocket the cake given him the day before by the Jewess, and asked him:

"And how much do you charge for cakes like this?"

The shopman took the cake in his hands, looked at it from all sides, and raised one eyebrow.

"Like that?" he asked.

Then he raised the other eyebrow, thought a minute, and answered:

"Two for three farthings. . . ."

A silence followed.

"Whose boy are you?" the shopman asked, pouring himself out some tea from a red copper teapot.

"The nephew of Ivan Ivanitch."

"There are all sorts of Ivan Ivanitchs," the shopkeeper sighed. He looked over Yegorushka's head towards the door, paused a minute and asked:

"Would you like some tea?"

"Please. . . ." Yegorushka assented not very readily, though he felt an intense longing for his usual morning tea.

The shopkeeper poured him out a glass and gave him with it a bit of sugar that looked as though it had been nibbled. Yegorushka sat down on the folding chair and began drinking it. He wanted to ask the price of a pound of sugar almonds, and had just broached the subject when a customer walked in, and the shopkeeper, leaving his glass of tea, attended to his business. He led the customer into the other half, where there was a smell of tar, and was there a long time discussing something with him. The customer, a man apparently very obstinate and pig-headed, was continually shaking his head to signify his disapproval, and retreating towards the door. The shopkeeper tried to persuade him of something and began pouring some oats into a big sack for him.

"Do you call those oats?" the customer said gloomily. "Those are not oats, but chaff. It's a mockery to give that to the hens; enough to make the hens laugh. . . . No, I will go to Bondarenko."

When Yegorushka went back to the river a small camp fire was smoking on the bank. The waggoners were cooking their dinner. Styopka was standing in the smoke, stirring the cauldron with a big notched spoon. A little on one side Kiruha and Vassya, with eyes reddened from the smoke, were sitting cleaning the fish. Before them lay the net covered with slime and water weeds, and on it lay gleaming fish and crawling crayfish.

Emelyan, who had not long been back from the church, was sitting beside Panteley, waving his arm and humming just audibly in a husky voice: "To Thee we sing. . . ." Dymov was moving about by the horses.

When they had finished cleaning them, Kiruha and Vassya put the fish and the living crayfish together in the pail, rinsed them, and from the pail poured them all into the boiling water.

"Shall I put in some fat?" asked Styopka, skimming off the froth.

"No need. The fish will make its own gravy," answered Kiruha.

Before taking the cauldron off the fire Styopka scattered into the water three big handfuls of millet and a spoonful of salt; finally he tried it, smacked his lips, licked the spoon, and gave a self-satisfied grunt, which meant that the grain was done.

All except Panteley sat down near the cauldron and set to work with their spoons.

"You there! Give the little lad a spoon!" Panteley observed sternly. "I dare say he is hungry too!"

"Ours is peasant fare," sighed Kiruha.

"Peasant fare is welcome, too, when one is hungry."

They gave Yegorushka a spoon. He began eating, not sitting, but standing close to the cauldron and looking down into it as in a hole. The grain smelt of fish and fish-scales were mixed up with the millet. The crayfish could not be hooked out with a spoon, and the men simply picked them out of the cauldron with their hands; Vassya did so particularly freely, and wetted his sleeves as well as his hands in the mess. But yet the stew seemed to Yegorushka very nice, and reminded him of the crayfish soup which his mother used to make at home on fast-days. Panteley was sitting apart munching bread.

"Grandfather, why aren't you eating?" Emelyan asked him.

"I don't eat crayfish. . . . Nasty things," the old man said, and turned away with disgust.

While they were eating they all talked. From this conversation Yegorushka gathered that all his new acquaintances, in spite of the differences of their ages and their characters, had one point in common which made them all alike: they were all people with a splendid past and a very poor present. Of their past they all -- everyone of them -- spoke with enthusiasm; their attitude to the present was almost one of contempt. The Russian loves recalling life, but he does not love living. Yegorushka did not yet know that, and before the stew had been all eaten he firmly believed that the men sitting round the cauldron were the injured victims of fate. Panteley told them that in the past, before there were railways, he used to go with trains of waggons to Moscow and to Nizhni, and used to earn so much that he did not know what to do with his money; and what merchants there used to be in those days! what fish! how cheap everything was! Now the roads were shorter, the merchants were stingier, the peasants were poorer, the bread was dearer, everything had shrunk and was on a smaller scale. Emelyan told them that in old days he had been in the choir in the Lugansky works, and that he had a remarkable voice and read music splendidly, while now he had become a peasant and lived on the charity of his brother, who sent him out with his horses and took half his earnings. Vassya had once worked in a match factory; Kiruha had been a coachman in a good family, and had been reckoned the smartest driver of a three-in-hand in the whole district. Dymov, the son of a well-to-do peasant, lived at ease, enjoyed himself and had known no trouble till he was twenty, when his stern harsh father, anxious to train him to work, and afraid he would be spoiled at home, had sent him to a carrier's to work as a hired labourer. Styopka was the only one who said nothing, but from his beardless face it was evident that his life had been a much better one in the past.

Thinking of his father, Dymov frowned and left off eating. Sullenly from under his brows he looked round at his companions and his eye rested upon Yegorushka.

"You heathen, take off your cap," he said rudely. "You can't eat with your cap on, and you a gentleman too!"

Yegorushka took off his hat and did not say a word, but the stew lost all savour for him, and he did not hear Panteley and Vassya intervening on his behalf. A feeling of anger with the insulting fellow was rankling oppressively in his breast, and he made up his mind that he would do him some injury, whatever it cost him.

After dinner everyone sauntered to the waggons and lay down in the shade.

"Are we going to start soon, grandfather?" Yegorushka asked Panteley.

"In God's good time we shall set off. There's no starting yet; it is too hot. . . . O Lord, Thy will be done. Holy Mother. . . Lie down, little lad."

Soon there was a sound of snoring from under the waggons. Yegorushka meant to go back to the village, but on consideration, yawned and lay down by the old man.

VI

The waggons remained by the river the whole day, and set off again when the sun was setting.

Yegorushka was lying on the bales again; the waggon creaked softly and swayed from side to side. Panteley walked below, stamping his feet, slapping himself on his thighs and muttering. The air was full of the churring music of the steppes, as it had been the day before.

Yegorushka lay on his back, and, putting his hands under his head, gazed upwards at the sky. He watched the glow of sunset kindle, then fade away; guardian angels covering the horizon with their gold wings disposed themselves to slumber. The day had passed peacefully; the quiet peaceful night had come, and they could stay tranquilly at home in heaven. . . . Yegorushka saw the sky by degrees grow dark and the mist fall over the earth -- saw the stars light up, one after the other. . . .

When you gaze a long while fixedly at the deep sky thoughts and feelings for some reason merge in a sense of loneliness. One begins to feel hopelessly solitary, and everything one used to look upon as near and akin becomes infinitely remote and valueless; the stars that have looked down from the sky thousands of years already, the mists and the incomprehensible sky itself, indifferent to the brief life of man, oppress the soul with their silence when one is left face to face with them and tries to grasp their significance. One is reminded of the solitude awaiting each one of us in the grave, and the reality of life seems awful . . . full of despair. . . .

Yegorushka thought of his grandmother, who was sleeping now under the cherry-trees in the cemetery. He remembered how she lay in her coffin with pennies on her eyes, how afterwards she was shut in and let down into the grave; he even recalled the hollow sound of the clods of earth on the coffin lid. . . . He pictured his granny in the dark and narrow coffin, helpless and deserted by everyone. His imagination pictured his granny suddenly awakening, not understanding where she was, knocking upon the lid and calling for help, and in the end swooning with horror and dying again. He imagined his mother dead, Father Christopher, Countess Dranitsky, Solomon. But however much he tried to imagine himself in the dark tomb, far from home, outcast, helpless and dead, he could not succeed; for himself personally he could not admit the possibility of death, and felt that he would never die. . . .

Panteley, for whom death could not be far away, walked below and went on reckoning up his thoughts.

"All right. . . . Nice gentlefolk, . . ." he muttered. "Took his little lad to school -- but how he is doing now I haven't heard say -- in Slavyanoserbsk. I say there is no establishment for teaching them to be very clever. . . . No, that's true -- a nice little lad, no harm in him. . . . He'll grow up and be a help to his father. . . . You, Yegory, are little now, but you'll grow big and will keep your father and mother. . . . So it is ordained of God, 'Honour your father and your mother.' . . . I had children myself, but they were burnt. . . . My wife was burnt and my children, . . . that's true. . . . The hut caught fire on the night of Epiphany. . . . I was not at home, I was driving in Oryol. In Oryol. . . . Marya dashed out into the street, but remembering that the children were asleep in the hut, ran back and was burnt with her children. . . . Next day they found nothing but bones."

About midnight Yegorushka and the waggoners were again sitting round a small camp fire. While the dry twigs and stems were burning up, Kiruha and Vassya went off somewhere to get water from a creek; they vanished into the darkness, but could be heard all the time talking and clinking their pails; so the creek was not far away. The light from the fire lay a great flickering patch on the earth; though the moon was bright, yet everything seemed impenetrably black beyond that red patch. The light was in the waggoners' eyes, and they saw only part of the great road; almost unseen in the darkness the waggons with the bales and the horses looked like a mountain of undefined shape. Twenty paces from the camp fire at the edge of the road stood a wooden cross that had fallen aslant. Before the camp fire had been lighted, when he could still see things at a distance, Yegorushka had noticed that there was a similar old slanting cross on the other side of the great road.

Coming back with the water, Kiruha and Vassya filled the cauldron and fixed it over the fire. Styopka, with the notched spoon in his hand, took his place in the smoke by the cauldron, gazing dreamily into the water for the scum to rise. Panteley and Emelyan were sitting side by side in silence, brooding over something. Dymov was lying on his stomach, with his head propped on his fists, looking into the fire. . . . Styopka's shadow was dancing over him, so that his handsome face was at one minute covered with darkness, at the next lighted up. . . . Kiruha and Vassya were wandering about at a little distance gathering dry grass and bark for the fire. Yegorushka, with his hands in his pockets, was standing by Panteley, watching how the fire devoured the grass.

All were resting, musing on something, and they glanced cursorily at the cross over which patches of red light were dancing. There is something melancholy, pensive, and extremely poetical about a solitary tomb; one feels its silence, and the silence gives one the sense of the presence of the soul of the unknown man who lies under the cross. Is that soul at peace on the steppe? Does it grieve in the moonlight? Near the tomb the steppe seems melancholy, dreary and mournful; the grass seems more sorrowful, and one fancies the grasshoppers chirrup less freely, and there is no passer-by who would not remember that lonely soul and keep looking back at the tomb, till it was left far behind and hidden in the mists. . . .

"Grandfather, what is that cross for?" asked Yegorushka.

Panteley looked at the cross and then at Dymov and asked:

"Nikola, isn't this the place where the mowers killed the merchants?"

Dymov not very readily raised himself on his elbow, looked at the road and said:

"Yes, it is. . . ."

A silence followed. Kiruha broke up some dry stalks, crushed them up together and thrust them under the cauldron. The fire flared up brightly; Styopka was enveloped in black smoke, and the shadow cast by the cross danced along the road in the dusk beside the waggons.

"Yes, they were killed," Dymov said reluctantly. "Two merchants, father and son, were travelling, selling holy images. They put up in the inn not far from here that is now kept by Ignat Fomin. The old man had a drop too much, and began boasting that he had a lot of money with him. We all know merchants are a boastful set, God preserve us. . . . They can't resist showing off before the likes of us. And at the time some mowers were staying the night at the inn. So they overheard what the merchants said and took note of it."

"O Lord! . . . Holy Mother!" sighed Panteley.

"Next day, as soon as it was light," Dymov went on, "the merchants were preparing to set off and the mowers tried to join them. 'Let us go together, your worships. It will be more cheerful and there will be less danger, for this is an out-of-the-way place. . . .' The merchants had to travel at a walking pace to avoid breaking the images, and that just suited the mowers. . . ."

Dymov rose into a kneeling position and stretched.

"Yes," he went on, yawning. "Everything went all right till they reached this spot, and then the mowers let fly at them with their scythes. The son, he was a fine young fellow, snatched the scythe from one of them, and he used it, too. . . . Well, of course, they got the best of it because there were eight of them. They hacked at the merchants so that there was not a sound place left on their bodies; when they had finished they dragged both of them off the road, the father to one side and the son to the other. Opposite that cross there is another cross on this side. . . . Whether it is still standing, I don't know. . . . I can't see from here. . . ."

"It is," said Kiruha.

"They say they did not find much money afterwards."

"No," Panteley confirmed; "they only found a hundred roubles."

"And three of them died afterwards, for the merchant had cut them badly with the scythe, too. They died from loss of blood. One had his hand cut off, so that they say he ran three miles without his hand, and they found him on a mound close to Kurikovo. He was squatting on his heels, with his head on his knees, as though he were lost in thought, but when they looked at him there was no life in him and he was dead. . . ."

"They found him by the track of blood," said Panteley.

Everyone looked at the cross, and again there was a hush. From somewhere, most likely from the creek, floated the mournful cry of the bird: "Sleep! sleep! sleep!"

"There are a great many wicked people in the world," said Emelyan.

"A great many," assented Panteley, and he moved up closer to the fire as though he were frightened. "A great many," he went on in a low voice. "I've seen lots and lots of them. . . . Wicked people! . . . I have seen a great many holy and just, too. . . . Queen of Heaven, save us and have mercy on us. I remember once thirty years ago, or maybe more, I was driving a merchant from Morshansk. The merchant was a jolly handsome fellow, with money, too . . . the merchant was . . . a nice man, no harm in him. . . . So we put up for the night at an inn. And in Russia the inns are not what they are in these parts. There the yards are roofed in and look like the ground floor, or let us say like barns in good farms. Only a barn would be a bit higher. So we put up there and were all right. My merchant was in a room, while I was with the horses, and everything was as it should be. So, lads, I said my prayers before going to sleep and began walking about the yard. And it was a dark night, I couldn't see anything; it was no good trying. So I walked about a bit up to the waggons, or nearly, when I saw a light gleaming. What could it mean? I thought the people of the inn had gone to bed long ago, and besides the merchant and me there were no other guests in the inn. . . . Where could the light have come from? I felt suspicious. . . . I went closer . . . towards the light. . . . The Lord have mercy upon me! and save me, Queen of Heaven! I looked and there was a little window with a grating, . . . close to the ground, in the house. . . I lay down on the ground and looked in; as soon as I looked in a cold chill ran all down me. . . ."

Kiruha, trying not to make a noise, thrust a handful of twigs into the fire. After waiting for it to leave off crackling and hissing, the old man went on:

"I looked in and there was a big cellar, black and dark. . . . There was a lighted lantern on a tub. In the middle of the cellar were about a dozen men in red shirts with their sleeves turned up, sharpening long knives. . . . Ugh! So we had fallen into a nest of robbers. . . . What's to be done? I ran to the merchant, waked him up quietly, and said: 'Don't be frightened, merchant,' said I, 'but we are in a bad way. We have fallen into a nest of robbers,' I said. He turned pale and asked: 'What are we to do now, Panteley? I have a lot of money that belongs to orphans. As for my life,' he said, 'that's in God's hands. I am not afraid to die, but it's dreadful to lose the orphans' money,' said he. . . . What were we to do? The gates were locked; there was no getting out. If there had been a fence one could have climbed over it, but with the yard shut up! . . . 'Come, don't be frightened, merchant,' said I; 'but pray to God. Maybe the Lord will not let the orphans suffer. Stay still.' said I, 'and make no sign, and meanwhile, maybe, I shall think of something. . . .' Right! . . . I prayed to God and the Lord put the thought into my mind. . . . I clambered up on my chaise and softly, . . . softly so that no one should hear, began pulling out the straw in the thatch, made a hole and crept out, crept out. . . . Then I jumped off the roof and ran along the road as fast as I could. I ran and ran till I was nearly dead. . . . I ran maybe four miles without taking breath, if not more. Thank God I saw a village. I ran up to a hut and began tapping at a window. 'Good Christian people,' I said, and told them all about it, 'do not let a Christian soul perish. . . .' I waked them all up. . . . The peasants gathered together and went with me, . . one with a cord, one with an oakstick, others with pitchforks. . . . We broke in the gates of the inn-yard and went straight to the cellar. . . . And the robbers had just finished sharpening their knives and were going to kill the merchant. The peasants took them, everyone of them, bound them and carried them to the police. The merchant gave them three hundred roubles in his joy, and gave me five gold pieces and put my name down. They said that they found human bones in the cellar afterwards, heaps and heaps of them. . . . Bones! . . . So they robbed people and then buried them, so that there should be no traces. . . . Well, afterwards they were punished at Morshansk."

Panteley had finished his story, and he looked round at his listeners. They were gazing at him in silence. The water was boiling by now and Styopka was skimming off the froth.

"Is the fat ready?" Kiruha asked him in a whisper.

"Wait a little. . . . Directly."

Styopka, his eyes fixed on Panteley as though he were afraid that the latter might begin some story before he was back, ran to the waggons; soon he came back with a little wooden bowl and began pounding some lard in it.

"I went another journey with a merchant, too, . . ." Panteley went on again, speaking as before in a low voice and with fixed unblinking eyes. "His name, as I remember now, was Pyotr Grigoritch. He was a nice man, . . . the merchant was. We stopped in the same way at an inn. . . . He indoors and me with the horses. . . . The people of the house, the innkeeper and his wife, seemed friendly good sort of people; the labourers, too, seemed all right; but yet, lads, I couldn't sleep. I had a queer feeling in my heart, . . . a queer feeling, that was just it. The gates were open and there were plenty of people about, and yet I felt afraid and not myself. Everyone had been asleep long ago. It was the middle of the night; it would soon be time to get up, and I was lying alone in my chaise and could not close my eyes, as though I were some owl. And then, lads, I heard this sound, 'Toop! toop! toop!' Someone was creeping up to the chaise. I poke my head out, and there was a peasant woman in nothing but her shift and with her feet bare. . . . 'What do you want, good woman?' I asked. And she was all of a tremble; her face was terror-stricken. . . 'Get up, good man,' said she; 'the people are plotting evil. . . . They mean to kill your merchant. With my own ears I heard the master whispering with his wife. . . .' So it was not for nothing, the foreboding of my heart! 'And who are you?' I asked. 'I am their cook,' she said. . . . Right! . . . So I got out of the chaise and went to the merchant. I waked him up and said: 'Things aren't quite right, Pyotr Grigoritch. . . . Make haste and rouse yourself from sleep, your worship, and dress now while there is still time,' I said; 'and to save our skins, let us get away from trouble.' He had no sooner begun dressing when the door opened and, mercy on us! I saw, Holy Mother! the innkeeper and his wife come into the room with three labourers. . . . So they had persuaded the labourers to join them. 'The merchant has a lot of money, and we'll go shares,' they told them. Everyone of the five had a long knife in their hand each a knife. The innkeeper locked the door and said: 'Say your prayers, travellers, . . . and if you begin screaming,' they said, 'we won't let you say your prayers before you die. . . .' As though we could scream! I had such a lump in my throat I could not cry out. . . . The merchant wept and said: 'Good Christian people! you have resolved to kill me because my money tempts you. Well, so be it; I shall not be the first nor shall I be the last. Many of us merchants have been murdered at inns. But why, good Christian brothers,' says he, 'murder my driver? Why should he have to suffer for my money?' And he said that so pitifully! And the innkeeper answered him: 'If we leave him alive,' said he, 'he will be the first to bear witness against us. One may just as well kill two as one. You can but answer once for seven misdeeds. . . Say your prayers, that's all you can do, and it is no good talking!' The merchant and I knelt down side by side and wept and said our prayers. He thought of his children. I was young in those days; I wanted to live. . . . We looked at the images and prayed, and so pitifully that it brings a tear even now. . . . And the innkeeper's wife looks at us and says: 'Good people,' said she, 'don't bear a grudge against us in the other world and pray to God for our punishment, for it is want that drives us to it.' We prayed and wept and prayed and wept, and God heard us. He had pity on us, I suppose. . . . At the very minute when the innkeeper had taken the merchant by the beard to rip open his throat with his knife suddenly someone seemed to tap at the window from the yard! We all started, and the innkeeper's hands dropped. . . . Someone was tapping at the window and shouting: 'Pyotr

Grigoritch,' he shouted, 'are you here? Get ready and let's go!' The people saw that someone had come for the merchant; they were terrified and took to their heels. . . . And we made haste into the yard, harnessed the horses, and were out of sight in a minute. . ."

"Who was it knocked at the window?" asked Dymov.

"At the window? It must have been a holy saint or angel, for there was no one else. . . . When we drove out of the yard there wasn't a soul in the street. . . . It was the Lord's doing."

Panteley told other stories, and in all of them "long knives" figured and all alike sounded made up. Had he heard these stories from someone else, or had he made them up himself in the remote past, and afterwards, as his memory grew weaker, mixed up his experiences with his imaginations and become unable to distinguish one from the other? Anything is possible, but it is strange that on this occasion and for the rest of the journey, whenever he happened to tell a story, he gave unmistakable preference to fiction, and never told of what he really had experienced. At the time Yegorushka took it all for the genuine thing, and believed every word; later on it seemed to him strange that a man who in his day had travelled all over Russia and seen and known so much, whose wife and children had been burnt to death, so failed to appreciate the wealth of his life that whenever he was sitting by the camp fire he was either silent or talked of what had never been.

Over their porridge they were all silent, thinking of what they had just heard. Life is terrible and marvellous, and so, however terrible a story you tell in Russia, however you embroider it with nests of robbers, long knives and such marvels, it always finds an echo of reality in the soul of the listener, and only a man who has been a good deal affected by education looks askance distrustfully, and even he will be silent. The cross by the roadside, the dark bales of wool, the wide expanse of the plain, and the lot of the men gathered together by the camp fire -- all this was of itself so marvellous and terrible that the fantastic colours of legend and fairy-tale were pale and blended with life.

All the others ate out of the cauldron, but Panteley sat apart and ate his porridge out of a wooden bowl. His spoon was not like those the others had, but was made of cypress wood, with a little cross on it. Yegorushka, looking at him, thought of the little ikon glass and asked Styopka softly:

"Why does Grandfather sit apart?"

"He is an Old Believer," Styopka and Vassya answered in a whisper. And as they said it they looked as though they were speaking of some secret vice or weakness.

All sat silent, thinking. After the terrible stories there was no inclination to speak of ordinary things. All at once in the midst of the silence Vassya drew himself up and, fixing his lustreless eyes on one point, pricked up his ears.

"What is it?" Dymov asked him.

"Someone is coming," answered Vassya.

"Where do you see him?"

"Yo-on-der! There's something white. . ."

There was nothing to be seen but darkness in the direction in which Vassya was looking; everyone listened, but they could hear no sound of steps.

"Is he coming by the highroad?" asked Dymov.

"No, over the open country. . . . He is coming this way."

A minute passed in silence.

"And maybe it's the merchant who was buried here walking over the steppe," said Dymov.

All looked askance at the cross, exchanged glances and suddenly broke into a laugh. They felt ashamed of their terror.

"Why should he walk?" asked Panteley. "It's only those walk at night whom the earth will not take to herself. And the merchants were all right. . . . The merchants have received the crown of martyrs."

But all at once they heard the sound of steps; someone was coming in haste.

"He's carrying something," said Vassya.

They could hear the grass rustling and the dry twigs crackling under the feet of the approaching wayfarer. But from the glare of the camp fire nothing could be seen. At last the steps sounded close by, and someone coughed. The flickering light seemed to part; a veil dropped from the waggoners' eyes, and they saw a man facing them.

Whether it was due to the flickering light or because everyone wanted to make out the man's face first of all, it happened, strangely enough, that at the first glance at him they all saw, first of all, not his face nor his clothes, but his smile. It was an extraordinarily good-natured, broad, soft smile, like that of a baby on waking, one of those infectious smiles to which it is difficult not to respond by smiling too. The stranger, when they did get a good look at him, turned out to be a man of thirty, ugly and in no way remarkable. He was a tall Little Russian, with a long nose, long arms and long legs; everything about him seemed long except his neck, which was so short that it made him seem stooping. He was wearing a clean white shirt with an embroidered collar, white trousers, and new high boots, and in comparison with the waggoners he looked quite a dandy. In his arms he was carrying something big, white, and at the first glance strange-looking, and the stock of a gun also peeped out from behind his shoulder.

Coming from the darkness into the circle of light, he stopped short as though petrified, and for half a minute looked at the waggoners as though he would have said: "Just look what a smile I have!"

Then he took a step towards the fire, smiled still more radiantly and said:

"Bread and salt, friends!"

"You are very welcome!" Panteley answered for them all.

The stranger put down by the fire what he was carrying in his arms -- it was a dead bustard -- and greeted them once more.

They all went up to the bustard and began examining it.

"A fine big bird; what did you kill it with?" asked Dymov.

"Grape-shot. You can't get him with small shot, he won't let you get near enough. Buy it, friends! I will let you have it for twenty kopecks."

"What use would it be to us? It's good roast, but I bet it would be tough boiled; you could not get your teeth into it. . . ."

"Oh, what a pity! I would take it to the gentry at the farm; they would give me half a rouble for it. But it's a long way to go -- twelve miles!"

The stranger sat down, took off his gun and laid it beside him.

He seemed sleepy and languid; he sat smiling, and, screwing up his eyes at the firelight, apparently thinking of something very agreeable. They gave him a spoon; he began eating.

"Who are you?" Dymov asked him.

The stranger did not hear the question; he made no answer, and did not even glance at Dymov. Most likely this smiling man did not taste the flavour of the porridge either, for he seemed to eat it mechanically, lifting the spoon to his lips sometimes very full and sometimes quite empty. He was not drunk, but he seemed to have something nonsensical in his head.

"I ask you who you are?" repeated Dymov.

"I?" said the unknown, starting. "Konstantin Zvonik from Rovno. It's three miles from here."

And anxious to show straight off that he was not quite an ordinary peasant, but something better, Konstantin hastened to add:

"We keep bees and fatten pigs."

"Do you live with your father or in a house of your own?"

"No; now I am living in a house of my own. I have parted. This month, just after St. Peter's Day, I got married. I am a married man now!. . . It's eighteen days since the wedding."

"That's a good thing," said Panteley. "Marriage is a good thing. . . . God's blessing is on it."

"His young wife sits at home while he rambles about the steppe," laughed Kiruha. "Queer chap!"

As though he had been pinched on the tenderest spot, Konstantin started, laughed and flushed crimson.

"But, Lord, she is not at home!" he said quickly, taking the spoon out of his mouth and looking round at everyone with an expression of delight and wonder. "She is not; she has gone to her mother's for three days! Yes, indeed, she has gone away, and I feel as though I were not married. . . ."

Konstantin waved his hand and turned his head; he wanted to go on thinking, but the joy which beamed in his face prevented him. As though he were not comfortable, he changed his attitude, laughed, and again waved his hand. He was ashamed to share his happy thoughts with strangers, but at the same time he had an irresistible longing to communicate his joy.

"She has gone to Demidovo to see her mother," he said, blushing and moving his gun. "She'll be back to-morrow. . . . She said she would be back to dinner."

"And do you miss her?" said Dymov.

"Oh, Lord, yes; I should think so. We have only been married such a little while, and she has gone away. . . . Eh! Oh, but she is a tricky one, God strike me dead! She is such a fine, splendid girl, such a one for laughing and singing, full of life and fire! When she is there your brain is in a whirl, and now she is away I wander about the steppe like a fool, as though I had lost something. I have been walking since dinner."

Konstantin rubbed his eyes, looked at the fire and laughed.

"You love her, then, . . ." said Panteley.

"She is so fine and splendid," Konstantin repeated, not hearing him; "such a housewife, clever and sensible. You wouldn't find another like her among simple folk in the whole province. She has gone away. . . . But she is missing me, I kno-ow! I know the little magpie. She said she would be back to-morrow by dinner-time. . . . And just think how queer!" Konstantin almost shouted, speaking a note higher and shifting his position. "Now she loves me and is sad without me, and yet she would not marry me."

"But eat," said Kiruha.

"She would not marry me," Konstantin went on, not heeding him. "I have been struggling with her for three years! I saw her at the Kalatchik fair; I fell madly in love with her, was ready to hang myself. . . . I live at Rovno, she at Demidovo, more than twenty miles apart, and there was nothing I could do. I sent match-makers to her, and all she said was: 'I won't!' Ah, the magpie! I sent her one thing and another, earrings and cakes, and twenty pounds of honey -- but still she said: 'I won't!' And there it was. If you come to think of it, I was not a match for her! She was young and lovely, full of fire, while I am old: I shall soon be thirty, and a regular beauty, too; a fine beard like a goat's, a clear complexion all covered with pimples -- how could I be compared with her! The only thing to be said is that we are well off, but then the Vahramenkys are well off, too. They've six oxen, and they keep a couple of labourers. I was in love, friends, as though I were plague-stricken. I couldn't sleep or eat; my brain was full of thoughts, and in such a maze, Lord preserve us! I longed to see her, and she was in Demidovo. What do you think? God be my witness, I am not lying, three times a week I walked over there on foot just to have a look at her. I gave up my work! I was so frantic that I even wanted to get taken on as a labourer in Demidovo, so as to be near her. I was in misery! My mother called in a witch a dozen times; my father tried thrashing me. For three years I was in this torment, and then I made up my mind. 'Damn my soul!' I said. 'I will go to the town and be a cabman. . . . It seems it is fated not to be.' At Easter I went to Demidovo to have a last look at her. . . ."

Konstantin threw back his head and went off into a mirthful tinkling laugh, as though he had just taken someone in very cleverly.

"I saw her by the river with the lads," he went on. "I was overcome with anger. . . . I called her aside and maybe for a full hour I said all manner of things to her. She fell in love with me! For three years she did not like me! she fell in love with me for what I said to her. . . ."

"What did you say to her?" asked Dymov.

"What did I say? I don't remember. . . How could one remember? My words flowed at the time like water from a tap, without stopping to take breath. Ta-ta-ta! And now I can't utter a word. . . . Well, so she married me. . . . She's gone now to her mother's, the magpie, and while she is away here I wander over the steppe. I can't stay at home. It's more than I can do!"

Konstantin awkwardly released his feet, on which he was sitting, stretched himself on the earth, and propped his head in his fists, then got up and sat down again. Everyone by now thoroughly understood that he was in love and happy, poignantly happy; his smile, his eyes, and every movement, expressed fervent happiness. He could not find a place for himself, and did not know what attitude to take to keep himself from being overwhelmed by the multitude of his delightful thoughts. Having poured out his soul before these strangers, he settled down quietly at last, and, looking at the fire, sank into thought.

At the sight of this happy man everyone felt depressed and longed to be happy, too. Everyone was dreamy. Dymov got up, walked about softly by the fire, and from his walk, from the movement of his shoulder-blades, it could be seen that he was weighed down by depression and yearning. He stood still for a moment, looked at Konstantin and sat down.

The camp fire had died down by now; there was no flicker, and the patch of red had grown small and dim. . . . And as the fire went out the moonlight grew clearer and clearer. Now they could see the full width of the road, the bales of wool, the shafts of the waggons, the munching horses; on the further side of the road there was the dim outline of the second cross. . . .

Dymov leaned his cheek on his hand and softly hummed some plaintive song. Konstantin smiled drowsily and chimed in with a thin voice. They sang for half a minute, then sank into silence. Emelyan started, jerked his elbows and wriggled his fingers.

"Lads," he said in an imploring voice, "let's sing something sacred!" Tears came into his eyes. "Lads," he repeated, pressing his hands on his heart, "let's sing something sacred!"

"I don't know anything," said Konstantin.

Everyone refused, then Emelyan sang alone. He waved both arms, nodded his head, opened his mouth, but nothing came from his throat but a discordant gasp. He sang with his arms, with his head, with his eyes, even with the swelling on his face; he sang passionately with anguish, and the more he strained his chest to extract at least one note from it, the more discordant were his gasps.

Yegorushka, like the rest, was overcome with depression. He went to his waggon, clambered up on the bales and lay down. He looked at the sky, and thought of happy Konstantin and his wife. Why did people get married? What were women in the world for? Yegorushka put the vague questions to himself, and thought that a man would certainly be happy if he had an affectionate, merry and beautiful woman continually living at his side. For some reason he remembered the Countess Dranitsky, and thought it would probably be very pleasant to live with a woman like that; he would perhaps have married her with pleasure if that idea had not been so shameful. He recalled her eyebrows, the pupils of her eyes, her carriage, the clock with the horseman. . . . The soft warm night moved softly down upon him and whispered something in his ear, and it seemed to him that it was that lovely woman bending over him, looking at him with a smile and meaning to kiss him. . . .

Nothing was left of the fire but two little red eyes, which kept on growing smaller and smaller. Konstantin and the waggoners were sitting by it, dark motionless figures, and it seemed as though there were many more of them than before. The twin crosses were equally visible, and far, far away, somewhere by the highroad there gleamed a red light -- other people cooking their porridge, most likely.

"Our Mother Russia is the he-ad of all the world!" Kiruha sang out suddenly in a harsh voice, choked and subsided. The steppe echo caught up his voice, carried it on, and it seemed as though stupidity itself were rolling on heavy wheels over the steppe.

"It's time to go," said Panteley. "Get up, lads."

While they were putting the horses in, Konstantin walked by the waggons and talked rapturously of his wife.

"Good-bye, mates!" he cried when the waggons started. "Thank you for your hospitality. I shall go on again towards that light. It's more than I can stand."

And he quickly vanished in the mist, and for a long time they could hear him striding in the direction of the light to tell those other strangers of his happiness.

When Yegorushka woke up next day it was early morning; the sun had not yet risen. The waggons were at a standstill. A man in a white cap and a suit of cheap grey material, mounted on a little Cossack stallion, was talking to Dymov and Kiruha beside the foremost waggon. A mile and a half ahead there were long low white barns and little houses with tiled roofs; there were neither yards nor trees to be seen beside the little houses.

"What village is that, Grandfather?" asked Yegorushka.

"That's the Armenian Settlement, youngster," answered Panteley. "The Armenians live there. They are a good sort of people, . . . the Arnienians are."

The man in grey had finished talking to Dymov and Kiruha; he pulled up his little stallion and looked across towards the settlement.

"What a business, only think!" sighed Panteley, looking towards the settlement, too, and shuddering at the morning freshness. "He has sent a man to the settlement for some papers, and he doesn't come. . . . He should have sent Styopka."

"Who is that, Grandfather?" asked Yegorushka.

"Varlamov."

My goodness! Yegorushka jumped up quickly, getting upon his knees, and looked at the white cap. It was hard to recognize the mysterious elusive Varlamov, who was sought by everyone, who was always "on his rounds," and who had far more money than Countess Dranitsky, in the short, grey little man in big boots, who was sitting on an ugly little nag and talking to peasants at an hour when all decent people were asleep.

"He is all right, a good man," said Panteley, looking towards the settlement. "God give him health -- a splendid gentleman, Semyon Alexandritch. . . . It's people like that the earth rests upon. That's true. . . . The cocks are not crowing yet, and he is already up and about. . . . Another man would be asleep, or gallivanting with visitors at home, but he is on the steppe all day, . . . on his rounds. . . . He does not let things slip. . . . No-o! He's a fine fellow. . ."

Varlamov was talking about something, while he kept his eyes fixed. The little stallion shifted from one leg to another impatiently.

"Semyon Alexandritch!" cried Panteley, taking off his hat. "Allow us to send Styopka! Emelyan, call out that Styopka should be sent."

But now at last a man on horseback could be seen coming from the settlement. Bending very much to one side and brandishing his whip above his head like a gallant young Caucasian, and wanting to astonish everyone by his horsemanship, he flew towards the waggons with the swiftness of a bird.

"That must be one of his circuit men," said Panteley. "He must have a hundred such horsemen or maybe more."

Reaching the first waggon, he pulled up his horse, and taking off his hat, handed Varlamov a little book. Varlamov took several papers out of the book, read them and cried:

"And where is Ivantchuk's letter?"

The horseman took the book back, looked at the papers and shrugged his shoulders. He began saying something, probably justifying himself and asking to be allowed to ride back to the settlement again. The little stallion suddenly stirred as though Varlamov had grown heavier. Varlamov stirred too.

"Go along!" he cried angrily, and he waved his whip at the man.

Then he turned his horse round and, looking through the papers in the book, moved at a walking pace alongside the waggons. When he reached the hindmost, Yegorushka strained his eyes to get a better look at him. Varlamov was an elderly man. His face, a simple Russian sunburnt face with a small grey beard, was red, wet with dew and covered with little blue veins; it had the same expression of businesslike coldness as Ivan Ivanitch's face, the same look of fanatical zeal for business. But yet what a difference could be felt between him and Kuzmitchov! Uncle Ivan Ivanitch always had on his face, together with his business-like reserve, a look of anxiety and apprehension that he would not find Varlamov, that he would be late, that he would miss a good price; nothing of that sort, so characteristic of small and dependent persons, could be seen in the face or figure of Varlamov. This man made the price himself, was not looking for anyone, and did not depend on anyone; however ordinary his exterior, yet in everything, even in the manner of holding his whip, there was a sense of power and habitual authority over the steppe.

As he rode by Yegorushka he did not glance at him. Only the little stallion deigned to notice Yegorushka; he looked at him with his large foolish eyes, and even he showed no interest. Panteley bowed to Varlamov; the latter noticed it, and without taking his eyes off the sheets of paper, said lisping:

"How are you, old man?"

Varlamov's conversation with the horseman and the way he had brandished his whip had evidently made an overwhelming impression on the whole party. Everyone looked grave. The man on horseback, cast down at the anger of the great man, remained stationary, with his hat off, and the rein loose by the foremost waggon; he was silent, and seemed unable to grasp that the day had begun so badly for him.

"He is a harsh old man, . ." muttered Panteley. "It's a pity he is so harsh! But he is all right, a good man. . . . He doesn't abuse men for nothing. . . . It's no matter. . . ."

After examining the papers, Varlamov thrust the book into his pocket; the little stallion, as though he knew what was in his mind, without waiting for orders, started and dashed along the highroad.

VII

On the following night the waggoners had halted and were cooking their porridge. On this occasion there was a sense of overwhelming oppression over everyone. It was sultry; they all drank a great deal, but could not quench their thirst. The moon was intensely crimson and sullen, as though it were sick. The stars, too, were sullen, the mist was thicker, the distance more clouded. Nature seemed as though languid and weighed down by some foreboding.

There was not the same liveliness and talk round the camp fire as there had been the day before. All were dreary and spoke listlessly and without interest. Panteley did nothing but sigh and complain of his feet, and continually alluded to impenitent deathbeds.

Dymov was lying on his stomach, chewing a straw in silence; there was an expression of disgust on his face as though the straw smelt unpleasant, a spiteful and exhausted look. . . . Vassya complained that his jaw ached, and prophesied bad weather; Emelyan was not waving his arms, but sitting still and looking gloomily at the fire. Yegorushka, too, was weary. This slow travelling exhausted him, and the sultriness of the day had given him a headache.

While they were cooking the porridge, Dymov, to relieve his boredom, began quarrelling with his companions.

"Here he lolls, the lumpy face, and is the first to put his spoon in," he said, looking spitefully at Emelyan. "Greedy! always contrives to sit next the cauldron. He's been a church-singer, so he thinks he is a gentleman! There are a lot of singers like you begging along the highroad!"

"What are you pestering me for?" asked Emelyan, looking at him angrily.

"To teach you not to be the first to dip into the cauldron. Don't think too much of yourself!"

"You are a fool, and that is all about it!" wheezed out Emelyan.

Knowing by experience how such conversations usually ended, Panteley and Vassya intervened and tried to persuade Dymov not to quarrel about nothing.

"A church-singer!" The bully would not desist, but laughed contemptuously. "Anyone can sing like that -- sit in the church porch and sing 'Give me alms, for Christ's sake!' Ugh! you are a nice fellow!"

Emelyan did not speak. His silence had an irritating effect on Dymov. He looked with still greater hatred at the ex-singer and said:

"I don't care to have anything to do with you, or I would show you what to think of yourself."

"But why are you pushing me, you Mazeppa?" Emelyan cried, flaring up. "Am I interfering with you?"

"What did you call me?" asked Dymov, drawing himself up, and his eyes were suffused with blood. "Eh! I am a Mazeppa? Yes? Take that, then; go and look for it."

Dymov snatched the spoon out of Emelyan's hand and flung it far away. Kiruha, Vassya, and Styopka ran to look for it, while Emelyan fixed an imploring and questioning look on Panteley. His face suddenly became small and wrinkled; it began twitching, and the ex-singer began to cry like a child.

Yegorushka, who had long hated Dymov, felt as though the air all at once were unbearably stifling, as though the fire were scorching his face; he longed to run quickly to the waggons in the darkness, but the bully's angry bored eyes drew the boy to him. With a passionate desire to say something extremely offensive, he took a step towards Dymov and brought out, gasping for breath:

"You are the worst of the lot; I can't bear you!"

After this he ought to have run to the waggons, but he could not stir from the spot and went on:

"In the next world you will burn in hell! I'll complain to Ivan Ivanitch. Don't you dare insult Emelyan!"

"Say this too, please," laughed Dyrnov: " 'every little sucking-pig wants to lay down the law.' Shall I pull your ear?"

Yegorushka felt that he could not breathe; and something which had never happened to him before -- he suddenly began shaking all over, stamping his feet and crying shrilly:

"Beat him, beat him!"

Tears gushed from his eyes; he felt ashamed, and ran staggering back to the waggon. The effect produced by his outburst he did not see. Lying on the bales and twitching his arms and legs, he whispered:

"Mother, mother!"

And these men and the shadows round the camp fire, and the dark bales and the far-away lightning, which was flashing every minute in the distance -- all struck him now as terrible and unfriendly. He was overcome with terror and asked himself in despair why and how he had come into this unknown land in the company of terrible peasants? Where was his uncle now, where was Father Christopher, where was Deniska? Why were they so long in coming? Hadn't they forgotten him? At the thought that he was forgotten and cast out to the mercy of fate, he felt such a cold chill of dread that he had several times an impulse to jump off the bales of wool, and run back full speed along the road; but the thought of the huge dark crosses, which would certainly meet him on the way, and the lightning flashing in the distance, stopped him. . . . And only when he whispered, "Mother, mother!" he felt as it were a little better.

The waggoners must have been full of dread, too. After Yegorushka had run away from the camp fire they sat at first for a long time in silence, then they began speaking in hollow undertones about something, saying that it was coming and that they must make haste and get away from it. . . . They quickly finished supper, put out the fire and began harnessing the horses in silence. From their fluster and the broken phrases they uttered it was apparent they foresaw some trouble. Before they set off on their way, Dymov went up to Panteley and asked softly:

"What's his name?"

"Yegory," answered Panteley.

Dymov put one foot on the wheel, caught hold of the cord which was tied round the bales and pulled himself up. Yegorushka saw his face and curly head. The face was pale and looked grave and exhausted, but there was no expression of spite in it.

"Yera!" he said softly, "here, hit me!"

Yegorushka looked at him in surprise. At that instant there was a flash of lightning.

"It's all right, hit me," repeated Dymov. And without waiting for Yegorushka to hit him or to speak to him, he jumped down and said: "How dreary I am!"

Then, swaying from one leg to the other and moving his shoulder-blades, he sauntered lazily alongside the string of waggons and repeated in a voice half weeping, half angry:

"How dreary I am! O Lord! Don't you take offence, Emelyan," he said as he passed Emelyan. "Ours is a wretched cruel life!"

There was a flash of lightning on the right, and, like a reflection in the looking-glass, at once a second flash in the distance.

"Yegory, take this," cried Panteley, throwing up something big and dark.

"What is it?" asked Yegorushka.

"A mat. There will be rain, so cover yourself up."

Yegorushka sat up and looked about him. The distance had grown perceptibly blacker, and now oftener than every minute winked with a pale light. The blackness was being bent towards the right as though by its own weight.

"Will there be a storm, Grandfather?" asked Yegorushka.

"Ah, my poor feet, how they ache!" Panteley said in a high-pitched voice, stamping his feet and not hearing the boy.

On the left someone seemed to strike a match in the sky; a pale phosphorescent streak gleamed and went out. There was a sound as though someone very far away were walking over an iron roof, probably barefoot, for the iron gave a hollow rumble.

"It's set in!" cried Kiruha.

Between the distance and the horizon on the right there was a flash of lightning so vivid that it lighted up part of the steppe and the spot where the clear sky met the blackness. A terrible cloud was swooping down, without haste, a compact mass; big black shreds hung from its edge; similar shreds pressing one upon another were piling up on the right and left horizon. The tattered, ragged look of the storm-cloud gave it a drunken disorderly air. There was a distinct, not smothered, growl of thunder. Yegorushka crossed himself and began quickly putting on his great-coat.

"I am dreary!" Dymov's shout floated from the foremost waggon, and it could be told from his voice that he was beginning to be ill-humoured again. "I am so dreary!"

All at once there was a squall of wind, so violent that it almost snatched away Yegorushka's bundle and mat; the mat fluttered in all directions and flapped on the bale and on Yegorushka's face. The wind dashed whistling over the steppe, whirled round in disorder and raised such an uproar from the grass that neither the thunder nor the creaking of the wheels could be heard; it blew from the black storm-cloud, carrying with it clouds of dust and the scent of rain and wet earth. The moonlight grew mistier, as it were dirtier; the stars were even more overcast; and clouds of dust could be seen hurrying along the edge of the road, followed by their shadows. By now, most likely, the whirlwind eddying round and lifting from the earth dust, dry grass and feathers, was mounting to the very sky; uprooted plants must have been flying by that very black storm-cloud, and how frightened they must have been! But through the dust that clogged the eyes nothing could be seen but the flash of lightning.

Yegorushka, thinking it would pour with rain in a minute, knelt up and covered himself with the mat.

"Panteley-ey!" someone shouted in the front. "A. . . a. . . va!"

"I can't!" Panteley answered in a loud high voice. "A . . . a . . . va! Arya . . . a!"

There was an angry clap of thunder, which rolled across the sky from right to left, then back again, and died away near the foremost waggon.

"Holy, holy, holy, Lord of Sabaoth," whispered Yegorushka, crossing himself. "Fill heaven and earth with Thy glory."

The blackness in the sky yawned wide and breathed white fire. At once there was another clap of thunder. It had scarcely ceased when there was a flash of lightning so broad that Yegorushka suddenly saw through a slit in the mat the whole highroad to the very horizon, all the waggoners and even Kiruha's waistcoat. The black shreds had by now moved upwards from the left, and one of them, a coarse, clumsy monster like a claw with fingers, stretched to the moon. Yegorushka made up his mind to shut his eyes tight, to pay no attention to it, and to wait till it was all over.

The rain was for some reason long in coming. Yegorushka peeped out from the mat in the hope that perhaps the storm-cloud was passing over. It was fearfully dark. Yegorushka could see neither Panteley, nor the bale of wool, nor himself; he looked sideways towards the place where the moon had lately been, but there was the same black darkness there as over the waggons. And in the darkness the flashes of lightning seemed more violent and blinding, so that they hurt his eyes.

"Panteley!" called Yegorushka.

No answer followed. But now a gust of wind for the last time flung up the mat and hurried away. A quiet regular sound was heard. A big cold drop fell on Yegorushka's knee, another trickled over his hand. He noticed that his knees were not covered, and tried to rearrange the mat, but at that moment something began pattering on the road, then on the shafts and the bales. It was the rain. As though they understood one another, the rain and the mat began prattling of something rapidly, gaily and most annoyingly like two magpies.

Yegorushka knelt up or rather squatted on his boots. While the rain was pattering on the mat, he leaned forward to screen his knees, which were suddenly wet. He succeeded in covering his knees, but in less than a minute was aware of a penetrating, unpleasant dampness behind on his back and the calves of his legs. He returned to his former position, exposing his knees to the rain, and wondered what to do to rearrange the mat which he could not see in the darkness. But his arms were already wet, the water was trickling up his sleeves and down his collar, and his shoulder-blades felt chilly. And he made up his mind to do nothing but sit motionless and wait till it was all over.

"Holy, holy, holy!" he whispered.

Suddenly, exactly over his head, the sky cracked with a fearful deafening din; he huddled up and held his breath, waiting for the fragments to fall upon his head and back. He inadvertently opened his eyes and saw a blinding intense light flare out and flash five times on his fingers, his wet sleeves, and on the trickles of water running from the mat upon the bales and down to the ground. There was a fresh peal of thunder as violent and awful; the sky was not growling and rumbling now, but uttering short crashing sounds like the crackling of dry wood.

"Trrah! tah! tah! tah!" the thunder rang out distinctly, rolled over the sky, seemed to stumble, and somewhere by the foremost waggons or far behind to fall with an abrupt angry "Trrra!"

The flashes of lightning had at first been only terrible, but with such thunder they seemed sinister and menacing. Their magic light pierced through closed eyelids and sent a chill all over the body. What could he do not to see them? Yegorushka made up his mind to turn over on his face. Cautiously, as though afraid of being watched, he got on all fours, and his hands slipping on the wet bale, he turned back again.

"Trrah! tah! tah!" floated over his head, rolled under the waggons and exploded "Kraa!"

Again he inadvertently opened his eyes and saw a new danger: three huge giants with long pikes were following the waggon! A flash of lightning gleamed on the points of their pikes and lighted up their figures very distinctly. They were men of huge proportions, with covered faces, bowed heads, and heavy footsteps. They seemed gloomy and dispirited and lost in thought. Perhaps they were not following the waggons with any harmful intent, and yet there was something awful in their proximity.

Yegorushka turned quickly forward, and trembling all over cried: "Panteley! Grandfather!"

"Trrah! tah! tah!" the sky answered him.

He opened his eyes to see if the waggoners were there. There were flashes of lightning in two places, which lighted up the road to the far distance, the whole string of waggons and all the waggoners. Streams of water were flowing along the road and bubbles were dancing. Panteley was walking beside the waggon; his tall hat and his shoulder were covered with a small mat; his figure expressed neither terror nor uneasiness, as though he were deafened by the thunder and blinded by the lightning.

"Grandfather, the giants!" Yegorushka shouted to him in tears.

But the old man did not hear. Further away walked Emelyan. He was covered from head to foot with a big mat and was triangular in shape. Vassya, without anything over him, was walking with the same wooden step as usual, lifting his feet high and not bending his knees. In the flash of lightning it seemed as though the waggons were not moving and the men were motionless, that Vassya's lifted foot was rigid in the same position. . . .

Yegorushka called the old man once more. Getting no answer, he sat motionless, and no longer waited for it all to end. He was convinced that the thunder would kill him in another minute, that he would accidentally open his eyes and see the terrible giants, and he left off crossing himself, calling the old man and thinking of his mother, and was simply numb with cold and the conviction that the storm would never end.

But at last there was the sound of voices.

"Yegory, are you asleep?" Panteley cried below. "Get down! Is he deaf, the silly little thing? . . ."

"Something like a storm!" said an unfamiliar bass voice, and the stranger cleared his throat as though he had just tossed off a good glass of vodka.

Yegorushka opened his eyes. Close to the waggon stood Panteley, Emelyan, looking like a triangle, and the giants. The latter were by now much shorter, and when Yegorushka looked more closely at them they turned out to be ordinary peasants, carrying on their shoulders not pikes but pitchforks. In the space between Panteley and the triangular figure, gleamed the window of a low-pitched hut. So the waggons were halting in the village. Yegorushka flung off the mat, took his bundle and made haste to get off the waggon. Now when close to him there were people talking and a lighted window he no longer felt afraid, though the thunder was crashing as before and the whole sky was streaked with lightning.

"It was a good storm, all right, . . ." Panteley was muttering. "Thank God, . . . my feet are a little softened by the rain. It was all right. . . . Have you got down, Yegory? Well, go into the hut; it is all right. . . ."

"Holy, holy, holy!" wheezed Emelyan, "it must have struck something. . . . Are you of these parts?" he asked the giants.

"No, from Glinovo. We belong to Glinovo. We are working at the Platers'."

"Threshing?"

"All sorts. Just now we are getting in the wheat. The lightning, the lightning! It is long since we have had such a storm. . . ."

Yegorushka went into the hut. He was met by a lean hunchbacked old woman with a sharp chin. She stood holding a tallow candle in her hands, screwing up her eyes and heaving prolonged sighs.

"What a storm God has sent us!" she said. "And our lads are out for the night on the steppe; they'll have a bad time, poor dears! Take off your things, little sir, take off your things."

Shivering with cold and shrugging squeamishly, Yegorushka pulled off his drenched overcoat, then stretched out his arms and straddled his legs, and stood a long time without moving. The slightest movement caused an unpleasant sensation of cold and wetness. His sleeves and the back of his shirt were sopped, his trousers stuck to his legs, his head was dripping.

"What's the use of standing there, with your legs apart, little lad?" said the old woman. "Come, sit down."

Holding his legs wide apart, Yegorushka went up to the table and sat down on a bench near somebody's head. The head moved, puffed a stream of air through its nose, made a chewing sound and subsided. A mound covered with a sheepskin stretched from the head along the bench; it was a peasant woman asleep.

The old woman went out sighing, and came back with a big water melon and a little sweet melon.

"Have something to eat, my dear! I have nothing else to offer you, . . ." she said, yawning. She rummaged in the table and took out a long sharp knife, very much like the one with which the brigands killed the merchants in the inn. "Have some, my dear!"

Yegorushka, shivering as though he were in a fever, ate a slice of sweet melon with black bread and then a slice of water melon, and that made him feel colder still.

"Our lads are out on the steppe for the night, . . ." sighed the old woman while he was eating. "The terror of the Lord! I'd light the candle under the ikon, but I don't know where Stepanida has put it. Have some more, little sir, have some more. . . ."

The old woman gave a yawn and, putting her right hand behind her, scratched her left shoulder.

"It must be two o'clock now," she said; "it will soon be time to get up. Our lads are out on the steppe for the night; they are all wet through for sure. . . ."

"Granny," said Yegorushka. "I am sleepy."

"Lie down, my dear, lie down," the old woman sighed, yawning. "Lord Jesus Christ! I was asleep, when I heard a noise as though someone were knocking. I woke up and looked, and it was the storm God had sent us. . . . I'd have lighted the candle, but I couldn't find it."

Talking to herself, she pulled some rags, probably her own bed, off the bench, took two sheepskins off a nail by the stove, and began laying them out for a bed for Yegorushka. "The storm doesn't grow less," she muttered. "If only nothing's struck in an unlucky hour. Our lads are out on the steppe for the night. Lie down and sleep, my dear. . . . Christ be with you, my child. . . . I won't take away the melon; maybe you'll have a bit when you get up."

The sighs and yawns of the old woman, the even breathing of the sleeping woman, the half-darkness of the hut, and the sound of the rain outside, made one sleepy. Yegorushka was shy of undressing before the old woman. He only took off his boots, lay down and covered himself with the sheepskin.

"Is the little lad lying down?" he heard Panteley whisper a little later.

"Yes," answered the old woman in a whisper. "The terror of the Lord! It thunders and thunders, and there is no end to it."

"It will soon be over," wheezed Panteley, sitting down; "it's getting quieter. . . . The lads have gone into the huts, and two have stayed with the horses. The lads have. . . . They can't; . . . the horses would be taken away. . . . I'll sit here a bit and then go and take my turn. . . . We can't leave them; they would be taken. . . ."

Panteley and the old woman sat side by side at Yegorushka's feet, talking in hissing whispers and interspersing their speech with sighs and yawns. And Yegorushka could not get warm. The warm heavy sheepskin lay on him, but he was trembling all over; his arms and legs were twitching, and his whole inside was shivering. . . . He undressed under the sheepskin, but that was no good. His shivering grew more and more acute.

Panteley went out to take his turn with the horses, and afterwards came back again, and still Yegorushka was shivering all over and could not get to sleep. Something weighed upon his head and chest and oppressed him, and he did not know what it was, whether it was the old people whispering, or the heavy smell of the sheepskin. The melon he had eaten had left an unpleasant metallic taste in his mouth. Moreover he was being bitten by fleas.

"Grandfather, I am cold," he said, and did not know his own voice.

"Go to sleep, my child, go to sleep," sighed the old woman.

Tit came up to the bedside on his thin little legs and waved his arms, then grew up to the ceiling and turned into a windmill. . . . Father Christopher, not as he was in the chaise, but in his full vestments with the sprinkler in his hand, walked round the mill, sprinkling it with holy water, and it left off waving. Yegorushka, knowing this was delirium, opened his eyes.

"Grandfather," he called, "give me some water."

No one answered. Yegorushka felt it insufferably stifling and uncomfortable lying down. He got up, dressed, and went out of the hut. Morning was beginning. The sky was overcast, but it was no longer raining. Shivering and wrapping himself in his wet overcoat, Yegorushka walked about the muddy yard and listened to the silence; he caught sight of a little shed with a half-open door made of reeds. He looked into this shed, went into it, and sat down in a dark corner on a heap of dry dung.

There was a tangle of thoughts in his heavy head; his mouth was dry and unpleasant from the metallic taste. He looked at his hat, straightened the peacock's feather on it, and thought how he had gone with his mother to buy the hat. He put his hand into his pocket and took out a lump of brownish sticky paste. How had that paste come into his pocket? He thought a minute, smelt it; it smelt of honey. Aha! it was the Jewish cake! How sopped it was, poor thing!

Yegorushka examined his coat. It was a little grey overcoat with big bone buttons, cut in the shape of a frock-coat. At home, being a new and expensive article, it had not been hung in the hall, but with his mother's dresses in her bedroom; he was only allowed to wear it on holidays. Looking at it, Yegorushka felt sorry for it. He thought that he and the great-coat were both abandoned to the mercy of destiny; he thought that he would never get back home, and began sobbing so violently that he almost fell off the heap of dung.

A big white dog with woolly tufts like curl-papers about its face, sopping from the rain, came into the shed and stared with curiosity at Yegorushka. It seemed to be hesitating whether to bark or not. Deciding that there was no need to bark, it went cautiously up to Yegorushka, ate the sticky plaster and went out again.

"There are Varlamov's men!" someone shouted in the street.

After having his cry out, Yegorushka went out of the shed and, walking round a big puddle, made his way towards the street. The waggons were standing exactly opposite the gateway. The drenched waggoners, with their muddy feet, were sauntering beside them or sitting on the shafts, as listless and drowsy as flies in autumn. Yegorushka looked at them and thought: "How dreary and comfortless to be a peasant!" He went up to Panteley and sat down beside him on the shaft.

"Grandfather, I'm cold," he said, shivering and thrusting his hands up his sleeves.

"Never mind, we shall soon be there," yawned Panteley. "Never mind, you will get warm."

It must have been early when the waggons set off, for it was not hot. Yegorushka lay on the bales of wool and shivered with cold, though the sun soon came out and dried his clothes, the bales, and the earth. As soon as he closed his eyes he saw Tit and the windmill again. Feeling a sickness and heaviness all over, he did his utmost to drive away these images, but as soon as they vanished the dare-devil Dymov, with red eyes and lifted fists, rushed at Yegorushka with a roar, or there was the sound of his complaint: "I am so dreary!" Varlamov rode by on his little Cossack stallion; happy Konstantin passed, with a smile and the bustard in his arms. And how tedious these people were, how sickening and unbearable!

Once -- it was towards evening -- he raised his head to ask for water. The waggons were standing on a big bridge across a broad river. There was black smoke below over the river, and through it could be seen a steamer with a barge in tow. Ahead of them, beyond the river, was a huge mountain dotted with houses and churches; at the foot of the mountain an engine was being shunted along beside some goods trucks.

Yegorushka had never before seen steamers, nor engines, nor broad rivers. Glancing at them now, he was not alarmed or surprised; there was not even a look of anything like curiosity in his face. He merely felt sick, and made haste to turn over to the edge of the bale. He was sick. Panteley, seeing this, cleared his throat and shook his head.

"Our little lad's taken ill," he said. "He must have got a chill to the stomach. The little lad must. . . away from home; it's a bad lookout!"

VIII

The waggons stopped at a big inn for merchants, not far from the quay. As Yegorushka climbed down from the waggon he heard a very familiar voice. Someone was helping him to get down, and saying:

"We arrived yesterday evening. . . . We have been expecting you all day. We meant to overtake you yesterday, but it was out of our way; we came by the other road. I say, how you have crumpled your coat! You'll catch it from your uncle!"

Yegorushka looked into the speaker's mottled face and remembered that this was Deniska.

"Your uncle and Father Christopher are in the inn now, drinking tea; come along!"

And he led Yegorushka to a big two-storied building, dark and gloomy like the almshouse at N. After going across the entry, up a dark staircase and through a narrow corridor, Yegorushka and Deniska reached a little room in which Ivan Ivanitch and Father Christopher were sitting at the tea-table. Seeing the boy, both the old men showed surprise and pleasure.

"Aha! Yegor Ni-ko-la-aitch!" chanted Father Christopher. "Mr. Lomonosov!"

"Ah, our gentleman that is to be," said Kuzmitchov, "pleased to see you!"

Yegorushka took off his great-coat, kissed his uncle's hand and Father Christopher's, and sat down to the table.

"Well, how did you like the journey, puer bone?" Father Christopher pelted him with questions as he poured him out some tea, with his radiant smile. "Sick of it, I've no doubt? God save us all from having to travel by waggon or with oxen. You go on and on, God forgive us; you look ahead and the steppe is always lying stretched out the same as it was -- you can't see the end of it! It's not travelling but regular torture. Why don't you drink your tea? Drink it up; and in your absence, while you have been trailing along with the waggons, we have settled all our business capitally. Thank God we have sold our wool to Tcherepahin, and no one could wish to have done better. . . . We have made a good bargain."

At the first sight of his own people Yegorushka felt an overwhelming desire to complain. He did not listen to Father Christopher, but thought how to begin and what exactly to complain of. But Father Christopher's voice, which seemed to him harsh and unpleasant, prevented him from concentrating his attention and confused his thoughts. He had not sat at the table five minutes before he got up, went to the sofa and lay down.

"Well, well," said Father Christopher in surprise. "What about your tea?"

Still thinking what to complain of, Yegorushka leaned his head against the wall and broke into sobs.

"Well, well!" repeated Father Christopher, getting up and going to the sofa. "Yegory, what is the matter with you? Why are you crying?"

"I'm . . . I'm ill," Yegorushka brought out.

"Ill?" said Father Christopher in amazement. "That's not the right thing, my boy. . . . One mustn't be ill on a journey. Aie, aie, what are you thinking about, boy . . . eh?"

He put his hand to Yegorushka's head, touched his cheek and said:

"Yes, your head's feverish. . . . You must have caught cold or else have eaten something. . . . Pray to God."

"Should we give him quinine? . . ." said Ivan Ivanitch, troubled.

"No; he ought to have something hot. . . . Yegory, have a little drop of soup? Eh?"

"I . . . don't want any," said Yegorushka.

"Are you feeling chilly?"

"I was chilly before, but now . . . now I am hot. And I ache all over. . . ."

Ivan Ivanitch went up to the sofa, touched Yegorushka on the head, cleared his throat with a perplexed air, and went back to the table.

"I tell you what, you undress and go to bed," said Father Christopher. "What you want is sleep now."

He helped Yegorushka to undress, gave him a pillow and covered him with a quilt, and over that Ivan Ivanitch's great-coat. Then he walked away on tiptoe and sat down to the table. Yegorushka shut his eyes, and at once it seemed to him that he was not in the hotel room, but on the highroad beside the camp fire. Emelyan waved his hands, and Dymov with red eyes lay on his stomach and looked mockingly at Yegorushka.

"Beat him, beat him!" shouted Yegorushka.

"He is delirious," said Father Christopher in an undertone.

"It's a nuisance!" sighed Ivan Ivanitch.

"He must be rubbed with oil and vinegar. Please God, he will be better to-morrow."

To be rid of bad dreams, Yegorushka opened his eyes and began looking towards the fire. Father Christopher and Ivan Ivanitch had now finished their tea and were talking in a whisper. The first was smiling with delight, and evidently could not forget that he had made a good bargain over his wool; what delighted him was not so much the actual profit he had made as the thought that on getting home he would gather round him his big family, wink slyly and go off into a chuckle; at first he would deceive them all, and say that he had sold the wool at a price below its value, then he would give his son-in-law, Mihail, a fat pocket-book and say: "Well, take it! that's the way to do business!" Kuzmitchov did not seem pleased; his face expressed, as before, a business-like reserve and anxiety.

"If I could have known that Tcherepahin would give such a price," he said in a low voice, "I wouldn't have sold Makarov those five tons at home. It is vexatious! But who could have told that the price had gone up here?"

A man in a white shirt cleared away the samovar and lighted the little lamp before the ikon in the corner. Father Christopher whispered something in his ear; the man looked, made a serious face like a conspirator, as though to say, "I understand," went out, and returned a little while afterwards and put something under the sofa. Ivan Ivanitch made himself a bed on the floor, yawned several times, said his prayers lazily, and lay down.

"I think of going to the cathedral to-morrow," said Father Christopher. "I know the sacristan there. I ought to go and see the bishop after mass, but they say he is ill."

He yawned and put out the lamp. Now there was no light in the room but the little lamp before the ikon.

"They say he can't receive visitors," Father Christopher went on, undressing. "So I shall go away without seeing him."

He took off his full coat, and Yegorushka saw Robinson Crusoe reappear. Robinson stirred something in a saucer, went up to Yegorushka and whispered:

"Lomonosov, are you asleep? Sit up; I'm going to rub you with oil and vinegar. It's a good thing, only you must say a prayer."

Yegorushka roused himself quickly and sat up. Father Christopher pulled down the boy's shirt, and shrinking and breathing jerkily, as though he were being tickled himself, began rubbing Yegorushka's chest.

"In the name of the Father, the Son, and the Holy Ghost," he whispered, "lie with your back upwards -- that's it. . . . You'll be all right to-morrow, but don't do it again. . . . You are as hot as fire. I suppose you were on the road in the storm."

"Yes."

"You might well fall ill! In the name of the Father, the Son, and the Holy Ghost, . . . you might well fall ill!"

After rubbing Yegorushka, Father Christopher put on his shirt again, covered him, made the sign of the cross over him, and walked away. Then Yegorushka saw him saying his prayers. Probably the old man knew a great many prayers by heart, for he stood a long time before the ikon murmuring. After saying his prayers he made the sign of the cross over the window, the door, Yegorushka, and Ivan Ivanitch, lay down on the little sofa without a pillow, and covered himself with his full coat. A clock in the corridor struck ten. Yegorushka thought how long a time it would be before morning; feeling miserable, he pressed his forehead against the back of the sofa and left off trying to get rid of the oppressive misty dreams. But morning came much sooner than he expected.

It seemed to him that he had not been lying long with his head pressed to the back of the sofa, but when he opened his eyes slanting rays of sunlight were already shining on the floor through the two windows of the little hotel room. Father Christopher and Ivan Ivanitch were not in the room. The room had been tidied; it was bright, snug, and smelt of Father Christopher, who always smelt of cypress and dried cornflowers (at home he used to make the holy-water sprinklers and decorations for the ikonstands out of cornflowers, and so he was saturated with the smell of them). Yegorushka looked at the pillow, at the slanting sunbeams, at his boots, which had been cleaned and were standing side by side near the sofa, and laughed. It seemed strange to him that he was not on the bales of wool, that everything was dry around him, and that there was no thunder and lightning on the ceiling.

He jumped off the sofa and began dressing. He felt splendid; nothing was left of his yesterday's illness but a slight weakness in his legs and neck. So the vinegar and oil had done good. He remembered the steamer, the railway engine, and the broad river, which he had dimly seen the day before, and now he made haste to dress, to run to the quay and have a look at them. When he had washed and was putting on his red shirt, the latch of the door clicked, and Father Christopher appeared in the doorway, wearing his top-hat and a brown silk cassock over his canvas coat and carrying his staff in his hand. Smiling and radiant (old men are always radiant when they come back from church), he put a roll of holy bread and a parcel of some sort on the table, prayed before the ikon, and said:

"God has sent us blessings -- well, how are you?"

"Quite well now," answered Yegorushka, kissing his hand.

"Thank God. . . . I have come from mass. I've been to see a sacristan I know. He invited me to breakfast with him, but I didn't go. I don't like visiting people too early, God bless them!"

He took off his cassock, stroked himself on the chest, and without haste undid the parcel. Yegorushka saw a little tin of caviare, a piece of dry sturgeon, and a French loaf.

"See; I passed a fish-shop and brought this," said Father Christopher. "There is no need to indulge in luxuries on an ordinary weekday; but I thought, I've an invalid at home, so it is excusable. And the caviare is good, real sturgeon. . . ."

The man in the white shirt brought in the samovar and a tray with tea-things.

"Eat some," said Father Christopher, spreading the caviare on a slice of bread and handing it to Yegorushka. "Eat now and enjoy yourself, but the time will soon come for you to be studying. Mind you study with attention and application, so that good may come of it. What you have to learn by heart, learn by heart, but when you have to tell the inner sense in your own words, without regard to the outer form, then say it in your own words. And try to master all subjects. One man knows mathematics excellently, but has never heard of Pyotr Mogila; another knows about Pyotr Mogila, but cannot explain about the moon. But you study so as to understand everything. Study Latin, French, German, . . . geography, of course, history, theology, philosophy, mathematics, . . . and when you have mastered everything, not with haste but with prayer and with zeal, then go into the service. When you know everything it will be easy for you in any line of life. . . . You study and strive for the divine blessing, and God will show you what to be. Whether a doctor, a judge or an engineer. . . ."

Father Christopher spread a little caviare on a piece of bread, put it in his mouth and said:

"The Apostle Paul says: 'Do not apply yourself to strange and diverse studies.' Of course, if it is black magic, unlawful arts, or calling up spirits from the other world, like Saul, or studying subjects that can be of no use to yourself or others, better not learn them. You must undertake only what God has blessed. Take example . . . the Holy Apostles spoke in all languages, so you study languages. Basil the Great studied mathematics and philosophy -- so you study them; St. Nestor wrote history -- so you study and write history. Take example from the saints."

Father Christopher sipped the tea from his saucer, wiped his moustaches, and shook his head.

"Good!" he said. "I was educated in the old-fashioned way; I have forgotten a great deal by now, but still I live differently from other people. Indeed, there is no comparison. For instance, in company at a dinner, or at an assembly, one says something in Latin, or makes some allusion from history or philosophy, and it pleases people, and it pleases me myself. . . . Or when the circuit court comes and one has to take the oath, all the other priests are shy, but I am quite at home with the judges, the prosecutors, and the lawyers. I talk intellectually, drink a cup of tea with them, laugh, ask them what I don't know, . . . and they like it. So that's how it is, my boy. Learning is light and ignorance is darkness. Study! It's hard, of course; nowadays study is expensive. . . . Your mother is a widow; she lives on her pension, but there, of course . . ."

Father Christopher glanced apprehensively towards the door, and went on in a whisper:

"Ivan Ivanitch will assist. He won't desert you. He has no children of his own, and he will help you. Don't be uneasy."

He looked grave, and whispered still more softly:

"Only mind, Yegory, don't forget your mother and Ivan Ivanitch, God preserve you from it. The commandment bids you honour your mother, and Ivan Ivanitch is your benefactor and takes the place of a father to you. If you become learned, God forbid you should be impatient and scornful with people because they are not so clever as you, then woe, woe to you!"

Father Christopher raised his hand and repeated in a thin voice:

"Woe to you! Woe to you!"

Father Christopher's tongue was loosened, and he was, as they say, warming to his subject; he would not have finished till dinnertime but the door opened and Ivan Ivanitch walked in. He said good-morning hurriedly, sat down to the table, and began rapidly swallowing his tea.

"Well, I have settled all our business," he said. "We might have gone home to-day, but we have still to think about Yegor. We must arrange for him. My sister told me that Nastasya Petrovna, a friend of hers, lives somewhere here, so perhaps she will take him in as a boarder."

He rummaged in his pocket-book, found a crumpled note and read:

" 'Little Lower Street: Nastasya Petrovna Toskunov, living in a house of her own.' We must go at once and try to find her. It's a nuisance!"

Soon after breakfast Ivan Ivanitch and Yegorushka left the inn.

"It's a nuisance," muttered his uncle. "You are sticking to me like a burr. You and your mother want education and gentlemanly breeding and I have nothing but worry with you both. . . ."

When they crossed the yard, the waggons and the drivers were not there. They had all gone off to the quay early in the morning. In a far-off dark corner of the yard stood the chaise.

"Good-bye, chaise!" thought Yegorushka.

At first they had to go a long way uphill by a broad street, then they had to cross a big marketplace; here Ivan Ivanitch asked a policeman for Little Lower Street.

"I say," said the policeman, with a grin, "it's a long way off, out that way towards the town grazing ground."

They met several cabs but Ivan Ivanitch only permitted himself such a weakness as taking a cab in exceptional cases and on great holidays. Yegorushka and he walked for a long while through paved streets, then along streets where there were only wooden planks at the sides and no pavements, and in the end got to streets where there were neither planks nor pavements. When their legs and their tongues had brought them to Little Lower Street they were both red in the face, and taking off their hats, wiped away the perspiration.

"Tell me, please," said Ivan Ivanitch, addressing an old man sitting on a little bench by a gate, "where is Nastasya Petrovna Toskunov's house?"

"There is no one called Toskunov here," said the old man, after pondering a moment. "Perhaps it's Timoshenko you want."

"No, Toskunov. . . ."

"Excuse me, there's no one called Toskunov. . . ."

Ivan Ivanitch shrugged his shoulders and trudged on farther.

"You needn't look," the old man called after them. "I tell you there isn't, and there isn't."

"Listen, auntie," said Ivan Ivanitch, addressing an old woman who was sitting at a corner with a tray of pears and sunflower seeds, "where is Nastasya Petrovna Toskunov's house?"

The old woman looked at him with surprise and laughed.

"Why, Nastasya Petrovna live in her own house now!" she cried. "Lord! it is eight years since she married her daughter and gave up the house to her son-in-law! It's her son-in-law lives there now."

And her eyes expressed: "How is it you didn't know a simple thing like that, you fools?"

"And where does she live now?" Ivan Ivanitch asked.

"Oh, Lord!" cried the old woman, flinging up her hands in surprise. "She moved ever so long ago! It's eight years since she gave up her house to her son-in-law! Upon my word!"

She probably expected Ivan Ivanitch to be surprised, too, and to exclaim: "You don't say so," but Ivan Ivanitch asked very calmly:

"Where does she live now?"

The old woman tucked up her sleeves and, stretching out her bare arm to point, shouted in a shrill piercing voice:

"Go straight on, straight on, straight on. You will pass a little red house, then you will see a little alley on your left. Turn down that little alley, and it will be the third gate on the right. . . ."

Ivan Ivanitch and Yegorushka reached the little red house, turned to the left down the little alley, and made for the third gate on the right. On both sides of this very old grey gate there was a grey fence with big gaps in it. The first part of the fence was tilting forwards and threatened to fall, while on the left of the gate it sloped backwards towards the yard. The gate itself stood upright and seemed to be still undecided which would suit it best -- to fall forwards or backwards. Ivan Ivanitch opened the little gate at the side, and he and Yegorushka saw a big yard overgrown with weeds and burdocks. A hundred paces from the gate stood a little house with a red roof and green shutters. A stout woman with her sleeves tucked up and her apron held out was standing in the middle of the yard, scattering something on the ground and shouting in a voice as shrill as that of the woman selling fruit:

"Chick! . . . Chick! . . . Chick!"

Behind her sat a red dog with pointed ears. Seeing the strangers, he ran to the little gate and broke into a tenor bark (all red dogs have a tenor bark).

"Whom do you want?" asked the woman, putting up her hand to shade her eyes from the sun.

"Good-morning!" Ivan Ivanitch shouted, too, waving off the red dog with his stick. "Tell me, please, does Nastasya Petrovna Toskunov live here?"

"Yes! But what do you want with her?"

"Perhaps you are Nastasya Petrovna?"

"Well, yes, I am!"

"Very pleased to see you. . . . You see, your old friend Olga Ivanovna Knyasev sends her love to you. This is her little son. And I, perhaps you remember, am her brother Ivan Ivanitch. . . . You are one of us from N. . . . You were born among us and married there. . . ."

A silence followed. The stout woman stared blankly at Ivan Ivanitch, as though not believing or not understanding him, then she flushed all over, and flung up her hands; the oats were scattered out of her apron and tears spurted from her eyes.

"Olga Ivanovna!" she screamed, breathless with excitement. "My own darling! Ah, holy saints, why am I standing here like a fool? My pretty little angel. . . ."

She embraced Yegorushka, wetted his face with her tears, and broke down completely.

"Heavens!" she said, wringing her hands, "Olga's little boy! How delightful! He is his mother all over! The image of his mother! But why are you standing in the yard? Come indoors."

Crying, gasping for breath and talking as she went, she hurried towards the house. Her visitors trudged after her.

"The room has not been done yet," she said, ushering the visitors into a stuffy little drawing-room adorned with many ikons and pots of flowers. "Oh, Mother of God! Vassilisa, go and open the shutters anyway! My little angel! My little beauty! I did not know that Olitchka had a boy like that!"

When she had calmed down and got over her first surprise Ivan Ivanitch asked to speak to her alone. Yegorushka went into another room; there was a sewing-machine; in the window was a cage with a starling in it, and there were as many ikons and flowers as in the drawing-room. Near the machine stood a little girl with a sunburnt face and chubby cheeks like Tit's, and a clean cotton dress. She stared at Yegorushka without blinking, and apparently felt very awkward. Yegorushka looked at her and after a pause asked:

"What's your name?"

The little girl moved her lips, looked as if she were going to cry, and answered softly:

"Atka. . . ."

This meant Katka.

"He will live with you," Ivan Ivanitch was whispering in the drawing-room, "if you will be so kind, and we will pay ten roubles a month for his keep. He is not a spoilt boy; he is quiet. . . ."

"I really don't know what to say, Ivan Ivanitch!" Nastasya Petrovna sighed tearfully. "Ten roubles a month is very good, but it is a dreadful thing to take another person's child! He may fall ill or something. . . ."

When Yegorushka was summoned back to the drawing-room Ivan Ivanitch was standing with his hat in his hands, saying good-bye.

"Well, let him stay with you now, then," he said. "Good-bye! You stay, Yegor!" he said, addressing his nephew. "Don't be troublesome; mind you obey Nastasya Petrovna. . . . Good-bye; I am coming again to-morrow."

And he went away. Nastasya once more embraced Yegorushka, called him a little angel, and with a tear-stained face began preparing for dinner. Three minutes later Yegorushka was sitting beside her, answering her endless questions and eating hot savoury cabbage soup.

In the evening he sat again at the same table and, resting his head on his hand, listened to Nastasya Petrovna. Alternately laughing and crying, she talked of his mother's young days, her own marriage, her children. . . . A cricket chirruped in the stove, and there was a faint humming from the burner of the lamp. Nastasya Petrovna talked in a low voice, and was continually dropping her thimble in her excitement; and Katka her granddaughter, crawled under the table after it and each time sat a long while under the table, probably examining Yegorushka's feet; and Yegorushka listened, half dozing and looking at the old woman's face, her wart with hairs on it, and the stains of tears, and he felt sad, very sad. He was put to sleep on a chest and told that if he were hungry in the night he must go out into the little passage and take some chicken, put there under a plate in the window.

Next morning Ivan Ivanitch and Father Christopher came to say good-bye. Nastasya Petrovna was delighted to see them, and was about to set the samovar; but Ivan Ivanitch, who was in a great hurry, waved his hands and said:

"We have no time for tea! We are just setting off."

Before parting they all sat down and were silent for a minute. Nastasya Petrovna heaved a deep sigh and looked towards the ikon with tear-stained eyes.

"Well," began Ivan Ivanitch, getting up, "so you will stay. . . ."

All at once the look of business-like reserve vanished from his face; he flushed a little and said with a mournful smile:

"Mind you work hard. . . . Don't forget your mother, and obey Nastasya Petrovna. . . . If you are diligent at school, Yegor, I'll stand by you."

He took his purse out of his pocket, turned his back to Yegorushka, fumbled for a long time among the smaller coins, and, finding a ten-kopeck piece, gave it to Yegorushka.

Father Christopher, without haste, blessed Yegorushka.

"In the name of the Father, the Son, and the Holy Ghost. . . . Study," he said. "Work hard, my lad. If I die, remember me in your prayers. Here is a ten-kopeck piece from me, too. . . ."

Yegorushka kissed his hand, and shed tears; something whispered in his heart that he would never see the old man again.

"I have applied at the high school already," said Ivan Ivanitch in a voice as though there were a corpse in the room. "You will take him for the entrance examination on the seventh of August. . . . Well, good-bye; God bless you, good-bye, Yegor!"

"You might at least have had a cup of tea," wailed Nastasya Petrovna.

Through the tears that filled his eyes Yegorushka could not see his uncle and Father Christopher go out. He rushed to the window, but they were not in the yard, and the red dog, who had just been barking, was running back from the gate with the air of having done his duty. When Yegorushka ran out of the gate Ivan Ivanitch and Father Christopher, the former waving his stick with the crook, the latter his staff, were just turning the corner. Yegorushka felt that with these people all that he had known till then had vanished from him forever.

He sank helplessly on to the little bench, and with bitter tears greeted the new unknown life that was beginning for him now. . . .

What would that life be like?

LIGHTS

The dog was barking excitedly outside. And Ananyev the engineer, his assistant called Von Schtenberg, and I went out of the hut to see at whom it was barking. I was the visitor, and might have remained indoors, but I must confess my head was a little dizzy from the wine I had drunk, and I was glad to get a breath of fresh air.

"There is nobody here," said Ananyev when we went out. "Why are you telling stories, Azorka? You fool!"

There was not a soul in sight.

"The fool," Azorka, a black house-dog, probably conscious of his guilt in barking for nothing and anxious to propitiate us, approached us, diffidently wagging his tail. The engineer bent down and touched him between his ears.

"Why are you barking for nothing, creature?" he said in the tone in which good-natured people talk to children and dogs. "Have you had a bad dream or what? Here, doctor, let me commend to your attention," he said, turning to me, "a wonderfully nervous subject! Would you believe it, he can't endure solitude -- he is always having terrible dreams and suffering from nightmares; and when you shout at him he has something like an attack of hysterics."

"Yes, a dog of refined feelings," the student chimed in.

Azorka must have understood that the conversation was concerning him. He turned his head upwards and grinned plaintively, as though to say, "Yes, at times I suffer unbearably, but please excuse it!"

It was an August night, there were stars, but it was dark. Owing to the fact that I had never in my life been in such exceptional surroundings, as I had chanced to come into now, the starry night seemed to me gloomy, inhospitable, and darker than it was in reality. I was on a railway line which was still in process of construction. The high, half-finished embankment, the mounds of sand, clay, and rubble, the holes, the wheel-barrows standing here and there, the flat tops of the mud huts in which the workmen lived -- all this muddle, coloured to one tint by the darkness, gave the earth a strange, wild aspect that suggested the times of chaos. There was so little order in all that lay before me that it was somehow strange in the midst of the hideously excavated, grotesque-looking earth to see the silhouettes of human beings and the slender telegraph posts. Both spoiled the ensemble of the picture, and seemed to belong to a different world. It was still, and the only sound came from the telegraph wire droning its wearisome refrain somewhere very high above our heads.

We climbed up on the embankment and from its height looked down upon the earth. A hundred yards away where the pits, holes, and mounds melted into the darkness of the night, a dim light was twinkling. Beyond it gleamed another light, beyond that a third, then a hundred paces away two red eyes glowed side by side -- probably the windows of some hut -- and a long series of such lights, growing continually closer and dimmer, stretched along the line to the very horizon, then turned in a semicircle to the left and disappeared in the darkness of the distance. The lights were motionless. There seemed to be something in common between them and the stillness of the night and the disconsolate song of the telegraph wire. It seemed as though some weighty secret were buried under the embankment and only the lights, the night, and the wires knew of it.

"How glorious, O Lord!" sighed Ananyev; "such space and beauty that one can't tear oneself away! And what an embankment! It's not an embankment, my dear fellow, but a regular Mont Blanc. It's costing millions. . . ."

Going into ecstasies over the lights and the embankment that was costing millions, intoxicated by the wine and his sentimental mood, the engineer slapped Von Schtenberg on the shoulder and went on in a jocose tone:

"Well, Mihail Mihailitch, lost in reveries? No doubt it is pleasant to look at the work of one's own hands, eh? Last year this very spot was bare steppe, not a sight of human life, and now look: life . . . civilisation. . . And how splendid it all is, upon my soul! You and I are building a railway, and after we are gone, in another century or two, good men will build a factory, a school, a hospital, and things will begin to move! Eh!"

The student stood motionless with his hands thrust in his pockets, and did not take his eyes off the lights. He was not listening to the engineer, but was thinking, and was apparently in the mood in which one does not want to speak or to listen. After a prolonged silence he turned to me and said quietly:

"Do you know what those endless lights are like? They make me think of something long dead, that lived thousands of years ago, something like the camps of the Amalekites or the Philistines. It is as though some people of the Old Testament had pitched their camp and were waiting for morning to fight with Saul or David. All that is wanting to complete the illusion is the blare of trumpets and sentries calling to one another in some Ethiopian language."

And, as though of design, the wind fluttered over the line and brought a sound like the clank of weapons. A silence followed. I don't know what the engineer and the student were thinking of, but it seemed to me already that I actually saw before me something long dead and even heard the sentry talking in an unknown tongue. My imagination hastened to picture the tents, the strange people, their clothes, their armour.

"Yes," muttered the student pensively, "once Philistines and Amalekites were living in this world, making wars, playing their part, and now no trace of them remains. So it will be with us. Now we are making a railway, are standing here philosophising, but two thousand years will pass -- and of this embankment and of all those men, asleep after their hard work, not one grain of dust will remain. In reality, it's awful!"

"You must drop those thoughts . . ." said the engineer gravely and admonishingly.

"Why?"

"Because. . . . Thoughts like that are for the end of life, not for the beginning of it. You are too young for them."

"Why so?" repeated the student.

"All these thoughts of the transitoriness, the insignificance and the aimlessness of life, of the inevitability of death, of the shadows of the grave, and so on, all such lofty thoughts, I tell you, my dear fellow, are good and natural in old age when they come as the product of years of inner travail, and are won by suffering and really are intellectual riches; for a youthful brain on the threshold of real life they are simply a calamity! A calamity!" Ananyev repeated with a wave of his hand. "To my mind it is better at your age to have no head on your shoulders at all than to think on these lines. I am speaking seriously, Baron. And I have been meaning to speak to you about it for a long time, for I noticed from the very first day of our acquaintance your partiality for these damnable ideas!"

"Good gracious, why are they damnable?" the student asked with a smile, and from his voice and his face I could see that he asked the question from simple politeness, and that the discussion raised by the engineer did not interest him in the least.

I could hardly keep my eyes open. I was dreaming that immediately after our walk we should wish each other good-night and go to bed, but my dream was not quickly realised. When we had returned to the hut the engineer put away the empty bottles and took out of a large wicker hamper two full ones, and uncorking them, sat down to his work-table with the evident intention of going on drinking, talking, and working. Sipping a little from his glass, he made pencil notes on some plans and went on pointing out to the student that the latter's way of thinking was not what it should be. The student sat beside him checking accounts and saying nothing. He, like me, had no inclination to speak or to listen. That I might not interfere with their work, I sat away from the table on the engineer's crooked-legged travelling bedstead, feeling bored and expecting every moment that they would suggest I should go to bed. It was going on for one o'clock.

Having nothing to do, I watched my new acquaintances. I had never seen Ananyev or the student before. I had only made their acquaintance on the night I have described. Late in the evening I was returning on horseback from a fair to the house of a landowner with whom I was staying, had got on the wrong road in the dark and lost my way. Going round and round by the railway line and seeing how dark the night was becoming, I thought of the "barefoot railway roughs," who lie in wait for travellers on foot and on horseback, was frightened, and knocked at the first hut I came to. There I was cordially received by Ananyev and the student. As is usually the case with strangers casually brought together, we quickly became acquainted, grew friendly and at first over the tea and afterward over the wine, began to feel as though we had known each other for years. At the end of an hour or so, I knew who they were and how fate had brought them from town to the far-away steppe; and they knew who I was, what my occupation and my way of thinking.

Nikolay Anastasyevitch Ananyev, the engineer, was a broad-shouldered, thick-set man, and, judging from his appearance, he had, like Othello, begun the "descent into the vale of years," and was growing rather too stout. He was just at that stage which old match-making women mean when they speak of "a man in the prime of his age," that is, he was neither young nor old, was fond of good fare, good liquor, and praising the past, panted a little as he walked, snored loudly when he was asleep, and in his manner with those surrounding him displayed that calm imperturbable good humour which is always acquired by decent people by the time they have reached the grade of a staff officer and begun to grow stout. His hair and beard were far from being grey, but already, with a condescension of which he was unconscious, he addressed young men as "my dear boy" and felt himself entitled to lecture them good-humouredly about their way of thinking. His movements and his voice were calm, smooth, and self-confident, as they are in a man who is thoroughly well aware that he has got his feet firmly planted on the right road, that he has definite work, a secure living, a settled outlook. . . . His sunburnt, thicknosed face and muscular neck seemed to say: "I am well fed, healthy, satisfied with myself, and the time will come when you young people too, will be wellfed, healthy, and satisfied with yourselves. . . ." He was dressed in a cotton shirt with the collar awry and in full linen trousers thrust into his high boots. From certain trifles, as for instance, from his coloured worsted girdle, his embroidered collar, and the patch on his elbow, I was able to guess that he was married and in all probability tenderly loved by his wife.

Baron Von Schtenberg, a student of the Institute of Transport, was a young man of about three or four and twenty. Only his fair hair and scanty beard, and, perhaps, a certain coarseness and frigidity in his features showed traces of his descent from Barons of the Baltic provinces; everything else -- his name, Mihail Mihailovitch, his religion, his ideas, his manners, and the expression of his face were purely Russian. Wearing, like Ananyev, a cotton shirt and high boots, with his round shoulders, his hair left uncut, and his sunburnt face, he did not look like a student or a Baron, but like an ordinary Russian workman. His words and gestures were few, he drank reluctantly without relish, checked the accounts mechanically, and seemed all the while to be thinking of something else. His movements and voice were calm, and smooth too, but his calmness was of a different kind from the engineer's. His sunburnt, slightly ironical, dreamy face, his eyes which looked up from under his brows, and his whole figure were expressive of spiritual stagnation -- mental sloth. He looked as though it did not matter to him in the least whether the light were burning before him or not, whether the wine were nice or nasty, and whether the accounts he was checking were correct or not. . . . And on his intelligent, calm face I read: "I don't see so far any good in definite work, a secure living, and a settled outlook. It's all nonsense. I was in Petersburg, now I am sitting here in this hut, in the autumn I shall go back to Petersburg, then in the spring here again. . . . What sense there is in all that I don't know, and no one knows. . . . And so it's no use talking about it. . . ."

He listened to the engineer without interest, with the condescending indifference with which cadets in the senior classes listen to an effusive and good-natured old attendant. It seemed as though there were nothing new to him in what the engineer said, and that if he had not himself been too lazy to talk, he would have said something newer and cleverer. Meanwhile Ananyev would not desist. He had by now laid aside his good-humoured, jocose tone and spoke seriously, even with a fervour which was quite out of keeping with his expression of calmness. Apparently he had no distaste for abstract subjects, was fond of them, indeed, but had neither skill nor practice in the handling of them. And this lack of practice was so pronounced in his talk that I did not always grasp his meaning at once.

"I hate those ideas with all my heart!" he said, "I was infected by them myself in my youth, I have not quite got rid of them even now, and I tell you -- perhaps because I am stupid and such thoughts were not the right food for my mind -- they did me nothing but harm. That's easy to understand! Thoughts of the aimlessness of life, of the insignificance and transitoriness of the visible world, Solomon's 'vanity of vanities' have been, and are to this day, the highest and final stage in the realm of thought. The thinker reaches that stage and -- comes to a halt! There is nowhere further to go. The activity of the normal brain is completed with this, and that is natural and in the order of things. Our misfortune is that we begin thinking at that end. What normal people end with we begin with. From the first start, as soon as the brain begins working independently, we mount to the very topmost, final step and refuse to know anything about the steps below."

"What harm is there in that?" said the student.

"But you must understand that it's abnormal," shouted Ananyev, looking at him almost wrathfully. "If we find means of mounting to the topmost step without the help of the lower ones, then the whole long ladder, that is the whole of life, with its colours, sounds, and thoughts, loses all meaning for us. That at your age such reflections are harmful and absurd, you can see from every step of your rational independent life. Let us suppose you sit down this minute to read Darwin or Shakespeare, you have scarcely read a page before the poison shows itself; and your long life, and Shakespeare, and Darwin, seem to you nonsense, absurdity, because you know you will die, that Shakespeare and Darwin have died too, that their thoughts have not saved them, nor the earth, nor you, and that if life is deprived of meaning in that way, all science, poetry, and exalted thoughts seem only useless diversions, the idle playthings of grown up people; and you leave off reading at the second page. Now, let us suppose that people come to you as an intelligent man and ask your opinion about war, for instance: whether it is desirable, whether it is morally justifiable or not. In answer to that terrible question you merely shrug your shoulders and confine yourself to some commonplace, because for you, with your way of thinking, it makes absolutely no difference whether hundreds of thousands of people die a violent death, or a natural one: the results are the same -- ashes and oblivion. You and I are building a railway line. What's the use, one may ask, of our worrying our heads, inventing, rising above the hackneyed thing, feeling for the workmen, stealing or not stealing, when we know that this railway line will turn to dust within two thousand years, and so on, and so on. . . . You must admit that with such a disastrous way of looking at things there can be no progress, no science, no art, nor even thought itself. We fancy that we are cleverer than the crowd, and than Shakespeare. In reality our thinking leads to nothing because we have no inclination to go down to the lower steps and there is nowhere higher to go, so our brain stands at the freezing point -- neither up nor down; I was in bondage to these ideas for six years, and by all that is holy, I never read a sensible book all that time, did not gain a ha'porth of wisdom, and did not raise my moral standard an inch. Was not that disastrous? Moreover, besides being corrupted ourselves, we bring poison into the lives of those surrounding us. It would be all right if, with our pessimism, we renounced life, went to live in a cave, or made haste to die, but, as it is, in obedience to the universal law, we live, feel, love women, bring up children, construct railways!"

"Our thoughts make no one hot or cold," the student said reluctantly.

"Ah! there you are again! -- do stop it! You have not yet had a good sniff at life. But when you have lived as long as I have you will know a thing or two! Our theory of life is not so innocent as you suppose. In practical life, in contact with human beings, it leads to nothing but horrors and follies. It has been my lot to pass through experiences which I would not wish a wicked Tatar to endure."

"For instance?" I asked.

"For instance?" repeated the engineer.

He thought a minute, smiled and said:

"For instance, take this example. More correctly, it is not an example, but a regular drama, with a plot and a dénouement. An excellent lesson! Ah, what a lesson!"

He poured out wine for himself and us, emptied his glass, stroked his broad chest with his open hands, and went on, addressing himself more to me than to the student.

"It was in the year 187--, soon after the war, and when I had just left the University. I was going to the Caucasus, and on the way stopped for five days in the seaside town of N. I must tell you that I was born and grew up in that town, and so there is nothing odd in my thinking N. extraordinarily snug, cosy, and beautiful, though for a man from Petersburg or Moscow, life in it would be as dreary and comfortless as in any Tchuhloma or Kashira. With melancholy I passed by the high school where I had been a pupil; with melancholy I walked about the very familiar park, I made a melancholy attempt to get a nearer look at people I had not seen for a long time -- all with the same melancholy.

"Among other things, I drove out one evening to the so-called Quarantine. It was a small mangy copse in which, at some forgotten time of plague, there really had been a quarantine station, and which was now the resort of summer visitors. It was a drive of three miles from the town along a good soft road. As one drove along one saw on the left the blue sea, on the right the unending gloomy steppe; there was plenty of air to breathe, and wide views for the eyes to rest on. The copse itself lay on the seashore. Dismissing my cabman, I went in at the familiar gates and first turned along an avenue leading to a little stone summer-house which I had been fond of in my childhood. In my opinion that round, heavy summer-house on its clumsy columns, which combined the romantic charm of an old tomb with the ungainliness of a Sobakevitch,* was the most poetical nook in the whole town. It stood at the edge above the cliff, and from it there was a splendid view of the sea.

"I sat down on the seat, and, bending over the parapet, looked down. A path ran from the summer-house along the steep, almost overhanging cliff, between the lumps of clay and tussocks of burdock. Where it ended, far below on the sandy shore, low waves were languidly foaming and softly purring. The sea was as majestic, as infinite, and as forbidding as seven years before when I left the high school and went from my native town to the capital; in the distance there was a dark streak of smoke -- a steamer was passing -- and except for this hardly visible and motionless streak and the sea-swallows that flitted over the water, there was nothing to give life to the monotonous view of sea and sky. To right and left of the summer-house stretched uneven clay cliffs.

"You know that when a man in a melancholy mood is left *tête-à-tête* with the sea, or any landscape which seems to him grandiose, there is always, for some reason, mixed with melancholy, a conviction that he will live and die in obscurity, and he reflectively snatches up a pencil and hastens to write his name on the first thing that comes handy. And that, I suppose, is why all convenient solitary nooks like my summer-house are always scrawled over in pencil or carved with penknives. I remember as though it were to-day; looking at the parapet I read: 'Ivan Korolkov, May 16, 1876.' Beside Korolkov some local dreamer had scribbled freely, adding:

" 'He stood on the desolate ocean's strand,
While his soul was filled with imaginings grand.'

And his handwriting was dreamy, limp like wet silk. An individual called Kross, probably an insignificant, little man, felt his unimportance so deeply that he gave full licence to his penknife and carved his name in deep letters an inch high. I took a pencil out of my pocket mechanically, and I too scribbled on one of the columns. All that is irrelevant, however. . . You must forgive me -- I don't know how to tell a story briefly.

"I was sad and a little bored. Boredom, the stillness, and the purring of the sea gradually brought me to the line of thought we have been discussing. At that period, towards the end of the 'seventies, it had begun to be fashionable with the public, and later, at the beginning of the 'eighties, it gradually passed from the general public into literature, science, and politics. I was no more than twenty-six at the time, but I knew perfectly well that life was aimless and had no meaning, that everything was a deception and an illusion, that in its essential nature and results a life of penal servitude in Sahalin was not in any way different from a life spent in Nice, that the difference between the brain of a Kant and the brain of a fly was of no real significance, that no one in this world is righteous or guilty, that everything was stuff and nonsense and damn it all! I lived as though I were doing a favour to some unseen power which compelled me to live, and to which I seemed to say: 'Look, I don't care a straw for life, but I am living!' I thought on one definite line, but in all sorts of keys, and in that respect I was like the subtle gourmand who could prepare a hundred appetising dishes from nothing but potatoes. There is no doubt that I was one-sided and even to some extent narrow, but I fancied at the time that my intellectual horizon had neither beginning nor end, and that my thought was as boundless as the sea. Well, as far as I can judge by myself, the philosophy of which we are speaking has something alluring, narcotic in its nature, like tobacco or morphia. It becomes a habit, a craving. You take advantage of every minute of solitude to gloat over thoughts of the aimlessness of life and the darkness of the grave. While I was sitting in the summer-house, Greek children with long noses were decorously walking about the avenues. I took advantage of the occasion and, looking at them, began reflecting in this style:

"'Why are these children born, and what are they living for? Is there any sort of meaning in their existence? They grow up, without themselves knowing what for; they will live in this God-forsaken, comfortless hole for no sort of reason, and then they will die. . . .'

"And I actually felt vexed with those children because they were walking about decorously and talking with dignity, as though they did not hold their little colourless lives so cheap and knew what they were living for. . . . I remember that far away at the end of an avenue three feminine figures came into sight. Three young ladies, one in a pink dress, two in white, were walking arm-in-arm, talking and laughing. Looking after them, I thought:

" 'It wouldn't be bad to have an affair with some woman for a couple of days in this dull place.'

"I recalled by the way that it was three weeks since I had visited my Petersburg lady, and thought that a passing love affair would come in very appropriately for me just now. The young lady in white in the middle was rather younger and better looking than her companions, and judging by her manners and her laugh, she was a high-school girl in an upper form. I looked, not without impure thoughts, at her bust, and at the same time reflected about her: 'She will be trained in music and manners, she will be married to some Greek -- God help us! -- will lead a grey, stupid, comfortless life, will bring into the world a crowd of children without knowing why, and then will die. An absurd life!'

"I must say that as a rule I was a great hand at combining my lofty ideas with the lowest prose.

Thoughts of the darkness of the grave did not prevent me from giving busts and legs their full due. Our dear Baron's exalted ideas do not prevent him from going on Saturdays to Vukolovka on amatory expeditions. To tell the honest truth, as far as I remember, my attitude to women was most insulting. Now, when I think of that high-school girl, I blush for my thoughts then, but at the time my conscience was perfectly untroubled. I, the son of honourable parents, a Christian, who had received a superior education, not naturally wicked or stupid, felt not the slightest uneasiness when I paid women *Blutgeld,* as the Germans call it, or when I followed highschool girls with insulting looks. . . . The trouble is that youth makes its demands, and our philosophy has nothing in principle against those demands, whether they are good or whether they are loathsome. One who knows that life is aimless and death inevitable is not interested in the struggle against nature or the conception of sin: whether you struggle or whether you don't, you will die and rot just the same. . . . Secondly, my friends, our philosophy instils even into very young people what is called reasonableness. The predominance of reason over the heart is simply overwhelming amongst us. Direct feeling, inspiration -- everything is choked by petty analysis. Where there is reasonableness there is coldness, and cold people -- it's no use to disguise it -- know nothing of chastity. That virtue is only known to those who are warm, affectionate, and capable of love. Thirdly, our philosophy denies the significance of each individual personality. It's easy to see that if I deny the personality of some Natalya Stepanovna, it's absolutely nothing to me whether she is insulted or not. To-day one insults her dignity as a human being and pays her *Blutgeld,* and next day thinks no more of her.

"So I sat in the summer-house and watched the young ladies. Another woman's figure appeared in the avenue, with fair hair, her head uncovered and a white knitted shawl on her shoulders. She walked along the avenue, then came into the summer-house, and taking hold of the parapet, looked indifferently below and into the distance over the sea. As she came in she paid no attention to me, as though she did not notice me. I scrutinised her from foot to head (not from head to foot, as one scrutinises men) and found that she was young, not more than five-and-twenty, nice-looking, with a good figure, in all probability married and belonging to the class of respectable women. She was dressed as though she were at home, but fashionably and with taste, as ladies are, as a rule, in N.

" 'This one would do nicely,' I thought, looking at her handsome figure and her arms; 'she is all right. . . . She is probably the wife of some doctor or schoolmaster. . . .'

"But to make up to her -- that is, to make her the heroine of one of those impromptu affairs to which tourists are so prone -- was not easy and, indeed, hardly possible. I felt that as I gazed at her face. The way she looked, and the expression of her face, suggested that the sea, the smoke in the distance, and the sky had bored her long, long ago, and wearied her sight. She seemed to be tired, bored, and thinking about something dreary, and her face had not even that fussy, affectedly indifferent expression which one sees in the face of almost every woman when she is conscious of the presence of an unknown man in her vicinity.

"The fair-haired lady took a bored and passing glance at me, sat down on a seat and sank into reverie, and from her face I saw that she had no thoughts for me, and that I, with my Petersburg appearance, did not arouse in her even simple curiosity. But yet I made up my mind to speak to her, and asked: 'Madam, allow me to ask you at what time do the waggonettes go from here to the town?'

" 'At ten or eleven, I believe. . . .' "

"I thanked her. She glanced at me once or twice, and suddenly there was a gleam of curiosity, then of something like wonder on her passionless face. . . . I made haste to assume an indifferent expression and to fall into a suitable attitude; she was catching on! She suddenly jumped up from the seat, as though something had bitten her, and examining me hurriedly, with a gentle smile, asked timidly:

" 'Oh, aren't you Ananyev?'

"'Yes, I am Ananyev,' I answered.

"'And don't you recognise me? No?'

"I was a little confused. I looked intently at her, and -- would you believe it? -- I recognised her not from her face nor her figure, but from her gentle, weary smile. It was Natalya Stepanovna, or, as she was called, Kisotchka, the very girl I had been head over ears in love with seven or eight years before, when I was wearing the uniform of a high-school boy. The doings of far, vanished days, the days of long ago. . . . I remember this Kisotchka, a thin little high-school girl of fifteen or sixteen, when she was something just for a schoolboy's taste, created by nature especially for Platonic love. What a charming little girl she was! Pale, fragile, light -- she looked as though a breath would send her flying like a feather to the skies -- a gentle, perplexed face, little hands, soft long hair to her belt, a waist as thin as a wasp's -- altogether something ethereal, transparent like moonlight -- in fact, from the point of view of a high-school boy a peerless beauty. . . . Wasn't I in love with her! I did not sleep at night. I wrote verses. . . . Sometimes in the evenings she would sit on a seat in the park while we schoolboys crowded round her, gazing reverently; in response to our compliments, our sighing, and attitudinising, she would shrink nervously from the evening damp, screw up her eyes, and smile gently, and at such times she was awfully like a pretty little kitten. As we gazed at her everyone of us had a desire to caress her and stroke her like a cat, hence her nickname of Kisotchka.

"In the course of the seven or eight years since we had met, Kisotchka had greatly changed. She had grown more robust and stouter, and had quite lost the resemblance to a soft, fluffy kitten. It was not that her features looked old or faded, but they had somehow lost their brilliance and looked sterner, her hair seemed shorter, she looked taller, and her shoulders were quite twice as broad, and what was most striking, there was already in her face the expression of motherliness and resignation commonly seen in respectable women of her age, and this, of course, I had never seen in her before. . . . In short, of the school-girlish and the Platonic her face had kept the gentle smile and nothing more. . . .

"We got into conversation. Learning that I was already an engineer, Kisotchka was immensely delighted.

"'How good that is!' she said, looking joyfully into my face. 'Ah, how good! And how splendid you all are! Of all who left with you, not one has been a failure -- they have all turned out well. One an engineer, another a doctor, a third a teacher, another, they say, is a celebrated singer in Petersburg. . . . You are all splendid, all of you. . . . Ah, how good that is!'

"Kisotchka's eyes shone with genuine goodwill and gladness. She was admiring me like an elder sister or a former governess. 'While I looked at her sweet face and thought, 'It wouldn't be bad to get hold of her to-day!'

"'Do you remember, Natalya Stepanovna,' I asked her, 'how I once brought you in the park a bouquet with a note in it? You read my note, and such a look of bewilderment came into your face. . . .'

"'No, I don't remember that,' she said, laughing. 'But I remember how you wanted to challenge Florens to a duel over me. . . .'

"'Well, would you believe it, I don't remember that. . . .'

"'Well, that's all over and done with . . .' sighed Kisotchka. 'At one time I was your idol, and now it is my turn to look up to all of you. . . .'

"From further conversation I learned that two years after leaving the high school, Kisotchka had been married to a resident in the town who was half Greek, half Russian, had a post either in the bank or in the insurance society, and also carried on a trade in corn. He had a strange surname, something in the style of Populaki or Skarandopulo. . . . Goodness only knows -- I have forgotten. . . . As a matter of fact, Kisotchka spoke little and with reluctance about herself. The conversation was only about me. She asked me about the College of

Engineering, about my comrades, about Petersburg, about my plans, and everything I said moved her to eager delight and exclamations of, 'Oh, how good that is!'

"We went down to the sea and walked over the sands; then when the night air began to blow chill and damp from the sea we climbed up again. All the while our talk was of me and of the past. We walked about until the reflection of the sunset had died away from the windows of the summer villas.

"'Come in and have some tea,' Kisotchka suggested. 'The samovar must have been on the table long ago. . . . I am alone at home,' she said, as her villa came into sight through the green of the acacias. 'My husband is always in the town and only comes home at night, and not always then, and I must own that I am so dull that it's simply deadly.'

"I followed her in, admiring her back and shoulders. I was glad that she was married. Married women are better material for temporary love affairs than girls. I was also pleased that her husband was not at home. At the same time I felt that the affair would not come off. . . .

"We went into the house. The rooms were smallish and had low ceilings, and the furniture was typical of the summer villa (Russians like having at their summer villas uncomfortable heavy, dingy furniture which they are sorry to throw away and have nowhere to put), but from certain details I could observe that Kisotchka and her husband were not badly off, and must be spending five or six thousand roubles a year. I remember that in the middle of the room which Kisotchka called the dining-room there was a round table, supported for some reason on six legs, and on it a samovar and cups. At the edge of the table lay an open book, a pencil, and an exercise book. I glanced at the book and recognised it as 'Malinin and Burenin's Arithmetical Examples.' It was open, as I now remember, at the 'Rules of Compound Interest.'

"'To whom are you giving lessons?' I asked Kisotchka.'

"'Nobody,' she answered. 'I am just doing some. . . . I have nothing to do, and am so bored that I think of the old days and do sums.'

"'Have you any children?'

"'I had a baby boy, but he only lived a week.'

"We began drinking tea. Admiring me, Kisotchka said again how good it was that I was an engineer, and how glad she was of my success. And the more she talked and the more genuinely she smiled, the stronger was my conviction that I should go away without having gained my object. I was a connoisseur in love affairs in those days, and could accurately gauge my chances of success. You can boldly reckon on success if you are tracking down a fool or a woman as much on the look out for new experiences and sensations as yourself, or an adventuress to whom you are a stranger. If you come across a sensible and serious woman, whose face has an expression of weary submission and goodwill, who is genuinely delighted at your presence, and, above all, respects you, you may as well turn back. To succeed in that case needs longer than one day.

"And by evening light Kisotchka seemed even more charming than by day. She attracted me more and more, and apparently she liked me too, and the surroundings were most appropriate: the husband not at home, no servants visible, stillness around. . . . Though I had little confidence in success, I made up my mind to begin the attack anyway. First of all it was necessary to get into a familiar tone and to change Kisotchka's lyrically earnest mood into a more frivolous one.

"'Let us change the conversation, Natalya Stepanovna,' I began. 'Let us talk of something amusing. First of all, allow me, for the sake of old times, to call you Kisotchka.'

"She allowed me.

"'Tell me, please, Kisotchka,' I went on, 'what is the matter with all the fair sex here. What has happened to them? In old days they were all so moral and virtuous, and now, upon my word, if one asks about anyone, one is told such things that one is quite shocked at human nature. . . . One young lady has eloped with an officer; another has run away and carried off a high-school boy with her; another -- a married woman -- has run away from her husband with an actor; a fourth has left her husband and gone off with an officer, and so on and so on. It's a regular epidemic! If it goes on like this there won't be a girl or a young woman left in your town!'

"I spoke in a vulgar, playful tone. If Kisotchka had laughed in response I should have gone on in this style: 'You had better look out, Kisotchka, or some officer or actor will be carrying you off!' She would have dropped her eyes and said: 'As though anyone would care to carry me off; there are plenty younger and better looking. . . .' And I should have said: 'Nonsense, Kisotchka -- I for one should be delighted!' And so on in that style, and it would all have gone swimmingly. But Kisotchka did not laugh in response; on the contrary, she looked grave and sighed.

"'All you have been told is true,' she said. 'My cousin Sonya ran away from her husband with an actor. Of course, it is wrong. . . . Everyone ought to bear the lot that fate has laid on him, but I do not condemn them or blame them. . . . Circumstances are sometimes too strong for anyone!'

"'That is so, Kisotchka, but what circumstances can produce a regular epidemic?'

"'It's very simple and easy to understand,' replied Kisotchka, raising her eyebrows. 'There is absolutely nothing for us educated girls and women to do with ourselves. Not everyone is able to go to the University, to become a teacher, to live for ideas, in fact, as men do. They have to be married. . . . And whom would you have them marry? You boys leave the high-school and go away to the University, never to return to your native town again, and you marry in Petersburg or Moscow, while the girls remain. . . . To whom are they to be married? Why, in the absence of decent cultured men, goodness knows what sort of men they marry -- stockbrokers and such people of all kinds, who can do nothing but drink and get into rows at the club. . . . A girl married like that, at random. . . . And what is her life like afterwards? You can understand: a well-educated, cultured woman is living with a stupid, boorish man; if she meets a cultivated man, an officer, an actor, or a doctor -- well, she gets to love him, her life becomes unbearable to her, and she runs away from her husband. And one can't condemn her!'

"'If that is so, Kisotchka, why get married?' I asked.

"'Yes, of course,' said Kisotchka with a sigh, 'but you know every girl fancies that any husband is better than nothing. . . . Altogether life is horrid here, Nikolay Anastasyevitch, very horrid! Life is stifling for a girl and stifling when one is married. . . . Here they laugh at Sonya for having run away from her husband, but if they could see into her soul they would not laugh. . . .' "

Azorka began barking outside again. He growled angrily at someone, then howled miserably and dashed with all his force against the wall of the hut. . . . Ananyev's face was puckered with pity; he broke off his story and went out. For two minutes he could be heard outside comforting his dog. "Good dog! poor dog!"

"Our Nikolay Anastasyevitch is fond of talking," said Von Schtenberg, laughing. "He is a good fellow," he added after a brief silence.

Returning to the hut, the engineer filled up our glasses and, smiling and stroking his chest, went on:

"And so my attack was unsuccessful. There was nothing for it, I put off my unclean thoughts to a more favourable occasion, resigned myself to my failure and, as the saying is, waved my hand. What is more, under the influence of Kisotchka's voice, the evening air, and the stillness, I gradually myself fell into a quiet sentimental mood. I remember I sat in an easy chair by the wide-open window and glanced at the trees and darkened sky. The outlines of the acacias and the lime trees were just the same as they had been eight years before; just as then, in the days of my childhood, somewhere far away there was the tinkling of a wretched piano, and the public had just the same habit of sauntering to and fro along the avenues, but the people were not the same. Along the avenues there walked now not my comrades and I and the object of my adoration, but schoolboys and young ladies who were strangers. And I felt melancholy. When to my inquiries about acquaintances I five times received from Kisotchka the answer, 'He is dead,' my melancholy changed into the feeling one has at the funeral service of a good man. And sitting there at the window, looking at the promenading public and listening to the tinkling piano, I saw with my own eyes for the first time in my life with what eagerness one generation hastens to replace another, and what a momentous significance even some seven or eight years may have in a man's life!

"Kisotchka put a bottle of red wine on the table. I drank it off, grew sentimental, and began telling a long story about something or other. Kisotchka listened as before, admiring me and my cleverness. And time passed. The sky was by now so dark that the outlines of the acacias and lime trees melted into one, the public was no longer walking up and down the avenues, the piano was silent and the only sound was the even murmur of the sea.

"Young people are all alike. Be friendly to a young man, make much of him, regale him with wine, let him understand that he is attractive and he will sit on and on, forget that it is time to go, and talk and talk and talk. . . . His hosts cannot keep their eyes open, it's past their bedtime, and he still stays and talks. That was what I did. Once I chanced to look at the clock; it was half-past ten. I began saying good-bye.

"'Have another glass before your walk,' said Kisotchka.

"I took another glass, again I began talking at length, forgot it was time to go, and sat down. Then there came the sound of men's voices, footsteps and the clank of spurs.

"'I think my husband has come in. . . .' said Kisotchka listening.

"The door creaked, two voices came now from the passage and I saw two men pass the door that led into the dining-room: one a stout, solid, dark man with a hooked nose, wearing a straw hat, and the other a young officer in a white tunic. As they passed the door they both glanced casually and indifferently at Kisotchka and me, and I fancied both of them were drunk.

"'She told you a lie then, and you believed her!' we heard a loud voice with a marked nasal twang say a minute later. 'To begin with, it wasn't at the big club but at the little one.'

"'You are angry, Jupiter, so you are wrong . . . .' said another voice, obviously the officer's, laughing and coughing. 'I say, can I stay the night? Tell me honestly, shall I be in your way?'

"'What a question! Not only you can, but you must. What will you have, beer or wine?'

"They were sitting two rooms away from us, talking loudly, and apparently feeling no interest in Kisotchka or her visitor. A perceptible change came over Kisotchka on her husband's arrival. At first she flushed red, then her face wore a timid, guilty expression; she seemed to be troubled by some anxiety, and I began to fancy that she was ashamed to show me her husband and wanted me to go.

"I began taking leave. Kisotchka saw me to the front door. I remember well her gentle mournful smile and kind patient eyes as she pressed my hand and said:

"'Most likely we shall never see each other again. Well, God give you every blessing. Thank you!'

"Not one sigh, not one fine phrase. As she said good-bye she was holding the candle in her hand; patches of light danced over her face and neck, as though chasing her mournful smile. I pictured to myself the old Kisotchka whom one used to want to stroke like a cat, I looked intently at the present Kisotchka, and for some reason recalled her words: 'Everyone ought to bear the lot that fate has laid on him.' And I had a pang at my heart. I instinctively guessed how it was, and my conscience whispered to me that I, in my happiness and indifference, was face to face with a good, warm-hearted, loving creature, who was broken by suffering.

"I said good-bye and went to the gate. By now it was quite dark. In the south the evenings draw in early in July and it gets dark rapidly. Towards ten o'clock it is so dark that you can't see an inch before your nose. I lighted a couple of dozen matches before, almost groping, I found my way to the gate.

"'Cab!' I shouted, going out of the gate; not a sound, not a sigh in answer. . . . 'Cab,' I repeated, 'hey, Cab!'

"But there was no cab of any description. The silence of the grave. I could hear nothing but the murmur of the drowsy sea and the beating of my heart from the wine. Lifting my eyes to the sky I found not a single star. It was dark and sullen. Evidently the sky was covered with clouds. For some reason I shrugged my shoulders, smiling foolishly, and once more, not quite so resolutely, shouted for a cab.

"The echo answered me. A walk of three miles across open country and in the pitch dark was not an agreeable prospect. Before making up my mind to walk, I spent a long time deliberating and shouting for a cab; then, shrugging my shoulders, I walked lazily back to the copse, with no definite object in my mind. It was dreadfully dark in the copse. Here and there between the trees the windows of the summer villas glowed a dull red. A raven, disturbed by my steps and the matches with which I lighted my way to the summer-house, flew from tree to tree and rustled among the leaves. I felt vexed and ashamed, and the raven seemed to understand this, and croaked 'krrra!' I was vexed that I had to walk, and ashamed that I had stayed on at Kisotchka's, chatting like a boy.

"I made my way to the summer-house, felt for the seat and sat down. Far below me, behind a veil of thick darkness, the sea kept up a low angry growl. I remember that, as though I were blind, I could see neither sky nor sea, nor even the summer-house in which I was sitting. And it seemed to me as though the whole world consisted only of the thoughts that were straying through my head, dizzy from the wine, and of an unseen power murmuring monotonously somewhere below. And afterwards, as I sank into a doze, it began to seem that it was not the sea murmuring, but my thoughts, and that the whole world consisted of nothing but me. And concentrating the whole world in myself in this way, I thought no more of cabs, of the town, and of Kisotchka, and abandoned myself to the sensation I was so fond of: that is, the sensation of fearful isolation when you feel that in the whole universe, dark and formless, you alone exist. It is a proud, demoniac sensation, only possible to Russians whose thoughts and sensations are as large, boundless, and gloomy as their plains, their forests, and their snow. If I had been an artist I should certainly have depicted the expression of a Russian's face when he sits motionless and, with his legs under him and his head clasped in his hands, abandons himself to this sensation. . . . And together with this sensation come thoughts of the aimlessness of life, of death, and of the darkness of the grave. . . . The thoughts are not worth a brass farthing, but the expression of face must be fine. . . .

"While I was sitting and dozing, unable to bring myself to get up -- I was warm and comfortable -- all at once, against the even monotonous murmur of the sea, as though upon a canvas, sounds began to grow distinct which drew my attention from myself. . . . Someone was coming hurriedly along the avenue. Reaching the summer-house this someone stopped, gave a sob like a little girl, and said in the voice of a weeping child: 'My God, when will it all end! Merciful Heavens!'

"Judging from the voice and the weeping I took it to be a little girl of ten or twelve. She walked irresolutely into the summer-house, sat down, and began half-praying, half-complaining aloud. . . .

"'Merciful God!' she said, crying, 'it's unbearable. It's beyond all endurance! I suffer in silence, but I want to live too. . . . Oh, my God! My God!'

"And so on in the same style.

"I wanted to look at the child and speak to her. So as not to frighten her I first gave a loud sigh and coughed, then cautiously struck a match. . . . There was a flash of bright light in the darkness, which lighted up the weeping figure. It was Kisotchka!"

"Marvels upon marvels!" said Von Schtenberg with a sigh. "Black night, the murmur of the sea; she in grief, he with a sensation of world -- solitude. . . . It's too much of a good thing. . . . You only want Circassians with daggers to complete it."

"I am not telling you a tale, but fact."

"Well, even if it is a fact . . . it all proves nothing, and there is nothing new in it. . . ."

"Wait a little before you find fault! Let me finish," said Ananyev, waving his hand with vexation; "don't interfere, please! I am not telling you, but the doctor. . . . Well," he went on, addressing me and glancing askance at the student who bent over his books and seemed very well satisfied at having gibed at the engineer -- "well, Kisotchka was not surprised or frightened at seeing me. It seemed as though she had known beforehand that she would find me in the summer-house. She was breathing in gasps and trembling all over as though in a fever, while her tear-stained face, so far as I could distinguish it as I struck match after match, was not the intelligent, submissive weary face I had seen before, but something different, which I cannot understand to this day. It did not express pain, nor anxiety, nor misery -- nothing of what was expressed by her words and her tears. . . . I must own that, probably because I did not understand it, it looked to me senseless and as though she were drunk.

"'I can't bear it,' muttered Kisotchka in the voice of a crying child. 'It's too much for me, Nikolay Anastasyitch. Forgive me, Nikolav Anastasyitch. I can't go on living like this. . . . I am going to the town to my mother's. . . . Take me there. . . . Take me there, for God's sake!'

"In the presence of tears I can neither speak nor be silent. I was flustered and muttered some nonsense. trying to comfort her.

"'No, no; I will go to my mother's,' said Kisotchka resolutely, getting up and clutching my arm convulsively (her hands and her sleeves were wet with tears). 'Forgive me, Nikolay Anastasyitch, I am going. . . . I can bear no more. . . .'

"'Kisotchka, but there isn't a single cab,' I said. 'How can you go?'

"'No matter, I'll walk. . . . It's not far. I can't bear it. . . .'

"I was embarrassed, but not touched. Kisotchka's tears, her trembling, and the blank expression of her face suggested to me a trivial, French or Little Russian melodrama, in which every ounce of cheap shallow feeling is washed down with pints of tears.

I didn t understand her, and knew I did not understand her; I ought to have been silent, but for some reason, most likely for fear my silence might be taken for stupidity, I thought fit to try to persuade her not to go to her mother's, but to stay at home. When people cry, they don't like their tears to be seen. And I lighted match after match and went on striking till the box was empty. What I wanted with this ungenerous illumination, I can't conceive to this day. Cold-hearted people are apt to be awkward, and even stupid.

"In the end Kisotchka took my arm and we set off. Going out of the gate, we turned to the right and sauntered slowly along the soft dusty road. It was dark. As my eyes grew gradually accustomed to the darkness, I began to distinguish the silhouettes of the old gaunt oaks and lime trees which bordered the road. The jagged, precipitous cliffs, intersected here and there by deep, narrow ravines and creeks, soon showed indistinctly, a black streak on the right. Low bushes nestled by the hollows, looking like sitting figures. It was uncanny. I looked sideways suspiciously at the cliffs, and the murmur of the sea and the stillness of the country alarmed my imagination. Kisotchka did not speak. She was still trembling, and before she had gone half a mile she was exhausted with walking and was out of breath. I too was silent.

"Three-quarters of a mile from the Quarantine Station there was a deserted building of four storeys, with a very high chimney in which there had once been a steam flour mill. It stood solitary on the cliff, and by day it could be seen for a long distance, both by sea and by land. Because it was deserted and no one lived in it, and because there was an echo in it which distinctly repeated the steps and voices of passers-by, it seemed mysterious. Picture me in the dark night arm-in-arm with a woman who was running away from her husband near this tall long monster which repeated the sound of every step I took and stared at me fixedly with its hundred black windows. A normal young man would have been moved to romantic feelings in such surroundings, but I looked at the dark windows and thought: 'All this is very impressive, but time will come when of that building and of Kisntchka and her troubles and of me with my thoughts, not one grain of dust will remain. . . . All is nonsense and vanity. . . .'

"When we reached the flour mill Kisotchka suddenly stopped, took her arm out of mine, and said, no longer in a childish voice, but in her own:

"'Nikolay Anastasvitch, I know all this seems strange to you. But I am terribly unhappy! And you cannot even imagine how unhappy! It's impossible to imagine it! I don't tell you about it because one can't talk about it. . . . Such a life, such a life! . . .'

"Kisotchka did not finish. She clenched her teeth and moaned as though she were doing her utmost not to scream with pain.

"'Such a life!' she repeated with horror, with the cadence and the southern, rather Ukrainian accent which particularly in women gives to emotional speech the effect of singing. 'It is a life! Ah, my God, my God! what does it mean? Oh, my God, my God!'

"As though trying to solve the riddle of her fate, she shrugged her shoulders in perplexity, shook her head, and clasped her hands. She spoke as though she were singing, moved gracefully, and reminded me of a celebrated Little Russian actress.

"'Great God, it is as though I were in a pit,' she went on. 'If one could live for one minute in happiness as other people live! Oh, my God, my God! I have come to such disgrace that before a stranger I am running away from my husband by night, like some disreputable creature! Can I expect anything good after that?'

"As I admired her movements and her voice, I began to feel annoyed that she was not on good terms with her husband. 'It would be nice to have got on into relations with her!' flitted through my mind; and this pitiless thought stayed in my brain, haunted me all the way and grew more and more alluring.

"About a mile from the flour mill we had to turn to the left by the cemetery. At the turning by the corner of the cemetery there stood a stone windmill, and by it a little hut in which the miller lived. We passed the mill and the hut, turned to the left and reached the gates of the cemetery. There Kisotchka stopped and said:

"'I am going back, Nikolay Anastasyitch! You go home, and God bless you, but I am going back. I am not frightened.'

"'Well, what next!' I said, disconcerted. 'If you are going, you had better go!'

"'I have been too hasty. . . . It was all about nothing that mattered. You and your talk took me back to the past and put all sort of ideas into my head. . . . I was sad and wanted to cry, and my husband said rude things to me before that officer, and I could not bear it. . . . And what's the good of my going to the town to my mother's? Will that make me any happier? I must go back. . . . But never mind . . . let us go on,' said Kisotchka, and she laughed. 'It makes no difference!'

"I remembered that over the gate of the cemetery there was an inscription: 'The hour will come wherein all they that lie in the grave will hear the voice of the Son of God.' I knew very well that sooner of later I and Kisotchka and her husband and the officer in the white tunic would lie under the dark trees in the churchyard; I knew that an unhappy and insulted fellow-creature was walking beside me. All this I recognised distinctly, but at the same time I was troubled by an oppressive and unpleasant dread that Kisotchka would turn back, and that I should not manage to say to her what had to be said. Never at any other time in my life have thoughts of a higher order been so closely interwoven with the basest animal prose as on that night. . . . It was horrible!

"Not far from the cemetery we found a cab. When we reached the High Street, where Kisotchka's mother lived, we dismissed the cab and walked along the pavement. Kisotchka was silent all the while, while I looked at her, and I raged at myself, 'Why don't you begin? Now's the time!' About twenty paces from the hotel where I was staying, Kisotchka stopped by the lamp-post and burst into tears.

"'Nikolay Anastasyitch!' she said, crying and laughing and looking at me with wet shining eyes, 'I shall never forget your sympathy. . . . How good you are! All of you are so splendid -- all of you! Honest, great-hearted, kind, clever. . . . Ah, how good that is!'

"She saw in me a highly educated man, advanced in every sense of the word, and on her tear-stained laughing face, together with the emotion and enthusiasm aroused by my personality, there was clearly written regret that she so rarely saw such people, and that God had not vouchsafed her the bliss of being the wife of one of them. She muttered, 'Ah, how splendid it is!' The childish gladness on her face, the tears, the gentle smile, the soft hair, which had escaped from under the kerchief, and the kerchief itself thrown carelessly over her head, in the light of the street lamp reminded me of the old Kisotchka whom one had wanted to stroke like a kitten.

"I could not restrain myself, and began stroking her hair, her shoulders, and her hands.

"'Kisotchka, what do you want?' I muttered. 'I'll go to the ends of the earth with you if you like! I will take you out of this hole and give you happiness. I love you. . . . Let us go, my sweet? Yes? Will you?'

"Kisotchka's face was flooded with bewilderment. She stepped back from the street lamp and, completely overwhelmed, gazed at me with wide-open eyes. I gripped her by the arm, began showering kisses on her face, her neck, her shoulders, and went on making vows and promises. In love affairs vows and promises are almost a physiological necessity. There's no getting on without them. Sometimes you know you are lying and that promises are not necessary, but still you vow and protest. Kisotchka, utterly overwhelmed, kept staggering back and gazing at me with round eyes.

"'Please don't! Please don't!' she muttered, holding me off with her hands.

"I clasped her tightly in my arms. All at once she broke into hysterical tears. And her face had the same senseless blank expression that I had seen in the summer-house when I lighted the matches. Without asking her consent, preventing her from speaking, I dragged her forcibly towards my hotel. She seemed almost swooning and did not walk, but I took her under the arms and almost carried her. . . . I remember, as we were going up the stairs, some man with a red band in his cap looked wonderingly at me and bowed to Kisotchka. . . ."

Ananvev flushed crimson and paused. He walked up and down near the table in silence, scratched the back of his head with an air of vexation, and several times shrugged his shoulders and twitched his shoulder-blades, while a shiver ran down his huge back. The memory was painful and made him ashamed, and he was struggling with himself.

"It's horrible!" he said, draining a glass of wine and shaking his head. "I am told that in every introductory lecture on women's diseases the medical students are admonished to remember that each one of them has a mother, a sister, a fiancée, before undressing and examining a female patient. . . . That advice would be very good not only for medical students but foreveryone who in one way or another has to deal with a woman's life. Now that I have a wife and a little daughter, oh, how well I understand that advice! How I understand it, my God! You may as well hear the rest, though. . . . As soon as she had become my mistress, Kisotchka's view of the position was very different from mine. First of all she felt for me a deep and passionate love. What was for me an ordinary amatory episode was for her an absolute revolution in her life. I remember, it seemed to me that she had gone out of her mind. Happy for the first time in her life, looking five years younger, with an inspired enthusiastic face, not knowing what to do with herself for happiness, she laughed and cried and never ceased dreaming aloud how next day we would set off for the Caucasus, then in the autumn to Petersburg; how we would live afterwards.

"'Don't worry yourself about my husband,' she said to reassure me. 'He is bound to give me a divorce. Everyone in the town knows that he is living with the elder Kostovitch. We will get a divorce and be married.'

"When women love they become acclimatised and at home with people very quickly, like cats. Kisotchka had only spent an hour and a half in my room when she already felt as though she were at home and was ready to treat my property as though it were her own. She packed my things in my portmanteau, scolded me for not hanging my new expensive overcoat on a peg instead of flinging it on a chair, and so on.

"I looked at her, listened, and felt weariness and vexation. I was conscious of a slight twinge of horror at the thought that a respectable, honest, and unhappy woman had so easily, after some three or four hours, succumbed to the first man she met. As a respectable man, you see, I didn't like it. Then, too, I was unpleasantly impressed by the fact that women of Kisotchka's sort, not deep or serious, are too much in love with life, and exalt what is in reality such a trifle as love for a man to the level of bliss, misery, a complete revolution in life. . . . Moreover, now that I was satisfied, I was vexed with myself for having been so stupid as to get entangled with a woman whom I should have to deceive. And in spite of my disorderly life I must observe that I could not bear telling lies.

"I remember that Kisotchka sat down at my feet, laid her head on my knees, and, looking at me with shining, loving eyes, asked:

"'Kolya, do you love me? Very, very much?'

"And she laughed with happiness. . . . This struck me as sentimental, affected, and not clever; and meanwhile I was already inclined to look for 'depth of thought' before everything.

"'Kisotchka, you had better go home,' I said, or else your people will be sure to miss you and will be looking for you all over the town; and it would be awkward for you to go to your mother in the morning.'

"Kisotchka agreed. At parting we arranged to meet at midday next morning in the park, and the day after to set off together to Pyatigorsk. I went into the street to see her home, and I remember that I caressed her with genuine tenderness on the way. There was a minute when I felt unbearably sorry for her, for trusting me so implicitly, and I made up my mind that I would really take her to Pyatigorsk, but remembering that I had only six hundred roubles in my portmanteau, and that it would be far more difficult to break it off with her in the autumn than now, I made haste to suppress my compassion.

"We reached the house where Kisotchka's mother lived. I pulled at the bell. When footsteps were heard at the other side of the door Kisotchka suddenly looked grave, glanced upwards to the sky, made the sign of the Cross over me several times and, clutching my hand, pressed it to her lips.

"'Till to-morrow,' she said, and disappeared into the house.

"I crossed to the opposite pavement and from there looked at the house. At first the windows were in darkness, then in one of the windows there was the glimmer of the faint bluish flame of a newly lighted candle; the flame grew, gave more light, and I saw shadows moving about the rooms together with it.

"'They did not expect her,' I thought.

"Returning to my hotel room I undressed, drank off a glass of red wine, ate some fresh caviare which I had bought that day in the bazaar, went to bed in a leisurely way, and slept the sound, untroubled sleep of a tourist.

"In the morning I woke up with a headache and in a bad humour. Something worried me.

"'What's the matter?' I asked myself, trying to explain my uneasiness. 'What's upsetting me?'

"And I put down my uneasiness to the dread that Kisotchka might turn up any minute and prevent my going away, and that I should have to tell lies and act a part before her. I hurriedly dressed, packed my things, and left the hotel, giving instructions to the porter to take my luggage to the station for the seven o'clock train in the evening. I spent the whole day with a doctor friend and left the town that evening. As you see, my philosophy did not prevent me from taking to my heels in a mean and treacherous flight. . . .

"All the while that I was at my friend's, and afterwards driving to the station, I was tormented by anxiety. I fancied that I was afraid of meeting with Kisotchka and a scene. In the station I purposely remained in the toilet room till the second bell rang, and while I was making my way to my compartment, I was oppressed by a feeling as though I were covered all over with stolen things. With what impatience and terror I waited for the third bell!

"At last the third bell that brought my deliverance rang at last, the train moved; we passed the prison, the barracks, came out into the open country, and yet, to my surprise, the feeling of uneasiness still persisted, and still I felt like a thief passionately longing to escape. It was queer. To distract my mind and calm myself I looked out of the window. The train ran along the coast. The sea was smooth, and the turquoise sky, almost half covered with the tender, golden crimson light of sunset, was gaily and serenely mirrored in it. Here and there fishing boats and rafts made black patches on its surface. The town, as clean and beautiful as a toy, stood on the high cliff, and was already shrouded in the mist of evening. The golden domes of its churches, the windows and the greenery reflected the setting sun, glowing and melting like shimmering gold. . . . The scent of the fields mingled with the soft damp air from the sea.

"The train flew rapidly along. I heard the laughter of passengers and guards. Everyone was good-humoured and light-hearted, yet my unaccountable uneasiness grew greater and greater. . . . I looked at the white mist that covered the town and I imagined how a woman with a senseless blank face was hurrying up and down in that mist by the churches and the houses, looking for me and moaning, 'Oh, my God! Oh, my God!' in the voice of a little girl or the cadences of a Little Russian actress. I recalled her grave face and big anxious eyes as she made the sign of the Cross over me, as though I belonged to her, and mechanically I looked at the hand which she had kissed the day before.

"'Surely I am not in love?' I asked myself, scratching my hand.

"Only as night came on when the passengers were asleep and I was left *tête-à-tête* with my conscience, I began to understand what I had not been able to grasp before. In the twilight of the railway carriage the image of Kisotchka rose before me, haunted me and I recognised clearly that I had committed a crime as bad as murder. My conscience tormented me. To stifle this unbearable feeling, I assured myself that everything was nonsense and vanity, that Kisotchka and I would die and decay, that her grief was nothing in comparison with death, and so on and so on . . . and that if you come to that, there is no such thing as freewill, and that therefore I was not to blame. But all these arguments only irritated me and were extraordinarily quickly crowded out by other thoughts. There was a miserable feeling in the hand that Kisotchka had kissed. . . . I kept lying down and getting up again, drank vodka at the stations, forced myself to eat bread and butter, fell to assuring myself again that life had no meaning, but nothing was of any use. A strange and if you like absurd ferment was going on in my brain. The most incongruous ideas crowded one after another in disorder, getting more and more tangled, thwarting each other, and I, the thinker, 'with my brow bent on the earth,' could make out nothing and could not find my bearings in this mass of essential and non-essential ideas. It appeared that I, the thinker, had not mastered the technique of thinking, and that I was no more capable of managing my own brain than mending a watch. For the first time in my life I was really thinking eagerly and intensely, and that seemed to me so monstrous that I said to myself: 'I am going off my head.' A man whose brain does not work at all times, but only at painful moments, is often haunted by the thought of madness.

"I spent a day and a night in this misery, then a second night, and learning from experience how little my philosophy was to me, I came to my senses and realised at last what sort of a creature I was. I saw that my ideas were not worth a brass farthing, and that before meeting Kisotchka I had not begun to think and had not even a conception of what thinking in earnest meant; now through suffering I realised that I had neither convictions nor a definite moral standard, nor heart, nor reason; my whole intellectual and moral wealth consisted of specialist knowledge, fragments, useless memories, other people's ideas -- and nothing else; and my mental processes were as lacking in complexity, as useless and as rudimentary as a Yakut's. . . . If I had disliked lying, had not stolen, had not murdered, and, in fact, made obviously gross mistakes, that was not owing to my convictions -- I had none, but because I was in bondage, hand and foot, to my nurse's fairy tales and to copy-book morals, which had entered into my flesh and blood and without my noticing it guided me in life, though I looked on them as absurd. . . .

"I realised that I was not a thinker, not a philosopher, but simply a dilettante. God had given me a strong healthy Russian brain with promise of talent. And, only fancy, here was that brain at twenty-six, undisciplined, completely free from principles, not weighed down by any stores of knowledge, but only lightly sprinkled with information of a sort in the engineering line; it was young and had a physiological craving for exercise, it was on the look-out for it, when all at once quite casually the fine juicy idea of the aimlessness of life and the darkness beyond the tomb descends upon it. It greedily sucks it in, puts its whole outlook at its disposal and begins playing with it, like a cat with a mouse. There is neither learning nor system in the brain, but that does not matter. It deals with the great ideas with its own innate powers, like a self-educated man, and before a month has passed the owner of the brain can turn a potato into a hundred dainty dishes, and fancies himself a philosopher. . . .

"Our generation has carried this dilettantism, this playing with serious ideas into science, into literature, into politics, and into everything which it is not too lazy to go into, and with its dilettantism has introduced, too, its coldness, its boredom, and its one-sidedness and, as it seems to me, it has already succeeded in developing in the masses a new hitherto non-existent attitude to serious ideas.

"I realised and appreciated my abnormality and utter ignorance, thanks to a misfortune. My normal thinking, so it seems to me now, dates from the day when I began again from the A, B, C, when my conscience sent me flying back to N., when with no philosophical subleties I repented, besought Kisotchka's forgiveness like a naughty boy and wept with her. . . ."

Ananyev briefly described his last interview with Kisotchka.

"H'm. . . ." the student filtered through his teeth when the engineer had finished. "That's the sort of thing that happens."

His face still expressed mental inertia, and apparently Ananyev's story had not touched him in the least. Only when the engineer after a moment's pause, began expounding his view again and repeating what he had said at first, the student frowned irritably, got up from the table and walked away to his bed. He made his bed and began undressing.

"You look as though you have really convinced someone this time," he said irritably.

"Me convince anybody!" said the engineer. "My dear soul, do you suppose I claim to do that? God bless you! To convince you is impossible. You can reach conviction only by way of personal experience and suffering!"

"And then -- it's queer logic!" grumbled the student as he put on his nightshirt. "The ideas which you so dislike, which are so ruinous for the young are, according to you, the normal thing for the old; it's as though it were a question of grey hairs. . . . Where do the old get this privilege? What is it based upon? If these ideas are poison, they are equally poisonous for all?"

"Oh, no, my dear soul, don't say so!" said the engineer with a sly wink. "Don't say so. In the first place, old men are not dilettanti. Their pessimism comes to them not casually from outside, but from the depths of their own brains, and only after they have exhaustively studied the Hegels and Kants of all sorts, have suffered, have made no end of mistakes, in fact -- when they have climbed the whole ladder from bottom to top. Their pessimism has both personal experience and sound philosophic training behind it. Secondly, the pessimism of old thinkers does not take the form of idle talk, as it does with you and me, but of *Weltschmertz*, of suffering; it rests in them on a Christian foundation because it is derived from love for humanity and from thoughts about humanity, and is entirely free from the egoism which is noticeable in dilettanti. You despise life because its meaning and its object are hidden just from you, and you are only afraid of your own death, while the real thinker is unhappy because the truth is hidden from all and he is afraid for all men. For instance, there is living not far from here the Crown forester, Ivan Alexandritch. He is a nice old man. At one time he was a teacher somewhere, and used to write something; the devil only knows what he was, but anyway he is a remarkably clever fellow and in philosophy he is A1. He has read a great deal and he is continually reading now. Well, we came across him lately in the Gruzovsky district. . . . They were laying the sleepers and rails just at the time. It's not a difficult job, but Ivan Alexandritch, not being a specialist, looked at it as though it were a conjuring trick. It takes an experienced workman less than a minute to lay a sleeper and fix a rail on it. The workmen were in good form and really were working smartly and rapidly; one rascal in particular brought his hammer down with exceptional smartness on the head of the nail and drove it in at one blow, though the handle of the hammer was two yards or more in length and each nail was a foot long. Ivan Alexandritch watched the workmen a long time, was moved, and said to me with tears in his eyes:

" 'What a pity that these splendid men will die!' Such pessimism I understand."

"All that proves nothing and explains nothing," said the student, covering himself up with a sheet; "all that is simply pounding liquid in a mortar. No one knows anything and nothing can be proved by words."

He peeped out from under the sheet, lifted up his head and, frowning irritably, said quickly:

"One must be very naïve to believe in human words and logic and to ascribe any determining value to them. You can prove and disprove anything you like with words, and people will soon perfect the technique of language to such a point that they will prove with mathematical certainty that twice two is seven. I am fond of reading and listening, but as to believing, no thank you; I can't, and I don't want to. I believe only in God, but as for you, if you talk to me till the Second Coming and seduce another five hundred Kisothchkas, I shall believe in you only when I go out of my mind. . . . Goodnight."

The student hid his head under the sheet and turned his face towards the wall, meaning by this action to let us know that he did not want to speak or listen. The argument ended at that.

Before going to bed the engineer and I went out of the hut, and I saw the lights once more.

"We have tired you out with our chatter," said Ananyev, yawning and looking at the sky. "Well, my good sir! The only pleasure we have in this dull hole is drinking and philosophising. . . . What an embankment, Lord have mercy on us!" he said admiringly, as we approached the embankment; "it is more like Mount Ararat than an embankment."

He paused for a little, then said: "Those lights remind the Baron of the Amalekites, but it seems to me that they are like the thoughts of man. . . . You know the thoughts of each individual man are scattered like that in disorder, stretch in a straight line towards some goal in the midst of the darkness and, without shedding light on anything, without lighting up the night, they vanish somewhere far beyond old age. But enough philosophising! It's time to go bye-bye."

When we were back in the hut the engineer began begging me to take his bed.

"Oh please!" he said imploringly, pressing both hands on his heart. "I entreat you, and don't worry about me! I can sleep anywhere, and, besides, I am not going to bed just yet. Please do -- it's a favour!"

I agreed, undressed, and went to bed, while he sat down to the table and set to work on the plans.

"We fellows have no time for sleep," he said in a low voice when I had got into bed and shut my eyes. "When a man has a wife and two children he can't think of sleep. One must think now of food and clothes and saving for the future. And I have two of them, a little son and a daughter. . . . The boy, little rascal, has a jolly little face. He's not six yet, and already he shows remarkable abilities, I assure you. . . . I have their photographs here, somewhere. . . . Ah, my children, my children!"

He rummaged among his papers, found their photographs, and began looking at them. I fell asleep.

I was awakened by the barking of Azorka and loud voices. Von Schtenberg with bare feet and ruffled hair was standing in the doorway dressed in his underclothes, talking loudly with someone . . . . It was getting light. A gloomy dark blue dawn was peeping in at the door, at the windows, and through the crevices in the hut walls, and casting a faint light on my bed, on the table with the papers, and on Ananyev. Stretched on the floor on a cloak, with a leather pillow under his head, the engineer lay asleep with his fleshy, hairy chest uppermost; he was snoring so loudly that I pitied the student from the bottom of my heart for having to sleep in the same room with him every night.

"Why on earth are we to take them?" shouted Von Schtenberg. "It has nothing to do with us! Go to Tchalisov! From whom do the cauldrons come?"

"From Nikitin . . ." a bass voice answered gruffly.

"Well, then, take them to Tchalisov. . . . That's not in our department. What the devil are you standing there for? Drive on!"

"Your honour, we have been to Tchalisov already," said the bass voice still more gruffly. "Yesterday we were the whole day looking for him down the line, and were told at his hut that he had gone to the Dymkovsky section. Please take them, your honour! How much longer are we to go carting them about? We go carting them on and on along the line, and see no end to it."

"What is it?" Ananyev asked huskily, waking up and lifting his head quickly.

"They have brought some cauldrons from Nikitin's," said the student, "and he is begging us to take them. And what business is it of ours to take them?"

"Do be so kind, your honour, and set things right! The horses have been two days without food and the master, for sure, will be angry. Are we to take them back, or what? The railway ordered the cauldrons, so it ought to take them. . . ."

"Can't you understand, you blockhead, that it has nothing to do with us? Go on to Tchalisov!"

"What is it? Who's there?" Ananyev asked huskily again. "Damnation take them all," he said, getting up and going to the door. "What is it?"

I dressed, and two minutes later went out of the hut. Ananyev and the student, both in their underclothes and barefooted, were angrily and impatiently explaining to a peasant who was standing before them bare-headed, with his whip in his hand, apparently not understanding them. Both faces looked preoccupied with workaday cares.

"What use are your cauldrons to me," shouted Ananyev. "Am I to put them on my head, or what? If you can't find Tchalisov, find his assistant, and leave us in peace!"

Seeing me, the student probably recalled the conversation of the previous night. The workaday expression vanished from his sleepy face and a look of mental inertia came into it. He waved the peasant off and walked away absorbed in thought.

It was a cloudy morning. On the line where the lights had been gleaming the night before, the workmen, just roused from sleep, were swarming. There was a sound of voices and the squeaking of wheelbarrows. The working day was beginning. One poor little nag harnessed with cord was already plodding towards the embankment, tugging with its neck, and dragging along a cartful of sand.

I began saying good-bye. . . . A great deal had been said in the night, but I carried away with me no answer to any question, and in the morning, of the whole conversation there remained in my memory, as in a filter, only the lights and the image of Kisotchka. As I got on the horse, I looked at the student and Ananyev for the last time, at the hysterical dog with the lustreless, tipsy-looking eyes, at the workmen flitting to and fro in the morning fog, at the embankment, at the little nag straining with its neck, and thought:

"There is no making out anything in this world."

And when I lashed my horse and galloped along the line, and when a little later I saw nothing before me but the endless gloomy plain and the cold overcast sky, I recalled the questions which were discussed in the night. I pondered while the sun-scorched plain, the immense sky, the oak forest, dark on the horizon and the hazy distance, seemed saying to me:

"Yes, there's no understanding anything in this world!"

The sun began to rise. . . .

THE BEAUTIES

I

I remember, when I was a high school boy in the fifth or sixth class, I was driving with my grandfather from the village of Bolshoe Kryepkoe in the Don region to Rostov-on-the-Don. It was a sultry, languidly dreary day of August. Our eyes were glued together, and our mouths were parched from the heat and the dry burning wind which drove clouds of dust to meet us; one did not want to look or speak or think, and when our drowsy driver, a Little Russian called Karpo, swung his whip at the horses and lashed me on my cap, I did not protest or utter a sound, but only, rousing myself from half-slumber, gazed mildly and dejectedly into the distance to see whether there was a village visible through the dust. We stopped to feed the horses in a big Armenian village at a rich Armenian's whom my grandfather knew. Never in my life have I seen a greater caricature than that Armenian. Imagine a little shaven head with thick overhanging eyebrows, a beak of a nose, long gray mustaches, and a wide mouth with a long cherry-wood chibouk sticking out of it. This little head was clumsily attached to a lean hunch-back carcass attired in a fantastic garb, a short red jacket, and full bright blue trousers. This figure walked straddling its legs and shuffling with its slippers, spoke without taking the chibouk out of its mouth, and behaved with truly Armenian dignity, not smiling, but staring with wide-open eyes and trying to take as little notice as possible of its guests.

There was neither wind nor dust in the Armenian's rooms, but it was just as unpleasant, stifling, and dreary as in the steppe and on the road. I remember, dusty and exhausted by the heat, I sat in the corner on a green box. The unpainted wooden walls, the furniture, and the floors colored with yellow ocher smelt of dry wood baked by the sun. Wherever I looked there were flies and flies and flies. . . . Grandfather and the Armenian were talking about grazing, about manure, and about oats. . . . I knew that they would be a good hour getting the samovar; that grandfather would be not less than an hour drinking his tea, and then would lie down to sleep for two or three hours; that I should waste a quarter of the day waiting, after which there would be again the heat, the dust, the jolting cart. I heard the muttering of the two voices, and it began to seem to me that I had been seeing the Armenian, the cupboard with the crockery, the flies, the windows with the burning sun beating on them, for ages and ages, and should only cease to see them in the far-off future, and I was seized with hatred for the steppe, the sun, the flies.. . .

A Little Russian peasant woman in a kerchief brought in a tray of tea-things, then the samovar. The Armenian went slowly out into the passage and shouted: "Mashya, come and pour out tea! Where are you, Mashya?"

Hurried footsteps were heard, and there came into the room a girl of sixteen in a simple cotton dress and a white kerchief. As she washed the crockery and poured out the tea, she was standing with her back to me, and all I could see was that she was of a slender figure, barefooted, and that her little bare heels were covered by long trousers.

The Armenian invited me to have tea. Sitting down to the table, I glanced at the girl, who was handing me a glass of tea, and felt all at once as though a wind were blowing over my soul and blowing away all the impressions of the day with their dust and dreariness. I saw the bewitching features of the most beautiful face I have ever met in real life or in my dreams. Before me stood a beauty, and I recognized that at the first glance as I should have recognized lightning.

I am ready to swear that Masha -- or, as her father called her, Mashya -- was a real beauty, but I don't know how to prove it. It sometimes happens that clouds are huddled together in disorder on the horizon, and the sun hiding behind them colors them and the sky with tints of every possible shade--crimson, orange, gold, lilac, muddy pink; one cloud is like a monk, another like a fish, a third like a Turk in a turban. The glow of sunset enveloping a third of the sky gleams on the cross on the church, flashes on the windows of the manor house, is reflected in the river and the puddles, quivers on the trees; far, far away against the background of the sunset, a flock of wild ducks is flying homewards. . . . And the boy herding the cows, and the surveyor driving in his chaise over the dam, and the gentleman out for a walk, all gaze at the sunset, and everyone of them thinks it terribly beautiful, but no one knows or can say in what its beauty lies.

I was not the only one to think the Armenian girl beautiful. My grandfather, an old man of seventy, gruff and indifferent to women and the beauties of nature, looked caressingly at Masha for a full minute, and asked:

"Is that your daughter, Avert Nazaritch?"

"Yes, she is my daughter," answered the Armenian.

"A fine young lady," said my grandfather approvingly.

An artist would have called the Armenian girl's beauty classical and severe, it was just that beauty, the contemplation of which -- God knows why!-- inspires in one the conviction that one is seeing correct features; that hair, eyes, nose, mouth, neck, bosom, and every movement of the young body all go together in one complete harmonious accord in which nature has not blundered over the smallest line. You fancy for some reason that the ideally beautiful woman must have such a nose as Masha's, straight and slightly aquiline, just such great dark eyes, such long lashes, such a languid glance; you fancy that her black curly hair and eyebrows go with the soft white tint of her brow and cheeks as the green reeds go with the quiet stream. Masha's white neck and her youthful bosom were not fully developed, but you fancy the sculptor would need a great creative genius to mold them. You gaze, and little by little the desire comes over you to say to Masha something extraordinarily pleasant, sincere, beautiful, as beautiful as she herself was.

At first I felt hurt and abashed that Masha took no notice of me, but was all the time looking down; it seemed to me as though a peculiar atmosphere, proud and happy, separated her from me and jealously screened her from my eyes.

"That's because I am covered with dust," I thought, "am sunburnt, and am still a boy."

But little by little I forgot myself, and gave myself up entirely to the consciousness of beauty. I thought no more now of the dreary steppe, of the dust, no longer heard the buzzing of the flies, no longer tasted the tea, and felt nothing except that a beautiful girl was standing only the other side of the table.

I felt this beauty rather strangely. It was not desire, nor ecstacy, nor enjoyment that Masha excited in me, but a painful though pleasant sadness. It was a sadness vague and undefined as a dream. For some reason I felt sorry for myself, for my grandfather and for the Armenian, even for the girl herself, and I had a feeling as though we all four had lost something important and essential to life which we should never find again. My grandfather, too, grew melancholy; he talked no more about manure or about oats, but sat silent, looking pensively at Masha.

After tea my grandfather lay down for a nap while I went out of the house into the porch. The house, like all the houses in the Armenian village stood in the full sun; there was not a tree, not an awning, no shade. The Armenian's great courtyard, overgrown with goosefoot and wild mallows, was lively and full of gaiety in spite of the great heat. Threshing was going on behind one of the low hurdles which intersected the big yard here and there. Round a post stuck into the middle of the threshing-floor ran a dozen horses harnessed side by side, so that they formed one long radius. A Little Russian in a long waistcoat and full trousers was walking beside them, cracking a whip and shouting in a tone that sounded as though he were jeering at the horses and showing off his power over them.

"A--a--a, you damned brutes! . . . A--a--a, plague take you! Are you frightened?"

The horses, sorrel, white, and piebald, not understanding why they were made to run round in one place and to crush the wheat straw, ran unwillingly as though with effort, swinging their tails with an offended air. The wind raised up perfect clouds of golden chaff from under their hoofs and carried it away far beyond the hurdle. Near the tall fresh stacks peasant women were swarming with rakes, and carts were moving, and beyond the stacks in another yard another dozen similar horses were running round a post, and a similar Little Russian was cracking his whip and jeering at the horses.

The steps on which I was sitting were hot; on the thin rails and here and there on the window-frames sap was oozing out of the wood from the heat; red ladybirds were huddling together in the streaks of shadow under the steps and under the shutters. The sun was baking me on my head, on my chest, and on my back, but I did not notice it, and was conscious only of the thud of bare feet on the uneven floor in the passage and in the rooms behind me. After clearing away the tea-things, Masha ran down the steps, fluttering the air as she passed, and like a bird flew into a little grimy outhouse--I suppose the kitchen--from which came the smell of roast mutton and the sound of angry talk in Armenian. She vanished into the dark doorway, and in her place there appeared on the threshold an old bent, red-faced Armenian woman wearing green trousers. The old woman was angry and was scolding someone. Soon afterwards Masha appeared in the doorway, flushed with the heat of the kitchen and carrying a big black loaf on her shoulder; swaying gracefully under the weight of the bread, she ran across the yard to the threshing-floor, darted over the hurdle, and, wrapt in a cloud of golden chaff, vanished behind the carts. The Little Russian who was driving the horses lowered his whip, sank into silence, and gazed for a minute in the direction of the carts. Then when the Armenian girl darted again by the horses and leaped over the hurdle, he followed her with his eyes, and shouted to the horses in a tone as though he were greatly disappointed:

"Plague take you, unclean devils!"

And all the while I was unceasingly hearing her bare feet, and seeing how she walked across the yard with a grave, preoccupied face. She ran now down the steps, swishing the air about me, now into the kitchen, now to the threshing-floor, now through the gate, and I could hardly turn my head quickly enough to watch her.

And the oftener she fluttered by me with her beauty, the more acute became my sadness. I felt sorry both for her and for myself and for the Little Russian, who mournfully watched her every time she ran through the cloud of chaff to the carts. Whether it was envy of her beauty, or that I was regretting that the girl was not mine, and never would be, or that I was a stranger to her; or whether I vaguely felt that her rare beauty was accidental, unnecessary, and, like everything on earth, of short duration; or whether, perhaps, my sadness was that peculiar feeling which is excited in man by the contemplation of real beauty, God only knows.

The three hours of waiting passed unnoticed. It seemed to me that I had not had time to look properly at Masha when Karpo drove up to the river, bathed the horse, and began to put it in the shafts. The wet horse snorted with pleasure and kicked his hoofs against the shafts. Karpo shouted to it: "Ba--ack!" My grandfather woke up. Masha opened the creaking gates for us, we got into the chaise and drove out of the yard. We drove in silence as though we were angry with one another.

When, two or three hours later, Rostov and Nahitchevan appeared in the distance, Karpo, who had been silent the whole time, looked round quickly, and said:

"A fine wench, that at the Armenian's."

And he lashed his horses.

II

Another time, after I had become a student, I was traveling by rail to the south. It was May. At one of the stations, I believe it was between Byelgorod and Harkov, I got out of the tram to walk about the platform.

The shades of evening were already lying on the station garden, on the platform, and on the fields; the station screened off the sunset, but on the topmost clouds of smoke from the engine, which were tinged with rosy light, one could see the sun had not yet quite vanished.

As I walked up and down the platform I noticed that the greater number of the passengers were standing or walking near a second-class compartment, and that they looked as though some celebrated person were in that compartment. Among the curious whom I met near this compartment I saw, however, an artillery officer who had been my fellow-traveler, an intelligent, cordial, and sympathetic fellow--as people mostly are whom we meet on our travels by chance and with whom we are not long acquainted.

"What are you looking at there?" I asked.

He made no answer, but only indicated with his eyes a feminine figure. It was a young girl of seventeen or eighteen, wearing a Russian dress, with her head bare and a little shawl flung carelessly on one shoulder; not a passenger, but I suppose a sister or daughter of the station-master. She was standing near the carriage window, talking to an elderly woman who was in the train. Before I had time to realize what I was seeing, I was suddenly overwhelmed by the feeling I had once experienced in the Armenian village.

The girl was remarkably beautiful, and that was unmistakable to me and to those who were looking at her as I was.

If one is to describe her appearance feature by feature, as the practice is, the only really lovely thing was her thick wavy fair hair, which hung loose with a black ribbon tied round her head; all the other features were either irregular or very ordinary. Either from a peculiar form of coquettishness, or from short-sightedness, her eyes were screwed up, her nose had an undecided tilt, her mouth was small, her profile was feebly and insipidly drawn, her shoulders were narrow and undeveloped for her age -- and yet the girl made the impression of being really beautiful, and looking at her, I was able to feel convinced that the Russian face does not need strict regularity in order to be lovely; what is more, that if instead of her turn-up nose the girl had been given a different one, correct and plastically irreproachable like the Armenian girl's, I fancy her face would have lost all its charm from the change.

Standing at the window talking, the girl, shrugging at the evening damp, continually looking round at us, at one moment put her arms akimbo, at the next raised her hands to her head to straighten her hair, talked, laughed, while her face at one moment wore an expression of wonder, the next of horror, and I don't remember a moment when her face and body were at rest. The whole secret and magic of her beauty lay just in these tiny, infinitely elegant movements, in her smile, in the play of her face, in her rapid glances at us, in the combination of the subtle grace of her movements with her youth, her freshness, the purity of her soul that sounded in her laugh and voice, and with the weakness we love so much in children, in birds, in fawns, and in young trees.

It was that butterfly's beauty so in keeping with waltzing, darting about the garden, laughter and gaiety, and incongruous with serious thought, grief, and repose; and it seemed as though a gust of wind blowing over the platform, or a fall of rain, would be enough to wither the fragile body and scatter the capricious beauty like the pollen of a flower.

"So--o! . . ." the officer muttered with a sigh when, after the second bell, we went back to our compartment.

And what that "So--o" meant I will not undertake to decide.

Perhaps he was sad, and did not want to go away from the beauty and the spring evening into the stuffy train; or perhaps he, like me, was unaccountably sorry for the beauty, for himself, and for me, and for all the passengers, who were listlessly and reluctantly sauntering back to their compartments. As we passed the station window, at which a pale, red-haired telegraphist with upstanding curls and a faded, broad-cheeked face was sitting beside his apparatus, the officer heaved a sigh and said:

"I bet that telegraphist is in love with that pretty girl. To live out in the wilds under one roof with that ethereal creature and not fall in love is beyond the power of man. And what a calamity, my friend! what an ironical fate, to be stooping, unkempt, gray, a decent fellow and not a fool, and to be in love with that pretty, stupid little girl who would never take a scrap of notice of you! Or worse still: imagine that telegraphist is in love, and at the same time married, and that his wife is as stooping, as unkempt, and as decent a person as himself."

On the platform between our carriage and the next the guard was standing with his elbows on the railing, looking in the direction of the beautiful girl, and his battered, wrinkled, unpleasantly beefy face, exhausted by sleepless nights and the jolting of the train, wore a look of tenderness and of the deepest sadness, as though in that girl he saw happiness, his own youth, soberness, purity, wife, children; as though he were repenting and feeling in his whole being that that girl was not his, and that for him, with his premature old age, his uncouthness, and his beefy face, the ordinary happiness of a man and a passenger was as far away as heaven. . . .

The third bell rang, the whistles sounded, and the train slowly moved off. First the guard, the station-master, then the garden, the beautiful girl with her exquisitely sly smile, passed before our windows. . . .

Putting my head out and looking back, I saw how, looking after the train, she walked along the platform by the window where the telegraph clerk was sitting, smoothed her hair, and ran into the garden. The station no longer screened off the sunset, the plain lay open before us, but the sun had already set and the smoke lay in black clouds over the green, velvety young corn. It was melancholy in the spring air, and in the darkening sky, and in the railway carriage.

The familiar figure of the guard came into the carriage, and he began lighting the candles.

THE PARTY

I

After the festive dinner with its eight courses and its endless conversation, Olga Mihalovna, whose husband's name-day was being celebrated, went out into the garden. The duty of smiling and talking incessantly, the clatter of the crockery, the stupidity of the servants, the long intervals between the courses, and the stays she had put on to conceal her condition from the visitors, wearied her to exhaustion. She longed to get away from the house, to sit in the shade and rest her heart with thoughts of the baby which was to be born to her in another two months. She was used to these thoughts coming to her as she turned to the left out of the big avenue into the narrow path. Here in the thick shade of the plums and cherry-trees the dry branches used to scratch her neck and shoulders; a spider's web would settle on her face, and there would rise up in her mind the image of a little creature of undetermined sex and undefined features, and it began to seem as though it were not the spider's web that tickled her face and neck caressingly, but that little creature. When, at the end of the path, a thin wicker hurdle came into sight, and behind it podgy beehives with tiled roofs; when in the motionless, stagnant air there came a smell of hay and honey, and a soft buzzing of bees was audible, then the little creature would take complete possession of Olga Mihalovna. She used to sit down on a bench near the shanty woven of branches, and fall to thinking.

This time, too, she went on as far as the seat, sat down, and began thinking; but instead of the little creature there rose up in her imagination the figures of the grown-up people whom she had just left. She felt dreadfully uneasy that she, the hostess, had deserted her guests, and she remembered how her husband, Pyotr Dmitritch, and her uncle, Nikolay Nikolaitch, had argued at dinner about trial by jury, about the press, and about the higher education of women. Her husband, as usual, argued in order to show off his Conservative ideas before his visitors -- and still more in order to disagree with her uncle, whom he disliked. Her uncle contradicted him and wrangled over every word he uttered, so as to show the company that he, Uncle Nikolay Nikolaitch, still retained his youthful freshness of spirit and free-thinking in spite of his fifty-nine years. And towards the end of dinner even Olga Mihalovna herself could not resist taking part and unskilfully attempting to defend university education for women -- not that that education stood in need of her defence, but simply because she wanted to annoy her husband, who to her mind was unfair. The guests were wearied by this discussion, but they all thought it necessary to take part in it, and talked a great deal, although none of them took any interest in trial by jury or the higher education of women. . . .

Olga Mihalovna was sitting on the nearest side of the hurdle near the shanty. The sun was hidden behind the clouds. The trees and the air were overcast as before rain, but in spite of that it was hot and stifling. The hay cut under the trees on the previous day was lying ungathered, looking melancholy, with here and there a patch of colour from the faded flowers, and from it came a heavy, sickly scent. It was still. The other side of the hurdle there was a monotonous hum of bees. . . .

Suddenly she heard footsteps and voices; someone was coming along the path towards the beehouse.

"How stifling it is!" said a feminine voice. "What do you think -- is it going to rain, or not?"

"It is going to rain, my charmer, but not before night," a very familiar male voice answered languidly. "There will be a good rain."

Olga Mihalovna calculated that if she made haste to hide in the shanty they would pass by without seeing her, and she would not have to talk and to force herself to smile. She picked up her skirts, bent down and crept into the shanty. At once she felt upon her face, her neck, her arms, the hot air as heavy as steam. If it had not been for the stuffiness and the close smell of rye bread, fennel, and brushwood, which prevented her from breathing freely, it would have been delightful to hide from her visitors here under the thatched roof in the dusk, and to think about the little creature. It was cosy and quiet.

"What a pretty spot!" said a feminine voice. "Let us sit here, Pyotr Dmitritch."

Olga Mihalovna began peeping through a crack between two branches. She saw her husband, Pyotr Dmitritch, and Lubotchka Sheller, a girl of seventeen who had not long left boarding-school. Pyotr Dmitritch, with his hat on the back of his head, languid and indolent from having drunk so much at dinner, slouched by the hurdle and raked the hay into a heap with his foot; Lubotchka, pink with the heat and pretty as ever, stood with her hands behind her, watching the lazy movements of his big handsome person.

Olga Mihalovna knew that her husband was attractive to women, and did not like to see him with them. There was nothing out of the way in Pyotr Dmitritch's lazily raking together the hay in order to sit down on it with Lubotchka and chatter to her of trivialities; there was nothing out of the way, either, in pretty Lubotchka's looking at him with her soft eyes; but yet Olga Mihalovna felt vexed with her husband and frightened and pleased that she could listen to them.

"Sit down, enchantress," said Pyotr Dmitritch, sinking down on the hay and stretching. "That's right. Come, tell me something."

"What next! If I begin telling you anything you will go to sleep."

"Me go to sleep? Allah forbid! Can I go to sleep while eyes like yours are watching me?"

In her husband's words, and in the fact that he was lolling with his hat on the back of his head in the presence of a lady, there was nothing out of the way either. He was spoilt by women, knew that they found him attractive, and had adopted with them a special tone which everyone said suited him. With Lubotchka he behaved as with all women. But, all the same, Olga Mihalovna was jealous.

"Tell me, please," said Lubotchka, after a brief silence -- "is it true that you are to be tried for something?"

"I? Yes, I am . . . numbered among the transgressors, my charmer."

"But what for?"

"For nothing, but just . . . it's chiefly a question of politics," yawned Pyotr Dmitritch -- "the antagonisms of Left and Right. I, an obscurantist and reactionary, ventured in an official paper to make use of an expression offensive in the eyes of such immaculate Gladstones as Vladimir Pavlovitch Vladimirov and our local justice of the peace -- Kuzma Grigoritch Vostryakov."

Pytor Dmitritch yawned again and went on:

"And it is the way with us that you may express disapproval of the sun or the moon, or anything you like, but God preserve you from touching the Liberals! Heaven forbid! A Liberal is like the poisonous dry fungus which covers you with a cloud of dust if you accidentally touch it with your finger."

"What happened to you?"

"Nothing particular. The whole flare-up started from the merest trifle. A teacher, a detestable person of clerical associations, hands to Vostryakov a petition against a tavern-keeper, charging him with insulting language and behaviour in a public place. Everything showed that both the teacher and the tavern-keeper were drunk as cobblers, and that they behaved equally badly. If there had been insulting behaviour, the insult had anyway been mutual. Vostryakov ought to have fined them both for a breach of the peace and have turned them out of the court -- that is all. But that's not our way of doing things. With us what stands first is not the person -- not the fact itself, but the trade-mark and label. However great a rascal a teacher may be, he is always in the right because he is a teacher; a tavern-keeper is always in the wrong because he is a tavern-keeper and a money-grubber. Vostryakov placed the tavern-keeper under arrest. The man appealed to the Circuit Court; the Circuit Court triumphantly upheld Vostryakov's decision. Well, I stuck to my own opinion. . . . Got a little hot. . . . That was all."

Pyotr Dmitritch spoke calmly with careless irony. In reality the trial that was hanging over him worried him extremely. Olga Mihalovna remembered how on his return from the unfortunate session he had tried to conceal from his household how troubled he was, and how dissatisfied with himself. As an intelligent man he could not help feeling that he had gone too far in expressing his disagreement; and how much lying had been needful to conceal that feeling from himself and from others! How many unnecessary conversations there had been! How much grumbling and insincere laughter at what was not laughable! When he learned that he was to be brought up before the Court, he seemed at once harassed and depressed; he began to sleep badly, stood oftener than ever at the windows, drumming on the panes with his fingers. And he was ashamed to let his wife see that he was worried, and it vexed her.

"They say you have been in the province of Poltava?" Lubotchka questioned him.

"Yes," answered Pyotr Dmitritch. "I came back the day before yesterday."

"I expect it is very nice there."

"Yes, it is very nice, very nice indeed; in fact, I arrived just in time for the haymaking, I must tell you, and in the Ukraine the haymaking is the most poetical moment of the year. Here we have a big house, a big garden, a lot of servants, and a lot going on, so that you don't see the haymaking; here it all passes unnoticed. There, at the farm, I have a meadow of forty-five acres as flat as my hand. You can see the men mowing from any window you stand at. They are mowing in the meadow, they are mowing in the garden. There are no visitors, no fuss nor hurry either, so that you can't help seeing, feeling, hearing nothing but the haymaking. There is a smell of hay indoors and outdoors. There's the sound of the scythes from sunrise to sunset. Altogether Little Russia is a charming country. Would you believe it, when I was drinking water from the rustic wells and filthy vodka in some Jew's tavern, when on quiet evenings the strains of the Little Russian fiddle and the tambourines reached me, I was tempted by a fascinating idea -- to settle down on my place and live there as long as I chose, far away from Circuit Courts, intellectual conversations, philosophizing women, long dinners. . . ."

Pyotr Dmitritch was not lying. He was unhappy and really longed to rest. And he had visited his Poltava property simply to avoid seeing his study, his servants, his acquaintances, and everything that could remind him of his wounded vanity and his mistakes.

Lubotchka suddenly jumped up and waved her hands about in horror.

"Oh! A bee, a bee!" she shrieked. "It will sting!"

"Nonsense; it won't sting," said Pyotr Dmitritch. "What a coward you are!"

"No, no, no," cried Lubotchka; and looking round at the bees, she walked rapidly back.

Pyotr Dmitritch walked away after her, looking at her with a softened and melancholy face. He was probably thinking, as he looked at her, of his farm, of solitude, and -- who knows? -- perhaps he was even thinking how snug and cosy life would be at the farm if his wife had been this girl - young, pure, fresh, not corrupted by higher education, not with child. . . .

When the sound of their footsteps had died away, Olga Mihalovna came out of the shanty and turned towards the house. She wanted to cry. She was by now acutely jealous. She could understand that her husband was worried, dissatisfied with himself and ashamed, and when people are ashamed they hold aloof, above all from those nearest to them, and are unreserved with strangers; she could understand, also, that she had nothing to fear from Lubotchka or from those women who were now drinking coffee indoors. But everything in general was terrible, incomprehensible, and it already seemed to Olga Mihalovna that Pyotr Dmitritch only half belonged to her.

"He has no right to do it!" she muttered, trying to formulate her jealousy and her vexation with her husband. "He has no right at all. I will tell him so plainly!"

She made up her mind to find her husband at once and tell him all about it: it was disgusting, absolutely disgusting, that he was attractive to other women and sought their admiration as though it were some heavenly manna; it was unjust and dishonourable that he should give to others what belonged by right to his wife, that he should hide his soul and his conscience from his wife to reveal them to the first pretty face he came across. What harm had his wife done him? How was she to blame? Long ago she had been sickened by his lying: he was forever posing, flirting, saying what he did not think, and trying to seem different from what he was and what he ought to be. Why this falsity? Was it seemly in a decent man? If he lied he was demeaning himself and those to whom he lied, and slighting what he lied about. Could he not understand that if he swaggered and posed at the judicial table, or held forth at dinner on the prerogatives of Government, that he, simply to provoke her uncle, was showing thereby that he had not a ha'p'orth of respect for the Court, or himself, or any of the people who were listening and looking at him?

Coming out into the big avenue, Olga Mihalovna assumed an expression of face as though she had just gone away to look after some domestic matter. In the verandah the gentlemen were drinking liqueur and eating strawberries: one of them, the Examining Magistrate -- a stout elderly man, *blagueur* and wit -- must have been telling some rather free anecdote, for, seeing their hostess, he suddenly clapped his hands over his fat lips, rolled his eyes, and sat down. Olga Mihalovna did not like the local officials. She did not care for their clumsy, ceremonious wives, their scandal-mongering, their frequent visits, their flattery of her husband, whom they all hated. Now, when they were drinking, were replete with food and showed no signs of going away, she felt their presence an agonizing weariness; but not to appear impolite, she smiled cordially to the Magistrate, and shook her finger at him. She walked across the dining-room and drawing-room smiling, and looking as though she had gone to give some order and make some arrangement. "God grant no one stops me," she thought, but she forced herself to stop in the drawing-room to listen from politeness to a young man who was sitting at the piano playing: after standing for a minute, she cried, "Bravo, bravo, M. Georges!" and clapping her hands twice, she went on.

She found her husband in his study. He was sitting at the table, thinking of something. His face looked stern, thoughtful, and guilty. This was not the same Pyotr Dmitritch who had been arguing at dinner and whom his guests knew, but a different man -- wearied, feeling guilty and dissatisfied with himself, whom nobody knew but his wife. He must have come to the study to get cigarettes. Before him lay an open cigarette-case full of cigarettes, and one of his hands was in the table drawer; he had paused and sunk into thought as he was taking the cigarettes.

Olga Mihalovna felt sorry for him. It was as clear as day that this man was harassed, could find no rest, and was perhaps struggling with himself. Olga Mihalovna went up to the table in silence: wanting to show that she had forgotten the argument at dinner and was not cross, she shut the cigarette-case and put it in her husband's coat pocket.

"What should I say to him?" she wondered; "I shall say that lying is like a forest -- the further one goes into it the more difficult it is to get out of it. I will say to him, 'You have been carried away by the false part you are playing; you have insulted people who were attached to you and have done you no harm. Go and apologize to them, laugh at yourself, and you will feel better. And if you want peace and solitude, let us go away together.' "

Meeting his wife's gaze, Pyotr Dmitritch's face immediately assumed the expression it had worn at dinner and in the garden -- indifferent and slightly ironical. He yawned and got up.

"It's past five," he said, looking at his watch. "If our visitors are merciful and leave us at eleven, even then we have another six hours of it. It's a cheerful prospect, there's no denying!"

And whistling something, he walked slowly out of the study with his usual dignified gait. She could hear him with dignified firmness cross the dining-room, then the drawing-room, laugh with dignified assurance, and say to the young man who was playing, "Bravo! bravo!" Soon his footsteps died away: he must have gone out into the garden. And now not jealousy, not vexation, but real hatred of his footsteps, his insincere laugh and voice, took possession of Olga Mihalovna. She went to the window and looked out into the garden. Pyotr Dmitritch was already walking along the avenue. Putting one hand in his pocket and snapping the fingers of the other, he walked with confident swinging steps, throwing his head back a little, and looking as though he were very well satisfied with himself, with his dinner, with his digestion, and with nature. . . .

Two little schoolboys, the children of Madame Tchizhevsky, who had only just arrived, made their appearance in the avenue, accompanied by their tutor, a student wearing a white tunic and very narrow trousers. When they reached Pyotr Dmitritch, the boys and the student stopped, and probably congratulated him on his name-day. With a graceful swing of his shoulders, he patted the children on their cheeks, and carelessly offered the student his hand without looking at him. The student must have praised the weather and compared it with the climate of Petersburg, for Pyotr Dmitritch said in a loud voice, in a tone as though he were not speaking to a guest, but to an usher of the court or a witness:

"What! It's cold in Petersburg? And here, my good sir, we have a salubrious atmosphere and the fruits of the earth in abundance. Eh? What?"

And thrusting one hand in his pocket and snapping the fingers of the other, he walked on. Till he had disappeared behind the nut bushes, Olga Mihalovna watched the back of his head in perplexity. How had this man of thirty-four come by the dignified deportment of a general? How had he come by that impressive, elegant manner? Where had he got that vibration of authority in his voice? Where had he got these "what's," "to be sure's," and "my good sir's"?

Olga Mihalovna remembered how in the first months of her marriage she had felt dreary at home alone and had driven into the town to the Circuit Court, at which Pyotr Dmitritch had sometimes presided in place of her godfather, Count Alexey Petrovitch. In the presidential chair, wearing his uniform and a chain on his breast, he was completely changed. Stately gestures, a voice of thunder, "what," "to be sure," careless tones. . . . Everything, all that was ordinary and human, all that was individual and personal to himself that Olga Mihalovna was accustomed to seeing in him at home, vanished in grandeur, and in the presidential chair there sat not Pyotr Dmitritch, but another man whom everyone called Mr. President. This consciousness of power prevented him from sitting still in his place, and he seized every opportunity to ring his bell, to glance sternly at the public, to shout. . . . Where had he got his short-sight and his deafness when he suddenly began to see and hear with difficulty, and, frowning majestically, insisted on people speaking louder and coming closer to the table? From the height of his grandeur he could hardly distinguish faces or sounds, so that it seemed that if Olga Mihalovna herself had gone up to him he would have shouted even to her, "Your name?" Peasant witnesses he addressed familiarly, he shouted at the public so that his voice could be heard even in the street, and behaved incredibly with the lawyers. If a lawyer had to speak to him, Pyotr Dmitritch, turning a little away from him, looked with half-closed eyes at the ceiling, meaning to signify thereby that the lawyer was utterly superfluous and that he was neither recognizing him nor listening to him; if a badly-dressed lawyer spoke, Pyotr Dmitritch pricked up his ears and looked the man up and down with a sarcastic, annihilating stare as though to say: "Queer sort of lawyers nowadays!"

"What do you mean by that?" he would interrupt.

If a would-be eloquent lawyer mispronounced a foreign word, saying, for instance, "factitious" instead of "fictitious," Pyotr Dmitritch brightened up at once and asked, "What? How? Factitious? What does that mean?" and then observed impressively: "Don't make use of words you do not understand." And the lawyer, finishing his speech, would walk away from the table, red and perspiring, while Pyotr Dmitritch; with a self-satisfied smile, would lean back in his chair triumphant. In his manner with the lawyers he imitated Count Alexey Petrovitch a little, but when the latter said, for instance, "Counsel for the defence, you keep quiet for a little!" it sounded paternally good-natured and natural, while the same words in Pyotr Dmitritch's mouth were rude and artificial.

II

There were sounds of applause. The young man had finished playing. Olga Mihalovna remembered her guests and hurried into the drawing-room.

"I have so enjoyed your playing," she said, going up to the piano. "I have so enjoyed it. You have a wonderful talent! But don't you think our piano's out of tune?"

At that moment the two schoolboys walked into the room, accompanied by the student.

"My goodness! Mitya and Kolya," Olga Mihalovna drawled joyfully, going to meet them: "How big they have grown! One would not know you! But where is your mamma?"

"I congratulate you on the name-day," the student began in a free-and-easy tone, "and I wish you all happiness. Ekaterina Andreyevna sends her congratulations and begs you to excuse her. She is not very well."

"How unkind of her! I have been expecting her all day. Is it long since you left Petersburg?" Olga Mihalovna asked the student. "What kind of weather have you there now?" And without waiting for an answer, she looked cordially at the schoolboys and repeated:

"How tall they have grown! It is not long since they used to come with their nurse, and they are at school already! The old grow older while the young grow up. . . . Have you had dinner?"

"Oh, please don't trouble!" said the student.

"Why, you have not had dinner?"

"For goodness' sake, don't trouble!"

"But I suppose you are hungry?" Olga Mihalovna said it in a harsh, rude voice, with impatience and vexation -- it escaped her unawares, but at once she coughed, smiled, and flushed crimson. "How tall they have grown!" she said softly.

"Please don't trouble!" the student said once more.

The student begged her not to trouble; the boys said nothing; obviously all three of them were hungry. Olga Mihalovna took them into the dining-room and told Vassily to lay the table.

"How unkind of your mamma!" she said as she made them sit down. "She has quite forgotten me. Unkind, unkind, unkind . . . you must tell her so. What are you studying?" she asked the student.

"Medicine."

"Well, I have a weakness for doctors, only fancy. I am very sorry my husband is not a doctor. What courage anyone must have to perform an operation or dissect a corpse, for instance! Horrible! Aren't you frightened? I believe I should die of terror! Of course, you drink vodka?"

"Please don't trouble."

"After your journey you must have something to drink. Though I am a woman, even I drink sometimes. And Mitya and Kolya will drink Malaga. It's not a strong wine; you need not be afraid of it. What fine fellows they are, really! They'll be thinking of getting married next."

Olga Mihalovna talked without ceasing; she knew by experience that when she had guests to entertain it was far easier and more comfortable to talk than to listen. When you talk there is no need to strain your attention to think of answers to questions, and to change your expression of face. But unawares she asked the student a serious question; the student began a lengthy speech and she was forced to listen. The student knew that she had once been at the University, and so tried to seem a serious person as he talked to her.

"What subject are you studying?" she asked, forgetting that she had already put that question to him.

"Medicine."

Olga Mihalovna now remembered that she had been away from the ladies for a long while.

"Yes? Then I suppose you are going to be a doctor?" she said, getting up. "That's splendid. I am sorry I did not go in for medicine myself. So you will finish your dinner here, gentlemen, and then come into the garden. I will introduce you to the young ladies."

She went out and glanced at her watch: it was five minutes to six. And she wondered that the time had gone so slowly, and thought with horror that there were six more hours before midnight, when the party would break up. How could she get through those six hours? What phrases could she utter? How should she behave to her husband?

There was not a soul in the drawing-room or on the verandah. All the guests were sauntering about the garden.

"I shall have to suggest a walk in the birchwood before tea, or else a row in the boats," thought Olga Mihalovna, hurrying to the croquet ground, from which came the sounds of voices and laughter.

"And sit the old people down to *vint*. . . ." She met Grigory the footman coming from the croquet ground with empty bottles.

"Where are the ladies?" she asked.

"Among the raspberry-bushes. The master's there, too."

"Oh, good heavens!" someone on the croquet lawn shouted with exasperation. "I have told you a thousand times over! To know the Bulgarians you must see them! You can't judge from the papers!"

Either because of the outburst or for some other reason, Olga Mihalovna was suddenly aware of a terrible weakness all over, especially in her legs and in her shoulders. She felt she could not bear to speak, to listen, or to move.

"Grigory," she said faintly and with an effort, "when you have to serve tea or anything, please don't appeal to me, don't ask me anything, don't speak of anything. . . . Do it all yourself, and . . . and don't make a noise with your feet, I entreat you. . . . I can't, because . . ."

Without finishing, she walked on towards the croquet lawn, but on the way she thought of the ladies, and turned towards the raspberry-bushes. The sky, the air, and the trees looked gloomy again and threatened rain; it was hot and stifling. An immense flock of crows, foreseeing a storm, flew cawing over the garden. The paths. were more overgrown, darker, and narrower as they got nearer the kitchen garden. In one of them, buried in a thick tangle of wild pear, crab-apple, sorrel, young oaks, and hopbine, clouds of tiny black flies swarmed round Olga Mihalovna. She covered her face with her hands and began forcing herself to think of the little creature. . . . There floated through her imagination the figures of Grigory, Mitya, Kolya, the faces of the peasants who had come in the morning to present their congratulations.

She heard footsteps, and she opened her eyes. Uncle Nikolay Nikolaitch was coming rapidly towards her.

"It's you, dear? I am very glad . . ." he began, breathless. "A couple of words. . . ." He mopped with his handkerchief his red shaven chin, then suddenly stepped back a pace, flung up his hands and opened his eyes wide. "My dear girl, how long is this going on?" he said rapidly, spluttering. "I ask you: is there no limit to it? I say nothing of the demoralizing effect of his martinet views on all around him, of the way he insults all that is sacred and best in me and in every honest thinking man -- I will say nothing about that, but he might at least behave decently! Why, he shouts, he bellows, gives himself airs, poses as a sort of Bonaparte, does not let one say a word. . . . I don't know what the devil's the matter with him! These lordly gestures, this condescending tone; and laughing like a general! Who is he, allow me to ask you? I ask you, who is he? The husband of his wife, with a few paltry acres and the rank of a titular who has had the luck to marry an heiress! An upstart and a *junker,* like so many others! A type out of Shtchedrin! Upon my word, it's either that he's suffering from megalomania, or that old rat in his dotage, Count Alexey Petrovitch, is right when he says that children and young people are a long time growing up nowadays, and go on playing they are cabmen and generals till they are forty!"

"That's true, that's true," Olga Mihalovna assented. "Let me pass."

"Now just consider: what is it leading to?" her uncle went on, barring her way. "How will this playing at being a general and a Conservative end? Already he has got into trouble! Yes, to stand his trial! I am very glad of it! That's what his noise and shouting has brought him to -- to stand in the prisoner's dock. And it's not as though it were the Circuit Court or something: it's the Central Court! Nothing worse could be imagined, I think! And then he has quarrelled with everyone! He is celebrating his name-day, and look, Vostryakov's not here, nor Yahontov, nor Vladimirov, nor Shevud, nor the Count. . . . There is no one, I imagine, more Conservative than Count Alexey Petrovitch, yet even he has not come. And he never will come again. He won't come, you will see!"

"My God! but what has it to do with me?" asked Olga Mihalovna.

"What has it to do with you? Why, you are his wife! You are clever, you have had a university education, and it was in your power to make him an honest worker!"

"At the lectures I went to they did not teach us how to influence tiresome people. It seems as though I should have to apologize to all of you for having been at the University," said Olga Mihalovna sharply. "Listen, uncle. If people played the same scales over and over again the whole day long in your hearing, you wouldn't be able to sit still and listen, but would run away. I hear the same thing over again for days together all the year round. You must have pity on me at last."

Her uncle pulled a very long face, then looked at her searchingly and twisted his lips into a mocking smile.

"So that's how it is," he piped in a voice like an old woman's. "I beg your pardon!" he said, and made a ceremonious bow. "If you have fallen under his influence yourself, and have abandoned your convictions, you should have said so before. I beg your pardon!"

"Yes, I have abandoned my convictions," she cried. "There; make the most of it!"

"I beg your pardon!"

Her uncle for the last time made her a ceremonious bow, a little on one side, and, shrinking into himself, made a scrape with his foot and walked back.

"Idiot!" thought Olga Mihalovna. "I hope he will go home."

She found the ladies and the young people among the raspberries in the kitchen garden. Some were eating raspberries; others, tired of eating raspberries, were strolling about the strawberry beds or foraging among the sugar-peas. A little on one side of the raspberry bed, near a branching appletree propped up by posts which had been pulled out of an old fence, Pyotr Dmitritch was mowing the grass. His hair was falling over his forehead, his cravat was untied. His watch-chain was hanging loose. Every step and every swing of the scythe showed skill and the possession of immense physical strength. Near him were standing Lubotchka and the daughters of a neighbour, Colonel Bukryeev -- two anaemic and unhealthily stout fair girls, Natalya and Valentina, or, as they were always called, Nata and Vata, both wearing white frocks and strikingly like each other. Pyotr Dmitritch was teaching them to mow.

"It's very simple," he said. "You have only to know how to hold the scythe and not to get too hot over it -- that is, not to use more force than is necessary! Like this. . . . Wouldn't you like to try?" he said, offering the scythe to Lubotchka. Come!"

Lubotchka took the scythe clumsily, blushed crimson, and laughed.

"Don't be afraid, Lubov Alexandrovna!" cried Olga Mihalovna, loud enough for all the ladies to hear that she was with them. "Don't be afraid! You must learn! If you marry a Tolstoyan he will make you mow."

Lubotchka raised the scythe, but began laughing again, and, helpless with laughter, let go of it at once. She was ashamed and pleased at being talked to as though grown up. Nata, with a cold, serious face, with no trace of smiling or shyness, took the scythe, swung it and caught it in the grass; Vata, also without a smile, as cold and serious as her sister, took the scythe, and silently thrust it into the earth. Having done this, the two sisters linked arms and walked in silence to the raspberries.

Pyotr Dmitritch laughed and played about like a boy, and this childish, frolicsome mood in which he became exceedingly good-natured suited him far better than any other. Olga Mihalovna loved him when he was like that. But his boyishness did not usually last long. It did not this time; after playing with the scythe, he for some reason thought it necessary to take a serious tone about it.

"When I am mowing, I feel, do you know, healthier and more normal," he said. "If I were forced to confine myself to an intellectual life I believe I should go out of my mind. I feel that I was not born to be a man of culture! I ought to mow, plough, sow, drive out the horses."

And Pyotr Dmitritch began a conversation with the ladies about the advantages of physical labour, about culture, and then about the pernicious effects of money, of property. Listening to her husband, Olga Mihalovna, for some reason, thought of her dowry.

"And the time will come, I suppose," she thought, "when he will not forgive me for being richer than he. He is proud and vain. Maybe he will hate me because he owes so much to me."

She stopped near Colonel Bukryeev, who was eating raspberries and also taking part in the conversation.

"Come," he said, making room for Olga Mihalovna and Pyotr Dmitritch. "The ripest are here. . . . And so, according to Proudhon," he went on, raising his voice, "property is robbery. But I must confess I don't believe in Proudhon, and don't consider him a philosopher. The French are not authorities, to my thinking -- God bless them!"

"Well, as for Proudhons and Buckles and the rest of them, I am weak in that department," said Pyotr Dmitritch. "For philosophy you must apply to my wife. She has been at University lectures and knows all yourSchopenhauers and Proudhons by heart. . . ."

Olga Mihalovna felt bored again. She walked again along a little path by apple and pear trees, and looked again as though she was on some very important errand. She reached the gardener's cottage. In the doorway the gardener's wife, Varvara, was sitting together with her four little children with big shaven heads. Varvara, too, was with child and expecting to be confined on Elijah's Day. After greeting her, Olga Mihalovna looked at her and the children in silence and asked:

"Well, how do you feel?"

"Oh, all right. . . ."

A silence followed. The two women seemed to understand each other without words.

"It's dreadful having one's first baby," said Olga Mihalovna after a moment's thought. "I keep feeling as though I shall not get through it, as though I shall die."

"I fancied that, too, but here I am alive. One has all sorts of fancies."

Varvara, who was just going to have her fifth, looked down a little on her mistress from the height of her experience and spoke in a rather didactic tone, and Olga Mihalovna could not help feeling her authority; she would have liked to have talked of her fears, of the child, of her sensations, but she was afraid it might strike Varvara as naïve and trivial. And she waited in silence for Varvara to say something herself.

"Olya, we are going indoors," Pyotr Dmitritch called from the raspberries.

Olga Mihalovna liked being silent, waiting and watching Varvara. She would have been ready to stay like that till night without speaking or having any duty to perform. But she had to go. She had hardly left the cottage when Lubotchka, Nata, and Vata came running to meet her. The sisters stopped short abruptly a couple of yards away; Lubotchka ran right up to her and flung herself on her neck.

"You dear, darling, precious," she said, kissing her face and her neck. "Let us go and have tea on the island!"

"On the island, on the island!" said the precisely similar Nata and Vata, both at once, without a smile.

"But it's going to rain, my dears."

"It's not, it's not," cried Lubotchka with a woebegone face. "They've all agreed to go. Dear! darling!"

"They are all getting ready to have tea on the island," said Pyotr Dmitritch, coming up. "See to arranging things. . . . We will all go in the boats, and the samovars and all the rest of it must be sent in the carriage with the servants."

He walked beside his wife and gave her his arm. Olga Mihalovna had a desire to say something disagreeable to her husband, something biting, even about her dowry perhaps -- the crueller the better, she felt. She thought a little, and said:

"Why is it Count Alexey Petrovitch hasn't come? What a pity!"

"I am very glad he hasn't come," said Pyotr Dmitritch, lying. "I'm sick to death of that old lunatic."

"But yet before dinner you were expecting him so eagerly!"

III

Half an hour later all the guests were crowding on the bank near the pile to which the boats were fastened. They were all talking and laughing, and were in such excitement and commotion that they could hardly get into the boats. Three boats were crammed with passengers, while two stood empty. The keys for unfastening these two boats had been somehow mislaid, and messengers were continually running from the river to the house to look for them. Some said Grigory had the keys, others that the bailiff had them, while others suggested sending for a blacksmith and breaking the padlocks. And all talked at once, interrupting and shouting one another down. Pyotr Dmitritch paced impatiently to and fro on the bank, shouting:

"What the devil's the meaning of it! The keys ought always to be lying in the hall window! Who has dared to take them away? The bailiff can get a boat of his own if he wants one!"

At last the keys were found. Then it appeared that two oars were missing. Again there was a great hullabaloo. Pyotr Dmitritch, who was weary of pacing about the bank, jumped into a long, narrow boat hollowed out of the trunk of a poplar, and, lurching from side to side and almost falling into the water, pushed off from the bank. The other boats followed him one after another, amid loud laughter and the shrieks of the young ladies.

The white cloudy sky, the trees on the riverside, the boats with the people in them, and the oars, were reflected in the water as in a mirror; under the boats, far away below in the bottomless depths, was a second sky with the birds flying across it. The bank on which the house and gardens stood was high, steep, and covered with trees; on the other, which was sloping, stretched broad green water-meadows with sheets of water glistening in them. The boats had floated a hundred yards when, behind the mournfully drooping willows on the sloping banks, huts and a herd of cows came into sight; they began to hear songs, drunken shouts, and the strains of a concertina.

Here and there on the river fishing-boats were scattered about, setting their nets for the night. In one of these boats was the festive party, playing on home-made violins and violoncellos.

Olga Mihalovna was sitting at the rudder; she was smiling affably and talking a great deal to entertain her visitors, while she glanced stealthily at her husband. He was ahead of them all, standing up punting with one oar. The light sharp-nosed canoe, which all the guests called the "death-trap" -- while Pyotr Dmitritch, for some reason, called it *Penderaklia* -- flew along quickly; it had a brisk, crafty expression, as though it hated its heavy occupant and was looking out for a favourable moment to glide away from under his feet. Olga Mihalovna kept looking at her husband, and she loathed his good looks which attracted everyone, the back of his head, his attitude, his familiar manner with women; she hated all the women sitting in the boat with her, was jealous, and at the same time was trembling every minute in terror that the frail craft would upset and cause an accident.

"Take care, Pyotr!" she cried, while her heart fluttered with terror. "Sit down! We believe in your courage without all that!"

She was worried, too, by the people who were in the boat with her. They were all ordinary good sort of people like thousands of others, but now each one of them struck her as exceptional and evil. In each one of them she saw nothing but falsity. "That young man," she thought, "rowing, in gold-rimmed spectacles, with chestnut hair and a nice-looking beard: he is a mamma's darling, rich, and well-fed, and always fortunate, and everyone considers him an honourable, free-thinking, advanced man. It's not a year since he left the University and came to live in the district, but he already talks of himself as 'we active members of the Zemstvo.' But in another year he will be bored like so many others and go off to Petersburg, and to justify running away, will tell everyone that the Zemstvos are good-for-nothing, and that he has been deceived in them. While from the other boat his young wife keeps her eyes fixed on him, and believes that he is 'an active member of the Zemstvo,' just as in a year she will believe that the Zemstvo is good-for-nothing. And that stout, carefully shaven gentleman in the straw hat with the broad ribbon, with an expensive cigar in his mouth: he is fond of saying, 'It is time to put away dreams and set to work!' He has Yorkshire pigs, Butler's hives, rape-seed, pine-apples, a dairy, a cheese factory, Italian bookkeeping by double entry; but every summer he sells his timber and mortgages part of his land to spend the autumn with his mistress in the Crimea. And there's Uncle Nikolay Nikolaitch, who has quarrelled with Pyotr Dmitritch, and yet for some reason does not go home."

Olga Mihalovna looked at the other boats, and there, too, she saw only uninteresting, queer creatures, affected or stupid people. She thought of all the people she knew in the district, and could not remember one person of whom one could say or think anything good. They all seemed to her mediocre, insipid, unintelligent, narrow, false, heartless; they all said what they did not think, and did what they did not want to. Dreariness and despair were stifling her; she longed to leave off smiling, to leap up and cry out, "I am sick of you," and then jump out and swim to the bank.

"I say, let's take Pyotr Dmitritch in tow!" someone shouted.

"In tow, in tow!" the others chimed in. "Olga Mihalovna, take your husband in tow."

To take him in tow, Olga Mihalovna, who was steering, had to seize the right moment and to catch bold of his boat by the chain at the beak. When she bent over to the chain Pyotr Dmitritch frowned and looked at her in alarm.

"I hope you won't catch cold," he said.

"If you are uneasy about me and the child, why do you torment me?" thought Olga Mihalovna.

Pyotr Dmitritch acknowledged himself vanquished, and, not caring to be towed, jumped from the *Penderaklia* into the boat which was overful already, and jumped so carelessly that the boat lurched violently, and everyone cried out in terror.

"He did that to please the ladies," thought Olga Mihalovna; "he knows it's charming." Her hands and feet began trembling, as she supposed, from boredom, vexation from the strain of smiling and the discomfort she felt all over her body. And to conceal this trembling from her guests, she tried to talk more loudly, to laugh, to move.

"If I suddenly begin to cry," she thought, "I shall say I have toothache. . . ."

But at last the boats reached the "Island of Good Hope," as they called the peninsula formed by a bend in the river at an acute angle, covered with a copse of old birch-trees, oaks, willows, and poplars. The tables were already laid under the trees; the samovars were smoking, and Vassily and Grigory, in their swallow-tails and white knitted gloves, were already busy with the tea-things. On the other bank, opposite the "Island of Good Hope," there stood the carriages which had come with the provisions. The baskets and parcels of provisions were carried across to the island in a little boat like the *Penderaklia*. The footmen, the coachmen, and even the peasant who was sitting in the boat, had the solemn expression befitting a name-day such as one only sees in children and servants.

While Olga Mihalovna was making the tea and pouring out the first glasses, the visitors were busy with the liqueurs and sweet things. Then there was the general commotion usual at picnics over drinking tea, very wearisome and exhausting for the hostess. Grigory and Vassily had hardly had time to take the glasses round before hands were being stretched out to Olga Mihalovna with empty glasses. One asked for no sugar, another wanted it stronger, another weak, a fourth declined another glass. And all this Olga Mihalovna had to remember, and then to call, "Ivan Petrovitch, is it without sugar for you?" or, "Gentlemen, which of you wanted it weak?" But the guest who had asked for weak tea, or no sugar, had by now forgotten it, and, absorbed in agreeable conversation, took the first glass that came. Depressed-looking figures wandered like shadows at a little distance from the table, pretending to look for mushrooms in the grass, or reading the labels on the boxes -- these were those for whom there were not glasses enough. "Have you had tea?" Olga Mihalovna kept asking, and the guest so addressed begged her not to trouble, and said, "I will wait," though it would have suited her better for the visitors not to wait but to make haste.

Some, absorbed in conversation, drank their tea slowly, keeping their glasses for half an hour; others, especially some who had drunk a good deal at dinner, would not leave the table, and kept on drinking glass after glass, so that Olga Mihalovna scarcely had time to fill them. One jocular young man sipped his tea through a lump of sugar, and kept saying, "Sinful man that I am, I love to indulge myself with the Chinese herb." He kept asking with a heavy sigh: "Another tiny dish of tea more, if you please." He drank a great deal, nibbled his sugar, and thought it all very amusing and original, and imagined that he was doing a clever imitation of a Russian merchant. None of them understood that these trifles were agonizing to their hostess, and, indeed, it was hard to understand it, as Olga Mihalovna went on all the time smiling affably and talking nonsense.

But she felt ill. . . . She was irritated by the crowd of people, the laughter, the questions, the jocular young man, the footmen harassed and run off their legs, the children who hung round the table; she was irritated at Vata's being like Nata, at Kolya's being like Mitya, so that one could not tell which of them had had tea and which of them had not. She felt that her smile of forced affability was passing into an expression of anger, and she felt every minute as though she would burst into tears.

"Rain, my friends," cried someone.

Everyone looked at the sky.

"Yes, it really is rain . . ." Pyotr Dmitritch assented, and wiped his cheek.

Only a few drops were falling from the sky -- the real rain had not begun yet; but the company abandoned their tea and made haste to get off. At first they all wanted to drive home in the carriages, but changed their minds and made for the boats. On the pretext that she had to hasten home to give directions about the supper, Olga Mihalovna asked to be excused for leaving the others, and went home in the carriage.

When she got into the carriage, she first of all let her face rest from smiling. With an angry face she drove through the village, and with an angry face acknowledged the bows of the peasants she met. When she got home, she went to the bedroom by the back way and lay down on her husband's bed.

"Merciful God!" she whispered. "What is all this hard labour for? Why do all these people hustle each other here and pretend that they are enjoying themselves? Why do I smile and lie? I don't understand it."

She heard steps and voices. The visitors had come back.

"Let them come," thought Olga Mihalovna; "I shall lie a little longer."

But a maid-servant came and said:

"Marya Grigoryevna is going, madam."

Olga Mihalovna jumped up, tidied her hair and hurried out of the room.

"Marya Grigoryevna, what is the meaning of this?" she began in an injured voice, going to meet Marya Grigoryevna. "Why are you in such a hurry?"

"I can't help it, darling! I've stayed too long as it is; my children are expecting me home."

"It's too bad of you! Why didn't you bring your children with you?"

"If you will let me, dear, I will bring them on some ordinary day, but to-day . . ."

"Oh, please do," Olga Mihalovna interrupted; "I shall be delighted! Your children are so sweet! Kiss them all for me. . . . But, really, I am offended with you! I don't understand why you are in such a hurry!"

"I really must, I really must. . . . Good-bye, dear. Take care of yourself. In your condition, you know . . ."

And the ladies kissed each other. After seeing the departing guest to her carriage, Olga Mihalovna went in to the ladies in the drawing-room. There the lamps were already lighted and the gentlemen were sitting down to cards.

IV

The party broke up after supper about a quarter past twelve. Seeing her visitors off, Olga Mihalovna stood at the door and said:

"You really ought to take a shawl! It's turning a little chilly. Please God, you don't catch cold!"

"Don't trouble, Olga Mihalovna," the ladies answered as they got into the carriage. "Well, good-bye. Mind now, we are expecting you; don't play us false!"

"Wo-o-o!" the coachman checked the horses.

"Ready, Denis! Good-bye, Olga Mihalovna!"

"Kiss the children for me!"

The carriage started and immediately disappeared into the darkness. In the red circle of light cast by the lamp in the road, a fresh pair or trio of impatient horses, and the silhouette of a coachman with his hands held out stiffly before him, would come into view. Again there began kisses, reproaches, and entreaties to come again or to take a shawl. Pyotr Dmitritch kept running out and helping the ladies into their carriages.

"You go now by Efremovshtchina," he directed the coachman; "it's nearer through Mankino, but the road is worse that way. You might have an upset. . . . Good-bye, my charmer. *Mille compliments* to your artist!"

"Good-bye, Olga Mihalovna, darling! Go indoors, or you will catch cold! It's damp!"

"Wo-o-o! you rascal!"

"What horses have you got here?" Pyotr Dmitritch asked.

"They were bought from Haidorov, in Lent," answered the coachman.

"Capital horses. . . ."

And Pyotr Dmitritch patted the trace horse on the haunch.

"Well, you can start! God give you good luck!"

The last visitor was gone at last; the red circle on the road quivered, moved aside, contracted and went out, as Vassily carried away the lamp from the entrance. On previous occasions when they had seen off their visitors, Pyotr Dmitritch and Olga Mihalovna had begun dancing about the drawing-room, facing each other, clapping their hands and singing: "They've gone! They've gone!" But now Olga Mihalovna was not equal to that. She went to her bedroom, undressed, and got into bed.

She fancied she would fall asleep at once and sleep soundly. Her legs and her shoulders ached painfully, her head was heavy from the strain of talking, and she was conscious, as before, of discomfort all over her body. Covering her head over, she lay still for three or four minutes, then peeped out from under the bed-clothes at the lamp before the ikon, listened to the silence, and smiled.

"It's nice, it's nice," she whispered, curling up her legs, which felt as if they had grown longer from so much walking. "Sleep, sleep . . . ."

Her legs would not get into a comfortable position; she felt uneasy all over, and she turned on the other side. A big fly blew buzzing about the bedroom and thumped against the ceiling. She could hear, too, Grigory and Vassily stepping cautiously about the drawing-room, putting the chairs back in their places; it seemed to Olga Mihalovna that she could not go to sleep, nor be comfortable till those sounds were hushed. And again she turned over on the other side impatiently.

She heard her husband's voice in the drawing-room. Someone must be staying the night, as Pyotr Dmitritch was addressing someone and speaking loudly:

"I don't say that Count Alexey Petrovitch is an impostor. But he can't help seeming to be one, because all of you gentlemen attempt to see in him something different from what he really is. His craziness is looked upon as originality, his familiar manners as good-nature, and his complete absence of opinions as Conservatism. Even granted that he is a Conservative of the stamp of '84, what after all is Conservatism?"

Pyotr Dmitritch, angry with Count Alexey Petrovitch, his visitors, and himself, was relieving his heart. He abused both the Count and his visitors, and in his vexation with himself was ready to speak out and to hold forth upon anything. After seeing his guest to his room, he walked up and down the drawing-room, walked through the dining-room, down the corridor, then into his study, then again went into the drawing-room, and came into the bedroom. Olga Mihalovna was lying on her back, with the bed-clothes only to her waist (by now she felt hot), and with an angry face, watched the fly that was thumping against the ceiling.

"Is someone staying the night?" she asked.

"Yegorov."

Pyotr Dmitritch undressed and got into his bed.

Without speaking, he lighted a cigarette, and he, too, fell to watching the fly. There was an uneasy and forbidding look in his eyes. Olga Mihalovna looked at his handsome profile for five minutes in silence. It seemed to her for some reason that if her husband were suddenly to turn facing her, and to say, "Olga, I am unhappy," she would cry or laugh, and she would be at ease. She fancied that her legs were aching and her body was uncomfortable all over because of the strain on her feelings.

"Pyotr, what are you thinking of?" she said.

"Oh, nothing . . ." her husband answered.

"You have taken to having secrets from me of late: that's not right."

"Why is it not right?" answered Pyotr Dmitritch drily and not at once. "We all have our personal life, everyone of us, and we are bound to have our secrets."

"Personal life, our secrets . . . that's all words! Understand you are wounding me!" said Olga Mihalovna, sitting up in bed. "If you have a load on your heart, why do you hide it from me? And why do you find it more suitable to open your heart to women who are nothing to you, instead of to your wife? I overheard your outpourings to Lubotchka by the bee-house to-day."

"Well, I congratulate you. I am glad you did overhear it."

This meant "Leave me alone and let me think." Olga Mihalovna was indignant. Vexation, hatred, and wrath, which had been accumulating within her during the whole day, suddenly boiled over; she wanted at once to speak out, to hurt her husband without putting it off till to-morrow, to wound him, to punish him. . . . Making an effort to control herself and not to scream, she said:

"Let me tell you, then, that it's all loathsome, loathsome, loathsome! I've been hating you all day; you see what you've done."

Pyotr Dmitritch, too, got up and sat on the bed.

"It's loathsome, loathsome, loathsome," Olga Mihalovna went on, beginning to tremble all over. "There's no need to congratulate me; you had better congratulate yourself! It's a shame, a disgrace. You have wrapped yourself in lies till you are ashamed to be alone in the room with your wife! You are a deceitful man! I see through you and understand every step you take!"

"Olya, I wish you would please warn me when you are out of humour. Then I will sleep in the study."

Saying this, Pyotr Dmitritch picked up his pillow and walked out of the bedroom. Olga Mihalovna had not foreseen this. For some minutes she remained silent with her mouth open, trembling all over and looking at the door by which her husband had gone out, and trying to understand what it meant. Was this one of the devices to which deceitful people have recourse when they are in the wrong, or was it a deliberate insult aimed at her pride? How was she to take it? Olga Mihalovna remembered her cousin, a lively young officer, who often used to tell her, laughing, that when "his spouse nagged at him" at night, he usually picked up his pillow and went whistling to spend the night in his study, leaving his wife in a foolish and ridiculous position. This officer was married to a rich, capricious, and foolish woman whom he did not respect but simply put up with.

Olga Mihalovna jumped out of bed. To her mind there was only one thing left for her to do now; to dress with all possible haste and to leave the house forever. The house was her own, but so much the worse for Pyotr Dmitritch. Without pausing to consider whether this was necessary or not, she went quickly to the study to inform her husband of her intention ("Feminine logic!" flashed through her mind), and to say something wounding and sarcastic at parting. . . .

Pyotr Dmitritch was lying on the sofa and pretending to read a newspaper. There was a candle burning on a chair near him. His face could not be seen behind the newspaper.

"Be so kind as to tell me what this means? I am asking you."

"Be so kind . . . " Pyotr Dmitritch mimicked her, not showing his face. "It's sickening, Olga! Upon my honour, I am exhausted and not up to it. . . . Let us do our quarrelling to-morrow."

"No, I understand you perfectly!" Olga Mihalovna went on. "You hate me! Yes, yes! You hate me because I am richer than you! You will never forgive me for that, and will always be lying to me!" (" Feminine logic!" flashed through her mind again.) "You are laughing at me now. . . . I am convinced, in fact, that you only married me in order to have property qualifications and those wretched horses. . . . Oh, I am miserable!"

Pyotr Dmitritch dropped the newspaper and got up. The unexpected insult overwhelmed him. With a childishly helpless smile he looked desperately at his wife, and holding out his hands to her as though to ward off blows, he said imploringly:

"Olya!"

And expecting her to say something else awful, he leaned back in his chair, and his huge figure seemed as helplessly childish as his smile.

"Olya, how could you say it?" he whispered.

Olga Mihalovna came to herself. She was suddenly aware of her passionate love for this man, remembered that he was her husband, Pyotr Dmitritch, without whom she could not live for a day, and who loved her passionately, too. She burst into loud sobs that sounded strange and unlike her, and ran back to her bedroom.

She fell on the bed, and short hysterical sobs, choking her and making her arms and legs twitch, filled the bedroom. Remembering there was a visitor sleeping three or four rooms away, she buried her head under the pillow to stifle her sobs, but the pillow rolled on to the floor, and she almost fell on the floor herself when she stooped to pick it up. She pulled the quilt up to her face, but her hands would not obey her, but tore convulsively at everything she clutched.

She thought that everything was lost, that the falsehood she had told to wound her husband had shattered her life into fragments. Her husband would not forgive her. The insult she had hurled at him was not one that could be effaced by any caresses, by any vows. . . . How could she convince her husband that she did not believe what she had said?

"It's all over, it's all over!" she cried, not noticing that the pillow had slipped on to the floor again. "For God's sake, for God's sake!"

Probably roused by her cries, the guest and the servants were now awake; next day all the neighbourhood would know that she had been in hysterics and would blame Pyotr Dmitritch. She made an effort to restrain herself, but her sobs grew louder and louder every minute.

"For God's sake," she cried in a voice not like her own, and not knowing why she cried it. "For God's sake!"

She felt as though the bed were heaving under her and her feet were entangled in the bed-clothes. Pyotr Dmitritch, in his dressing-gown, with a candle in his hand, came into the bedroom.

"Olya, hush!" he said.

She raised herself, and kneeling up in bed, screwing up her eyes at the light, articulated through her sobs:

"Understand . . . understand! . . . ."

She wanted to tell him that she was tired to death by the party, by his falsity, by her own falsity, that it had all worked together, but she could only articulate:

"Understand . . . understand!"

"Come, drink!" he said, handing her some water.

She took the glass obediently and began drinking, but the water splashed over and was spilt on her arms, her throat and knees.

"I must look horribly unseemly," she thought.

Pyotr Dmitritch put her back in bed without a word, and covered her with the quilt, then he took the candle and went out.

"For God's sake!" Olga Mihalovna cried again. "Pyotr, understand, understand!"

Suddenly something gripped her in the lower part of her body and back with such violence that her wailing was cut short, and she bit the pillow from the pain. But the pain let her go again at once, and she began sobbing again.

The maid came in, and arranging the quilt over her, asked in alarm:

"Mistress, darling, what is the matter?"

"Go out of the room," said Pyotr Dmitritch sternly, going up to the bed.

"Understand . . . understand! . . ." Olga Mihalovna began.

"Olya, I entreat you, calm yourself," he said. "I did not mean to hurt you. I would not have gone out of the room if I had known it would have hurt you so much; I simply felt depressed. I tell you, on my honour . . ."

"Understand! . . . You were lying, I was lying. . . ."

"I understand. . . . Come, come, that's enough! I understand," said Pyotr Dmitritch tenderly, sitting down on her bed. "You said that in anger; I quite understand. I swear to God I love you beyond anything on earth, and when I married you I never once thought of your being rich. I loved you immensely, and that's all . . . I assure you. I have never been in want of money or felt the value of it, and so I cannot feel the difference between your fortune and mine. It always seemed to me we were equally well off. And that I have been deceitful in little things, that . . . of course, is true. My life has hitherto been arranged in such a frivolous way that it has somehow been impossible to get on without paltry lying. It weighs on me, too, now. . . . Let us leave off talking about it, for goodness' sake!"

Olga Mihalovna again felt in acute pain, and clutched her husband by the sleeve.

"I am in pain, in pain, in pain . . ." she said rapidly. "Oh, what pain!"

"Damnation take those visitors!" muttered Pyotr Dmitritch, getting up. "You ought not to have gone to the island to-day!" he cried. "What an idiot I was not to prevent you! Oh, my God!"

He scratched his head in vexation, and, with a wave of his hand, walked out of the room.

Then he came into the room several times, sat down on the bed beside her, and talked a great deal, sometimes tenderly, sometimes angrily, but she hardly heard him. Her sobs were continually interrupted by fearful attacks of pain, and each time the pain was more acute and prolonged. At first she held her breath and bit the pillow during the pain, but then she began screaming on an unseemly piercing note. Once seeing her husband near her, she remembered that she had insulted him, and without pausing to think whether it were really Pyotr Dmitritch or whether she were in delirium, clutched his hand in both hers and began kissing it.

"You were lying, I was lying . . ." she began justifying herself. "Understand, understand. . . . They have exhausted me, driven me out of all patience."

"Olya, we are not alone," said Pyotr Dmitritch.

Olga Mihalovna raised her head and saw Varvara, who was kneeling by the chest of drawers and pulling out the bottom drawer. The top drawers were already open. Then Varvara got up, red from the strained position, and with a cold, solemn face began trying to unlock a box.

"Marya, I can't unlock it! "she said in a whisper. "You unlock it, won't you?"

Marya, the maid, was digging a candle end out of the candlestick with a pair of scissors, so as to put in a new candle; she went up to Varvara and helped her to unlock the box.

"There should be nothing locked . . ." whispered Varvara. "Unlock this basket, too, my good girl. Master," she said, "you should send to Father Mihail to unlock the holy gates! You must!"

"Do what you like," said Pyotr Dmitritch, breathing hard, "only, for God's sake, make haste and fetch the doctor or the midwife! Has Vassily gone? Send someone else. Send your husband!"

"It's the birth," Olga Mihalovna thought. "Varvara," she moaned, "but he won't be born alive!"

"It's all right, it's all right, mistress," whispered Varvara. "Please God, he will be alive! he will be alive!"

When Olga Mihalovna came to herself again after a pain she was no longer sobbing nor tossing from side to side, but moaning. She could not refrain from moaning even in the intervals between the pains. The candles were still burning, but the morning light was coming through the blinds. It was probably about five o'clock in the morning. At the round table there was sitting some unknown woman with a very discreet air, wearing a white apron. From her whole appearance it was evident she had been sitting there a long time. Olga Mihalovna guessed that she was the midwife.

"Will it soon be over?" she asked, and in her voice she heard a peculiar and unfamiliar note which had never been there before. "I must be dying in childbirth," she thought.

Pyotr Dmitritch came cautiously into the bedroom, dressed for the day, and stood at the window with his back to his wife. He lifted the blind and looked out of window.

"What rain!" he said.

"What time is it?" asked Olga Mihalovna, in order to hear the unfamiliar note in her voice again.

"A quarter to six," answered the midwife.

"And what if I really am dying?" thought Olga Mihalovna, looking at her husband's head and the window-panes on which the rain was beating. "How will he live without me? With whom will he have tea and dinner, talk in the evenings, sleep?"

And he seemed to her like a forlorn child; she felt sorry for him and wanted to say something nice, caressing and consolatory. She remembered how in the spring he had meant to buy himself some harriers, and she, thinking it a cruel and dangerous sport, had prevented him from doing it.

"Pyotr, buy yourself harriers," she moaned.

He dropped the blind and went up to the bed, and would have said something; but at that moment the pain came back, and Olga Mihalovna uttered an unseemly, piercing scream.

The pain and the constant screaming and moaning stupefied her. She heard, saw, and sometimes spoke, but hardly understood anything, and was only conscious that she was in pain or was just going to be in pain. It seemed to her that the nameday party had been long, long ago -- not yesterday, but a year ago perhaps; and that her new life of agony had lasted longer than her childhood, her school-days, her time at the University, and her marriage, and would go on for a long, long time, endlessly. She saw them bring tea to the midwife, and summon her at midday to lunch and afterwards to dinner; she saw Pyotr Dmitritch grow used to coming in, standing for long intervals by the window, and going out again; saw strange men, the maid, Varvara, come in as though they were at home. . . . Varvara said nothing but, "He will, he will," and was angry when anyone closed the drawers and the chest. Olga Mihalovna saw the light change in the room and in the windows: at one time it was twilight, then thick like fog, then bright daylight as it had been at dinner-time the day before, then again twilight . . . and each of these changes lasted as long as her childhood, her school-days, her life at the University. . . .

In the evening two doctors -- one bony, bald, with a big red beard; the other with a swarthy Jewish face and cheap spectacles -- performed some sort of operation on Olga Mihalovna. To these unknown men touching her body she felt utterly indifferent. By now she had no feeling of shame, no will, and anyone might do what he would with her. If anyone had rushed at her with a knife, or had insulted Pyotr Dmitritch, or had robbed her of her right to the little creature, she would not have said a word.

They gave her chloroform during the operation. When she came to again, the pain was still there and insufferable. It was night. And Olga Mihalovna remembered that there had been just such a night with the stillness, the lamp, with the midwife sitting motionless by the bed, with the drawers of the chest pulled out, with Pyotr Dmitritch standing by the window, but some time very, very long ago. . . .

V

"I am not dead . . ." thought Olga Mihalovna when she began to understand her surroundings again, and when the pain was over.

A bright summer day looked in at the widely open windows; in the garden below the windows, the sparrows and the magpies never ceased chattering for one instant.

The drawers were shut now, her husband's bed had been made. There was no sign of the midwife or of the maid, or of Varvara in the room, only Pyotr Dmitritch was standing, as before, motionless by the window looking into the garden. There was no sound of a child's crying, no one was congratulating her or rejoicing, it was evident that the little creature had not been born alive.

"Pyotr!"

Olga Mihalovna called to her husband.

Pyotr Dmitritch looked round. It seemed as though a long time must have passed since the last guest had departed and Olga Mihalovna had insulted her husband, for Pyotr Dmitritch was perceptibly thinner and hollow-eyed.

"What is it?" he asked, coming up to the bed.

He looked away, moved his lips and smiled with childlike helplessness.

"Is it all over?" asked Olga Mihalovna.

Pyotr Dmitritch tried to make some answer, but his lips quivered and his mouth worked like a toothless old man's, like Uncle Nikolay Nikolaitch's.

"Olya," he said, wringing his hands; big tears suddenly dropping from his eyes. "Olya, I don't care about your property qualification, nor the Circuit Courts . . ." (he gave a sob) "nor particular views, nor those visitors, nor your fortune. . . . I don't care about anything! Why didn't we take care of our child? Oh, it's no good talking!"

With a despairing gesture he went out of the bedroom.

But nothing mattered to Olga Mihalovna now, there was a mistiness in her brain from the chloroform, an emptiness in her soul. . . . The dull indifference to life which had overcome her when the two doctors were performing the operation still had possession of her.

A NERVOUS BREAKDOWN

A medical student called Mayer, and a pupil of the Moscow School of Painting, Sculpture, and Architecture called Rybnikov, went one evening to see their friend Vassilyev, a law student, and suggested that he should go with them to S. Street. For a long time Vassilyev would not consent to go, but in the end he put on his greatcoat and went with them.

He knew nothing of fallen women except by hearsay and from books, and he had never in his life been in the houses in which they live. He knew that there are immoral women who, under the pressure of fatal circumstances -- environment, bad education, poverty, and so on -- are forced to sell their honor for money.

They know nothing of pure love, have no children, have no civil rights; their mothers and sisters weep over them as though they were dead, science treats of them as an evil, men address them with contemptuous familiarity. But in spite of all that, they do not lose the semblance and image of God. They all acknowledge their sin and hope for salvation. Of the means that lead to salvation they can avail themselves to the fullest extent. Society, it is true, will not forgive people their past, but in the sight of God St. Mary of Egypt is no lower than the other saints. When it had happened to Vassilyev in the street to recognize a fallen woman as such, by her dress or her manners, or to see a picture of one in a comic paper, he always remembered a story he had once read: a young man, pure and self-sacrificing, loves a fallen woman and urges her to become his wife; she, considering herself unworthy of such happiness, takes poison.

Vassilyev lived in one of the side streets turning out of Tverskoy Boulevard. When he came out of the house with his two friends it was about eleven o'clock. The first snow had not long fallen, and all nature was under the spell of the fresh snow. There was the smell of snow in the air, the snow crunched softly under the feet; the earth, the roofs, the trees, the seats on the boulevard, everything was soft, white, young, and this made the houses look quite different from the day before; the street lamps burned more brightly, the air was more transparent, the carriages rumbled with a deeper note, and with the fresh, light, frosty air a feeling stirred in the soul akin to the white, youthful, feathery snow. "Against my will an unknown force," hummed the medical student in his agreeable tenor, "has led me to these mournful shores."

"Behold the mill . . ." the artist seconded him, "in ruins now. . . ."

"Behold the mill . . . in ruins now," the medical student repeated, raising his eyebrows and shaking his head mournfully.

He paused, rubbed his forehead, trying to remember the words, and then sang aloud, so well that passers-by looked round:

"Here in old days when I was free,
Love, free, unfettered, greeted me."

The three of them went into a restaurant and, without taking off their greatcoats, drank a couple of glasses of vodka each. Before drinking the second glass, Vassilyev noticed a bit of cork in his vodka, raised the glass to his eyes, and gazed into it for a long time, screwing up his shortsighted eyes. The medical student did not understand his expression, and said:

"Come, why look at it? No philosophizing, please. Vodka is given us to be drunk, sturgeon to be eaten, women to be visited, snow to be walked upon. For one evening anyway live like a human being!"

"But I haven't said anything . . ." said Vassilyev, laughing. "Am I refusing to?"

There was a warmth inside him from the vodka. He looked with softened feelings at his friends, admired them and envied them. In these strong, healthy, cheerful people how wonderfully balanced everything is, how finished and smooth is everything in their minds and souls! They sing, and have a passion for the theatre, and draw, and talk a great deal, and drink, and they don't have headaches the day after; they are both poetical and debauched, both soft and hard; they can work, too, and be indignant, and laugh without reason, and talk nonsense; they are warm, honest, self-sacrificing, and as men are in no way inferior to himself, Vassilyev, who watched over every step he took and every word he uttered, who was fastidious and cautious, and ready to raise every trifle to the level of a problem. And he longed for one evening to live as his friends did, to open out, to let himself loose from his own control. If vodka had to be drunk, he would drink it, though his head would be splitting next morning. If he were taken to the women he would go. He would laugh, play the fool, gaily respond to the passing advances of strangers in the street. . . .

He went out of the restaurant laughing. He liked his friends -- one in a crushed broad-brimmed hat, with an affectation of artistic untidiness; the other in a sealskin cap, a man not poor, though he affected to belong to the Bohemia of learning. He liked the snow, the pale street lamps, the sharp black tracks left in the first snow by the feet of the passers-by. He liked the air, and especially that limpid, tender, naïve, as it were virginal tone, which can be seen in nature only twice in the year -- when everything is covered with snow, and in spring on bright days and moonlight evenings when the ice breaks on the river.

"Against my will an unknown force,
Has led me to these mournful shores,"

he hummed in an undertone.

And the tune for some reason haunted him and his friends all the way, and all three of them hummed it mechanically, not in time with one another.

Vassilyev's imagination was picturing how, in another ten minutes, he and his friends would knock at a door; how by little dark passages and dark rooms they would steal in to the women; how, taking advantage of the darkness, he would strike a match, would light up and see the face of a martyr and a guilty smile. The unknown, fair or dark, would certainly have her hair down and be wearing a white dressing-jacket; she would be panic-stricken by the light, would be fearfully confused, and would say: "For God's sake, what are you doing! Put it out!" It would all be dreadful, but interesting and new.

II

The friends turned out of Trubnoy Square into Gratchevka, and soon reached the side street which Vassilyev only knew by reputation. Seeing two rows of houses with brightly lighted windows and wide-open doors, and hearing gay strains of pianos and violins, sounds which floated out from every door and mingled in a strange chaos, as though an unseen orchestra were tuning up in the darkness above the roofs, Vassilyev was surprised and said:

"What a lot of houses!"

"That's nothing," said the medical student. "In London there are ten times as many. There are about a hundred thousand such women there."

The cabmen were sitting on their boxes as calmly and indifferently as in any other side street; the same passers-by were walking along the pavement as in other streets. No one was hurrying, no one was hiding his face in his coat-collar, no one shook his head reproachfully. . . . And in this indifference to the noisy chaos of pianos and violins, to the bright windows and wide-open doors, there was a feeling of something very open, insolent, reckless, and devil-may-care. Probably it was as gay and noisy at the slave-markets in their day, and people's faces and movements showed the same indifference.

"Let us begin from the beginning," said the artist.

The friends went into a narrow passage lighted by a lamp with a reflector. When they opened the door a man in a black coat, with an unshaven face like a flunkey's, and sleepy-looking eyes, got up lazily from a yellow sofa in the hall. The place smelt like a laundry with an odor of vinegar in addition. A door from the hall led into a brightly lighted room. The medical student and the artist stopped at this door and, craning their necks, peeped into the room.

"Buona sera, signori, rigolleto -- hugenotti -- traviata!" began the artist, with a theatrical bow.

"Havanna -- tarakano -- pistoleto!" said the medical student, pressing his cap to his breast and bowing low.

Vassilyev was standing behind them. He would have liked to make a theatrical bow and say something silly, too, but he only smiled, felt an awkwardness that was like shame, and waited impatiently for what would happen next.

A little fair girl of seventeen or eighteen, with short hair, in a short light-blue frock with a bunch of white ribbon on her bosom, appeared in the doorway.

"Why do you stand at the door?" she said. "Take off your coats and come into the drawing-room."

The medical student and the artist, still talking Italian, went into the drawing-room. Vassilyev followed them irresolutely.

"Gentlemen, take off your coats!" the flunkey said sternly; "you can't go in like that."

In the drawing-room there was, besides the girl, another woman, very stout and tall, with a foreign face and bare arms. She was sitting near the piano, laying out a game of patience on her lap. She took no notice whatever of the visitors.

"Where are the other young ladies?" asked the medical student.

"They are having their tea," said the fair girl. "Stepan," she called, "go and tell the young ladies some students have come!"

A little later a third young lady came into the room. She was wearing a bright red dress with blue stripes. Her face was painted thickly and unskillfully, her brow was hidden under her hair, and there was an unblinking, frightened stare in her eyes. As she came in, she began at once singing some song in a coarse, powerful contralto. After her a fourth appeared, and after her a fifth. . . .

In all this Vassilyev saw nothing new or interesting. It seemed to him that that room, the piano, the looking-glass in its cheap gilt frame, the bunch of white ribbon, the dress with the blue stripes, and the blank indifferent faces, he had seen before and more than once. Of the darkness, the silence, the secrecy, the guilty smile, of all that he had expected to meet here and had dreaded, he saw no trace.

Everything was ordinary, prosaic, and uninteresting. Only one thing faintly stirred his curiosity -- the terrible, as it were intentionally designed, bad taste which was visible in the cornices, in the absurd pictures, in the dresses, in the bunch of ribbons. There was something characteristic and peculiar in this bad taste.

"How poor and stupid it all is!" thought Vassilyev. "What is there in all this trumpery I see now that can tempt a normal man and excite him to commit the horrible sin of buying a human being for a rouble? I understand any sin for the sake of splendor, beauty, grace, passion, taste; but what is there here? What is there here worth sinning for? But . . . one mustn't think!"

"Beardy, treat me to some porter!" said the fair girl, addressing him.

Vassilyev was at once overcome with confusion.

"With pleasure," he said, bowing politely. "Only excuse me, madam, I . . . I won't drink with you. I don't drink.

Five minutes later the friends went off into another house.

"Why did you ask for porter?" said the medical student angrily. "What a millionaire! You have thrown away six roubles for no reason whatever -- simply waste!"

"If she wants it, why not let her have the pleasure?" said Vassilyev, justifying himself.

"You did not give pleasure to her, but to the 'Madam.' They are told to ask the visitors to stand them treat because it is a profit to the keeper."

"Behold the mill . . ." hummed the artist, "in ruins now. . . ."

Going into the next house, the friends stopped in the hall and did not go into the drawing-room. Here, as in the first house, a figure in a black coat, with a sleepy face like a flunkey's, got up from a sofa in the hall. Looking at this flunkey, at his face and his shabby black coat, Vassilyev thought: "What must an ordinary simple Russian have gone through before fate flung him down as a flunkey here? Where had he been before and what had he done? What was awaiting him? Was he married? Where was his mother, and did she know that he was a servant here?" And Vassilyev could not help particularly noticing the flunkey in each house. In one of the houses -- he thought it was the fourth -- there was a little spare, frail-looking flunkey with a watch-chain on his waistcoat. He was reading a newspaper, and took no notice of them when they went in. Looking at his face Vassilyev, for some reason, thought that a man with such a face might steal, might murder, might bear false witness. But the face was really interesting: a big forehead, gray eyes, a little flattened nose, thin compressed lips, and a blankly stupid and at the same time insolent expression like that of a young harrier overtaking a hare. Vassilyev thought it would be nice to touch this man's hair, to see whether it was soft or coarse. It must be coarse like a dog's.

III

Having drunk two glasses of porter, the artist became suddenly tipsy and grew unnaturally lively.

"Let's go to another!" he said peremptorily, waving his hands. "I will take you to the best one."

When he had brought his friends to the house which in his opinion was the best, he declared his firm intention of dancing a quadrille. The medical student grumbled something about their having to pay the musicians a rouble, but agreed to be his *vis-à-vis.* They began dancing.

It was just as nasty in the best house as in the worst. Here there were just the same looking-glasses and pictures, the same styles of coiffure and dress. Looking round at the furnishing of the rooms and the costumes, Vassilyev realized that this was not lack of taste, but something that might be called the taste, and even the style, of S. Street, which could not be found elsewhere--something intentional in its ugliness, not accidental, but elaborated in the course of years. After he had been in eight houses he was no longer surprised at the color of the dresses, at the long trains, the gaudy ribbons, the sailor dresses, and the thick purplish rouge on the cheeks; he saw that it all had to be like this, that if a single one of the women had been dressed like a human being, or if there had been one decent engraving on the wall, the general tone of the whole street would have suffered.

"How unskillfully they sell themselves!" he thought. "How can they fail to understand that vice is only alluring when it is beautiful and hidden, when it wears the mask of virtue? Modest black dresses, pale faces, mournful smiles, and darkness would be far more effective than this clumsy tawdriness. Stupid things! If they don't understand it of themselves, their visitors might surely have taught them. . . ."

A young lady in a Polish dress edged with white fur came up to him and sat down beside him.

"You nice dark man, why aren't you dancing?" she asked. "Why are you so dull?"

"Because it is dull."

"Treat me to some Lafitte. Then it won't be dull."

Vassilyev made no answer. He was silent for a little, and then asked:

"What time do you get to sleep?"

"At six o'clock."

"And what time do you get up?"

"Sometimes at two and sometimes at three."

"And what do you do when you get up?"

"We have coffee, and at six o'clock we have dinner."

"And what do you have for dinner?"

"Usually soup, beefsteak, and dessert. Our madam keeps the girls well. But why do you ask all this?"

"Oh, just to talk. . . ."

Vassilyev longed to talk to the young lady about many things. He felt an intense desire to find out where she came from, whether her parents were living, and whether they knew that she was here; how she had come into this house; whether she were cheerful and satisfied, or sad and oppressed by gloomy thoughts; whether she hoped some day to get out of her present position. . . . But he could not think how to begin or in what shape to put his questions so as not to seem impertinent. He thought for a long time, and asked:

"How old are you?"

"Eighty," the young lady jested, looking with a laugh at the antics of the artist as he danced.

All at once she burst out laughing at something, and uttered a long cynical sentence loud enough to be heard by everyone. Vassilyev was aghast, and not knowing how to look, gave a constrained smile. He was the only one who smiled; all the others, his friends, the musicians, the women, did not even glance towards his neighbor, but seemed not to have heard her.

"Stand me some Lafitte," his neighbor said again.

Vassilyev felt a repulsion for her white fur and for her voice, and walked away from her. It seemed to him hot and stifling, and his heart began throbbing slowly but violently, like a hammer -- one! two! three!

"Let us go away!" he said, pulling the artist by his sleeve.

"Wait a little; let me finish."

While the artist and the medical student were finishing the quadrille, to avoid looking at the women, Vassilyev scrutinized the musicians. A respectable-looking old man in spectacles, rather like Marshal Bazaine, was playing the piano; a young man with a fair beard, dressed in the latest fashion, was playing the violin. The young man had a face that did not look stupid nor exhausted, but intelligent, youthful, and fresh. He was dressed fancifully and with taste; he played with feeling. It was a mystery how he and the respectable-looking old man had come here. How was it they were not ashamed to sit here? What were they thinking about when they looked at the women?

If the violin and the piano had been played by men in rags, looking hungry, gloomy, drunken, with dissipated or stupid faces, then one could have understood their presence, perhaps. As it was, Vassilyev could not understand it at all. He recalled the story of the fallen woman he had once read, and he thought now that that human figure with the guilty smile had nothing in common with what he was seeing now. It seemed to him that he was seeing not fallen women, but some different world quite apart, alien to him and incomprehensible; if he had seen this world before on the stage, or read of it in a book, he would not have believed in it. . . .

The woman with the white fur burst out laughing again and uttered a loathsome sentence in a loud voice. A feeling of disgust took possession of him. He flushed crimson and went out of the room.

"Wait a minute, we are coming too!" the artist shouted to him.

IV

"While we were dancing," said the medical student, as they all three went out into the street, "I had a conversation with my partner. We talked about her first romance. He, the hero, was an accountant at Smolensk with a wife and five children. She was seventeen, and she lived with her papa and mamma, who sold soap and candles."

"How did he win her heart?" asked Vassilyev.

"By spending fifty roubles on underclothes for her. What next!"

"So he knew how to get his partner's story out of her," thought Vassilyev about the medical student. "But I don't know how to."

"I say, I am going home!" he said.

"What for?"

"Because I don't know how to behave here. Besides, I am bored, disgusted. What is there amusing in it? If they were human beings -- but they are savages and animals. I am going; do as you like."

"Come, Grisha, Grigory, darling. . ." said the artist in a tearful voice, hugging Vassilyev, "come along! Let's go to one more together and damnation take them! . . . Please do, Grisha!"

They persuaded Vassilyev and led him up a staircase. In the carpet and the gilt banisters, in the porter who opened the door, and in the panels that decorated the hall, the same S. Street style was apparent, but carried to a greater perfection, more imposing.

"I really will go home!" said Vassilyev as he was taking off his coat.

"Come, come, dear boy," said the artist, and he kissed him on the neck. "Don't be tiresome. . . . Gri-gri, be a good comrade! We came together, we will go back together. What a beast you are, really!"

"I can wait for you in the street. I think it's loathsome, really!"

"Come, come, Grisha. . . . If it is loathsome, you can observe it! Do you understand? You can observe!"

"One must take an objective view of things," said the medical student gravely.

Vassilyev went into the drawing-room and sat down. There were a number of visitors in the room besides him and his friends: two infantry officers, a bald, gray-haired gentleman in spectacles, two beardless youths from the institute of land-surveying, and a very tipsy man who looked like an actor. All the young ladies were taken up with these visitors and paid no attention to Vassilyev.

Only one of them, dressed *à la Aïda,* glanced sideways at him, smiled, and said, yawning: "A dark one has come. . . ."

Vassilyev's heart was throbbing and his face burned. He felt ashamed before these visitors of his presence here, and he felt disgusted and miserable. He was tormented by the thought that he, a decent and loving man (such as he had hitherto considered himself), hated these women and felt nothing but repulsion towards them. He felt pity neither for the women nor the musicians nor the flunkeys.

"It is because I am not trying to understand them," he thought. "They are all more like animals than human beings, but of course they are human beings all the same, they have souls. One must understand them and then judge. . . ."

"Grisha, don't go, wait for us," the artist shouted to him and disappeared.

The medical student disappeared soon after.

"Yes, one must make an effort to understand, one mustn't be like this. . ." Vassilyev went on thinking.

And he began gazing at each of the women with strained attention, looking for a guilty smile. But either he did not know how to read their faces, or not one of these women felt herself to be guilty; he read on every face nothing but a blank expression of everyday vulgar boredom and complacency. Stupid faces, stupid smiles, harsh, stupid voices, insolent movements, and nothing else. Apparently each of them had in the past a romance with an accountant based on underclothes for fifty roubles, and looked for no other charm in the present but coffee, a dinner of three courses, wines, quadrilles, sleeping till two in the afternoon. . . .

Finding no guilty smile, Vassilyev began to look whether there was not one intelligent face. And his attention was caught by one pale, rather sleepy, exhausted-looking face. . . . It was a dark woman, not very young, wearing a dress covered with spangles; she was sitting in an easy-chair, looking at the floor lost in thought. Vassilyev walked from one corner of the room to the other, and, as though casually, sat down beside her.

"I must begin with something trivial," he thought, "and pass to what is serious. . . ."

"What a pretty dress you have," and with his finger he touched the gold fringe of her fichu.

"Oh, is it? . . ." said the dark woman listlessly.

"What province do you come from?"

"I? From a distance. . . . From Tchernigov."

"A fine province. It's nice there."

"Any place seems nice when one is not in it."

"It's a pity I cannot describe nature," thought Vassilyev. "I might touch her by a description of nature in Tchernigov. No doubt she loves the place if she has been born there."

"Are you dull here?" he asked.

"Of course I am dull."

"Why don't you go away from here if you are dull?"

"Where should I go to? Go begging or what?"

"Begging would be easier than living here."

How do you know that? Have you begged?"

"Yes, when I hadn't the money to study. Even if I hadn't anyone could understand that. A beggar is anyway a free man, and you are a slave."

The dark woman stretched, and watched with sleepy eyes the footman who was bringing a trayful of glasses and seltzer water.

"Stand me a glass of porter," she said, and yawned again.

"Porter," thought Vassilyev. "And what if your brother or mother walked in at this moment? What would you say? And what would they say? There would be porter then, I imagine. . . ."

All at once there was the sound of weeping. From the adjoining room, from which the footman had brought the seltzer water, a fair man with a red face and angry eyes ran in quickly. He was followed by the tall, stout "madam," who was shouting in a shrill voice:

"Nobody has given you leave to slap girls on the cheeks! We have visitors better than you, and they don't fight! Impostor!"

A hubbub arose. Vassilyev was frightened and turned pale. In the next room there was the sound of bitter, genuine weeping, as though of someone insulted. And he realized that there were real people living here who, like people everywhere else, felt insulted, suffered, wept, and cried for help. The feeling of oppressive hate and disgust gave way to an acute feeling of pity and anger against the aggressor. He rushed into the room where there was weeping. Across rows of bottles on a marble-top table he distinguished a suffering face, wet with tears, stretched out his hands towards that face, took a step towards the table, but at once drew back in horror. The weeping girl was drunk.

As he made his way though the noisy crowd gathered about the fair man, his heart sank and he felt frightened like a child; and it seemed to him that in this alien, incomprehensible world people wanted to pursue him, to beat him, to pelt him with filthy words. . . . He tore down his coat from the hatstand and ran headlong downstairs.

V

Leaning against the fence, he stood near the house waiting for his friends to come out. The sounds of the pianos and violins, gay, reckless, insolent, and mournful, mingled in the air in a sort of chaos, and this tangle of sounds seemed again like an unseen orchestra tuning up on the roofs. If one looked upwards into the darkness, the black background was all spangled with white, moving spots: it was snow falling. As the snowflakes came into the light they floated round lazily in the air like down, and still more lazily fell to the ground. The snowflakes whirled thickly round Vassilyev and hung upon his beard, his eyelashes, his eyebrows. . . . The cabmen, the horses, and the passers-by were white.

"And how can the snow fall in this street!" thought Vassilyev. "Damnation take these houses!"

His legs seemed to be giving way from fatigue, simply from having run down the stairs; he gasped for breath as though he had been climbing uphill, his heart beat so loudly that he could hear it. He was consumed by a desire to get out of the street as quickly as possible and to go home, but even stronger was his desire to wait for his companions and vent upon them his oppressive feeling.

There was much he did not understand in these houses, the souls of ruined women were a mystery to him as before; but it was clear to him that the thing was far worse than could have been believed. If that sinful woman who had poisoned herself was called fallen, it was difficult to find a fitting name for all these who were dancing now to this tangle of sound and uttering long, loathsome sentences. They were not on the road to ruin, but ruined.

"There is vice," he thought, "but neither consciousness of sin nor hope of salvation. They are sold and bought, steeped in wine and abominations, while they, like sheep, are stupid, indifferent, and don't understand. My God! My God!"

It was clear to him, too, that everything that is called human dignity, personal rights, the Divine image and semblance, were defiled to their very foundations -- "to the very marrow," as drunkards say -- and that not only the street and the stupid women were responsible for it.

A group of students, white with snow, passed him laughing and talking gaily; one, a tall thin fellow, stopped, glanced into Vassilyev's face, and said in a drunken voice:

"One of us! A bit on, old man? Aha-ha! Never mind, have a good time! Don't be down-hearted, old chap!"

He took Vassilyev by the shoulder and pressed his cold wet mustache against his cheek, then he slipped, staggered, and, waving both hands, cried:

"Hold on! Don't upset!"

And laughing, he ran to overtake his companions.

Through the noise came the sound of the artist's voice:

"Don't you dare to hit the women! I won't let you, damnation take you! You scoundrels!"

The medical student appeared in the doorway. He looked from side to side, and seeing Vassilyev, said in an agitated voice:

"You here! I tell you it's really impossible to go anywhere with Yegor! What a fellow he is! I don't understand him! He has got up a scene! Do you hear? Yegor!" he shouted at the door. Yegor!"

"I won't allow you to hit women!" the artist's piercing voice sounded from above. Something heavy and lumbering rolled down the stairs. It was the artist falling headlong. Evidently he had been pushed downstairs.

He picked himself up from the ground, shook his hat, and, with an angry and indignant face, brandished his fist towards the top of the stairs and shouted:

"Scoundrels! Torturers! Bloodsuckers! I won't allow you to hit them! To hit a weak, drunken woman! Oh, you brutes! . . ."

"Yegor! . . . Come, Yegor! . . ." the medical student began imploring him. "I give you my word of honor I'll never come with you again. On my word of honor I won't!"

Little by little the artist was pacified and the friends went homewards.

"Against my will an unknown force," hummed the medical student, "has led me to these mournful shores."

"Behold the mill," the artist chimed in a little later, "in ruins now. What a lot of snow, Holy Mother! Grisha, why did you go? You are a funk, a regular old woman."

Vassilyev walked behind his companions, looked at their backs, and thought:

"One of two things: either we only fancy prostitution is an evil, and we exaggerate it; or, if prostitution really is as great an evil as is generally assumed, these dear friends of mine are as much slaveowners, violators, and murderers, as the inhabitants of Syria and Cairo, that are described in the 'Neva.' Now they are singing, laughing, talking sense, but haven't they just been exploiting hunger, ignorance, and stupidity? They have -- I have been a witness of it. What is the use of their humanity, their medicine, their painting? The science, art, and lofty sentiments of these soul-destroyers remind me of the piece of bacon in the story. Two brigands murdered a beggar in a forest; they began sharing his clothes between them, and found in his wallet a piece of bacon. 'Well found,' said one of them, 'let us have a bit.' 'What do you mean? How can you?' cried the other in horror. 'Have you forgotten that to-day is Wednesday?' And they would not eat it. After murdering a man, they came out of the forest in the firm conviction that they were keeping the fast. In the same way these men, after buying women, go their way imagining that they are artists and men of science. . . ."

"Listen!" he said sharply and angrily. "Why do you come here? Is it possible -- is it possible you don't understand how horrible it is? Your medical books tell you that everyone of these women dies prematurely of consumption or something; art tells you that morally they are dead even earlier. Everyone of them dies because she has in her time to entertain five hundred men on an average, let us say. Each one of them is killed by five hundred men. You are among those five hundred! If each of you in the course of your lives visits this place or others like it two hundred and fifty times, it follows that one woman is killed forevery two of you! Can't you understand that? Isn't it horrible to murder, two of you, three of you, five of you, a foolish, hungry woman! Ah! isn't it awful, my God!"

"I knew it would end like that," the artist said frowning. "We ought not to have gone with this fool and ass! You imagine you have grand notions in your head now, ideas, don't you? No, it's the devil knows what, but not ideas. You are looking at me now with hatred and repulsion, but I tell you it's better you should set up twenty more houses like those than look like that. There's more vice in your expression than in the whole street! Come along, Volodya, let him go to the devil! He's a fool and an ass, and that's all. . . ."

"We human beings do murder each other," said the medical student. "It's immoral, of course, but philosophizing doesn't help it. Good-by!"

At Trubnoy Square the friends said good-by and parted. When he was left alone, Vassilyev strode rapidly along the boulevard. He felt frightened of the darkness, of the snow which was falling in heavy flakes on the ground, and seemed as though it would cover up the whole world; he felt frightened of the street lamps shining with pale light through the clouds of snow. His soul was possessed by an unaccountable, faint-hearted terror. Passers-by came towards him from time to time, but he timidly moved to one side; it seemed to him that women, none but women, were coming from all sides and staring at him. . . .

"It's beginning," he thought, "I am going to have a breakdown."

VI

At home he lay on his bed and said, shuddering all over: "They are alive! Alive! My God, those women are alive!"

He encouraged his imagination in all sorts of ways to picture himself the brother of a fallen woman, or her father; then a fallen woman herself, with her painted cheeks; and it all moved him to horror.

It seemed to him that he must settle the question at once at all costs, and that this question was not one that did not concern him, but was his own personal problem. He made an immense effort, repressed his despair, and, sitting on the bed, holding his head in his hands, began thinking how one could save all the women he had seen that day. The method for attacking problems of all kinds was, as he was an educated man, well known to him. And, however excited he was, he strictly adhered to that method. He recalled the history of the problem and its literature, and for a quarter of an hour he paced from one end of the room to the other trying to remember all the methods practiced at the present time for saving women. He had very many good friends and acquaintances who lived in lodgings in Petersburg. . . . Among them were a good many honest and self-sacrificing men. Some of them had attempted to save women. . . .

"All these not very numerous attempts," thought Vassilyev, "can be divided into three groups. Some, after buying the woman out of the brothel, took a room for her, bought her a sewing-machine, and she became a semptress. And whether he wanted to or not, after having bought her out he made her his mistress; then when he had taken his degree, he went away and handed her into the keeping of some other decent man as though she were a thing. And the fallen woman remained a fallen woman. Others, after buying her out, took a lodging apart for her, bought the inevitable sewing-machine, and tried teaching her to read, preaching at her and giving her books. The woman lived and sewed as long as it was interesting and a novelty to her, then getting bored, began receiving men on the sly, or ran away and went back where she could sleep till three o'clock, drink coffee, and have good dinners. The third class, the most ardent and self-sacrificing, had taken a bold, resolute step. They had married them. And when the insolent and spoilt, or stupid and crushed animal became a wife, the head of a household, and afterwards a mother, it turned her whole existence and attitude to life upside down, so that it was hard to recognize the fallen woman afterwards in the wife and the mother. Yes, marriage was the best and perhaps the only means."

"But it is impossible!" Vassilyev said aloud, and he sank upon his bed. "I, to begin with, could not marry one! To do that one must be a saint and be unable to feel hatred or repulsion. But supposing that I, the medical student, and the artist mastered ourselves and did marry them -- suppose they were all married. What would be the result? The result would be that while here in Moscow they were being married, some Smolensk accountant would be debauching another lot, and that lot would be streaming here to fill the vacant places, together with others from Saratov, Nizhni-Novgorod, Warsaw. . . . And what is one to do with the hundred thousand in London? What's one to do with those in Hamburg?"

The lamp in which the oil had burnt down began to smoke. Vassilyev did not notice it. He began pacing to and fro again, still thinking. Now he put the question differently: what must be done that fallen women should not be needed? For that, it was essential that the men who buy them and do them to death should feel all the immorality of their share in enslaving them and should be horrified. One must save the men.

"One won't do anything by art and science, that is clear . . ." thought Vassilyev. "The only way out of it is missionary work."

And he began to dream how he would the next evening stand at the corner of the street and say to every passer-by: "Where are you going and what for? Have some fear of God!"

He would turn to the apathetic cabmen and say to them: "Why are you staying here? Why aren't you revolted? Why aren't you indignant? I suppose you believe in God and know that it is a sin, that people go to hell for it? Why don't you speak? It is true that they are strangers to you, but you know even they have fathers, brothers like yourselves. . . ."

One of Vassilyev's friends had once said of him that he was a talented man. There are all sorts of talents -- talent for writing, talent for the stage, talent for art; but he had a peculiar talent -- a talent for *humanity*. He possessed an extraordinarily fine delicate scent for pain in general. As a good actor reflects in himself the movements and voice of others, so Vassilyev could reflect in his soul the sufferings of others. When he saw tears, he wept; beside a sick man, he felt sick himself and moaned; if he saw an act of violence, he felt as though he himself were the victim of it, he was frightened as a child, and in his fright ran to help. The pain of others worked on his nerves, excited him, roused him to a state of frenzy, and so on.

Whether this friend were right I don't know, but what Vassilyev experienced when he thought this question was settled was something like inspiration. He cried and laughed, spoke aloud the words that he should say next day, felt a fervent love for those who would listen to him and would stand beside him at the corner of the street to preach; he sat down to write letters, made vows to himself. . . .

All this was like inspiration also from the fact that it did not last long. Vassilyev was soon tired. The cases in London, in Hamburg, in Warsaw, weighed upon him by their mass as a mountain weighs upon the earth; he felt dispirited, bewildered, in the face of this mass; he remembered that he had not a gift for words, that he was cowardly and timid, that indifferent people would not be willing to listen and understand him, a law student in his third year, a timid and insignificant person; that genuine missionary work included not only teaching but deeds. . . .

When it was daylight and carriages were already beginning to rumble in the street, Vassilyev was lying motionless on the sofa, staring into space. He was no longer thinking of the women, nor of the men, nor of missionary work. His whole attention was turned upon the spiritual agony which was torturing him. It was a dull, vague, undefined anguish akin to misery, to an extreme form of terror and to despair. He could point to the place where the pain was, in his breast under his heart; but he could not compare it with anything. In the past he had had acute toothache, he had had pleurisy and neuralgia, but all that was insignificant compared with this spiritual anguish. In the presence of that pain life seemed loathsome. The dissertation, the excellent work he had written already, the people he loved, the salvation of fallen women -- everything that only the day before he had cared about or been indifferent to, now when he thought of them irritated him in the same way as the noise of the carriages, the scurrying footsteps of the waiters in the passage, the daylight. . . . If at that moment someone had performed a great deed of mercy or had committed a revolting outrage, he would have felt the same repulsion for both actions. Of all the thoughts that strayed through his mind only two did not irritate him: one was that at every moment he had the power to kill himself, the other that this agony would not last more than three days. This last he knew by experience.

After lying for a while he got up and, wringing his hands, walked about the room, not as usual from corner to corner, but round the room beside the walls. As he passed he glanced at himself in the looking-glass. His face looked pale and sunken, his temples looked hollow, his eyes were bigger, darker, more staring, as though they belonged to someone else, and they had an expression of insufferable mental agony.

At midday the artist knocked at the door.

"Grigory, are you at home?" he asked.

Getting no answer, he stood for a minute, pondered, and answered himself in Little Russian: "Nay. The confounded fellow has gone to the University."

And he went away. Vassilyev lay down on the bed and, thrusting his head under the pillow, began crying with agony, and the more freely his tears flowed the more terrible his mental anguish became. As it began to get dark, he thought of the agonizing night awaiting him, and was overcome by a horrible despair. He dressed quickly, ran out of his room, and, leaving his door wide open, for no object or reason, went out into the street. Without asking himself where he should go, he walked quickly along Sadovoy Street.

Snow was falling as heavily as the day before; it was thawing. Thrusting his hands into his sleeves, shuddering and frightened at the noises, at the trambells, and at the passers-by, Vassilyev walked along Sadovoy Street as far as Suharev Tower; then to the Red Gate; from there he turned off to Basmannya Street. He went into a tavern and drank off a big glass of vodka, but that did not make him feel better. When he reached Razgulya he turned to the right, and strode along side streets in which he had never been before in his life. He reached the old bridge by which the Yauza runs gurgling, and from which one can see long rows of lights in the windows of the Red Barracks. To distract his spiritual anguish by some new sensation or some other pain, Vassilyev, not knowing what to do, crying and shuddering, undid his greatcoat and jacket and exposed his bare chest to the wet snow and the wind. But that did not lessen his suffering either. Then he bent down over the rail of the bridge and looked down into the black, yeasty Yauza, and he longed to plunge down head foremost; not from loathing for life, not for the sake of suicide, but in order to bruise himself at least, and by one pain to ease the other. But the black water, the darkness, the deserted banks covered with snow were terrifying. He shivered and walked on. He walked up and down by the Red Barracks, then turned back and went down to a copse, from the copse back to the bridge again

"No, home, home!" he thought. "At home I believe it's better. . . ."

And he went back. When he reached home he pulled off his wet coat and cap, began pacing round the room, and went on pacing round and round without stopping till morning.

VII

When next morning the artist and the medical student went in to him, he was moving about the room with his shirt torn, biting his hands and moaning with pain.

"For God's sake!" he sobbed when he saw his friends, "take me where you please, do what you can; but for God's sake, save me quickly! I shall kill myself!"

The artist turned pale and was helpless. The medical student, too, almost shed tears, but considering that doctors ought to be cool and composed in every emergency said coldly:

"It's a nervous breakdown. But it's nothing. Let us go at once to the doctor."

"Wherever you like, only for God's sake, make haste"

"Don't excite yourself. You must try and control yourself."

The artist and the medical student with trembling hands put Vassilyev's coat and hat on and led him out into the street.

"Mihail Sergeyitch has been wanting to make your acquaintance for a long time," the medical student said on the way. "He is a very nice man and thoroughly good at his work. He took his degree in 1882, and he has an immense practice already. He treats students as though he were one himself."

"Make haste, make haste! . . ." Vassilyev urged.

Mihail Sergeyitch, a stout, fair-haired doctor, received the friends with politeness and frigid dignity, and smiled only on one side of his face.

"Rybnikov and Mayer have spoken to me of your illness already," he said. "Very glad to be of service to you. Well? Sit down, I beg. . . ."

He made Vassilyev sit down in a big armchair near the table, and moved a box of cigarettes towards him.

"Now then!" he began, stroking his knees. "Let us get to work. . . . How old are you?"

He asked questions and the medical student answered them. He asked whether Vassilyev's father had suffered from certain special diseases, whether he drank to excess, whether he were remarkable for cruelty or any peculiarities. He made similar inquiries about his grandfather, mother, sisters, and brothers. On learning that his mother had a beautiful voice and sometimes acted on the stage, he grew more animated at once, and asked:

"Excuse me, but don't you remember, perhaps, your mother had a passion for the stage?"

Twenty minutes passed. Vassilyev was annoyed by the way the doctor kept stroking his knees and talking of the same thing.

"So far as I understand your questions, doctor," he said, "you want to know whether my illness is hereditary or not. It is not."

The doctor proceeded to ask Vassilyev whether he had had any secret vices as a boy, or had received injuries to his head; whether he had had any aberrations, any peculiarities, or exceptional propensities. Half the questions usually asked by doctors of their patients can be left unanswered without the slightest ill effect on the health, but Mihail Sergeyitch, the medical student, and the artist all looked as though if Vassilyev failed to answer one question all would be lost. As he received answers, the doctor for some reason noted them down on a slip of paper. On learning that Vassilyev had taken his degree in natural science, and was now studying law, the doctor pondered.

"He wrote a first-rate piece of original work last year, . . ." said the medical student.

"I beg your pardon, but don't interrupt me; you prevent me from concentrating," said the doctor, and he smiled on one side of his face. "Though, of course, that does enter into the diagnosis. Intense intellectual work, nervous exhaustion. . . . Yes, yes. . . . And do you drink vodka?" he said, addressing Vassilyev.

"Very rarely."

Another twenty minutes passed. The medical student began telling the doctor in a low voice his opinion as to the immediate cause of the attack, and described how the day before yesterday the artist, Vassilyev, and he had visited S. Street.

The indifferent, reserved, and frigid tone in which his friends and the doctor spoke of the women and that miserable street struck Vassilyev as strange in the extreme. . . .

"Doctor, tell me one thing only," he said, controlling himself so as not to speak rudely. "Is prostitution an evil or not?"

"My dear fellow, who disputes it?" said the doctor, with an expression that suggested that he had settled all such questions for himself long ago. "Who disputes it?"

"You are a mental doctor, aren't you?" Vassilyev asked curtly.

"Yes, a mental doctor."

"Perhaps all of you are right!" said Vassilyev, getting up and beginning to walk from one end of the room to the other. "Perhaps! But it all seems marvelous to me! That I should have taken my degree in two faculties you look upon as a great achievement; because I have written a work which in three years will be thrown aside and forgotten, I am praised up to the skies; but because I cannot speak of fallen women as unconcernedly as of these chairs, I am being examined by a doctor, I am called mad, I am pitied!"

Vassilyev for some reason felt all at once unutterably sorry for himself, and his companions, and all the people he had seen two days before, and for the doctor; he burst into tears and sank into a chair.

His friends looked inquiringly at the doctor. The latter, with the air of completely comprehending the tears and the despair, of feeling himself a specialist in that line, went up to Vassilyev and, without a word, gave him some medicine to drink; and then, when he was calmer, undressed him and began to investigate the degree of sensibility of the skin, the reflex action of the knees, and so on.

And Vassilyev felt easier. When he came out from the doctor's he was beginning to feel ashamed; the rattle of the carriages no longer irritated him, and the load at his heart grew lighter and lighter as though it were melting away. He had two prescriptions in his hand: one was for bromide, one was for morphia. . . . He had taken all these remedies before.

In the street he stood still and, saying good-by to his friends, dragged himself languidly to the University.

THE SHOEMAKER AND THE DEVIL

It was Christmas Eve. Marya had long been snoring on the stove; all the paraffin in the little lamp had burnt out, but Fyodor Nilov still sat at work. He would long ago have flung aside his work and gone out into the street, but a customer from Kolokolny Lane, who had a fortnight before ordered some boots, had been in the previous day, had abused him roundly, and had ordered him to finish the boots at once before the morning service.

"It's a convict's life!" Fyodor grumbled as he worked. "Some people have been asleep long ago, others are enjoying themselves, while you sit here like some Cain and sew for the devil knows whom. . . ."

To save himself from accidentally falling asleep, he kept taking a bottle from under the table and drinking out of it, and after every pull at it he twisted his head and said aloud:

"What is the reason, kindly tell me, that customers enjoy themselves while I am forced to sit and work for them? Because they have money and I am a beggar?"

He hated all his customers, especially the one who lived in Kolokolny Lane. He was a gentleman of gloomy appearance, with long hair, a yellow face, blue spectacles, and a husky voice. He had a German name which one could not pronounce. It was impossible to tell what was his calling and what he did. When, a fortnight before, Fyodor had gone to take his measure, he, the customer, was sitting on the floor pounding something in a mortar. Before Fyodor had time to say good-morning the contents of the mortar suddenly flared up and burned with a bright red flame; there was a stink of sulphur and burnt feathers, and the room was filled with a thick pink smoke, so that Fyodor sneezed five times; and as he returned home afterwards, he thought: "Anyone who feared God would not have anything to do with things like that."

When there was nothing left in the bottle Fyodor put the boots on the table and sank into thought. He leaned his heavy head on his fist and began thinking of his poverty, of his hard life with no glimmer of light in it. Then he thought of the rich, of their big houses and their carriages, of their hundred-rouble notes. . . . How nice it would be if the houses of these rich men -- the devil flay them! -- were smashed, if their horses died, if their fur coats and sable caps got shabby! How splendid it would be if the rich, little by little, changed into beggars having nothing, and he, a poor shoemaker, were to become rich, and were to lord it over some other poor shoemaker on Christmas Eve.

Dreaming like this, Fyodor suddenly thought of his work, and opened his eyes.

"Here's a go," he thought, looking at the boots. "The job has been finished ever so long ago, and I go on sitting here. I must take the boots to the gentleman."

He wrapped up the work in a red handkerchief, put on his things, and went out into the street. A fine hard snow was falling, pricking the face as though with needles. It was cold, slippery, dark, the gas-lamps burned dimly, and for some reason there was a smell of paraffin in the street, so that Fyodor coughed and cleared his throat. Rich men were driving to and fro on the road, and every rich man had a ham and a bottle of vodka in his hands. Rich young ladies peeped at Fyodor out of the carriages and sledges, put out their tongues and shouted, laughing:

"Beggar! Beggar!"

Students, officers, and merchants walked behind Fyodor, jeering at him and crying:

"Drunkard! Drunkard! Infidel cobbler! Soul of a boot-leg! Beggar!"

All this was insulting, but Fyodor held his tongue and only spat in disgust. But when Kuzma Lebyodkin from Warsaw, a master-bootmaker, met him and said: "I've married a rich woman and I have men working under me, while you are a beggar and have nothing to eat," Fyodor could not refrain from running after him. He pursued him till he found himself in Kolokolny Lane. His customer lived in the fourth house from the corner on the very top floor. To reach him one had to go through a long, dark courtyard, and then to climb up a very high slippery stair-case which tottered under one's feet. When Fyodor went in to him he was sitting on the floor pounding something in a mortar, just as he had been the fortnight before.

"Your honor, I have brought your boots," said Fyodor sullenly.

The customer got up and began trying on the boots in silence. Desiring to help him, Fyodor went down on one knee and pulled off his old, boot, but at once jumped up and staggered towards the door in horror. The customer had not a foot, but a hoof like a horse's.

"Aha!" thought Fyodor; "here's a go!"

The first thing should have been to cross himself, then to leave everything and run downstairs; but he immediately reflected that he was meeting a devil for the first and probably the last time, and not to take advantage of his services would be foolish. He controlled himself and determined to try his luck. Clasping his hands behind him to avoid making the sign of the cross, he coughed respectfully and began:

"They say that there is nothing on earth more evil and impure than the devil, but I am of the opinion, your honor, that the devil is highly educated. He has -- excuse my saying it -- hoofs and a tail behind, but he has more brains than many a student."

"I like you for what you say," said the devil, flattered. "Thank you, shoemaker! What do you want?"

And without loss of time the shoemaker began complaining of his lot. He began by saying that from his childhood up he had envied the rich. He had always resented it that all people did not live alike in big houses and drive with good horses. Why, he asked, was he poor? How was he worse than Kuzma Lebyodkin from Warsaw, who had his own house, and whose wife wore a hat? He had the same sort of nose, the same hands, feet, head, and back, as the rich, and so why was he forced to work when others were enjoying themselves? Why was he married to Marya and not to a lady smelling of scent? He had often seen beautiful young ladies in the houses of rich customers, but they either took no notice of him whatever, or else sometimes laughed and whispered to each other: "What a red nose that shoemaker has!" It was true that Marya was a good, kind, hard-working woman, but she was not educated; her hand was heavy and hit hard, and if one had occasion to speak of politics or anything intellectual before her, she would put her spoke in and talk the most awful nonsense.

"What do you want, then?" his customer interrupted him.

"I beg you, your honor Satan Ivanitch, to be graciously pleased to make me a rich man."

"Certainly. Only for that you must give me up your soul! Before the cocks crow, go and sign on this paper here that you give me up your soul."

"Your honor," said Fyodor politely, "when you ordered a pair of boots from me I did not ask for the money in advance. One has first to carry out the order and then ask for payment."

"Oh, very well!" the customer assented.

A bright flame suddenly flared up in the mortar, a pink thick smoke came puffing out, and there was a smell of burnt feathers and sulphur. When the smoke had subsided, Fyodor rubbed his eyes and saw that he was no longer Fyodor, no longer a shoemaker, but quite a different man, wearing a waistcoat and a watch-chain, in a new pair of trousers, and that he was sitting in an armchair at a big table. Two foot men were handing him dishes, bowing low and saying:

"Kindly eat, your honor, and may it do you good!"

What wealth! The footmen handed him a big piece of roast mutton and a dish of cucumbers, and then brought in a frying-pan a roast goose, and a little afterwards boiled pork with horse-radish cream. And how dignified, how genteel it all was! Fyodor ate, and before each dish drank a big glass of excellent vodka, like some general or some count. After the pork he was handed some boiled grain moistened with goose fat, then an omelette with bacon fat, then fried liver, and he went on eating and was delighted. What more? They served, too, a pie with onion and steamed turnip with kvass.

"How is it the gentry don't burst with such meals?" he thought.

In conclusion they handed him a big pot of honey. After dinner the devil appeared in blue spectacles and asked with a low bow:

"Are you satisfied with your dinner, Fyodor Pantelyeitch?"

But Fyodor could not answer one word, he was so stuffed after his dinner. The feeling of repletion was unpleasant, oppressive, and to distract his thoughts he looked at the boot on his left foot.

"For a boot like that I used not to take less than seven and a half roubles. What shoemaker made it?" he asked.

"Kuzma Lebyodkin," answered the footman.

"Send for him, the fool!"

Kuzma Lebyodkin from Warsaw soon made his appearance. He stopped in a respectful attitude at the door and asked:

"What are your orders, your honor?"

"Hold your tongue!" cried Fyodor, and stamped his foot. "Don't dare to argue; remember your place as a cobbler! Blockhead! You don't know how to make boots! I'll beat your ugly phiz to a jelly! Why have you come?"

"For money."

"What money? Be off! Come on Saturday! Boy, give him a cuff!"

But he at once recalled what a life the customers used to lead him, too, and he felt heavy at heart, and to distract his attention he took a fat pocketbook out of his pocket and began counting his money. There was a great deal of money, but Fyodor wanted more still. The devil in the blue spectacles brought him another notebook fatter still, but he wanted even more; and the more he counted it, the more discontented he became.

In the evening the evil one brought him a full-bosomed lady in a red dress, and said that this was his new wife. He spent the whole evening kissing her and eating gingerbreads, and at night he went to bed on a soft, downy feather-bed, turned from side to side, and could not go to sleep. He felt uncanny.

"We have a great deal of money," he said to his wife; "we must look out or thieves will be breaking in. You had better go and look with a candle."

He did not sleep all night, and kept getting up to see if his box was all right. In the morning he had to go to church to matins. In church the same honor is done to rich and poor alike. When Fyodor was poor he used to pray in church like this: "God, forgive me, a sinner!" He said the same thing now though he had become rich. What difference was there? And after death Fyodor rich would not be buried in gold, not in diamonds, but in the same black earth as the poorest beggar. Fyodor would burn in the same fire as cobblers. Fyodor resented all this, and, too, he felt weighed down all over by his dinner, and instead of prayer he had all sorts of thoughts in his head about his box of money, about thieves, about his bartered, ruined soul.

He came out of church in a bad temper. To drive away his unpleasant thoughts as he had often done before, he struck up a song at the top of his voice. But as soon as he began a policeman ran up and said, with his fingers to the peak of his cap:

"Your honor, gentlefolk must not sing in the street! You are not a shoemaker!"

Fyodor leaned his back against a fence and fell to thinking: what could he do to amuse himself?

"Your honor," a porter shouted to him, "don't lean against the fence, you will spoil your fur coat!"

Fyodor went into a shop and bought himself the very best concertina, then went out into the street playing it. Everybody pointed at him and laughed.

"And a gentleman, too," the cabmen jeered at him; "like some cobbler. . . ."

"Is it the proper thing for gentlefolk to be disorderly in the street?" a policeman said to him. "You had better go into a tavern!"

"Your honor, give us a trifle, for Christ's sake," the beggars wailed, surrounding Fyodor on all sides.

In earlier days when he was a shoemaker the beggars took no notice of him, now they wouldn't let him pass.

And at home his new wife, the lady, was waiting for him, dressed in a green blouse and a red skirt. He meant to be attentive to her, and had just lifted his arm to give her a good clout on the back, but she said angrily:

"Peasant! Ignorant lout! You don't know how to behave with ladies! If you love me you will kiss my hand; I don't allow you to beat me."

"This is a blasted existence!" thought Fyodor. "People do lead a life! You mustn't sing, you mustn't play the concertina, you mustn't have a lark with a lady. . . . Pfoo!"

He had no sooner sat down to tea with the lady when the evil spirit in the blue spectacles appeared and said:

"Come, Fyodor Pantelyeitch, I have performed my part of the bargain. Now sign your paper and come along with me!"

And he dragged Fyodor to hell, straight to the furnace, and devils flew up from all directions and shouted:

"Fool! Blockhead! Ass!"

There was a fearful smell of paraffin in hell, enough to suffocate one. And suddenly it all vanished. Fyodor opened his eyes and saw his table, the boots, and the tin lamp. The lamp-glass was black, and from the faint light on the wick came clouds of stinking smoke as from a chimney. Near the table stood the customer in the blue spectacles, shouting angrily:

"Fool! Blockhead! Ass! I'll give you a lesson, you scoundrel! You took the order a fortnight ago and the boots aren't ready yet! Do you suppose I want to come trapesing round here half a dozen times a day for my boots? You wretch! you brute!"

Fyodor shook his head and set to work on the boots. The customer went on swearing and threatening him for a long time. At last when he subsided, Fyodor asked sullenly:

"And what is your occupation, sir?"

"I make Bengal lights and fireworks. I am a pyrotechnician."

They began ringing for matins. Fyodor gave the customer the boots, took the money for them, and went to church.

Carriages and sledges with bearskin rugs were dashing to and fro in the street; merchants, ladies, officers were walking along the pavement together with the humbler folk. . . . But Fyodor did not envy them nor repine at his lot. It seemed to him now that rich and poor were equally badly off. Some were able to drive in a carriage, and others to sing songs at the top of their voice and to play the concertina, but one and the same thing, the same grave, was awaiting all alike, and there was nothing in life for which one would give the devil even a tiny scrap of one's soul.

THE BET

I

It was a dark autumn night. The old banker was walking up and down his study and remembering how, fifteen years before, he had given a party one autumn evening. There had been many clever men there, and there had been interesting conversations. Among other things they had talked of capital punishment. The majority of the guests, among whom were many journalists and intellectual men, disapproved of the death penalty. They considered that form of punishment out of date, immoral, and unsuitable for Christian States. In the opinion of some of them the death penalty ought to be replaced everywhere by imprisonment for life.

"I don't agree with you," said their host the banker. "I have not tried either the death penalty or imprisonment for life, but if one may judge *à priori,* the death penalty is more moral and more humane than imprisonment for life. Capital punishment kills a man at once, but lifelong imprisonment kills him slowly. Which executioner is the more humane, he who kills you in a few minutes or he who drags the life out of you in the course of many years?"

"Both are equally immoral," observed one of the guests, "for they both have the same object -- to take away life. The State is not God. It has not the right to take away what it cannot restore when it wants to."

Among the guests was a young lawyer, a young man of five-and-twenty. When he was asked his opinion, he said:

"The death sentence and the life sentence are equally immoral, but if I had to choose between the death penalty and imprisonment for life, I would certainly choose the second. To live anyhow is better than not at all."

A lively discussion arose. The banker, who was younger and more nervous in those days, was suddenly carried away by excitement; he struck the table with his fist and shouted at the young man:

"It's not true! I'll bet you two millions you wouldn't stay in solitary confinement for five years."

"If you mean that in earnest," said the young man, "I'll take the bet, but I would stay not five but fifteen years."

"Fifteen? Done!" cried the banker. "Gentlemen, I stake two millions!"

"Agreed! You stake your millions and I stake my freedom!" said the young man.

And this wild, senseless bet was carried out! The banker, spoilt and frivolous, with millions beyond his reckoning, was delighted at the bet. At supper he made fun of the young man, and said:

"Think better of it, young man, while there is still time. To me two millions are a trifle, but you are losing three or four of the best years of your life. I say three or four, because you won't stay longer. Don't forget either, you unhappy man, that voluntary confinement is a great deal harder to bear than compulsory. The thought that you have the right to step out in liberty at any moment will poison your whole existence in prison. I am sorry for you."

And now the banker, walking to and fro, remembered all this, and asked himself: "What was the object of that bet? What is the good of that man's losing fifteen years of his life and my throwing away two millions? Can it prove that the death penalty is better or worse than imprisonment for life? No, no. It was all nonsensical and meaningless. On my part it was the caprice of a pampered man, and on his part simple greed for money. . . ."

Then he remembered what followed that evening. It was decided that the young man should spend the years of his captivity under the strictest supervision in one of the lodges in the banker's garden. It was agreed that for fifteen years he should not be free to cross the threshold of the lodge, to see human beings, to hear the human voice, or to receive letters and newspapers. He was allowed to have a musical instrument and books, and was allowed to write letters, to drink wine, and to smoke. By the terms of the agreement, the only relations he could have with the outer world were by a little window made purposely for that object. He might have anything he wanted -- books, music, wine, and so on -- in any quantity he desired by writing an order, but could only receive them through the window. The agreement provided forevery detail and every trifle that would make his imprisonment strictly solitary, and bound the young man to stay there *exactly* fifteen years, beginning from twelve o'clock of November 14, 1870, and ending at twelve o'clock of November 14, 1885. The slightest attempt on his part to break the conditions, if only two minutes before the end, released the banker from the obligation to pay him two millions.

For the first year of his confinement, as far as one could judge from his brief notes, the prisoner suffered severely from loneliness and depression. The sounds of the piano could be heard continually day and night from his lodge. He refused wine and tobacco. Wine, he wrote, excites the desires, and desires are the worst foes of the prisoner; and besides, nothing could be more dreary than drinking good wine and seeing no one. And tobacco spoilt the air of his room. In the first year the books he sent for were principally of a light character; novels with a complicated love plot, sensational and fantastic stories, and so on.

In the second year the piano was silent in the lodge, and the prisoner asked only for the classics. In the fifth year music was audible again, and the prisoner asked for wine. Those who watched him through the window said that all that year he spent doing nothing but eating and drinking and lying on his bed, frequently yawning and angrily talking to himself. He did not read books. Sometimes at night he would sit down to write; he would spend hours writing, and in the morning tear up all that he had written. More than once he could be heard crying.

In the second half of the sixth year the prisoner began zealously studying languages, philosophy, and history. He threw himself eagerly into these studies -- so much so that the banker had enough to do to get him the books he ordered. In the course of four years some six hundred volumes were procured at his request. It was during this period that the banker received the following letter from his prisoner:

"My dear Jailer, I write you these lines in six languages. Show them to people who know the languages. Let them read them. If they find not one mistake I implore you to fire a shot in the garden. That shot will show me that my efforts have not been thrown away. The geniuses of all ages and of all lands speak different languages, but the same flame burns in them all. Oh, if you only knew what unearthly happiness my soul feels now from being able to understand them!" The prisoner's desire was fulfilled. The banker ordered two shots to be fired in the garden.

Then after the tenth year, the prisoner sat immovably at the table and read nothing but the Gospel. It seemed strange to the banker that a man who in four years had mastered six hundred learned volumes should waste nearly a year over one thin book easy of comprehension. Theology and histories of religion followed the Gospels.

In the last two years of his confinement the prisoner read an immense quantity of books quite indiscriminately. At one time he was busy with the natural sciences, then he would ask for Byron or Shakespeare. There were notes in which he demanded at the same time books on chemistry, and a manual of medicine, and a novel, and some treatise on philosophy or theology. His reading suggested a man swimming in the sea among the wreckage of his ship, and trying to save his life by greedily clutching first at one spar and then at another.

II

The old banker remembered all this, and thought:

"To-morrow at twelve o'clock he will regain his freedom. By our agreement I ought to pay him two millions. If I do pay him, it is all over with me: I shall be utterly ruined."

Fifteen years before, his millions had been beyond his reckoning; now he was afraid to ask himself which were greater, his debts or his assets. Desperate gambling on the Stock Exchange, wild speculation and the excitability which he could not get over even in advancing years, had by degrees led to the decline of his fortune and the proud, fearless, self-confident millionaire had become a banker of middling rank, trembling at every rise and fall in his investments. "Cursed bet!" muttered the old man, clutching his head in despair "Why didn't the man die? He is only forty now. He will take my last penny from me, he will marry, will enjoy life, will gamble on the Exchange; while I shall look at him with envy like a beggar, and hear from him every day the same sentence: 'I am indebted to you for the happiness of my life, let me help you!' No, it is too much! The one means of being saved from bankruptcy and disgrace is the death of that man!"

It struck three o'clock, the banker listened; everyone was asleep in the house and nothing could be heard outside but the rustling of the chilled trees. Trying to make no noise, he took from a fireproof safe the key of the door which had not been opened for fifteen years, put on his overcoat, and went out of the house.

It was dark and cold in the garden. Rain was falling. A damp cutting wind was racing about the garden, howling and giving the trees no rest. The banker strained his eyes, but could see neither the earth nor the white statues, nor the lodge, nor the trees. Going to the spot where the lodge stood, he twice called the watchman. No answer followed. Evidently the watchman had sought shelter from the weather, and was now asleep somewhere either in the kitchen or in the greenhouse.

"If I had the pluck to carry out my intention," thought the old man, "Suspicion would fall first upon the watchman."

He felt in the darkness for the steps and the door, and went into the entry of the lodge. Then he groped his way into a little passage and lighted a match. There was not a soul there. There was a bedstead with no bedding on it, and in the corner there was a dark cast-iron stove. The seals on the door leading to the prisoner's rooms were intact.

When the match went out the old man, trembling with emotion, peeped through the little window. A candle was burning dimly in the prisoner's room. He was sitting at the table. Nothing could be seen but his back, the hair on his head, and his hands. Open books were lying on the table, on the two easy-chairs, and on the carpet near the table.

Five minutes passed and the prisoner did not once stir. Fifteen years' imprisonment had taught him to sit still. The banker tapped at the window with his finger, and the prisoner made no movement whatever in response. Then the banker cautiously broke the seals off the door and put the key in the keyhole. The rusty lock gave a grating sound and the door creaked. The banker expected to hear at once footsteps and a cry of astonishment, but three minutes passed and it was as quiet as ever in the room. He made up his mind to go in.

At the table a man unlike ordinary people was sitting motionless. He was a skeleton with the skin drawn tight over his bones, with long curls like a woman's and a shaggy beard. His face was yellow with an earthy tint in it, his cheeks were hollow, his back long and narrow, and the hand on which his shaggy head was propped was so thin and delicate that it was dreadful to look at it. His hair was already streaked with silver, and seeing his emaciated, aged-looking face, no one would have believed that he was only forty. He was asleep. . . . In front of his bowed head there lay on the table a sheet of paper on which there was something written in fine handwriting.

"Poor creature!" thought the banker, "he is asleep and most likely dreaming of the millions. And I have only to take this half-dead man, throw him on the bed, stifle him a little with the pillow, and the most conscientious expert would find no sign of a violent death. But let us first read what he has written here. . . ."

The banker took the page from the table and read as follows:

"To-morrow at twelve o'clock I regain my freedom and the right to associate with other men, but before I leave this room and see the sunshine, I think it necessary to say a few words to you. With a clear conscience I tell you, as before God, who beholds me, that I despise freedom and life and health, and all that in your books is called the good things of the world.

"For fifteen years I have been intently studying earthly life. It is true I have not seen the earth nor men, but in your books I have drunk fragrant wine, I have sung songs, I have hunted stags and wild boars in the forests, have loved women. . . . Beauties as ethereal as clouds, created by the magic of your poets and geniuses, have visited me at night, and have whispered in my ears wonderful tales that have set my brain in a whirl. In your books I have climbed to the peaks of Elburz and Mont Blanc, and from there I have seen the sun rise and have watched it at evening flood the sky, the ocean, and the mountain-tops with gold and crimson. I have watched from there the lightning flashing over my head and cleaving the storm-clouds. I have seen green forests, fields, rivers, lakes, towns. I have heard the singing of the sirens, and the strains of the shepherds' pipes; I have touched the wings of comely devils who flew down to converse with me of God. . . . In your books I have flung myself into the bottomless pit, performed miracles, slain, burned towns, preached new religions, conquered whole kingdoms. . . .

"Your books have given me wisdom. All that the unresting thought of man has created in the ages is compressed into a small compass in my brain. I know that I am wiser than all of you.

"And I despise your books, I despise wisdom and the blessings of this world. It is all worthless, fleeting, illusory, and deceptive, like a mirage. You may be proud, wise, and fine, but death will wipe you off the face of the earth as though you were no more than mice burrowing under the floor, and your posterity, your history, your immortal geniuses will burn or freeze together with the earthly globe.

"You have lost your reason and taken the wrong path. You have taken lies for truth, and hideousness for beauty. You would marvel if, owing to strange events of some sorts, frogs and lizards suddenly grew on apple and orange trees instead of fruit, or if roses began to smell like a sweating horse; so I marvel at you who exchange heaven for earth. I don't want to understand you.

"To prove to you in action how I despise all that you live by, I renounce the two millions of which I once dreamed as of paradise and which now I despise. To deprive myself of the right to the money I shall go out from here five hours before the time fixed, and so break the compact. . . ."

When the banker had read this he laid the page on the table, kissed the strange man on the head, and went out of the lodge, weeping. At no other time, even when he had lost heavily on the Stock Exchange, had he felt so great a contempt for himself. When he got home he lay on his bed, but his tears and emotion kept him for hours from sleeping.

Next morning the watchmen ran in with pale faces, and told him they had seen the man who lived in the lodge climb out of the window into the garden, go to the gate, and disappear. The banker went at once with the servants to the lodge and made sure of the flight of his prisoner. To avoid arousing unnecessary talk, he took from the table the writing in which the millions were renounced, and when he got home locked it up in the fireproof safe.

THE PRINCESS

A carriage with four fine sleek horses drove in at the big so-called Red Gate of the N--- Monastery. While it was still at a distance, the priests and monks who were standing in a group round the part of the hostel allotted to the gentry, recognised by the coachman and horses that the lady in the carriage was Princess Vera Gavrilovna, whom they knew very well.

An old man in livery jumped off the box and helped the princess to get out of the carriage. She raised her dark veil and moved in a leisurely way up to the priests to receive their blessing; then she nodded pleasantly to the rest of the monks and went into the hostel.

"Well, have you missed your princess?" she said to the monk who brought in her things. "It's a whole month since I've been to see you. But here I am; behold your princess. And where is the Father Superior? My goodness, I am burning with impatience! Wonderful, wonderful old man! You must be proud of having such a Superior."

When the Father Superior came in, the princess uttered a shriek of delight, crossed her arms over her bosom, and went up to receive his blessing.

"No, no, let me kiss your hand," she said, snatching it and eagerly kissing it three times. "How glad I am to see you at last, holy Father! I'm sure you've forgotten your princess, but my thoughts have been in your dear monastery every moment. How delightful it is here! This living for God far from the busy, giddy world has a special charm of its own, holy Father, which I feel with my whole soul although I cannot express it!"

The princess's cheeks glowed and tears came into her eyes. She talked incessantly, fervently, while the Father Superior, a grave, plain, shy old man of seventy, remained mute or uttered abruptly, like a soldier on duty, phrases such as:

"Certainly, Your Excellency. . . . Quite so. I understand."

"Has Your Excellency come for a long stay?" he inquired.

"I shall stay the night here, and to-morrow I'm going on to Klavdia Nikolaevna's -- it's a long time since I've seen her -- and the day after to-morrow I'll come back to you and stay three or four days. I want to rest my soul here among you, holy Father. . . ."

The princess liked being at the monastery at N---. For the last two years it had been a favourite resort of hers; she used to go there almost every month in the summer and stay two or three days, even sometimes a week. The shy novices, the stillness, the low ceilings, the smell of cypress, the modest fare, the cheap curtains on the windows -- all this touched her, softened her, and disposed her to contemplation and good thoughts. It was enough for her to be half an hour in the hostel for her to feel that she, too, was timid and modest, and that she, too, smelt of cypress-wood. The past retreated into the background, lost its significance, and the princess began to imagine that in spite of her twenty-nine years she was very much like the old Father Superior, and that, like him, she was created not for wealth, not for earthly grandeur and love, but for a peaceful life secluded from the world, a life in twilight like the hostel.

It happens that a ray of light gleams in the dark cell of the anchorite absorbed in prayer, or a bird alights on the window and sings its song; the stern anchorite will smile in spite of himself, and a gentle, sinless joy will pierce through the load of grief over his sins, like water flowing from under a stone. The princess fancied she brought from the outside world just such comfort as the ray of light or the bird. Her gay, friendly smile, her gentle eyes, her voice, her jests, her whole personality in fact, her little graceful figure always dressed in simple black, must arouse in simple, austere people a feeling of tenderness and joy. Everyone, looking at her, must think: "God has sent us an angel. . . ." And feeling that no one could help thinking this, she smiled still more cordially, and tried to look like a bird.

After drinking tea and resting, she went for a walk. The sun was already setting. From the monastery garden came a moist fragrance of freshly watered mignonette, and from the church floated the soft singing of men's voices, which seemed very pleasant and mournful in the distance. It was the evening service. In the dark windows where the little lamps glowed gently, in the shadows, in the figure of the old monk sitting at the church door with a collecting-box, there was such unruffled peace that the princess felt moved to tears.

Outside the gate, in the walk between the wall and the birch-trees where there were benches, it was quite evening. The air grew rapidly darker and darker. The princess went along the walk, sat on a seat, and sank into thought.

She thought how good it would be to settle down for her whole life in this monastery where life was as still and unruffled as a summer evening; how good it would be to forget the ungrateful, dissipated prince; to forget her immense estates, the creditors who worried her every day, her misfortunes, her maid Dasha, who had looked at her impertinently that morning. It would be nice to sit here on the bench all her life and watch through the trunks of the birch-trees the evening mist gathering in wreaths in the valley below; the rooks flying home in a black cloud like a veil far, far away above the forest; two novices, one astride a piebald horse, another on foot driving out the horses for the night and rejoicing in their freedom, playing pranks like little children; their youthful voices rang out musically in the still air, and she could distinguish every word. It is nice to sit and listen to the silence: at one moment the wind blows and stirs the tops of the birch-trees, then a frog rustles in last year's leaves, then the clock on the belfry strikes the quarter. . . . One might sit without moving, listen and think, and think. . . .

An old woman passed by with a wallet on her back. The princess thought that it would be nice to stop the old woman and to say something friendly and cordial to her, to help her. . . . But the old woman turned the corner without once looking round.

Not long afterwards a tall man with a grey beard and a straw hat came along the walk. When he came up to the princess, he took off his hat and bowed. From the bald patch on his head and his sharp, hooked nose the princess recognised him as the doctor, Mihail Ivanovitch, who had been in her service at Dubovki. She remembered that someone had told her that his wife had died the year before, and she wanted to sympathise with him, to console him.

"Doctor, I expect you don't recognise me?" she said with an affable smile.

"Yes, Princess, I recognised you," said the doctor, taking off his hat again.

"Oh, thank you; I was afraid that you, too, had forgotten your princess. People only remember their enemies, but they forget their friends. Have you, too, come to pray?"

"I am the doctor here, and I have to spend the night at the monastery every Saturday."

"Well, how are you?" said the princess, sighing. "I hear that you have lost your wife. What a calamity!"

"Yes, Princess, for me it is a great calamity."

"There's nothing for it! We must bear our troubles with resignation. Not one hair of a man's head is lost without the Divine Will."

"Yes, Princess."

To the princess's friendly, gentle smile and her sighs the doctor responded coldly and dryly: "Yes, Princess." And the expression of his face was cold and dry.

"What else can I say to him?" she wondered.

"How long it is since we met!" she said. "Five years! How much water has flowed under the bridge, how many changes in that time; it quite frightens one to think of it! You know, I am married. . . . I am not a countess now, but a princess. And by now I am separated from my husband too."

"Yes, I heard so."

"God has sent me many trials. No doubt you have heard, too, that I am almost ruined. My Dubovki, Sofyino, and Kiryakovo have all been sold for my unhappy husband's debts. And I have only Baranovo and Mihaltsevo left. It's terrible to look back: how many changes and misfortunes of all kinds, how many mistakes!"

"Yes, Princess, many mistakes."

The princess was a little disconcerted. She knew her mistakes; they were all of such a private character that no one but she could think or speak of them. She could not resist asking:

"What mistakes are you thinking about?"

"You referred to them, so you know them . . ." answered the doctor, and he smiled. "Why talk about them!"

"No; tell me, doctor. I shall be very grateful to you. And please don't stand on ceremony with me. I love to hear the truth."

"I am not your judge, Princess."

"Not my judge! What a tone you take! You must know something about me. Tell me!"

"If you really wish it, very well. Only I regret to say I'm not clever at talking, and people can't always understand me."

The doctor thought a moment and began:

"A lot of mistakes; but the most important of them, in my opinion, was the general spirit that prevailed on all your estates. You see, I don't know how to express myself. I mean chiefly the lack of love, the aversion for people that was felt in absolutely everything. Your whole system of life was built upon that aversion. Aversion for the human voice, for faces, for heads, steps . . . in fact, foreverything that makes up a human being. At all the doors and on the stairs there stand sleek, rude, and lazy grooms in livery to prevent badly dressed persons from entering the house; in the hall there are chairs with high backs so that the footmen waiting there, during balls and receptions, may not soil the walls with their heads; in every room there are thick carpets that no human step may be heard; everyone who comes in is infallibly warned to speak as softly and as little as possible, and to say nothing that might have a disagreeable effect on the nerves or the imagination. And in your room you don't shake hands with anyone or ask him to sit down -- just as you didn't shake hands with me or ask me to sit down. . . ."

"By all means, if you like," said the princess, smiling and holding out her hand. "Really, to be cross about such trifles. . . ."

"But I am not cross," laughed the doctor, but at once he flushed, took off his hat, and waving it about, began hotly: "To be candid, I've long wanted an opportunity to tell you all I think. . . . That is, I want to tell you that you look upon the mass of mankind from the Napoleonic standpoint as food for the cannon. But Napoleon had at least some idea; you have nothing except aversion."

"I have an aversion for people?" smiled the princess, shrugging her shoulders in astonishment. "I have!"

"Yes, you! You want facts? By all means. In Mihaltsevo three former cooks of yours, who have gone blind in your kitchens from the heat of the stove, are living upon charity. All the health and strength and good looks that is found on your hundreds of thousands of acres is taken by you and your parasites for your grooms, your footmen, and your coachmen. All these two-legged cattle are trained to be flunkeys, overeat themselves, grow coarse, lose the 'image and likeness,' in fact. . . . Young doctors, agricultural experts, teachers, intellectual workers generally -- think of it! -- are torn away from their honest work and forced for a crust of bread to take part in all sorts of mummeries which make every decent man feel ashamed! Some young men cannot be in your service for three years without becoming hypocrites, toadies, sneaks. . . . Is that a good thing? Your Polish superintendents, those abject spies, all those Kazimers and Kaetans, go hunting about on your hundreds of thousands of acres from morning to night, and to please you try to get three skins off one ox. Excuse me, I speak disconnectedly, but that doesn't matter. You don't look upon the simple people as human beings. And even the princes, counts, and bishops who used to come and see you, you looked upon simply as decorative figures, not as living beings. But the worst of all, the thing that most revolts me, is having a fortune of over a million and doing nothing for other people, nothing!"

The princess sat amazed, aghast, offended, not knowing what to say or how to behave. She had never before been spoken to in such a tone. The doctor's unpleasant, angry voice and his clumsy, faltering phrases made a harsh clattering noise in her ears and her head. Then she began to feel as though the gesticulating doctor was hitting her on the head with his hat.

"It's not true!" she articulated softly, in an imploring voice. "I've done a great deal of good for other people; you know it yourself!"

"Nonsense!" cried the doctor. "Can you possibly go on thinking of your philanthropic work as something genuine and useful, and not a mere mummery? It was a farce from beginning to end; it was playing at loving your neighbour, the most open farce which even children and stupid peasant women saw through! Take for instance your -- what was it called? -- house for homeless old women without relations, of which you made me something like a head doctor, and of which you were the patroness. Mercy on us! What a charming institution it was! A house was built with parquet floors and a weathercock on the roof; a dozen old women were collected from the villages and made to sleep under blankets and sheets of Dutch linen, and given toffee to eat."

The doctor gave a malignant chuckle into his hat, and went on speaking rapidly and stammering:

"It was a farce! The attendants kept the sheets and the blankets under lock and key, for fear the old women should soil them -- 'Let the old devil's pepper-pots sleep on the floor.' The old women did not dare to sit down on the beds, to put on their jackets, to walk over the polished floors. Everything was kept for show and hidden away from the old women as though they were thieves, and the old women were clothed and fed on the sly by other people's charity, and prayed to God night and day to be released from their prison and from the canting exhortations of the sleek rascals to whose care you committed them. And what did the managers do? It was simply charming! About twice a week there would be thirty-five thousand messages to say that the princess -- that is, you -- were coming to the home next day. That meant that next day I had to abandon my patients, dress up and be on parade. Very good; I arrive. The old women, in everything clean and new, are already drawn up in a row, waiting. Near them struts the old garrison rat -- the superintendent with his mawkish, sneaking smile. The old women yawn and exchange glances, but are afraid to complain. We wait. The junior steward gallops up. Half an hour later the senior steward; then the superintendent of the accounts' office, then another, and then another of them . . . they keep arriving endlessly. They all have mysterious, solemn faces. We wait and wait, shift from one leg to another, look at the clock -- all this in monumental silence because we all hate each other like poison. One hour passes, then a second, and then at last the carriage is seen in the distance, and . . . and . . ."

The doctor went off into a shrill laugh and brought out in a shrill voice:

"You get out of the carriage, and the old hags, at the word of command from the old garrison rat, begin chanting: 'The Glory of our Lord in Zion the tongue of man cannot express. . .' A pretty scene, wasn't it?"

The doctor went off into a bass chuckle, and waved his hand as though to signify that he could not utter another word for laughing. He laughed heavily, harshly, with clenched teeth, as ill-natured people laugh; and from his voice, from his face, from his glittering, rather insolent eyes it could be seen that he had a profound contempt for the princess, for the home, and for the old women. There was nothing amusing or laughable in all that he described so clumsily and coarsely, but he laughed with satisfaction, even with delight.

"And the school?" he went on, panting from laughter. "Do you remember how you wanted to teach peasant children yourself? You must have taught them very well, for very soon the children all ran away, so that they had to be thrashed and bribed to come and be taught. And you remember how you wanted to feed with your own hands the infants whose mothers were working in the fields. You went about the village crying because the infants were not at your disposal, as the mothers would take them to the fields with them. Then the village foreman ordered the mothers by turns to leave their infants behind for your entertainment. A strange thing! They all ran away from your benevolence like mice from a cat! And why was it? It's very simple. Not because our people are ignorant and ungrateful, as you always explained it to yourself, but because in all your fads, if you'll excuse the word, there wasn't a ha'p'orth of love and kindness! There was nothing but the desire to amuse yourself with living puppets, nothing else. . . . A person who does not feel the difference between a human being and a lap-dog ought not to go in for philanthropy. I assure you, there's a great difference between human beings and lap-dogs!"

The princess's heart was beating dreadfully; there was a thudding in her ears, and she still felt as though the doctor were beating her on the head with his hat. The doctor talked quickly, excitedly, and uncouthly, stammering and gesticulating unnecessarily. All she grasped was that she was spoken to by a coarse, ill-bred, spiteful, and ungrateful man; but what he wanted of her and what he was talking about, she could not understand.

"Go away!" she said in a tearful voice, putting up her hands to protect her head from the doctor's hat; "go away!"

"And how you treat your servants!" the doctor went on, indignantly. "You treat them as the lowest scoundrels, and don't look upon them as human beings. For example, allow me to ask, why did you dismiss me? For ten years I worked for your father and afterwards for you, honestly, without vacations or holidays. I gained the love of all for more than seventy miles round, and suddenly one fine day I am informed that I am no longer wanted. What for? I've no idea to this day. I, a doctor of medicine, a gentleman by birth, a student of the Moscow University, father of a family -- am such a petty, insignificant insect that you can kick me out without explaining the reason! Why stand on ceremony with me! I heard afterwards that my wife went without my knowledge three times to intercede with you for me -- you wouldn't receive her. I am told she cried in your hall. And I shall never forgive her for it, never!"

The doctor paused and clenched his teeth, making an intense effort to think of something more to say, very unpleasant and vindictive. He thought of something, and his cold, frowning face suddenly brightened.

"Take your attitude to this monastery!" he said with avidity. "You've never spared anyone, and the holier the place, the more chance of its suffering from your loving-kindness and angelic sweetness. Why do you come here? What do you want with the monks here, allow me to ask you? What is Hecuba to you or you to Hecuba? It's another farce, another amusement for you, another sacrilege against human dignity, and nothing more. Why, you don't believe in the monks' God; you've a God of your own in your heart, whom you've evolved for yourself at spiritualist séances. You look with condescension upon the ritual of the Church; you don't go to mass or vespers; you sleep till midday. . . . Why do you come here? . . . You come with a God of your own into a monastery you have nothing to do with, and you imagine that the monks look upon it as a very great honour. To be sure they do! You'd better ask, by the way, what your visits cost the monastery. You were graciously pleased to arrive here this evening, and a messenger from your estate arrived on horseback the day before yesterday to warn them of your coming. They were the whole day yesterday getting the rooms ready and expecting you. This morning your advance-guard arrived -- an insolent maid, who keeps running across the courtyard, rustling her skirts, pestering them with questions, giving orders. . . . I can't endure it! The monks have been on the lookout all day, for if you were not met with due ceremony, there would be trouble! You'd complain to the bishop! 'The monks don't like me, your holiness; I don't know what I've done to displease them. It's true I'm a great sinner, but I'm so unhappy!' Already one monastery has been in hot water over you. The Father Superior is a busy, learned man; he hasn't a free moment, and you keep sending for him to come to your rooms. Not a trace of respect for age or for rank! If at least you were a bountiful giver to the monastery, one wouldn't resent it so much, but all this time the monks have not received a hundred roubles from you!"

Whenever people worried the princess, misunderstood her, or mortified her, and when she did not know what to say or do, she usually began to cry. And on this occasion, too, she ended by hiding her face in her hands and crying aloud in a thin treble like a child. The doctor suddenly stopped and looked at her. His face darkened and grew stern.

"Forgive me, Princess," he said in a hollow voice. "I've given way to a malicious feeling and forgotten myself. It was not right."

And coughing in an embarrassed way, he walked away quickly, without remembering to put his hat on.

Stars were already twinkling in the sky. The moon must have been rising on the further side of the monastery, for the sky was clear, soft, and transparent. Bats were flitting noiselessly along the white monastery wall.

The clock slowly struck three quarters, probably a quarter to nine. The princess got up and walked slowly to the gate. She felt wounded and was crying, and she felt that the trees and the stars and even the bats were pitying her, and that the clock struck musically only to express its sympathy with her. She cried and thought how nice it would be to go into a monastery for the rest of her life. On still summer evenings she would walk alone through the avenues, insulted, injured, misunderstood by people, and only God and the starry heavens would see the martyr's tears. The evening service was still going on in the church. The princess stopped and listened to the singing; how beautiful the singing sounded in the still darkness! How sweet to weep and suffer to the sound of that singing!

Going into her rooms, she looked at her tear-stained face in the glass and powdered it, then she sat down to supper. The monks knew that she liked pickled sturgeon, little mushrooms, Malaga and plain honey-cakes that left a taste of cypress in the mouth, and every time she came they gave her all these dishes. As she ate the mushrooms and drank the Malaga, the princess dreamed of how she would be finally ruined and deserted -- how all her stewards, bailiffs, clerks, and maid-servants for whom she had done so much, would be false to her, and begin to say rude things; how people all the world over would set upon her, speak ill of her, jeer at her. She would renounce her title, would renounce society and luxury, and would go into a convent without one word of reproach to anyone; she would pray for her enemies -- and then they would all understand her and come to beg her forgiveness, but by that time it would be too late. . . .

After supper she knelt down in the corner before the ikon and read two chapters of the Gospel. Then her maid made her bed and she got into it. Stretching herself under the white quilt, she heaved a sweet, deep sigh, as one sighs after crying, closed her eyes, and began to fall asleep.

In the morning she waked up and glanced at her watch. It was half-past nine. On the carpet near the bed was a bright, narrow streak of sunlight from a ray which came in at the window and dimly lighted up the room. Flies were buzzing behind the black curtain at the window. "It's early," thought the princess, and she closed her eyes.

Stretching and lying snug in her bed, she recalled her meeting yesterday with the doctor and all the thoughts with which she had gone to sleep the night before: she remembered she was unhappy. Then she thought of her husband living in Petersburg, her stewards, doctors, neighbours, the officials of her acquaintance . . . a long procession of familiar masculine faces passed before her imagination. She smiled and thought, if only these people could see into her heart and understand her, they would all be at her feet.

At a quarter past eleven she called her maid.

"Help me to dress, Dasha," she said languidly. "But go first and tell them to get out the horses. I must set off for Klavdia Nikolaevna's."

Going out to get into the carriage, she blinked at the glaring daylight and laughed with pleasure: it was a wonderfully fine day! As she scanned from her half-closed eyes the monks who had gathered round the steps to see her off, she nodded graciously and said:

"Good-bye, my friends! Till the day after tomorrow."

It was an agreeable surprise to her that the doctor was with the monks by the steps. His face was pale and severe.

"Princess," he said with a guilty smile, taking off his hat, "I've been waiting here a long time to see you. Forgive me, for God's sake. . . . I was carried away yesterday by an evil, vindictive feeling and I talked . . . nonsense. In short, I beg your pardon."

The princess smiled graciously, and held out her hand for him to kiss. He kissed it, turning red.

Trying to look like a bird, the princess fluttered into the carriage and nodded in all directions. There was a gay, warm, serene feeling in her heart, and she felt herself that her smile was particularly soft and friendly. As the carriage rolled towards the gates, and afterwards along the dusty road past huts and gardens, past long trains of waggons and strings of pilgrims on their way to the monastery, she still screwed up her eyes and smiled softly. She was thinking there was no higher bliss than to bring warmth, light, and joy wherever one went, to forgive injuries, to smile graciously on one's enemies. The peasants she passed bowed to her, the carriage rustled softly, clouds of dust rose from under the wheels and floated over the golden rye, and it seemed to the princess that her body was swaying not on carriage cushions but on clouds, and that she herself was like a light, transparent little cloud. . . .

"How happy I am!" she murmured, shutting her eyes. "How happy I am!"

A DREARY STORY

From the Notebook of an Old Man

I

There is in Russia an emeritus Professor Nikolay Stepanovitch, a chevalier and privy councillor; he has so many Russian and foreign decorations that when he has occasion to put them on the students nickname him "TheIkonstand." His acquaintances are of the most aristocratic; for the last twenty-five or thirty years, at any rate, there has not been one single distinguished man of learning in Russia with whom he has not been intimately acquainted. There is no one for him to make friends with nowadays; but if we turn to the past, the long list of his famous friends winds up with such names as Pirogov, Kavelin, and the poet Nekrasov, all of whom bestowed upon him a warm and sincere affection. He is a member of all the Russian and of three foreign universities. And so on, and so on. All that and a great deal more that might be said makes up what is called my "name."

That is my name as known to the public. In Russia it is known to every educated man, and abroad it is mentioned in the lecture-room with the addition "honoured and distinguished." It is one of those fortunate names to abuse which or to take which in vain, in public or in print, is considered a sign of bad taste. And that is as it should be. You see, my name is closely associated with the conception of a highly distinguished man of great gifts and unquestionable usefulness. I have the industry and power of endurance of a camel, and that is important, and I have talent, which is even more important. Moreover, while I am on this subject, I am a well-educated, modest, and honest fellow. I have never poked my nose into literature or politics; I have never sought popularity in polemics with the ignorant; I have never made speeches either at public dinners or at the funerals of my friends. . . . In fact, there is no slur on my learned name, and there is no complaint one can make against it. It is fortunate.

The bearer of that name, that is I, see myself as a man of sixty-two, with a bald head, with false teeth, and with an incurable tic douloureux. I am myself as dingy and unsightly as my name is brilliant and splendid. My head and my hands tremble with weakness; my neck, as Turgenev says of one of his heroines, is like the handle of a double bass; my chest is hollow; my shoulders narrow; when I talk or lecture, my mouth turns down at one corner; when I smile, my whole face is covered with aged-looking, deathly wrinkles. There is nothing impressive about my pitiful figure; only, perhaps, when I have an attack of tic douloureux my face wears a peculiar expression, the sight of which must have roused in everyone the grim and impressive thought, "Evidently that man will soon die."

I still, as in the past, lecture fairly well; I can still, as in the past, hold the attention of my listeners for a couple of hours. My fervour, the literary skill of my exposition, and my humour, almost efface the defects of my voice, though it is harsh, dry, and monotonous as a praying beggar's. I write poorly. That bit of my brain which presides over the faculty of authorship refuses to work. My memory has grown weak; there is a lack of sequence in my ideas, and when I put them on paper it always seems to me that I have lost the instinct for their organic connection; my construction is monotonous; my language is poor and timid. Often I write what I do not mean; I have forgotten the beginning when I am writing the end. Often I forget ordinary words, and I always have to waste a great deal of energy in avoiding superfluous phrases and unnecessary parentheses in my letters, both unmistakable proofs of a decline in mental activity. And it is noteworthy that the simpler the letter the more painful the effort to write it. At a scientific article I feel far more intelligent and at ease than at a letter of congratulation or a minute of proceedings. Another point: I find it easier to write German or English than to write Russian.

As regards my present manner of life, I must give a foremost place to the insomnia from which I have suffered of late. If I were asked what constituted the chief and fundamental feature of my existence now, I should answer, Insomnia. As in the past, from habit I undress and go to bed exactly at midnight. I fall asleep quickly, but before two o'clock I wake up and feel as though I had not slept at all. Sometimes I get out of bed and light a lamp. For an hour or two I walk up and down the room looking at the familiar photographs and pictures. When I am weary of walking about, I sit down to my table. I sit motionless, thinking of nothing, conscious of no inclination; if a book is lying before me, I mechanically move it closer and read it without any interest -- in that way not long ago I mechanically read through in one night a whole novel, with the strange title "The Song the Lark was Singing"; or to occupy my attention I force myself to count to a thousand; or I imagine the face of one of my colleagues and begin trying to remember in what year and under what circumstances he entered the service. I like listening to sounds. Two rooms away from me my daughter Liza says something rapidly in her sleep, or my wife crosses the drawing-room with a candle and invariably drops the matchbox; or a warped cupboard creaks; or the burner of the lamp suddenly begins to hum -- and all these sounds, for some reason, excite me.

To lie awake at night means to be at every moment conscious of being abnormal, and so I look forward with impatience to the morning and the day when I have a right to be awake. Many wearisome hours pass before the cock crows in the yard. He is my first bringer of good tidings. As soon as he crows I know that within an hour the porter will wake up below, and, coughing angrily, will go upstairs to fetch something. And then a pale light will begin gradually glimmering at the windows, voices will sound in the street. . . .

The day begins for me with the entrance of my wife. She comes in to me in her petticoat, before she has done her hair, but after she has washed, smelling of flower-scented eau-de-Cologne, looking as though she had come in by chance. Every time she says exactly the same thing: "Excuse me, I have just come in for a minute. . . . Have you had a bad night again?"

Then she puts out the lamp, sits down near the table, and begins talking. I am no prophet, but I know what she will talk about. Every morning it is exactly the same thing. Usually, after anxious inquiries concerning my health, she suddenly mentions our son who is an officer serving at Warsaw. After the twentieth of each month we send him fifty roubles, and that serves as the chief topic of our conversation.

"Of course it is difficult for us," my wife would sigh, "but until he is completely on his own feet it is our duty to help him. The boy is among strangers, his pay is small. . . . However, if you like, next month we won't send him fifty, but forty. What do you think?"

Daily experience might have taught my wife that constantly talking of our expenses does not reduce them, but my wife refuses to learn by experience, and regularly every morning discusses our officer son, and tells me that bread, thank God, is cheaper, while sugar is a halfpenny dearer -- with a tone and an air as though she were communicating interesting news.

I listen, mechanically assent, and probably because I have had a bad night, strange and inappropriate thoughts intrude themselves upon me. I gaze at my wife and wonder like a child. I ask myself in perplexity, is it possible that this old, very stout, ungainly woman, with her dull expression of petty anxiety and alarm about daily bread, with eyes dimmed by continual brooding over debts and money difficulties, who can talk of nothing but expenses and who smiles at nothing but things getting cheaper -- is it possible that this woman is no other than the slender Varya whom I fell in love with so passionately for her fine, clear intelligence, for her pure soul, her beauty, and, as Othello his Desdemona, for her "sympathy" for my studies? Could that woman be no other than the Varya who had once borne me a son?

I look with strained attention into the face of this flabby, spiritless, clumsy old woman, seeking in her my Varya, but of her past self nothing is left but her anxiety over my health and her manner of calling my salary "our salary," and my cap "our cap." It is painful for me to look at her, and, to give her what little comfort I can, I let her say what she likes, and say nothing even when she passes unjust criticisms on other people or pitches into me for not having a private practice or not publishing text-books.

Our conversation always ends in the same way. My wife suddenly remembers with dismay that I have not had my tea.

"What am I thinking about, sitting here?" she says, getting up. "The samovar has been on the table ever so long, and here I stay gossiping. My goodness! how forgetful I am growing!"

She goes out quickly, and stops in the doorway to say:

"We owe Yegor five months' wages. Did you know it? You mustn't let the servants' wages run on; how many times I have said it! It's much easier to pay ten roubles a month than fifty roubles every five months!"

As she goes out, she stops to say:

"The person I am sorriest for is our Liza. The girl studies at the Conservatoire, always mixes with people of good position, and goodness knows how she is dressed. Her fur coat is in such a state she is ashamed to show herself in the street. If she were somebody else's daughter it wouldn't matter, but of course everyone knows that her father is a distinguished professor, a privy councillor."

And having reproached me with my rank and reputation, she goes away at last. That is how my day begins. It does not improve as it goes on.

As I am drinking my tea, my Liza comes in wearing her fur coat and her cap, with her music in her hand, already quite ready to go to the Conservatoire. She is two-and-twenty. She looks younger, is pretty, and rather like my wife in her young days. She kisses me tenderly on my forehead and on my hand, and says:

"Good-morning, papa; are you quite well?"

As a child she was very fond of ice-cream, and I used often to take her to a confectioner's. Ice-cream was for her the type of everything delightful. If she wanted to praise me she would say: "You are as nice as cream, papa." We used to call one of her little fingers "pistachio ice," the next, "cream ice," the third "raspberry," and so on. Usually when she came in to say good-morning to me I used to sit her on my knee, kiss her little fingers, and say:

"Creamy ice . . . pistachio . . . lemon. . . ."

And now, from old habit, I kiss Liza's fingers and mutter: "Pistachio . . . cream . . . lemon. . ." but the effect is utterly different. I am cold as ice and I am ashamed. When my daughter comes in to me and touches my forehead with her lips I start as though a bee had stung me on the head, give a forced smile, and turn my face away. Ever since I have been suffering from sleeplessness, a question sticks in my brain like a nail. My daughter often sees me, an old man and a distinguished man, blush painfully at being in debt to my footman; she sees how often anxiety over petty debts forces me to lay aside my work and to walk up and down the room for hours together, thinking; but why is it she never comes to me in secret to whisper in my ear: "Father, here is my watch, here are my bracelets, my earrings, my dresses. . . . Pawn them all; you want money . . ."? How is it that, seeing how her mother and I are placed in a false position and do our utmost to hide our poverty from people, she does not give up her expensive pleasure of music lessons? I would not accept her watch nor her bracelets, nor the sacrifice of her lessons -- God forbid! That isn't what I want.

I think at the same time of my son, the officer at Warsaw. He is a clever, honest, and sober fellow. But that is not enough for me. I think if I had an old father, and if I knew there were moments when he was put to shame by his poverty, I should give up my officer's commission to somebody else, and should go out to earn my living as a workman. Such thoughts about my children poison me. What is the use of them? It is only a narrow-minded or embittered man who can harbour evil thoughts about ordinary people because they are not heroes. But enough of that!

At a quarter to ten I have to go and give a lecture to my dear boys. I dress and walk along the road which I have known for thirty years, and which has its history for me. Here is the big grey house with the chemist's shop; at this point there used to stand a little house, and in it was a beershop; in that beershop I thought out my thesis and wrote my first love-letter to Varya. I wrote it in pencil, on a page headed "Historia morbi." Here there is a grocer's shop; at one time it was kept by a little Jew, who sold me cigarettes on credit; then by a fat peasant woman, who liked the students because "everyone of them has a mother"; now there is a red-haired shopkeeper sitting in it, a very stolid man who drinks tea from a copper teapot. And here are the gloomy gates of the University, which have long needed doing up; I see the bored porter in his sheep-skin, the broom, the drifts of snow. . . . On a boy coming fresh from the provinces and imagining that the temple of science must really be a temple, such gates cannot make a healthy impression. Altogether the dilapidated condition of the University buildings, the gloominess of the corridors, the griminess of the walls, the lack of light, the dejected aspect of the steps, the hat-stands and the benches, take a prominent position among predisposing causes in the history of Russian pessimism. . . . Here is our garden . . . I fancy it has grown neither better nor worse since I was a student. I don't like it. It would be far more sensible if there were tall pines and fine oaks growing here instead of sickly-looking lime-trees, yellow acacias, and skimpy pollard lilacs. The student whose state of mind is in the majority of cases created by his surroundings, ought in the place where he is studying to see facing him at every turn nothing but what is lofty, strong and elegant. . . . God preserve him from gaunt trees, broken windows, grey walls, and doors covered with torn American leather!

When I go to my own entrance the door is flung wide open, and I am met by my colleague, contemporary, and namesake, the porter Nikolay. As he lets me in he clears his throat and says:

"A frost, your Excellency!"

Or, if my great-coat is wet:

"Rain, your Excellency!"

Then he runs on ahead of me and opens all the doors on my way. In my study he carefully takes off my fur coat, and while doing so manages to tell me some bit of University news. Thanks to the close intimacy existing between all the University porters and beadles, he knows everything that goes on in the four faculties, in the office, in the rector's private room, in the library. What does he not know? When in an evil day a rector or dean, for instance, retires, I hear him in conversation with the young porters mention the candidates for the post, explain that such a one would not be confirmed by the minister, that another would himself refuse to accept it, then drop into fantastic details concerning mysterious papers received in the office, secret conversations alleged to have taken place between the minister and the trustee, and so on. With the exception of these details, he almost always turns out to be right. His estimates of the candidates, though original, are very correct, too. If one wants to know in what year someone read his thesis, entered the service, retired, or died, then summon to your assistance the vast memory of that soldier, and he will not only tell you the year, the month and the day, but will furnish you also with the details that accompanied this or that event. Only one who loves can remember like that.

He is the guardian of the University traditions. From the porters who were his predecessors he has inherited many legends of University life, has added to that wealth much of his own gained during his time of service, and if you care to hear he will tell you many long and intimate stories. He can tell one about extraordinary sages who knew *everything,* about remarkable students who did not sleep for weeks, about numerous martyrs and victims of science; with him good triumphs over evil, the weak always vanquishes the strong, the wise man the fool, the humble the proud, the young the old. There is no need to take all these fables and legends for sterling coin; but filter them, and you will have left what is wanted: our fine traditions and the names of real heroes, recognized as such by all.

In our society the knowledge of the learned world consists of anecdotes of the extraordinary absentmindedness of certain old professors, and two or three witticisms variously ascribed to Gruber, to me, and to Babukin. For the educated public that is not much. If it loved science, learned men, and students, as Nikolay does, its literature would long ago have contained whole epics, records of sayings and doings such as, unfortunately, it cannot boast of now.

After telling me a piece of news, Nikolay assumes a severe expression, and conversation about business begins. If any outsider could at such times overhear Nikolay's free use of our terminology, he might perhaps imagine that he was a learned man disguised as a soldier. And, by the way, the rumours of the erudition of the University porters are greatly exaggerated. It is true that Nikolay knows more than a hundred Latin words, knows how to put the skeleton together, sometimes prepares the apparatus and amuses the students by some long, learned quotation, but the by no means complicated theory of the circulation of the blood, for instance, is as much a mystery to him now as it was twenty years ago.

At the table in my study, bending low over some book or preparation, sits Pyotr Ignatyevitch, my demonstrator, a modest and industrious but by no means clever man of five-and-thirty, already bald and corpulent; he works from morning to night, reads a lot, remembers well everything he has read -- and in that way he is not a man, but pure gold; in all else he is a carthorse or, in other words, a learned dullard. The carthorse characteristics that show his lack of talent are these: his outlook is narrow and sharply limited by his specialty; outside his special branch he is simple as a child.

"Fancy! what a misfortune! They say Skobelev is dead."

Nikolay crosses himself, but Pyotr Ignatyevitch turns to me and asks:

"What Skobelev is that?"

Another time -- somewhat earlier -- I told him that Professor Perov was dead. Good Pyotr Ignatyevitch asked:

"What did he lecture on?"

I believe if Patti had sung in his very ear, if a horde of Chinese had invaded Russia, if there had been an earthquake, he would not have stirred a limb, but screwing up his eye, would have gone on calmly looking through his microscope. What is he to Hecuba or Hecuba to him, in fact? I would give a good deal to see how this dry stick sleeps with his wife at night.

Another characteristic is his fanatical faith in the infallibility of science, and, above all, of everything written by the Germans. He believes in himself, in his preparations; knows the object of life, and knows nothing of the doubts and disappointments that turn the hair of talent grey. He has a slavish reverence for authorities and a complete lack of any desire for independent thought. To change his convictions is difficult, to argue with him impossible. How is one to argue with a man who is firmly persuaded that medicine is the finest of sciences, that doctors are the best of men, and that the traditions of the medical profession are superior to those of any other? Of the evil past of medicine only one tradition has been preserved -- the white tie still worn by doctors; for a learned -- in fact, for any educated man the only traditions that can exist are those of the University as a whole, with no distinction between medicine, law, etc. But it would be hard for Pyotr Ignatyevitch to accept these facts, and he is ready to argue with you till the day of judgment.

I have a clear picture in my mind of his future. In the course of his life he will prepare many hundreds of chemicals of exceptional purity; he will write a number of dry and very accurate memoranda, will make some dozen conscientious translations, but he won't do anything striking. To do that one must have imagination, inventiveness, the gift of insight, and Pyotr Ignatyevitch has nothing of the kind. In short, he is not a master in science, but a journeyman.

Pyotr Ignatyevitch, Nikolay, and I, talk in subdued tones. We are not quite ourselves. There is always a peculiar feeling when one hears through the doors a murmur as of the sea from the lecture-theatre. In the course of thirty years I have not grown accustomed to this feeling, and I experience it every morning. I nervously button up my coat, ask Nikolay unnecessary questions, lose my temper. . . . It is just as though I were frightened; it is not timidity, though, but something different which I can neither describe nor find a name for.

Quite unnecessarily, I look at my watch and say: "Well, it's time to go in."

And we march into the room in the following order: foremost goes Nikolay, with the chemicals and apparatus or with a chart; after him I come; and then the carthorse follows humbly, with hanging head; or, when necessary, a dead body is carried in first on a stretcher, followed by Nikolay, and so on. On my entrance the students all stand up, then they sit down, and the sound as of the sea is suddenly hushed. Stillness reigns.

I know what I am going to lecture about, but I don't know how I am going to lecture, where I am going to begin or with what I am going to end. I haven't a single sentence ready in my head. But I have only to look round the lecture-hall (it is built in the form of an amphitheatre) and utter the stereotyped phrase, "Last lecture we stopped at . . ." when sentences spring up from my soul in a long string, and I am carried away by my own eloquence. I speak with irresistible rapidity and passion, and it seems as though there were no force which could check the flow of my words. To lecture well -- that is, with profit to the listeners and without boring them -- one must have, besides talent, experience and a special knack; one must possess a clear conception of one's own powers, of the audience to which one is lecturing, and of the subject of one's lecture. Moreover, one must be a man who knows what he is doing; one must keep a sharp lookout, and not for one second lose sight of what lies before one.

A good conductor, interpreting the thought of the composer, does twenty things at once: reads the score, waves his baton, watches the singer, makes a motion sideways, first to the drum then to the wind-instruments, and so on. I do just the same when I lecture. Before me a hundred and fifty faces, all unlike one another; three hundred eyes all looking straight into my face. My object is to dominate this many-headed monster. If every moment as I lecture I have a clear vision of the degree of its attention and its power of comprehension, it is in my power. The other foe I have to overcome is in myself. It is the infinite variety of forms, phenomena, laws, and the multitude of ideas of my own and other people's conditioned by them. Every moment I must have the skill to snatch out of that vast mass of material what is most important and necessary, and, as rapidly as my words flow, clothe my thought in a form in which it can be grasped by the monster's intelligence, and may arouse its attention, and at the same time one must keep a sharp lookout that one's thoughts are conveyed, not just as they come, but in a certain order, essential for the correct composition of the picture I wish to sketch. Further, I endeavour to make my diction literary, my definitions brief and precise, my wording, as far as possible, simple and eloquent. Every minute I have to pull myself up and remember that I have only an hour and forty minutes at my disposal. In short, one has one's work cut out. At one and the same minute one has to play the part of savant and teacher and orator, and it's a bad thing if the orator gets the upper hand of the savant or of the teacher in one, or *vice versa.*

You lecture for a quarter of an hour, for half an hour, when you notice that the students are beginning to look at the ceiling, at Pyotr Ignatyevitch; one is feeling for his handkerchief, another shifts in his seat, another smiles at his thoughts. . . . That means that their attention is flagging. Something must be done. Taking advantage of the first opportunity, I make some pun. A broad grin comes on to a hundred and fifty faces, the eyes shine brightly, the sound of the sea is audible for a brief moment. . . . I laugh too. Their attention is refreshed, and I can go on.

No kind of sport, no kind of game or diversion, has ever given me such enjoyment as lecturing. Only at lectures have I been able to abandon myself entirely to passion, and have understood that inspiration is not an invention of the poets, but exists in real life, and I imagine Hercules after the most piquant of his exploits felt just such voluptuous exhaustion as I experience after every lecture.

That was in old times. Now at lectures I feel nothing but torture. Before half an hour is over I am conscious of an overwhelming weakness in my legs and my shoulders. I sit down in my chair, but I am not accustomed to lecture sitting down; a minute later I get up and go on standing, then sit down again. There is a dryness in my mouth, my voice grows husky, my head begins to go round. . . . To conceal my condition from my audience I continually drink water, cough, often blow my nose as though I were hindered by a cold, make puns inappropriately, and in the end break off earlier than I ought to. But above all I am ashamed.

My conscience and my intelligence tell me that the very best thing I could do now would be to deliver a farewell lecture to the boys, to say my last word to them, to bless them, and give up my post to a man younger and stronger than me. But, God, be my judge, I have not manly courage enough to act according to my conscience.

Unfortunately, I am not a philosopher and not a theologian. I know perfectly well that I cannot live more than another six months; it might be supposed that I ought now to be chiefly concerned with the question of the shadowy life beyond the grave, and the visions that will visit my slumbers in the tomb. But for some reason my soul refuses to recognize these questions, though my mind is fully alive to their importance. Just as twenty, thirty years ago, so now, on the threshold of death, I am interested in nothing but science. As I yield up my last breath I shall still believe that science is the most important, the most splendid, the most essential thing in the life of man; that it always has been and will be the highest manifestation of love, and that only by means of it will man conquer himself and nature. This faith is perhaps naive and may rest on false assumptions, but it is not my fault that I believe that and nothing else; I cannot overcome in myself this belief.

But that is not the point. I only ask people to be indulgent to my weakness, and to realize that to tear from the lecture-theatre and his pupils a man who is more interested in the history of the development of the bone medulla than in the final object of creation would be equivalent to taking him and nailing him up in his coffin without waiting for him to be dead.

Sleeplessness and the consequent strain of combating increasing weakness leads to something strange in me. In the middle of my lecture tears suddenly rise in my throat, my eyes begin to smart, and I feel a passionate, hysterical desire to stretch out my hands before me and break into loud lamentation. I want to cry out in a loud voice that I, a famous man, have been sentenced by fate to the death penalty, that within some six months another man will be in control here in the lecture-theatre. I want to shriek that I am poisoned; new ideas such as I have not known before have poisoned the last days of my life, and are still stinging my brain like mosquitoes. And at that moment my position seems to me so awful that I want all my listeners to be horrified, to leap up from their seats and to rush in panic terror, with desperate screams, to the exit.

It is not easy to get through such moments.

II

After my lecture I sit at home and work. I read journals and monographs, or prepare my next lecture; sometimes I write something. I work with interruptions, as I have from time to time to see visitors.

There is a ring at the bell. It is a colleague come to discuss some business matter with me. He comes in to me with his hat and his stick, and, holding out both these objects to me, says:

"Only for a minute! Only for a minute! Sit down, *collega!* Only a couple of words."

To begin with, we both try to show each other that we are extraordinarily polite and highly delighted to see each other. I make him sit down in an easy-chair, and he makes me sit down; as we do so, we cautiously pat each other on the back, touch each other's buttons, and it looks as though we were feeling each other and afraid of scorching our fingers. Both of us laugh, though we say nothing amusing. When we are seated we bow our heads towards each other and begin talking in subdued voices. However affectionately disposed we may be to one another, we cannot help adorning our conversation with all sorts of Chinese mannerisms, such as "As you so justly observed," or "I have already had the honour to inform you"; we cannot help laughing if one of us makes a joke, however unsuccessfully. When we have finished with business my colleague gets up impulsively and, waving his hat in the direction of my work, begins to say good-bye. Again we paw one another and laugh. I see him into the hall; when I assist my colleague to put on his coat, while he does all he can to decline this high honour. Then when Yegor opens the door my colleague declares that I shall catch cold, while I make a show of being ready to go even into the street with him. And when at last I go back into my study my face still goes on smiling, I suppose from inertia.

A little later another ring at the bell. Somebody comes into the hall, and is a long time coughing and taking off his things. Yegor announces a student. I tell him to ask him in. A minute later a young man of agreeable appearance comes in. For the last year he and I have been on strained relations; he answers me disgracefully at the examinations, and I mark him one. Every year I have some seven such hopefuls whom, to express it in the students' slang, I "chivy" or "floor." Those of them who fail in their examination through incapacity or illness usually bear their cross patiently and do not haggle with me; those who come to the house and haggle with me are always youths of sanguine temperament, broad natures, whose failure at examinations spoils their appetites and hinders them from visiting the opera with their usual regularity. I let the first class off easily, but the second I chivy through a whole year.

"Sit down," I say to my visitor; "what have you to tell me?"

"Excuse me, professor, for troubling you," he begins, hesitating, and not looking me in the face. "I would not have ventured to trouble you if it had not been . . . I have been up for your examination five times, and have been ploughed. . . . I beg you, be so good as to mark me for a pass, because . . ."

The argument which all the sluggards bring forward on their own behalf is always the same; they have passed well in all their subjects and have only come to grief in mine, and that is the more surprising because they have always been particularly interested in my subject and knew it so well; their failure has always been entirely owing to some incomprehensible misunderstanding.

"Excuse me, my friend," I say to the visitor; "I cannot mark you for a pass. Go and read up the lectures and come to me again. Then we shall see."

A pause. I feel an impulse to torment the student a little for liking beer and the opera better than science, and I say, with a sigh:

"To my mind, the best thing you can do now is to give up medicine altogether. If, with your abilities, you cannot succeed in passing the examination, it's evident that you have neither the desire nor the vocation for a doctor's calling."

The sanguine youth's face lengthens.

"Excuse me, professor," he laughs, "but that would be odd of me, to say the least of it. After studying for five years, all at once to give it up."

"Oh, well! Better to have lost your five years than have to spend the rest of your life in doing work you do not care for."

But at once I feel sorry for him, and I hasten to add:

"However, as you think best. And so read a little more and come again."

"When?" the idle youth asks in a hollow voice.

"When you like. Tomorrow if you like."

And in his good-natured eyes I read:

"I can come all right, but of course you will plough me again, you beast!"

"Of course," I say, "you won't know more science for going in for my examination another fifteen times, but it is training your character, and you must be thankful for that."

Silence follows. I get up and wait for my visitor to go, but he stands and looks towards the window, fingers his beard, and thinks. It grows boring.

The sanguine youth's voice is pleasant and mellow, his eyes are clever and ironical, his face is genial, though a little bloated from frequent indulgence in beer and overlong lying on the sofa; he looks as though he could tell me a lot of interesting things about the opera, about his affairs of the heart, and about comrades whom he likes. Unluckily, it is not the thing to discuss these subjects, or else I should have been glad to listen to him.

"Professor, I give you my word of honour that if you mark me for a pass I . . . I'll . . ."

As soon as we reach the "word of honour" I wave my hands and sit down to the table. The student ponders a minute longer, and says dejectedly:

"In that case, good-bye. . . I beg your pardon."

"Good-bye, my friend. Good luck to you."

He goes irresolutely into the hall, slowly puts on his outdoor things, and, going out into the street, probably ponders for some time longer; unable to think of anything, except "old devil," inwardly addressed to me, he goes into a wretched restaurant to dine and drink beer, and then home to bed. "Peace be to thy ashes, honest toiler."

A third ring at the bell. A young doctor, in a pair of new black trousers, gold spectacles, and of course a white tie, walks in. He introduces himself. I beg him to be seated, and ask what I can do for him. Not without emotion, the young devotee of science begins telling me that he has passed his examination as a doctor of medicine, and that he has now only to write his dissertation. He would like to work with me under my guidance, and he would be greatly obliged to me if I would give him a subject for his dissertation.

"Very glad to be of use to you, colleague," I say, "but just let us come to an understanding as to the meaning of a dissertation. That word is taken to mean a composition which is a product of independent creative effort. Is that not so? A work written on another man's subject and under another man's guidance is called something different. . . ."

The doctor says nothing. I fly into a rage and jump up from my seat.

"Why is it you all come to me?" I cry angrily. "Do I keep a shop? I don't deal in subjects. For the thousand and oneth time I ask you all to leave me in peace! Excuse my brutality, but I am quite sick of it!"

The doctor remains silent, but a faint flush is apparent on his cheek-bones. His face expresses a profound reverence for my fame and my learning, but from his eyes I can see he feels a contempt for my voice, my pitiful figure, and my nervous gesticulation. I impress him in my anger as a queer fish.

"I don't keep a shop," I go on angrily. "And it is a strange thing! Why don't you want to be independent? Why have you such a distaste for independence?"

I say a great deal, but he still remains silent. By degrees I calm down, and of course give in. The doctor gets a subject from me for his theme not worth a halfpenny, writes under my supervision a dissertation of no use to anyone, with dignity defends it in a dreary discussion, and receives a degree of no use to him.

The rings at the bell may follow one another endlessly, but I will confine my description here to four of them. The bell rings for the fourth time, and I hear familiar footsteps, the rustle of a dress, a dear voice. . . .

Eighteen years ago a colleague of mine, an oculist, died leaving a little daughter Katya, a child of seven, and sixty thousand roubles. In his will he made me the child's guardian. Till she was ten years old Katya lived with us as one of the family, then she was sent to a boarding-school, and only spent the summer holidays with us. I never had time to look after her education. I only superintended it at leisure moments, and so I can say very little about her childhood.

The first thing I remember, and like so much in remembrance, is the extraordinary trustfulness with which she came into our house and let herself be treated by the doctors, a trustfulness which was always shining in her little face. She would sit somewhere out of the way, with her face tied up, invariably watching something with attention; whether she watched me writing or turning over the pages of a book, or watched my wife bustling about, or the cook scrubbing a potato in the kitchen, or the dog playing, her eyes invariably expressed the same thought -- that is, "Everything that is done in this world is nice and sensible." She was curious, and very fond of talking to me. Sometimes she would sit at the table opposite me, watching my movements and asking questions. It interested her to know what I was reading, what I did at the University, whether I was not afraid of the dead bodies, what I did with my salary.

"Do the students fight at the University?" she would ask.

"They do, dear."

"And do you make them go down on their knees?"

"Yes, I do."

And she thought it funny that the students fought and I made them go down on their knees, and she laughed. She was a gentle, patient, good child. It happened not infrequently that I saw something taken away from her, saw her punished without reason, or her curiosity repressed; at such times a look of sadness was mixed with the invariable expression of trustfulness on her face -- that was all. I did not know how to take her part; only when I saw her sad I had an inclination to draw her to me and to commiserate her like some old nurse: "My poor little orphan one!"

I remember, too, that she was fond of fine clothes and of sprinkling herself with scent. In that respect she was like me. I, too, am fond of pretty clothes and nice scent.

I regret that I had not time nor inclination to watch over the rise and development of the passion which took complete possession of Katya when she was fourteen or fifteen. I mean her passionate love for the theatre. When she used to come from boarding-school and stay with us for the summer holidays, she talked of nothing with such pleasure and such warmth as of plays and actors. She bored us with her continual talk of the theatre. My wife and children would not listen to her. I was the only one who had not the courage to refuse to attend to her. When she had a longing to share her transports, she used to come into my study and say in an imploring tone:

"Nikolay Stepanovitch, do let me talk to you about the theatre!"

I pointed to the clock, and said:

"I'll give you half an hour -- begin."

Later on she used to bring with her dozens of portraits of actors and actresses which she worshipped; then she attempted several times to take part in private theatricals, and the upshot of it all was that when she left school she came to me and announced that she was born to be an actress.

I had never shared Katya's inclinations for the theatre. To my mind, if a play is good there is no need to trouble the actors in order that it may make the right impression; it is enough to read it. If the play is poor, no acting will make it good.

In my youth I often visited the theatre, and now my family takes a box twice a year and carries me off for a little distraction. Of course, that is not enough to give me the right to judge of the theatre. In my opinion the theatre has become no better than it was thirty or forty years ago. Just as in the past, I can never find a glass of clean water in the corridors or foyers of the theatre. Just as in the past, the attendants fine me twenty kopecks for my fur coat, though there is nothing reprehensible in wearing a warm coat in winter. As in the past, for no sort of reason, music is played in the intervals, which adds something new and uncalled-for to the impression made by the play. As in the past, men go in the intervals and drink spirits in the buffet. If no progress can be seen in trifles, I should look for it in vain in what is more important. When an actor wrapped from head to foot in stage traditions and conventions tries to recite a simple ordinary speech, "To be or not to be," not simply, but invariably with the accompaniment of hissing and convulsive movements all over his body, or when he tries to convince me at all costs that Tchatsky, who talks so much with fools and is so fond of folly, is a very clever man, and that "Woe from Wit" is not a dull play, the stage gives me the same feeling of conventionality which bored me so much forty years ago when I was regaled with the classical howling and beating on the breast. And every time I come out of the theatre more conservative than I go in.

The sentimental and confiding public may be persuaded that the stage, even in its present form, is a school; but anyone who is familiar with a school in its true sense will not be caught with that bait. I cannot say what will happen in fifty or a hundred years, but in its actual condition the theatre can serve only as an entertainment. But this entertainment is too costly to be frequently enjoyed. It robs the state of thousands of healthy and talented young men and women, who, if they had not devoted themselves to the theatre, might have been good doctors, farmers, schoolmistresses, officers; it robs the public of the evening hours -- the best time for intellectual work and social intercourse. I say nothing of the waste of money and the moral damage to the spectator when he sees murder, fornication, or false witness unsuitably treated on the stage.

Katya was of an entirely different opinion. She assured me that the theatre, even in its present condition, was superior to the lecture-hall, to books, or to anything in the world. The stage was a power that united in itself all the arts, and actors were missionaries. No art nor science was capable of producing so strong and so certain an effect on the soul of man as the stage, and it was with good reason that an actor of medium quality enjoys greater popularity than the greatest savant or artist. And no sort of public service could provide such enjoyment and gratification as the theatre.

And one fine day Katya joined a troupe of actors, and went off, I believe to Ufa, taking away with her a good supply of money, a store of rainbow hopes, and the most aristocratic views of her work.

Her first letters on the journey were marvellous. I read them, and was simply amazed that those small sheets of paper could contain so much youth, purity of spirit, holy innocence, and at the same time subtle and apt judgments which would have done credit to a fine masculine intellect. It was more like a rapturous paean of praise she sent me than a mere description of the Volga, the country, the towns she visited, her companions, her failures and successes; every sentence was fragrant with that confiding trustfulness I was accustomed to read in her face -- and at the same time there were a great many grammatical mistakes, and there was scarcely any punctuation at all.

Before six months had passed I received a highly poetical and enthusiastic letter beginning with the words, "I have come to love . . ." This letter was accompanied by a photograph representing a young man with a shaven face, a wide-brimmed hat, and a plaid flung over his shoulder. The letters that followed were as splendid as before, but now commas and stops made their appearance in them, the grammatical mistakes disappeared, and there was a distinctly masculine flavour about them. Katya began writing to me how splendid it would be to build a great theatre somewhere on the Volga, on a cooperative system, and to attract to the enterprise the rich merchants and the steamer owners; there would be a great deal of money in it; there would be vast audiences; the actors would play on co-operative terms. . . . Possibly all this was really excellent, but it seemed to me that such schemes could only originate from a man's mind.

However that may have been, for a year and a half everything seemed to go well: Katya was in love, believed in her work, and was happy; but then I began to notice in her letters unmistakable signs of falling off. It began with Katya's complaining of her companions -- this was the first and most ominous symptom; if a young scientific or literary man begins his career with bitter complaints of scientific and literary men, it is a sure sign that he is worn out and not fit for his work. Katya wrote to me that her companions did not attend the rehearsals and never knew their parts; that one could see in everyone of them an utter disrespect for the public in the production of absurd plays, and in their behaviour on the stage; that for the benefit of the Actors' Fund, which they only talked about, actresses of the serious drama demeaned themselves by singing chansonettes, while tragic actors sang comic songs making fun of deceived husbands and the pregnant condition of unfaithful wives, and so on. In fact, it was amazing that all this had not yet ruined the provincial stage, and that it could still maintain itself on such a rotten and unsubstantial footing.

In answer I wrote Katya a long and, I must confess, a very boring letter. Among other things, I wrote to her:

"I have more than once happened to converse with old actors, very worthy men, who showed a friendly disposition towards me; from my conversations with them I could understand that their work was controlled not so much by their own intelligence and free choice as by fashion and the mood of the public. The best of them had had to play in their day in tragedy, in operetta, in Parisian farces, and in extravaganzas, and they always seemed equally sure that they were on the right path and that they were of use. So, as you see, the cause of the evil must be sought, not in the actors, but, more deeply, in the art itself and in the attitude of the whole of society to it."

This letter of mine only irritated Katya. She answered me:

"You and I are singing parts out of different operas. I wrote to you, not of the worthy men who showed a friendly disposition to you, but of a band of knaves who have nothing worthy about them. They are a horde of savages who have got on the stage simply because no one would have taken them elsewhere, and who call themselves artists simply because they are impudent. There are numbers of dull-witted creatures, drunkards, intriguing schemers and slanderers, but there is not one person of talent among them. I cannot tell you how bitter it is to me that the art I love has fallen into the hands of people I detest; how bitter it is that the best men look on at evil from afar, not caring to come closer, and, instead of intervening, write ponderous commonplaces and utterly useless sermons. . . ." And so on, all in the same style.

A little time passed, and I got this letter: "I have been brutally deceived. I cannot go on living. Dispose of my money as you think best. I loved you as my father and my only friend. Good-bye."

It turned out that *he,* too, belonged to the "horde of savages." Later on, from certain hints, I gathered that there had been an attempt at suicide. I believe Katya tried to poison herself. I imagine that she must have been seriously ill afterwards, as the next letter I got was from Yalta, where she had most probably been sent by the doctors. Her last letter contained a request to send her a thousand roubles to Yalta as quickly as possible, and ended with these words:

"Excuse the gloominess of this letter; yesterday I buried my child." After spending about a year in the Crimea, she returned home.

She had been about four years on her travels, and during those four years, I must confess, I had played a rather strange and unenviable part in regard to her. When in earlier days she had told me she was going on the stage, and then wrote to me of her love; when she was periodically overcome by extravagance, and I continually had to send her first one and then two thousand roubles; when she wrote to me of her intention of suicide, and then of the death of her baby, every time I lost my head, and all my sympathy for her sufferings found no expression except that, after prolonged reflection, I wrote long, boring letters which I might just as well not have written. And yet I took a father's place with her and loved her like a daughter!

Now Katya is living less than half a mile off. She has taken a flat of five rooms, and has installed herself fairly comfortably and in the taste of the day. If anyone were to undertake to describe her surroundings, the most characteristic note in the picture would be indolence. For the indolent body there are soft lounges, soft stools; for indolent feet soft rugs; for indolent eyes faded, dingy, or flat colours; for the indolent soul the walls are hung with a number of cheap fans and trivial pictures, in which the originality of the execution is more conspicuous than the subject; and the room contains a multitude of little tables and shelves filled with utterly useless articles of no value, and shapeless rags in place of curtains. . . . All this, together with the dread of bright colours, of symmetry, and of empty space, bears witness not only to spiritual indolence, but also to a corruption of natural taste. For days together Katya lies on the lounge reading, principally novels and stories. She only goes out of the house once a day, in the afternoon, to see me.

I go on working while Katya sits silent not far from me on the sofa, wrapping herself in her shawl, as though she were cold. Either because I find her sympathetic or because I was used to her frequent visits when she was a little girl, her presence does not prevent me from concentrating my attention. From time to time I mechanically ask her some question; she gives very brief replies; or, to rest for a minute, I turn round and watch her as she looks dreamily at some medical journal or review. And at such moments I notice that her face has lost the old look of confiding trustfulness. Her expression now is cold, apathetic, and absent-minded, like that of passengers who had to wait too long for a train. She is dressed, as in old days, simply and beautifully, but carelessly; her dress and her hair show visible traces of the sofas and rocking-chairs in which she spends whole days at a stretch. And she has lost the curiosity she had in old days. She has ceased to ask me questions now, as though she had experienced everything in life and looked for nothing new from it.

Towards four o'clock there begins to be sounds of movement in the hall and in the drawing-room. Liza has come back from the Conservatoire, and has brought some girl-friends in with her. We hear them playing on the piano, trying their voices and laughing; in the dining-room Yegor is laying the table, with the clatter of crockery.

"Good-bye," said Katya. "I won't go in and see your people today. They must excuse me. I haven't time. Come and see me."

While I am seeing her to the door, she looks me up and down grimly, and says with vexation:

"You are getting thinner and thinner! Why don't you consult a doctor? I'll call at Sergey Fyodorovitch's and ask him to have a look at you."

"There's no need, Katya."

"I can't think where your people's eyes are! They are a nice lot, I must say!"

She puts on her fur coat abruptly, and as she does so two or three hairpins drop unnoticed on the floor from her carelessly arranged hair. She is too lazy and in too great a hurry to do her hair up; she carelessly stuffs the falling curls under her hat, and goes away.

When I go into the dining-room my wife asks me:

"Was Katya with you just now? Why didn't she come in to see us? It's really strange . . . ."

"Mamma," Liza says to her reproachfully, "let her alone, if she doesn't want to. We are not going down on our knees to her."

"It's very neglectful, anyway. To sit for three hours in the study without remembering our existence! But of course she must do as she likes."

Varya and Liza both hate Katya. This hatred is beyond my comprehension, and probably one would have to be a woman in order to understand it. I am ready to stake my life that of the hundred and fifty young men I see every day in the lecture-theatre, and of the hundred elderly ones I meet every week, hardly one could be found capable of understanding their hatred and aversion for Katya's past -- that is, for her having been a mother without being a wife, and for her having had an illegitimate child; and at the same time I cannot recall one woman or girl of my acquaintance who would not consciously or unconsciously harbour such feelings. And this is not because woman is purer or more virtuous than man: why, virtue and purity are not very different from vice if they are not free from evil feeling. I attribute this simply to the backwardness of woman. The mournful feeling of compassion and the pang of conscience experienced by a modern man at the sight of suffering is, to my mind, far greater proof of culture and moral elevation than hatred and aversion. Woman is as tearful and as coarse in her feelings now as she was in the Middle Ages, and to my thinking those who advise that she should be educated like a man are quite right.

My wife also dislikes Katya for having been an actress, for ingratitude, for pride, for eccentricity, and for the numerous vices which one woman can always find in another.

Besides my wife and daughter and me, there are dining with us two or three of my daughter's friends and Alexandr Adolfovitch Gnekker, her admirer and suitor. He is a fair-haired young man under thirty, of medium height, very stout and broad-shouldered, with red whiskers near his ears, and little waxed moustaches which make his plump smooth face look like a toy. He is dressed in a very short reefer jacket, a flowered waistcoat, breeches very full at the top and very narrow at the ankle, with a large check pattern on them, and yellow boots without heels. He has prominent eyes like a crab's, his cravat is like a crab's neck, and I even fancy there is a smell of crab-soup about the young man's whole person. He visits us every day, but no one in my family knows anything of his origin nor of the place of his education, nor of his means of livelihood. He neither plays nor sings, but has some connection with music and singing, sells somebody's pianos somewhere, is frequently at the Conservatoire, is acquainted with all the celebrities, and is a steward at the concerts; he criticizes music with great authority, and I have noticed that people are eager to agree with him.

Rich people always have dependents hanging about them; the arts and sciences have the same. I believe there is not an art nor a science in the world free from "foreign bodies" after the style of this Mr. Gnekker. I am not a musician, and possibly I am mistaken in regard to Mr. Gnekker, of whom, indeed, I know very little. But his air of authority and the dignity with which he takes his stand beside the piano when anyone is playing or singing strike me as very suspicious.

You may be ever so much of a gentleman and a privy councillor, but if you have a daughter you cannot be secure of immunity from that petty bourgeois atmosphere which is so often brought into your house and into your mood by the attentions of suitors, by matchmaking and marriage. I can never reconcile myself, for instance, to the expression of triumph on my wife's face every time Gnekker is in our company, nor can I reconcile myself to the bottles of Lafitte, port and sherry which are only brought out on his account, that he may see with his own eyes the liberal and luxurious way in which we live. I cannot tolerate the habit of spasmodic laughter Liza has picked up at the Conservatoire, and her way of screwing up her eyes whenever there are men in the room. Above all, I cannot understand why a creature utterly alien to my habits, my studies, my whole manner of life, completely different from the people I like, should come and see me every day, and every day should dine with me. My wife and my servants mysteriously whisper that he is a suitor, but still I don't understand his presence; it rouses in me the same wonder and perplexity as if they were to set a Zulu beside me at the table. And it seems strange to me, too, that my daughter, whom I am used to thinking of as a child, should love that cravat, those eyes, those soft cheeks. . . .

In the old days I used to like my dinner, or at least was indifferent about it; now it excites in me no feeling but weariness and irritation. Ever since I became an "Excellency" and one of the Deans of the Faculty my family has for some reason found it necessary to make a complete change in our menu and dining habits. Instead of the simple dishes to which I was accustomed when I was a student and when I was in practice, now they feed me with a puree with little white things like circles floating about in it, and kidneys stewed in madeira. My rank as a general and my fame have robbed me forever of cabbage-soup and savoury pies, and goose with apple-sauce, and bream with boiled grain. They have robbed me of our maid-servant Agasha, a chatty and laughter-loving old woman, instead of whom Yegor, a dull-witted and conceited fellow with a white glove on his right hand, waits at dinner. The intervals between the courses are short, but they seem immensely long because there is nothing to occupy them. There is none of the gaiety of the old days, the spontaneous talk, the jokes, the laughter; there is nothing of mutual affection and the joy which used to animate the children, my wife, and me when in old days we met together at meals. For me, the celebrated man of science, dinner was a time of rest and reunion, and for my wife and children a fete -- brief indeed, but bright and joyous -- in which they knew that for half an hour I belonged, not to science, not to students, but to them alone. Our real exhilaration from one glass of wine is gone forever, gone is Agasha, gone the bream with boiled grain, gone the uproar that greeted every little startling incident at dinner, such as the cat and dog fighting under the table, or Katya's bandage falling off her face into her soup-plate.

To describe our dinner nowadays is as uninteresting as to eat it. My wife's face wears a look of triumph and affected dignity, and her habitual expression of anxiety. She looks at our plates and says, "I see you don't care for the joint. Tell me; you don't like it, do you?" and I am obliged to answer: "There is no need for you to trouble, my dear; the meat is very nice." And she will say: "You always stand up for me, Nikolay Stepanovitch, and you never tell the truth. Why is Alexandr Adolfovitch eating so little?" And so on in the same style all through dinner. Liza laughs spasmodically and screws up her eyes. I watch them both, and it is only now at dinner that it becomes absolutely evident to me that the inner life of these two has slipped away out of my ken. I have a feeling as though I had once lived at home with a real wife and children and that now I am dining with visitors, in the house of a sham wife who is not the real one, and am looking at a Liza who is not the real Liza. A startling change has taken place in both of them; I have missed the long process by which that change was effected, and it is no wonder that I can make nothing of it. Why did that change take place? I don't know. Perhaps the whole trouble is that God has not given my wife and daughter the same strength of character as me. From childhood I have been accustomed to resisting external influences, and have steeled myself pretty thoroughly. Such catastrophes in life as fame, the rank of a general, the transition from comfort to living beyond our means, acquaintance with celebrities, etc., have scarcely affected me, and I have remained intact and unashamed; but on my wife and Liza, who have not been through the same hardening process and are weak, all this has fallen like an avalanche of snow, overwhelming them. Gnekker and the young ladies talk of fugues, of counterpoint, of singers and pianists, of Bach and Brahms, while my wife, afraid of their suspecting her of ignorance of music, smiles to them sympathetically and mutters: "That's exquisite . . . really! You don't say so! . . . Gnekker eats with solid dignity, jests with solid dignity, and condescendingly listens to the remarks of the young ladies. From time to time he is moved to speak in bad French, and then, for some reason or other, he thinks it necessary to address me as *"Votre Excellence."*

And I am glum. Evidently I am a constraint to them and they are a constraint to me. I have never in my earlier days had a close knowledge of class antagonism, but now I am tormented by something of that sort. I am on the lookout for nothing but bad qualities in Gnekker; I quickly find them, and am fretted at the thought that a man not of my circle is sitting here as my daughter's suitor. His presence has a bad influence on me in other ways, too. As a rule, when I am alone or in the society of people I like, never think of my own achievements, or, if I do recall them, they seem to me as trivial as though I had only completed my studies yesterday; but in the presence of people like Gnekker my achievements in science seem to be a lofty mountain the top of which vanishes into the clouds, while at its foot Gnekkers are running about scarcely visible to the naked eye.

After dinner I go into my study and there smoke my pipe, the only one in the whole day, the sole relic of my old bad habit of smoking from morning till night. While I am smoking my wife comes in and sits down to talk to me. Just as in the morning, I know beforehand what our conversation is going to be about.

"I must talk to you seriously, Nikolay Stepanovitch," she begins. "I mean about Liza. . . . Why don't you pay attention to it?"

"To what?"

"You pretend to notice nothing. But that is not right. We can't shirk responsibility. . . . Gnekker has intentions in regard to Liza. . . . What do you say?"

"That he is a bad man I can't say, because I don't know him, but that I don't like him I have told you a thousand times already."

"But you can't . . . you can't!"

She gets up and walks about in excitement.

"You can't take up that attitude to a serious step," she says. "When it is a question of our daughter's happiness we must lay aside all personal feeling. I know you do not like him. . . . Very good . . . if we refuse him now, if we break it all off, how can you be sure that Liza will not have a grievance against us all her life? Suitors are not plentiful nowadays, goodness knows, and it may happen that no other match will turn up. . . . He is very much in love with Liza, and she seems to like him. . . . Of course, he has no settled position, but that can't be helped. Please God, in time he will get one. He is of good family and well off."

"Where did you learn that?"

"He told us so. His father has a large house in Harkov and an estate in the neighbourhood. In short, Nikolay Stepanovitch, you absolutely must go to Harkov."

"What for?"

"You will find out all about him there. . . . You know the professors there; they will help you. I would go myself, but I am a woman. I cannot. . . ."

"I am not going to Harkov," I say morosely.

My wife is frightened, and a look of intense suffering comes into her face.

"For God's sake, Nikolay Stepanovitch," she implores me, with tears in her voice --"for God's sake, take this burden off me! I am so worried!"

It is painful for me to look at her.

"Very well, Varya," I say affectionately, "if you wish it, then certainly I will go to Harkov and do all you want."

She presses her handkerchief to her eyes and goes off to her room to cry, and I am left alone.

A little later lights are brought in. The armchair and the lamp-shade cast familiar shadows that have long grown wearisome on the walls and on the floor, and when I look at them I feel as though the night had come and with it my accursed sleeplessness. I lie on my bed, then get up and walk about the room, then lie down again. As a rule it is after dinner, at the approach of evening, that my nervous excitement reaches its highest pitch. For no reason I begin crying and burying my head in the pillow. At such times I am afraid that someone may come in; I am afraid of suddenly dying; I am ashamed of my tears, and altogether there is something insufferable in my soul. I feel that I can no longer bear the sight of my lamp, of my books, of the shadows on the floor. I cannot bear the sound of the voices coming from the drawing-room. Some force unseen, uncomprehended, is roughly thrusting me out of my flat. I leap up hurriedly, dress, and cautiously, that my family may not notice, slip out into the street. Where am I to go?

The answer to that question has long been ready in my brain. To Katya.

III

As a rule she is lying on the sofa or in a lounge-chair reading. Seeing me, she raises her head languidly, sits up, and shakes hands.

"You are always lying down," I say, after pausing and taking breath. "That's not good for you. You ought to occupy yourself with something."

"What?"

"I say you ought to occupy yourself in some way."

"With what? A woman can be nothing but a simple workwoman or an actress."

"Well, if you can't be a workwoman, be an actress."

She says nothing.

"You ought to get married," I say, half in jest.

"There is no one to marry. There's no reason to, either."

"You can't live like this."

"Without a husband? Much that matters; I could have as many men as I like if I wanted to."

"That's ugly, Katya."

"What is ugly?"

"Why, what you have just said."

Noticing that I am hurt and wishing to efface the disagreeable impression, Katya says:

"Let us go; come this way."

She takes me into a very snug little room, and says, pointing to the writing-table:

"Look . . . I have got that ready for you. You shall work here. Come here every day and bring your work with you. They only hinder you there at home. Will you work here? Will you like to?"

Not to wound her by refusing, I answer that I will work here, and that I like the room very much. Then we both sit down in the snug little room and begin talking.

The warm, snug surroundings and the presence of a sympathetic person does not, as in old days, arouse in me a feeling of pleasure, but an intense impulse to complain and grumble. I feel for some reason that if I lament and complain I shall feel better.

"Things are in a bad way with me, my dear -- very bad. . . ."

"What is it?"

"You see how it is, my dear; the best and holiest right of kings is the right of mercy. And I have always felt myself a king, since I have made unlimited use of that right. I have never judged, I have been indulgent, I have readily forgiven everyone, right and left. Where others have protested and expressed indignation, I have only advised and persuaded. All my life it has been my endeavour that my society should not be a burden to my family, to my students, to my colleagues, to my servants. And I know that this attitude to people has had a good influence on all who have chanced to come into contact with me. But now I am not a king. Something is happening to me that is only excusable in a slave; day and night my brain is haunted by evil thoughts, and feelings such as I never knew before are brooding in my soul. I am full of hatred, and contempt, and indignation, and loathing, and dread. I have become excessively severe, exacting, irritable, ungracious, suspicious. Even things that in old days would have provoked me only to an unnecessary jest and a good-natured laugh now arouse an oppressive feeling in me. My reasoning, too, has undergone a change: in old days I despised money; now I harbour an evil feeling, not towards money, but towards the rich as though they were to blame: in old days I hated violence and tyranny, but now I hate the men who make use of violence, as though they were alone to blame, and not all of us who do not know how to educate each other. What is the meaning of it? If these new ideas and new feelings have come from a change of convictions, what is that change due to? Can the world have grown worse and I better, or was I blind before and indifferent? If this change is the result of a general decline of physical and intellectual powers -- I am ill, you know, and every day I am losing weight -- my position is pitiable; it means that my new ideas are morbid and abnormal; I ought to be ashamed of them and think them of no consequence. . . ."

"Illness has nothing to do with it," Katya interrupts me; "it's simply that your eyes are opened, that's all. You have seen what in old days, for some reason, you refused to see. To my thinking, what you ought to do first of all, is to break with your family for good, and go away."

"You are talking nonsense."

"You don't love them; why should you force your feelings? Can you call them a family? Nonentities! If they died today, no one would notice their absence tomorrow."

Katya despises my wife and Liza as much as they hate her. One can hardly talk at this date of people's having a right to despise one another. But if one looks at it from Katya's standpoint and recognizes such a right, one can see she has as much right to despise my wife and Liza as they have to hate her.

"Nonentities," she goes on. "Have you had dinner today? How was it they did not forget to tell you it was ready? How is it they still remember your existence?"

"Katya," I say sternly, "I beg you to be silent."

"You think I enjoy talking about them? I should be glad not to know them at all. Listen, my dear: give it all up and go away. Go abroad. The sooner the better."

"What nonsense! What about the University?"

"The University, too. What is it to you? There's no sense in it, anyway. You have been lecturing for thirty years, and where are your pupils? Are many of them celebrated scientific men? Count them up! And to multiply the doctors who exploit ignorance and pile up hundreds of thousands for themselves, there is no need to be a good and talented man. You are not wanted."

"Good heavens! how harsh you are!" I cry in horror. "How harsh you are! Be quiet or I will go away! I don't know how to answer the harsh things you say!"

The maid comes in and summons us to tea. At the samovar our conversation, thank God, changes. After having had my grumble out, I have a longing to give way to another weakness of old age, reminiscences. I tell Katya about my past, and to my great astonishment tell her incidents which, till then, I did not suspect of being still preserved in my memory, and she listens to me with tenderness, with pride, holding her breath. I am particularly fond of telling her how I was educated in a seminary and dreamed of going to the University.

"At times I used to walk about our seminary garden . . ." I would tell her. "If from some faraway tavern the wind floated sounds of a song and the squeaking of an accordion, or a sledge with bells dashed by the garden-fence, it was quite enough to send a rush of happiness, filling not only my heart, but even my stomach, my legs, my arms. . . . I would listen to the accordion or the bells dying away in the distance and imagine myself a doctor, and paint pictures, one better than another. And here, as you see, my dreams have come true. I have had more than I dared to dream of. For thirty years I have been the favourite professor, I have had splendid comrades, I have enjoyed fame and honour. I have loved, married from passionate love, have had children. In fact, looking back upon it, I see my whole life as a fine composition arranged with talent. Now all that is left to me is not to spoil the end. For that I must die like a man. If death is really a thing to dread, I must meet it as a teacher, a man of science, and a citizen of a Christian country ought to meet it, with courage and untroubled soul. But I am spoiling the end; I am sinking, I fly to you, I beg for help, and you tell me 'Sink; that is what you ought to do.' "

But here there comes a ring at the front-door. Katya and I recognize it, and say:

"It must be Mihail Fyodorovitch."

And a minute later my colleague, the philologist Mihail Fyodorovitch, a tall, well-built man of fifty, clean-shaven, with thick grey hair and black eyebrows, walks in. He is a good-natured man and an excellent comrade. He comes of a fortunate and talented old noble family which has played a prominent part in the history of literature and enlightenment. He is himself intelligent, talented, and very highly educated, but has his oddities. To a certain extent we are all odd and all queer fish, but in his oddities there is something exceptional, apt to cause anxiety among his acquaintances. I know a good many people for whom his oddities completely obscure his good qualities.

Coming in to us, he slowly takes off his gloves and says in his velvety bass:

"Good-evening. Are you having tea? That's just right. It's diabolically cold."

Then he sits down to the table, takes a glass, and at once begins talking. What is most characteristic in his manner of talking is the continually jesting tone, a sort of mixture of philosophy and drollery as in Shakespeare's gravediggers. He is always talking about serious things, but he never speaks seriously. His judgments are always harsh and railing, but, thanks to his soft, even, jesting tone, the harshness and abuse do not jar upon the ear, and one soon grows used to them. Every evening he brings with him five or six anecdotes from the University, and he usually begins with them when he sits down to table.

"Oh, Lord!" he sighs, twitching his black eyebrows ironically. "What comic people there are in the world!"

"Well?" asks Katya.

"As I was coming from my lecture this morning I met that old idiot N. N---- on the stairs. . . . He was going along as usual, sticking out his chin like a horse, looking for someone to listen to his grumblings at his migraine, at his wife, and his students who won't attend his lectures. 'Oh,' I thought, 'he has seen me -- I am done for now; it is all up. . . .' "

And so on in the same style. Or he will begin like this:

"I was yesterday at our friend Z. Z----'s public lecture. I wonder how it is our alma mater -- don't speak of it after dark -- dare display in public such noodles and patent dullards as that Z. Z---- Why, he is a European fool! Upon my word, you could not find another like him all over Europe! He lectures -- can you imagine? -- as though he were sucking a sugar-stick -- sue, sue, sue; . . . he is in a nervous funk; he can hardly decipher his own manuscript; his poor little thoughts crawl along like a bishop on a bicycle, and, what's worse, you can never make out what he is trying to say. The deadly dulness is awful, the very flies expire. It can only be compared with the boredom in the assembly-hall at the yearly meeting when the traditional address is read -- damn it!"

And at once an abrupt transition:

"Three years ago -- Nikolay Stepanovitch here will remember it -- I had to deliver that address. It was hot, stifling, my uniform cut me under the arms -- it was deadly! I read for half an hour, for an hour, for an hour and a half, for two hours. . . . 'Come,' I thought; 'thank God, there are only ten pages left!' And at the end there were four pages that there was no need to read, and I reckoned to leave them out. 'So there are only six really,' I thought; 'that is, only six pages left to read.' But, only fancy, I chanced to glance before me, and, sitting in the front row, side by side, were a general with a ribbon on his breast and a bishop. The poor beggars were numb with boredom; they were staring with their eyes wide open to keep awake, and yet they were trying to put on an expression of attention and to pretend that they understood what I was saying and liked it. 'Well,' I thought, 'since you like it you shall have it! I'll pay you out;' so I just gave them those four pages too."

As is usual with ironical people, when he talks nothing in his face smiles but his eyes and eyebrows. At such times there is no trace of hatred or spite in his eyes, but a great deal of humour, and that peculiar fox-like slyness which is only to be noticed in very observant people. Since I am speaking about his eyes, I notice another peculiarity in them. When he takes a glass from Katya, or listens to her speaking, or looks after her as she goes out of the room for a moment, I notice in his eyes something gentle, beseeching, pure. . . .

The maid-servant takes away the samovar and puts on the table a large piece of cheese, some fruit, and a bottle of Crimean champagne -- a rather poor wine of which Katya had grown fond in the Crimea. Mihail Fyodorovitch takes two packs of cards off the whatnot and begins to play patience. According to him, some varieties of patience require great concentration and attention, yet while he lays out the cards he does not leave off distracting his attention with talk. Katya watches his cards attentively, and more by gesture than by words helps him in his play. She drinks no more than a couple of wine-glasses of wine the whole evening; I drink four glasses, and the rest of the bottle falls to the share of Mihail Fyodorovitch, who can drink a great deal and never get drunk.

Over our patience we settle various questions, principally of the higher order, and what we care for most of all -- that is, science and learning -- is more roughly handled than anything.

"Science, thank God, has outlived its day," says Mihail Fyodorovitch emphatically. "Its song is sung. Yes, indeed. Mankind begins to feel impelled to replace it by something different. It has grown on the soil of superstition, been nourished by superstition, and is now just as much the quintessence of superstition as its defunct granddames, alchemy, metaphysics, and philosophy. And, after all, what has it given to mankind? Why, the difference between the learned Europeans and the Chinese who have no science is trifling, purely external. The Chinese know nothing of science, but what have they lost thereby?"

"Flies know nothing of science, either," I observe, "but what of that?"

"There is no need to be angry, Nikolay Stepanovitch. I only say this here between ourselves. . . I am more careful than you think, and I am not going to say this in public -- God forbid! The superstition exists in the multitude that the arts and sciences are superior to agriculture, commerce, superior to handicrafts. Our sect is maintained by that superstition, and it is not for you and me to destroy it. God forbid!"

After patience the younger generation comes in for a dressing too.

"Our audiences have degenerated," sighs Mihail Fyodorovitch. "Not to speak of ideals and all the rest of it, if only they were capable of work and rational thought! In fact, it's a case of 'I look with mournful eyes on the young men of today.' "

"Yes; they have degenerated horribly," Katya agrees. "Tell me, have you had one man of distinction among them for the last five or ten years?"

"I don't know how it is with the other professors, but I can't remember any among mine."

"I have seen in my day many of your students and young scientific men and many actors -- well, I have never once been so fortunate as to meet -- I won't say a hero or a man of talent, but even an interesting man. It's all the same grey mediocrity, puffed up with self-conceit."

All this talk of degeneration always affects me as though I had accidentally overheard offensive talk about my own daughter. It offends me that these charges are wholesale, and rest on such worn-out commonplaces, on such wordy vapourings as degeneration and absence of ideals, or on references to the splendours of the past. Every accusation, even if it is uttered in ladies' society, ought to be formulated with all possible definiteness, or it is not an accusation, but idle disparagement, unworthy of decent people.

I am an old man, I have been lecturing for thirty years, but I notice neither degeneration nor lack of ideals, and I don't find that the present is worse than the past. My porter Nikolay, whose experience of this subject has its value, says that the students of today are neither better nor worse than those of the past.

If I were asked what I don't like in my pupils of today, I should answer the question, not straight off and not at length, but with sufficient definiteness. I know their failings, and so have no need to resort to vague generalities. I don't like their smoking, using spirituous beverages, marrying late, and often being so irresponsible and careless that they will let one of their number be starving in their midst while they neglect to pay their subscriptions to the Students' Aid Society. They don't know modern languages, and they don't express themselves correctly in Russian; no longer ago than yesterday my colleague, the professor of hygiene, complained to me that he had to give twice as many lectures, because the students had a very poor knowledge of physics and were utterly ignorant of meteorology. They are readily carried away by the influence of the last new writers, even when they are not first-rate, but they take absolutely no interest in classics such as Shakespeare, Marcus Aurelius, Epictetus, or Pascal, and this inability to distinguish the great from the small betrays their ignorance of practical life more than anything. All difficult questions that have more or less a social character (for instance the migration question) they settle by studying monographs on the subject, but not by way of scientific investigation or experiment, though that method is at their disposal and is more in keeping with their calling. They gladly become ward-surgeons, assistants, demonstrators, external teachers, and are ready to fill such posts until they are forty, though independence, a sense of freedom and personal initiative, are no less necessary in science than, for instance, in art or commerce. I have pupils and listeners, but no successors and helpers, and so I love them and am touched by them, but am not proud of them. And so on, and so on. . . .

Such shortcomings, however numerous they may be, can only give rise to a pessimistic or fault-finding temper in a faint-hearted and timid man. All these failings have a casual, transitory character, and are completely dependent on conditions of life; in some ten years they will have disappeared or given place to other fresh defects, which are all inevitable and will in their turn alarm the faint-hearted. The students' sins often vex me, but that vexation is nothing in comparison with the joy I have been experiencing now for the last thirty years when I talk to my pupils, lecture to them, watch their relations, and compare them with people not of their circle.

Mihail Fyodorovitch speaks evil of everything. Katya listens, and neither of them notices into what depths the apparently innocent diversion of finding fault with their neighbours is gradually drawing them. They are not conscious how by degrees simple talk passes into malicious mockery and jeering, and how they are both beginning to drop into the habits and methods of slander.

"Killing types one meets with," says Mihail Fyodorovitch. "I went yesterday to our friend Yegor Petrovitch's, and there I found a studious gentleman, one of your medicals in his third year, I believe. Such a face! . . . in theDobrolubov style, the imprint of profound thought on his brow; we got into talk. 'Such doings, young man,' said I. 'I've read,' said I, 'that some German -- I've forgotten his name -- has created from the human brain a new kind of alkaloid, idiotine.' What do you think? He believed it, and there was positively an expression of respect on his face, as though to say, 'See what we fellows can do!' And the other day I went to the theatre. I took my seat. In the next row directly in front of me were sitting two men: one of 'us fellows' and apparently a law student, the other a shaggy-looking figure, a medical student. The latter was as drunk as a cobbler. He did not look at the stage at all. He was dozing with his nose on his shirt-front. But as soon as an actor begins loudly reciting a monologue, or simply raises his voice, our friend starts, pokes his neighbour in the ribs, and asks, 'What is he saying? Is it elevating?' 'Yes,' answers one of our fellows. 'B-r-r-ravo!' roars the medical student. 'Elevating! Bravo!' He had gone to the theatre, you see, the drunken blockhead, not for the sake of art, the play, but for elevation! He wanted noble sentiments."

Katya listens and laughs. She has a strange laugh; she catches her breath in rhythmically regular gasps, very much as though she were playing the accordion, and nothing in her face is laughing but her nostrils. I grow depressed and don't know what to say. Beside myself, I fire up, leap up from my seat, and cry:

"Do leave off! Why are you sitting here like two toads, poisoning the air with your breath? Give over!"

And without waiting for them to finish their gossip I prepare to go home. And, indeed, it is high time: it is past ten.

"I will stay a little longer," says Mihail Fyodorovitch. "Will you allow me, Ekaterina Vladimirovna?"

"I will," answers Katya.

"*Bene!* In that case have up another little bottle."

They both accompany me with candles to the hall, and while I put on my fur coat, Mihail Fyodorovitch says:

"You have grown dreadfully thin and older looking, Nikolay Stepanovitch. What's the matter with you? Are you ill?"

"Yes; I am not very well."

"And you are not doing anything for it. . ." Katya puts in grimly.

"Why don't you? You can't go on like that! God helps those who help themselves, my dear fellow. Remember me to your wife and daughter, and make my apologies for not having been to see them. In a day or two, before I go abroad, I shall come to say good-bye. I shall be sure to. I am going away next week."

I come away from Katya, irritated and alarmed by what has been said about my being ill, and dissatisfied with myself. I ask myself whether I really ought not to consult one of my colleagues. And at once I imagine how my colleague, after listening to me, would walk away to the window without speaking, would think a moment, then would turn round to me and, trying to prevent my reading the truth in his face, would say in a careless tone: "So far I see nothing serious, but at the same time, *collega,* I advise you to lay aside your work. . . ." And that would deprive me of my last hope.

Who is without hope? Now that I am diagnosing my illness and prescribing for myself, from time to time I hope that I am deceived by my own illness, that I am mistaken in regard to the albumen and the sugar I find, and in regard to my heart, and in regard to the swellings I have twice noticed in the mornings; when with the fervour of the hypochondriac I look through the textbooks of therapeutics and take a different medicine every day, I keep fancying that I shall hit upon something comforting. All that is petty.

Whether the sky is covered with clouds or the moon and the stars are shining, I turn my eyes towards it every evening and think that death is taking me soon. One would think that my thoughts at such times ought to be deep as the sky, brilliant, striking. . . . But no! I think about myself, about my wife, about Liza, Gnekker, the students, people in general; my thoughts are evil, petty, I am insincere with myself, and at such times my theory of life may be expressed in the words the celebrated Araktcheev said in one of his intimate letters: "Nothing good can exist in the world without evil, and there is more evil than good." That is, everything is disgusting; there is nothing to live for, and the sixty-two years I have already lived must be reckoned as wasted. I catch myself in these thoughts, and try to persuade myself that they are accidental, temporary, and not deeply rooted in me, but at once I think:

"If so, what drives me every evening to those two toads?"

And I vow to myself that I will never go to Katya's again, though I know I shall go next evening.

Ringing the bell at the door and going upstairs, I feel that I have no family now and no desire to bring it back again. It is clear that the new Araktcheev thoughts are not casual, temporary visitors, but have possession of my whole being. With my conscience ill at ease, dejected, languid, hardly able to move my limbs, feeling as though tons were added to my weight, I get into bed and quickly drop asleep.

And then -- insomnia!

IV

Summer comes on and life is changed.

One fine morning Liza comes in to me and says in a jesting tone:

"Come, your Excellency! We are ready."

My Excellency is conducted into the street, and seated in a cab. As I go along, having nothing to do, I read the signboards from right to left. The word "Traktir" reads "Ritkart"; that would just suit some baron's family: Baroness Ritkart. Farther on I drive through fields, by the graveyard, which makes absolutely no impression on me, though I shall soon lie in it; then I drive by forests and again by fields. There is nothing of interest. After two hours of driving, my Excellency is conducted into the lower storey of a summer villa and installed in a small, very cheerful little room with light blue hangings.

At night there is sleeplessness as before, but in the morning I do not put a good face upon it and listen to my wife, but lie in bed. I do not sleep, but lie in the drowsy, half-conscious condition in which you know you are not asleep, but dreaming. At midday I get up and from habit sit down at my table, but I do not work now; I amuse myself with French books in yellow covers, sent me by Katya. Of course, it would be more patriotic to read Russian authors, but I must confess I cherish no particular liking for them. With the exception of two or three of the older writers, all our literature of today strikes me as not being literature, but a special sort of home industry, which exists simply in order to be encouraged, though people do not readily make use of its products. The very best of these home products cannot be called remarkable and cannot be sincerely praised without qualification. I must say the same of all the literary novelties I have read during the last ten or fifteen years; not one of them is remarkable, and not one of them can be praised without a "but." Cleverness, a good tone, but no talent; talent, a good tone, but no cleverness; or talent, cleverness, but not a good tone.

I don't say the French books have talent, cleverness, and a good tone. They don't satisfy me, either. But they are not so tedious as the Russian, and it is not unusual to find in them the chief element of artistic creation -- the feeling of personal freedom which is lacking in the Russian authors. I don't remember one new book in which the author does not try from the first page to entangle himself in all sorts of conditions and contracts with his conscience. One is afraid to speak of the naked body; another ties himself up hand and foot in psychological analysis; a third must have a "warm attitude to man"; a fourth purposely scrawls whole descriptions of nature that he may not be suspected of writing with a purpose. . . . One is bent upon being middle-class in his work, another must be a nobleman, and so on. There is intentionalness, circumspection, and self-will, but they have neither the independence nor the manliness to write as they like, and therefore there is no creativeness.

All this applies to what is called belles-lettres.

As for serious treatises in Russian on sociology, for instance, on art, and so on, I do not read them simply from timidity. In my childhood and early youth I had for some reason a terror of doorkeepers and attendants at the theatre, and that terror has remained with me to this day. I am afraid of them even now. It is said that we are only afraid of what we do not understand. And, indeed, it is very difficult to understand why doorkeepers and theatre attendants are so dignified, haughty, and majestically rude. I feel exactly the same terror when I read serious articles. Their extraordinary dignity, their bantering lordly tone, their familiar manner to foreign authors, their ability to split straws with dignity -- all that is beyond my understanding; it is intimidating and utterly unlike the quiet, gentlemanly tone to which I am accustomed when I read the works of our medical and scientific writers. It oppresses me to read not only the articles written by serious Russians, but even works translated or edited by them. The pretentious, edifying tone of the preface; the redundancy of remarks made by the translator, which prevent me from concentrating my attention; the question marks and "sic" in parenthesis scattered all over the book or article by the liberal translator, are to my mind an outrage on the author and on my independence as a reader.

Once I was summoned as an expert to a circuit court; in an interval one of my fellow-experts drew my attention to the rudeness of the public prosecutor to the defendants, among whom there were two ladies of good education. I believe I did not exaggerate at all when I told him that the prosecutor s manner was no ruder than that of the authors of serious articles to one another. Their manners are, indeed, so rude that I cannot speak of them without distaste. They treat one another and the writers they criticize either with superfluous respect, at the sacrifice of their own dignity, or, on the contrary, with far more ruthlessness than I have shown in my notes and my thoughts in regard to my future son-in-law Gnekker. Accusations of irrationality, of evil intentions, and, indeed, of every sort of crime, form an habitual ornament of serious articles. And that, as young medical men are fond of saying in their monographs, is the *ultima ratio!* Such ways must infallibly have an effect on the morals of the younger generation of writers, and so I am not at all surprised that in the new works with which our literature has been enriched during the last ten or fifteen years the heroes drink too much vodka and the heroines are not over-chaste.

I read French books, and I look out of the window which is open; I can see the spikes of my garden-fence, two or three scraggy trees, and beyond the fence the road, the fields, and beyond them a broad stretch of pine-wood. Often I admire a boy and girl, both flaxen-headed and ragged, who clamber on the fence and laugh at my baldness. In their shining little eyes I read, "Go up, go up, thou baldhead!" They are almost the only people who care nothing for my celebrity or my rank.

Visitors do not come to me every day now. I will only mention the visits of Nikolay and Pyotr Ignatyevitch. Nikolay usually comes to me on holidays, with some pretext of business, though really to see me. He arrives very much exhilarated, a thing which never occurs to him in the winter.

"What have you to tell me?" I ask, going out to him in the hall.

"Your Excellency!" he says, pressing his hand to his heart and looking at me with the ecstasy of a lover -- "your Excellency! God be my witness! Strike me dead on the spot! *Gaudeamus egitur juventus!*"

And he greedily kisses me on the shoulder, on the sleeve, and on the buttons.

"Is everything going well?" I ask him.

"Your Excellency! So help me God! . . ."

He persists in grovelling before me for no sort of reason, and soon bores me, so I send him away to the kitchen, where they give him dinner.

Pyotr Ignatyevitch comes to see me on holidays, too, with the special object of seeing me and sharing his thoughts with me. He usually sits down near my table, modest, neat, and reasonable, and does not venture to cross his legs or put his elbows on the table. All the time, in a soft, even, little voice, in rounded bookish phrases, he tells me various, to his mind, very interesting and piquant items of news which he has read in the magazines and journals. They are all alike and may be reduced to this type: "A Frenchman has made a discovery; someone else, a German, has denounced him, proving that the discovery was made in 1870 by some American; while a third person, also a German, trumps them both by proving they both had made fools of themselves, mistaking bubbles of air for dark pigment under the microscope. Even when he wants to amuse me, Pyotr Ignatyevitch tells me things in the same lengthy, circumstantial manner as though he were defending a thesis, enumerating in detail the literary sources from which he is deriving his narrative, doing his utmost to be accurate as to the date and number of the journals and the name of everyone concerned, invariably mentioning it in full -- Jean Jacques Petit, never simply Petit. Sometimes he stays to dinner with us, and then during the whole of dinner-time he goes on telling me the same sort of piquant anecdotes, reducing everyone at table to a state of dejected boredom. If Gnekker and Liza begin talking before him of fugues and counterpoint, Brahms and Bach, he drops his eyes modestly, and is overcome with embarrassment; he is ashamed that such trivial subjects should be discussed before such serious people as him and me.

In my present state of mind five minutes of him is enough to sicken me as though I had been seeing and hearing him for an eternity. I hate the poor fellow. His soft, smooth voice and bookish language exhaust me, and his stories stupefy me. . . . He cherishes the best of feelings for me, and talks to me simply in order to give me pleasure, and I repay him by looking at him as though I wanted to hypnotize him, and think, "Go, go, go! . . ." But he is not amenable to thought-suggestion, and sits on and on and on. . . .

While he is with me I can never shake off the thought, "It's possible when I die he will be appointed to succeed me," and my poor lecture-hall presents itself to me as an oasis in which the spring is died up; and I am ungracious, silent, and surly with Pyotr Ignatyevitch, as though he were to blame for such thoughts, and not I myself. When he begins, as usual, praising up the German savants, instead of making fun of him good-humouredly, as I used to do, I mutter sullenly:

"Asses, your Germans! . . ."

That is like the late Professor Nikita Krylov, who once, when he was bathing with Pirogov at Revel and vexed at the water's being very cold, burst out with, "Scoundrels, these Germans!" I behave badly with Pyotr Ignatyevitch, and only when he is going away, and from the window I catch a glimpse of his grey hat behind the garden-fence, I want to call out and say, "Forgive me, my dear fellow!"

Dinner is even drearier than in the winter. Gnekker, whom now I hate and despise, dines with us almost every day. I used to endure his presence in silence, now I aim biting remarks at him which make my wife and daughter blush. Carried away by evil feeling, I often say things that are simply stupid, and I don't know why I say them. So on one occasion it happened that I stared a long time at Gnekker, and, *a propos* of nothing, I fired off:

"An eagle may perchance swoop down below a cock,
But never will the fowl soar upwards to the clouds. . .

And the most vexatious thing is that the fowl Gnekker shows himself much cleverer than the eagle professor. Knowing that my wife and daughter are on his side, he takes up the line of meeting my gibes with condescending silence, as though to say:

"The old chap is in his dotage; what's the use of talking to him?"

Or he makes fun of me good-naturedly. It is wonderful how petty a man may become! I am capable of dreaming all dinner-time of how Gnekker will turn out to be an adventurer, how my wife and Liza will come to see their mistake, and how I will taunt them -- and such absurd thoughts at the time when I am standing with one foot in the grave!

There are now, too, misunderstandings of which in the old days I had no idea except from hearsay. Though I am ashamed of it, I will describe one that occurred the other day after dinner.

I was sitting in my room smoking a pipe; my wife came in as usual, sat down, and began saying what a good thing it would be for me to go to Harkov now while it is warm and I have free time, and there find out what sort of person our Gnekker is.

"Very good; I will go," I assented.

My wife, pleased with me, got up and was going to the door, but turned back and said:

"By the way, I have another favour to ask of you. I know you will be angry, but it is my duty to warn you. . . . Forgive my saying it, Nikolay Stepanovitch, but all our neighbours and acquaintances have begun talking about your being so often at Katya's. She is clever and well-educated; I don't deny that her company may be agreeable; but at your age and with your social position it seems strange that you should find pleasure in her society. . . . Besides, she has such a reputation that . . ."

All the blood suddenly rushed to my brain, my eyes flashed fire, I leaped up and, clutching at my head and stamping my feet, shouted in a voice unlike my own:

"Let me alone! let me alone! let me alone!"

Probably my face was terrible, my voice was strange, for my wife suddenly turned pale and began shrieking aloud in a despairing voice that was utterly unlike her own. Liza, Gnekker, then Yegor, came running in at our shouts. . . .

"Let me alone!" I cried; "let me alone! Go away!"

My legs turned numb as though they had ceased to exist; I felt myself falling into someone's arms; for a little while I still heard weeping, then sank into a swoon which lasted two or three hours.

Now about Katya; she comes to see me every day towards evening, and of course neither the neighbours nor our acquaintances can avoid noticing it. She comes in for a minute and carries me off for a drive with her. She has her own horse and a new chaise bought this summer. Altogether she lives in an expensive style; she has taken a big detached villa with a large garden, and has taken all her town retinue with her -- two maids, a coachman . . . I often ask her:

"Katya, what will you live on when you have spent your father's money?"

"Then we shall see," she answers.

"That money, my dear, deserves to be treated more seriously. It was earned by a good man, by honest labour."

"You have told me that already. I know it."

At first we drive through the open country, then through the pine-wood which is visible from my window. Nature seems to me as beautiful as it always has been, though some evil spirit whispers to me that these pines and fir trees, birds, and white clouds on the sky, will not notice my absence when in three or four months I am dead. Katya loves driving, and she is pleased that it is fine weather and that I am sitting beside her. She is in good spirits and does not say harsh things.

"You are a very good man, Nikolay Stepanovitch," she says. "You are a rare specimen, and there isn't an actor who would understand how to play you. Me or Mihail Fyodorovitch, for instance, any poor actor could do, but not you. And I envy you, I envy you horribly! Do you know what I stand for? What?"

She ponders for a minute, and then asks me:

"Nikolay Stepanovitch, I am a negative phenomenon! Yes?"

"Yes," I answer.

"H'm! what am I to do?"

What answer was I to make her? It is easy to say "work," or "give your possessions to the poor," or "know yourself," and because it is so easy to say that, I don't know what to answer.

My colleagues when they teach therapeutics advise "the individual study of each separate case." One has but to obey this advice to gain the conviction that the methods recommended in the textbooks as the best and as providing a safe basis for treatment turn out to be quite unsuitable in individual cases. It is just the same in moral ailments.

But I must make some answer, and I say:

"You have too much free time, my dear; you absolutely must take up some occupation. After all, why shouldn't you be an actress again if it is your vocation?"

"I cannot!"

"Your tone and manner suggest that you are a victim. I don't like that, my dear; it is your own fault. Remember, you began with falling out with people and methods, but you have done nothing to make either better. You did not struggle with evil, but were cast down by it, and you are not the victim of the struggle, but of your own impotence. Well, of course you were young and inexperienced then; now it may all be different. Yes, really, go on the stage. You will work, you will serve a sacred art."

"Don't pretend, Nikolay Stepanovitch," Katya interrupts me. "Let us make a compact once for all; we will talk about actors, actresses, and authors, but we will let art alone. You are a splendid and rare person, but you don't know enough about art sincerely to think it sacred. You have no instinct or feeling for art. You have been hard at work all your life, and have not had time to acquire that feeling. Altogether . . . I don't like talk about art," she goes on nervously. "I don't like it! And, my goodness, how they have vulgarized it!"

"Who has vulgarized it?"

"They have vulgarized it by drunkenness, the newspapers by their familiar attitude, clever people by philosophy."

"Philosophy has nothing to do with it."

"Yes, it has. If anyone philosophizes about it, it shows he does not understand it."

To avoid bitterness I hasten to change the subject, and then sit a long time silent. Only when we are driving out of the wood and turning towards Katya's villa I go back to my former question, and say:

"You have still not answered me, why you don't want to go on the stage."

"Nikolay Stepanovitch, this is cruel!" she cries, and suddenly flushes all over. "You want me to tell you the truth aloud? Very well, if . . . if you like it! I have no talent! No talent and . . . and a great deal of vanity! So there!"

After making this confession she turns her face away from me, and to hide the trembling of her hands tugs violently at the reins.

As we are driving towards her villa we see Mihail Fyodorovitch walking near the gate, impatiently awaiting us.

"That Mihail Fyodorovitch again!" says Katya with vexation. "Do rid me of him, please! I am sick and tired of him . . . bother him!"

Mihail Fyodorovitch ought to have gone abroad long ago, but he puts off going from week to. week. Of late there have been certain changes in him. He looks, as it were, sunken, has taken to drinking until he is tipsy, a thing which never used to happen to him, and his black eyebrows are beginning to turn grey. When our chaise stops at the gate he does not conceal his joy and his impatience. He fussily helps me and Katya out, hurriedly asks questions, laughs, rubs his hands, and that gentle, imploring, pure expression, which I used to notice only in his eyes, is now suffused all over his face. He is glad and at the same time he is ashamed of his gladness, ashamed of his habit of spending every evening with Katya. And he thinks it necessary to explain his visit by some obvious absurdity such as: "I was driving by, and I thought I would just look in for a minute."

We all three go indoors; first we drink tea, then the familiar packs of cards, the big piece of cheese, the fruit, and the bottle of Crimean champagne are put upon the table. The subjects of our conversation are not new; they are just the same as in the winter. We fall foul of the University, the students, and literature and the theatre; the air grows thick and stifling with evil speaking, and poisoned by the breath, not of two toads as in the winter, but of three. Besides the velvety baritone laugh and the giggle like the gasp of a concertina, the maid who waits upon us hears an unpleasant cracked "He, he!" like the chuckle of a general in a vaudeville.

V

There are terrible nights with thunder, lightning, rain, and wind, such as are called among the people "sparrow nights." There has been one such night in my personal life.

I woke up after midnight and leaped suddenly out of bed. It seemed to me for some reason that I was just immediately going to die. Why did it seem so? I had no sensation in my body that suggested my immediate death, but my soul was oppressed with terror, as though I had suddenly seen a vast menacing glow of fire.

I rapidly struck a light, drank some water straight out of the decanter, then hurried to the open window. The weather outside was magnificent. There was a smell of hay and some other very sweet scent. I could see the spikes of the fence, the gaunt, drowsy trees by the window, the road, the dark streak of woodland, there was a serene, very bright moon in the sky and not a single cloud, perfect stillness, not one leaf stirring. I felt that everything was looking at me and waiting for me to die. . . .

It was uncanny. I closed the window and ran to my bed. I felt for my pulse, and not finding it in my wrist, tried to find it in my temple, then in my chin, and again in my wrist, and everything I touched was cold and clammy with sweat. My breathing came more and more rapidly, my body was shivering, all my inside was in commotion; I had a sensation on my face and on my bald head as though they were covered with spiders' webs.

What should I do? Call my family? No; it would be no use. I could not imagine what my wife and Liza would do when they came in to me.

I hid my head under the pillow, closed my eyes, and waited and waited. . . . My spine was cold; it seemed to be drawn inwards, and I felt as though death were coming upon me stealthily from behind

"Kee-vee! kee-vee!" I heard a sudden shriek in the night's stillness, and did not know where it was -- in my breast or in the street -- "Kee-vee! kee-vee!"

"My God, how terrible!" I would have drunk some more water, but by then it was fearful to open my eyes and I was afraid to raise my head. I was possessed by unaccountable animal terror, and I cannot understand why I was so frightened: was it that I wanted to live, or that some new unknown pain was in store for me?

Upstairs, overhead, someone moaned or laughed. I listened. Soon afterwards there was a sound of footsteps on the stairs. Someone came hurriedly down, then went up again. A minute later there was a sound of steps downstairs again; someone stopped near my door and listened.

"Who is there?" I cried.

The door opened. I boldly opened my eyes, and saw my wife. Her face was pale and her eyes were tear-stained.

"You are not asleep, Nikolay Stepanovitch?" she asked.

"What is it? "

"For God's sake, go up and have a look at Liza; there is something the matter with her. . . ."

"Very good, with pleasure," I muttered, greatly relieved at not being alone. "Very good, this minute. . . ."

I followed my wife, heard what she said to me, and was too agitated to understand a word. Patches of light from her candle danced about the stairs, our long shadows trembled. My feet caught in the skirts of my dressing-gown; I gasped for breath, and felt as though something were pursuing me and trying to catch me from behind.

"I shall die on the spot, here on the staircase," I thought. "On the spot. . . ." But we passed the staircase, the dark corridor with the Italian windows, and went into Liza's room. She was sitting on the bed in her nightdress, with her bare feet hanging down, and she was moaning.

"Oh, my God! Oh, my God!" she was muttering, screwing up her eyes at our candle. "I can't bear it."

"Liza, my child," I said, "what is it?"

Seeing me, she began crying out, and flung herself on my neck.

"My kind papa! . . ." she sobbed -- "my dear, good papa . . . my darling, my pet, I don't know what is the matter with me. . . . I am miserable!"

She hugged me, kissed me, and babbled fond words I used to hear from her when she was a child.

"Calm yourself, my child. God be with you," I said. "There is no need to cry. I am miserable, too."

I tried to tuck her in; my wife gave her water, and we awkwardly stumbled by her bedside; my shoulder jostled against her shoulder, and meanwhile I was thinking how we used to give our children their bath together.

"Help her! help her!" my wife implored me. "Do something!"

What could I do? I could do nothing. There was some load on the girl's heart; but I did not understand, I knew nothing about it, and could only mutter:

"It's nothing, it's nothing; it will pass. Sleep, sleep!"

To make things worse, there was a sudden sound of dogs howling, at first subdued and uncertain, then loud, two dogs howling together. I had never attached significance to such omens as the howling of dogs or the shrieking of owls, but on that occasion it sent a pang to my heart, and I hastened to explain the howl to myself.

"It's nonsense," I thought, "the influence of one organism on another. The intensely strained condition of my nerves has infected my wife, Liza, the dog -- that is all. . . . Such infection explains presentiments, forebodings. . . ."

When a little later I went back to my room to write a prescription for Liza, I no longer thought I should die at once, but only had such a weight, such a feeling of oppression in my soul that I felt actually sorry that I had not died on the spot. For a long time I stood motionless in the middle of the room, pondering what to prescribe for Liza. But the moans overhead ceased, and I decided to prescribe nothing, and yet I went on standing there. . . .

There was a deathlike stillness, such a stillness, as some author has expressed it, "it rang in one's ears." Time passed slowly; the streaks of moonlight on the window-sill did not shift their position, but seemed as though frozen. . . . It was still some time before dawn.

But the gate in the fence creaked, someone stole in and, breaking a twig from one of those scraggy trees, cautiously tapped on the window with it.

"Nikolay Stepanovitch," I heard a whisper. "Nikolay Stepanovitch."

I opened the window, and fancied I was dreaming: under the window, huddled against the wall, stood a woman in a black dress, with the moonlight bright upon her, looking at me with great eyes. Her face was pale, stern, and weird-looking in the moonlight, like marble, her chin was quivering.

"It is I," she said -- " I . . . Katya."

In the moonlight all women's eyes look big and black, all people look taller and paler, and that was probably why I had not recognized her for the first minute.

"What is it?"

"Forgive me! " she said. "I suddenly felt unbearably miserable . . . I couldn't stand it, so came here. There was a light in your window and . . . and I ventured to knock. . . . I beg your pardon. Ah! if you knew how miserable I am! What are you doing just now?"

"Nothing. . . . I can't sleep."

"I had a feeling that there was something wrong, but that is nonsense."

Her brows were lifted, her eyes shone with tears, and her whole face was lighted up with the familiar look of trustfulness which I had not seen for so long.

"Nikolay Stepanovitch," she said imploringly, stretching out both hands to me, "my precious friend, I beg you, I implore you. . . . If you don't despise my affection and respect for you, consent to what I ask of you."

"What is it?"

"Take my money from me!"

"Come! what an idea! What do I want with your money?"

"You'll go away somewhere for your health. . . . You ought to go for your health. Will you take it? Yes? Nikolay Stepanovitch darling, yes?"

She looked greedily into my face and repeated: "Yes, you will take it?"

"No, my dear, I won't take it . . " I said. "Thank you."

She turned her back upon me and bowed her head. Probably I refused her in a tone which made further conversation about money impossible.

"Go home to bed," I said. "We will see each other tomorrow."

"So you don't consider me your friend?" she asked dejectedly.

"I don't say that. But your money would be no use to me now."

"I beg your pardon . . ." she said, dropping her voice a whole octave. "I understand you . . . to be indebted to a person like me . . . a retired actress. . . . But, good-bye. . . ."

And she went away so quickly that I had not time even to say good-bye.

VI

I am in Harkov.

As it would be useless to contend against my present mood and, indeed, beyond my power, I have made up my mind that the last days of my life shall at least be irreproachable externally. If I am unjust in regard to my wife and daughter, which I fully recognize, I will try and do as she wishes; since she wants me to go to Harkov, I go to Harkov. Besides, I have become of late so indifferent to everything that it is really all the same to me where I go, to Harkov, or to Paris, or to Berditchev.

I arrived here at midday, and have put up at the hotel not far from the cathedral. The train was jolting, there were draughts, and now I am sitting on my bed, holding my head and expecting tic douloureux. I ought to have gone today to see some professors of my acquaintance, but I have neither strength nor inclination.

The old corridor attendant comes in and asks whether I have brought my bed-linen. I detain him for five minutes, and put several questions to him about Gnekker, on whose account I have come here. The attendant turns out to be a native of Harkov; he knows the town like the fingers of his hand, but does not remember any household of the surname of Gnekker. I question him about the estate -- the same answer.

The clock in the corridor strikes one, then two, then three. . . . These last months in which I am waiting for death seem much longer than the whole of my life. And I have never before been so ready to resign myself to the slowness of time as now. In the old days, when one sat in the station and waited for a train, or presided in an examination-room, a quarter of an hour would seem an eternity. Now I can sit all night on my bed without moving, and quite unconcernedly reflect that tomorrow will be followed by another night as long and colourless, and the day after tomorrow.

In the corridor it strikes five, six, seven. . . . It grows dark.

There is a dull pain in my cheek, the tic beginning. To occupy myself with thoughts, I go back to my old point of view, when I was not so indifferent, and ask myself why I, a distinguished man, a privy councillor, am sitting in this little hotel room, on this bed with the unfamiliar grey quilt. Why am I looking at that cheap tin washing-stand and listening to the whirr of the wretched clock in the corridor? Is all this in keeping with my fame and my lofty position? And I answer these questions with a jeer. I am amused by the naïveté with which I used in my youth to exaggerate the value of renown and of the exceptional position which celebrities are supposed to enjoy. I am famous, my name is pronounced with reverence, my portrait has been both in the *Niva* and in the *Illustrated News of the World;* I have read my biography even in a German magazine. And what of all that? Here I am sitting utterly alone in a strange town, on a strange bed, rubbing my aching cheek with my hand. . . . Domestic worries, the hard-heartedness of creditors, the rudeness of the railway servants, the inconveniences of thepassport system, the expensive and unwholesome food in the refreshment-rooms, the general rudeness and coarseness in social intercourse -- all this, and a great deal more which would take too long to reckon up, affects me as much as any working man who is famous only in his alley. In what way, does my exceptional position find expression? Admitting that I am celebrated a thousand times over, that I am a hero of whom my country is proud. They publish bulletins of my illness in every paper, letters of sympathy come to me by post from my colleagues, my pupils, the general public; but all that does not prevent me from dying in a strange bed, in misery, in utter loneliness. Of course, no one is to blame for that; but I in my foolishness dislike my popularity. I feel as though it had cheated me.

At ten o'clock I fall asleep, and in spite of the tic I sleep soundly, and should have gone on sleeping if I had not been awakened. Soon after one came a sudden knock at the door.

"Who is there?"

"A telegram."

"You might have waited till tomorrow," I say angrily, taking the telegram from the attendant. "Now I shall not get to sleep again."

"I am sorry. Your light was burning, so I thought you were not asleep."

I tear open the telegram and look first at the signature. From my wife.

"What does she want?"

"Gnekker was secretly married to Liza yesterday. Return."

I read the telegram, and my dismay does not last long. I am dismayed, not by what Liza and Gnekker have done, but by the indifference with which I hear of their marriage. They say philosophers and the truly wise are indifferent. It is false: indifference is the paralysis of the soul; it is premature death.

I go to bed again, and begin trying to think of something to occupy my mind. What am I to think about? I feel as though everything had been thought over already and there is nothing which could hold my attention now.

When daylight comes I sit up in bed with my arms round my knees, and to pass the time I try to know myself. "Know thyself" is excellent and useful advice; it is only a pity that the ancients never thought to indicate the means of following this precept.

When I have wanted to understand somebody or myself I have considered, not the actions, in which everything is relative, but the desires.

"Tell me what you want, and I will tell you what manner of man you are."

And now I examine myself: what do I want?

I want our wives, our children, our friends, our pupils, to love in us, not our fame, not the brand and not the label, but to love us as ordinary men. Anything else? I should like to have had helpers and successors. Anything else? I should like to wake up in a hundred years' time and to have just a peep out of one eye at what is happening in science. I should have liked to have lived another ten years. . . What further? Why, nothing further. I think and think, and can think of nothing more. And however much I might think, and however far my thoughts might travel, it is clear to me that there is nothing vital, nothing of great importance in my desires. In my passion for science, in my desire to live, in this sitting on a strange bed, and in this striving to know myself -- in all the thoughts, feelings, and ideas I form about everything, there is no common bond to connect it all into one whole. Every feeling and every thought exists apart in me; and in all my criticisms of science, the theatre, literature, my pupils, and in all the pictures my imagination draws, even the most skilful analyst could not find what is called a general idea, or the god of a living man.

And if there is not that, then there is nothing.

In a state so poverty-stricken, a serious ailment, the fear of death, the influences of circumstance and men were enough to turn upside down and scatter in fragments all which I had once looked upon as my theory of life, and in which I had seen the meaning and joy of my existence. So there is nothing surprising in the fact that I have over-shadowed the last months of my life with thoughts and feelings only worthy of a slave and barbarian, and that now I am indifferent and take no heed of the dawn. When a man has not in him what is loftier and mightier than all external impressions a bad cold is really enough to upset his equilibrium and make him begin to see an owl in every bird, to hear a dog howling in every sound. And all his pessimism or optimism with his thoughts great and small have at such times significance as symptoms and nothing more.

I am vanquished. If it is so, it is useless to think, it is useless to talk. I will sit and wait in silence for what is to come.

In the morning the corridor attendant brings me tea and a copy of the local newspaper. Mechanically I read the advertisements on the first page, the leading article, the extracts from the newspapers and journals, the chronicle of events. . . . In the latter I find, among other things, the following paragraph: "Our distinguished savant, Professor Nikolay Stepanovitch So-and-so, arrived yesterday in Harkov, and is staying in the So-and-so Hotel."

Apparently, illustrious names are created to live on their own account, apart from those that bear them. Now my name is promenading tranquilly about Harkov; in another three months, printed in gold letters on my monument, it will shine bright as the sun itself, while I shall be already under the moss.

A light tap at the door. Somebody wants me.

"Who is there? Come in."

The door opens, and I step back surprised and hurriedly wrap my dressing-gown round me. Before me stands Katya.

"How do you do?" she says, breathless with running upstairs. "You didn't expect me? I have come here, too. . . . I have come, too!"

She sits down and goes on, hesitating and not looking at me.

"Why don't you speak to me? I have come, too . . . today. . . . I found out that you were in this hotel, and have come to you."

"Very glad to see you," I say, shrugging my shoulders, "but I am surprised. You seem to have dropped from the skies. What have you come for?"

"Oh . . . I've simply come."

Silence. Suddenly she jumps up impulsively and comes to me.

"Nikolay Stepanovitch," she says, turning pale and pressing her hands on her bosom -- "Nikolay Stepanovitch, I cannot go on living like this! I cannot! For God's sake tell me quickly, this minute, what I am to do! Tell me, what am I to do?"

"What can I tell you?" I ask in perplexity. "I can do nothing."

"Tell me, I beseech you," she goes on, breathing hard and trembling all over. "I swear that I cannot go on living like this. It's too much for me!"

She sinks on a chair and begins sobbing. She flings her head back, wrings her hands, taps with her feet; her hat falls off and hangs bobbing on its elastic; her hair is ruffled.

"Help me! help me! "she implores me. "I cannot go on!"

She takes her handkerchief out of her travelling-bag, and with it pulls out several letters, which fall from her lap to the floor. I pick them up, and on one of them I recognize the handwriting of Mihail Fyodorovitch and accidentally read a bit of a word "passionat. . ."

"There is nothing I can tell you, Katya," I say.

"Help me!" she sobs, clutching at my hand and kissing it. "You are my father, you know, my only friend! You are clever, educated; you have lived so long; you have been a teacher! Tell me, what am I to do?"

"Upon my word, Katya, I don't know. . . ."

I am utterly at a loss and confused, touched by her sobs, and hardly able to stand.

"Let us have lunch, Katya," I say, with a forced smile. "Give over crying."

And at once I add in a sinking voice:

"I shall soon be gone, Katya. . . ."

"Only one word, only one word!" she weeps, stretching out her hands to me.

"What am I to do?"

"You are a queer girl, really . . ." I mutter. "I don't understand it! So sensible, and all at once crying your eyes out. . . ."

A silence follows. Katya straightens her hair, puts on her hat, then crumples up the letters and stuffs them in her bag -- and all this deliberately, in silence. Her face, her bosom, and her gloves are wet with tears, but her expression now is cold and forbidding. . . . I look at her, and feel ashamed that I am happier than she. The absence of what my philosophic colleagues call a general idea I have detected in myself only just before death, in the decline of my days, while the soul of this poor girl has known and will know no refuge all her life, all her life!

"Let us have lunch, Katya," I say.

"No, thank you," she answers coldly. Another minute passes in silence. "I don't like Harkov," I say; "it's so grey here -- such a grey town."

"Yes, perhaps. . . . It's ugly. I am here not for long, passing through. I am going on today."

"Where?"

"To the Crimea . . . that is, to the Caucasus."

"Oh! For long?"

"I don't know."

Katya gets up, and, with a cold smile, holds out her hand without looking at me.

I want to ask her, "Then, you won't be at my funeral?" but she does not look at me; her hand is cold and, as it were, strange. I escort her to the door in silence. She goes out, walks down the long corridor without looking back; she knows that I am looking after her, and most likely she will look back at the turn.

No, she did not look back. I've seen her black dress for the last time: her steps have died away. Farewell, my treasure!

THE HORSE-STEALERS

A hospital assistant, called Yergunov, an empty-headed fellow, known throughout the district as a great braggart and drunkard, was returning one evening in Christmas week from the hamlet of Ryepino, where he had been to make some purchases for the hospital. That he might get home in good time and not be late, the doctor had lent him his very best horse.

At first it had been a still day, but at eight o'clock a violent snow-storm came on, and when he was only about four miles from home Yergunov completely lost his way.

He did not know how to drive, he did not know the road, and he drove on at random, hoping that the horse would find the way of itself. Two hours passed; the horse was exhausted, he himself was chilled, and already began to fancy that he was not going home, but back towards Ryepino. But at last above the uproar of the storm he heard the far-away barking of a dog, and a murky red blur came into sight ahead of him: little by little, the outlines of a high gate could be discerned, then a long fence on which there were nails with their points uppermost, and beyond the fence there stood the slanting crane of a well. The wind drove away the mist of snow from before the eyes, and where there had been a red blur, there sprang up a small, squat little house with a steep thatched roof. Of the three little windows one, covered on the inside with something red, was lighted up.

What sort of place was it? Yergunov remembered that to the right of the road, three and a half or four miles from the hospital, there was Andrey Tchirikov's tavern. He remembered, too, that this Tchirikov, who had been lately killed by some sledge-drivers, had left a wife and a daughter called Lyubka, who had come to the hospital two years before as a patient. The inn had a bad reputation, and to visit it late in the evening, and especially with someone else's horse, was not free from risk. But there was no help for it. Yergunov fumbled in his knapsack for his revolver, and, coughing sternly, tapped at the window-frame with his whip.

"Hey! who is within?" he cried. "Hey, granny! let me come in and get warm!"

With a hoarse bark a black dog rolled like a ball under the horse's feet, then another white one, then another black one -- there must have been a dozen of them. Yergunov looked to see which was the biggest, swung his whip and lashed at it with all his might. A small, long-legged puppy turned its sharp muzzle upwards and set up a shrill, piercing howl.

Yergunov stood for a long while at the window, tapping. But at last the hoar-frost on the trees near the house glowed red, and a muffled female figure appeared with a lantern in her hands.

"Let me in to get warm, granny," said Yergunov. "I was driving to the hospital, and I have lost my way. It's such weather, God preserve us. Don't be afraid; we are your own people, granny."

"All my own people are at home, and we didn't invite strangers," said the figure grimly. "And what are you knocking for? The gate is not locked."

Yergunov drove into the yard and stopped at the steps.

"Bid your labourer take my horse out, granny," said he.

"I am not granny."

And indeed she was not a granny. While she was putting out the lantern the light fell on her face, and Yergunov saw black eyebrows, and recognized Lyubka.

"There are no labourers about now," she said as she went into the house. "Some are drunk and asleep, and some have been gone to Ryepino since the morning. It's a holiday. . . ."

As he fastened his horse up in the shed, Yergunov heard a neigh, and distinguished in the darkness another horse, and felt on it a Cossack saddle. So there must be someone else in the house besides the woman and her daughter. For greater security Yergunov unsaddled his horse, and when he went into the house, took with him both his purchases and his saddle.

The first room into which he went was large and very hot, and smelt of freshly washed floors. A short, lean peasant of about forty, with a small, fair beard, wearing a dark blue shirt, was sitting at the table under the holy images. It was Kalashnikov, an arrant scoundrel and horse-stealer, whose father and uncle kept a tavern in Bogalyovka, and disposed of the stolen horses where they could. He too had been to the hospital more than once, not for medical treatment, but to see the doctor about horses -- to ask whether he had not one for sale, and whether his honour would not like to swop his bay mare for a dun-coloured gelding. Now his head was pomaded and a silver ear-ring glittered in his ear, and altogether he had a holiday air. Frowning and dropping his lower lip, he was looking intently at a big dog's-eared picture-book. Another peasant lay stretched on the floor near the stove; his head, his shoulders, and his chest were covered with a sheepskin -- he was probably asleep; beside his new boots, with shining bits of metal on the heels, there were two dark pools of melted snow.

Seeing the hospital assistant, Kalashnikov greeted him.

"Yes, it is weather," said Yergunov, rubbing his chilled knees with his open hands. "The snow is up to one's neck; I am soaked to the skin, I can tell you. And I believe my revolver is, too. . . ."

He took out his revolver, looked it all over, and put it back in his knapsack. But the revolver made no impression at all; the peasant went on looking at the book.

"Yes, it is weather. . . . I lost my way, and if it had not been for the dogs here, I do believe it would have been my death. There would have been a nice to-do. And where are the women?"

"The old woman has gone to Ryepino, and the girl is getting supper ready . . ." answered Kalashnikov.

Silence followed. Yergunov, shivering and gasping, breathed on his hands, huddled up, and made a show of being very cold and exhausted. The still angry dogs could be heard howling outside. It was dreary.

"You come from Bogalyovka, don't you?" he asked the peasant sternly.

"Yes, from Bogalyovka."

And to while away the time Yergunov began to think about Bogalyovka. It was a big village and it lay in a deep ravine, so that when one drove along the highroad on a moonlight night, and looked down into the dark ravine and then up at the sky, it seemed as though the moon were hanging over a bottomless abyss and it were the end of the world. The path going down was steep, winding, and so narrow that when one drove down to Bogalyovka on account of some epidemic or to vaccinate the people, one had to shout at the top of one's voice, or whistle all the way, for if one met a cart coming up one could not pass. The peasants of Bogalyovka had the reputation of being good gardeners and horse-stealers. They had well-stocked gardens. In spring the whole village was buried in white cherry-blossom, and in the summer they sold cherries at three kopecks a pail. One could pay three kopecks and pick as one liked. Their women were handsome and looked well fed, they were fond of finery, and never did anything even on working-days, but spent all their time sitting on the ledge in front of their houses and searching in each other's heads.

But at last there was the sound of footsteps. Lyubka, a girl of twenty, with bare feet and a red dress, came into the room. . . . She looked sideways at Yergunov and walked twice from one end of the room to the other. She did not move simply, but with tiny steps, thrusting forward her bosom; evidently she enjoyed padding about with her bare feet on the freshly washed floor, and had taken off her shoes on purpose.

Kalashnikov laughed at something and beckoned her with his finger. She went up to the table, and he showed her a picture of the Prophet Elijah, who, driving three horses abreast, was dashing up to the sky. Lyubka put her elbow on the table; her plait fell across her shoulder -- a long chestnut plait tied with red ribbon at the end -- and it almost touched the floor. She, too, smiled.

"A splendid, wonderful picture," said Kalashnikov. "Wonderful," he repeated, and motioned with his hand as though he wanted to take the reins instead of Elijah.

The wind howled in the stove; something growled and squeaked as though a big dog had strangled a rat.

"Ugh! the unclean spirits are abroad!" said Lyubka.

"That's the wind," said Kalashnikov; and after a pause he raised his eyes to Yergunov and asked:

"And what is your learned opinion, Osip Vassilyitch -- are there devils in this world or not? "

"What's one to say, brother?" said Yergunov, and he shrugged one shoulder. "If one reasons from science, of course there are no devils, for it's a superstition; but if one looks at it simply, as you and I do now, there are devils, to put it shortly. . . . I have seen a great deal in my life. . . . When I finished my studies I served as medical assistant in the army in a regiment of the dragoons, and I have been in the war, of course. I have a medal and a decoration from the Red Cross, but after the treaty of San Stefano I returned to Russia and went into the service of the Zemstvo. And in consequence of my enormous circulation about the world, I may say I have seen more than many another has dreamed of. It has happened to me to see devils, too; that is, not devils with horns and a tail -- that is all nonsense -- but just, to speak precisely, something of the sort."

"Where?" asked Kalashnikov.

"In various places. There is no need to go far. Last year I met him here -- speak of him not at night -- near this very inn. I was driving, I remember, to Golyshino; I was going there to vaccinate. Of course, as usual, I had the racing droshky and a horse, and all the necessary paraphernalia, and, what's more, I had a watch and all the rest of it, so I was on my guard as I drove along, for fear of some mischance. There are lots of tramps of all sorts. I came up to the Zmeinoy Ravine -- damnation take it -- and was just going down it, when all at once somebody comes up to me -- such a fellow! Black hair, black eyes, and his whole face looked smutted with soot. . . . He comes straight up to the horse and takes hold of the left rein: 'Stop!' He looked at the horse, then at me, then dropped the reins, and without saying a bad word, 'Where are you going?' says he. And he showed his teeth in a grin, and his eyes were spiteful-looking.

'Ah,' thought I, 'you are a queer customer!' 'I am going to vaccinate for the smallpox,' said I. 'And what is that to you?' 'Well, if that's so,' says he, 'vaccinate me. He bared his arm and thrust it under my nose. Of course, I did not bandy words with him; I just vaccinated him to get rid of him. Afterwards I looked at my lancet and it had gone rusty."

The peasant who was asleep near the stove suddenly turned over and flung off the sheepskin; to his great surprise, Yergunov recognized the stranger he had met that day at Zmeinoy Ravine. This peasant's hair, beard, and eyes were black as soot; his face was swarthy; and, to add to the effect, there was a black spot the size of a lentil on his right cheek. He looked mockingly at the hospital assistant and said:

"I did take hold of the left rein -- that was so; but about the smallpox you are lying, sir. And there was not a word said about the smallpox between us."

Yergunov was disconcerted.

"I'm not talking about you," he said. "Lie down, since you are lying down."

The dark-skinned peasant had never been to the hospital, and Yergunov did not know who he was or where he came from; and now, looking at him, he made up his mind that the man must be a gypsy. The peasant got up and, stretching and yawning loudly, went up to Lyubka and Kalashnikov, and sat down beside them, and he, too, began looking at the book. His sleepy face softened and a look of envy came into it.

"Look, Merik," Lyubka said to him; "get me such horses and I will drive to heaven."

"Sinners can't drive to heaven," said Kalashnikov. "That's for holiness."

Then Lyubka laid the table and brought in a big piece of fat bacon, salted cucumbers, a wooden platter of boiled meat cut up into little pieces, then a frying-pan, in which there were sausages and cabbage spluttering. A cut-glass decanter of vodka, which diffused a smell of orange-peel all over the room when it was poured out, was put on the table also.

Yergunov was annoyed that Kalashnikov and the dark fellow Merik talked together and took no notice of him at all, behaving exactly as though he were not in the room. And he wanted to talk to them, to brag, to drink, to have a good meal, and if possible to have a little fun with Lyubka, who sat down near him half a dozen times while they were at supper, and, as though by accident, brushed against him with her handsome shoulders and passed her hands over her broad hips. She was a healthy, active girl, always laughing and never still: she would sit down, then get up, and when she was sitting down she would keep turning first her face and then her back to her neighbour, like a fidgety child, and never failed to brush against him with her elbows or her knees.

And he was displeased, too, that the peasants drank only a glass each and no more, and it was awkward for him to drink alone. But he could not refrain from taking a second glass, all the same, then a third, and he ate all the sausage. He brought himself to flatter the peasants, that they might accept him as one of the party instead of holding him at arm's length.

"You are a fine set of fellows in Bogalyovka!" he said, and wagged his head.

"In what way fine fellows?" enquired Kalashnikov.

"Why, about horses, for instance. Fine fellows at stealing!"

"H'm! fine fellows, you call them. Nothing but thieves and drunkards."

"They have had their day, but it is over," said Merik, after a pause. "But now they have only Filya left, and he is blind."

"Yes, there is no one but Filya," said Kalashnikov, with a sigh. "Reckon it up, he must be seventy; the German settlers knocked out one of his eyes, and he does not see well with the other. It is cataract. In old days the police officer would shout as soon as he saw him: 'Hey, you Shamil!' and all the peasants called him that -- he was Shamil all over the place; and now his only name is One-eyed Filya. But he was a fine fellow! Lyuba's father, Andrey Grigoritch, and he stole one night into Rozhnovo -- there were cavalry regiments stationed there -- and carried off nine of the soldiers' horses, the very best of them. They weren't frightened of the sentry, and in the morning they sold all the horses for twenty roubles to the gypsy Afonka. Yes! But nowadays a man contrives to carry off a horse whose rider is drunk or asleep, and has no fear of God, but will take the very boots from a drunkard, and then slinks off and goes away a hundred and fifty miles with a horse, and haggles at the market, haggles like a Jew, till the policeman catches him, the fool. There is no fun in it; it is simply a disgrace! A paltry set of people, I must say."

"What about Merik?" asked Lyubka.

"Merik is not one of us," said Kalashnikov. "He is a Harkov man from Mizhiritch. But that he is a bold fellow, that's the truth; there's no gainsaying that he is a fine fellow."

Lyubka looked slily and gleefully at Merik, and said:

"It wasn't for nothing they dipped him in a hole in the ice."

"How was that?" asked Yergunov.

"It was like this . . ." said Merik, and he laughed. "Filya carried off three horses from the Samoylenka tenants, and they pitched upon me. There were ten of the tenants at Samoylenka, and with their labourers there were thirty altogether, and all of them Molokans. . . . So one of them says to me at the market: 'Come and have a look, Merik; we have brought some new horses from the fair.' I was interested, of course. I went up to them, and the whole lot of them, thirty men, tied my hands behind me and led me to the river. 'We'll show you fine horses,' they said. One hole in the ice was there already; they cut another beside it seven feet away. Then, to be sure, they took a cord and put a noose under my armpits, and tied a crooked stick to the other end, long enough to reach both holes. They thrust the stick in and dragged it through. I went plop into the ice-hole just as I was, in my fur coat and my high boots, while they stood and shoved me, one with his foot and one with his stick, then dragged me under the ice and pulled me out of the other hole."

Lyubka shuddered and shrugged.

"At first I was in a fever from the cold," Merik went on, "but when they pulled me out I was helpless, and lay in the snow, and the Molokans stood round and hit me with sticks on my knees and my elbows. It hurt fearfully. They beat me and they went away . . . and everything on me was frozen, my clothes were covered with ice. I got up, but I couldn't move. Thank God, a woman drove by and gave me a lift."

Meanwhile Yergunov had drunk five or six glasses of vodka; his heart felt lighter, and he longed to tell some extraordinary, wonderful story too, and to show that he, too, was a bold fellow and not afraid of anything.

"I'll tell you what happened to us in Penza Province . . ." he began.

Either because he had drunk a great deal and was a little tipsy, or perhaps because he had twice been detected in a lie, the peasants took not the slightest notice of him, and even left off answering his questions. What was worse, they permitted themselves a frankness in his presence that made him feel uncomfortable and cold all over, and that meant that they took no notice of him.

Kalashnikov had the dignified manners of a sedate and sensible man; he spoke weightily, and made the sign of the cross over his mouth every time he yawned, and no one could have supposed that this was a thief, a heartless thief who had stripped poor creatures, who had already been twice in prison, and who had been sentenced by the commune to exile in Siberia, and had been bought off by his father and uncle, who were as great thieves and rogues as he was. Merik gave himself the airs of a bravo. He saw that Lyubka and Kalashnikov were admiring him, and looked upon himself as a very fine fellow, and put his arms akimbo, squared his chest, or stretched so that the bench creaked under him. . . .

After supper Kalashnikov prayed to the holy image without getting up from his seat, and shook hands with Merik; the latter prayed too, and shook Kalashnikov's hand. Lyubka cleared away the supper, shook out on the table some peppermint biscuits, dried nuts, and pumpkin seeds, and placed two bottles of sweet wine.

"The kingdom of heaven and peace everlasting to Andrey Grigoritch," said Kalashnikov, clinking glasses with Merik. "When he was alive we used to gather together here or at his brother Martin's, and -- my word! my word! what men, what talks! Remarkable conversations! Martin used to be here, and Filya, and Fyodor Stukotey. . . . It was all done in style, it was all in keeping. . . . And what fun we had! We did have fun, we did have fun!"

Lyubka went out and soon afterwards came back wearing a green kerchief and beads.

"Look, Merik, what Kalashnikov brought me to-day," she said.

She looked at herself in the looking-glass, and tossed her head several times to make the beads jingle. And then she opened a chest and began taking out, first, a cotton dress with red and blue flowers on it, and then a red one with flounces which rustled and crackled like paper, then a new kerchief, dark blue, shot with many colours -- and all these things she showed and flung up her hands, laughing as though astonished that she had such treasures.

Kalashnikov tuned the balalaika and began playing it, but Yergunov could not make out what sort of song he was singing, and whether it was gay or melancholy, because at one moment it was so mournful he wanted to cry, and at the next it would be merry. Merik suddenly jumped up and began tapping with his heels on the same spot, then, brandishing his arms, he moved on his heels from the table to the stove, from the stove to the chest, then he bounded up as though he had been stung, clicked the heels of his boots together in the air, and began going round and round in a crouching position. Lyubka waved both her arms, uttered a desperate shriek, and followed him. At first she moved sideways, like a snake, as though she wanted to steal up to someone and strike him from behind. She tapped rapidly with her bare heels as Merik had done with the heels of his boots, then she turned round and round like a top and crouched down, and her red dress was blown out like a bell. Merik, looking angrily at her, and showing his teeth in a grin, flew towards her in the same crouching posture as though he wanted to crush her with his terrible legs, while she jumped up, flung back her head, and waving her arms as a big bird does its wings, floated across the room scarcely touching the floor. . . .

"What a flame of a girl!" thought Yergunov, sitting on the chest, and from there watching the dance. "What fire! Give up everything for her, and it would be too little . . . ."

And he regretted that he was a hospital assistant, and not a simple peasant, that he wore a reefer coat and a chain with a gilt key on it instead of a blue shirt with a cord tied round the waist. Then he could boldly have sung, danced, flung both arms round Lyubka as Merik did. . . .

The sharp tapping, shouts, and whoops set the crockery ringing in the cupboard and the flame of the candle dancing.

The thread broke and the beads were scattered all over the floor, the green kerchief slipped off, and Lyubka was transformed into a red cloud flitting by and flashing black eyes, and it seemed as though in another second Merik's arms and legs would drop off.

But finally Merik stamped for the last time, and stood still as though turned to stone. Exhausted and almost breathless, Lyubka sank on to his bosom and leaned against him as against a post, and he put his arms round her, and looking into her eyes, said tenderly and caressingly, as though in jest:

"I'll find out where your old mother's money is hidden, I'll murder her and cut your little throat for you, and after that I will set fire to the inn. . . . People will think you have perished in the fire, and with your money I shall go to Kuban. I'll keep droves of horses and flocks of sheep. . . ."

Lyubka made no answer, but only looked at him with a guilty air, and asked:

"And is it nice in Kuban, Merik?"

He said nothing, but went to the chest, sat down, and sank into thought; most likely he was dreaming of Kuban.

"It's time for me to be going," said Kalashnikov, getting up. "Filya must be waiting for me. Goodbye, Lyuba."

Yergunov went out into the yard to see that Kalashnikov did not go off with his horse. The snowstorm still persisted. White clouds were floating about the yard, their long tails clinging to the rough grass and the bushes, while on the other side of the fence in the open country huge giants in white robes with wide sleeves were whirling round and falling to the ground, and getting up again to wave their arms and fight. And the wind, the wind! The bare birches and cherry-trees, unable to endure its rude caresses, bowed low down to the ground and wailed: "God, for what sin hast Thou bound us to the earth and will not let us go free?"

"Wo!" said Kalashnikov sternly, and he got on his horse; one half of the gate was opened, and by it lay a high snowdrift. "Well, get on!" shouted Kalashnikov. His little short-legged nag set off, and sank up to its stomach in the drift at once. Kalashnikov was white all over with the snow, and soon vanished from sight with his horse.

When Yergunov went back into the room, Lyubka was creeping about the floor picking up her beads; Merik was not there.

"A splendid girl!" thought Yergunov, as he lay down on the bench and put his coat under his head. "Oh, if only Merik were not here." Lyubka excited him as she crept about the floor by the bench, and he thought that if Merik had not been there he would certainly have got up and embraced her, and then one would see what would happen. It was true she was only a girl, but not likely to be chaste; and even if she were -- need one stand on ceremony in a den of thieves? Lyubka collected her beads and went out. The candle burnt down and the flame caught the paper in the candlestick. Yergunov laid his revolver and matches beside him, and put out the candle. The light before the holy images flickered so much that it hurt his eyes, and patches of light danced on the ceiling, on the floor, and on the cupboard, and among them he had visions of Lyubka, buxom, full-bosomed: now she was turning round like a top, now she was exhausted and breathless. . . .

"Oh, if the devils would carry off that Merik," he thought.

The little lamp gave a last flicker, spluttered, and went out. Someone, it must have been Merik, came into the room and sat down on the bench. He puffed at his pipe, and for an instant lighted up a dark cheek with a patch on it. Yergunov's throat was irritated by the horrible fumes of the tobacco smoke.

"What filthy tobacco you have got -- damnation take it!" said Yergunov. "It makes me positively sick."

"I mix my tobacco with the flowers of the oats," answered Merik after a pause. "It is better for the chest."

He smoked, spat, and went out again. Half an hour passed, and all at once there was the gleam of a light in the passage. Merik appeared in a coat and cap, then Lyubka with a candle in her hand.

"Do stay, Merik," said Lyubka in an imploring voice.

"No, Lyuba, don't keep me."

"Listen, Merik," said Lyubka, and her voice grew soft and tender. "I know you will find mother's money, and will do for her and for me, and will go to Kuban and love other girls; but God be with you. I only ask you one thing, sweetheart: do stay!"

"No, I want some fun . . ." said Merik, fastening his belt.

"But you have nothing to go on. . . . You came on foot; what are you going on?"

Merik bent down to Lyubka and whispered something in her ear; she looked towards the door and laughed through her tears.

"He is asleep, the puffed-up devil . . ." she said.

Merik embraced her, kissed her vigorously, and went out. Yergunov thrust his revolver into his pocket, jumped up, and ran after him.

"Get out of the way!" he said to Lyubka, who hurriedly bolted the door of the entry and stood across the threshold. "Let me pass! Why are you standing here?"

"What do you want to go out for?"

"To have a look at my horse."

Lyubka gazed up at him with a sly and caressing look.

"Why look at it? You had better look at me . . . ." she said, then she bent down and touched with her finger the gilt watch-key that hung on his chain.

"Let me pass, or he will go off on my horse," said Yergunov. "Let me go, you devil!" he shouted, and giving her an angry blow on the shoulder, he pressed his chest against her with all his might to push her away from the door, but she kept tight hold of the bolt, and was like iron.

"Let me go!" he shouted, exhausted; "he will go off with it, I tell you."

"Why should he? He won't." Breathing hard and rubbing her shoulder, which hurt, she looked up at him again, flushed a little and laughed. "Don't go away, dear heart," she said; "I am dull alone."

Yergunov looked into her eyes, hesitated, and put his arms round her; she did not resist.

"Come, no nonsense; let me go," he begged her. She did not speak.

"I heard you just now," he said, "telling Merik that you love him.

"I dare say. . . . My heart knows who it is I love."

She put her finger on the key again, and said softly: "Give me that."

Yergunov unfastened the key and gave it to her. She suddenly craned her neck and listened with a grave face, and her expression struck Yergunov as cold and cunning; he thought of his horse, and now easily pushed her aside and ran out into the yard. In the shed a sleepy pig was grunting with lazy regularity and a cow was knocking her horn. Yergunov lighted a match and saw the pig, and the cow, and the dogs, which rushed at him on all sides at seeing the light, but there was no trace of the horse. Shouting and waving his arms at the dogs, stumbling over the drifts and sticking in the snow, he ran out at the gate and fell to gazing into the darkness. He strained his eyes to the utmost, and saw only the snow flying and the snowflakes distinctly forming into all sorts of shapes; at one moment the white, laughing face of a corpse would peep out of the darkness, at the next a white horse would gallop by with an Amazon in a muslin dress upon it, at the next a string of white swans would fly overhead. . . . Shaking with anger and cold, and not knowing what to do, Yergunov fired his revolver at the dogs, and did not hit one of them; then he rushed back to the house.

When he went into the entry he distinctly heard someone scurry out of the room and bang the door. It was dark in the room. Yergunov pushed against the door; it was locked. Then, lighting match after match, he rushed back into the entry, from there into the kitchen, and from the kitchen into a little room where all the walls were hung with petticoats and dresses, where there was a smell of cornflowers and fennel, and a bedstead with a perfect mountain of pillows, standing in the corner by the stove; this must have been the old mother's room. From there he passed into another little room, and here he saw Lyubka. She was lying on a chest, covered with a gay-coloured patchwork cotton quilt, pretending to be asleep. A little ikon-lamp was burning in the corner above the pillow.

"Where is my horse?" Yergunov asked.

Lyubka did not stir.

"Where is my horse, I am asking you?" Yergunov repeated still more sternly, and he tore the quilt off her. "I am asking you, she-devil!" he shouted.

She jumped up on her knees, and with one hand holding her shift and with the other trying to clutch the quilt, huddled against the wall. . . . She looked at Yergunov with repulsion and terror in her eyes, and, like a wild beast in a trap, kept cunning watch on his faintest movement.

"Tell me where my horse is, or I'll knock the life out of you," shouted Yergunov.

"Get away, dirty brute!" she said in a hoarse voice.

Yergunov seized her by the shift near the neck and tore it. And then he could not restrain himself, and with all his might embraced the girl. But hissing with fury, she slipped out of his arms, and freeing one hand -- the other was tangled in the torn shift -- hit him a blow with her fist on the skull.

His head was dizzy with the pain, there was a ringing and rattling in his ears, he staggered back, and at that moment received another blow -- this time on the temple. Reeling and clutching at the doorposts, that he might not fall, he made his way to the room where his things were, and lay down on the bench; then after lying for a little time, took the matchbox out of his pocket and began lighting match after match for no object: he lit it, blew it out, and threw it under the table, and went on till all the matches were gone.

Meanwhile the air began to turn blue outside, the cocks began to crow, but his head still ached, and there was an uproar in his ears as though he were sitting under a railway bridge and hearing the trains passing over his head. He got, somehow, into his coat and cap; the saddle and the bundle of his purchases he could not find, his knapsack was empty: it was not for nothing that someone had scurried out of the room when he came in from the yard.

He took a poker from the kitchen to keep off the dogs, and went out into the yard, leaving the door open. The snow-storm had subsided and it was calm outside. . . . When he went out at the gate, the white plain looked dead, and there was not a single bird in the morning sky. On both sides of the road and in the distance there were bluish patches of young copse.

Yergunov began thinking how he would be greeted at the hospital and what the doctor would say to him; it was absolutely necessary to think of that, and to prepare beforehand to answer questions he would be asked, but this thought grew blurred and slipped away. He walked along thinking of nothing but Lyubka, of the peasants with whom he had passed the night; he remembered how, after Lyubka struck him the second time, she had bent down to the floor for the quilt, and how her loose hair had fallen on the floor. His mind was in a maze, and he wondered why there were in the world doctors, hospital assistants, merchants, clerks, and peasants instead of simple free men? There are, to be sure, free birds, free beasts, a free Merik, and they are not afraid of anyone, and don't need anyone! And whose idea was it, who had decreed that one must get up in the morning, dine at midday, go to bed in the evening; that a doctor takes precedence of a hospital assistant; that one must live in rooms and love only one's wife? And why not the contrary -- dine at night and sleep in the day? Ah, to jump on a horse without enquiring whose it is, to ride races with the wind like a devil, over fields and forests and ravines, to make love to girls, to mock at everyone. . . .

Yergunov thrust the poker into the snow, pressed his forehead to the cold white trunk of a birch-tree, and sank into thought; and his grey, monotonous life, his wages, his subordinate position, the dispensary, the everlasting to-do with the bottles and blisters, struck him as contemptible, sickening.

"Who says it's a sin to enjoy oneself?" he asked himself with vexation. "Those who say that have never lived in freedom like Merik and Kalashnikov, and have never loved Lyubka; they have been beggars all their lives, have lived without any pleasure, and have only loved their wives, who are like frogs."

And he thought about himself that he had not hitherto been a thief, a swindler, or even a brigand, simply because he could not, or had not yet met with a suitable opportunity.

A year and a half passed. In spring, after Easter, Yergunov, who had long before been dismissed from the hospital and was hanging about without a job, came out of the tavern in Ryepino and sauntered aimlessly along the street.

He went out into the open country. Here there was the scent of spring, and a warm caressing wind was blowing. The calm, starry night looked down from the sky on the earth. My God, how infinite the depth of the sky, and with what fathomless immensity it stretched over the world! The world is created well enough, only why and with what right do people, thought Yergunov, divide their fellows into the sober and the drunken, the employed and the dismissed, and so on. Why do the sober and well fed sleep comfortably in their homes while the drunken and the hungry must wander about the country without a refuge? Why was it that if anyone had not a job and did not get a salary he had to go hungry, without clothes and boots? Whose idea was it? Why was it the birds and the wild beasts in the woods did not have jobs and get salaries, but lived as they pleased?

Far away in the sky a beautiful crimson glow lay quivering, stretched wide over the horizon. Yergunov stopped, and for a long time he gazed at it, and kept wondering why was it that if he had carried off someone else's samovar the day before and sold it for drink in the taverns it would be a sin? Why was it?

Two carts drove by on the road; in one of them there was a woman asleep, in the other sat an old man without a cap on.

"Grandfather, where is that fire?" asked Yergunov.

"Andrey Tchirikov's inn," answered the old man.

And Yergunov recalled what had happened to him eighteen months before in the winter, in that very inn, and how Merik had boasted; and he imagined the old woman and Lyubka, with their throats cut, burning, and he envied Merik. And when he walked back to the tavern, looking at the houses of the rich publicans, cattle-dealers, and blacksmiths, he reflected how nice it would be to steal by night into some rich man's house!

GUSEV

I

It was getting dark; it would soon be night.

Gusev, a discharged soldier, sat up in his hammock and said in an undertone:

"I say, Pavel Ivanitch. A soldier at Sutchan told me: while they were sailing a big fish came into collision with their ship and stove a hole in it."

The nondescript individual whom he was addressing, and whom everyone in the ship's hospital called Pavel Ivanitch, was silent, as though he had not heard.

And again a stillness followed. . . The wind frolicked with the rigging, the screw throbbed, the waves lashed, the hammocks creaked, but the ear had long ago become accustomed to these sounds, and it seemed that everything around was asleep and silent. It was dreary. The three invalids -- two soldiers and a sailor -- who had been playing cards all the day were asleep and talking in their dreams.

It seemed as though the ship were beginning to rock. The hammock slowly rose and fell under Gusev, as though it were heaving a sigh, and this was repeated once, twice, three times. . . . Something crashed on to the floor with a clang: it must have been a jug falling down.

"The wind has broken loose from its chain. . ." said Gusev, listening.

This time Pavel Ivanitch cleared his throat and answered irritably:

"One minute a vessel's running into a fish, the next, the wind's breaking loose from its chain. Is the wind a beast that it can break loose from its chain?"

"That's how christened folk talk."

"They are as ignorant as you are then. They say all sorts of things. One must keep a head on one's shoulders and use one's reason. You are a senseless creature."

Pavel Ivanitch was subject to sea-sickness. When the sea was rough he was usually ill-humoured, and the merest trifle would make him irritable. And in Gusev's opinion there was absolutely nothing to be vexed about. What was there strange or wonderful, for instance, in the fish or in the wind's breaking loose from its chain? Suppose the fish were as big as a mountain and its back were as hard as a sturgeon: and in the same way, supposing that away yonder at the end of the world there stood great stone walls and the fierce winds were chained up to the walls . . . if they had not broken loose, why did they tear about all over the sea like maniacs, and struggle to escape like dogs? If they were not chained up, what did become of them when it was calm?

Gusev pondered for a long time about fishes as big as a mountain and stout, rusty chains, then he began to feel dull and thought of his native place to which he was returning after five years' service in the East. He pictured an immense pond covered with snow. . . . On one side of the pond the red-brick building of the potteries with a tall chimney and clouds of black smoke; on the other side -- a village. . . . His brother Alexey comes out in a sledge from the fifth yard from the end; behind him sits his little son Vanka in big felt over-boots, and his little girl Akulka, also in big felt boots. Alexey has been drinking, Vanka is laughing, Akulka's face he could not see, she had muffled herself up.

"You never know, he'll get the children frozen . . ." thought Gusev. "Lord send them sense and judgment that they may honour their father and mother and not be wiser than their parents."

"They want re-soleing," a delirious sailor says in a bass voice. "Yes, yes!"

Gusev's thoughts break off, and instead of a pond there suddenly appears apropos of nothing a huge bull's head without eyes, and the horse and sledge are not driving along, but are whirling round and round in a cloud of smoke. But still he was glad he had seen his own folks. He held his breath from delight, shudders ran all over him, and his fingers twitched.

"The Lord let us meet again," he muttered feverishly, but he at once opened his eyes and sought in the darkness for water.

He drank and lay back, and again the sledge was moving, then again the bull's head without eyes, smoke, clouds. . . . And so on till daybreak.

II

The first outline visible in the darkness was a blue circle -- the little round window; then little by little Gusev could distinguish his neighbour in the next hammock, Pavel Ivanitch. The man slept sitting up, as he could not breathe lying down. His face was grey, his nose was long and sharp, his eyes looked huge from the terrible thinness of his face, his temples were sunken, his beard was skimpy, his hair was long. . . . Looking at him you could not make out of what class he was, whether he were a gentleman, a merchant, or a peasant. Judging from his expression and his long hair he might have been a hermit or a lay brother in a monastery -- but if one listened to what he said it seemed that he could not be a monk. He was worn out by his cough and his illness and by the stifling heat, and breathed with difficulty, moving his parched lips. Noticing that Gusev was looking at him he turned his face towards him and said:

"I begin to guess. . . . Yes. . . . I understand it all perfectly now."

"What do you understand, Pavel Ivanitch?"

"I'll tell you. . . . It has always seemed to me strange that terribly ill as you are you should be here in a steamer where it is so hot and stifling and we are always being tossed up and down, where, in fact, everything threatens you with death; now it is all clear to me. . . . Yes. . . . Your doctors put you on the steamer to get rid of you. They get sick of looking after poor brutes like you. . . . You don't pay them anything, they have a bother with you, and you damage their records with your deaths -- so, of course, you are brutes! It's not difficult to get rid of you. . . . All that is necessary is, in the first place, to have no conscience or humanity, and, secondly, to deceive the steamer authorities. The first condition need hardly be considered, in that respect we are artists; and one can always succeed in the second with a little practice. In a crowd of four hundred healthy soldiers and sailors half a dozen sick ones are not conspicuous; well, they drove you all on to the steamer, mixed you with the healthy ones, hurriedly counted you over, and in the confusion nothing amiss was noticed, and when the steamer had started they saw that there were paralytics and consumptives in the last stage lying about on the deck. . . ."

Gusev did not understand Pavel Ivanitch; but supposing he was being blamed, he said in self-defence:

"I lay on the deck because I had not the strength to stand; when we were unloaded from the barge on to the ship I caught a fearful chill."

"It's revolting," Pavel Ivanitch went on. "The worst of it is they know perfectly well that you can't last out the long journey, and yet they put you here. Supposing you get as far as the Indian Ocean, what then? It's horrible to think of it. . . . And that's their gratitude for your faithful, irreproachable service!"

Pavel Ivanitch's eyes looked angry; he frowned contemptuously and said, gasping:

"Those are the people who ought to be plucked in the newspapers till the feathers fly in all directions."

The two sick soldiers and the sailor were awake and already playing cards. The sailor was half reclining in his hammock, the soldiers were sitting near him on the floor in the most uncomfortable attitudes. One of the soldiers had his right arm in a sling, and the hand was swathed up in a regular bundle so that he held his cards under his right arm or in the crook of his elbow while he played with the left. The ship was rolling heavily. They could not stand up, nor drink tea, nor take their medicines.

"Were you an officer's servant?" Pavel Ivanitch asked Gusev.

"Yes, an officer's servant."

"My God, my God!" said Pavel Ivanitch, and he shook his head mournfully. "To tear a man out of his home, drag him twelve thousand miles away, then to drive him into consumption and. . . and what is it all for, one wonders? To turn him into a servant for some Captain Kopeikin or midshipman Dirka! How logical!"

"It's not hard work, Pavel Ivanitch. You get up in the morning and clean the boots, get the samovar, sweep the rooms, and then you have nothing more to do. The lieutenant is all the day drawing plans, and if you like you can say your prayers, if you like you can read a book or go out into the street. God grant everyone such a life."

"Yes, very nice, the lieutenant draws plans all the day and you sit in the kitchen and pine for home. . . . Plans indeed! . . . It is not plans that matter, but a human life. Life is not given twice, it must be treated mercifully."

"Of course, Pavel Ivanitch, a bad man gets no mercy anywhere, neither at home nor in the army, but if you live as you ought and obey orders, who has any need to insult you? The officers are educated gentlemen, they understand. . . . In five years I was never once in prison, and I was never struck a blow, so help me God, but once."

"What for?"

"For fighting. I have a heavy hand, Pavel Ivanitch. Four Chinamen came into our yard; they were bringing firewood or something, I don't remember. Well, I was bored and I knocked them about a bit, one's nose began bleeding, damn the fellow. . . . The lieutenant saw it through the little window, he was angry and gave me a box on the ear."

"Foolish, pitiful man . . ." whispered Pavel Ivanitch. "You don't understand anything."

He was utterly exhausted by the tossing of the ship and closed his eyes; his head alternately fell back and dropped forward on his breast. Several times he tried to lie down but nothing came of it; his difficulty in breathing prevented it.

"And what did you hit the four Chinamen for?" he asked a little while afterwards.

"Oh, nothing. They came into the yard and I hit them."

And a stillness followed. . . . The card-players had been playing for two hours with enthusiasm and loud abuse of one another, but the motion of the ship overcame them, too; they threw aside the cards and lay down. Again Gusev saw the big pond, the brick building, the village. . . . Again the sledge was coming along, again Vanka was laughing and Akulka, silly little thing, threw open her fur coat and stuck her feet out, as much as to say: "Look, good people, my snowboots are not like Vanka's, they are new ones."

"Five years old, and she has no sense yet," Gusev muttered in delirium. "Instead of kicking your legs you had better come and get your soldier uncle a drink. I will give you something nice."

Then Andron with a flintlock gun on his shoulder was carrying a hare he had killed, and he was followed by the decrepit old Jew Isaitchik, who offers to barter the hare for a piece of soap; then the black calf in the shed, then Domna sewing at a shirt and crying about something, and then again the bull's head without eyes, black smoke. . . .

Overhead someone gave a loud shout, several sailors ran by, they seemed to be dragging something bulky over the deck, something fell with a crash. Again they ran by. . . . Had something gone wrong? Gusev raised his head, listened, and saw that the two soldiers and the sailor were playing cards again; Pavel Ivanitch was sitting up moving his lips. It was stifling, one hadn't strength to breathe, one was thirsty, the water was warm, disgusting. The ship heaved as much as ever.

Suddenly something strange happened to one of the soldiers playing cards. . . . He called hearts diamonds, got muddled in his score, and dropped his cards, then with a frightened, foolish smile looked round at all of them.

"I shan't be a minute, mates, I'll . . ." he said, and lay down on the floor.

Everybody was amazed. They called to him, he did not answer.

"Stephan, maybe you are feeling bad, eh?" the soldier with his arm in a sling asked him. "Perhaps we had better bring the priest, eh?"

"Have a drink of water, Stepan . . ." said the sailor. "Here, lad, drink."

"Why are you knocking the jug against his teeth?" said Gusev angrily. " Don't you see, turnip head?'

"What?"

"What?" Gusev repeated, mimicking him. "There is no breath in him, he is dead! That's what! What nonsensical people, Lord have mercy on us. . . !"

III

The ship was not rocking and Pavel Ivanitch was more cheerful. He was no longer ill-humoured. His face had a boastful, defiant, mocking expression. He looked as though he wanted to say: "Yes, in a minute I will tell you something that will make you split your sides with laughing." The little round window was open and a soft breeze was blowing on Pavel Ivanitch. There was a sound of voices, of the plash of oars in the water. . . .

Just under the little window someone began droning in a high, unpleasant voice: no doubt it was a Chinaman singing.

"Here we are in the harbour," said Pavel Ivanitch, smiling ironically. "Only another month and we shall be in Russia. Well, worthy gentlemen and warriors! I shall arrive at Odessa and from there go straight to Harkov. In Harkov I have a friend, a literary man. I shall go to him and say, 'Come, old man, put aside your horrid subjects, ladies' amours and the beauties of nature, and show up human depravity.' "

For a minute he pondered, then said:

"Gusev, do you know how I took them in?"

"Took in whom, Pavel Ivanitch?"

"Why, these fellows. . . . You know that on this steamer there is only a first-class and a third-class, and they only allow peasants -- that is the rift-raft -- to go in the third. If you have got on a reefer jacket and have the faintest resemblance to a gentleman or a bourgeois you must go first-class, if you please. You must fork out five hundred roubles if you die for it. Why, I ask, have you made such a rule? Do you want to raise the prestige of educated Russians thereby? Not a bit of it. We don't let you go third-class simply because a decent person can't go third-class; it is very horrible and disgusting. Yes, indeed. I am very grateful for such solicitude for decent people's welfare. But in any case, whether it is nasty there or nice, five hundred roubles I haven't got. I haven't pilfered government money. I haven't exploited the natives, I haven't trafficked in contraband, I have flogged no one to death, so judge whether I have the right to travel first-class and even less to reckon myself of the educated class? But you won't catch them with logic. . . . One has to resort to deception. I put on a workman's coat and high boots, I assumed a drunken, servile mug and went to the agents: 'Give us a little ticket, your honour,' said I. . . ."

"Why, what class do you belong to?" asked a sailor.

"Clerical. My father was an honest priest, he always told the great ones of the world the truth to their faces; and he had a great deal to put up with in consequence."

Pavel Ivanitch was exhausted with talking and gasped for breath, but still went on:

"Yes, I always tell people the truth to their faces. I am not afraid of anyone or anything. There is a vast difference between me and all of you in that respect. You are in darkness, you are blind, crushed; you see nothing and what you do see you don't understand. . . . You are told the wind breaks loose from its chain, that you are beasts, Petchenyegs, and you believe it; they punch you in the neck, you kiss their hands; some animal in a sable-lined coat robs you and then tips you fifteen kopecks and you: 'Let me kiss your hand, sir.' You are pariahs, pitiful people. . . . I am a different sort. My eyes are open, I see it all as clearly as a hawk or an eagle when it floats over the earth, and I understand it all. I am a living protest. I see irresponsible tyranny -- I protest. I see cant and hypocrisy -- I protest. I see swine triumphant -- I protest. And I cannot be suppressed, no Spanish Inquisition can make me hold my tongue. No. . . . Cut out my tongue and I would protest in dumb show; shut me up in a cellar -- I will shout from it to be heard half a mile away, or I will starve myself to death that they may have another weight on their black consciences. Kill me and I will haunt them with my ghost. All my acquaintances say to me: 'You are a most insufferable person, Pavel Ivanitch.' I am proud of such a reputation. I have served three years in the far East, and I shall be remembered there for a hundred years: I had rows with everyone. My friends write to me from Russia, 'Don't come back,' but here I am going back to spite them . . . yes. . . . That is life as I understand it. That is what one can call life."

Gusev was looking at the little window and was not listening. A boat was swaying on the transparent, soft, turquoise water all bathed in hot, dazzling sunshine. In it there were naked Chinamen holding up cages with canaries and calling out:

"It sings, it sings!"

Another boat knocked against the first; the steam cutter darted by. And then there came another boat with a fat Chinaman sitting in it, eating rice with little sticks.

Languidly the water heaved, languidly the white seagulls floated over it.

"I should like to give that fat fellow one in the neck," thought Gusev, gazing at the stout Chinaman, with a yawn.

He dozed off, and it seemed to him that all nature was dozing, too. Time flew swiftly by; imperceptibly the day passed, imperceptibly the darkness came on. . . . The steamer was no longer standing still, but moving on further.

IV

Two days passed, Pavel Ivanitch lay down instead of sitting up; his eyes were closed, his nose seemed to have grown sharper.

"Pavel Ivanitch," Gusev called to him. "Hey, Pavel Ivanitch."

Pavel Ivanitch opened his eyes and moved his lips.

"Are you feeling bad?"

"No . . . it's nothing . . ." answered Pavel Ivanitch, gasping. "Nothing; on the contrary -- I am rather better. . . . You see I can lie down. I am a little easier. . . ."

"Well, thank God for that, Pavel Ivanitch."

"When I compare myself with you I am sorry for you . . . poor fellow. My lungs are all right, it is only a stomach cough. . . . I can stand hell, let alone the Red Sea. Besides I take a critical attitude to my illness and to the medicines they give me for it. While you . . . you are in darkness. . . . It's hard for you, very, very hard!"

The ship was not rolling, it was calm, but as hot and stifling as a bath-house; it was not only hard to speak but even hard to listen. Gusev hugged his knees, laid his head on them and thought of his home. Good heavens, what a relief it was to think of snow and cold in that stifling heat! You drive in a sledge, all at once the horses take fright at something and bolt. . . . Regardless of the road, the ditches, the ravines, they dash like mad things, right through the village, over the pond by the pottery works, out across the open fields. "Hold on," the pottery hands and the peasants shout, meeting them. "Hold on." But why? Let the keen, cold wind beat in one's face and bite one's hands; let the lumps of snow, kicked up by the horses' hoofs, fall on one's cap, on one's back, down one's collar, on one's chest; let the runners ring on the snow, and the traces and the sledge be smashed, deuce take them one and all! And how delightful when the sledge upsets and you go flying full tilt into a drift, face downwards in the snow, and then you get up white all over with icicles on your moustaches; no cap, no gloves, your belt undone. . . . People laugh, the dogs bark. . . .

Pavel Ivanitch half opened one eye, looked at Gusev with it, and asked softly:

"Gusev, did your commanding officer steal?"

"Who can tell, Pavel Ivanitch! We can't say, it didn't reach us."

And after that a long time passed in silence. Gusev brooded, muttered something in delirium, and kept drinking water; it was hard for him to talk and hard to listen, and he was afraid of being talked to. An hour passed, a second, a third; evening came on, then night, but he did not notice it. He still sat dreaming of the frost.

There was a sound as though someone came into the hospital, and voices were audible, but a few minutes passed and all was still again.

"The Kingdom of Heaven and eternal peace," said the soldier with his arm in a sling. "He was an uncomfortable man."

"What?" asked Gusev. "Who?"

"He is dead, they have just carried him up."

"Oh, well," muttered Gusev, yawning, "the Kingdom of Heaven be his."

"What do you think?" the soldier with his arm in a sling asked Gusev. "Will he be in the Kingdom of Heaven or not?"

"Who is it you are talking about?"

"Pavel Ivanitch."

"He will be . . . he suffered so long. And there is another thing, he belonged to the clergy, and the priests always have a lot of relations. Their prayers will save him."

The soldier with the sling sat down on a hammock near Gusev and said in an undertone:

"And you, Gusev, are not long for this world. You will never get to Russia."

"Did the doctor or his assistant say so?" asked Gusev.

"It isn't that they said so, but one can see it. . . . One can see directly when a man's going to die. You don't eat, you don't drink; it's dreadful to see how thin you've got. It's consumption, in fact. I say it, not to upset you, but because maybe you would like to have the sacrament and extreme unction. And if you have any money you had better give it to the senior officer."

"I haven't written home . . ." Gusev sighed. "I shall die and they won't know."

"They'll hear of it," the sick sailor brought out in a bass voice. "When you die they will put it down in the *Gazette*, at Odessa they will send in a report to the commanding officer there and he will send it to the parish or somewhere. .

Gusev began to be uneasy after such a conversation and to feel a vague yearning. He drank water -- it was not that; he dragged himself to the window and breathed the hot, moist air -- it was not that; he tried to think of home, of the frost -- it was not that. . . . At last it seemed to him one minute longer in the ward and he would certainly expire.

"It's stifling, mates . . ." he said. "I'll go on deck. Help me up, for Christ's sake."

"All right," assented the soldier with the sling. "I'll carry you, you can't walk, hold on to my neck."

Gusev put his arm round the soldier's neck, the latter put his unhurt arm round him and carried him up. On the deck sailors and time-expired soldiers were lying asleep side by side; there were so many of them it was difficult to pass.

"Stand down," the soldier with the sling said softly. "Follow me quietly, hold on to my shirt. . . ."

It was dark. There was no light on deck, nor on the masts, nor anywhere on the sea around. At the furthest end of the ship the man on watch was standing perfectly still like a statue, and it looked as though he were asleep. It seemed as though the steamer were abandoned to itself and were going at its own will.

"Now they will throw Pavel Ivanitch into the sea," said the soldier with the sling. "In a sack and then into the water."

"Yes, that's the rule."

"But it's better to lie at home in the earth. Anyway, your mother comes to the grave and weeps."

"Of course."

There was a smell of hay and of dung. There were oxen standing with drooping heads by the ship's rail. One, two, three; eight of them! And there was a little horse. Gusev put out his hand to stroke it, but it shook its head, showed its teeth, and tried to bite his sleeve.

"Damned brute . . ." said Gusev angrily.

The two of them, he and the soldier, threaded their way to the head of the ship, then stood at the rail and looked up and down. Overhead deep sky, bright stars, peace and stillness, exactly as at home in the village, below darkness and disorder. The tall waves were resounding, no one could tell why. Whichever wave you looked at each one was trying to rise higher than all the rest and to chase and crush the next one; after it a third as fierce and hideous flew noisily, with a glint of light on its white crest.

The sea has no sense and no pity. If the steamer had been smaller and not made of thick iron, the waves would have crushed it to pieces without the slightest compunction, and would have devoured all the people in it with no distinction of saints or sinners. The steamer had the same cruel and meaningless expression. This monster with its huge beak was dashing onwards, cutting millions of waves in its path; it had no fear of the darkness nor the wind, nor of space, nor of solitude, caring for nothing, and if the ocean had its people, this monster would have crushed them, too, without distinction of saints or sinners.

"Where are we now?" asked Gusev.

"I don't know. We must be in the ocean."

"There is no sight of land. . ."

"No indeed! They say we shan't see it for seven days."

The two soldiers watched the white foam with the phosphorus light on it and were silent, thinking. Gusev was the first to break the silence.

"There is nothing to be afraid of," he said, "only one is full of dread as though one were sitting in a dark forest; but if, for instance, they let a boat down on to the water this minute and an officer ordered me to go a hundred miles over the sea to catch fish, I'd go. Or, let's say, if a Christian were to fall into the water this minute, I'd go in after him. A German or a Chinaman I wouldn't save, but I'd go in after a Christian."

"And are you afraid to die?"

"Yes. I am sorry for the folks at home. My brother at home, you know, isn't steady; he drinks, he beats his wife for nothing, he does not honour his parents. Everything will go to ruin without me, and father and my old mother will be begging their bread, I shouldn't wonder. But my legs won't bear me, brother, and it's hot here. Let's go to sleep."

V

Gusev went back to the ward and got into his hammock. He was again tormented by a vague craving, and he could not make out what he wanted. There was an oppression on his chest, a throbbing in his head, his mouth was so dry that it was difficult for him to move his tongue. He dozed, and murmured in his sleep, and, worn out with nightmares, his cough, and the stifling heat, towards morning he fell into a sound sleep. He dreamed that they were just taking the bread out of the oven in the barracks and he climbed into the stove and had a steam bath in it, lashing himself with a bunch of birch twigs. He slept for two days, and at midday on the third two sailors came down and carried him out.

He was sewn up in sailcloth and to make him heavier they put with him two iron weights. Sewn up in the sailcloth he looked like a carrot or a radish: broad at the head and narrow at the feet. . . . Before sunset they brought him up to the deck and put him on a plank; one end of the plank lay on the side of the ship, the other on a box, placed on a stool. Round him stood the soldiers and the officers with their caps off.

"Blessed be the Name of the Lord . . ." the priest began. "As it was in the beginning, is now, and ever shall be."

"Amen," chanted three sailors.

The soldiers and the officers crossed themselves and looked away at the waves. It was strange that a man should be sewn up in sailcloth and should soon be flying into the sea. Was it possible that such a thing might happen to anyone?

The priest strewed earth upon Gusev and bowed down. They sang "Eternal Memory."

The man on watch duty tilted up the end of the plank, Gusev slid off and flew head foremost, turned a somersault in the air and splashed into the sea. He was covered with foam and for a moment looked as though he were wrapped in lace, but the minute passed and he disappeared in the waves.

He went rapidly towards the bottom. Did he reach it? It was said to be three miles to the bottom. After sinking sixty or seventy feet, he began moving more and more slowly, swaying rhythmically, as though he were hesitating and, carried along by the current, moved more rapidly sideways than downwards.

Then he was met by a shoal of the fish called harbour pilots. Seeing the dark body the fish stopped as though petrified, and suddenly turned round and disappeared. In less than a minute they flew back swift as an arrow to Gusev, and began zig-zagging round him in the water.

After that another dark body appeared. It was a shark. It swam under Gusev with dignity and no show of interest, as though it did not notice him, and sank down upon its back, then it turned belly upwards, basking in the warm, transparent water and languidly opened its jaws with two rows of teeth. The harbour pilots are delighted, they stop to see what will come next. After playing a little with the body the shark nonchalantly puts its jaws under it, cautiously touches it with its teeth, and the sailcloth is rent its full length from head to foot; one of the weights falls out and frightens the harbour pilots, and striking the shark on the ribs goes rapidly to the bottom.

Overhead at this time the clouds are massed together on the side where the sun is setting; one cloud like a triumphal arch, another like a lion, a third like a pair of scissors. . . . From behind the clouds a broad, green shaft of light pierces through and stretches to the middle of the sky; a little later another, violet-coloured, lies beside it; next that, one of gold, then one rose-coloured. . . . The sky turns a soft lilac. Looking at this gorgeous, enchanted sky, at first the ocean scowls, but soon it, too, takes tender, joyous, passionate colours for which it is hard to find a name in human speech.

PEASANT WIVES

In the village of Reybuzh, just facing the church, stands a two-storeyed house with a stone foundation and an iron roof. In the lower storey the owner himself, Filip Ivanov Kashin, nicknamed Dyudya, lives with his family, and on the upper floor, where it is apt to be very hot in summer and very cold in winter, they put up government officials, merchants, or landowners, who chance to be travelling that way. Dyudya rents some bits of land, keeps a tavern on the highroad, does a trade in tar, honey, cattle, and jackdaws, and has already something like eight thousand roubles put by in the bank in the town.

His elder son, Fyodor, is head engineer in the factory, and, as the peasants say of him, he has risen so high in the world that he is quite out of reach now. Fyodor's wife, Sofya, a plain, ailing woman, lives at home at her father-in-law's. She is forever crying, and every Sunday she goes over to the hospital for medicine. Dyudya's second son, the hunchback Alyoshka, is living at home at his father's. He has only lately been married to Varvara, whom they singled out for him from a poor family. She is a handsome young woman, smart and buxom. When officials or merchants put up at the house, they always insist on having Varvara to bring in the samovar and make their beds.

One June evening when the sun was setting and the air was full of the smell of hay, of steaming dung-heaps and new milk, a plain-looking cart drove into Dyudya's yard with three people in it: a man of about thirty in a canvas suit, beside him a little boy of seven or eight in a long black coat with big bone buttons, and on the driver's seat a young fellow in a red shirt.

The young fellow took out the horses and led them out into the street to walk them up and down a bit, while the traveller washed, said a prayer, turning towards the church, then spread a rug near the cart and sat down with the boy to supper. He ate without haste, sedately, and Dyudya, who had seen a good many travellers in his time, knew him from his manners for a businesslike man, serious and aware of his own value.

Dyudya was sitting on the step in his waistcoat without a cap on, waiting for the visitor to speak first. He was used to hearing all kinds of stories from the travellers in the evening, and he liked listening to them before going to bed. His old wife, Afanasyevna, and his daughter-in-law Sofya, were milking in the cowshed. The other daughter-in-law, Varvara, was sitting at the open window of the upper storey, eating sunflower seeds.

"The little chap will be your son, I'm thinking?" Dyudya asked the traveller.

"No; adopted. An orphan. I took him for my soul's salvation."

They got into conversation. The stranger seemed to be a man fond of talking and ready of speech, and Dyudya learned from him that he was from the town, was of the tradesman class, and had a house of his own, that his name was Matvey Savitch, that he was on his way now to look at some gardens that he was renting from some German colonists, and that the boy's name was Kuzka. The evening was hot and close, no one felt inclined for sleep. When it was getting dark and pale stars began to twinkle here and there in the sky, Matvey Savitch began to tell how he had come by Kuzka. Afanasyevna and Sofya stood a little way off, listening. Kuzka had gone to the gate.

"It's a complicated story, old man," began Matvey Savitch, "and if I were to tell you all just as it happened, it would take all night and more. Ten years ago in a little house in our street, next door to me, where now there's a tallow and oil factory, there was living an old widow, Marfa Semyonovna Kapluntsev, and she had two sons: one was a guard on the railway, but the other, Vasya, who was just my own age, lived at home with his mother. Old Kapluntsev had kept five pair of horses and sent carriers all over the town; his widow had not given up the business, but managed the carriers as well as her husband had done, so that some days they would bring in as much as five roubles from their rounds.

"The young fellow, too, made a trifle on his own account. He used to breed fancy pigeons and sell them to fanciers; at times he would stand for hours on the roof, waving a broom in the air and whistling; his pigeons were right up in the clouds, but it wasn't enough for him, and he'd want them to go higher yet. Siskins and starlings, too, he used to catch, and he made cages for sale. All trifles, but, mind you, he'd pick up some ten roubles a month over such trifles. Well, as time went on, the old lady lost the use of her legs and took to her bed. In consequence of which event the house was left without a woman to look after it, and that's for all the world like a man without an eye. The old lady bestirred herself and made up her mind to marry Vasya. They called in a matchmaker at once, the women got to talking of one thing and another, and Vasya went off to have a look at the girls. He picked out Mashenka, a widow's daughter. They made up their minds without loss of time and in a week it was all settled. The girl was a little slip of a thing, seventeen, but fair-skinned and pretty-looking, and like a lady in all her ways; and a decent dowry with her, five hundred roubles, a cow, a bed. . . . Well, the old lady -- it seemed as though she had known it was coming -- three days after the wedding, departed to the Heavenly Jerusalem where is neither sickness nor sighing. The young people gave her a good funeral and began their life together. For just six months they got on splendidly, and then all of a sudden another misfortune. It never rains but it pours: Vasya was summoned to the recruiting office to draw lots for the service. He was taken, poor chap, for a soldier, and not even granted exemption. They shaved his head and packed him off to Poland. It was God's will; there was nothing to be done. When he said good-bye to his wife in the yard, he bore it all right; but as he glanced up at the hay-loft and his pigeons for the last time, he burst out crying. It was pitiful to see him.

"At first Mashenka got her mother to stay with her, that she mightn't be dull all alone; she stayed till the baby -- this very Kuzka here -- was born, and then she went off to Oboyan to another married daughter's and left Mashenka alone with the baby. There were five peasants -- the carriers -- a drunken saucy lot; horses, too, and dray-carts to see to, and then the fence would be broken or the soot afire in the chimney -- jobs beyond a woman, and through our being neighbours, she got into the way of turning to me forevery little thing. . . . Well, I'd go over, set things to rights, and give advice. . . . Naturally, not without going indoors, drinking a cup of tea and having a little chat with her. I was a young fellow, intellectual, and fond of talking on all sorts of subjects; she, too, was well-bred and educated. She was always neatly dressed, and in summer she walked out with a sunshade. Sometimes I would begin upon religion or politics with her, and she was flattered and would entertain me with tea and jam. . . . In a word, not to make a long story of it, I must tell you, old man, a year had not passed before the Evil One, the enemy of all mankind, confounded me. I began to notice that any day I didn't go to see her, I seemed out of sorts and dull. And I'd be continually making up something that I must see her about: 'It's high time,' I'd say to myself, 'to put the double windows in for the winter,' and the whole day I'd idle away over at her place putting in the windows and take good care to leave a couple of them over for the next day too.

" 'I ought to count over Vasya's pigeons, to see none of them have strayed,' and so on. I used always to be talking to her across the fence, and in the end I made a little gate in the fence so as not to have to go so far round. From womankind comes much evil into the world and every kind of abomination. Not we sinners only; even the saints themselves have been led astray by them. Mashenka did not try to keep me at a distance. Instead of thinking of her husband and being on her guard, she fell in love with me. I began to notice that she was dull without me, and was always walking to and fro by the fence looking into my yard through the cracks.

"My brains were going round in my head in a sort of frenzy. On Thursday in Holy Week I was going early in the morning -- it was scarcely light -- to market. I passed close by her gate, and the Evil One was by me -- at my elbow. I looked -- she had a gate with open trellis work at the top -- and there she was, up already, standing in the middle of the yard, feeding the ducks. I could not restrain myself, and I called her name. She came up and looked at me through the trellis. . . . Her little face was white, her eyes soft and sleepy-looking. . . . I liked her looks immensely, and I began paying her compliments, as though we were not at the gate, but just as one does on namedays, while she blushed, and laughed, and kept looking straight into my eyes without winking. . . . I lost all sense and began to declare my love to her. . . . She opened the gate, and from that morning we began to live as man and wife. . . ."

The hunchback Alyoshka came into the yard from the street and ran out of breath into the house, not looking at anyone. A minute later he ran out of the house with a concertina. Jingling some coppers in his pocket, and cracking sunflower seeds as he ran, he went out at the gate.

"And who's that, pray?" asked Matvey Savitch.

"My son Alexey," answered Dyudya. "He's off on a spree, the rascal. God has afflicted him with a hump, so we are not very hard on him."

"And he's always drinking with the other fellows, always drinking," sighed Afanasyevna. "Before Carnival we married him, thinking he'd be steadier, but there! he's worse than ever."

"It's been no use. Simply keeping another man's daughter for nothing," said Dyudya.

Somewhere behind the church they began to sing a glorious, mournful song. The words they could not catch and only the voices could be heard -- two tenors and a bass. All were listening; there was complete stillness in the yard. . . . Two voices suddenly broke off with a loud roar of laughter, but the third, a tenor, still sang on, and took so high a note that everyone instinctively looked upwards, as though the voice had soared to heaven itself.

Varvara came out of the house, and screening her eyes with her hand, as though from the sun, she looked towards the church.

"It's the priest's sons with the schoolmaster," she said.

Again all the three voices began to sing together. Matvey Savitch sighed and went on:

"Well, that's how it was, old man. Two years later we got a letter from Vasya from Warsaw. He wrote that he was being sent home sick. He was ill. By that time I had put all that foolishness out of my head, and I had a fine match picked out all ready for me, only I didn't know how to break it off with my sweetheart. Every day I'd make up my mind to have it out with Mashenka, but I didn't know how to approach her so as not to have a woman's screeching about my ears. The letter freed my hands. I read it through with Mashenka; she turned white as a sheet, while I said to her: 'Thank God; now,' says I, 'you'll be a married woman again.' But says she: 'I'm not going to live with him.' 'Why, isn't he your husband?' said I. 'Is it an easy thing? . . . I never loved him and I married him not of my own free will. My mother made me.' 'Don't try to get out of it, silly,' said I, 'but tell me this: were you married to him in church or not?' 'I was married,' she said, 'but it's you that I love, and I will stay with you to the day of my death. Folks may jeer. I don't care. . . .' 'You're a Christian woman,' said I, 'and have read the Scriptures; what is written there?'

"Once married, with her husband she must live," said Dyudya.

" 'Man and wife are one flesh. We have sinned,' I said, 'you and I, and it is enough; we must repent and fear God. We must confess it all to Vasya,' said I; 'he's a quiet fellow and soft -- he won't kill you. And indeed,' said

I, 'better to suffer torments in this world at the hands of your lawful master than to gnash your teeth at the dread Seat of Judgment.' The wench wouldn't listen; she stuck to her silly, 'It's you I love!' and nothing more could I get out of her.

"Vasya came back on the Saturday before Trinity, early in the morning. From my fence I could see everything; he ran into the house, and came back a minute later with Kuzka in his arms, and he was laughing and crying all at once; he was kissing Kuzka and looking up at the hay-loft, and hadn't the heart to put the child down, and yet he was longing to go to his pigeons. He was always a soft sort of chap -- sentimental. That day passed off very well, all quiet and proper. They had begun ringing the church bells for the evening service, when the thought struck me: 'To-morrow's Trinity Sunday; how is it they are not decking the gates and the fence with green? Something's wrong,' I thought. I went over to them. I peeped in, and there he was, sitting on the floor in the middle of the room, his eyes staring like a drunken man's, the tears streaming down his cheeks and his hands shaking; he was pulling cracknels, necklaces, gingerbread nuts, and all sorts of little presents out of his bundle and flinging them on the floor. Kuzka -- he was three years old -- was crawling on the floor, munching the gingerbreads, while Mashenka stood by the stove, white and shivering all over, muttering: 'I'm not your wife; I can't live with you,' and all sorts of foolishness. I bowed down at Vasya's feet, and said: 'We have sinned against you, Vassily Maximitch; forgive us, for Christ's sake!' Then I got up and spoke to Mashenka: 'You, Marya Semyonovna, ought now to wash Vassily Maximitch's feet and drink the water. Do you be an obedient wife to him, and pray to God for me, that He in His mercy may forgive my transgression.' It came to me like an inspiration from an angel of Heaven; I gave her solemn counsel and spoke with such feeling that my own tears flowed too. And so two days later Vasya comes to me: 'Matyusha,' says he, 'I forgive you and my wife; God have mercy on you! She was a soldier's wife, a young thing all alone; it was hard for her to be on her guard. She's not the first, nor will she be the last. Only,' he says, 'I beg you to behave as though there had never been anything between you, and to make no sign, while I,' says he, 'will do my best to please her in every way, so that she may come to love me again.' He gave me his hand on it, drank a cup of tea, and went away more cheerful.

" 'Well,' thought I, 'thank God!' and I did feel glad that everything had gone off so well. But no sooner had Vasya gone out of the yard, when in came Mashenka. Ah! What I had to suffer! She hung on my neck, weeping and praying: 'For God's sake, don't cast me off; I can't live without you!' "

"The vile hussy!" sighed Dyudya.

"I swore at her, stamped my foot, and dragging her into the passage, I fastened the door with the hook. 'Go to your husband,' I cried. 'Don't shame me before folks. Fear God!' And every day there was a scene of that sort.

"One morning I was standing in my yard near the stable cleaning a bridle. All at once I saw her running through the little gate into my yard, with bare feet, in her petticoat, and straight towards me; she clutched at the bridle, getting all smeared with the pitch, and shaking and weeping, she cried: 'I can't stand him; I loathe him; I can't bear it! If you don't love me, better kill me!' I was angry, and I struck her twice with the bridle, but at that instant Vasya ran in at the gate, and in a despairing voice he shouted: 'Don't beat her! Don't beat her!' But he ran up himself, and waving his arms, as though he were mad, he let fly with his fists at her with all his might, then flung her on the ground and kicked her. I tried to defend her, but he snatched up the reins and thrashed her with them, and all the while, like a colt's whinny, he went: 'He -- he-- he!' "

"I'd take the reins and let you feel them," muttered Varvara, moving away; "murdering our sister, the damned brutes! . . ."

"Hold your tongue, you jade!" Dyudya shouted at her.

" 'He -- he -- he!' " Matvey Savitch went on. "A carrier ran out of his yard; I called to my workman, and the three of us got Mashenka away from him and carried her home in our arms. The disgrace of it! The same day I went over in the evening to see how things were. She was lying in bed, all wrapped up in bandages, nothing but her eyes and nose to be seen; she was looking at the ceiling. I said: 'Good-evening, Marya Semyonovna!' She did not speak. And Vasya was sitting in the next room, his head in his hands, crying and saying: 'Brute that I am! I've ruined my life! O God, let me die!' I sat for half an hour by Mashenka and gave her a good talking-to. I tried to frighten her a bit. 'The righteous,' said I, 'after this life go to Paradise, but you will go to a Gehenna of fire, like all adulteresses. Don't strive against your husband, go and lay yourself at his feet.' But never a word from her; she didn't so much as blink an eyelid, for all the world as though I were talking to a post. The next day Vasya fell ill with something like cholera, and in the evening I heard that he was dead. Well, so they buried him, and Mashenka did not go to the funeral; she didn't care to show her shameless face and her bruises. And soon there began to be talk all over the district that Vasya had not died a natural death, that Mashenka had made away with him. It got to the ears of the police; they had Vasya dug up and cut open, and in his stomach they found arsenic. It was clear he had been poisoned; the police came and took Mashenka away, and with her the innocent Kuzka. They were put in prison. . . . The woman had gone too far -- God punished her. . . . Eight months later they tried her. She sat, I remember, on a low stool, with a little white kerchief on her head, wearing a grey gown, and she was so thin, so pale, so sharp-eyed it made one sad to look at her. Behind her stood a soldier with a gun. She would not confess her guilt. Some in the court said she had poisoned her husband and others declared he had poisoned himself for grief. I was one of the witnesses. When they questioned me, I told the whole truth according to my oath. 'Hers,' said I, 'is the guilt. It's no good to conceal it; she did not love her husband, and she had a will of her own. . . .' The trial began in the morning and towards night they passed this sentence: to send her to hard labour in Siberia for thirteen years. After that sentence Mashenka remained three months longer in prison. I went to see her, and from Christian charity I took her a little tea and sugar. But as soon as she set eyes on me she began to shake all over, wringing her hands and muttering: 'Go away! go away!' And Kuzka she clasped to her as though she were afraid I would take him away. 'See,' said I, 'what you have come to! Ah, Masha, Masha! you would not listen to me when I gave you good advice, and now you must repent it. You are yourself to blame,' said I; 'blame yourself!' I was giving her good counsel, but she: 'Go away, go away!' huddling herself and Kuzka against the wall, and trembling all over.

"When they were taking her away to the chief town of our province, I walked by the escort as far as the station and slipped a rouble into her bundle for my soul's salvation. But she did not get as far as Siberia. . . . She fell sick of fever and died in prison."

"Live like a dog and you must die a dog's death," said Dyudya.

"Kuzka was sent back home. . . . I thought it over and took him to bring up. After all -- though a convict's child -- still he was a living soul, a Christian. . . . I was sorry for him. I shall make him my clerk, and if I have no children of my own, I'll make a merchant of him. Wherever I go now, I take him with me; let him learn his work."

All the while Matvey Savitch had been telling his story, Kuzka had sat on a little stone near the gate. His head propped in both hands, he gazed at the sky, and in the distance he looked in the dark like a stump of wood.

"Kuzka, come to bed," Matvey Savitch bawled to him.

"Yes, it's time," said Dyudya, getting up; he yawned loudly and added:

"Folks will go their own way, and that's what comes of it."

Over the yard the moon was floating now in the heavens; she was moving one way, while the clouds beneath moved the other way; the clouds were disappearing into the darkness, but still the moon could be seen high above the yard.

Matvey Savitch said a prayer, facing the church, and saying good-night, he lay down on the ground near his cart. Kuzka, too, said a prayer, lay down in the cart, and covered himself with his little overcoat; he made himself a little hole in the hay so as to be more comfortable, and curled up so that his elbows looked like knees. From the yard Dyudya could be seen lighting a candle in his room below, putting on his spectacles and standing in the corner with a book. He was a long while reading and crossing himself.

The travellers fell asleep. Afanasyevna and Sofya came up to the cart and began looking at Kuzka.

"The little orphan's asleep," said the old woman. "He's thin and frail, nothing but bones. No mother and no one to care for him properly."

"My Grishutka must be two years older," said Sofya. "Up at the factory he lives like a slave without his mother. The foreman beats him, I dare say. When I looked at this poor mite just now, I thought of my own Grishutka, and my heart went cold within me."

A minute passed in silence.

"Doesn't remember his mother, I suppose," said the old woman.

"How could he remember?"

And big tears began dropping from Sofya's eyes.

"He's curled himself up like a cat," she said, sobbing and laughing with tenderness and sorrow. . . . "Poor motherless mite!

Kuzka started and opened his eyes. He saw before him an ugly, wrinkled, tear-stained face, and beside it another, aged and toothless, with a sharp chin and hooked nose, and high above them the infinite sky with the flying clouds and the moon. He cried out in fright, and Sofya, too, uttered a cry; both were answered by the echo, and a faint stir passed over the stifling air; a watchman tapped somewhere near, a dog barked. Matvey Savitch muttered something in his sleep and turned over on the other side.

Late at night when Dyudya and the old woman and the neighbouring watchman were all asleep, Sofya went out to the gate and sat down on the bench. She felt stifled and her head ached from weeping. The street was a wide and long one; it stretched for nearly two miles to the right and as far to the left, and the end of it was out of sight. The moon was now not over the yard, but behind the church. One side of the street was flooded with moonlight, while the other side lay in black shadow. The long shadows of the poplars and the starling-cotes stretched right across the street, while the church cast a broad shadow, black and terrible that enfolded Dyudya's gates and half his house. The street was still and deserted. From time to time the strains of music floated faintly from the end of the street -- Alyoshka, most likely, playing his concertina.

Someone moved in the shadow near the church enclosure, and Sofya could not make out whether it were a man or a cow, or perhaps merely a big bird rustling in the trees. But then a figure stepped out of the shadow, halted, and said something in a man's voice, then vanished down the turning by the church. A little later, not three yards from the gate, another figure came into sight; it walked straight from the church to the gate and stopped short, seeing Sofya on the bench.

"Varvara, is that you?" said Sofya.

"And if it were?"

It was Varvara. She stood still a minute, then came up to the bench and sat down.

"Where have you been?" asked Sofya.

Varvara made no answer.

"You'd better mind you don't get into trouble with such goings-on, my girl," said Sofya. "Did you hear how Mashenka was kicked and lashed with the reins? You'd better look out, or they'll treat you the same."

"Well, let them!"

Varvara laughed into her kerchief and whispered:

"I have just been with the priest's son."

"Nonsense!"

"I have!"

"It's a sin!" whispered Sofya.

"Well, let it be. . . . What do I care? If it's a sin, then it is a sin, but better be struck dead by thunder than live like this. I'm young and strong, and I've a filthy crooked hunchback for a husband, worse than Dyudya himself, curse him! When I was a girl, I hadn't bread to eat, or a shoe to my foot, and to get away from that wretchedness I was tempted by Alyoshka's money, and got caught like a fish in a net, and I'd rather have a viper for my bedfellow than that scurvy Alyoshka. And what's your life? It makes me sick to look at it. Your Fyodor sent you packing from the factory and he's taken up with another woman. They have robbed you of your boy and made a slave of him. You work like a horse, and never hear a kind word. I'd rather pine all my days an old maid, I'd rather get half a rouble from the priest's son, I'd rather beg my bread, or throw myself into the well. . .

"It's a sin!" whispered Sofya again.

"Well, let it be."

Somewhere behind the church the same three voices, two tenors and a bass, began singing again a mournful song. And again the words could not be distinguished.

"They are not early to bed," Varvara said, laughing.

And she began telling in a whisper of her midnight walks with the priest's son, and of the stories he had told her, and of his comrades, and of the fun she had with the travellers who stayed in the house. The mournful song stirred a longing for life and freedom. Sofya began to laugh; she thought it sinful and terrible and sweet to hear about, and she felt envious and sorry that she, too, had not been a sinner when she was young and pretty.

In the churchyard they heard twelve strokes beaten on the watchman's board.

"It's time we were asleep," said Sofya, getting up, "or, maybe, we shall catch it from Dyudya."

They both went softly into the yard.

"I went away without hearing what he was telling about Mashenka," said Varvara, making herself a bed under the window.

"She died in prison, he said. She poisoned her husband."

Varvara lay down beside Sofya a while, and said softly:

"I'd make away with my Alyoshka and never regret it."

"You talk nonsense; God forgive you."

When Sofya was just dropping asleep, Varvara, coming close, whispered in her ear:

"Let us get rid of Dyudya and Alyoshka!"

Sofya started and said nothing. Then she opened her eyes and gazed a long while steadily at the sky.

"People would find out," she said.

"No, they wouldn't. Dyudya's an old man, it's time he did die; and they'd say Alyoshka died of drink."

"I'm afraid . . . God would chastise us."

"Well, let Him. . . ."

Both lay awake thinking in silence.

"It's cold," said Sofya, beginning to shiver all over. "It will soon be morning. . . . Are you asleep?"

"No. . . . Don't you mind what I say, dear," whispered Varvara; "I get so mad with the damned brutes, I don't know what I do say. Go to sleep, or it will be daylight directly. . . . Go to sleep."

Both were quiet and soon they fell asleep.

Earlier than all woke the old woman. She waked up Sofya and they went together into the cowshed to milk the cows. The hunchback Alyoshka came in hopelessly drunk without his concertina; his breast and knees had been in the dust and straw -- he must have fallen down in the road. Staggering, he went into the cowshed, and without undressing he rolled into a sledge and began to snore at once. When first the crosses on the church and then the windows were flashing in the light of the rising sun, and shadows stretched across the yard over the dewy grass from the trees and the top of the well, Matvey Savitch jumped up and began hurrying about:

"Kuzka! get up!" he shouted. "It's time to put in the horses! Look sharp!"

The bustle of morning was beginning. A young Jewess in a brown gown with flounces led a horse into the yard to drink. The pulley of the well creaked plaintively, the bucket knocked as it went down. . . .

Kuzka, sleepy, tired, covered with dew, sat up in the cart, lazily putting on his little overcoat, and listening to the drip of the water from the bucket into the well as he shivered with the cold.

"Auntie!" shouted Matvey Savitch to Sofya, "tell my lad to hurry up and to harness the horses!"

And Dyudya at the same instant shouted from the window:

"Sofya, take a farthing from the Jewess for the horse's drink! They're always in here, the mangy creatures!

In the street sheep were running up and down, baaing; the peasant women were shouting at the shepherd, while he played his pipes, cracked his whip, or answered them in a thick sleepy bass. Three sheep strayed into the yard, and not finding the gate again, pushed at the fence.

Varvara was waked by the noise, and bundling her bedding up in her arms, she went into the house.

"You might at least drive the sheep out!" the old woman bawled after her, "my lady!"

"I dare say! As if I were going to slave for you Herods!" muttered Varvara, going into the house.

Dyudya came out of the house with his accounts in his hands, sat down on the step, and began reckoning how much the traveller owed him for the night's lodging, oats, and watering his horses.

"You charge pretty heavily for the oats, my good man," said Matvey Savitch.

"If it's too much, don't take them. There's no compulsion, merchant."

When the travellers were ready to start, they were detained for a minute. Kuzka had lost his cap.

"Little swine, where did you put it?" Matvey Savitch roared angrily. "Where is it?"

Kuzka's face was working with terror; he ran up and down near the cart, and not finding it there, ran to the gate and then to the shed. The old woman and Sofya helped him look.

"I'll pull your ears off!" yelled Matvey Savitch. "Dirty brat!"

The cap was found at the bottom of the cart.

Kuzka brushed the hay off it with his sleeve, put it on, and timidly he crawled into the cart, still with an expression of terror on his face as though he were afraid of a blow from behind.

Matvey Savitch crossed himself. The driver gave a tug at the reins and the cart rolled out of the yard.

THE DUEL

I

It was eight o'clock in the morning -- the time when the officers, the local officials, and the visitors usually took their morning dip in the sea after the hot, stifling night, and then went into the pavilion to drink tea or coffee. Ivan Andreitch Laevsky, a thin, fair young man of twenty-eight, wearing the cap of a clerk in the Ministry of Finance and with slippers on his feet, coming down to bathe, found a number of acquaintances on the beach, and among them his friend Samoylenko, the army doctor.

With his big cropped head, short neck, his red face, his big nose, his shaggy black eyebrows and grey whiskers, his stout puffy figure and his hoarse military bass, this Samoylenko made on every newcomer the unpleasant impression of a gruff bully; but two or three days after making his acquaintance, one began to think his face extraordinarily good-natured, kind, and even handsome. In spite of his clumsiness and rough manner, he was a peaceable man, of infinite kindliness and goodness of heart, always ready to be of use. He was on familiar terms with everyone in the town, lent everyone money, doctored everyone, made matches, patched up quarrels, arranged picnics at which he cooked *shashlik* and an awfully good soup of grey mullets. He was always looking after other people's affairs and trying to interest someone on their behalf, and was always delighted about something. The general opinion about him was that he was without faults of character. He had only two weaknesses: he was ashamed of his own good nature, and tried to disguise it by a surly expression and an assumed gruffness; and he liked his assistants and his soldiers to call him "Your Excellency," although he was only a civil councillor.

"Answer one question for me, Alexandr Daviditch," Laevsky began, when both he and Samoylenko were in the water up to their shoulders. "Suppose you had loved a woman and had been living with her for two or three years, and then left off caring for her, as one does, and began to feel that you had nothing in common with her. How would you behave in that case?"

"It's very simple. 'You go where you please, madam' -- and that would be the end of it."

"It's easy to say that! But if she has nowhere to go? A woman with no friends or relations, without a farthing, who can't work . . ."

"Well? Five hundred roubles down or an allowance of twenty-five roubles a month -- and nothing more. It's very simple."

"Even supposing you have five hundred roubles and can pay twenty-five roubles a month, the woman I am speaking of is an educated woman and proud. Could you really bring yourself to offer her money? And how would you do it?"

Samoylenko was going to answer, but at that moment a big wave covered them both, then broke on the beach and rolled back noisily over the shingle. The friends got out and began dressing.

"Of course, it is difficult to live with a woman if you don't love her," said Samoylenko, shaking the sand out of his boots. "But one must look at the thing humanely, Vanya. If it were my case, I should never show a sign that I did not love her, and I should go on living with her till I died."

He was at once ashamed of his own words; he pulled himself up and said:

"But for aught I care, there might be no females at all. Let them all go to the devil!"

The friends dressed and went into the pavilion. There Samoylenko was quite at home, and even had a special cup and saucer. Every morning they brought him on a tray a cup of coffee, a tall cut glass of iced water, and a tiny glass of brandy. He would first drink the brandy, then the hot coffee, then the iced water, and this must have been very nice, for after drinking it his eyes looked moist with pleasure, he would stroke his whiskers with both hands, and say, looking at the sea:

"A wonderfully magnificent view!"

After a long night spent in cheerless, unprofitable thoughts which prevented him from sleeping, and seemed to intensify the darkness and sultriness of the night, Laevsky felt listless and shattered. He felt no better for the bathe and the coffee.

"Let us go on with our talk, Alexandr Daviditch," he said. "I won't make a secret of it; I'll speak to you openly as to a friend. Things are in a bad way with Nadyezhda Fyodorovna and me . . . a very bad way! Forgive me for forcing my private affairs upon you, but I must speak out."

Samoylenko, who had a misgiving of what he was going to speak about, dropped his eyes and drummed with his fingers on the table.

"I've lived with her for two years and have ceased to love her," Laevsky went on; "or, rather, I realised that I never had felt any love for her. . . . These two years have been a mistake."

It was Laevsky's habit as he talked to gaze attentively at the pink palms of his hands, to bite his nails, or to pinch his cuffs. And he did so now.

"I know very well you can't help me," he said. "But I tell you, because unsuccessful and superfluous people like me find their salvation in talking. I have to generalise about everything I do. I'm bound to look for an explanation and justification of my absurd existence in somebody else's theories, in literary types -- in the idea that we, upper-class Russians, are degenerating, for instance, and so on. Last night, for example, I comforted myself by thinking all the time: 'Ah, how true Tolstoy is, how mercilessly true!' And that did me good. Yes, really, brother, he is a great writer, say what you like!"

Samoylenko, who had never read Tolstoy and was intending to do so every day of his life, was a little embarrassed, and said:

"Yes, all other authors write from imagination, but he writes straight from nature."

"My God!" sighed Laevsky; "how distorted we all are by civilisation! I fell in love with a married woman and she with me. . . . To begin with, we had kisses, and calm evenings, and vows, and Spencer, and ideals, and interests in common. . . . What a deception! We really ran away from her husband, but we lied to ourselves and made out that we ran away from the emptiness of the life of the educated class. We pictured our future like this: to begin with, in the Caucasus, while we were getting to know the people and the place, I would put on the Government uniform and enter the service; then at our leisure we would pick out a plot of ground, would toil in the sweat of our brow, would have a vineyard and a field, and so on. If you were in my place, or that zoologist of yours, Von Koren, you might live with Nadyezhda Fyodorovna for thirty years, perhaps, and might leave your heirs a rich vineyard and three thousand acres of maize; but I felt like a bankrupt from the first day. In the town you have insufferable heat, boredom, and no society; if you go out into the country, you fancy poisonous spiders, scorpions, or snakes lurking under every stone and behind every bush, and beyond the fields -- mountains and the desert. Alien people, an alien country, a wretched form of civilisation -- all that is not so easy, brother, as walking on the Nevsky Prospect in one's fur coat, arm-in-arm with Nadyezhda Fyodorovna, dreaming of the sunny South. What is needed here is a life and death struggle, and I'm not a fighting man. A wretched neurasthenic, an idle gentleman. . . . From the first day I knew that my dreams of a life of labour and of a vineyard were worthless. As for love, I ought to tell you that living with a woman who has read Spencer and has followed you to the ends of the earth is no more interesting than living with any Anfissa or Akulina. There's the same smell of ironing, of powder, and of medicines, the same curl-papers every morning, the same self-deception."

"You can't get on in the house without an iron," said Samoylenko, blushing at Laevsky's speaking to him so openly of a lady he knew. "You are out of humour to-day, Vanya, I notice. Nadyezhda Fyodorovna is a splendid woman, highly educated, and you are a man of the highest intellect. Of course, you are not married," Samoylenko went on, glancing round at the adjacent tables, "but that's not your fault; and besides . . . one ought to be above conventional prejudices and rise to the level of modern ideas. I believe in free love myself, yes. . . . But to my thinking, once you have settled together, you ought to go on living together all your life."

"Without love?"

"I will tell you directly," said Samoylenko. "Eight years ago there was an old fellow, an agent, here -- a man of very great intelligence. Well, he used to say that the great thing in married life was patience. Do you hear, Vanya? Not love, but patience. Love cannot last long. You have lived two years in love, and now evidently your married life has reached the period when, in order to preserve equilibrium, so to speak, you ought to exercise all your patience. . . ."

"You believe in your old agent; to me his words are meaningless. Your old man could be a hypocrite; he could exercise himself in the virtue of patience, and, as he did so, look upon a person he did not love as an object indispensable for his moral exercises; but I have not yet fallen so low. If I want to exercise myself in patience, I will buy dumb-bells or a frisky horse, but I'll leave human beings alone."

Samoylenko asked for some white wine with ice. When they had drunk a glass each, Laevsky suddenly asked:

"Tell me, please, what is the meaning of softening of the brain?"

"How can I explain it to you? . . . It's a disease in which the brain becomes softer . . . as it were, dissolves."

"Is it curable?"

"Yes, if the disease is not neglected. Cold douches, blisters. . . . Something internal, too."

"Oh! . . . Well, you see my position; I can't live with her: it is more than I can do. While I'm with you I can be philosophical about it and smile, but at home I lose heart completely; I am so utterly miserable, that if I were told, for instance, that I should have to live another month with her, I should blow out my brains. At the same time, parting with her is out of the question. She has no friends or relations; she cannot work, and neither she nor I have any money. . . . What could become of her? To whom could she go? There is nothing one can think of. . . . Come, tell me, what am I to do?"

"H'm! . . ." growled Samoylenko, not knowing what to answer. "Does she love you?"

"Yes, she loves me in so far as at her age and with her temperament she wants a man. It would be as difficult for her to do without me as to do without her powder or her curl-papers. I am for her an indispensable, integral part of her boudoir."

Samoylenko was embarrassed.

"You are out of humour to-day, Vanya," he said. "You must have had a bad night."

"Yes, I slept badly. . . . Altogether, I feel horribly out of sorts, brother. My head feels empty; there's a sinking at my heart, a weakness. . . . I must run away."

"Run where?"

"There, to the North. To the pines and the mushrooms, to people and ideas. . . . I'd give half my life to bathe now in some little stream in the province of Moscow or Tula; to feel chilly, you know, and then to stroll for three hours even with the feeblest student, and to talk and talk endlessly. . . . And the scent of the hay! Do you remember it? And in the evening, when one walks in the garden, sounds of the piano float from the house; one hears the train passing. . . ."

Laevsky laughed with pleasure; tears came into his eyes, and to cover them, without getting up, he stretched across the next table for the matches.

"I have not been in Russia for eighteen years," said Samoylenko. "I've forgotten what it is like. To my mind, there is not a country more splendid than the Caucasus."

"Vereshtchagin has a picture in which some men condemned to death are languishing at the bottom of a very deep well. Your magnificent Caucasus strikes me as just like that well. If I were offered the choice of a chimney-sweep in Petersburg or a prince in the Caucasus, I should choose the job of chimney-sweep."

Laevsky grew pensive. Looking at his stooping figure, at his eyes fixed dreamily at one spot, at his pale, perspiring face and sunken temples, at his bitten nails, at the slipper which had dropped off his heel, displaying a badly darned sock, Samoylenko was moved to pity, and probably because Laevsky reminded him of a helpless child, he asked:

"Is your mother living?"

"Yes, but we are on bad terms. She could not forgive me for this affair."

Samoylenko was fond of his friend. He looked upon Laevsky as a good-natured fellow, a student, a man with no nonsense about him, with whom one could drink, and laugh, and talk without reserve. What he understood in him he disliked extremely. Laevsky drank a great deal and at unsuitable times; he played cards, despised his work, lived beyond his means, frequently made use of unseemly expressions in conversation, walked about the streets in his slippers, and quarrelled with Nadyezhda Fyodorovna before other people -- and Samoylenko did not like this. But the fact that Laevsky had once been a student in the Faculty of Arts, subscribed to two fat reviews, often talked so cleverly that only a few people understood him, was living with a well-educated woman -- all this Samoylenko did not understand, and he liked this and respected Laevsky, thinking him superior to himself.

"There is another point," said Laevsky, shaking his head. "Only it is between ourselves. I'm concealing it from Nadyezhda Fyodorovna for the time. . . . Don't let it out before her. . . . I got a letter the day before yesterday, telling me that her husband has died from softening of the brain."

"The Kingdom of Heaven be his!" sighed Samoylenko. "Why are you concealing it from her?"

"To show her that letter would be equivalent to 'Come to church to be married.' And we should first have to make our relations clear. When she understands that we can't go on living together, I will show her the letter. Then there will be no danger in it."

"Do you know what, Vanya," said Samoylenko, and a sad and imploring expression came into his face, as though he were going to ask him about something very touching and were afraid of being refused. "Marry her, my dear boy!"

"Why?"

"Do your duty to that splendid woman! Her husband is dead, and so Providence itself shows you what to do!"

"But do understand, you queer fellow, that it is impossible. To marry without love is as base and unworthy of a man as to perform mass without believing in it."

"But it's your duty to."

"Why is it my duty?" Laevsky asked irritably.

"Because you took her away from her husband and made yourself responsible for her."

"But now I tell you in plain Russian, I don't love her!"

"Well, if you've no love, show her proper respect, consider her wishes. . . ."

" 'Show her respect, consider her wishes,' " Laevsky mimicked him. "As though she were some Mother Superior! . . . You are a poor psychologist and physiologist if you think that living with a woman one can get off with nothing but respect and consideration. What a woman thinks most of is her bedroom."

"Vanya, Vanya!" said Samoylenko, overcome with confusion.

"You are an elderly child, a theorist, while I am an old man in spite of my years, and practical, and we shall never understand one another. We had better drop this conversation. Mustapha!" Laevsky shouted to the waiter. "What's our bill?"

"No, no . . ." the doctor cried in dismay, clutching Laevsky's arm. "It is for me to pay. I ordered it. Make it out to me," he cried to Mustapha.

The friends got up and walked in silence along the sea-front. When they reached the boulevard, they stopped and shook hands at parting.

"You are awfully spoilt, my friend!" Samoylenko sighed. "Fate has sent you a young, beautiful, cultured woman, and you refuse the gift, while if God were to give me a crooked old woman, how pleased I should be if only she were kind and affectionate! I would live with her in my vineyard and . . ."

Samoylenko caught himself up and said:

"And she might get the samovar ready for me there, the old hag."

After parting with Laevsky he walked along the boulevard. When, bulky and majestic, with a stern expression on his face, he walked along the boulevard in his snow-white tunic and superbly polished boots, squaring his chest, decorated with the Vladimir cross on a ribbon, he was very much pleased with himself, and it seemed as though the whole world were looking at him with pleasure. Without turning his head, he looked to each side and thought that the boulevard was extremely well laid out; that the young cypress-trees, the eucalyptuses, and the ugly, anemic palm-trees were very handsome and would in time give abundant shade; that the Circassianswere an honest and hospitable people.

"It's strange that Laevsky does not like the Caucasus," he thought, "very strange."

Five soldiers, carrying rifles, met him and saluted him. On the right side of the boulevard the wife of a local official was walking along the pavement with her son, a schoolboy.

"Good-morning, Marya Konstantinovna," Samoylenko shouted to her with a pleasant smile. "Have you been to bathe? Ha, ha, ha! . . . My respects to Nikodim Alexandritch!"

And he went on, still smiling pleasantly, but seeing an assistant of the military hospital coming towards him, he suddenly frowned, stopped him, and asked:

"Is there anyone in the hospital?"

"No one, Your Excellency."

"Eh?"

"No one, Your Excellency."

"Very well, run along. . . ."

Swaying majestically, he made for the lemonade stall, where sat a full-bosomed old Jewess, who gave herself out to be a Georgian, and said to her as loudly as though he were giving the word of command to a regiment:

"Be so good as to give me some soda-water!"

II

Laevsky's not loving Nadyezhda Fyodorovna showed itself chiefly in the fact that everything she said or did seemed to him a lie, or equivalent to a lie, and everything he read against women and love seemed to him to apply perfectly to himself, to Nadyezhda Fyodorovna and her husband. When he returned home, she was sitting at the window, dressed and with her hair done, and with a preoccupied face was drinking coffee and turning over the leaves of a fat magazine; and he thought the drinking of coffee was not such a remarkable event that she need put on a preoccupied expression over it, and that she had been wasting her time doing her hair in a fashionable style, as there was no one here to attract and no need to be attractive. And in the magazine he saw nothing but falsity. He thought she had dressed and done her hair so as to look handsomer, and was reading in order to seem clever.

"Will it be all right for me to go to bathe to-day?" she said.

"Why? There won't be an earthquake whether you go or not, I suppose. . . ."

"No, I only ask in case the doctor should be vexed."

"Well, ask the doctor, then; I'm not a doctor."

On this occasion what displeased Laevsky most in Nadyezhda Fyodorovna was her white open neck and the little curls at the back of her head. And he remembered that when Anna Karenin got tired of her husband, what she disliked most of all was his ears, and thought: "How true it is, how true!"

Feeling weak and as though his head were perfectly empty, he went into his study, lay down on his sofa, and covered his face with a handkerchief that he might not be bothered by the flies. Despondent and oppressive thoughts always about the same thing trailed slowly across his brain like a long string of waggons on a gloomy autumn evening, and he sank into a state of drowsy oppression. It seemed to him that he had wronged Nadyezhda Fyodorovna and her husband, and that it was through his fault that her husband had died. It seemed to him that he had sinned against his own life, which he had ruined, against the world of lofty ideas, of learning, and of work, and he conceived that wonderful world as real and possible, not on this sea-front with hungry Turks and lazy mountaineers sauntering upon it, but there in the North, where there were operas, theatres, newspapers, and all kinds of intellectual activity. One could only there -- not here -- be honest, intelligent, lofty, and pure. He accused himself of having no ideal, no guiding principle in life, though he had a dim understanding now what it meant. Two years before, when he fell in love with Nadyezhda Fyodorovna, it seemed to him that he had only to go with her as his wife to the Caucasus, and he would be saved from vulgarity and emptiness; in the same way now, he was convinced that he had only to part from Nadyezhda Fyodorovna and to go to Petersburg, and he would get everything he wanted.

"Run away," he muttered to himself, sitting up and biting his nails. "Run away!"

He pictured in his imagination how he would go aboard the steamer and then would have some lunch, would drink some cold beer, would talk on deck with ladies, then would get into the train at Sevastopol and set off. Hurrah for freedom! One station after another would flash by, the air would keep growing colder and keener, then the birches and the fir-trees, then Kursk, Moscow. . . . In the restaurants cabbage soup, mutton with kasha, sturgeon, beer, no more Asiaticism, but Russia, real Russia. The passengers in the train would talk about trade, new singers, the Franco-Russian *entente;* on all sides there would be the feeling of keen, cultured, intellectual, eager life. . . . Hasten on, on! At last Nevsky Prospect, and Great Morskaya Street, and then Kovensky Place, where he used to live at one time when he was a student, the dear grey sky, the drizzling rain, the drenched cabmen. . . .

"Ivan Andreitch!" someone called from the next room. "Are you at home?"

"I'm here," Laevsky responded. "What do you want?"

"Papers."

Laevsky got up languidly, feeling giddy, walked into the other room, yawning and shuffling with his slippers. There, at the open window that looked into the street, stood one of his young fellow-clerks, laying out some government documents on the window-sill.

"One minute, my dear fellow," Laevsky said softly, and he went to look for the ink; returning to the window, he signed the papers without looking at them, and said: "It's hot!"

"Yes. Are you coming to-day?"

"I don't think so. . . . I'm not quite well. Tell Sheshkovsky that I will come and see him after dinner."

The clerk went away. Laevsky lay down on his sofa again and began thinking:

"And so I must weigh all the circumstances and reflect on them. Before I go away from here I ought to pay up my debts. I owe about two thousand roubles. I have no money. . . . Of course, that's not important; I shall pay part now, somehow, and I shall send the rest, later, from Petersburg. The chief point is Nadyezhda Fyodorovna. . . . First of all we must define our relations. . . . Yes."

A little later he was considering whether it would not be better to go to Samoylenko for advice.

"I might go," he thought, "but what use would there be in it? I shall only say something inappropriate about boudoirs, about women, about what is honest or dishonest. What's the use of talking about what is honest or dishonest, if I must make haste to save my life, if I am suffocating in this cursed slavery and am killing myself? . . . One must realise at last that to go on leading the life I do is something so base and so cruel that everything else seems petty and trivial beside it. To run away," he muttered, sitting down, "to run away."

The deserted seashore, the insatiable heat, and the monotony of the smoky lilac mountains, ever the same and silent, everlastingly solitary, overwhelmed him with depression, and, as it were, made him drowsy and sapped his energy. He was perhaps very clever, talented, remarkably honest; perhaps if the sea and the mountains had not closed him in on all sides, he might have become an excellent Zemstvo leader, a statesman, an orator, a political writer, a saint. Who knows? If so, was it not stupid to argue whether it were honest or dishonest when a gifted and useful man -- an artist or musician, for instance -- to escape from prison, breaks a wall and deceives his jailers? Anything is honest when a man is in such a position.

At two o'clock Laevsky and Nadyezhda Fyodorovna sat down to dinner. When the cook gave them rice and tomato soup, Laevsky said:

"The same thing every day. Why not have cabbage soup?"

"There are no cabbages."

"It's strange. Samoylenko has cabbage soup and Marya Konstantinovna has cabbage soup, and only I am obliged to eat this mawkish mess. We can't go on like this, darling."

As is common with the vast majority of husbands and wives, not a single dinner had in earlier days passed without scenes and fault-finding between Nadyezhda Fyodorovna and Laevsky; but ever since Laevsky had made up his mind that he did not love her, he had tried to give way to Nadyezhda Fyodorovna in everything, spoke to her gently and politely, smiled, and called her " darling."

"This soup tastes like liquorice," he said, smiling; he made an effort to control himself and seem amiable, but could not refrain from saying: "Nobody looks after the housekeeping. . . . If you are too ill or busy with reading, let me look after the cooking."

In earlier days she would have said to him, "Do by all means," or, "I see you want to turn me into a cook"; but now she only looked at him timidly and flushed crimson.

"Well, how do you feel to-day?" he asked kindly.

"I am all right to-day. There is nothing but a little weakness."

"You must take care of yourself, darling. I am awfully anxious about you."

Nadyezhda Fyodorovna was ill in some way. Samoylenko said she had intermittent fever, and gave her quinine; the other doctor, Ustimovitch, a tall, lean, unsociable man, who used to sit at home in the daytime, and in the evenings walk slowly up and down on the sea-front coughing, with his hands folded behind him and a cane stretched along his back, was of opinion that she had a female complaint, and prescribed warm compresses. In old days, when Laevsky loved her, Nadyezhda Fyodorovna's illness had excited his pity and terror; now he saw falsity even in her illness. Her yellow, sleepy face, her lustreless eyes, her apathetic expression, and the yawning that always followed her attacks of fever, and the fact that during them she lay under a shawl and looked more like a boy than a woman, and that it was close and stuffy in her room -- all this, in his opinion, destroyed the illusion and was an argument against love and marriage.

The next dish given him was spinach with hard-boiled eggs, while Nadyezhda Fyodorovna, as an invalid, had jelly and milk. When with a preoccupied face she touched the jelly with a spoon and then began languidly eating it, sipping milk, and he heard her swallowing, he was possessed by such an overwhelming aversion that it made his head tingle. He recognised that such a feeling would be an insult even to a dog, but he was angry, not with himself but with Nadyezhda Fyodorovna, for arousing such a feeling, and he understood why lovers sometimes murder their mistresses. He would not murder her, of course, but if he had been on a jury now, he would have acquitted the murderer.

"Merci, darling," he said after dinner, and kissed Nadyezhda Fyodorovna on the forehead.

Going back into his study, he spent five minutes in walking to and fro, looking at his boots; then he sat down on his sofa and muttered:

"Run away, run away! We must define the position and run away!"

He lay down on the sofa and recalled again that Nadyezhda Fyodorovna's husband had died, perhaps, by his fault.

"To blame a man for loving a woman, or ceasing to love a woman, is stupid," he persuaded himself, lying down and raising his legs in order to put on his high boots. "Love and hatred are not under our control. As for her husband, maybe I was in an indirect way one of the causes of his death; but again, is it my fault that I fell in love with his wife and she with me?"

Then he got up, and finding his cap, set off to the lodgings of his colleague, Sheshkovsky, where the Government clerks met every day to play *vint* and drink beer.

"My indecision reminds me of Hamlet," thought Laevsky on the way. "How truly Shakespeare describes it! Ah, how truly!"

III

For the sake of sociability and from sympathy for the hard plight of newcomers without families, who, as there was not an hotel in the town, had nowhere to dine, Dr. Samoylenko kept a sort of table dÕhôte. At this time there were only two men who habitually dined with him: a young zoologist called Von Koren, who had come for the summer to the Black Sea to study the embryology of the medusa, and a deacon called Pobyedov, who had only just left the seminary and been sent to the town to take the duty of the old deacon who had gone away for a cure. Each of them paid twelve roubles a month for their dinner and supper, and Samoylenko made them promise to turn up at two o'clock punctually.

Von Koren was usually the first to appear. He sat down in the drawing-room in silence, and taking an album from the table, began attentively scrutinising the faded photographs of unknown men in full trousers and top-hats, and ladies in crinolines and caps. Samoylenko only remembered a few of them by name, and of those whom he had forgotten he said with a sigh: "A very fine fellow, remarkably intelligent!" When he had finished with the album, Von Koren took a pistol from the whatnot, and screwing up his left eye, took deliberate aim at the portrait of Prince Vorontsov, or stood still at the looking-glass and gazed a long time at his swarthy face, his big forehead, and his black hair, which curled like a negro's, and his shirt of dull-coloured cotton with big flowers on it like a Persian rug, and the broad leather belt he wore instead of a waistcoat. The contemplation of his own image seemed to afford him almost more satisfaction than looking at photographs or playing with the pistols. He was very well satisfied with his face, and his becomingly clipped beard, and the broad shoulders, which were unmistakable evidence of his excellent health and physical strength. He was satisfied, too, with his stylish get-up, from the cravat, which matched the colour of his shirt, down to his brown boots.

While he was looking at the album and standing before the glass, at that moment, in the kitchen and in the passage near, Samoylenko, without his coat and waistcoat, with his neck bare, excited and bathed in perspiration, was bustling about the tables, mixing the salad, or making some sauce, or preparing meat, cucumbers, and onion for the cold soup, while he glared fiercely at the orderly who was helping him, and brandished first a knife and then a spoon at him.

"Give me the vinegar!" he said. "That's not the vinegar -- it's the salad oil!" he shouted, stamping. "Where are you off to, you brute?"

"To get the butter, Your Excellency," answered the flustered orderly in a cracked voice.

"Make haste; it's in the cupboard! And tell Daria to put some fennel in the jar with the cucumbers! Fennel! Cover the cream up, gaping laggard, or the flies will get into it!

And the whole house seemed resounding with his shouts. When it was ten or fifteen minutes to two the deacon would come in; he was a lanky young man of twenty-two, with long hair, with no beard and a hardly perceptible moustache. Going into the drawing-room, he crossed himself before the ikon, smiled, and held out his hand to Von Koren.

"Good-morning," the zoologist said coldly. "Where have you been?"

"I've been catching sea-gudgeon in the harbour."

"Oh, of course. . . . Evidently, deacon, you will never be busy with work."

"Why not? Work is not like a bear; it doesn't run off into the woods," said the deacon, smiling and thrusting his hands into the very deep pockets of his white cassock.

"There's no one to whip you!" sighed the zoologist.

Another fifteen or twenty minutes passed and they were not called to dinner, and they could still hear the orderly running into the kitchen and back again, noisily treading with his boots, and Samoylenko shouting:

"Put it on the table! Where are your wits? Wash it first."

The famished deacon and Von Koren began tapping on the floor with their heels, expressing in this way their impatience like the audience at a theatre. At last the door opened and the harassed orderly announced that dinner was ready! In the dining-room they were met by Samoylenko, crimson in the face, wrathful, perspiring from the heat of the kitchen; he looked at them furiously, and with an expression of horror, took the lid off the soup tureen and helped each of them to a plateful; and only when he was convinced that they were eating it with relish and liked it, he gave a sigh of relief and settled himself in his deep arm-chair. His face looked blissful and his eyes grew moist. . . . He deliberately poured himself out a glass of vodka and said:

"To the health of the younger generation."

After his conversation with Laevsky, from early morning till dinner Samoylenko had been conscious of a load at his heart, although he was in the best of humours; he felt sorry for Laevsky and wanted to help him. After drinking a glass of vodka before the soup, he heaved a sigh and said:

"I saw Vanya Laevsky to-day. He is having a hard time of it, poor fellow! The material side of life is not encouraging for him, and the worst of it is all this psychology is too much for him. I'm sorry for the lad."

"Well, that is a person I am not sorry for," said Von Koren. "If that charming individual were drowning, I would push him under with a stick and say, 'Drown, brother, drown away.' . . ."

"That's untrue. You wouldn't do it."

"Why do you think that?" The zoologist shrugged his shoulders. "I'm just as capable of a good action as you are."

"Is drowning a man a good action?" asked the deacon, and he laughed.

"Laevsky? Yes."

I think there is something amiss with the soup . . ." said Samoylenko, anxious to change the conversation.

"Laevsky is absolutely pernicious and is as dangerous to society as the cholera microbe," Von Koren went on. "To drown him would be a service."

"It does not do you credit to talk like that about your neighbour. Tell us: what do you hate him for?"

"Don't talk nonsense, doctor. To hate and despise a microbe is stupid, but to look upon everybody one meets without distinction as one's neighbour, whatever happens -- thanks very much, that is equivalent to giving up criticism, renouncing a straightforward attitude to people, washing one's hands of responsibility, in fact! I consider your Laevsky a blackguard; I do not conceal it, and I am perfectly conscientious in treating him as such. Well, you look upon him as your neighbour -- and you may kiss him if you like: you look upon him as your neighbour, and that means that your attitude to him is the same as to me and to the deacon; that is no attitude at all. You are equally indifferent to all."

"To call a man a blackguard!" muttered Samoylenko, frowning with distaste -- "that is so wrong that I can't find words for it!"

"People are judged by their actions," Von Koren continued. "Now you decide, deacon. . . . I am going to talk to you, deacon. Mr. Laevsky's career lies open before you, like a long Chinese puzzle, and you can read it from beginning to end. What has he been doing these two years that he has been living here? We will reckon his doings on our fingers. First, he has taught the inhabitants of the town to play *vint*: two years ago that game was unknown here; now they all play it from morning till late at night, even the women and the boys. Secondly, he has taught the residents to drink beer, which was not known here either; the inhabitants are indebted to him for the knowledge of various sorts of spirits, so that now they can distinguish Kospelov's vodka from Smirnov's No. 21, blindfold. Thirdly, in former days, people here made love to other men's wives in secret, from the same motives as thieves steal in secret and not openly; adultery was considered something they were ashamed to make a public display of. Laevsky has come as a pioneer in that line; he lives with another man's wife openly. . . . Fourthly . . ."

Von Koren hurriedly ate up his soup and gave his plate to the orderly.

"I understood Laevsky from the first month of our acquaintance," he went on, addressing the deacon. "We arrived here at the same time. Men like him are very fond of friendship, intimacy, solidarity, and all the rest of it, because they always want company for *vint*, drinking, and eating; besides, they are talkative and must have listeners. We made friends -- that is, he turned up every day, hindered me working, and indulged in confidences in regard to his mistress. From the first he struck me by his exceptional falsity, which simply made me sick. As a friend I pitched into him, asking him why he drank too much, why he lived beyond his means and got into debt, why he did nothing and read nothing, why he had so little culture and so little knowledge; and in answer to all my questions he used to smile bitterly, sigh, and say: 'I am a failure, a superfluous man'; or: 'What do you expect, my dear fellow, from us, the debris of the serf-owning class?' or: 'We are degenerate. . . .' Or he would begin a long rigmarole about Onyegin, Petchorin, Byron's Cain, and Bazarov, of whom he would say: 'They are our fathers in flesh and in spirit.' So we are to understand that it was not his fault that Government envelopes lay unopened in his office for weeks together, and that he drank and taught others to drink, but Onyegin, Petchorin, and Turgenev, who had invented the failure and the superfluous man, were responsible for it. The cause of his extreme dissoluteness and unseemliness lies, do you see, not in himself, but somewhere outside in space. And so -- an ingenious idea! -- it is not only he who is dissolute, false, and disgusting, but we . . . 'we men of the eighties,' 'we the spiritless, nervous offspring of the serf-owning class'; 'civilisation has crippled us' . . . in fact, we are to understand that such a great man as Laevsky is great even in his fall: that his dissoluteness, his lack of culture and of moral purity, is a phenomenon of natural history, sanctified by inevitability; that the causes of it are world-wide, elemental; and that we ought to hang up a lamp before Laevsky, since he is the fated victim of the age, of influences, of heredity, and so on. All the officials and their ladies were in ecstasies when they listened to him, and I could not make out for a long time what sort of man I had to deal with, a cynic or a clever rogue. Such types as he, on the surface intellectual with a smattering of education and a great deal of talk about their own nobility, are very clever in posing as exceptionally complex natures."

"Hold your tongue!" Samoylenko flared up. "I will not allow a splendid fellow to be spoken ill of in my presence!"

"Don't interrupt, Alexandr Daviditch," said Von Koren coldly; "I am just finishing. Laevsky is by no means a complex organism. Here is his moral skeleton: in the morning, slippers, a bathe, and coffee; then till dinner-time, slippers, a constitutional, and conversation; at two o'clock slippers, dinner, and wine; at five o'clock a bathe, tea and wine, then *vint* and lying; at ten o'clock supper and wine; and after midnight sleep and *la femme.* His existence is confined within this narrow programme like an egg within its shell. Whether he walks or sits, is angry, writes, rejoices, it may all be reduced to wine, cards, slippers, and women. Woman plays a fatal, overwhelming part in his life. He tells us himself that at thirteen he was in love; that when he was a student in his first year he was living with a lady who had a good influence over him, and to whom he was indebted for his musical education. In his second year he bought a prostitute from a brothel and raised her to his level -- that is, took her as his kept mistress, and she lived with him for six months and then ran away back to the brothel-keeper, and her flight caused him much spiritual suffering. Alas! his sufferings were so great that he had to leave the university and spend two years at home doing nothing. But this was all for the best. At home he made friends with a widow who advised him to leave the Faculty of Jurisprudence and go into the Faculty of Arts. And so he did. When he had taken his degree, he fell passionately in love with his present . . . what's her name? . . . married lady, and was obliged to flee with her here to the Caucasus for the sake of his ideals, he would have us believe, seeing that . . . to-morrow, if not to-day, he will be tired of her and flee back again to Petersburg, and that, too, will be for the sake of his ideals."

"How do you know?" growled Samoylenko, looking angrily at the zoologist. "You had better eat your dinner."

The next course consisted of boiled mullet with Polish sauce. Samoylenko helped each of his companions to a whole mullet and poured out the sauce with his own hand. Two minutes passed in silence.

"Woman plays an essential part in the life of every man," said the deacon. "You can't help that."

"Yes, but to what degree? For each of us woman means mother, sister, wife, friend. To Laevsky she is everything, and at the same time nothing but a mistress. She -- that is, cohabitation with her -- is the happiness and object of his life; he is gay, sad, bored, disenchanted -- on account of woman; his life grows disagreeable -- woman is to blame; the dawn of a new life begins to glow, ideals turn up -- and again look for the woman. . . . He only derives enjoyment from books and pictures in which there is woman. Our age is, to his thinking, poor and inferior to the forties and the sixties only because we do not know how to abandon ourselves obviously to the passion and ecstasy of love. These voluptuaries must have in their brains a special growth of the nature of sarcoma, which stifles the brain and directs their whole psychology. Watch Laevsky when he is sitting anywhere in company. You notice: when one raises any general question in his presence, for instance, about the cell or instinct, he sits apart, and neither speaks nor listens; he looks languid and disillusioned; nothing has any interest for him, everything is vulgar and trivial. But as soon as you speak of male and female -- for instance, of the fact that the female spider, after fertilisation, devours the male -- his eyes glow with curiosity, his face brightens, and the man revives, in fact. All his thoughts, however noble, lofty, or neutral they may be, they all have one point of resemblance. You walk along the street with him and meet a donkey, for instance. . . . 'Tell me, please,' he asks, 'what would happen if you mated a donkey with a camel?' And his dreams! Has he told you of his dreams? It is magnificent! First, he dreams that he is married to the moon, then that he is summoned before the police and ordered to live with a guitar . . ."

The deacon burst into resounding laughter; Samoylenko frowned and wrinkled up his face angrily so as not to laugh, but could not restrain himself, and laughed.

"And it's all nonsense!" he said, wiping his tears. "Yes, by Jove, it's nonsense!"

IV

The deacon was very easily amused, and laughed at every trifle till he got a stitch in his side, till he was helpless. It seemed as though he only liked to be in people's company because there was a ridiculous side to them, and because they might be given ridiculous nicknames. He had nicknamed Samoylenko "the tarantula," his orderly "the drake," and was in ecstasies when on one occasion Von Koren spoke of Laevsky and Nadyezhda Fyodorovna as "Japanese monkeys." He watched people's faces greedily, listened without blinking, and it could be seen that his eyes filled with laughter and his face was tense with expectation of the moment when he could let himself go and burst into laughter.

"He is a corrupt and depraved type," the zoologist continued, while the deacon kept his eyes riveted on his face, expecting he would say something funny. "It is not often one can meet with such a nonentity. In body he is inert, feeble, prematurely old, while in intellect he differs in no respect from a fat shopkeeper's wife who does nothing but eat, drink, and sleep on a feather-bed, and who keeps her coachman as a lover."

The deacon began guffawing again.

"Don't laugh, deacon," said Von Koren. "It grows stupid, at last. I should not have paid attention to his insignificance," he went on, after waiting till the deacon had left off laughing; "I should have passed him by if he were not so noxious and dangerous. His noxiousness lies first of all in the fact that he has great success with women, and so threatens to leave descendants -- that is, to present the world with a dozen Laevskys as feeble and as depraved as himself. Secondly, he is in the highest degree contaminating. I have spoken to you already of *vint* and beer. In another year or two he will dominate the whole Caucasian coast. You know how the mass, especially its middle stratum, believe in intellectuality, in a university education, in gentlemanly manners, and in literary language. Whatever filthy thing he did, they would all believe that it was as it should be, since he is an intellectual man, of liberal ideas and university education. What is more, he is a failure, a superfluous man, a neurasthenic, a victim of the age, and that means he can do anything. He is a charming fellow, a regular good sort, he is so genuinely indulgent to human weaknesses; he is compliant, accommodating, easy and not proud; one can drink with him and gossip and talk evil of people. . . . The masses, always inclined to anthropomorphism in religion and morals, like best of all the little gods who have the same weaknesses as themselves. Only think what a wide field he has for contamination! Besides, he is not a bad actor and is a clever hypocrite, and knows very well how to twist things round. Only take his little shifts and dodges, his attitude to civilisation, for instance. He has scarcely sniffed at civilisation, yet: 'Ah, how we have been crippled by civilisation! Ah, how I envy those savages, those children of nature, who know nothing of civilisation!' We are to understand, you see, that at one time, in ancient days, he has been devoted to civilisation with his whole soul, has served it, has sounded it to its depths, but it has exhausted him, disillusioned him, deceived him; he is a Faust, do you see? -- a second Tolstoy. . . . As for Schopenhauer and Spencer, he treats them like small boys and slaps them on the shoulder in a fatherly way: 'Well, what do you say, old Spencer?' He has not read Spencer, of course, but how charming he is when with light, careless irony he says of his lady friend: 'She has read Spencer!' And they all listen to him, and no one cares to understand that this charlatan has not the right to kiss the sole of Spencer's foot, let alone speaking about him in that tone! Sapping the foundations of civilisation, of authority, of other people's altars, spattering them with filth, winking jocosely at them only to justify and conceal one's own rottenness and moral poverty is only possible for a very vain, base, and nasty creature."

"I don't know what it is you expect of him, Kolya," said Samoylenko, looking at the zoologist, not with anger now, but with a guilty air. "He is a man the same as everyone else. Of course, he has his weaknesses, but he is abreast of modern ideas, is in the service, is of use to his country. Ten years ago there was an old fellow serving as agent here, a man of the greatest intelligence . . . and he used to say . . ."

"Nonsense, nonsense!" the zoologist interrupted. "You say he is in the service; but how does he serve? Do you mean to tell me that things have been done better because he is here, and the officials are more punctual, honest, and civil? On the contrary, he has only sanctioned their slackness by his prestige as an intellectual university man. He is only punctual on the 20th of the month, when he gets his salary; on the other days he lounges about at home in slippers and tries to look as if he were doing the Government a great service by living in the Caucasus. No, Alexandr Daviditch, don't stick up for him. You are insincere from beginning to end. If you really loved him and considered him your neighbour, you would above all not be indifferent to his weaknesses, you would not be indulgent to them, but for his own sake would try to make him innocuous."

"That is?"

"Innocuous. Since he is incorrigible, he can only be made innocuous in one way. . . ." Von Koren passed his finger round his throat. "Or he might be drowned . . .," he added. "In the interests of humanity and in their own interests, such people ought to be destroyed. They certainly ought."

"What are you saying?" muttered Samoylenko, getting up and looking with amazement at the zoologist's calm, cold face. " Deacon, what is he saying? Why -- are you in your senses?"

"I don't insist on the death penalty," said Von Koren. "If it is proved that it is pernicious, devise something else. If we can't destroy Laevsky, why then, isolate him, make him harmless, send him to hard labour."

"What are you saying!" said Samoylenko in horror. "With pepper, with pepper," he cried in a voice of despair, seeing that the deacon was eating stuffed aubergines without pepper. "You with your great intellect, what are you saying! Send our friend, a proud intellectual man, to penal servitude!"

"Well, if he is proud and tries to resist, put him in fetters!"

Samoylenko could not utter a word, and only twiddled his fingers; the deacon looked at his flabbergasted and really absurd face, and laughed.

"Let us leave off talking of that," said the zoologist. "Only remember one thing, Alexandr Daviditch: primitive man was preserved from such as Laevsky by the struggle for existence and by natural selection; now our civilisation has considerably weakened the struggle and the selection, and we ought to look after the destruction of the rotten and worthless for ourselves; otherwise, when the Laevskys multiply, civilisation will perish and mankind will degenerate utterly. It will be our fault."

"If it depends on drowning and hanging," said Samoylenko, "damnation take your civilisation, damnation take your humanity! Damnation take it! I tell you what: you are a very learned and intelligent man and the pride of your country, but the Germans have ruined you. Yes, the Germans! The Germans!

Since Samoylenko had left Dorpat, where he had studied medicine, he had rarely seen a German and had not read a single German book, but, in his opinion, every harmful idea in politics or science was due to the Germans. Where he had got this notion he could not have said himself, but he held it firmly.

"Yes, the Germans!" he repeated once more. "Come and have some tea."

All three stood up, and putting on their hats, went out into the little garden, and sat there under the shade of the light green maples, the pear-trees, and a chestnut-tree. The zoologist and the deacon sat on a bench by the table, while Samoylenko sank into a deep wicker chair with a sloping back. The orderly handed them tea, jam, and a bottle of syrup.

It was very hot, thirty degrees Réaumur in the shade. The sultry air was stagnant and motionless, and a long spider-web, stretching from the chestnut-tree to the ground, hung limply and did not stir.

The deacon took up the guitar, which was constantly lying on the ground near the table, tuned it, and began singing softly in a thin voice:

"'Gathered round the tavern were the seminary lads,' "

but instantly subsided, overcome by the heat, mopped his brow and glanced upwards at the blazing blue sky. Samoylenko grew drowsy; the sultry heat, the stillness and the delicious after-dinner languor, which quickly pervaded all his limbs, made him feel heavy and sleepy; his arms dropped at his sides, his eyes grew small, his head sank on his breast. He looked with almost tearful tenderness at Von Koren and the deacon, and muttered:

"The younger generation. . . A scientific star and a luminary of the Church. . . . I shouldn't wonder if the long-skirted alleluia will be shooting up into a bishop; I dare say I may come to kissing his hand. . . . Well . . . please God. . . ."

Soon a snore was heard. Von Koren and the deacon finished their tea and went out into the street.

"Are you going to the harbour again to catch sea-gudgeon?" asked the zoologist.

"No, it's too hot."

"Come and see me. You can pack up a parcel and copy something for me. By the way, we must have a talk about what you are to do. You must work, deacon. You can't go on like this."

"Your words are just and logical," said the deacon. "But my laziness finds an excuse in the circumstances of my present life. You know yourself that an uncertain position has a great tendency to make people apathetic. God only knows whether I have been sent here for a time or permanently. I am living here in uncertainty, while my wife is vegetating at her father's and is missing me. And I must confess my brain is melting with the heat."

"That's all nonsense," said the zoologist. "You can get used to the heat, and you can get used to being without the deaconess. You mustn't be slack; you must pull yourself together."

V

Nadyezhda Fyodorovna went to bathe in the morning, and her cook, Olga, followed her with a jug, a copper basin, towels, and a sponge. In the bay stood two unknown steamers with dirty white funnels, obviously foreign cargo vessels. Some men dressed in white and wearing white shoes were walking along the harbour, shouting loudly in French, and were answered from the steamers. The bells were ringing briskly in the little church of the town.

"To-day is Sunday!" Nadyezhda Fyodorovna remembered with pleasure.

She felt perfectly well, and was in a gay holiday humour. In a new loose-fitting dress of coarse thick tussore silk, and a big wide-brimmed straw hat which was bent down over her ears, so that her face looked out as though from a basket, she fancied she looked very charming. She thought that in the whole town there was only one young, pretty, intellectual woman, and that was herself, and that she was the only one who knew how to dress herself cheaply, elegantly, and with taste. That dress, for example, cost only twenty-two roubles, and yet how charming it was! In the whole town she was the only one who could be attractive, while there were numbers of men, so they must all, whether they would or not, be envious of Laevsky.

She was glad that of late Laevsky had been cold to her, reserved and polite, and at times even harsh and rude; in the past she had met all his outbursts, all his contemptuous, cold or strange incomprehensible glances, with tears, reproaches, and threats to leave him or to starve herself to death; now she only blushed, looked guiltily at him, and was glad he was not affectionate to her. If he had abused her, threatened her, it would have been better and pleasanter, since she felt hopelessly guilty towards him. She felt she was to blame, in the first place, for not sympathising with the dreams of a life of hard work, for the sake of which he had given up Petersburg and had come here to the Caucasus, and she was convinced that he had been angry with her of late for precisely that. When she was travelling to the Caucasus, it seemed that she would find here on the first day a cosy nook by the sea, a snug little garden with shade, with birds, with little brooks, where she could grow flowers and vegetables, rear ducks and hens, entertain her neighbours, doctor poor peasants and distribute little books amongst them. It had turned out that the Caucasus was nothing but bare mountains, forests, and huge valleys, where it took a long time and a great deal of effort to find anything and settle down; that there were no neighbours of any sort; that it was very hot and one might be robbed. Laevsky had been in no hurry to obtain a piece of land; she was glad of it, and they seemed to be in a tacit compact never to allude to a life of hard work. He was silent about it, she thought, because he was angry with her for being silent about it.

In the second place, she had without his knowledge during those two years bought various trifles to the value of three hundred roubles at Atchmianov's shop. She had bought the things by degrees, at one time materials, at another time silk or a parasol, and the debt had grown imperceptibly.

"I will tell him about it to-day . . .," she used to decide, but at once reflected that in Laevsky's present mood it would hardly be convenient to talk to him of debts.

Thirdly, she had on two occasions in Laevsky's absence received a visit from Kirilin, the police captain: once in the morning when Laevsky had gone to bathe, and another time at midnight when he was playing cards. Remembering this, Nadyezhda Fyodorovna flushed crimson, and looked round at the cook as though she might overhear her thoughts. The long, insufferably hot, wearisome days, beautiful languorous evenings and stifling nights, and the whole manner of living, when from morning to night one is at a loss to fill up the useless hours, and the persistent thought that she was the prettiest young woman in the town, and that her youth was passing and being wasted, and Laevsky himself, though honest and idealistic, always the same, always lounging about in his slippers, biting his nails, and wearying her with his caprices, led by degrees to her becoming possessed by desire, and as though she were mad, she thought of nothing else day and night. Breathing, looking, walking, she felt nothing but desire. The sound of the sea told her she must love; the darkness of evening -- the same; the mountains -- the same. . . . And when Kirilin began paying her attentions, she had neither the power nor the wish to resist, and surrendered to him. . . .

Now the foreign steamers and the men in white reminded her for some reason of a huge hall; together with the shouts of French she heard the strains of a waltz, and her bosom heaved with unaccountable delight. She longed to dance and talk French.

She reflected joyfully that there was nothing terrible about her infidelity. Her soul had no part in her infidelity; she still loved Laevsky, and that was proved by the fact that she was jealous of him, was sorry for him, and missed him when he was away. Kirilin had turned out to be very mediocre, rather coarse though handsome; everything was broken off with him already and there would never be anything more. What had happened was over; it had nothing to do with anyone, and if Laevsky found it out he would not believe in it.

There was only one bathing-house for ladies on the sea-front; men bathed under the open sky. Going into the bathing-house, Nadyezhda Fyodorovna found there an elderly lady, Marya Konstantinovna Bityugov, and her daughter Katya, a schoolgirl of fifteen; both of them were sitting on a bench undressing. Marya Konstantinovna was a good-natured, enthusiastic, and genteel person, who talked in a drawling and pathetic voice. She had been a governess until she was thirty-two, and then had married Bityugov, a Government official -- a bald little man with his hair combed on to his temples and with a very meek disposition. She was still in love with him, was jealous, blushed at the word "love," and told everyone she was very happy.

"My dear," she cried enthusiastically, on seeing Nadyezhda Fyodorovna, assuming an expression which all her acquaintances called "almond-oily." "My dear, how delightful that you have come! We'll bathe together -- that's enchanting!"

Olga quickly flung off her dress and chemise, and began undressing her mistress.

"It's not quite so hot to-day as yesterday?" said Nadyezhda Fyodorovna, shrinking at the coarse touch of the naked cook. "Yesterday I almost died of the heat."

"Oh, yes, my dear; I could hardly breathe myself. Would you believe it? I bathed yesterday three times! Just imagine, my dear, three times! Nikodim Alexandritch was quite uneasy."

"Is it possible to be so ugly?" thought Nadyezhda Fyodorovna, looking at Olga and the official's wife; she glanced at Katya and thought: "The little girl's not badly made."

"Your Nikodim Alexandritch is very charming!" she said. "I'm simply in love with him."

"Ha, ha, ha!" cried Marya Konstantinovna, with a forced laugh; "that's quite enchanting."

Free from her clothes, Nadyezhda Fyodorovna felt a desire to fly. And it seemed to her that if she were to wave her hands she would fly upwards. When she was undressed, she noticed that Olga looked scornfully at her white body. Olga, a young soldier's wife, was living with her lawful husband, and so considered herself superior to her mistress. Marya Konstantinovna and Katya were afraid of her, and did not respect her. This was disagreeable, and to raise herself in their opinion, Nadyezhda Fyodorovna said:

"At home, in Petersburg, summer villa life is at its height now. My husband and I have so many friends! We ought to go and see them."

"I believe your husband is an engineer?" said Marya Konstantinovna timidly.

"I am speaking of Laevsky. He has a great many acquaintances. But unfortunately his mother is a proud aristocrat, not very intelligent. . . ."

Nadyezhda Fyodorovna threw herself into the water without finishing; Marya Konstantinovna and Katya made their way in after her.

"There are so many conventional ideas in the world," Nadyezhda Fyodorovna went on, "and life is not so easy as it seems."

Marya Konstantinovna, who had been a governess in aristocratic families and who was an authority on social matters, said:

"Oh yes! Would you believe me, my dear, at the Garatynskys' I was expected to dress for lunch as well as for dinner, so that, like an actress, I received a special allowance for my wardrobe in addition to my salary."

She stood between Nadyezhda Fyodorovna and Katya as though to screen her daughter from the water that washed the former.

Through the open doors looking out to the sea they could see someone swimming a hundred paces from their bathing-place.

"Mother, it's our Kostya," said Katya.

"Ach, ach!" Marya Konstantinovna cackled in her dismay. "Ach, Kostya!" she shouted, "Come back! Kostya, come back!"

Kostya, a boy of fourteen, to show off his prowess before his mother and sister, dived and swam farther, but began to be exhausted and hurried back, and from his strained and serious face it could be seen that he could not trust his own strength.

"The trouble one has with these boys, my dear! said Marya Konstantinovna, growing calmer. "Before you can turn round, he will break his neck. Ah, my dear, how sweet it is, and yet at the same time how difficult, to be a mother! One's afraid of everything."

Nadyezhda Fyodorovna put on her straw hat and dashed out into the open sea. She swam some thirty feet and then turned on her back. She could see the sea to the horizon, the steamers, the people on the sea-front, the town; and all this, together with the sultry heat and the soft, transparent waves, excited her and whispered that she must live, live. . . . A sailing-boat darted by her rapidly and vigorously, cleaving the waves and the air; the man sitting at the helm looked at her, and she liked being looked at. . . .

After bathing, the ladies dressed and went away together.

"I have fever every alternate day, and yet I don't get thin," said Nadyezhda Fyodorovna, licking her lips, which were salt from the bathe, and responding with a smile to the bows of her acquaintances. "I've always been plump, and now I believe I'm plumper than ever."

"That, my dear, is constitutional. If, like me, one has no constitutional tendency to stoutness, no diet is of any use. . . . But you've wetted your hat, my dear."

"It doesn't matter; it will dry."

Nadyezhda Fyodorovna saw again the men in white who were walking on the sea-front and talking French; and again she felt a sudden thrill of joy, and had a vague memory of some big hall in which she had once danced, or of which, perhaps, she had once dreamed. And something at the bottom of her soul dimly and obscurely whispered to her that she was a pretty, common, miserable, worthless woman. . . .

Marya Konstantinovna stopped at her gate and asked her to come in and sit down for a little while.

"Come in, my dear," she said in an imploring voice, and at the same time she looked at Nadyezhda Fyodorovna with anxiety and hope; perhaps she would refuse and not come in!

"With pleasure," said Nadyezhda Fyodorovna, accepting. "You know how I love being with you!"

And she went into the house. Marya Konstantinovna sat her down and gave her coffee, regaled her with milk rolls, then showed her photographs of her former pupils, the Garatynskys, who were by now married. She showed her, too, the examination reports of Kostya and Katya. The reports were very good, but to make them seem even better, she complained, with a sigh, how difficult the lessons at school were now. . . . She made much of her visitor, and was sorry for her, though at the same time she was harassed by the thought that Nadyezhda Fyodorovna might have a corrupting influence on the morals of Kostya and Katya, and was glad that her Nikodim Alexandritch was not at home. Seeing that in her opinion all men are fond of "women like that," Nadyezhda Fyodorovna might have a bad effect on Nikodim Alexandritch too.

As she talked to her visitor, Marya Konstantinovna kept remembering that they were to have a picnic that evening, and that Von Koren had particularly begged her to say nothing about it to the "Japanese monkeys" -- that is, Laevsky and Nadyezhda Fyodorovna; but she dropped a word about it unawares, crimsoned, and said in confusion:

"I hope you will come too!"

VI

It was agreed to drive about five miles out of town on the road to the south, to stop near a *duhan* at the junction of two streams -- the Black River and the Yellow River -- and to cook fish soup. They started out soon after five. Foremost of the party in a char-à-banc drove Samoylenko and Laevsky; they were followed by Marya Konstantinovna, Nadyezhda Fyodorovna, Katya and Kostya, in a coach with three horses, carrying with them the crockery and a basket with provisions. In the next carriage came the police captain, Kirilin, and the young Atchmianov, the son of the shopkeeper to whom Nadyezhda Fyodorovna owed three hundred roubles; opposite them, huddled up on the little seat with his feet tucked under him, sat Nikodim Alexandritch, a neat little man with hair combed on to his temples. Last of all came Von Koren and the deacon; at the deacon's feet stood a basket of fish.

"R-r-right!" Samoylenko shouted at the top of his voice when he met a cart or a mountaineer riding on a donkey.

"In two years' time, when I shall have the means and the people ready, I shall set off on an expedition," Von Koren was telling the deacon. " I shall go by the sea-coast from Vladivostok to the Behring Straits, and then from the Straits to the mouth of the Yenisei. We shall make the map, study the fauna and the flora, and make detailed geological, anthropological, and ethnographical researches. It depends upon you to go with me or not."

"It's impossible," said the deacon.

"Why?"

"I'm a man with ties and a family."

"Your wife will let you go; we will provide for her. Better still if you were to persuade her for the public benefit to go into a nunnery; that would make it possible for you to become a monk, too, and join the expedition as a priest. I can arrange it for you."

The deacon was silent.

"Do you know your theology well?" asked the zoologist.

"No, rather badly."

"H'm! . . . I can't give you any advice on that score, because I don't know much about theology myself. You give me a list of books you need, and I will send them to you from Petersburg in the winter. It will be necessary for you to read the notes of religious travellers, too; among them are some good ethnologists and Oriental scholars. When you are familiar with their methods, it will be easier for you to set to work. And you needn't waste your time till you get the books; come to me, and we will study the compass and go through a course of meteorology. All that's indispensable."

"To be sure . . ." muttered the deacon, and he laughed. "I was trying to get a place in Central Russia, and my uncle, the head priest, promised to help me. If I go with you I shall have troubled them for nothing."

"I don't understand your hesitation. If you go on being an ordinary deacon, who is only obliged to hold a service on holidays, and on the other days can rest from work, you will be exactly the same as you are now in ten years' time, and will have gained nothing but a beard and moustache; while on returning from this expedition in ten years' time you will be a different man, you will be enriched by the consciousness that something has been done by you."

From the ladies' carriage came shrieks of terror and delight. The carriages were driving along a road hollowed in a literally overhanging precipitous cliff, and it seemed to everyone that they were galloping along a shelf on a steep wall, and that in a moment the carriages would drop into the abyss. On the right stretched the sea; on the left was a rough brown wall with black blotches and red veins and with climbing roots; while on the summit stood shaggy fir-trees bent over, as though looking down in terror and curiosity. A minute later there were shrieks and laughter again: they had to drive under a huge overhanging rock.

"I don't know why the devil I'm coming with you," said Laevsky. "How stupid and vulgar it is! I want to go to the North, to run away, to escape; but here I am, for some reason, going to this stupid picnic."

"But look, what a view!" said Samoylenko as the horses turned to the left, and the valley of the Yellow River came into sight and the stream itself gleamed in the sunlight, yellow, turbid, frantic.

"I see nothing fine in that, Sasha," answered Laevsky. "To be in continual ecstasies over nature shows poverty of imagination. In comparison with what my imagination can give me, all these streams and rocks are trash, and nothing else."

The carriages now were by the banks of the stream. The high mountain banks gradually grew closer, the valley shrank together and ended in a gorge; the rocky mountain round which they were driving had been piled together by nature out of huge rocks, pressing upon each other with such terrible weight, that Samoylenko could not help gasping every time he looked at them. The dark and beautiful mountain was cleft in places by narrow fissures and gorges from which came a breath of dewy moisture and mystery; through the gorges could be seen other mountains, brown, pink, lilac, smoky, or bathed in vivid sunlight. From time to time as they passed a gorge they caught the sound of water falling from the heights and splashing on the stones.

"Ach, the damned mountains!" sighed Laevsky. "How sick I am of them!"

At the place where the Black River falls into the Yellow, and the water black as ink stains the yellow and struggles with it, stood the Tatar Kerbalay's *duhan*, with the Russian flag on the roof and with an inscription written in chalk: "The Pleasant *duhan*." Near it was a little garden, enclosed in a hurdle fence, with tables and chairs set out in it, and in the midst of a thicket of wretched thornbushes stood a single solitary cypress, dark and beautiful.

Kerbalay, a nimble little Tatar in a blue shirt and a white apron, was standing in the road, and, holding his stomach, he bowed low to welcome the carriages, and smiled, showing his glistening white teeth.

"Good-evening, Kerbalay," shouted Samoylenko. "We are driving on a little further, and you take along the samovar and chairs! Look sharp!"

Kerbalay nodded his shaven head and muttered something, and only those sitting in the last carriage could hear: "We've got trout, your Excellency."

"Bring them, bring them!" said Von Koren.

Five hundred paces from the *duhan* the carriages stopped. Samoylenko selected a small meadow round which there were scattered stones convenient for sitting on, and a fallen tree blown down by the storm with roots overgrown by moss and dry yellow needles. Here there was a fragile wooden bridge over the stream, and just opposite on the other bank there was a little barn for drying maize, standing on four low piles, and looking like the hut on hen's legs in the fairy tale; a little ladder sloped from its door.

The first impression in all was a feeling that they would never get out of that place again. On all sides wherever they looked, the mountains rose up and towered above them, and the shadows of evening were stealing rapidly, rapidly from the *duhan* and dark cypress, making the narrow winding valley of the Black River narrower and the mountains higher. They could hear the river murmuring and the unceasing chirrup of the grasshoppers.

"Enchanting!" said Marya Konstantinovna, heaving deep sighs of ecstasy. "Children, look how fine! What peace!"

"Yes, it really is fine," assented Laevsky, who liked the view, and for some reason felt sad as he looked at the sky and then at the blue smoke rising from the chimney of the *duhan*. "Yes, it is fine," he repeated.

"Ivan Andreitch, describe this view," Marya Konstantinovna said tearfully.

"Why?" asked Laevsky. "The impression is better than any description. The wealth of sights and sounds which everyone receives from nature by direct impression is ranted about by authors in a hideous and unrecognisable way."

"Really?" Von Koren asked coldly, choosing the biggest stone by the side of the water, and trying to clamber up and sit upon it. "Really?" he repeated, looking directly at Laevsky. "What of 'Romeo and Juliet'? Or, for instance, Pushkin's 'Night in the Ukraine'? Nature ought to come and bow down at their feet."

"Perhaps," said Laevsky, who was too lazy to think and oppose him. "Though what is 'Romeo and Juliet' after all? " he added after a short pause. "The beauty of poetry and holiness of love are simply the roses under which they try to hide its rottenness. Romeo is just the same sort of animal as all the rest of us."

"Whatever one talks to you about, you always bring it round to . . ." Von Koren glanced round at Katya and broke off.

"What do I bring it round to?" asked Laevsky.

"One tells you, for instance, how beautiful a bunch of grapes is, and you answer: 'Yes, but how ugly it is when it is chewed and digested in one's stomach!' Why say that? It's not new, and . . . altogether it is a queer habit."

Laevsky knew that Von Koren did not like him, and so was afraid of him, and felt in his presence as though everyone were constrained and someone were standing behind his back. He made no answer and walked away, feeling sorry he had come.

"Gentlemen, quick march for brushwood for the fire!" commanded Samoylenko.

They all wandered off in different directions, and no one was left but Kirilin, Atchmianov, and Nikodim Alexandritch. Kerbalay brought chairs, spread a rug on the ground, and set a few bottles of wine.

The police captain, Kirilin, a tall, good-looking man, who in all weathers wore his great-coat over his tunic, with his haughty deportment, stately carriage, and thick, rather hoarse voice, looked like a young provincial chief of police; his expression was mournful and sleepy, as though he had just been waked against his will.

"What have you brought this for, you brute?" he asked Kerbalay, deliberately articulating each word. "I ordered you to give us *kvarel,* and what have you brought, you ugly Tatar? Eh? What?"

"We have plenty of wine of our own, Yegor Alekseitch," Nikodim Alexandritch observed, timidly and politely.

"What? But I want us to have my wine, too; I'm taking part in the picnic and I imagine I have full right to contribute my share. I im-ma-gine so! Bring ten bottles of *kvarel."*

"Why so many?" asked Nikodim Alexandritch, in wonder, knowing Kirilin had no money.

"Twenty bottles! Thirty!" shouted Kirilin.

"Never mind, let him," Atchmianov whispered to Nikodim Alexandritch; "I'll pay."

Nadyezhda Fyodorovna was in a light-hearted, mischievous mood; she wanted to skip and jump, to laugh, to shout, to tease, to flirt. In her cheap cotton dress with blue pansies on it, in her red shoes and the same straw hat, she seemed to herself, little, simple, light, ethereal as a butterfly. She ran over the rickety bridge and looked for a minute into the water, in order to feel giddy; then, shrieking and laughing, ran to the other side to the drying-shed, and she fancied that all the men were admiring her, even Kerbalay. When in the rapidly falling darkness the trees began to melt into the mountains and the horses into the carriages, and a light gleamed in the windows of the *duhan,* she climbed up the mountain by the little path which zigzagged between stones and thorn-bushes and sat on a stone. Down below, the camp-fire was burning. Near the fire, with his sleeves tucked up, the deacon was moving to and fro, and his long black shadow kept describing a circle round it; he put on wood, and with a spoon tied to a long stick he stirred the cauldron. Samoylenko, with a copper-red face, was fussing round the fire just as though he were in his own kitchen, shouting furiously:

"Where's the salt, gentlemen? I bet you've forgotten it. Why are you all sitting about like lords while I do the work?"

Laevsky and Nikodim Alexandritch were sitting side by side on the fallen tree looking pensively at the fire. Marya Konstantinovna, Katya, and Kostya were taking the cups, saucers, and plates out of the baskets. Von Koren, with his arms folded and one foot on a stone, was standing on a bank at the very edge of the water, thinking about something. Patches of red light from the fire moved together with the shadows over the ground near the dark human figures, and quivered on the mountain, on the trees, on the bridge, on the drying-shed; on the other side the steep, scooped-out bank was all lighted up and glimmering in the stream, and the rushing turbid water broke its reflection into little bits.

The deacon went for the fish which Kerbalay was cleaning and washing on the bank, but he stood still half-way and looked about him.

"My God, how nice it is!" he thought. "People, rocks, the fire, the twilight, a monstrous tree -- nothing more, and yet how fine it is!"

On the further bank some unknown persons made their appearance near the drying-shed. The flickering light and the smoke from the camp-fire puffing in that direction made it impossible to get a full view of them all at once, but glimpses were caught now of a shaggy hat and a grey beard, now of a blue shirt, now of a figure, ragged from shoulder to knee, with a dagger across the body; then a swarthy young face with black eyebrows, as thick and bold as though they had been drawn in charcoal. Five of them sat in a circle on the ground, and the other five went into the drying-shed. One was standing at the door with his back to the fire, and with his hands behind his back was telling something, which must have been very interesting, for when Samoylenko threw on twigs and the fire flared up, and scattered sparks and threw a glaring light on the shed, two calm countenances with an expression on them of deep attention could be seen, looking out of the door, while those who were sitting in a circle turned round and began listening to the speaker. Soon after, those sitting in a circle began softly singing something slow and melodious, that sounded like Lenten Church music. . . . Listening to them, the deacon imagined how it would be with him in ten years' time, when he would come back from the expedition: he would be a young priest and monk, an author with a name and a splendid past; he would be consecrated an archimandrite, then a bishop; and he would serve mass in the cathedral; in a golden mitre he would come out into the body of the church with the ikon on his breast, and blessing the mass of the people with the triple and the double candelabra, would proclaim: "Look down from Heaven, O God, behold and visit this vineyard which Thy Hand has planted," and the children with their angel voices would sing in response: "Holy God. . ."

"Deacon, where is that fish?" he heard Samoylenko's voice.

As he went back to the fire, the deacon imagined the Church procession going along a dusty road on a hot July day; in front the peasants carrying the banners and the women and children the ikons, then the boy choristers and the sacristan with his face tied up and a straw in his hair, then in due order himself, the deacon, and behind him the priest wearing his *calotte* and carrying a cross, and behind them, tramping in the dust, a crowd of peasants -- men, women, and children; in the crowd his wife and the priest's wife with kerchiefs on their heads. The choristers sing, the babies cry, the corncrakes call, the lark carols. . . . Then they make a stand and sprinkle the herd with holy water. . . . They go on again, and then kneeling pray for rain. Then lunch and talk. . . .

"And that's nice too . . ." thought the deacon.

VII

Kirilin and Atchmianov climbed up the mountain by the path. Atchmianov dropped behind and stopped, while Kirilin went up to Nadyezhda Fyodorovna.

"Good-evening," he said, touching his cap.

"Good-evening."

"Yes!" said Kirilin, looking at the sky and pondering.

"Why 'yes'?" asked Nadyezhda Fyodorovna after a brief pause, noticing that Atchmianov was watching them both.

"And so it seems," said the officer, slowly, "that our love has withered before it has blossomed, so to speak. How do you wish me to understand it? Is it a sort of coquetry on your part, or do you look upon me as a nincompoop who can be treated as you choose."

"It was a mistake! Leave me alone!" Nadyezhda Fyodorovna said sharply, on that beautiful, marvellous evening, looking at him with terror and asking herself with bewilderment, could there really have been a moment when that man attracted her and had been near to her?

"So that's it!" said Kirilin; he thought in silence for a few minutes and said: "Well, I'll wait till you are in a better humour, and meanwhile I venture to assure you I am a gentleman, and I don't allow anyone to doubt it. Adieu!"

He touched his cap again and walked off, making his way between the bushes. After a short interval Atchmianov approached hesitatingly.

"What a fine evening!" he said with a slight Armenian accent.

He was nice-looking, fashionably dressed, and behaved unaffectedly like a well-bred youth, but Nadyezhda Fyodorovna did not like him because she owed his father three hundred roubles; it was displeasing to her, too, that a shopkeeper had been asked to the picnic, and she was vexed at his coming up to her that evening when her heart felt so pure.

The picnic is a success altogether," he said, after a pause.

"Yes," she agreed, and as though suddenly remembering her debt, she said carelessly: "Oh, tell them in your shop that Ivan Andreitch will come round in a day or two and will pay three hundred roubles. . . . I don't remember exactly what it is."

"I would give another three hundred if you would not mention that debt every day. Why be prosaic?"

Nadyezhda Fyodorovna laughed; the amusing idea occurred to her that if she had been willing and sufficiently immoral she might in one minute be free from her debt. If she, for instance, were to turn the head of this handsome young fool! How amusing, absurd, wild it would be really! And she suddenly felt a longing to make him love her, to plunder him, throw him over, and then to see what would come of it.

"Allow me to give you one piece of advice," Atchmianov said timidly. "I beg you to beware of Kirilin. He says horrible things about you everywhere."

"It doesn't interest me to know what every fool says of me," Nadyezhda Fyodorovna said coldly, and the amusing thought of playing with handsome young Atchmianov suddenly lost its charm.

"We must go down," she said; "they're calling us."

The fish soup was ready by now. They were ladling it out by platefuls, and eating it with the religious solemnity with which this is only done at a picnic; and everyone thought the fish soup very good, and thought that at home they had never eaten anything so nice. As is always the case at picnics, in the mass of dinner napkins, parcels, useless greasy papers fluttering in the wind, no one knew where was his glass or where his bread. They poured the wine on the carpet and on their own knees, spilt the salt, while it was dark all round them and the fire burnt more dimly, and everyone was too lazy to get up and put wood on. They all drank wine, and even gave Kostya and Katya half a glass each. Nadyezhda Fyodorovna drank one glass and then another, got a little drunk and forgot about Kirilin.

"A splendid picnic, an enchanting evening," said Laevsky, growing lively with the wine. "But I should prefer a fine winter to all this. 'His beaver collar is silver with hoar-frost.'

"Everyone to his taste," observed Von Koren.

Laevsky felt uncomfortable; the heat of the campfire was beating upon his back, and the hatred of Von Koren upon his breast and face: this hatred on the part of a decent, clever man, a feeling in which there probably lay hid a well-grounded reason, humiliated him and enervated him, and unable to stand up against it, he said in a propitiatory tone:

"I am passionately fond of nature, and I regret that I'm not a naturalist. I envy you."

"Well, I don't envy you, and don't regret it," said Nadyezhda Fyodorovna. "I don't understand how anyone can seriously interest himself in beetles and ladybirds while the people are suffering."

Laevsky shared her opinion. He was absolutely ignorant of natural science, and so could never reconcile himself to the authoritative tone and the learned and profound air of the people who devoted themselves to the whiskers of ants and the claws of beetles, and he always felt vexed that these people, relying on these whiskers, claws, and something they called protoplasm (he always imagined it in the form of an oyster), should undertake to decide questions involving the origin and life of man. But in Nadyezhda Fyodorovna's words he heard a note of falsity, and simply to contradict her he said: "The point is not the ladybirds, but the deductions made from them."

VIII

It was late, eleven o'clock, when they began to get into the carriages to go home. They took their seats, and the only ones missing were Nadyezhda Fyodorovna and Atchmianov, who were running after one another, laughing, the other side of the stream.

"Make haste, my friends," shouted Samoylenko.

"You oughtn't to give ladies wine," said Von Koren in a low voice.

Laevsky, exhausted by the picnic, by the hatred of Von Koren, and by his own thoughts, went to meet Nadyezhda Fyodorovna, and when, gay and happy, feeling light as a feather, breathless and laughing, she took him by both hands and laid her head on his breast, he stepped back and said dryly:

"You are behaving like a . . . cocotte."

It sounded horribly coarse, so that he felt sorry for her at once. On his angry, exhausted face she read hatred, pity and vexation with himself, and her heart sank at once. She realised instantly that she had gone too far, had been too free and easy in her behaviour, and overcome with misery, feeling herself heavy, stout, coarse, and drunk, she got into the first empty carriage together with Atchmianov. Laevsky got in with Kirilin, the zoologist with Samoylenko, the deacon with the ladies, and the party set off.

"You see what the Japanese monkeys are like," Von Koren began, rolling himself up in his cloak and shutting his eyes. "You heard she doesn't care to take an interest in beetles and ladybirds because the people are suffering. That's how all the Japanese monkeys look upon people like us. They're a slavish, cunning race, terrified by the whip and the fist for ten generations; they tremble and burn incense only before violence; but let the monkey into a free state where there's no one to take it by the collar, and it relaxes at once and shows itself in its true colours. Look how bold they are in picture galleries, in museums, in theatres, or when they talk of science: they puff themselves out and get excited, they are abusive and critical . . . they are bound to criticise -- it's the sign of the slave. You listen: men of the liberal professions are more often sworn at than pickpockets -- that's because three-quarters of society are made up of slaves, of just such monkeys. It never happens that a slave holds out his hand to you and sincerely says 'Thank you' to you for your work."

"I don't know what you want," said Samoylenko, yawning; "the poor thing, in the simplicity of her heart, wanted to talk to you of scientific subjects, and you draw a conclusion from that. You're cross with him for something or other, and with her, too, to keep him company. She's a splendid woman."

"Ah, nonsense! An ordinary kept woman, depraved and vulgar. Listen, Alexandr Daviditch; when you meet a simple peasant woman, who isn't living with her husband, who does nothing but giggle, you tell her to go and work. Why are you timid in this case and afraid to tell the truth? Simply because Nadyezhda Fyodorovna is kept, not by a sailor, but by an official."

"What am I to do with her?" said Samoylenko, getting angry. "Beat her or what?

"Not flatter vice. We curse vice only behind its back, and that's like making a long nose at it round a corner. I am a zoologist or a sociologist, which is the same thing; you are a doctor; society believes in us; we ought to point out the terrible harm which threatens it and the next generation from the existence of ladies like Nadyezhda Ivanovna."

"Fyodorovna," Samoylenko corrected. "But what ought society to do?"

"Society? That's its affair. To my thinking the surest and most direct method is -- compulsion. *Manu militari* she ought to be returned to her husband; and if her husband won't take her in, then she ought to be sent to penal servitude or some house of correction."

"Ouf!" sighed Samoylenko. He paused and asked quietly: "You said the other day that people like Laevsky ought to be destroyed. . . . Tell me, if you . . . if the State or society commissioned you to destroy him, could you . . . bring yourself to it?"

"My hand would not tremble."

IX

When they got home, Laevsky and Nadyezhda Fyodorovna went into their dark, stuffy, dull rooms. Both were silent. Laevsky lighted a candle, while Nadyezhda Fyodorovna sat down, and without taking off her cloak and hat, lifted her melancholy, guilty eyes to him.

He knew that she expected an explanation from him, but an explanation would be wearisome, useless and exhausting, and his heart was heavy because he had lost control over himself and been rude to her. He chanced to feel in his pocket the letter which he had been intending every day to read to her, and thought if he were to show her that letter now, it would turn her thoughts in another direction.

"It is time to define our relations," he thought. "I will give it her; what is to be will be."

He took out the letter and gave it her.

"Read it. It concerns you."

Saying this, he went into his own room and lay down on the sofa in the dark without a pillow. Nadyezhda Fyodorovna read the letter, and it seemed to her as though the ceiling were falling and the walls were closing in on her. It seemed suddenly dark and shut in and terrible. She crossed herself quickly three times and said:

"Give him peace, O Lord . . . give him peace. . . ."

And she began crying.

"Vanya," she called. "Ivan Andreitch!"

There was no answer. Thinking that Laevsky had come in and was standing behind her chair, she sobbed like a child, and said:

"Why did you not tell me before that he was dead? I wouldn't have gone to the picnic; I shouldn't have laughed so horribly. . . . The men said horrid things to me. What a sin, what a sin! Save me, Vanya, save me. . . . I have been mad. . . . I am lost. . . ."

Laevsky heard her sobs. He felt stifled and his heart was beating violently. In his misery he got up, stood in the middle of the room, groped his way in the dark to an easy-chair by the table, and sat down.

"This is a prison . . ." he thought. "I must get away . . . I can't bear it."

It was too late to go and play cards; there were no restaurants in the town. He lay down again and covered his ears that he might not hear her sobbing, and he suddenly remembered that he could go to Samoylenko. To avoid going near Nadyezhda Fyodorovna, he got out of the window into the garden, climbed over the garden fence and went along the street. It was dark. A steamer, judging by its lights, a big passenger one, had just come in. He heard the clank of the anchor chain. A red light was moving rapidly from the shore in the direction of the steamer: it was the Customs boat going out to it.

"The passengers are asleep in their cabins . . ." thought Laevsky, and he envied the peace of mind of other people.

The windows in Samoylenko's house were open. Laevsky looked in at one of them, then in at another; it was dark and still in the rooms.

"Alexandr Daviditch, are you asleep?" he called. "Alexandr Daviditch!"

He heard a cough and an uneasy shout:

"Who's there? What the devil?"

"It is I, Alexandr Daviditch; excuse me."

A little later the door opened; there was a glow of soft light from the lamp, and Samoylenko's huge figure appeared all in white, with a white nightcap on his head.

"What now?" he asked, scratching himself and breathing hard from sleepiness. "Wait a minute; I'll open the door directly."

"Don't trouble; I'll get in at the window. . . ."

Laevsky climbed in at the window, and when he reached Samoylenko, seized him by the hand.

"Alexandr Daviditch," he said in a shaking voice, "save me! I beseech you, I implore you. Understand me! My position is agonising. If it goes on for another two days I shall strangle myself like . . . like a dog."

"Wait a bit. . . . What are you talking about exactly?"

"Light a candle."

"Oh . . . oh! . . ." sighed Samoylenko, lighting a candle. "My God! My God! . . . Why, it's past one, brother."

"Excuse me, but I can't stay at home," said Laevsky, feeling great comfort from the light and the presence of Samoylenko. "You are my best, my only friend, Alexandr Daviditch. . . . You are my only hope. For God's sake, come to my rescue, whether you want to or not. I must get away from here, come what may! . . . Lend me the money!"

"Oh, my God, my God! . . . sighed Samoylenko, scratching himself. "I was dropping asleep and I hear the whistle of the steamer, and now you . . . Do you want much?"

"Three hundred roubles at least. I must leave her a hundred, and I need two hundred for the journey. . . . I owe you about four hundred already, but I will send it you all . . . all. . . ."

Samoylenko took hold of both his whiskers in one hand, and standing with his legs wide apart, pondered.

"Yes . . ." he muttered, musing. "Three hundred. . . . Yes. . . . But I haven't got so much. I shall have to borrow it from someone."

"Borrow it, for God's sake!" said Laevsky, seeing from Samoylenko's face that he wanted to lend him the money and certainly would lend it. "Borrow it, and I'll be sure to pay you back. I will send it from Petersburg as soon as I get there. You can set your mind at rest about that. I'll tell you what, Sasha," he said, growing more animated; "let us have some wine."

"Yes . . . we can have some wine, too."

They both went into the dining-room.

"And how about Nadyezhda Fyodorovna?" asked Samoylenko, setting three bottles and a plate of peaches on the table. "Surely she's not remaining?"

"I will arrange it all, I will arrange it all," said Laevsky, feeling an unexpected rush of joy. "I will send her the money afterwards and she will join me. . . . Then we will define our relations. To your health, friend."

"Wait a bit," said Samoylenko. "Drink this first. . . . This is from my vineyard. This bottle is from Navaridze's vineyard and this one is from Ahatulov's. . . . Try all three kinds and tell me candidly. . . . There seems a little acidity about mine. Eh? Don't you taste it?"

"Yes. You have comforted me, Alexandr Daviditch. Thank you. . . . I feel better."

"Is there any acidity?"

"Goodness only knows, I don't know. But you are a splendid, wonderful man!"

Looking at his pale, excited, good-natured face, Samoylenko remembered Von Koren's view that men like that ought to be destroyed, and Laevsky seemed to him a weak, defenceless child, whom anyone could injure and destroy.

"And when you go, make it up with your mother," he said. "It's not right."

"Yes, yes; I certainly shall."

They were silent for a while. When they had emptied the first bottle, Samoylenko said:

"You ought to make it up with Von Koren too. You are both such splendid, clever fellows, and you glare at each other like wolves."

"Yes, he's a fine, very intelligent fellow," Laevsky assented, ready now to praise and forgive everyone. "He's a remarkable man, but it's impossible for me to get on with him. No! Our natures are too different. I'm an indolent, weak, submissive nature. Perhaps in a good minute I might hold out my hand to him, but he would turn away from me . . . with contempt."

Laevsky took a sip of wine, walked from corner to corner and went on, standing in the middle of the room:

"I understand Von Koren very well. His is a resolute, strong, despotic nature. You have heard him continually talking of 'the expedition,' and it's not mere talk. He wants the wilderness, the moonlit night: all around in little tents, under the open sky, lie sleeping his sick and hungry Cossacks, guides, porters, doctor, priest, all exhausted with their weary marches, while only he is awake, sitting like Stanley on a camp-stool, feeling himself the monarch of the desert and the master of these men. He goes on and on and on, his men groan and die, one after another, and he goes on and on, and in the end perishes himself, but still is monarch and ruler of the desert, since the cross upon his tomb can be seen by the caravans for thirty or forty miles over the desert. I am sorry the man is not in the army. He would have made a splendid military genius. He would not have hesitated to drown his cavalry in the river and make a bridge out of dead bodies. And such hardihood is more needed in war than any kind of fortification or strategy. Oh, I understand him perfectly! Tell me: why is he wasting his substance here? What does he want here?"

"He is studying the marine fauna."

"No, no, brother, no!" Laevsky sighed. "A scientific man who was on the steamer told me the Black Sea was poor in animal life, and that in its depths, thanks to the abundance of sulphuric hydrogen, organic life was impossible. All the serious zoologists work at the biological station at Naples or Villefranche. But Von Koren is independent and obstinate: he works on the Black Sea because nobody else is working there; he is at loggerheads with the university, does not care to know his comrades and other scientific men because he is first of all a despot and only secondly a zoologist. And you'll see he'll do something. He is already dreaming that when he comes back from his expedition he will purify our universities from intrigue and mediocrity, and will make the scientific men mind their ps and qs. Despotism is just as strong in science as in the army. And he is spending his second summer in this stinking little town because he would rather be first in a village than second in a town. Here he is a king and an eagle; he keeps all the inhabitants under his thumb and oppresses them with his authority. He has appropriated everyone, he meddles in other people's affairs; everything is of use to him, and everyone is afraid of him. I am slipping out of his clutches, he feels that and hates me. Hasn't he told you that I ought to be destroyed or sent to hard labour?"

"Yes," laughed Samoylenko.

Laevsky laughed too, and drank some wine.

"His ideals are despotic too," he said, laughing, and biting a peach. "Ordinary mortals think of their neighbour -- me, you, man in fact -- if they work for the common weal. To Von Koren men are puppets and nonentities, too trivial to be the object of his life. He works, will go for his expedition and break his neck there, not for the sake of love for his neighbour, but for the sake of such abstractions as humanity, future generations, an ideal race of men. He exerts himself for the improvement of the human race, and we are in his eyes only slaves, food for the cannon, beasts of burden; some he would destroy or stow away in Siberia, others he would break by discipline, would, like Araktcheev, force them to get up and go to bed to the sound of the drum; would appoint eunuchs to preserve our chastity and morality, would order them to fire at anyone who steps out of the circle of our narrow conservative morality; and all this in the name of the improvement of the human race. . . . And what is the human race? Illusion, mirage . . . despots have always been illusionists. I understand him very well, brother. I appreciate him and don't deny his importance; this world rests on men like him, and if the world were left only to such men as us, for all our good-nature and good intentions, we should make as great a mess of it as the flies have of that picture. Yes."

Laevsky sat down beside Samoylenko, and said with genuine feeling: "I'm a foolish, worthless, depraved man. The air I breathe, this wine, love, life in fact -- for all that, I have given nothing in exchange so far but lying, idleness, and cowardice. Till now I have deceived myself and other people; I have been miserable about it, and my misery was cheap and common. I bow my back humbly before Von Koren's hatred because at times I hate and despise myself."

Laevsky began again pacing from one end of the room to the other in excitement, and said:

"I'm glad I see my faults clearly and am conscious of them. That will help me to reform and become a different man. My dear fellow, if only you knew how passionately, with what anguish, I long for such a change. And I swear to you I'll be a man! I will! I don't know whether it is the wine that is speaking in me, or whether it really is so, but it seems to me that it is long since I have spent such pure and lucid moments as I have just now with you."

It's time to sleep, brother," said Samoylenko.

"Yes, yes. . . . Excuse me; I'll go directly."

Laevsky moved hurriedly about the furniture and windows, looking for his cap.

"Thank you," he muttered, sighing. "Thank you. . . . Kind and friendly words are better than charity. You have given me new life."

He found his cap, stopped, and looked guiltily at Samoylenko.

"Alexandr Daviditch," he said in an imploring voice.

"What is it?"

"Let me stay the night with you, my dear fellow!"

"Certainly. . . . Why not?"

Laevsky lay down on the sofa, and went on talking to the doctor for a long time.

X

Three days after the picnic, Marya Konstantinovna unexpectedly called on Nadyezhda Fyodorovna, and without greeting her or taking off her hat, seized her by both hands, pressed them to her breast and said in great excitement:

"My dear, I am deeply touched and moved: our dear kind-hearted doctor told my Nikodim Alexandritch yesterday that your husband was dead. Tell me, my dear . . . tell me, is it true?

"Yes, it's true; he is dead," answered Nadyezhda Fyodorovna.

"That is awful, awful, my dear! But there's no evil without some compensation; your husband was no doubt a noble, wonderful, holy man, and such are more needed in Heaven than on earth."

Every line and feature in Marya Konstantinovna's face began quivering as though little needles were jumping up and down under her skin; she gave an almond-oily smile and said, breathlessly, enthusiastically:

"And so you are free, my dear. You can hold your head high now, and look people boldly in the face. Henceforth God and man will bless your union with Ivan Andreitch. It's enchanting. I am trembling with joy, I can find no words. My dear, I will give you away. . . . Nikodim Alexandritch and I have been so fond of you, you will allow us to give our blessing to your pure, lawful union. When, when do you think of being married?"

"I haven't thought of it," said Nadyezhda Fyodorovna, freeing her hands.

"That's impossible, my dear. You have thought of it, you have."

"Upon my word, I haven't," said Nadyezhda Fyodorovna, laughing. "What should we be married for? I see no necessity for it. We'll go on living as we have lived."

"What are you saying!" cried Marya Konstantinovna in horror. "For God's sake, what are you saying!"

"Our getting married won't make things any better. On the contrary, it will make them even worse. We shall lose our freedom."

"My dear, my dear, what are you saying!" exclaimed Marya Konstantinovna, stepping back and flinging up her hands. "You are talking wildly! Think what you are saying. You must settle down!"

"'Settle down.' How do you mean? I have not lived yet, and you tell me to settle down."

Nadyezhda Fyodorovna reflected that she really had not lived. She had finished her studies in a boarding-school and had been married to a man she did not love; then she had thrown in her lot with Laevsky, and had spent all her time with him on this empty, desolate coast, always expecting something better. Was that life?

"I ought to be married though," she thought, but remembering Kirilin and Atchmianov she flushed and said:

"No, it's impossible. Even if Ivan Andreitch begged me to on his knees -- even then I would refuse."

Marya Konstantinovna sat on the sofa for a minute in silence, grave and mournful, gazing fixedly into space; then she got up and said coldly:

"Good-bye, my dear! Forgive me for having troubled you. Though it's not easy for me, it's my duty to tell you that from this day all is over between us, and, in spite of my profound respect for Ivan Andreitch, the door of my house is closed to you henceforth."

She uttered these words with great solemnity and was herself overwhelmed by her solemn tone. Her face began quivering again; it assumed a soft almond-oily expression. She held out both hands to Nadyezhda Fyodorovna, who was overcome with alarm and confusion, and said in an imploring voice:

"My dear, allow me if only for a moment to be a mother or an elder sister to you! I will be as frank with you as a mother."

Nadyezhda Fyodorovna felt in her bosom warmth, gladness, and pity for herself, as though her own mother had really risen up and were standing before her. She impulsively embraced Marya Konstantinovna and pressed her face to her shoulder. Both of them shed tears. They sat down on the sofa and for a few minutes sobbed without looking at one another or being able to utter a word.

"My dear child," began Marya Konstantinovna, "I will tell you some harsh truths, without sparing you."

"For God's sake, for God's sake, do!

"Trust me, my dear. You remember of all the ladies here, I was the only one to receive you. You horrified me from the very first day, but I had not the heart to treat you with disdain like all the rest. I grieved over dear, good Ivan Andreitch as though he were my son -- a young man in a strange place, inexperienced, weak, with no mother; and I was worried, dreadfully worried. . . . My husband was opposed to our making his acquaintance, but I talked him over . . . persuaded him. . . . We began receiving Ivan Andreitch, and with him, of course, you. If we had not, he would have been insulted. I have a daughter, a son. . . . You understand the tender mind, the pure heart of childhood . . . 'who so offendeth one of these little ones.' . . . I received you into my house and trembled for my children. Oh, when you become a mother, you will understand my fears. And everyone was surprised at my receiving you, excuse my saying so, as a respectable woman, and hinted to me . . . well, of course, slanders, suppositions. . . . At the bottom of my heart I blamed you, but you were unhappy, flighty, to be pitied, and my heart was wrung with pity for you."

"But why, why?" asked Nadyezhda Fyodorovna, trembling all over. "What harm have I done anyone?"

"You are a terrible sinner. You broke the vow you made your husband at the altar. You seduced a fine young man, who perhaps had he not met you might have taken a lawful partner for life from a good family in his own circle, and would have been like everyone else now. You have ruined his youth. Don't speak, don't speak, my dear! I never believe that man is to blame for our sins. It is always the woman's fault. Men are frivolous in domestic life; they are guided by their minds, and not by their hearts. There's a great deal they don't understand; woman understands it all. Everything depends on her. To her much is given and from her much will be required. Oh, my dear, if she had been more foolish or weaker than man on that side, God would not have entrusted her with the education of boys and girls. And then, my dear, you entered on the path of vice, forgetting all modesty; any other woman in your place would have hidden herself from people, would have sat shut up at home, and would only have been seen in the temple of God, pale, dressed all in black and weeping, and everyone would have said in genuine compassion: 'O Lord, this erring angel is coming back again to Thee. . . .' But you, my dear, have forgotten all discretion; have lived openly, extravagantly; have seemed to be proud of your sin; you have been gay and laughing, and I, looking at you, shuddered with horror, and have been afraid that thunder from Heaven would strike our house while you were sitting with us. My dear, don't speak, don't speak," cried Marya Konstantinovna, observing that Nadyezhda Fyodorovna wanted to speak. "Trust me, I will not deceive you, I will not hide one truth from the eyes of your soul. Listen to me, my dear. . . . God marks great sinners, and you have been marked-out: only think -- your costumes have always been appalling."

Nadyezhda Fyodorovna, who had always had the highest opinion of her costumes, left off crying and looked at her with surprise.

"Yes, appalling," Marya Konstantinovna went on. "Anyone could judge of your behaviour from the elaboration and gaudiness of your attire. People laughed and shrugged their shoulders as they looked at you, and I grieved, I grieved. . . . And forgive me, my dear; you are not nice in your person! When we met in the bathing-place, you made me tremble. Your outer clothing was decent enough, but your petticoat, your chemise. . . . My dear, I blushed! Poor Ivan Andreitch! No one ever ties his cravat properly, and from his linen and his boots, poor fellow! one can see he has no one at home to look after him. And he is always hungry, my darling, and of course, if there is no one at home to think of the samovar and the coffee, one is forced to spend half one's salary at the pavilion. And it's simply awful, awful in your home! No one else in the town has flies, but there's no getting rid of them in your rooms: all the plates and dishes are black with them. If you look at the windows and the chairs, there's nothing but dust, dead flies, and glasses. . . . What do you want glasses standing about for? And, my dear, the table's not cleared till this time in the day. And one's ashamed to go into your bedroom: underclothes flung about everywhere, india-rubber tubes hanging on the walls, pails and basins standing about. . . . My dear! A husband ought to know nothing, and his wife ought to be as neat as a little angel in his presence. I wake up every morning before it is light, and wash my face with cold water that my Nikodim Alexandritch may not see me looking drowsy."

"That's all nonsense," Nadyezhda Fyodorovna sobbed. "If only I were happy, but I am so unhappy!"

"Yes, yes; you are very unhappy!" Marya Konstantinovna sighed, hardly able to restrain herself from weeping. "And there's terrible grief in store for you in the future! A solitary old age, ill-health; and then you will have to answer at the dread judgment seat. . . It's awful, awful. Now fate itself holds out to you a helping hand, and you madly thrust it from you. Be married, make haste and be married!"

"Yes, we must, we must," said Nadyezhda Fyodorovna; "but it's impossible!"

"Why?"

"It's impossible. Oh, if only you knew!"

Nadyezhda Fyodorovna had an impulse to tell her about Kirilin, and how the evening before she had met handsome young Atchmianov at the harbour, and how the mad, ridiculous idea had occurred to her of cancelling her debt for three hundred; it had amused her very much, and she returned home late in the evening feeling that she had sold herself and was irrevocably lost. She did not know herself how it had happened. And she longed to swear to Marya Konstantinovna that she would certainly pay that debt, but sobs and shame prevented her from speaking.

"I am going away," she said. "Ivan Andreitch may stay, but I am going."

"Where?"

"To Russia."

"But how will you live there? Why, you have nothing."

"I will do translation, or . . . or I will open a library . . . ."

"Don't let your fancy run away with you, my dear. You must have money for a library. Well, I will leave you now, and you calm yourself and think things over, and to-morrow come and see me, bright and happy. That will be enchanting! Well, good-bye, my angel. Let me kiss you."

Marya Konstantinovna kissed Nadyezhda Fyodorovna on the forehead, made the sign of the cross over her, and softly withdrew. It was getting dark, and Olga lighted up in the kitchen. Still crying, Nadyezhda Fyodorovna went into the bedroom and lay down on the bed. She began to be very feverish. She undressed without getting up, crumpled up her clothes at her feet, and curled herself up under the bedclothes. She was thirsty, and there was no one to give her something to drink.

"I'll pay it back!" she said to herself, and it seemed to her in delirium that she was sitting beside some sick woman, and recognised her as herself. "I'll pay it back. It would be stupid to imagine that it was for money I . . . I will go away and send him the money from Petersburg. At first a hundred . . . then another hundred . . . and then the third hundred. . . ."

It was late at night when Laevsky came in.

"At first a hundred . . ." Nadyezhda Fyodorovna said to him, "then another hundred . . ."

"You ought to take some quinine," he said, and thought, "To-morrow is Wednesday; the steamer goes and I am not going in it. So I shall have to go on living here till Saturday."

Nadyezhda Fyodorovna knelt up in bed.

"I didn't say anything just now, did I?" she asked, smiling and screwing up her eyes at the light.

"No, nothing. We shall have to send for the doctor to-morrow morning. Go to sleep."

He took his pillow and went to the door. Ever since he had finally made up his mind to go away and leave Nadyezhda Fyodorovna, she had begun to raise in him pity and a sense of guilt; he felt a little ashamed in her presence, as though in the presence of a sick or old horse whom one has decided to kill. He stopped in the doorway and looked round at her.

"I was out of humour at the picnic and said something rude to you. Forgive me, for God's sake!"

Saying this, he went off to his study, lay down, and for a long while could not get to sleep.

Next morning when Samoylenko, attired, as it was a holiday, in full-dress uniform with epaulettes on his shoulders and decorations on his breast, came out of the bedroom after feeling Nadyezhda Fyodorovna's pulse and looking at her tongue, Laevsky, who was standing in the doorway, asked him anxiously: "Well? Well?"

There was an expression of terror, of extreme uneasiness, and of hope on his face.

"Don't worry yourself; there's nothing dangerous," said Samoylenko; "it's the usual fever."

"I don't mean that." Laevsky frowned impatiently. "Have you got the money?"

"My dear soul, forgive me," he whispered, looking round at the door and overcome with confusion.

"For God's sake, forgive me! No one has anything to spare, and I've only been able to collect by five- and by ten-rouble notes. . . . Only a hundred and ten in all. To-day I'll speak to someone else. Have patience."

"But Saturday is the latest date," whispered Laevsky, trembling with impatience. "By all that's sacred, get it by Saturday! If I don't get away by Saturday, nothing's any use, nothing! I can't understand how a doctor can be without money!"

"Lord have mercy on us!" Samoylenko whispered rapidly and intensely, and there was positively a breaking note in his throat. "I've been stripped of everything; I am owed seven thousand, and I'm in debt all round. Is it my fault?"

"Then you'll get it by Saturday? Yes?"

"I'll try."

"I implore you, my dear fellow! So that the money may be in my hands by Friday morning!"

Samoylenko sat down and prescribed solution of quinine and kalii bromati and tincture of rhubarb, tincturæ gentianæ, aquæ foeniculi -- all in one mixture, added some pink syrup to sweeten it, and went away.

XI

"You look as though you were coming to arrest me," said Von Koren, seeing Samoylenko coming in, in his full-dress uniform.

"I was passing by and thought: 'Suppose I go in and pay my respects to zoology,' " said Samoylenko, sitting down at the big table, knocked together by the zoologist himself out of plain boards. "Good-morning, holy father," he said to the deacon, who was sitting in the window, copying something. "I'll stay a minute and then run home to see about dinner. It's time. . . . I'm not hindering you?"

"Not in the least," answered the zoologist, laying out over the table slips of paper covered with small writing. "We are busy copying."

"Ah! . . . Oh, my goodness, my goodness! . . ." sighed Samoylenko. He cautiously took up from the table a dusty book on which there was lying a dead dried spider, and said: "Only fancy, though; some little green beetle is going about its business, when suddenly a monster like this swoops down upon it. I can fancy its terror."

"Yes, I suppose so."

"Is poison given it to protect it from its enemies?"

"Yes, to protect it and enable it to attack."

"To be sure, to be sure. . . . And everything in nature, my dear fellows, is consistent and can be explained," sighed Samoylenko; "only I tell you what I don't understand. You're a man of very great intellect, so explain it to me, please. There are, you know, little beasts no bigger than rats, rather handsome to look at, but nasty and immoral in the extreme, let me tell you. Suppose such a little beast is running in the woods. He sees a bird; he catches it and devours it. He goes on and sees in the grass a nest of eggs; he does not want to eat them -- he is not hungry, but yet he tastes one egg and scatters the others out of the nest with his paw. Then he meets a frog and begins to play with it; when he has tormented the frog he goes on licking himself and meets a beetle; he crushes the beetle with his paw . . . and so he spoils and destroys everything on his way. . . . He creeps into other beasts' holes, tears up the anthills, cracks the snail's shell. If he meets a rat, he fights with it; if he meets a snake or a mouse, he must strangle it; and so the whole day long. Come, tell me: what is the use of a beast like that? Why was he created?"

"I don't know what animal you are talking of," said Von Koren; "most likely one of the insectivora. Well, he got hold of the bird because it was incautious; he broke the nest of eggs because the bird was not skilful, had made the nest badly and did not know how to conceal it. The frog probably had some defect in its colouring or he would not have seen it, and so on. Your little beast only destroys the weak, the unskilful, the careless -- in fact, those who have defects which nature does not think fit to hand on to posterity. Only the cleverer, the stronger, the more careful and developed survive; and so your little beast, without suspecting it, is serving the great ends of perfecting creation."

"Yes, yes, yes. . . . By the way, brother," said Samoylenko carelessly, "lend me a hundred roubles."

"Very good. There are some very interesting types among the insectivorous mammals. For instance, the mole is said to be useful because he devours noxious insects. There is a story that some German sent William I. a fur coat made of moleskins, and the Emperor ordered him to be reproved for having destroyed so great a number of useful animals. And yet the mole is not a bit less cruel than your little beast, and is very mischievous besides, as he spoils meadows terribly."

Von Koren opened a box and took out a hundred-rouble note.

"The mole has a powerful thorax, just like the bat," he went on, shutting the box; "the bones and muscles are tremendously developed, the mouth is extraordinarily powerfully furnished. If it had the proportions of an elephant, it would be an all-destructive, invincible animal. It is interesting when two moles meet underground; they begin at once as though by agreement digging a little platform; they need the platform in order to have a battle more conveniently. When they have made it they enter upon a ferocious struggle and fight till the weaker one falls. Take the hundred roubles," said Von Koren, dropping his voice, "but only on condition that you're not borrowing it for Laevsky."

"And if it were for Laevsky," cried Samoylenko, flaring up, "what is that to you?"

"I can't give it to you for Laevsky. I know you like lending people money. You would give it to Kerim, the brigand, if he were to ask you; but, excuse me, I can't assist you in that direction."

"Yes, it is for Laevsky I am asking it," said Samoylenko, standing up and waving his right arm. "Yes! For Laevsky! And no one, fiend or devil, has a right to dictate to me how to dispose of my own money. It doesn't suit you to lend it me? No?"

The deacon began laughing.

"Don't get excited, but be reasonable," said the zoologist. "To shower benefits on Mr. Laevsky is, to my thinking, as senseless as to water weeds or to feed locusts."

"To my thinking, it is our duty to help our neighbours!" cried Samoylenko.

"In that case, help that hungry Turk who is lying under the fence! He is a workman and more useful and indispensable than your Laevsky. Give him that hundred-rouble note! Or subscribe a hundred roubles to my expedition!"

"Will you give me the money or not? I ask you!"

"Tell me openly: what does he want money for?

"It's not a secret; he wants to go to Petersburg on Saturday."

"So that is it!" Von Koren drawled out. "Aha! . . . We understand. And is she going with him, or how is it to be?"

"She's staying here for the time. He'll arrange his affairs in Petersburg and send her the money, and then she'll go."

"That's smart!" said the zoologist, and he gave a short tenor laugh. "Smart, well planned."

He went rapidly up to Samoylenko, and standing face to face with him, and looking him in the eyes, asked: "Tell me now honestly: is he tired of her? Yes? tell me: is he tired of her? Yes?"

"Yes," Samoylenko articulated, beginning to perspire.

"How repulsive it is!" said Von Koren, and from his face it could be seen that he felt repulsion. "One of two things, Alexandr Daviditch: either you are in the plot with him, or, excuse my saying so, you are a simpleton. Surely you must see that he is taking you in like a child in the most shameless way? Why, it's as clear as day that he wants to get rid of her and abandon her here. She'll be left a burden on you. It is as clear as day that you will have to send her to Petersburg at your expense. Surely your fine friend can't have so blinded you by his dazzling qualities that you can't see the simplest thing?"

"That's all supposition," said Samoylenko, sitting down.

"Supposition? But why is he going alone instead of taking her with him? And ask him why he doesn't send her off first. The sly beast!"

Overcome with sudden doubts and suspicions about his friend, Samoylenko weakened and took a humbler tone.

"But it's impossible," he said, recalling the night Laevsky had spent at his house. "He is so unhappy!"

"What of that? Thieves and incendiaries are unhappy too!"

"Even supposing you are right . . ." said Samoylenko, hesitating. " Let us admit it. . . . Still, he's a young man in a strange place . . . a student. We have been students, too, and there is no one but us to come to his assistance."

"To help him to do abominable things, because he and you at different times have been at universities, and neither of you did anything there! What nonsense!"

"Stop; let us talk it over coolly. I imagine it will be possible to make some arrangement. . . ." Samoylenko reflected, twiddling his fingers. "I'll give him the money, you see, but make him promise on his honour that within a week he'll send Nadyezhda Fyodorovna the money for the journey."

"And he'll give you his word of honour -- in fact, he'll shed tears and believe in it himself; but what's his word of honour worth? He won't keep it, and when in a year or two you meet him on the Nevsky Prospect with a new mistress on his arm, he'll excuse himself on the ground that he has been crippled by civilisation, and that he is made after the pattern of Rudin. Drop him, for God's sake! Keep away from the filth; don't stir it up with both hands!"

Samoylenko thought for a minute and said resolutely:

"But I shall give him the money all the same. As you please. I can't bring myself to refuse a man simply on an assumption."

"Very fine, too. You can kiss him if you like."

"Give me the hundred roubles, then," Samoylenko asked timidly.

"I won't."

A silence followed. Samoylenko was quite crushed; his face wore a guilty, abashed, and ingratiating expression, and it was strange to see this pitiful, childish, shamefaced countenance on a huge man wearing epaulettes and orders of merit.

"The bishop here goes the round of his diocese on horseback instead of in a carriage," said the deacon, laying down his pen. "It's extremely touching to see him sit on his horse. His simplicity and humility are full of Biblical grandeur."

"Is he a good man?" asked Von Koren, who was glad to change the conversation.

"Of course! If he hadn't been a good man, do you suppose he would have been consecrated a bishop?"

"Among the bishops are to be found good and gifted men," said Von Koren. "The only drawback is that some of them have the weakness to imagine themselves statesmen. One busies himself with Russification, another criticises the sciences. That's not their business. They had much better look into their consistory a little."

"A layman cannot judge of bishops."

"Why so, deacon? A bishop is a man just the same as you or I."

"The same, but not the same." The deacon was offended and took up his pen. "If you had been the same, the Divine Grace would have rested upon you, and you would have been bishop yourself; and since you are not bishop, it follows you are not the same."

"Don't talk nonsense, deacon," said Samoylenko dejectedly. " Listen to what I suggest," he said, turning to Von Koren. "Don't give me that hundred roubles. You'll be having your dinners with me for three months before the winter, so let me have the money beforehand for three months."

"I won't."

Samoylenko blinked and turned crimson; he mechanically drew towards him the book with the spider on it and looked at it, then he got up and took his hat.

Von Koren felt sorry for him.

"What it is to have to live and do with people like this," said the zoologist, and he kicked a paper into the corner with indignation. "You must understand that this is not kindness, it is not love, but cowardice, slackness, poison! What's gained by reason is lost by your flabby good-for-nothing hearts! When I was ill with typhoid as a schoolboy, my aunt in her sympathy gave me pickled mushrooms to eat, and I very nearly died. You, and my aunt too, must understand that love for man is not to be found in the heart or the stomach or the bowels, but here!"

Von Koren slapped himself on the forehead.

"Take it," he said, and thrust a hundred-rouble note into his hand.

"You've no need to be angry, Kolya," said Samoylenko mildly, folding up the note. "I quite understand you, but . . . you must put yourself in my place."

"You are an old woman, that's what you are."

The deacon burst out laughing.

"Hear my last request, Alexandr Daviditch," said Von Koren hotly. "When you give that scoundrel the money, make it a condition that he takes his lady with him, or sends her on ahead, and don't give it him without. There's no need to stand on ceremony with him. Tell him so, or, if you don't, I give you my word I'll go to his office and kick him downstairs, and I'll break off all acquaintance with you. So you'd better know it."

"Well! To go with her or send her on beforehand will be more convenient for him," said Samoylenko. "He'll be delighted indeed. Well, goodbye."

He said good-bye affectionately and went out, but before shutting the door after him, he looked round at Von Koren and, with a ferocious face, said:

"It's the Germans who have ruined you, brother! Yes! The Germans!"

XII

Next day, Thursday, Marya Konstantinovna was celebrating the birthday of her Kostya. All were invited to come at midday and eat pies, and in the evening to drink chocolate. When Laevsky and Nadyezhda Fyodorovna arrived in the evening, the zoologist, who was already sitting in the drawing-room, drinking chocolate, asked Samoylenko:

"Have you talked to him?"

"Not yet."

"Mind now, don't stand on ceremony. I can't understand the insolence of these people! Why, they know perfectly well the view taken by this family of their cohabitation, and yet they force themselves in here."

"If one is to pay attention to every prejudice," said Samoylenko, "one could go nowhere."

"Do you mean to say that the repugnance felt by the masses for illicit love and moral laxity is a prejudice?"

"Of course it is. It's prejudice and hate. When the soldiers see a girl of light behaviour, they laugh and whistle; but just ask them what they are themselves."

"It's not for nothing they whistle. The fact that girls strangle their illegitimate children and go to prison for it, and that Anna Karenin flung herself under the train, and that in the villages they smear the gates with tar, and that you and I, without knowing why, are pleased by Katya's purity, and that everyone of us feels a vague craving for pure love, though he knows there is no such love -- is all that prejudice? That is the one thing, brother, which has survived intact from natural selection, and, if it were not for that obscure force regulating the relations of the sexes, the Laevskys would have it all their own way, and mankind would degenerate in two years."

Laevsky came into the drawing-room, greeted everyone, and shaking hands with Von Koren, smiled ingratiatingly. He waited for a favourable moment and said to Samoylenko:

"Excuse me, Alexandr Daviditch, I must say two words to you."

Samoylenko got up, put his arm round Laevsky's waist, and both of them went into Nikodim Alexandritch's study.

"To-morrow's Friday," said Laevsky, biting his nails. "Have you got what you promised?"

"I've only got two hundred. I'll get the rest to-day or to-morrow. Don't worry yourself."

"Thank God . . ." sighed Laevsky, and his hands began trembling with joy. "You are saving me, Alexandr Daviditch, and I swear to you by God, by my happiness and anything you like, I'll send you the money as soon as I arrive. And I'll send you my old debt too."

"Look here, Vanya . . ." said Samoylenko, turning crimson and taking him by the button. "You must forgive my meddling in your private affairs, but . . . why shouldn't you take Nadyezhda Fyodorovna with you?"

"You queer fellow. How is that possible? One of us must stay, or our creditors will raise an outcry. You see, I owe seven hundred or more to the shops. Only wait, and I will send them the money. I'll stop their mouths, and then she can come away."

"I see. . . . But why shouldn't you send her on first?"

"My goodness, as though that were possible!" Laevsky was horrified. "Why, she's a woman; what would she do there alone? What does she know about it? That would only be a loss of time and a useless waste of money."

"That's reasonable . . ." thought Samoylenko, but remembering his conversation with Von Koren, he looked down and said sullenly: "I can't agree with you. Either go with her or send her first; otherwise . . . otherwise I won't give you the money. Those are my last words. . ."

He staggered back, lurched backwards against the door, and went into the drawing-room, crimson, and overcome with confusion.

"Friday . . . Friday," thought Laevsky, going back into the drawing-room. "Friday. . . ."

He was handed a cup of chocolate; he burnt his lips and tongue with the scalding chocolate and thought: "Friday . . . Friday. . . ."

For some reason he could not get the word "Friday" out of his head; he could think of nothing but Friday, and the only thing that was clear to him, not in his brain but somewhere in his heart, was that he would not get off on Saturday. Before him stood Nikodim Alexandritch, very neat, with his hair combed over his temples, saying:

"Please take something to eat. . . ."

Marya Konstantinovna showed the visitors Katya's school report and said, drawling:

"It's very, very difficult to do well at school nowadays! So much is expected . . ."

"Mamma!" groaned Katya, not knowing where to hide her confusion at the praises of the company.

Laevsky, too, looked at the report and praised it. Scripture, Russian language, conduct, fives and fours, danced before his eyes, and all this, mixed with the haunting refrain of " Friday," with the carefully combed locks of Nikodim Alexandritch and the red cheeks of Katya, produced on him a sensation of such immense overwhelming boredom that he almost shrieked with despair and asked himself: "Is it possible, is it possible I shall not get away?"

They put two card tables side by side and sat down to play post. Laevsky sat down too.

"Friday . . . Friday . . ." he kept thinking, as he smiled and took a pencil out of his pocket. "Friday. . . ."

He wanted to think over his position, and was afraid to think. It was terrible to him to realise that the doctor had detected him in the deception which he had so long and carefully concealed from himself. Every time he thought of his future he would not let his thoughts have full rein. He would get into the train and set off, and thereby the problem of his life would be solved, and he did not let his thoughts go farther. Like a far-away dim light in the fields, the thought sometimes flickered in his mind that in one of the side-streets of Petersburg, in the remote future, he would have to have recourse to a tiny lie in order to get rid of Nadyezhda Fyodorovna and pay his debts; he would tell a lie only once, and then a completely new life would begin. And that was right: at the price of a small lie he would win so much truth.

Now when by his blunt refusal the doctor had crudely hinted at his deception, he began to understand that he would need deception not only in the remote future, but to-day, and to-morrow, and in a month's time, and perhaps up to the very end of his life. In fact, in order to get away he would have to lie to Nadyezhda Fyodorovna, to his creditors, and to his superiors in the Service; then, in order to get money in Petersburg, he would have to lie to his mother, to tell her that he had already broken with Nadyezhda Fyodorovna; and his mother would not give him more than five hundred roubles, so he had already deceived the doctor, as he would not be in a position to pay him back the money within a short time. Afterwards, when Nadyezhda Fyodorovna came to Petersburg, he would have to resort to a regular series of deceptions, little and big, in order to get free of her; and again there would be tears, boredom, a disgusting existence, remorse, and so there would be no new life. Deception and nothing more. A whole mountain of lies rose before Laevsky's imagination. To leap over it at one bound and not to do his lying piecemeal, he would have to bring himself to stern, uncompromising action; for instance, to getting up without saying a word, putting on his hat, and at once setting off without money and without explanation. But Laevsky felt that was impossible for him.

"Friday, Friday . . ." he thought. "Friday. . . ."

They wrote little notes, folded them in two, and put them in Nikodim Alexandritch's old top-hat. When there were a sufficient heap of notes, Kostya, who acted the part of postman, walked round the table and delivered them. The deacon, Katya, and Kostya, who received amusing notes and tried to write as funnily as they could, were highly delighted.

"We must have a little talk," Nadyezhda Fyodorovna read in a little note; she glanced at Marya Konstantinovna, who gave her an almond-oily smile and nodded.

"Talk of what?" thought Nadyezhda Fyodorovna. "If one can't tell the whole, it's no use talking."

Before going out for the evening she had tied Laevsky's cravat for him, and that simple action filled her soul with tenderness and sorrow. The anxiety in his face, his absent-minded looks, his pallor, and the incomprehensible change that had taken place in him of late, and the fact that she had a terrible revolting secret from him, and the fact that her hands trembled when she tied his cravat -- all this seemed to tell her that they had not long left to be together. She looked at him as though he were an ikon, with terror and penitence, and thought: "Forgive, forgive."

Opposite her was sitting Atchmianov, and he never took his black, love-sick eyes off her. She was stirred by passion; she was ashamed of herself, and afraid that even her misery and sorrow would not prevent her from yielding to impure desire to-morrow, if not to-day -- and that, like a drunkard, she would not have the strength to stop herself.

She made up her mind to go away that she might not continue this life, shameful for herself, and humiliating for Laevsky. She would beseech him with tears to let her go; and if he opposed her, she would go away secretly. She would not tell him what had happened; let him keep a pure memory of her.

"I love you, I love you, I love you," she read. It was from Atchmianov.

She would live in some far remote place, would work and send Laevsky, "anonymously," money, embroidered shirts, and tobacco, and would return to him only in old age or if he were dangerously ill and needed a nurse. When in his old age he learned what were her reasons for leaving him and refusing to be his wife, he would appreciate her sacrifice and forgive.

"You've got a long nose." That must be from the deacon or Kostya.

Nadyezhda Fyodorovna imagined how, parting from Laevsky, she would embrace him warmly, would kiss his hand, and would swear to love him all her life, all her life, and then, living in obscurity among strangers, she would every day think that somewhere she had a friend, someone she loved -- a pure, noble, lofty man who kept a pure memory of her.

"If you don't give me an interview to-day, I shall take measures, I assure you on my word of honour. You can't treat decent people like this; you must understand that." That was from Kirilin.

XIII

Laevsky received two notes; he opened one and read: "Don't go away, my darling."

"Who could have written that?" he thought. "Not Samoylenko, of course. And not the deacon, for he doesn't know I want to go away. Von Koren, perhaps?"

The zoologist bent over the table and drew a pyramid. Laevsky fancied that his eyes were smiling.

"Most likely Samoylenko . . . has been gossiping," thought Laevsky.

In the other note, in the same disguised angular handwriting with long tails to the letters, was written: "Somebody won't go away on Saturday."

"A stupid gibe," thought Laevsky. "Friday, Friday. . . ."

Something rose in his throat. He touched his collar and coughed, but instead of a cough a laugh broke from his throat.

"Ha-ha-ha!" he laughed. "Ha-ha-ha! What am I laughing at? Ha-ha-ha!"

He tried to restrain himself, covered his mouth with his hand, but the laugh choked his chest and throat, and his hand could not cover his mouth.

"How stupid it is!" he thought, rolling with laughter. "Have I gone out of my mind?"

The laugh grew shriller and shriller, and became something like the bark of a lap-dog. Laevsky tried to get up from the table, but his legs would not obey him and his right hand was strangely, without his volition, dancing on the table, convulsively clutching and crumpling up the bits of paper. He saw looks of wonder, Samoylenko's grave, frightened face, and the eyes of the zoologist full of cold irony and disgust, and realised that he was in hysterics.

"How hideous, how shameful!" he thought, feeling the warmth of tears on his face. ". . . Oh, oh, what a disgrace! It has never happened to me. . . ."

They took him under his arms, and supporting his head from behind, led him away; a glass gleamed before his eyes and knocked against his teeth, and the water was spilt on his breast; he was in a little room, with two beds in the middle, side by side, covered by two snow-white quilts. He dropped on one of the beds and sobbed.

"It's nothing, it's nothing," Samoylenko kept saying; "it does happen . . . it does happen. . . ."

Chill with horror, trembling all over and dreading something awful, Nadyezhda Fyodorovna stood by the bedside and kept asking:

"What is it? What is it? For God's sake, tell me."

"Can Kirilin have written him something?" she thought.

"It's nothing," said Laevsky, laughing and crying; "go away, darling."

His face expressed neither hatred nor repulsion: so he knew nothing; Nadyezhda Fyodorovna was somewhat reassured, and she went into the drawing-room.

"Don't agitate yourself, my dear!" said Marya Konstantinovna, sitting down beside her and taking her hand. "It will pass. Men are just as weak as we poor sinners. You are both going through a crisis. . . . One can so well understand it! Well, my dear, I am waiting for an answer. Let us have a little talk."

"No, we are not going to talk," said Nadyezhda Fyodorovna, listening to Laevsky's sobs. "I feel depressed. . . . You must allow me to go home."

"What do you mean, what do you mean, my dear?" cried Marya Konstantinovna in alarm. "Do you think I could let you go without supper? We will have something to eat, and then you may go with my blessing."

"I feel miserable . . ." whispered Nadyezhda Fyodorovna, and she caught at the arm of the chair with both hands to avoid falling.

"He's got a touch of hysterics," said Von Koren gaily, coming into the drawing-room, but seeing Nadyezhda Fyodorovna, he was taken aback and retreated.

When the attack was over, Laevsky sat on the strange bed and thought.

"Disgraceful! I've been howling like some wretched girl! I must have been absurd and disgusting. I will go away by the back stairs. . . . But that would seem as though I took my hysterics too seriously. I ought to take it as a joke. . . ."

He looked in the looking-glass, sat there for some time, and went back into the drawing-room.

"Here I am," he said, smiling; he felt agonisingly ashamed, and he felt others were ashamed in his presence. "Fancy such a thing happening," he said, sitting down. "I was sitting here, and all of a sudden, do you know, I felt a terrible piercing pain in my side . . . unendurable, my nerves could not stand it, and . . . and it led to this silly performance. This is the age of nerves; there is no help for it."

At supper he drank some wine, and, from time to time, with an abrupt sigh rubbed his side as though to suggest that he still felt the pain. And no one, except Nadyezhda Fyodorovna, believed him, and he saw that.

After nine o'clock they went for a walk on the boulevard. Nadyezhda Fyodorovna, afraid that Kirilin would speak to her, did her best to keep all the time beside Marya Konstantinovna and the children. She felt weak with fear and misery, and felt she was going to be feverish; she was exhausted and her legs would hardly move, but she did not go home, because she felt sure that she would be followed by Kirilin or Atchmianov or both at once. Kirilin walked behind her with Nikodim Alexandritch, and kept humming in an undertone:

"I don't al-low people to play with me! I don't al-low it."

From the boulevard they went back to the pavilion and walked along the beach, and looked for a long time at the phosphorescence on the water. Von Koren began telling them why it looked phosphorescent.

XIV

"It's time I went to my *vint*. . . . They will be waiting for me," said Laevsky. "Good-bye, my friends."

"I'll come with you; wait a minute," said Nadyezhda Fyodorovna, and she took his arm.

They said good-bye to the company and went away. Kirilin took leave too, and saying that he was going the same way, went along beside them.

"What will be, will be," thought Nadyezhda Fyodorovna. "So be it. . . ."

And it seemed to her that all the evil memories in her head had taken shape and were walking beside her in the darkness, breathing heavily, while she, like a fly that had fallen into the inkpot, was crawling painfully along the pavement and smirching Laevsky's side and arm with blackness.

If Kirilin should do anything horrid, she thought, not he but she would be to blame for it. There was a time when no man would have talked to her as Kirilin had done, and she had torn up her security like a thread and destroyed it irrevocably -- who was to blame for it? Intoxicated by her passions she had smiled at a complete stranger, probably just because he was tall and a fine figure. After two meetings she was weary of him, had thrown him over, and did not that, she thought now, give him the right to treat her as he chose?

"Here I'll say good-bye to you, darling," said Laevsky. "Ilya Mihalitch will see you home."

He nodded to Kirilin, and, quickly crossing the boulevard, walked along the street to Sheshkovsky's, where there were lights in the windows, and then they heard the gate bang as he went in.

"Allow me to have an explanation with you," said Kirilin. "I'm not a boy, not some Atchkasov or Latchkasov, Zatchkasov. . . . I demand serious attention."

Nadyezhda Fyodorovna's heart began beating violently. She made no reply.

"The abrupt change in your behaviour to me I put down at first to coquetry," Kirilin went on; "now I see that you don't know how to behave with gentlemanly people. You simply wanted to play with me, as you are playing with that wretched Armenian boy; but I'm a gentleman and I insist on being treated like a gentleman. And so I am at your service. . . ."

"I'm miserable," said Nadyezhda Fyodorovna beginning to cry, and to hide her tears she turned away.

"I'm miserable too," said Kirilin, "but what of that?"

Kirilin was silent for a space, then he said distinctly and emphatically:

"I repeat, madam, that if you do not give me an interview this evening, I'll make a scandal this very evening."

"Let me off this evening," said Nadyezhda Fyodorovna, and she did not recognise her own voice, it was so weak and pitiful.

"I must give you a lesson. . . . Excuse me for the roughness of my tone, but it's necessary to give you a lesson. Yes, I regret to say I must give you a lesson. I insist on two interviews -- to-day and to-morrow. After to-morrow you are perfectly free and can go wherever you like with anyone you choose. To-day and to-morrow."

Nadyezhda Fyodorovna went up to her gate and stopped.

"Let me go," she murmured, trembling all over and seeing nothing before her in the darkness but his white tunic. "You're right: I'm a horrible woman. . . . I'm to blame, but let me go . . . I beg you." She touched his cold hand and shuddered. "I beseech you. . . ."

"Alas!" sighed Kirilin, "alas! it's not part of my plan to let you go; I only mean to give you a lesson and make you realise. And what's more, madam, I've too little faith in women."

"I'm miserable. . . ."

Nadyezhda Fyodorovna listened to the even splash of the sea, looked at the sky studded with stars, and longed to make haste and end it all, and get away from the cursed sensation of life, with its sea, stars, men, fever.

"Only not in my home," she said coldly. "Take me somewhere else."

"Come to Muridov's. That's better."

"Where's that?"

"Near the old wall."

She walked quickly along the street and then turned into the side-street that led towards the mountains. It was dark. There were pale streaks of light here and there on the pavement, from the lighted windows, and it seemed to her that, like a fly, she kept falling into the ink and crawling out into the light again. At one point he stumbled, almost fell down and burst out laughing.

"He's drunk," thought Nadyezhda Fyodorovna. "Never mind. . . . Never mind. . . . So be it."

Atchmianov, too, soon took leave of the party and followed Nadyezhda Fyodorovna to ask her to go for a row. He went to her house and looked over the fence: the windows were wide open, there were no lights.

"Nadyezhda Fyodorovna!" he called.

A moment passed, he called again.

"Who's there?" he heard Olga's voice.

"Is Nadyezhda Fyodorovna at home?"

"No, she has not come in yet."

"Strange . . . very strange," thought Atchmianov, feeling very uneasy. "She went home. . . ."

He walked along the boulevard, then along the street, and glanced in at the windows of Sheshkovsky's. Laevsky was sitting at the table without his coat on, looking attentively at his cards.

"Strange, strange," muttered Atchmianov, and remembering Laevsky's hysterics, he felt ashamed. "If she is not at home, where is she?"

He went to Nadyezhda Fyodorovna's lodgings again, and looked at the dark windows.

"It's a cheat, a cheat . . ." he thought, remembering that, meeting him at midday at Marya Konstantinovna's, she had promised to go in a boat with him that evening.

The windows of the house where Kirilin lived were dark, and there was a policeman sitting asleep on a little bench at the gate. Everything was clear to Atchmianov when he looked at the windows and the policeman. He made up his mind to go home, and set off in that direction, but somehow found himself near Nadyezhda Fyodorovna's lodgings again. He sat down on the bench near the gate and took off his hat, feeling that his head was burning with jealousy and resentment.

The clock in the town church only struck twice in the twenty-four hours -- at midday and midnight. Soon after it struck midnight he heard hurried footsteps.

"To-morrow evening, then, again at Muridov's," Atchmianov heard, and he recognised Kirilin' s voice. "At eight o'clock; good-bye!"

Nadyezhda Fyodorovna made her appearance near the garden. Without noticing that Atchmianov was sitting on the bench, she passed beside him like a shadow, opened the gate, and leaving it open, went into the house. In her own room she lighted the candle and quickly undressed, but instead of getting into bed, she sank on her knees before a chair, flung her arms round it, and rested her head on it.

It was past two when Laevsky came home.

XV

Having made up his mind to lie, not all at once but piecemeal, Laevsky went soon after one o'clock next day to Samoylenko to ask for the money that he might be sure to get off on Saturday. After his hysterical attack, which had added an acute feeling of shame to his depressed state of mind, it was unthinkable to remain in the town. If Samoylenko should insist on his conditions, he thought it would be possible to agree to them and take the money, and next day, just as he was starting, to say that Nadyezhda Fyodorovna refused to go. He would be able to persuade her that evening that the whole arrangement would be for her benefit. If Samoylenko, who was obviously under the influence of Von Koren, should refuse the money altogether or make fresh conditions, then he, Laevsky, would go off that very evening in a cargo vessel, or even in a sailing-boat, to Novy Athon or Novorossiisk, would send from there an humiliating telegram, and would stay there till his mother sent him the money for the journey.

When he went into Samoylenko's, he found Von Koren in the drawing-room. The zoologist had just arrived for dinner, and, as usual, was turning over the album and scrutinising the gentlemen in top-hats and the ladies in caps.

"How very unlucky!" thought Laevsky, seeing him. "He may be in the way. Good-morning."

"Good-morning," answered Von Koren, without looking at him.

"Is Alexandr Daviditch at home?"

"Yes, in the kitchen."

Laevsky went into the kitchen, but seeing from the door that Samoylenko was busy over the salad, he went back into the drawing-room and sat down. He always had a feeling of awkwardness in the zoologist's presence, and now he was afraid there would be talk about his attack of hysterics. There was more than a minute of silence. Von Koren suddenly raised his eyes to Laevsky and asked:

"How do you feel after yesterday?"

"Very well indeed," said Laevsky, flushing. "It really was nothing much. . .

"Until yesterday I thought it was only ladies who had hysterics, and so at first I thought you had St. Vitus's dance."

Laevsky smiled ingratiatingly, and thought:

"How indelicate on his part! He knows quite well how unpleasant it is for me. . . ."

"Yes, it was a ridiculous performance," he said, still smiling. "I've been laughing over it the whole morning. What's so curious in an attack of hysterics is that you know it is absurd, and are laughing at it in your heart, and at the same time you sob. In our neurotic age we are the slaves of our nerves; they are our masters and do as they like with us. Civilisation has done us a bad turn in that way. . . ."

As Laevsky talked, he felt it disagreeable that Von Koren listened to him gravely, and looked at him steadily and attentively as though studying him; and he was vexed with himself that in spite of his dislike of Von Koren, he could not banish the ingratiating smile from his face.

"I must admit, though," he added, "that there were immediate causes for the attack, and quite sufficient ones too. My health has been terribly shaky of late. To which one must add boredom, constantly being hard up . . . the absence of people and general interests. . . . My position is worse than a governor's."

"Yes, your position is a hopeless one," answered Von Koren.

These calm, cold words, implying something between a jeer and an uninvited prediction, offended Laevsky. He recalled the zoologist's eyes the evening before, full of mockery and disgust. He was silent for a space and then asked, no longer smiling:

"How do you know anything of my position?"

"You were only just speaking of it yourself. Besides, your friends take such a warm interest in you, that I am hearing about you all day long."

"What friends? Samoylenko, I suppose?"

"Yes, he too."

"I would ask Alexandr Daviditch and my friends in general not to trouble so much about me."

"Here is Samoylenko; you had better ask him not to trouble so much about you."

"I don't understand your tone," Laevsky muttered, suddenly feeling as though he had only just realised that the zoologist hated and despised him, and was jeering at him, and was his bitterest and most inveterate enemy.

"Keep that tone for someone else," he said softly, unable to speak aloud for the hatred with which his chest and throat were choking, as they had been the night before with laughter.

Samoylenko came in in his shirt-sleeves, crimson and perspiring from the stifling kitchen.

"Ah, you here?" he said. "Good-morning, my dear boy. Have you had dinner? Don't stand on ceremony. Have you had dinner?"

"Alexandr Daviditch," said Laevsky, standing up, "though I did appeal to you to help me in a private matter, it did not follow that I released you from the obligation of discretion and respect for other people's private affairs."

"What's this?" asked Samoylenko, in astonishment.

"If you have no money," Laevsky went on, raising his voice and shifting from one foot to the other in his excitement, "don't give it; refuse it. But why spread abroad in every back street that my position is hopeless, and all the rest of it? I can't endure such benevolence and friend's assistance where there's a shilling-worth of talk for a ha'p'orth of help! You can boast of your benevolence as much as you please, but no one has given you the right to gossip about my private affairs!"

"What private affairs?" asked Samoylenko, puzzled and beginning to be angry. "If you've come here to be abusive, you had better clear out. You can come again afterwards!"

He remembered the rule that when one is angry with one's neighbour, one must begin to count a hundred, and one will grow calm again; and he began rapidly counting.

"I beg you not to trouble yourself about me," Laevsky went on. "Don't pay any attention to me, and whose business is it what I do and how I live? Yes, I want to go away. Yes, I get into debt, I drink, I am living with another man's wife, I'm hysterical, I'm ordinary. I am not so profound as some people, but whose business is that? Respect other people's privacy."

"Excuse me, brother," said Samoylenko, who had counted up to thirty-five, "but . . ."

"Respect other people's individuality!" interrupted Laevsky. "This continual gossip about other people's affairs, this sighing and groaning and everlasting prying, this eavesdropping, this friendly sympathy . . . damn it all! They lend me money and make conditions as though I were a schoolboy! I am treated as the devil knows what! I don't want anything," shouted Laevsky, staggering with excitement and afraid that it might end in another attack of hysterics. "I shan't get away on Saturday, then," flashed through his mind. "I want nothing. All I ask of you is to spare me your protecting care. I'm not a boy, and I'm not mad, and I beg you to leave off looking after me."

The deacon came in, and seeing Laevsky pale and gesticulating, addressing his strange speech to the portrait of Prince Vorontsov, stood still by the door as though petrified.

"This continual prying into my soul," Laevsky went on, "is insulting to my human dignity, and I beg these volunteer detectives to give up their spying! Enough!"

"What's that . . . what did you say?" said Samoylenko, who had counted up to a hundred. He turned crimson and went up to Laevsky.

"It's enough," said Laevsky, breathing hard and snatching up his cap.

"I'm a Russian doctor, a nobleman by birth, and a civil councillor," said Samoylenko emphatically. "I've never been a spy, and I allow no one to insult me!" he shouted in a breaking voice, emphasising the last word. "Hold your tongue!"

The deacon, who had never seen the doctor so majestic, so swelling with dignity, so crimson and so ferocious, shut his mouth, ran out into the entry and there exploded with laughter.

As though through a fog, Laevsky saw Von Koren get up and, putting his hands in his trouser-pockets, stand still in an attitude of expectancy, as though waiting to see what would happen. This calm attitude struck Laevsky as insolent and insulting to the last degree.

"Kindly take back your words," shouted Samoylenko.

Laevsky, who did not by now remember what his words were, answered:

"Leave me alone! I ask for nothing. All I ask is that you and German upstarts of Jewish origin should let me alone! Or I shall take steps to make you! I will fight you!"

"Now we understand," said Von Koren, coming from behind the table. "Mr. Laevsky wants to amuse himself with a duel before he goes away. I can give him that pleasure. Mr. Laevsky, I accept your challenge."

"A challenge," said Laevsky, in a low voice, going up to the zoologist and looking with hatred at his swarthy brow and curly hair. "A challenge? By all means! I hate you! I hate you!"

"Delighted. To-morrow morning early near Kerbalay's. I leave all details to your taste. And now, clear out!"

"I hate you," Laevsky said softly, breathing hard. "I have hated you a long while! A duel! Yes!"

"Get rid of him, Alexandr Daviditch, or else I'm going," said Von Koren. "He'll bite me."

Von Koren's cool tone calmed the doctor; he seemed suddenly to come to himself, to recover his reason; he put both arms round Laevsky's waist, and, leading him away from the zoologist, muttered in a friendly voice that shook with emotion:

"My friends . . . dear, good . . . you've lost your tempers and that's enough . . . and that's enough, my friends."

Hearing his soft, friendly voice, Laevsky felt that something unheard of, monstrous, had just happened to him, as though he had been nearly run over by a train; he almost burst into tears, waved his hand, and ran out of the room.

"To feel that one is hated, to expose oneself before the man who hates one, in the most pitiful, contemptible, helpless state. My God, how hard it is!" he thought a little while afterwards as he sat in the pavilion, feeling as though his body were scarred by the hatred of which he had just been the object.

"How coarse it is, my God!"

Cold water with brandy in it revived him. He vividly pictured Von Koren's calm, haughty face; his eyes the day before, his shirt like a rug, his voice, his white hand; and heavy, passionate, hungry hatred rankled in his breast and clamoured for satisfaction. In his thoughts he felled Von Koren to the ground, and trampled him underfoot. He remembered to the minutest detail all that had happened, and wondered how he could have smiled ingratiatingly to that insignificant man, and how he could care for the opinion of wretched petty people whom nobody knew, living in a miserable little town which was not, it seemed, even on the map, and of which not one decent person in Petersburg had heard. If this wretched little town suddenly fell into ruins or caught fire, the telegram with the news would be read in Russia with no more interest than an advertisement of the sale of second-hand furniture. Whether he killed Von Koren next day or left him alive, it would be just the same, equally useless and uninteresting. Better to shoot him in the leg or hand, wound him, then laugh at him, and let him, like an insect with a broken leg lost in the grass -- let him be lost with his obscure sufferings in the crowd of insignificant people like himself.

Laevsky went to Sheshkovsky, told him all about it, and asked him to be his second; then they both went to the superintendent of the postal telegraph department, and asked him, too, to be a second, and stayed to dinner with him. At dinner there was a great deal of joking and laughing. Laevsky made jests at his own expense, saying he hardly knew how to fire off a pistol, calling himself a royal archer and William Tell.

"We must give this gentleman a lesson . . ." he said.

After dinner they sat down to cards. Laevsky played, drank wine, and thought that duelling was stupid and senseless, as it did not decide the question but only complicated it, but that it was sometimes impossible to get on without it. In the given case, for instance, one could not, of course, bring an action against Von Koren. And this duel was so far good in that it made it impossible for Laevsky to remain in the town afterwards. He got a little drunk and interested in the game, and felt at ease.

But when the sun had set and it grew dark, he was possessed by a feeling of uneasiness. It was not fear at the thought of death, because while he was dining and playing cards, he had for some reason a confident belief that the duel would end in nothing; it was dread at the thought of something unknown which was to happen next morning for the first time in his life, and dread of the coming night. . . . He knew that the night would be long and sleepless, and that he would have to think not only of Von Koren and his hatred, but also of the mountain of lies which he had to get through, and which he had not strength or ability to dispense with. It was as though he had been taken suddenly ill; all at once he lost all interest in the cards and in people, grew restless, and began asking them to let him go home. He was eager to get into bed, to lie without moving, and to prepare his thoughts for the night. Sheshkovsky and the postal superintendent saw him home and went on to Von Koren's to arrange about the duel.

Near his lodgings Laevsky met Atchmianov. The young man was breathless and excited.

"I am looking for you, Ivan Andreitch," he said. "I beg you to come quickly. . . ."

"Where?"

"Someone wants to see you, someone you don't know, about very important business; he earnestly begs you to come for a minute. He wants to speak to you of something. . . . For him it's a question of life and death. . . ." In his excitement Atchmianov spoke in a strong Armenian accent.

"Who is it?" asked Laevsky.

"He asked me not to tell you his name."

"Tell him I'm busy; to-morrow, if he likes. . . ."

"How can you!" Atchmianov was aghast. "He wants to tell you something very important for you . . . very important! If you don't come, something dreadful will happen."

"Strange . . ." muttered Laevsky, unable to understand why Atchmianov was so excited and what mysteries there could be in this dull, useless little town.

"Strange," he repeated in hesitation. "Come along, though; I don't care."

Atchmianov walked rapidly on ahead and Laevsky followed him. They walked down a street, then turned into an alley.

"What a bore this is!" said Laevsky.

"One minute, one minute . . . it's near."

Near the old rampart they went down a narrow alley between two empty enclosures, then they came into a sort of large yard and went towards a small house.

"That's Muridov's, isn't it?" asked Laevsky.

"Yes."

"But why we've come by the back yards I don't understand. We might have come by the street; it's nearer. . . ."

"Never mind, never mind. . . ."

It struck Laevsky as strange, too, that Atchmianov led him to a back entrance, and motioned to him as though bidding him go quietly and hold his tongue.

"This way, this way . . ." said Atchmianov, cautiously opening the door and going into the passage on tiptoe. "Quietly, quietly, I beg you . . . they may hear."

He listened, drew a deep breath and said in a whisper:

"Open that door, and go in . . . don't be afraid."

Laevsky, puzzled, opened the door and went into a room with a low ceiling and curtained windows.

There was a candle on the table.

"What do you want?" asked someone in the next room. "Is it you, Muridov?"

Laevsky turned into that room and saw Kirilin, and beside him Nadyezhda Fyodorovna.

He didn't hear what was said to him; he staggered back, and did not know how he found himself in the street. His hatred for Von Koren and his uneasiness -- all had vanished from his soul. As he went home he waved his right arm awkwardly and looked carefully at the ground under his feet, trying to step where it was smooth. At home in his study he walked backwards and forwards, rubbing his hands, and awkwardly shrugging his shoulders and neck, as though his jacket and shirt were too tight; then he lighted a candle and sat down to the table. . . .

XVI

"The 'humane studies' of which you speak will only satisfy human thought when, as they advance, they meet the exact sciences and progress side by side with them. Whether they will meet under a new microscope, or in the monologues of a new Hamlet, or in a new religion, I do not know, but I expect the earth will be covered with a crust of ice before it comes to pass. Of all humane learning the most durable and living is, of course, the teaching of Christ; but look how differently even that is interpreted! Some teach that we must love all our neighbours but make an exception of soldiers, criminals, and lunatics. They allow the first to be killed in war, the second to be isolated or executed, and the third they forbid to marry. Other interpreters teach that we must love all our neighbours without exception, with no distinction of *plus* or minus. According to their teaching, if a consumptive or a murderer or an epileptic asks your daughter in marriage, you must let him have her. If *crêtins* go to war against the physically and mentally healthy, don't defend yourselves. This advocacy of love for love's sake, like art for art's sake, if it could have power, would bring mankind in the long run to complete extinction, and so would become the vastest crime that has ever been committed upon earth. There are very many interpretations, and since there are many of them, serious thought is not satisfied by anyone of them, and hastens to add its own individual interpretation to the mass. For that reason you should never put a question on a philosophical or so-called Christian basis; by so doing you only remove the question further from solution."

The deacon listened to the zoologist attentively, thought a little, and asked:

"Have the philosophers invented the moral law which is innate in every man, or did God create it together with the body?"

"I don't know. But that law is so universal among all peoples and all ages that I fancy we ought to recognise it as organically connected with man. It is not invented, but exists and will exist. I don't tell you that one day it will be seen under the microscope, but its organic connection is shown, indeed, by evidence: serious affections of the brain and all so-called mental diseases, to the best of my belief, show themselves first of all in the perversion of the moral law."

"Good. So then, just as our stomach bids us eat, our moral sense bids us love our neighbours. Is that it? But our natural man through self-love opposes the voice of conscience and reason, and this gives rise to many brain-racking questions. To whom ought we to turn for the solution of those questions if you forbid us to put them on the philosophic basis?"

"Turn to what little exact science we have. Trust to evidence and the logic of facts. It is true it is but little, but, on the other hand, it is less fluid and shifting than philosophy. The moral law, let us suppose, demands that you love your neighbour. Well? Love ought to show itself in the removal of everything which in one way or another is injurious to men and threatens them with danger in the present or in the future. Our knowledge and the evidence tells us that the morally and physically abnormal are a menace to humanity. If so you must struggle against the abnormal; if you are not able to raise them to the normal standard you must have strength and ability to render them harmless -- that is, to destroy them."

"So love consists in the strong overcoming the weak."

"Undoubtedly."

"But you know the strong crucified our Lord Jesus Christ," said the deacon hotly.

"The fact is that those who crucified Him were not the strong but the weak. Human culture weakens and strives to nullify the struggle for existence and natural selection; hence the rapid advancement of the weak and their predominance over the strong. Imagine that you succeeded in instilling into bees humanitarian ideas in their crude and elementary form. What would come of it? The drones who ought to be killed would remain alive, would devour the honey, would corrupt and stifle the bees, resulting in the predominance of the weak over the strong and the degeneration of the latter. The same process is taking place now with humanity; the weak are oppressing the strong. Among savages untouched by civilisation the strongest, cleverest, and most moral takes the lead; he is the chief and the master. But we civilised men have crucified Christ, and we go on crucifying Him, so there is something lacking in us. . . . And that something one ought to raise up in ourselves, or there will be no end to these errors."

"But what criterion have you to distinguish the strong from the weak?"

"Knowledge and evidence. The tuberculous and the scrofulous are recognised by their diseases, and the insane and the immoral by their actions."

"But mistakes may be made!"

"Yes, but it's no use to be afraid of getting your feet wet when you are threatened with the deluge!"

"That's philosophy," laughed the deacon.

"Not a bit of it. You are so corrupted by your seminary philosophy that you want to see nothing but fog in everything. The abstract studies with which your youthful head is stuffed are called abstract just because they abstract your minds from what is obvious. Look the devil straight in the eye, and if he's the devil, tell him he's the devil, and don't go calling to Kant or Hegel for explanations."

The zoologist paused and went on:

"Twice two's four, and a stone's a stone. Here to-morrow we have a duel. You and I will say it's stupid and absurd, that the duel is out of date, that there is no real difference between the aristocratic duel and the drunken brawl in the pot-house, and yet we shall not stop, we shall go there and fight. So there is some force stronger than our reasoning. We shout that war is plunder, robbery, atrocity, fratricide; we cannot look upon blood without fainting; but the French or the Germans have only to insult us for us to feel at once an exaltation of spirit; in the most genuine way we shout 'Hurrah!' and rush to attack the foe. You will invoke the blessing of God on our weapons, and our valour will arouse universal and general enthusiasm. Again it follows that there is a force, if not higher, at any rate stronger, than us and our philosophy. We can no more stop it than that cloud which is moving upwards over the sea. Don't be hypocritical, don't make a long nose at it on the sly; and don't say, 'Ah, old-fashioned, stupid! Ah, it's inconsistent with Scripture!' but look it straight in the face, recognise its rational lawfulness, and when, for instance, it wants to destroy a rotten, scrofulous, corrupt race, don't hinder it with your pilules and misunderstood quotations from the Gospel. Leskov has a story of a conscientious Danila who found a leper outside the town, and fed and warmed him in the name of love and of Christ. If that Danila had really loved humanity, he would have dragged the leper as far as possible from the town, and would have flung him in a pit, and would have gone to save the healthy. Christ, I hope, taught us a rational, intelligent, practical love."

"What a fellow you are!" laughed the deacon. "You don't believe in Christ. Why do you mention His name so often?"

"Yes, I do believe in Him. Only, of course, in my own way, not in yours. Oh, deacon, deacon!" laughed the zoologist; he put his arm round the deacon's waist, and said gaily: "Well? Are you coming with us to the duel to-morrow?"

"My orders don't allow it, or else I should come."

"What do you mean by 'orders'?"

"I have been consecrated. I am in a state of grace."

"Oh, deacon, deacon," repeated Von Koren, laughing, "I love talking to you."

"You say you have faith," said the deacon. "What sort of faith is it? Why, I have an uncle, a priest, and he believes so that when in time of drought he goes out into the fields to pray for rain, he takes his umbrella and leather overcoat for fear of getting wet through on his way home. That's faith! When he speaks of Christ, his face is full of radiance, and all the peasants, men and women, weep floods of tears. He would stop that cloud and put all those forces you talk about to flight. Yes . . . faith moves mountains."

The deacon laughed and slapped the zoologist on the shoulder.

"Yes . . ." he went on; "here you are teaching all the time, fathoming the depths of the ocean, dividing the weak and the strong, writing books and challenging to duels -- and everything remains as it is; but, behold! some feeble old man will mutter just one word with a holy spirit, or a new Mahomet, with a sword, will gallop from Arabia, and everything will be topsy-turvy, and in Europe not one stone will be left standing upon another."

"Well, deacon, that's on the knees of the gods."

"Faith without works is dead, but works without faith are worse still -- mere waste of time and nothing more."

The doctor came into sight on the sea-front. He saw the deacon and the zoologist, and went up to them.

"I believe everything is ready," he said, breathing hard. "Govorovsky and Boyko will be the seconds. They will start at five o'clock in the morning. How it has clouded over," he said, looking at the sky. "One can see nothing; there will be rain directly."

"I hope you are coming with us?" said the zoologist.

"No, God preserve me; I'm worried enough as it is. Ustimovitch is going instead of me. I've spoken to him already."

Far over the sea was a flash of lightning, followed by a hollow roll of thunder.

"How stifling it is before a storm!" said Von Koren. "I bet you've been to Laevsky already and have been weeping on his bosom."

"Why should I go to him?" answered the doctor in confusion. "What next?"

Before sunset he had walked several times along the boulevard and the street in the hope of meeting Laevsky. He was ashamed of his hastiness and the sudden outburst of friendliness which had followed it. He wanted to apologise to Laevsky in a joking tone, to give him a good talking to, to soothe him and to tell him that the duel was a survival of mediæval barbarism, but that Providence itself had brought them to the duel as a means of reconciliation; that the next day, both being splendid and highly intelligent people, they would, after exchanging shots, appreciate each other's noble qualities and would become friends. But he could not come across Laevsky.

"What should I go and see him for?" repeated Samoylenko. "I did not insult him; he insulted me. Tell me, please, why he attacked me. What harm had I done him? I go into the drawing-room, and, all of a sudden, without the least provocation: 'Spy!' There's a nice thing! Tell me, how did it begin? What did you say to him?"

"I told him his position was hopeless. And I was right. It is only honest men or scoundrels who can find an escape from any position, but one who wants to be at the same time an honest man and a scoundrel -- it is a hopeless position. But it's eleven o'clock, gentlemen, and we have to be up early to-morrow."

There was a sudden gust of wind; it blew up the dust on the sea-front, whirled it round in eddies, with a howl that drowned the roar of the sea.

"A squall," said the deacon. "We must go in, our eyes are getting full of dust."

As they went, Samoylenko sighed and, holding his hat, said:

"I suppose I shan't sleep to-night."

"Don't you agitate yourself," laughed the zoologist. "You can set your mind at rest; the duel will end in nothing. Laevsky will magnanimously fire into the air -- he can do nothing else; and I daresay I shall not fire at all. To be arrested and lose my time on Laevsky's account -- the game's not worth the candle. By the way, what is the punishment for duelling?"

"Arrest, and in the case of the death of your opponent a maximum of three years' imprisonment in the fortress."

"The fortress of St. Peter and St. Paul?"

"No, in a military fortress, I believe."

"Though this fine gentleman ought to have a lesson!"

Behind them on the sea, there was a flash of lightning, which for an instant lighted up the roofs of the houses and the mountains. The friends parted near the boulevard. When the doctor disappeared in the darkness and his steps had died away, Von Koren shouted to him:

"I only hope the weather won't interfere with us to-morrow!"

"Very likely it will! Please God it may!"

"Good-night!"

"What about the night? What do you say?"

In the roar of the wind and the sea and the crashes of thunder, it was difficult to hear.

"It's nothing," shouted the zoologist, and hurried home.

XVII

"Upon my mind, weighed down with woe,
Crowd thoughts, a heavy multitude:
In silence memory unfolds
Her long, long scroll before my eyes.
Loathing and shuddering I curse
And bitterly lament in vain,
And bitter though the tears I weep
I do not wash those lines away."

PUSHKIN.

Whether they killed him next morning, or mocked at him -- that is, left him his life -- he was ruined, anyway. Whether this disgraced woman killed herself in her shame and despair, or dragged on her pitiful existence, she was ruined anyway.

So thought Laevsky as he sat at the table late in the evening, still rubbing his hands. The windows suddenly blew open with a bang; a violent gust of wind burst into the room, and the papers fluttered from the table. Laevsky closed the windows and bent down to pick up the papers. He was aware of something new in his body, a sort of awkwardness he had not felt before, and his movements were strange to him. He moved timidly, jerking with his elbows and shrugging his shoulders; and when he sat down to the table again, he again began rubbing his hands. His body had lost its suppleness.

On the eve of death one ought to write to one's nearest relation. Laevsky thought of this. He took a pen and wrote with a tremulous hand:

"Mother!"

He wanted to write to beg his mother, for the sake of the merciful God in whom she believed, that she would give shelter and bring a little warmth and kindness into the life of the unhappy woman who, by his doing, had been disgraced and was in solitude, poverty, and weakness, that she would forgive and forget everything, everything, everything, and by her sacrifice atone to some extent for her son's terrible sin. But he remembered how his mother, a stout, heavily-built old woman in a lace cap, used to go out into the garden in the morning, followed by her companion with the lap-dog; how she used to shout in a peremptory way to the gardener and the servants, and how proud and haughty her face was -- he remembered all this and scratched out the word he had written.

There was a vivid flash of lightning at all three windows, and it was followed by a prolonged, deafening roll of thunder, beginning with a hollow rumble and ending with a crash so violent that all the window-panes rattled. Laevsky got up, went to the window, and pressed his forehead against the pane. There was a fierce, magnificent storm. On the horizon lightning-flashes were flung in white streams from the storm-clouds into the sea, lighting up the high, dark waves over the far-away expanse. And to right and to left, and, no doubt, over the house too, the lightning flashed.

"The storm!" whispered Laevsky; he had a longing to pray to someone or to something, if only to the lightning or the storm-clouds. "Dear storm!"

He remembered how as a boy he used to run out into the garden without a hat on when there was a storm, and how two fair-haired girls with blue eyes used to run after him, and how they got wet through with the rain; they laughed with delight, but when there was a loud peal of thunder, the girls used to nestle up to the boy confidingly, while he crossed himself and made haste to repeat: "Holy, holy, holy. . . ." Oh, where had they vanished to! In what sea were they drowned, those dawning days of pure, fair life? He had no fear of the storm, no love of nature now; he had no God. All the confiding girls he had ever known had by now been ruined by him and those like him. All his life he had not planted one tree in his own garden, nor grown one blade of grass; and living among the living, he had not saved one fly; he had done nothing but destroy and ruin, and lie, lie. . . .

"What in my past was not vice?" he asked himself, trying to clutch at some bright memory as a man falling down a precipice clutches at the bushes.

School? The university? But that was a sham. He had neglected his work and forgotten what he had learnt. The service of his country? That, too, was a sham, for he did nothing in the Service, took a salary for doing nothing, and it was an abominable swindling of the State for which one was not punished.

He had no craving for truth, and had not sought it; spellbound by vice and lying, his conscience had slept or been silent. Like a stranger, like an alien from another planet, he had taken no part in the common life of men, had been indifferent to their sufferings, their ideas, their religion, their sciences, their strivings, and their struggles. He had not said one good word, not written one line that was not useless and vulgar; he had not done his fellows one ha'p'orth of service, but had eaten their bread, drunk their wine, seduced their wives, lived on their thoughts, and to justify his contemptible, parasitic life in their eyes and in his own, he had always tried to assume an air of being higher and better than they. Lies, lies, lies. . . .

He vividly remembered what he had seen that evening at Muridov's, and he was in an insufferable anguish of loathing and misery. Kirilin and Atchmianov were loathsome, but they were only continuing what he had begun; they were his accomplices and his disciples. This young weak woman had trusted him more than a brother, and he had deprived her of her husband, of her friends and of her country, and had brought her here -- to the heat, to fever, and to boredom; and from day to day she was bound to reflect, like a mirror, his idleness, his viciousness and falsity -- and that was all she had had to fill her weak, listless, pitiable life. Then he had grown sick of her, had begun to hate her, but had not had the pluck to abandon her, and he had tried to entangle her more and more closely in a web of lies. . . . These men had done the rest.

Laevsky sat at the table, then got up and went to the window; at one minute he put out the candle and then he lighted it again. He cursed himself aloud, wept and wailed, and asked forgiveness; several times he ran to the table in despair, and wrote:

"Mother!"

Except his mother, he had no relations or near friends; but how could his mother help him? And where was she? He had an impulse to run to Nadyezhda Fyodorovna, to fall at her feet, to kiss her hands and feet, to beg her forgiveness; but she was his victim, and he was afraid of her as though she were dead.

"My life is ruined," he repeated, rubbing his hands. "Why am I still alive, my God! . . ."

He had cast out of heaven his dim star; it had fallen, and its track was lost in the darkness of night. It would never return to the sky again, because life was given only once and never came a second time. If he could have turned back the days and years of the past, he would have replaced the falsity with truth, the idleness with work, the boredom with happiness; he would have given back purity to those whom he had robbed of it. He would have found God and goodness, but that was as impossible as to put back the fallen star into the sky, and because it was impossible he was in despair.

When the storm was over, he sat by the open window and thought calmly of what was before him. Von Koren would most likely kill him. The man's clear, cold theory of life justified the destruction of the rotten and the useless; if it changed at the crucial moment, it would be the hatred and the repugnance that Laevsky inspired in him that would save him. If he missed his aim or, in mockery of his hated opponent, only wounded him, or fired in the air, what could he do then? Where could he go?

"Go to Petersburg?" Laevsky asked himself. But that would mean beginning over again the old life which he cursed. And the man who seeks salvation in change of place like a migrating bird would find nothing anywhere, for all the world is alike to him. Seek salvation in men? In whom and how? Samoylenko's kindness and generosity could no more save him than the deacon's laughter or Von Koren's hatred. He must look for salvation in himself alone, and if there were no finding it, why waste time? He must kill himself, that was all. . . .

He heard the sound of a carriage. It was getting light. The carriage passed by, turned, and crunching on the wet sand, stopped near the house. There were two men in the carriage.

"Wait a minute; I'm coming directly," Laevsky said to them out of the window. "I'm not asleep. Surely it's not time yet?"

"Yes, it's four o'clock. By the time we get there . . . ."

Laevsky put on his overcoat and cap, put some cigarettes in his pocket, and stood still hesitating. He felt as though there was something else he must do. In the street the seconds talked in low voices and the horses snorted, and this sound in the damp, early morning, when everybody was asleep and light was hardly dawning in the sky, filled Laevsky's soul with a disconsolate feeling which was like a presentiment of evil. He stood for a little, hesitating, and went into the bedroom.

Nadyezhda Fyodorovna was lying stretched out on the bed, wrapped from head to foot in a rug. She did not stir, and her whole appearance, especially her head, suggested an Egyptian mummy. Looking at her in silence, Laevsky mentally asked her forgiveness, and thought that if the heavens were not empty and there really were a God, then He would save her; if there were no God, then she had better perish -- there was nothing for her to live for.

All at once she jumped up, and sat up in bed. Lifting her pale face and looking with horror at Laevsky, she asked:

"Is it you? Is the storm over?"

"Yes."

She remembered; put both hands to her head and shuddered all over.

"How miserable I am!" she said. "If only you knew how miserable I am! I expected," she went on, half closing her eyes, "that you would kill me or turn me out of the house into the rain and storm, but you delay . . . delay . . ."

Warmly and impulsively he put his arms round her and covered her knees and hands with kisses. Then when she muttered something and shuddered with the thought of the past, he stroked her hair, and looking into her face, realised that this unhappy, sinful woman was the one creature near and dear to him, whom no one could replace.

When he went out of the house and got into the carriage he wanted to return home alive.

XVIII

The deacon got up, dressed, took his thick, gnarled stick and slipped quietly out of the house. It was dark, and for the first minute when he went into the street, he could not even see his white stick. There was not a single star in the sky, and it looked as though there would be rain again. There was a smell of wet sand and sea.

"It's to be hoped that the mountaineers won't attack us," thought the deacon, hearing the tap of the stick on the pavement, and noticing how loud and lonely the taps sounded in the stillness of the night.

When he got out of town, he began to see both the road and his stick. Here and there in the black sky there were dark cloudy patches, and soon a star peeped out and timidly blinked its one eye. The deacon walked along the high rocky coast and did not see the sea; it was slumbering below, and its unseen waves broke languidly and heavily on the shore, as though sighing "Ouf!" and how slowly! One wave broke -- the deacon had time to count eight steps; then another broke, and six steps; later a third. As before, nothing could be seen, and in the darkness one could hear the languid, drowsy drone of the sea. One could hear the infinitely faraway, inconceivable time when God moved above chaos.

The deacon felt uncanny. He hoped God would not punish him for keeping company with infidels, and even going to look at their duels. The duel would be nonsensical, bloodless, absurd, but however that might be, it was a heathen spectacle, and it was altogether unseemly for an ecclesiastical person to be present at it. He stopped and wondered -- should he go back? But an intense, restless curiosity triumphed over his doubts, and he went on.

"Though they are infidels they are good people, and will be saved," he assured himself. "They are sure to be saved," he said aloud, lighting a cigarette.

By what standard must one measure men's qualities, to judge rightly of them? The deacon remembered his enemy, the inspector of the clerical school, who believed in God, lived in chastity, and did not fight duels; but he used to feed the deacon on bread with sand in it, and on one occasion almost pulled off the deacon's ear. If human life was so artlessly constructed that everyone respected this cruel and dishonest inspector who stole the Government flour, and his health and salvation were prayed for in the schools, was it just to shun such men as Von Koren and Laevsky, simply because they were unbelievers? The deacon was weighing this question, but he recalled how absurd Samoylenko had looked yesterday, and that broke the thread of his ideas. What fun they would have next day! The deacon imagined how he would sit under a bush and look on, and when Von Koren began boasting next day at dinner, he, the deacon, would begin laughing and telling him all the details of the duel.

"How do you know all about it?" the zoologist would ask.

"Well, there you are! I stayed at home, but I know all about it."

It would be nice to write a comic description of the duel. His father-in-law would read it and laugh. A good story, told or written, was more than meat and drink to his father-in-law.

The valley of the Yellow River opened before him. The stream was broader and fiercer for the rain, and instead of murmuring as before, it was raging. It began to get light. The grey, dingy morning, and the clouds racing towards the west to overtake the storm-clouds, the mountains girt with mist, and the wet trees, all struck the deacon as ugly and sinister. He washed at the brook, repeated his morning prayer, and felt a longing for tea and hot rolls, with sour cream, which were served every morning at his father-in-law's. He remembered his wife and the "Days past Recall," which she played on the piano. What sort of woman was she? His wife had been introduced, betrothed, and married to him all in one week: he had lived with her less than a month when he was ordered here, so that he had not had time to find out what she was like. All the same, he rather missed her.

"I must write her a nice letter . . ." he thought. The flag on the *duhan* hung limp, soaked by the rain, and the *duhan* itself with its wet roof seemed darker and lower than it had been before. Near the door was standing a cart; Kerbalay, with two mountaineers and a young Tatar woman in trousers -- no doubt Kerbalay's wife or daughter -- were bringing sacks of something out of the *duhan,* and putting them on maize straw in the cart.

Near the cart stood a pair of asses hanging their heads. When they had put in all the sacks, the mountaineers and the Tatar woman began covering them over with straw, while Kerbalay began hurriedly harnessing the asses.

"Smuggling, perhaps," thought the deacon.

Here was the fallen tree with the dried pine-needles, here was the blackened patch from the fire. He remembered the picnic and all its incidents, the fire, the singing of the mountaineers, his sweet dreams of becoming a bishop, and of the Church procession. . . . The Black River had grown blacker and broader with the rain. The deacon walked cautiously over the narrow bridge, which by now was reached by the topmost crests of the dirty water, and went up through the little copse to the drying-shed.

"A splendid head," he thought, stretching himself on the straw, and thinking of Von Koren. "A fine head -- God grant him health; only there is cruelty in him. . . ."

Why did he hate Laevsky and Laevsky hate him? Why were they going to fight a duel? If from their childhood they had known poverty as the deacon had; if they had been brought up among ignorant, hard-hearted, grasping, coarse and ill-mannered people who grudged you a crust of bread, who spat on the floor and hiccoughed at dinner and at prayers; if they had not been spoilt from childhood by the pleasant surroundings and the select circle of friends they lived in -- how they would have rushed at each other, how readily they would have overlooked each other's shortcomings and would have prized each other's strong points! Why, how few even outwardly decent people there were in the world! It was true that Laevsky was flighty, dissipated, queer, but he did not steal, did not spit loudly on the floor; he did not abuse his wife and say, "You'll eat till you burst, but you don't want to work;" he would not beat a child with reins, or give his servants stinking meat to eat -- surely this was reason enough to be indulgent to him? Besides, he was the chief sufferer from his failings, like a sick man from his sores. Instead of being led by boredom and some sort of misunderstanding to look for degeneracy, extinction, heredity, and other such incomprehensible things in each other, would they not do better to stoop a little lower and turn their hatred and anger where whole streets resounded with moanings from coarse ignorance, greed, scolding, impurity, swearing, the shrieks of women. . . .

The sound of a carriage interrupted the deacon's thoughts. He glanced out of the door and saw a carriage and in it three persons: Laevsky, Sheshkovsky, and the superintendent of the post-office.

"Stop!" said Sheshkovsky.

All three got out of the carriage and looked at one another.

"They are not here yet," said Sheshkovsky, shaking the mud off. "Well? Till the show begins, let us go and find a suitable spot; there's not room to turn round here."

They went further up the river and soon vanished from sight. The Tatar driver sat in the carriage with his head resting on his shoulder and fell asleep. After waiting ten minutes the deacon came out of the drying-shed, and taking off his black hat that he might not be noticed, he began threading his way among the bushes and strips of maize along the bank, crouching and looking about him. The grass and maize were wet, and big drops fell on his head from the trees and bushes. "Disgraceful!" he muttered, picking up his wet and muddy skirt. "Had I realised it, I would not have come."

Soon he heard voices and caught sight of them. Laevsky was walking rapidly to and fro in the small glade with bowed back and hands thrust in his sleeves; his seconds were standing at the water's edge, rolling cigarettes.

"Strange," thought the deacon, not recognising Laevsky's walk; "he looks like an old man. . . ."

"How rude it is of them!" said the superintendent of the post-office, looking at his watch. "It may be learned manners to be late, but to my thinking it's hoggish."

Sheshkovsky, a stout man with a black beard, listened and said:

"They're coming!"

XIX

"It's the first time in my life I've seen it! How glorious!" said Von Koren, pointing to the glade and stretching out his hands to the east. "Look: green rays!"

In the east behind the mountains rose two green streaks of light, and it really was beautiful. The sun was rising.

"Good-morning!" the zoologist went on, nodding to Laevsky's seconds. "I'm not late, am I?"

He was followed by his seconds, Boyko and Govorovsky, two very young officers of the same height, wearing white tunics, and Ustimovitch, the thin, unsociable doctor; in one hand he had a bag of some sort, and in the other hand, as usual, a cane which he held behind him. Laying the bag on the ground and greeting no one, he put the other hand, too, behind his back and began pacing up and down the glade.

Laevsky felt the exhaustion and awkwardness of a man who is soon perhaps to die, and is for that reason an object of general attention. He wanted to be killed as soon as possible or taken home. He saw the sunrise now for the first time in his life; the early morning, the green rays of light, the dampness, and the men in wet boots, seemed to him to have nothing to do with his life, to be superfluous and embarrassing. All this had no connection with the night he had been through, with his thoughts and his feeling of guilt, and so he would have gladly gone away without waiting for the duel.

Von Koren was noticeably excited and tried to conceal it, pretending that he was more interested in the green light than anything. The seconds were confused, and looked at one another as though wondering why they were here and what they were to do.

"I imagine, gentlemen, there is no need for us to go further," said Sheshkovsky. "This place will do."

"Yes, of course," Von Koren agreed.

A silence followed. Ustimovitch, pacing to and fro, suddenly turned sharply to Laevsky and said in a low voice, breathing into his face:

"They have very likely not told you my terms yet. Each side is to pay me fifteen roubles, and in the case of the death of one party, the survivor is to pay thirty."

Laevsky was already acquainted with the man, but now for the first time he had a distinct view of his lustreless eyes, his stiff moustaches, and wasted, consumptive neck; he was a money-grubber, not a doctor; his breath had an unpleasant smell of beef.

"What people there are in the world!" thought Laevsky, and answered: "Very good."

The doctor nodded and began pacing to and fro again, and it was evident he did not need the money at all, but simply asked for it from hatred. Everyone felt it was time to begin, or to end what had been begun, but instead of beginning or ending, they stood about, moved to and fro and smoked. The young officers, who were present at a duel for the first time in their lives, and even now hardly believed in this civilian and, to their thinking, unnecessary duel, looked critically at their tunics and stroked their sleeves. Sheshkovsky went up to them and said softly: "Gentlemen, we must use every effort to prevent this duel; they ought to be reconciled."

He flushed crimson and added:

"Kirilin was at my rooms last night complaining that Laevsky had found him with Nadyezhda Fyodorovna, and all that sort of thing."

"Yes, we know that too," said Boyko.

"Well, you see, then . . . Laevsky's hands are trembling and all that sort of thing . . . he can scarcely hold a pistol now. To fight with him is as inhuman as to fight a man who is drunk or who has typhoid. If a reconciliation cannot be arranged, we ought to put off the duel, gentlemen, or something. . . . It's such a sickening business, I can't bear to see it.

"Talk to Von Koren."

"I don't know the rules of duelling, damnation take them, and I don't want to either; perhaps he'll imagine Laevsky funks it and has sent me to him, but he can think what he likes -- I'll speak to him."

Sheshkovsky hesitatingly walked up to Von Koren with a slight limp, as though his leg had gone to sleep; and as he went towards him, clearing his throat, his whole figure was a picture of indolence.

"There's something I must say to you, sir," he began, carefully scrutinising the flowers on the zoologist's shirt. "It's confidential. I don't know the rules of duelling, damnation take them, and I don't want to, and I look on the matter not as a second and that sort of thing, but as a man, and that's all about it."

"Yes. Well?"

"When seconds suggest reconciliation they are usually not listened to; it is looked upon as a formality. *Amour propre* and all that. But I humbly beg you to look carefully at Ivan Andreitch. He's not in a normal state, so to speak, to-day -- not in his right mind, and a pitiable object. He has had a misfortune. I can't endure gossip. . .."

Sheshkovsky flushed crimson and looked round.

"But in view of the duel, I think it necessary to inform you, Laevsky found his madam last night at Muridov's with . . . another gentleman."

"How disgusting!" muttered the zoologist; he turned pale, frowned, and spat loudly. "Tfoo!"

His lower lip quivered, he walked away from Sheshkovsky, unwilling to hear more, and as though he had accidentally tasted something bitter, spat loudly again, and for the first time that morning looked with hatred at Laevsky. His excitement and awkwardness passed off; he tossed his head and said aloud:

"Gentlemen, what are we waiting for, I should like to know? Why don't we begin?"

Sheshkovsky glanced at the officers and shrugged his shoulders.

"Gentlemen," he said aloud, addressing no one in particular. "Gentlemen, we propose that you should be reconciled."

"Let us make haste and get the formalities over," said Von Koren. "Reconciliation has been discussed already. What is the next formality? Make haste, gentlemen, time won't wait for us."

"But we insist on reconciliation all the same," said Sheshkovsky in a guilty voice, as a man compelled to interfere in another man's business; he flushed, laid his hand on his heart, and went on: "Gentlemen, we see no grounds for associating the offence with the duel. There's nothing in common between duelling and offences against one another of which we are sometimes guilty through human weakness. You are university men and men of culture, and no doubt you see in the duel nothing but a foolish and out-of-date formality, and all that sort of thing. That's how we look at it ourselves, or we shouldn't have come, for we cannot allow that in our presence men should fire at one another, and all that." Sheshkovsky wiped the perspiration off his face and went on: "Make an end to your misunderstanding, gentlemen; shake hands, and let us go home and drink to peace. Upon my honour, gentlemen!"

Von Koren did not speak. Laevsky, seeing that they were looking at him, said:

"I have nothing against Nikolay Vassilitch; if he considers I'm to blame, I'm ready to apologise to him."

Von Koren was offended.

"It is evident, gentlemen," he said, "you want Mr. Laevsky to return home a magnanimous and chivalrous figure, but I cannot give you and him that satisfaction. And there was no need to get up early and drive eight miles out of town simply to drink to peace, to have breakfast, and to explain to me that the duel is an out-of-date formality. A duel is a duel, and there is no need to make it more false and stupid than it is in reality. I want to fight!"

A silence followed. Boyko took a pair of pistols out of a box; one was given to Von Koren and one to Laevsky, and then there followed a difficulty which afforded a brief amusement to the zoologist and the seconds. It appeared that of all the people present not one had ever in his life been at a duel, and no one knew precisely how they ought to stand, and what the seconds ought to say and do. But then Boyko remembered and began, with a smile, to explain.

"Gentlemen, who remembers the description in Lermontov?" asked Von Koren, laughing. "In Turgenev, too, Bazarov had a duel with someone. . . ."

"There's no need to remember," said Ustimovitch impatiently. "Measure the distance, that's all."

And he took three steps as though to show how to measure it. Boyko counted out the steps while his companion drew his sabre and scratched the earth at the extreme points to mark the barrier. In complete silence the opponents took their places.

"Moles," the deacon thought, sitting in the bushes.

Sheshkovsky said something, Boyko explained something again, but Laevsky did not hear -- or rather heard, but did not understand. He cocked his pistol when the time came to do so, and raised the cold, heavy weapon with the barrel upwards. He forgot to unbutton his overcoat, and it felt very tight over his shoulder and under his arm, and his arm rose as awkwardly as though the sleeve had been cut out of tin. He remembered the hatred he had felt the night before for the swarthy brow and curly hair, and felt that even yesterday at the moment of intense hatred and anger he could not have shot a man. Fearing that the bullet might somehow hit Von Koren by accident, he raised the pistol higher and higher, and felt that this too obvious magnanimity was indelicate and anything but magnanimous, but he did not know how else to do and could do nothing else. Looking at the pale, ironically smiling face of Von Koren, who evidently had been convinced from the beginning that his opponent would fire in the air, Laevsky thought that, thank God, everything would be over directly, and all that he had to do was to press the trigger rather hard. . . .

He felt a violent shock on the shoulder; there was the sound of a shot and an answering echo in the mountains: ping-ting!

Von Koren cocked his pistol and looked at Ustimovitch, who was pacing as before with his hands behind his back, taking no notice of anyone.

"Doctor," said the zoologist, "be so good as not to move to and fro like a pendulum. You make me dizzy."

The doctor stood still. Von Koren began to take aim at Laevsky.

"It's all over!" thought Laevsky.

The barrel of the pistol aimed straight at his face, the expression of hatred and contempt in Von Koren's attitude and whole figure, and the murder just about to be committed by a decent man in broad daylight, in the presence of decent men, and the stillness and the unknown force that compelled Laevsky to stand still and not to run -- how mysterious it all was, how incomprehensible and terrible!

The moment while Von Koren was taking aim seemed to Laevsky longer than a night: he glanced imploringly at the seconds; they were pale and did not stir.

"Make haste and fire," thought Laevsky, and felt that his pale, quivering, and pitiful face must arouse even greater hatred in Von Koren.

"I'll kill him directly," thought Von Koren, aiming at his forehead, with his finger already on the catch. "Yes, of course I'll kill him."

"He'll kill him!" A despairing shout was suddenly heard somewhere very close at hand.

A shot rang out at once. Seeing that Laevsky remained standing where he was and did not fall, they all looked in the direction from which the shout had come, and saw the deacon. With pale face and wet hair sticking to his forehead and his cheeks, wet through and muddy, he was standing in the maize on the further bank, smiling rather queerly and waving his wet hat. Sheshkovsky laughed with joy, burst into tears, and moved away. . . .

XX

A little while afterwards, Von Koren and the deacon met near the little bridge. The deacon was excited; he breathed hard, and avoided looking in people's faces. He felt ashamed both of his terror and his muddy, wet garments.

"I thought you meant to kill him . . ." he muttered. "How contrary to human nature it is! How utterly unnatural it is!"

"But how did you come here?" asked the zoologist.

"Don't ask," said the deacon, waving his hand. "The evil one tempted me, saying: 'Go, go. . . .' So I went and almost died of fright in the maize. But now, thank God, thank God. . . . I am awfully pleased with you," muttered the deacon. "Old Grandad Tarantula will be glad. . . . It's funny, it's too funny! Only I beg of you most earnestly don't tell anybody I was there, or I may get into hot water with the authorities. They will say: 'The deacon was a second.' "

"Gentlemen," said Von Koren, "the deacon asks you not to tell anyone you've seen him here. He might get into trouble."

"How contrary to human nature it is!" sighed the deacon. "Excuse my saying so, but your face was so dreadful that I thought you were going to kill him."

"I was very much tempted to put an end to that scoundrel," said Von Koren, "but you shouted close by, and I missed my aim. The whole procedure is revolting to anyone who is not used to it, and it has exhausted me, deacon. I feel awfully tired. Come along. . . ."

"No, you must let me walk back. I must get dry, for I am wet and cold."

"Well, as you like," said the zoologist, in a weary tone, feeling dispirited, and, getting into the carriage, he closed his eyes. "As you like. . . ."

While they were moving about the carriages and taking their seats, Kerbalay stood in the road, and, laying his hands on his stomach, he bowed low, showing his teeth; he imagined that the gentry had come to enjoy the beauties of nature and drink tea, and could not understand why they were getting into the carriages. The party set off in complete silence and only the deacon was left by the *duhan.*

"Come to the *duhan,* drink tea," he said to Kerbalay. "Me wants to eat."

Kerbalay spoke good Russian, but the deacon imagined that the Tatar would understand him better if he talked to him in broken Russian. "Cook omelette, give cheese. . . ."

"Come, come, father," said Kerbalay, bowing. "I'll give you everything. . . . I've cheese and wine. . . . Eat what you like."

"What is 'God' in Tatar?" asked the deacon, going into the *duhan.*

"Your God and my God are the same," said Kerbalay, not understanding him. "God is the same for all men, only men are different. Some are Russian, some are Turks, some are English -- there are many sorts of men, but God is one."

"Very good. If all men worship the same God, why do you Mohammedans look upon Christians as your everlasting enemies?"

"Why are you angry?" said Kerbalay, laying both hands on his stomach. "You are a priest; I am a Mussulman: you say, 'I want to eat' -- I give it you. . . . Only the rich man distinguishes your God from my God; for the poor man it is all the same. If you please, it is ready."

While this theological conversation was taking place at the *duhan,* Laevsky was driving home thinking how dreadful it had been driving there at daybreak, when the roads, the rocks, and the mountains were wet and dark, and the uncertain future seemed like a terrible abyss, of which one could not see the bottom; while now the raindrops hanging on the grass and on the stones were sparkling in the sun like diamonds, nature was smiling joyfully, and the terrible future was left behind. He looked at Sheshkovsky's sullen, tear-stained face, and at the two carriages ahead of them in which Von Koren, his seconds, and the doctor were sitting, and it seemed to him as though they were all coming back from a graveyard in which a wearisome, insufferable man who was a burden to others had just been buried.

"Everything is over," he thought of his past. cautiously touching his neck with his fingers.

On the right side of his neck was a small swelling, of the length and breadth of his little finger, and he felt a pain, as though someone had passed a hot iron over his neck. The bullet had bruised it.

Afterwards, when he got home, a strange, long, sweet day began for him, misty as forgetfulness. Like a man released from prison or from hospital, he stared at the long-familiar objects and wondered that the tables, the windows, the chairs, the light, and the sea stirred in him a keen, childish delight such as he had not known for long, long years. Nadyezhda Fyodorovna, pale and haggard, could not understand his gentle voice and strange movements; she made haste to tell him everything that had happened to her. . . . It seemed to her that very likely he scarcely heard and did not understand her, and that if he did know everything he would curse her and kill her, but he listened to her, stroked her face and hair, looked into her eyes and said:

"I have nobody but you. . . ."

Then they sat a long while in the garden, huddled close together, saying nothing, or dreaming aloud of their happy life in the future, in brief, broken sentences, while it seemed to him that he had never spoken at such length or so eloquently.

XXI

More than three months had passed.

The day came that Von Koren had fixed on for his departure. A cold, heavy rain had been falling from early morning, a north-east wind was blowing, and the waves were high on the sea. It was said that the steamer would hardly be able to come into the harbour in such weather. By the time-table it should have arrived at ten o'clock in the morning, but Von Koren, who had gone on to the sea-front at midday and again after dinner, could see nothing through the field-glass but grey waves and rain covering the horizon.

Towards the end of the day the rain ceased and the wind began to drop perceptibly. Von Koren had already made up his mind that he would not be able to get off that day, and had settled down to play chess with Samoylenko; but after dark the orderly announced that there were lights on the sea and that a rocket had been seen.

Von Koren made haste. He put his satchel over his shoulder, and kissed Samoylenko and the deacon. Though there was not the slightest necessity, he went through the rooms again, said good-bye to the orderly and the cook, and went out into the street, feeling that he had left something behind, either at the doctor's or his lodging. In the street he walked beside Samoylenko, behind them came the deacon with a box, and last of all the orderly with two portmanteaus. Only Samoylenko and the orderly could distinguish the dim lights on the sea. The others gazed into the darkness and saw nothing. The steamer had stopped a long way from the coast.

"Make haste, make haste," Von Koren hurried them. "I am afraid it will set off."

As they passed the little house with three windows, into which Laevsky had moved soon after the duel, Von Koren could not resist peeping in at the window. Laevsky was sitting, writing, bent over the table, with his back to the window.

"I wonder at him!" said the zoologist softly. "What a screw he has put on himself!"

"Yes, one may well wonder," said Samoylenko. "He sits from morning till night, he's always at work. He works to pay off his debts. And he lives, brother, worse than a beggar!"

Half a minute of silence followed. The zoologist, the doctor, and the deacon stood at the window and went on looking at Laevsky.

"So he didn't get away from here, poor fellow," said Samoylenko. "Do you remember how hard he tried?"

"Yes, he has put a screw on himself," Von Koren repeated. "His marriage, the way he works all day long for his daily bread, a new expression in his face, and even in his walk -- it's all so extraordinary that I don't know what to call it."

The zoologist took Samoylenko's sleeve and went on with emotion in his voice:

"You tell him and his wife that when I went away I was full of admiration for them and wished them all happiness . . . and I beg him, if he can, not to remember evil against me. He knows me. He knows that if I could have foreseen this change, then I might have become his best friend."

"Go in and say good-bye to him."

"No, that wouldn't do."

"Why? God knows, perhaps you'll never see him again."

The zoologist reflected, and said:

"That's true."

Samoylenko tapped softly at the window. Laevsky started and looked round.

"Vanya, Nikolay Vassilitch wants to say goodbye to you," said Samoylenko. "He is just going away."

Laevsky got up from the table, and went into the passage to open the door. Samoylenko, the zoologist, and the deacon went into the house.

"I can only come for one minute," began the zoologist, taking off his goloshes in the passage, and already wishing he had not given way to his feelings and come in, uninvited. "It is as though I were forcing myself on him," he thought, "and that's stupid."

"Forgive me for disturbing you," he said as he went into the room with Laevsky, "but I'm just going away, and I had an impulse to see you. God knows whether we shall ever meet again."

"I am very glad to see you. . . . Please come in," said Laevsky, and he awkwardly set chairs for his visitors as though he wanted to bar their way, and stood in the middle of the room, rubbing his hands.

"I should have done better to have left my audience in the street," thought Von Koren, and he said firmly: "Don't remember evil against me, Ivan Andreitch. To forget the past is, of course, impossible -- it is too painful, and I've not come here to apologise or to declare that I was not to blame. I acted sincerely, and I have not changed my convictions since then. . . . It is true that I see, to my great delight, that I was mistaken in regard to you, but it's easy to make a false step even on a smooth road, and, in fact, it's the natural human lot: if one is not mistaken in the main, one is mistaken in the details. Nobody knows the real truth."

"No, no one knows the truth," said Laevsky.

"Well, good-bye. . . . God give you all happiness."

Von Koren gave Laevsky his hand; the latter took it and bowed.

"Don't remember evil against me," said Von Koren. "Give my greetings to your wife, and say I am very sorry not to say good-bye to her."

"She is at home."

Laevsky went to the door of the next room, and said:

"Nadya, Nikolay Vassilitch wants to say goodbye to you."

Nadyezhda Fyodorovna came in; she stopped near the doorway and looked shyly at the visitors. There was a look of guilt and dismay on her face, and she held her hands like a schoolgirl receiving a scolding.

"I'm just going away, Nadyezhda Fyodorovna," said Von Koren, "and have come to say good-bye."

She held out her hand uncertainly, while Laevsky bowed.

"What pitiful figures they are, though!" thought Von Koren. "The life they are living does not come easy to them. I shall be in Moscow and Petersburg; can I send you anything?" he asked.

"Oh!" said Nadyezhda Fyodorovna, and she looked anxiously at her husband. "I don't think there's anything. . . ."

"No, nothing . . ." said Laevsky, rubbing his hands. "Our greetings."

Von Koren did not know what he could or ought to say, though as he went in he thought he would say a very great deal that would be warm and good and important. He shook hands with Laevsky and his wife in silence, and left them with a depressed feeling.

"What people!" said the deacon in a low voice, as he walked behind them. "My God, what people! Of a truth, the right hand of God has planted this vine! Lord! Lord! One man vanquishes thousands and another tens of thousands. Nikolay Vassilitch," he said ecstatically, "let me tell you that to-day you have conquered the greatest of man's enemies -- pride."

"Hush, deacon! Fine conquerors we are! Conquerors ought to look like eagles, while he's a pitiful figure, timid, crushed; he bows like a Chinese idol, and I, I am sad. . . ."

They heard steps behind them. It was Laevsky, hurrying after them to see him off. The orderly was standing on the quay with the two portmanteaus, and at a little distance stood four boatmen.

"There is a wind, though. . . . Brrr!" said Samoylenko. "There must be a pretty stiff storm on the sea now! You are not going off at a nice time, Koyla."

"I'm not afraid of sea-sickness."

"That's not the point. . . . I only hope these rascals won't upset you. You ought to have crossed in the agent's sloop. Where's the agent's sloop?" he shouted to the boatmen.

"It has gone, Your Excellency."

"And the Customs-house boat?"

"That's gone, too."

"Why didn't you let us know," said Samoylenko angrily. "You dolts!"

"It's all the same, don't worry yourself . . ." said Von Koren. "Well, good-bye. God keep you."

Samoylenko embraced Von Koren and made the sign of the cross over him three times.

"Don't forget us, Kolya. . . . Write. . . . We shall look out for you next spring."

"Good-bye, deacon," said Von Koren, shaking hands with the deacon. "Thank you for your company and for your pleasant conversation. Think about the expedition."

"Oh Lord, yes! to the ends of the earth," laughed the deacon. "I've nothing against it."

Von Koren recognised Laevsky in the darkness, and held out his hand without speaking. The boatmen were by now below, holding the boat, which was beating against the piles, though the breakwater screened it from the breakers. Von Koren went down the ladder, jumped into the boat, and sat at the helm.

"Write!" Samoylenko shouted to him. "Take care of yourself."

"No one knows the real truth," thought Laevsky, turning up the collar of his coat and thrusting his hands into his sleeves.

The boat turned briskly out of the harbour into the open sea. It vanished in the waves, but at once from a deep hollow glided up onto a high breaker, so that they could distinguish the men and even the oars. The boat moved three yards forward and was sucked two yards back.

"Write! " shouted Samoylenko; "it's devilish weather for you to go in."

"Yes, no one knows the real truth . . ." thought Laevsky, looking wearily at the dark, restless sea.

"It flings the boat back," he thought; "she makes two steps forward and one step back; but the boatmen are stubborn, they work the oars unceasingly, and are not afraid of the high waves. The boat goes on and on.

Now she is out of sight, but in half an hour the boatmen will see the steamer lights distinctly, and within an hour they will be by the steamer ladder. So it is in life. . . . In the search for truth man makes two steps forward and one step back. Suffering, mistakes, and weariness of life thrust them back, but the thirst for truth and stubborn will drive them on and on. And who knows? Perhaps they will reach the real truth at last."

"Go--o--od-by--e," shouted Samoylenko.

"There's no sight or sound of them," said the deacon. "Good luck on the journey!"

It began to spot with rain.

THE WIFE

I

I received the following letter:

"DEAR SIR, PAVEL ANDREITCH!

"Not far from you -- that is to say, in the village of Pestrovo -- very distressing incidents are taking place, concerning which I feel it my duty to write to you. All the peasants of that village sold their cottages and all their belongings, and set off for the province of Tomsk, but did not succeed in getting there, and have come back. Here, of course, they have nothing now; everything belongs to other people. They have settled three or four families in a hut, so that there are no less than fifteen persons of both sexes in each hut, not counting the young children; and the long and the short of it is, there is nothing to eat. There is famine and there is a terrible pestilence of hunger, or spotted, typhus; literally everyone is stricken. The doctor's assistant says one goes into a cottage and what does one see? Everyone is sick, everyone delirious, some laughing, others frantic; the huts are filthy; there is no one to fetch them water, no one to give them a drink, and nothing to eat but frozen potatoes. What can Sobol (our Zemstvo doctor) and his lady assistant do when more than medicine the peasants need bread which they have not? The District Zemstvo refuses to assist them, on the ground that their names have been taken off the register of this district, and that they are now reckoned as inhabitants of Tomsk; and, besides, the Zemstvo has no money.

"Laying these facts before you, and knowing your humanity, I beg you not to refuse immediate help.

"Your well-wisher."

Obviously the letter was written by the doctor with the animal name* or his lady assistant. Zemstvo doctors and their assistants go on for years growing more and more convinced every day that they can do *nothing*, and yet continue to receive their salaries from people who are living upon frozen potatoes, and consider they have a right to judge whether I am humane or not.

Worried by the anonymous letter and by the fact that peasants came every morning to the servants' kitchen and went down on their knees there, and that twenty sacks of rye had been stolen at night out of the barn, the wall having first been broken in, and by the general depression which was fostered by conversations, newspapers, and horrible weather -- worried by all this, I worked listlessly and ineffectively. I was writing "A History of Railways"; I had to read a great number of Russian and foreign books, pamphlets, and articles in the magazines, to make calculations, to refer to logarithms, to think and to write; then again to read, calculate, and think; but as soon as I took up a book or began to think, my thoughts were in a muddle, my eyes began blinking, I would get up from the table with a sigh and begin walking about the big rooms of my deserted country-house. When I was tired of walking about I would stand still at my study window, and, looking across the wide courtyard, over the pond and the bare young birch-trees and the great fields covered with recently fallen, thawing snow, I saw on a low hill on the horizon a group of mud-coloured huts from which a black muddy road ran down in an irregular streak through the white field. That was Pestrovo, concerning which my anonymous correspondent had written to me. If it had not been for the crows who, foreseeing rain or snowy weather, floated cawing over the pond and the fields, and the tapping in the carpenter's shed, this bit of the world about which such a fuss was being made would have seemed like the Dead Sea; it was all so still, motionless, lifeless, and dreary!

My uneasiness hindered me from working and concentrating myself; I did not know what it was, and chose to believe it was disappointment. I had actually given up my post in the Department of Ways and Communications, and had come here into the country expressly to live in peace and to devote myself to writing on social questions. It had long been my cherished dream. And now I had to say good-bye both to peace and to literature, to give up everything and think only of the peasants. And that was inevitable, because I was convinced that there was absolutely nobody in the district except me to help the starving. The people surrounding me were uneducated, unintellectual, callous, for the most part dishonest, or if they were honest, they were unreasonable and unpractical like my wife, for instance. It was impossible to rely on such people, it was impossible to leave the peasants to their fate, so that the only thing left to do was to submit to necessity and see to setting the peasants to rights myself.

I began by making up my mind to give five thousand roubles to the assistance of the starving peasants. And that did not decrease, but only aggravated my uneasiness. As I stood by the window or walked about the rooms I was tormented by the question which had not occurred to me before: how this money was to be spent. To have bread bought and to go from hut to hut distributing it was more than one man could do, to say nothing of the risk that in your haste you might give twice as much to one who was well-fed or to one who was making. money out of his fellows as to the hungry. I had no faith in the local officials. All these district captains and tax inspectors were young men, and I distrusted them as I do all young people of today, who are materialistic and without ideals. The District Zemstvo, the Peasant Courts, and all the local institutions, inspired in me not the slightest desire to appeal to them for assistance. I knew that all these institutions who were busily engaged in picking out plums from the Zemstvo and the Government pie had their mouths always wide open for a bite at any other pie that might turn up.

The idea occurred to me to invite the neighbouring landowners and suggest to them to organize in my house something like a committee or a centre to which all subscriptions could be forwarded, and from which assistance and instructions could be distributed throughout the district; such an organization, which would render possible frequent consultations and free control on a big scale, would completely meet my views. But I imagined the lunches, the dinners, the suppers and the noise, the waste of time, the verbosity and the bad taste which that mixed provincial company would inevitably bring into my house, and I made haste to reject my idea.

As for the members of my own household, the last thing I could look for was help or support from them. Of my father's household, of the household of my childhood, once a big and noisy family, no one remained but the governess Mademoiselle Marie, or, as she was now called, Marya Gerasimovna, an absolutely insignificant person. She was a precise little old lady of seventy, who wore a light grey dress and a cap with white ribbons, and looked like a china doll. She always sat in the drawing-room reading.

Whenever I passed by her, she would say, knowing the reason for my brooding:

"What can you expect, Pasha? I told you how it would be before. You can judge from our servants."

My wife, Natalya Gavrilovna, lived on the lower storey, all the rooms of which she occupied. She slept, had her meals, and received her visitors downstairs in her own rooms, and took not the slightest interest in how I dined, or slept, or whom I saw. Our relations with one another were simple and not strained, but cold, empty, and dreary as relations are between people who have been so long estranged, that even living under the same roof gives no semblance of nearness. There was no trace now of the passionate and tormenting love -- at one time sweet, at another bitter as wormwood -- which I had once felt for Natalya Gavrilovna. There was nothing left, either, of the outbursts of the past -- the loud altercations, upbraidings, complaints, and gusts of hatred which had usually ended in my wife's going abroad or to her own people, and in my sending money in small but frequent instalments that I might sting her pride oftener. (My proud and sensitive wife and her family live at my expense, and much as she would have liked to do so, my wife could not refuse my money: that afforded me satisfaction and was one comfort in my sorrow.) Now when we chanced to meet in the corridor downstairs or in the yard, I bowed, she smiled graciously. We spoke of the weather, said that it seemed time to put in the double windows, and that someone with bells on their harness had driven over the dam. And at such times I read in her face: "I am faithful to you and am not disgracing your good name which you think so much about; you are sensible and do not worry me; we are quits."

I assured myself that my love had died long ago, that I was too much absorbed in my work to think seriously of my relations with my wife. But, alas! that was only what I imagined. When my wife talked aloud downstairs I listened intently to her voice, though I could not distinguish one word. When she played the piano downstairs I stood up and listened. When her carriage or her saddlehorse was brought to the door, I went to the window and waited to see her out of the house; then I watched her get into her carriage or mount her horse and ride out of the yard. I felt that there was something wrong with me, and was afraid the expression of my eyes or my face might betray me. I looked after my wife and then watched for her to come back that I might see again from the window her face, her shoulders, her fur coat, her hat. I felt dreary, sad, infinitely regretful, and felt inclined in her absence to walk through her rooms, and longed that the problem that my wife and I had not been able to solve because our characters were incompatible, should solve itself in the natural way as soon as possible -- that is, that this beautiful woman of twenty-seven might make haste and grow old, and that my head might be grey and bald.

One day at lunch my bailiff informed me that the Pestrovo peasants had begun to pull the thatch off the roofs to feed their cattle. Marya Gerasimovna looked at me in alarm and perplexity.

"What can I do?" I said to her. "One cannot fight single-handed, and I have never experienced such loneliness as I do now. I would give a great deal to find one man in the whole province on whom I could rely."

"Invite Ivan Ivanitch," said Marya Gerasimovna.

"To be sure!" I thought, delighted. "That is an idea! *C'est raison,*" I hummed, going to my study to write to Ivan Ivanitch. "*C'est raison, c'est raison.*"

II

Of all the mass of acquaintances who, in this house twenty-five to thirty-five years ago, had eaten, drunk, masqueraded, fallen in love, married, bored us with accounts of their splendid packs of hounds and horses, the only one still living was Ivan Ivanitch Bragin. At one time he had been very active, talkative, noisy, and given to falling in love, and had been famous for his extreme views and for the peculiar charm of his face, which fascinated men as well as women; now he was an old man, had grown corpulent, and was living out his days with neither views nor charm. He came the day after getting my letter, in the evening just as the samovar was brought into the dining-room and little Marya Gerasimovna had begun slicing the lemon.

"I am very glad to see you, my dear fellow," I said gaily, meeting him. "Why, you are stouter than ever. . . ."

"It isn't getting stout; it's swelling," he answered. "The bees must have stung me."

With the familiarity of a man laughing at his own fatness, he put his arms round my waist and laid on my breast his big soft head, with the hair combed down on the forehead like a Little Russian's, and went off into a thin, aged laugh.

"And you go on getting younger," he said through his laugh. "I wonder what dye you use for your hair and beard; you might let me have some of it." Sniffing and gasping, he embraced me and kissed me on the cheek. "You might give me some of it," he repeated. "Why, you are not forty, are you?"

"Alas, I am forty-six!" I said, laughing.

Ivan Ivanitch smelt of tallow candles and cooking, and that suited him. His big, puffy, slow-moving body was swathed in a long frock-coat like a coachman's full coat, with a high waist, and with hooks and eyes instead of buttons, and it would have been strange if he had smelt of eau-de-Cologne, for instance. In his long, unshaven, bluish double chin, which looked like a thistle, his goggle eyes, his shortness of breath, and in the whole of his clumsy, slovenly figure, in his voice, his laugh, and his words, it was difficult to recognize the graceful, interesting talker who used in old days to make the husbands of the district jealous on account of their wives.

"I am in great need of your assistance, my friend," I said, when we were sitting in the dining-room, drinking tea. "I want to organize relief for the starving peasants, and I don't know how to set about it. So perhaps you will be so kind as to advise me."

"Yes, yes, yes," said Ivan Ivanitch, sighing. "To be sure, to be sure, to be sure. . . ."

"I would not have worried you, my dear fellow, but really there is no one here but you I can appeal to. You know what people are like about here."

"To be sure, to be sure, to be sure. . . . Yes."

I thought that as we were going to have a serious, business consultation in which anyone might take part, regardless of their position or personal relations, why should I not invite Natalya Gavrilovna.

"*Tres faciunt collegium*," I said gaily. "What if we were to ask Natalya Gavrilovna? What do you think? Fenya," I said, turning to the maid, "ask Natalya Gavrilovna to come upstairs to us, if possible at once. Tell her it's a very important matter."

A little later Natalya Gavrilovna came in. I got up to meet her and said:

"Excuse us for troubling you, Natalie. We are discussing a very important matter, and we had the happy thought that we might take advantage of your good advice, which you will not refuse to give us. Please sit down."

Ivan Ivanitch kissed her hand while she kissed his forehead; then, when we all sat down to the table, he, looking at her tearfully and blissfully, craned forward to her and kissed her hand again. She was dressed in black, her hair was carefully arranged, and she smelt of fresh scent. She had evidently dressed to go out or was expecting somebody. Coming into the dining-room, she held out her hand to me with simple friendliness, and smiled to me as graciously as she did to Ivan Ivanitch -- that pleased me; but as she talked she moved her fingers, often and abruptly leaned back in her chair and talked rapidly, and this jerkiness in her words and movements irritated me and reminded me of her native town -- Odessa, where the society, men and women alike, had wearied me by its bad taste.

"I want to do something for the famine-stricken peasants," I began, and after a brief pause I went on: " Money, of course, is a great thing, but to confine oneself to subscribing money, and with that to be satisfied, would be evading the worst of the trouble. Help must take the form of money, but the most important thing is a proper and sound organization. Let us think it over, my friends, and do something."

Natalya Gavrilovna looked at me inquiringly and shrugged her shoulders as though to say, "What do I know about it?"

"Yes, yes, famine . . ." muttered Ivan Ivanitch. "Certainly . . . yes."

"It's a serious position," I said, "and assistance is needed as soon as possible. I imagine the first point among the principles which we must work out ought to be promptitude. We must act on the military principles of judgment, promptitude, and energy."

"Yes, promptitude . . ." repeated Ivan Ivanitch in a drowsy and listless voice, as though he were dropping asleep. "Only one can't do anything. The crops have failed, and so what's the use of all your judgment and energy? . . . It's the elements. . . . You can't go against God and fate."

"Yes, but that's what man has a head for, to contend against the elements."

"Eh? Yes . . . that's so, to be sure. . . . Yes."

Ivan Ivanitch sneezed into his handkerchief, brightened up, and as though he had just woken up, looked round at my wife and me.

"My crops have failed, too." He laughed a thin little laugh and gave a sly wink as though this were really funny. "No money, no corn, and a yard full of labourers like Count Sheremetyev's. I want to kick them out, but I haven't the heart to."

Natalya Gavrilovna laughed, and began questioning him about his private affairs. Her presence gave me a pleasure such as I had not felt for a long time, and I was afraid to look at her for fear my eyes would betray my secret feeling. Our relations were such that that feeling might seem surprising and ridiculous.

She laughed and talked with Ivan Ivanitch without being in the least disturbed that she was in my room and that I was not laughing.

"And so, my friends, what are we to do?" I asked after waiting for a pause. "I suppose before we do anything else we had better immediately open a subscription-list. We will write to our friends in the capitals and in Odessa, Natalie, and ask them to subscribe. When we have got together a little sum we will begin buying corn and fodder for the cattle; and you, Ivan Ivanitch, will you be so kind as to undertake distributing the relief? Entirely relying on your characteristic tact and efficiency, we will only venture to express a desire that before you give any relief you make acquaintance with the details of the case on the spot, and also, which is very important, you should be careful that corn should be distributed only to those who are in genuine need, and not to the drunken, the idle, or the dishonest."

"Yes, yes, yes . . ." muttered Ivan Ivanitch. "To be sure, to be sure."

"Well, one won't get much done with that slobbering wreck," I thought, and I felt irritated.

"I am sick of these famine-stricken peasants, bother them! It's nothing but grievances with them!" Ivan Ivanitch went on, sucking the rind of the lemon. "The hungry have a grievance against those who have enough, and those who have enough have a grievance against the hungry. Yes . . . hunger stupefies and maddens a man and makes him savage; hunger is not a potato. When a man is starving he uses bad language, and steals, and may do worse. . . . One must realize that."

Ivan Ivanitch choked over his tea, coughed, and shook all over with a squeaky, smothered laughter.

" 'There was a battle at Pol . . . Poltava,' " he brought out, gesticulating with both hands in protest against the laughter and coughing which prevented him from speaking. " 'There was a battle at Poltava!' When three years after the Emancipation we had famine in two districts here, Fyodor Fyodoritch came and invited me to go to him. 'Come along, come along,' he persisted, and nothing else would satisfy him. 'Very well, let us go,' I said. And, so we set off. It was in the evening; there was snow falling. Towards night we were getting near his place, and suddenly from the wood came 'bang!' and another time 'bang!' 'Oh, damn it all!' . . . I jumped out of the sledge, and I saw in the darkness a man running up to me, knee-deep in the snow. I put my arm round his shoulder, like this, and knocked the gun out of his hand. Then another one turned up; I fetched him a knock on the back of his head so that he grunted and flopped with his nose in the snow. I was a sturdy chap then, my fist was heavy; I disposed of two of them, and when I turned round Fyodor was sitting astride of a third. We did not let our three fine fellows go; we tied their hands behind their backs so that they might not do us or themselves any harm, and took the fools into the kitchen. We were angry with them and at the same time ashamed to look at them; they were peasants we knew, and were good fellows; we were sorry for them. They were quite stupid with terror. One was crying and begging our pardon, the second looked like a wild beast and kept swearing, the third knelt down and began to pray. I said to Fedya: 'Don't bear them a grudge; let them go, the rascals!' He fed them, gave them a bushel of flour each, and let them go: 'Get along with you,' he said. So that's what he did.. . . The Kingdom of Heaven be his and everlasting peace! He understood and did not bear them a grudge; but there were some who did, and how many people they ruined! Yes. . . Why, over the affair at the Klotchkovs' tavern eleven men were sent to the disciplinary battalion. Yes. . . . And now, look, it's the same thing. Anisyin, the investigating magistrate, stayed the night with me last Thursday, and he told me about some landowner. . . . Yes. . . . They took the wall of his barn to pieces at night and carried off twenty sacks of rye. When the gentleman heard that such a crime had been committed, he sent a telegram to the Governor and another to the police captain, another to the investigating magistrate! . . . Of course, everyone is afraid of a man who is fond of litigation. The authorities were in a flutter and there was a general hubbub. Two villages were searched."

"Excuse me, Ivan Ivanitch," I said. "Twenty sacks of rye were stolen from me, and it was I who telegraphed to the Governor. I telegraphed to Petersburg, too. But it was by no means out of love for litigation, as you are pleased to express it, and not because I bore them a grudge. I look at every subject from the point of view of principle. From the point of view of the law, theft is the same whether a man is hungry or not."

"Yes, yes. . ." muttered Ivan Ivanitch in confusion. "Of course. . . To be sure, yes."

Natalya Gavrilovna blushed.

"There are people. . ." she said and stopped; she made an effort to seem indifferent, but she could not keep it up, and looked into my eyes with the hatred that I know so well. "There are people," she said, "for whom famine and human suffering exist simply that they may vent their hateful and despicable temperaments upon them."

I was confused and shrugged my shoulders.

"I meant to say generally," she went on, "that there are people who are quite indifferent and completely devoid of all feeling of sympathy, yet who do not pass human suffering by, but insist on meddling for fear people should be able to do without them. Nothing is sacred for their vanity."

"There are people," I said softly, "who have an angelic character, but who express their glorious ideas in such a form that it is difficult to distinguish the angel from an Odessa market-woman."

I must confess it was not happily expressed.

My wife looked at me as though it cost her a great effort to hold her tongue. Her sudden outburst, and then her inappropriate eloquence on the subject of my desire to help the famine-stricken peasants, were, to say the least, out of place; when I had invited her to come upstairs I had expected quite a different attitude to me and my intentions. I cannot say definitely what I had expected, but I had been agreeably agitated by the expectation. Now I saw that to go on speaking about the famine would be difficult and perhaps stupid.

"Yes . . ." Ivan Ivanitch muttered inappropriately. "Burov, the merchant, must have four hundred thousand at least. I said to him: 'Hand over one or two thousand to the famine. You can't take it with you when you die, anyway.' He was offended. But we all have to die, you know. Death is not a potato."

A silence followed again.

"So there's nothing left for me but to reconcile myself to loneliness," I sighed. "One cannot fight single-handed. Well, I will try single-handed. Let us hope that my campaign against the famine will be more successful than my campaign against indifference."

"I am expected downstairs," said Natalya Gavrilovna.

She got up from the table and turned to Ivan Ivanitch.

"So you will look in upon me downstairs for a minute? I won't say good-bye to you."

And she went away.

Ivan Ivanitch was now drinking his seventh glass of tea, choking, smacking his lips, and sucking sometimes his moustache, sometimes the lemon. He was muttering something drowsily and listlessly, and I did not listen but waited for him to go. At last, with an expression that suggested that he had only come to me to take a cup of tea, he got up and began to take leave. As I saw him out I said:

"And so you have given me no advice."

"Eh? I am a feeble, stupid old man," he answered. "What use would my advice be? You shouldn't worry yourself. . . . I really don't know why you worry yourself. Don't disturb yourself, my dear fellow! Upon my word, there's no need," he whispered genuinely and affectionately, soothing me as though I were a child. "Upon my word, there's no need."

"No need? Why, the peasants are pulling the thatch off their huts, and they say there is typhus somewhere already."

"Well, what of it? If there are good crops next year, they'll thatch them again, and if we die of typhus others will live after us. Anyway, we have to die -- if not now, later. Don't worry yourself, my dear."

"I can't help worrying myself," I said irritably.

We were standing in the dimly lighted vestibule. Ivan Ivanitch suddenly took me by the elbow, and, preparing to say something evidently very important, looked at me in silence for a couple of minutes.

"Pavel Andreitch!" he said softly, and suddenly in his puffy, set face and dark eyes there was a gleam of the expression for which he had once been famous and which was truly charming. "Pavel Andreitch, I speak to you as a friend: try to be different! One is ill at ease with you, my dear fellow, one really is!"

He looked intently into my face; the charming expression faded away, his eyes grew dim again, and he sniffed and muttered feebly:

"Yes, yes. . . . Excuse an old man. . . . It's all nonsense . . . yes."

As he slowly descended the staircase, spreading out his hands to balance himself and showing me his huge, bulky back and red neck, he gave me the unpleasant impression of a sort of crab.

"You ought to go away, your Excellency," he muttered. "To Petersburg or abroad. . . . Why should you live here and waste your golden days? You are young, wealthy, and healthy. . . . Yes. . . . Ah, if I were younger I would whisk away like a hare, and snap my fingers at everything."

III

My wife's outburst reminded me of our married life together. In old days after every such outburst we felt irresistibly drawn to each other; we would meet and let off all the dynamite that had accumulated in our souls. And now after Ivan Ivanitch had gone away I had a strong impulse to go to my wife. I wanted to go downstairs and tell her that her behaviour at tea had been an insult to me, that she was cruel, petty, and that her plebeian mind had never risen to a comprehension of what *I* was saying and of what *I* was doing. I walked about the rooms a long time thinking of what I would say to her and trying to guess what she would say to me.

That evening, after Ivan Ivanitch went away, I felt in a peculiarly irritating form the uneasiness which had worried me of late. I could not sit down or sit still, but kept walking about in the rooms that were lighted up and keeping near to the one in which Marya Gerasimovna was sitting. I had a feeling very much like that which I had on the North Sea during a storm when everyone thought that our ship, which had no freight nor ballast, would overturn. And that evening I understood that my uneasiness was not disappointment, as I had supposed, but a different feeling, though what exactly I could not say, and that irritated me more than ever.

"I will go to her," I decided. "I can think of a pretext. I shall say that I want to see Ivan Ivanitch; that will be all."

I went downstairs and walked without haste over the carpeted floor through the vestibule and the hall. Ivan Ivanitch was sitting on the sofa in the drawing-room; he was drinking tea again and muttering something. My wife was standing opposite to him and holding on to the back of a chair. There was a gentle, sweet, and docile expression on her face, such as one sees on the faces of people listening to crazy saints or holy men when a peculiar hidden significance is imagined in their vague words and mutterings. There was something morbid, something of a nun's exaltation, in my wife's expression and attitude; and her low-pitched, half-dark rooms with their old-fashioned furniture, with her birds asleep in their cages, and with a smell of geranium, reminded me of the rooms of some abbess or pious old lady.

I went into the drawing-room. My wife showed neither surprise nor confusion, and looked at me calmly and serenely, as though she had known I should come.

"I beg your pardon," I said softly. "I am so glad you have not gone yet, Ivan Ivanitch. I forgot to ask you, do you know the Christian name of the president of our Zemstvo?"

"Andrey Stanislavovitch. Yes. . . ."

"*Merci,*" I said, took out my notebook, and wrote it down.

There followed a silence during which my wife and Ivan Ivanitch were probably waiting for me to go; my wife did not believe that I wanted to know the president's name -- I saw that from her eyes.

"Well, I must be going, my beauty," muttered Ivan Ivanitch, after I had walked once or twice across the drawing-room and sat down by the fireplace.

"No," said Natalya Gavrilovna quickly, touching his hand. "Stay another quarter of an hour. . . . Please do!"

Evidently she did not wish to be left alone with me without a witness.

"Oh, well, I'll wait a quarter of an hour, too," I thought.

"Why, it's snowing!" I said, getting up and looking out of window. "A good fall of snow! Ivan Ivanitch"-- I went on walking about the room -- "I do regret not being a sportsman. I can imagine what a pleasure it must be coursing hares or hunting wolves in snow like this!"

My wife, standing still, watched my movements, looking out of the corner of her eyes without turning her head. She looked as though she thought I had a sharp knife or a revolver in my pocket.

"Ivan Ivanitch, do take me out hunting some day," I went on softly. "I shall be very, very grateful to you."

At that moment a visitor came into the room. He was a tall, thick-set gentleman whom I did not know, with a bald head, a big fair beard, and little eyes. From his baggy, crumpled clothes and his manners I took him to be a parish clerk or a teacher, but my wife introduced him to me as Dr. Sobol.

"Very, very glad to make your acquaintance," said the doctor in a loud tenor voice, shaking hands with me warmly, with a naïve smile. "Very glad!"

He sat down at the table, took a glass of tea, and said in a loud voice:

"Do you happen to have a drop of rum or brandy? Have pity on me, Olya, and look in the cupboard; I am frozen," he said, addressing the maid.

I sat down by the fire again, looked on, listened, and from time to time put in a word in the general conversation. My wife smiled graciously to the visitors and kept a sharp lookout on me, as though I were a wild beast. She was oppressed by my presence, and this aroused in me jealousy, annoyance, and an obstinate desire to wound her. "Wife, these snug rooms, the place by the fire," I thought, "are mine, have been mine for years, but some crazy Ivan Ivanitch or Sobol has for some reason more right to them than I. Now I see my wife, not out of window, but close at hand, in ordinary home surroundings that I feel the want of now I am growing older, and, in spite of her hatred for me, I miss her as years ago in my childhood I used to miss my mother and my nurse. And I feel that now, on the verge of old age, my love for her is purer and loftier than it was in the past; and that is why I want to go up to her, to stamp hard on her toe with my heel, to hurt her and smile as I do it."

"Monsieur Marten," I said, addressing the doctor, "how many hospitals have we in the district?"

"Sobol," my wife corrected.

"Two," answered Sobol.

"And how many deaths are there every year in each hospital?"

"Pavel Andreitch, I want to speak to you," said my wife.

She apologized to the visitors and went to the next room. I got up and followed her.

"You will go upstairs to your own rooms this minute," she said.

"You are ill-bred," I said to her.

"You will go upstairs to your own rooms this very minute," she repeated sharply, and she looked into my face with hatred.

She was standing so near that if I had stooped a little my beard would have touched her face.

"What is the matter?" I asked. "What harm have I done all at once?"

Her chin quivered, she hastily wiped her eyes, and, with a cursory glance at the looking-glass, whispered:

"The old story is beginning all over again. Of course you won't go away. Well, do as you like. I'll go away myself, and you stay."

We returned to the drawing-room, she with a resolute face, while I shrugged my shoulders and tried to smile. There were some more visitors -- an elderly lady and a young man in spectacles. Without greeting the new arrivals or taking leave of the others, I went off to my own rooms.

After what had happened at tea and then again downstairs, it became clear to me that our "family happiness," which we had begun to forget about in the course of the last two years, was through some absurd and trivial reason beginning all over again, and that neither I nor my wife could now stop ourselves; and that next day or the day after, the outburst of hatred would, as I knew by experience of past years, be followed by something revolting which would upset the whole order of our lives. "So it seems that during these two years we have grown no wiser, colder, or calmer," I thought as I began walking about the rooms. "So there will again be tears, outcries, curses, packing up, going abroad, then the continual sickly fear that she will disgrace me with some coxcomb out there, Italian or Russian, refusing a passport, letters, utter loneliness, missing her, and in five years old age, grey hairs." I walked about, imagining what was really impossible -- her, grown handsomer, stouter, embracing a man I did not know. By now convinced that that would certainly happen, "'Why," I asked myself, "Why, in one of our long past quarrels, had not I given her a divorce, or why had she not at that time left me altogether? I should not have had this yearning for her now, this hatred, this anxiety; and I should have lived out my life quietly, working and not worrying about anything."

A carriage with two lamps drove into the yard, then a big sledge with three horses. My wife was evidently having a party.

Till midnight everything was quiet downstairs and I heard nothing, but at midnight there was a sound of moving chairs and a clatter of crockery. So there was supper. Then the chairs moved again, and through the floor I heard a noise; they seemed to be shouting hurrah. Marya Gerasimovna was already asleep and I was quite alone in the whole upper storey; the portraits of my forefathers, cruel, insignificant people, looked at me from the walls of the drawing-room, and the reflection of my lamp in the window winked unpleasantly. And with a feeling of jealousy and envy for what was going on downstairs, I listened and thought: "I am master here; if I like, I can in a moment turn out all that fine crew." But I knew that all that was nonsense, that I could not turn out anyone, and the word "master" had no meaning. One may think oneself master, married, rich, a kammer-junker, as much as one likes, and at the same time not know what it means.

After supper someone downstairs began singing in a tenor voice.

"Why, nothing special has happened," I tried to persuade myself. "Why am I so upset? I won't go downstairs tomorrow, that's all; and that will be the end of our quarrel."

At a quarter past one I went to bed.

"Have the visitors downstairs gone?" I asked Alexey as he was undressing me.

"Yes, sir, they've gone."

"And why were they shouting hurrah?"

"Alexey Dmitritch Mahonov subscribed for the famine fund a thousand bushels of flour and a thousand roubles. And the old lady -- I don't know her name -- promised to set up a soup kitchen on her estate to feed a hundred and fifty people. Thank God . . . Natalya Gavrilovna has been pleased to arrange that all the gentry should assemble every Friday."

"To assemble here, downstairs?"

"Yes, sir. Before supper they read a list: since August up to today Natalya Gavrilovna has collected eight thousand roubles, besides corn. Thank God. . . . What I think is that if our mistress does take trouble for the salvation of her soul, she will soon collect a lot. There are plenty of rich people here."

Dismissing Alexey, I put out the light and drew the bedclothes over my head.

"After all, why am I so troubled?" I thought. "What force draws me to the starving peasants like a butterfly to a flame? I don't know them, I don't understand them; I have never seen them and I don't like them. Why this uneasiness?"

I suddenly crossed myself under the quilt.

"But what a woman she is!" I said to myself, thinking of my wife. "There's a regular committee held in the house without my knowing. Why this secrecy? Why this conspiracy? What have I done to them? Ivan Ivanitch is right -- I must go away."

Next morning I woke up firmly resolved to go away. The events of the previous day -- the conversation at tea, my wife, Sobol, the supper, my apprehensions -- worried me, and I felt glad to think of getting away from the surroundings which reminded me of all that. While I was drinking my coffee the bailiff gave me a long report on various matters. The most agreeable item he saved for the last.

"The thieves who stole our rye have been found," he announced with a smile. "The magistrate arrested three peasants at Pestrovo yesterday."

"Go away!" I shouted at him; and a propos of nothing, I picked up the cake-basket and flung it on the floor.

IV

After lunch I rubbed my hands, and thought I must go to my wife and tell her that I was going away. Why? Who cared? Nobody cares, I answered, but why shouldn't I tell her, especially as it would give her nothing but pleasure? Besides, to go away after our yesterday's quarrel without saying a word would not be quite tactful: she might think that I was frightened of her, and perhaps the thought that she has driven me out of my house may weigh upon her. It would be just as well, too, to tell her that I subscribe five thousand, and to give her some advice about the organization, and to warn her that her inexperience in such a complicated and responsible matter might lead to most lamentable results. In short, I wanted to see my wife, and while I thought of various pretexts for going to her, I had a firm conviction in my heart that I should do so.

It was still light when I went in to her, and the lamps had not yet been lighted. She was sitting in her study, which led from the drawing-room to her bedroom, and, bending low over the table, was writing something quickly. Seeing me, she started, got up from the table, and remained standing in an attitude such as to screen her papers from me.

"I beg your pardon, I have only come for a minute," I said, and, I don't know why, I was overcome with embarrassment. "I have learnt by chance that you are organizing relief for the famine, Natalie."

"Yes, I am. But that's my business," she answered.

"Yes, it is your business," I said softly. "I am glad of it, for it just fits in with my intentions. I beg your permission to take part in it."

"Forgive me, I cannot let you do it," she said in response, and looked away.

"Why not, Natalie?" I said quietly. "Why not? I, too, am well fed and I, too, want to help the hungry."

"I don't know what it has to do with you," she said with a contemptuous smile, shrugging her shoulders. "Nobody asks you."

"Nobody asks you, either, and yet you have got up a regular committee in *my* house," I said.

"I am asked, but you can have my word for it no one will ever ask you. Go and help where you are not known."

"For God's sake, don't talk to me in that tone." I tried to be mild, and besought myself most earnestly not to lose my temper. For the first few minutes I felt glad to be with my wife. I felt an atmosphere of youth, of home, of feminine softness, of the most refined elegance -- exactly what was lacking on my floor and in my life altogether. My wife was wearing a pink flannel dressing-gown; it made her look much younger, and gave a softness to her rapid and sometimes abrupt movements. Her beautiful dark hair, the mere sight of which at one time stirred me to passion, had from sitting so long with her head bent come loose from the comb and was untidy, but, to my eyes, that only made it look more rich and luxuriant. All this, though is banal to the point of vulgarity. Before me stood an ordinary woman, perhaps neither beautiful nor elegant, but this was my wife with whom I had once lived, and with whom I should have been living to this day if it had not been for her unfortunate character; she was the one human being on the terrestrial globe whom I loved. At this moment, just before going away, when I knew that I should no longer see her even through the window, she seemed to me fascinating even as she was, cold and forbidding, answering me with a proud and contemptuous mockery. I was proud of her, and confessed to myself that to go away from her was terrible and impossible.

"Pavel Andreitch," she said after a brief silence, "for two years we have not interfered with each other but have lived quietly. Why do you suddenly feel it necessary to go back to the past? Yesterday you came to insult and humiliate me," she went on, raising her voice, and her face flushed and her eyes flamed with hatred; "but restrain yourself; do not do it, Pavel Andreitch! Tomorrow I will send in a petition and they will give me a passport, and I will go away; I will go! I will go! I'll go into a convent, into a widows' home, into an almshouse. . . ."

"Into a lunatic asylum!" I cried, not able to restrain myself.

"Well, even into a lunatic asylum! That would be better, that would be better," she cried, with flashing eyes. "When I was in Pestrovo today I envied the sick and starving peasant women because they are not living with a man like you. They are free and honest, while, thanks to you, I am a parasite, I am perishing in idleness, I eat your bread, I spend your money, and I repay you with my liberty and a fidelity which is of no use to anyone. Because you won't give me a passport, I must respect your good name, though it doesn't exist."

I had to keep silent. Clenching my teeth, I walked quickly into the drawing-room, but turned back at once and said:

"I beg you earnestly that there should be no more assemblies, plots, and meetings of conspirators in my house! I only admit to my house those with whom I am acquainted, and let all your crew find another place to do it if they want to take up philanthropy. I can't allow people at midnight in my house to be shouting hurrah at successfully exploiting an hysterical woman like you!"

My wife, pale and wringing her hands, took a rapid stride across the room, uttering a prolonged moan as though she had toothache. With a wave of my hand, I went into the drawing-room. I was choking with rage, and at the same time I was trembling with terror that I might not restrain myself, and that I might say or do something which I might regret all my life. And I clenched my hands tight, hoping to hold myself in.

After drinking some water and recovering my calm a little, I went back to my wife. She was standing in the same attitude as before, as though barring my approach to the table with the papers. Tears were slowly trickling down her pale, cold face. I paused then and said to her bitterly but without anger:

"How you misunderstand me! How unjust you are to me! I swear upon my honour I came to you with the best of motives, with nothing but the desire to do good!"

"Pavel Andreitch!" she said, clasping her hands on her bosom, and her face took on the agonized, imploring expression with which frightened, weeping children beg not to be punished, "I know perfectly well that you will refuse me, but still I beg you. Force yourself to do one kind action in your life. I entreat you, go away from here! That's the only thing you can do for the starving peasants. Go away, and I will forgive you everything, everything!"

"There is no need for you to insult me, Natalie," I sighed, feeling a sudden rush of humility. "I had already made up my mind to go away, but I won't go until I have done something for the peasants. It's my duty!"

"Ach!" she said softly with an impatient frown. "You can make an excellent bridge or railway, but you can do nothing for the starving peasants. Do understand!"

"Indeed? Yesterday you reproached me with indifference and with being devoid of the feeling of compassion. How well you know me!" I laughed. "You believe in God -- well, God is my witness that I am worried day and night. . . ."

"I see that you are worried, but the famine and compassion have nothing to do with it. You are worried because the starving peasants can get on without you, and because the Zemstvo, and in fact everyone who is helping them, does not need your guidance."

I was silent, trying to suppress my irritation. Then I said:

"I came to speak to you on business. Sit down. Please sit down."

She did not sit down.

"I beg you to sit down," I repeated, and I motioned her to a chair.

She sat down. I sat down, too, thought a little, and said:

"I beg you to consider earnestly what I am saying. Listen. . . . Moved by love for your fellow-creatures, you have undertaken the organization of famine relief. I have nothing against that, of course; I am completely in sympathy with you, and am prepared to co-operate with you in every way, whatever our relations may be. But, with all my respect for your mind and your heart . . . and your heart," I repeated, "I cannot allow such a difficult, complex, and responsible matter as the organization of relief to be left in your hands entirely. You are a woman, you are inexperienced, you know nothing of life, you are too confiding and expansive. You have surrounded yourself with assistants whom you know nothing about. I am not exaggerating if I say that under these conditions your work will inevitably lead to two deplorable consequences. To begin with, our district will be left unrelieved; and, secondly, you will have to pay for your mistakes and those of your assistants, not only with your purse, but with your reputation. The money deficit and other losses I could, no doubt, make good, but who could restore you your good name? When through lack of proper supervision and oversight there is a rumour that you, and consequently I, have made two hundred thousand over the famine fund, will your assistants come to your aid?"

She said nothing.

"Not from vanity, as you say," I went on, "but simply that the starving peasants may not be left unrelieved and your reputation may not be injured, I feel it my moral duty to take part in your work."

"Speak more briefly," said my wife.

"You will be so kind," I went on, "as to show me what has been subscribed so far and what you have spent. Then inform me daily of every fresh subscription in money or kind, and of every fresh outlay. You will also give me, Natalie, the list of your helpers. Perhaps they are quite decent people; I don't doubt it; but, still, it is absolutely necessary to make inquiries."

She was silent. I got up, and walked up and down the room.

"Let us set to work, then," I said, and I sat down to her table.

"Are you in earnest?" she asked, looking at me in alarm and bewilderment.

"Natalie, do be reasonable!" I said appealingly, seeing from her face that she meant to protest. "I beg you, trust my experience and my sense of honour."

"I don't understand what you want."

"Show me how much you have collected and how much you have spent."

"I have no secrets. Anyone may see. Look."

On the table lay five or six school exercise books, several sheets of notepaper covered with writing, a map of the district, and a number of pieces of paper of different sizes. It was getting dusk. I lighted a candle.

"Excuse me, I don't see anything yet," I said, turning over the leaves of the exercise books. "Where is the account of the receipt of money subscriptions?"

"That can be seen from the subscription lists."

"Yes, but you must have an account," I said, smiling at her naïveté. "Where are the letters accompanying the subscriptions in money or in kind? *Pardon,* a little practical advice, Natalie: it's absolutely necessary to keep those letters. You ought to number each letter and make a special note of it in a special record. You ought to do the same with your own letters. But I will do all that myself."

"Do so, do so . . ." she said.

I was very much pleased with myself. Attracted by this living interesting work, by the little table, the naïve exercise books and the charm of doing this work in my wife's society, I was afraid that my wife would suddenly hinder me and upset everything by some sudden whim, and so I was in haste and made an effort to attach no consequence to the fact that her lips were quivering, and that she was looking about her with a helpless and frightened air like a wild creature in a trap.

"I tell you what, Natalie," I said without looking at her; "let me take all these papers and exercise books upstairs to my study. There I will look through them and tell you what I think about it tomorrow. Have you any more papers?" I asked, arranging the exercise books and sheets of papers in piles.

"Take them, take them all!" said my wife, helping me to arrange them, and big tears ran down her cheeks. "Take it all! That's all that was left me in life. . . . Take the last."

"Ach! Natalie, Natalie!" I sighed reproachfully.

She opened the drawer in the table and began flinging the papers out of it on the table at random, poking me in the chest with her elbow and brushing my face with her hair; as she did so, copper coins kept dropping upon my knees and on the floor.

"Take everything!" she said in a husky voice.

When she had thrown out the papers she walked away from me, and putting both hands to her head, she flung herself on the couch. I picked up the money, put it back in the drawer, and locked it up that the servants might not be led into dishonesty; then I gathered up all the papers and went off with them. As I passed my wife I stopped. and, looking at her back and shaking shoulders, I said:

"What a baby you are, Natalie! Fie, fie! Listen, Natalie: when you realize how serious and responsible a business it is you will be the first to thank me. I assure you you will."

In my own room I set to work without haste. The exercise books were not bound, the pages were not numbered. The entries were put in all sorts of handwritings; evidently anyone who liked had a hand in managing the books. In the record of the subscriptions in kind there was no note of their money value. But, excuse me, I thought, the rye which is now worth one rouble fifteen kopecks may be worth two roubles fifteen kopecks in two months' time! Was that the way to do things? Then, "Given to A. M. Sobol 32 roubles." When was it given? For what purpose was it given? Where was the receipt? There was nothing to show, and no making anything of it. In case of legal proceedings, these papers would only obscure the case.

"How naïve she is!" I thought with surprise. "What a child!"

I felt both vexed and amused.

V

My wife had already collected eight thousand; with my five it would be thirteen thousand. For a start that was very good. The business which had so worried and interested me was at last in my hands; I was doing what the others would not and could not do; I was doing my duty, organizing the relief fund in a practical and businesslike way

Everything seemed to be going in accordance with my desires and intentions; but why did my feeling of uneasiness persist? I spent four hours over my wife's papers, making out their meaning and correcting her mistakes, but instead of feeling soothed, I felt as though someone were standing behind me and rubbing my back with a rough hand. What was it I wanted? The organization of the relief fund had come into trustworthy hands, the hungry would be fed -- what more was wanted?

The four hours of this light work for some reason exhausted me, so that I could not sit bending over the table nor write. From below I heard from time to time a smothered moan; it was my wife sobbing. Alexey, invariably meek, sleepy, and sanctimonious, kept coming up to the table to see to the candles, and looked at me somewhat strangely.

"Yes, I must go away," I decided at last, feeling utterly exhausted. "As far as possible from these agreeable impressions! I will set off tomorrow."

I gathered together the papers and exercise books, and went down to my wife. As, feeling quite worn out and shattered, I held the papers and the exercise books to my breast with both hands, and passing through my bedroom saw my trunks, the sound of weeping reached me through the floor.

"Are you a kammer-junker?" a voice whispered in my ear. "That's a very pleasant thing. But yet you are a reptile."

"It's all nonsense, nonsense, nonsense," I muttered as I went downstairs. "Nonsense . . . and it's nonsense, too, that I am actuated by vanity or a love of display. . . . What rubbish! Am I going to get a decoration for working for the peasants or be made the director of a department? Nonsense, nonsense! And who is there to show off to here in the country?"

I was tired, frightfully tired, and something kept whispering in my ear: "Very pleasant. But, still, you are a reptile." For some reason I remembered a line out of an old poem I knew as a child: "How pleasant it is to be good!"

My wife was lying on the couch in the same attitude, on her face and with her hands clutching her head. She was crying. A maid was standing beside her with a perplexed and frightened face. I sent the maid away, laid the papers on the table, thought a moment and said:

"Here are all your papers, Natalie. It's all in order, it's all capital, and I am very much pleased. I am going away tomorrow."

She went on crying. I went into the drawing-room and sat there in the dark. My wife's sobs, her sighs, accused me of something, and to justify myself I remembered the whole of our quarrel, starting from my unhappy idea of inviting my wife to our consultation and ending with the exercise books and these tears. It was an ordinary attack of our conjugal hatred, senseless and unseemly, such as had been frequent during our married life, but what had the starving peasants to do with it? How could it have happened that they had become a bone of contention between us? It was just as though pursuing one another we had accidentally run up to the altar and had carried on a quarrel there.

"Natalie," I said softly from the drawing-room, "hush, hush!"

To cut short her weeping and make an end of this agonizing state of affairs, I ought to have gone up to my wife and comforted her, caressed her, or apologized; but how could I do it so that she would believe me? How could I persuade the wild duck, living in captivity and hating me, that it was dear to me, and that I felt for its sufferings? I had never known my wife, so I had never known how to talk to her or what to talk about. Her appearance I knew very well and appreciated it as it deserved, but her spiritual, moral world, her mind, her outlook on life, her frequent changes of mood, her eyes full of hatred, her disdain, the scope and variety of her reading which sometimes struck me, or, for instance, the nun-like expression I had seen on her face the day before -- all that was unknown and incomprehensible to me. When in my collisions with her I tried to define what sort of a person she was, my psychology went no farther than deciding that she was giddy, impractical, ill-tempered, guided by feminine logic; and it seemed to me that that was quite sufficient. But now that she was crying I had a passionate desire to know more.

The weeping ceased. I went up to my wife. She sat up on the couch, and, with her head propped in both hands, looked fixedly and dreamily at the fire.

"I am going away tomorrow morning," I said.

She said nothing. I walked across the room, sighed, and said:

"Natalie, when you begged me to go away, you said: 'I will forgive you everything, everything' . . . . So you think I have wronged you. I beg you calmly and in brief terms to formulate the wrong I've done you."

"I am worn out. Afterwards, some time. . ." said my wife.

"How am I to blame?" I went on. "What have I done? Tell me: you are young and beautiful, you want to live, and I am nearly twice your age and hated by you, but is that my fault? I didn't marry you by force. But if you want to live in freedom, go; I'll give you your liberty. You can go and love whom you please. . . . I will give you a divorce."

"That's not what I want," she said. "You know I used to love you and always thought of myself as older than you. That's all nonsense. . . . You are not to blame for being older or for my being younger, or that I might be able to love someone else if I were free; but because you are a difficult person, an egoist, and hate everyone."

"Perhaps so. I don't know," I said.

"Please go away. You want to go on at me till the morning, but I warn you I am quite worn out and cannot answer you. You promised me to go to town. I am very grateful; I ask nothing more."

My wife wanted me to go away, but it was not easy for me to do that. I was dispirited and I dreaded the big, cheerless, chill rooms that I was so weary of. Sometimes when I had an ache or a pain as a child, I used to huddle up to my mother or my nurse, and when I hid my face in the warm folds of their dress, it seemed to me as though I were hiding from the pain. And in the same way it seemed to me now that I could only hide from my uneasiness in this little room beside my wife. I sat down and screened away the light from my eyes with my hand. . . . There was a stillness.

"How are you to blame?" my wife said after a long silence, looking at me with red eyes that gleamed with tears. "You are very well educated and very well bred, very honest, just, and high-principled, but in you the effect of all that is that wherever you go you bring suffocation, oppression, something insulting and humiliating to the utmost degree. You have a straightforward way of looking at things, and so you hate the whole world. You hate those who have faith, because faith is an expression of ignorance and lack of culture, and at the same time you hate those who have no faith for having no faith and no ideals; you hate old people for being conservative and behind the times, and young people for free-thinking. The interests of the peasantry and of Russia are dear to you, and so you hate the peasants because you suspect everyone of them of being a thief and a robber. You hate everyone. You are just, and always take your stand on your legal rights, and so you are always at law with the peasants and your neighbours. You have had twenty bushels of rye stolen, and your love of order has made you complain of the peasants to the Governor and all the local authorities, and to send a complaint of the local authorities to Petersburg. Legal justice!" said my wife, and she laughed. "On the ground of your legal rights and in the interests of morality, you refuse to give me a passport. Law and morality is such that a self-respecting healthy young woman has to spend her life in idleness, in depression, and in continual apprehension, and to receive in return board and lodging from a man she does not love. You have a thorough knowledge of the law, you are very honest and just, you respect marriage and family life, and the effect of all that is that all your life you have not done one kind action, that everyone hates you, that you are on bad terms with everyone, and the seven years that you have been married you've only lived seven months with your wife. You've had no wife and I've had no husband. To live with a man like you is impossible; there is no way of doing it. In the early years I was frightened with you, and now I am ashamed. . . . That's how my best years have been wasted. When I fought with you I ruined my temper, grew shrewish, coarse, timid, mistrustful. . . . Oh, but what's the use of talking! As though you wanted to understand! Go upstairs, and God be with you!"

My wife lay down on the couch and sank into thought.

"And how splendid, how enviable life might have been!" she said softly, looking reflectively into the fire. "What a life it might have been! There's no bringing it back now."

Anyone who has lived in the country in winter and knows those long dreary, still evenings when even the dogs are too bored to bark and even the clocks seem weary of ticking, and anyone who on such evenings has been troubled by awakening conscience and has moved restlessly about, trying now to smother his conscience, now to interpret it, will understand the distraction and the pleasure my wife's voice gave me as it sounded in the snug little room, telling me I was a bad man. I did not understand what was wanted of me by my conscience, and my wife, translating it in her feminine way, made clear to me in the meaning of my agitation. As often before in the moments of intense uneasiness, I guessed that the whole secret lay, not in the starving peasants, but in my not being the sort of a man I ought to be.

My wife got up with an effort and came up to me.

"Pavel Andreitch," she said, smiling mournfully, "forgive me, I don't believe you: you are not going away, but I will ask you one more favour. Call this" -- she pointed to her papers -- "self-deception, feminine logic, a mistake, as you like; but do not hinder me. It's all that is left me in life." She turned away and paused. "Before this I had nothing. I have wasted my youth in fighting with you. Now I have caught at this and am living; I am happy. . . . It seems to me that I have found in this a means of justifying my existence."

"Natalie, you are a good woman, a woman of ideas," I said, looking at my wife enthusiastically, and everything you say and do is intelligent and fine."

I walked about the room to conceal my emotion.

"Natalie," I went on a minute later, "before I go away, I beg of you as a special favour, help me to do something for the starving peasants!"

"What can I do?" said my wife, shrugging her shoulders. "Here's the subscription list."

She rummaged among the papers and found the subscription list.

"Subscribe some money," she said, and from her tone I could see that she did not attach great importance to her subscription list; "that is the only way in which you can take part in the work."

I took the list and wrote: "Anonymous, 5,000."

In this "anonymous" there was something wrong, false, conceited, but I only realized that when I noticed that my wife flushed very red and hurriedly thrust the list into the heap of papers. We both felt ashamed; I felt that I must at all costs efface this clumsiness at once, or else I should feel ashamed afterwards, in the train and at Petersburg. But how efface it? What was I to say?

"I fully approve of what you are doing, Natalie," I said genuinely, "and I wish you every success. But allow me at parting to give you one piece of advice, Natalie; be on your guard with Sobol, and with your assistants generally, and don't trust them blindly. I don't say they are not honest, but they are not gentlefolks; they are people with no ideas, no ideals, no faith, with no aim in life, no definite principles, and the whole object of their life is comprised in the rouble. Rouble, rouble, rouble!" I sighed. "They are fond of getting money easily, for nothing, and in that respect the better educated they are the more they are to be dreaded."

My wife went to the couch and lay down.

"Ideas," she brought out, listlessly and reluctantly, "ideas, ideals, objects of life, principles . . . .you always used to use those words when you wanted to insult or humiliate someone, or say something unpleasant. Yes, that's your way: if with your views and such an attitude to people you are allowed to take part in anything, you would destroy it from the first day. It's time you understand that."

She sighed and paused.

"It's coarseness of character, Pavel Andreitch," she said. "You are well-bred and educated, but what a . . . Scythian you are in reality! That's because you lead a cramped life full of hatred, see no one, and read nothing but your engineering books. And, you know, there are good people, good books! Yes . . . but I am exhausted and it wearies me to talk. I ought to be in bed."

"So I am going away, Natalie," I said.

"Yes . . . yes. . . . *Merci*. . . ."

I stood still for a little while, then went upstairs. An hour later -- it was half-past one -- I went downstairs again with a candle in my hand to speak to my wife. I didn't know what I was going to say to her, but I felt that I must say something very important and necessary. She was not in her study, the door leading to her bedroom was closed.

"Natalie, are you asleep?" I asked softly.

There was no answer.

I stood near the door, sighed, and went into the drawing-room. There I sat down on the sofa, put out the candle, and remained sitting in the dark till the dawn.

VI

I went to the station at ten o'clock in the morning. There was no frost, but snow was falling in big wet flakes and an unpleasant damp wind was blowing.

We passed a pond and then a birch copse, and then began going uphill along the road which I could see from my window. I turned round to take a last look at my house, but I could see nothing for the snow. Soon afterwards dark huts came into sight ahead of us as in a fog. It was Pestrovo.

"If I ever go out of my mind, Pestrovo will be the cause of it," I thought. "It persecutes me."

We came out into the village street. All the roofs were intact, not one of them had been pulled to pieces; so my bailiff had told a lie. A boy was pulling along a little girl and a baby in a sledge. Another boy of three, with his head wrapped up like a peasant woman's and with huge mufflers on his hands, was trying to catch the flying snowflakes on his tongue, and laughing. Then a wagon loaded with fagots came toward us and a peasant walking beside it, and there was no telling whether his beard was white or whether it was covered with snow. He recognized my coachman, smiled at him and said something, and mechanically took off his hat to me. The dogs ran out of the yards and looked inquisitively at my horses. Everything was quiet, ordinary, as usual. The emigrants had returned, there was no bread; in the huts "some were laughing, some were delirious"; but it all looked so ordinary that one could not believe it really was so. There were no distracted faces, no voices whining for help, no weeping, nor abuse, but all around was stillness, order, life, children, sledges, dogs with dishevelled tails. Neither the children nor the peasant we met were troubled; why was I so troubled?

Looking at the smiling peasant, at the boy with the huge mufflers, at the huts, remembering my wife, I realized there was no calamity that could daunt this people; I felt as though there were already a breath of victory in the air. I felt proud and felt ready to cry out that I was with them too; but the horses were carrying us away from the village into the open country, the snow was whirling, the wind was howling, and I was left alone with my thoughts. Of the million people working for the peasantry, life itself had cast me out as a useless, incompetent, bad man. I was a hindrance, a part of the people's calamity; I was vanquished, cast out, and I was hurrying to the station to go away and hide myself in Petersburg in a hotel in Bolshaya Morskaya.

An hour later we reached the station. The coachman and a porter with a disc on his breast carried my trunks into the ladies' room. My coachman Nikanor, wearing high felt boots and the skirt of his coat tucked up through his belt, all wet with the snow and glad I was going away, gave me a friendly smile and said:

"A fortunate journey, your Excellency. God give you luck."

Everyone, by the way, calls me "your Excellency," though I am only a collegiate councillor and a kammer-junker. The porter told me the train had not yet left the next station; I had to wait. I went outside, and with my head heavy from my sleepless night, and so exhausted I could hardly move my legs, I walked aimlessly towards the pump. There was not a soul anywhere near.

"Why am I going?" I kept asking myself. "What is there awaiting me there? The acquaintances from whom I have come away, loneliness, restaurant dinners, noise, the electric light, which makes my eyes ache. Where am I going, and what am I going for? What am I going for?"

And it seemed somehow strange to go away without speaking to my wife. I felt that I was leaving her in uncertainty. Going away, I ought to have told that she was right, that I really was a bad man.

When I turned away from the pump, I saw in the doorway the station-master, of whom I had twice made complaints to his superiors, turning up the collar of his coat, shrinking from the wind and the snow. He came up to me, and putting two fingers to the peak of his cap, told me with an expression of helpless confusion, strained respectfulness, and hatred on his face, that the train was twenty minutes late, and asked me would I not like to wait in the warm?

"Thank you," I answered, "but I am probably not going. Send word to my coachman to wait; I have not made up my mind."

I walked to and fro on the platform and thought, should I go away or not? When the train came in I decided not to go. At home I had to expect my wife's amazement and perhaps her mockery, the dismal upper storey and my uneasiness; but, still, at my age that was easier and as it were more homelike than travelling for two days and nights with strangers to Petersburg, where I should be conscious every minute that my life was of no use to anyone or to anything, and that it was approaching its end. No, better at home whatever awaited me there. . . . I went out of the station. It was awkward by daylight to return home, where everyone was so glad at my going. I might spend the rest of the day till evening at some neighbour's, but with whom? With some of them I was on strained relations, others I did not know at all. I considered and thought of Ivan Ivanitch.

"We are going to Bragino!" I said to the coachman, getting into the sledge.

"It's a long way," sighed Nikanor; "it will be twenty miles, or maybe twenty-five."

"Oh, please, my dear fellow," I said in a tone as though Nikanor had the right to refuse. "Please let us go!"

Nikanor shook his head doubtfully and said slowly that we really ought to have put in the shafts, not Circassian, but Peasant or Siskin; and uncertainly, as though expecting I should change my mind, took the reins in his gloves, stood up, thought a moment, and then raised his whip.

"A whole series of inconsistent actions . . ." I thought, screening my face from the snow. "I must have gone out of my mind. Well, I don't care. . . ."

In one place, on a very high and steep slope, Nikanor carefully held the horses in to the middle of the descent, but in the middle the horses suddenly bolted and dashed downhill at a fearful rate; he raised his elbows and shouted in a wild, frantic voice such as I had never heard from him before:

"Hey! Let's give the general a drive! If you come to grief he'll buy new ones, my darlings! Hey! look out! We'll run you down!"

Only now, when the extraordinary pace we were going at took my breath away, I noticed that he was very drunk. He must have been drinking at the station. At the bottom of the descent there was the crash of ice; a piece of dirty frozen snow thrown up from the road hit me a painful blow in the face.

The runaway horses ran up the hill as rapidly as they had downhill, and before I had time to shout to Nikanor my sledge was flying along on the level in an old pine forest, and the tall pines were stretching out their shaggy white paws to me from all directions.

"I have gone out of my mind, and the coachman's drunk," I thought. "Good!"

I found Ivan Ivanitch at home. He laughed till he coughed, laid his head on my breast, and said what he always did say on meeting me:

"You grow younger and younger. I don't know what dye you use for your hair and your beard; you might give me some of it."

"I've come to return your call, Ivan Ivanitch," I said untruthfully. "Don't be hard on me; I'm a townsman, conventional; I do keep count of calls."

"I am delighted, my dear fellow. I am an old man; I like respect. . . . Yes."

From his voice and his blissfully smiling face, I could see that he was greatly flattered by my visit. Two peasant women helped me off with my coat in the entry, and a peasant in a red shirt hung it on a hook, and when Ivan Ivanitch and I went into his little study, two barefooted little girls were sitting on the floor looking at a picture-book; when they saw us they jumped up and ran away, and a tall, thin old woman in spectacles came in at once, bowed gravely to me, and picking up a pillow from the sofa and a picture-book from the floor, went away. From the adjoining rooms we heard incessant whispering and the patter of bare feet.

"I am expecting the doctor to dinner," said Ivan Ivanitch. "He promised to come from the relief centre. Yes. He dines with me every Wednesday, God bless him." He craned towards me and kissed me on the neck. "You have come, my dear fellow, so you are not vexed," he whispered, sniffing. "Don't be vexed, my dear creature. Yes. Perhaps it is annoying, but don't be cross. My only prayer to God before I die is to live in peace and harmony with all in the true way. Yes."

"Forgive me, Ivan Ivanitch, I will put my feet on a chair," I said, feeling that I was so exhausted I could not be myself; I sat further back on the sofa and put up my feet on an arm-chair. My face was burning from the snow and the wind, and I felt as though my whole body were basking in the warmth and growing weaker from it.

"It's very nice here," I went on -- "warm, soft, snug . . . and goose-feather pens," I laughed, looking at the writing-table; "sand instead of blotting-paper."

"Eh? Yes . . . yes. . . . The writing-table and the mahogany cupboard here were made for my father by a self-taught cabinet-maker -- Glyeb Butyga, a serf of General Zhukov's. Yes . . . a great artist in his own way."

Listlessly and in the tone of a man dropping asleep, he began telling me about cabinet-maker Butyga. I listened. Then Ivan Ivanitch went into the next room to show me a polisander wood chest of drawers remarkable for its beauty and cheapness. He tapped the chest with his fingers, then called my attention to a stove of patterned tiles, such as one never sees now. He tapped the stove, too, with his fingers. There was an atmosphere of good-natured simplicity and well-fed abundance about the chest of drawers, the tiled stove, the low chairs, the pictures embroidered in wool and silk on canvas in solid, ugly frames. When one remembers that all those objects were standing in the same places and precisely in the same order when I was a little child, and used to come here to name-day parties with my mother, it is simply unbelievable that they could ever cease to exist.

I thought what a fearful difference between Butyga and me! Butyga who made things, above all, solidly and substantially, and seeing in that his chief object, gave to length of life peculiar significance, had no thought of death, and probably hardly believed in its possibility; I, when I built my bridges of iron and stone which would last a thousand years, could not keep from me the thought, "It's not for long . . . .it's no use." If in time Butyga's cupboard and my bridge should come under the notice of some sensible historian of art, he would say: "These were two men remarkable in their own way: Butyga loved his fellow-creatures and would not admit the thought that they might die and be annihilated, and so when he made his furniture he had the immortal man in his mind. The engineer Asorin did not love life or his fellow-creatures; even in the happy moments of creation, thoughts of death, of finiteness and dissolution, were not alien to him, and we see how insignificant and finite, how timid and poor, are these lines of his. . . ."

"I only heat these rooms," muttered Ivan Ivanitch, showing me his rooms. "Ever since my wife died and my son was killed in the war, I have kept the best rooms shut up. Yes . . . see. . ."

He opened a door, and I saw a big room with four columns, an old piano, and a heap of peas on the floor; it smelt cold and damp.

"The garden seats are in the next room . . ." muttered Ivan Ivanitch. "There's no one to dance the mazurka now. . . . I've shut them up."

We heard a noise. It was Dr. Sobol arriving. While he was rubbing his cold hands and stroking his wet beard, I had time to notice in the first place that he had a very dull life, and so was pleased to see Ivan Ivanitch and me; and, secondly, that he was a naïve and simple-hearted man. He looked at me as though I were very glad to see him and very much interested in him.

"I have not slept for two nights," he said, looking at me naïvely and stroking his beard. "One night with a confinement, and the next I stayed at a peasant's with the bugs biting me all night. I am as sleepy as Satan, do you know."

With an expression on his face as though it could not afford me anything but pleasure, he took me by the arm and led me to the dining-room. His naïve eyes, his crumpled coat, his cheap tie and the smell of iodoform made an unpleasant impression upon me; I felt as though I were in vulgar company. When we sat down to table he filled my glass with vodka, and, smiling helplessly, I drank it; he put a piece of ham on my plate and I ate it submissively.

"*Repetitia est mater studiorum,*" said Sobol, hastening to drink off another wineglassful. "Would you believe it, the joy of seeing good people has driven away my sleepiness? I have turned into a peasant, a savage in the wilds; I've grown coarse, but I am still an educated man, and I tell you in good earnest, it's tedious without company."

They served first for a cold course white sucking-pig with horse-radish cream, then a rich and very hot cabbage soup with pork on it, with boiled buckwheat, from which rose a column of steam. The doctor went on talking, and I was soon convinced that he was a weak, unfortunate man, disorderly in external life. Three glasses of vodka made him drunk; he grew unnaturally lively, ate a great deal, kept clearing his throat and smacking his lips, and already addressed me in Italian, "Eccellenza." Looking naïvely at me as though he were convinced that I was very glad to see and hear him, he informed me that he had long been separated from his wife and gave her three-quarters of his salary; that she lived in the town with his children, a boy and a girl, whom he adored; that he loved another woman, a widow, well educated, with an estate in the country, but was rarely able to see her, as he was busy with his work from morning till night and had not a free moment.

"The whole day long, first at the hospital, then on my rounds," he told us; "and I assure you, Eccellenza, I have not time to read a book, let alone going to see the woman I love. I've read nothing for ten years! For ten years, Eccellenza. As for the financial side of the question, ask Ivan Ivanitch: I have often no money to buy tobacco."

"On the other hand, you have the moral satisfaction of your work," I said.

"What?" he asked, and he winked. "No," he said, "better let us drink."

I listened to the doctor, and, after my invariable habit, tried to take his measure by my usual classification -- materialist, idealist, filthy lucre, gregarious instincts, and so on; but no classification fitted him even approximately; and strange to say, while I simply listened and looked at him, he seemed perfectly clear to me as a person, but as soon as I began trying to classify him he became an exceptionally complex, intricate, and incomprehensible character in spite of all his candour and simplicity. "Is that man," I asked myself, "capable of wasting other people's money, abusing their confidence, being disposed to sponge on them?" And now this question, which had once seemed to me grave and important, struck me as crude, petty, and coarse.

Pie was served; then, I remember, with long intervals between, during which we drank home-made liquors, they gave us a stew of pigeons, some dish of giblets, roast sucking-pig, partridges, cauliflower, curd dumplings, curd cheese and milk, jelly, and finally pancakes and jam. At first I ate with great relish, especially the cabbage soup and the buckwheat, but afterwards I munched and swallowed mechanically, smiling helplessly and unconscious of the taste of anything. My face was burning from the hot cabbage soup and the heat of the room. Ivan Ivanitch and Sobol, too, were crimson.

"To the health of your wife," said Sobol. "She likes me. Tell her her doctor sends her his respects."

"She's fortunate, upon my word," sighed Ivan Ivanitch. "Though she takes no trouble, does not fuss or worry herself, she has become the most important person in the whole district. Almost the whole business is in her hands, and they all gather round her, the doctor, the District Captains, and the ladies. With people of the right sort that happens of itself. Yes. . . . The apple-tree need take no thought for the apple to grow on it; it will grow of itself."

"It's only people who don't care who take no thought," said I.

"Eh? Yes . . . " muttered Ivan Ivanitch, not catching what I said, "that's true. . . . One must not worry oneself. Just so, just so. . . . Only do your duty towards God and your neighbour, and then never mind what happens."

"Eccellenza," said Sobol solemnly, "just look at nature about us: if you poke your nose or your ear out of your fur collar it will be frost-bitten; stay in the fields for one hour, you'll be buried in the snow; while the village is just the same as in the days of Rurik, the same Petchenyegs and Polovtsi. It's nothing but being burnt down, starving, and struggling against nature in every way. What was I saying? Yes! If one thinks about it, you know, looks into it and analyses all this hotchpotch, if you will allow me to call it so, it's not life but more like a fire in a theatre! Anyone who falls down or screams with terror, or rushes about, is the worst enemy of good order; one must stand up and look sharp, and not stir a hair! There's no time for whimpering and busying oneself with trifles. When you have to deal with elemental forces you must put out force against them, be firm and as unyielding as a stone. Isn't that right, grandfather?" He turned to Ivan Ivanitch and laughed. "I am no better than a woman myself; I am a limp rag, a flabby creature, so I hate flabbiness. I can't endure petty feelings! One mopes, another is frightened, a third will come straight in here and say: 'Fie on you! Here you've guzzled a dozen courses and you talk about the starving!' That's petty and stupid! A fourth will reproach you, Eccellenza, for being rich. Excuse me, Eccellenza," he went on in a loud voice, laying his hand on his heart, "but your having set our magistrate the task of hunting day and night for your thieves -- excuse me, that's also petty on your part. I am a little drunk, so that's why I say this now, but you know, it is petty!"

"Who's asking him to worry himself? I don't understand!" I said, getting up.

I suddenly felt unbearably ashamed and mortified, and I walked round the table.

"Who asks him to worry himself? I didn't ask him to. . . . Damn him!"

"They have arrested three men and let them go again. They turned out not to be the right ones, and now they are looking for a fresh lot," said Sobol, laughing. "It's too bad!"

"I did not ask him to worry himself," said I, almost crying with excitement. "What's it all for? What's it all for? Well, supposing I was wrong, supposing I have done wrong, why do they try to put me more in the wrong?"

"Come, come, come, come!" said Sobol, trying to soothe me. "Come! I have had a drop, that is why I said it. My tongue is my enemy. Come," he sighed, "we have eaten and drunk wine, and now for a nap."

He got up from the table, kissed Ivan Ivanitch on the head, and staggering from repletion, went out of the dining-room. Ivan Ivanitch and I smoked in silence.

I don't sleep after dinner, my dear," said Ivan Ivanitch, "but you have a rest in the lounge-room."

I agreed. In the half-dark and warmly heated room they called the lounge-room, there stood against the walls long, wide sofas, solid and heavy, the work of Butyga the cabinet maker; on them lay high, soft, white beds, probably made by the old woman in spectacles. On one of them Sobol, without his coat and boots, already lay asleep with his face to the back of the sofa; another bed was awaiting me. I took off my coat and boots, and, overcome by fatigue, by the spirit of Butyga which hovered over the quiet lounge-room, and by the light, caressing snore of Sobol, I lay down submissively.

And at once I began dreaming of my wife, of her room, of the station-master with his face full of hatred, the heaps of snow, a fire in the theatre. I dreamed of the peasants who had stolen twenty sacks of rye out of my barn.

"Anyway, it's a good thing the magistrate let them go," I said.

I woke up at the sound of my own voice, looked for a moment in perplexity at Sobol's broad back, at the buckles of his waistcoat, at his thick heels, then lay down again and fell asleep.

When I woke up the second time it was quite dark. Sobol was asleep. There was peace in my heart, and I longed to make haste home. I dressed and went out of the lounge-room. Ivan Ivanitch was sitting in a big arm-chair in his study, absolutely motionless, staring at a fixed point, and it was evident that he had been in the same state of petrifaction all the while I had been asleep.

"Good!" I said, yawning. "I feel as though I had woken up after breaking the fast at Easter. I shall often come and see you now. Tell me, did my wife ever dine here?"

"So-ome-ti-mes . . . sometimes,'" muttered Ivan Ivanitch, making an effort to stir. "She dined here last Saturday. Yes. . . . She likes me."

After a silence I said:

"Do you remember, Ivan Ivanitch, you told me I had a disagreeable character and that it was difficult to get on with me? But what am I to do to make my character different?"

"I don't know, my dear boy. . . . I'm a feeble old man, I can't advise you. . . . Yes. . . . But I said that to you at the time because I am fond of you and fond of your wife, and I was fond of your father. . . . Yes. I shall soon die, and what need have I to conceal things from you or to tell you lies? So I tell you: I am very fond of you, but I don't respect you. No, I don't respect you."

He turned towards me and said in a breathless whisper:

"It's impossible to respect you, my dear fellow. You look like a real man. You have the figure and deportment of the French President Carnot -- I saw a portrait of him the other day in an illustrated paper . . . yes. . . . You use lofty language, and you are clever, and you are high up in the service beyond all reach, but haven't real soul, my dear boy . . . there's no strength in it."

"A Scythian, in fact," I laughed. "But what about my wife? Tell me something about my wife; you know her better."

I wanted to talk about my wife, but Sobol came in and prevented me.

"I've had a sleep and a wash," he said, looking at me naïvely. "I'll have a cup of tea with some rum in it and go home."

VII

It was by now past seven. Besides Ivan Ivanitch, women servants, the old dame in spectacles, the little girls and the peasant, all accompanied us from the hall out on to the steps, wishing us good-bye and all sorts of blessings, while near the horses in the darkness there were standing and moving about men with lanterns, telling our coachmen how and which way to drive, and wishing us a lucky journey. The horses, the men, and the sledges were white.

"Where do all these people come from?" I asked as my three horses and the doctor's two moved at a walking pace out of the yard.

"They are all his serfs," said Sobol. "The new order has not reached him yet. Some of the old servants are living out their lives with him, and then there are orphans of all sorts who have nowhere to go; there are some, too, who insist on living there, there's no turning them out. A queer old man!"

Again the flying horses, the strange voice of drunken Nikanor, the wind and the persistent snow, which got into one's eyes, one's mouth, and every fold of one's fur coat. . . .

"Well, I am running a rig," I thought, while my bells chimed in with the doctor's, the wind whistled, the coachmen shouted; and while this frantic uproar was going on, I recalled all the details of that strange wild day, unique in my life, and it seemed to me that I really had gone out of my mind or become a different man. It was as though the man I had been till that day were already a stranger to me.

The doctor drove behind and kept talking loudly with his coachman. From time to time he overtook me, drove side by side, and always, with the same naïve confidence that it was very pleasant to me, offered me a cigarette or asked for the matches. Or, overtaking me, he would lean right out of his sledge, and waving about the sleeves of his fur coat, which were at least twice as long as his arms, shout:

"Go it, Vaska! Beat the thousand roublers! Hey, my kittens!"

And to the accompaniment of loud, malicious laughter from Sobol and his Vaska the doctor's kittens raced ahead. My Nikanor took it as an affront, and held in his three horses, but when the doctor's bells had passed out of hearing, he raised his elbows, shouted, and our horses flew like mad in pursuit. We drove into a village, there were glimpses of lights, the silhouettes of huts. Someone shouted:

"Ah, the devils!" We seemed to have galloped a mile and a half, and still it was the village street and there seemed no end to it. When we caught up the doctor and drove more quietly, he asked for matches and said:

"Now try and feed that street! And, you know, there are five streets like that, sir. Stay, stay," he shouted. "Turn in at the tavern! We must get warm and let the horses rest."

They stopped at the tavern.

"I have more than one village like that in my district," said the doctor, opening a heavy door with a squeaky block, and ushering me in front of him. "If you look in broad daylight you can't see to the end of the street, and there are side-streets, too, and one can do nothing but scratch one's head. It's hard to do anything."

We went into the best room where there was a strong smell of table-cloths, and at our entrance a sleepy peasant in a waistcoat and a shirt worn outside his trousers jumped up from a bench. Sobol asked for some beer and I asked for tea.

"It's hard to do anything," said Sobol. "Your wife has faith; I respect her and have the greatest reverence for her, but I have no great faith myself. As long as our relations to the people continue to have the character of ordinary philanthropy, as shown in orphan asylums and almshouses, so long we shall only be shuffling, shamming, and deceiving ourselves, and nothing more. Our relations ought to be businesslike, founded on calculation, knowledge, and justice. My Vaska has been working for me all his life; his crops have failed, he is sick and starving. If I give him fifteen kopecks a day, by so doing I try to restore him to his former condition as a workman; that is, I am first and foremost looking after my own interests, and yet for some reason I call that fifteen kopecks relief, charity, good works. Now let us put it like this. On the most modest computation, reckoning seven kopecks a soul and five souls a family, one needs three hundred and fifty roubles a day to feed a thousand families. That sum is fixed by our practical duty to a thousand families. Meanwhile we give not three hundred and fifty a day, but only ten, and say that that is relief, charity, that that makes your wife and all of us exceptionally good people and hurrah for our humaneness. That is it, my dear soul! Ah! if we would talk less of being humane and calculated more, reasoned, and took a conscientious attitude to our duties! How many such humane, sensitive people there are among us who tear about in all good faith with subscription lists, but don't pay their tailors or their cooks. There is no logic in our life; that's what it is! No logic!"

We were silent for a while. I was making a mental calculation and said:

"I will feed a thousand families for two hundred days. Come and see me tomorrow to talk it over."

I was pleased that this was said quite simply, and was glad that Sobol answered me still more simply:

"Right."

We paid for what we had and went out of the tavern.

"I like going on like this," said Sobol, getting into the sledge. "Eccellenza, oblige me with a match. I've forgotten mine in the tavern."

A quarter of an hour later his horses fell behind, and the sound of his bells was lost in the roar of the snow-storm. Reaching home, I walked about my rooms, trying to think things over and to define my position clearly to myself; I had not one word, one phrase, ready for my wife. My brain was not working.

But without thinking of anything, I went downstairs to my wife. She was in her room, in the same pink dressing-gown, and standing in the same attitude as though screening her papers from me. On her face was an expression of perplexity and irony, and it was evident that having heard of my arrival, she had prepared herself not to cry, not to entreat me, not to defend herself, as she had done the day before, but to laugh at me, to answer me contemptuously, and to act with decision. Her face was saying: "If that's how it is, good-bye."

"Natalie, I've not gone away," I said, "but it's not deception. I have gone out of my mind; I've grown old, I'm ill, I've become a different man -- think as you like. . . . I've shaken off my old self with horror, with horror; I despise him and am ashamed of him, and the new man who has been in me since yesterday will not let me go away. Do not drive me away, Natalie!"

She looked intently into my face and believed me, and there was a gleam of uneasiness in her eyes. Enchanted by her presence, warmed by the warmth of her room, I muttered as in delirium, holding out my hands to her:

"I tell you, I have no one near to me but you. I have never for one minute ceased to miss you, and only obstinate vanity prevented me from owning it. The past, when we lived as husband and wife, cannot be brought back, and there's no need; but make me your servant, take all my property, and give it away to anyone you like. I am at peace, Natalie, I am content. . . . I am at peace."

My wife, looking intently and with curiosity into my face, suddenly uttered a faint cry, burst into tears, and ran into the next room. I went upstairs to my own storey.

An hour later I was sitting at my table, writing my "History of Railways," and the starving peasants did not now hinder me from doing so. Now I feel no uneasiness. Neither the scenes of disorder which I saw when I went the round of the huts at Pestrovo with my wife and Sobol the other day, nor malignant rumours, nor the mistakes of the people around me, nor old age close upon me -- nothing disturbs me. Just as the flying bullets do not hinder soldiers from talking of their own affairs, eating and cleaning their boots, so the starving peasants do not hinder me from sleeping quietly and looking after my personal affairs. In my house and far around it there is in full swing the work which Dr. Sobol calls "an orgy of philanthropy." My wife often comes up to me and looks about my rooms uneasily, as though looking for what more she can give to the starving peasants "to justify her existence," and I see that, thanks to her, there will soon be nothing of our property left and we shall be poor; but that does not trouble me, and I smile at her gaily. What will happen in the future I don't know.

THE GRASSHOPPER

I

All Olga Ivanovna's friends and acquaintances were at her wedding.

"Look at him; isn't it true that there is something in him?" she said to her friends, with a nod towards her husband, as though she wanted to explain why she was marrying a simple, very ordinary, and in no way remarkable man.

Her husband, Osip Stepanitch Dymov, was a doctor, and only of the rank of a titular councillor. He was on the staff of two hospitals: in one a ward-surgeon and in the other a dissecting demonstrator. Every day from nine to twelve he saw patients and was busy in his ward, and after twelve o'clock he went by tram to the other hospital, where he dissected. His private practice was a small one, not worth more than five hundred roubles a year. That was all. What more could one say about him? Meanwhile, Olga Ivanovna and her friends and acquaintances were not quite ordinary people. Everyone of them was remarkable in some way, and more or less famous; already had made a reputation and was looked upon as a celebrity; or if not yet a celebrity, gave brilliant promise of becoming one. There was an actor from the Dramatic Theatre, who was a great talent of established reputation, as well as an elegant, intelligent, and modest man, and a capital elocutionist, and who taught Olga Ivanovna to recite; there was a singer from the opera, a good-natured, fat man who assured Olga Ivanovna, with a sigh, that she was ruining herself, that if she would take herself in hand and not be lazy she might make a remarkable singer; then there were several artists, and chief among them Ryabovsky, a very handsome, fair young man of five-and-twenty who painted genre pieces, animal studies, and landscapes, was successful at exhibitions, and had sold his last picture for five hundred roubles. He touched up Olga Ivanovna's sketches, and used to say she might do something. Then a violoncellist, whose instrument used to sob, and who openly declared that of all the ladies of his acquaintance the only one who could accompany him was Olga Ivanovna; then there was a literary man, young but already well known, who had written stories, novels, and plays. Who else? Why, Vassily Vassilyitch, a landowner and amateur illustrator and vignettist, with a great feeling for the old Russian style, the old ballad and epic. On paper, on china, and on smoked plates, he produced literally marvels. In the midst of this free artistic company, spoiled by fortune, though refined and modest, who recalled the existence of doctors only in times of illness, and to whom the name of Dymov sounded in no way different from Sidorov or Tarasov -- in the midst of this company Dymov seemed strange, not wanted, and small, though he was tall and broad-shouldered. He looked as though he had on somebody else's coat, and his beard was like a shopman's. Though if he had been a writer or an artist, they would have said that his beard reminded them of Zola.

An artist said to Olga Ivanovna that with her flaxen hair and in her wedding-dress she was very much like a graceful cherry-tree when it is covered all over with delicate white blossoms in spring.

"Oh, let me tell you," said Olga Ivanovna, taking his arm, "how it was it all came to pass so suddenly. Listen, listen! . . . I must tell you that my father was on the same staff at the hospital as Dymov. When my poor father was taken ill, Dymov watched for days and nights together at his bedside. Such self-sacrifice! Listen, Ryabovsky! You, my writer, listen; it is very interesting! Come nearer. Such self-sacrifice, such genuine sympathy! I sat up with my father, and did not sleep for nights, either. And all at once -- the princess had won the hero's heart -- my Dymov fell head over ears in love. Really, fate is so strange at times! Well, after my father's death he came to see me sometimes, met me in the street, and one fine evening, all at once he made me an offer . . . like snow upon my head. . . . I lay awake all night, crying, and fell hellishly in love myself. And here, as you see, I am his wife. There really is something strong, powerful, bearlike about him, isn't there? Now his face is turned three-quarters towards us in a bad light, but when he turns round look at his forehead. Ryabovsky, what do you say to that forehead? Dymov, we are talking about you!" she called to her husband. "Come here; hold out your honest hand to Ryabovsky. . . . That's right, be friends."

Dymov, with a naïve and good-natured smile, held out his hand to Ryabovsky, and said:

"Very glad to meet you. There was a Ryabovsky in my year at the medical school. Was he a relation of yours?"

II

Olga Ivanovna was twenty-two, Dymov was thirty-one. They got on splendidly together when they were married. Olga Ivanovna hung all her drawing-room walls with her own and other people's sketches, in frames and without frames, and near the piano and furniture arranged picturesque corners with Japanese parasols, easels, daggers, busts, photographs, and rags of many colours. . . . In the dining-room she papered the walls with peasant woodcuts, hung up bark shoes and sickles, stood in a corner a scythe and a rake, and so achieved a dining-room in the Russian style. In her bedroom she draped the ceiling and the walls with dark cloths to make it like a cavern, hung a Venetian lantern over the beds, and at the door set a figure with a halberd. And everyone thought that the young people had a very charming little home.

When she got up at eleven o'clock every morning, Olga Ivanovna played the piano or, if it were sunny, painted something in oils. Then between twelve and one she drove to her dressmaker's. As Dymov and she had very little money, only just enough, she and her dressmaker were often put to clever shifts to enable her to appear constantly in new dresses and make a sensation with them. Very often out of an old dyed dress, out of bits of tulle, lace, plush, and silk, costing nothing, perfect marvels were created, something bewitching -- not a dress, but a dream. From the dressmaker's Olga Ivanovna usually drove to some actress of her acquaintance to hear the latest theatrical gossip, and incidentally to try and get hold of tickets for the first night of some new play or for a benefit performance. From the actress's she had to go to some artist's studio or to some exhibition or to see some celebrity -- either to pay a visit or to give an invitation or simply to have a chat. And everywhere she met with a gay and friendly welcome, and was assured that she was good, that she was sweet, that she was rare. . . . Those whom she called great and famous received her as one of themselves, as an equal, and predicted with one voice that, with her talents, her taste, and her intelligence, she would do great things if she concentrated herself. She sang, she played the piano, she painted in oils, she carved, she took part in amateur performances; and all this not just anyhow, but all with talent, whether she made lanterns for an illumination or dressed up or tied somebody's cravat -- everything she did was exceptionally graceful, artistic, and charming. But her talents showed themselves in nothing so clearly as in her faculty for quickly becoming acquainted and on intimate terms with celebrated people. No sooner did anyone become ever so little celebrated, and set people talking about him, than she made his acquaintance, got on friendly terms the same day, and invited him to her house. Every new acquaintance she made was a veritable fête for her. She adored celebrated people, was proud of them, dreamed of them every night. She craved for them, and never could satisfy her craving. The old ones departed and were forgotten, new ones came to replace them, but to these, too, she soon grew accustomed or was disappointed in them, and began eagerly seeking for fresh great men, finding them and seeking for them again. What for?

Between four and five she dined at home with her husband. His simplicity, good sense, and kind-heartedness touched her and moved her up to enthusiasm. She was constantly jumping up, impulsively hugging his head and showering kisses on it.

"You are a clever, generous man, Dymov," she used to say, "but you have one very serious defect. You take absolutely no interest in art. You don't believe in music or painting."

"I don't understand them," he would say mildly. "I have spent all my life in working at natural science and medicine, and I have never had time to take an interest in the arts."

"But, you know, that's awful, Dymov!"

"Why so? Your friends don't know anything of science or medicine, but you don't reproach them with it. Everyone has his own line. I don't understand landscapes and operas, but the way I look at it is that if one set of sensible people devote their whole lives to them, and other sensible people pay immense sums for them, they must be of use. I don't understand them, but not understanding does not imply disbelieving in them."

"Let me shake your honest hand!"

After dinner Olga Ivanovna would drive off to see her friends, then to a theatre or to a concert, and she returned home after midnight. So it was every day.

On Wednesdays she had "At Homes." At these "At Homes" the hostess and her guests did not play cards and did not dance, but entertained themselves with various arts. An actor from the Dramatic Theatre recited, a singer sang, artists sketched in the albums of which Olga Ivanovna had a great number, the violoncellist played, and the hostess herself sketched, carved, sang, and played accompaniments. In the intervals between the recitations, music, and singing, they talked and argued about literature, the theatre, and painting. There were no ladies, for Olga Ivanovna considered all ladies wearisome and vulgar except actresses and her dressmaker. Not one of these entertainments passed without the hostess starting at every ring at the bell, and saying, with a triumphant expression, "It is he," meaning by "he," of course, some new celebrity. Dymov was not in the drawing-room, and no one remembered his existence. But exactly at half-past eleven the door leading into the dining-room opened, and Dymov would appear with his good-natured, gentle smile and say, rubbing his hands:

"Come to supper, gentlemen."

They all went into the dining-room, and every time found on the table exactly the same things: a dish of oysters, a piece of ham or veal, sardines, cheese, caviare, mushrooms, vodka, and two decanters of wine.

"My dear *maître d'hôtel!*" Olga Ivanovna would say, clasping her hands with enthusiasm, "you are simply fascinating! My friends, look at his forehead! Dymov, turn your profile. Look! he has the face of a Bengal tiger and an expression as kind and sweet as a gazelle. Ah, the darling!"

The visitors ate, and, looking at Dymov, thought, "He really is a nice fellow"; but they soon forgot about him, and went on talking about the theatre, music, and painting.

The young people were happy, and their life flowed on without a hitch.

The third week of their honeymoon was spent, however, not quite happily -- sadly, indeed. Dymov caught erysipelas in the hospital, was in bed for six days, and had to have his beautiful black hair cropped. Olga Ivanovna sat beside him and wept bitterly, but when he was better she put a white handkerchief on his shaven head and began to paint him as a Bedouin. And they were both in good spirits. Three days after he had begun to go back to the hospital he had another mischance.

"I have no luck, little mother," he said one day at dinner. "I had four dissections to do today, and I cut two of my fingers at one. And I did not notice it till I got home."

Olga Ivanovna was alarmed. He smiled, and told her that it did not matter, and that he often cut his hands when he was dissecting.

"I get absorbed, little mother, and grow careless."

Olga Ivanovna dreaded symptoms of blood-poisoning, and prayed about it every night, but all went well. And again life flowed on peaceful and happy, free from grief and anxiety. The present was happy, and to follow it spring was at hand, already smiling in the distance, and promising a thousand delights. There would be no end to their happiness. In April, May and June a summer villa a good distance out of town; walks, sketching, fishing, nightingales; and then from July right on to autumn an artist's tour on the Volga, and in this tour Olga Ivanovna would take part as an indispensable member of the society. She had already had made for her two travelling dresses of linen, had bought paints, brushes, canvases, and a new palette for the journey. Almost every day Ryabovsky visited her to see what progress she was making in her painting; when she showed him her painting, he used to thrust his hands deep into his pockets, compress his lips, sniff, and say:

"Ye -- es . . . ! That cloud of yours is screaming: it's not in the evening light. The foreground is somehow chewed up, and there is something, you know, not the thing. . . . And your cottage is weighed down and whines pitifully. That corner ought to have been taken more in shadow, but on the whole it is not bad; I like it."

And the more incomprehensible he talked, the more readily Olga Ivanovna understood him.

III

After dinner on the second day of Trinity week, Dymov bought some sweets and some savouries and went down to the villa to see his wife. He had not seen her for a fortnight, and missed her terribly. As he sat in the train and afterwards as he looked for his villa in a big wood, he felt all the while hungry and weary, and dreamed of how he would have supper in freedom with his wife, then tumble into bed and to sleep. And he was delighted as he looked at his parcel, in which there was caviare, cheese, and white salmon.

The sun was setting by the time he found his villa and recognized it. The old servant told him that her mistress was not at home, but that most likely she would soon be in. The villa, very uninviting in appearance, with low ceilings papered with writing-paper and with uneven floors full of crevices, consisted only of three rooms. In one there was a bed, in the second there were canvases, brushes, greasy papers, and men's overcoats and hats lying about on the chairs and in the windows, while in the third Dymov found three unknown men; two were dark-haired and had beards, the other was clean-shaven and fat, apparently an actor. There was a samovar boiling on the table.

"What do you want?" asked the actor in a bass voice, looking at Dymov ungraciously. "Do you want Olga Ivanovna? Wait a minute; she will be here directly."

Dymov sat down and waited. One of the dark-haired men, looking sleepily and listlessly at him, poured himself out a glass of tea, and asked:

"Perhaps you would like some tea?"

Dymov was both hungry and thirsty, but he refused tea for fear of spoiling his supper. Soon he heard footsteps and a familiar laugh; a door slammed, and Olga Ivanovna ran into the room, wearing a wide-brimmed hat and carrying a box in her hand; she was followed by Ryabovsky, rosy and good-humoured, carrying a big umbrella and a camp-stool.

"Dymov!" cried Olga Ivanovna, and she flushed crimson with pleasure. "Dymov!" she repeated, laying her head and both arms on his bosom. "Is that you? Why haven't you come for so long? Why? Why?"

"When could I, little mother? I am always busy, and whenever I am free it always happens somehow that the train does not fit."

"But how glad I am to see you! I have been dreaming about you the whole night, the whole night, and I was afraid you must be ill. Ah! if you only knew how sweet you are! You have come in the nick of time! You will be my salvation! You are the only person who can save me! There is to be a most original wedding here tomorrow," she went on, laughing, and tying her husband's cravat. "A young telegraph clerk at the station, called Tchikeldyeev, is going to be married. He is a handsome young man and -- well, not stupid, and you know there is something strong, bearlike in his face . . . you might paint him as a young Norman. We summer visitors take a great interest in him, and have promised to be at his wedding. . . . He is a lonely, timid man, not well off, and of course it would be a shame not to be sympathetic to him. Fancy! the wedding will be after the service; then we shall all walk from the church to the bride's lodgings . . . you see the wood, the birds singing, patches of sunlight on the grass, and all of us spots of different colours against the bright green background -- very original, in the style of the French impressionists. But, Dymov, what am I to go to the church in?" said Olga Ivanovna, and she looked as though she were going to cry. "I have nothing here, literally nothing! no dress, no flowers, no gloves . . . you must save me. Since you have come, fate itself bids you save me. Take the keys, my precious, go home and get my pink dress from the wardrobe. You remember it; it hangs in front. . . . Then, in the storeroom, on the floor, on the right side, you will see two cardboard boxes. When you open the top one you will see tulle, heaps of tulle and rags of all sorts, and under them flowers. Take out all the flowers carefully, try not to crush them, darling; I will choose among them later. . . . And buy me some gloves."

"Very well!" said Dymov; "I will go tomorrow and send them to you."

"Tomorrow?" asked Olga Ivanovna, and she looked at him surprised. "You won't have time tomorrow. The first train goes tomorrow at nine, and the wedding's at eleven. No, darling, it must be today; it absolutely must be today. If you won't be able to come tomorrow, send them by a messenger. Come, you must run along. . . . The passenger train will be in directly; don't miss it, darling."

"Very well."

"Oh, how sorry I am to let you go!" said Olga Ivanovna, and tears came into her eyes. "And why did I promise that telegraph clerk, like a silly?"

Dymov hurriedly drank a glass of tea, took a cracknel, and, smiling gently, went to the station. And the caviare, the cheese, and the white salmon were eaten by the two dark gentlemen and the fat actor.

IV

On a still moonlight night in July Olga Ivanovna was standing on the deck of a Volga steamer and looking alternately at the water and at the picturesque banks. Beside her was standing Ryabovsky, telling her the black shadows on the water were not shadows, but a dream, that it would be sweet to sink into forgetfulness, to die, to become a memory in the sight of that enchanted water with the fantastic glimmer, in sight of the fathomless sky and the mournful, dreamy shores that told of the vanity of our life and of the existence of something higher, blessed, and eternal. The past was vulgar and uninteresting, the future was trivial, and that marvellous night, unique in a lifetime, would soon be over, would blend with eternity; then, why live?

And Olga Ivanovna listened alternately to Ryabovsky's voice and the silence of the night, and thought of her being immortal and never dying. The turquoise colour of the water, such as she had never seen before, the sky, the river-banks, the black shadows, and the unaccountable joy that flooded her soul, all told her that she would make a great artist, and that somewhere in the distance, in the infinite space beyond the moonlight, success, glory, the love of the people, lay awaiting her. . . . When she gazed steadily without blinking into the distance, she seemed to see crowds of people, lights, triumphant strains of music, cries of enthusiasm, she herself in a white dress, and flowers showered upon her from all sides. She thought, too, that beside her, leaning with his elbows on the rail of the steamer, there was standing a real great man, a genius, one of God's elect. . . . All that he had created up to the present was fine, new, and extraordinary, but what he would create in time, when with maturity his rare talent reached its full development, would be astounding, immeasurably sublime; and that could be seen by his face, by his manner of expressing himself and his attitude to nature. He talked of shadows, of the tones of evening, of the moonlight, in a special way, in a language of his own, so that one could not help feeling the fascination of his power over nature. He was very handsome, original, and his life, free, independent, aloof from all common cares, was like the life of a bird.

"It's growing cooler," said Olga Ivanovna, and she gave a shudder.

Ryabovsky wrapped her in his cloak, and said mournfully:

"I feel that I am in your power; I am a slave. Why are you so enchanting today?"

He kept staring intently at her, and his eyes were terrible. And she was afraid to look at him.

"I love you madly," he whispered, breathing on her cheek. "Say one word to me and I will not go on living; I will give up art . . ." he muttered in violent emotion. "Love me, love . . ."

"Don't talk like that," said Olga Ivanovna, covering her eyes. "It's dreadful! How about Dymov?"

"What of Dymov? Why Dymov? What have I to do with Dymov? The Volga, the moon, beauty, my love, ecstasy, and there is no such thing as Dymov. . . . Ah! I don't know . . . I don't care about the past; give me one moment, one instant!"

Olga Ivanovna's heart began to throb. She tried to think about her husband, but all her past, with her wedding, with Dymov, and with her "At Homes," seemed to her petty, trivial, dingy, unnecessary, and far, far away. . . . Yes, really, what of Dymov? Why Dymov? What had she to do with Dymov? Had he any existence in nature, or was he only a dream?

"For him, a simple and ordinary man the happiness he has had already is enough," she thought, covering her face with her hands. "Let them condemn me, let them curse me, but in spite of them all I will go to my ruin; I will go to my ruin! . . . One must experience everything in life. My God! how terrible and how glorious!"

"Well? Well?" muttered the artist, embracing her, and greedily kissing the hands with which she feebly tried to thrust him from her. "You love me? Yes? Yes? Oh, what a night! marvellous night!"

"Yes, what a night!" she whispered, looking into his eyes, which were bright with tears.

Then she looked round quickly, put her arms round him, and kissed him on the lips.

"We are nearing Kineshmo!" said someone on the other side of the deck.

They heard heavy footsteps; it was a waiter from the refreshment-bar.

"Waiter," said Olga Ivanovna, laughing and crying with happiness, "bring us some wine."

The artist, pale with emotion, sat on the seat, looking at Olga Ivanovna with adoring, grateful eyes; then he closed his eyes, and said, smiling languidly:

"I am tired."

And he leaned his head against the rail.

V

On the second of September the day was warm and still, but overcast. In the early morning a light mist had hung over the Volga, and after nine o'clock it had begun to spout with rain. And there seemed no hope of the sky clearing. Over their morning tea Ryabovsky told Olga Ivanovna that painting was the most ungrateful and boring art, that he was not an artist, that none but fools thought that he had any talent, and all at once, for no rhyme or reason, he snatched up a knife and with it scraped over his very best sketch. After his tea he sat plunged in gloom at the window and gazed at the Volga. And now the Volga was dingy, all of one even colour without a gleam of light, cold-looking. Everything, everything recalled the approach of dreary, gloomy autumn. And it seemed as though nature had removed now from the Volga the sumptuous green covers from the banks, the brilliant reflections of the sunbeams, the transparent blue distance, and all its smart gala array, and had packed it away in boxes till the coming spring, and the crows were flying above the Volga and crying tauntingly, "Bare, bare!"

Ryabovsky heard their cawing, and thought he had already gone off and lost his talent, that everything in this world was relative, conditional, and stupid, and that he ought not to have taken up with this woman. . . . In short, he was out of humour and depressed.

Olga Ivanovna sat behind the screen on the bed, and, passing her fingers through her lovely flaxen hair, pictured herself first in the drawing-room, then in the bedroom, then in her husband's study; her imagination carried her to the theatre, to the dress-maker, to her distinguished friends. Were they getting something up now? Did they think of her? The season had begun by now, and it would be time to think about her "At Homes." And Dymov? Dear Dymov! with what gentleness and childlike pathos he kept begging her in his letters to make haste and come home! Every month he sent her seventy-five roubles, and when she wrote him that she had lent the artists a hundred roubles, he sent that hundred too. What a kind, generous-hearted man! The travelling wearied Olga Ivanovna; she was bored; and she longed to get away from the peasants, from the damp smell of the river, and to cast off the feeling of physical uncleanliness of which she was conscious all the time, living in the peasants' huts and wandering from village to village. If Ryabovsky had not given his word to the artists that he would stay with them till the twentieth of September, they might have gone away that very day. And how nice that would have been!

"My God!" moaned Ryabovsky. "Will the sun ever come out? I can't go on with a sunny landscape without the sun. . . ."

"But you have a sketch with a cloudy sky," said Olga Ivanovna, coming from behind the screen. "Do you remember, in the right foreground forest trees, on the left a herd of cows and geese? You might finish it now."

"Aie!" the artist scowled. "Finish it! Can you imagine I am such a fool that I don't know what I want to do?"

"How you have changed to me!" sighed Olga Ivanovna.

"Well, a good thing too!"

Olga Ivanovna's face quivered; she moved away to the stove and began to cry.

"Well, that's the last straw -- crying! Give over! I have a thousand reasons for tears, but I am not crying."

"A thousand reasons!" cried Olga Ivanovna. "The chief one is that you are weary of me. Yes!" she said, and broke into sobs. "If one is to tell the truth, you are ashamed of our love. You keep trying to prevent the artists from noticing it, though it is impossible to conceal it, and they have known all about it forever so long."

"Olga, one thing I beg you," said the artist in an imploring voice, laying his hand on his heart -- "one thing, don't worry me! I want nothing else from you!"

"But swear that you love me still!"

"This is agony!" the artist hissed through his teeth, and he jumped up. "It will end by my throwing myself in the Volga or going out of my mind! Let me alone!"

"Come, kill me, kill me!" cried Olga Ivanovna. "Kill me!"

She sobbed again, and went behind the screen. There was a swish of rain on the straw thatch of the hut. Ryabovsky clutched his head and strode up and down the hut; then with a resolute face, as though bent on proving something to somebody, put on his cap, slung his gun over his shoulder, and went out of the hut.

After he had gone, Olga Ivanovna lay a long time on the bed, crying. At first she thought it would be a good thing to poison herself, so that when Ryabovsky came back he would find her dead; then her imagination carried her to her drawing-room, to her husband's study, and she imagined herself sitting motionless beside Dymov and enjoying the physical peace and cleanliness, and in the evening sitting in the theatre, listening to Mazini. And a yearning for civilization, for the noise and bustle of the town, for celebrated people sent a pang to her heart. A peasant woman came into the hut and began in a leisurely way lighting the stove to get the dinner. There was a smell of charcoal fumes, and the air was filled with bluish smoke. The artists came in, in muddy high boots and with faces wet with rain, examined their sketches, and comforted themselves by saying that the Volga had its charms even in bad weather. On the wall the cheap clock went "tic-tic-tic." . . . The flies, feeling chilled, crowded round the ikon in the corner, buzzing, and one could hear the cockroaches scurrying about among the thick portfolios under the seats. . . .

Ryabovsky came home as the sun was setting. He flung his cap on the table, and, without removing his muddy boots, sank pale and exhausted on the bench and closed his eyes.

"I am tired . . ." he said, and twitched his eyebrows, trying to raise his eyelids.

To be nice to him and to show she was not cross, Olga Ivanovna went up to him, gave him a silent kiss, and passed the comb through his fair hair. She meant to comb it for him.

"What's that?" he said, starting as though something cold had touched him, and he opened his eyes. "What is it? Please let me alone."

He thrust her off, and moved away. And it seemed to her that there was a look of aversion and annoyance on his face.

At that time the peasant woman cautiously carried him, in both hands, a plate of cabbage-soup. And Olga Ivanovna saw how she wetted her fat fingers in it. And the dirty peasant woman, standing with her body thrust forward, and the cabbage-soup which Ryabovsky began eating greedily, and the hut, and their whole way of life, which she at first had so loved for its simplicity and artistic disorder, seemed horrible to her now. She suddenly felt insulted, and said coldly:

"We must part for a time, or else from boredom we shall quarrel in earnest. I am sick of this; I am going today."

"Going how? Astride on a broomstick?"

"Today is Thursday, so the steamer will be here at half-past nine."

"Eh? Yes, yes. . . . Well, go, then . . ." Ryabovsky said softly, wiping his mouth with a towel instead of a dinner napkin. "You are dull and have nothing to do here, and one would have to be a great egoist to try and keep you. Go home, and we shall meet again after the twentieth."

Olga Ivanovna packed in good spirits. Her cheeks positively glowed with pleasure. Could it really be true, she asked herself, that she would soon be writing in her drawing-room and sleeping in her bedroom, and dining with a cloth on the table? A weight was lifted from her heart, and she no longer felt angry with the artist.

"My paints and brushes I will leave with you, Ryabovsky," she said. "You can bring what's left. . . . Mind, now, don't be lazy here when I am gone; don't mope, but work. You are such a splendid fellow, Ryabovsky!"

At ten o'clock Ryabovsky gave her a farewell kiss, in order, as she thought, to avoid kissing her on the steamer before the artists, and went with her to the landing-stage. The steamer soon came up and carried her away.

She arrived home two and a half days later. Breathless with excitement, she went, without taking off her hat or waterproof, into the drawing-room and thence into the dining-room. Dymov, with his waistcoat unbuttoned and no coat, was sitting at the table sharpening a knife on a fork; before him lay a grouse on a plate. As Olga Ivanovna went into the flat she was convinced that it was essential to hide everything from her husband, and that she would have the strength and skill to do so; but now, when she saw his broad, mild, happy smile, and shining, joyful eyes, she felt that to deceive this man was as vile, as revolting, and as impossible and out of her power as to bear false witness, to steal, or to kill, and in a flash she resolved to tell him all that had happened. Letting him kiss and embrace her, she sank down on her knees before him and hid her face.

"What is it, what is it, little mother?" he asked tenderly. "Were you homesick?"

She raised her face, red with shame, and gazed at him with a guilty and imploring look, but fear and shame prevented her from telling him the truth.

"Nothing," she said; "it's just nothing. . . ."

"Let us sit down," he said, raising her and seating her at the table. "That's right, eat the grouse. You are starving, poor darling."

She eagerly breathed in the atmosphere of home and ate the grouse, while he watched her with tenderness and laughed with delight.

VI

Apparently, by the middle of the winter Dymov began to suspect that he was being deceived. As though his conscience was not clear, he could not look his wife straight in the face, did not smile with delight when he met her, and to avoid being left alone with her, he often brought in to dinner his colleague, Korostelev, a little close-cropped man with a wrinkled face, who kept buttoning and unbuttoning his reefer jacket with embarrassment when he talked with Olga Ivanovna, and then with his right hand nipped his left moustache. At dinner the two doctors talked about the fact that a displacement of the diaphragm was sometimes accompanied by irregularities of the heart, or that a great number of neurotic complaints were met with of late, or that Dymov had the day before found a cancer of the lower abdomen while dissecting a corpse with the diagnosis of pernicious anaemia. And it seemed as though they were talking of medicine to give Olga Ivanovna a chance of being silent -- that is, of not lying. After dinner Korostelev sat down to the piano, while Dymov sighed and said to him:

"Ech, brother -- well, well! Play something melancholy."

Hunching up his shoulders and stretching his fingers wide apart, Korostelev played some chords and began singing in a tenor voice, "Show me the abode where the Russian peasant would not groan," while Dymov sighed once more, propped his head on his fist, and sank into thought.

Olga Ivanovna had been extremely imprudent in her conduct of late. Every morning she woke up in a very bad humour and with the thought that she no longer cared for Ryabovsky, and that, thank God, it was all over now. But as she drank her coffee she reflected that Ryabovsky had robbed her of her husband, and that now she was left with neither her husband nor Ryabovsky; then she remembered talks she had heard among her acquaintances of a picture Ryabovsky was preparing for the exhibition, something striking, a mixture of genre and landscape, in the style of Polyenov, about which everyone who had been into his studio went into raptures; and this, of course, she mused, he had created under her influence, and altogether, thanks to her influence, he had greatly changed for the better. Her influence was so beneficent and essential that if she were to leave him he might perhaps go to ruin. And she remembered, too, that the last time he had come to see her in a great-coat with flecks on it and a new tie, he had asked her languidly:

"Am I beautiful?"

And with his elegance, his long curls, and his blue eyes, he really was very beautiful (or perhaps it only seemed so), and he had been affectionate to her.

Considering and remembering many things Olga Ivanovna dressed and in great agitation drove to Ryabovsky's studio. She found him in high spirits, and enchanted with his really magnificent picture. He was dancing about and playing the fool and answering serious questions with jokes. Olga Ivanovna was jealous of the picture and hated it, but from politeness she stood before the picture for five minutes in silence, and, heaving a sigh, as though before a holy shrine, said softly:

"Yes, you have never painted anything like it before. Do you know, it is positively awe-inspiring?"

And then she began beseeching him to love her and not to cast her off, to have pity on her in her misery and her wretchedness. She shed tears, kissed his hands, insisted on his swearing that he loved her, told him that without her good influence he would go astray and be ruined. And, when she had spoilt his good-humour, feeling herself humiliated, she would drive off to her dressmaker or to an actress of her acquaintance to try and get theatre tickets.

If she did not find him at his studio she left a letter in which she swore that if he did not come to see her that day she would poison herself. He was scared, came to see her, and stayed to dinner. Regardless of her husband's presence, he would say rude things to her, and she would answer him in the same way. Both felt they were a burden to each other, that they were tyrants and enemies, and were wrathful, and in their wrath did not notice that their behaviour was unseemly, and that even Korostelev, with his close-cropped head, saw it all. After dinner Ryabovsky made haste to say good-bye and get away.

"Where are you off to?" Olga Ivanovna would ask him in the hall, looking at him with hatred.

Scowling and screwing up his eyes, he mentioned some lady of their acquaintance, and it was evident that he was laughing at her jealousy and wanted to annoy her. She went to her bedroom and lay down on her bed; from jealousy, anger, a sense of humiliation and shame, she bit the pillow and began sobbing aloud. Dymov left Korostelev in the drawing-room, went into the bedroom, and with a desperate and embarrassed face said softly:

"Don't cry so loud, little mother; there's no need. You must be quiet about it. You must not let people see. . . . You know what is done is done, and can't be mended."

Not knowing how to ease the burden of her jealousy, which actually set her temples throbbing with pain, and thinking still that things might be set right, she would wash, powder her tear-stained face, and fly off to the lady mentioned.

Not finding Ryabovsky with her, she would drive off to a second, then to a third. At first she was ashamed to go about like this, but afterwards she got used to it, and it would happen that in one evening she would make the round of all her female acquaintances in search of Ryabovsky, and they all understood it.

One day she said to Ryabovsky of her husband:

"That man crushes me with his magnanimity."

This phrase pleased her so much that when she met the artists who knew of her affair with Ryabovsky she said every time of her husband, with a vigorous movement of her arm:

"That man crushes me with his magnanimity."

Their manner of life was the same as it had been the year before. On Wednesdays they were "At Home", an actor recited, the artists sketched. The violoncellist played, a singer sang, and invariably at half-past eleven the door leading to the dining-room opened and Dymov, smiling, said:

"Come to supper, gentlemen."

As before, Olga Ivanovna hunted celebrities, found them, was not satisfied, and went in pursuit of fresh ones. As before, she came back late every night; but now Dymov was not, as last year, asleep, but sitting in his study at work of some sort. He went to bed at three o'clock and got up at eight.

One evening when she was getting ready to go to the theatre and standing before the pier glass, Dymov came into her bedroom, wearing his dress-coat and a white tie. He was smiling gently and looked into his wife's face joyfully, as in old days; his face was radiant.

"I have just been defending my thesis," he said, sitting down and smoothing his knees.

"Defending?" asked Olga Ivanovna.

"Oh, oh!" he laughed, and he craned his neck to see his wife's face in the mirror, for she was still standing with her back to him, doing up her hair. "Oh, oh," he repeated, "do you know it's very possible they may offer me the Readership in General Pathology? It seems like it."

It was evident from his beaming, blissful face that if Olga Ivanovna had shared with him his joy and triumph he would have forgiven her everything, both the present and the future, and would have forgotten everything, but she did not understand what was meant by a "readership" or by "general pathology"; besides, she was afraid of being late for the theatre, and she said nothing.

He sat there another two minutes, and with a guilty smile went away.

VII

It had been a very troubled day.

Dymov had a very bad headache; he had no breakfast, and did not go to the hospital, but spent the whole time lying on his sofa in the study. Olga Ivanovna went as usual at midday to see Ryabovsky, to show him her still-life sketch, and to ask him why he had not been to see her the evening before. The sketch seemed to her worthless, and she had painted it only in order to have an additional reason for going to the artist.

She went in to him without ringing, and as she was taking off her goloshes in the entry she heard a sound as of something running softly in the studio, with a feminine rustle of skirts; and as she hastened to peep in she caught a momentary glimpse of a bit of brown petticoat, which vanished behind a big picture draped, together with the easel, with black calico, to the floor. There could be no doubt that a woman was hiding there. How often Olga Ivanovna herself had taken refuge behind that picture!

Ryabovsky, evidently much embarrassed, held out both hands to her, as though surprised at her arrival, and said with a forced smile:

"Aha! Very glad to see you! Anything nice to tell me?"

Olga Ivanovna's eyes filled with tears. She felt ashamed and bitter, and would not for a million roubles have consented to speak in the presence of the outsider, the rival, the deceitful woman who was standing now behind the picture, and probably giggling malignantly.

"I have brought you a sketch," she said timidly in a thin voice, and her lips quivered. "*Nature morte.*"

"Ah -- ah! . . . A sketch?"

The artist took the sketch in his hands, and as he examined it walked, as it were mechanically, into the other room.

Olga Ivanovna followed him humbly.

"*Nature morte* . . . first-rate sort," he muttered, falling into rhyme. "Kurort . . . sport . . . port . . ."

From the studio came the sound of hurried footsteps and the rustle of a skirt.

So she had gone. Olga Ivanovna wanted to scream aloud, to hit the artist on the head with something heavy, but she could see nothing through her tears, was crushed by her shame, and felt herself, not Olga Ivanovna, not an artist, but a little insect.

"I am tired . . ." said the artist languidly, looking at the sketch and tossing his head as though struggling with drowsiness. "It's very nice, of course, but here a sketch today, a sketch last year, another sketch in a month . . . I wonder you are not bored with them. If I were you I should give up painting and work seriously at music or something. You're not an artist, you know, but a musician. But you can't think how tired I am! I'll tell them to bring us some tea, shall I?"

He went out of the room, and Olga Ivanovna heard him give some order to his footman. To avoid farewells and explanations, and above all to avoid bursting into sobs, she ran as fast as she could, before Ryabovsky came back, to the entry, put on her goloshes, and went out into the street; then she breathed easily, and felt she was free forever from Ryabovsky and from painting and from the burden of shame which had so crushed her in the studio. It was all over!

She drove to her dressmaker's; then to see Barnay, who had only arrived the day before; from Barnay to a music-shop, and all the time she was thinking how she would write Ryabovsky a cold, cruel letter full of personal dignity, and how in the spring or the summer she would go with Dymov to the Crimea, free herself finally from the past there, and begin a new life.

On getting home late in the evening she sat down in the drawing-room, without taking off her things, to begin the letter. Ryabovsky had told her she was not an artist, and to pay him out she wrote to him now that he painted the same thing every year, and said exactly the same thing every day; that he was at a standstill, and that nothing more would come of him than had come already. She wanted to write, too, that he owed a great deal to her good influence, and that if he was going wrong it was only because her influence was paralysed by various dubious persons like the one who had been hiding behind the picture that day.

"Little mother!" Dymov called from the study, without opening the door.

"What is it?"

"Don't come in to me, but only come to the door -- that's right. . . . The day before yesterday I must have caught diphtheria at the hospital, and now . . . I am ill. Make haste and send for Korostelev."

Olga Ivanovna always called her husband by his surname, as she did all the men of her acquaintance; she disliked his Christian name, Osip, because it reminded her of the Osip in Gogol and the silly pun on his name. But now she cried:

"Osip, it cannot be!"

"Send for him; I feel ill," Dymov said behind the door, and she could hear him go back to the sofa and lie down. "Send!" she heard his voice faintly.

"Good Heavens!" thought Olga Ivanovna, turning chill with horror. "Why, it's dangerous!"

For no reason she took the candle and went into the bedroom, and there, reflecting what she must do, glanced casually at herself in the pier glass. With her pale, frightened face, in a jacket with sleeves high on the shoulders, with yellow ruches on her bosom, and with stripes running in unusual directions on her skirt, she seemed to herself horrible and disgusting. She suddenly felt poignantly sorry for Dymov, for his boundless love for her, for his young life, and even for the desolate little bed in which he had not slept for so long; and she remembered his habitual, gentle, submissive smile. She wept bitterly, and wrote an imploring letter to Korostelev. It was two o'clock in the night.

VIII

When towards eight o'clock in the morning Olga Ivanovna, her head heavy from want of sleep and her hair unbrushed, came out of her bedroom, looking unattractive and with a guilty expression on her face, a gentleman with a black beard, apparently the doctor, passed by her into the entry. There was a smell of drugs. Korostelev was standing near the study door, twisting his left moustache with his right hand.

"Excuse me, I can't let you go in," he said surlily to Olga Ivanovna; "it's catching. Besides, it's no use, really; he is delirious, anyway."

"Has he really got diphtheria?" Olga Ivanovna asked in a whisper.

"People who wantonly risk infection ought to be hauled up and punished for it," muttered Korostelev, not answering Olga Ivanovna's question. "Do you know why he caught it? On Tuesday he was sucking up the mucus through a pipette from a boy with diphtheria. And what for? It was stupid. . . . Just from folly. . . ."

"Is it dangerous, very?" asked Olga Ivanovna.

"Yes; they say it is the malignant form. We ought to send for Shrek really."

A little red-haired man with a long nose and a Jewish accent arrived; then a tall, stooping, shaggy individual, who looked like a head deacon; then a stout young man with a red face and spectacles. These were doctors who came to watch by turns beside their colleague. Korostelev did not go home when his turn was over, but remained and wandered about the rooms like an uneasy spirit. The maid kept getting tea for the various doctors, and was constantly running to the chemist, and there was no one to do the rooms. There was a dismal stillness in the flat.

Olga Ivanovna sat in her bedroom and thought that God was punishing her for having deceived her husband. That silent, unrepining, uncomprehended creature, robbed by his mildness of all personality and will, weak from excessive kindness, had been suffering in obscurity somewhere on his sofa, and had not complained. And if he were to complain even in delirium, the doctors watching by his bedside would learn that diphtheria was not the only cause of his sufferings. They would ask Korostelev. He knew all about it, and it was not for nothing that he looked at his friend's wife with eyes that seemed to say that she was the real chief criminal and diphtheria was only her accomplice. She did not think now of the moonlight evening on the Volga, nor the words of love, nor their poetical life in the peasant's hut. She thought only that from an idle whim, from self-indulgence, she had sullied herself all over from head to foot in something filthy, sticky, which one could never wash off. . . .

"Oh, how fearfully false I've been!" she thought, recalling the troubled passion she had known with Ryabovsky. "Curse it all! . . ."

At four o'clock she dined with Korostelev. He did nothing but scowl and drink red wine, and did not eat a morsel. She ate nothing, either. At one minute she was praying inwardly and vowing to God that if Dymov recovered she would love him again and be a faithful wife to him. Then, forgetting herself for a minute, she would look at Korostelev, and think: "Surely it must be dull to be a humble, obscure person, not remarkable in any way, especially with such a wrinkled face and bad manners!" Then it seemed to her that God would strike her dead that minute for not having once been in her husband's study, for fear of infection. And altogether she had a dull, despondent feeling and a conviction that her life was spoilt, and that there was no setting it right anyhow. . . .

After dinner darkness came on. When Olga Ivanovna went into the drawing-room Korostelev was asleep on the sofa, with a gold-embroidered silk cushion under his head.

"Khee-poo-ah," he snored -- "khee-poo-ah."

And the doctors as they came to sit up and went away again did not notice this disorder. The fact that a strange man was asleep and snoring in the drawing-room, and the sketches on the walls and the exquisite decoration of the room, and the fact that the lady of the house was dishevelled and untidy -- all that aroused not the slightest interest now. One of the doctors chanced to laugh at something, and the laugh had a strange and timid sound that made one's heart ache.

When Olga Ivanovna went into the drawing-room next time, Korostelev was not asleep, but sitting up and smoking.

"He has diphtheria of the nasal cavity," he said in a low voice, "and the heart is not working properly now. Things are in a bad way, really."

"But you will send for Shrek?" said Olga Ivanovna.

"He has been already. It was he noticed that the diphtheria had passed into the nose. What's the use of Shrek! Shrek's no use at all, really. He is Shrek, I am Korostelev, and nothing more."

The time dragged on fearfully slowly. Olga Ivanovna lay down in her clothes on her bed, that had not been made all day, and sank into a doze. She dreamed that the whole flat was filled up from floor to ceiling with a huge piece of iron, and that if they could only get the iron out they would all be light-hearted and happy. Waking, she realized that it was not the iron but Dymov's illness that was weighing on her.

"*Nature morte,* port . . ." she thought, sinking into forgetfulness again. "Sport . . . Kurort . . . and what of Shrek? Shrek . . . trek . . . wreck. . . . And where are my friends now? Do they know that we are in trouble? Lord, save . . . spare! Shrek . . . trek . . ."

And again the iron was there. . . . The time dragged on slowly, though the clock on the lower storey struck frequently. And bells were continually ringing as the doctors arrived. . . . The house-maid came in with an empty glass on a tray, and asked, "Shall I make the bed, madam?" and getting no answer, went away.

The clock below struck the hour. She dreamed of the rain on the Volga; and again someone came into her bedroom, she thought a stranger. Olga Ivanovna jumped up, and recognized Korostelev.

"What time is it?" she asked.

"About three."

"Well, what is it?"

"What, indeed! . . . I've come to tell you he is passing. . . ."

He gave a sob, sat down on the bed beside her, and wiped away the tears with his sleeve. She could not grasp it at once, but turned cold all over and began slowly crossing herself.

"He is passing," he repeated in a shrill voice, and again he gave a sob. "He is dying because he sacrificed himself. What a loss for science!" he said bitterly." Compare him with all of us. He was a great man, an extraordinary man! What gifts! What hopes we all had of him!" Korostelev went on, wringing his hands: "Merciful God, he was a man of science; we shall never look on his like again. Osip Dymov, what have you done -- aie, aie, my God!"

Korostelev covered his face with both hands in despair, and shook his head.

"And his moral force," he went on, seeming to grow more and more exasperated against someone. "Not a man, but a pure, good, loving soul, and clean as crystal. He served science and died for science. And he worked like an ox night and day -- no one spared him -- and with his youth and his learning he had to take a private practice and work at translations at night to pay for these . . . vile rags!"

Korostelev looked with hatred at Olga Ivanovna, snatched at the sheet with both hands and angrily tore it, as though it were to blame.

"He did not spare himself, and others did not spare him. Oh, what's the use of talking!"

"Yes, he was a rare man," said a bass voice in the drawing-room.

Olga Ivanovna remembered her whole life with him from the beginning to the end, with all its details, and suddenly she understood that he really was an extraordinary, rare, and, compared with everyone else she knew, a great man. And remembering how her father, now dead, and all the other doctors had behaved to him, she realized that they really had seen in him a future celebrity. The walls, the ceiling, the lamp, and the carpet on the floor, seemed to be winking at her sarcastically, as though they would say, "You were blind! you were blind!" With a wail she flung herself out of the bedroom, dashed by some unknown man in the drawing-room, and ran into her husband's study. He was lying motionless on the sofa, covered to the waist with a quilt. His face was fearfully thin and sunken, and was of a grayish-yellow colour such as is never seen in the living; only from the forehead, from the black eyebrows and from the familiar smile, could he be recognized as Dymov. Olga Ivanovna hurriedly felt his chest, his forehead, and his hands. The chest was still warm, but the forehead and hands were unpleasantly cold, and the half-open eyes looked, not at Olga Ivanovna, but at the quilt.

"Dymov!" she called aloud, "Dymov!" She wanted to explain to him that it had been a mistake, that all was not lost, that life might still be beautiful and happy, that he was an extraordinary, rare, great man, and that she would all her life worship him and bow down in homage and holy awe before him. . . .

"Dymov!" she called him, patting him on the shoulder, unable to believe that he would never wake again. "Dymov! Dymov!"

In the drawing-room Korostelev was saying to the housemaid:

"Why keep asking? Go to the church beadle and enquire where they live. They'll wash the body and lay it out, and do everything that is necessary."

AFTER THE THEATRE

Nadya Zelenin had just come back with her mamma from the theatre where she had seen a performance of "Yevgeny Onyegin." As soon as she reached her own room she threw off her dress, let down her hair, and in her petticoat and white dressing-jacket hastily sat down to the table to write a letter like Tatyana's.

"I love you," she wrote, "but you do not love me, do not love me!"

She wrote it and laughed.

She was only sixteen and did not yet love anyone. She knew that an officer called Gorny and a student called Gruzdev loved her, but now after the opera she wanted to be doubtful of their love. To be unloved and unhappy -- how interesting that was. There is something beautiful, touching, and poetical about it when one loves and the other is indifferent. Onyegin was interesting because he was not in love at all, and Tatyana was fascinating because she was so much in love; but if they had been equally in love with each other and had been happy, they would perhaps have seemed dull.

"Leave off declaring that you love me," Nadya went on writing, thinking of Gorny. "I cannot believe it. You are very clever, cultivated, serious, you have immense talent, and perhaps a brilliant future awaits you, while I am an uninteresting girl of no importance, and you know very well that I should be only a hindrance in your life. It is true that you were attracted by me and thought you had found your ideal in me, but that was a mistake, and now you are asking yourself in despair: 'Why did I meet that girl?' And only your goodness of heart prevents you from owning it to yourself. . . ."

Nadya felt sorry for herself, she began to cry, and went on:

"It is hard for me to leave my mother and my brother, or I should take a nun's veil and go whither chance may lead me. And you would be left free and would love another. Oh, if I were dead! "

She could not make out what she had written through her tears; little rainbows were quivering on the table, on the floor, on the ceiling, as though she were looking through a prism. She could not write, she sank back in her easy-chair and fell to thinking of Gorny.

My God! how interesting, how fascinating men were! Nadya recalled the fine expression, ingratiating, guilty, and soft, which came into the officer's face when one argued about music with him, and the effort he made to prevent his voice from betraying his passion. In a society where cold haughtiness and indifference are regarded as signs of good breeding and gentlemanly bearing, one must conceal one's passions. And he did try to conceal them, but he did not succeed, and everyone knew very well that he had a passionate love of music. The endless discussions about music and the bold criticisms of people who knew nothing about it kept him always on the strain; he was frightened, timid, and silent. He played the piano magnificently, like a professional pianist, and if he had not been in the army he would certainly have been a famous musician.

The tears on her eyes dried. Nadya remembered that Gorny had declared his love at a Symphony concert, and again downstairs by the hatstand where there was a tremendous draught blowing in all directions.

"I am very glad that you have at last made the acquaintance of Gruzdev, our student friend," she went on writing. "He is a very clever man, and you will be sure to like him. He came to see us yesterday and stayed till two o'clock. We were all delighted with him, and I regretted that you had not come. He said a great deal that was remarkable."

Nadya laid her arms on the table and leaned her head on them, and her hair covered the letter. She recalled that the student, too, loved her, and that he had as much right to a letter from her as Gorny. Wouldn't it be better after all to write to Gruzdev? There was a stir of joy in her bosom for no reason whatever; at first the joy was small, and rolled in her bosom like an india-rubber ball; then it became more massive, bigger, and rushed like a wave. Nadya forgot Gorny and Gruzdev; her thoughts were in a tangle and her joy grew and grew; from her bosom it passed into her arms and legs, and it seemed as though a light, cool breeze were breathing on her head and ruffling her hair. Her shoulders quivered with subdued laughter, the table and the lamp chimney shook, too, and tears from her eyes splashed on the letter. She could not stop laughing, and to prove to herself that she was not laughing about nothing she made haste to think of something funny.

"What a funny poodle," she said, feeling as though she would choke with laughter. "What a funny poodle! "

She thought how, after tea the evening before, Gruzdev had played with Maxim the poodle, and afterwards had told them about a very intelligent poodle who had run after a crow in the yard, and the crow had looked round at him and said: "Oh, you scamp! "

The poodle, not knowing he had to do with a learned crow, was fearfully confused and retreated in perplexity, then began barking. . . .

"No, I had better love Gruzdev," Nadya decided, and she tore up the letter to Gorny.

She fell to thinking of the student, of his love, of her love; but the thoughts in her head insisted on flowing in all directions, and she thought about everything -- about her mother, about the street, about the pencil, about the piano. . . . She thought of them joyfully, and felt that everything was good, splendid, and her joy told her that this was not all, that in a little while it would be better still. Soon it would be spring, summer, going with her mother to Gorbiki. Gorny would come for his furlough, would walk about the garden with her and make love to her. Gruzdev would come too. He would play croquet and skittles with her, and would tell her wonderful things. She had a passionate longing for the garden, the darkness, the pure sky, the stars. Again her shoulders shook with laughter, and it seemed to her that there was a scent of wormwood in the room and that a twig was tapping at the window.

She went to her bed, sat down, and not knowing what to do with the immense joy which filled her with yearning, she looked at the holy image hanging at the back of her bed, and said:

"Oh, Lord God! Oh, Lord God!"

IN EXILE

Old Semyon, nicknamed Canny, and a young Tatar, whom no one knew by name, were sitting on the river-bank by the camp-fire; the other three ferrymen were in the hut. Semyon, an old man of sixty, lean and toothless, but broad shouldered and still healthy-looking, was drunk; he would have gone in to sleep long before, but he had a bottle in his pocket and he was afraid that the fellows in the hut would ask him for vodka. The Tatar was ill and weary, and wrapping himself up in his rags was describing how nice it was in the Simbirsk province, and what a beautiful and clever wife he had left behind at home. He was not more than twenty five, and now by the light of the camp-fire, with his pale and sick, mournful face, he looked like a boy.

"To be sure, it is not paradise here," said Canny. "You can see for yourself, the water, the bare banks, clay, and nothing else. . . . Easter has long passed and yet there is ice on the river, and this morning there was snow. . ."

"It's bad! it's bad!" said the Tatar, and looked round him in terror.

The dark, cold river was flowing ten paces away; it grumbled, lapped against the hollow clay banks and raced on swiftly towards the far-away sea. Close to the bank there was the dark blur of a big barge, which the ferrymen called a "karbos." Far away on the further bank, lights, dying down and flickering up again, zigzagged like little snakes; they were burning last year's grass. And beyond the little snakes there was darkness again. There little icicles could be heard knocking against the barge It was damp and cold. . . .

The Tatar glanced at the sky. There were as many stars as at home, and the same blackness all round, but something was lacking. At home in the Simbirsk province the stars were quite different, and so was the sky.

"It's bad! it's bad!" he repeated.

"You will get used to it," said Semyon, and he laughed. "Now you are young and foolish, the milk is hardly dry on your lips, and it seems to you in your foolishness that you are more wretched than anyone; but the time will come when you will say to yourself: 'I wish no one a better life than mine.' You look at me. Within a week the floods will be over and we shall set up the ferry; you will all go wandering off about Siberia while I shall stay and shall begin going from bank to bank. I've been going like that for twenty-two years, day and night. The pike and the salmon are under the water while I am on the water. And thank God for it, I want nothing; God give everyone such a life."

The Tatar threw some dry twigs on the camp-fire, lay down closer to the blaze, and said:

"My father is a sick man. When he dies my mother and wife will come here. They have promised."

"And what do you want your wife and mother for?" asked Canny. "That's mere foolishness, my lad. It's the devil confounding you, damn his soul! Don't you listen to him, the cursed one. Don't let him have his way. He is at you about the women, but you spite him; say, 'I don't want them!' He is on at you about freedom, but you stand up to him and say: 'I don't want it!' I want nothing, neither father nor mother, nor wife, nor freedom, nor post, nor paddock; I want nothing, damn their souls!"

Semyon took a pull at the bottle and went on:

"I am not a simple peasant, not of the working class, but the son of a deacon, and when I was free I lived at Kursk; I used to wear a frockcoat, and now I have brought myself to such a pass that I can sleep naked on the ground and eat grass. And I wish no one a better life. I want nothing and I am afraid of nobody, and the way I look at it is that there is nobody richer and freer than I am. When they sent me here from Russia from the first day I stuck it out; I want nothing! The devil was at me about my wife and about my home and about freedom, but I told him: 'I want nothing.' I stuck to it, and here you see I live well, and I don't complain, and if anyone gives way to the devil and listens to him, if but once, he is lost, there is no salvation for him: he is sunk in the bog to the crown of his head and will never get out.

"It is not only a foolish peasant like you, but even gentlemen, well-educated people, are lost. Fifteen years ago they sent a gentleman here from Russia. He hadn't shared something with his brothers and had forged something in a will. They did say he was a prince or a baron, but maybe he was simply an official -- who knows? Well, the gentleman arrived here, and first thing he bought himself a house and land in Muhortinskoe. 'I want to live by my own work,' says he, 'in the sweat of my brow, for I am not a gentleman now,' says he, 'but a settler.' 'Well,' says I, 'God help you, that's the right thing.' He was a young man then, busy and careful; he used to mow himself and catch fish and ride sixty miles on horseback. Only this is what happened: from the very first year he took to riding to Gyrino for the post; he used to stand on my ferry and sigh: 'Ech, Semyon, how long it is since they sent me any money from home!' 'You don't want money, Vassily Sergeyitch,' says I. 'What use is it to you? You cast away the past, and forget it as though it had never been at all, as though it had been a dream, and begin to live anew. Don't listen to the devil,' says I; 'he will bring you to no good, he'll draw you into a snare. Now you want money,' says I, ' but in a very little while you'll be wanting something else, and then more and more. If you want to be happy,' says I, the chief thing is not to want anything. Yes. . . . If,' says I, 'if Fate has wronged you and me cruelly it's no good asking for her favor and bowing down to her, but you despise her and laugh at her, or else she will laugh at you.' That's what I said to him. . . .

"Two years later I ferried him across to this side, and he was rubbing his hands and laughing. ' I am going to Gyrino to meet my wife,' says he. 'She was sorry for me,' says he; 'she has come. She is good and kind.' And he was breathless with joy. So a day later he came with his wife. A beautiful young lady in a hat; in her arms was a baby girl. And lots of luggage of all sorts. And my Vassily Sergeyitch was fussing round her; he couldn't take his eyes off her and couldn't say enough in praise of her. 'Yes, brother Semyon, even in Siberia people can live!' 'Oh, all right,' thinks I, 'it will be a different tale presently.' And from that time forward he went almost every week to inquire whether money had not come from Russia. He wanted a lot of money. 'She is losing her youth and beauty here in Siberia for my sake,' says he, 'and sharing my bitter lot with me, and so I ought,' says he, 'to provide her with every comfort. . . .'

"To make it livelier for the lady he made acquaintance with the officials and all sorts of riff-raff. And of course he had to give food and drink to all that crew, and there had to be a piano and a shaggy lapdog on the sofa -- plague take it! . . . Luxury, in fact, self-indulgence. The lady did not stay with him long. How could she? The clay, the water, the cold, no vegetables for you, no fruit. All around you ignorant and drunken people and no sort of manners, and she was a spoilt lady from Petersburg or Moscow. . . . To be sure she moped. Besides, her husband, say what you like, was not a gentleman now, but a settler -- not the same rank.

"Three years later, I remember, on the eve of the Assumption, there was shouting from the further bank. I went over with the ferry, and what do I see but the lady, all wrapped up, and with her a young gentleman, an official. A sledge with three horses. . . . I ferried them across here, they got in and away like the wind. They were soon lost to sight. And towards morning Vassily Sergeyitch galloped down to the ferry. 'Didn't my wife come this way with a gentleman in spectacles, Semyon?' 'She did,' said I; 'you may look for the wind in the fields!' He galloped in pursuit of them. For five days and nights he was riding after them. When I ferried him over to the other side afterwards, he flung himself on the ferry and beat his head on the boards of the ferry and howled. 'So that's how it is,' says I. I laughed, and reminded him 'people can live even in Siberia!' And he beat his head harder than ever. . . .

"Then he began longing for freedom. His wife had slipped off to Russia, and of course he was drawn there to see her and to get her away from her lover. And he took, my lad, to galloping almost every day, either to the post or the town to see the commanding officer; he kept sending in petitions for them to have mercy on him and let him go back home; and he used to say that he had spent some two hundred roubles on telegrams alone. He sold his land and mortgaged his house to the Jews. He grew gray and bent, and yellow in the face, as though he was in consumption. If he talked to you he would go, khee--khee--khee,. . . and there were tears in his eyes. He kept rushing about like this with petitions for eight years, but now he has grown brighter and more cheerful again: he has found another whim to give way to. You see, his daughter has grown up. He looks at her, and she is the apple of his eye. And to tell the truth she is all right, good-looking, with black eyebrows and a lively disposition. Every Sunday he used to ride with her to church in Gyrino. They used to stand on the ferry, side by side, she would laugh and he could not take his eyes off her. 'Yes, Semyon,' says he, 'people can live even in Siberia. Even in Siberia there is happiness. Look,' says he, 'what a daughter I have got! I warrant you wouldn't find another like her for a thousand versts round.' 'Your daughter is all right,' says I, 'that's true, certainly.' But to myself I thought: 'Wait a bit, the wench is young, her blood is dancing, she wants to live, and there is no life here.' And she did begin to pine, my lad. . . . She faded and faded, and now she can hardly crawl about. Consumption.

"So you see what Siberian happiness is, damn its soul! You see how people can live in Siberia. . . . He has taken to going from one doctor to another and taking them home with him. As soon as he hears that two or three hundred miles away there is a doctor or a sorcerer, he will drive to fetch him. A terrible lot of money he spent on doctors, and to my thinking he had better have spent the money on drink. . . . She'll die just the same. She is certain to die, and then it will be all over with him. He'll hang himself from grief or run away to Russia -- that's a sure thing. He'll run away and they'll catch him, then he will be tried, sent to prison, he will have a taste of the lash. . . ."

"Good! good!" said the Tatar, shivering with cold.

"What is good?" asked Canny.

"His wife, his daughter. . . . What of prison and what of sorrow! -- anyway, he did see his wife and his daughter. . . . You say, want nothing. But 'nothing' is bad! His wife lived with him three years -- that was a gift from God. 'Nothing' is bad, but three years is good. How not understand?"

Shivering and hesitating, with effort picking out the Russian words of which he knew but few, the Tatar said that God forbid one should fall sick and die in a strange land, and be buried in the cold and dark earth; that if his wife came to him for one day, even for one hour, that for such happiness he would be ready to bear any suffering and to thank God. Better one day of happiness than nothing.

Then he described again what a beautiful and clever wife he had left at home. Then, clutching his head in both hands, he began crying and assuring Semyon that he was not guilty, and was suffering for nothing. His two brothers and an uncle had carried off a peasant's horses, and had beaten the old man till he was half dead, and the commune had not judged fairly, but had contrived a sentence by which all the three brothers were sent to Siberia, while the uncle, a rich man, was left at home.

"You will get used to it!" said Semyon.

The Tatar was silent, and stared with tear-stained eyes at the fire; his face expressed bewilderment and fear, as though he still did not understand why he was here in the darkness and the wet, beside strangers, and not in the Simbirsk province.

Canny lay near the fire, chuckled at something, and began humming a song in an undertone.

"What joy has she with her father?" he said a little later. "He loves her and he rejoices in her, that's true; but, mate, you must mind your ps and qs with him, he is a strict old man, a harsh old man. And young wenches don't want strictness. They want petting and ha-ha-ha! and ho-ho-ho! and scent and pomade. Yes. . . . Ech! life, life," sighed Semyon, and he got up heavily. "The vodka is all gone, so it is time to sleep. Eh? I am going, my lad. . . ."

Left alone, the Tatar put on more twigs, lay down and stared at the fire; he began thinking of his own village and of his wife. If his wife could only come for a month, for a day; and then if she liked she might go back again. Better a month or even a day than nothing. But if his wife kept her promise and came, what would he have to feed her on? Where could she live here?

"If there were not something to eat, how could she live?" the Tatar asked aloud.

He was paid only ten kopecks for working all day and all night at the oar; it is true that travelers gave him tips for tea and for vodkas but the men shared all they received among themselves, and gave nothing to the Tatar, but only laughed at him. And from poverty he was hungry, cold, and frightened. . . . Now, when his whole body was aching and shivering, he ought to go into the hut and lie down to sleep; but he had nothing to cover him there, and it was colder than on the river-bank; here he had nothing to cover him either, but at least he could make up the fire. . . .

In another week, when the floods were quite over and they set the ferry going, none of the ferrymen but Semyon would be wanted, and the Tatar would begin going from village to village begging for alms and for work. His wife was only seventeen; she was beautiful, spoilt, and shy; could she possibly go from village to village begging alms with her face unveiled? No, it was terrible even to think of that. . . .

It was already getting light; the barge, the bushes of willow on the water, and the waves could be clearly discerned, and if one looked round there was the steep clay slope; at the bottom of it the hut thatched with dingy brown straw, and the huts of the village lay clustered higher up. The cocks were already crowing in the village.

The rusty red clay slope, the barge, the river, the strange, unkind people, hunger, cold, illness, perhaps all that was not real. Most likely it was all a dream, thought the Tatar. He felt that he was asleep and heard his own snoring. . . . Of course he was at home in the Simbirsk province, and he had only to call his wife by name for her to answer; and in the next room was his mother. . . . What terrible dreams there are, though! What are they for? The Tatar smiled and opened his eyes. What river was this, the Volga?

Snow was falling.

"Boat!" was shouted on the further side. "Boat!"

The Tatar woke up, and went to wake his mates and row over to the other side. The ferrymen came on to the river-bank, putting on their torn sheepskins as they walked, swearing with voices husky from sleepiness and shivering from the cold. On waking from their sleep, the river, from which came a breath of piercing cold, seemed to strike them as revolting and horrible. They jumped into the barge without hurrying themselves. . . . The Tatar and the three ferrymen took the long, broad-bladed oars, which in the darkness looked like the claws of crabs; Semyon leaned his stomach against the tiller. The shout on the other side still continued, and two shots were fired from a revolver, probably with the idea that the ferrymen were asleep or had gone to the pot-house in the village.

"All right, you have plenty of time," said Semyon in the tone of a man convinced that there was no necessity in this world to hurry -- that it would lead to nothing, anyway.

The heavy, clumsy barge moved away from the bank and floated between the willow-bushes, and only the willows slowly moving back showed that the barge was not standing still but moving. The ferrymen swung the oars evenly in time; Semyon lay with his stomach on the tiller and, describing a semicircle in the air, flew from one side to the other. In the darkness it looked as though the men were sitting on some antediluvian animal with long paws, and were moving on it through a cold, desolate land, the land of which one sometimes dreams in nightmares.

They passed beyond the willows and floated out into the open. The creak and regular splash of the oars was heard on the further shore, and a shout came: "Make haste! make haste!"

Another ten minutes passed, and the barge banged heavily against the landing-stage.

"And it keeps sprinkling and sprinkling," muttered Semyon, wiping the snow from his face; "and where it all comes from God only knows."

On the bank stood a thin man of medium height in a jacket lined with fox fur and in a white lambskin cap. He was standing at a little distance from his horses and not moving; he had a gloomy, concentrated expression, as though he were trying to remember something and angry with his untrustworthy memory. When Semyon went up to him and took off his cap, smiling, he said:

"I am hastening to Anastasyevka. My daughter's worse again, and they say that there is a new doctor at Anastasyevka."

They dragged the carriage on to the barge and floated back. The man whom Semyon addressed as Vassily Sergeyitch stood all the time motionless, tightly compressing his thick lips and staring off into space; when his coachman asked permission to smoke in his presence he made no answer, as though he had not heard. Semyon, lying with his stomach on the tiller, looked mockingly at him and said:

"Even in Siberia people can live -- can li-ive!"

There was a triumphant expression on Canny's face, as though he had proved something and was delighted that things had happened as he had foretold. The unhappy helplessness of the man in the foxskin coat evidently afforded him great pleasure.

"It's muddy driving now, Vassily Sergeyitch," he said when the horses were harnessed again on the bank. "You should have put off going for another fortnight, when it will be drier. Or else not have gone at all. . . . If any good would come of your going -- but as you know yourself, people have been driving about for years and years, day and night, and it's alway's been no use. That's the truth."

Vassily Sergeyitch tipped him without a word, got into his carriage and drove off.

"There, he has galloped off for a doctor!" said Semyon, shrinking from the cold. "But looking for a good doctor is like chasing the wind in the fields or catching the devil by the tail, plague take your soul! What a queer chap, Lord forgive me a sinner!"

The Tatar went up to Canny, and, looking at him with hatred and repulsion, shivering, and mixing Tatar words with his broken Russian, said: "He is good . . . good; but you are bad! You are bad! The gentleman is a good soul, excellent, and you are a beast, bad! The gentleman is alive, but you are a dead carcass. . . . God created man to be alive, and to have joy and grief and sorrow; but you want nothing, so you are not alive, you are stone, clay! A stone wants nothing and you want nothing. You are a stone, and God does not love you, but He loves the gentleman!"

Everyone laughed; the Tatar frowned contemptuously, and with a wave of his hand wrapped himself in his rags and went to the campfire. The ferrymen and Semyon sauntered to the hut.

"It's cold," said one ferryman huskily as he stretched himself on the straw with which the damp clay floor was covered.

"Yes, its not warm," another assented. "It's a dog's life. . . ."

They all lay down. The door was thrown open by the wind and the snow drifted into the hut; nobody felt inclined to get up and shut the door: they were cold, and it was too much trouble.

"I am all right," said Semyon as he began to doze. "I wouldn't wish anyone a better life."

"You are a tough one, we all know. Even the devils won't take you!"

Sounds like a dog's howling came from outside.

"What's that? Who's there?"

"It's the Tatar crying."

"I say. . . . He's a queer one!"

"He'll get u-used to it!" said Semyon, and at once fell asleep.

The others were soon asleep too. The door remained unclosed.

NEIGHBOURS

Pyotr Mihalitch Ivashin was very much out of humour: his sister, a young girl, had gone away to live with Vlassitch, a married man. To shake off the despondency and depression which pursued him at home and in the fields, he called to his aid his sense of justice, his genuine and noble ideas -- he had always defended free-love! -- but this was of no avail, and he always came back to the same conclusion as their foolish old nurse, that his sister had acted wrongly and that Vlassitch had abducted his sister. And that was distressing.

His mother did not leave her room all day long; the old nurse kept sighing and speaking in whispers; his aunt had been on the point of taking her departure every day, and her trunks were continually being brought down to the hall and carried up again to her room. In the house, in the yard, and in the garden it was as still as though there were someone dead in the house. His aunt, the servants, and even the peasants, so it seemed to Pyotr Mihalitch, looked at him enigmatically and with perplexity, as though they wanted to say "Your sister has been seduced; why are you doing nothing?" And he reproached himself for inactivity, though he did not know precisely what action he ought to have taken.

So passed six days. On the seventh -- it was Sunday afternoon -- a messenger on horseback brought a letter. The address was in a familiar feminine handwriting: "Her Excy. Anna Nikolaevna Ivashin." Pyotr Mihalitch fancied that there was something defiant, provocative, in the handwriting and in the abbreviation "Excy." And advanced ideas in women are obstinate, ruthless, cruel.

"She'd rather die than make any concession to her unhappy mother, or beg her forgiveness," thought Pyotr Mihalitch, as he went to his mother with the letter.

His mother was lying on her bed, dressed. Seeing her son, she rose impulsively, and straightening her grey hair, which had fallen from under her cap, asked quickly:

"What is it? What is it?"

"This has come . . ." said her son, giving her the letter.

Zina's name, and even the pronoun "she" was not uttered in the house. Zina was spoken of impersonally: "this has come," "Gone away," and so on. . . . The mother recognised her daughter's handwriting, and her face grew ugly and unpleasant, and her grey hair escaped again from her cap.

"No!" she said, with a motion of her hands, as though the letter scorched her fingers. "No, no, never! Nothing would induce me!"

The mother broke into hysterical sobs of grief and shame; she evidently longed to read the letter, but her pride prevented her. Pyotr Mihalitch realised that he ought to open the letter himself and read it aloud, but he was overcome by anger such as he had never felt before; he ran out into the yard and shouted to the messenger:

"Say there will be no answer! There will be no answer! Tell them that, you beast!

And he tore up the letter; then tears came into his eyes, and feeling that he was cruel, miserable, and to blame, he went out into the fields.

He was only twenty-seven, but he was already stout. He dressed like an old man in loose, roomy clothes, and suffered from asthma. He already seemed to be developing the characteristics of an elderly country bachelor. He never fell in love, never thought of marriage, and loved no one but his mother, his sister, his old nurse, and the gardener, Vassilitch. He was fond of good fare, of his nap after dinner, and of talking about politics and exalted subjects. He had in his day taken his degree at the university, but he now looked upon his studies as though in them he had discharged a duty incumbent upon young men between the ages of eighteen and twenty-five; at any rate, the ideas which now strayed every day through his mind had nothing in common with the university or the subjects he had studied there.

In the fields it was hot and still, as though rain were coming. It was steaming in the wood, and there was a heavy fragrant scent from the pines and rotting leaves. Pyotr Mihalitch stopped several times and wiped his wet brow. He looked at his winter corn and his spring oats, walked round the clover-field, and twice drove away a partridge with its chicks which had strayed in from the wood. And all the while he was thinking that this insufferable state of things could not go on forever, and that he must end it one way or another. End it stupidly, madly, but he must end it.

"But how? What can I do?" he asked himself, and looked imploringly at the sky and at the trees, as though begging for their help.

But the sky and the trees were mute. His noble ideas were no help, and his common sense whispered that the agonising question could have no solution but a stupid one, and that to-day's scene with the messenger was not the last one of its kind. It was terrible to think what was in store for him!

As he returned home the sun was setting. By now it seemed to him that the problem was incapable of solution. He could not accept the accomplished fact, and he could not refuse to accept it, and there was no intermediate course. When, taking off his hat and fanning himself with his handkerchief, he was walking along the road, and had only another mile and a half to go before he would reach home, he heard bells behind him. It was a very choice and successful combination of bells, which gave a clear crystal note. No one had such bells on his horses but the police captain, Medovsky, formerly an officer in the hussars, a man in broken-down health, who had been a great rake and spendthrift, and was a distant relation of Pyotr Mihalitch. He was like one of the family at the Ivashins' and had a tender, fatherly affection for Zina, as well as a great admiration for her.

"I was coming to see you," he said, overtaking Pyotr Mihalitch. "Get in; I'll give you a lift."

He was smiling and looked cheerful. Evidently he did not yet know that Zina had gone to live with Vlassitch; perhaps he had been told of it already, but did not believe it. Pyotr Mihalitch felt in a difficult position.

"You are very welcome," he muttered, blushing till the tears came into his eyes, and not knowing how to lie or what to say. "I am delighted," he went on, trying to smile, "but . . . Zina is away and mother is ill."

"How annoying!" said the police captain, looking pensively at Pyotr Mihalitch. "And I was meaning to spend the evening with you. Where has Zinaida Mihalovna gone?"

"To the Sinitskys', and I believe she meant to go from there to the monastery. I don't quite know."

The police captain talked a little longer and then turned back. Pyotr Mihalitch walked home, and thought with horror what the police captain's feelings would be when he learned the truth. And Pyotr Mihalitch imagined his feelings, and actually experiencing them himself, went into the house.

"Lord help us," he thought, "Lord help us!"

At evening tea the only one at the table was his aunt. As usual, her face wore the expression that seemed to say that though she was a weak, defenceless woman, she would allow no one to insult her. Pyotr Mihalitch sat down at the other end of the table (he did not like his aunt) and began drinking tea in silence.

"Your mother has had no dinner again to-day," said his aunt. "You ought to do something about it, Petrusha. Starving oneself is no help in sorrow."

It struck Pyotr Mihalitch as absurd that his aunt should meddle in other people's business and should make her departure depend on Zina's having gone away. He was tempted to say something rude to her, but restrained himself. And as he restrained himself he felt the time had come for action, and that he could not bear it any longer. Either he must act at once or fall on the ground, and scream and bang his head upon the floor. He pictured Vlassitch and Zina, both of them progressive and self-satisfied, kissing each other somewhere under a maple tree, and all the anger and bitterness that had been accumulating in him for the last seven days fastened upon Vlassitch.

"One has seduced and abducted my sister," he thought, "another will come and murder my mother, a third will set fire to the house and sack the place. . . . And all this under the mask of friendship, lofty ideas, unhappiness!"

"No, it shall not be!" Pyotr Mihalitch cried suddenly, and he brought his fist down on the table.

He jumped up and ran out of the dining-room. In the stable the steward's horse was standing ready saddled. He got on it and galloped off to Vlassitch.

There was a perfect tempest within him. He felt a longing to do something extraordinary, startling, even if he had to repent of it all his life afterwards. Should he call Vlassitch a blackguard, slap him in the face, and then challenge him to a duel? But Vlassitch was not one of those men who do fight duels; being called a blackguard and slapped in the face would only make him more unhappy, and would make him shrink into himself more than ever. These unhappy, defenceless people are the most insufferable, the most tiresome creatures in the world. They can do anything with impunity. When the luckless man responds to well-deserved reproach by looking at you with eyes full of deep and guilty feeling, and with a sickly smile bends his head submissively, even justice itself could not lift its hand against him.

"No matter. I'll horsewhip him before her eyes and tell him what I think of him," Pyotr Mihalitch decided.

He was riding through his wood and waste land, and he imagined Zina would try to justify her conduct by talking about the rights of women and individual freedom, and about there being no difference between legal marriage and free union. Like a woman, she would argue about what she did not understand. And very likely at the end she would ask, "How do you come in? What right have you to interfere?"

"No, I have no right," muttered Pyotr Mihalitch. "But so much the better. . . . The harsher I am, the less right I have to interfere, the better."

It was sultry. Clouds of gnats hung over the ground and in the waste places the peewits called plaintively. Everything betokened rain, but he could not see a cloud in the sky. Pyotr Mihalitch crossed the boundary of his estate and galloped over a smooth, level field. He often went along this road and knew every bush, every hollow in it. What now in the far distance looked in the dusk like a dark cliff was a red church; he could picture it all down to the smallest detail, even the plaster on the gate and the calves that were always grazing in the church enclosure. Three-quarters of a mile to the right of the church there was a copse like a dark blur -- it was Count Koltonovitch's. And beyond the church Vlassitch's estate began.

From behind the church and the count's copse a huge black storm-cloud was rising, and there were ashes of white lightning.

"Here it is!" thought Pyotr Mihalitch. "Lord help us, Lord help us!"

The horse was soon tired after its quick gallop, and Pyotr Mihalitch was tired too. The storm-cloud looked at him angrily and seemed to advise him to go home. He felt a little scared.

"I will prove to them they are wrong," he tried to reassure himself. "They will say that it is free-love, individual freedom; but freedom means self-control and not subjection to passion. It's not liberty but license!"

He reached the count's big pond; it looked dark blue and frowning under the cloud, and a smell of damp and slime rose from it. Near the dam, two willows, one old and one young, drooped tenderly towards one another. Pyotr Mihalitch and Vlassitch had been walking near this very spot only a fortnight before, humming a students' song:

" 'Youth is wasted, life is nought, when the heart is cold and loveless.' "

A wretched song!

It was thundering as Pyotr Mihalitch rode through the copse, and the trees were bending and rustling in the wind. He had to make haste. It was only three-quarters of a mile through a meadow from the copse to Vlassitch's house. Here there were old birch-trees on each side of the road. They had the same melancholy and unhappy air as their owner Vlassitch, and looked as tall and lanky as he. Big drops of rain pattered on the birches and on the grass; the wind had suddenly dropped, and there was a smell of wet earth and poplars. Before him he saw Vlassitch's fence with a row of yellow acacias, which were tall and lanky too; where the fence was broken he could see the neglected orchard.

Pyotr Mihalitch was not thinking now of the horsewhip or of a slap in the face, and did not know what he would do at Vlassitch's. He felt nervous. He felt frightened on his own account and on his sister's, and was terrified at the thought of seeing her. How would she behave with her brother? What would they both talk about? And had he not better go back before it was too late? As he made these reflections, he galloped up the avenue of lime-trees to the house, rode round the big clumps of lilacs, and suddenly saw Vlassitch.

Vlassitch, wearing a cotton shirt, and top-boots, bending forward, with no hat on in the rain, was coming from the corner of the house to the front door. He was followed by a workman with a hammer and a box of nails. They must have been mending a shutter which had been banging in the wind. Seeing Pyotr Mihalitch, Vlassitch stopped.

"It's you!" he said, smiling. "That's nice."

"Yes, I've come, as you see," said Pyotr Mihalitch, brushing the rain off himself with both hands.

"Well, that's capital! I'm very glad," said Vlassitch, but he did not hold out his hand: evidently he did not venture, but waited for Pyotr Mihalitch to hold out his. "It will do the oats good," he said, looking at the sky.

"Yes."

They went into the house in silence. To the right of the hall was a door leading to another hall and then to the drawing-room, and on the left was a little room which in winter was used by the steward. Pyotr Mihalitch and Vlassitch went into this little room.

"Where were you caught in the rain?"

"Not far off, quite close to the house."

Pyotr Mihalitch sat down on the bed. He was glad of the noise of the rain and the darkness of the room. It was better: it made it less dreadful, and there was no need to see his companion's face. There was no anger in his heart now, nothing but fear and vexation with himself. He felt he had made a bad beginning, and that nothing would come of this visit.

Both were silent for some time and affected to be listening to the rain.

"Thank you, Petrusha," Vlassitch began, clearing his throat. "I am very grateful to you for coming. It's generous and noble of you. I understand it, and, believe me, I appreciate it. Believe me."

He looked out of the window and went on, standing in the middle of the room:

"Everything happened so secretly, as though we were concealing it all from you. The feeling that you might be wounded and angry has been a blot on our happiness all these days. But let me justify myself. We kept it secret not because we did not trust you. To begin with, it all happened suddenly, by a kind of inspiration; there was no time to discuss it. Besides, it's such a private, delicate matter, and it was awkward to bring a third person in, even someone as intimate as you. Above all, in all this we reckoned on your generosity. You are a very noble and generous person. I am infinitely grateful to you. If you ever need my life, come and take it."

Vlassitch talked in a quiet, hollow bass, always on the same droning note; he was evidently agitated. Pyotr Mihalitch felt it was his turn to speak, and that to listen and keep silent would really mean playing the part of a generous and noble simpleton, and that had not been his idea in coming. He got up quickly and said, breathlessly in an undertone:

"Listen, Grigory. You know I liked you and could have desired no better husband for my sister; but what has happened is awful! It's terrible to think of it!"

"Why is it terrible?" asked Vlassitch, with a quiver in his voice. "It would be terrible if we had done wrong, but that isn't so."

"Listen, Grigory. You know I have no prejudices; but, excuse my frankness, to my mind you have both acted selfishly. Of course, I shan't say so to my sister -- it will distress her; but you ought to know: mother is miserable beyond all description."

"Yes, that's sad," sighed Vlassitch. "We foresaw that, Petrusha, but what could we have done? Because one's actions hurt other people, it doesn't prove that they are wrong. What's to be done! Every important step one takes is bound to distress somebody. If you went to fight for freedom, that would distress your mother, too. What's to be done! Anyone who puts the peace of his family before everything has to renounce the life of ideas completely."

There was a vivid flash of lightning at the window, and the lightning seemed to change the course of Vlassitch's thoughts. He sat down beside Pyotr Mihalitch and began saying what was utterly beside the point.

"I have such a reverence for your sister, Petrusha," he said. "When I used to come and see you, I felt as though I were going to a holy shrine, and I really did worship Zina. Now my reverence for her grows every day. For me she is something higher than a wife -- yes, higher! " Vlassitch waved his hands. "She is my holy of holies. Since she is living with me, I enter my house as though it were a temple. She is an extraordinary, rare, most noble woman!"

"Well, he's off now!" thought Pyotr Mihalitch; he disliked the word "woman."

"Why shouldn't you be married properly?" he asked. "How much does your wife want for a divorce?"

"Seventy-five thousand."

"It's rather a lot. But if we were to negotiate with her?"

"She won't take a farthing less. She is an awful woman, brother," sighed Vlassitch. "I've never talked to you about her before -- it was unpleasant to think of her; but now that the subject has come up, I'll tell you about her. I married her on the impulse of the moment -- a fine, honourable impulse. An officer in command of a battalion of our regiment -- if you care to hear the details -- had an affair with a girl of eighteen; that is, to put it plainly, he seduced her, lived with her for two months, and abandoned her. She was in an awful position, brother. She was ashamed to go home to her parents; besides, they wouldn't have received her. Her lover had abandoned her; there was nothing left for her but to go to the barracks and sell herself. The other officers in the regiment were indignant. They were by no means saints themselves, but the baseness of it was so striking. Besides, no one in the regiment could endure the man. And to spite him, you understand, the indignant lieutenants and ensigns began getting up a subscription for the unfortunate girl. And when we subalterns met together and began to subscribe five or ten roubles each, I had a sudden inspiration. I felt it was an opportunity to do something fine. I hastened to the girl and warmly expressed my sympathy. And while I was on my way to her, and while I was talking to her, I loved her fervently as a woman insulted and injured. Yes. . . . Well, a week later I made her an offer. The colonel and my comrades thought my marriage out of keeping with the dignity of an officer. That roused me more than ever. I wrote a long letter, do you know, in which I proved that my action ought to be inscribed in the annals of the regiment in letters of gold, and so on. I sent the letter to my colonel and copies to my comrades. Well, I was excited, and, of course, I could not avoid being rude. I was asked to leave the regiment. I have a rough copy of it put away somewhere; I'll give it to you to read sometime. It was written with great feeling. You will see what lofty and noble sentiments I was experiencing. I resigned my commission and came here with my wife. My father had left a few debts, I had no money, and from the first day my wife began making acquaintances, dressing herself smartly, and playing cards, and I was obliged to mortgage the estate. She led a bad life, you understand, and you are the only one of the neighbours who hasn't been her lover. After two years I gave her all I had to set me free and she went off to town. Yes. . . . And now I pay her twelve hundred roubles a year. She is an awful woman! There is a fly, brother, which lays an egg in the back of a spider so that the spider can't shake it off: the grub fastens upon the spider and drinks its heart's blood. That was how this woman fastened upon me and sucks the blood of my heart. She hates and despises me for being so stupid; that is, for marrying a woman like her. My chivalry seems to her despicable. 'A wise man cast me off,' she says, 'and a fool picked me up.' To her thinking no one but a pitiful idiot could have behaved as I did. And that is insufferably bitter to me, brother. Altogether, I may say in parenthesis, fate has been hard upon me, very hard."

Pyotr Mihalitch listened to Vlassitch and wondered in perplexity what it was in this man that had so charmed his sister. He was not young -- he was forty-one -- lean and lanky, narrow-chested, with a long nose, and grey hairs in his beard. He talked in a droning voice, had a sickly smile, and waved his hands awkwardly as he talked. He had neither health, nor pleasant, manly manners, nor *savoir-faire,* nor gaiety, and in all his exterior there was something colourless and indefinite. He dressed without taste, his surroundings were depressing, he did not care for poetry or painting because "they have no answer to give to the questions of the day" -- that is, he did not understand them; music did not touch him. He was a poor farmer.

His estate was in a wretched condition and was mortgaged; he was paying twelve percent on the second mortgage and owed ten thousand on personal securities as well. When the time came to pay the interest on the mortgage or to send money to his wife, he asked everyone to lend him money with as much agitation as though his house were on fire, and, at the same time losing his head, he would sell the whole of his winter store of fuel for five roubles and a stack of straw for three roubles, and then have his garden fence or old cucumber-frames chopped up to heat his stoves. His meadows were ruined by pigs, the peasants' cattle strayed in the undergrowth in his woods, and every year the old trees were fewer and fewer: beehives and rusty pails lay about in his garden and kitchen-garden. He had neither talents nor abilities, nor even ordinary capacity for living like other people. In practical life he was a weak, naïve man, easy to deceive and to cheat, and the peasants with good reason called him "simple."

He was a Liberal, and in the district was regarded as a "Red," but even his progressiveness was a bore. There was no originality nor moving power about his independent views: he was revolted, indignant, and delighted always on the same note; it was always spiritless and ineffective. Even in moments of strong enthusiasm he never raised his head or stood upright. But the most tiresome thing of all was that he managed to express even his best and finest ideas so that they seemed in him commonplace and out of date. It reminded one of something old one had read long ago, when slowly and with an air of profundity he would begin discoursing of his noble, lofty moments, of his best years; or when he went into raptures over the younger generation, which has always been, and still is, in advance of society; or abused Russians for donning their dressing-gowns at thirty and forgetting the principles of their *alma mater.* If you stayed the night with him, he would put Pissarev or Darwin on your bedroom table; if you said you had read it, he would go and bring Dobrolubov.

In the district this was called free-thinking, and many people looked upon this free-thinking as an innocent and harmless eccentricity; it made him profoundly unhappy, however. It was for him the maggot of which he had just been speaking; it had fastened upon him and was sucking his life-blood. In his past there had been the strange marriage in the style of Dostoevsky; long letters and copies written in a bad, unintelligible hand-writing, but with great feeling, endless misunderstandings, explanations, disappointments, then debts, a second mortgage, the allowance to his wife, the monthly borrowing of money -- and all this for no benefit to anyone, either himself or others. And in the present, as in the past, he was still in a nervous flurry, on the lookout for heroic actions, and poking his nose into other people's affairs; as before, at every favourable opportunity there were long letters and copies, wearisome, stereotyped conversations about the village community, or the revival of handicrafts or the establishment of cheese factories -- conversations as like one another as though he had prepared them, not in his living brain, but by some mechanical process. And finally this scandal with Zina of which one could not see the end!

And meanwhile Zina was young -- she was only twenty-two -- good-looking, elegant, gay; she was fond of laughing, chatter, argument, a passionate musician; she had good taste in dress, in furniture, in books, and in her own home she would not have put up with a room like this, smelling of boots and cheap vodka. She, too, had advanced ideas, but in her free-thinking one felt the overflow of energy, the vanity of a young, strong, spirited girl, passionately eager to be better and more original than others. . . . How had it happened that she had fallen in love with Vlassitch?

"He is a Quixote, an obstinate fanatic, a maniac," thought Pyotr Mihalitch, "and she is as soft, yielding, and weak in character as I am. . . . She and I give in easily, without resistance. She loves him; but, then, I, too, love him in spite of everything."

Pyotr Mihalitch considered Vlassitch a good, straightforward man, but narrow and one-sided. In his perturbations and his sufferings, and in fact in his whole life, he saw no lofty aims, remote or immediate; he saw nothing but boredom and incapacity for life. His self-sacrifice and all that Vlassitch himself called heroic actions or noble impulses seemed to him a useless waste of force, unnecessary blank shots which consumed a great deal of powder. And Vlassitch's fanatical belief in the extraordinary loftiness and faultlessness of his own way of thinking struck him as naïve and even morbid; and the fact that Vlassitch all his life had contrived to mix the trivial with the exalted, that he had made a stupid marriage and looked upon it as an act of heroism, and then had affairs with other women and regarded that as a triumph of some idea or other was simply incomprehensible.

Nevertheless, Pyotr Mihalitch was fond of Vlassitch; he was conscious of a sort of power in him, and for some reason he had never had the heart to contradict him.

Vlassitch sat down quite close to him for a talk in the dark, to the accompaniment of the rain, and he had cleared his throat as a prelude to beginning on something lengthy, such as the history of his marriage. But it was intolerable for Pyotr Mihalitch to listen to him; he was tormented by the thought that he would see his sister directly.

"Yes, you've had bad luck," he said gently; "but, excuse me, we've been wandering from the point. That's not what we are talking about."

"Yes, yes, quite so. Well, let us come back to the point," said Vlassitch, and he stood up. "I tell you, Petrusha, our conscience is clear. We are not married, but there is no need for me to prove to you that our marriage is perfectly legitimate. You are as free in your ideas as I am, and, happily, there can be no disagreement between us on that point. As for our future, that ought not to alarm you. I'll work in the sweat of my brow, I'll work day and night -- in fact, I will strain every nerve to make Zina happy. Her life will be a splendid one! You may ask, am I able to do it. I am, brother! When a man devotes every minute to one thought, it's not difficult for him to attain his object. But let us go to Zina; it will be a joy to her to see you."

Pyotr Mihalitch's heart began to beat. He got up and followed Vlassitch into the hall, and from there into the drawing-room. There was nothing in the huge gloomy room but a piano and a long row of old chairs ornamented with bronze, on which no one ever sat. There was a candle alight on the piano. From the drawing-room they went in silence into the dining-room. This room, too, was large and comfortless; in the middle of the room there was a round table with two leaves with six thick legs, and only one candle. A clock in a large mahogany case like an ikon stand pointed to half-past two.

Vlassitch opened the door into the next room and said:

"Zina, here is Petrusha come to see us!"

At once there was the sound of hurried footsteps and Zina came into the dining-room. She was tall, plump, and very pale, and, just as when he had seen her for the last time at home, she was wearing a black skirt and a red blouse, with a large buckle on her belt. She flung one arm round her brother and kissed him on the temple.

"What a storm!" she said. "Grigory went off somewhere and I was left quite alone in the house."

She was not embarrassed, and looked at her brother as frankly and candidly as at home; looking at her, Pyotr Mihalitch, too, lost his embarrassment.

"But you are not afraid of storms," he said, sitting down at the table.

"No," she said, "but here the rooms are so big, the house is so old, and when there is thunder it all rattles like a cupboard full of crockery. It's a charming house altogether," she went on, sitting down opposite her brother. "There's some pleasant memory in every room. In my room, only fancy, Grigory's grandfather shot himself."

"In August we shall have the money to do up the lodge in the garden," said Vlassitch.

"For some reason when it thunders I think of that grandfather," Zina went on. "And in this dining-room somebody was flogged to death."

"That's an actual fact," said Vlassitch, and he looked with wide-open eyes at Pyotr Mihalitch. "Sometime in the forties this place was let to a Frenchman called Olivier. The portrait of his daughter is lying in an attic now -- a very pretty girl. This Olivier, so my father told me, despised Russians for their ignorance and treated them with cruel derision. Thus, for instance, he insisted on the priest walking without his hat for half a mile round his house, and on the church bells being rung when the Olivier family drove through the village. The serfs and altogether the humble of this world, of course, he treated with even less ceremony. Once there came along this road one of the simple-hearted sons of wandering Russia, somewhat after the style of Gogol's divinity student, Homa Brut. He asked for a night's lodging, pleased the bailiffs, and was given a job at the office of the estate. There are many variations of the story. Some say the divinity student stirred up the peasants, others that Olivier' s daughter fell in love with him. I don't know which is true, only one fine evening Olivier called him in here and cross-examined him, then ordered him to be beaten. Do you know, he sat here at this table drinking claret while the stable-boys beat the man. He must have tried to wring something out of him. Towards morning the divinity student died of the torture and his body was hidden. They say it was thrown into Koltovitch's pond. There was an inquiry, but the Frenchman paid some thousands to someone in authority and went away to Alsace. His lease was up just then, and so the matter ended."

"What scoundrels!" said Zina, shuddering.

"My father remembered Olivier and his daughter well. He used to say she was remarkably beautiful and eccentric. I imagine the divinity student had done both -- stirred up the peasants and won the daughter's heart. Perhaps he wasn't a divinity student at all, but someone travelling incognito."

Zina grew thoughtful; the story of the divinity student and the beautiful French girl had evidently carried her imagination far away. It seemed to Pyotr Mihalitch that she had not changed in the least during the last week, except that she was a little paler. She looked calm and just as usual, as though she had come with her brother to visit Vlassitch. But Pyotr Mihalitch felt that some change had taken place in himself. Before, when she was living at home, he could have spoken to her about anything, and now he did not feel equal to asking her the simple question, "How do you like being here?" The question seemed awkward and unnecessary. Probably the same change had taken place in her. She was in no haste to turn the conversation to her mother, to her home, to her relations with Vlassitch; she did not defend herself, she did not say that free unions are better than marriages in the church; she was not agitated, and calmly brooded over the story of Olivier. . . . And why had they suddenly begun talking of Olivier?

"You are both of you wet with the rain," said Zina, and she smiled joyfully; she was touched by this point of resemblance between her brother and Vlassitch.

And Pyotr Mihalitch felt all the bitterness and horror of his position. He thought of his deserted home, the closed piano, and Zina's bright little room into which no one went now; he thought there were no prints of little feet on the garden-paths, and that before tea no one went off, laughing gaily, to bathe. What he had clung to more and more from his childhood upwards, what he had loved thinking about when he used to sit in the stuffy class-room or the lecture theatre -- brightness, purity, and joy, everything that filled the house with life and light, had gone never to return, had vanished, and was mixed up with a coarse, clumsy story of some battalion officer, a chivalrous lieutenant, a depraved woman and a grandfather who had shot himself. . . . And to begin to talk about his mother or to think that the past could ever return would mean not understanding what was clear.

Pyotr Mihalitch's eyes filled with tears and his hand began to tremble as it lay on the table. Zina guessed what he was thinking about, and her eyes, too, glistened and looked red.

"Grigory, come here," she said to Vlassitch.

They walked away to the window and began talking of something in a whisper. From the way that Vlassitch stooped down to her and the way she looked at him, Pyotr Mihalitch realised again that everything was irreparably over, and that it was no use to talk of anything. Zina went out of the room.

"Well, brother!" Vlassitch began, after a brief silence, rubbing his hands and smiling. "I called our life happiness just now, but that was, so to speak, poetical license. In reality, there has not been a sense of happiness so far. Zina has been thinking all the time of you, of her mother, and has been worrying; looking at her, I, too, felt worried. Hers is a bold, free nature, but, you know, it's difficult when you're not used to it, and she is young, too. The servants call her 'Miss'; it seems a trifle, but it upsets her. There it is, brother."

Zina brought in a plateful of strawberries. She was followed by a little maidservant, looking crushed and humble, who set a jug of milk on the table and made a very low bow: she had something about her that was in keeping with the old furniture, something petrified and dreary.

The sound of the rain had ceased. Pyotr Mihalitch ate strawberries while Vlassitch and Zina looked at him in silence. The moment of the inevitable but useless conversation was approaching, and all three felt the burden of it. Pyotr Mihalitch's eyes filled with tears again; he pushed away his plate and said that he must be going home, or it would be getting late, and perhaps it would rain again. The time had come when common decency required Zina to speak of those at home and of her new life.

"How are things at home?" she asked rapidly, and her pale face quivered. "How is mother?"

"You know mother . . ." said Pyotr Mihalitch, not looking at her.

"Petrusha, you've thought a great deal about what has happened," she said, taking hold of her brother's sleeve, and he knew how hard it was for her to speak. "You've thought a great deal: tell me, can we reckon on mother's accepting Grigory . . . and the whole position, one day?"

She stood close to her brother, face to face with him, and he was astonished that she was so beautiful, and that he seemed not to have noticed it before. And it seemed to him utterly absurd that his sister, so like his mother, pampered, elegant, should be living with Vlassitch and in Vlassitch's house, with the petrified servant, and the table with six legs -- in the house where a man had been flogged to death, and that she was not going home with him, but was staying here to sleep.

"You know mother," he said, not answering her question. "I think you ought to have . . . to do something, to ask her forgiveness or something. . . ."

"But to ask her forgiveness would mean pretending we had done wrong. I'm ready to tell a lie to comfort mother, but it won't lead anywhere. I know mother. Well, what will be, must be!" said Zina, growing more cheerful now that the most unpleasant had been said. "We'll wait for five years, ten years, and be patient, and then God's will be done."

She took her brother's arm, and when she walked through the dark hall she squeezed close to him. They went out on the steps. Pyotr Mihalitch said good-bye, got on his horse, and set off at a walk; Zina and Vlassitch walked a little way with him. It was still and warm, with a delicious smell of hay; stars were twinkling brightly between the clouds. Vlassitch's old garden, which had seen so many gloomy stories in its time, lay slumbering in the darkness, and for some reason it was mournful riding through it.

"Zina and I to-day after dinner spent some really exalted moments," said Vlassitch. "I read aloud to her an excellent article on the question of emigration. You must read it, brother! You really must. It's remarkable for its lofty tone. I could not resist writing a letter to the editor to be forwarded to the author. I wrote only a single line: 'I thank you and warmly press your noble hand.' "

Pyotr Mihalitch was tempted to say, "Don't meddle in what does not concern you," but he held his tongue.

Vlassitch walked by his right stirrup and Zina by the left; both seemed to have forgotten that they had to go home. It was damp, and they had almost reached Koltovitch's copse. Pyotr Mihalitch felt that they were expecting something from him, though they hardly knew what it was, and he felt unbearably sorry for them. Now as they walked by the horse with submissive faces, lost in thought, he had a deep conviction that they were unhappy, and could not be happy, and their love seemed to him a melancholy, irreparable mistake. Pity and the sense that he could do nothing to help them reduced him to that state of spiritual softening when he was ready to make any sacrifice to get rid of the painful feeling of sympathy.

"I'll come over sometimes for a night," he said.

But it sounded as though he were making a concession, and did not satisfy him. When they stopped near Koltovitch's copse to say good-bye, he bent down to Zina, touched her shoulder, and said:

"You are right, Zina! You have done well." To avoid saying more and bursting into tears, he lashed his horse and galloped into the wood. As he rode into the darkness, he looked round and saw Vlassitch and Zina walking home along the road -- he taking long strides, while she walked with a hurried, jerky step beside him -- talking eagerly about something.

"I am an old woman!" thought Pyotr Mihalitch. "I went to solve the question and I have only made it more complicated -- there it is!"

He was heavy at heart. When he got out of the copse he rode at a walk and then stopped his horse near the pond. He wanted to sit and think without moving. The moon was rising and was reflected in a streak of red on the other side of the pond. There were low rumbles of thunder in the distance. Pyotr Mihalitch looked steadily at the water and imagined his sister's despair, her martyr-like pallor, the tearless eyes with which she would conceal her humiliation from others. He imagined her with child, imagined the death of their mother,

her funeral, Zina's horror. . . . The proud, superstitious old woman would be sure to die of grief. Terrible pictures of the future rose before him on the background of smooth, dark water, and among pale feminine figures he saw himself, a weak, cowardly man with a guilty face.

A hundred paces off on the right bank of the pond, something dark was standing motionless: was it a man or a tall post? Pyotr Mihalitch thought of the divinity student who had been killed and thrown into the pond.

"Olivier behaved inhumanly, but one way or another he did settle the question, while I have settled nothing and have only made it worse," he thought, gazing at the dark figure that looked like a ghost. "He said and did what he thought right while I say and do what I don't think right; and I don't know really what I do think. . . ."

He rode up to the dark figure: it was an old rotten post, the relic of some shed.

From Koltovitch's copse and garden there came a strong fragrant scent of lilies of the valley and honey-laden flowers. Pyotr Mihalitch rode along the bank of the pond and looked mournfully into the water. And thinking about his life, he came to the conclusion he had never said or acted upon what he really thought, and other people had repaid him in the same way. And so the whole of life seemed to him as dark as this water in which the night sky was reflected and water-weeds grew in a tangle. And it seemed to him that nothing could ever set it right.

WARD NO. 6

I

In the hospital yard there stands a small lodge surrounded by a perfect forest of burdocks, nettles, and wild hemp. Its roof is rusty, the chimney is tumbling down, the steps at the front-door are rotting away and overgrown with grass, and there are only traces left of the stucco. The front of the lodge faces the hospital; at the back it looks out into the open country, from which it is separated by the grey hospital fence with nails on it. These nails, with their points upwards, and the fence, and the lodge itself, have that peculiar, desolate, God-forsaken look which is only found in our hospital and prison buildings.

If you are not afraid of being stung by the nettles, come by the narrow footpath that leads to the lodge, and let us see what is going on inside. Opening the first door, we walk into the entry. Here along the walls and by the stove every sort of hospital rubbish lies littered about. Mattresses, old tattered dressing-gowns, trousers, blue striped shirts, boots and shoes no good for anything -- all these remnants are piled up in heaps, mixed up and crumpled, mouldering and giving out a sickly smell.

The porter, Nikita, an old soldier wearing rusty good-conduct stripes, is always lying on the litter with a pipe between his teeth. He has a grim, surly, battered-looking face, overhanging eyebrows which give him the expression of a sheep-dog of the steppes, and a red nose; he is short and looks thin and scraggy, but he is of imposing deportment and his fists are vigorous. He belongs to the class of simple-hearted, practical, and dull-witted people, prompt in carrying out orders, who like discipline better than anything in the world, and so are convinced that it is their duty to beat people. He showers blows on the face, on the chest, on the back, on whatever comes first, and is convinced that there would be no order in the place if he did not.

Next you come into a big, spacious room which fills up the whole lodge except for the entry. Here the walls are painted a dirty blue, the ceiling is as sooty as in a hut without a chimney -- it is evident that in the winter the stove smokes and the room is full of fumes. The windows are disfigured by iron gratings on the inside. The wooden floor is grey and full of splinters. There is a stench of sour cabbage, of smouldering wicks, of bugs, and of ammonia, and for the first minute this stench gives you the impression of having walked into a menagerie.

There are bedsteads screwed to the floor. Men in blue hospital dressing-gowns, and wearing nightcaps in the old style, are sitting and lying on them. These are the lunatics.

There are five of them in all here. Only one is of the upper class, the rest are all artisans. The one nearest the door -- a tall, lean workman with shining red whiskers and tear-stained eyes -- sits with his head propped on his hand, staring at the same point. Day and night he grieves, shaking his head, sighing and smiling bitterly. He takes a part in conversation and usually makes no answer to questions; he eats and drinks mechanically when food is offered him. From his agonizing, throbbing cough, his thinness, and the flush on his cheeks, one may judge that he is in the first stage of consumption. Next to him is a little, alert, very lively old man, with a pointed beard and curly black hair like a negro's. By day he walks up and down the ward from window to window, or sits on his bed, cross-legged like a Turk, and, ceaselessly as a bullfinch whistles, softly sings and titters. He shows his childish gaiety and lively character at night also when he gets up to say his prayers -- that is, to beat himself on the chest with his fists, and to scratch with his fingers at the door. This is the Jew Moiseika, an imbecile, who went crazy twenty years ago when his hat factory was burnt down.

And of all the inhabitants of Ward No. 6, he is the only one who is allowed to go out of the lodge, and even out of the yard into the street. He has enjoyed this privilege for years, probably because he is an old inhabitant of the hospital -- a quiet, harmless imbecile, the buffoon of the town, where people are used to seeing him surrounded by boys and dogs. In his wretched gown, in his absurd night-cap, and in slippers, sometimes with bare legs and even without trousers, he walks about the streets, stopping at the gates and little shops, and begging for a copper. In one place they will give him some kvass, in another some bread, in another a copper, so that he generally goes back to the ward feeling rich and well fed. Everything that he brings back Nikita takes from him for his own benefit. The soldier does this roughly, angrily turning the Jew's pockets inside out, and calling God to witness that he will not let him go into the street again, and that breach of the regulations is worse to him than anything in the world.

Moiseika likes to make himself useful. He gives his companions water, and covers them up when they are asleep; he promises each of them to bring him back a kopeck, and to make him a new cap; he feeds with a spoon his neighbour on the left, who is paralyzed. He acts in this way, not from compassion nor from any considerations of a humane kind, but through imitation, unconsciously dominated by Gromov, his neighbour on the right hand.

Ivan Dmitritch Gromov, a man of thirty-three, who is a gentleman by birth, and has been a court usher and provincial secretary, suffers from the mania of persecution. He either lies curled up in bed, or walks from corner to corner as though for exercise; he very rarely sits down. He is always excited, agitated, and overwrought by a sort of vague, undefined expectation. The faintest rustle in the entry or shout in the yard is enough to make him raise his head and begin listening: whether they are coming for him, whether they are looking for him. And at such times his face expresses the utmost uneasiness and repulsion.

I like his broad face with its high cheek-bones, always pale and unhappy, and reflecting, as though in a mirror, a soul tormented by conflict and long-continued terror. His grimaces are strange and abnormal, but the delicate lines traced on his face by profound, genuine suffering show intelligence and sense, and there is a warm and healthy light in his eyes. I like the man himself, courteous, anxious to be of use, and extraordinarily gentle to everyone except Nikita. When anyone drops a button or a spoon, he jumps up from his bed quickly and picks it up; every day he says good-morning to his companions, and when he goes to bed he wishes them good-night.

Besides his continually overwrought condition and his grimaces, his madness shows itself in the following way also. Sometimes in the evenings he wraps himself in his dressing-gown, and, trembling all over, with his teeth chattering, begins walking rapidly from corner to corner and between the bedsteads. It seems as though he is in a violent fever. From the way he suddenly stops and glances at his companions, it can be seen that he is longing to say something very important, but, apparently reflecting that they would not listen, or would not understand him, he shakes his head impatiently and goes on pacing up and down. But soon the desire to speak gets the upper hand of every consideration, and he will let himself go and speak fervently and passionately. His talk is disordered and feverish like delirium, disconnected, and not always intelligible, but, on the other hand, something extremely fine may be felt in it, both in the words and the voice. When he talks you recognize in him the lunatic and the man. It is difficult to reproduce on paper his insane talk. He speaks of the baseness of mankind, of violence trampling on justice, of the glorious life which will one day be upon earth, of the window-gratings, which remind him every minute of the stupidity and cruelty of oppressors. It makes a disorderly, incoherent potpourri of themes old but not yet out of date.

II

Some twelve or fifteen years ago an official called Gromov, a highly respectable and prosperous person, was living in his own house in the principal street of the town. He had two sons, Sergey and Ivan. When Sergey was a student in his fourth year he was taken ill with galloping consumption and died, and his death was, as it were, the first of a whole series of calamities which suddenly showered on the Gromov family. Within a week of Sergey's funeral the old father was put on trial for fraud and misappropriation, and he died of typhoid in the prison hospital soon afterwards. The house, with all their belongings, was sold by auction, and Ivan Dmitritch and his mother were left entirely without means.

Hitherto in his father's lifetime, Ivan Dmitritch, who was studying in the University of Petersburg, had received an allowance of sixty or seventy roubles a month, and had had no conception of poverty; now he had to make an abrupt change in his life. He had to spend his time from morning to night giving lessons for next to nothing, to work at copying, and with all that to go hungry, as all his earnings were sent to keep his mother. Ivan Dmitritch could not stand such a life; he lost heart and strength, and, giving up the university, went home.

Here, through interest, he obtained the post of teacher in the district school, but could not get on with his colleagues, was not liked by the boys, and soon gave up the post. His mother died. He was for six months without work, living on nothing but bread and water; then he became a court usher. He kept this post until he was dismissed owing to his illness.

He had never even in his young student days given the impression of being perfectly healthy. He had always been pale, thin, and given to catching cold; he ate little and slept badly. A single glass of wine went to his head and made him hysterical. He always had a craving for society, but, owing to his irritable temperament and suspiciousness, he never became very intimate with anyone, and had no friends. He always spoke with contempt of his fellow-townsmen, saying that their coarse ignorance and sleepy animal existence seemed to him loathsome and horrible. He spoke in a loud tenor, with heat, and invariably either with scorn and indignation, or with wonder and enthusiasm, and always with perfect sincerity. Whatever one talked to him about he always brought it round to the same subject: that life was dull and stifling in the town; that the townspeople had no lofty interests, but lived a dingy, meaningless life, diversified by violence, coarse profligacy, and hypocrisy; that scoundrels were well fed and clothed, while honest men lived from hand to mouth; that they needed schools, a progressive local paper, a theatre, public lectures, the co-ordination of the intellectual elements; that society must see its failings and be horrified. In his criticisms of people he laid on the colours thick, using only black and white, and no fine shades; mankind was divided for him into honest men and scoundrels: there was nothing in between. He always spoke with passion and enthusiasm of women and of love, but he had never been in love.

In spite of the severity of his judgments and his nervousness, he was liked, and behind his back was spoken of affectionately as Vanya. His innate refinement and readiness to be of service, his good breeding, his moral purity, and his shabby coat, his frail appearance and family misfortunes, aroused a kind, warm, sorrowful feeling. Moreover, he was well educated and well read; according to the townspeople's notions, he knew everything, and was in their eyes something like a walking encyclopedia.

He had read a great deal. He would sit at the club, nervously pulling at his beard and looking through the magazines and books; and from his face one could see that he was not reading, but devouring the pages without giving himself time to digest what he read. It must be supposed that reading was one of his morbid habits, as he fell upon anything that came into his hands with equal avidity, even last year's newspapers and calendars. At home he always read lying down.

III

One autumn morning Ivan Dmitritch, turning up the collar of his greatcoat and splashing through the mud, made his way by side-streets and back lanes to see some artisan, and to collect some payment that was owing. He was in a gloomy mood, as he always was in the morning. In one of the side-streets he was met by two convicts in fetters and four soldiers with rifles in charge of them. Ivan Dmitritch had very often met convicts before, and they had always excited feelings of compassion and discomfort in him; but now this meeting made a peculiar, strange impression on him. It suddenly seemed to him for some reason that he, too, might be put into fetters and led through the mud to prison like that. After visiting the artisan, on the way home he met near the post office a police superintendent of his acquaintance, who greeted him and walked a few paces along the street with him, and for some reason this seemed to him suspicious. At home he could not get the convicts or the soldiers with their rifles out of his head all day, and an unaccountable inward agitation prevented him from reading or concentrating his mind. In the evening he did not light his lamp, and at night he could not sleep, but kept thinking that he might be arrested, put into fetters, and thrown into prison. He did not know of any harm he had done, and could be certain that he would never be guilty of murder, arson, or theft in the future either; but was it not easy to commit a crime by accident, unconsciously, and was not false witness always possible, and, indeed, miscarriage of justice? It was not without good reason that the agelong experience of the simple people teaches that beggary and prison are ills none can be safe from. A judicial mistake is very possible as legal proceedings are conducted nowadays, and there is nothing to be wondered at in it. People who have an official, professional relation to other men's sufferings for instance, judges, police officers, doctors -- in course of time, through habit, grow so callous that they cannot, even if they wish it, take any but a formal attitude to their clients; in this respect they are not different from the peasant who slaughters sheep and calves in the back-yard, and does not notice the blood. With this formal, soulless attitude to human personality the judge needs but one thing -- time -- in order to deprive an innocent man of all rights of property, and to condemn him to penal servitude. Only the time spent on performing certain formalities for which the judge is paid his salary, and then -- it is all over. Then you may look in vain for justice and protection in this dirty, wretched little town a hundred and fifty miles from a railway station! And, indeed, is it not absurd even to think of justice when every kind of violence is accepted by society as a rational and consistent necessity, and every act of mercy -- for instance, a verdict of acquittal -- calls forth a perfect outburst of dissatisfied and revengeful feeling?

In the morning Ivan Dmitritch got up from his bed in a state of horror, with cold perspiration on his forehead, completely convinced that he might be arrested any minute. Since his gloomy thoughts of yesterday had haunted him so long, he thought, it must be that there was some truth in them. They could not, indeed, have come into his mind without any grounds whatever.

A policeman walking slowly passed by the windows: that was not for nothing. Here were two men standing still and silent near the house. Why were they silent? And agonizing days and nights followed for Ivan Dmitritch. Everyone who passed by the windows or came into the yard seemed to him a spy or a detective. At midday the chief of the police usually drove down the street with a pair of horses; he was going from his estate near the town to the police department; but Ivan Dmitritch fancied every time that he was driving especially quickly, and that he had a peculiar expression: it was evident that he was in haste to announce that there was a very important criminal in the town. Ivan Dmitritch started at every ring at the bell and knock at the gate, and was agitated whenever he came upon anyone new at his landlady's; when he met police officers and gendarmes he smiled and began whistling so as to seem unconcerned. He could not sleep for whole nights in succession expecting to be arrested, but he snored loudly and sighed as though in deep sleep, that his landlady might think he was asleep; for if he could not sleep it meant that he was tormented by the stings of conscience -- what a piece of evidence! Facts and common sense persuaded him that all these terrors were nonsense and morbidity, that if one looked at the matter more broadly there was nothing really terrible in arrest and imprisonment -- so long as the conscience is at ease; but the more sensibly and logically he reasoned, the more acute and agonizing his mental distress became. It might be compared with the story of a hermit who tried to cut a dwelling-place for himself in a virgin forest; the more zealously he worked with his axe, the thicker the forest grew. In the end Ivan Dmitritch, seeing it was useless, gave up reasoning altogether, and abandoned himself entirely to despair and terror.

He began to avoid people and to seek solitude. His official work had been distasteful to him before: now it became unbearable to him. He was afraid they would somehow get him into trouble, would put a bribe in his pocket unnoticed and then denounce him, or that he would accidentally make a mistake in official papers that would appear to be fraudulent, or would lose other people's money. It is strange that his imagination had never at other times been so agile and inventive as now, when every day he thought of thousands of different reasons for being seriously anxious over his freedom and honour; but, on the other hand, his interest in the outer world, in books in particular, grew sensibly fainter, and his memory began to fail him.

In the spring when the snow melted there were found in the ravine near the cemetery two half-decomposed corpses -- the bodies of an old woman and a boy bearing the traces of death by violence. Nothing was talked of but these bodies and their unknown murderers. That people might not think he had been guilty of the crime, Ivan Dmitritch walked about the streets, smiling, and when he met acquaintances he turned pale, flushed, and began declaring that there was no greater crime than the murder of the weak and defenceless. But this duplicity soon exhausted him, and after some reflection he decided that in his position the best thing to do was to hide in his landlady's cellar. He sat in the cellar all day and then all night, then another day, was fearfully cold, and waiting till dusk, stole secretly like a thief back to his room. He stood in the middle of the room till daybreak, listening without stirring. Very early in the morning, before sunrise, some workmen came into the house. Ivan Dmitritch knew perfectly well that they had come to mend the stove in the kitchen, but terror told him that they were police officers disguised as workmen. He slipped stealthily out of the flat, and, overcome by terror, ran along the street without his cap and coat. Dogs raced after him barking, a peasant shouted somewhere behind him, the wind whistled in his ears, and it seemed to Ivan Dmitritch that the force and violence of the whole world was massed together behind his back and was chasing after him.

He was stopped and brought home, and his landlady sent for a doctor. Doctor Andrey Yefimitch, of whom we shall have more to say hereafter, prescribed cold compresses on his head and laurel drops, shook his head, and went away, telling the landlady he should not come again, as one should not interfere with people who are going out of their minds. As he had not the means to live at home and be nursed, Ivan Dmitritch was soon sent to the hospital, and was there put into the ward for venereal patients. He could not sleep at night, was full of whims and fancies, and disturbed the patients, and was soon afterwards, by Andrey Yefimitch's orders, transferred to Ward No. 6.

Within a year Ivan Dmitritch was completely forgotten in the town, and his books, heaped up by his landlady in a sledge in the shed, were pulled to pieces by boys.

IV

Ivan Dmitritch's neighbour on the left hand is, as I have said already, the Jew Moiseika; his neighbour on the right hand is a peasant so rolling in fat that he is almost spherical, with a blankly stupid face, utterly devoid of thought. This is a motionless, gluttonous, unclean animal who has long ago lost all powers of thought or feeling. An acrid, stifling stench always comes from him.

Nikita, who has to clean up after him, beats him terribly with all his might, not sparing his fists; and what is dreadful is not his being beaten -- that one can get used to -- but the fact that this stupefied creature does not respond to the blows with a sound or a movement, nor by a look in the eyes, but only sways a little like a heavy barrel.

The fifth and last inhabitant of Ward No. 6 is a man of the artisan class who had once been a sorter in the post office, a thinnish, fair little man with a good-natured but rather sly face. To judge from the clear, cheerful look in his calm and intelligent eyes, he has some pleasant idea in his mind, and has some very important and agreeable secret. He has under his pillow and under his mattress something that he never shows anyone, not from fear of its being taken from him and stolen, but from modesty. Sometimes he goes to the window, and turning his back to his companions, puts something on his breast, and bending his head, looks at it; if you go up to him at such a moment, he is overcome with confusion and snatches something off his breast. But it is not difficult to guess his secret.

"Congratulate me," he often says to Ivan Dmitritch; "I have been presented with the Stanislav order of the second degree with the star. The second degree with the star is only given to foreigners, but for some reason they want to make an exception for me," he says with a smile, shrugging his shoulders in perplexity. "That I must confess I did not expect."

"I don't understand anything about that," Ivan Dmitritch replies morosely.

"But do you know what I shall attain to sooner or later?" the former sorter persists, screwing up his eyes slyly. "I shall certainly get the Swedish 'Polar Star.' That's an order it is worth working for, a white cross with a black ribbon. It's very beautiful."

Probably in no other place is life so monotonous as in this ward. In the morning the patients, except the paralytic and the fat peasant, wash in the entry at a big tab and wipe themselves with the skirts of their dressing-gowns; after that they drink tea out of tin mugs which Nikita brings them out of the main building. Everyone is allowed one mugful. At midday they have soup made out of sour cabbage and boiled grain, in the evening their supper consists of grain left from dinner. In the intervals they lie down, sleep, look out of window, and walk from one corner to the other. And so every day. Even the former sorter always talks of the same orders.

Fresh faces are rarely seen in Ward No. 6. The doctor has not taken in any new mental cases for a long time, and the people who are fond of visiting lunatic asylums are few in this world. Once every two months Semyon Lazaritch, the barber, appears in the ward. How he cuts the patients' hair, and how Nikita helps him to do it, and what a trepidation the lunatics are always thrown into by the arrival of the drunken, smiling barber, we will not describe.

No one even looks into the ward except the barber. The patients are condemned to see day after day no one but Nikita.

A rather strange rumour has, however, been circulating in the hospital of late.

It is rumoured that the doctor has begun to visit Ward No. 6.

V

A strange rumour!

Dr. Andrey Yefimitch Ragin is a strange man in his way. They say that when he was young he was very religious, and prepared himself for a clerical career, and that when he had finished his studies at the high school in 1863 he intended to enter a theological academy, but that his father, a surgeon and doctor of medicine, jeered at him and declared point-blank that he would disown him if he became a priest. How far this is true I don't know, but Andrey Yefimitch himself has more than once confessed that he has never had a natural bent for medicine or science in general.

However that may have been, when he finished his studies in the medical faculty he did not enter the priesthood. He showed no special devoutness, and was no more like a priest at the beginning of his medical career than he is now.

His exterior is heavy -- coarse like a peasant's, his face, his beard, his flat hair, and his coarse, clumsy figure, suggest an overfed, intemperate, and harsh innkeeper on the highroad. His face is surly-looking and covered with blue veins, his eyes are little and his nose is red. With his height and broad shoulders he has huge hands and feet; one would think that a blow from his fist would knock the life out of anyone, but his step is soft, and his walk is cautious and insinuating; when he meets anyone in a narrow passage he is always the first to stop and make way, and to say, not in a bass, as one would expect, but in a high, soft tenor: "I beg your pardon!" He has a little swelling on his neck which prevents him from wearing stiff starched collars, and so he always goes about in soft linen or cotton shirts. Altogether he does not dress like a doctor. He wears the same suit for ten years, and the new clothes, which he usually buys at a Jewish shop, look as shabby and crumpled on him as his old ones; he sees patients and dines and pays visits all in the same coat; but this is not due to niggardliness, but to complete carelessness about his appearance.

When Andrey Yefimitch came to the town to take up his duties the "institution founded to the glory of God" was in a terrible condition. One could hardly breathe for the stench in the wards, in the passages, and in the courtyards of the hospital. The hospital servants, the nurses, and their children slept in the wards together with the patients. They complained that there was no living for beetles, bugs, and mice. The surgical wards were never free from erysipelas. There were only two scalpels and not one thermometer in the whole hospital; potatoes were kept in the baths. The superintendent, the housekeeper, and the medical assistant robbed the patients, and of the old doctor, Andrey Yefimitch's predecessor, people declared that he secretly sold the hospital alcohol, and that he kept a regular harem consisting of nurses and female patients. These disorderly proceedings were perfectly well known in the town, and were even exaggerated, but people took them calmly; some justified them on the ground that there were only peasants and working men in the hospital, who could not be dissatisfied, since they were much worse off at home than in the hospital -- they couldn't be fed on woodcocks! Others said in excuse that the town alone, without help from the Zemstvo, was not equal to maintaining a good hospital; thank God for having one at all, even a poor one. And the newly formed Zemstvo did not open infirmaries either in the town or the neighbourhood, relying on the fact that the town already had its hospital.

After looking over the hospital Andrey Yefimitch came to the conclusion that it was an immoral institution and extremely prejudicial to the health of the townspeople. In his opinion the most sensible thing that could be done was to let out the patients and close the hospital. But he reflected that his will alone was not enough to do this, and that it would be useless; if physical and moral impurity were driven out of one place, they would only move to another; one must wait for it to wither away of itself Besides, if people open a hospital and put up with having it, it must be because they need it; superstition and all the nastiness and abominations of daily life were necessary, since in process of time they worked out to something sensible, just as manure turns into black earth. There was nothing on earth so good that it had not something nasty about its first origin.

When Andrey Yefimitch undertook his duties he was apparently not greatly concerned about the irregularities at the hospital. He only asked the attendants and nurses not to sleep in the wards, and had two cupboards of instruments put up; the superintendent, the housekeeper, the medical assistant, and the erysipelas remained unchanged.

Andrey Yefimitch loved intelligence and honesty intensely, but he had no strength of will nor belief in his right to organize an intelligent and honest life about him. He was absolutely unable to give orders, to forbid things, and to insist. It seemed as though he had taken a vow never to raise his voice and never to make use of the imperative. It was difficult for him to say. "Fetch" or "Bring"; when he wanted his meals he would cough hesitatingly and say to the cook, "How about tea?. . ." or "How about dinner? . . ." To dismiss the superintendent or to tell him to leave off stealing, or to abolish the unnecessary parasitic post altogether, was absolutely beyond his powers. When Andrey Yefimitch was deceived or flattered, or accounts he knew to be cooked were brought him to sign, he would turn as red as a crab and feel guilty, but yet he would sign the accounts. When the patients complained to him of being hungry or of the roughness of the nurses, he would be confused and mutter guiltily: "Very well, very well, I will go into it later. . . . Most likely there is some misunderstanding. . ."

At first Andrey Yefimitch worked very zealously. He saw patients every day from morning till dinner-time, performed operations, and even attended confinements. The ladies said of him that he was attentive and clever at diagnosing diseases, especially those of women and children. But in process of time the work unmistakably wearied him by its monotony and obvious uselessness. To-day one sees thirty patients, and to-morrow they have increased to thirty-five, the next day forty, and so on from day to day, from year to year, while the mortality in the town did not decrease and the patients did not leave off coming. To be any real help to forty patients between morning and dinner was not physically possible, so it could but lead to deception. If twelve thousand patients were seen in a year it meant, if one looked at it simply, that twelve thousand men were deceived. To put those who were seriously ill into wards, and to treat them according to the principles of science, was impossible, too, because though there were principles there was no science; if he were to put aside philosophy and pedantically follow the rules as other doctors did, the things above all necessary were cleanliness and ventilation instead of dirt, wholesome nourishment instead of broth made of stinking, sour cabbage, and good assistants instead of thieves; and, indeed, why hinder people dying if death is the normal and legitimate end of everyone? What is gained if some shop-keeper or clerk lives an extra five or ten years? If the aim of medicine is by drugs to alleviate suffering, the question forces itself on one: why alleviate it? In the first place, they say that suffering leads man to perfection; and in the second, if mankind really learns to alleviate its sufferings with pills and drops, it will completely abandon religion and philosophy, in which it has hitherto found not merely protection from all sorts of trouble, but even happiness. Pushkin suffered terrible agonies before his death, poor Heine lay paralyzed for several years; why, then, should not some Andrey Yefimitch or Matryona Savishna be ill, since their lives had nothing of importance in them, and would have been entirely empty and like the life of an amoeba except for suffering?

Oppressed by such reflections, Andrey Yefimitch relaxed his efforts and gave up visiting the hospital every day.

VI

His life was passed like this. As a rule he got up at eight o'clock in the morning, dressed, and drank his tea. Then he sat down in his study to read, or went to the hospital. At the hospital the out-patients were sitting in the dark, narrow little corridor waiting to be seen by the doctor. The nurses and the attendants, tramping with their boots over the brick floors, ran by them; gaunt-looking patients in dressing-gowns passed; dead bodies and vessels full of filth were carried by; the children were crying, and there was a cold draught. Andrey Yefimitch knew that such surroundings were torture to feverish, consumptive, and impressionable patients; but what could be done? In the consulting-room he was met by his assistant, Sergey Sergeyitch -- a fat little man with a plump, well-washed shaven face, with soft, smooth manners, wearing a new loosely cut suit, and looking more like asenator than a medical assistant. He had an immense practice in the town, wore a white tie, and considered himself more proficient than the doctor, who had no practice. In the corner of the consulting-room there stood a large ikon in a shrine with a heavy lamp in front of it, and near it a candle-stand with a white cover on it. On the walls hung portraits of bishops, a view of the Svyatogorsky Monastery, and wreaths of dried cornflowers. Sergey Sergeyitch was religious, and liked solemnity and decorum. The ikon had been put up at his expense; at his instructions someone of the patients read the hymns of praise in the consulting-room on Sundays, and after the reading Sergey Sergeyitch himself went through the wards with a censer and burned incense.

There were a great many patients, but the time was short, and so the work was confined to the asking of a few brief questions and the administration of some drugs, such as castor-oil or volatile ointment. Andrey Yefimitch would sit with his cheek resting in his hand, lost in thought and asking questions mechanically. Sergey Sergeyitch sat down too, rubbing his hands, and from time to time putting in his word.

"We suffer pain and poverty," he would say, "because we do not pray to the merciful God as we should. Yes!"

Andrey Yefimitch never performed any operation when he was seeing patients; he had long ago given up doing so, and the sight of blood upset him. When he had to open a child's mouth in order to look at its throat, and the child cried and tried to defend itself with its little hands, the noise in his ears made his head go round and brought tears to his eyes. He would make haste to prescribe a drug, and motion to the woman to take the child away.

He was soon wearied by the timidity of the patients and their incoherence, by the proximity of the pious Sergey Sergeyitch, by the portraits on the walls, and by his own questions which he had asked over and over again for twenty years. And he would go away after seeing five or six patients. The rest would be seen by his assistant in his absence.

With the agreeable thought that, thank God, he had no private practice now, and that no one would interrupt him, Andrey Yefimitch sat down to the table immediately on reaching home and took up a book. He read a great deal and always with enjoyment. Half his salary went on buying books, and of the six rooms that made up his abode three were heaped up with books and old magazines. He liked best of all works on history and philosophy; the only medical publication to which he subscribed was *The Doctor,* of which he always read the last pages first. He would always go on reading for several hours without a break and without being weary. He did not read as rapidly and impulsively as Ivan Dmitritch had done in the past, but slowly and with concentration, often pausing over a passage which he liked or did not find intelligible. Near the books there always stood a decanter of vodka, and a salted cucumber or a pickled apple lay beside it, not on a plate, but on the baize table-cloth. Every half-hour he would pour himself out a glass of vodka and drink it without taking his eyes off the book. Then without looking at it he would feel for the cucumber and bite off a bit.

At three o'clock he would go cautiously to the kitchen door; cough, and say, "Daryushka, what about dinner? . ."

After his dinner -- a rather poor and untidily served one -- Andrey Yefimitch would walk up and down his rooms with his arms folded, thinking. The clock would strike four, then five, and still he would be walking up and down thinking. Occasionally the kitchen door would creak, and the red and sleepy face of Daryushka would appear.

"Andrey Yefimitch, isn't it time for you to have your beer?" she would ask anxiously.

"No, it's not time yet . . ." he would answer. "I'll wait a little. . . . I'll wait a little. . ."

Towards the evening the postmaster, Mihail Averyanitch, the only man in town whose society did not bore Andrey Yefimitch, would come in. Mihail Averyanitch had once been a very rich landowner, and had served in the calvary, but had come to ruin, and was forced by poverty to take a job in the post office late in life. He had a hale and hearty appearance, luxuriant grey whiskers, the manners of a well-bred man, and a loud, pleasant voice. He was good-natured and emotional, but hot-tempered. When anyone in the post office made a protest, expressed disagreement, or even began to argue, Mihail Averyanitch would turn crimson, shake all over, and shout in a voice of thunder, "Hold your tongue!" so that the post office had long enjoyed the reputation of an institution which it was terrible to visit. Mihail Averyanitch liked and respected Andrey Yefimitch for his culture and the loftiness of his soul; he treated the other inhabitants of the town superciliously, as though they were his subordinates.

"Here I am," he would say, going in to Andrey Yefimitch. "Good evening, my dear fellow! I'll be bound, you are getting sick of me, aren't you?"

"On the contrary, I am delighted," said the doctor. "I am always glad to see you."

The friends would sit on the sofa in the study and for some time would smoke in silence.

"Daryushka, what about the beer?" Andrey Yefimitch would say.

They would drink their first bottle still in silence, the doctor brooding and Mihail Averyanitch with a gay and animated face, like a man who has something very interesting to tell. The doctor was always the one to begin the conversation.

"What a pity," he would say quietly and slowly, not looking his friend in the face (he never looked anyone in the face) -- "what a great pity it is that there are no people in our town who are capable of carrying on intelligent and interesting conversation, or care to do so. It is an immense privation for us. Even the educated class do not rise above vulgarity; the level of their development, I assure you, is not a bit higher than that of the lower orders."

"Perfectly true. I agree."

"You know, of course," the doctor went on quietly and deliberately, "that everything in this world is insignificant and uninteresting except the higher spiritual manifestations of the human mind. Intellect draws a sharp line between the animals and man, suggests the divinity of the latter, and to some extent even takes the place of the immortality which does not exist. Consequently the intellect is the only possible source of enjoyment. We see and hear of no trace of intellect about us, so we are deprived of enjoyment. We have books, it is true, but that is not at all the same as living talk and converse. If you will allow me to make a not quite apt comparison: books are the printed score, while talk is the singing."

"Perfectly true."

A silence would follow. Daryushka would come out of the kitchen and with an expression of blank dejection would stand in the doorway to listen, with her face propped on her fist.

"Eh!" Mihail Averyanitch would sigh. "To expect intelligence of this generation!"

And he would describe how wholesome, entertaining, and interesting life had been in the past. How intelligent the educated class in Russia used to be, and what lofty ideas it had of honour and friendship; how they used to lend money without an IOU, and it was thought a disgrace not to give a helping hand to a comrade in need; and what campaigns, what adventures, what skirmishes, what comrades, what women! And the Caucasus, what a marvellous country! The wife of a battalion commander, a queer woman, used to put on an officer's uniform and drive off into the mountains in the evening, alone, without a guide. It was said that she had a love affair with some princeling in the native village.

"Queen of Heaven, Holy Mother..." Daryushka would sigh.

"And how we drank! And how we ate! And what desperate liberals we were!"

Andrey Yefimitch would listen without hearing; he was musing as he sipped his beer.

"I often dream of intellectual people and conversation with them," he said suddenly, interrupting Mihail Averyanitch. "My father gave me an excellent education, but under the influence of the ideas of the sixties made me become a doctor. I believe if I had not obeyed him then, by now I should have been in the very centre of the intellectual movement. Most likely I should have become a member of some university. Of course, intellect, too, is transient and not eternal, but you know why I cherish a partiality for it. Life is a vexatious trap; when a thinking man reaches maturity and attains to full consciousness he cannot help feeling that he is in a trap from which there is no escape. Indeed, he is summoned without his choice by fortuitous circumstances from non-existence into life . . . what for? He tries to find out the meaning and object of his existence; he is told nothing, or he is told absurdities; he knocks and it is not opened to him; death comes to him -- also without his choice. And so, just as in prison men held together by common misfortune feel more at ease when they are together, so one does not notice the trap in life when people with a bent for analysis and generalization meet together and pass their time in the interchange of proud and free ideas. In that sense the intellect is the source of an enjoyment nothing can replace."

"Perfectly true."

Not looking his friend in the face, Andrey Yefimitch would go on, quietly and with pauses, talking about intellectual people and conversation with them, and Mihail Averyanitch would listen attentively and agree: "Perfectly true."

"And you do not believe in the immortality of the soul?" he would ask suddenly.

"No, honoured Mihail Averyanitch; I do not believe it, and have no grounds for believing it."

"I must own I doubt it too. And yet I have a feeling as though I should never die. Oh, I think to myself: 'Old fogey, it is time you were dead!' But there is a little voice in my soul says: 'Don't believe it; you won't die.' "

Soon after nine o'clock Mihail Averyanitch would go away. As he put on his fur coat in the entry he would say with a sigh:

"What a wilderness fate has carried us to, though, really! What's most vexatious of all is to have to die here. Ech! . ."

VII

After seeing his friend out Andrey Yefimitch would sit down at the table and begin reading again. The stillness of the evening, and afterwards of the night, was not broken by a single sound, and it seemed as though time were standing still and brooding with the doctor over the book, and as though there were nothing in existence but the books and the lamp with the green shade. The doctor's coarse peasant-like face was gradually lighted up by a smile of delight and enthusiasm over the progress of the human intellect. Oh, why is not man immortal? he thought. What is the good of the brain centres and convolutions, what is the good of sight, speech, self-consciousness, genius, if it is all destined to depart into the soil, and in the end to grow cold together with the earth's crust, and then for millions of years to fly with the earth round the sun with no meaning and no object? To do that there was no need at all to draw man with his lofty, almost godlike intellect out of non-existence, and then, as though in mockery, to turn him into clay. The transmutation of substances! But what cowardice to comfort oneself with that cheap substitute for immortality! The unconscious processes that take place in nature are lower even than the stupidity of man, since in stupidity there is, anyway, consciousness and will, while in those processes there is absolutely nothing. Only the coward who has more fear of death than dignity can comfort himself with the fact that his body will in time live again in the grass, in the stones, in the toad. To find one's immortality in the transmutation of substances is as strange as to prophesy a brilliant future for the case after a precious violin has been broken and become useless.

When the clock struck, Andrey Yefimitch would sink back into his chair and close his eyes to think a little. And under the influence of the fine ideas of which he had been reading he would, unawares, recall his past and his present. The past was hateful -- better not to think of it. And it was the same in the present as in the past. He knew that at the very time when his thoughts were floating together with the cooling earth round the sun, in the main building beside his abode people were suffering in sickness and physical impurity: someone perhaps could not sleep and was making war upon the insects, someone was being infected by erysipelas, or moaning over too tight a bandage; perhaps the patients were playing cards with the nurses and drinking vodka. According to the yearly return, twelve thousand people had been deceived; the whole hospital rested as it had done twenty years ago on thieving, filth, scandals, gossip, on gross quackery, and, as before, it was an immoral institution extremely injurious to the health of the inhabitants. He knew that Nikita knocked the patients about behind the barred windows of Ward No. 6, and that Moiseika went about the town every day begging alms.

On the other hand, he knew very well that a magical change had taken place in medicine during the last twenty-five years. When he was studying at the university he had fancied that medicine would soon be overtaken by the fate of alchemy and metaphysics; but now when he was reading at night the science of medicine touched him and excited his wonder, and even enthusiasm. What unexpected brilliance, what a revolution! Thanks to the antiseptic system operations were performed such as the great Pirogov had considered impossible even *in spe*. Ordinary Zemstvo doctors were venturing to perform the resection of the kneecap; of abdominal operations only one per cent. was fatal; while stone was considered such a trifle that they did not even write about it. A radical cure for syphilis had been discovered. And the theory of heredity, hypnotism, the discoveries of Pasteur and of Koch, hygiene based on statistics, and the work of Zemstvo doctors!

Psychiatry with its modern classification of mental diseases, methods of diagnosis, and treatment, was a perfect Elborus in comparison with what had been in the past. They no longer poured cold water on the heads of lunatics nor put strait-waistcoats upon them; they treated them with humanity, and even, so it was stated in the papers, got up balls and entertainments for them. Andrey Yefimitch knew that with modern tastes and views such an abomination as Ward No. 6 was possible only a hundred and fifty miles from a railway in a little town where the mayor and all the town council were half-illiterate tradesmen who looked upon the doctor as an oracle who must be believed without any criticism even if he had poured molten lead into their mouths; in any other place the public and the newspapers would long ago have torn this little Bastille to pieces.

"But, after all, what of it?" Andrey Yefimitch would ask himself, opening his eyes. "There is the antiseptic system, there is Koch, there is Pasteur, but the essential reality is not altered a bit; ill-health and mortality are still the same. They get up balls and entertainments for the mad, but still they don't let them go free; so it's all nonsense and vanity, and there is no difference in reality between the best Vienna clinic and my hospital." But depression and a feeling akin to envy prevented him from feeling indifferent; it must have been owing to exhaustion. His heavy head sank on to the book, he put his hands under his face to make it softer, and thought: "I serve in a pernicious institution and receive a salary from people whom I am deceiving. I am not honest, but then, I of myself am nothing, I am only part of an inevitable social evil: all local officials are pernicious and receive their salary for doing nothing. . . . And so for my dishonesty it is not I who am to blame, but the times.... If I had been born two hundred years later I should have been different. . ."

When it struck three he would put out his lamp and go into his bedroom; he was not sleepy.

VIII

Two years before, the Zemstvo in a liberal mood had decided to allow three hundred roubles a year to pay for additional medical service in the town till the Zemstvo hospital should be opened, and the district doctor, Yevgeny Fyodoritch Hobotov, was invited to the town to assist Andrey Yefimitch. He was a very young man

-- not yet thirty -- tall and dark, with broad cheek-bones and little eyes; his forefathers had probably come from one of the many alien races of Russia. He arrived in the town without a farthing, with a small portmanteau, and a plain young woman whom he called his cook. This woman had a baby at the breast. Yevgeny Fyodoritch used to go about in a cap with a peak, and in high boots, and in the winter wore a sheepskin. He made great friends with Sergey Sergeyitch, the medical assistant, and with the treasurer, but held aloof from the other officials, and for some reason called them aristocrats. He had only one book in his lodgings, "The Latest Prescriptions of the Vienna Clinic for 1881." When he went to a patient he always took this book with him. He played billiards in the evening at the club: he did not like cards. He was very fond of using in conversation such expressions as "endless bobbery," "canting soft soap," "shut up with your finicking. . ."

He visited the hospital twice a week, made the round of the wards, and saw out-patients. The complete absence of antiseptic treatment and the cupping roused his indignation, but he did not introduce any new system, being afraid of offending Andrey Yefimitch. He regarded his colleague as a sly old rascal, suspected him of being a man of large means, and secretly envied him. He would have been very glad to have his post.

IX

On a spring evening towards the end of March, when there was no snow left on the ground and the starlings were singing in the hospital garden, the doctor went out to see his friend the postmaster as far as the gate. At that very moment the Jew Moiseika, returning with his booty, came into the yard. He had no cap on, and his bare feet were thrust into goloshes; in his hand he had a little bag of coppers.

"Give me a kopeck!" he said to the doctor, smiling, and shivering with cold. Andrey Yefimitch, who could never refuse anyone anything, gave him a ten-kopeck piece.

"How bad that is!" he thought, looking at the Jew's bare feet with their thin red ankles. "Why, it's wet."

And stirred by a feeling akin both to pity and disgust, he went into the lodge behind the Jew, looking now at his bald head, now at his ankles. As the doctor went in, Nikita jumped up from his heap of litter and stood at attention.

"Good-day, Nikita," Andrey Yefimitch said mildly. "That Jew should be provided with boots or something, he will catch cold."

"Certainly, your honour. I'll inform the superintendent."

"Please do; ask him in my name. Tell him that I asked."

The door into the ward was open. Ivan Dmitritch, lying propped on his elbow on the bed, listened in alarm to the unfamiliar voice, and suddenly recognized the doctor. He trembled all over with anger, jumped up, and with a red and wrathful face, with his eyes starting out of his head, ran out into the middle of the road.

"The doctor has come!" he shouted, and broke into a laugh. "At last! Gentlemen, I congratulate you. The doctor is honouring us with a visit! Cursed reptile!" he shrieked, and stamped in a frenzy such as had never been seen in the ward before. "Kill the reptile! No, killing's too good. Drown him in the midden-pit!"

Andrey Yefimitch, hearing this, looked into the ward from the entry and asked gently: "What for?"

"What for?" shouted Ivan Dmitritch, going up to him with a menacing air and convulsively wrapping himself in his dressing-gown. "What for? Thief!" he said with a look of repulsion, moving his lips as though he would spit at him. "Quack! hangman!"

"Calm yourself," said Andrey Yefimitch, smiling guiltily. "I assure you I have never stolen anything; and as to the rest, most likely you greatly exaggerate. I see you are angry with me. Calm yourself, I beg, if you can, and tell me coolly what are you angry for?"

"What are you keeping me here for?"

"Because you are ill."

"Yes, I am ill. But you know dozens, hundreds of madmen are walking about in freedom because your ignorance is incapable of distinguishing them from the sane. Why am I and these poor wretches to be shut up here like scapegoats for all the rest? You, your assistant, the superintendent, and all your hospital rabble, are immeasurably inferior to everyone of us morally; why then are we shut up and you not? Where's the logic of it?"

"Morality and logic don't come in, it all depends on chance. If anyone is shut up he has to stay, and if anyone is not shut up he can walk about, that's all. There is neither morality nor logic in my being a doctor and your being a mental patient, there is nothing but idle chance."

"That twaddle I don't understand. . ." Ivan Dmitritch brought out in a hollow voice, and he sat down on his bed.

Moiseika, whom Nikita did not venture to search in the presence of the doctor, laid out on his bed pieces of bread, bits of paper, and little bones, and, still shivering with cold, began rapidly in a singsong voice saying something in Yiddish. He most likely imagined that he had opened a shop.

"Let me out," said Ivan Dmitritch, and his voice quivered.

"I cannot."

"But why, why?"

"Because it is not in my power. Think, what use will it be to you if I do let you out? Go. The townspeople or the police will detain you or bring you back."

"Yes, yes, that's true," said Ivan Dmitritch, and he rubbed his forehead. "It's awful! But what am I to do, what?"

Andrey Yefimitch liked Ivan Dmitritch's voice and his intelligent young face with its grimaces. He longed to be kind to the young man and soothe him; he sat down on the bed beside him, thought, and said:

"You ask me what to do. The very best thing in your position would be to run away. But, unhappily, that is useless. You would be taken up. When society protects itself from the criminal, mentally deranged, or otherwise inconvenient people, it is invincible. There is only one thing left for you: to resign yourself to the thought that your presence here is inevitable."

"It is no use to anyone."

"So long as prisons and madhouses exist someone must be shut up in them. If not you, I. If not I, some third person. Wait till in the distant future prisons and madhouses no longer exist, and there will be neither bars on the windows nor hospital gowns. Of course, that time will come sooner or later."

Ivan Dmitritch smiled ironically.

"You are jesting," he said, screwing up his eyes. "Such gentlemen as you and your assistant Nikita have nothing to do with the future, but you may be sure, sir, better days will come! I may express myself cheaply, you may laugh, but the dawn of a new life is at hand; truth and justice will triumph, and -- our turn will come! I shall not live to see it, I shall perish, but some people's great-grandsons will see it. I greet them with all my heart and rejoice, rejoice with them! Onward! God be your help, friends!"

With shining eyes Ivan Dmitritch got up, and stretching his hands towards the window, went on with emotion in his voice:

"From behind these bars I bless you! Hurrah for truth and justice! I rejoice!"

"I see no particular reason to rejoice," said Andrey Yefimitch, who thought Ivan Dmitritch's movement theatrical, though he was delighted by it. "Prisons and madhouses there will not be, and truth, as you have just expressed it, will triumph; but the reality of things, you know, will not change, the laws of nature will still remain the same. People will suffer pain, grow old, and die just as they do now. However magnificent a dawn lighted up your life, you would yet in the end be nailed up in a coffin and thrown into a hole."

"And immortality?"

"Oh, come, now!"

"You don't believe in it, but I do. Somebody in Dostoevsky or Voltaire said that if there had not been a God men would have invented him. And I firmly believe that if there is no immortality the great intellect of man will sooner or later invent it."

"Well said," observed Andrey Yefimitch, smiling with pleasure; its a good thing you have faith. With such a belief one may live happily even shut up within walls. You have studied somewhere, I presume?"

"Yes, I have been at the university, but did not complete my studies."

"You are a reflecting and a thoughtful man. In any surroundings you can find tranquillity in yourself. Free and deep thinking which strives for the comprehension of life, and complete contempt for the foolish bustle of the world -- those are two blessings beyond any that man has ever known. And you can possess them even though you lived behind threefold bars. Diogenes lived in a tub, yet he was happier than all the kings of the earth."

"Your Diogenes was a blockhead," said Ivan Dmitritch morosely. "Why do you talk to me about Diogenes and some foolish comprehension of life?" he cried, growing suddenly angry and leaping up. "I love life; I love it passionately. I have the mania of persecution, a continual agonizing terror; but I have moments when I am overwhelmed by the thirst for life, and then I am afraid of going mad. I want dreadfully to live, dreadfully!"

He walked up and down the ward in agitation, and said, dropping his voice:

"When I dream I am haunted by phantoms. People come to me, I hear voices and music, and I fancy I am walking through woods or by the seashore, and I long so passionately for movement, for interests. . . . Come, tell me, what news is there?" asked Ivan Dmitritch; "what's happening?"

"Do you wish to know about the town or in general?"

"Well, tell me first about the town, and then in general."

"Well, in the town it is appallingly dull. . . . There's no one to say a word to, no one to listen to. There are no new people. A young doctor called Hobotov has come here recently."

"He had come in my time. Well, he is a low cad, isn't he?"

"Yes, he is a man of no culture. It's strange, you know. . . . Judging by every sign, there is no intellectual stagnation in our capital cities; there is a movement -- so there must be real people there too; but for some reason they always send us such men as I would rather not see. It's an unlucky town!"

"Yes, it is an unlucky town," sighed Ivan Dmitritch, and he laughed. "And how are things in general? What are they writing in the papers and reviews?"

It was by now dark in the ward. The doctor got up, and, standing, began to describe what was being written abroad and in Russia, and the tendency of thought that could be noticed now. Ivan Dmitritch listened attentively and put questions, but suddenly, as though recalling something terrible, clutched at his head and lay down on the bed with his back to the doctor.

"What's the matter?" asked Andrey Yefimitch.

"You will not hear another word from me," said Ivan Dmitritch rudely. "Leave me alone."

"Why so?"

"I tell you, leave me alone. Why the devil do you persist?"

Andrey Yefimitch shrugged his shoulders, heaved a sigh, and went out. As he crossed the entry he said: "You might clear up here, Nikita . . . there's an awfully stuffy smell."

"Certainly, your honour."

"What an agreeable young man!" thought Andrey Yefimitch, going back to his flat. "In all the years I have been living here I do believe he is the first I have met with whom one can talk. He is capable of reasoning and is interested in just the right things."

While he was reading, and afterwards, while he was going to bed, he kept thinking about Ivan Dmitritch, and when he woke next morning he remembered that he had the day before made the acquaintance of an intelligent and interesting man, and determined to visit him again as soon as possible.

X

Ivan Dmitritch was lying in the same position as on the previous day, with his head clutched in both hands and his legs drawn up. His face was not visible.

"Good-day, my friend," said Andrey Yefimitch. "You are not asleep, are you?"

"In the first place, I am not your friend," Ivan Dmitritch articulated into the pillow; "and in the second, your efforts are useless; you will not get one word out of me."

"Strange," muttered Andrey Yefimitch in confusion. "Yesterday we talked peacefully, but suddenly for some reason you took offence and broke off all at once. . . . Probably I expressed myself awkwardly, or perhaps gave utterance to some idea which did not fit in with your convictions. . . ."

"Yes, a likely idea!" said Ivan Dmitritch, sitting up and looking at the doctor with irony and uneasiness. His eyes were red. "You can go and spy and probe somewhere else, it's no use your doing it here. I knew yesterday what you had come for."

"A strange fancy," laughed the doctor. "So you suppose me to be a spy?"

"Yes, I do. . . . A spy or a doctor who has been charged to test me -- it's all the same ---"

"Oh excuse me, what a queer fellow you are really!"

The doctor sat down on the stool near the bed and shook his head reproachfully.

"But let us suppose you are right," he said, "let us suppose that I am treacherously trying to trap you into saying something so as to betray you to the police. You would be arrested and then tried. But would you be any worse off being tried and in prison than you are here? If you are banished to a settlement, or even sent to penal servitude, would it be worse than being shut up in this ward? I imagine it would be no worse. . . . What, then, are you afraid of?"

These words evidently had an effect on Ivan Dmitritch. He sat down quietly.

It was between four and five in the afternoon -- the time when Andrey Yefimitch usually walked up and down his rooms, and Daryushka asked whether it was not time for his beer. It was a still, bright day.

"I came out for a walk after dinner, and here I have come, as you see," said the doctor. "It is quite spring."

"What month is it? March?" asked Ivan Dmitritch.

"Yes, the end of March."

"Is it very muddy?"

"No, not very. There are already paths in the garden."

"It would be nice now to drive in an open carriage somewhere into the country," said Ivan Dmitritch, rubbing his red eyes as though he were just awake, "then to come home to a warm, snug study, and . . . and to have a decent doctor to cure one's headache. . . . It's so long since I have lived like a human being. It's disgusting here! Insufferably disgusting!"

After his excitement of the previous day he was exhausted and listless, and spoke unwillingly. His fingers twitched, and from his face it could be seen that he had a splitting headache.

"There is no real difference between a warm, snug study and this ward," said Andrey Yefimitch. "A man's peace and contentment do not lie outside a man, but in himself."

"What do you mean?"

"The ordinary man looks for good and evil in external things -- that is, in carriages, in studies -- but a thinking man looks for it in himself."

"You should go and preach that philosophy in Greece, where it's warm and fragrant with the scent of pomegranates, but here it is not suited to the climate. With whom was it I was talking of Diogenes? Was it with you?"

"Yes, with me yesterday."

"Diogenes did not need a study or a warm habitation; it's hot there without. You can lie in your tub and eat oranges and olives. But bring him to Russia to live: he'd be begging to be let indoors in May, let alone December. He'd be doubled up with the cold."

"No. One can be insensible to cold as to every other pain. Marcus Aurelius says: 'A pain is a vivid idea of pain; make an effort of will to change that idea, dismiss it, cease to complain, and the pain will disappear.' That is true. The wise man, or simply the reflecting, thoughtful man, is distinguished precisely by his contempt for suffering; he is always contented and surprised at nothing."

"Then I am an idiot, since I suffer and am discontented and surprised at the baseness of mankind."

"You are wrong in that; if you will reflect more on the subject you will understand how insignificant is all that external world that agitates us. One must strive for the comprehension of life, and in that is true happiness."

"Comprehension . . ." repeated Ivan Dmitritch frowning. "External, internal. . . . Excuse me, but I don t understand it. I only know," he said, getting up and looking angrily at the doctor -- "I only know that God has created me of warm blood and nerves, yes, indeed! If organic tissue is capable of life it must react to every stimulus. And I do! To pain I respond with tears and outcries, to baseness with indignation, to filth with loathing. To my mind, that is just what is called life. The lower the organism, the less sensitive it is, and the more feebly it reacts to stimulus; and the higher it is, the more responsively and vigorously it reacts to reality. How is it you don't know that? A doctor, and not know such trifles! To despise suffering, to be always contented, and to be surprised at nothing, one must reach this condition" -- and Ivan Dmitritch pointed to the peasant who was a mass of fat -- "or to harden oneself by suffering to such a point that one loses all sensibility to it -- that is, in other words, to cease to live. You must excuse me, I am not a sage or a philosopher," Ivan Dmitritch continued with irritation, "and I don't understand anything about it. I am not capable of reasoning."

"On the contrary, your reasoning is excellent."

"The Stoics, whom you are parodying, were remarkable people, but their doctrine crystallized two thousand years ago and has not advanced, and will not advance, an inch forward, since it is not practical or living. It had a success only with the minority which spends its life in savouring all sorts of theories and ruminating over them; the majority did not understand it. A doctrine which advocates indifference to wealth and to the comforts of life, and a contempt for suffering and death, is quite unintelligible to the vast majority of men, since that majority has never known wealth or the comforts of life; and to despise suffering would mean to it despising life itself, since the whole existence of man is made up of the sensations of hunger, cold, injury, and a Hamlet-like dread of death. The whole of life lies in these sensations; one may be oppressed by it, one may hate it, but one cannot despise it. Yes, so, I repeat, the doctrine of the Stoics can never have a future; from the beginning of time up to to-day you see continually increasing the struggle, the sensibility to pain, the capacity of responding to stimulus."

Ivan Dmitritch suddenly lost the thread of his thoughts, stopped, and rubbed his forehead with vexation.

"I meant to say something important, but I have lost it," he said. "What was I saying? Oh, yes! This is what I mean: one of the Stoics sold himself into slavery to redeem his neighbour, so, you see, even a Stoic did react to stimulus, since, for such a generous act as the destruction of oneself for the sake of one's neighbour, he must have had a soul capable of pity and indignation. Here in prison I have forgotten everything I have learned, or else I could have recalled something else. Take Christ, for instance: Christ responded to reality by weeping, smiling, being sorrowful and moved to wrath, even overcome by misery. He did not go to meet His sufferings with a smile, He did not despise death, but prayed in the Garden of Gethsemane that this cup might pass Him by."

Ivan Dmitritch laughed and sat down.

"Granted that a man's peace and contentment lie not outside but in himself," he said, "granted that one must despise suffering and not be surprised at anything, yet on what ground do you preach the theory? Are you a sage? A philosopher?"

"No, I am not a philosopher, but everyone ought to preach it because it is reasonable."

"No, I want to know how it is that you consider yourself competent to judge of 'comprehension,' contempt for suffering, and so on. Have you ever suffered? Have you any idea of suffering? Allow me to ask you, were you ever thrashed in your childhood?"

"No, my parents had an aversion for corporal punishment."

"My father used to flog me cruelly; my father was a harsh, sickly Government clerk with a long nose and a yellow neck. But let us talk of you. No one has laid a finger on you all your life, no one has scared you nor beaten you; you are as strong as a bull. You grew up under your father's wing and studied at his expense, and then you dropped at once into a sinecure. For more than twenty years you have lived rent free with heating, lighting, and service all provided, and had the right to work how you pleased and as much as you pleased, even to do nothing. You were naturally a flabby, lazy man, and so you have tried to arrange your life so that nothing should disturb you or make you move. You have handed over your work to the assistant and the rest of the rabble while you sit in peace and warmth, save money, read, amuse yourself with reflections, with all sorts of lofty nonsense, and" (Ivan Dmitritch looked at the doctor's red nose) "with boozing; in fact, you have seen nothing of life, you know absolutely nothing of it, and are only theoretically acquainted with reality; you despise suffering and are surprised at nothing for a very simple reason: vanity of vanities, the external and the internal, contempt for life, for suffering and for death, comprehension, true happiness -- that's the philosophy that suits the Russian sluggard best. You see a peasant beating his wife, for instance. Why interfere? Let him beat her, they will both die sooner or later, anyway; and, besides, he who beats injures by his blows, not the person he is beating, but himself. To get drunk is stupid and unseemly, but if you drink you die, and if you don't drink you die. A peasant woman comes with toothache . . . well, what of it? Pain is the idea of pain, and besides 'there is no living in this world without illness; we shall all die, and so, go away, woman, don't hinder me from thinking and drinking vodka.' A young man asks advice, what he is to do, how he is to live; anyone else would think before answering, but you have got the answer ready: strive for 'comprehension' or for true happiness. And what is that fantastic 'true happiness'? There's no answer, of course. We are kept here behind barred windows, tortured, left to rot; but that is very good and reasonable, because there is no difference at all between this ward and a warm, snug study. A convenient philosophy. You can do nothing, and your conscience is clear, and you feel you are wise. . . . No, sir, it is not philosophy, it's not thinking, it's not breadth of vision, but laziness, fakirism, drowsy stupefaction. Yes," cried Ivan Dmitritch, getting angry again, "you despise suffering, but I'll be bound if you pinch your finger in the door you will howl at the top of your voice."

"And perhaps I shouldn't howl," said Andrey Yefimitch, with a gentle smile.

"Oh, I dare say! Well, if you had a stroke of paralysis, or supposing some fool or bully took advantage of his position and rank to insult you in public, and if you knew he could do it with impunity, then you would understand what it means to put people off with comprehension and true happiness."

"That's original," said Andrey Yefimitch, laughing with pleasure and rubbing his hands. "I am agreeably struck by your inclination for drawing generalizations, and the sketch of my character you have just drawn is simply brilliant. I must confess that talking to you gives me great pleasure. Well, I've listened to you, and now you must graciously listen to me."

XI

The conversation went on for about an hour longer, and apparently made a deep impression on Andrey Yefimitch. He began going to the ward every day. He went there in the mornings and after dinner, and often the dusk of evening found him in conversation with Ivan Dmitritch. At first Ivan Dmitritch held aloof from him, suspected him of evil designs, and openly expressed his hostility. But afterwards he got used to him, and his abrupt manner changed to one of condescending irony.

Soon it was all over the hospital that the doctor, Andrey Yefimitch, had taken to visiting Ward No. 6. No one -- neither Sergey Sergevitch, nor Nikita, nor the nurses -- could conceive why he went there, why he stayed there for hours together, what he was talking about, and why he did not write prescriptions. His actions seemed strange. Often Mihail Averyanitch did not find him at home, which had never happened in the past, and Daryushka was greatly perturbed, for the doctor drank his beer now at no definite time, and sometimes was even late for dinner.

One day -- it was at the end of June -- Dr. Hobotov went to see Andrey Yefimitch about something. Not finding him at home, he proceeded to look for him in the yard; there he was told that the old doctor had gone to see the mental patients. Going into the lodge and stopping in the entry, Hobotov heard the following conversation:

"We shall never agree, and you will not succeed in converting me to your faith," Ivan Dmitritch was saying irritably; "you are utterly ignorant of reality, and you have never known suffering, but have only like a leech fed beside the sufferings of others, while I have been in continual suffering from the day of my birth till to-day. For that reason, I tell you frankly, I consider myself superior to you and more competent in every respect. It's not for you to teach me."

"I have absolutely no ambition to convert you to my faith," said Andrey Yefimitch gently, and with regret that the other refused to understand him. "And that is not what matters, my friend; what matters is not that you have suffered and I have not. Joy and suffering are passing; let us leave them, never mind them. What matters is that you and I think; we see in each other people who are capable of thinking and reasoning, and that is a common bond between us however different our views. If you knew, my friend, how sick I am of the universal senselessness, ineptitude, stupidity, and with what delight I always talk with you! You are an intelligent man, and I enjoyed your company."

Hobotov opened the door an inch and glanced into the ward; Ivan Dmitritch in his night-cap and the doctor Andrey Yefimitch were sitting side by side on the bed. The madman was grimacing, twitching, and convulsively wrapping himself in his gown, while the doctor sat motionless with bowed head, and his face was red and look helpless and sorrowful. Hobotov shrugged his shoulders, grinned, and glanced at Nikita. Nikita shrugged his shoulders too.

Next day Hobotov went to the lodge, accompanied by the assistant. Both stood in the entry and listened.

"I fancy our old man has gone clean off his chump!" said Hobotov as he came out of the lodge.

"Lord have mercy upon us sinners!" sighed the decorous Sergey Sergeyitch, scrupulously avoiding the puddles that he might not muddy his polished boots. "I must own, honoured Yevgeny Fyodoritch, I have been expecting it for a long time."

XII

After this Andrey Yefimitch began to notice a mysterious air in all around him. The attendants, the nurses, and the patients looked at him inquisitively when they met him, and then whispered together. The superintendent's little daughter Masha, whom he liked to meet in the hospital garden, for some reason ran away from him now when he went up with a smile to stroke her on the head. The postmaster no longer said, "Perfectly true," as he listened to him, but in unaccountable confusion muttered, "Yes, yes, yes . . ." and looked at him with a grieved and thoughtful expression; for some reason he took to advising his friend to give up vodka and beer, but as a man of delicate feeling he did not say this directly, but hinted it, telling him first about the commanding officer of his battalion, an excellent man, and then about the priest of the regiment, a capital fellow, both of whom drank and fell ill, but on giving up drinking completely regained their health. On two or three occasions Andrey Yefimitch was visited by his colleague Hobotov, who also advised him to give up spirituous liquors, and for no apparent reason recommended him to take bromide.

In August Andrey Yefimitch got a letter from the mayor of the town asking him to come on very important business. On arriving at the town hall at the time fixed, Andrey Yefimitch found there the military commander, the superintendent of the district school, a member of the town council, Hobotov, and a plump, fair gentleman who was introduced to him as a doctor. This doctor, with a Polish surname difficult to pronounce, lived at a pedigree stud-farm twenty miles away, and was now on a visit to the town.

"There's something that concerns you," said the member of the town council, addressing Andrey Yefimitch after they had all greeted one another and sat down to the table. "Here Yevgeny Fyodoritch says that there is not room for the dispensary in the main building, and that it ought to be transferred to one of the lodges. That's of no consequence -- of course it can be transferred, but the point is that the lodge wants doing up."

"Yes, it would have to be done up," said Andrey Yefimitch after a moment's thought. "If the corner lodge, for instance, were fitted up as a dispensary, I imagine it would cost at least five hundred roubles. An unproductive expenditure!"

Everyone was silent for a space.

"I had the honour of submitting to you ten years ago," Andrey Yefimitch went on in a low voice, "that the hospital in its present form is a luxury for the town beyond its means. It was built in the forties, but things were different then. The town spends too much on unnecessary buildings and superfluous staff. I believe with a different system two model hospitals might be maintained for the same money."

"Well, let us have a different system, then!" the member of the town council said briskly.

"I have already had the honour of submitting to you that the medical department should be transferred to the supervision of the Zemstvo."

"Yes, transfer the money to the Zemstvo and they will steal it," laughed the fair-haired doctor.

"That's what it always comes to," the member of the council assented, and he also laughed.

Andrey Yefimitch looked with apathetic, lustreless eyes at the fair-haired doctor and said: "One should be just."

Again there was silence. Tea was brought in. The military commander, for some reason much embarrassed, touched Andrey Yefimitch's hand across the table and said: "You have quite forgotten us, doctor. But of course you are a hermit: you don't play cards and don't like women. You would be dull with fellows like us."

They all began saying how boring it was for a decent person to live in such a town. No theatre, no music, and at the last dance at the club there had been about twenty ladies and only two gentlemen. The young men did not dance, but spent all the time crowding round the refreshment bar or playing cards.

Not looking at anyone and speaking slowly in a low voice, Andrey Yefimitch began saying what a pity, what a terrible pity it was that the townspeople should waste their vital energy, their hearts, and their minds on cards and gossip, and should have neither the power nor the inclination to spend their time in interesting conversation and reading, and should refuse to take advantage of the enjoyments of the mind. The mind alone was interesting and worthy of attention, all the rest was low and petty. Hobotov listened to his colleague attentively and suddenly asked:

"Andrey Yefimitch, what day of the month is it?"

Having received an answer, the fair-haired doctor and he, in the tone of examiners conscious of their lack of skill, began asking Andrey Yefimitch what was the day of the week, how many days there were in the year, and whether it was true that there was a remarkable prophet living in Ward No. 6.

In response to the last question Andrey Yefimitch turned rather red and said: "Yes, he is mentally deranged, but he is an interesting young man."

They asked him no other questions.

When he was putting on his overcoat in the entry, the military commander laid a hand on his shoulder and said with a sigh:

"It's time for us old fellows to rest!"

As he came out of the hall, Andrey Yefimitch understood that it had been a committee appointed to enquire into his mental condition. He recalled the questions that had been asked him, flushed crimson, and for some reason, for the first time in his life, felt bitterly grieved for medical science.

"My God. . ." he thought, remembering how these doctors had just examined him; "why, they have only lately been hearing lectures on mental pathology; they had passed an examination -- what's the explanation of this crass ignorance? They have not a conception of mental pathology!"

And for the first time in his life he felt insulted and moved to anger.

In the evening of the same day Mihail Averyanitch came to see him. The postmaster went up to him without waiting to greet him, took him by both hands, and said in an agitated voice:

"My dear fellow, my dear friend, show me that you believe in my genuine affection and look on me as your friend!" And preventing Andrey Yefimitch from speaking, he went on, growing excited: "I love you for your culture and nobility of soul. Listen to me, my dear fellow. The rules of their profession compel the doctors to conceal the truth from you, but I blurt out the plain truth like a soldier. You are not well! Excuse me, my dear fellow, but it is the truth; everyone about you has been noticing it for a long time. Dr. Yevgeny Fyodoritch has just told me that it is essential for you to rest and distract your mind for the sake of your health. Perfectly true! Excellent! In a day or two I am taking a holiday and am going away for a sniff of a different atmosphere. Show that you are a friend to me, let us go together! Let us go for a jaunt as in the good old days."

"I feel perfectly well," said Andrey Yefimitch after a moment's thought. "I can't go away. Allow me to show you my friendship in some other way."

To go off with no object, without his books, without his Daryushka, without his beer, to break abruptly through the routine of life, established for twenty years -- the idea for the first minute struck him as wild and fantastic, but he remembered the conversation at the Zemstvo committee and the depressing feelings with which he had returned home, and the thought of a brief absence from the town in which stupid people looked on him as a madman was pleasant to him.

"And where precisely do you intend to go?" he asked.

"To Moscow, to Petersburg, to Warsaw. . . . I spent the five happiest years of my life in Warsaw. What a marvellous town! Let us go, my dear fellow!"

XIII

A week later it was suggested to Andrey Yefimitch that he should have a rest -- that is, send in his resignation -- a suggestion he received with indifference, and a week later still, Mihail Averyanitch and he were sitting in a posting carriage driving to the nearest railway station. The days were cool and bright, with a blue sky and a transparent distance. They were two days driving the hundred and fifty miles to the railway station, and stayed two nights on the way. When at the posting station the glasses given them for their tea had not been properly washed, or the drivers were slow in harnessing the horses, Mihail Averyanitch would turn crimson, and quivering all over would shout:

"Hold your tongue! Don't argue!"

And in the carriage he talked without ceasing for a moment, describing his campaigns in the Caucasus and in Poland. What adventures he had had, what meetings! He talked loudly and opened his eyes so wide with wonder that he might well be thought to be lying. Moreover, as he talked he breathed in Andrey Yefimitch's face and laughed into his ear. This bothered the doctor and prevented him from thinking or concentrating his mind.

In the train they travelled, from motives of economy, third-class in a non-smoking compartment. Half the passengers were decent people. Mihail Averyanitch soon made friends with everyone, and moving from one seat to another, kept saying loudly that they ought not to travel by these appalling lines. It was a regular swindle! A very different thing riding on a good horse: one could do over seventy miles a day and feel fresh and well after it. And our bad harvests were due to the draining of the Pinsk marshes; altogether, the way things were done was dreadful. He got excited, talked loudly, and would not let others speak. This endless chatter to the accompaniment of loud laughter and expressive gestures wearied Andrey Yefimitch.

"Which of us is the madman?" he thought with vexation. "I, who try not to disturb my fellow-passengers in any way, or this egoist who thinks that he is cleverer and more interesting than anyone here, and so will leave no one in peace?"

In Moscow Mihail Averyanitch put on a military coat without epaulettes and trousers with red braid on them. He wore a military cap and overcoat in the street, and soldiers saluted him. It seemed to Andrey Yefimitch, now, that his companion was a man who had flung away all that was good and kept only what was bad of all the characteristics of a country gentleman that he had once possessed. He liked to be waited on even when it was quite unnecessary. The matches would be lying before him on the table, and he would see them and shout to the waiter to give him the matches; he did not hesitate to appear before a maidservant in nothing but his underclothes; he used the familiar mode of address to all footmen indiscriminately, even old men, and when he was angry called them fools and blockheads. This, Andrey Yefimitch thought, was like a gentleman, but disgusting.

First of all Mihail Averyanitch led his friend to the Iversky Madonna. He prayed fervently, shedding tears and bowing down to the earth, and when he had finished, heaved a deep sigh and said:

"Even though one does not believe it makes one somehow easier when one prays a little. Kiss the ikon, my dear fellow."

Andrey Yefimitch was embarrassed and he kissed the image, while Mihail Averyanitch pursed up his lips and prayed in a whisper, and again tears came into his eyes. Then they went to the Kremlin and looked there at theTsar-cannon and the Tsar-bell, and even touched them with their fingers, admired the view over the river, visited St. Saviour's and the Rumyantsev museum.

They dined at Tyestov's. Mihail Averyanitch looked a long time at the menu, stroking his whiskers, and said in the tone of a gourmand accustomed to dine in restaurants:

"We shall see what you give us to eat to-day, angel!"

XIV

The doctor walked about, looked at things, ate and drank, but he had all the while one feeling: annoyance with Mihail Averyanitch. He longed to have a rest from his friend, to get away from him, to hide himself, while the friend thought it was his duty not to let the doctor move a step away from him, and to provide him with as many distractions as possible. When there was nothing to look at he entertained him with conversation. For two days Andrey Yefimitch endured it, but on the third he announced to his friend that he was ill and wanted to stay at home for the whole day; his friend replied that in that case he would stay too -- that really he needed rest, for he was run off his legs already. Andrey Yefimitch lay on the sofa, with his face to the back, and clenching his teeth, listened to his friend, who assured him with heat that sooner or later France would certainly thrash Germany, that there were a great many scoundrels in Moscow, and that it was impossible to judge of a horse's quality by its outward appearance. The doctor began to have a buzzing in his ears and palpitations of the heart, but out of delicacy could not bring himself to beg his friend to go away or hold his tongue. Fortunately Mihail Averyanitch grew weary of sitting in the hotel room, and after dinner he went out for a walk.

As soon as he was alone Andrey Yefimitch abandoned himself to a feeling of relief. How pleasant to lie motionless on the sofa and to know that one is alone in the room! Real happiness is impossible without solitude. The fallen angel betrayed God probably because he longed for solitude, of which the angels know nothing. Andrey Yefimitch wanted to think about what he had seen and heard during the last few days, but he could not get Mihail Averyanitch out of his head.

"Why, he has taken a holiday and come with me out of friendship, out of generosity," thought the doctor with vexation; "nothing could be worse than this friendly supervision. I suppose he is good-natured and generous and a lively fellow, but he is a bore. An insufferable bore. In the same way there are people who never say anything but what is clever and good, yet one feels that they are dull-witted people."

For the following days Andrey Yefimitch declared himself ill and would not leave the hotel room; he lay with his face to the back of the sofa, and suffered agonies of weariness when his friend entertained him with conversation, or rested when his friend was absent. He was vexed with himself for having come, and with his friend, who grew every day more talkative and more free-and-easy; he could not succeed in attuning his thoughts to a serious and lofty level.

"This is what I get from the real life Ivan Dmitritch talked about," he thought, angry at his own pettiness. "It's of no consequence, though. . . . I shall go home, and everything will go on as before. . . ."

It was the same thing in Petersburg too; for whole days together he did not leave the hotel room, but lay on the sofa and only got up to drink beer.

Mihail Averyanitch was all haste to get to Warsaw.

"My dear man, what should I go there for?" said Andrey Yefimitch in an imploring voice. "You go alone and let me get home! I entreat you!"

"On no account," protested Mihail Averyanitch. "It's a marvellous town."

Andrey Yefimitch had not the strength of will to insist on his own way, and much against his inclination went to Warsaw. There he did not leave the hotel room, but lay on the sofa, furious with himself, with his friend, and with the waiters, who obstinately refused to understand Russian; while Mihail Averyanitch, healthy, hearty, and full of spirits as usual, went about the town from morning to night, looking for his old acquaintances. Several times he did not return home at night. After one night spent in some unknown haunt he returned home early in the morning, in a violently excited condition, with a red face and tousled hair. For a long time he walked up and down the rooms muttering something to himself, then stopped and said:

"Honour before everything."

After walking up and down a little longer he clutched his head in both hands and pronounced in a tragic voice: "Yes, honour before everything! Accursed be the moment when the idea first entered my head to visit this Babylon! My dear friend," he added, addressing the doctor, "you may despise me, I have played and lost; lend me five hundred roubles!"

Andrey Yefimitch counted out five hundred roubles and gave them to his friend without a word. The latter, still crimson with shame and anger, incoherently articulated some useless vow, put on his cap, and went out. Returning two hours later he flopped into an easy-chair, heaved a loud sigh, and said:

"My honour is saved. Let us go, my friend; I do not care to remain another hour in this accursed town. Scoundrels! Austrian spies!"

By the time the friends were back in their own town it was November, and deep snow was lying in the streets. Dr. Hobotov had Andrey Yefimitch's post; he was still living in his old lodgings, waiting for Andrey Yefimitch to arrive and clear out of the hospital apartments. The plain woman whom he called his cook was already established in one of the lodges.

Fresh scandals about the hospital were going the round of the town. It was said that the plain woman had quarrelled with the superintendent, and that the latter had crawled on his knees before her begging forgiveness. On the very first day he arrived Andrey Yefimitch had to look out for lodgings.

"My friend," the postmaster said to him timidly, "excuse an indiscreet question: what means have you at your disposal?"

Andrey Yefimitch, without a word, counted out his money and said: "Eighty-six roubles."

"I don't mean that," Mihail Averyanitch brought out in confusion, misunderstanding him; "I mean, what have you to live on?"

"I tell you, eighty-six roubles . . . I have nothing else."

Mihail Averyanitch looked upon the doctor as an honourable man, yet he suspected that he had accumulated a fortune of at least twenty thousand. Now learning that Andrey Yefimitch was a beggar, that he had nothing to live on he was for some reason suddenly moved to tears and embraced his friend.

XV

Andrey Yefimitch now lodged in a little house with three windows. There were only three rooms besides the kitchen in the little house. The doctor lived in two of them which looked into the street, while Daryushka and the landlady with her three children lived in the third room and the kitchen. Sometimes the landlady's lover, a drunken peasant who was rowdy and reduced the children and Daryushka to terror, would come for the night. When he arrived and established himself in the kitchen and demanded vodka, they all felt very uncomfortable, and the doctor would be moved by pity to take the crying children into his room and let them lie on his floor, and this gave him great satisfaction.

He got up as before at eight o'clock, and after his morning tea sat down to read his old books and magazines: he had no money for new ones. Either because the books were old, or perhaps because of the change in his surroundings, reading exhausted him, and did not grip his attention as before. That he might not spend his time in idleness he made a detailed catalogue of his books and gummed little labels on their backs, and this mechanical, tedious work seemed to him more interesting than reading. The monotonous, tedious work lulled his thoughts to sleep in some unaccountable way, and the time passed quickly while he thought of nothing. Even sitting in the kitchen, peeling potatoes with Daryushka or picking over the buckwheat grain, seemed to him interesting. On Saturdays and Sundays he went to church. Standing near the wall and half closing his eyes, he listened to the singing and thought of his father, of his mother, of the university, of the religions of the world; he felt calm and melancholy, and as he went out of the church afterwards he regretted that the service was so soon over. He went twice to the hospital to talk to Ivan Dmitritch. But on both occasions Ivan Dmitritch was unusually excited and ill-humoured; he bade the doctor leave him in peace, as he had long been sick of empty chatter, and declared, to make up for all his sufferings, he asked from the damned scoundrels only one favour -- solitary confinement. Surely they would not refuse him even that? On both occasions when Andrey Yefimitch was taking leave of him and wishing him good-night, he answered rudely and said:

"Go to hell!"

And Andrey Yefimitch did not know now whether to go to him for the third time or not. He longed to go.

In old days Andrey Yefimitch used to walk about his rooms and think in the interval after dinner, but now from dinner-time till evening tea he lay on the sofa with his face to the back and gave himself up to trivial thoughts which he could not struggle against. He was mortified that after more than twenty years of service he had been given neither a pension nor any assistance. It is true that he had not done his work honestly, but, then, all who are in the Service get a pension without distinction whether they are honest or not. Contemporary justice lies precisely in the bestowal of grades, orders, and pensions, not for moral qualities or capacities, but for service whatever it may have been like. Why was he alone to be an exception? He had no money at all. He was ashamed to pass by the shop and look at the woman who owned it. He owed thirty-two roubles for beer already. There was money owing to the landlady also. Daryushka sold old clothes and books on the sly, and told lies to the landlady, saying that the doctor was just going to receive a large sum of money.

He was angry with himself for having wasted on travelling the thousand roubles he had saved up. How useful that thousand roubles would have been now! He was vexed that people would not leave him in peace. Hobotov thought it his duty to look in on his sick colleague from time to time. Everything about him was revolting to Andrey Yefimitch -- his well-fed face and vulgar, condescending tone, and his use of the word "colleague," and his high top-boots; the most revolting thing was that he thought it was his duty to treat Andrey Yefimitch, and thought that he really was treating him. On every visit he brought a bottle of bromide and rhubarb pills.

Mihail Averyanitch, too, thought it his duty to visit his friend and entertain him. Every time he went in to Andrey Yefimitch with an affectation of ease, laughed constrainedly, and began assuring him that he was looking very well to-day, and that, thank God, he was on the highroad to recovery, and from this it might be concluded that he looked on his friend's condition as hopeless. He had not yet repaid his Warsaw debt, and was overwhelmed by shame; he was constrained, and so tried to laugh louder and talk more amusingly. His anecdotes and descriptions seemed endless now, and were an agony both to Andrey Yefimitch and himself.

In his presence Andrey Yefimitch usually lay on the sofa with his face to the wall, and listened with his teeth clenched; his soul was oppressed with rankling disgust, and after every visit from his friend he felt as though this disgust had risen higher, and was mounting into his throat.

To stifle petty thoughts he made haste to reflect that he himself, and Hobotov, and Mihail Averyanitch, would all sooner or later perish without leaving any trace on the world. If one imagined some spirit flying by the earthly globe in space in a million years he would see nothing but clay and bare rocks. Everything -- culture and the moral law -- would pass away and not even a burdock would grow out of them. Of what consequence was shame in the presence of a shopkeeper, of what consequence was the insignificant Hobotov or the wearisome friendship of Mihail Averyanitch? It was all trivial and nonsensical.

But such reflections did not help him now. Scarcely had he imagined the earthly globe in a million years, when Hobotov in his high top-boots or Mihail Averyanitch with his forced laugh would appear from behind a bare rock, and he even heard the shamefaced whisper: "The Warsaw debt. . . . I will repay it in a day or two, my dear fellow, without fail. . . ."

XVI

One day Mihail Averyanitch came after dinner when Andrey Yefimitch was lying on the sofa. It so happened that Hobotov arrived at the same time with his bromide. Andrey Yefimitch got up heavily and sat down, leaning both arms on the sofa.

"You have a much better colour to-day than you had yesterday, my dear man," began Mihail Averyanitch. "Yes, you look jolly. Upon my soul, you do!"

"It's high time you were well, dear colleague," said Hobotov, yawning. "I'll be bound, you are sick of this bobbery."

"And we shall recover," said Mihail Averyanitch cheerfully. "We shall live another hundred years! To be sure!"

"Not a hundred years, but another twenty," Hobotov said reassuringly. "It's all right, all right, colleague; don't lose heart. . . . Don't go piling it on!"

"We'll show what we can do," laughed Mihail Averyanitch, and he slapped his friend on the knee. "We'll show them yet! Next summer, please God, we shall be off to the Caucasus, and we will ride all over it on horseback -- trot, trot, trot! And when we are back from the Caucasus I shouldn't wonder if we will all dance at the wedding." Mihail Averyanitch gave a sly wink. "We'll marry you, my dear boy, we'll marry you. . . ."

Andrey Yefimitch felt suddenly that the rising disgust had mounted to his throat, his heart began beating violently.

"That's vulgar," he said, getting up quickly and walking away to the window. "Don't you understand that you are talking vulgar nonsense?"

He meant to go on softly and politely, but against his will he suddenly clenched his fists and raised them above his head.

"Leave me alone," he shouted in a voice unlike his own, blushing crimson and shaking all over. "Go away, both of you!"

Mihail Averyanitch and Hobotov got up and stared at him first with amazement and then with alarm.

"Go away, both!" Andrey Yefimitch went on shouting. "Stupid people! Foolish people! I don't want either your friendship or your medicines, stupid man! Vulgar! Nasty!"

Hobotov and Mihail Averyanitch, looking at each other in bewilderment, staggered to the door and went out. Andrey Yefimitch snatched up the bottle of bromide and flung it after them; the bottle broke with a crash on the door-frame.

"Go to the devil!" he shouted in a tearful voice, running out into the passage. "To the devil!"

When his guests were gone Andrey Yefimitch lay down on the sofa, trembling as though in a fever, and went on for a long while repeating: "Stupid people! Foolish people!"

When he was calmer, what occurred to him first of all was the thought that poor Mihail Averyanitch must be feeling fearfully ashamed and depressed now, and that it was all dreadful. Nothing like this had ever happened to him before. Where was his intelligence and his tact? Where was his comprehension of things and his philosophical indifference?

The doctor could not sleep all night for shame and vexation with himself, and at ten o'clock next morning he went to the post office and apologized to the postmaster.

"We won't think again of what has happened," Mihail Averyanitch, greatly touched, said with a sigh, warmly pressing his hand. "Let bygones be bygones. Lyubavkin," he suddenly shouted so loud that all the postmen and other persons present started, "hand a chair; and you wait," he shouted to a peasant woman who was stretching out a registered letter to him through the grating. "Don't you see that I am busy? We will not remember the past," he went on, affectionately addressing Andrey Yefimitch; "sit down, I beg you, my dear fellow."

For a minute he stroked his knees in silence, and then said:

"I have never had a thought of taking offence. Illness is no joke, I understand. Your attack frightened the doctor and me yesterday, and we had a long talk about you afterwards. My dear friend, why won't you treat your illness seriously? You can't go on like this. . . . Excuse me speaking openly as a friend," whispered Mihail Averyanitch. "You live in the most unfavourable surroundings, in a crowd, in uncleanliness, no one to look after you, no money for proper treatment. . . . My dear friend, the doctor and I implore you with all our hearts, listen to our advice: go into the hospital! There you will have wholesome food and attendance and treatment. Though, between ourselves, Yevgeny Fyodoritch is *mauvais ton,* yet he does understand his work, you can fully rely upon him. He has promised me he will look after you.

Andrey Yefimitch was touched by the postmaster's genuine sympathy and the tears which suddenly glittered on his cheeks.

"My honoured friend, don't believe it!" he whispered, laying his hand on his heart; "don't believe them. It's all a sham. My illness is only that in twenty years I have only found one intelligent man in the whole town, and he is mad. I am not ill at all, it's simply that I have got into an enchanted circle which there is no getting out of. I don't care; I am ready for anything."

"Go into the hospital, my dear fellow."

"I don't care if it were into the pit."

"Give me your word, my dear man, that you will obey Yevgeny Fyodoritch in everything."

"Certainly I will give you my word. But I repeat, my honoured friend, I have got into an enchanted circle. Now everything, even the genuine sympathy of my friends, leads to the same thing -- to my ruin. I am going to my ruin, and I have the manliness to recognize it."

"My dear fellow, you will recover."

"What's the use of saying that?" said Andrey Yefimitch, with irritation. "There are few men who at the end of their lives do not experience what I am experiencing now. When you are told that you have something such as diseased kidneys or enlarged heart, and you begin being treated for it, or are told you are mad or a criminal -- that is, in fact, when people suddenly turn their attention to you -- you may be sure you have got into an enchanted circle from which you will not escape. You will try to escape and make things worse. You had better give in, for no human efforts can save you. So it seems to me."

Meanwhile the public was crowding at the grating. That he might not be in their way, Andrey Yefimitch got up and began to take leave. Mihail Averyanitch made him promise on his honour once more, and escorted him to the outer door.

Towards evening on the same day Hobotov, in his sheepskin and his high top-boots, suddenly made his appearance, and said to Andrey Yefimitch in a tone as though nothing had happened the day before:

"I have come on business, colleague. I have come to ask you whether you would not join me in a consultation. Eh?"

Thinking that Hobotov wanted to distract his mind with an outing, or perhaps really to enable him to earn something, Andrey Yefimitch put on his coat and hat, and went out with him into the street. He was glad of the opportunity to smooth over his fault of the previous day and to be reconciled, and in his heart thanked Hobotov, who did not even allude to yesterday's scene and was evidently sparing him. One would never have expected such delicacy from this uncultured man.

"Where is your invalid?" asked Andrey Yefimitch.

"In the hospital. . . . I have long wanted to show him to you. A very interesting case."

They went into the hospital yard, and going round the main building, turned towards the lodge where the mental cases were kept, and all this, for some reason, in silence. When they went into the lodge Nikita as usual jumped up and stood at attention.

"One of the patients here has a lung complication." Hobotov said in an undertone, going into the yard with Andrey Yefimitch. "You wait here, I'll be back directly. I am going for a stethoscope."

And he went away.

XVII

It was getting dusk. Ivan Dmitritch was lying on his bed with his face thrust unto his pillow; the paralytic was sitting motionless, crying quietly and moving his lips. The fat peasant and the former sorter were asleep. It was quiet.

Andrey Yefimitch sat down on Ivan Dmitritch's bed and waited. But half an hour passed, and instead of Hobotov, Nikita came into the ward with a dressing-gown, some underlinen, and a pair of slippers in a heap on his arm.

"Please change your things, your honour," he said softly. "Here is your bed; come this way," he added, pointing to an empty bedstead which had obviously recently been brought into the ward. "It's all right; please God, you will recover."

Andrey Yefimitch understood it all. Without saying a word he crossed to the bed to which Nikita pointed and sat down; seeing that Nikita was standing waiting, he undressed entirely and he felt ashamed. Then he put on the hospital clothes; the drawers were very short, the shirt was long, and the dressing-gown smelt of smoked fish.

"Please God, you will recover," repeated Nikita, and he gathered up Andrey Yefimitch's clothes into his arms, went out, and shut the door after him.

"No matter. . ." thought Andrey Yefimitch, wrapping himself in his dressing-gown in a shamefaced way and feeling that he looked like a convict in his new costume. "It's no matter. . . . It does not matter whether it's a dress-coat or a uniform or this dressing-gown."

But how about his watch? And the notebook that was in the side-pocket? And his cigarettes? Where had Nikita taken his clothes? Now perhaps to the day of his death he would not put on trousers, a waistcoat, and high boots. It was all somehow strange and even incomprehensible at first. Andrey Yefimitch was even now convinced that there was no difference between his landlady's house and Ward No. 6, that everything in this world was nonsense and vanity of vanities. And yet his hands were trembling, his feet were cold, and he was filled with dread at the thought that soon Ivan Dmitritch would get up and see that he was in a dressing-gown. He got up and walked across the room and sat down again.

Here he had been sitting already half an hour, an hour, and he was miserably sick of it: was it really possible to live here a day, a week, and even years like these people? Why, he had been sitting here, had walked about and sat down again; he could get up and look out of window and walk from corner to corner again, and then what? Sit so all the time, like a post, and think? No, that was scarcely possible.

Andrey Yefimitch lay down, but at once got up, wiped the cold sweat from his brow with his sleeve and felt that his whole face smelt of smoked fish. He walked about again.

"It's some misunderstanding. . ." he said, turning out the palms of his hands in perplexity. "It must be cleared up. There is a misunderstanding."

Meanwhile Ivan Dmitritch woke up; he sat up and propped his cheeks on his fists. He spat. Then he glanced lazily at the doctor, and apparently for the first minute did not understand; but soon his sleepy face grew malicious and mocking.

"Aha! so they have put you in here, too, old fellow?" he said in a voice husky from sleepiness, screwing up one eye. "Very glad to see you. You sucked the blood of others, and now they will suck yours. Excellent!"

"It's a misunderstanding . . ." Andrey Yefimitch brought out, frightened by Ivan Dmitritch's words; he shrugged his shoulders and repeated: "It's some misunderstanding."

Ivan Dmitritch spat again and lay down.

"Cursed life," he grumbled, "and what's bitter and insulting, this life will not end in compensation for our sufferings, it will not end with apotheosis as it would in an opera, but with death; peasants will come and drag one's dead body by the arms and the legs to the cellar. Ugh! Well, it does not matter. . . . We shall have our good time in the other world. . . . I shall come here as a ghost from the other world and frighten these reptiles. I'll turn their hair grey."

Moiseika returned, and, seeing the doctor, held out his hand.

"Give me one little kopeck," he said.

XVIII

Andrey Yefimitch walked away to the window and looked out into the open country. It was getting dark, and on the horizon to the right a cold crimson moon was mounting upwards. Not far from the hospital fence, not much more than two hundred yards away, stood a tall white house shut in by a stone wall. This was the prison.

"So this is real life," thought Andrey Yefimitch, and he felt frightened.

The moon and the prison, and the nails on the fence, and the far-away flames at the bone-charring factory were all terrible. Behind him there was the sound of a sigh. Andrey Yefimitch looked round and saw a man with glittering stars and orders on his breast, who was smiling and slyly winking. And this, too, seemed terrible.

Andrey Yefimitch assured himself that there was nothing special about the moon or the prison, that even sane persons wear orders, and that everything in time will decay and turn to earth, but he was suddenly overcome with desire; he clutched at the grating with both hands and shook it with all his might. The strong grating did not yield.

Then that it might not be so dreadful he went to Ivan Dmitritch's bed and sat down.

"I have lost heart, my dear fellow," he muttered, trembling and wiping away the cold sweat, "I have lost heart."

"You should be philosophical," said Ivan Dmitritch ironically.

"My God, my God. . . . Yes, yes. . . . You were pleased to say once that there was no philosophy in Russia, but that all people, even the paltriest, talk philosophy. But you know the philosophizing of the paltriest does not harm anyone," said Andrey Yefimitch in a tone as if he wanted to cry and complain. "Why, then, that malignant laugh, my friend, and how can these paltry creatures help philosophizing if they are not satisfied? For an intelligent, educated man, made in God's image, proud and loving freedom, to have no alternative but to be a doctor in a filthy, stupid, wretched little town, and to spend his whole life among bottles, leeches, mustard plasters! Quackery, narrowness, vulgarity! Oh, my God!"

"You are talking nonsense. If you don't like being a doctor you should have gone in for being a statesman."

"I could not, I could not do anything. We are weak, my dear friend. . . . I used to be indifferent. I reasoned boldly and soundly, but at the first coarse touch of life upon me I have lost heart. . . . Prostration. . . . . We are weak, we are poor creatures . . . and you, too, my dear friend, you are intelligent, generous, you drew in good impulses with your mother's milk, but you had hardly entered upon life when you were exhausted and fell ill. . . . Weak, weak!"

Andrey Yefimitch was all the while at the approach of evening tormented by another persistent sensation besides terror and the feeling of resentment. At last he realized that he was longing for a smoke and for beer.

"I am going out, my friend," he said. "I will tell them to bring a light; I can't put up with this. . . . I am not equal to it. . . ."

Andrey Yefimitch went to the door and opened it, but at once Nikita jumped up and barred his way.

"Where are you going? You can't, you can't!" he said. "It's bedtime."

"But I'm only going out for a minute to walk about the yard," said Andrey Yefimitch.

"You can't, you can't; it's forbidden. You know that yourself."

"But what difference will it make to anyone if I do go out?" asked Andrey Yefimitch, shrugging his shoulders. "I don't understand. Nikita, I must go out!" he said in a trembling voice. "I must."

"Don't be disorderly, it's not right," Nikita said peremptorily.

"This is beyond everything," Ivan Dmitritch cried suddenly, and he jumped up. "What right has he not to let you out? How dare they keep us here? I believe it is clearly laid down in the law that no one can be deprived of freedom without trial! It's an outrage! It's tyranny!"

"Of course it's tyranny," said Andrey Yefimitch, encouraged by Ivan Dmitritch's outburst. "I must go out, I want to. He has no right! Open, I tell you."

"Do you hear, you dull-witted brute?" cried Ivan Dmitritch, and he banged on the door with his fist. "Open the door, or I will break it open! Torturer!"

"Open the door," cried Andrey Yefimitch, trembling all over; "I insist!"

"Talk away!" Nikita answered through the door, "talk away. . . ."

"Anyhow, go and call Yevgeny Fyodoritch! Say that I beg him to come for a minute!"

"His honour will come of himself to-morrow."

"They will never let us out," Ivan Dmitritch was going on meanwhile. "They will leave us to rot here! Oh, Lord, can there really be no hell in the next world, and will these wretches be forgiven? Where is justice? Open the door, you wretch! I am choking!" he cried in a hoarse voice, and flung himself upon the door. "I'll dash out my brains, murderers!"

Nikita opened the door quickly, and roughly with both his hands and his knee shoved Andrey Yefimitch back, then swung his arm and punched him in the face with his fist. It seemed to Andrey Yefimitch as though a huge salt wave enveloped him from his head downwards and dragged him to the bed; there really was a salt taste in his mouth: most likely the blood was running from his teeth. He waved his arms as though he were trying to swim out and clutched at a bedstead, and at the same moment felt Nikita hit him twice on the back.

Ivan Dmitritch gave a loud scream. He must have been beaten too.

Then all was still, the faint moonlight came through the grating, and a shadow like a net lay on the floor. It was terrible. Andrey Yefimitch lay and held his breath: he was expecting with horror to be struck again. He felt as though someone had taken a sickle, thrust it into him, and turned it round several times in his breast and bowels. He bit the pillow from pain and clenched his teeth, and all at once through the chaos in his brain there flashed the terrible unbearable thought that these people, who seemed now like black shadows in the moonlight, had to endure such pain day by day for years. How could it have happened that for more than twenty years he had not known it and had refused to know it? He knew nothing of pain, had no conception of it, so he was not to blame, but his conscience, as inexorable and as rough as Nikita, made him turn cold from the crown of his head to his heels. He leaped up, tried to cry out with all his might, and to run in haste to kill Nikita, and then Hobotov, the superintendent and the assistant, and then himself; but no sound came from his chest, and his legs would not obey him. Gasping for breath, he tore at the dressing-gown and the shirt on his breast, rent them, and fell senseless on the bed.

XIX

Next morning his head ached, there was a droning in his ears and a feeling of utter weakness all over. He was not ashamed at recalling his weakness the day before. He had been cowardly, had even been afraid of the moon, had openly expressed thoughts and feelings such as he had not expected in himself before; for instance, the thought that the paltry people who philosophized were really dissatisfied. But now nothing mattered to him.

He ate nothing; he drank nothing. He lay motionless and silent.

"It is all the same to me, he thought when they asked him questions. "I am not going to answer. . . . It's all the same to me."

After dinner Mihail Averyanitch brought him a quarter pound of tea and a pound of fruit pastilles. Daryushka came too and stood for a whole hour by the bed with an expression of dull grief on her face. Dr. Hobotov visited him. He brought a bottle of bromide and told Nikita to fumigate the ward with something.

Towards evening Andrey Yefimitch died of an apoplectic stroke. At first he had a violent shivering fit and a feeling of sickness; something revolting as it seemed, penetrating through his whole body, even to his finger-tips, strained from his stomach to his head and flooded his eyes and ears. There was a greenness before his eyes. Andrey Yefimitch understood that his end had come, and remembered that Ivan Dmitritch, Mihail Averyanitch, and millions of people believed in immortality. And what if it really existed? But he did not want immortality -- and he thought of it only for one instant. A herd of deer, extraordinarily beautiful and graceful, of which he had been reading the day before, ran by him; then a peasant woman stretched out her hand to him with a registered letter. . . . Mihail Averyanitch said something, then it all vanished, and Andrey Yefimitch sank into oblivion forever.

The hospital porters came, took him by his arms and legs, and carried him away to the chapel.

There he lay on the table, with open eyes, and the moon shed its light upon him at night. In the morning Sergey Sergeyitch came, prayed piously before the crucifix, and closed his former chief's eyes.

Next day Andrey Yefimitch was buried. Mihail Averyanitch and Daryushka were the only people at the funeral.

TERROR

My Friend's Story

Dmitri Petrovitch Silin had taken his degree and entered the government service in Petersburg, but at thirty he gave up his post and went in for agriculture. His farming was fairly successful, and yet it always seemed to me that he was not in his proper place, and that he would do well to go back to Petersburg. When sunburnt, grey with dust, exhausted with toil, he met me near the gates or at the entrance, and then at supper struggled with sleepiness and his wife took him off to bed as though he were a baby; or when, overcoming his sleepiness, he began in his soft, cordial, almost imploring voice, to talk about his really excellent ideas, I saw him not as a farmer nor an agriculturist, but only as a worried and exhausted man, and it was clear to me that he did not really care for farming, but that all he wanted was for the day to be over and "Thank God for it."

I liked to be with him, and I used to stay on his farm for two or three days at a time. I liked his house, and his park, and his big fruit garden, and the river -- and his philosophy, which was clear, though rather spiritless and rhetorical. I suppose I was fond of him on his own account, though I can't say that for certain, as I have not up to now succeeded in analysing my feelings at that time. He was an intelligent, kind-hearted, genuine man, and not a bore, but I remember that when he confided to me his most treasured secrets and spoke of our relation to each other as friendship, it disturbed me unpleasantly, and I was conscious of awkwardness. In his affection for me there was something inappropriate, tiresome, and I should have greatly preferred commonplace friendly relations.

The fact is that I was extremely attracted by his wife, Marya Sergeyevna. I was not in love with her, but I was attracted by her face, her eyes, her voice, her walk. I missed her when I did not see her for a long time, and my imagination pictured no one at that time so eagerly as that young, beautiful, elegant woman. I had no definite designs in regard to her, and did not dream of anything of the sort, yet for some reason, whenever we were left alone, I remembered that her husband looked upon me as his friend, and I felt awkward. When she played my favourite pieces on the piano or told me something interesting, I listened with pleasure, and yet at the same time for some reason the reflection that she loved her husband, that he was my friend, and that she herself looked upon me as his friend, obtruded themselves upon me, my spirits flagged, and I became listless, awkward, and dull. She noticed this change and would usually say:

"You are dull without your friend. We must send out to the fields for him."

And when Dmitri Petrovitch came in, she would say:

"Well, here is your friend now. Rejoice."

So passed a year and a half.

It somehow happened one July Sunday that Dmitri Petrovitch and I, having nothing to do, drove to the big village of Klushino to buy things for supper. While we were going from one shop to another the sun set and the evening came on -- the evening which I shall probably never forget in my life. After buying cheese that smelt like soap, and petrified sausages that smelt of tar, we went to the tavern to ask whether they had any beer. Our coachman went off to the blacksmith to get our horses shod, and we told him we would wait for him near the church. We walked, talked, laughed over our purchases, while a man who was known in the district by a very strange nickname, "Forty Martyrs," followed us all the while in silence with a mysterious air like a detective. This Forty Martyrs was no other than Gavril Syeverov, or more simply Gavryushka, who had been for a short time in my service as a footman and had been dismissed by me for drunkenness. He had been in Dmitri Petrovitch's service, too, and by him had been dismissed for the same vice. He was an inveterate drunkard, and indeed his whole life was as drunk and disorderly as himself. His father had been a priest and his mother of noble rank, so by birth he belonged to the privileged class; but however carefully I scrutinized his exhausted, respectful, and always perspiring face, his red beard now turning grey, his pitifully torn reefer jacket and his red shirt, I could not discover in him the faintest trace of anything we associate with privilege. He spoke of himself as a man of education, and used to say that he had been in a clerical school, but had not finished his studies there, as he had been expelled for smoking; then he had sung in the bishop's choir and lived for two years in a monastery, from which he was also expelled, but this time not for smoking but for "his weakness." He had walked all over two provinces, had presented petitions to the Consistory, and to various government offices, and had been four times on his trial. At last, being stranded in our district, he had served as a footman, as a forester, as a kennelman, as a sexton, had married a cook who was a widow and rather a loose character, and had so hopelessly sunk into a menial position, and had grown so used to filth and dirt, that he even spoke of his privileged origin with a certain scepticism, as of some myth. At the time I am describing, he was hanging about without a job, calling himself a carrier and a huntsman, and his wife had disappeared and made no sign.

From the tavern we went to the church and sat in the porch, waiting for the coachman. Forty Martyrs stood a little way off and put his hand before his mouth in order to cough in it respectfully if need be. By now it was dark; there was a strong smell of evening dampness, and the moon was on the point of rising. There were only two clouds in the clear starry sky exactly over our heads: one big one and one smaller; alone in the sky they were racing after one another like mother and child, in the direction where the sunset was glowing.

"What a glorious day!" said Dmitri Petrovitch.

"In the extreme . . ." Forty Martyrs assented, and he coughed respectfully into his hand. "How was it, Dmitri Petrovitch, you thought to visit these parts?" he asked in an ingratiating voice, evidently anxious to get up a conversation.

Dmitri Petrovitch made no answer. Forty Martyrs heaved a deep sigh and said softly, not looking at us:

"I suffer solely through a cause to which I must answer to Almighty God. No doubt about it, I am a hopeless and incompetent man; but believe me, on my conscience, I am without a crust of bread and worse off than a dog. . . . Forgive me, Dmitri Petrovitch."

Silin was not listening, but sat musing with his head propped on his fists. The church stood at the end of the street on the high river-bank, and through the trellis gate of the enclosure we could see the river, the water-meadows on the near side of it, and the crimson glare of a camp fire about which black figures of men and horses were moving. And beyond the fire, further away, there were other lights, where there was a little village. They were singing there. On the river, and here and there on the meadows, a mist was rising. High narrow coils of mist, thick and white as milk, were trailing over the river, hiding the reflection of the stars and hovering over the willows. Every minute they changed their form, and it seemed as though some were embracing, others were bowing, others lifting up their arms to heaven with wide sleeves like priests, as though they were praying. . . . Probably they reminded Dmitri Petrovitch of ghosts and of the dead, for he turned facing me and asked with a mournful smile:

"Tell me, my dear fellow, why is it that when we want to tell some terrible, mysterious, and fantastic story, we draw our material, not from life, but invariably from the world of ghosts and of the shadows beyond the grave."

"We are frightened of what we don't understand."

"And do you understand life? Tell me: do you understand life better than the world beyond the grave?"

Dmitri Petrovitch was sitting quite close to me, so that I felt his breath upon my cheek. In the evening twilight his pale, lean face seemed paler than ever and his dark beard was black as soot. His eyes were sad, truthful, and a little frightened, as though he were about to tell me something horrible. He looked into my eyes and went on in his habitual imploring voice:

"Our life and the life beyond the grave are equally incomprehensible and horrible. If anyone is afraid of ghosts he ought to be afraid, too, of me, and of those lights and of the sky, seeing that, if you come to reflect, all that is no less fantastic and beyond our grasp than apparitions from the other world. Prince Hamlet did not kill himself because he was afraid of the visions that might haunt his dreams after death. I like that famous soliloquy of his, but, to be candid, it never touched my soul. I will confess to you as a friend that in moments of depression I have sometimes pictured to myself the hour of my death. My fancy invented thousands of the gloomiest visions, and I have succeeded in working myself up to an agonizing exaltation, to a state of nightmare, and I assure you that that did not seem to me more terrible than reality. What I mean is, apparitions are terrible, but life is terrible, too. I don't understand life and I am afraid of it, my dear boy; I don't know. Perhaps I am a morbid person, unhinged. It seems to a sound, healthy man that he understands everything he sees and hears, but that 'seeming' is lost to me, and from day to day I am poisoning myself with terror. There is a disease, the fear of open spaces, but my disease is the fear of life. When I lie on the grass and watch a little beetle which was born yesterday and understands nothing, it seems to me that its life consists of nothing else but fear, and in it I see myself."

"What is it exactly you are frightened of?" I asked.

"I am afraid of everything. I am not by nature a profound thinker, and I take little interest in such questions as the life beyond the grave, the destiny of humanity, and, in fact, I am rarely carried away to the heights. What chiefly frightens me is the common routine of life from which none of us can escape. I am incapable of distinguishing what is true and what is false in my actions, and they worry me. I recognize that education and the conditions of life have imprisoned me in a narrow circle of falsity, that my whole life is nothing else than a daily effort to deceive myself and other people, and to avoid noticing it; and I am frightened at the thought that to the day of my death I shall not escape from this falsity. To-day I do something and to-morrow I do not understand why I did it. I entered the service in Petersburg and took fright; I came here to work on the land, and here, too, I am frightened. . . . I see that we know very little and so make mistakes every day. We are unjust, we slander one another and spoil each other's lives, we waste all our powers on trash which we do not need and which hinders us from living; and that frightens me, because I don't understand why and for whom it is necessary. I don't understand men, my dear fellow, and I am afraid of them. It frightens me to look at the peasants, and I don't know for what higher objects they are suffering and what they are living for. If life is an enjoyment, then they are unnecessary, superfluous people; if the object and meaning of life is to be found in poverty and unending, hopeless ignorance, I can't understand for whom and what this torture is necessary. I understand no one and nothing. Kindly try to understand this specimen, for instance," said Dmitri Petrovitch, pointing to Forty Martyrs. "Think of him!"

Noticing that we were looking at him, Forty Martyrs coughed deferentially into his fist and said:

"I was always a faithful servant with good masters, but the great trouble has been spirituous liquor. If a poor fellow like me were shown consideration and given a place, I would kiss the ikon. My word's my bond."

The sexton walked by, looked at us in amazement, and began pulling the rope. The bell, abruptly breaking upon the stillness of the evening, struck ten with a slow and prolonged note.

"It's ten o'clock, though," said Dmitri Petrovitch. "It's time we were going. Yes, my dear fellow," he sighed, "if only you knew how afraid I am of my ordinary everyday thoughts, in which one would have thought there should be nothing dreadful. To prevent myself thinking I distract my mind with work and try to tire myself out that I may sleep sound at night. Children, a wife -- all that seems ordinary with other people; but how that weighs upon me, my dear fellow!"

He rubbed his face with his hands, cleared his throat, and laughed.

"If I could only tell you how I have played the fool in my life! " he said. "They all tell me that I have a sweet wife, charming children, and that I am a good husband and father. They think I am very happy and envy me. But since it has come to that, I will tell you in secret: my happy family life is only a grievous misunderstanding, and I am afraid of it." His pale face was distorted by a wry smile. He put his arm round my waist and went on in an undertone:

"You are my true friend; I believe in you and have a deep respect for you. Heaven gave us friendship that we may open our hearts and escape from the secrets that weigh upon us. Let me take advantage of your friendly feeling for me and tell you the whole truth. My home life, which seems to you so enchanting, is my chief misery and my chief terror. I got married in a strange and stupid way. I must tell you that I was madly in love with Masha before I married her, and was courting her for two years. I asked her to marry me five times, and she refused me because she did not care for me in the least. The sixth, when burning with passion I crawled on my knees before her and implored her to take a beggar and marry me, she consented. . . . What she said to me was: 'I don't love you, but I will be true to you. . . .' I accepted that condition with rapture. At the time I understood what that meant, but I swear to God I don't understand it now. 'I don't love you, but I will be true to you.' What does that mean? It's a fog, a darkness. I love her now as intensely as I did the day we were married, while she, I believe, is as indifferent as ever, and I believe she is glad when I go away from home. I don't know for certain whether she cares for me or not -- I don't know, I don't know; but, as you see, we live under the same roof, call each other 'thou,' sleep together, have children, our property is in common. . . . What does it mean, what does it mean? What is the object of it? And do you understand it at all, my dear fellow? It's cruel torture! Because I don't understand our relations, I hate, sometimes her, sometimes myself, sometimes both at once. Everything is in a tangle in my brain; I torment myself and grow stupid. And as though to spite me, she grows more beautiful every day, she is getting more wonderful. . . I fancy her hair is marvellous, and her smile is like no other woman's. I love her, and I know that my love is hopeless. Hopeless love for a woman by whom one has two children! Is that intelligible? And isn't it terrible? Isn't it more terrible than ghosts?"

He was in the mood to have talked on a good deal longer, but luckily we heard the coachman's voice. Our horses had arrived. We got into the carriage, and Forty Martyrs, taking off his cap, helped us both into the carriage with an expression that suggested that he had long been waiting for an opportunity to come in contact with our precious persons.

"Dmitri Petrovitch, let me come to you," he said, blinking furiously and tilting his head on one side. "Show divine mercy! I am dying of hunger!"

"Very well," said Silin. "Come, you shall stay three days, and then we shall see."

"Certainly, sir," said Forty Martyrs, overjoyed. "I'll come today, sir."

It was a five miles' drive home. Dmitri Petrovitch, glad that he had at last opened his heart to his friend, kept his arm round my waist all the way; and speaking now, not with bitterness and not with apprehension, but quite cheerfully, told me that if everything had been satisfactory in his home life, he should have returned to Petersburg and taken up scientific work there. The movement which had driven so many gifted young men into the country was, he said, a deplorable movement. We had plenty of rye and wheat in Russia, but absolutely no cultured people. The strong and gifted among the young ought to take up science, art, and politics; to act otherwise meant being wasteful. He generalized with pleasure and expressed regret that he would be parting from me early next morning, as he had to go to a sale of timber.

And I felt awkward and depressed, and it seemed to me that I was deceiving the man. And at the same time it was pleasant to me. I gazed at the immense crimson moon which was rising, and pictured the tall, graceful, fair woman, with her pale face, always well-dressed and fragrant with some special scent, rather like musk, and for some reason it pleased me to think she did not love her husband.

On reaching home, we sat down to supper. Marya Sergeyevna, laughing, regaled us with our purchases, and I thought that she certainly had wonderful hair and that her smile was unlike any other woman's. I watched her, and I wanted to detect in every look and movement that she did not love her husband, and I fancied that I did see it.

Dmitri Petrovitch was soon struggling with sleep. After supper he sat with us for ten minutes and said:

"Do as you please, my friends, but I have to be up at three o'clock tomorrow morning. Excuse my leaving you."

He kissed his wife tenderly, pressed my hand with warmth and gratitude, and made me promise that I would certainly come the following week. That he might not oversleep next morning, he went to spend the night in the lodge.

Marya Sergeyevna always sat up late, in the Petersburg fashion, and for some reason on this occasion I was glad of it.

"And now," I began when we were left alone, "and now you'll be kind and play me something."

I felt no desire for music, but I did not know how to begin the conversation. She sat down to the piano and played, I don't remember what. I sat down beside her and looked at her plump white hands and tried to read something on her cold, indifferent face. Then she smiled at something and looked at me.

"You are dull without your friend," she said.

I laughed.

"It would be enough for friendship to be here once a month, but I turn up oftener than once a week."

Saying this, I got up and walked from one end of the room to the other. She too got up and walked away to the fireplace.

"What do you mean to say by that?" she said, raising her large, clear eyes and looking at me.

I made no answer.

"What you say is not true," she went on, after a moment's thought. "You only come here on account of Dmitri Petrovitch. Well, I am very glad. One does not often see such friendships nowadays."

"Aha!" I thought, and, not knowing what to say, I asked: "Would you care for a turn in the garden?"

I went out upon the verandah. Nervous shudders were running over my head and I felt chilly with excitement. I was convinced now that our conversation would be utterly trivial, and that there was nothing particular we should be able to say to one another, but that, that night, what I did not dare to dream of was bound to happen -- that it was bound to be that night or never.

"What lovely weather!" I said aloud.

"It makes absolutely no difference to me," she answered.

I went into the drawing-room. Marya Sergeyevna was standing, as before, near the fireplace, with her hands behind her back, looking away and thinking of something.

"Why does it make no difference to you?" I asked.

"Because I am bored. You are only bored without your friend, but I am always bored. However . . . that is of no interest to you."

I sat down to the piano and struck a few chords, waiting to hear what she would say.

"Please don't stand on ceremony," she said, looking angrily at me, and she seemed as though on the point of crying with vexation. "If you are sleepy, go to bed. Because you are Dmitri Petrovitch's friend, you are not in duty bound to be bored with his wife's company. I don't want a sacrifice. Please go."

I did not, of course, go to bed. She went out on the verandah while I remained in the drawing-room and spent five minutes turning over the music. Then I went out, too. We stood close together in the shadow of the curtains, and below us were the steps bathed in moonlight. The black shadows of the trees stretched across the flower beds and the yellow sand of the paths.

"I shall have to go away tomorrow, too," I said.

"Of course, if my husband's not at home you can't stay here," she said sarcastically. "I can imagine how miserable you would be if you were in love with me! Wait a bit: one day I shall throw myself on your neck. . . . I shall see with what horror you will run away from me. That would be interesting."

Her words and her pale face were angry, but her eyes were full of tender passionate love. I already looked upon this lovely creature as my property, and then for the first time I noticed that she had golden eyebrows, exquisite eyebrows. I had never seen such eyebrows before. The thought that I might at once press her to my heart, caress her, touch her wonderful hair, seemed to me such a miracle that I laughed and shut my eyes.

"It's bed-time now. . . . A peaceful night," she said.

"I don't want a peaceful night," I said, laughing, following her into the drawing-room. "I shall curse this night if it is a peaceful one."

Pressing her hand, and escorting her to the door, I saw by her face that she understood me, and was glad that I understood her, too.

I went to my room. Near the books on the table lay Dmitri Petrovitch's cap, and that reminded me of his affection for me. I took my stick and went out into the garden. The mist had risen here, too, and the same tall, narrow, ghostly shapes which I had seen earlier on the river were trailing round the trees and bushes and wrapping about them. What a pity I could not talk to them!

In the extraordinarily transparent air, each leaf, each drop of dew stood out distinctly; it was all smiling at me in the stillness half asleep, and as I passed the green seats I recalled the words in some play of Shakespeare's: "How sweetly falls the moonlight on yon seat!"

There was a mound in the garden; I went up it and sat down. I was tormented by a delicious feeling. I knew for certain that in a moment I should hold in my arms, should press to my heart her magnificent body, should kiss her golden eyebrows; and I wanted to disbelieve it, to tantalize myself, and was sorry that she had cost me so little trouble and had yielded so soon.

But suddenly I heard heavy footsteps. A man of medium height appeared in the avenue, and I recognized him at once as Forty Martyrs. He sat down on the bench and heaved a deep sigh, then crossed himself three times and lay down. A minute later he got up and lay on the other side. The gnats and the dampness of the night prevented his sleeping.

"Oh, life!" he said. "Wretched, bitter life!"

Looking at his bent, wasted body and hearing his heavy, noisy sighs, I thought of an unhappy, bitter life of which the confession had been made to me that day, and I felt uneasy and frightened at my blissful mood. I came down the knoll and went to the house.

"Life, as he thinks, is terrible," I thought, "so don't stand on ceremony with it, bend it to your will, and until it crushes you, snatch all you can wring from it."

Marya Sergeyevna was standing on the verandah. I put my arms round her without a word, and began greedily kissing her eyebrows, her temples, her neck. . . .

In my room she told me she had loved me for a long time, more than a year. She vowed eternal love, cried and begged me to take her away with me. I repeatedly took her to the window to look at her face in the moonlight, and she seemed to me a lovely dream, and I made haste to hold her tight to convince myself of the truth of it. It was long since I had known such raptures. . . . Yet somewhere far away at the bottom of my heart I felt an awkwardness, and I was ill at ease. In her love for me there was something incongruous and burdensome, just as in Dmitri Petrovitch's friendship. It was a great, serious passion with tears and vows, and I wanted nothing serious in it -- no tears, no vows, no talk of the future. Let that moonlight night flash through our lives like a meteor and -- *basta!*

At three o'clock she went out of my room, and, while I was standing in the doorway, looking after her, at the end of the corridor Dmitri Petrovitch suddenly made his appearance; she started and stood aside to let him pass, and her whole figure was expressive of repulsion. He gave a strange smile, coughed, and came into my room.

"I forgot my cap here yesterday," he said without looking at me.

He found it and, holding it in both hands, put it on his head; then he looked at my confused face, at my slippers, and said in a strange, husky voice unlike his own:

"I suppose it must be my fate that I should understand nothing. . . . If you understand anything, I congratulate you. It's all darkness before my eyes."

And he went out, clearing his throat. Afterwards from the window I saw him by the stable, harnessing the horses with his own hands. His hands were trembling, he was in nervous haste and kept looking round at the house; probably he was feeling terror. Then he got into the gig, and, with a strange expression as though afraid of being pursued, lashed the horses.

Shortly afterwards I set off, too. The sun was already rising, and the mist of the previous day clung timidly to the bushes and the hillocks. On the box of the carriage was sitting Forty Martyrs; he had already succeeded in getting drunk and was muttering tipsy nonsense.

"I am a free man," he shouted to the horses. "Ah, my honeys, I am a nobleman in my own right, if you care to know!"

The terror of Dmitri Petrovitch, the thought of whom I could not get out of my head, infected me. I thought of what had happened and could make nothing of it. I looked at the rooks, and it seemed so strange and terrible that they were flying.

"Why have I done this?" I kept asking myself in bewilderment and despair. "Why has it turned out like this and not differently? To whom and for what was it necessary that she should love me in earnest, and that he should come into my room to fetch his cap? What had a cap to do with it?

I set off for Petersburg that day, and I have not seen Dmitri Petrovitch nor his wife since. I am told that they are still living together.

AN ANONYMOUS STORY

I

Through causes which it is not the time to go into in detail, I had to enter the service of a Petersburg official called Orlov, in the capacity of a footman. He was about five and thirty, and was called Georgy* Ivanitch.

*Both *g's* hard, as in "Gorgon"; *e* like *ai* in *rain.*

I entered this Orlov's service on account of his father, a prominent political man, whom I looked upon as a serious enemy of my cause. I reckoned that, living with the son, I should -- from the conversations I should hear, and from the letters and papers I should find on the table -- learn every detail of the father's plans and intentions.

As a rule at eleven o'clock in the morning the electric bell rang in my footman's quarters to let me know that my master was awake. When I went into the bedroom with his polished shoes and brushed clothes, Georgy Ivanitch would be sitting in his bed with a face that looked, not drowsy, but rather exhausted by sleep, and he would gaze off in one direction without any sign of satisfaction at having waked. I helped him to dress, and he let me do it with an air of reluctance without speaking or noticing my presence; then with his head wet with washing, smelling of fresh scent, he used to go into the dining-room to drink his coffee. He used to sit at the table, sipping his coffee and glancing through the newspapers, while the maid Polya and I stood respectfully at the door gazing at him. Two grown-up persons had to stand watching with the gravest attention a third drinking coffee and munching rusks. It was probably ludicrous and grotesque, but I saw nothing humiliating in having to stand near the door, though I was quite as well born and well educated as Orlov himself.

I was in the first stage of consumption, and was suffering from something else, possibly even more serious than consumption. I don't know whether it was the effect of my illness or of an incipient change in my philosophy of life of which I was not conscious at the time, but I was, day by day, more possessed by a passionate, irritating longing for ordinary everyday life. I yearned for mental tranquillity, health, fresh air, good food. I was becoming a dreamer, and, like a dreamer, I did not know exactly what I wanted. Sometimes I felt inclined to go into a monastery, to sit there for days together by the window and gaze at the trees and the fields; sometimes I fancied I would buy fifteen acres of land and settle down as a country gentleman; sometimes I inwardly vowed to take up science and become a professor at some provincial university. I was a retired navy lieutenant; I dreamed of the sea, of our squadron, and of the corvette in which I had made the cruise round the world. I longed to experience again the indescribable feeling when, walking in the tropical forest or looking at the sunset in the Bay of Bengal, one is thrilled with ecstasy and at the same time homesick. I dreamed of mountains, women, music, and, with the curiosity of a child, I looked into people's faces, listened to their voices. And when I stood at the door and watched Orlov sipping his coffee, I felt not a footman, but a man interested in everything in the world, even in Orlov.

In appearance Orlov was a typical Petersburger, with narrow shoulders, a long waist, sunken temples, eyes of an indefinite colour, and scanty, dingy-coloured hair, beard and moustaches. His face had a stale, unpleasant look, though it was studiously cared for. It was particularly unpleasant when he was asleep or lost in thought. It is not worth while describing a quite ordinary appearance; besides, Petersburg is not Spain, and a man's appearance is not of much consequence even in love affairs, and is only of value to a handsome footman or coachman. I have spoken of Orlov's face and hair only because there was something in his appearance worth mentioning. When Orlov took a newspaper or book, whatever it might be, or met people, whoever they be, an ironical smile began to come into his eyes, and his whole countenance assumed an expression of light mockery in which there was no malice. Before reading or hearing anything he always had his irony in readiness, as a savage has his shield. It was an habitual irony, like some old liquor brewed years ago, and now it came into his face probably without any participation of his will, as it were by reflex action. But of that later.

Soon after midday he took his portfolio, full of papers, and drove to his office. He dined away from home and returned after eight o'clock. I used to light the lamp and candles in his study, and he would sit down in a low chair with his legs stretched out on another chair, and, reclining in that position, would begin reading. Almost every day he brought in new books with him or received parcels of them from the shops, and there were heaps of books in three languages, to say nothing of Russian, which he had read and thrown away, in the corners of my room and under my bed. He read with extraordinary rapidity. They say: "Tell me what you read, and I'll tell you who you are." That may be true, but it was absolutely impossible to judge of Orlov by what he read. It was a regular hotchpotch. Philosophy, French novels, political economy, finance, new poets, and publications of the firm *Posrednik** -- and he read it all with the same rapidity and with the same ironical expression in his eyes.

* I.e., Tchertkov and others, publishers of Tolstoy, who issued good literature for peasants' reading.

After ten o'clock he carefully dressed, often in evening dress, very rarely in his *kammer-junker*'s uniform, and went out, returning in the morning.

Our relations were quiet and peaceful, and we never had any misunderstanding. As a rule he did not notice my presence, and when he talked to me there was no expression of irony on his face -- he evidently did not look upon me as a human being.

I only once saw him angry. One day -- it was a week after I had entered his service -- he came back from some dinner at nine o'clock; his face looked ill-humoured and exhausted. When I followed him into his study to light the candles, he said to me:

"There's a nasty smell in the flat."

"No, the air is fresh," I answered.

"I tell you, there's a bad smell," he answered irritably.

"I open the movable panes every day."

"Don't argue, blockhead!" he shouted.

I was offended, and was on the point of answering, and goodness knows how it would have ended if Polya, who knew her master better than I did, had not intervened.

"There really is a disagreeable smell," she said, raising her eyebrows. "What can it be from? Stepan, open the pane in the drawing-room, and light the fire."

With much bustle and many exclamations, she went through all the rooms, rustling her skirts and squeezing the sprayer with a hissing sound. And Orlov was still out of humour; he was obviously restraining himself not to vent his ill-temper aloud. He was sitting at the table and rapidly writing a letter. After writing a few lines he snorted angrily and tore it up, then he began writing again.

"Damn them all!" he muttered. "They expect me to have an abnormal memory!"

At last the letter was written; he got up from the table and said, turning to me:

"Go to Znamensky Street and deliver this letter to Zinaida Fyodorovna Krasnovsky in person. But first ask the porter whether her husband -- that is, Mr. Krasnovsky -- has returned yet. If he has returned, don't deliver the letter, but come back. Wait a minute! . . . If she asks whether I have anyone here, tell her that there have been two gentlemen here since eight o'clock, writing something."

I drove to Znamensky Street. The porter told me that Mr. Krasnovsky had not yet come in, and I made my way up to the third storey. The door was opened by a tall, stout, drab-coloured flunkey with black whiskers, who in a sleepy, churlish, and apathetic voice, such as only flunkeys use in addressing other flunkeys, asked me what I wanted. Before I had time to answer, a lady dressed in black came hurriedly into the hall. She screwed up her eyes and looked at me.

"Is Zinaida Fyodorovna at home?" I asked.

"That is me," said the lady.

"A letter from Georgy Ivanitch."

She tore the letter open impatiently, and holding it in both hands, so that I saw her sparkling diamond rings, she began reading. I made out a pale face with soft lines, a prominent chin, and long dark lashes. From her appearance I should not have judged the lady to be more than five and twenty.

"Give him my thanks and my greetings," she said when she had finished the letter. "Is there anyone with Georgy Ivanitch?" she asked softly, joyfully, and as though ashamed of her mistrust.

"Two gentlemen," I answered. "They're writing something."

"Give him my greetings and thanks," she repeated, bending her head sideways, and, reading the letter as she walked, she went noiselessly out. I saw few women at that time, and this lady of whom I had a passing glimpse made an impression on me. As I walked home I recalled her face and the delicate fragrance about her, and fell to dreaming. By the time I got home Orlov had gone out.

II

And so my relations with my employer were quiet and peaceful, but still the unclean and degrading element which I so dreaded on becoming a footman was conspicuous and made itself felt every day. I did not get on with Polya. She was a well-fed and pampered hussy who adored Orlov because he was a gentleman and despised me because I was a footman. Probably, from the point of view of a real flunkey or cook, she was fascinating, with her red cheeks, her turned-up nose, her coquettish glances, and the plumpness, one might almost say fatness, of her person. She powdered her face, coloured her lips and eyebrows, laced herself in, and wore a bustle, and a bangle made of coins. She walked with little ripping steps; as she walked she swayed, or, as they say, wriggled her shoulders and back. The rustle of her skirts, the creaking of her stays, the jingle her bangle and the vulgar smell of lip salve, toilet vinegar, and scent stolen from her master, aroused me whilst I was doing the rooms with her in the morning a sensation as though I were taking part with her in some abomination.

Either because I did not steal as she did, or because I displayed no desire to become her lover, which she probably looked upon as an insult, or perhaps because she felt that I was a man of a different order, she hated me from the first day. My inexperience, my appearance -- so unlike a flunkey -- and my illness, seemed to her pitiful and excited her disgust. I had a bad cough at that time, and sometimes at night I prevented her from sleeping, as our rooms were only divided by a wooden partition, and every morning she said to me:

"Again you didn't let me sleep. You ought to be in hospital instead of in service."

She so genuinely believed that I was hardly a human being, but something infinitely below her, that, like the Roman matrons who were not ashamed to bathe before their slaves, she sometimes went about in my presence in nothing but her chemise.

Once when I was in a happy, dreamy mood, I asked her at dinner (we had soup and roast meat sent in from a restaurant every day)

"Polya, do you believe in God?"

"Why, of course!"

"Then," I went on, "you believe there will be a day of judgment, and that we shall have to answer to God forevery evil action?"

She gave me no reply, but simply made a contemptuous grimace, and, looking that time at her cold eyes and over-fed expression, I realised that for her complete and finished personality no God, no conscience, no laws existed, and that if I had had to set fire to the house, to murder or to rob, I could not have hired a better accomplice.

In my novel surroundings I felt very uncomfortable for the first week at Orlov's before I got used to being addressed as "thou," and being constantly obliged to tell lies (saying "My master is not at home" when he was). In my flunkey's swallow-tail I felt as though I were in armour. But I grew accustomed to it in time. Like a genuine footman, I waited at table, tidied the rooms, ran and drove about on errands of all sorts. When Orlov did not want to keep an appointment with Zinaida Fyodorovna, or when he forgot that he had promised to go and see her, I drove to Znamensky Street, put a letter into her hands and told a lie. And the result of it all was quite different from what I had expected when I became a footman. Every day of this new life of mine was wasted for me and my cause, as Orlov never spoke of his father, nor did his visitors, and all I could learn of the stateman's doings was, as before, what I could glean from the newspapers or from correspondence with my comrades. The hundreds of notes and papers I used to find in the study and read had not the remotest connection with what I was looking for. Orlov was absolutely uninterested in his father's political work, and looked as though he had never heard of it, or as though his father had long been dead.

III

Every Thursday we had visitors.

I ordered a piece of roast beef from the restaurant and telephoned to Eliseyev's to send us caviare, cheese, oysters, and so on. I bought playing-cards. Polya was busy all day getting ready the tea-things and the dinner service. To tell the truth, this spurt of activity came as a pleasant change in our idle life, and Thursdays were for us the most interesting days.

Only three visitors used to come. The most important and perhaps the most interesting was the one called Pekarsky -- a tall, lean man of five and forty, with a long hooked nose, with a big black beard, and a bald patch on his head. His eyes were large and prominent, and his expression was grave and thoughtful like that of a Greek philosopher. He was on the board of management of some railway, and also had some post in a bank; he was a consulting lawyer in some important Government institution, and had business relations with a large number of private persons as a trustee, chairman of committees, and so on. He was of quite a low grade in the service, and modestly spoke of himself as a lawyer, but he had a vast influence. A note or card from him was enough to make a celebrated doctor, a director of a railway, or a great dignitary see anyone without waiting; and it was said that through his protection one might obtain even a post of the Fourth Class, and get any sort of unpleasant business hushed up. He was looked upon as a very intelligent man, but his was a strange, peculiar intelligence. He was able to multiply 213 by 373 in his head instantaneously, or turn English pounds into German marks without help of pencil or paper; he understood finance and railway business thoroughly, and the machinery of Russian administration had no secrets for him; he was a most skilful pleader in civil suits, and it was not easy to get the better of him at law. But that exceptional intelligence could not grasp many things which are understood even by some stupid people. For instance, he was absolutely unable to understand why people are depressed, why they weep, shoot themselves, and even kill others; why they fret about things that do not affect them personally, and why they laugh when they read Gogol or Shtchedrin. . . . Everything abstract, everything belonging to the domain of thought and feeling, was to him boring and incomprehensible, like music to one who has no ear. He looked at people simply from the business point of view, and divided them into competent and incompetent. No other classification existed for him. Honesty and rectitude were only signs of competence. Drinking, gambling, and debauchery were permissible, but must not be allowed to interfere with business. Believing in God was rather stupid, but religion ought be safeguarded, as the common people must have some principle to restrain them, otherwise they would not work. Punishment is only necessary as deterrent. There was no need to go away for holidays, as it was just as nice in town. And so on. He was a widower and had no children, but lived on a large scale, as though he had a family, and paid thousand roubles a year for his flat.

The second visitor, Kukushkin, an actual civil councillor though a young man, was short, and was conspicuous for his extremely unpleasant appearance, which was due to the disproportion between his fat, puffy body and his lean little face. His lips were puckered up suavely, and his little trimmed moustaches looked as though they had been fixed on with glue. He was a man with the manners of a lizard. He did not walk, but, as it were, crept along with tiny steps, squirming and sniggering, and when he laughed he showed his teeth. He was a clerk on special commissions, and did nothing, though he received a good salary, especially in the summer, when special and lucrative jobs were found for him. He was a man of personal ambition, not only to the marrow of his bones, but more fundamentally -- to the last drop of his blood; but even in his ambitions he was petty and did not rely on himself, but was building his career on the chance favour flung him by his superiors. For the sake of obtaining some foreign decoration, or for the sake of having his name mentioned in the newspapers as having been present at some special service in the company of other great personages, he was ready to submit to any kind of humiliation, to beg, to flatter, to promise. He flattered Orlov and Pekarsky from cowardice, because he thought they were powerful; he flattered Polya and me because we were in the service of a powerful man. Whenever I took off his fur coat he tittered and asked me: "Stepan, are you married?" and then unseemly vulgarities followed -- by way of showing me special attention. Kukushkin flattered Orlov's weaknesses, humoured his corrupted and blasé ways; to please him he affected malicious raillery and atheism, in his company criticised persons before whom in other places he would slavishly grovel. When at supper they talked of love and women, he pretended to be a subtle and perverse voluptuary. As a rule, one may say, Petersburg rakes are fond of talking of their abnormal tastes. Some young actual civil councillor is perfectly satisfied with the embraces of his cook or of some unhappy street-walker on the Nevsky Prospect, but to listen to him you would think he was contaminated by all the vices of East and West combined, that he was an honourary member of a dozen iniquitous secret societies and was already marked by the police. Kukushkin lied about himself in an unconscionable way, and they did not exactly disbelieve him, but paid little heed to his incredible stories.

The third guest was Gruzin, the son of a worthy and learned general; a man of Orlov's age, with long hair, short-sighted eyes, and gold spectacles. I remember his long white fingers, that looked like a pianist's; and, indeed, there was something of a musician, of a virtuoso, about his whole figure. The first violins in orchestras look just like that. He used to cough, suffered from migraine, and seemed invalidish and delicate. Probably at home he was dressed and undressed like a baby. He had finished at the College of Jurisprudence, and had at first served in the Department of Justice, then he was transferred to the Senate; he left that, and through patronage had received a post in the Department of Crown Estates, and had soon afterwards given that up. In my time he was serving in Orlov's department; he was his head-clerk, but he said that he should soon exchange into the Department of Justice again. He took his duties and his shifting about from one post to another with exceptional levity, and when people talked before him seriously of grades in the service, decorations, salaries, he smiled good-naturedly and repeated Prutkov's aphorism: "It's only in the Government service you learn the truth." He had a little wife with a wrinkled face, who was very jealous of him, and five weedy-looking children. He was unfaithful to his wife, he was only fond of his children when he saw them, and on the whole was rather indifferent to his family, and made fun of them. He and his family existed on credit, borrowing wherever they could at every opportunity, even from his superiors in the office and porters in people's houses. His was a flabby nature; he was so lazy that he did not care what became of himself, and drifted along heedless where or why he was going. He went where he was taken. If he was taken to some low haunt, he went; if wine was set before him, he drank -- if it were not put before him, he abstained; if wives were abused in his presence, he abused his wife, declaring she had ruined his life -- when wives were praised, he praised his and said quite sincerely: "I am very fond of her, poor thing!" He had no fur coat and always wore a rug which smelt of the nursery. When at supper he rolled balls of bread and drank a great deal of red wine, absorbed in thought, strange to say, I used to feel almost certain that there was something in him of which perhaps he had a vague sense, though in the bustle and vulgarity of his daily life he had not time to understand and appreciate it. He played a little on the piano. Sometimes he would sit down at the piano, play a chord or two, and begin singing softly:

"What does the coming day bring to me?"

But at once, as though afraid, he would get up and walk from the piano.

The visitors usually arrived about ten o'clock. They played cards in Orlov's study, and Polya and I handed them tea. It was only on these occasions that I could gauge the full sweetness of a flunkey's life. Standing for four or five hours at the door, watching that no one's glass should be empty, changing the ash-trays, running to the table to pick up the chalk or a card when it was dropped, and, above all, standing, waiting, being attentive without venturing to speak, to cough, to smile -- is harder, I assure you, is harder than the hardest of field labour. I have stood on watch at sea for four hours at a stretch on stormy winter nights, and to my thinking it is an infinitely easier duty.

They used to play cards till two, sometimes till three o'clock at night, and then, stretching, they would go into the dining-room to supper, or, as Orlov said, for a snack of something. At supper there was conversation. It usually began by Orlov's speaking with laughing eyes of some acquaintance, of some book he had lately been reading, of a new appointment or Government scheme. Kukushkin, always ingratiating, would fall into his tone, and what followed was to me, in my mood at that time, a revolting exhibition. The irony of Orlov and his friends knew no bounds, and spared no one and nothing. If they spoke of religion, it was with irony; they spoke of philosophy, of the significance and object of life -- irony again, if anyone began about the peasantry, it was with irony.

There is in Petersburg a species of men whose specialty it is to jeer at every aspect of life; they cannot even pass by a starving man or a suicide without saying something vulgar. But Orlov and his friends did not jeer or make jokes, they talked ironically. They used to say that there was no God, and personality was completely lost at death; the immortals only existed in the French Academy. Real good did not and could not possibly exist, as its existence was conditional upon human perfection, which was a logical absurdity. Russia was a country as poor and dull as Persia. The intellectual class was hopeless; in Pekarsky's opinion the overwhelming majority in it were incompetent persons, good for nothing. The people were drunken, lazy, thievish, and degenerate. We had no science, our literature was uncouth, our commerce rested on swindling -- "No selling without cheating." And everything was in that style, and everything was a subject for laughter.

Towards the end of supper the wine made them more good-humoured, and they passed to more lively conversation. They laughed over Gruzin's family life, over Kukushkin's conquests, or at Pekarsky, who had, they said, in his account book one page headed *Charity* and another *Physiological Necessities.* They said that no wife was faithful; that there was no wife from whom one could not, with practice, obtain caresses without leaving her drawing-room while her husband was sitting in his study close by; that girls in their teens were perverted and knew everything. Orlov had preserved a letter of a schoolgirl of fourteen: on her way home from school she had "hooked an officer on the Nevsky," who had, it appears, taken her home with him, and had only let her go late in the evening; and she hastened to write about this to her school friend to share her joy with her. They maintained that there was not and never had been such a thing as moral purity, and that evidently it was unnecessary; mankind had so far done very well without it. The harm done by so-called vice was undoubtedly exaggerated. Vices which are punished by our legal code had not prevented Diogenes from being a philosopher and a teacher. Cæsar and Cicero were profligates and at the same time great men. Cato in his old age married a young girl, and yet he was regarded as a great ascetic and a pillar of morality.

At three or four o'clock the party broke up or they went off together out of town, or to Officers' Street, to the house of a certain Varvara Ossipovna, while I retired to my quarters, and was kept awake a long while by coughing and headache.

IV

Three weeks after I entered Orlov's service -- it was Sunday morning, I remember -- somebody rang the bell. It was not yet eleven, and Orlov was still asleep. I went to open the door. You can imagine my astonishment when I found a lady in a veil standing at the door on the landing.

"Is Georgy Ivanitch up?" she asked.

From her voice I recognised Zinaida Fyodorovna, to whom I had taken letters in Znamensky Street. I don't remember whether I had time or self-possession to answer her -- I was taken aback at seeing her. And, indeed, she did not need my answer. In a flash she had darted by me, and, filling the hall with the fragrance of her perfume, which I remember to this day, she went on, and her footsteps died away. For at least half an hour afterwards I heard nothing. But again someone rang. This time it was a smartly dressed girl, who looked like a maid in a wealthy family, accompanied by our house porter. Both were out of breath, carrying two trunks and a dress-basket.

"These are for Zinaida Fyodorovna," said the girl.

And she went down without saying another word. All this was mysterious, and made Polya, who had a deep admiration for the pranks of her betters, smile slyly to herself; she looked as though she would like to say, "So that's what we're up to," and she walked about the whole time on tiptoe. At last we heard footsteps; Zinaida Fyodorovna came quickly into the hall, and seeing me at the door of my room, said:

"Stepan, take Georgy Ivanitch his things."

When I went in to Orlov with his clothes and his boots, he was sitting on the bed with his feet on the bearskin rug. There was an air of embarrassment about his whole figure. He did not notice me, and my menial opinion did not interest him; he was evidently perturbed and embarrassed before himself, before his inner eye. He dressed, washed, and used his combs and brushes silently and deliberately, as though allowing himself time to think over his position and to reflect, and even from his back one could see he was troubled and dissatisfied with himself.

They drank coffee together. Zinaida Fyodorovna poured out coffee for herself and for Orlov, then she put her elbows on the table and laughed.

"I still can't believe it," she said. "When one has been a long while on onc's travels and reaches a hotel at last, it's difficult to believe that one hasn't to go on. It is pleasant to breathe freely."

With the expression of a child who very much wants to be mischievous, she sighed with relief and laughed again.

"You will excuse me," said Orlov, nodding towards the coffee. "Reading at breakfast is a habit I can't get over. But I can do two things at once -- read and listen."

"Read away. . . . You shall keep your habits and your freedom. But why do you look so solemn? Are you always like that in the morning, or is it only to-day? Aren't you glad?"

"Yes, I am. But I must own I am a little overwhelmed."

"Why? You had plenty of time to prepare yourself for my descent upon you. I've been threatening to come every day."

"Yes, but I didn't expect you to carry out your threat to-day."

"I didn't expect it myself, but that's all the better. It's all the better, my dear. It's best to have an aching tooth out and have done with it."

"Yes, of course."

"Oh, my dear," she said, closing her eyes, "all is well that ends well; but before this happy ending, what suffering there has been! My laughing means nothing; I am glad, I am happy, but I feel more like crying than laughing. Yesterday I had to fight a regular battle," she went on in French. "God alone knows how wretched I was. But I laugh because I can't believe in it. I keep fancying that my sitting here drinking coffee with you is not real, but a dream."

Then, still speaking French, she described how she had broken with her husband the day before and her eyes were alternately full of tears and of laughter while she gazed with rapture at Orlov. She told him her husband had long suspected her, but had avoided explanations; they had frequent quarrels, and usually at the most heated moment he would suddenly subside into silence and depart to his study for fear that in his exasperation he might give utterance to his suspicions or she might herself begin to speak openly. And she had felt guilty, worthless, incapable of taking a bold and serious step, and that had made her hate herself and her husband more every day, and she had suffered the torments of hell. But the day before, when during a quarrel he had cried out in a tearful voice, "My God, when will it end?" and had walked off to his study, she had run after him like a cat after a mouse, and, preventing him from shutting the door, she had cried that she hated him with her whole soul. Then he let her come into the study and she had told him everything, had confessed that she loved someone else, that that someone else was her real, most lawful husband, and that she thought it her true duty to go away to him that very day, whatever might happen, if she were to be shot for it.

"There's a very romantic streak in you," Orlov interrupted, keeping his eyes fixed on the newspaper.

She laughed and went on talking without touching her coffee. Her cheeks glowed and she was a little embarrassed by it, and she looked in confusion at Polya and me. From what she went on to say I learnt that her husband had answered her with threats, reproaches, and finally tears, and that it would have been more accurate to say that she, and not he, had been the attacking party.

"Yes, my dear, so long as I was worked up, everything went all right," she told Orlov; "but as night came on, my spirits sank. You don't believe in God, *George,* but I do believe a little, and I fear retribution. God requires of us patience, magnanimity, self-sacrifice, and here I am refusing to be patient and want to remodel my life to suit myself. Is that right? What if from the point of view of God it's wrong? At two o'clock in the night my husband came to me and said: 'You dare not go away. I'll fetch you back through the police and make a scandal.' And soon afterwards I saw him like a shadow at my door. 'Have mercy on me! Your elopement may injure me in the service. Those words had a coarse effect upon me and made me feel stiff all over. I felt as though the retribution were beginning already; I began crying and trembling with terror. I felt as though the ceiling would fall upon me, that I should be dragged off to the police-station at once, that you would grow cold to me -- all sorts of things, in fact! I thought I would go into a nunnery or become a nurse, and give up all thought of happiness, but then I remembered that you loved me, and that I had no right to dispose of myself without your knowledge; and everything in my mind was in a tangle -- I was in despair and did not know what to do or think. But the sun rose and I grew happier. As soon as it was morning I dashed off to you. Ah, what I've been through, dear one! I haven't slept for two nights!

She was tired out and excited. She was sleepy, and at the same time she wanted to talk endlessly, to laugh and to cry, and to go to a restaurant to lunch that she might feel her freedom.

"You have a cosy flat, but I am afraid it may be small for the two of us," she said, walking rapidly through all the rooms when they had finished breakfast. "What room will you give me? I like this one because it is next to your study."

At one o'clock she changed her dress in the room next to the study, which from that time she called hers, and she went off with Orlov to lunch. They dined, too, at a restaurant, and spent the long interval between lunch and dinner in shopping. Till late at night I was opening the door to messengers and errand-boys from the shops. They bought, among other things, a splendid pier-glass, a dressing-table, a bedstead, and a gorgeous tea service which we did not need. They bought a regular collection of copper saucepans, which we set in a row on the shelf in our cold, empty kitchen. As we were unpacking the tea service Polya's eyes gleamed, and she looked at me two or three times with hatred and fear that I, not she, would be the first to steal one of these charming cups. A lady's writing-table, very expensive and inconvenient, came too. It was evident that Zinaida Fyodorovna contemplated settling with us for good, and meant to make the flat her home.

She came back with Orlov between nine and ten. Full of proud consciousness that she had done something bold and out of the common, passionately in love, and, as she imagined, passionately loved, exhausted, looking forward to a sweet sound sleep, Zinaida Fyodorovna was revelling in her new life. She squeezed her hands together in the excess of her joy, declared that everything was delightful, and swore that she would love Orlov forever; and these vows, and the naïve, almost childish confidence that she too was deeply loved and would be loved forever, made her at least five years younger. She talked charming nonsense and laughed at herself.

"There's no other blessing greater than freedom!" she said, forcing herself to say something serious and edifying. "How absurd it is when you think of it! We attach no value to our own opinion even when it is wise, but tremble before the opinion of all sorts of stupid people. Up to the last minute I was afraid of what other people would say, but as soon as I followed my own instinct and made up my mind to go my own way, my eyes were opened, I overcame my silly fears, and now I am happy and wish everyone could be as happy!"

But her thoughts immediately took another turn, and she began talking of another flat, of wallpapers, horses, a trip to Switzerland and Italy. Orlov was tired by the restaurants and the shops, and was still suffering from the same uneasiness that I had noticed in the morning. He smiled, but more from politeness than pleasure, and when she spoke of anything seriously, he agreed ironically: "Oh, yes."

"Stepan, make haste and find us a good cook," she said to me.

"There's no need to be in a hurry over the kitchen arrangements," said Orlov, looking at me coldly. "We must first move into another flat."

We had never had cooking done at home nor kept horses, because, as he said, "he did not like disorder about him," and only put up with having Polya and me in his flat from necessity. The so-called domestic hearth with its everyday joys and its petty cares offended his taste as vulgarity; to be with child, or to have children and talk about them, was bad form, like a petty bourgeois. And I began to feel very curious to see how these two creatures would get on together in one flat -- she, domestic and home-loving with her copper saucepans and her dreams of a good cook and horses; and he, fond of saying to his friends that a decent and orderly man's flat ought, like a warship, to have nothing in it superfluous -- no women, no children, no rags, no kitchen utensils.

V

Then I will tell you what happened the following Thursday. That day Zinaida Fyodorovna dined at Content's or Donon's. Orlov returned home alone, and Zinaida Fyodorovna, as I learnt afterwards, went to the Petersburg Side to spend with her old governess the time visitors were with us. Orlov did not care to show her to his friends. I realised that at breakfast, when he began assuring her that for the sake of her peace of mind it was essential to give up his Thursday evenings.

As usual the visitors arrived at almost the same time.

"Is your mistress at home, too?" Kukushkin asked me in a whisper.

"No, sir," I answered.

He went in with a sly, oily look in his eyes, smiling mysteriously, rubbing his hands, which were cold from the frost.

"I have the honour to congratulate you," he said to Orlov, shaking all over with ingratiating, obsequious laughter. "May you increase and multiply like the cedars of Lebanon."

The visitors went into the bedroom, and were extremely jocose on the subject of a pair of feminine slippers, the rug that had been put down between the two beds, and a grey dressing-jacket that hung at the foot of the bedstead. They were amused that the obstinate man who despised all the common place details of love had been caught in feminine snares in such a simple and ordinary way.

"He who pointed the finger of scorn is bowing the knee in homage," Kukushkin repeated several times. He had, I may say in parenthesis, an unpleasant habit of adorning his conversation with texts in Church Slavonic. "Sh-sh!" he said as they went from the bedroom into the room next to the study. "Sh-sh! Here Gretchen is dreaming of her Faust."

He went off into a peal of laughter as though he had said something very amusing. I watched Gruzin, expecting that his musical soul would not endure this laughter, but I was mistaken. His thin, good-natured face beamed with pleasure. When they sat down to play cards, he, lisping and choking with laughter, said that all that "dear *George*" wanted to complete his domestic felicity was a cherry-wood pipe and a guitar. Pekarsky laughed sedately, but from his serious expression one could see that Orlov's new love affair was distasteful to him. He did not understand what had happened exactly.

"But how about the husband?" he asked in perplexity, after they had played three rubbers.

"I don't know," answered Orlov.

Pekarsky combed his big beard with his fingers and sank into thought, and he did not speak again till supper-time. When they were seated at supper, he began deliberately, drawling every word:

"Altogether, excuse my saying so, I don't understand either of you. You might love each other and break the seventh commandment to your heart's content -- that I understand. Yes, that's comprehensible. But why make the husband a party to your secrets? Was there any need for that?"

"But does it make any difference?"

"Hm! . . . ." Pekarsky mused. "Well, then, let me tell you this, my friend," he went on, evidently thinking hard: "if I ever marry again and you take it into your head to seduce my wife, please do it so that I don't notice it. It's much more honest to deceive a man than to break up his family life and injure his reputation. I understand. You both imagine that in living together openly you are doing something exceptionally honourable and advanced, but I can't agree with that . . . what shall I call it? . . . romantic attitude?"

Orlov made no reply. He was out of humour and disinclined to talk. Pekarsky, still perplexed, drummed on the table with his fingers, thought a little, and said:

"I don't understand you, all the same. You are not a student and she is not a dressmaker. You are both of you people with means. I should have thought you might have arranged a separate flat for her."

"No, I couldn't. Read Turgenev."

"Why should I read him? I have read him already."

"Turgenev teaches us in his novels that every exalted, noble-minded girl should follow the man she loves to the ends of the earth, and should serve his idea," said Orlov, screwing up his eyes ironically. "The ends of the earth are poetic license; the earth and all its ends can be reduced to the flat of the man she loves. . . . And so not to live in the same flat with the woman who loves you is to deny her her exalted vocation and to refuse to share her ideals. Yes, my dear fellow, Turgenev wrote, and I have to suffer for it."

"What Turgenev has got to do with it I don't understand," said Gruzin softly, and he shrugged his shoulders. "Do you remember, *George,* how in 'Three Meetings' he is walking late in the evening somewhere in Italy, and suddenly hears, *'Vieni pensando a me segretamente,'*" Gruzin hummed. "It's fine."

But she hasn't come to settle with you by force," said Pekarsky. "It was your own wish."

"What next! Far from wishing it, I never imagined that this would ever happen. When she said she was coming to live with me, I thought it was a charming joke on her part."

Everybody laughed.

"I couldn't have wished for such a thing," said Orlov in the tone of a man compelled to justify himself. "I am not a Turgenev hero, and if I ever wanted to free Bulgaria I shouldn't need a lady's company. I look upon love primarily as a necessity of my physical nature, degrading and antagonistic to my spirit; it must either be satisfied with discretion or renounced altogether, otherwise it will bring into one's life elements as unclean as itself. For it to be an enjoyment and not a torment, I will try to make it beautiful and to surround it with a mass of illusions. I should never go and see a woman unless I were sure beforehand that she would be beautiful and fascinating; and I should never go unless I were in the mood. And it is only in that way that we succeed in deceiving one another, and fancying that we are in love and happy. But can I wish for copper saucepans and untidy hair, or like to be seen myself when I am unwashed or out of humour? Zinaida Fyodorovna in the simplicity of her heart wants me to love what I have been shunning all my life. She wants my flat to smell of cooking and washing up; she wants all the fuss of moving into another flat, of driving about with her own horses; she wants to count over my linen and to look after my health; she wants to meddle in my personal life at every instant, and to watch over every step; and at the same time she assures me genuinely that my habits and my freedom will be untouched. She is persuaded that, like a young couple, we shall very soon go for a honeymoon -- that is, she wants to be with me all the time in trains and hotels, while I like to read on the journey and cannot endure talking in trains."

"You should give her a talking to," said Pekarsky.

"What! Do you suppose she would understand me? Why, we think so differently. In her opinion, to leave one's papa and mamma or one's husband for the sake of the man one loves is the height of civic virtue, while I look upon it as childish. To fall in love and run away with a man to her means beginning a new life, while to my mind it means nothing at all. Love and man constitute the chief interest of her life, and possibly it is the philosophy of the unconscious at work in her. Try and make her believe that love is only a simple physical need, like the need of food or clothes; that it doesn't mean the end of the world if wives and husbands are unsatisfactory; that a man may be a profligate and a libertine, and yet a man of honour and a genius; and that, on the other hand, one may abstain from the pleasures of love and at the same time be a stupid, vicious animal! The civilised man of to-day, even among the lower classes -- for instance, the French workman -- spends ten *sous* on dinner, five *sous* on his wine, and five or ten *sous* on woman, and devotes his brain and nerves entirely to his work. But Zinaida Fyodorovna assigns to love not so many *sous,* but her whole soul. I might give her a talking to, but she would raise a wail in answer, and declare in all sincerity that I had ruined her, that she had nothing left to live for."

"Don't say anything to her," said Pekarsky, "but simply take a separate flat for her, that's all."

"That's easy to say."

There was a brief silence.

"But she is charming," said Kukushkin. "She is exquisite. Such women imagine that they will be in love forever, and abandon themselves with tragic intensity."

"But one must keep a head on one's shoulders," said Orlov; "one must be reasonable. All experience gained from everyday life and handed down in innumerable novels and plays, uniformly confirms the fact that adultery and cohabitation of any sort between decent people never lasts longer than two or at most three years, however great the love may have been at the beginning. That she ought to know. And so all this business of moving, of saucepans, hopes of eternal love and harmony, are nothing but a desire to delude herself and me. She is charming and exquisite -- who denies it? But she has turned my life upside down; what I have regarded as trivial and nonsensical till now she has forced me to raise to the level of a serious problem; I serve an idol whom I have never looked upon as God. She is charming -- exquisite, but for some reason now when I am going home, I feel uneasy, as though I expected to meet with something inconvenient at home, such as workmen pulling the stove to pieces and blocking up the place with heaps of bricks. In fact, I am no longer giving up to love a *sous,* but part of my peace of mind and my nerves. And that's bad."

"And she doesn't hear this villain!" sighed Kukushkin. "My dear sir," he said theatrically, "I will relieve you from the burdensome obligation to love that adorable creature! I will wrest Zinaida Fyodorovna from you!"

"You may . . ." said Orlov carelessly.

For half a minute Kukushkin laughed a shrill little laugh, shaking all over, then he said:

"Look out; I am in earnest! Don't you play the Othello afterwards!"

They all began talking of Kukushkin's indefatigable energy in love affairs, how irresistible he was to women, and what a danger he was to husbands; and how the devil would roast him in the other world for his immorality in this. He screwed up his eyes and remained silent, and when the names of ladies of their acquaintance were mentioned, he held up his little finger -- as though to say they mustn't give away other people's secrets.

Orlov suddenly looked at his watch.

His friends understood, and began to take their leave. I remember that Gruzin, who was a little drunk, was wearisomely long in getting off. He put on his coat, which was cut like children's coats in poor families, pulled up the collar, and began telling some long-winded story; then, seeing he was not listened to, he flung the rug that smelt of the nursery over one shoulder, and with a guilty and imploring face begged me to find his hat.

"*George*, my angel," he said tenderly. "Do as I ask you, dear boy; come out of town with us!"

"You can go, but I can't. I am in the position of a married man now."

"She is a dear, she won't be angry. My dear chief, come along! It's glorious weather; there's snow and frost. . . . Upon my word, you want shaking up a bit; you are out of humour. I don't know what the devil is the matter with you. . . ."

Orlov stretched, yawned, and looked at Pekarsky.

"Are you going?" he said, hesitating.

"I don't know. Perhaps."

"Shall I get drunk? All right, I'll come," said Orlov after some hesitation. "Wait a minute; I'll get some money."

He went into the study, and Gruzin slouched in, too, dragging his rug after him. A minute later both came back into the hall. Gruzin, a little drunk and very pleased, was crumpling a ten-rouble note in his hands.

"We'll settle up to-morrow," he said. "And she is kind, she won't be cross. . . . She is my Lisotchka's godmother; I am fond of her, poor thing! Ah, my dear fellow!" he laughed joyfully, and pressing his forehead on Pekarsky's back. "Ah, Pekarsky, my dear soul! Advocatissimus -- as dry as a biscuit, but you bet he is fond of women. . . ."

"Fat ones," said Orlov, putting on his fur coat. "But let us get off, or we shall be meeting her on the doorstep."

"'*Vieni pensando a me segretamente*,'" hummed Gruzin.

At last they drove off: Orlov did not sleep at home, and returned next day at dinner-time.

VI

Zinaida Fyodorovna had lost her gold watch, a present from her father. This loss surprised and alarmed her. She spent half a day going through the rooms, looking helplessly on all the tables and on all the windows. But the watch had disappeared completely.

Only three days afterwards Zinaida Fyodorovna, on coming in, left her purse in the hall. Luckily for me, on that occasion it was not I but Polya who helped her off with her coat. When the purse was missed, it could not be found in the hall.

"Strange," said Zinaida Fyodorovna in bewilderment. "I distinctly remember taking it out of my pocket to pay the cabman . . . and then I put it here near the looking-glass. It's very odd!"

I had not stolen it, but I felt as though I had stolen it and had been caught in the theft. Tears actually came into my eyes. When they were seated at dinner, Zinaida Fyodorovna said to Orlov in French:

"There seem to be spirits in the flat. I lost my purse in the hall to-day, and now, lo and behold, it is on my table. But it's not quite a disinterested trick of the spirits. They took out a gold coin and twenty roubles in notes."

"You are always losing something; first it's your watch and then it's your money . . ." said Orlov. "Why is it nothing of the sort ever happens to me?"

A minute later Zinaida Fyodorovna had forgotten the trick played by the spirits, and was telling with a laugh how the week before she had ordered some notepaper and had forgotten to give her new address, and the shop had sent the paper to her old home at her husband's, who had to pay twelve roubles for it. And suddenly she turned her eyes on Polya and looked at her intently. She blushed as she did so, and was so confused that she began talking of something else.

When I took in the coffee to the study, Orlov was standing with his back to the fire and she was sitting in an arm-chair facing him.

"I am not in a bad temper at all," she was saying in French. "But I have been putting things together, and now I see it clearly. I can give you the day and the hour when she stole my watch. And the purse? There can be no doubt about it. Oh!" she laughed as she took the coffee from me. "Now I understand why I am always losing my handkerchiefs and gloves. Whatever you say, I shall dismiss the magpie to-morrow and send Stepan for my Sofya. She is not a thief and has not got such a repulsive appearance."

"You are out of humour. To-morrow you will feel differently, and will realise that you can't discharge people simply because you suspect them."

"It's not suspicion; it's certainty," said Zinaida Fyodorovna. "So long as I suspected that unhappy-faced, poor-looking valet of yours, I said nothing. It's too bad of you not to believe me, *George*."

"If we think differently about anything, it doesn't follow that I don't believe you. You may be right," said Orlov, turning round and flinging his cigarette-end into the fire, "but there is no need to be excited about it, anyway. In fact, I must say, I never expected my humble establishment would cause you so much serious worry and agitation. You've lost a gold coin: never mind -- you may have a hundred of mine; but to change my habits, to pick up a new housemaid, to wait till she is used to the place -- all that's a tedious, tiring business and does not suit me. Our present maid certainly is fat, and has, perhaps, a weakness for gloves and handkerchiefs, but she is perfectly well behaved, well trained, and does not shriek when Kukushkin pinches her."

"You mean that you can't part with her? . . . Why don't you say so?"

"Are you jealous?"

"Yes, I am," said Zinaida Fyodorovna, decidedly.

"Thank you."

"Yes, I am jealous," she repeated, and tears glistened in her eyes. "No, it's something worse . . . which I find it difficult to find a name for." She pressed her hands on her temples, and went on impulsively. "You men are so disgusting! It's horrible!"

"I see nothing horrible about it."

"I've not seen it; I don't know; but they say that you men begin with housemaids as boys, and get so used to it that you feel no repugnance. I don't know, I don't know, but I have actually read . . .*George,* of course you are right," she said, going up to Orlov and changing to a caressing and imploring tone. "I really am out of humour to-day. But, you must understand, I can't help it. She disgusts me and I am afraid of her. It makes me miserable to see her."

"Surely you can rise above such paltriness?" said Orlov, shrugging his shoulders in perplexity, and walking away from the fire. "Nothing could be simpler: take no notice of her, and then she won't disgust you, and you won't need to make a regular tragedy out of a trifle."

I went out of the study, and I don't know what answer Orlov received. Whatever it was, Polya remained. After that Zinaida Fyodorovna never applied to her for anything, and evidently tried to dispense with her services. When Polya handed her anything or even passed by her, jingling her bangle and rustling her skirts, she shuddered.

I believe that if Gruzin or Pekarsky had asked Orlov to dismiss Polya he would have done so without the slightest hesitation, without troubling about any explanations. He was easily persuaded, like all indifferent people. But in his relations with Zinaida Fyodorovna he displayed for some reason, even in trifles, an obstinacy which sometimes was almost irrational. I knew beforehand that if Zinaida Fyodorovna liked anything, it would be certain not to please Orlov. When on coming in from shopping she made haste to show him with pride some new purchase, he would glance at it and say coldly that the more unnecessary objects they had in the flat, the less airy it would be. It sometimes happened that after putting on his dress clothes to go out somewhere, and after saying good-bye to Zinaida Fyodorovna, he would suddenly change his mind and remain at home from sheer perversity. I used to think that he remained at home then simply in order to feel injured.

"Why are you staying?" said Zinaida Fyodorovna, with a show of vexation, though at the same time she was radiant with delight. "Why do you? You are not accustomed to spending your evenings at home, and I don't want you to alter your habits on my account. Do go out as usual, if you don't want me to feel guilty."

"No one is blaming you," said Orlov.

With the air of a victim he stretched himself in his easy-chair in the study, and shading his eyes with his hand, took up a book. But soon the book dropped from his hand, he turned heavily in his chair, and again screened his eyes as though from the sun. Now he felt annoyed that he had not gone out.

"May I come in?" Zinaida Fyodorovna would say, coming irresolutely into the study. "Are you reading? I felt dull by myself, and have come just for a minute . . . to have a peep at you."

I remember one evening she went in like that, irresolutely and inappropriately, and sank on the rug at Orlov's feet, and from her soft, timid movements one could see that she did not understand his mood and was afraid.

"You are always reading . . ." she said cajolingly, evidently wishing to flatter him. "Do you know, *George,* what is one of the secrets of your success? You are very clever and well-read. What book have you there?"

Orlov answered. A silence followed for some minutes which seemed to me very long. I was standing in the drawing-room, from which I could watch them, and was afraid of coughing.

"There is something I wanted to tell you," said Zinaida Fyodorovna, and she laughed; "shall I? Very likely you'll laugh and say that I flatter myself. You know I want, I want horribly to believe that you are staying at home to-night for my sake . . . that we might spend the evening together. Yes? May I think so?"

"Do," he said, screening his eyes. "The really happy man is he who thinks not only of what is, but of what is not."

"That was a long sentence which I did not quite understand. You mean happy people live in their imagination. Yes, that's true. I love to sit in your study in the evening and let my thoughts carry me far, far away. . . . It's pleasant sometimes to dream. Let us dream aloud, *George.*"

"I've never been at a girls' boarding-school; I never learnt the art."

"You are out of humour?" said Zinaida Fyodorovna, taking Orlov's hand. "Tell me why. When you are like that, I'm afraid. I don't know whether your head aches or whether you are angry with me. . . ."

Again there was a silence lasting several long minutes.

"Why have you changed?" she said softly. "Why are you never so tender or so gay as you used to be at Znamensky Street? I've been with you almost a month, but it seems to me as though we had not yet begun to live, and have not yet talked of anything as we ought to. You always answer me with jokes or else with a long cold lecture like a teacher. And there is something cold in your jokes. . . . Why have you given up talking to me seriously?"

"I always talk seriously."

"Well, then, let us talk. For God's sake, *George*. . . . Shall we?"

"Certainly, but about what?"

"Let us talk of our life, of our future," said Zinaida Fyodorovna dreamily. "I keep making plans for our life, plans and plans -- and I enjoy doing it so! *George,* I'll begin with the question, when are you going to give up your post?"

"What for?" asked Orlov, taking his hand from his forehead.

"With your views you cannot remain in the service. You are out of place there."

"My views?" Orlov repeated. "My views? In conviction and temperament I am an ordinary official, one of Shtchedrin's heroes. You take me for something different, I venture to assure you."

"Joking again, *George!*"

"Not in the least. The service does not satisfy me, perhaps; but, anyway, it is better for me than anything else. I am used to it, and in it I meet men of my own sort; I am in my place there and find it tolerable."

"You hate the service and it revolts you."

"Indeed? If I resign my post, take to dreaming aloud and letting myself be carried away into another world, do you suppose that that world would be less hateful to me than the service?"

"You are ready to libel yourself in order to contradict me." Zinaida Fyodorovna was offended and got up. "I am sorry I began this talk."

"Why are you angry? I am not angry with you for not being an official. Everyone lives as he likes best."

"Why, do you live as you like best? Are you free? To spend your life writing documents that are opposed to your own ideas," Zinaida Fyodorovna went on, clasping her hands in despair: "to submit to authority, congratulate your superiors at the New Year, and then cards and nothing but cards: worst of all, to be working for a system which must be distasteful to you -- no, *George,* no! You should not make such horrid jokes. It's dreadful. You are a man of ideas, and you ought to be working for your ideas and nothing else."

"You really take me for quite a different person from what I am," sighed Orlov.

"Say simply that you don't want to talk to me. You dislike me, that's all," said Zinaida Fyodorovna through her tears.

"Look here, my dear," said Orlov admonishingly, sitting up in his chair. "You were pleased to observe yourself that I am a clever, well-read man, and to teach one who knows does nothing but harm. I know very well all the ideas, great and small, which you mean when you call me a man of ideas. So if I prefer the service and cards to those ideas, you may be sure I have good grounds for it. That's one thing. Secondly, you have, so far as I know, never been in the service, and can only have drawn your ideas of Government service from anecdotes and indifferent novels. So it would not be amiss for us to make a compact, once for all, not to talk of things we know already or of things about which we are not competent to speak."

"Why do you speak to me like that?" said Zinaida Fyodorovna, stepping back as though in horror. "What for? *George,* for God's sake, think what you are saying!"

Her voice quivered and broke; she was evidently trying to restrain her tears, but she suddenly broke into sobs.

"*George,* my darling, I am perishing!" she said in French, dropping down before Orlov, and laying her head on his knees. "I am miserable, I am exhausted. I can't bear it, I can't bear it. . . . In my childhood my hateful, depraved stepmother, then my husband, now you . . . you! . . . You meet my mad love with coldness and irony. . . . And that horrible, insolent servant," she went on, sobbing. "Yes, yes, I see: I am not your wife nor your friend, but a woman you don't respect because she has become your mistress. . . . I shall kill myself!"

I had not expected that her words and her tears would make such an impression on Orlov. He flushed, moved uneasily in his chair, and instead of irony, his face wore a look of stupid, schoolboyish dismay.

"My darling, you misunderstood me," he muttered helplessly, touching her hair and her shoulders. "Forgive me, I entreat you. I was unjust and I hate myself."

"I insult you with my whining and complaints. You are a true, generous . . . rare man -- I am conscious of it every minute; but I've been horribly depressed for the last few days. . ."

Zinaida Fyodorovna impulsively embraced Orlov and kissed him on the cheek.

"Only please don't cry," he said.

"No, no. . . . I've had my cry, and now I am better."

"As for the servant, she shall be gone to-morrow," he said, still moving uneasily in his chair.

"No, she must stay, *George!* Do you hear? I am not afraid of her now. . . . One must rise above trifles and not imagine silly things. You are right! You are a wonderful, rare person!"

She soon left off crying. With tears glistening on her eyelashes, sitting on Orlov's knee, she told him in a low voice something touching, something like a reminiscence of childhood and youth. She stroked his face, kissed him, and carefully examined his hands with the rings on them and the charms on his watch-chain. She was carried away by what she was saying, and by being near the man she loved, and probably because her tears had cleared and refreshed her soul, there was a note of wonderful candour and sincerity in her voice. And Orlov played with her chestnut hair and kissed her hands, noiselessly pressing them to his lips.

Then they had tea in the study, and Zinaida Fyodorovna read aloud some letters. Soon after midnight they went to bed. I had a fearful pain in my side that night, and I not get warm or go to sleep till morning. I could hear Orlov go from the bedroom into his study. After sitting there about an hour, he rang the bell. In my pain and exhaustion I forgot all the rules and conventions, and went to his study in my night attire, barefooted. Orlov, in his dressing-gown and cap, was standing in the doorway, waiting for me.

"When you are sent for you should come dressed," he said sternly. "Bring some fresh candles."

I was about to apologise, but suddenly broke into a violent cough, and clutched at the side of the door to save myself from falling.

"Are you ill?" said Orlov.

I believe it was the first time of our acquaintance that he addressed me not in the singular -- goodness knows why. Most likely, in my night clothes and with my face distorted by coughing, I played my part poorly, and was very little like a flunkey.

"If you are ill, why do you take a place?" he said.

"That I may not die of starvation," I answered.

"How disgusting it all is, really!" he said softly, going up to his table.

While hurriedly getting into my coat, I put up and lighted fresh candles. He was sitting at the table, with feet stretched out on a low chair, cutting a book.

I left him deeply engrossed, and the book did not drop out of his hands as it had done in the evening.

VII

Now that I am writing these lines I am restrained by that dread of appearing sentimental and ridiculous, in which I have been trained from childhood; when I want to be affectionate or to say anything tender, I don't know how to be natural. And it is that dread, together with lack of practice, that prevents me from being able to express with perfect clearness what was passing in my soul at that time.

I was not in love with Zinaida Fyodorovna, but in the ordinary human feeling I had for her, there was far more youth, freshness, and joyousness than in Orlov's love.

As I worked in the morning, cleaning boots or sweeping the rooms, I waited with a thrill at my heart for the moment when I should hear her voice and her footsteps. To stand watching her as she drank her coffee in the morning or ate her lunch, to hold her fur coat for her in the hall, and to put the goloshes on her little feet while she rested her hand on my shoulder; then to wait till the hall porter rang up for me, to meet her at the door, cold, and rosy, powdered with the snow, to listen to her brief exclamations about the frost or the cabman -- if only you knew how much all that meant to me! I longed to be in love, to have a wife and child of my own. I wanted my future wife to have just such a face, such a voice. I dreamed of it at dinner, and in the street when I was sent on some errand, and when I lay awake at night. Orlov rejected with disgust children, cooking, copper saucepans, and feminine knicknacks and I gathered them all up, tenderly cherished them in my dreams, loved them, and begged them of destiny. I had visions of a wife, a nursery, a little house with garden paths. . . .

I knew that if I did love her I could never dare hope for the miracle of her returning my love, but that reflection did not worry me. In my quiet, modest feeling akin to ordinary affection, there was no jealousy of Orlov or even envy of him, since I realised that for a wreck like me happiness was only to be found in dreams.

When Zinaida Fyodorovna sat up night after night for her *George,* looking immovably at a book of which she never turned a page, or when she shuddered and turned pale at Polya's crossing the room, I suffered with her, and the idea occurred to me to lance this festering wound as quickly as possible by letting her know what was said here at supper on Thursdays; but -- how was it to be done? More and more often I saw her tears. For the first weeks she laughed and sang to herself, even when Orlov was not at home, but by the second month there was a mournful stillness in our flat broken only on Thursday evenings.

She flattered Orlov, and to wring from him a counterfeit smile or kiss, was ready to go on her knees to him, to fawn on him like a dog. Even when her heart was heaviest, she could not resist glancing into a looking-glass if she passed one and straightening her hair. It seemed strange to me that she could still take an interest in clothes and go into ecstasies over her purchases. It did not seem in keeping with her genuine grief. She paid attention to the fashions and ordered expensive dresses. What for? On whose account? I particularly remember one dress which cost four hundred roubles. To give four hundred roubles for an unnecessary, useless dress while women for their hard day's work get only twenty kopecks a day without food, and the makers of Venice and Brussels lace are only paid half a franc a day on the supposition that they can earn the rest by immorality! And it seemed strange to me that Zinaida Fyodorovna was not conscious of it; it vexed me. But she had only to go out of the house for me to find excuses and explanations foreverything, and to be waiting eagerly for the hall porter to ring for me.

She treated me as a flunkey, a being of a lower order. One may pat a dog, and yet not notice it; I was given orders and asked questions, but my presence was not observed. My master and mistress thought it unseemly to say more to me than is usually said to servants; if when waiting at dinner I had laughed or put in my word in the conversation, they would certainly have thought I was mad and have dismissed me. Zinaida Fyodorovna was favourably disposed to me, all the same. When she was sending me on some errand or explaining to me the working of a new lamp or anything of that sort, her face was extraordinarily kind, frank, and cordial, and her eyes looked me straight in the face. At such moments I always fancied she remembered with gratitude how I used to bring her letters to Znamensky Street. When she rang the bell, Polya, who considered me her favourite and hated me for it, used to say with a jeering smile:

"Go along, *your* mistress wants you."

Zinaida Fyodorovna considered me as a being of a lower order, and did not suspect that if anyone in the house were in a humiliating position it was she. She did not know that I, a footman, was unhappy on her account, and used to ask myself twenty times a day what was in store for her and how it would all end. Things were growing visibly worse day by day. After the evening on which they had talked of his official work, Orlov, who could not endure tears, unmistakably began to avoid conversation with her; whenever Zinaida Fyodorovna began to argue, or to beseech him, or seemed on the point of crying, he seized some plausible excuse for retreating to his study or going out. He more and more rarely slept at home, and still more rarely dined there: on Thursdays he was the one to suggest some expedition to his friends. Zinaida Fyodorovna was still dreaming of having the cooking done at home, of moving to a new flat, of travelling abroad, but her dreams remained dreams. Dinner was sent in from the restaurant. Orlov asked her not to broach the question of moving until after they had come back from abroad, and apropos of their foreign tour, declared that they could not go till his hair had grown long, as one could not go trailing from hotel to hotel and serving the idea without long hair.

To crown it all, in Orlov's absence, Kukushkin began calling at the flat in the evening. There was nothing exceptional in his behaviour, but I could never forget the conversation in which he had offered to cut Orlov out. He was regaled with tea and red wine, and he used to titter and, anxious to say something pleasant, would declare that a free union was superior in every respect to legal marriage, and that all decent people ought really to come to Zinaida Fyodorovna and fall at her feet.

VIII

Christmas was spent drearily in vague anticipations of calamity. On New Year's Eve Orlov unexpectedly announced at breakfast that he was being sent to assist a senator who was on a revising commission in a certain province.

"I don't want to go, but I can't find an excuse to get off," he said with vexation. "I must go; there's nothing for it."

Such news instantly made Zinaida Fyodorovna's eyes look red. "Is it for long?" she asked.

"Five days or so."

"I am glad, really, you are going," she said after a moment's thought. "It will be a change for you. You will fall in love with someone on the way, and tell me about it afterwards."

At every opportunity she tried to make Orlov feel that she did not restrict his liberty in any way, and that he could do exactly as he liked, and this artless, transparent strategy deceived no one, and only unnecessarily reminded Orlov that he was not free.

"I am going this evening," he said, and began reading the paper.

Zinaida Fyodorovna wanted to see him off at the station, but he dissuaded her, saying that he was not going to America, and not going to be away five years, but only five days -- possibly less.

The parting took place between seven and eight. He put one arm round her, and kissed her on the lips and on the forehead.

"Be a good girl, and don't be depressed while I am away," he said in a warm, affectionate tone which touched even me. "God keep you!"

She looked greedily into his face, to stamp his dear features on her memory, then she put her arms gracefully round his neck and laid her head on his breast.

"Forgive me our misunderstandings," she said in French. "Husband and wife cannot help quarrelling if they love each other, and I love you madly. Don't forget me. . . . Wire to me often and fully."

Orlov kissed her once more, and, without saying a word, went out in confusion. When he heard the click of the lock as the door closed, he stood still in the middle of the staircase in hesitation and glanced upwards. It seemed to me that if a sound had reached him at that moment from above, he would have turned back. But all was quiet. He straightened his coat and went downstairs irresolutely.

The sledges had been waiting a long while at the door. Orlov got into one, I got into the other with two portmanteaus. It was a hard frost and there were fires smoking at the cross-roads. The cold wind nipped my face and hands, and took my breath away as we drove rapidly along; and, closing my eyes, I thought what a splendid woman she was. How she loved him! Even useless rubbish is collected in the courtyards nowadays and used for some purpose, even broken glass is considered a useful commodity, but something so precious, so rare, as the love of a refined, young, intelligent, and good woman is utterly thrown away and wasted. One of the early sociologists regarded every evil passion as a force which might by judicious management be turned to good, while among us even a fine, noble passion springs up and dies away in impotence, turned to no account, misunderstood or vulgarised. Why is it?

The sledges stopped unexpectedly. I opened my eyes and I saw that we had come to a standstill in Sergievsky Street, near a big house where Pekarsky lived. Orlov got out of the sledge and vanished into the entry. Five minutes later Pekarsky's footman came out, bareheaded, and, angry with the frost, shouted to me:

"Are you deaf? Pay the cabmen and go upstairs. You are wanted!"

At a complete loss, I went to the first storey. I had been to Pekarsky's flat before -- that is, I had stood in the hall and looked into the drawing-room, and, after the damp, gloomy street, it always struck me by the brilliance of its picture-frames, its bronzes and expensive furniture. To-day in the midst of this splendour I saw Gruzin, Kukushkin, and, after a minute, Orlov.

"Look here, Stepan," he said, coming up to me. "I shall be staying here till Friday or Saturday. If any letters or telegrams come, you must bring them here every day. At home, of course you will say that I have gone, and send my greetings. Now you can go."

When I reached home Zinaida Fyodorovna was lying on the sofa in the drawing-room, eating a pear. There was only one candle burning in the candelabra.

"Did you catch the train?" asked Zinaida Fyodorovna.

"Yes, madam. His honour sends his greetings."

I went into my room and I, too, lay down. I had nothing to do, and I did not want to read. I was not surprised and I was not indignant. I only racked my brains to think why this deception was necessary. It is only boys in their teens who deceive their mistresses like that. How was it that a man who had thought and read so much could not imagine anything more sensible? I must confess I had by no means a poor opinion of his intelligence. I believe if he had had to deceive his minister or any other influential person he would have put a great deal of skill and energy into doing so; but to deceive a woman, the first idea that occurred to him was evidently good enough. If it succeeded -- well and good; if it did not, there would be no harm done -- he could tell some other lie just as quickly and simply, with no mental effort.

At midnight when the people on the floor overhead were moving their chairs and shouting hurrah to welcome the New Year, Zinaida Fyodorovna rang for me from the room next to the study. Languid from lying down so long, she was sitting at the table, writing something on a scrap of paper.

"I must send a telegram," she said, with a smile. "Go to the station as quick as you can and ask them to send it after him."

Going out into the street, I read on the scrap of paper:

"May the New Year bring new happiness. Make haste and telegraph; I miss you dreadfully. It seems an eternity. I am only sorry I can't send a thousand kisses and my very heart by telegraph. Enjoy yourself, my darling.-- ZINA."

I sent the telegram, and next morning I gave her the receipt.

IX

The worst of it was that Orlov had thoughtlessly let Polya, too, into the secret of his deception, telling her to bring his shirts to Sergievsky Street. After that, she looked at Zinaida Fyodorovna with a malignant joy and hatred I could not understand, and was never tired of snorting with delight to herself in her own room and in the hall.

"She's outstayed her welcome; it's time she took herself off!" she would say with zest. "She ought to realise that herself. . . ."

She already divined by instinct that Zinaida Fyodorovna would not be with us much longer, and, not to let the chance slip, carried off everything she set her eyes on -- smelling-bottles, tortoise-shell hairpins, handkerchiefs, shoes! On the day after New Year's Day, Zinaida Fyodorovna summoned me to her room and told me in a low voice that she missed her black dress. And then she walked through all the rooms, with a pale, frightened, and indignant face, talking to herself:

"It's too much! It's beyond everything. Why, it's unheard-of insolence!"

At dinner she tried to help herself to soup, but could not -- her hands were trembling. Her lips were trembling, too. She looked helplessly at the soup and at the little pies, waiting for the trembling to pass off, and suddenly she could not resist looking at Polya.

"You can go, Polya," she said. "Stepan is enough by himself."

"I'll stay; I don't mind," answered Polya.

"There's no need for you to stay. You go away altogether," Zinaida Fyodorovna went on, getting up in great agitation. "You may look out for another place. You can go at once."

"I can't go away without the master's orders. He engaged me. It must be as he orders."

"You can take orders from me, too! I am mistress here!" said Zinaida Fyodorovna, and she flushed crimson.

"You may be the mistress, but only the master can dismiss me. It was he engaged me."

"You dare not stay here another minute!" cried Zinaida Fyodorovna, and she struck the plate with her knife. "You are a thief! Do you hear?"

Zinaida Fyodorovna flung her dinner-napkin on the table, and with a pitiful, suffering face, went quickly out of the room. Loudly sobbing and wailing something indistinct, Polya, too, went away. The soup and the grouse got cold. And for some reason all the restaurant dainties on the table struck me as poor, thievish, like Polya. Two pies on a plate had a particularly miserable and guilty air. "We shall be taken back to the restaurant to-day," they seemed to be saying, "and to-morrow we shall be put on the table again for some official or celebrated singer."

"She is a fine lady, indeed," I heard uttered in Polya's room. "I could have been a lady like that long ago, but I have some self-respect! We'll see which of us will be the first to go!"

Zinaida Fyodorovna rang the bell. She was sitting in her room, in the corner, looking as though she had been put in the corner as a punishment.

"No telegram has come?" she asked.

"No, madam."

"Ask the porter; perhaps there is a telegram. And don't leave the house," she called after me. "I am afraid to be left alone."

After that I had to run down almost every hour to ask the porter whether a telegram had come. I must own it was a dreadful time! To avoid seeing Polya, Zinaida Fyodorovna dined and had tea in her own room; it was here that she slept, too, on a short sofa like a half-moon, and she made her own bed. For the first days I took the telegrams; but, getting no answer, she lost her faith in me and began telegraphing herself. Looking at her, I, too, began impatiently hoping for a telegram. I hoped he would contrive some deception, would make arrangements, for instance, that a telegram should be sent to her from some station. If he were too much engrossed with cards or had been attracted by some other woman, I thought that both Gruzin and Kukushkin would remind him of us. But our expectations were vain. Five times a day I would go in to Zinaida Fyodorovna, intending to tell her the truth, But her eyes looked piteous as a fawn's, her shoulders seemed to droop, her lips were moving, and I went away again without saying a word. Pity and sympathy seemed to rob me of all manliness. Polya, as cheerful and well satisfied with herself as though nothing had happened, was tidying the master's study and the bedroom, rummaging in the cupboards, and making the crockery jingle, and when she passed Zinaida Fyodorovna's door, she hummed something and coughed. She was pleased that her mistress was hiding from her. In the evening she would go out somewhere, and rang at two or three o'clock in the morning, and I had to open the door to her and listen to remarks about my cough. Immediately afterwards I would hear another ring; I would run to the room next to the study, and Zinaida Fyodorovna, putting her head out of the door, would ask, "Who was it rung?" while she looked at my hands to see whether I had a telegram.

When at last on Saturday the bell rang below and she heard the familiar voice on the stairs, she was so delighted that she broke into sobs. She rushed to meet him, embraced him, kissed him on the breast and sleeves, said something one could not understand. The hall porter brought up the portmanteaus; Polya's cheerful voice was heard. It was as though someone had come home for the holidays.

"Why didn't you wire?" asked Zinaida Fyodorovna, breathless with joy. "Why was it? I have been in misery; I don't know how I've lived through it. . . . Oh, my God!"

"It was very simple! I returned with the senator to Moscow the very first day, and didn't get your telegrams," said Orlov. "After dinner, my love, I'll give you a full account of my doings, but now I must sleep and sleep. . . . I am worn out with the journey."

It was evident that he had not slept all night; he had probably been playing cards and drinking freely. Zinaida Fyodorovna put him to bed, and we all walked about on tiptoe all that day. The dinner went off quite satisfactorily, but when they went into the study and had coffee the explanation began. Zinaida Fyodorovna began talking of something rapidly in a low voice; she spoke in French, and her words flowed like a stream. Then I heard a loud sigh from Orlov, and his voice.

"My God!" he said in French. "Have you really nothing fresher to tell me than this everlasting tale of your servant's misdeeds?"

"But, my dear, she robbed me and said insulting things to me."

"But why is it she doesn't rob me or say insulting things to me? Why is it I never notice the maids nor the porters nor the footmen? My dear, you are simply capricious and refuse to know your own mind. . . . I really begin to suspect that you must be in a certain condition. When I offered to let her go, you insisted on her remaining, and now you want me to turn her away. I can be obstinate, too, in such cases. You want her to go, but I want her to remain. That's the only way to cure you of your nerves."

"Oh, very well, very well," said Zinaida Fyodorovna in alarm. "Let us say no more about that. . . . Let us put it off till to-morrow. . . . Now tell me about Moscow. . . . What is going on in Moscow?"

X

After lunch next day -- it was the seventh of January, St. John the Baptist's Day -- Orlov put on his black dress coat and his decoration to go to visit his father and congratulate him on his name day. He had to go at two o'clock, and it was only half-past one when he had finished dressing. What was he to do for that half-hour? He walked about the drawing-room, declaiming some congratulatory verses which he had recited as a child to his father and mother.

Zinaida Fyodorovna, who was just going out to a dressmaker's or to the shops, was sitting, listening to him with a smile. I don't know how their conversation began, but when I took Orlov his gloves, he was standing before her with a capricious, beseeching face, saying:

"For God's sake, in the name of everything that's holy, don't talk of things that everybody knows! What an unfortunate gift our intellectual thoughtful ladies have for talking with enthusiasm and an air of profundity of things that every schoolboy is sick to death of! Ah, if only you would exclude from our conjugal programme all these serious questions! How grateful I should be to you!"

"We women may not dare, it seems, to have views of our own."

"I give you full liberty to be as liberal as you like, and quote from any authors you choose, but make me one concession: don't hold forth in my presence on either of two subjects: the corruption of the upper classes and the evils of the marriage system. Do understand me, at last. The upper class is always abused in contrast with the world of tradesmen, priests, workmen and peasants, Sidors and Nikitas of all sorts. I detest both classes, but if I had honestly to choose between the two, I should without hesitation, prefer the upper class, and there would be no falsity or affectation about it, since all my tastes are in that direction. Our world is trivial and empty, but at any rate we speak French decently, read something, and don't punch each other in the ribs even in our most violent quarrels, while the Sidors and the Nikitas and their worships in trade talk about 'being quite agreeable,' 'in a jiffy,' 'blast your eyes,' and display the utmost license of pothouse manners and the most degrading superstition."

"The peasant and the tradesman feed you."

"Yes, but what of it? That's not only to my discredit, but to theirs too. They feed me and take off their caps to me, so it seems they have not the intelligence and honesty to do otherwise. I don't blame or praise anyone: I only mean that the upper class and the lower are as bad as one another. My feelings and my intelligence are opposed to both, but my tastes lie more in the direction of the former. Well, now for the evils of marriage," Orlov went on, glancing at his watch. "It's high time for you to understand that there are no evils in the system itself; what is the matter is that you don't know yourselves what you want from marriage. What is it you want? In legal and illegal cohabitation, in every sort of union and cohabitation, good or bad, the underlying reality is the same. You ladies live for that underlying reality alone: for you it's everything; your existence would have no meaning for you without it. You want nothing but that, and you get it; but since you've taken to reading novels you are ashamed of it: you rush from pillar to post, you recklessly change your men, and to justify this turmoil you have begun talking of the evils of marriage. So long as you can't and won't renounce what underlies it all, your chief foe, your devil -- so long as you serve that slavishly, what use is there in discussing the matter seriously? Everything you may say to me will be falsity and affectation. I shall not believe you."

I went to find out from the hall porter whether the sledge was at the door, and when I came back I found it had become a quarrel. As sailors say, a squall had blown up.

"I see you want to shock me by your cynicism today," said Zinaida Fyodorovna, walking about the drawing-room in great emotion. "It revolts me to listen to you. I am pure before God and man, and have nothing to repent of. I left my husband and came to you, and am proud of it. I swear, on my honour, I am proud of it!"

"Well, that's all right, then!"

"If you are a decent, honest man, you, too, ought to be proud of what I did. It raises you and me above thousands of people who would like to do as we have done, but do not venture through cowardice or petty prudence. But you are not a decent man. You are afraid of freedom, and you mock the promptings of genuine feeling, from fear that some ignoramus may suspect you of being sincere. You are afraid to show me to your friends; there's no greater infliction for you than to go about with me in the street. . . . Isn't that true? Why haven't you introduced me to your father or your cousin all this time? Why is it? No, I am sick of it at last," cried Zinaida Fyodorovna, stamping. "I demand what is mine by right. You must present me to your father."

"If you want to know him, go and present yourself. He receives visitors every morning from ten till half-past."

"How base you are!" said Zinaida Fyodorovna, wringing her hands in despair. "Even if you are not sincere, and are not saying what you think, I might hate you for your cruelty. Oh, how base you are!"

"We keep going round and round and never reach the real point. The real point is that you made a mistake, and you won't acknowledge it aloud. You imagined that I was a hero, and that I had some extraordinary ideas and ideals, and it has turned out that I am a most ordinary official, a cardplayer, and have no partiality for ideas of any sort. I am a worthy representative of the rotten world from which you have run away because you were revolted with its triviality and emptiness. Recognise it and be just: don't be indignant with me, but with yourself, as it is your mistake, and not mine."

"Yes, I admit I was mistaken."

"Well, that's all right, then. We've reached that point at last, thank God. Now hear something more, if you please: I can't rise to your level -- I am too depraved; you can't descend to my level, either, for you are too exalted. So there is only one thing left to do. . . ."

"What?" Zinaida Fyodorovna asked quickly, holding her breath and turning suddenly as white as a sheet of paper.

"To call logic to our aid. . . ."

"Georgy, why are you torturing me?" Zinaida Fyodorovna said suddenly in Russian in a breaking voice. "What is it for? Think of my misery. . . ."

Orlov, afraid of tears, went quickly into his study, and I don't know why -- whether it was that he wished to cause her extra pain, or whether he remembered it was usually done in such cases -- he locked the door after him. She cried out and ran after him with a rustle of her skirt.

"What does this mean?" she cried, knocking at his door. "What . . . what does this mean?" she repeated in a shrill voice breaking with indignation. "Ah, so this is what you do! Then let me tell you I hate you, I despise you! Everything is over between us now."

I heard hysterical weeping mingled with laughter. Something small in the drawing-room fell off the table and was broken. Orlov went out into the hall by another door, and, looking round him nervously, he hurriedly put on his great-coat and went out.

Half an hour passed, an hour, and she was still weeping. I remembered that she had no father or mother, no relations, and here she was living between a man who hated her and Polya, who robbed her -- and how desolate her life seemed to me! I do not know why, but I went into the drawing-room to her. Weak and helpless, looking with her lovely hair like an embodiment of tenderness and grace, she was in anguish, as though she were ill; she was lying on a couch, hiding her face, and quivering all over.

"Madam, shouldn't I fetch a doctor?" I asked gently.

"No, there's no need . . . it's nothing," she said, and she looked at me with her tear-stained eyes. "I have a little headache. . . . Thank you."

I went out, and in the evening she was writing letter after letter, and sent me out first to Pekarsky, then to Gruzin, then to Kukushkin, and finally anywhere I chose, if only I could find Orlov and give him the letter. Every time I came back with the letter she scolded me, entreated me, thrust money into my hand -- as though she were in a fever. And all the night she did not sleep, but sat in the drawing-room, talking to herself.

Orlov returned to dinner next day, and they were reconciled.

The first Thursday afterwards Orlov complained to his friends of the intolerable life he led; he smoked a great deal, and said with irritation:

"It is no life at all; it's the rack. Tears, wailing, intellectual conversations, begging for forgiveness, again tears and wailing; and the long and the short of it is that I have no flat of my own now. I am wretched, and I make her wretched. Surely I haven't to live another month or two like this? How can I? But yet I may have to."

"Why don't you speak, then?" said Pekarsky.

"I've tried, but I can't. One can boldly tell the truth, whatever it may be, to an independent, rational man; but in this case one has to do with a creature who has no will, no strength of character, and no logic. I cannot endure tears; they disarm me. When she cries, I am ready to swear eternal love and cry myself."

Pekarsky did not understand; he scratched his broad forehead in perplexity and said:

"You really had better take another flat for her. It's so simple!"

"She wants me, not the flat. But what's the good of talking?" sighed Orlov. "I only hear endless conversations, but no way out of my position. It certainly is a case of 'being guilty without guilt.' I don't claim to be a mushroom, but it seems I've got to go into the basket. The last thing I've ever set out to be is a hero. I never could endure Turgenev's novels; and now, all of a sudden, as though to spite me, I've heroism forced upon me. I assure her on my honour that I'm not a hero at all, I adduce irrefutable proofs of the same, but she doesn't believe me. Why doesn't she believe me? I suppose I really must have something of the appearance of a hero."

"You go off on a tour of inspection in the provinces," said Kukushkin, laughing.

"Yes, that's the only thing left for me."

A week after this conversation Orlov announced that he was again ordered to attend the senator, and the same evening he went off with his portmanteaus to Pekarsky.

XI

An old man of sixty, in a long fur coat reaching to the ground, and a beaver cap, was standing at the door.

"Is Georgy Ivanitch at home?" he asked.

At first I thought it was one of the moneylenders, Gruzin's creditors, who sometimes used to come to Orlov for small payments on account; but when he came into the hall and flung open his coat, I saw the thick brows and the characteristically compressed lips which I knew so well from the photographs, and two rows of stars on the uniform. I recognised him: it was Orlov's father, the distinguished statesman.

I answered that Georgy Ivanitch was not at home. The old man pursed up his lips tightly and looked into space, reflecting, showing me his dried-up, toothless profile.

"I'll leave a note," he said; "show me in."

He left his goloshes in the hall, and, without taking off his long, heavy fur coat, went into the study. There he sat down before the table, and, before taking up the pen, for three minutes he pondered, shading his eyes with his hand as though from the sun -- exactly as his son did when he was out of humour. His face was sad, thoughtful, with that look of resignation which I have only seen on the faces of the old and religious. I stood behind him, gazed at his bald head and at the hollow at the nape of his neck, and it was clear as daylight to me that this weak old man was now in my power. There was not a soul in the flat except my enemy and me. I had only to use a little physical violence, then snatch his watch to disguise the object of the crime, and to get off by the back way, and I should have gained infinitely more than I could have imagined possible when I took up the part of a footman. I thought that I could hardly get a better opportunity. But instead of acting, I looked quite unconcernedly, first at his bald patch and then at his fur, and calmly meditated on this man's relation to his only son, and on the fact that people spoiled by power and wealth probably don't want to die. . . .

"Have you been long in my son's service?" he asked, writing a large hand on the paper.

"Three months, your High Excellency."

He finished the letter and stood up. I still had time. I urged myself on and clenched my fists, trying to wring out of my soul some trace of my former hatred; I recalled what a passionate, implacable, obstinate hate I had felt for him only a little while before. . . . But it is difficult to strike a match against a crumbling stone. The sad old face and the cold glitter of his stars roused in me nothing but petty, cheap, unnecessary thoughts of the transitoriness of everything earthly, of the nearness of death. . . .

"Good-day, brother," said the old man. He put on his cap and went out.

There could be no doubt about it: I had undergone a change; I had become different. To convince myself, I began to recall the past, but at once I felt uneasy, as though I had accidentally peeped into a dark, damp corner. I remembered my comrades and friends, and my first thought was how I should blush in confusion if ever I met any of them. What was I now? What had I to think of and to do? Where was I to go? What was I living for?

I could make nothing of it. I only knew one thing -- that I must make haste to pack my things and be off. Before the old man's visit my position as a flunkey had a meaning; now it was absurd. Tears dropped into my open portmanteau; I felt insufferably sad; but how I longed to live! I was ready to embrace and include in my short life every possibility open to man. I wanted to speak, to read, and to hammer in some big factory, and to stand on watch, and to plough. I yearned for the Nevsky Prospect, for the sea and the fields -- forevery place to which my imagination travelled. When Zinaida Fyodorovna came in, I rushed to open the door for her, and with peculiar tenderness took off her fur coat. The last time!

We had two other visitors that day besides the old man. In the evening when it was quite dark, Gruzin came to fetch some papers for Orlov. He opened the table-drawer, took the necessary papers, and, rolling them up, told me to put them in the hall beside his cap while he went in to see Zinaida Fyodorovna. She was lying on the sofa in the drawing-room, with her arms behind her head. Five or six days had already passed since Orlov went on his tour of inspection, and no one knew when he would be back, but this time she did not send telegrams and did not expect them. She did not seem to notice the presence of Polya, who was still living with us. "So be it, then," was what I read on her passionless and very pale face. Like Orlov, she wanted to be unhappy out of obstinacy. To spite herself and everything in the world, she lay for days together on the sofa, desiring and expecting nothing but evil for herself. Probably she was picturing to herself Orlov's return and the inevitable quarrels with him; then his growing indifference to her, his infidelities; then how they would separate; and perhaps these agonising thoughts gave her satisfaction. But what would she have said if she found out the actual truth?

"I love you, Godmother," said Gruzin, greeting her and kissing her hand. "You are so kind! And so dear *George* has gone away," he lied. "He has gone away, the rascal!"

He sat down with a sigh and tenderly stroked her hand.

"Let me spend an hour with you, my dear," he said. "I don't want to go home, and it's too early to go to the Birshovs'. The Birshovs are keeping their Katya's birthday to-day. She is a nice child!"

I brought him a glass of tea and a decanter of brandy. He slowly and with obvious reluctance drank the tea, and returning the glass to me, asked timidly:

"Can you give me . . . something to eat, my friend? I have had no dinner."

We had nothing in the flat. I went to the restaurant and brought him the ordinary rouble dinner.

"To your health, my dear," he said to Zinaida Fyodorovna, and he tossed off a glass of vodka. "My little girl, your godchild, sends you her love. Poor child! she's rickety. Ah, children, children!" he sighed. "Whatever you may say, Godmother, it is nice to be a father. Dear *George* can't understand that feeling."

He drank some more. Pale and lean, with his dinner-napkin over his chest like a little pinafore, he ate greedily, and raising his eyebrows, kept looking guiltily, like a little boy, first at Zinaida Fyodorovna and then at me. It seemed as though he would have begun crying if I had not given him the grouse or the jelly. When he had satisfied his hunger he grew more lively, and began laughingly telling some story about the Birshov household, but perceiving that it was tiresome and that Zinaida Fyodorovna was not laughing, he ceased. And there was a sudden feeling of dreariness. After he had finished his dinner they sat in the drawing-room by the light of a single lamp, and did not speak; it was painful to him to lie to her, and she wanted to ask him something, but could not make up her mind to. So passed half an hour. Gruzin glanced at his watch.

"I suppose it's time for me to go."

"No, stay a little. . . . We must have a talk."

Again they were silent. He sat down to the piano, struck one chord, then began playing, and sang softly, "What does the coming day bring me?" but as usual he got up suddenly and tossed his head.

"Play something," Zinaida Fyodorovna asked him.

"What shall I play?" he asked, shrugging his shoulders. "I have forgotten everything. I've given it up long ago."

Looking at the ceiling as though trying to remember, he played two pieces of Tchaikovsky with exquisite expression, with such warmth, such insight! His face was just as usual -- neither stupid nor intelligent -- and it seemed to me a perfect marvel that a man whom I was accustomed to see in the midst of the most degrading, impure surroundings, was capable of such purity, of rising to a feeling so lofty, so far beyond my reach. Zinaida Fyodorovna's face glowed, and she walked about the drawing-room in emotion.

"Wait a bit, Godmother; if I can remember it, I will play you something," he said; "I heard it played on the violoncello."

Beginning timidly and picking out the notes, and then gathering confidence, he played Saint-Saëns's "Swan Song." He played it through, and then played it a second time.

"It's nice, isn't it?" he said.

Moved by the music, Zinaida Fyodorovna stood beside him and asked:

"Tell me honestly, as a friend, what do you think about me?"

"What am I to say?" he said, raising his eyebrows. "I love you and think nothing but good of you. But if you wish that I should speak generally about the question that interests you," he went on, rubbing his sleeve near the elbow and frowning, "then, my dear, you know. . . . To follow freely the promptings of the heart does not always give good people happiness. To feel free and at the same time to be happy, it seems to me, one must not conceal from oneself that life is coarse, cruel, and merciless in its conservatism, and one must retaliate with what it deserves -- that is, be as coarse and as merciless in one's striving for freedom. That's what I think."

"That's beyond me," said Zinaida Fyodorovna, with a mournful smile. "I am exhausted already. I am so exhausted that I wouldn't stir a finger for my own salvation."

"Go into a nunnery."

He said this in jest, but after he had said it, tears glistened in Zinaida Fyodorovna's eyes and then in his.

"Well," he said, "we've been sitting and sitting, and now we must go. Good-bye, dear Godmother. God give you health."

He kissed both her hands, and stroking them tenderly, said that he should certainly come to see her again in a day or two. In the hall, as he was putting on his overcoat, that was so like a child's pelisse, he fumbled long in his pockets to find a tip for me, but found nothing there.

"Good-bye, my dear fellow," he said sadly, and went away.

I shall never forget the feeling that this man left behind him.

Zinaida Fyodorovna still walked about the room in her excitement. That she was walking about and not still lying down was so much to the good. I wanted to take advantage of this mood to speak to her openly and then to go away, but I had hardly seen Gruzin out when I heard a ring. It was Kukushkin.

"Is Georgy Ivanitch at home?" he said. "Has he come back? You say no? What a pity! In that case, I'll go in and kiss your mistress's hand, and so away. Zinaida Fyodorovna, may I come in?" he cried. "I want to kiss your hand. Excuse my being so late."

He was not long in the drawing-room, not more than ten minutes, but I felt as though he were staying a long while and would never go away. I bit my lips from indignation and annoyance, and already hated Zinaida Fyodorovna. "Why does she not turn him out?" I thought indignantly, though it was evident that she was bored by his company.

When I held his fur coat for him he asked me, as a mark of special good-will, how I managed to get on without a wife.

"But I don't suppose you waste your time," he said, laughingly. "I've no doubt Polya and you are as thick as thieves. . . . You rascal!"

In spite of my experience of life, I knew very little of mankind at that time, and it is very likely that I often exaggerated what was of little consequence and failed to observe what was important. It seemed to me it was not without motive that Kukushkin tittered and flattered me. Could it be that he was hoping that I, like a flunkey, would gossip in other kitchens and servants' quarters of his coming to see us in the evenings when Orlov was away, and staying with Zinaida Fyodorovna till late at night? And when my tittle-tattle came to the ears of his acquaintance, he would drop his eyes in confusion and shake his little finger. And would not he, I thought, looking at his little honeyed face, this very evening at cards pretend and perhaps declare that he had already won Zinaida Fyodorovna from Orlov?

That hatred which failed me at midday when the old father had come, took possession of me now. Kukushkin went away at last, and as I listened to the shuffle of his leather goloshes, I felt greatly tempted to fling after him, as a parting shot, some coarse word of abuse, but I restrained myself. And when the steps had died away on the stairs, I went back to the hall, and, hardly conscious of what I was doing, took up the roll of papers that Gruzin had left behind, and ran headlong downstairs. Without cap or overcoat, I ran down into the street. It was not cold, but big flakes of snow were falling and it was windy.

"Your Excellency!" I cried, catching up Kukushkin. "Your Excellency!

He stopped under a lamp-post and looked round with surprise. "Your Excellency!" I said breathless, "your Excellency!"

And not able to think of anything to say, I hit him two or three times on the face with the roll of paper. Completely at a loss, and hardly wondering-- I had so completely taken him by surprise -- he leaned his back against the lamp-post and put up his hands to protect his face. At that moment an army doctor passed, and saw how I was beating the man, but he merely looked at us in astonishment and went on. I felt ashamed and I ran back to the house.

XII

With my head wet from the snow, and gasping for breath, I ran to my room, and immediately flung off my swallow-tails, put on a reefer jacket and an overcoat, and carried my portmanteau out into the passage; I must get away! But before going I hurriedly sat down and began writing to Orlov:

"I leave you my false passport," I began. "I beg you to keep it as a memento, you false man, you Petersburg official!

"To steal into another man's house under a false name, to watch under the mask of a flunkey this person's intimate life, to hear everything, to see everything in order later on, unasked, to accuse a man of lying -- all this, you will say, is on a level with theft. Yes, but I care nothing for fine feelings now. I have endured dozens of your dinners and suppers when you said and did what you liked, and I had to hear, to look on, and be silent. I don't want to make you a present of my silence. Besides, if there is not a living soul at hand who dares to tell you the truth without flattery, let your flunkey Stepan wash your magnificent countenance for you."

I did not like this beginning, but I did not care to alter it. Besides, what did it matter?

The big windows with their dark curtains, the bed, the crumpled dress coat on the floor, and my wet footprints, looked gloomy and forbidding. And there was a peculiar stillness.

Possibly because I had run out into the street without my cap and goloshes I was in a high fever. My face burned, my legs ached. . . . My heavy head drooped over the table, and there was that kind of division in my thought when every idea in the brain seemed dogged by its shadow.

"I am ill, weak, morally cast down," I went on; "I cannot write to you as I should like to. From the first moment I desired to insult and humiliate you, but now I do not feel that I have the right to do so. You and I have both fallen, and neither of us will ever rise up again; and even if my letter were eloquent, terrible, and passionate, it would still seem like beating on the lid of a coffin: however one knocks upon it, one will not wake up the dead! No efforts could warm your accursed cold blood, and you know that better than I do. Why write? But my mind and heart are burning, and I go on writing; for some reason I am moved as though this letter still might save you and me. I am so feverish that my thoughts are disconnected, and my pen scratches the paper without meaning; but the question I want to put to you stands before me as clear as though in letters of flame.

"Why I am prematurely weak and fallen is not hard to explain. Like Samson of old, I have taken the gates of Gaza on my shoulders to carry them to the top of the mountain, and only when I was exhausted, when youth and health were quenched in me forever, I noticed that that burden was not for my shoulders, and that I had deceived myself. I have been, moreover, in cruel and continual pain. I have endured cold, hunger, illness, and loss of liberty. Of personal happiness I know and have known nothing. I have no home; my memories are bitter, and my conscience is often in dread of them. But why have you fallen -- you? What fatal, diabolical causes hindered your life from blossoming into full flower? Why, almost before beginning life, were you in such haste to cast off the image and likeness of God, and to become a cowardly beast who backs and scares others because he is afraid himself? You are afraid of life -- as afraid of it as an Oriental who sits all day on a cushion smoking his hookah. Yes, you read a great deal, and a European coat fits you well, but yet with what tender, purely Oriental, pasha-like care you protect yourself from hunger, cold, physical effort, from pain and uneasiness! How early your soul has taken to its dressing-gown! What a cowardly part you have played towards real life and nature, with which every healthy and normal man struggles! How soft, how snug, how warm, how comfortable -- and how bored you are! Yes, it is deathly boredom, unrelieved by one ray of light, as in solitary confinement; but you try to hide from that enemy, too, you play cards eight hours out of twenty-four.

"And your irony? Oh, but how well I understand it! Free, bold, living thought is searching and dominating; for an indolent, sluggish mind it is intolerable. That it may not disturb your peace, like thousands of your contemporaries, you made haste in youth to put it under bar and bolt. Your ironical attitude to life, or whatever you like to call it, is your armour; and your thought, fettered and frightened, dare not leap over the fence you have put round it; and when you jeer at ideas which you pretend to know all about, you are like the deserter fleeing from the field of battle, and, to stifle his shame, sneering at war and at valour. Cynicism stifles pain. In some novel of Dostoevsky's an old man tramples underfoot the portrait of his dearly loved daughter because he had been unjust to her, and you vent your foul and vulgar jeers upon the ideas of goodness and truth because you have not the strength to follow them. You are frightened of every honest and truthful hint at your degradation, and you purposely surround yourself with people who do nothing but flatter your weaknesses. And you may well, you may well dread the sight of tears!

"By the way, your attitude to women. Shamelessness has been handed down to us in our flesh and blood, and we are trained to shamelessness; but that is what we are men for -- to subdue the beast in us. When you reached manhood and *all* ideas became known to you, you could not have failed to see the truth; you knew it, but you did not follow it; you were afraid of it, and to deceive your conscience you began loudly assuring yourself that it was not you but woman that was to blame, that she was as degraded as your attitude to her. Your cold, scabrous anecdotes, your coarse laughter, all your innumerable theories concerning the underlying reality of marriage and the definite demands made upon it, concerning the ten *sous* the French workman pays his woman; your everlasting attacks on female logic, lying, weakness and so on -- doesn't it all look like a desire at all costs to force woman down into the mud that she may be on the same level as your attitude to her? You are a weak, unhappy, unpleasant person!"

Zinaida Fyodorovna began playing the piano in the drawing-room, trying to recall the song of Saint Saëns that Gruzin had played. I went and lay on my bed, but remembering that it was time for me to go, I got up with an effort and with a heavy, burning head went to the table again.

"But this is the question," I went on. "Why are we worn out? Why are we, at first so passionate so bold, so noble, and so full of faith, complete bankrupts at thirty or thirty-five? Why does one waste in consumption, another put a bullet through his brains, a third seeks forgetfulness in vodka and cards, while the fourth tries to stifle his fear and misery by cynically trampling underfoot the pure image of his fair youth? Why is it that, having once fallen, we do not try to rise up again, and, losing one thing, do not seek something else? Why is it?

"The thief hanging on the Cross could bring back the joy of life and the courage of confident hope, though perhaps he had not more than an hour to live. You have long years before you, and I shall probably not die so soon as one might suppose. What if by a miracle the present turned out to be a dream, a horrible nightmare, and we should wake up renewed, pure, strong, proud of our righteousness? Sweet visions fire me, and I am almost breathless with emotion. I have a terrible longing to live. I long for our life to be holy, lofty, and majestic as the heavens above. Let us live! The sun doesn't rise twice a day, and life is not given us again -- clutch at what is left of your life and save it. . . ."

I did not write another word. I had a multitude of thoughts in my mind, but I could not connect them and get them on to paper. Without finishing the letter, I signed it with my name and rank, and went into the study. It was dark. I felt for the table and put the letter on it. I must have stumbled against the furniture in the dark and made a noise.

"Who is there?" I heard an alarmed voice in the drawing-room.

And the clock on the table softly struck one at the moment.

XIII

For at least half a minute I fumbled at the door in the dark, feeling for the handle; then I slowly opened it and walked into the drawing-room. Zinaida Fyodorovna was lying on the couch, and raising herself on her elbow, she looked towards me. Unable to bring myself to speak, I walked slowly by, and she followed me with her eyes. I stood for a little time in the dining-room and then walked by her again, and she looked at me intently and with perplexity, even with alarm. At last I stood still and said with an effort:

"He is not coming back."

She quickly got on to her feet, and looked at me without understanding.

"He is not coming back," I repeated, and my heart beat violently. "He will not come back, for he has not left Petersburg. He is staying at Pekarsky's."

She understood and believed me -- I saw that from her sudden pallor, and from the way she laid her arms upon her bosom in terror and entreaty. In one instant all that had happened of late flashed through her mind; she reflected, and with pitiless clarity she saw the whole truth. But at the same time she remembered that I was a flunkey, a being of a lower order. . . . A casual stranger, with hair ruffled, with face flushed with fever, perhaps drunk, in a common overcoat, was coarsely intruding into her intimate life, and that offended her. She said to me sternly:

"It's not your business: go away."

"Oh, believe me!" I cried impetuously, holding out my hands to her. "I am not a footman; I am as free as you."

I mentioned my name, and, speaking very rapidly that she might not interrupt me or go away, explained to her who I was and why I was living there. This new discovery struck her more than the first. Till then she had hoped that her footman had lied or made a mistake or been silly, but now after my confession she had no doubts left. From the expression of her unhappy eyes and face, which suddenly lost its softness and beauty and looked old, I saw that she was insufferably miserable, and that the conversation would lead to no good; but I went on impetuously:

"The senator and the tour of inspection were invented to deceive you. In January, just as now, he did not go away, but stayed at Pekarsky's, and I saw him every day and took part in the deception. He was weary of you, he hated your presence here, he mocked at you. . . . If you could have heard how he and his friends here jeered at you and your love, you would not have remained here one minute! Go away from here! Go away."

"Well," she said in a shaking voice, and moved her hand over her hair. "Well, so be it."

Her eyes were full of tears, her lips were quivering, and her whole face was strikingly pale and distorted with anger. Orlov's coarse, petty lying revolted her and seemed to her contemptible, ridiculous: she smiled and I did not like that smile.

"Well," she repeated, passing her hand over her hair again, "so be it. He imagines that I shall die of humiliation, and instead of that I am . . . amused by it. There's no need for him to hide." She walked away from the piano and said, shrugging her shoulders: "There's no need. . . . It would have been simpler to have it out with me instead of keeping in hiding in other people's flats. I have eyes; I saw it myself long ago. . . . I was only waiting for him to come back to have things out once for all."

Then she sat down on a low chair by the table, and, leaning her head on the arm of the sofa, wept bitterly. In the drawing-room there was only one candle burning in the candelabra, and the chair where she was sitting was in darkness; but I saw how her head and shoulders were quivering, and how her hair, escaping from her combs, covered her neck, her face, her arms. . . . Her quiet, steady weeping, which was not hysterical but a woman's ordinary weeping, expressed a sense of insult, of wounded pride, of injury, and of something helpless, hopeless, which one could not set right and to which one could not get used. Her tears stirred an echo in my troubled and suffering heart; I forgot my illness and everything else in the world; I walked about the drawing-room and muttered distractedly:

"Is this life? . . . Oh, one can't go on living like this, one can't. . . . Oh, it's madness, wickedness, not life."

"What humiliation!" she said through her tears. "To live together, to smile at me at the very time when I was burdensome to him, ridiculous in his eyes! Oh, how humiliating!"

She lifted up her head, and looking at me with tear-stained eyes through her hair, wet with her tears, and pushing it back as it prevented her seeing me, she asked:

"They laughed at me?"

"To these men you were laughable -- you and your love and Turgenev; they said your head was full of him. And if we both die at once in despair, that will amuse them, too; they will make a funny anecdote of it and tell it at your requiem service. But why talk of them?" I said impatiently. "We must get away from here -- I cannot stay here one minute longer.

She began crying again, while I walked to the piano and sat down.

"What are we waiting for?" I asked dejectedly. "It's two o'clock."

"I am not waiting for anything," she said. "I am utterly lost."

"Why do you talk like that? We had better consider together what we are to do. Neither you nor I can stay here. Where do you intend to go?"

Suddenly there was a ring at the bell. My heart stood still. Could it be Orlov, to whom perhaps Kukushkin had complained of me? How should we meet? I went to open the door. It was Polya. She came in shaking the snow off her pelisse, and went into her room without saying a word to me. When I went back to the drawing-room, Zinaida Fyodorovna, pale as death, was standing in the middle of the room, looking towards me with big eyes.

"Who was it?" she asked softly.

"Polya," I answered.

She passed her hand over her hair and closed her eyes wearily.

"I will go away at once," she said. "Will you be kind and take me to the Petersburg Side? What time is it now?"

"A quarter to three."

XIV

When, a little afterwards, we went out of the house, it was dark and deserted in the street. Wet snow was falling and a damp wind lashed in one's face. I remember it was the beginning of March; a thaw had set in, and for some days past the cabmen had been driving on wheels. Under the impression of the back stairs, of the cold, of the midnight darkness, and the porter in his sheepskin who had questioned us before letting us out of the gate, Zinaida Fyodorovna was utterly cast down and dispirited. When we got into the cab and the hood was put up, trembling all over, she began hurriedly saying how grateful she was to me.

"I do not doubt your good-will, but I am ashamed that you should be troubled," she muttered. "Oh, I understand, I understand. . . . When Gruzin was here to-day, I felt that he was lying and concealing something. Well, so be it. But I am ashamed, anyway, that you should be troubled."

She still had her doubts. To dispel them finally, I asked the cabman to drive through Sergievsky Street; stopping him at Pekarsky's door, I got out of the cab and rang. When the porter came to the door, I asked aloud, that Zinaida Fyodorovna might hear, whether Georgy Ivanitch was at home.

"Yes," was the answer, "he came in half an hour ago. He must be in bed by now. What do you want?"

Zinaida Fyodorovna could not refrain from putting her head out.

"Has Georgy Ivanitch been staying here long?" she asked.

"Going on for three weeks."

"And he's not been away?"

"No," answered the porter, looking at me with surprise.

"Tell him, early to-morrow," I said, "that his sister has arrived from Warsaw. Good-bye."

Then we drove on. The cab had no apron, the snow fell on us in big flakes, and the wind, especially on the Neva, pierced us through and through. I began to feel as though we had been driving for a long time, that for ages we had been suffering, and that for ages I had been listening to Zinaida Fyodorovna's shuddering breath. In semi-delirium, as though half asleep, I looked back upon my strange, incoherent life, and for some reason recalled a melodrama, "The Parisian Beggars," which I had seen once or twice in my childhood. And when to shake off that semi-delirium I peeped out from the hood and saw the dawn, all the images of the past, all my misty thoughts, for some reason, blended in me into one distinct, overpowering thought: everything was irrevocably over for Zinaida Fyodorovna and for me. This was as certain a conviction as though the cold blue sky contained a prophecy, but a minute later I was already thinking of something else and believed differently.

"What am I now?" said Zinaida Fyodorovna, in a voice husky with the cold and the damp. "Where am I to go? What am I to do? Gruzin told me to go into a nunnery. Oh, I would! I would change my dress, my face, my name, my thoughts . . . everything -- everything, and would hide myself forever. But they will not take me into a nunnery. I am with child."

"We will go abroad together to-morrow," I said.

"That's impossible. My husband won't give me a passport."

"I will take you without a passport."

The cabman stopped at a wooden house of two storeys, painted a dark colour. I rang. Taking from me her small light basket -- the only luggage we had brought with us -- Zinaida Fyodorovna gave a wry smile and said:

"These are my *bijoux*."

But she was so weak that she could not carry these *bijoux*.

It was a long while before the door was opened. After the third or fourth ring a light gleamed in the windows, and there was a sound of steps, coughing and whispering; at last the key grated in the lock, and a stout peasant woman with a frightened red face appeared at the door. Some distance behind her stood a thin little old woman with short grey hair, carrying a candle in her hand. Zinaida Fyodorovna ran into the passage and flung her arms round the old woman's neck.

"Nina, I've been deceived," she sobbed loudly. "I've been coarsely, foully deceived! Nina, Nina!"

I handed the basket to the peasant woman. The door was closed, but still I heard her sobs and the cry "Nina!"

I got into the cab and told the man to drive slowly to the Nevsky Prospect. I had to think of a night's lodging for myself.

Next day towards evening I went to see Zinaida Fyodorovna. She was terribly changed. There were no traces of tears on her pale, terribly sunken face, and her expression was different. I don't know whether it was that I saw her now in different surroundings, far from luxurious, and that our relations were by now different, or perhaps that intense grief had already set its mark upon her; she did not strike me as so elegant and well dressed as before. Her figure seemed smaller; there was an abruptness and excessive nervousness about her as though she were in a hurry, and there was not the same softness even in her smile. I was dressed in an expensive suit which I had bought during the day. She looked first of all at that suit and at the hat in my hand, then turned an impatient, searching glance upon my face as though studying it.

"Your transformation still seems to me a sort of miracle," she said. "Forgive me for looking at you with such curiosity. You are an extraordinary man, you know."

I told her again who I was, and why I was living at Orlov's, and I told her at greater length and in more detail than the day before. She listened with great attention, and said without letting me finish:

"Everything there is over for me. You know, I could not refrain from writing a letter. Here is the answer."

On the sheet which she gave there was written in Orlov's hand:

"I am not going to justify myself. But you must own that it was your mistake, not mine. I wish you happiness, and beg you to make haste and forget.

Yours sincerely,

"G. O.

"P. S. -- I am sending on your things."

The trunks and baskets despatched by Orlov were standing in the passage, and my poor little portmanteau was there beside them.

"So . . ." Zinaida Fyodorovna began, but she did not finish.

We were silent. She took the note and held it for a couple of minutes before her eyes, and during that time her face wore the same haughty, contemptuous, proud, and harsh expression as the day before at the beginning of our explanation; tears came into her eyes -- not timid, bitter tears, but proud, angry tears.

"Listen," she said, getting up abruptly and moving away to the window that I might not see her face. "I have made up my mind to go abroad with you tomorrow."

"I am very glad. I am ready to go to-day."

"Accept me as a recruit. Have you read Balzac?" she asked suddenly, turning round. "Have you? At the end of his novel 'Père Goriot' the hero looks down upon Paris from the top of a hill and threatens the town: 'Now we shall settle our account,' and after this he begins a new life. So when I look out of the train window at Petersburg for the last time, I shall say, 'Now we shall settle our account!' "

Saying this, she smiled at her jest, and for some reason shuddered all over.

XV

At Venice I had an attack of pleurisy. Probably I had caught cold in the evening when we were rowing from the station to the Hotel Bauer. I had to take to my bed and stay there for a fortnight. Every morning while I was ill Zinaida Fyodorovna came from her room to drink coffee with me, and afterwards read aloud to me French and Russian books, of which we had bought a number at Vienna. These books were either long, long familiar to me or else had no interest for me, but I had the sound of a sweet, kind voice beside me, so that the meaning of all of them was summed up for me in the one thing -- I was not alone. She would go out for a walk, come back in her light grey dress, her light straw hat, gay, warmed by the spring sun; and sitting by my bed, bending low down over me, would tell me something about Venice or read me those books -- and I was happy.

At night I was cold, ill, and dreary, but by day I revelled in life -- I can find no better expression for it. The brilliant warm sunshine beating in at the open windows and at the door upon the balcony, the shouts below, the splash of oars, the tinkle of bells, the prolonged boom of the cannon at midday, and the feeling of perfect, perfect freedom, did wonders with me; I felt as though I were growing strong, broad wings which were bearing me God knows whither. And what charm, what joy at times at the thought that another life was so close to mine! that I was the servant, the guardian, the friend, the indispensable fellow-traveller of a creature, young, beautiful, wealthy, but weak, lonely, and insulted! It is pleasant even to be ill when you know that there are people who are looking forward to your convalescence as to a holiday. One day I heard her whispering behind the door with my doctor, and then she came in to me with tear-stained eyes. It was a bad sign, but I was touched, and there was a wonderful lightness in my heart.

But at last they allowed me to go out on the balcony. The sunshine and the breeze from the sea caressed and fondled my sick body. I looked down at the familiar gondolas, which glide with feminine grace smoothly and majestically as though they were alive, and felt all the luxury of this original, fascinating civilisation. There was a smell of the sea. Someone was playing a stringed instrument and two voices were singing. How delightful it was! How unlike it was to that Petersburg night when the wet snow was falling and beating so rudely on our faces. If one looks straight across the canal, one sees the sea, and on the wide expanse towards the horizon the sun glittered on the water so dazzlingly that it hurt one's eyes to look at it. My soul yearned towards that lovely sea, which was so akin to me and to which I had given up my youth. I longed to live -- to live -- and nothing more.

A fortnight later I began walking freely. I loved to sit in the sun, and to listen to the gondoliers without understanding them, and for hours together to gaze at the little house where, they said, Desdemona lived -- a naïve, mournful little house with a demure expression, as light as lace, so light that it looked as though one could lift it from its place with one hand. I stood for a long time by the tomb of Canova, and could not take my eyes off the melancholy lion. And in the Palace of the Doges I was always drawn to the corner where the portrait of the unhappy Marino Faliero was painted over with black. "It is fine to be an artist, a poet, a dramatist," I thought, "but since that is not vouchsafed to me, if only I could go in for mysticism! If only I had a grain of some faith to add to the unruffled peace and serenity that fills the soul!"

In the evening we ate oysters, drank wine, and went out in a gondola. I remember our black gondola swayed softly in the same place while the water faintly gurgled under it. Here and there the reflection of the stars and the lights on the bank quivered and trembled. Not far from us in a gondola, hung with coloured lanterns which were reflected in the water, there were people singing. The sounds of guitars, of violins, of mandolins, of men's and women's voices, were audible in the dark. Zinaida Fyodorovna, pale, with a grave, almost stern face, was sitting beside me, compressing her lips and clenching her hands. She was thinking about something; she did not stir an eyelash, nor hear me. Her face, her attitude, and her fixed, expressionless gaze, and her incredibly miserable, dreadful, and icy-cold memories, and around her the gondolas, the lights, the music, the song with its vigorous passionate cry of "*Jam-mo! Jam-mo!*" -- what contrasts in life! When she sat like that, with tightly clasped hands, stony, mournful, I used to feel as though we were both characters in some novel in the old-fashioned style called "The Ill-fated," "The Abandoned," or something of the sort. Both of us: she -- the ill-fated, the abandoned; and I -- the faithful, devoted friend, the dreamer, and, if you like it, a superfluous man, a failure capable of nothing but coughing and dreaming, and perhaps sacrificing myself.

But who and what needed my sacrifices now? And what had I to sacrifice, indeed?

When we came in in the evening we always drank tea in her room and talked. We did not shrink from touching on old, unhealed wounds -- on the contrary, for some reason I felt a positive pleasure in telling her about my life at Orlov's, or referring openly to relations which I knew and which could not have been concealed from me.

"At moments I hated you," I said to her. "When he was capricious, condescending, told you lies, I marvelled how it was you did not see, did not understand, when it was all so clear! You kissed his hands, you knelt to him, you flattered him. . ."

"When I . . . kissed his hands and knelt to him, I loved him . . ." she said, blushing crimson.

"Can it have been so difficult to see through him? A fine sphinx! A sphinx indeed -- a *kammer-junker!* I reproach you for nothing, God forbid," I went on, feeling I was coarse, that I had not the tact, the delicacy which are so essential when you have to do with a fellow-creature's soul; in early days before I knew her I had not noticed this defect in myself. "But how could you fail to see what he was," I went on, speaking more softly and more diffidently, however.

"You mean to say you despise my past, and you are right," she said, deeply stirred. " You belong to a special class of men who cannot be judged by ordinary standards; your moral requirements are exceptionally rigorous, and I understand you can't forgive things. I understand you, and if sometimes I say the opposite, it doesn't mean that I look at things differently from you; I speak the same old nonsense simply because I haven't had time yet to wear out my old clothes and prejudices. I, too, hate and despise my past, and Orlov and my love. . . . What was that love? It's positively absurd now," she said, going to the window and looking down at the canal. "All this love only clouds the conscience and confuses the mind. The meaning of life is to be found only in one thing -- fighting. To get one's heel on the vile head of the serpent and to crush it! That's the meaning of life. In that alone or in nothing."

I told her long stories of my past, and described my really astounding adventures. But of the change that had taken place in me I did not say one word. She always listened to me with great attention, and at interesting places she rubbed her hands as though vexed that it had not yet been her lot to experience such adventures, such joys and terrors. Then she would suddenly fall to musing and retreat into herself, and I could see from her face that she was not attending to me.

I closed the windows that looked out on the canal and asked whether we should not have the fire lighted.

"No, never mind. I am not cold," she said, smiling listlessly. "I only feel weak. Do you know, I fancy I have grown much wiser lately. I have extraordinary, original ideas now. When I think of my past, of my life then . . . people in general, in fact, it is all summed up for me in the image of my stepmother. Coarse, insolent, soulless, false, depraved, and a morphia maniac too. My father, who was feeble and weak-willed, married my mother for her money and drove her into consumption; but his second wife, my stepmother, he loved passionately, insanely. . . . What I had to put up with! But what is the use of talking! And so, as I say, it is all summed up in her image. . . . And it vexes me that my stepmother is dead. I should like to meet her now!"

"Why?"

"I don't know," she answered with a laugh and a graceful movement of her head. "Good-night. You must get well. As soon as you are well, we'll take up our work. . . It's time to begin."

After I had said good-night and had my hand on the door-handle, she said:

"What do you think? Is Polya still living there?"

"Probably."

And I went off to my room. So we spent a whole month. One grey morning when we both stood at my window, looking at the clouds which were moving up from the sea, and at the darkening canal, expecting every minute that it would pour with rain, and when a thick, narrow streak of rain covered the sea as though with a muslin veil, we both felt suddenly dreary. The same day we both set off for Florence.

XVI

It was autumn, at Nice. One morning when I went into her room she was sitting on a low chair, bent together and huddled up, with her legs crossed and her face hidden in her hands. She was weeping bitterly, with sobs, and her long, unbrushed hair fell on her knees. The impression of the exquisite marvellous sea which I had only just seen and of which I wanted to tell her, left me all at once, and my heart ached.

"What is it?" I asked; she took one hand from her face and motioned me to go away. "What is it?" I repeated, and for the first time during our acquaintance I kissed her hand.

"No, it's nothing, nothing," she said quickly. "Oh, it's nothing, nothing. . . . Go away. . . . You see, I am not dressed."

I went out overwhelmed. The calm and serene mood in which I had been for so long was poisoned by compassion. I had a passionate longing to fall at her feet, to entreat her not to weep in solitude, but to share her grief with me, and the monotonous murmur of the sea already sounded a gloomy prophecy in my ears, and I foresaw fresh tears, fresh troubles, and fresh losses in the future. "What is she crying about? What is it?" I wondered, recalling her face and her agonised look. I remembered she was with child. She tried to conceal her condition from other people, and also from herself. At home she went about in a loose wrapper or in a blouse with extremely full folds over the bosom, and when she went out anywhere she laced herself in so tightly that on two occasions she fainted when we were out. She never spoke to me of her condition, and when I hinted that it might be as well to see a doctor, she flushed crimson and said not a word.

When I went to see her next time she was already dressed and had her hair done.

"There, there," I said, seeing that she was ready to cry again. "We had better go to the sea and have a talk."

"I can't talk. Forgive me, I am in the mood now when one wants to be alone. And, if you please, Vladimir Ivanitch, another time you want to come into my room, be so good as to give a knock at the door."

That "be so good" had a peculiar, unfeminine sound. I went away. My accursed Petersburg mood came back, and all my dreams were crushed and crumpled up like leaves by the heat. I felt I was alone again and there was no nearness between us. I was no more to her than that cobweb to that palm-tree, which hangs on it by chance and which will be torn off and carried away by the wind. I walked about the square where the band was playing, went into the Casino; there I looked at overdressed and heavily perfumed women, and everyone of them glanced at me as though she would say: "You are alone; that's all right." Then I went out on the terrace and looked for a long time at the sea. There was not one sail on the horizon. On the left bank, in the lilac-coloured mist, there were mountains, gardens, towers, and houses, the sun was sparkling over it all, but it was all alien, indifferent, an incomprehensible tangle.

XVII

She used as before to come into my room in the morning to coffee, but we no longer dined together, as she said she was not hungry; and she lived only on coffee, tea, and various trifles such as oranges and caramels.

And we no longer had conversations in the evening. I don't know why it was like this. Ever since the day when I had found her in tears she had treated me somehow lightly, at times casually, even ironically, and for some reason called me "My good sir." What had before seemed to her terrible, heroic, marvellous, and had stirred her envy and enthusiasm, did not touch her now at all, and usually after listening to me, she stretched and said:

"Yes, 'great things were done in days of yore,' my good sir."

It sometimes happened even that I did not see her for days together. I would knock timidly and guiltily at her door and get no answer; I would knock again -- still silence. . . . I would stand near the door and listen; then the chambermaid would pass and say coldly, "*Madame est partie.*" Then I would walk about the passages of the hotel, walk and walk. . . . English people, full-bosomed ladies, waiters in swallow-tails. . . . And as I keep gazing at the long striped rug that stretches the whole length of the corridor, the idea occurs to me that I am playing in the life of this woman a strange, probably false part, and that it is beyond my power to alter that part. I run to my room and fall on my bed, and think and think, and can come to no conclusion; and all that is clear to me is that I want to live, and that the plainer and the colder and the harder her face grows, the nearer she is to me, and the more intensely and painfully I feel our kinship. Never mind "My good sir," never mind her light careless tone, never mind anything you like, only don't leave me, my treasure. I am afraid to be alone.

Then I go out into the corridor again, listen in a tremor. . . . I have no dinner; I don't notice the approach of evening. At last about eleven I hear the familiar footstep, and at the turn near the stairs Zinaida Fyodorovna comes into sight.

"Are you taking a walk?" she would ask as she passes me. "You had better go out into the air. . . . Good-night!"

"But shall we not meet again to-day?"

"I think it's late. But as you like."

"Tell me, where have you been?" I would ask, following her into the room.

"Where? To Monte Carlo." She took ten gold coins out of her pocket and said: "Look, my good sir; I have won. That's at roulette."

"Nonsense! As though you would gamble."

"Why not? I am going again to-morrow."

I imagined her with a sick and morbid face, in her condition, tightly laced, standing near the gaming-table in a crowd of cocottes, of old women in their dotage who swarm round the gold like flies round the honey. I remembered she had gone off to Monte Carlo for some reason in secret from me.

"I don't believe you," I said one day. "You wouldn't go there."

"Don't agitate yourself. I can't lose much."

"It's not the question of what you lose," I said with annoyance. "Has it never occurred to you while you were playing there that the glitter of gold, all these women, young and old, the croupiers, all the surroundings -- that it is all a vile, loathsome mockery at the toiler's labour, at his bloody sweat?

"If one doesn't play, what is one to do here?" she asked. "The toiler's labour and his bloody sweat -- all that eloquence you can put off till another time; but now, since you have begun, let me go on. Let me ask you bluntly, what is there for me to do here, and what am I to do?"

"What are you to do?" I said, shrugging my shoulders. "That's a question that can't be answered straight off."

"I beg you to answer me honestly, Vladimir Ivanitch," she said, and her face looked angry. "Once I have brought myself to ask you this question, I am not going to listen to stock phrases. I am asking you," she went on, beating her hand on the table, as though marking time, "what ought I to do here? And not only here at Nice, but in general?"

I did not speak, but looked out of window to the sea. My heart was beating terribly.

"Vladimir Ivanitch," she said softly and breathlessly; it was hard for her to speak -- "Vladimir Ivanitch, if you do not believe in the cause yourself, if you no longer think of going back to it, why . . . why did you drag me out of Petersburg? Why did you make me promises, why did you rouse mad hopes? Your convictions have changed; you have become a different man, and nobody blames you for it -- our convictions are not always in our power. But . . . but, Vladimir Ivanitch, for God's sake, why are you not sincere?" she went on softly, coming up to me. "All these months when I have been dreaming aloud, raving, going into raptures over my plans, remodelling my life on a new pattern, why didn't you tell me the truth? Why were you silent or encouraged me by your stories, and behaved as though you were in complete sympathy with me? Why was it? Why was it necessary?"

"It's difficult to acknowledge one's bankruptcy," I said, turning round, but not looking at her. "Yes, I have no faith; I am worn out. I have lost heart. . . . It is difficult to be truthful -- very difficult, and I held my tongue. God forbid that anyone should have to go through what I have been through."

I felt that I was on the point of tears, and ceased speaking.

"Vladimir Ivanitch," she said, and took me by both hands, "you have been through so much and seen so much of life, you know more than I do; think seriously, and tell me, what am I to do? Teach me! If you haven't the strength to go forward yourself and take others with you, at least show me where to go. After all, I am a living, feeling, thinking being. To sink into a false position . . . to play an absurd part . . . is painful to me. I don't reproach you, I don't blame you; I only ask you."

Tea was brought in.

"Well?" said Zinaida Fyodorovna, giving me a glass. "What do you say to me?"

"There is more light in the world than you see through your window," I answered. "And there are other people besides me, Zinaida Fyodorovna."

"Then tell me who they are," she said eagerly. "That's all I ask of you."

"And I want to say, too, I went on, "one can serve an idea in more than one calling. If one has made a mistake and lost faith in one, one may find another. The world of ideas is large and cannot be exhausted."

"The world of ideas!" she said, and she looked into my face sarcastically. "Then we had better leave off talking. What's the use? . . ."

She flushed.

"The world of ideas!" she repeated. She threw her dinner-napkin aside, and an expression of indignation and contempt came into her face. "All your fine ideas, I see, lead up to one inevitable, essential step: I ought to become your mistress. That's what's wanted. To be taken up with ideas without being the mistress of an honourable, progressive man, is as good as not understanding the ideas. One has to begin with that . . . that is, with being your mistress, and the rest will come of itself."

"You are irritated, Zinaida Fyodorovna," I said.

"No, I am sincere!" she cried, breathing hard. "I am sincere!"

"You are sincere, perhaps, but you are in error, and it hurts me to hear you."

"I am in error?" she laughed. "Anyone else might say that, but not you, my dear sir! I may seem to you indelicate, cruel, but I don't care: you love me? You love me, don't you?"

I shrugged my shoulders.

"Yes, shrug your shoulders!" she went on sarcastically. "When you were ill I heard you in your delirium, and ever since these adoring eyes, these sighs, and edifying conversations about friendship, about spiritual kinship. . . . But the point is, why haven't you been sincere? Why have you concealed what is and talked about what isn't? Had you said from the beginning what ideas exactly led you to drag me from Petersburg, I should have known. I should have poisoned myself then as I meant to, and there would have been none of this tedious farce. . . . But what's the use of talking!"

With a wave of the hand she sat down.

"You speak to me as though you suspected me of dishonourable intentions," I said, offended.

"Oh, very well. What's the use of talking! I don't suspect you of intentions, but of having no intentions. If you had any, I should have known them by now. You had nothing but ideas and love. For the present -- ideas and love, and in prospect -- me as your mistress. That's in the order of things both in life and in novels. . . . Here you abused him," she said, and she slapped the table with her hand, "but one can't help agreeing with him. He has good reasons for despising these ideas."

"He does not despise ideas; he is afraid of them," I cried. "He is a coward and a liar."

"Oh, very well. He is a coward and a liar, and deceived me. And you? Excuse my frankness; what are you? He deceived me and left me to take my chance in Petersburg, and you have deceived me and abandoned me here. But he did not mix up ideas with his deceit, and you . . ."

"For goodness' sake, why are you saying this?" I cried in horror, wringing my hands and going up to her quickly. "No, Zinaida Fyodorovna, this is cynicism. You must not be so despairing; listen to me," I went on, catching at a thought which flashed dimly upon me, and which seemed to me might still save us both. "Listen. I have passed through so many experiences in my time that my head goes round at the thought of them, and I have realised with my mind, with my racked soul, that man finds his true destiny in nothing if not in self-sacrificing love for his neighbour. It is towards that we must strive, and that is our destination! That is my faith!"

I wanted to go on to speak of mercy, of forgiveness, but there was an insincere note in my voice, and I was embarrassed.

"I want to live!" I said genuinely. "To live, to live! I want peace, tranquillity; I want warmth -- this sea here -- to have you near. Oh, how I wish I could rouse in you the same thirst for life! You spoke just now of love, but it would be enough for me to have you near, to hear your voice, to watch the look in your face . . . !"

She flushed crimson, and to hinder my speaking, said quickly:

"You love life, and I hate it. So our ways lie apart."

She poured herself out some tea, but did not touch it, went into the bedroom, and lay down.

"I imagine it is better to cut short this conversation," she said to me from within. "Everything is over for me, and I want nothing. . . . What more is there to say?"

"No, it's not all over!"

"Oh, very well! . . . I know! I am sick of it. . . . That's enough."

I got up, took a turn from one end of the room to the other, and went out into the corridor. When late at night I went to her door and listened, I distinctly heard her crying.

Next morning the waiter, handing me my clothes, informed me, with a smile, that the lady in number thirteen was confined. I dressed somehow, and almost fainting with terror ran to Zinaida Fyodorovna. In her room I found a doctor, a midwife, and an elderly Russian lady from Harkov, called Darya Milhailovna. There was a smell of ether. I had scarcely crossed the threshold when from the room where she was lying I heard a low, plaintive moan, and, as though it had been wafted me by the wind from Russia, I thought of Orlov, his irony, Polya, the Neva, the drifting snow, then the cab without an apron, the prediction I had read in the cold morning sky, and the despairing cry "Nina! Nina!"

"Go in to her," said the lady.

I went in to see Zinaida Fyodorovna, feeling as though I were the father of the child. She was lying with her eyes closed, looking thin and pale, wearing a white cap edged with lace. I remember there were two expressions on her face: one -- cold, indifferent, apathetic; the other -- a look of childish helplessness given her by the white cap. She did not hear me come in, or heard, perhaps, but did not pay attention. I stood, looked at her, and waited.

But her face was contorted with pain; she opened her eyes and gazed at the ceiling, as though wondering what was happening to her. . . . There was a look of loathing on her face.

"It's horrible . . ." she whispered.

"Zinaida Fyodorovna." I spoke her name softly. She looked at me indifferently, listlessly, and closed her eyes. I stood there a little while, then went away.

At night, Darya Mihailovna informed me that the child, a girl, was born, but that the mother was in a dangerous condition. Then I heard noise and bustle in the passage. Darya Mihailovna came to me again and with a face of despair, wringing her hands, said:

"Oh, this is awful! The doctor suspects that she has taken poison! Oh, how badly Russians do behave here!"

And at twelve o'clock the next day Zinaida Fyodorovna died.

XVIII

Two years had passed. Circumstances had changed; I had come to Petersburg again and could live here openly. I was no longer afraid of being and seeming sentimental, and gave myself up entirely to the fatherly, or rather idolatrous feeling roused in me by Sonya, Zinaida Fyodorovna's child. I fed her with my own hands, gave her her bath, put her to bed, never took my eyes off her for nights together, and screamed when it seemed to me that the nurse was just going to drop her. My thirst for normal ordinary life became stronger and more acute as time went on, but wider visions stopped short at Sonya, as though I had found in her at last just what I needed. I loved the child madly. In her I saw the continuation of my life, and it was not exactly that I fancied, but I felt, I almost believed, that when I had cast off at last my long, bony, bearded frame, I should go on living in those little blue eyes, that silky flaxen hair, those dimpled pink hands which stroked my face so lovingly and were clasped round my neck.

Sonya's future made me anxious. Orlov was her father; in her birth certificate she was called Krasnovsky, and the only person who knew of her existence, and took interest in her -- that is, I -- was at death's door. I had to think about her seriously.

The day after I arrived in Petersburg I went to see Orlov. The door was opened to me by a stout old fellow with red whiskers and no moustache, who looked like a German. Polya, who was tidying the drawing-room, did not recognise me, but Orlov knew me at once.

"Ah, Mr. Revolutionist!" he said, looking at me with curiosity, and laughing. "What fate has brought you?"

He was not changed in the least: the same well-groomed, unpleasant face, the same irony. And a new book was lying on the table just as of old, with an ivory paper-knife thrust in it. He had evidently been reading before I came in. He made me sit down, offered me a cigar, and with a delicacy only found in well-bred people, concealing the unpleasant feeling aroused by my face and my wasted figure, observed casually that I was not in the least changed, and that he would have known me anywhere in spite of my having grown a beard. We talked of the weather, of Paris. To dispose as quickly as possible of the oppressive, inevitable question, which weighed upon him and me, he asked:

"Zinaida Fyodorovna is dead?"

"Yes," I answered.

"In childbirth?"

"Yes, in childbirth. The doctor suspected another cause of death, but . . . it is more comforting for you and for me to think that she died in childbirth."

He sighed decorously and was silent. The angel of silence passed over us, as they say.

"Yes. And here everything is as it used to be -- no changes," he said briskly, seeing that I was looking about the room. "My father, as you know, has left the service and is living in retirement; I am still in the same department. Do you remember Pekarsky? He is just the same as ever. Gruzin died of diphtheria a year ago. . . . Kukushkin is alive, and often speaks of you. By the way," said Orlov, dropping his eyes with an air of reserve, "when Kukushkin heard who you were, he began telling everyone you had attacked him and tried to murder him . . . and that he only just escaped with his life."

I did not speak.

"Old servants do not forget their masters. . . . It's very nice of you," said Orlov jocosely. "Will you have some wine and some coffee, though? I will tell them to make some."

"No, thank you. I have come to see you about a very important matter, Georgy Ivanitch."

"I am not very fond of important matters, but I shall be glad to be of service to you. What do you want?"

"You see," I began, growing agitated, "I have here with me Zinaida Fyodorovna's daughter. . . . Hitherto I have brought her up, but, as you see, before many days I shall be an empty sound. I should like to die with the thought that she is provided for."

Orlov coloured a little, frowned a little, and took a cursory and sullen glance at me. He was unpleasantly affected, not so much by the "important matter" as by my words about death, about becoming an empty sound.

"Yes, it must be thought about," he said, screening his eyes as though from the sun. "Thank you. You say it's a girl?"

"Yes, a girl. A wonderful child!"

"Yes. Of course, it's not a lap-dog, but a human being. I understand we must consider it seriously. I am prepared to do my part, and am very grateful to you."

He got up, walked about, biting his nails, and stopped before a picture.

"We must think about it," he said in a hollow voice, standing with his back to me. "I shall go to Pekarsky's to-day and will ask him to go to Krasnovsky's. I don't think he will make much ado about consenting to take the child."

"But, excuse me, I don't see what Krasnovsky has got to do with it," I said, also getting up and walking to a picture at the other end of the room.

"But she bears his name, of course!" said Orlov.

"Yes, he may be legally obliged to accept the child -- I don't know; but I came to you, Georgy Ivanitch, not to discuss the legal aspect."

"Yes, yes, you are right," he agreed briskly. "I believe I am talking nonsense. But don't excite yourself. We will decide the matter to our mutual satisfaction. If one thing won't do, we'll try another; and if that won't do, we'll try a third -- one way or another this delicate question shall be settled. Pekarsky will arrange it all. Be so good as to leave me your address and I will let you know at once what we decide. Where are you living?"

Orlov wrote down my address, sighed, and said with a smile:

"Oh, Lord, what a job it is to be the father of a little daughter! But Pekarsky will arrange it all. He is a sensible man. Did you stay long in Paris?"

"Two months."

We were silent. Orlov was evidently afraid I should begin talking of the child again, and to turn my attention in another direction, said:

"You have probably forgotten your letter by now. But I have kept it. I understand your mood at the time, and, I must own, I respect that letter. 'Damnable cold blood,' 'Asiatic,' 'coarse laugh' -- that was charming and characteristic," he went on with an ironical smile. "And the fundamental thought is perhaps near the truth, though one might dispute the question endlessly. That is," he hesitated, "not dispute the thought itself, but your attitude to the question -- your temperament, so to say. Yes, my life is abnormal, corrupted, of no use to anyone, and what prevents me from beginning a new life is cowardice -- there you are quite right. But that you take it so much to heart, are troubled, and reduced to despair by it -- that's irrational; there you are quite wrong."

"A living man cannot help being troubled and reduced to despair when he sees that he himself is going to ruin and others are going to ruin round him."

"Who doubts it! I am not advocating indifference; all I ask for is an objective attitude to life. The more objective, the less danger of falling into error. One must look into the root of things, and try to see in every phenomenon a cause of all the other causes. We have grown feeble, slack -- degraded, in fact. Our generation is entirely composed of neurasthenics and whimperers; we do nothing but talk of fatigue and exhaustion. But the fault is neither yours nor mine; we are of too little consequence to affect the destiny of a whole generation. We must suppose for that larger, more general causes with a solid *raison d'être* from the biological point of view. We are neurasthenics, flabby, renegades, but perhaps it's necessary and of service for generations that will come after us. Not one hair falls from the head without the will of the Heavenly Father -- in other words, nothing happens by chance in Nature and in human environment. Everything has its cause and is inevitable. And if so, why should we worry and write despairing letters?"

"That's all very well," I said, thinking a little. "I believe it will be easier and clearer for the generations to come; our experience will be at their service. But one wants to live apart from future generations and not only for their sake. Life is only given us once, and one wants to live it boldly, with full consciousness and beauty. One wants to play a striking, independent, noble part; one wants to make history so that those generations may not have the right to say of each of us that we were nonentities or worse. . . . I believe what is going on about us is inevitable and not without a purpose, but what have I to do with that inevitability? Why should my ego be lost?"

"Well, there's no help for it," sighed Orlov, getting up and, as it were, giving me to understand that our conversation was over.

I took my hat.

"We've only been sitting here half an hour, and how many questions we have settled, when you come to think of it!" said Orlov, seeing me into the hall. "So I will see to that matter. . . . I will see Pekarsky to-day. . . . Don't be uneasy."

He stood waiting while I put on my coat, and was obviously relieved at the feeling that I was going away.

"Georgy Ivanitch, give me back my letter," I said.

"Certainly."

He went to his study, and a minute later returned with the letter. I thanked him and went away.

The next day I got a letter from him. He congratulated me on the satisfactory settlement of the question. Pekarsky knew a lady, he wrote, who kept a school, something like a kindergarten, where she took quite little children. The lady could be entirely depended upon, but before concluding anything with her it would be as well to discuss the matter with Krasnovsky -- it was a matter of form. He advised me to see Pekarsky at once and to take the birth certificate with me, if I had it. "Rest assured of the sincere respect and devotion of your humble servant. . . ."

I read this letter, and Sonya sat on the table and gazed at me attentively without blinking, as though she knew her fate was being decided.

THE TWO VOLODYAS

"Let me; I want to drive myself! I'll sit by the driver!" Sofya Lvovna said in a loud voice. "Wait a minute, driver; I'll get up on the box beside you."

She stood up in the sledge, and her husband, Vladimir Nikititch, and the friend of her childhood, Vladimir Mihalovitch, held her arms to prevent her falling. The three horses were galloping fast.

"I said you ought not to have given her brandy," Vladimir Nikititch whispered to his companion with vexation. "What a fellow you are, really!"

The Colonel knew by experience that in women like his wife, Sofya Lvovna, after a little too much wine, turbulent gaiety was followed by hysterical laughter and then tears. He was afraid that when they got home, instead of being able to sleep, he would have to be administering compresses and drops.

"Wo!" cried Sofya Lvovna. "I want to drive myself!"

She felt genuinely gay and triumphant. For the last two months, ever since her wedding, she had been tortured by the thought that she had married Colonel Yagitch from worldly motives and, as it is said, *par dépit;* but that evening, at the restaurant, she had suddenly become convinced that she loved him passionately. In spite of his fifty-four years, he was so slim, agile, supple, he made puns and hummed to the gipsies' tunes so charmingly. Really, the older men were nowadays a thousand times more interesting than the young. It seemed as though age and youth had changed parts. The Colonel was two years older than her father, but could there be any importance in that if, honestly speaking, there were infinitely more vitality, go, and freshness in him than in herself, though she was only twenty-three?

"Oh, my darling!" she thought. "You are wonderful!"

She had become convinced in the restaurant, too, that not a spark of her old feeling remained. For the friend of her childhood, Vladimir Mihalovitch, or simply Volodya, with whom only the day before she had been madly, miserably in love, she now felt nothing but complete indifference. All that evening he had seemed to her spiritless, torpid, uninteresting, and insignificant, and the *sangfroid* with which he habitually avoided paying at restaurants on this occasion revolted her, and she had hardly been able to resist saying, "If you are poor, you should stay at home." The Colonel paid for all.

Perhaps because trees, telegraph posts, and drifts of snow kept flitting past her eyes, all sorts of disconnected ideas came rushing into her mind. She reflected: the bill at the restaurant had been a hundred and twenty roubles, and a hundred had gone to the gipsies, and to-morrow she could fling away a thousand roubles if she liked; and only two months ago, before her wedding, she had not had three roubles of her own, and had to ask her father forevery trifle. What a change in her life!

Her thoughts were in a tangle. She recalled, how, when she was a child of ten, Colonel Yagitch, now her husband, used to make love to her aunt, and everyone in the house said that he had ruined her. And her aunt had, in fact, often come down to dinner with her eyes red from crying, and was always going off somewhere; and people used to say of her that the poor thing could find no peace anywhere. He had been very handsome in those days, and had an extraordinary reputation as a lady-killer. So much so that he was known all over the town, and it was said of him that he paid a round of visits to his adorers every day like a doctor visiting his patients. And even now, in spite of his grey hair, his wrinkles, and his spectacles, his thin face looked handsome, especially in profile.

Sofya Lvovna's father was an army doctor, and had at one time served in the same regiment with Colonel Yagitch. Volodya's father was an army doctor too, and he, too, had once been in the same regiment as her father and Colonel Yagitch. In spite of many amatory adventures, often very complicated and disturbing, Volodya had done splendidly at the university, and had taken a very good degree. Now he was specialising in foreign literature, and was said to be writing a thesis. He lived with his father, the army doctor, in the barracks, and had no means of his own, though he was thirty. As children Sofya and he had lived under the same roof, though in different flats. He often came to play with her, and they had dancing and French lessons together. But when he grew up into a graceful, remarkably handsome young man, she began to feel shy of him, and then fell madly in love with him, and had loved him right up to the time when she was married to Yagitch. He, too, had been renowned for his success with women almost from the age of fourteen, and the ladies who deceived their husbands on his account excused themselves by saying that he was only a boy. Someone had told a story of him lately that when he was a student living in lodgings so as to be near the university, it always happened if one knocked at his door, that one heard his footstep, and then a whispered apology: "*Pardon, je ne suis pas setul.*" Yagitch was delighted with him, and blessed him as a worthy successor, as Derchavin blessed Pushkin; he appeared to be fond of him. They would play billiards or picquet by the hour together without uttering a word, if Yagitch drove out on any expedition he always took Volodya with him, and Yagitch was the only person Volodya initiated into the mysteries of his thesis. In earlier days, when Yagitch was rather younger, they had often been in the position of rivals, but they had never been jealous of one another. In the circle in which they moved Yagitch was nicknamed Big Volodya, and his friend Little Volodya.

Besides Big Volodya, Little Volodya, and Sofya Lvovna, there was a fourth person in the sledge -- Margarita Alexandrovna, or, as everyone called her, Rita, a cousin of Madame Yagitch -- a very pale girl over thirty, with black eyebrows and a pince-nez, who was forever smoking cigarettes, even in the bitterest frost, and who always had her knees and the front of her blouse covered with cigarette ash. She spoke through her nose, drawling every word, was of a cold temperament, could drink any amount of wine and liquor without being drunk, and used to tell scandalous anecdotes in a languid and tasteless way. At home she spent her days reading thick magazines, covering them with cigarette ash, or eating frozen apples.

"Sonia, give over fooling," she said, drawling. "It's really silly."

As they drew near the city gates they went more slowly, and began to pass people and houses. Sofya Lvovna subsided, nestled up to her husband, and gave herself up to her thoughts. Little Volodya sat opposite. By now her light-hearted and cheerful thoughts were mingled with gloomy ones. She thought that the man sitting opposite knew that she loved him, and no doubt he believed the gossip that she married the Colonel *par dépit.* She had never told him of her love; she had not wanted him to know, and had done her best to hide her feeling, but from her face she knew that he understood her perfectly -- and her pride suffered. But what was most humiliating in her position was that, since her wedding, Volodya had suddenly begun to pay her attention, which he had never done before, spending hours with her, sitting silent or chattering about trifles; and even now in the sledge, though he did not talk to her, he touched her foot with his and pressed her hand a little. Evidently that was all he wanted, that she should be married; and it was evident that he despised her and that she only excited in him an interest of a special kind as though she were an immoral and disreputable woman. And when the feeling of triumph and love for her husband were mingled in her soul with humiliation and wounded pride, she was overcome by a spirit of defiance, and longed to sit on the box, to shout and whistle to the horses.

Just as they passed the nunnery the huge hundred-ton bell rang out. Rita crossed herself.

"Our Olga is in that nunnery," said Sofya Lvovna, and she, too, crossed herself and shuddered.

"Why did she go into the nunnery?" said the Colonel.

"*Par dépit,*" Rita answered crossly, with obvious allusion to Sofya's marrying Yagitch. "*Par dépit* is all the fashion nowadays. Defiance of all the world. She was always laughing, a desperate flirt, fond of nothing but balls and young men, and all of a sudden off she went -- to surprise everyone!"

"That's not true," said Volodya, turning down the collar of his fur coat and showing his handsome face. "It wasn't a case of *par dépit;* it was simply horrible, if you like. Her brother Dmitri was sent to penal servitude, and they don't know where he is now. And her mother died of grief."

He turned up his collar again.

"Olga did well," he added in a muffled voice. "Living as an adopted child, and with such a paragon as Sofya Lvovna, -- one must take that into consideration too!"

Sofya Lvovna heard a tone of contempt in his voice, and longed to say something rude to him, but she said nothing. The spirit of defiance came over her again; she stood up again and shouted in a tearful voice:

"I want to go to the early service! Driver, back! I want to see Olga."

They turned back. The nunnery bell had a deep note, and Sofya Lvovna fancied there was something in it that reminded her of Olga and her life. The other church bells began ringing too. When the driver stopped the horses, Sofya Lvovna jumped out of the sledge and, unescorted and alone, went quickly up to the gate.

"Make haste, please!" her husband called to her. "It's late already."

She went in at the dark gateway, then by the avenue that led from the gate to the chief church. The snow crunched under her feet, and the ringing was just above her head, and seemed to vibrate through her whole being. Here was the church door, then three steps down, and an ante-room with ikons of the saints on both sides, a fragrance of juniper and incense, another door, and a dark figure opening it and bowing very low. The service had not yet begun. One nun was walking by the ikon-screen and lighting the candles on the tall standard candlesticks, another was lighting the chandelier. Here and there, by the columns and the side chapels, there stood black, motionless figures. "I suppose they must remain standing as they are now till the morning," thought Sofya Lvovna, and it seemed to her dark, cold, and dreary -- drearier than a graveyard. She looked with a feeling of dreariness at the still, motionless figures and suddenly felt a pang at her heart. For some reason, in one short nun, with thin shoulders and a black kerchief on her head, she recognised Olga, though when Olga went into the nunnery she had been plump and had looked taller. Hesitating and extremely agitated, Sofya Lvovna went up to the nun, and looking over her shoulder into her face, recognised her as Olga.

"Olga!" she cried, throwing up her hands, and could not speak from emotion. "Olga!"

The nun knew her at once; she raised her eyebrows in surprise, and her pale, freshly washed face, and even, it seemed, the white headcloth that she wore under her wimple, beamed with pleasure.

"What a miracle from God!" she said, and she, too, threw up her thin, pale little hands.

Sofya Lvovna hugged her and kissed her warmly, and was afraid as she did so that she might smell of spirits.

"We were just driving past, and we thought of you," she said, breathing hard, as though she had been running. "Dear me! How pale you are! I . . . I'm very glad to see you. Well, tell me how are you? Are you dull?"

Sofya Lvovna looked round at the other nuns, and went on in a subdued voice:

"There've been so many changes at home . . . you know, I'm married to Colonel Yagitch. You remember him, no doubt. . . . I am very happy with him."

"Well, thank God for that. And is your father quite well?

"Yes, he is quite well. He often speaks of you. You must come and see us during the holidays, Olga, won't you?"

"I will come," said Olga, and she smiled. "I'll come on the second day."

Sofya Lvovna began crying, she did not know why, and for a minute she shed tears in silence, then she wiped her eyes and said:

"Rita will be very sorry not to have seen you. She is with us too. And Volodya's here. They are close to the gate. How pleased they'd be if you'd come out and see them. Let's go out to them; the service hasn't begun yet."

"Let us," Olga agreed. She crossed herself three times and went out with Sofya Lvovna to the entrance.

"So you say you're happy, Sonitchka?" she asked when they came out at the gate.

"Very."

"Well, thank God for that."

The two Volodyas, seeing the nun, got out of the sledge and greeted her respectfully. Both were visibly touched by her pale face and her black monastic dress, and both were pleased that she had remembered them and come to greet them. That she might not be cold, Sofya Lvovna wrapped her up in a rug and put one half of her fur coat round her. Her tears had relieved and purified her heart, and she was glad that this noisy, restless, and, in reality, impure night should unexpectedly end so purely and serenely. And to keep Olga by her a little longer she suggested:

"Let us take her for a drive! Get in, Olga; we'll go a little way."

The men expected the nun to refuse -- saints don't dash about in three-horse sledges; but to their surprise, she consented and got into the sledge. And while the horses were galloping to the city gate all were silent, and only tried to make her warm and comfortable, and each of them was thinking of what she had been in the past and what she was now. Her face was now passionless, inexpressive, cold, pale, and transparent, as though there were water, not blood, in her veins. And two or three years ago she had been plump and rosy, talking about her suitors and laughing at every trifle.

Near the city gate the sledge turned back; when it stopped ten minutes later near the nunnery, Olga got out of the sledge. The bell had begun to ring more rapidly.

"The Lord save you," said Olga, and she bowed low as nuns do.

"Mind you come, Olga."

"I will, I will."

She went and quickly disappeared through the gateway. And when after that they drove on again, Sofya Lvovna felt very sad. Everyone was silent. She felt dispirited and weak all over. That she should have made a nun get into a sledge and drive in a company hardly sober seemed to her now stupid, tactless, and almost sacrilegious. As the intoxication passed off, the desire to deceive herself passed away also. It was clear to her now that she did not love her husband, and never could love him, and that it all had been foolishness and nonsense. She had married him from interested motives, because, in the words of her school friends, he was madly rich, and because she was afraid of becoming an old maid like Rita, and because she was sick of her father, the doctor, and wanted to annoy Volodya.

If she could have imagined when she got married, that it would be so oppressive, so dreadful, and so hideous, she would not have consented to the marriage for all the wealth in the world. But now there was no setting it right. She must make up her mind to it.

They reached home. Getting into her warm, soft bed, and pulling the bed-clothes over her, Sofya Lvovna recalled the dark church, the smell of incense, and the figures by the columns, and she felt frightened at the thought that these figures would be standing there all the while she was asleep. The early service would be very, very long; then there would be "the hours," then the mass, then the service of the day.

"But of course there is a God -- there certainly is a God; and I shall have to die, so that sooner or later one must think of one's soul, of eternal life, like Olga. Olga is saved now; she has settled all questions for herself. . . . But if there is no God? Then her life is wasted. But how is it wasted? Why is it wasted?"

And a minute later the thought came into her mind again:

"There is a God; death must come; one must think of one's soul. If Olga were to see death before her this minute she would not be afraid. She is prepared. And the great thing is that she has already solved the problem of life for herself. There is a God . . . yes. . . . But is there no other solution except going into a monastery? To go into the monastery means to renounce life, to spoil it . . . ."

Sofya Lvovna began to feel rather frightened; she hid her head under her pillow.

"I mustn't think about it," she whispered. "I mustn't. . . ."

Yagitch was walking about on the carpet in the next room with a soft jingle of spurs, thinking about something. The thought occurred to Sofya Lvovna that this man was near and dear to her only for one reason -- that his name, too, was Vladimir. She sat up in bed and called tenderly:

"Volodya!"

"What is it?" her husband responded.

"Nothing."

She lay down again. She heard a bell, perhaps the same nunnery bell. Again she thought of the vestibule and the dark figures, and thoughts of God and of inevitable death strayed through her mind, and she covered her ears that she might not hear the bell. She thought that before old age and death there would be a long, long life before her, and that day by day she would have to put up with being close to a man she did not love, who had just now come into the bedroom and was getting into bed, and would have to stifle in her heart her hopeless love for the other young, fascinating, and, as she thought, exceptional man. She looked at her husband and tried to say good-night to him, but suddenly burst out crying instead. She was vexed with herself.

"Well, now then for the music!" said Yagitch.

She was not pacified till ten o'clock in the morning. She left off crying and trembling all over, but she began to have a splitting headache. Yagitch was in haste to go to the late mass, and in the next room was grumbling at his orderly, who was helping him to dress. He came into the bedroom once with the soft jingle of his spurs to fetch something, and then a second time wearing his epaulettes, and his orders on his breast, limping slightly from rheumatism; and it struck Sofya Lvovna that he looked and walked like a bird of prey.

She heard Yagitch ring the telephone bell.

"Be so good as to put me on to the Vassilevsky barracks," he said; and a minute later: "Vassilevsky barracks? Please ask Doctor Salimovitch to come to the telephone . . ." And a minute later: "With whom am I speaking? Is it you, Volodya? Delighted. Ask your father to come to us at once, dear boy; my wife is rather shattered after yesterday. Not at home, you say? H'm! . . . Thank you. Very good. I shall be much obliged . . . *Merci.*"

Yagitch came into the bedroom for the third time, bent down to his wife, made the sign of the cross over her, gave her his hand to kiss (the women who had been in love with him used to kiss his hand and he had got into the habit of it), and saying that he should be back to dinner, went out.

At twelve o'clock the maid came in to announce that Vladimir Mihalovitch had arrived. Sofya Lvovna, staggering with fatigue and headache, hurriedly put on her marvellous new lilac dressing-gown trimmed with fur, and hastily did up her hair after a fashion. She was conscious of an inexpressible tenderness in her heart, and was trembling with joy and with fear that he might go away. She wanted nothing but to look at him.

Volodya came dressed correctly for calling, in a swallow-tail coat and white tie. When Sofya Lvovna came in he kissed her hand and expressed his genuine regret that she was ill. Then when they had sat down, he admired her dressing-gown.

"I was upset by seeing Olga yesterday," she said. "At first I felt it dreadful, but now I envy her. She is like a rock that cannot be shattered; there is no moving her. But was there no other solution for her, Volodya? Is burying oneself alive the only solution of the problem of life? Why, it's death, not life!"

At the thought of Olga, Volodya's face softened.

"Here, you are a clever man, Volodya," said Sofya Lvovna. "Show me how to do what Olga has done. Of course, I am not a believer and should not go into a nunnery, but one can do something equivalent. Life isn't easy for me," she added after a brief pause. "Tell me what to do. . . . Tell me something I can believe in. Tell me something, if it's only one word."

"One word? By all means: tararaboomdeeay."

"Volodya, why do you despise me?" she asked hotly. "You talk to me in a special, fatuous way, if you'll excuse me, not as one talks to one's friends and women one respects. You are so good at your work, you are fond of science; why do you never talk of it to me? Why is it? Am I not good enough?"

Volodya frowned with annoyance and said:

"Why do you want science all of a sudden? Don't you perhaps want constitutional government? Or sturgeon and horse-radish?"

"Very well, I am a worthless, trivial, silly woman with no convictions. I have a mass, a mass of defects. I am neurotic, corrupt, and I ought to be despised for it. But you, Volodya, are ten years older than I am, and my husband is thirty years older. I've grown up before your eyes, and if you would, you could have made anything you liked of me -- an angel. But you" -- her voice quivered -- "treat me horribly. Yagitch has married me in his old age, and you . . ."

"Come, come," said Volodya, sitting nearer her and kissing both her hands. "Let the Schopenhauers philosophise and prove whatever they like, while we'll kiss these little hands."

"You despise me, and if only you knew how miserable it makes me," she said uncertainly, knowing beforehand that he would not believe her. "And if you only knew how I want to change, to begin another life! I think of it with enthusiasm!" and tears of enthusiasm actually came into her eyes. "To be good, honest, pure, not to be lying; to have an object in life."

"Come, come, come, please don't be affected! I don't like it!" said Volodya, and an ill-humoured expression came into his face. "Upon my word, you might be on the stage. Let us behave like simple people."

To prevent him from getting cross and going away, she began defending herself, and forced herself to smile to please him; and again she began talking of Olga, and of how she longed to solve the problem of her life and to become something real.

"Ta-ra-ra-boomdee-ay," he hummed. "Ta-ra-ra-boom-dee-ay!"

And all at once he put his arm round her waist, while she, without knowing what she was doing, laid her hands on his shoulders and for a minute gazed with ecstasy, almost intoxication, at his clever, ironical face, his brow, his eyes, his handsome beard.

"You have known that I love you forever so long," she confessed to him, and she blushed painfully, and felt that her lips were twitching with shame. "I love you. Why do you torture me?"

She shut her eyes and kissed him passionately on the lips, and for a long while, a full minute, could not take her lips away, though she knew it was unseemly, that he might be thinking the worse of her, that a servant might come in.

"Oh, how you torture me!" she repeated.

When half an hour later, having got all that he wanted, he was sitting at lunch in the dining-room, she was kneeling before him, gazing greedily into his face, and he told her that she was like a little dog waiting for a bit of ham to be thrown to it. Then he sat her on his knee, and dancing her up and down like a child, hummed:

"Tara-raboom-dee-ay. . . . Tara-raboom-dee-ay." And when he was getting ready to go she asked him in a passionate whisper:

"When? To-day? Where?" And held out both hands to his mouth as though she wanted to seize his answer in them.

"To-day it will hardly be convenient," he said after a minute's thought. "To-morrow, perhaps."

And they parted. Before dinner Sofya Lvovna went to the nunnery to see Olga, but there she was told that Olga was reading the psalter somewhere over the dead. From the nunnery she went to her father's and found that he, too, was out. Then she took another sledge and drove aimlessly about the streets till evening. And for some reason she kept thinking of the aunt whose eyes were red with crying, and who could find no peace anywhere.

And at night they drove out again with three horses to a restaurant out of town and listened to the gipsies. And driving back past the nunnery again, Sofya Lvovna thought of Olga, and she felt aghast at the thought that for the girls and women of her class there was no solution but to go on driving about and telling lies, or going into a nunnery to mortify the flesh. . . . And next day she met her lover, and again Sofya Lvovna drove about the town alone in a hired sledge thinking about her aunt.

A week later Volodya threw her over. And after that life went on as before, uninteresting, miserable, and sometimes even agonising. The Colonel and Volodya spent hours playing billiards and picquet, Rita told anecdotes in the same languid, tasteless way, and Sofya Lvovna went about alone in hired sledges and kept begging her husband to take her for a good drive with three horses.

Going almost every day to the nunnery, she wearied Olga, complaining of her unbearable misery, weeping, and feeling as she did so that she brought with her into the cell something impure, pitiful, shabby. And Olga repeated to her mechanically as though a lesson learnt by rote, that all this was of no consequence, that it would all pass and God would forgive her.

THE BLACK MONK

I

Andrey Vassilitch Kovrin, who held a master's degree at the University, had exhausted himself, and had upset his nerves. He did not send for a doctor, but casually, over a bottle of wine, he spoke to a friend who was a doctor, and the latter advised him to spend the spring and summer in the country. Very opportunely a long letter came from Tanya Pesotsky, who asked him to come and stay with them at Borissovka. And he made up his mind that he really must go.

To begin with -- that was in April -- he went to his own home, Kovrinka, and there spent three weeks in solitude; then, as soon as the roads were in good condition, he set off, driving in a carriage, to visit Pesotsky, his former guardian, who had brought him up, and was a horticulturist well known all over Russia. The distance from Kovrinka to Borissovka was reckoned only a little over fifty miles. To drive along a soft road in May in a comfortable carriage with springs was a real pleasure.

Pesotsky had an immense house with columns and lions, off which the stucco was peeling, and with a footman in swallow-tails at the entrance. The old park, laid out in the English style, gloomy and severe, stretched for almost three-quarters of a mile to the river, and there ended in a steep, precipitous clay bank, where pines grew with bare roots that looked like shaggy paws; the water shone below with an unfriendly gleam, and the peewits flew up with a plaintive cry, and there one always felt that one must sit down and write a ballad. But near the house itself, in the courtyard and orchard, which together with the nurseries covered ninety acres, it was all life and gaiety even in bad weather. Such marvellous roses, lilies, camellias; such tulips of all possible shades, from glistening white to sooty black -- such a wealth of flowers, in fact, Kovrin had never seen anywhere as at Pesotsky's. It was only the beginning of spring, and the real glory of the flower-beds was still hidden away in the hot-houses. But even the flowers along the avenues, and here and there in the flower-beds, were enough to make one feel, as one walked about the garden, as though one were in a realm of tender colours, especially in the early morning when the dew was glistening on every petal.

What was the decorative part of the garden, and what Pesotsky contemptuously spoke of as rubbish, had at one time in his childhood given Kovrin an impression of fairyland.

Every sort of caprice, of elaborate monstrosity and mockery at Nature was here. There were espaliers of fruit-trees, a pear-tree in the shape of a pyramidal poplar, spherical oaks and lime-trees, an apple-tree in the shape of an umbrella, plum-trees trained into arches, crests, candelabra, and even into the number 1862 -- the year when Pesotsky first took up horticulture. One came across, too, lovely, graceful trees with strong, straight stems like palms, and it was only by looking intently that one could recognise these trees as gooseberries or currants. But what made the garden most cheerful and gave it a lively air, was the continual coming and going in it, from early morning till evening; people with wheelbarrows, shovels, and watering-cans swarmed round the trees and bushes, in the avenues and the flower-beds, like ants. . . .

Kovrin arrived at Pesotsky's at ten o'clock in the evening. He found Tanya and her father, Yegor Semyonitch, in great anxiety. The clear starlight sky and the thermometer foretold a frost towards morning, and meanwhile Ivan Karlovitch, the gardener, had gone to the town, and they had no one to rely upon. At supper they talked of nothing but the morning frost, and it was settled that Tanya should not go to bed, and between twelve and one should walk through the garden, and see that everything was done properly, and Yegor Semyonitch should get up at three o'clock or even earlier.

Kovrin sat with Tanya all the evening, and after midnight went out with her into the garden. It was cold. There was a strong smell of burning already in the garden. In the big orchard, which was called the commercial garden, and which brought Yegor Semyonitch several thousand clear profit, a thick, black, acrid smoke was creeping over the ground and, curling around the trees, was saving those thousands from the frost. Here the trees were arranged as on a chessboard, in straight and regular rows like ranks of soldiers, and this severe pedantic regularity, and the fact that all the trees were of the same size, and had tops and trunks all exactly alike, made them look monotonous and even dreary. Kovrin and Tanya walked along the rows where fires of dung, straw, and all sorts of refuse were smouldering, and from time to time they were met by labourers who wandered in the smoke like shadows. The only trees in flower were the cherries, plums, and certain sorts of apples, but the whole garden was plunged in smoke, and it was only near the nurseries that Kovrin could breathe freely.

"Even as a child I used to sneeze from the smoke here," he said, shrugging his shoulders, "but to this day I don't understand how smoke can keep off frost."

"Smoke takes the place of clouds when there are none . . ." answered Tanya.

"And what do you want clouds for?"

"In overcast and cloudy weather there is no frost."

"You don't say so."

He laughed and took her arm. Her broad, very earnest face, chilled with the frost, with her delicate black eyebrows, the turned-up collar of her coat, which prevented her moving her head freely, and the whole of her thin, graceful figure, with her skirts tucked up on account of the dew, touched him.

"Good heavens! she is grown up," he said. "When I went away from here last, five years ago, you were still a child. You were such a thin, longlegged creature, with your hair hanging on your shoulders; you used to wear short frocks, and I used to tease you, calling you a heron. . . . What time does!"

"Yes, five years!" sighed Tanya. "Much water has flowed since then. Tell me, Andryusha, honestly," she began eagerly, looking him in the face: "do you feel strange with us now? But why do I ask you? You are a man, you live your own interesting life, you are somebody. . . . To grow apart is so natural! But however that may be, Andryusha, I want you to think of us as your people. We have a right to that."

"I do, Tanya."

"On your word of honour?"

"Yes, on my word of honour."

"You were surprised this evening that we have so many of your photographs. You know my father adores you. Sometimes it seems to me that he loves you more than he does me. He is proud of you. You are a clever, extraordinary man, you have made a brilliant career for yourself, and he is persuaded that you have turned out like this because he brought you up. I don't try to prevent him from thinking so. Let him."

Dawn was already beginning, and that was especially perceptible from the distinctness with which the coils of smoke and the tops of the trees began to stand out in the air.

"It's time we were asleep, though," said Tanya, "and it's cold, too." She took his arm. "Thank you for coming, Andryusha. We have only uninteresting acquaintances, and not many of them. We have only the garden, the garden, the garden, and nothing else. Standards, half-standards," she laughed. "Aports, Reinettes, Borovinkas, budded stocks, grafted stocks. . . . All, all our life has gone into the garden. I never even dream of anything but apples and pears. Of course, it is very nice and useful, but sometimes one longs for something else for variety. I remember that when you used to come to us for the summer holidays, or simply a visit, it always seemed to be fresher and brighter in the house, as though the covers had been taken off the lustres and the furniture. I was only a little girl then, but yet I understood it."

She talked a long while and with great feeling. For some reason the idea came into his head that in the course of the summer he might grow fond of this little, weak, talkative creature, might be carried away and fall in love; in their position it was so possible and natural! This thought touched and amused him; he bent down to her sweet, preoccupied face and hummed softly:

> "'Onyegin, I won't conceal it;
> I madly love Tatiana. . . .' "

By the time they reached the house, Yegor Semyonitch had got up. Kovrin did not feel sleepy; he talked to the old man and went to the garden with him. Yegor Semyonitch was a tall, broad-shouldered, corpulent man, and he suffered from asthma, yet he walked so fast that it was hard work to hurry after him. He had an extremely preoccupied air; he was always hurrying somewhere, with an expression that suggested that if he were one minute late all would be ruined!

"Here is a business, brother . . ." he began, standing still to take breath. "On the surface of the ground, as you see, is frost; but if you raise the thermometer on a stick fourteen feet above the ground, there it is warm. . . . Why is that?"

"I really don't know," said Kovrin, and he laughed.

"H'm! . . . One can't know everything, of course. . . . However large the intellect may be, you can't find room foreverything in it. I suppose you still go in chiefly for philosophy?"

"Yes, I lecture in psychology; I am working at philosophy in general."

"And it does not bore you?"

"On the contrary, it's all I live for."

"Well, God bless you! . . ." said Yegor Semyonitch, meditatively stroking his grey whiskers. "God bless you! . . . I am delighted about you . . . delighted, my boy. . . ."

But suddenly he listened, and, with a terrible face, ran off and quickly disappeared behind the trees in a cloud of smoke.

"Who tied this horse to an apple-tree?" Kovrin heard his despairing, heart-rending cry. "Who is the low scoundrel who has dared to tie this horse to an apple-tree? My God, my God! They have ruined everything; they have spoilt everything; they have done everything filthy, horrible, and abominable. The orchard's done for, the orchard's ruined. My God!"

When he came back to Kovrin, his face looked exhausted and mortified.

"What is one to do with these accursed people?" he said in a tearful voice, flinging up his hands. "Styopka was carting dung at night, and tied the horse to an apple-tree! He twisted the reins round it, the rascal, as tightly as he could, so that the bark is rubbed off in three places. What do you think of that! I spoke to him and he stands like a post and only blinks his eyes. Hanging is too good for him."

Growing calmer, he embraced Kovrin and kissed him on the cheek.

"Well, God bless you! . . . God bless you! . . ." he muttered. "I am very glad you have come. Unutterably glad. . . . Thank you."

Then, with the same rapid step and preoccupied face, he made the round of the whole garden, and showed his former ward all his greenhouses and hot-houses, his covered-in garden, and two apiaries which he called the marvel of our century.

While they were walking the sun rose, flooding the garden with brilliant light. It grew warm. Foreseeing a long, bright, cheerful day, Kovrin recollected that it was only the beginning of May, and that he had before him a whole summer as bright, cheerful, and long; and suddenly there stirred in his bosom a joyous, youthful feeling, such as he used to experience in his childhood, running about in that garden. And he hugged the old man and kissed him affectionately. Both of them, feeling touched, went indoors and drank tea out of old-fashioned china cups, with cream and satisfying krendels made with milk and eggs; and these trifles reminded Kovrin again of his childhood and boyhood. The delightful present was blended with the impressions of the past that stirred within him; there was a tightness at his heart; yet he was happy.

He waited till Tanya was awake and had coffee with her, went for a walk, then went to his room and sat down to work. He read attentively, making notes, and from time to time raised his eyes to look out at the open windows or at the fresh, still dewy flowers in the vases on the table; and again he dropped his eyes to his book, and it seemed to him as though every vein in his body was quivering and fluttering with pleasure.

II

In the country he led just as nervous and restless a life as in town. He read and wrote a great deal, he studied Italian, and when he was out for a walk, thought with pleasure that he would soon sit down to work again. He slept so little that everyone wondered at him; if he accidentally dozed for half an hour in the daytime, he would lie awake all night, and, after a sleepless night, would feel cheerful and vigorous as though nothing had happened.

He talked a great deal, drank wine, and smoked expensive cigars. Very often, almost every day, young ladies of neighbouring families would come to the Pesotskys', and would sing and play the piano with Tanya; sometimes a young neighbour who was a good violinist would come, too. Kovrin listened with eagerness to the music and singing, and was exhausted by it, and this showed itself by his eyes closing and his head falling to one side.

One day he was sitting on the balcony after evening tea, reading. At the same time, in the drawing-room, Tanya taking soprano, one of the young ladies a contralto, and the young man with his violin, were practising a well-known serenade of Braga's. Kovrin listened to the words -- they were Russian -- and could not understand their meaning. At last, leaving his book and listening attentively, he understood: a maiden, full of sick fancies, heard one night in her garden mysterious sounds, so strange and lovely that she was obliged to recognise them as a holy harmony which is unintelligible to us mortals, and so flies back to heaven. Kovrin's eyes began to close. He got up, and in exhaustion walked up and down the drawing-room, and then the dining-room. When the singing was over he took Tanya's arm, and with her went out on the balcony.

"I have been all day thinking of a legend," he said. "I don't remember whether I have read it somewhere or heard it, but it is a strange and almost grotesque legend. To begin with, it is somewhat obscure. A thousand years ago a monk, dressed in black, wandered about the desert, somewhere in Syria or Arabia. . . . Some miles from where he was, some fisherman saw another black monk, who was moving slowly over the surface of a lake. This second monk was a mirage. Now forget all the laws of optics, which the legend does not recognise, and listen to the rest. From that mirage there was cast another mirage, then from that other a third, so that the image of the black monk began to be repeated endlessly from one layer of the atmosphere to another. So that he was seen at one time in Africa, at another in Spain, then in Italy, then in the Far North. . . . Then he passed out of the atmosphere of the earth, and now he is wandering all over the universe, still never coming into conditions in which he might disappear. Possibly he may be seen now in Mars or in some star of the Southern Cross. But, my dear, the real point on which the whole legend hangs lies in the fact that, exactly a thousand years from the day when the monk walked in the desert, the mirage will return to the atmosphere of the earth again and will appear to men. And it seems that the thousand years is almost up. . . . According to the legend, we may look out for the black monk to-day or to-morrow."

"A queer mirage," said Tanya, who did not like the legend.

"But the most wonderful part of it all," laughed Kovrin, "is that I simply cannot recall where I got this legend from. Have I read it somewhere? Have I heard it? Or perhaps I dreamed of the black monk. I swear I don't remember. But the legend interests me. I have been thinking about it all day."

Letting Tanya go back to her visitors, he went out of the house, and, lost in meditation, walked by the flower-beds. The sun was already setting. The flowers, having just been watered, gave forth a damp, irritating fragrance. Indoors they began singing again, and in the distance the violin had the effect of a human voice. Kovrin, racking his brains to remember where he had read or heard the legend, turned slowly towards the park, and unconsciously went as far as the river. By a little path that ran along the steep bank, between the bare roots, he went down to the water, disturbed the peewits there and frightened two ducks. The last rays of the setting sun still threw light here and there on the gloomy pines, but it was quite dark on the surface of the river. Kovrin crossed to the other side by the narrow bridge. Before him lay a wide field covered with young rye not yet in blossom. There was no living habitation, no living soul in the distance, and it seemed as though the little path, if one went along it, would take one to the unknown, mysterious place where the sun had just gone down, and where the evening glow was flaming in immensity and splendour.

"How open, how free, how still it is here!" thought Kovrin, walking along the path. "And it feels as though all the world were watching me, hiding and waiting for me to understand it. . . ."

But then waves began running across the rye, and a light evening breeze softly touched his uncovered head. A minute later there was another gust of wind, but stronger -- the rye began rustling, and he heard behind him the hollow murmur of the pines. Kovrin stood still in amazement. From the horizon there rose up to the sky, like a whirlwind or a waterspout, a tall black column. Its outline was indistinct, but from the first instant it could be seen that it was not standing still, but moving with fearful rapidity, moving straight towards Kovrin, and the nearer it came the smaller and the more distinct it was. Kovrin moved aside into the rye to make way for it, and only just had time to do so.

A monk, dressed in black, with a grey head and black eyebrows, his arms crossed over his breast, floated by him. . . . His bare feet did not touch the earth. After he had floated twenty feet beyond him, he looked round at Kovrin, and nodded to him with a friendly but sly smile. But what a pale, fearfully pale, thin face! Beginning to grow larger again, he flew across the river, collided noiselessly with the clay bank and pines, and passing through them, vanished like smoke.

"Why, you see," muttered Kovrin, "there must be truth in the legend."

Without trying to explain to himself the strange apparition, glad that he had succeeded in seeing so near and so distinctly, not only the monk's black garments, but even his face and eyes, agreeably excited, he went back to the house.

In the park and in the garden people were moving about quietly, in the house they were playing -- so he alone had seen the monk. He had an intense desire to tell Tanya and Yegor Semyonitch, but he reflected that they would certainly think his words the ravings of delirium, and that would frighten them; he had better say nothing.

He laughed aloud, sang, and danced the mazurka; he was in high spirits, and all of them, the visitors and Tanya, thought he had a peculiar look, radiant and inspired, and that he was very interesting.

III

After supper, when the visitors had gone, he went to his room and lay down on the sofa: he wanted to think about the monk. But a minute later Tanya came in.

"Here, Andryusha; read father's articles," she said, giving him a bundle of pamphlets and proofs. "They are splendid articles. He writes capitally."

"Capitally, indeed!" said Yegor Semyonitch, following her and smiling constrainedly; he was ashamed. "Don't listen to her, please; don't read them! Though, if you want to go to sleep, read them by all means; they are a fine soporific."

"I think they are splendid articles," said Tanya, with deep conviction. "You read them, Andryusha, and persuade father to write oftener. He could write a complete manual of horticulture."

Yegor Semyonitch gave a forced laugh, blushed, and began uttering the phrases usually made us of by an embarrassed author. At last he began to give way.

"In that case, begin with Gaucher's article and these Russian articles," he muttered, turning over the pamphlets with a trembling hand, "or else you won't understand. Before you read my objections, you must know what I am objecting to. But it's all nonsense . . . tiresome stuff. Besides, I believe it's bedtime."

Tanya went away. Yegor Semyonitch sat down on the sofa by Kovrin and heaved a deep sigh.

"Yes, my boy . . ." he began after a pause. "That's how it is, my dear lecturer. Here I write articles, and take part in exhibitions, and receive medals. . . . Pesotsky, they say, has apples the size of a head, and Pesotsky, they say, has made his fortune with his garden. In short, 'Kotcheby is rich and glorious.' But one asks oneself: what is it all for? The garden is certainly fine, a model. It's not really a garden, but a regular institution, which is of the greatest public importance because it marks, so to say, a new era in Russian agriculture and Russian industry. But, what's it for? What's the object of it?"

"The fact speaks for itself."

"I do not mean in that sense. I meant to ask: what will happen to the garden when I die? In the condition in which you see it now, it would not be maintained for one month without me. The whole secret of success lies not in its being a big garden or a great number of labourers being employed in it, but in the fact that I love the work. Do you understand? I love it perhaps more than myself. Look at me; I do everything myself. I work from morning to night: I do all the grafting myself, the pruning myself, the planting myself. I do it all myself: when anyone helps me I am jealous and irritable till I am rude. The whole secret lies in loving it -- that is, in the sharp eye of the master; yes, and in the master's hands, and in the feeling that makes one, when one goes anywhere for an hour's visit, sit, ill at ease, with one's heart far away, afraid that something may have happened in the garden. But when I die, who will look after it? Who will work? The gardener? The labourers? Yes? But I will tell you, my dear fellow, the worst enemy in the garden is not a hare, not a cockchafer, and not the frost, but any outside person."

"And Tanya?" asked Kovrin, laughing. "She can't be more harmful than a hare? She loves the work and understands it."

"Yes, she loves it and understands it. If after my death the garden goes to her and she is the mistress, of course nothing better could be wished. But if, which God forbid, she should marry," Yegor Semyonitch whispered, and looked with a frightened look at Kovrin, "that's just it. If she marries and children come, she will have no time to think about the garden. What I fear most is: she will marry some fine gentleman, and he will be greedy, and he will let the garden to people who will run it for profit, and everything will go to the devil the very first year! In our work females are the scourge of God!"

Yegor Semyonitch sighed and paused for a while.

"Perhaps it is egoism, but I tell you frankly: I don't want Tanya to get married. I am afraid of it! There is one young dandy comes to see us, bringing his violin and scraping on it; I know Tanya will not marry him, I know it quite well; but I can't bear to see him! Altogether, my boy, I am very queer. I know that."

Yegor Semyonitch got up and walked about the room in excitement, and it was evident that he wanted to say something very important, but could not bring himself to it.

"I am very fond of you, and so I am going to speak to you openly," he decided at last, thrusting his hands into his pockets. "I deal plainly with certain delicate questions, and say exactly what I think, and I cannot endure so-called hidden thoughts. I will speak plainly: you are the only man to whom I should not be afraid to marry my daughter. You are a clever man with a good heart, and would not let my beloved work go to ruin; and the chief reason is that I love you as a son, and I am proud of you. If Tanya and you could get up a romance somehow, then -- well! I should be very glad and even happy. I tell you this plainly, without mincing matters, like an honest man."

Kovrin laughed. Yegor Semyonitch opened the door to go out, and stood in the doorway.

"If Tanya and you had a son, I would make a horticulturist of him," he said, after a moment's thought. "However, this is idle dreaming. Goodnight."

Left alone, Kovrin settled himself more comfortably on the sofa and took up the articles. The title of one was "On Intercropping"; of another, "A few Words on the Remarks of Monsieur Z. concerning the Trenching of the Soil for a New Garden"; a third, "Additional Matter concerning Grafting with a Dormant Bud"; and they were all of the same sort. But what a restless, jerky tone! What nervous, almost hysterical passion! Here was an article, one would have thought, with most peaceable and impersonal contents: the subject of it was the Russian Antonovsky Apple. But Yegor Semyonitch began it with "Audiatur altera pars," and finished it with "Sapienti sat"; and between these two quotations a perfect torrent of venomous phrases directed "at the learned ignorance of our recognised horticultural authorities, who observe Nature from the height of their university chairs," or at Monsieur Gaucher, "whose success has been the work of the vulgar and the dilettanti." "And then followed an inappropriate, affected, and insincere regret that peasants who stole fruit and broke the branches could not nowadays be flogged.

"It is beautiful, charming, healthy work, but even in this there is strife and passion," thought Kovrin, "I suppose that everywhere and in all careers men of ideas are nervous, and marked by exaggerated sensitiveness. Most likely it must be so."

He thought of Tanya, who was so pleased with Yegor Semyonitch's articles. Small, pale, and so thin that her shoulder-blades stuck out, her eyes, wide and open, dark and intelligent, had an intent gaze, as though looking for something. She walked like her father with a little hurried step. She talked a great deal and was fond of arguing, accompanying every phrase, however insignificant, with expressive mimicry and gesticulation. No doubt she was nervous in the extreme.

Kovrin went on reading the articles, but he understood nothing of them, and flung them aside. The same pleasant excitement with which he had earlier in the evening danced the mazurka and listened to the music was now mastering him again and rousing a multitude of thoughts. He got up and began walking about the room, thinking about the black monk. It occurred to him that if this strange, supernatural monk had appeared to him only, that meant that he was ill and had reached the point of having hallucinations. This reflection frightened him, but not for long.

"But I am all right, and I am doing no harm to anyone; so there is no harm in my hallucinations," he thought; and he felt happy again.

He sat down on the sofa and clasped his hands round his head. Restraining the unaccountable joy which filled his whole being, he then paced up and down again, and sat down to his work. But the thought that he read in the book did not satisfy him. He wanted something gigantic, unfathomable, stupendous. Towards morning he undressed and reluctantly went to bed: he ought to sleep.

When he heard the footsteps of Yegor Semyonitch going out into the garden, Kovrin rang the bell and asked the footman to bring him some wine. He drank several glasses of Lafitte, then wrapped himself up, head and all; his consciousness grew clouded and he fell asleep.

IV

Yegor Semyonitch and Tanya often quarrelled and said nasty things to each other.

They quarrelled about something that morning. Tanya burst out crying and went to her room. She would not come down to dinner nor to tea. At first Yegor Semyonitch went about looking sulky and dignified, as though to give everyone to understand that for him the claims of justice and good order were more important than anything else in the world; but he could not keep it up for long, and soon sank into depression. He walked about the park dejectedly, continually sighing: "Oh, my God! My God!" and at dinner did not eat a morsel. At last, guilty and conscience-stricken, he knocked at the locked door and called timidly:

"Tanya! Tanya!"

And from behind the door came a faint voice, weak with crying but still determined:

"Leave me alone, if you please."

The depression of the master and mistress was reflected in the whole household, even in the labourers working in the garden. Kovrin was absorbed in his interesting work, but at last he, too, felt dreary and uncomfortable. To dissipate the general ill-humour in some way, he made up his mind to intervene, and towards evening he knocked at Tanya's door. He was admitted.

"Fie, fie, for shame!" he began playfully, looking with surprise at Tanya's tear-stained, woebegone face, flushed in patches with crying. "Is it really so serious? Fie, fie!"

"But if you knew how he tortures me!" she said, and floods of scalding tears streamed from her big eyes. "He torments me to death," she went on, wringing her hands. "I said nothing to him . . . nothing . . . I only said that there was no need to keep . . . too many labourers . . . if we could hire them by the day when we wanted them. You know . . . you know the labourers have been doing nothing for a whole week. . . . I . . . I . . . only said that, and he shouted and . . . said . . . a lot of horrible insulting things to me. What for?"

"There, there," said Kovrin, smoothing her hair. "You've quarrelled with each other, you've cried, and that's enough. You must not be angry for long -- that's wrong . . . all the more as he loves you beyond everything."

"He has . . . has spoiled my whole life," Tanya went on, sobbing. "I hear nothing but abuse and . . . insults. He thinks I am of no use in the house. Well! He is right. I shall go away to-morrow; I shall become a telegraph clerk. . . . I don't care. . . ."

"Come, come, come. . . . You mustn't cry, Tanya. You mustn't, dear. . . . You are both hot-tempered and irritable, and you are both to blame. Come along; I will reconcile you."

Kovrin talked affectionately and persuasively, while she went on crying, twitching her shoulders and wringing her hands, as though some terrible misfortune had really befallen her. He felt all the sorrier for her because her grief was not a serious one, yet she suffered extremely. What trivialities were enough to make this little creature miserable for a whole day, perhaps for her whole life! Comforting Tanya, Kovrin thought that, apart from this girl and her father, he might hunt the world over and would not find people who would love him as one of themselves, as one of their kindred. If it had not been for those two he might very likely, having lost his father and mother in early childhood, never to the day of his death have known what was meant by genuine affection and that naïve, uncritical love which is only lavished on very close blood relations; and he felt that the nerves of this weeping, shaking girl responded to his half-sick, overstrained nerves like iron to a magnet. He never could have loved a healthy, strong, rosy-cheeked woman, but pale, weak, unhappy Tanya attracted him.

And he liked stroking her hair and her shoulders, pressing her hand and wiping away her tears. . . . At last she left off crying. She went on for a long time complaining of her father and her hard, insufferable life in that house, entreating Kovrin to put himself in her place; then she began, little by little, smiling, and sighing that God had given her such a bad temper. At last, laughing aloud, she called herself a fool, and ran out of the room.

When a little later Kovrin went into the garden, Yegor Semyonitch and Tanya were walking side by side along an avenue as though nothing had happened, and both were eating rye bread with salt on it, as both were hungry.

V

Glad that he had been so successful in the part of peacemaker, Kovrin went into the park. Sitting on a garden seat, thinking, he heard the rattle of a carriage and a feminine laugh -- visitors were arriving. When the shades of evening began falling on the garden, the sounds of the violin and singing voices reached him indistinctly, and that reminded him of the black monk. Where, in what land or in what planet, was that optical absurdity moving now?

Hardly had he recalled the legend and pictured in his imagination the dark apparition he had seen in the rye-field, when, from behind a pine-tree exactly opposite, there came out noiselessly, without the slightest rustle, a man of medium height with uncovered grey head, all in black, and barefooted like a beggar, and his black eyebrows stood out conspicuously on his pale, death-like face. Nodding his head graciously, this beggar or pilgrim came noiselessly to the seat and sat down, and Kovrin recognised him as the black monk.

For a minute they looked at one another, Kovrin with amazement, and the monk with friendliness, and, just as before, a little slyness, as though he were thinking something to himself.

"But you are a mirage," said Kovrin. "Why are you here and sitting still? That does not fit in with the legend."

"That does not matter," the monk answered in a low voice, not immediately turning his face towards him. "The legend, the mirage, and I are all the products of your excited imagination. I am a phantom."

"Then you don't exist?" said Kovrin.

"You can think as you like," said the monk, with a faint smile. "I exist in your imagination, and your imagination is part of nature, so I exist in nature."

"You have a very old, wise, and extremely expressive face, as though you really had lived more than a thousand years," said Kovrin. "I did not know that my imagination was capable of creating such phenomena. But why do you look at me with such enthusiasm? Do you like me?"

"Yes, you are one of those few who are justly called the chosen of God. You do the service of eternal truth. Your thoughts, your designs, the marvellous studies you are engaged in, and all your life, bear the Divine, the heavenly stamp, seeing that they are consecrated to the rational and the beautiful -- that is, to what is eternal."

"You said 'eternal truth.' . . . But is eternal truth of use to man and within his reach, if there is no eternal life?"

"There is eternal life," said the monk.

"Do you believe in the immortality of man?"

"Yes, of course. A grand, brilliant future is in store for you men. And the more there are like you on earth, the sooner will this future be realised. Without you who serve the higher principle and live in full understanding and freedom, mankind would be of little account; developing in a natural way, it would have to wait a long time for the end of its earthly history. You will lead it some thousands of years earlier into the kingdom of eternal truth -- and therein lies your supreme service. You are the incarnation of the blessing of God, which rests upon men."

"And what is the object of eternal life?" asked Kovrin.

"As of all life -- enjoyment. True enjoyment lies in knowledge, and eternal life provides innumerable and inexhaustible sources of knowledge, and in that sense it has been said: 'In My Father's house there are many mansions.' "

"If only you knew how pleasant it is to hear you!" said Kovrin, rubbing his hands with satisfaction.

"I am very glad."

"But I know that when you go away I shall be worried by the question of your reality. You are a phantom, an hallucination. So I am mentally deranged, not normal?"

"What if you are? Why trouble yourself? You are ill because you have overworked and exhausted yourself, and that means that you have sacrificed your health to the idea, and the time is near at hand when you will give up life itself to it. What could be better? That is the goal towards which all divinely endowed, noble natures strive."

"If I know I am mentally affected, can I trust myself?"

"And are you sure that the men of genius, whom all men trust, did not see phantoms, too? The learned say now that genius is allied to madness. My friend, healthy and normal people are only the common herd. Reflections upon the neurasthenia of the age, nervous exhaustion and degeneracy, et cetera, can only seriously agitate those who place the object of life in the present -- that is, the common herd."

"The Romans used to say: *Mens sana in corpore sano.*"

"Not everything the Greeks and the Romans said is true. Exaltation, enthusiasm, ecstasy -- all that distinguishes prophets, poets, martyrs for the idea, from the common folk -- is repellent to the animal side of man -- that is, his physical health. I repeat, if you want to be healthy and normal, go to the common herd."

"Strange that you repeat what often comes into my mind," said Kovrin. "It is as though you had seen and overheard my secret thoughts. But don't let us talk about me. What do you mean by 'eternal truth'?"

The monk did not answer. Kovrin looked at him and could not distinguish his face. His features grew blurred and misty. Then the monk's head and arms disappeared; his body seemed merged into the seat and the evening twilight, and he vanished altogether.

"The hallucination is over," said Kovrin; and he laughed. "It's a pity."

He went back to the house, light-hearted and happy. The little the monk had said to him had flattered, not his vanity, but his whole soul, his whole being. To be one of the chosen, to serve eternal truth, to stand in the ranks of those who could make mankind worthy of the kingdom of God some thousands of years sooner -- that is, to free men from some thousands of years of unnecessary struggle, sin, and suffering; to sacrifice to the idea everything -- youth, strength, health; to be ready to die for the common weal -- what an exalted, what a happy lot! He recalled his past -- pure, chaste, laborious; he remembered what he had learned himself and what he had taught to others, and decided that there was no exaggeration in the monk's words.

Tanya came to meet him in the park: she was by now wearing a different dress.

"Are you here?" she said. "And we have been looking and looking for you. . . . But what is the matter with you?" she asked in wonder, glancing at his radiant, ecstatic face and eyes full of tears. "How strange you are, Andryusha!"

"I am pleased, Tanya," said Kovrin, laying his hand on her shoulders. "I am more than pleased: I am happy. Tanya, darling Tanya, you are an extraordinary, nice creature. Dear Tanya, I am so glad, I am so glad!"

He kissed both her hands ardently, and went on:

"I have just passed through an exalted, wonderful, unearthly moment. But I can't tell you all about it or you would call me mad and not believe me. Let us talk of you. Dear, delightful Tanya! I love you, and am used to loving you. To have you near me, to meet you a dozen times a day, has become a necessity of my existence; I don't know how I shall get on without you when I go back home."

"Oh," laughed Tanya, "you will forget about us in two days. We are humble people and you are a great man."

"No; let us talk in earnest!" he said. "I shall take you with me, Tanya. Yes? Will you come with me? Will you be mine?"

"Come," said Tanya, and tried to laugh again, but the laugh would not come, and patches of colour came into her face.

She began breathing quickly and walked very quickly, but not to the house, but further into the park.

"I was not thinking of it . . . I was not thinking of it," she said, wringing her hands in despair.

And Kovrin followed her and went on talking, with the same radiant, enthusiastic face:

"I want a love that will dominate me altogether; and that love only you, Tanya, can give me. I am happy! I am happy!"

She was overwhelmed, and huddling and shrinking together, seemed ten years older all at once, while he thought her beautiful and expressed his rapture aloud:

"How lovely she is!"

VI

Learning from Kovrin that not only a romance had been got up, but that there would even be a wedding, Yegor Semyonitch spent a long time in pacing from one corner of the room to the other, trying to conceal his agitation. His hands began trembling, his neck swelled and turned purple, he ordered his racing droshky and drove off somewhere. Tanya, seeing how he lashed the horse, and seeing how he pulled his cap over his ears, understood what he was feeling, shut herself up in her room, and cried the whole day.

In the hot-houses the peaches and plums were already ripe; the packing and sending off of these tender and fragile goods to Moscow took a great deal of care, work, and trouble. Owing to the fact that the summer was very hot and dry, it was necessary to water every tree, and a great deal of time and labour was spent on doing it. Numbers of caterpillars made their appearance, which, to Kovrin's disgust, the labourers and even Yegor Semyonitch and Tanya squashed with their fingers. In spite of all that, they had already to book autumn orders for fruit and trees, and to carry on a great deal of correspondence. And at the very busiest time, when no one seemed to have a free moment, the work of the fields carried off more than half their labourers from the garden. Yegor Semyonitch, sunburnt, exhausted, ill-humoured, galloped from the fields to the garden and back again; cried that he was being torn to pieces, and that he should put a bullet through his brains.

Then came the fuss and worry of the trousseau, to which the Pesotskys attached a good deal of importance. Everyone's head was in a whirl from the snipping of the scissors, the rattle of the sewing-machine, the smell of hot irons, and the caprices of the dressmaker, a huffy and nervous lady. And, as ill-luck would have it, visitors came every day, who had to be entertained, fed, and even put up for the night. But all this hard labour passed unnoticed as though in a fog. Tanya felt that love and happiness had taken her unawares, though she had, since she was fourteen, for some reason been convinced that Kovrin would marry her and no one else. She was bewildered, could not grasp it, could not believe herself. . . . At one minute such joy would swoop down upon her that she longed to fly away to the clouds and there pray to God, at another moment she would remember that in August she would have to part from her home and leave her father; or, goodness knows why, the idea would occur to her that she was worthless -- insignificant and unworthy of a great man like Kovrin -- and she would go to her room, lock herself in, and cry bitterly for several hours. When there were visitors, she would suddenly fancy that Kovrin looked extraordinarily handsome, and that all the women were in love with him and envying her, and her soul was filled with pride and rapture, as though she had vanquished the whole world; but he had only to smile politely at any young lady for her to be trembling with jealousy, to retreat to her room -- and tears again. These new sensations mastered her completely; she helped her father mechanically, without noticing peaches, caterpillars or labourers, or how rapidly the time was passing.

It was almost the same with Yegor Semyonitch. He worked from morning till night, was always in a hurry, was irritable, and flew into rages, but all of this was in a sort of spellbound dream. It seemed as though there were two men in him: one was the real Yegor Semyonitch, who was moved to indignation, and clutched his head in despair when he heard of some irregularity from Ivan Karlovitch the gardener; and another -- not the real one -- who seemed as though he were half drunk, would interrupt a business conversation at half a word, touch the gardener on the shoulder, and begin muttering:

"Say what you like, there is a great deal in blood. His mother was a wonderful woman, most high-minded and intelligent. It was a pleasure to look at her good, candid, pure face; it was like the face of an angel. She drew splendidly, wrote verses, spoke five foreign languages, sang. . . . Poor thing! she died of consumption. The Kingdom of Heaven be hers."

The unreal Yegor Semyonitch sighed, and after a pause went on:

"When he was a boy and growing up in my house, he had the same angelic face, good and candid. The way he looks and talks and moves is as soft and elegant as his mother's. And his intellect! We were always struck with his intelligence. To be sure, it's not for nothing he's a Master of Arts! It's not for nothing! And wait a bit, Ivan Karlovitch, what will he be in ten years' time? He will be far above us!"

But at this point the real Yegor Semyonitch, suddenly coming to himself, would make a terrible face, would clutch his head and cry:

"The devils! They have spoilt everything! They have ruined everything! They have spoilt everything! The garden's done for, the garden's ruined!"

Kovrin, meanwhile, worked with the same ardour as before, and did not notice the general commotion. Love only added fuel to the flames. After every talk with Tanya he went to his room, happy and triumphant, took up his book or his manuscript with the same passion with which he had just kissed Tanya and told her of his love. What the black monk had told him of the chosen of God, of eternal truth, of the brilliant future of mankind and so on, gave peculiar and extraordinary significance to his work, and filled his soul with pride and the consciousness of his own exalted consequence. Once or twice a week, in the park or in the house, he met the black monk and had long conversations with him, but this did not alarm him, but, on the contrary, delighted him, as he was now firmly persuaded that such apparitions only visited the elect few who rise up above their fellows and devote themselves to the service of the idea.

One day the monk appeared at dinner-time and sat in the dining-room window. Kovrin was delighted, and very adroitly began a conversation with Yegor Semyonitch and Tanya of what might be of interest to the monk; the black-robed visitor listened and nodded his head graciously, and Yegor Semyonitch and Tanya listened, too, and smiled gaily without suspecting that Kovrin was not talking to them but to his hallucination.

Imperceptibly the fast of the Assumption was approaching, and soon after came the wedding, which, at Yegor Semyonitch's urgent desire, was celebrated with "a flourish" -- that is, with senseless festivities that lasted for two whole days and nights. Three thousand roubles' worth of food and drink was consumed, but the music of the wretched hired band, the noisy toasts, the scurrying to and fro of the footmen, the uproar and crowding, prevented them from appreciating the taste of the expensive wines and wonderful delicacies ordered from Moscow.

VII

One long winter night Kovrin was lying in bed, reading a French novel. Poor Tanya, who had headaches in the evenings from living in town, to which she was not accustomed, had been asleep a long while, and, from time to time, articulated some incoherent phrase in her restless dreams.

It struck three o'clock. Kovrin put out the light and lay down to sleep, lay for a long time with his eyes closed, but could not get to sleep because, as he fancied, the room was very hot and Tanya talked in her sleep. At half-past four he lighted the candle again, and this time he saw the black monk sitting in an arm-chair near the bed.

"Good-morning," said the monk, and after a brief pause he asked: "What are you thinking of now?"

"Of fame," answered Kovrin. "In the French novel I have just been reading, there is a description of a young *savant,* who does silly things and pines away through worrying about fame. I can't understand such anxiety."

"Because you are wise. Your attitude towards fame is one of indifference, as towards a toy which no longer interests you."

"Yes, that is true."

"Renown does not allure you now. What is there flattering, amusing, or edifying in their carving your name on a tombstone, then time rubbing off the inscription together with the gilding? Moreover, happily there are too many of you for the weak memory of mankind to be able to retain your names."

"Of course," assented Kovrin. "Besides, why should they be remembered? But let us talk of something else. Of happiness, for instance. What is happiness?'

When the clock struck five, he was sitting on the bed, dangling his feet to the carpet, talking to the monk:

"In ancient times a happy man grew at last frightened of his happiness -- it was so great! -- and to propitiate the gods he brought as a sacrifice his favourite ring. Do you know, I, too, like Polykrates, begin to be uneasy of my happiness. It seems strange to me that from morning to night I feel nothing but joy; it fills my whole being and smothers all other feelings. I don't know what sadness, grief, or boredom is. Here I am not asleep; I suffer from sleeplessness, but I am not dull. I say it in earnest; I begin to feel perplexed."

"But why?" the monk asked in wonder. "Is joy a supernatural feeling? Ought it not to be the normal state of man? The more highly a man is developed on the intellectual and moral side, the more independent he is, the more pleasure life gives him. Socrates, Diogenes, and Marcus Aurelius, were joyful, not sorrowful. And the Apostle tells us: 'Rejoice continually'; 'Rejoice and be glad.' "

"But will the gods be suddenly wrathful?" Kovrin jested; and he laughed. "If they take from me comfort and make me go cold and hungry, it won't be very much to my taste."

Meanwhile Tanya woke up and looked with amazement and horror at her husband. He was talking, addressing the arm-chair, laughing and gesticulating; his eyes were gleaming, and there was something strange in his laugh.

"Andryusha, whom are you talking to?" she asked, clutching the hand he stretched out to the monk. "Andryusha! Whom?"

"Oh! Whom?" said Kovrin in confusion. "Why, to him. . . . He is sitting here," he said, pointing to the black monk.

"There is no one here . . . no one! Andryusha, you are ill!"

Tanya put her arm round her husband and held him tight, as though protecting him from the apparition, and put her hand over his eyes.

"You are ill!" she sobbed, trembling all over. "Forgive me, my precious, my dear one, but I have noticed for a long time that your mind is clouded in some way. . . . You are mentally ill, Andryusha. . . ."

Her trembling infected him, too. He glanced once more at the arm-chair, which was now empty, felt a sudden weakness in his arms and legs, was frightened, and began dressing.

"It's nothing, Tanya; it's nothing," he muttered, shivering. "I really am not quite well . . . it's time to admit that."

"I have noticed it for a long time . . . and father has noticed it," she said, trying to suppress her sobs. "You talk to yourself, smile somehow strangely . . . and can't sleep. Oh, my God, my God, save us!" she said in terror. "But don't be frightened, Andryusha; for God's sake don't be frightened. . . ."

She began dressing, too. Only now, looking at her, Kovrin realised the danger of his position -- realised the meaning of the black monk and his conversations with him. It was clear to him now that he was mad.

Neither of them knew why they dressed and went into the dining-room: she in front and he following her. There they found Yegor Semyonitch standing in his dressing-gown and with a candle in his hand. He was staying with them, and had been awakened by Tanya's sobs.

"Don't be frightened, Andryusha," Tanya was saying, shivering as though in a fever; "don't be frightened. . . . Father, it will all pass over . . . it will all pass over. . . ."

Kovrin was too much agitated to speak. He wanted to say to his father-in-law in a playful tone: "Congratulate me; it appears I have gone out of my mind"; but he could only move his lips and smile bitterly.

At nine o'clock in the morning they put on his jacket and fur coat, wrapped him up in a shawl, and took him in a carriage to a doctor.

VIII

Summer had come again, and the doctor advised their going into the country. Kovrin had recovered; he had left off seeing the black monk, and he had only to get up his strength. Staying at his father-in-law's, he drank a great deal of milk, worked for only two hours out of the twenty-four, and neither smoked nor drank wine.

On the evening before Elijah's Day they had an evening service in the house. When the deacon was handing the priest the censer the immense old room smelt like a graveyard, and Kovrin felt bored. He went out into the garden. Without noticing the gorgeous flowers, he walked about the garden, sat down on a seat, then strolled about the park; reaching the river, he went down and then stood lost in thought, looking at the water. The sullen pines with their shaggy roots, which had seen him a year before so young, so joyful and confident, were not whispering now, but standing mute and motionless, as though they did not recognise him. And, indeed, his head was closely cropped, his beautiful long hair was gone, his step was lagging, his face was fuller and paler than last summer.

He crossed by the footbridge to the other side. Where the year before there had been rye the oats stood, reaped, and lay in rows. The sun had set and there was a broad stretch of glowing red on the horizon, a sign of windy weather next day. It was still. Looking in the direction from which the year before the black monk had first appeared, Kovrin stood for twenty minutes, till the evening glow had begun to fade. . . .

When, listless and dissatisfied, he returned home the service was over. Yegor Semyonitch and Tanya were sitting on the steps of the verandah, drinking tea. They were talking of something, but, seeing Kovrin, ceased at once, and he concluded from their faces that their talk had been about him.

"I believe it is time for you to have your milk," Tanya said to her husband.

"No, it is not time yet . . ." he said, sitting down on the bottom step. "Drink it yourself; I don't want it."

Tanya exchanged a troubled glance with her father, and said in a guilty voice:

"You notice yourself that milk does you good."

"Yes, a great deal of good!" Kovrin laughed. "I congratulate you: I have gained a pound in weight since Friday." He pressed his head tightly in his hands and said miserably: "Why, why have you cured me? Preparations ofbromide, idleness, hot baths, supervision, cowardly consternation at every mouthful, at every step -- all this will reduce me at last to idiocy. I went out of my mind, I had megalomania; but then I was cheerful, confident, and even happy; I was interesting and original. Now I have become more sensible and stolid, but I am just like everyone else: I am -- mediocrity; I am weary of life. . . . Oh, how cruelly you have treated me! . . . I saw hallucinations, but what harm did that do to anyone? I ask, what harm did that do anyone?"

"Goodness knows what you are saying!" sighed Yegor Semyonitch. "It's positively wearisome to listen to it."

"Then don't listen."

The presence of other people, especially Yegor Semyonitch, irritated Kovrin now; he answered him drily, coldly, and even rudely, never looked at him but with irony and hatred, while Yegor Semyonitch was overcome with confusion and cleared his throat guiltily, though he was not conscious of any fault in himself. At a loss to understand why their charming and affectionate relations had changed so abruptly, Tanya huddled up to her father and looked anxiously in his face; she wanted to understand and could not understand, and all that was clear to her was that their relations were growing worse and worse every day, that of late her father had begun to look much older, and her husband had grown irritable, capricious, quarrelsome and uninteresting. She could not laugh or sing; at dinner she ate nothing; did not sleep for nights together, expecting something awful, and was so worn out that on one occasion she lay in a dead faint from dinner-time till evening. During the service she thought her father was crying, and now while the three of them were sitting together on the terrace she made an effort not to think of it.

"How fortunate Buddha, Mahomed, and Shakespeare were that their kind relations and doctors did not cure them of their ecstasy and their inspiration," said Kovrin. "If Mahomed had taken bromide for his nerves, had worked only two hours out of the twenty-four, and had drunk milk, that remarkable man would have left no more trace after him than his dog. Doctors and kind relations will succeed in stupefying mankind, in making mediocrity pass for genius and in bringing civilisation to ruin. If only you knew," Kovrin said with annoyance, "how grateful I am to you."

He felt intense irritation, and to avoid saying too much, he got up quickly and went into the house. It was still, and the fragrance of the tobacco plant and the marvel of Peru floated in at the open window. The moonlight lay in green patches on the floor and on the piano in the big dark dining-room. Kovrin remembered the raptures of the previous summer when there had been the same scent of the marvel of Peru and the moon had shone in at the window. To bring back the mood of last year he went quickly to his study, lighted a strong cigar, and told the footman to bring him some wine. But the cigar left a bitter and disgusting taste in his mouth, and the wine had not the same flavour as it had the year before. And so great is the effect of giving up a habit, the cigar and the two gulps of wine made him giddy, and brought on palpitations of the heart, so that he was obliged to take bromide.

Before going to bed, Tanya said to him:

"Father adores you. You are cross with him about something, and it is killing him. Look at him; he is ageing, not from day to day, but from hour to hour. I entreat you, Andryusha, for God's sake, for the sake of your dead father, for the sake of my peace of mind, be affectionate to him."

"I can't, I don't want to."

"But why?" asked Tanya, beginning to tremble all over. "Explain why."

"Because he is antipathetic to me, that's all," said Kovrin carelessly; and he shrugged his shoulders. "But we won't talk about him: he is your father."

"I can't understand, I can't," said Tanya, pressing her hands to her temples and staring at a fixed point. "Something incomprehensible, awful, is going on in the house. You have changed, grown unlike yourself. . . . You, clever, extraordinary man as you are, are irritated over trifles, meddle in paltry nonsense. . . . Such trivial things excite you, that sometimes one is simply amazed and can't believe that it is you. Come, come, don't be angry, don't be angry," she went on, kissing his hands, frightened of her own words. "You are clever, kind, noble. You will be just to father. He is so good."

"He is not good; he is just good-natured. Burlesque old uncles like your father, with well-fed, good-natured faces, extraordinarily hospitable and queer, at one time used to touch me and amuse me in novels and in farces and in life; now I dislike them. They are egoists to the marrow of their bones. What disgusts me most of all is their being so well-fed, and that purely bovine, purely hoggish optimism of a full stomach."

Tanya sat down on the bed and laid her head on the pillow.

"This is torture," she said, and from her voice it was evident that she was utterly exhausted, and that it was hard for her to speak. "Not one moment of peace since the winter. . . . Why, it's awful! My God! I am wretched."

"Oh, of course, I am Herod, and you and your father are the innocents. Of course."

His face seemed to Tanya ugly and unpleasant. Hatred and an ironical expression did not suit him. And, indeed, she had noticed before that there was something lacking in his face, as though ever since his hair had been cut his face had changed, too. She wanted to say something wounding to him, but immediately she caught herself in this antagonistic feeling, she was frightened and went out of the bedroom.

IX

Kovrin received a professorship at the University. The inaugural address was fixed for the second of December, and a notice to that effect was hung up in the corridor at the University. But on the day appointed he informed the students' inspector, by telegram, that he was prevented by illness from giving the lecture.

He had hæmorrhage from the throat. He was often spitting blood, but it happened two or three times a month that there was a considerable loss of blood, and then he grew extremely weak and sank into a drowsy condition. This illness did not particularly frighten him, as he knew that his mother had lived for ten years or longer suffering from the same disease, and the doctors assured him that there was no danger, and had only advised him to avoid excitement, to lead a regular life, and to speak as little as possible.

In January again his lecture did not take place owing to the same reason, and in February it was too late to begin the course. It had to be postponed to the following year.

By now he was living not with Tanya, but with another woman, who was two years older than he was, and who looked after him as though he were a baby. He was in a calm and tranquil state of mind; he readily gave in to her, and when Varvara Nikolaevna -- that was the name of his friend -- decided to take him to the Crimea, he agreed, though he had a presentiment that no good would come of the trip.

They reached Sevastopol in the evening and stopped at an hotel to rest and go on the next day to Yalta. They were both exhausted by the journey. Varvara Nikolaevna had some tea, went to bed and was soon asleep. But Kovrin did not go to bed. An hour before starting for the station, he had received a letter from Tanya, and had not brought himself to open it, and now it was lying in his coat pocket, and the thought of it excited him disagreeably. At the bottom of his heart he genuinely considered now that his marriage to Tanya had been a mistake. He was glad that their separation was final, and the thought of that woman who in the end had turned into a living relic, still walking about though everything seemed dead in her except her big, staring, intelligent eyes -- the thought of her roused in him nothing but pity and disgust with himself. The handwriting on the envelope reminded him how cruel and unjust he had been two years before, how he had worked off his anger at his spiritual emptiness, his boredom, his loneliness, and his dissatisfaction with life by revenging himself on people in no way to blame. He remembered, also, how he had torn up his dissertation and all the articles he had written during his illness, and how he had thrown them out of window, and the bits of paper had fluttered in the wind and caught on the trees and flowers. In every line of them he saw strange, utterly groundless pretension, shallow defiance, arrogance, megalomania; and they made him feel as though he were reading a description of his vices. But when the last manuscript had been torn up and sent flying out of window, he felt, for some reason, suddenly bitter and angry; he went to his wife and said a great many unpleasant things to her. My God, how he had tormented her! One day, wanting to cause her pain, he told her that her father had played a very unattractive part in their romance, that he had asked him to marry her. Yegor Semyonitch accidentally overheard this, ran into the room, and, in his despair, could not utter a word, could only stamp and make a strange, bellowing sound as though he had lost the power of speech, and Tanya, looking at her father, had uttered a heart-rending shriek and had fallen into a swoon. It was hideous.

All this came back into his memory as he looked at the familiar writing. Kovrin went out on to the balcony; it was still warm weather and there was a smell of the sea. The wonderful bay reflected the moonshine and the lights, and was of a colour for which it was difficult to find a name. It was a soft and tender blending of dark blue and green; in places the water was like blue vitriol, and in places it seemed as though the moonlight were liquefied and filling the bay instead of water. And what harmony of colours, what an atmosphere of peace, calm, and sublimity!

In the lower storey under the balcony the windows were probably open, for women's voices and laughter could be heard distinctly. Apparently there was an evening party.

Kovrin made an effort, tore open the envelope, and, going back into his room, read:

"My father is just dead. I owe that to you, for you have killed him. Our garden is being ruined; strangers are managing it already -- that is, the very thing is happening that poor father dreaded. That, too, I owe to you. I hate you with my whole soul, and I hope you may soon perish. Oh, how wretched I am! Insufferable anguish is burning my soul. . . . My curses on you. I took you for an extraordinary man, a genius; I loved you, and you have turned out a madman. . . ."

Kovrin could read no more, he tore up the letter and threw it away. He was overcome by an uneasiness that was akin to terror. Varvara Nikolaevna was asleep behind the screen, and he could hear her breathing. From the lower storey came the sounds of laughter and women's voices, but he felt as though in the whole hotel there were no living soul but him. Because Tanya, unhappy, broken by sorrow, had cursed him in her letter and hoped for his perdition, he felt eerie and kept glancing hurriedly at the door, as though he were afraid that the uncomprehended force which two years before had wrought such havoc in his life and in the life of those near him might come into the room and master him once more.

He knew by experience that when his nerves were out of hand the best thing for him to do was to work. He must sit down to the table and force himself, at all costs, to concentrate his mind on someone thought. He took from his red portfolio a manuscript containing a sketch of a small work of the nature of a compilation, which he had planned in case he should find it dull in the Crimea without work. He sat down to the table and began working at this plan, and it seemed to him that his calm, peaceful, indifferent mood was coming back. The manuscript with the sketch even led him to meditation on the vanity of the world. He thought how much life exacts for the worthless or very commonplace blessings it can give a man. For instance, to gain, before forty, a university chair, to be an ordinary professor, to expound ordinary and second-hand thoughts in dull, heavy, insipid language -- in fact, to gain the position of a mediocre learned man, he, Kovrin, had had to study for fifteen years, to work day and night, to endure a terrible mental illness, to experience an unhappy marriage, and to do a great number of stupid and unjust things which it would have been pleasant not to remember. Kovrin recognised clearly, now, that he was a mediocrity, and readily resigned himself to it, as he considered that every man ought to be satisfied with what he is.

The plan of the volume would have soothed him completely, but the torn letter showed white on the floor and prevented him from concentrating his attention. He got up from the table, picked up the pieces of the letter and threw them out of window, but there was a light wind blowing from the sea, and the bits of paper were scattered on the windowsill. Again he was overcome by uneasiness akin to terror, and he felt as though in the whole hotel there were no living soul but himself. . . . He went out on the balcony. The bay, like a living thing, looked at him with its multitude of light blue, dark blue, turquoise and fiery eyes, and seemed beckoning to him. And it really was hot and oppressive, and it would not have been amiss to have a bathe.

Suddenly in the lower storey under the balcony a violin began playing, and two soft feminine voices began singing. It was something familiar. The song was about a maiden, full of sick fancies, who heard one night in her garden mysterious sounds, so strange and lovely that she was obliged to recognise them as a holy harmony which is unintelligible to us mortals, and so flies back to heaven. . . . Kovrin caught his breath and there was a pang of sadness at his heart, and a thrill of the sweet, exquisite delight he had so long forgotten began to stir in his breast.

A tall black column, like a whirlwind or a waterspout, appeared on the further side of the bay. It moved with fearful rapidity across the bay, towards the hotel, growing smaller and darker as it came, and Kovrin only just had time to get out of the way to let it pass. . . . The monk with bare grey head, black eyebrows, barefoot, his arms crossed over his breast, floated by him, and stood still in the middle of the room.

"Why did you not believe me?" he asked reproachfully, looking affectionately at Kovrin. "If you had believed me then, that you were a genius, you would not have spent these two years so gloomily and so wretchedly."

Kovrin already believed that he was one of God's chosen and a genius; he vividly recalled his conversations with the monk in the past and tried to speak, but the blood flowed from his throat on to his breast, and not knowing what he was doing, he passed his hands over his breast, and his cuffs were soaked with blood. He tried to call Varvara Nikolaevna, who was asleep behind the screen; he made an effort and said:

"Tanya!"

He fell on the floor, and propping himself on his arms, called again:

"Tanya!"

He called Tanya, called to the great garden with the gorgeous flowers sprinkled with dew, called to the park, the pines with their shaggy roots, the rye-field, his marvellous learning, his youth, courage, joy -- called to life, which was so lovely. He saw on the floor near his face a great pool of blood, and was too weak to utter a word, but an unspeakable, infinite happiness flooded his whole being. Below, under the balcony, they were playing the serenade, and the black monk whispered to him that he was a genius, and that he was dying only because his frail human body had lost its balance and could no longer serve as the mortal garb of genius.

When Varvara Nikolaevna woke up and came out from behind the screen, Kovrin was dead, and a blissful smile was set upon his face.

A WOMAN'S KINGDOM

I

Christmas Eve

HERE was a thick roll of notes. It came from the bailiff at the forest villa; he wrote that he was sending fifteen hundred roubles, which he had been awarded as damages, having won an appeal. Anna Akimovna disliked and feared such words as "awarded damages" and "won the suit." She knew that it was impossible to do without the law, but for some reason, whenever Nazaritch, the manager of the factory, or the bailiff of her villa in the country, both of whom frequently went to law, used to win lawsuits of some sort for her benefit, she always felt uneasy and, as it were, ashamed. On this occasion, too, she felt uneasy and awkward, and wanted to put that fifteen hundred roubles further away that it might be out of her sight.

She thought with vexation that other girls of her age -- she was in her twenty-sixth year -- were now busy looking after their households, were weary and would sleep sound, and would wake up tomorrow morning in holiday mood; many of them had long been married and had children. Only she, for some reason, was compelled to sit like an old woman over these letters, to make notes upon them, to write answers, then to do nothing the whole evening till midnight, but wait till she was sleepy; and tomorrow they would all day long be coming with Christmas greetings and asking for favours; and the day after tomorrow there would certainly be some scandal at the factory -- someone would be beaten or would die of drinking too much vodka, and she would be fretted by pangs of conscience; and after the holidays Nazaritch would turn off some twenty of the workpeople for absence from work, and all of the twenty would hang about at the front door, without their caps on, and she would be ashamed to go out to them, and they would be driven away like dogs. And all her acquaintances would say behind her back, and write to her in anonymous letters, that she was a millionaire and exploiter -- that she was devouring other men's lives and sucking the blood of the workers.

Here there lay a heap of letters read through and laid aside already. They were all begging letters. They were from people who were hungry, drunken, dragged down by large families, sick, degraded, despised. . . . Anna Akimovna had already noted on each letter, three roubles to be paid to one, five to another; these letters would go the same day to the office, and next the distribution of assistance would take place, or, as the clerks used to say, the beasts would be fed.

They would distribute also in small sums four hundred and seventy roubles -- the interest on a sum bequeathed by the late Akim Ivanovitch for the relief of the poor and needy. There would be a hideous crush. From the gates to the doors of the office there would stretch a long file of strange people with brutal faces, in rags, numb with cold, hungry and already drunk, in husky voices calling down blessings upon Anna Akimovna, their benefactress, and her parents: those at the back would press upon those in front, and those in front would abuse them with bad language. The clerk would get tired of the noise, the swearing, and the sing-song whining and blessing; would fly out and give someone a box on the ear to the delight of all. And her own people, the factory hands, who received nothing at Christmas but their wages, and had already spent every farthing of it, would stand in the middle of the yard, looking on and laughing -- some enviously, others ironically.

"Merchants, and still more their wives, are fonder of beggars than they are of their own workpeople," thought Anna Akimovna. "It's always so."

Her eye fell upon the roll of money. It would be nice to distribute that hateful, useless money among the workpeople tomorrow, but it did not do to give the workpeople anything for nothing, or they would demand it again next time. And what would be the good of fifteen hundred roubles when there were eighteen hundred workmen in the factory besides their wives and children? Or she might, perhaps, pick out one of the writers of those begging letters -- some luckless man who had long ago lost all hope of anything better, and give him the fifteen hundred. The money would come upon the poor creature like a thunder-clap, and perhaps for the first time in his life he would feel happy. This idea struck Anna Akimovna as original and amusing, and it fascinated her. She took one letter at random out of the pile and read it. Some petty official called Tchalikov had long been out of a situation, was ill, and living in Gushtchin's Buildings; his wife was in consumption, and he had five little girls. Anna Akimovna knew well the four-storeyed house, Gushtchin's Buildings, in which Tchalikov lived. Oh, it was a horrid, foul, unhealthy house!

"Well, I will give it to that Tchalikov," she decided. "I won't send it; I had better take it myself to prevent unnecessary talk. Yes," she reflected, as she put the fifteen hundred roubles in her pocket, "and I'll have a look at them, and perhaps I can do something for the little girls."

She felt light-hearted; she rang the bell and ordered the horses to be brought round.

When she got into the sledge it was past six o'clock in the evening. The windows in all the blocks of buildings were brightly lighted up, and that made the huge courtyard seem very dark: at the gates, and at the far end of the yard near the warehouses and the workpeople's barracks, electric lamps were gleaming.

Anna Akimovna disliked and feared those huge dark buildings, warehouses, and barracks where the workmen lived. She had only once been in the main building since her father's death. The high ceilings with iron girders; the multitude of huge, rapidly turning wheels, connecting straps and levers; the shrill hissing; the clank of steel; the rattle of the trolleys; the harsh puffing of steam; the faces -- pale, crimson, or black with coal-dust; the shirts soaked with sweat; the gleam of steel, of copper, and of fire; the smell of oil and coal; and the draught, at times very hot and at times very cold -- gave her an impression of hell. It seemed to her as though the wheels, the levers, and the hot hissing cylinders were trying to tear themselves away from their fastenings to crush the men, while the men, not hearing one another, ran about with anxious faces, and busied themselves about the machines, trying to stop their terrible movement. They showed Anna Akimovna something and respectfully explained it to her. She remembered how in the forge a piece of red-hot iron was pulled out of the furnace; and how an old man with a strap round his head, and another, a young man in a blue shirt with a chain on his breast, and an angry face, probably one of the foremen, struck the piece of iron with hammers; and how the golden sparks had been scattered in all directions; and how, a little afterwards, they had dragged out a huge piece of sheet-iron with a clang. The old man had stood erect and smiled, while the young man had wiped his face with his sleeve and explained something to her. And she remembered, too, how in another department an old man with one eye had been filing a piece of iron, and how the iron filings were scattered about; and how a red-haired man in black spectacles, with holes in his shirt, had been working at a lathe, making something out of a piece of steel: the lathe roared and hissed and squeaked, and Anna Akimovna felt sick at the sound, and it seemed as though they were boring into her ears. She looked, listened, did not understand, smiled graciously, and felt ashamed. To get hundreds of thousands of roubles from a business which one does not understand and cannot like -- how strange it is!

And she had not once been in the workpeople's barracks. There, she was told, it was damp; there were bugs, debauchery, anarchy. It was an astonishing thing: a thousand roubles were spent annually on keeping the barracks in good order, yet, if she were to believe the anonymous letters, the condition of the workpeople was growing worse and worse every year.

"There was more order in my father's day," thought Anna Akimovna, as she drove out of the yard, "because he had been a workman himself. I know nothing about it and only do silly things."

She felt depressed again, and was no longer glad that she had come, and the thought of the lucky man upon whom fifteen hundred roubles would drop from heaven no longer struck her as original and amusing. To go to some Tchalikov or other, when at home a business worth a million was gradually going to pieces and being ruined, and the workpeople in the barracks were living worse than convicts, meant doing something silly and cheating her conscience. Along the highroad and across the fields near it, workpeople from the neighbouring cotton and paper factories were walking towards the lights of the town. There was the sound of talk and laughter in the frosty air. Anna Akimovna looked at the women and young people, and she suddenly felt a longing for a plain rough life among a crowd. She recalled vividly that far-away time when she used to be called Anyutka, when she was a little girl and used to lie under the same quilt with her mother, while a washerwoman who lodged with them used to wash clothes in the next room; while through the thin walls there came from the neighbouring flats sounds of laughter, swearing, children's crying, the accordion, and the whirr of carpenters' lathes and sewing-machines; while her father, Akim Ivanovitch, who was clever at almost every craft, would be soldering something near the stove, or drawing or planing, taking no notice whatever of the noise and stuffiness. And she longed to wash, to iron, to run to the shop and the tavern as she used to do every day when she lived with her mother. She ought to have been a work-girl and not the factory owner! Her big house with its chandeliers and pictures; her footman Mishenka, with his glossy moustache and swallowtail coat; the devout and dignified Varvarushka, and smooth-tongued Agafyushka; and the young people of both sexes who came almost every day to ask her for money, and with whom she always for some reason felt guilty; and the clerks, the doctors, and the ladies who were charitable at her expense, who flattered her and secretly despised her for her humble origin -- how wearisome and alien it all was to her!

Here was the railway crossing and the city gate; then came houses alternating with kitchen gardens; and at last the broad street where stood the renowned Gushtchin's Buildings. The street, usually quiet, was now on Christmas Eve full of life and movement. The eating-houses and beer-shops were noisy. If someone who did not belong to that quarter but lived in the centre of the town had driven through the street now, he would have noticed nothing but dirty, drunken, and abusive people; but Anna Akimovna, who had lived in those parts all her life, was constantly recognizing in the crowd her own father or mother or uncle. Her father was a soft fluid character, a little fantastical, frivolous, and irresponsible. He did not care for money, respectability, or power; he used to say that a working man had no time to keep the holy-days and go to church; and if it had not been for his wife, he would probably never have gone to confession, taken the sacrament or kept the fasts. While her uncle, Ivan Ivanovitch, on the contrary, was like flint; in everything relating to religion, politics, and morality, he was harsh and relentless, and kept a strict watch, not only over himself, but also over all his servants and acquaintances. God forbid that one should go into his room without crossing oneself before the ikon! The luxurious mansion in which Anna Akimovna now lived he had always kept locked up, and only opened it on great holidays for important visitors, while he lived himself in the office, in a little room covered with ikons. He had leanings towards the Old Believers, and was continually entertaining priests and bishops of the old ritual, though he had been christened, and married, and had buried his wife in accordance with the Orthodox rites. He disliked Akim, his only brother and his heir, for his frivolity, which he called simpleness and folly, and for his indifference to religion. He treated him as an inferior, kept him in the position of a workman, paid him sixteen roubles a month. Akim addressed his brother with formal respect, and on the days of asking forgiveness, he and his wife and daughter bowed down to the ground before him. But three years before his death Ivan Ivanovitch had drawn closer to his brother, forgave his shortcomings, and ordered him to get a governess for Anyutka.

There was a dark, deep, evil-smelling archway under Gushtchin's Buildings; there was a sound of men coughing near the walls. Leaving the sledge in the street, Anna Akimovna went in at the gate and there inquired how to get to No. 46 to see a clerk called Tchalikov. She was directed to the furthest door on the right in the third story. And in the courtyard and near the outer door, and even on the stairs, there was still the same loathsome smell as under the archway. In Anna Akimovna's childhood, when her father was a simple workman, she used to live in a building like that, and afterwards, when their circumstances were different, she had often visited them in the character of a Lady Bountiful. The narrow stone staircase with its steep dirty steps, with landings at every story; the greasy swinging lanterns; the stench; the troughs, pots, and rags on the landings near the doors, -- all this had been familiar to her long ago. . . . One door was open, and within could be seen Jewish tailors in caps, sewing. Anna Akimovna met people on the stairs, but it never entered her head that people might be rude to her. She was no more afraid of peasants or workpeople, drunk or sober, than of her acquaintances of the educated class.

There was no entry at No. 46; the door opened straight into the kitchen. As a rule the dwellings of workmen and mechanics smell of varnish, tar, hides, smoke, according to the occupation of the tenant; the dwellings of persons of noble or official class who have come to poverty may be known by a peculiar rancid, sour smell. This disgusting smell enveloped Anna Akimovna on all sides, and as yet she was only on the threshold. A man in a black coat, no doubt Tchalikov himself, was sitting in a corner at the table with his back to the door, and with him were five little girls. The eldest, a broad-faced thin girl with a comb in her hair, looked about fifteen, while the youngest, a chubby child with hair that stood up like a hedge-hog, was not more than three. All the six were eating. Near the stove stood a very thin little woman with a yellow face, far gone in pregnancy. She was wearing a skirt and a white blouse, and had an oven fork in her hand.

"I did not expect you to be so disobedient, Liza," the man was saying reproachfully. "Fie, fie, for shame! Do you want papa to whip you -- eh?"

Seeing an unknown lady in the doorway, the thin woman started, and put down the fork.

"Vassily Nikititch!" she cried, after a pause, in a hollow voice, as though she could not believe her eyes.

The man looked round and jumped up. He was a flat-chested, bony man with narrow shoulders and sunken temples. His eyes were small and hollow with dark rings round them, he had a wide mouth, and a long nose like a bird's beak -- a little bit bent to the right. His beard was parted in the middle, his moustache was shaven, and this made him look more like a hired footman than a government clerk.

"Does Mr. Tchalikov live here?" asked Anna Akimovna.

"Yes, madam," Tchalikov answered severely, but immediately recognizing Anna Akimovna, he cried: "Anna Akimovna!" and all at once he gasped and clasped his hands as though in terrible alarm. "Benefactress!"

With a moan he ran to her, grunting inarticulately as though he were paralyzed -- there was cabbage on his beard and he smelt of vodka -- pressed his forehead to her muff, and seemed as though he were in a swoon.

"Your hand, your holy hand!" he brought out breathlessly. "It's a dream, a glorious dream! Children, awaken me!"

He turned towards the table and said in a sobbing voice, shaking his fists:

"Providence has heard us! Our saviour, our angel, has come! We are saved! Children, down on your knees! on your knees!"

Madame Tchalikov and the little girls, except the youngest one, began for some reason rapidly clearing the table.

"You wrote that your wife was very ill," said Anna Akimovna, and she felt ashamed and annoyed. "I am not going to give them the fifteen hundred," she thought.

"Here she is, my wife," said Tchalikov in a thin feminine voice, as though his tears had gone to his head. "Here she is, unhappy creature! With one foot in the grave! But we do not complain, madam. Better death than such a life. Better die, unhappy woman!"

"Why is he playing these antics?" thought Anna Akimovna with annoyance. "One can see at once he is used to dealing with merchants."

"Speak to me like a human being," she said. "I don't care for farces."

"Yes, madam; five bereaved children round their mother's coffin with funeral candles -- that's a farce? Eh?" said Tchalikov bitterly, and turned away.

"Hold your tongue," whispered his wife, and she pulled at his sleeve. "The place has not been tidied up, madam," she said, addressing Anna Akimovna; "please excuse it . . . you know what it is where there are children. A crowded hearth, but harmony."

"I am not going to give them the fifteen hundred," Anna Akimovna thought again.

And to escape as soon as possible from these people and from the sour smell, she brought out her purse and made up her mind to leave them twenty-five roubles, not more; but she suddenly felt ashamed that she had come so far and disturbed people for so little.

"If you give me paper and ink, I will write at once to a doctor who is a friend of mine to come and see you," she said, flushing red. "He is a very good doctor. And I will leave you some money for medicine."

Madame Tchalikov was hastening to wipe the table.

"It's messy here! What are you doing?" hissed Tchalikov, looking at her wrathfully. "Take her to the lodger's room! I make bold to ask you, madam, to step into the lodger's room," he said, addressing Anna Akimovna. "It's clean there."

"Osip Ilyitch told us not to go into his room!" said one of the little girls, sternly.

But they had already led Anna Akimovna out of the kitchen, through a narrow passage room between two bedsteads: it was evident from the arrangement of the beds that in one two slept lengthwise, and in the other three slept across the bed. In the lodger's room, that came next, it really was clean. A neat-looking bed with a red woollen quilt, a pillow in a white pillow-case, even a slipper for the watch, a table covered with a hempen cloth and on it, an inkstand of milky-looking glass, pens, paper, photographs in frames -- everything as it ought to be; and another table for rough work, on which lay tidily arranged a watchmaker's tools and watches taken to pieces. On the walls hung hammers, pliers, awls, chisels, nippers, and so on, and there were three hanging clocks which were ticking; one was a big clock with thick weights, such as one sees in eating-houses.

As she sat down to write the letter, Anna Akimovna saw facing her on the table the photographs of her father and of herself. That surprised her.

"Who lives here with you?" she asked.

"Our lodger, madam, Pimenov. He works in your factory."

"Oh, I thought he must be a watchmaker."

"He repairs watches privately, in his leisure hours. He is an amateur."

After a brief silence during which nothing could be heard but the ticking of the clocks and the scratching of the pen on the paper, Tchalikov heaved a sigh and said ironically, with indignation:

"It's a true saying: gentle birth and a grade in the service won't put a coat on your back. A cockade in your cap and a noble title, but nothing to eat. To my thinking, if anyone of humble class helps the poor he is much more of a gentleman than any Tchalikov who has sunk into poverty and vice."

To flatter Anna Akimovna, he uttered a few more disparaging phrases about his gentle birth, and it was evident that he was humbling himself because he considered himself superior to her. Meanwhile she had finished her letter and had sealed it up. The letter would be thrown away and the money would not be spent on medicine -- that she knew, but she put twenty-five roubles on the table all the same, and after a moment's thought, added two more red notes. She saw the wasted, yellow hand of Madame Tchalikov, like the claw of a hen, dart out and clutch the money tight.

"You have graciously given this for medicine," said Tchalikov in a quivering voice, "but hold out a helping hand to me also . . . and the children!" he added with a sob. "My unhappy children! I am not afraid for myself; it is for my daughters I fear! It's the hydra of vice that I fear!"

Trying to open her purse, the catch of which had gone wrong, Anna Akimovna was confused and turned red. She felt ashamed that people should be standing before her, looking at her hands and waiting, and most likely at the bottom of their hearts laughing at her. At that instant someone came into the kitchen and stamped his feet, knocking the snow off.

"The lodger has come in," said Madame Tchalikov.

Anna Akimovna grew even more confused. She did not want anyone from the factory to find her in this ridiculous position. As ill-luck would have it, the lodger came in at the very moment when, having broken the catch at last, she was giving Tchalikov some notes, and Tchalikov, grunting as though he were paraylzed, was feeling about with his lips where he could kiss her. In the lodger she recognized the workman who had once clanked the sheet-iron before her in the forge, and had explained things to her. Evidently he had come in straight from the factory; his face looked dark and grimy, and on one cheek near his nose was a smudge of soot. His hands were perfectly black, and his unbelted shirt shone with oil and grease. He was a man of thirty, of medium height, with black hair and broad shoulders, and a look of great physical strength. At the first glance Anna Akimovna perceived that he must be a foreman, who must be receiving at least thirty-five roubles a month, and a stern, loud-voiced man who struck the workmen in the face; all this was evident from his manner of standing, from the attitude he involuntarily assumed at once on seeing a lady in his room, and most of all from the fact that he did not wear top-boots, that he had breast pockets, and a pointed, picturesquely clipped beard. Her father, Akim Ivanovitch, had been the brother of the factory owner, and yet he had been afraid of foremen like this lodger and had tried to win their favour.

"Excuse me for having come in here in your absence," said Anna Akimovna.

The workman looked at her in surprise, smiled in confusion and did not speak.

"You must speak a little louder, madam . . . ." said Tchalikov softly. "When Mr. Pimenov comes home from the factory in the evenings he is a little hard of hearing."

But Anna Akimovna was by now relieved that there was nothing more for her to do here; she nodded to them and went rapidly out of the room. Pimenov went to see her out.

"Have you been long in our employment?" she asked in a loud voice, without turning to him.

"From nine years old. I entered the factory in your uncle's time."

"That's a long while! My uncle and my father knew all the workpeople, and I know hardly any of them. I had seen you before, but I did not know your name was Pimenov."

Anna Akimovna felt a desire to justify herself before him, to pretend that she had just given the money not seriously, but as a joke.

"Oh, this poverty," she sighed. "We give charity on holidays and working days, and still there is no sense in it. I believe it is useless to help such people as this Tchalikov."

"Of course it is useless," he agreed. "However much you give him, he will drink it all away. And now the husband and wife will be snatching it from one another and fighting all night," he added with a laugh.

"Yes, one must admit that our philanthropy is useless, boring, and absurd. But still, you must agree, one can't sit with one's hand in one's lap; one must do something. What's to be done with the Tchalikovs, for instance?"

She turned to Pimenov and stopped, expecting an answer from him; he, too, stopped and slowly, without speaking, shrugged his shoulders. Obviously he knew what to do with the Tchalikovs, but the treatment would have been so coarse and inhuman that he did not venture to put it into words. And the Tchalikovs were to him so utterly uninteresting and worthless, that a moment later he had forgotten them; looking into Anna Akimovna's eyes, he smiled with pleasure, and his face wore an expression as though he were dreaming about something very pleasant. Only, now standing close to him, Anna Akimovna saw from his face, and especially from his eyes, how exhausted and sleepy he was.

"Here, I ought to give him the fifteen hundred roubles!" she thought, but for some reason this idea seemed to her incongruous and insulting to Pimenov.

"I am sure you are aching all over after your work, and you come to the door with me," she said as they went down the stairs. "Go home."

But he did not catch her words. When they came out into the street, he ran on ahead, unfastened the cover of the sledge, and helping Anna Akimovna in, said:

"I wish you a happy Christmas!"

II

Christmas Morning

"They have left off ringing ever so long! It's dreadful; you won't be there before the service is over! Get up!"

"Two horses are racing, racing . . ." said Anna Akimovna, and she woke up; before her, candle in hand, stood her maid, red-haired Masha. "Well, what is it?"

"Service is over already," said Masha with despair. "I have called you three times! Sleep till evening for me, but you told me yourself to call you!"

Anna Akimovna raised herself on her elbow and glanced towards the window. It was still quite dark outside, and only the lower edge of the window-frame was white with snow. She could hear a low, mellow chime of bells; it was not the parish church, but somewhere further away. The watch on the little table showed three minutes past six.

"Very well, Masha. . . . In three minutes . . ." said Anna Akimovna in an imploring voice, and she snuggled under the bed-clothes.

She imagined the snow at the front door, the sledge, the dark sky, the crowd in the church, and the smell of juniper, and she felt dread at the thought; but all the same, she made up her mind that she would get up at once and go to early service. And while she was warm in bed and struggling with sleep -- which seems, as though to spite one, particularly sweet when one ought to get up -- and while she had visions of an immense garden on a mountain and then Gushtchin's Buildings, she was worried all the time by the thought that she ought to get up that very minute and go to church.

But when she got up it was quite light, and it turned out to be half-past nine. There had been a heavy fall of snow in the night; the trees were clothed in white, and the air was particularly light, transparent, and tender, so that when Anna Akimovna looked out of the window her first impulse was to draw a deep, deep breath. And when she had washed, a relic of far-away childish feelings -- joy that today was Christmas -- suddenly stirred within her; after that she felt light-hearted, free and pure in soul, as though her soul, too, had been washed or plunged in the white snow. Masha came in, dressed up and tightly laced, and wished her a happy Christmas; then she spent a long time combing her mistress's hair and helping her to dress. The fragrance and feeling of the new, gorgeous, splendid dress, its faint rustle, and the smell of fresh scent, excited Anna Akimoyna.

"Well, it's Christmas," she said gaily to Masha. "Now we will try our fortunes."

"Last year, I was to marry an old man. It turned up three times the same."

"Well, God is merciful."

"Well, Anna Akimovna, what I think is, rather than neither one thing nor the other, I'd marry an old man," said Masha mournfully, and she heaved a sigh. "I am turned twenty; it's no joke."

Everyone in the house knew that red-haired Masha was in love with Mishenka, the footman, and this genuine, passionate, hopeless love had already lasted three years.

"Come, don't talk nonsense," Anna Akimovna consoled her. "I am going on for thirty, but I am still meaning to marry a young man."

While his mistress was dressing, Mishenka, in a new swallow-tail and polished boots, walked about the hall and drawing-room and waited for her to come out, to wish her a happy Christmas. He had a peculiar walk, stepping softly and delicately; looking at his feet, his hands, and the bend of his head, it might be imagined that he was not simply walking, but learning to dance the first figure of a quadrille. In spite of his fine velvety moustache and handsome, rather flashy appearance, he was steady, prudent, and devout as an old man. He said his prayers, bowing down to the ground, and liked burning incense in his room. He respected people of wealth and rank and had a reverence for them; he despised poor people, and all who came to ask favours of any kind, with all the strength of his cleanly flunkey soul. Under his starched shirt he wore a flannel, winter and summer alike, being very careful of his health; his ears were plugged with cotton-wool.

When Anna Akimovna crossed the hall with Masha, he bent his head downwards a little and said in his agreeable, honeyed voice:

"I have the honour to congratulate you, Anna Akimovna, on the most solemn feast of the birth of our Lord."

Anna Akimovna gave him five roubles, while poor Masha was numb with ecstasy. His holiday get-up, his attitude, his voice, and what he said, impressed her by their beauty and elegance; as she followed her mistress she could think of nothing, could see nothing, she could only smile, first blissfully and then bitterly. The upper story of the house was called the best or visitors' half, while the name of the business part -- old people's or simply women's part -- was given to the rooms on the lower story where Aunt Tatyana Ivanovna kept house. In the upper part the gentry and educated visitors were entertained; in the lower story, simpler folk and the aunt's personal friends. Handsome, plump, and healthy, still young and fresh, and feeling she had on a magnificent dress which seemed to her to diffuse a sort of radiance all about her, Anna Akimovna went down to the lower story. Here she was met with reproaches for forgetting God now that she was so highly educated, for sleeping too late for the service, and for not coming downstairs to break the fast, and they all clasped their hands and exclaimed with perfect sincerity that she was lovely, wonderful; and she believed it, laughed, kissed them, gave one a rouble, another three or five according to their position. She liked being downstairs. Wherever one looked there were shrines, ikons, little lamps, portraits of ecclesiastical personages -- the place smelt of monks; there was a rattle of knives in the kitchen, and already a smell of something savoury, exceedingly appetizing, was pervading all the rooms. The yellow-painted floors shone, and from the doors narrow rugs with bright blue stripes ran like little paths to the ikon corner, and the sunshine was simply pouring in at the windows.

In the dining-room some old women, strangers, were sitting; in Varvarushka's room, too, there were old women, and with them a deaf and dumb girl, who seemed abashed about something and kept saying, "Bli, bli! . . ." Two skinny-looking little girls who had been brought out of the orphanage for Christmas came up to kiss Anna Akimovna's hand, and stood before her transfixed with admiration of her splendid dress; she noticed that one of the girls squinted, and in the midst of her light-hearted holiday mood she felt a sick pang at her heart at the thought that young men would despise the girl, and that she would never marry. In the cook Agafya's room, five huge peasants in new shirts were sitting round the samovar; these were not workmen from the factory, but relations of the cook. Seeing Anna Akimovna, all the peasants jumped up from their seats, and from regard for decorum, ceased munching, though their mouths were full. The cook Stepan, in a white cap, with a knife in his hand, came into the room and gave her his greetings; porters in high felt boots came in, and they, too, offered their greetings. The water-carrier peeped in with icicles on his beard, but did not venture to come in.

Anna Akimovna walked through the rooms followed by her retinue -- the aunt, Varvarushka, Nikandrovna, the sewing-maid Marfa Petrovna, and the downstairs Masha. Varvarushka -- a tall, thin, slender woman, taller than anyone in the house, dressed all in black, smelling of cypress and coffee -- crossed herself in each room before the ikon, bowing down from the waist. And whenever one looked at her one was reminded that she had already prepared her shroud and that lottery tickets were hidden away by her in the same box.

"Anyutinka, be merciful at Christmas," she said, opening the door into the kitchen. "Forgive him, bless the man! Have done with it!"

The coachman Panteley, who had been dismissed for drunkenness in November, was on his knees in the middle of the kitchen. He was a good-natured man, but he used to be unruly when he was drunk, and could not go to sleep, but persisted in wandering about the buildings and shouting in a threatening voice, "I know all about it!" Now from his beefy and bloated face and from his bloodshot eyes it could be seen that he had been drinking continually from November till Christmas.

"Forgive me, Anna Akimovna," he brought out in a hoarse voice, striking his forehead on the floor and showing his bull-like neck.

"It was Auntie dismissed you; ask her."

"What about auntie?" said her aunt, walking into the kitchen, breathing heavily; she was very stout, and on her bosom one might have stood a tray of teacups and a samovar. "What about auntie now? You are mistress here, give your own orders; though these rascals might be all dead for all I care. Come, get up, you hog!" she shouted at Panteley, losing patience. "Get out of my sight! It's the last time I forgive you, but if you transgress again -- don't ask for mercy!"

Then they went into the dining-room to coffee. But they had hardly sat down, when the downstairs Masha rushed headlong in, saying with horror, "The singers!" And ran back again. They heard someone blowing his nose, a low bass cough, and footsteps that sounded like horses' iron-shod hoofs tramping about the entry near the hall. For half a minute all was hushed. . . . The singers burst out so suddenly and loudly that everyone started. While they were singing, the priest from the almshouses with the deacon and the sexton arrived. Putting on the stole, the priest slowly said that when they were ringing for matins it was snowing and not cold, but that the frost was sharper towards morning, God bless it! and now there must be twenty degrees of frost.

"Many people maintain, though, that winter is healthier than summer," said the deacon; then immediately assumed an austere expression and chanted after the priest. "Thy Birth, O Christ our Lord. . . ."

Soon the priest from the workmen's hospital came with the deacon, then the Sisters from the hospital, children from the orphanage, and then singing could be heard almost uninterruptedly. They sang, had lunch, and went away.

About twenty men from the factory came to offer their Christmas greetings. They were only the foremen, mechanicians, and their assistants, the pattern-makers, the accountant, and so on -- all of good appearance, in new black coats. They were all first-rate men, as it were picked men; each one knew his value -- that is, knew that if he lost his berth today, people would be glad to take him on at another factory. Evidently they liked Auntie, as they behaved freely in her presence and even smoked, and when they had all trooped in to have something to eat, the accountant put his arm round her immense waist. They were free-and-easy, perhaps, partly also because Varvarushka, who under the old masters had wielded great power and had kept watch over the morals of the clerks, had now no authority whatever in the house; and perhaps because many of them still remembered the time when Auntie Tatyana Ivanovna, whose brothers kept a strict hand over her, had been dressed like a simple peasant woman like Agafya, and when Anna Akimovna used to run about the yard near the factory buildings and everyone used to call her Anyutya.

The foremen ate, talked, and kept looking with amazement at Anna Akimovna, how she had grown up and how handsome she had become! But this elegant girl, educated by governesses and teachers, was a stranger to them; they could not understand her, and they instinctively kept closer to "Auntie," who called them by their names, continually pressed them to eat and drink, and, clinking glasses with them, had already drunk two wineglasses of rowanberry wine with them. Anna Akimovna was always afraid of their thinking her proud, an upstart, or a crow in peacock's feathers; and now while the foremen were crowding round the food, she did not leave the dining-room, but took part in the conversation. She asked Pimenov, her acquaintance of the previous day:

"Why have you so many clocks in your room?"

"I mend clocks," he answered. "I take the work up between times, on holidays, or when I can't sleep."

"So if my watch goes wrong I can bring it to you to be repaired?" Anna Akimovna asked, laughing.

"To be sure, I will do it with pleasure," said Pimenov, and there was an expression of tender devotion in his face, when, not herself knowing why, she unfastened her magnificent watch from its chain and handed it to him; he looked at it in silence and gave it back. "To be sure, I will do it with pleasure," he repeated. "I don't mend watches now. My eyes are weak, and the doctors have forbidden me to do fine work. But for you I can make an exception."

"Doctors talk nonsense," said the accountant. They all laughed. "Don't you believe them," he went on, flattered by the laughing; "last year a tooth flew out of a cylinder and hit old Kalmykov such a crack on the head that you could see his brains, and the doctor said he would die; but he is alive and working to this day, only he has taken to stammering since that mishap."

"Doctors do talk nonsense, they do, but not so much," sighed Auntie. "Pyotr Andreyitch, poor dear, lost his sight. Just like you, he used to work day in day out at the factory near the hot furnace, and he went blind. The eyes don't like heat. But what are we talking about?" she said, rousing herself. "Come and have a drink. My best wishes for Christmas, my dears. I never drink with anyone else, but I drink with you, sinful woman as I am. Please God!"

Anna Akimovna fancied that after yesterday Pimenov despised her as a philanthropist, but was fascinated by her as a woman. She looked at him and thought that he behaved very charmingly and was nicely dressed. It is true that the sleeves of his coat were not quite long enough, and the coat itself seemed short-waisted, and his trousers were not wide and fashionable, but his tie was tied carelessly and with taste and was not as gaudy as the others'. And he seemed to be a good-natured man, for he ate submissively whatever Auntie put on his plate. She remembered how black he had been the day before, and how sleepy, and the thought of it for some reason touched her.

When the men were preparing to go, Anna Akimovna put out her hand to Pimenov. She wanted to ask him to come in sometimes to see her, without ceremony, but she did not know how to -- her tongue would not obey her; and that they might not think she was attracted by Pimenov, she shook hands with his companions, too.

Then the boys from the school of which she was a patroness came. They all had their heads closely cropped and all wore grey blouses of the same pattern. The teacher -- a tall, beardless young man with patches of red on his face -- was visibly agitated as he formed the boys into rows; the boys sang in tune, but with harsh, disagreeable voices. The manager of the factory, Nazaritch, a bald, sharp-eyed Old Believer, could never get on with the teachers, but the one who was now anxiously waving his hands he despised and hated, though he could not have said why. He behaved rudely and condescendingly to the young man, kept back his salary, meddled with the teaching, and had finally tried to dislodge him by appointing, a fortnight before Christmas, as porter to the school a drunken peasant, a distant relation of his wife's, who disobeyed the teacher and said rude things to him before the boys.

Anna Akimovna was aware of all this, but she could be of no help, for she was afraid of Nazaritch herself. Now she wanted at least to be very nice to the schoolmaster, to tell him she was very much pleased with him; but when after the singing he began apologizing for something in great confusion, and Auntie began to address him familiarly as she drew him without ceremony to the table, she felt, for some reason, bored and awkward, and giving orders that the children should be given sweets, went upstairs.

"In reality there is something cruel in these Christmas customs," she said a little while afterwards, as it were to herself, looking out of window at the boys, who were flocking from the house to the gates and shivering with cold, putting their coats on as they ran. "At Christmas one wants to rest, to sit at home with one's own people, and the poor boys, the teacher, and the clerks and foremen, are obliged for some reason to go through the frost, then to offer their greetings, show their respect, be put to confusion . . ."

Mishenka, who was standing at the door of the drawing-room and overheard this, said:

"It has not come from us, and it will not end with us. Of course, I am not an educated man, Anna Akimovna, but I do understand that the poor must always respect the rich. It is well said, 'God marks the rogue.' In prisons, night refuges, and pot-houses you never see any but the poor, while decent people, you may notice, are always rich. It has been said of the rich, 'Deep calls to deep.' "

"You always express yourself so tediously and incomprehensibly," said Anna Akimovna, and she walked to the other end of the big drawing-room.

It was only just past eleven. The stillness of the big room, only broken by the singing that floated up from below, made her yawn. The bronzes, the albums, and the pictures on the walls, representing a ship at sea, cows in a meadow, and views of the Rhine, were so absolutely stale that her eyes simply glided over them without observing them. The holiday mood was already growing tedious. As before, Anna Akimovna felt that she was beautiful, good-natured, and wonderful, but now it seemed to her that that was of no use to anyone; it seemed to her that she did not know for whom and for what she had put on this expensive dress, too, and, as always happened on all holidays, she began to be fretted by loneliness and the persistent thought that her beauty, her health, and her wealth, were a mere cheat, since she was not wanted, was of no use to anyone, and nobody loved her. She walked through all the rooms, humming and looking out of window; stopping in the drawing-room, she could not resist beginning to talk to Mishenka.

"I don't know what you think of yourself, Misha," she said, and heaved a sigh. "Really, God might punish you for it."

"What do you mean?"

"You know what I mean. Excuse my meddling in your affairs. But it seems you are spoiling your own life out of obstinacy. You'll admit that it is high time you got married, and she is an excellent and deserving girl. You will never find anyone better. She's a beauty, clever, gentle, and devoted. . . . And her appearance! . . . If she belonged to our circle or a higher one, people would be falling in love with her for her red hair alone. See how beautifully her hair goes with her complexion. Oh, goodness! You don't understand anything, and don't know what you want," Anna Akimovna said bitterly, and tears came into her eyes. "Poor girl, I am so sorry for her! I know you want a wife with money, but I have told you already I will give Masha a dowry."

Mishenka could not picture his future spouse in his imagination except as a tall, plump, substantial, pious woman, stepping like a peacock, and, for some reason, with a long shawl over her shoulders; while Masha was thin, slender, tightly laced, and walked with little steps, and, worst of all, she was too fascinating and at times extremely attractive to Mishenka, and that, in his opinion, was incongruous with matrimony and only in keeping with loose behaviour. When Anna Akimovna had promised to give Masha a dowry, he had hesitated for a time; but once a poor student in a brown overcoat over his uniform, coming with a letter for Anna Akimovna, was fascinated by Masha, and could not resist embracing her near the hat-stand, and she had uttered a faint shriek; Mishenka, standing on the stairs above, had seen this, and from that time had begun to cherish a feeling of disgust for Masha. A poor student! Who knows, if she had been embraced by a rich student or an officer the consequences might have been different.

"Why don't you wish it?" Anna Akimovna asked. "What more do you want?"

Mishenka was silent and looked at the arm-chair fixedly, and raised his eyebrows.

"Do you love someone else?"

Silence. The red-haired Masha came in with letters and visiting cards on a tray. Guessing that they were talking about her, she blushed to tears.

"The postmen have come," she muttered. "And there is a clerk called Tchalikov waiting below. He says you told him to come to-day for something."

"What insolence!" said Anna Akimovna, moved to anger. "I gave him no orders. Tell him to take himself off; say I am not at home!"

A ring was heard. It was the priests from her parish. They were always shown into the aristocratic part of the house -- that is, upstairs. After the priests, Nazaritch, the manager of the factory, came to pay his visit, and then the factory doctor; then Mishenka announced the inspector of the elementary schools. Visitors kept arriving.

When there was a moment free, Anna Akimovna sat down in a deep arm-chair in the drawing-room, and shutting her eyes, thought that her loneliness was quite natural because she had not married and never would marry. . . . But that was not her fault. Fate itself had flung her out of the simple working-class surroundings in which, if she could trust her memory, she had felt so snug and at home, into these immense rooms, where she could never think what to do with herself, and could not understand why so many people kept passing before her eyes. What was happening now seemed to her trivial, useless, since it did not and could not give her happiness for one minute.

"If I could fall in love," she thought, stretching; the very thought of this sent a rush of warmth to her heart. "And if I could escape from the factory . . ." she mused, imagining how the weight of those factory buildings, barracks, and schools would roll off her conscience, roll off her mind. . . . Then she remembered her father, and thought if he had lived longer he would certainly have married her to a working man -- to Pimenov, for instance. He would have told her to marry, and that would have been all about it. And it would have been a good thing; then the factory would have passed into capable hands.

She pictured his curly head, his bold profile, his delicate, ironical lips and the strength, the tremendous strength, in his shoulders, in his arms, in his chest, and the tenderness with which he had looked at her watch that day.

"Well," she said, "it would have been all right. I would have married him."

"Anna Akimovna," said Mishenka, coming noiselessly into the drawing-room.

"How you frightened me!" she said, trembling all over. "What do you want?"

"Anna Akimovna," he said, laying his hand on his heart and raising his eyebrows, "you are my mistress and my benefactress, and no one but you can tell me what I ought to do about marriage, for you are as good as a mother to me. . . . But kindly forbid them to laugh and jeer at me downstairs. They won't let me pass without it."

"How do they jeer at you?"

"They call me Mashenka's Mishenka."

"Pooh, what nonsense!" cried Anna Akimovna indignantly. "How stupid you all are! What a stupid you are, Misha! How sick I am of you! I can't bear the sight of you."

III

Dinner

Just as the year before, the last to pay her visits were Krylin, an actual civil councillor, and Lysevitch, a well-known barrister. It was already dark when they arrived. Krylin, a man of sixty, with a wide mouth and with grey whiskers close to his ears, with a face like a lynx, was wearing a uniform with an Anna ribbon, and white trousers. He held Anna Akimovna's hand in both of his for a long while, looked intently in her face, moved his lips, and at last said, drawling upon one note:

"I used to respect your uncle . . . and your father, and enjoyed the privilege of their friendship. Now I feel it an agreeable duty, as you see, to present my Christmas wishes to their honoured heiress in spite of my infirmities and the distance I have to come. . . . And I am very glad to see you in good health."

The lawyer Lysevitch, a tall, handsome fair man, with a slight sprinkling of grey on his temples and beard, was distinguished by exceptionally elegant manners; he walked with a swaying step, bowed as it were reluctantly, and shrugged his shoulders as he talked, and all this with an indolent grace, like a spoiled horse fresh from the stable. He was well fed, extremely healthy, and very well off; on one occasion he had won forty thousand roubles, but concealed the fact from his friends. He was fond of good fare, especially cheese, truffles, and grated radish with hemp oil; while in Paris he had eaten, so he said, baked but unwashed guts. He spoke smoothly, fluently, without hesitation, and only occasionally, for the sake of effect, permitted himself to hesitate and snap his fingers as if picking up a word. He had long ceased to believe in anything he had to say in the law courts, or perhaps he did believe in it, but attached no kind of significance to it; it had all so long been familiar, stale, ordinary. . . . He believed in nothing but what was original and unusual. A copy-book moral in an original form would move him to tears. Both his notebooks were filled with extraordinary expressions which he had read in various authors; and when he needed to look up any expression, he would search nervously in both books, and usually failed to find it. Anna Akimovna's father had in a good-humoured moment ostentatiously appointed him legal adviser in matters concerning the factory, and had assigned him a salary of twelve thousand roubles. The legal business of the factory had been confined to two or three trivial actions for recovering debts, which Lysevitch handed to his assistants.

Anna Akimovna knew that he had nothing to do at the factory, but she could not dismiss him -- she had not the moral courage; and besides, she was used to him. He used to call himself her legal adviser, and his salary, which he invariably sent for on the first of the month punctually, he used to call "stern prose." Anna Akimovna knew that when, after her father's death, the timber of her forest was sold for railway sleepers, Lysevitch had made more than fifteen thousand out of the transaction, and had shared it with Nazaritch. When first she found out they had cheated her she had wept bitterly, but afterwards she had grown used to it.

Wishing her a happy Christmas, and kissing both her hands, he looked her up and down, and frowned.

"You mustn't," he said with genuine disappointment. "I have told you, my dear, you mustn't!"

"What do you mean, Viktor Nikolaitch?"

"I have told you you mustn't get fat. All your family have an unfortunate tendency to grow fat. You mustn't," he repeated in an imploring voice, and kissed her hand. "You are so handsome! You are so splendid! Here, your Excellency, let me introduce the one woman in the world whom I have ever seriously loved."

"There is nothing surprising in that. To know Anna Akimovna at your age and not to be in love with her, that would be impossible."

"I adore her," the lawyer continued with perfect sincerity, but with his usual indolent grace. "I love her, but not because I am a man and she is a woman. When I am with her I always feel as though she belongs to some third sex, and I to a fourth, and we float away together into the domain of the subtlest shades, and there we blend into the spectrum. Leconte de Lisle defines such relations better than anyone. He has a superb passage, a marvellous passage. . . ."

Lysevitch rummaged in one notebook, then in the other, and, not finding the quotation, subsided. They began talking of the weather, of the opera, of the arrival, expected shortly, of Duse. Anna Akimovna remembered that the year before Lysevitch and, she fancied, Krylin had dined with her, and now when they were getting ready to go away, she began with perfect sincerity pointing out to them in an imploring voice that as they had no more visits to pay, they ought to remain to dinner with her. After some hesitation the visitors agreed.

In addition to the family dinner, consisting of cabbage soup, sucking pig, goose with apples, and so on, a so-called "French" or "chef's" dinner used to be prepared in the kitchen on great holidays, in case any visitor in the upper story wanted a meal. When they heard the clatter of crockery in the dining-room, Lysevitch began to betray a noticeable excitement; he rubbed his hands, shrugged his shoulders, screwed up his eyes, and described with feeling what dinners her father and uncle used to give at one time, and a marvellous *matelote* of turbots the cook here could make: it was not a *matelote*, but a veritable revelation! He was already gloating over the dinner, already eating it in imagination and enjoying it. When Anna Akimovna took his arm and led him to the dining-room, he tossed off a glass of vodka and put a piece of salmon in his mouth; he positively purred with pleasure. He munched loudly, disgustingly, emitting sounds from his nose, while his eyes grew oily and rapacious.

The *hors d'oeuvres* were superb; among other things, there were fresh white mushrooms stewed in cream, and *sauce provençale* made of fried oysters and crayfish, strongly flavoured with some bitter pickles. The dinner, consisting of elaborate holiday dishes, was excellent, and so were the wines. Mishenka waited at table with enthusiasm. When he laid some new dish on the table and lifted the shining cover, or poured out the wine, he did it with the solemnity of a professor of black magic, and, looking at his face and his movements suggesting the first figure of a quadrille, the lawyer thought several times, "What a fool!"

After the third course Lysevitch said, turning to Anna Akimovna:

"The *fin de siècle* woman -- I mean when she is young, and of course wealthy -- must be independent, clever, elegant, intellectual, bold, and a little depraved. Depraved within limits, a little; for excess, you know, is wearisome. You ought not to vegetate, my dear; you ought not to live like everyone else, but to get the full savour of life, and a slight flavour of depravity is the sauce of life. Revel among flowers of intoxicating fragrance, breathe the perfume of musk, eat hashish, and best of all, love, love, love. . . . To begin with, in your place I would set up seven lovers -- one for each day of the week; and one I would call Monday, one Tuesday, the third Wednesday, and so on, so that each might know his day."

This conversation troubled Anna Akimovna; she ate nothing and only drank a glass of wine.

"Let me speak at last," she said. "For myself personally, I can't conceive of love without family life. I am lonely, lonely as the moon in the sky, and a waning moon, too; and whatever you may say, I am convinced, I feel that this waning can only be restored by love in its ordinary sense. It seems to me that such love would define my duties, my work, make clear my conception of life. I want from love peace of soul, tranquillity; I want the very opposite of musk, and spiritualism, and *fin de siècle* . . . in short" -- she grew embarrassed -- "a husband and children."

"You want to be married? Well, you can do that, too," Lysevitch assented. "You ought to have all experiences: marriage, and jealousy, and the sweetness of the first infidelity, and even children. . . . But make haste and live -- make haste, my dear: time is passing; it won't wait."

"Yes, I'll go and get married!" she said, looking angrily at his well-fed, satisfied face. "I will marry in the simplest, most ordinary way and be radiant with happiness. And, would you believe it, I will marry some plain working man, some mechanic or draughtsman."

"There is no harm in that, either. The Duchess Josiana loved Gwinplin, and that was permissible for her because she was a grand duchess. Everything is permissible for you, too, because you are an exceptional woman: if, my dear, you want to love a negro or an Arab, don't scruple; send for a negro. Don't deny yourself anything. You ought to be as bold as your desires; don't fall short of them."

"Can it be so hard to understand me?" Anna Akimovna asked with amazement, and her eyes were bright with tears. "Understand, I have an immense business on my hands -- two thousand workmen, for whom I must answer before God. The men who work for me grow blind and deaf. I am afraid to go on like this; I am afraid! I am wretched, and you have the cruelty to talk to me of negroes and . . . and you smile!" Anna Akimovna brought her fist down on the table. "To go on living the life I am living now, or to marry someone as idle and incompetent as myself, would be a crime. I can't go on living like this," she said hotly, "I cannot!"

"How handsome she is!" said Lysevitch, fascinated by her. "My God, how handsome she is! But why are you angry, my dear? Perhaps I am wrong; but surely you don't imagine that if, for the sake of ideas for which I have the deepest respect, you renounce the joys of life and lead a dreary existence, your workmen will be any the better for it? Not a scrap! No, frivolity, frivolity!" he said decisively. "It's essential for you; it's your duty to be frivolous and depraved! Ponder that, my dear, ponder it."

Anna Akimovna was glad she had spoken out, and her spirits rose. She was pleased she had spoken so well, and that her ideas were so fine and just, and she was already convinced that if Pimenov, for instance, loved her, she would marry him with pleasure.

Mishenka began to pour out champagne.

"You make me angry, Viktor Nikolaitch," she said, clinking glasses with the lawyer. "It seems to me you give advice and know nothing of life yourself. According to you, if a man be a mechanic or a draughtsman, he is bound to be a peasant and an ignoramus! But they are the cleverest people! Extraordinary people!"

"Your uncle and father . . . I knew them and respected them . . ." Krylin said, pausing for emphasis (he had been sitting upright as a post, and had been eating steadily the whole time), "were people of considerable intelligence and . . . of lofty spiritual qualities."

"Oh, to be sure, we know all about their qualities," the lawyer muttered, and asked permission to smoke.

When dinner was over Krylin was led away for a nap. Lysevitch finished his cigar, and, staggering from repletion, followed Anna Akimovna into her study. Cosy corners with photographs and fans on the walls, and the inevitable pink or pale blue lanterns in the middle of the ceiling, he did not like, as the expression of an insipid and unoriginal character; besides, the memory of certain of his love affairs of which he was now ashamed was associated with such lanterns. Anna Akimovna's study with its bare walls and tasteless furniture pleased him exceedingly. It was snug and comfortable for him to sit on a Turkish divan and look at Anna Akimovna, who usually sat on the rug before the fire, clasping her knees and looking into the fire and thinking of something; and at such moments it seemed to him that her peasant Old Believer blood was stirring within her.

Every time after dinner when coffee and liqueurs were handed, he grew livelier and began telling her various bits of literary gossip. He spoke with eloquence and inspiration, and was carried away by his own stories; and she listened to him and thought every time that for such enjoyment it was worth paying not only twelve thousand, but three times that sum, and forgave him everything she disliked in him. He sometimes told her the story of some tale or novel he had been reading, and then two or three hours passed unnoticed like a minute. Now he began rather dolefully in a failing voice with his eyes shut.

"It's ages, my dear, since I have read anything," he said when she asked him to tell her something. "Though I do sometimes read Jules Verne."

"I was expecting you to tell me something new."

"H'm! . . . new," Lysevitch muttered sleepily, and he settled himself further back in the corner of the sofa. "None of the new literature, my dear, is any use for you or me. Of course, it is bound to be such as it is, and to refuse to recognize it is to refuse to recognize -- would mean refusing to recognize the natural order of things, and I do recognize it, but . . ." Lysevitch seemed to have fallen asleep. But a minute later his voice was heard again:

"All the new literature moans and howls like the autumn wind in the chimney. 'Ah, unhappy wretch! Ah, your life may be likened to a prison! Ah, how damp and dark it is in your prison! Ah, you will certainly come to ruin, and there is no chance of escape for you!' That's very fine, but I should prefer a literature that would tell us how to escape from prison. Of all contemporary writers, however, I prefer Maupassant." Lysevitch opened his eyes. "A fine writer, a perfect writer!" Lysevitch shifted in his seat. "A wonderful artist! A terrible, prodigious, supernatural artist!" Lysevitch got up from the sofa and raised his right arm. "Maupassant!" he said rapturously. "My dear, read Maupassant! one page of his gives you more than all the riches of the earth! Every line is a new horizon. The softest, tenderest impulses of the soul alternate with violent tempestuous sensations; your soul, as though under the weight of forty thousand atmospheres, is transformed into the most insignificant little bit of some great thing of an undefined rosy hue which I fancy, if one could put it on one's tongue, would yield a pungent, voluptuous taste. What a fury of transitions, of motives, of melodies! You rest peacefully on the lilies and the roses, and suddenly a thought -- a terrible, splendid, irresistible thought -- swoops down upon you like a locomotive, and bathes you in hot steam and deafens you with its whistle. Read Maupassant, dear girl; I insist on it."

Lysevitch waved his arms and paced from corner to corner in violent excitement.

"Yes, it is inconceivable," he pronounced, as though in despair; "his last thing overwhelmed me, intoxicated me! But I am afraid you will not care for it. To be carried away by it you must savour it, slowly suck the juice from each line, drink it in. . . . You must drink it in! . . ."

After a long introduction, containing many words such as dæmonic sensuality, a network of the most delicate nerves, simoom, crystal, and so on, he began at last telling the story of the novel. He did not tell the story so whimsically, but told it in minute detail, quoting from memory whole descriptions and conversations; the characters of the novel fascinated him, and to describe them he threw himself into attitudes, changed the expression of his face and voice like a real actor. He laughed with delight at one moment in a deep bass, and at another, on a high shrill note, clasped his hands and clutched at his head with an expression which suggested that it was just going to burst. Anna Akimovna listened enthralled, though she had already read the novel, and it seemed to her ever so much finer and more subtle in the lawyer's version than in the book itself. He drew her attention to various subtleties, and emphasized the felicitous expressions and the profound thoughts, but she saw in it, only life, life, life and herself, as though she had been a character in the novel. Her spirits rose, and she, too, laughing and clasping her hands, thought that she could not go on living such a life, that there was no need to have a wretched life when one might have a splendid one. She remembered her words and thoughts at dinner, and was proud of them; and when Pimenov suddenly rose up in her imagination, she felt happy and longed for him to love her.

When he had finished the story, Lysevitch sat down on the sofa, exhausted.

"How splendid you are! How handsome!" he began, a little while afterwards in a faint voice as if he were ill. "I am happy near you, dear girl, but why am I forty-two instead of thirty? Your tastes and mine do not coincide: you ought to be depraved, and I have long passed that phase, and want a love as delicate and immaterial as a ray of sunshine -- that is, from the point of view of a woman of your age, I am of no earthly use."

In his own words, he loved Turgenev, the singer of virginal love and purity, of youth, and of the melancholy Russian landscape; but he loved virginal love, not from knowledge but from hearsay, as something abstract, existing outside real life. Now he assured himself that he loved Anna Akimovna platonically, ideally, though he did not know what those words meant. But he felt comfortable, snug, warm. Anna Akimovna seemed to him enchanting, original, and he imagined that the pleasant sensation that was aroused in him by these surroundings was the very thing that was called platonic love.

He laid his cheek on her hand and said in the tone commonly used in coaxing little children:

"My precious, why have you punished me?"

"How? When?"

"I have had no Christmas present from you."

Anna Akimovna had never heard before of their sending a Christmas box to the lawyer, and now she was at a loss how much to give him. But she must give him something, for he was expecting it, though he looked at her with eyes full of love.

"I suppose Nazaritch forgot it," she said, "but it is not too late to set it right."

She suddenly remembered the fifteen hundred she had received the day before, which was now lying in the toilet drawer in her bedroom. And when she brought that ungrateful money and gave it to the lawyer, and he put it in his coat pocket with indolent grace, the whole incident passed off charmingly and naturally. The sudden reminder of a Christmas box and this fifteen hundred was not unbecoming in Lysevitch.

"Merci," he said, and kissed her finger.

Krylin came in with blissful, sleepy face, but without his decorations.

Lysevitch and he stayed a little longer and drank a glass of tea each, and began to get ready to go. Anna Akimovna was a little embarrassed. . . . She had utterly forgotten in what department Krylin served, and whether she had to give him money or not; and if she had to, whether to give it now or send it afterwards in an envelope.

"Where does he serve?" she whispered to Lysevitch.

"Goodness knows," muttered Lysevitch, yawning.

She reflected that if Krylin used to visit her father and her uncle and respected them, it was probably not for nothing: apparently he had been charitable at their expense, serving in some charitable institution. As she said good-bye she slipped three hundred roubles into his hand; he seemed taken aback, and looked at her for a minute in silence with his pewtery eyes, but then seemed to understand and said:

"The receipt, honoured Anna Akimovna, you can only receive on the New Year."

Lysevitch had become utterly limp and heavy, and he staggered when Mishenka put on his overcoat.

As he went downstairs he looked like a man in the last stage of exhaustion, and it was evident that he would drop asleep as soon as he got into his sledge.

"Your Excellency," he said languidly to Krylin, stopping in the middle of the staircase, "has it ever happened to you to experience a feeling as though some unseen force were drawing you out longer and longer? You are drawn out and turn into the finest wire. Subjectively this finds expression in a curious voluptuous feeling which is impossible to compare with anything."

Anna Akimovna, standing at the top of the stairs, saw each of them give Mishenka a note.

"Good-bye! Come again!" she called to them, and ran into her bedroom.

She quickly threw off her dress, that she was weary of already, put on a dressing-gown, and ran downstairs; and as she ran downstairs she laughed and thumped with her feet like a school-boy; she had a great desire for mischief.

IV

Evening

Auntie, in a loose print blouse, Varvarushka and two old women, were sitting in the dining-room having supper. A big piece of salt meat, a ham, and various savouries, were lying on the table before them, and clouds of steam were rising from the meat, which looked particularly fat and appetizing. Wine was not served on the lower story, but they made up for it with a great number of spirits and home-made liqueurs. Agafyushka, the fat, white-skinned, well-fed cook, was standing with her arms crossed in the doorway and talking to the old women, and the dishes were being handed by the downstairs Masha, a dark girl with a crimson ribbon in her hair. The old women had had enough to eat before the morning was over, and an hour before supper had had tea and buns, and so they were now eating with effort -- as it were, from a sense of duty.

"Oh, my girl!" sighed Auntie, as Anna Akimovna ran into the dining-room and sat down beside her. "You've frightened me to death!"

Everyone in the house was pleased when Anna Akimovna was in good spirits and played pranks; this always reminded them that the old men were dead and that the old women had no authority in the house, and anyone could do as he liked without any fear of being sharply called to account for it. Only the two old women glanced askance at Anna Akimovna with amazement: she was humming, and it was a sin to sing at table.

"Our mistress, our beauty, our picture," Agafyushka began chanting with sugary sweetness. "Our precious jewel! The people, the people that have come to-day to look at our queen. Lord have mercy upon us! Generals, and officers and gentlemen. . . . I kept looking out of window and counting and counting till I gave it up."

"I'd as soon they did not come at all," said Auntie; she looked sadly at her niece and added: "They only waste the time for my poor orphan girl."

Anna Akimovna felt hungry, as she had eaten nothing since the morning. They poured her out some very bitter liqueur; she drank it off, and tasted the salt meat with mustard, and thought it extraordinarily nice. Then the downstairs Masha brought in the turkey, the pickled apples and the gooseberries. And that pleased her, too. There was only one thing that was disagreeable: there was a draught of hot air from the tiled stove; it was stiflingly close and everyone's cheeks were burning. After supper the cloth was taken off and plates of peppermint biscuits, walnuts, and raisins were brought in.

"You sit down, too . . . no need to stand there!" said Auntie to the cook.

Agafyushka sighed and sat down to the table; Masha set a wineglass of liqueur before her, too, and Anna Akimovna began to feel as though Agafyushka's white neck were giving out heat like the stove. They were all talking of how difficult it was nowadays to get married, and saying that in old days, if men did not court beauty, they paid attention to money, but now there was no making out what they wanted; and while hunchbacks and cripples used to be left old maids, nowadays men would not have even the beautiful and wealthy. Auntie began to set this down to immorality, and said that people had no fear of God, but she suddenly remembered that Ivan Ivanitch, her brother, and Varvarushka -- both people of holy life -- had feared God, but all the same had had children on the sly, and had sent them to the Foundling Asylum. She pulled herself up and changed the conversation, telling them about a suitor she had once had, a factory hand, and how she had loved him, but her brothers had forced her to marry a widower, an ikon-painter, who, thank God, had died two years after. The downstairs Masha sat down to the table, too, and told them with a mysterious air that for the last week some unknown man with a black moustache, in a great-coat with an astrachan collar, had made his appearance every morning in the yard, had stared at the windows of the big house, and had gone on further -- to the buildings; the man was all right, nice-looking.

All this conversation made Anna Akimovna suddenly long to be married -- long intensely, painfully; she felt as though she would give half her life and all her fortune only to know that upstairs there was a man who was closer to her than anyone in the world, that he loved her warmly and was missing her; and the thought of such closeness, ecstatic and inexpressible in words, troubled her soul. And the instinct of youth and health flattered her with lying assurances that the real poetry of life was not over but still to come, and she believed it, and leaning back in her chair (her hair fell down as she did so), she began laughing, and, looking at her, the others laughed, too. And it was a long time before this causeless laughter died down in the dining-room.

She was informed that the Stinging Beetle had come. This was a pilgrim woman called Pasha or Spiridonovna -- a thin little woman of fifty, in a black dress with a white kerchief, with keen eyes, sharp nose, and a sharp chin; she had sly, viperish eyes and she looked as though she could see right through everyone. Her lips were shaped like a heart. Her viperishness and hostility to everyone had earned her the nickname of the Stinging Beetle.

Going into the dining-room without looking at anyone, she made for the ikons and chanted in a high voice "Thy Holy Birth," then she sang "The Virgin today gives birth to the Son," then "Christ is born," then she turned round and bent a piercing gaze upon all of them.

"A happy Christmas," she said, and she kissed Anna Akimovna on the shoulder. "It's all I could do, all I could do to get to you, my kind friends." She kissed Auntie on the shoulder. "I should have come to you this morning, but I went in to some good people to rest on the way. 'Stay, Spiridonovna, stay,' they said, and I did not notice that evening was coming on."

As she did not eat meat, they gave her salmon and caviare. She ate looking from under her eyelids at the company, and drank three glasses of vodka. When she had finished she said a prayer and bowed down to Anna Akimovna's feet.

They began to play a game of "kings," as they had done the year before, and the year before that, and all the servants in both stories crowded in at the doors to watch the game. Anna Akimovna fancied she caught a glimpse once or twice of Mishenka, with a patronizing smile on his face, among the crowd of peasant men and women. The first to be king was Stinging Beetle, and Anna Akimovna as the soldier paid her tribute; and then Auntie was king and Anna Akimovna was peasant, which excited general delight, and Agafyushka was prince, and was quite abashed with pleasure. Another game was got up at the other end of the table -- played by the two Mashas, Varvarushka, and the sewing-maid Marfa Ptrovna, who was waked on purpose to play "kings," and whose face looked cross and sleepy.

While they were playing they talked of men, and of how difficult it was to get a good husband nowadays, and which state was to be preferred -- that of an old maid or a widow.

"You are a handsome, healthy, sturdy lass," said Stinging Beetle to Anna Akimovna. "But I can't make out for whose sake you are holding back."

"What's to be done if nobody will have me?"

"Or maybe you have taken a vow to remain a maid?" Stinging Beetle went on, as though she did not hear. "Well, that's a good deed. . . . Remain one," she repeated, looking intently and maliciously at her cards. "All right, my dear, remain one. . . . Yes . . . only maids, these saintly maids, are not all alike." She heaved a sigh and played the king. "Oh, no, my girl, they are not all alike! Some really watch over themselves like nuns, and butter would not melt in their mouths; and if such a one does sin in an hour of weakness, she is worried to death, poor thing! so it would be a sin to condemn her. While others will go dressed in black and sew their shroud, and yet love rich old men on the sly. Yes, y-es, my canary birds, some hussies will bewitch an old man and rule over him, my doves, rule over him and turn his head; and when they've saved up money and lottery tickets enough, they will bewitch him to his death."

Varvarushka's only response to these hints was to heave a sigh and look towards the ikons. There was an expression of Christian meekness on her countenance.

"I know a maid like that, my bitterest enemy," Stinging Beetle went on, looking round at everyone in triumph; "she is always sighing, too, and looking at the ikons, the she-devil. When she used to rule in a certain old man's house, if one went to her she would give one a crust, and bid one bow down to the ikons while she would sing: 'In conception Thou dost abide a Virgin . . .!' On holidays she will give one a bite, and on working days she will reproach one for it. But nowadays I will make merry over her! I will make as merry as I please, my jewel."

Varvarushka glanced at the ikons again and crossed herself.

"But no one will have me, Spiridonovna," said Anna Akimovna to change the conversation. "What's to be done?"

"It's your own fault. You keep waiting for highly educated gentlemen, but you ought to marry one of your own sort, a merchant."

"We don't want a merchant," said Auntie, all in a flutter. "Queen of Heaven, preserve us! A gentleman will spend your money, but then he will be kind to you, you poor little fool. But a merchant will be so strict that you won't feel at home in your own house. You'll be wanting to fondle him and he will be counting his money, and when you sit down to meals with him, he'll grudge you every mouthful, though it's your own, the lout! . . . Marry a gentleman."

They all talked at once, loudly interrupting one another, and Auntie tapped on the table with the nutcrackers and said, flushed and angry:

"We won't have a merchant; we won't have one! If you choose a merchant I shall go to an almshouse."

"Sh . . . Sh! . . . Hush!" cried Stinging Beetle; when all were silent she screwed up one eye and said: "Do you know what, Annushka, my birdie . . .? There is no need for you to get married really like everyone else. You're rich and free, you are your own mistress; but yet, my child, it doesn't seem the right thing for you to be an old maid. I'll find you, you know, some trumpery and simple-witted man. You'll marry him for appearances and then have your fling, bonny lass! You can hand him five thousand or ten maybe, and pack him off where he came from, and you will be mistress in your own house -- you can love whom you like and no one can say anything to you. And then you can love your highly educated gentleman. You'll have a jolly time!" Stinging Beetle snapped her fingers and gave a whistle.

"It's sinful," said Auntie.

"Oh, sinful," laughed Stinging Beetle. "She is educated, she understands. To cut someone's throat or bewitch an old man -- that's a sin, that's true; but to love some charming young friend is not a sin at all. And what is there in it, really? There's no sin in it at all! The old pilgrim women have invented all that to make fools of simple folk. I, too, say everywhere it's a sin; I don't know myself why it's a sin." Stinging Beetle emptied her glass and cleared her throat. "Have your fling, bonny lass," this time evidently addressing herself. "For thirty years, wenches, I have thought of nothing but sins and been afraid, but now I see I have wasted my time, I've let it slip by like a ninny! Ah, I have been a fool, a fool!" She sighed. "A woman's time is short and every day is precious. You are handsome, Annushka, and very rich; but as soon as thirty-five or forty strikes for you your time is up. Don't listen to anyone, my girl; live, have your fling till you are forty, and then you will have time to pray forgiveness -- there will be plenty of time to bow down and to sew your shroud. A candle to God and a poker to the devil! You can do both at once! Well, how is it to be? Will you make some little man happy?"

"I will," laughed Anna Akimovna. "I don't care now; I would marry a working man."

"Well, that would do all right! Oh, what a fine fellow you would choose then!" Stinging Beetle screwed up her eyes and shook her head. "O--o--oh!"

"I tell her myself," said Auntie, "it's no good waiting for a gentleman, so she had better marry, not a gentleman, but someone humbler; anyway we should have a man in the house to look after things. And there are lots of good men. She might have someone out of the factory. They are all sober, steady men. . . ."

"I should think so," Stinging Beetle agreed. "They are capital fellows. If you like, Aunt, I will make a match for her with Vassily Lebedinsky?"

"Oh, Vasya's legs are so long," said Auntie seriously. "He is so lanky. He has no looks."

There was laughter in the crowd by the door.

"Well, Pimenov? Would you like to marry Pimenov?" Stinging Beetle asked Anna Akimovna.

"Very good. Make a match for me with Pimenov."

"Really?"

"Yes, do!" Anna Akimovna said resolutely, and she struck her fist on the table. "On my honour, I will marry him."

"Really?"

Anna Akimovna suddenly felt ashamed that her cheeks were burning and that everyone was looking at her; she flung the cards together on the table and ran out of the room. As she ran up the stairs and, reaching the upper story, sat down to the piano in the drawing-room, a murmur of sound reached her from below like the roar of the sea; most likely they were talking of her and of Pimenov, and perhaps Stinging Beetle was taking advantage of her absence to insult Varvarushka and was putting no check on her language.

The lamp in the big room was the only light burning in the upper story, and it sent a glimmer through the door into the dark drawing-room. It was between nine and ten, not later. Anna Akimovna played a waltz, then another, then a third; she went on playing without stopping. She looked into the dark corner beyond the piano, smiled, and inwardly called to it, and the idea occurred to her that she might drive off to the town to see someone, Lysevitch for instance, and tell him what was passing in her heart. She wanted to talk without ceasing, to laugh, to play the fool, but the dark corner was sullenly silent, and all round in all the rooms of the upper story it was still and desolate.

She was fond of sentimental songs, but she had a harsh, untrained voice, and so she only played the accompaniment and sang hardly audibly, just above her breath. She sang in a whisper one song after another, for the most part about love, separation, and frustrated hopes, and she imagined how she would hold out her hands to him and say with entreaty, with tears, "Pimenov, take this burden from me!" And then, just as though her sins had been forgiven, there would be joy and comfort in her soul, and perhaps a free, happy life would begin. In an anguish of anticipation she leant over the keys, with a passionate longing for the change in her life to come at once without delay, and was terrified at the thought that her old life would go on for some time longer. Then she played again and sang hardly above her breath, and all was stillness about her. There was no noise coming from downstairs now, they must have gone to bed. It had struck ten some time before. A long, solitary, wearisome night was approaching.

Anna Akimovna walked through all the rooms, lay down for a while on the sofa, and read in her study the letters that had come that evening; there were twelve letters of Christmas greetings and three anonymous letters. In one of them some workman complained in a horrible, almost illegible handwriting that Lenten oil sold in the factory shop was rancid and smelt of paraffin; in another, someone respectfully informed her that over a purchase of iron Nazaritch had lately taken a bribe of a thousand roubles from someone; in a third she was abused for her inhumanity.

The excitement of Christmas was passing off, and to keep it up Anna Akimovna sat down at the piano again and softly played one of the new waltzes, then she remembered how cleverly and creditably she had spoken at dinner today. She looked round at the dark windows, at the walls with the pictures, at the faint light that came from the big room, and all at once she began suddenly crying, and she felt vexed that she was so lonely, and that she had no one to talk to and consult. To cheer herself she tried to picture Pimenov in her imagination, but it was unsuccessful.

It struck twelve. Mishenka, no longer wearing his swallow-tail but in his reefer jacket, came in, and without speaking lighted two candles; then he went out and returned a minute later with a cup of tea on a tray.

"What are you laughing at?" she asked, noticing a smile on his face.

"I was downstairs and heard the jokes you were making about Pimenov . . ." he said, and put his hand before his laughing mouth. "If he were sat down to dinner today with Viktor Nikolaevitch and the general, he'd have died of fright." Mishenka's shoulders were shaking with laughter. "He doesn't know even how to hold his fork, I bet."

The footman's laughter and words, his reefer jacket and moustache, gave Anna Akimovna a feeling of uncleanness. She shut her eyes to avoid seeing him, and, against her own will, imagined Pimenov dining with Lysevitch and Krylin, and his timid, unintellectual figure seemed to her pitiful and helpless, and she felt repelled by it. And only now, for the first time in the whole day, she realized clearly that all she had said and thought about Pimenov and marrying a workman was nonsense, folly, and wilfulness. To convince herself of the opposite, to overcome her repulsion, she tried to recall what she had said at dinner, but now she could not see anything in it: shame at her own thoughts and actions, and the fear that she had said something improper during the day, and disgust at her own lack of spirit, overwhelmed her completely. She took up a candle and, as rapidly as if someone were pursuing her, ran downstairs, woke Spiridonovna, and began assuring her she had been joking. Then she went to her bedroom. Red-haired Masha, who was dozing in an arm-chair near the bed, jumped up and began shaking up the pillows. Her face was exhausted and sleepy, and her magnificent hair had fallen on one side.

"Tchalikov came again this evening," she said, yawning, "but I did not dare to announce him; he was very drunk. He says he will come again tomorrow."

"What does he want with me?" said Anna Akimovna, and she flung her comb on the floor. "I won't see him, I won't."

She made up her mind she had no one left in life but this Tchalikov, that he would never leave off persecuting her, and would remind her every day how uninteresting and absurd her life was. So all she was fit for was to help the poor. Oh, how stupid it was!

She lay down without undressing, and sobbed with shame and depression: what seemed to her most vexatious and stupid of all was that her dreams that day about Pimenov had been right, lofty, honourable, but at the same time she felt that Lysevitch and even Krylin were nearer to her than Pimenov and all the workpeople taken together. She thought that if the long day she had just spent could have been represented in a picture, all that had been bad and vulgar -- as, for instance, the dinner, the lawyer's talk, the game of "kings" -- would have been true, while her dreams and talk about Pimenov would have stood out from the whole as something false, as out of drawing; and she thought, too, that it was too late to dream of happiness, that everything was over for her, and it was impossible to go back to the life when she had slept under the same quilt with her mother, or to devise some new special sort of life.

Red-haired Masha was kneeling before the bed, gazing at her in mournful perplexity; then she, too, began crying, and laid her face against her mistress's arm, and without words it was clear why she was so wretched.

"We are fools!" said Anna Akimovna, laughing and crying. "We are fools! Oh, what fools we are!"

ROTHSCHILD'S FIDDLE

The town was a little one, worse than a village, and it was inhabited by scarcely any but old people who died with an infrequency that was really annoying. In the hospital and in the prison fortress very few coffins were needed. In fact business was bad. If Yakov Ivanov had been an undertaker in the chief town of the province he would certainly have had a house of his own, and people would have addressed him as Yakov Matveyitch; here in this wretched little town people called him simply Yakov; his nickname in the street was for some reason Bronze, and he lived in a poor way like a humble peasant, in a little old hut in which there was only one room, and in this room he and Marfa, the stove, a double bed, the coffins, his bench, and all their belongings were crowded together.

Yakov made good, solid coffins. For peasants and working people he made them to fit himself, and this was never unsuccessful, for there were none taller and stronger than he, even in the prison, though he was seventy. For gentry and for women he made them to measure, and used an iron foot-rule for the purpose. He was very unwilling to take orders for children's coffins, and made them straight off without measurements, contemptuously, and when he was paid for the work he always said:

"I must confess I don't like trumpery jobs."

Apart from his trade, playing the fiddle brought him in a small income.

The Jews' orchestra conducted by Moisey Ilyitch Shahkes, the tinsmith, who took more than half their receipts for himself, played as a rule at weddings in the town. As Yakov played very well on the fiddle, especially Russian songs, Shahkes sometimes invited him to join the orchestra at a fee of half a rouble a day, in addition to tips from the visitors. When Bronze sat in the orchestra first of all his face became crimson and perspiring; it was hot, there was a suffocating smell of garlic, the fiddle squeaked, the double bass wheezed close to his right ear, while the flute wailed at his left, played by a gaunt, red-haired Jew who had a perfect network of red and blue veins all over his face, and who bore the name of the famous millionaire Rothschild. And this accursed Jew contrived to play even the liveliest things plaintively. For no apparent reason Yakov little by little became possessed by hatred and contempt for the Jews, and especially for Rothschild; he began to pick quarrels with him, rail at him in unseemly language and once even tried to strike him, and Rothschild was offended and said, looking at him ferociously:

"If it were not that I respect you for your talent, I would have sent you flying out of the window."

Then he began to weep. And because of this Yakov was not often asked to play in the orchestra; he was only sent for in case of extreme necessity in the absence of one of the Jews.

Yakov was never in a good temper, as he was continually having to put up with terrible losses. For instance, it was a sin to work on Sundays or Saints' days, and Monday was an unlucky day, so that in the course of the year there were some two hundred days on which, whether he liked it or not, he had to sit with his hands folded. And only think, what a loss that meant. If anyone in the town had a wedding without music, or if Shahkes did not send for Yakov, that was a loss, too. The superintendent of the prison was ill for two years and was wasting away, and Yakov was impatiently waiting for him to die, but the superintendent went away to the chief town of the province to be doctored, and there took and died. There's a loss for you, ten roubles at least, as there would have been an expensive coffin to make, lined with brocade. The thought of his losses haunted Yakov, especially at night; he laid his fiddle on the bed beside him, and when all sorts of nonsensical ideas came into his mind he touched a string; the fiddle gave out a sound in the darkness, and he felt better.

On the sixth of May of the previous year Marfa had suddenly been taken ill. The old woman's breathing was laboured, she drank a great deal of water, and she staggered as she walked, yet she lighted the stove in the morning and even went herself to get water. Towards evening she lay down. Yakov played his fiddle all day; when it was quite dark he took the book in which he used every day to put down his losses, and, feeling dull, he began adding up the total for the year. It came to more than a thousand roubles. This so agitated him that he flung the reckoning beads down, and trampled them under his feet. Then he picked up the reckoning beads, and again spent a long time clicking with them and heaving deep, strained sighs. His face was crimson and wet with perspiration. He thought that if he had put that lost thousand roubles in the bank, the interest for a year would have been at least forty roubles, so that forty roubles was a loss too. In fact, wherever one turned there were losses and nothing else.

"Yakov!" Marfa called unexpectedly. "I am dying."

He looked round at his wife. Her face was rosy with fever, unusually bright and joyful-looking. Bronze, accustomed to seeing her face always pale, timid, and unhappy-looking, was bewildered. It looked as if she really were dying and were glad that she was going away forever from that hut, from the coffins, and from Yakov. . . . And she gazed at the ceiling and moved her lips, and her expression was one of happiness, as though she saw death as her deliverer and were whispering with him.

It was daybreak; from the windows one could see the flush of dawn. Looking at the old woman, Yakov for some reason reflected that he had not once in his life been affectionate to her, had had no feeling for her, had never once thought to buy her a kerchief, or to bring her home some dainty from a wedding, but had done nothing but shout at her, scold her for his losses, shake his fists at her; it is true he had never actually beaten her, but he had frightened her, and at such times she had always been numb with terror. Why, he had forbidden her to drink tea because they spent too much without that, and she drank only hot water. And he understood why she had such a strange, joyful face now, and he was overcome with dread.

As soon as it was morning he borrowed a horse from a neighbour and took Marfa to the hospital. There were not many patients there, and so he had not long to wait, only three hours. To his great satisfaction the patients were not being received by the doctor, who was himself ill, but by the assistant, Maxim Nikolaitch, an old man of whom everyone in the town used to say that, though he drank and was quarrelsome, he knew more than the doctor.

"I wish you good-day," said Yakov, leading his old woman into the consulting room. "You must excuse us, Maxim Nikolaitch, we are always troubling you with our trumpery affairs. Here you see my better half is ailing, the partner of my life, as they say, excuse the expression. . . ."

Knitting his grizzled brows and stroking his whiskers the assistant began to examine the old woman, and she sat on a stool, a wasted, bent figure with a sharp nose and open mouth, looking like a bird that wants to drink.

"H------m . . . Ah! . . ." the assistant said slowly, and he heaved a sigh. "Influenza and possibly fever. There's typhus in the town now. Well, the old woman has lived her life, thank God. . . . How old is she?"

"She'll be seventy in another year, Maxim Nikolaitch."

"Well, the old woman has lived her life, it's time to say good-bye."

"You are quite right in what you say, of course, Maxim Nikolaitch," said Yakov, smiling from politeness, "and we thank you feelingly for your kindness, but allow me to say every insect wants to live."

"To be sure," said the assistant, in a tone which suggested that it depended upon him whether the woman lived or died. "Well, then, my good fellow, put a cold compress on her head, and give her these powders twice a day, and so good-bye. Bonjour."

From the expression of his face Yakov saw that it was a bad case, and that no sort of powders would be any help; it was clear to him that Marfa would die very soon, if not to-day, to-morrow. He nudged the assistant's elbow, winked at him, and said in a low voice:

"If you would just cup her, Maxim Nikolaitch."

"I have no time, I have no time, my good fellow. Take your old woman and go in God's name. Goodbye."

"Be so gracious," Yakov besought him. "You know yourself that if, let us say, it were her stomach or her inside that were bad, then powders or drops, but you see she had got a chill! In a chill the first thing is to let blood, Maxim Nikolaitch."

But the assistant had already sent for the next patient, and a peasant woman came into the consulting room with a boy.

"Go along! go along," he said to Yakov, frowning. "It's no use to --"

"In that case put on leeches, anyway! Make us pray for you forever."

The assistant flew into a rage and shouted:

"You speak to me again! You blockhead. . . ."

Yakov flew into a rage too, and he turned crimson all over, but he did not utter a word. He took Marfa on his arm and led her out of the room. Only when they were sitting in the cart he looked morosely and ironically at the hospital, and said:

"A nice set of artists they have settled here! No fear, but he would have cupped a rich man, but even a leech he grudges to the poor. The Herods!"

When they got home and went into the hut, Marfa stood for ten minutes holding on to the stove. It seemed to her that if she were to lie down Yakov would talk to her about his losses, and scold her for lying down and not wanting to work. Yakov looked at her drearily and thought that to-morrow was St. John the Divine's, and next day St. Nikolay the Wonder-worker's, and the day after that was Sunday, and then Monday, an unlucky day. For four days he would not be able to work, and most likely Marfa would die on one of those days; so he would have to make the coffin to-day. He picked up his iron rule, went up to the old woman and took her measure. Then she lay down, and he crossed himself and began making the coffin.

When the coffin was finished Bronze put on his spectacles and wrote in his book: "Marfa Ivanov's coffin, two roubles, forty kopecks."

And he heaved a sigh. The old woman lay all the time silent with her eyes closed. But in the evening, when it got dark, she suddenly called the old man.

"Do you remember, Yakov," she asked, looking at him joyfully. "Do you remember fifty years ago God gave us a little baby with flaxen hair? We used always to be sitting by the river then, singing songs . . . under the willows," and laughing bitterly, she added: "The baby girl died."

Yakov racked his memory, but could not remember the baby or the willows.

"It's your fancy," he said.

The priest arrived; he administered the sacrament and extreme unction. Then Marfa began muttering something unintelligible, and towards morning she died. Old women, neighbours, washed her, dressed her, and laid her in the coffin. To avoid paying the sacristan, Yakov read the psalms over the body himself, and they got nothing out of him for the grave, as the grave-digger was a crony of his. Four peasants carried the coffin to the graveyard, not for money, but from respect. The coffin was followed by old women, beggars, and a couple of crazy saints, and the people who met it crossed themselves piously. . . . And Yakov was very much pleased that it was so creditable, so decorous, and so cheap, and no offence to anyone. As he took his last leave of Marfa he touched the coffin and thought: "A good piece of work!"

But as he was going back from the cemetery he was overcome by acute depression. He didn't feel quite well: his breathing was laboured and feverish, his legs felt weak, and he had a craving for drink. And thoughts of all sorts forced themselves on his mind. He remembered again that all his life he had never felt for Marfa, had never been affectionate to her. The fifty-two years they had lived in the same hut had dragged on a long, long time, but it had somehow happened that in all that time he had never once thought of her, had paid no attention to her, as though she had been a cat or a dog. And yet, every day, she had lighted the stove had cooked and baked, had gone for the water, had chopped the wood, had slept with him in the same bed, and when he came home drunk from the weddings always reverently hung his fiddle on the wall and put him to bed, and all this in silence, with a timid, anxious expression.

Rothschild, smiling and bowing, came to meet Yakov.

"I was looking for you, uncle," he said. "Moisey Ilyitch sends you his greetings and bids you come to him at once."

Yakov felt in no mood for this. He wanted to cry.

"Leave me alone," he said, and walked on.

"How can you," Rothschild said, fluttered, running on in front. "Moisey Ilyitch will be offended! He bade you come at once!"

Yakov was revolted at the Jew's gasping for breath and blinking, and having so many red freckles on his face. And it was disgusting to look at his green coat with black patches on it, and all his fragile, refined figure.

"Why are you pestering me, garlic?" shouted Yakov. "Don't persist!"

The Jew got angry and shouted too:

"Not so noisy, please, or I'll send you flying over the fence!"

"Get out of my sight!" roared Yakov, and rushed at him with his fists. "One can't live for you scabby Jews!"

Rothschild, half dead with terror, crouched down and waved his hands over his head, as though to ward off a blow; then he leapt up and ran away as fast as his legs could carry him: as he ran he gave little skips and kept clasping his hands, and Yakov could see how his long thin spine wriggled. Some boys, delighted at the incident, ran after him shouting "Jew! Jew!" Some dogs joined in the chase barking. Someone burst into a roar of laughter, then gave a whistle; the dogs barked with even more noise and unanimity. Then a dog must have bitten Rothschild, as a desperate, sickly scream was heard.

Yakov went for a walk on the grazing ground, then wandered on at random in the outskirts of the town, while the street boys shouted:

"Here's Bronze! Here's Bronze!"

He came to the river, where the curlews floated in the air uttering shrill cries and the ducks quacked. The sun was blazing hot, and there was a glitter from the water, so that it hurt the eyes to look at it. Yakov walked by a path along the bank and saw a plump, rosy-cheeked lady come out of the bathing-shed, and thought about her: "Ugh! you otter!"

Not far from the bathing-shed boys were catching crayfish with bits of meat; seeing him, they began shouting spitefully, "Bronze! Bronze!" And then he saw an old spreading willow-tree with a big hollow in it, and a crow's nest on it. . . . And suddenly there rose up vividly in Yakov's memory a baby with flaxen hair, and the willow-tree Marfa had spoken of. Why, that is it, the same willow-tree -- green, still, and sorrowful. . . . How old it has grown, poor thing!

He sat down under it and began to recall the past. On the other bank, where now there was the water meadow, in those days there stood a big birchwood, and yonder on the bare hillside that could be seen on the horizon an old, old pine forest used to be a bluish patch in the distance. Big boats used to sail on the river. But now it was all smooth and unruffled, and on the other bank there stood now only one birch-tree, youthful and slender like a young lady, and there was nothing on the river but ducks and geese, and it didn't look as though there had ever been boats on it. It seemed as though even the geese were fewer than of old. Yakov shut his eyes, and in his imagination huge flocks of white geese soared, meeting one another.

He wondered how it had happened that for the last forty or fifty years of his life he had never once been to the river, or if he had been by it he had not paid attention to it. Why, it was a decent sized river, not a trumpery one; he might have gone in for fishing and sold the fish to merchants, officials, and the bar-keeper at the station, and then have put money in the bank; he might have sailed in a boat from one house to another, playing the fiddle, and people of all classes would have paid to hear him; he might have tried getting big boats afloat again -- that would be better than making coffins; he might have bred geese, killed them and sent them in the winter to Moscow Why, the feathers alone would very likely mount up to ten roubles in the year. But he had wasted his time, he had done nothing of this. What losses! Ah! What losses! And if he had gone in for all those things at once -- catching fish and playing the fiddle, and running boats and killing geese -- what a fortune he would have made! But nothing of this had happened, even in his dreams; life had passed uselessly without any pleasure, had been wasted for nothing, not even a pinch of snuff; there was nothing left in front, and if one looked back -- there was nothing there but losses, and such terrible ones, it made one cold all over. And why was it a man could not live so as to avoid these losses and misfortunes? One wondered why they had cut down the birch copse and the pine forest. Why was he walking with no reason on the grazing ground? Why do people always do what isn't needful? Why had Yakov all his life scolded, bellowed, shaken his fists, ill-treated his wife, and, one might ask, what necessity was there for him to frighten and insult the Jew that day? Why did people in general hinder each other from living? What losses were due to it! what terrible losses! If it were not for hatred and malice people would get immense benefit from one another.

In the evening and the night he had visions of the baby, of the willow, of fish, of slaughtered geese, and Marfa looking in profile like a bird that wants to drink, and the pale, pitiful face of Rothschild, and faces moved down from all sides and muttered of losses. He tossed from side to side, and got out of bed five times to play the fiddle.

In the morning he got up with an effort and went to the hospital. The same Maxim Nikolaitch told him to put a cold compress on his head, and gave him some powders, and from his tone and expression of face Yakov realized that it was a bad case and that no powders would be any use. As he went home afterwards, he reflected that death would be nothing but a benefit; he would not have to eat or drink, or pay taxes or offend people, and, as a man lies in his grave not for one year but for hundreds and thousands, if one reckoned it up the gain would be enormous. A man's life meant loss: death meant gain. This reflection was, of course, a just one, but yet it was bitter and mortifying; why was the order of the world so strange, that life, which is given to man only once, passes away without benefit?

He was not sorry to die, but at home, as soon as he saw his fiddle, it sent a pang to his heart and he felt sorry. He could not take the fiddle with him to the grave, and now it would be left forlorn, and the same thing would happen to it as to the birch copse and the pine forest. Everything in this world was wasted and would be wasted! Yakov went out of the hut and sat in the doorway, pressing the fiddle to his bosom. Thinking of his wasted, profitless life, he began to play, he did not know what, but it was plaintive and touching, and tears trickled down his cheeks. And the harder he thought, the more mournfully the fiddle wailed.

The latch clicked once and again, and Rothschild appeared at the gate. He walked across half the yard boldly, but seeing Yakov he stopped short, and seemed to shrink together, and probably from terror, began making signs with his hands as though he wanted to show on his fingers what o'clock it was.

"Come along, it's all right," said Yakov in a friendly tone, and he beckoned him to come up. "Come along!"

Looking at him mistrustfully and apprehensively, Rothschild began to advance, and stopped seven feet off.

"Be so good as not to beat me," he said, ducking. "Moisey Ilyitch has sent me again. 'Don't be afraid,' he said; 'go to Yakov again and tell him,' he said, 'we can't get on without him.' There is a wedding on Wednesday. . . . Ye---es! Mr. Shapovalov is marrying his daughter to a good man. . . . And it will be a grand wedding, oo-oo!" added the Jew, screwing up one eye.

"I can't come," said Yakov, breathing hard. "I'm ill, brother."

And he began playing again, and the tears gushed from his eyes on to the fiddle. Rothschild listened attentively, standing sideways to him and folding his arms on his chest. The scared and perplexed expression on his face, little by little, changed to a look of woe and suffering; he rolled his eyes as though he were experiencing an agonizing ecstasy, and articulated, "Vachhh!" and tears slowly ran down his cheeks and trickled on his greenish coat.

And Yakov lay in bed all the rest of the day grieving. In the evening, when the priest confessing him asked, Did he remember any special sin he had committed? straining his failing memory he thought again of Marfa's unhappy face, and the despairing shriek of the Jew when the dog bit him, and said, hardly audibly, "Give the fiddle to Rothschild."

"Very well," answered the priest.

And now everyone in the town asks where Rothschild got such a fine fiddle. Did he buy it or steal it? Or perhaps it had come to him as a pledge. He gave up the flute long ago, and now plays nothing but the fiddle. As plaintive sounds flow now from his bow, as came once from his flute, but when he tries to repeat what Yakov played, sitting in the doorway, the effect is something so sad and sorrowful that his audience weep, and he himself rolls his eyes and articulates "Vachhh! . . ." And this new air was so much liked in the town that the merchants and officials used to be continually sending for Rothschild and making him play it over and over again a dozen times.

THE STUDENT

At first the weather was fine and still. The thrushes were calling, and in the swamps close by something alive droned pitifully with a sound like blowing into an empty bottle. A snipe flew by, and the shot aimed at it rang out with a gay, resounding note in the spring air. But when it began to get dark in the forest a cold, penetrating wind blew inappropriately from the east, and everything sank into silence. Needles of ice stretched across the pools, and it felt cheerless, remote, and lonely in the forest. There was a whiff of winter.

Ivan Velikopolsky, the son of a sacristan, and a student of the clerical academy, returning home from shooting, kept walking on the path by the water-logged meadows. His fingers were numb and his face was burning with the wind. It seemed to him that the cold that had suddenly come on had destroyed the order and harmony of things, that nature itself felt ill at ease, and that was why the evening darkness was falling more rapidly than usual. All around it was deserted and peculiarly gloomy. The only light was one gleaming in the widows' gardens near the river; the village, over three miles away, and everything in the distance all round was plunged in the cold evening mist. The student remembered that, as he had left the house, his mother was sitting barefoot on the floor in the entryway, cleaning the samovar, while his father lay on the stove coughing; as it was Good Friday nothing had been cooked, and the student was terribly hungry. And now, shrinking from the cold, he thought that just such a wind had blown in the days of Rurik and in the time of Ivan the Terrible and Peter, and in their time there had been just the same desperate poverty and hunger, the same thatched roofs with holes in them, ignorance, misery, the same desolation around, the same darkness, the same feeling of oppression -- all these had existed, did exist, and would exist, and the lapse of a thousand years would make life no better. And he did not want to go home.

The gardens were called the widows' because they were kept by two widows, mother and daughter. A campfire was burning brightly with a crackling sound, throwing out light far around on the ploughed earth. The widow Vasilisa, a tall, fat old woman in a man's coat, was standing by and looking thoughtfully into the fire; her daughter Lukerya, a little pockmarked woman with a stupid-looking face, was sitting on the ground, washing a cauldron and spoons. Apparently they had just had supper. There was a sound of men's voices; it was the laborers watering their horses at the river.

"Here you have winter back again," said the student, going up to the campfire. "Good evening."

Vasilisa started, but at once recognized him and smiled cordially.

"I did not know you; God bless you," she said. "You'll be rich."

They talked. Vasilisa, a woman of experience who had been in service with the gentry, first as a wet-nurse, afterwards as a children's nurse expressed herself with refinement, and a soft, sedate smile never left her face; her daughter Lukerya, a village peasant woman who had been beaten by her husband, simply screwed up her eyes at the student and said nothing, and she had a strange expression like that of a deaf-mute.

"At just such a fire the Apostle Peter warmed himself," said the student, stretching out his hands to the fire, "so it must have been cold then, too. Ah, what a terrible night it must have been, granny! An utterly dismal long night!"

He looked round at the darkness, shook his head abruptly and asked:

"No doubt you have heard the reading of the Twelve Apostles?"

"Yes, I have," answered Vasilisa.

"If you remember, at the Last Supper Peter said to Jesus, 'I am ready to go with Thee into darkness and unto death.' And our Lord answered him thus: 'I say unto thee, Peter, before the cock croweth thou wilt have denied Me thrice.' After the supper Jesus went through the agony of death in the garden and prayed, and poor Peter was weary in spirit and faint, his eyelids were heavy and he could not struggle against sleep. He fell asleep. Then you heard how Judas the same night kissed Jesus and betrayed Him to His tormentors. They took Him bound to the high priest and beat Him, while Peter, exhausted, worn out with misery and alarm, hardly awake, you know, feeling that something awful was just going to happen on earth, followed behind. . . . He loved Jesus passionately, intensely, and now he saw from far off how He was beaten. . . . "

Lukerya left the spoons and fixed an immovable stare upon the student.

"They came to the high priest's," he went on; "they began to question Jesus, and meantime the laborers made a fire in the yard as it was cold, and warmed themselves. Peter, too, stood with them near the fire and warmed himself as I am doing. A woman, seeing him, said: 'He was with Jesus, too' -- that is as much as to say that he, too, should be taken to be questioned. And all the laborers that were standing near the fire must have looked sourly and suspiciously at him, because he was confused and said: 'I don't know Him.' A little while after again someone recognized him as one of Jesus' disciples and said: 'Thou, too, art one of them,' but again he denied it. And for the third time someone turned to him: 'Why, did I not see thee with Him in the garden today?' For the third time he denied it. And immediately after that time the cock crowed, and Peter, looking from afar off at Jesus, remembered the words He had said to him in the evening. . . . He remembered, he came to himself, went out of the yard and wept bitterly -- bitterly. In the Gospel it is written: 'He went out and wept bitterly.' I imagine it: the still, still, dark, dark garden, and in the stillness, faintly audible, smothered sobbing.. . . ."

The student sighed and sank into thought. Still smiling, Vasilisa suddenly gave a gulp, big tears flowed freely down her cheeks, and she screened her face from the fire with her sleeve as though ashamed of her tears, and Lukerya, staring immovably at the student, flushed crimson, and her expression became strained and heavy like that of someone enduring intense pain.

The laborers came back from the river, and one of them riding a horse was quite near, and the light from the fire quivered upon him. The student said good-night to the widows and went on. And again the darkness was about him and his fingers began to be numb. A cruel wind was blowing, winter really had come back and it did not feel as though Easter would be the day after tomorrow.

Now the student was thinking about Vasilisa: since she had shed tears all that had happened to Peter the night before the Crucifixion must have some relation to her. . . .

He looked round. The solitary light was still gleaming in the darkness and no figures could be seen near it now. The student thought again that if Vasilisa had shed tears, and her daughter had been troubled, it was evident that what he had just been telling them about, which had happened nineteen centuries ago, had a relation to the present -- to both women, to the desolate village, to himself, to all people. The old woman had wept, not because he could tell the story touchingly, but because Peter was near to her, because her whole being was interested in what was passing in Peter's soul.

And joy suddenly stirred in his soul, and he even stopped for a minute to take breath. "The past," he thought, "is linked with the present by an unbroken chain of events flowing one out of another." And it seemed to him that he had just seen both ends of that chain; that when he touched one end the other quivered.

When he crossed the river by the ferryboat and afterwards, mounting the hill, looked at his village and towards the west where the cold crimson sunset lay a narrow streak of light, he thought that truth and beauty which had guided human life there in the garden and in the yard of the high priest had continued without interruption to this day, and had evidently always been the chief thing in human life and in all earthly life, indeed; and the feeling of youth, health, vigor -- he was only twenty-two -- and the inexpressible sweet expectation of happiness, of unknown mysterious happiness, took possession of him little by little, and life seemed to him enchanting, marvellous, and full of lofty meaning.

THE TEACHER OF LITERATURE

I

There was the thud of horses' hoofs on the wooden floor; they brought out of the stable the black horse, Count Nulin; then the white, Giant; then his sister Maika. They were all magnificent, expensive horses. Old Shelestov saddled Giant and said, addressing his daughter Masha:

"Well, Marie Godefroi, come, get on! Hopla!"

Masha Shelestov was the youngest of the family; she was eighteen, but her family could not get used to thinking that she was not a little girl, and so they still called her Manya and Manyusa; and after there had been a circus in the town which she had eagerly visited, everyone began to call her Marie Godefroi.

"Hop-la!" she cried, mounting Giant. Her sister Varya got on Maika, Nikitin on Count Nulin, the officers on their horses, and the long picturesque cavalcade, with the officers in white tunics and the ladies in their riding habits, moved at a walking pace out of the yard.

Nikitin noticed that when they were mounting the horses and afterwards riding out into the street, Masha for some reason paid attention to no one but himself. She looked anxiously at him and at Count Nulin and said:

"You must hold him all the time on the curb, Sergey Vassilitch. Don't let him shy. He's pretending."

And either because her Giant was very friendly with Count Nulin, or perhaps by chance, she rode all the time beside Nikitin, as she had done the day before, and the day before that. And he looked at her graceful little figure sitting on the proud white beast, at her delicate profile, at the chimney-pot hat, which did not suit her at all and made her look older than her age -- looked at her with joy, with tenderness, with rapture; listened to her, taking in little of what she said, and thought:

"I promise on my honour, I swear to God, I won't be afraid and I'll speak to her today."

It was seven o'clock in the evening -- the time when the scent of white acacia and lilac is so strong that the air and the very trees seem heavy with the fragrance. The band was already playing in the town gardens. The horses made a resounding thud on the pavement, on all sides there were sounds of laughter, talk, and the banging of gates. The soldiers they met saluted the officers, the schoolboys bowed to Nikitin, and all the people who were hurrying to the gardens to hear the band were pleased at the sight of the party. And how warm it was! How soft-looking were the clouds scattered carelessly about the sky, how kindly and comforting the shadows of the poplars and the acacias, which stretched across the street and reached as far as the balconies and second stories of the houses on the other side.

They rode on out of the town and set off at a trot along the highroad. Here there was no scent of lilac and acacia, no music of the band, but there was the fragrance of the fields, there was the green of young rye and wheat, the marmots were squeaking, the rooks were cawing. Wherever one looked it was green, with only here and there black patches of bare ground, and far away to the left in the cemetery a white streak of apple-blossom.

They passed the slaughter-houses, then the brewery, and overtook a military band hastening to the suburban gardens.

"Polyansky has a very fine horse, I don't deny that," Masha said to Nikitin, with a glance towards the officer who was riding beside Varya. "But it has blemishes. That white patch on its left leg ought not to be there, and, look, it tosses its head. You can't train it not to now; it will toss its head till the end of its days."

Masha was as passionate a lover of horses as her father. She felt a pang when she saw other people with fine horses, and was pleased when she saw defects in them. Nikitin knew nothing about horses; it made absolutely no difference to him whether he held his horse on the bridle or on the curb, whether he trotted or galloped; he only felt that his position was strained and unnatural, and that consequently the officers who knew how to sit in their saddles must please Masha more than he could. And he was jealous of the officers.

As they rode by the suburban gardens someone suggested their going in and getting some seltzer-water. They went in. There were no trees but oaks in the gardens; they had only just come into leaf, so that through the young foliage the whole garden could still be seen with its platform, little tables, and swings, and the crows' nests were visible, looking like big hats. The party dismounted near a table and asked for seltzer-water. People they knew, walking about the garden, came up to them. Among them the army doctor in high boots, and the conductor of the band, waiting for the musicians. The doctor must have taken Nikitin for a student, for he asked: "Have you come for the summer holidays?"

"No, I am here permanently," answered Nikitin. "I am a teacher at the school."

"You don't say so?" said the doctor, with surprise. "So young and already a teacher?"

"Young, indeed! My goodness, I'm twenty-six!

"You have a beard and moustache, but yet one would never guess you were more than twenty-two or twenty-three. How young-looking you are!"

"What a beast!" thought Nikitin. "He, too, takes me for a whipper-snapper!"

He disliked it extremely when people referred to his youth, especially in the presence of women or the schoolboys. Ever since he had come to the town as a master in the school he had detested his own youthful appearance. The schoolboys were not afraid of him, old people called him "young man," ladies preferred dancing with him to listening to his long arguments, and he would have given a great deal to be ten years older.

From the garden they went on to the Shelestovs' farm. There they stopped at the gate and asked the bailiff's wife, Praskovya, to bring some new milk. Nobody drank the milk; they all looked at one another, laughed, and galloped back. As they rode back the band was playing in the suburban garden; the sun was setting behind the cemetery, and half the sky was crimson from the sunset.

Masha again rode beside Nikitin. He wanted to tell her how passionately he loved her, but he was afraid he would be overheard by the officers and Varya, and he was silent. Masha was silent, too, and he felt why she was silent and why she was riding beside him, and was so happy that the earth, the sky, the lights of the town, the black outline of the brewery -- all blended for him into something very pleasant and comforting, and it seemed to him as though Count Nulin were stepping on air and would climb up into the crimson sky.

They arrived home. The samovar was already boiling on the table, old Shelestov was sitting with his friends, officials in the Circuit Court, and as usual he was criticizing something.

"It's loutishness! " he said. "Loutishness and nothing more. Yes!"

Since Nikitin had been in love with Masha, everything at the Shelestovs' pleased him: the house, the garden, and the evening tea, and the wickerwork chairs, and the old nurse, and even the word "loutishness," which the old man was fond of using. The only thing he did not like was the number of cats and dogs and the Egyptian pigeons, who moaned disconsolately in a big cage in the verandah. There were so many house-dogs and yard-dogs that he had only learnt to recognize two of them in the course of his acquaintance with the Shelestovs: Mushka and Som. Mushka was a little mangy dog with a shaggy face, spiteful and spoiled. She hated Nikitin: when she saw him she put her head on one side, showed her teeth, and began: "Rrr . . . nga-nga-nga . . . rrr . . . !" Then she would get under his chair, and when he would try to drive her away she would go off into piercing yaps, and the family would say: "Don't be frightened. She doesn't bite. She is a good dog."

Som was a tall black dog with long legs and a tail as hard as a stick. At dinner and tea he usually moved about under the table, and thumped on people's boots and on the legs of the table with his tail. He was a good-natured, stupid dog, but Nikitin could not endure him because he had the habit of putting his head on people's knees at dinner and messing their trousers with saliva. Nikitin had more than once tried to hit him on his head with a knife-handle, to flip him on the nose, had abused him, had complained of him, but nothing saved his trousers.

After their ride the tea, jam, rusks, and butter seemed very nice. They all drank their first glass in silence and with great relish; over the second they began an argument. It was always Varya who started the arguments at tea; she was good-looking, handsomer than Masha, and was considered the cleverest and most cultured person in the house, and she behaved with dignity and severity, as an eldest daughter should who has taken the place of her dead mother in the house. As the mistress of the house, she felt herself entitled to wear a dressing-gown in the presence of her guests, and to call the officers by their surnames; she looked on Masha as a little girl, and talked to her as though she were a schoolmistress. She used to speak of herself as an old maid -- so she was certain she would marry.

Every conversation, even about the weather, she invariably turned into an argument. She had a passion for catching at words, pouncing on contradictions, quibbling over phrases. You would begin talking to her, and she would stare at you and suddenly interrupt: "Excuse me, excuse me, Petrov, the other day you said the very opposite!"

Or she would smile ironically and say: "I notice, though, you begin to advocate the principles of the secret police. I congratulate you."

If you jested or made a pun, you would hear her voice at once: "That's stale," "That's pointless." If an officer ventured on a joke, she would make a contemptuous grimace and say, "An army joke!"

And she rolled the *r* so impressively that Mushka invariably answered from under a chair, "Rrr . . . nga-nga-nga . . . !"

On this occasion at tea the argument began with Nikitin's mentioning the school examinations.

"Excuse me, Sergey Vassilitch," Varya interrupted him. "You say it's difficult for the boys. And whose fault is that, let me ask you? For instance, you set the boys in the eighth class an essay on 'Pushkin as a Psychologist.' To begin with, you shouldn't set such a difficult subject; and, secondly, Pushkin was not a psychologist. Shtchedrin now, or Dostoevsky let us say, is a different matter, but Pushkin is a great poet and nothing more."

"Shtchedrin is one thing, and Pushkin is another," Nikitin answered sulkily.

"I know you don't think much of Shtchedrin at the high school, but that's not the point. Tell me, in what sense is Pushkin a psychologist?"

"Why, do you mean to say he was not a psychologist? If you like, I'll give you examples."

And Nikitin recited several passages from "Onyegin" and then from "Boris Godunov."

"I see no psychology in that." Varya sighed. "The psychologist is the man who describes the recesses of the human soul, and that's fine poetry and nothing more."

"I know the sort of psychology you want," said Nikitin, offended. "You want someone to saw my finger with a blunt saw while I howl at the top of my voice -- that's what you mean by psychology."

"That's poor! But still you haven't shown me in what sense Pushkin is a psychologist?"

When Nikitin had to argue against anything that seemed to him narrow, conventional, or something of that kind, he usually leaped up from his seat, clutched at his head with both hands, and began with a moan, running from one end of the room to another. And it was the same now: he jumped up, clutched his head in his hands, and with a moan walked round the table, then he sat down a little way off.

The officers took his part. Captain Polyansky began assuring Varya that Pushkin really was a psychologist, and to prove it quoted two lines from Lermontov; Lieutenant Gernet said that if Pushkin had not been a psychologist they would not have erected a monument to him in Moscow.

"That's loutishness!" was heard from the other end of the table. "I said as much to the governor: 'It's loutishness, your Excellency,' I said."

"I won't argue any more," cried Nikitin. "It's unending. . . . Enough! Ach, get away, you nasty dog!" he cried to Som, who laid his head and paw on his knee.

"Rrr . . . nga-nga-nga!" came from under the table.

"Admit that you are wrong!" cried Varya. "Own up!"

But some young ladies came in, and the argument dropped of itself. They all went into the drawing-room. Varya sat down at the piano and began playing dances. They danced first a waltz, then a polka, then a quadrille with a grand chain which Captain Polyansky led through all the rooms, then a waltz again.

During the dancing the old men sat in the drawing-room, smoking and looking at the young people. Among them was Shebaldin, the director of the municipal bank, who was famed for his love of literature and dramatic art. He had founded the local Musical and Dramatic Society, and took part in the performances himself, confining himself, for some reason, to playing comic footmen or to reading in a sing-song voice "The Woman who was a Sinner." His nickname in the town was "the Mummy," as he was tall, very lean and scraggy, and always had a solemn air and a fixed, lustreless eye. He was so devoted to the dramatic art that he even shaved his moustache and beard, and this made him still more like a mummy.

After the grand chain, he shuffled up to Nikitin sideways, coughed, and said:

"I had the pleasure of being present during the argument at tea. I fully share your opinion. We are of one mind, and it would be a great pleasure to me to talk to you. Have you read Lessing on the dramatic art of Hamburg?"

"No, I haven't."

Shebaldin was horrified, and waved his hands as though he had burnt his fingers, and saying nothing more, staggered back from Nikitin. Shebaldin's appearance, his question, and his surprise, struck Nikitin as funny, but he thought none the less:

"It really is awkward. I am a teacher of literature, and to this day I've not read Lessing. I must read him."

Before supper the whole company, old and young, sat down to play "fate." They took two packs of cards: one pack was dealt round to the company, the other was laid on the table face downwards.

"The one who has this card in his hand," old Shelestov began solemnly, lifting the top card of the second pack, "is fated to go into the nursery and kiss nurse.

The pleasure of kissing the nurse fell to the lot of Shebaldin. They all crowded round him, took him to the nursery, and laughing and clapping their hands, made him kiss the nurse. There was a great uproar and shouting.

"Not so ardently!" cried Shelestov with tears of laughter. "Not so ardently!"

It was Nikitin's "fate" to hear the confessions of all. He sat on a chair in the middle of the drawing-room. A shawl was brought and put over his head. The first who came to confess to him was Varya.

"I know your sins," Nikitin began, looking in the darkness at her stern profile. "Tell me, madam, how do you explain your walking with Polyansky every day? Oh, it's not for nothing she walks with an hussar!"

"That's poor," said Varya, and walked away.

Then under the shawl he saw the shine of big motionless eyes, caught the lines of a dear profile in the dark, together with a familiar, precious fragrance which reminded Nikitin of Masha's room.

"Marie Godefroi," he said, and did not know his own voice, it was so soft and tender, "what are your sins?"

Masha screwed up her eyes and put out the tip of her tongue at him, then she laughed and went away. And a minute later she was standing in the middle of the room, clapping her hands and crying:

"Supper, supper, supper!"

And they all streamed into the dining-room. At supper Varya had another argument, and this time with her father. Polyansky ate stolidly, drank red wine, and described to Nikitin how once in a winter campaign he had stood all night up to his knees in a bog; the enemy was so near that they were not allowed to speak or smoke, the night was cold and dark, a piercing wind was blowing. Nikitin listened and stole side-glances at Masha. She was gazing at him immovably, without blinking, as though she was pondering something or was lost in a reverie. . . . It was pleasure and agony to him both at once.

"Why does she look at me like that?" was the question that fretted him. "It's awkward. People may notice it. Oh, how young, how naïve she is!"

The party broke up at midnight. When Nikitin went out at the gate, a window opened on the first-floor, and Masha showed herself at it.

"Sergey Vassilitch!" she called.

"What is it?"

"I tell you what . . ." said Masha, evidently thinking of something to say. "I tell you what. . . Polyansky said he would come in a day or two with his camera and take us all. We must meet here."

"Very well."

Masha vanished, the window was slammed, and someone immediately began playing the piano in the house.

"Well, it is a house!" thought Nikitin while he crossed the street. "A house in which there is no moaning except from Egyptian pigeons, and they only do it because they have no other means of expressing their joy!"

But the Shelestovs were not the only festive household. Nikitin had not gone two hundred paces before he heard the strains of a piano from another house. A little further he met a peasant playing the balalaika at the gate. In the gardens the band struck up a potpourri of Russian songs.

Nikitin lived nearly half a mile from the Shelestoys' in a flat of eight rooms at the rent of three hundred roubles a year, which he shared with his colleague Ippolit Ippolititch, a teacher of geography and history. When Nikitin went in this Ippolit Ippolititch, a snub-nosed, middle-aged man with a reddish beard, with a coarse, good-natured, unintellectual face like a workman's, was sitting at the table correcting his pupils' maps. He considered that the most important and necessary part of the study of geography was the drawing of maps, and of the study of history the learning of dates: he would sit for nights together correcting in blue pencil the maps drawn by the boys and girls he taught, or making chronological tables.

"What a lovely day it has been!" said Nikitin, going in to him. "I wonder at you -- how can you sit indoors?"

Ippolit Ippolititch was not a talkative person; he either remained silent or talked of things which everybody knew already. Now what he answered was:

"Yes, very fine weather. It's May now; we soon shall have real summer. And summer's a very different thing from winter. In the winter you have to heat the stoves, but in summer you can keep warm without. In summer you have your window open at night and still are warm, and in winter you are cold even with the double frames in."

Nikitin had not sat at the table for more than one minute before he was bored.

"Good-night!" he said, getting up and yawning. "I wanted to tell you something romantic concerning myself, but you are -- geography! If one talks to you of love, you will ask one at once, 'What was the date of the Battle of Kalka?' Confound you, with your battles and your capes in Siberia!"

"What are you cross about?"

"Why, it is vexatious!"

And vexed that he had not spoken to Masha, and that he had no one to talk to of his love, he went to his study and lay down upon the sofa. It was dark and still in the study. Lying gazing into the darkness, Nikitin for some reason began thinking how in two or three years he would go to Petersburg, how Masha would see him off at the station and would cry; in Petersburg he would get a long letter from her in which she would entreat him to come home as quickly as possible. And he would write to her. . . . He would begin his letter like that: "My dear little rat!"

"Yes, my dear little rat!" he said, and he laughed.

He was lying in an uncomfortable position. He put his arms under his head and put his left leg over the back of the sofa. He felt more comfortable. Meanwhile a pale light was more and more perceptible at the windows, sleepy cocks crowed in the yard. Nikitin went on thinking how he would come back from Petersburg, how Masha would meet him at the station, and with a shriek of delight would fling herself on his neck; or, better still, he would cheat her and come home by stealth late at night: the cook would open the door, then he would go on tiptoe to the bedroom, undress noiselessly, and jump into bed! And she would wake up and be overjoyed.

It was beginning to get quite light. By now there were no windows, no study. On the steps of the brewery by which they had ridden that day Masha was sitting, saying something. Then she took Nikitin by the arm and went with him to the suburban garden. There he saw the oaks and, the crows' nests like hats. One of the nests rocked; out of it peeped Shebaldin, shouting loudly: "You have not read Lessing!"

Nikitin shuddered all over and opened his eyes. Ippolit Ippolititch was standing before the sofa, and throwing back his head, was putting on his cravat.

"Get up; it's time for school," he said. "You shouldn't sleep in your clothes; it spoils your clothes. You should sleep in your bed, undressed."

And as usual he began slowly and emphatically saying what everybody knew.

Nikitin's first lesson was on Russian language in the second class. When at nine o'clock punctually he went into the classroom, he saw written on the blackboard two large letters -- *M. S.* That, no doubt, meant Masha Shelestov.

"They've scented it out already, the rascals . . ." thought Nikitin. "How is it they know everything?"

The second lesson was in the fifth class. And there two letters, *M. S.*, were written on the blackboard; and when he went out of the classroom at the end of the lesson, he heard the shout behind him as though from a theatre gallery:

"Hurrah for Masha Shelestov!"

His head was heavy from sleeping in his clothes, his limbs were weighted down with inertia. The boys, who were expecting every day to break up before the examinations, did nothing, were restless, and so bored that they got into mischief. Nikitin, too, was restless, did not notice their pranks, and was continually going to the window. He could see the street brilliantly lighted up with the sun; above the houses the blue limpid sky, the birds, and far, far away, beyond the gardens and the houses, vast indefinite distance, the forests in the blue haze, the smoke from a passing train. . . .

Here two officers in white tunics, playing with their whips, passed in the street in the shade of the acacias. Here a lot of Jews, with grey beards, and caps on, drove past in a waggonette. . . . The governess walked by with the director's granddaughter. Som ran by in the company of two other dogs. . . . And then Varya, wearing a simple grey dress and red stockings, carrying the "Vyestnik Evropi" in her hand, passed by. She must have been to the town library. . . .

And it would be a long time before lessons were over at three o'clock! And after school he could not go home nor to the Shelestovs', but must go to give a lesson at Wolf's. This Wolf, a wealthy Jew who had turned Lutheran, did not send his children to the high school, but had them taught at home by the high-school masters, and paid five roubles a lesson.

He was bored, bored, bored.

At three o'clock he went to Wolf's and spent there, as it seemed to him, an eternity. He left there at five o'clock, and before seven he had to be at the high school again to a meeting of the masters -- to draw up the plan for the *viva voce* examination of the fourth and sixth classes.

When late in the evening he left the high school and went to the Shelestovs', his heart was beating and his face was flushed. A month before, even a week before, he had, every time that he made up his mind to speak to her, prepared a whole speech, with an introduction and a conclusion. Now he had not one word ready;

everything was in a muddle in his head, and all he knew was that today he would *certainly* declare himself, and that it was utterly impossible to wait any longer.

"I will ask her to come to the garden," he thought; "we'll walk about a little and I'll speak."

There was not a soul in the hall; he went into the dining-room and then into the drawing-room. . . . There was no one there either. He could hear Varya arguing with someone upstairs and the clink of the dressmaker's scissors in the nursery.

There was a little room in the house which had three names: the little room, the passage room, and the dark room. There was a big cupboard in it where they kept medicines, gunpowder, and their hunting gear. Leading from this room to the first floor was a narrow wooden staircase where cats were always asleep. There were two doors in it -- one leading to the nursery, one to the drawing-room. When Nikitin went into this room to go upstairs, the door from the nursery opened and shut with such a bang that it made the stairs and the cupboard tremble; Masha, in a dark dress, ran in with a piece of blue material in her hand, and, not noticing Nikitin, darted towards the stairs.

"Stay . . ." said Nikitin, stopping her. "Good-evening, Godefroi. . . . Allow me. . . ."

He gasped, he did not know what to say; with one hand he held her hand and with the other the blue material. And she was half frightened, half surprised, and looked at him with big eyes.

"Allow me . . ." Nikitin went on, afraid she would go away. "There's something I must say to you. . . . Only . . . it's inconvenient here. I cannot, I am incapable. . . . Understand, Godefroi, I can't -- that's all . . . ."

The blue material slipped on to the floor, and Nikitin took Masha by the other hand. She turned pale, moved her lips, then stepped back from Nikitin and found herself in the corner between the wall and the cupboard.

"On my honour, I assure you . . ." he said softly. "Masha, on my honour. . . ."

She threw back her head and he kissed her lips, and that the kiss might last longer he put his fingers to her cheeks; and it somehow happened that he found himself in the corner between the cupboard and the wall, and she put her arms round his neck and pressed her head against his chin.

Then they both ran into the garden. The Shelestoys had a garden of nine acres. There were about twenty old maples and lime-trees in it; there was one fir-tree, and all the rest were fruit-trees: cherries, apples, pears, horse-chestnuts, silvery olive-trees. . . . There were heaps of flowers, too.

Nikitin and Masha ran along the avenues in silence, laughed, asked each other from time to time disconnected questions which they did not answer. A crescent moon was shining over the garden, and drowsy tulips and irises were stretching up from the dark grass in its faint light, as though entreating for words of love for them, too.

When Nikitin and Masha went back to the house, the officers and the young ladies were already assembled and dancing the mazurka. Again Polyansky led the grand chain through all the rooms, again after dancing they played "fate." Before supper, when the visitors had gone into the dining-room, Masha, left alone with Nikitin, pressed close to him and said:

"You must speak to papa and Varya yourself; I am ashamed."

After supper he talked to the old father. After listening to him, Shelestov thought a little and said:

"I am very grateful for the honour you do me and my daughter, but let me speak to you as a friend. I will speak to you, not as a father, but as one gentleman to another. Tell me, why do you want to be married so young? Only peasants are married so young, and that, of course, is loutishness. But why should you? Where's the satisfaction of putting on the fetters at your age?"

"I am not young!" said Nikitin, offended. "I am in my twenty-seventh year."

"Papa, the farrier has come!" cried Varya from the other room.

And the conversation broke off. Varya, Masha, and Polyansky saw Nikitin home. When they reached his gate, Varya said:

"Why is it your mysterious Metropolit Metropolititch never shows himself anywhere? He might come and see us."

The mysterious Ippolit Ippolititch was sitting on his bed, taking off his trousers, when Nikitin went in to him.

"Don't go to bed, my dear fellow," said Nikitin breathlessly. "Stop a minute; don't go to bed!"

Ippolit Ippolititch put on his trousers hurriedly and asked in a flutter:

"What is it?"

"I am going to be married."

Nikitin sat down beside his companion, and looking at him wonderingly, as though surprised at himself, said:

"Only fancy, I am going to be married! To Masha Shelestov! I made an offer today."

"Well? She seems a good sort of girl. Only she is very young."

"Yes, she is young," sighed Nikitin, and shrugged his shoulders with a careworn air. "Very, very young!"

"She was my pupil at the high school. I know her. She wasn't bad at geography, but she was no good at history. And she was inattentive in class, too."

Nikitin for some reason felt suddenly sorry for his companion, and longed to say something kind and comforting to him.

"My dear fellow, why don't you get married?" he asked. "Why don't you marry Varya, for instance? She is a splendid, first-rate girl! It's true she is very fond of arguing, but a heart . . . what a heart! She was just asking about you. Marry her, my dear boy! Eh?"

He knew perfectly well that Varya would not marry this dull, snub-nosed man, but still persuaded him to marry her -- why?

"Marriage is a serious step," said Ippolit Ippolititch after a moment's thought. "One has to look at it all round and weigh things thoroughly; it's not to be done rashly. Prudence is always a good thing, and especially in marriage, when a man, ceasing to be a bachelor, begins a new life."

And he talked of what everyone has known for ages. Nikitin did not stay to listen, said goodnight, and went to his own room. He undressed quickly and quickly got into bed, in order to be able to think the sooner of his happiness, of Masha, of the future; he smiled, then suddenly recalled that he had not read Lessing.

"I must read him," he thought. "Though, after all, why should I? Bother him!"

And exhausted by his happiness, he fell asleep at once and went on smiling till the morning.

He dreamed of the thud of horses' hoofs on a wooden floor; he dreamed of the black horse Count Nulin, then of the white Giant and its sister Maika, being led out of the stable.

II

"It was very crowded and noisy in the church, and once someone cried out, and the head priest, who was marrying Masha and me, looked through his spectacles at the crowd, and said severely: 'Don't move about the church, and don't make a noise, but stand quietly and pray. You should have the fear of God in your hearts.'

"My best men were two of my colleagues, and Masha's best men were Captain Polyansky and Lieutenant Gernet. The bishop's choir sang superbly. The sputtering of the candles, the brilliant light, the gorgeous dresses, the officers, the numbers of gay, happy faces, and a special ethereal look in Masha, everything together -- the surroundings and the words of the wedding prayers -- moved me to tears and filled me with triumph. I thought how my life had blossomed, how poetically it was shaping itself! Two years ago I was still a student, I was living in cheap furnished rooms, without money, without relations, and, as I fancied then, with nothing to look forward to. Now I am a teacher in the high school in one of the best provincial towns, with a secure income, loved, spoiled. It is for my sake, I thought, this crowd is collected, for my sake three candelabra have been lighted, the deacon is booming, the choir is doing its best; and it's for my sake that this young creature, whom I soon shall call my wife, is so young, so elegant, and so joyful. I recalled our first meetings, our rides into the country, my declaration of love and the weather, which, as though expressly, was so exquisitely fine all the summer; and the happiness which at one time in my old rooms seemed to me possible only in novels and stories, I was now experiencing in reality -- I was now, as it were, holding it in my hands.

"After the ceremony they all crowded in disorder round Masha and me, expressed their genuine pleasure, congratulated us and wished us joy. The brigadier-general, an old man of seventy, confined himself to congratulating Masha, and said to her in a squeaky, aged voice, so loud that it could be heard all over the church:

" 'I hope that even after you are married you may remain the rose you are now, my dear.'

"The officers, the director, and all the teachers smiled from politeness, and I was conscious of an agreeable artificial smile on my face, too. Dear Ippolit Ippolititch, the teacher of history and geography, who always says what everyone has heard before, pressed my hand warmly and said with feeling:

" 'Hitherto you have been unmarried and have lived alone, and now you are married and no longer single.'

"From the church we went to a two-storied house which I am receiving as part of the dowry. Besides that house Masha is bringing me twenty thousand roubles, as well as a piece of waste land with a shanty on it, where I am told there are numbers of hens and ducks which are not looked after and are turning wild. When I got home from the church, I stretched myself at full length on the low sofa in my new study and began to smoke; I felt snug, cosy, and comfortable, as I never had in my life before. And meanwhile the wedding party were shouting 'Hurrah!' while a wretched band in the hall played flourishes and all sorts of trash. Varya, Masha's sister, ran into the study with a wineglass in her hand, and with a queer, strained expression, as though her mouth were full of water; apparently she had meant to go on further, but she suddenly burst out laughing and sobbing, and the wineglass crashed on the floor. We took her by the arms and led her away.

" 'Nobody can understand!' she muttered afterwards, lying on the old nurse's bed in a back room. 'Nobody, nobody! My God, nobody can understand!'

"But everyone understood very well that she was four years older than her sister Masha, and still unmarried, and that she was crying, not from envy, but from the melancholy consciousness that her time was passing, and perhaps had passed. When they danced the quadrille, she was back in the drawing-room with a tear-stained and heavily powdered face, and I saw Captain Polyansky holding a plate of ice before her while she ate it with a spoon.

"It is past five o'clock in the morning. I took up my diary to describe my complete and perfect happiness, and thought I would write a good six pages, and read it tomorrow to Masha; but, strange to say, everything is muddled in my head and as misty as a dream, and I can remember vividly nothing but that episode with Varya, and I want to write, 'Poor Varya!' I could go on sitting here and writing 'Poor Varya!' By the way, the trees have begun rustling; it will rain. The crows are cawing, and my Masha, who has just gone to sleep, has for some reason a sorrowful face."

For a long while afterwards Nikitin did not write his diary. At the beginning of August he had the school examinations, and after the fifteenth the classes began. As a rule he set off for school before nine in the morning, and before ten o'clock he was looking at his watch and pining for his Masha and his new house. In the lower forms he would set some boy to dictate, and while the boys were writing, would sit in the window with his eyes shut, dreaming; whether he dreamed of the future or recalled the past, everything seemed to him equally delightful, like a fairy tale. In the senior classes they were reading aloud Gogol or Pushkin's prose works, and that made him sleepy; people, trees, fields, horses, rose before his imagination, and he would say with a sigh, as though fascinated by the author:

"How lovely!"

At the midday recess Masha used to send him lunch in a snow-white napkin, and he would eat it slowly, with pauses, to prolong the enjoyment of it; and Ippolit Ippolititch, whose lunch as a rule consisted of nothing but bread, looked at him with respect and envy, and gave expression to some familiar fact, such as:

"Men cannot live without food."

After school Nikitin went straight to give his private lessons, and when at last by six o'clock he got home, he felt excited and anxious, as though he had been away for a year. He would run upstairs breathless, find Masha, throw his arms round her, and kiss her and swear that he loved her, that he could not live without her, declare that he had missed her fearfully, and ask her in trepidation how she was and why she looked so depressed. Then they would dine together. After dinner he would lie on the sofa in his study and smoke, while she sat beside him and talked in a low voice.

His happiest days now were Sundays and holidays, when he was at home from morning till evening. On those days he took part in the naïve but extraordinarily pleasant life which reminded him of a pastoral idyl. He was never weary of watching how his sensible and practical Masha was arranging her nest, and anxious to show that he was of some use in the house, he would do something useless -- for instance, bring the chaise out of the stable and look at it from every side. Masha had installed a regular dairy with three cows, and in her cellar she had many jugs of milk and pots of sour cream, and she kept it all for butter. Sometimes, by way of a joke, Nikitin would ask her for a glass of milk, and she would be quite upset because it was against her rules; but he would laugh and throw his arms round her, saying:

"There, there; I was joking, my darling! I was joking!"

Or he would laugh at her strictness when, finding in the cupboard some stale bit of cheese or sausage as hard as a stone, she would say seriously:

"They will eat that in the kitchen."

He would observe that such a scrap was only fit for a mousetrap, and she would reply warmly that men knew nothing about housekeeping, and that it was just the same to the servants if you were to send down a hundredweight of savouries to the kitchen. He would agree, and embrace her enthusiastically. Everything that was just in what she said seemed to him extraordinary and amazing; and what did not fit in with his convictions seemed to him naïve and touching.

Sometimes he was in a philosophical mood, and he would begin to discuss some abstract subject while she listened and looked at his face with curiosity.

"I am immensely happy with you, my joy," he used to say, playing with her fingers or plaiting and unplaiting her hair. "But I don't look upon this happiness of mine as something that has come to me by chance, as though it had dropped from heaven. This happiness is a perfectly natural, consistent, logical consequence. I believe that man is the creator of his own happiness, and now I am enjoying just what I have myself created. Yes, I speak without false modesty: I have created this happiness myself and I have a right to it. You know my past. My unhappy childhood, without father or mother; my depressing youth, poverty -- all this was a struggle, all this was the path by which I made my way to happiness. . . ."

In October the school sustained a heavy loss: Ippolit Ippolititch was taken ill with erysipelas on the head and died. For two days before his death he was unconscious and delirious, but even in his delirium he said nothing that was not perfectly well known to everyone.

"The Volga flows into the Caspian Sea. . . . Horses eat oats and hay. . . ."

There were no lessons at the high school on the day of his funeral. His colleagues and pupils were the coffin-bearers, and the school choir sang all the way to the grave the anthem "Holy God." Three priests, two deacons, all his pupils and the staff of the boys' high school, and the bishop's choir in their best kaftans, took part in the procession. And passers-by who met the solemn procession, crossed themselves and said:

"God grant us all such a death."

Returning home from the cemetery much moved, Nikitin got out his diary from the table and wrote:

"We have just consigned to the tomb Ippolit Ippolititch Ryzhitsky. Peace to your ashes, modest worker! Masha, Varya, and all the women at the funeral, wept from genuine feeling, perhaps because they knew this uninteresting, humble man had never been loved by a woman. I wanted to say a warm word at my colleague's grave, but I was warned that this might displease the director, as he did not like our poor friend. I believe that this is the first day since my marriage that my heart has been heavy."

There was no other event of note in the scholastic year.

The winter was mild, with wet snow and no frost; on Epiphany Eve, for instance, the wind howled all night as though it were autumn, and water trickled off the roofs; and in the morning, at the ceremony of the blessing of the water, the police allowed no one to go on the river, because they said the ice was swelling up and looked dark. But in spite of bad weather Nikitin's life was as happy as in summer. And, indeed, he acquired another source of pleasure; he learned to play *vint*. Only one thing troubled him, moved him to anger, and seemed to prevent him from being perfectly happy: the cats and dogs which formed part of his wife's dowry. The rooms, especially in the morning, always smelt like a menagerie, and nothing could destroy the odour; the cats frequently fought with the dogs. The spiteful beast Mushka was fed a dozen times a day; she still refused to recognize Nikitin and growled at him: "Rrr . . . nga-nga-nga!"

One night in Lent he was returning home from the club where he had been playing cards. It was dark, raining, and muddy. Nikitin had an unpleasant feeling at the bottom of his heart and could not account for it. He did not know whether it was because he had lost twelve roubles at cards, or whether because one of the players, when they were settling up, had said that of course Nikitin had pots of money, with obvious reference to his wife's portion. He did not regret the twelve roubles, and there was nothing offensive in what had been said; but, still, there was the unpleasant feeling. He did not even feel a desire to go home.

"Foo, how horrid!" he said, standing still at a lamp-post.

It occurred to him that he did not regret the twelve roubles because he got them for nothing. If he had been a working man he would have known the value of every farthing, and would not have been so careless whether he lost or won. And his good-fortune had all, he reflected, come to him by chance, for nothing, and really was as superfluous for him as medicine for the healthy. If, like the vast majority of people, he had been harassed by anxiety for his daily bread, had been struggling for existence, if his back and chest had ached from work, then supper, a warm snug home, and domestic happiness, would have been the necessity, the compensation, the crown of his life; as it was, all this had a strange, indefinite significance for him.

"Foo, how horrid!" he repeated, knowing perfectly well that these reflections were in themselves a bad sign.

When he got home Masha was in bed: she was breathing evenly and smiling, and was evidently sleeping with great enjoyment. Near her the white cat lay curled up, purring. While Nikitin lit the candle and lighted his cigarette, Masha woke up and greedily drank a glass of water.

"I ate too many sweets," she said, and laughed. "Have you been home?" she asked after a pause.

"No."

Nikitin knew already that Captain Polyansky, on whom Varya had been building great hopes of late, was being transferred to one of the western provinces, and was already making his farewell visits in the town, and so it was depressing at his father-in-law's.

"Varya looked in this evening," said Masha, sitting up. "She did not say anything, but one could see from her face how wretched she is, poor darling! I can't bear Polyansky. He is fat and bloated, and when he walks or dances his cheeks shake. . . . He is not a man I would choose. But, still, I did think he was a decent person."

"I think he is a decent person now," said Nikitin.

"Then why has he treated Varya so badly?"

"Why badly?" asked Nikitin, beginning to feel irritation against the white cat, who was stretching and arching its back. "As far as I know, he has made no proposal and has given her no promises."

"Then why was he so often at the house? If he didn't mean to marry her, he oughtn't to have come."

Nikitin put out the candle and got into bed. But he felt disinclined to lie down and to sleep. He felt as though his head were immense and empty as a barn, and that new, peculiar thoughts were wandering about in it like tall shadows. He thought that, apart from the soft light of the ikon lamp, that beamed upon their quiet domestic happiness, that apart from this little world in which he and this cat lived so peacefully and happily, there was another world. . . . And he had a passionate, poignant longing to be in that other world, to work himself at some factory or big workshop, to address big audiences, to write, to publish, to raise a stir, to exhaust himself, to suffer. . . . He wanted something that would engross him till he forgot himself, ceased to care for the personal happiness which yielded him only sensations so monotonous. And suddenly there rose vividly before his imagination the figure of Shebaldin with his clean-shaven face, saying to him with horror: "You haven't even read Lessing! You are quite behind the times! How you have gone to seed!"

Masha woke up and again drank some water. He glanced at her neck, at her plump shoulders and throat, and remembered the word the brigadier-general had used in church -- "rose."

"Rose," he muttered, and laughed.

His laugh was answered by a sleepy growl from Mushka under the bed: "Rrr . . . nga-nga-nga . . . !"

A heavy anger sank like a cold weight on his heart, and he felt tempted to say something rude to Masha, and even to jump up and hit her; his heart began throbbing.

"So then," he asked, restraining himself, "since I went to your house, I was bound in duty to marry you?"

"Of course. You know that very well."

"That's nice." And a minute later he repeated: "That's nice."

To relieve the throbbing of his heart, and to avoid saying too much, Nikitin went to his study and lay down on the sofa, without a pillow; then he lay on the floor on the carpet.

"What nonsense it is!" he said to reassure himself. "You are a teacher, you are working in the noblest of callings. . . . What need have you of any other world? What rubbish!"

But almost immediately he told himself with conviction that he was not a real teacher, but simply a government employé, as commonplace and mediocre as the Czech who taught Greek. He had never had a vocation for teaching, he knew nothing of the theory of teaching, and never had been interested in the subject; he did not know how to treat children; he did not understand the significance of what he taught, and perhaps did not teach the right things. Poor Ippolit Ippolititch had been frankly stupid, and all the boys, as well as his colleagues, knew what he was and what to expect from him; but he, Nikitin, like the Czech, knew how to conceal his stupidity and cleverly deceived everyone by pretending that, thank God, his teaching was a success. These new ideas frightened Nikitin; he rejected them, called them stupid, and believed that all this was due to his nerves, that he would laugh at himself.

And he did, in fact, by the morning laugh at himself and call himself an old woman; but it was clear to him that his peace of mind was lost, perhaps, forever, and that in that little two-story house happiness was henceforth impossible for him. He realized that the illusion had evaporated, and that a new life of unrest and clear sight was beginning which was incompatible with peace and personal happiness.

Next day, which was Sunday, he was at the school chapel, and there met his colleagues and the director. It seemed to him that they were entirely preoccupied with concealing their ignorance and discontent with life, and he, too, to conceal his uneasiness, smiled affably and talked of trivialities. Then he went to the station and saw the mail train come in and go out, and it was agreeable to him to be alone and not to have to talk to anyone.

At home he found Varya and his father-in-law, who had come to dinner. Varya's eyes were red with crying, and she complained of a headache, while Shelestov ate a great deal, saying that young men nowadays were unreliable, and that there was very little gentlemanly feeling among them.

"It's loutishness!" he said. "I shall tell him so to his face: 'It's loutishness, sir,' I shall say."

Nikitin smiled affably and helped Masha to look after their guests, but after dinner he went to his study and shut the door.

The March sun was shining brightly in at the windows and shedding its warm rays on the table. It was only the twentieth of the month, but already the cabmen were driving with wheels, and the starlings were noisy in the garden. It was just the weather in which Masha would come in, put one arm round his neck, tell him the horses were saddled or the chaise was at the door, and ask him what she should put on to keep warm. Spring was beginning as exquisitely as last spring, and it promised the same joys. . . . But Nikitin was thinking that it would be nice to take a holiday and go to Moscow, and stay at his old lodgings there. In the next room they were drinking coffee and talking of Captain Polyansky, while he tried not to listen and wrote in his diary: "Where am I, my God? I am surrounded by vulgarity and vulgarity. Wearisome, insignificant people, pots of sour cream, jugs of milk, cockroaches, stupid women. . . . There is nothing more terrible, mortifying, and distressing than vulgarity. I must escape from here, I must escape today, or I shall go out of my mind!"

AT A COUNTRY HOUSE

Pavel Ilyitch Rashevitch walked up and down, stepping softly on the floor covered with little Russian plaids, and casting a long shadow on the wall and ceiling while his guest, Meier, the deputy examining magistrate, sat on the sofa with one leg drawn up under him smoking and listening. The clock already pointed to eleven, and there were sounds of the table being laid in the room next to the study.

"Say what you like," Rashevitch was saying, "from the standpoint of fraternity, equality, and the rest of it, Mitka, the swineherd, is perhaps a man the same as Goethe and Frederick the Great; but take your stand on a scientific basis, have the courage to look facts in the face, and it will be obvious to you that blue blood is not a mere prejudice, that it is not a feminine invention. Blue blood, my dear fellow, has an historical justification, and to refuse to recognize it is, to my thinking, as strange as to refuse to recognize the antlers on a stag. One must reckon with facts! You are a law student and have confined your attention to the humane studies, and you can still flatter yourself with illusions of equality, fraternity, and so on; I am an incorrigible Darwinian, and for me words such as lineage, aristocracy, noble blood, are not empty sounds."

Rashevitch was roused and spoke with feeling. His eyes sparkled, his pince-nez would not stay on his nose, he kept nervously shrugging his shoulders and blinking, and at the word " Darwinian" he looked jauntily in the looking-glass and combed his grey beard with both hands. He was wearing a very short and shabby reefer jacket and narrow trousers; the rapidity of his movements, his jaunty air, and his abbreviated jacket all seemed out of keeping with him, and his big comely head, with long hair suggestive of a bishop or a veteran poet, seemed to have been fixed on to the body of a tall, lanky, affected youth. When he stood with his legs wide apart, his long shadow looked like a pair of scissors.

He was fond of talking, and he always fancied that he was saying something new and original. In the presence of Meier he was conscious of an unusual flow of spirits and rush of ideas. He found the examining magistrate sympathetic, and was stimulated by his youth, his health, his good manners, his dignity, and, above all, by his cordial attitude to himself and his family. Rashevitch was not a favourite with his acquaintances; as a rule they fought shy of him, and, as he knew, declared that he had driven his wife into her grave with his talking, and they called him, behind his back, a spiteful creature and a toad. Meier, a man new to the district and unprejudiced, visited him often and readily and had even been known to say that Rashevitch and his daughters were the only people in the district with whom he felt as much at home as with his own people. Rashevitch liked him too, because he was a young man who might be a good match for his elder daughter, Genya.

And now, enjoying his ideas and the sound of his own voice, and looking with pleasure at the plump but well-proportioned, neatly cropped, correct Meier, Rashevitch dreamed of how he would arrange his daughter's marriage with a good man, and then how all his worries over the estate would pass to his son-in-law. Hateful worries! The interest owing to the bank had not been paid for the last two quarters, and fines and arrears of all sorts had mounted up to more than two thousand.

"To my mind there can be no doubt," Rashevitch went on, growing more and more enthusiastic, "that if a Richard Coeur-de-Lion, or Frederick Barbarossa, for instance, is brave and noble those qualities will pass by heredity to his son, together with the convolutions and bumps of the brain, and if that courage and nobility of soul are preserved in the son by means of education and exercise, and if he marries a princess who is also noble and brave, those qualities will be transmitted to his grandson, and so on, until they become a generic characteristic and pass organically into the flesh and blood. Thanks to a strict sexual selection, to the fact that high-born families have instinctively guarded themselves against marriage with their inferiors, and young men of high rank have not married just anybody, lofty, spiritual qualities have been transmitted from generation to generation in their full purity, have been preserved, and as time goes on have, through exercise, become more exalted and lofty. For the fact that there is good in humanity we are indebted to nature, to the normal, natural, consistent order of things, which has throughout the ages scrupulously segregated blue blood from plebeian. Yes, my dear boy, no low lout, no cook's son has given us literature, science, art, law, conceptions of honour and duty. . . . For all these things mankind is indebted exclusively to the aristocracy, and from that point of view, the point of view of natural history, an inferior Sobakevitch by the very fact of his blue blood is superior and more useful than the very best merchant, even though the latter may have built fifteen museums. Say what you like! And when I refuse to shake hands with a low lout or a cook's son, or to let him sit down to table with me, by that very act I am safeguarding what is the best thing on earth, and am carrying out one of Mother Nature's finest designs for leading us up to perfection. . ."

Rashevitch stood still, combing his beard with both hands; his shadow, too, stood still on the wall, looking like a pair of scissors.

"Take Mother-Russia now," he went on, thrusting his hands in his pockets and standing first on his heels and then on his toes. "Who are her best people? Take our first-rate painters, writers, composers. . . . Who are they? They were all of aristocratic origin. Pushkin, Lermontov, Turgenev, Gontcharov, Tolstoy, they were not sexton's children."

"Gontcharov was a merchant," said Meier.

"Well, the exception only proves the rule. Besides, Gontcharov's genius is quite open to dispute. But let us drop names and turn to facts. What would you say, my good sir, for instance, to this eloquent fact: when one of the mob forces his way where he has not been permitted before, into society, into the world of learning, of literature, into the Zemstvo or the law courts, observe, Nature herself, first of all, champions the higher rights of humanity, and is the first to wage war on the rabble. As soon as the plebeian forces himself into a place he is not fit for he begins to ail, to go into consumption, to go out of his mind, and to degenerate, and nowhere do we find so many puny, neurotic wrecks, consumptives, and starvelings of all sorts as among these darlings. They die like flies in autumn. If it were not for this providential degeneration there would not have been a stone left standing of our civilization, the rabble would have demolished everything. Tell me, if you please, what has the inroad of the barbarians given us so far? What has the rabble brought with it?" Rashevitch assumed a mysterious, frightened expression, and went on: "Never has literature and learning been at such low ebb among us as now. The men of to-day, my good sir, have neither ideas nor ideals, and all their sayings and doings are permeated by one spirit--to get all they can and to strip someone to his last thread. All these men of to-day who give themselves out as honest and progressive people can be bought at a rouble a piece, and the distinguishing mark of the 'intellectual' of to-day is that you have to keep strict watch over your pocket when you talk to him, or else he will run off with your purse." Rashevitch winked and burst out laughing. "Upon my soul, he will! he said, in a thin, gleeful voice. "And morals! What of their morals?" Rashevitch looked round towards the door. "No one is surprised nowadays when a wife robs and leaves her husband. What's that, a trifle! Nowadays, my dear boy, a chit of a girl of twelve is scheming to get a lover, and all these amateur theatricals and literary evenings are only invented to make it easier to get a rich merchant to take a girl on as his mistress. . . . Mothers sell their daughters, and people make no bones about asking a husband at what price he sells his wife, and one can haggle over the bargain, you know, my dear. . . ."

Meier, who had been sitting motionless and silent all the time, suddenly got up from the sofa and looked at his watch.

"I beg your pardon, Pavel Ilyitch," he said, "it is time for me to be going."

But Pavel Ilyitch, who had not finished his remarks, put his arm round him and, forcibly reseating him on the sofa, vowed that he would not let him go without supper. And again Meier sat and listened, but he looked at

Rashevitch with perplexity and uneasiness, as though he were only now beginning to understand him. Patches of red came into his face. And when at last a maidservant came in to tell them that the young ladies asked them to go to supper, he gave a sigh of relief and was the first to walk out of the study.

At the table in the next room were Rashevitch's daughters, Genya and Iraida, girls of four-and-twenty and two-and-twenty respectively, both very pale, with black eyes, and exactly the same height. Genya had her hair down, and Iraida had hers done up high on her head. Before eating anything they each drank a wineglassful of bitter liqueur, with an air as though they had drunk it by accident for the first time in their lives and both were overcome with confusion and burst out laughing.

"Don't be naughty, girls," said Rashevitch.

Genya and Iraida talked French with each other, and Russian with their father and their visitor. Interrupting one another, and mixing up French words with Russian, they began rapidly describing how just at this time in August, in previous years, they had set off to the hoarding school and what fun it had been. Now there was nowhere to go, and they had to stay at their home in the country, summer and winter without change. Such dreariness!

"Don't be naughty, girls," Rashevitch said again.

He wanted to be talking himself. If other people talked in his presence, he suffered from a feeling like jealousy.

"So that's how it is, my dear boy," he began, looking affectionately at Meier. "In the simplicity and goodness of our hearts, and from fear of being suspected of being behind the times, we fraternize with, excuse me, all sorts of riff-raff, we preach fraternity and equality with money-lenders and innkeepers; but if we would only think, we should see how criminal that good-nature is. We have brought things to such a pass, that the fate of civilization is hanging on a hair. My dear fellow, what our forefathers gained in the course of ages will be to-morrow, if not to-day, outraged and destroyed by these modern Huns. . . ."

After supper they all went into the drawing-room. Genya and Iraida lighted the candles on the piano, got out their music. . . . But their father still went on talking, and there was no telling when he would leave off. They looked with misery and vexation at their egoist-father, to whom the pleasure of chattering and displaying his intelligence was evidently more precious and important than his daughters' happiness. Meier, the only young man who ever came to their house, came--they knew--for the sake of their charming, feminine society, but the irrepressible old man had taken possession of him, and would not let him move a step away.

"Just as the knights of the west repelled the invasions of the Mongols, so we, before it is too late, ought to unite and strike together against our foe," Rashevitch went on in the tone of a preacher, holding up his right hand. "May I appear to the riff-raff not as Pavel Ilyitch, but as a mighty, menacing Richard Coeur-de-Lion. Let us give up sloppy sentimentality; enough of it! Let us all make a compact, that as soon as a plebeian comes near us we fling some careless phrase straight in his ugly face: 'Paws off! Go back to your kennel, you cur!' straight in his ugly face," Rashevitch went on gleefully, flicking his crooked finger in front of him. "In his ugly face!"

"I can't do that," Meier brought out, turning away.

"Why not?" Rashevitch answered briskly, anticipating a prolonged and interesting argument. "Why not?"

"Because I am of the artisan class myself!"

As he said this Meier turned crimson, and his neck seemed to swell, and tears actually gleamed in his eyes.

"My father was a simple workman," he said, in a rough, jerky voice, "but I see no harm in that."

Rashevitch was fearfully confused. Dumbfounded, as though he had been caught in the act of a crime, he gazed helplessly at Meier, and did not know what to say. Genya and Iraida flushed crimson, and bent over their music; they were ashamed of their tactless father. A minute passed in silence, and there was a feeling of unbearable discomfort, when all at once with a sort of painful stiffness and inappropriateness, there sounded in the air the words:

"Yes, I am of the artisan class, and I am proud of it!"

Thereupon Meier, stumbling awkwardly among the furniture, took his leave, and walked rapidly into the hall, though his carriage was not yet at the door.

"You'll have a dark drive to-night," Rashevitch muttered, following him. "The moon does not rise till late to-night."

They stood together on the steps in the dark, and waited for the horses to be brought. It was cool.

"There's a falling star," said Meier, wrapping himself in his overcoat.

"There are a great many in August."

When the horses were at the door, Rashevitch gazed intently at the sky, and said with a sigh:

"A phenomenon worthy of the pen of Flammarion. . . ."

After seeing his visitor off, he walked up and down the garden, gesticulating in the darkness, reluctant to believe that such a queer, stupid misunderstanding had only just occurred. He was ashamed and vexed with himself. In the first place it had been extremely incautious and tactless on his part to raise the damnable subject of blue blood, without finding out beforehand what his visitor's position was. Something of the same sort had happened to him before; he had, on one occasion in a railway carriage, begun abusing the Germans, and it had afterwards appeared that all the persons he had been conversing with were German. In the second place he felt that Meier would never come and see him again. These intellectuals who have risen from the people are morbidly sensitive, obstinate and slow to forgive.

"It's bad, it's bad," muttered Rashevitch, spitting; he had a feeling of discomfort and loathing as though he had eaten soap. "Ah, it's bad!"

He could see from the garden, through the drawing-room window, Genya by the piano, very pale, and looking scared, with her hair down. She was talking very, very rapidly. . . . Iraida was walking up and down the room, lost in thought; hut now she, too, began talking rapidly with her face full of indignation. They were both talking at once. Rashevitch could not hear a word, but he guessed what they were talking about. Genya was probably complaining that her father drove away every decent person from the house with his talk, and to-day he had driven away from them their one acquaintance, perhaps a suitor, and now the poor young man would not have one place in the whole district where he could find rest for his soul. And judging by the despairing way in which she threw up her arms, Iraida was talking probably on the subject of their dreary existence, their wasted youth. . . .

When he reached his own room, Rashevitch sat down on his bed and began to undress. He felt oppressed, and he was still haunted by the same feeling as though he had eaten soap. He was ashamed. As he undressed he looked at his long, sinewy, elderly legs, and remembered that in the district they called him the "toad," and after every long conversation he always felt ashamed. Somehow or other, by some fatality, it always happened that he began mildly, amicably, with good intentions, calling himself an old student, an idealist, a Quixote, but without being himself aware of it, gradually passed into abuse and slander, and what was most surprising, with perfect sincerity criticized science, art and morals, though he had not read a book for the last twenty years, had been nowhere farther than their provincial town, and did not really know what was going on in the world. If he sat down to write anything, if it were only a letter of congratulation, there would somehow be abuse in the letter. And all this was strange, because in reality he was a man of feeling, given to tears, Could he be possessed by some devil which hated and slandered in him, apart from his own will?

"It's bad," he sighed, as he lay down under the quilt. "It's bad."

His daughters did not sleep either. There was a sound of laughter and screaming, as though someone was being pursued; it was Genya in hysterics. A little later Iraida was sobbing too. A maidservant ran barefoot up and down the passage several times. . . .

"What a business! Good Lord! . . ." muttered Rashevitch, sighing and tossing from side to side. "It's bad."

He had a nightmare. He dreamt he was standing naked, as tall as a giraffe, in the middle of the room, and saying, as he flicked his finger before him:

"In his ugly face! his ugly face! his ugly face!"

He woke up in a fright, and first of all remembered that a misunderstanding had happened in the evening, and that Meier would certainly not come again. He remembered, too, that he had to pay the interest at the bank, to find husbands for his daughters, that one must have food and drink, and close at hand were illness, old age, unpleasantnesses, that soon it would be winter, and that there was no wood. . . .

It was past nine o'clock in the morning. Rashevitch slowly dressed, drank his tea and ate two hunks of bread and butter. His daughters did not come down to breakfast; they did not want to meet him, and that wounded him. He lay down on his sofa in his study, then sat down to his table and began writing a letter to his daughters. His hand shook and his eyes smarted. He wrote that he was old, and no use to anyone and that nobody loved him, and he begged his daughters to forget him, and when he died to bury him in a plain, deal coffin without ceremony, or to send his body to Harkov to the dissecting theatre. He felt that every line he wrote reeked of malice and affectation, but he could not stop, and went on writing and writing.

"The toad!" he suddenly heard from the next room; it was the voice of his elder daughter, a voice with a hiss of indignation. "The toad!"

"The toad!" the younger one repeated like an echo. "The toad!"

THE HEAD-GARDENER'S STORY

A sale of flowers was taking place in Count N.'s greenhouses. The purchasers were few in number -- a landowner who was a neighbor of mine, a young timber-merchant, and myself. While the workmen were carrying out our magnificent purchases and packing them into the carts, we sat at the entry of the greenhouse and chatted about one thing and another. It is extremely pleasant to sit in a garden on a still April morning, listening to the birds, and watching the flowers brought out into the open air and basking in the sunshine.

The head-gardener, Mihail Karlovitch, a venerable old man with a full shaven face, wearing a fur waistcoat and no coat, superintended the packing of the plants himself, but at the same time he listened to our conversation in the hope of hearing something new. He was an intelligent, very good-hearted man, respected by everyone. He was for some reason looked upon by everyone as a German, though he was in reality on his father's side Swedish, on his mother's side Russian, and attended the Orthodox church. He knew Russian,

Swedish, and German. He had read a good deal in those languages, and nothing one could do gave him greater pleasure than lending him some new book or talking to him, for instance, about Ibsen.

He had his weaknesses, but they were innocent ones: he called himself the head gardener, though there were no under-gardeners; the expression of his face was unusually dignified and haughty; he could not endure to be contradicted, and liked to be listened to with respect and attention.

"That young fellow there I can recommend to you as an awful rascal," said my neighbor, pointing to a laborer with a swarthy, gipsy face, who drove by with the water-barrel. "Last week he was tried in the town for burglary and was acquitted; they pronounced him mentally deranged, and yet look at him, he is the picture of health. Scoundrels are very often acquitted nowadays in Russia on grounds of abnormality and aberration, yet these acquittals, these unmistakable proofs of an indulgent attitude to crime, lead to no good. They demoralize the masses, the sense of justice is blunted in all as they become accustomed to seeing vice unpunished, and you know in our age one may boldly say in the words of Shakespeare that in our evil and corrupt age virtue must ask forgiveness of vice."

"That's very true," the merchant assented. "Owing to these frequent acquittals, murder and arson have become much more common. Ask the peasants."

Mihail Karlovitch turned towards us and said:

"As far as I am concerned, gentlemen, I am always delighted to meet with these verdicts of not guilty. I am not afraid for morality and justice when they say 'Not guilty,' but on the contrary I feel pleased. Even when my conscience tells me the jury have made a mistake in acquitting the criminal, even then I am triumphant. Judge for yourselves, gentlemen; if the judges and the jury have more faith in *man* than in evidence, material proofs, and speeches for the prosecution, is not that faith *in man* in itself higher than any ordinary considerations? Such faith is only attainable by those few who understand and feel Christ."

"A fine thought," I said.

"But it's not a new one. I remember a very long time ago I heard a legend on that subject. A very charming legend," said the gardener, and he smiled. "I was told it by my grandmother, my father's mother, an excellent old lady. She told me it in Swedish, and it does not sound so fine, so classical, in Russian."

But we begged him to tell it and not to be put off by the coarseness of the Russian language. Much gratified, he deliberately lighted his pipe, looked angrily at the laborers, and began:

"There settled in a certain little town a solitary, plain, elderly gentleman called Thomson or Wilson -- but that does not matter; the surname is not the point. He followed an honorable profession: he was a doctor. He was always morose and unsociable, and only spoke when required by his profession. He never visited anyone, never extended his acquaintance beyond a silent bow, and lived as humbly as a hermit. The fact was, he was a learned man, and in those days learned men were not like other people. They spent their days and nights in contemplation, in reading and in healing disease, looked upon everything else as trivial, and had no time to waste a word. The inhabitants of the town understood this, and tried not to worry him with their visits and empty chatter. They were very glad that God had sent them at last a man who could heal diseases, and were proud that such a remarkable man was living in their town. 'He knows everything,' they said about him.

"But that was not enough. They ought to have also said, 'He loves everyone.' In the breast of that learned man there beat a wonderful angelic heart. Though the people of that town were strangers and not his own people, yet he loved them like children, and did not spare himself for them. He was himself ill with consumption, he had a cough, but when he was summoned to the sick he forgot his own illness he did not spare himself and, gasping for breath, climbed up the hills however high they might be. He disregarded the sultry heat and the cold, despised thirst and hunger. He would accept no money and strange to say, when one of his patients died, he would follow the coffin with the relations, weeping.

"And soon he became so necessary to the town that the inhabitants wondered how they could have got on before without the man. Their gratitude knew no bounds. Grown-up people and children, good and bad alike, honest men and cheats -- all in fact, respected him and knew his value. In the little town and all the surrounding neighborhood there was no man who would allow himself to do anything disagreeable to him; indeed, they would never have dreamed of it. When he came out of his lodging, he never fastened the doors or windows, in complete confidence that there was no thief who could bring himself to do him wrong. He often had in the course of his medical duties to walk along the highroads, through the forests and mountains haunted by numbers of hungry vagrants; but he felt that he was in perfect security.

"One night he was returning from a patient when robbers fell upon him in the forest, but when they recognized him, they took off their hats respectfully and offered him something to eat. When he answered that he was not hungry, they gave him a warm wrap and accompanied him as far as the town, happy that fate had given them the chance in some small way to show their gratitude to the benevolent man. Well, to be sure, my grandmother told me that even the horses and the cows and the dogs knew him and expressed their joy when they met him.

"And this man who seemed by his sanctity to have guarded himself from every evil, to whom even brigands and frenzied men wished nothing but good, was one fine morning found murdered. Covered with blood, with his skull broken, he was lying in a ravine, and his pale face wore an expression of amazement. Yes, not horror but amazement was the emotion that had been fixed upon his face when he saw the murderer before him. You can imagine the grief that overwhelmed the inhabitants of the town and the surrounding districts. All were in despair, unable to believe their eyes, wondering who could have killed the man. The judges who conducted the inquiry and examined the doctor's body said: 'Here we have all the signs of a murder, but as there is not a man in the world capable of murdering our doctor, obviously it was not a case of murder, and the combination of evidence is due to simple chance. We must suppose that in the darkness he fell into the ravine of himself and was mortally injured.'

"The whole town agreed with this opinion. The doctor was buried, and nothing more was said about a violent death. The existence of a man who could have the baseness and wickedness to kill the doctor seemed incredible. There is a limit even to wickedness, isn't there?

"All at once, would you believe it, chance led them to discovering the murderer. A vagrant who had been many times convicted, notorious for his vicious life, was seen selling for drink a snuff-box and watch that had belonged to the doctor. When he was questioned he was confused, and answered with an obvious lie. A search was made, and in his bed was found a shirt with stains of blood on the sleeves, and a doctor's lancet set in gold. What more evidence was wanted? They put the criminal in prison. The inhabitants were indignant, and at the same time said:

" 'It's incredible! It can't be so! Take care that a mistake is not made; it does happen, you know, that evidence tells a false tale.'

"At his trial the murderer obstinately denied his guilt. Everything was against him, and to be convinced of his guilt was as easy as to believe that this earth is black; but the judges seem to have gone mad: they weighed every proof ten times, looked distrustfully at the witnesses, flushed crimson and sipped water. . . . The trial began early in the morning and was only finished in the evening.

"'Accused!' the chief judge said, addressing the murderer, 'the court has found you guilty of murdering Dr. So-and-so, and has sentenced you to. . . .'

"The chief judge meant to say 'to the death penalty,' but he dropped from his hands the paper on which the sentence was written, wiped the cold sweat from his face, and cried out:

" 'No! May God punish me if I judge wrongly, but I swear he is not guilty. I cannot admit the thought that there exists a man who would dare to murder our friend the doctor! A man could not sink so low!'

" 'There cannot be such a man!' the other judges assented.

" 'No,' the crowd cried. 'Let him go!'

"The murderer was set free to go where he chose, and not one soul blamed the court for an unjust verdict. And my grandmother used to say that for such faith in humanity God forgave the sins of all the inhabitants of that town. He rejoices when people believe that man is His image and semblance, and grieves if, forgetful of human dignity, they judge worse of men than of dogs. The sentence of acquittal may bring harm to the inhabitants of the town, but on the other hand, think of the beneficial influence upon them of that faith in man -- a faith which does not remain dead, you know; it raises up generous feelings in us, and always impels us to love and respect every man. Every man! And that is important."

Mihail Karlovitch had finished. My neighbor would have urged some objection, but the head-gardener made a gesture that signified that he did not like objections; then he walked away to the carts, and, with an expression of dignity, went on looking after the packing.

THREE YEARS

I

It was dark, and already lights had begun to gleam here and there in the houses, and a pale moon was rising behind the barracks at the end of the street. Laptev was sitting on a bench by the gate waiting for the end of the evening service at the Church of St. Peter and St. Paul. He was reckoning that Yulia Sergeyevna would pass by on her way from the service, and then he would speak to her, and perhaps spend the whole evening with her.

He had been sitting there for an hour and a half already, and all that time his imagination had been busy picturing his Moscow rooms, his Moscow friends, his man Pyotr, and his writing-table. He gazed half wonderingly at the dark, motionless trees, and it seemed strange to him that he was living now, not in his summer villa at Sokolniki, but in a provincial town in a house by which a great herd of cattle was driven every morning and evening, accompanied by terrible clouds of dust and the blowing of a horn. He thought of long conversations in which he had taken part quite lately in Moscow -- conversations in which it had been maintained that one could live without love, that passionate love was an obsession, that finally there is no such love, but only a physical attraction between the sexes -- and so on, in the same style; he remembered them and thought mournfully that if he were asked now what love was, he could not have found an answer.

The service was over, the people began to appear. Laptev strained his eyes gazing at the dark figures. The bishop had been driven by in his carriage, the bells had stopped ringing, and the red and green lights in the belfry were one after another extinguished -- there had been an illumination, as it was dedication day -- but the people were still coming out, lingering, talking, and standing under the windows. But at last Laptev heard a familiar voice, his heart began beating violently, and he was overcome with despair on seeing that Yulia Sergeyevna was not alone, but walking with two ladies.

"It's awful, awful!" he whispered, feeling jealous. "It's awful!"

At the corner of the lane, she stopped to say good-bye to the ladies, and while doing so glanced at Laptev.

"I was coming to see you," he said. "I'm coming for a chat with your father. Is he at home?"

"Most likely," she answered. "It's early for him to have gone to the club."

There were gardens all along the lane, and a row of lime-trees growing by the fence cast a broad patch of shadow in the moonlight, so that the gate and the fences were completely plunged in darkness on one side, from which came the sounds of women whispering, smothered laughter, and someone playing softly on a balalaika. There was a fragrance of lime-flowers and of hay. This fragrance and the murmur of the unseen whispers worked upon Laptev. He was all at once overwhelmed with a passionate longing to throw his arms round his companion, to shower kisses on her face, her hands, her shoulders, to burst into sobs, to fall at her feet and to tell her how long he had been waiting for her. A faint scarcely perceptible scent of incense hung about her; and that scent reminded him of the time when he, too, believed in God and used to go to evening service, and when he used to dream so much of pure romantic love. And it seemed to him that, because this girl did not love him, all possibility of the happiness he had dreamed of then was lost to him forever.

She began speaking sympathetically of the illness of his sister, Nina Fyodorovna. Two months before his sister had undergone an operation for cancer, and now everyone was expecting a return of the disease.

"I went to see her this morning," said Yulia Sergeyevna, "and it seemed to me that during the last week she has, not exactly grown thin, but has, as it were, faded."

"Yes, yes," Laptev agreed. "There's no return of the symptoms, but every day I notice she grows weaker and weaker, and is wasting before my eyes. I don't understand what's the matter with her."

"Oh dear! And how strong she used to be, plump and rosy!" said Yulia Sergeyevna after a moment's silence. "Everyone here used to call her the Moscow lady. How she used to laugh! On holidays she used to dress up like a peasant girl, and it suited her so well."

Doctor Sergey Borisovitch was at home; he was a stout, red-faced man, wearing a long coat that reached below his knees, and looking as though he had short legs. He was pacing up and down his study, with his hands in his pockets, and humming to himself in an undertone, "Ru-ru-ru-ru." His grey whiskers looked unkempt, and his hair was unbrushed, as though he had just got out of bed. And his study with pillows on the sofa, with stacks of papers in the corners, and with a dirty invalid poodle lying under the table, produced the same impression of unkemptness and untidiness as himself.

"M. Laptev wants to see you," his daughter said to him, going into his study.

"Ru-ru-ru-ru," he hummed louder than ever, and turning into the drawing-room, gave his hand to Laptev, and asked: "What good news have you to tell me?"

It was dark in the drawing-room. Laptev, still standing with his hat in his hand, began apologising for disturbing him; he asked what was to be done to make his sister sleep at night, and why she was growing so thin; and he was embarrassed by the thought that he had asked those very questions at his visit that morning.

"Tell me," he said, "wouldn't it be as well to send for some specialist on internal diseases from Moscow? What do you think of it?"

The doctor sighed, shrugged his shoulders, and made a vague gesture with his hands.

It was evident that he was offended. He was a very huffy man, prone to take offence, and always ready to suspect that people did not believe in him, that he was not recognised or properly respected, that his patients exploited him, and that his colleagues showed him ill-will. He was always jeering at himself, saying that fools like him were only made for the public to ride rough-shod over them.

Yulia Sergeyevna lighted the lamp. She was tired out with the service, and that was evident from her pale, exhausted face, and her weary step. She wanted to rest. She sat down on the sofa, put her hands on her lap, and sank into thought. Laptev knew that he was ugly, and now he felt as though he were conscious of his ugliness all over his body. He was short, thin, with ruddy cheeks, and his hair had grown so thin that his head felt cold. In his expression there was none of that refined simplicity which makes even rough, ugly faces attractive; in the society of women, he was awkward, over-talkative, affected. And now he almost despised himself for it. He must talk that Yulia Sergeyevna might not be bored in his company. But what about? About his sister's illness again?

And he began to talk about medicine, saying what is usually said. He approved of hygiene, and said that he had long ago wanted to found a night-refuge in Moscow -- in fact, he had already calculated the cost of it. According to his plan the workmen who came in the evening to the night-refuge were to receive a supper of hot cabbage soup with bread, a warm, dry bed with a rug, and a place for drying their clothes and their boots.

Yulia Sergeyevna was usually silent in his presence, and in a strange way, perhaps by the instinct of a lover, he divined her thoughts and intentions. And now, from the fact that after the evening service she had not gone to her room to change her dress and drink tea, he deduced that she was going to pay some visit elsewhere.

"But I'm in no hurry with the night-refuge," he went on, speaking with vexation and irritability, and addressing the doctor, who looked at him, as it were, blankly and in perplexity, evidently unable to understand what induced him to raise the question of medicine and hygiene. "And most likely it will be a long time, too, before I make use of our estimate. I fear our night-shelter will fall into the hands of our pious humbugs and philanthropic ladies, who always ruin any undertaking."

Yulia Sergeyevna got up and held out her hand to Laptev.

"Excuse me," she said, "it's time for me to go. Please give my love to your sister."

"Ru-ru-ru-ru," hummed the doctor. "Ru-ru-ru-ru."

Yulia Sergeyevna went out, and after staying a little longer, Laptev said good-bye to the doctor and went home. When a man is dissatisfied and feels unhappy, how trivial seem to him the shapes of the lime-trees, the shadows, the clouds, all the beauties of nature, so complacent, so indifferent! By now the moon was high up in the sky, and the clouds were scudding quickly below. "But how naïve and provincial the moon is, how threadbare and paltry the clouds!" thought Laptev. He felt ashamed of the way he had talked just now about medicine, and the night-refuge. He felt with horror that next day he would not have will enough to resist trying to see her and talk to her again, and would again be convinced that he was nothing to her. And the day after -- it would be the same. With what object? And how and when would it all end?

At home he went in to see his sister. Nina Fyodorovna still looked strong and gave the impression of being a well-built, vigorous woman, but her striking pallor made her look like a corpse, especially when, as now, she was lying on her back with her eyes closed; her eldest daughter Sasha, a girl of ten years old, was sitting beside her reading aloud from her reading-book.

"Alyosha has come," the invalid said softly to herself.

There had long been established between Sasha and her uncle a tacit compact, to take turns in sitting with the patient. On this occasion Sasha closed her reading-book, and without uttering a word, went softly out of the room. Laptev took an historical novel from the chest of drawers, and looking for the right page, sat down and began reading it aloud.

Nina Fyodorovna was born in Moscow of a merchant family. She and her two brothers had spent their childhood and early youth, living at home in Pyatnitsky Street. Their childhood was long and wearisome; her father treated her sternly, and had even on two or three occasions flogged her, and her mother had had a long illness and died. The servants were coarse, dirty, and hypocritical; the house was frequented by priests and monks, also hypocritical; they ate and drank and coarsely flattered her father, whom they did not like. The boys had the good-fortune to go to school, while Nina was left practically uneducated. All her life she wrote an illegible scrawl, and had read nothing but historical novels. Seventeen years ago, when she was twenty-two, on a summer holiday at Himki, she made the acquaintance of her present husband, a landowner called Panaurov, had fallen in love with him, and married him secretly against her father's will. Panaurov, a handsome, rather impudent fellow, who whistled and lighted his cigarette from the holy lamp, struck the father as an absolutely worthless person. And when the son-in-law began in his letters demanding a dowry, the old man wrote to his daughter that he would send her furs, silver, and various articles that had been left at her mother's death, as well as thirty thousand roubles, but without his paternal blessing. Later he sent another twenty thousand. This money, as well as the dowry, was spent; the estate had been sold and Panaurov moved with his family to the town and got a job in a provincial government office. In the town he formed another tie, and had a second family, and this was the subject of much talk, as his illicit family was not a secret.

Nina Fyodorovna adored her husband. And now, listening to the historical novel, she was thinking how much she had gone through in her life, how much she had suffered, and that if anyone were to describe her life it would make a very pathetic story. As the tumour was in her breast, she was persuaded that love and her domestic grief were the cause of her illness, and that jealousy and tears had brought her to her hopeless state.

At last Alexey Fyodorovitch closed the book and said:

"That's the end, and thank God for it. To-morrow we'll begin a new one."

Nina Fyodorovna laughed. She had always been given to laughter, but of late Laptev had begun to notice that at moments her mind seemed weakened by illness, and she would laugh at the smallest trifle, and even without any cause at all.

"Yulia came before dinner while you were out," she said. "So far as I can see, she hasn't much faith in her papa. 'Let papa go on treating you,' she said, 'but write in secret to the holy elder to pray for you, too.' There is a holy man somewhere here. Yulia forgot her parasol here; you must take it to her to-morrow," she went on after a brief pause. "No, when the end comes, neither doctors nor holy men are any help."

"Nina, why can't you sleep at night?" Laptev asked, to change the subject.

"Oh, well, I don't go to sleep -- that's all. I lie and think."

"What do you think about, dear?"

"About the children, about you . . . about my life. I've gone through a great deal, Alyosha, you know. When one begins to remember and remember. . . . My God!" She laughed. "It's no joke to have borne five children as I have, to have buried three. . . Sometimes I was expecting to be confined while my Grigory Nikolaitch would be sitting at that very time with another woman. There would be no one to send for the doctor or the midwife. I would go into the passage or the kitchen for the servant, and there Jews, tradesmen, moneylenders, would be waiting for him to come home. My head used to go round. . . . He did not love me, though he never said so openly. Now I've grown calmer -- it doesn't weigh on my heart; but in old days, when I was younger, it hurt me -- ach! how it hurt me, darling! Once -- while we were still in the country -- I found him in the garden with a lady, and I walked away. . . I walked on aimlessly, and I don't know how, but I found myself in the church porch. I fell on my knees: 'Queen of Heaven!' I said. And it was night, the moon was shining. . . ."

She was exhausted, she began gasping for breath. Then, after resting a little, she took her brother's hand and went on in a weak, toneless voice:

"How kind you are, Alyosha! . . . And how clever! . . . What a good man you've grown up into!"

At midnight Laptev said good-night to her, and as he went away he took with him the parasol that Yulia Sergeyevna had forgotten. In spite of the late hour, the servants, male and female, were drinking tea in the dining-room. How disorderly! The children were not in bed, but were there in the dining-room, too. They were all talking softly in undertones, and had not noticed that the lamp was smoking and would soon go out. All these people, big and little, were disturbed by a whole succession of bad omens and were in an oppressed mood. The glass in the hall had been broken, the samovar had been buzzing every day, and, as though on purpose, was even buzzing now. They were describing how a mouse had jumped out of Nina Fyodorovna's boot when she was dressing. And the children were quite aware of the terrible significance of these omens. The elder girl, Sasha, a thin little brunette, was sitting motionless at the table, and her face looked scared and woebegone, while the younger, Lida, a chubby fair child of seven, stood beside her sister looking from under her brows at the light.

Laptev went downstairs to his own rooms in the lower storey, where under the low ceilings it was always close and smelt of geraniums. In his sitting-room, Panaurov, Nina Fyodorovna's husband, was sitting reading the newspaper. Laptev nodded to him and sat down opposite. Both sat still and said nothing. They used to spend whole evenings like this without speaking, and neither of them was in the least put out by this silence.

The little girls came down from upstairs to say good-night. Deliberately and in silence, Panaurov made the sign of the cross over them several times, and gave them his hand to kiss. They dropped curtsies, and then went up to Laptev, who had to make the sign of the cross and give them his hand to kiss also. This ceremony with the hand-kissing and curtsying was repeated every evening.

When the children had gone out Panaurov laid aside the newspaper and said:

"It's not very lively in our God-fearing town! I must confess, my dear fellow," he added with a sigh, "I'm very glad that at last you've found some distraction."

"What do you mean?" asked Laptev.

"I saw you coming out of Dr. Byelavin's Just now. I expect you don't go there for the sake of the papa."

"Of course not," said Laptev, and he blushed.

"Well, of course not. And by the way, you wouldn't find such another old brute as that papa if you hunted by daylight with a candle. You can't imagine what a foul, stupid, clumsy beast he is! You cultured people in the capitals are still interested in the provinces only on the lyrical side, only from the *paysage* and *Poor Anton* point of view, but I can assure you, my boy, there's nothing logical about it; there's nothing but barbarism, meanness, and nastiness -- that's all. Take the local devotees of science -- the local intellectuals, so to speak. Can you imagine there are here in this town twenty-eight doctors? They've all made their fortunes, and they are living in houses of their own, and meanwhile the population is in just as helpless a condition as ever. Here, Nina had to have an operation, quite an ordinary one really, yet we were obliged to get a surgeon from Moscow; not one doctor here would undertake it. It's beyond all conception. They know nothing, they understand nothing. They take no interest in anything. Ask them, for instance, what cancer is -- what it is, what it comes from."

And Panaurov began to explain what cancer was. He was a specialist on all scientific subjects, and explained from a scientific point of view everything that was discussed. But he explained it all in his own way. He had a theory of his own about the circulation of the blood, about chemistry, about astronomy. He talked slowly, softly, convincingly.

"It's beyond all conception," he pronounced in an imploring voice, screwing up his eyes, sighing languidly, and smiling as graciously as a king, and it was evident that he was very well satisfied with himself, and never gave a thought to the fact that he was fifty.

"I am rather hungry," said Laptev. "I should like something savoury."

"Well, that can easily be managed."

Not long afterwards Laptev and his brother-in-law were sitting upstairs in the dining-room having supper. Laptev had a glass of vodka, and then began drinking wine. Panaurov drank nothing. He never drank, and never gambled, yet in spite of that he had squandered all his own and his wife's property, and had accumulated debts. To squander so much in such a short time, one must have, not passions, but a special talent. Panaurov liked dainty fare, liked a handsome dinner service, liked music after dinner, speeches, bowing footmen, to whom he would carelessly fling tips of ten, even twenty-five roubles. He always took part in all lotteries and subscriptions, sent bouquets to ladies of his acquaintance on their birthdays, bought cups, stands for glasses, studs, ties, walking-sticks, scents, cigarette-holders, pipes, lap-dogs, parrots, Japanese bric-à-brac, antiques; he had silk nightshirts, and a bedstead made of ebony inlaid with mother-of-pearl. His dressing-gown was a genuine Bokhara, and everything was to correspond; and on all this there went every day, as he himself expressed, "a deluge" of money.

At supper he kept sighing and shaking his head.

"Yes, everything on this earth has an end," he said softly, screwing up his dark eyes. "You will fall in love and suffer. You will fall out of love; you'll be deceived, for there is no woman who will not deceive; you will suffer, will be brought to despair, and will be faithless too. But the time will come when all this will be a memory, and when you will reason about it coldly and look upon it as utterly trivial. . . ."

Laptev, tired, a little drunk, looked at his handsome head, his clipped black beard, and seemed to understand why women so loved this pampered, conceited, and physically handsome creature.

After supper Panaurov did not stay in the house, but went off to his other lodgings. Laptev went out to see him on his way. Panaurov was the only man in the town who wore a top-hat, and his elegant, dandified figure, his top-hat and tan gloves, beside the grey fences, the pitiful little houses, with their three windows and the thickets of nettles, always made a strange and mournful impression.

After saying good-bye to him Laptev returned home without hurrying. The moon was shining brightly; one could distinguish every straw on the ground, and Laptev felt as though the moonlight were caressing his bare head, as though someone were passing a feather over his hair.

"I love!" he pronounced aloud, and he had a sudden longing to run to overtake Panaurov, to embrace him, to forgive him, to make him a present of a lot of money, and then to run off into the open country, into a wood, to run on and on without looking back.

At home he saw lying on the chair the parasol Yulia Sergeyevna had forgotten; he snatched it up and kissed it greedily. The parasol was a silk one, no longer new, tied round with old elastic. The handle was a cheap one, of white bone. Laptev opened it over him, and he felt as though there were the fragrance of happiness about him.

He settled himself more comfortably in his chair, and still keeping hold of the parasol, began writing to Moscow to one of his friends:

"DEAR PRECIOUS KOSTYA,

"Here is news for you: I'm in love again! I say *again,* because six years ago I fell in love with a Moscow actress, though I didn't even succeed in making her acquaintance, and for the last year and a half I have been living with a certain person you know -- a woman neither young nor good-looking. Ah, my dear boy, how unlucky I am in love. I've never had any success with women, and if I say *again* it's simply because it's rather sad and mortifying to acknowledge even to myself that my youth has passed entirely without love, and that I'm in love in a real sense now for the first time in my life, at thirty-four. Let it stand that I love *again.*

"If only you knew what a girl she was! She couldn't be called a beauty -- she has a broad face, she is very thin, but what a wonderful expression of goodness she has when she smiles! When she speaks, her voice is as clear as a bell. She never carries on a conversation with me -- I don't know her; but when I'm beside her I feel she's a striking, exceptional creature, full of intelligence and lofty aspirations. She is religious, and you cannot imagine how deeply this touches me and exalts her in my eyes. On that point I am ready to argue with you endlessly. You may be right, to your thinking; but, still, I love to see her praying in church. She is a provincial, but she was educated in Moscow. She loves our Moscow; she dresses in the Moscow style, and I love her for that -- love her, love her. . . . I see you frowning and getting up to read me a long lecture on what love is, and what sort of woman one can love, and what sort one cannot, and so on, and so on. But, dear Kostya, before I was in love I, too, knew quite well what love was.

"My sister thanks you for your message. She often recalls how she used to take Kostya Kotchevoy to the preparatory class, and never speaks of you except as *poor Kostya,* as she still thinks of you as the little orphan boy she remembers. And so, poor orphan, I'm in love. While it's a secret, don't say anything to a 'certain person.' I think it will all come right of itself, or, as the footman says in Tolstoy, will 'come round.' "

When he had finished his letter Laptev went to bed. He was so tired that he couldn't keep his eyes open, but for some reason he could not get to sleep; the noise in the street seemed to prevent him. The cattle were driven by to the blowing of a horn, and soon afterwards the bells began ringing for early mass. At one minute a cart drove by creaking; at the next, he heard the voice of some woman going to market. And the sparrows twittered the whole time.

II

The next morning was a cheerful one; it was a holiday. At ten o'clock Nina Fyodorovna, wearing a brown dress and with her hair neatly arranged, was led into the drawing-room, supported on each side. There she walked about a little and stood by the open window, and her smile was broad and naïve, and, looking at her, one recalled a local artist, a great drunkard, who wanted her to sit to him for a picture of the Russian carnival. And all of them -- the children, the servants, her brother, Alexey Fyodorovitch, and she herself -- were suddenly convinced, that she was certainly going to get well. With shrieks of laughter the children ran after their uncle, chasing him and catching him, and filling the house with noise.

People called to ask how she was, brought her holy bread, told her that in almost all the churches they were offering up prayers for her that day. She had been conspicuous for her benevolence in the town, and was liked. She was very ready with her charity, like her brother Alexey, who gave away his money freely, without considering whether it was necessary to give it or not. Nina Fyodorovna used to pay the school fees for poor children; used to give away tea, sugar, and jam to old women; used to provide trousseaux for poor brides; and if she picked up a newspaper, she always looked first of all to see if there were any appeals for charity or a paragraph about somebody's being in a destitute condition.

She was holding now in her hand a bundle of notes, by means of which various poor people, her protégés, had procured goods from a grocer's shop.

They had been sent her the evening before by the shopkeeper with a request for the payment of the total -- eighty-two roubles.

"My goodness, what a lot they've had! They've no conscience!" she said, deciphering with difficulty her ugly handwriting. "It's no joke! Eighty-two roubles! I declare I won't pay it."

"I'll pay it to-day," said Laptev.

"Why should you? Why should you?" cried Nina Fyodorovna in agitation. "It's quite enough for me to take two hundred and fifty every month from you and our brother. God bless you!" she added, speaking softly, so as not to be overheard by the servants.

"Well, but I spend two thousand five hundred a month," he said. "I tell you again, dear: you have just as much right to spend it as I or Fyodor. Do understand that, once for all. There are three of us, and of every three kopecks of our father's money, one belongs to you."

But Nina Fyodorovna did not understand, and her expression looked as though she were mentally solving some very difficult problem. And this lack of comprehension in pecuniary matters, always made Laptev feel uneasy and troubled. He suspected that she had private debts in addition which worried her and of which she scrupled to tell him.

Then came the sound of footsteps and heavy breathing; it was the doctor coming up the stairs, dishevelled and unkempt as usual.

"Ru-ru-ru," he was humming. "Ru-ru."

To avoid meeting him, Laptev went into the dining-room, and then went downstairs to his own room. It was clear to him that to get on with the doctor and to drop in at his house without formalities was impossible; and to meet the "old brute," as Panaurov called him, was distasteful. That was why he so rarely saw Yulia. He reflected now that the father was not at home, that if he were to take Yulia Sergeyevna her parasol, he would be sure to find her at home alone, and his heart ached with joy. Haste, haste!

He took the parasol and, violently agitated, flew on the wings of love. It was hot in the street. In the big courtyard of the doctor's house, overgrown with coarse grass and nettles, some twenty urchins were playing ball. These were all the children of working-class families who tenanted the three disreputable-looking lodges, which the doctor was always meaning to have done up, though he put it off from year to year. The yard resounded with ringing, healthy voices. At some distance on one side, Yulia Sergeyevna was standing at her porch, her hands folded, watching the game.

"Good-morning!" Laptev called to her.

She looked round. Usually he saw her indifferent, cold, or tired as she had been the evening before. Now her face looked full of life and frolic, like the faces of the boys who were playing ball.

"Look, they never play so merrily in Moscow," she said, going to meet him. "There are no such big yards there, though; they've no place to run there. Papa has only just gone to you," she added, looking round at the children.

"I know; but I've not come to see him, but to see you," said Laptev, admiring her youthfulness, which he had not noticed till then, and seemed only that day to have discovered in her; it seemed to him as though he were seeing her slender white neck with the gold chain for the first time. "I've come to see you . . ." he repeated. "My sister has sent you your parasol; you forgot it yesterday."

She put out her hand to take the parasol, but he pressed it to his bosom and spoke passionately, without restraint, yielding again to the sweet ecstasy he had felt the night before, sitting under the parasol.

"I entreat you, give it me. I shall keep it in memory of you . . . of our acquaintance. It's so wonderful!"

"Take it," she said, and blushed; "but there's nothing wonderful about it."

He looked at her in ecstasy, in silence, not knowing what to say.

"Why am I keeping you here in the heat?" she said after a brief pause, laughing. "Let us go indoors."

"I am not disturbing you?"

They went into the hall. Yulia Sergeyevna ran upstairs, her white dress with blue flowers on it rustling as she went.

"I can't be disturbed," she answered, stopping on the landing. "I never do anything. Every day is a holiday for me, from morning till night."

"What you say is inconceivable to me," he said, going up to her. "I grew up in a world in which everyone without exception, men and women alike, worked hard every day."

"But if one has nothing to do?" she asked. "One has to arrange one's life under such conditions, that work is inevitable. There can be no clean and happy life without work."

Again he pressed the parasol to his bosom, and to his own surprise spoke softly, in a voice unlike his own:

"If you would consent to be my wife I would give everything -- I would give everything. There's no price I would not pay, no sacrifice I would not make."

She started and looked at him with wonder and alarm.

"What are you saying!" she brought out, turning pale. "It's impossible, I assure you. Forgive me."

Then with the same rustle of her skirts she went up higher, and vanished through the doorway.

Laptev grasped what this meant, and his mood was transformed, completely, abruptly, as though a light in his soul had suddenly been extinguished. Filled with the shame of a man humiliated, of a man who is disdained, who is not liked, who is distasteful, perhaps disgusting, who is shunned, he walked out of the house.

"I would give everything," he thought, mimicking himself as he went home through the heat and recalled the details of his declaration. "I would give everything -- like a regular tradesman. As though she wanted your *everything!*"

All he had just said seemed to him repulsively stupid. Why had he lied, saying that he had grown up in a world where everyone worked, without exception? Why had he talked to her in a lecturing tone about a clean and happy life? It was not clever, not interesting; it was false -- false in the Moscow style. But by degrees there followed that mood of indifference into which criminals sink after a severe sentence. He began thinking that, thank God! everything was at an end and that the terrible uncertainty was over; that now there was no need to spend whole days in anticipation, in pining, in thinking always of the same thing. Now everything was clear; he must give up all hope of personal happiness, live without desires, without hopes, without dreams, or expectations, and to escape that dreary sadness which he was so sick of trying to soothe, he could busy himself with other people's affairs, other people's happiness, and old age would come on imperceptibly, and life would reach its end -- and nothing more was wanted. He did not care, he wished for nothing, and could reason about it coolly, but there was a sort of heaviness in his face especially under his eyes, his forehead felt drawn tight like elastic -- and tears were almost starting into his eyes. Feeling weak all over, he lay down on his bed, and in five minutes was sound asleep.

III

The proposal Laptev had made so suddenly threw Yulia Sergeyevna into despair.

She knew Laptev very little, had made his acquaintance by chance; he was a rich man, a partner in the well-known Moscow firm of "Fyodor Laptev and Sons"; always serious, apparently clever, and anxious about his sister s illness. It had seemed to her that he took no notice of her whatever, and she did not care about him in the least -- and then all of a sudden that declaration on the stairs, that pitiful, ecstatic face. . . .

The offer had overwhelmed her by its suddenness and by the fact that the word wife had been uttered, and by the necessity of rejecting it. She could not remember what she had said to Laptev, but she still felt traces of the sudden, unpleasant feeling with which she had rejected him. He did not attract her; he looked like a shopman; he was not interesting; she could not have answered him except with a refusal, and yet she felt uncomfortable, as though she had done wrong.

"My God! without waiting to get into the room, on the stairs," she said to herself in despair, addressing the ikon which hung over her pillow; "and no courting beforehand, but so strangely, so oddly. . . ."

In her solitude her agitation grew more intense every hour, and it was beyond her strength to master this oppressive feeling alone. She needed someone to listen to her story and to tell her that she had done right. But she had no one to talk to. She had lost her mother long before; she thought her father a queer man, and could not talk to him seriously. He worried her with his whims, his extreme readiness to take offence, and his meaningless gestures; and as soon as one began to talk to him, he promptly turned the conversation on himself. And in her prayer she was not perfectly open, because she did not know for certain what she ought to pray for.

The samovar was brought in. Yulia Sergeyevna, very pale and tired, looking dejected, came into the dining-room to make tea -- it was one of her duties -- and poured out a glass for her father. Sergey Borisovitch, in his long coat that reached below his knees, with his red face and unkempt hair, walked up and down the room with his hands in his pockets, pacing, not from corner to corner, but backwards and forwards at random, like a wild beast in its cage. He would stand still by the table, sip his glass of tea with relish, and pace about again, lost in thought.

"Laptev made me an offer to-day," said Yulia Sergeyevna, and she flushed crimson.

The doctor looked at her and did not seem to understand.

"Laptev?" he queried. "Panaurov's brother-in-law?"

He was fond of his daughter; it was most likely that she would sooner or later be married, and leave him, but he tried not to think about that. He was afraid of being alone, and for some reason fancied, that if he were left alone in that great house, he would have an apoplectic stroke, but he did not like to speak of this directly.

"Well, I'm delighted to hear it," he said, shrugging his shoulders. "I congratulate you with all my heart. It offers you a splendid opportunity for leaving me, to your great satisfaction. And I quite understand your feelings. To live with an old father, an invalid, half crazy, must be very irksome at your age. I quite understand you. And the sooner I'm laid out and in the devil's clutches, the better everyone will be pleased. I congratulate you with all my heart."

"I refused him."

The doctor felt relieved, but he was unable to stop himself and went on:

"I wonder, I've long wondered, why I've not yet been put into a madhouse -- why I'm still wearing this coat instead of a strait-waistcoat? I still have faith in justice, in goodness. I am a fool, an idealist, and nowadays that's insanity, isn't it? And how do they repay me for my honesty? They almost throw stones at me and ride rough-shod over me. And even my nearest kith and kin do nothing but try to get the better of me. It's high time the devil fetched an old fool like me. . . ."

"There's no talking to you like a rational being!" said Yulia.

She got up from the table impulsively, and went to her room in great wrath, remembering how often her father had been unjust to her. But a little while afterwards she felt sorry for her father, too, and when he was going to the club she went downstairs with him, and shut the door after him. It was a rough and stormy night; the door shook with the violence of the wind, and there were draughts in all directions in the passage, so that the candle was almost blown out. In her own domain upstairs Yulia Sergeyevna went the round of all the rooms, making the sign of the cross over every door and window; the wind howled, and it sounded as though someone were walking on the roof. Never had it been so dreary, never had she felt so lonely.

She asked herself whether she had done right in rejecting a man, simply because his appearance did not attract her. It was true he was a man she did not love, and to marry him would mean renouncing forever her dreams, her conceptions of happiness in married life, but would she ever meet the man of whom she dreamed, and would he love her? She was twenty-one already. There were no eligible young men in the town. She pictured all the men she knew -- government clerks, schoolmasters, officers, and some of them were married already, and their domestic life was conspicuous for its dreariness and triviality; others were uninteresting, colourless, unintelligent, immoral. Laptev was, anyway, a Moscow man, had taken his degree at the university, spoke French. He lived in the capital, where there were lots of clever, noble, remarkable people; where there was noise and bustle, splendid theatres, musical evenings, first-rate dressmakers, confectioners. . . . In the Bible it was written that a wife must love her husband, and great importance was given to love in novels, but wasn't there exaggeration in it? Was it out of the question to enter upon married life without love? It was said, of course, that love soon passed away, and that nothing was left but habit, and that the object of married life was not to be found in love, nor in happiness, but in duties, such as the bringing up of one's children, the care of one's household, and so on. And perhaps what was meant in the Bible was love for one's husband as one's neighbour, respect for him, charity.

At night Yulia Sergeyevna read the evening prayers attentively, then knelt down, and pressing her hands to her bosom, gazing at the flame of the lamp before the ikon, said with feeling:

"Give me understanding, Holy Mother, our Defender! Give me understanding, O Lord!"

She had in the course of her life come across elderly maiden ladies, poor and of no consequence in the world, who bitterly repented and openly confessed their regret that they had refused suitors in the past. Would not the same thing happen to her? Had not she better go into a convent or become a Sister of Mercy?

She undressed and got into bed, crossing herself and crossing the air around her. Suddenly the bell rang sharply and plaintively in the corridor.

"Oh, my God!" she said, feeling a nervous irritation all over her at the sound. She lay still and kept thinking how poor this provincial life was in events, monotonous and yet not peaceful. One was constantly having to tremble, to feel apprehensive, angry or guilty, and in the end one's nerves were so strained, that one was afraid to peep out of the bedclothes.

A little while afterwards the bell rang just as sharply again. The servant must have been asleep and had not heard. Yulia Sergeyevna lighted a candle, and feeling vexed with the servant, began with a shiver to dress, and when she went out into the corridor, the maid was already closing the door downstairs.

"I thought it was the master, but it's someone from a patient," she said.

Yulia Sergeyevna went back to her room. She took a pack of cards out of the chest of drawers, and decided that if after shuffling the cards well and cutting, the bottom card turned out to be a red one, it would mean *yes* -- that is, she would accept Laptev's offer; and that if it was a black, it would mean *no*. The card turned out to be the ten of spades.

That relieved her mind -- she fell asleep; but in the morning, she was wavering again between *yes* and *no,* and she was dwelling on the thought that she could, if she chose, change her life. The thought harassed her, she felt exhausted and unwell; but yet, soon after eleven, she dressed and went to see Nina Fyodorovna. She wanted to see Laptev: perhaps now he would seem more attractive to her; perhaps she had been wrong about him hitherto. . . .

She found it hard to walk against the wind. She struggled along, holding her hat on with both hands, and could see nothing for the dust.

IV

Going into his sister's room, and seeing to his surprise Yulia Sergeyevna, Laptev had again the humiliating sensation of a man who feels himself an object of repulsion. He concluded that if after what had happened yesterday she could bring herself so easily to visit his sister and meet him, it must be because she was not concerned about him, and regarded him as a complete nonentity. But when he greeted her, and with a pale face and dust under her eyes she looked at him mournfully and remorsefully, he saw that she, too, was miserable.

She did not feel well. She only stayed ten minutes, and began saying good-bye. And as she went out she said to Laptev:

"Will you see me home, Alexey Fyodorovitch?"

They walked along the street in silence, holding their hats, and he, walking a little behind, tried to screen her from the wind. In the lane it was more sheltered, and they walked side by side.

"Forgive me if I was not nice yesterday;" and her voice quavered as though she were going to cry. "I was so wretched! I did not sleep all night."

"I slept well all night," said Laptev, without looking at her; "but that doesn't mean that I was happy. My life is broken. I'm deeply unhappy, and after your refusal yesterday I go about like a man poisoned. The most difficult thing was said yesterday. To-day I feel no embarrassment and can talk to you frankly. I love you more than my sister, more than my dead mother. . . . I can live without my sister, and without my mother, and I have lived without them, but life without you -- is meaningless to me; I can't face it. . . ."

And now too, as usual, he guessed her intention.

He realised that she wanted to go back to what had happened the day before, and with that object had asked him to accompany her, and now was taking him home with her. But what could she add to her refusal? What new idea had she in her head? From everything, from her glances, from her smile, and even from her tone, from the way she held her head and shoulders as she walked beside him, he saw that, as before, she did not love him, that he was a stranger to her. What more did she want to say?

Doctor Sergey Borisovitch was at home.

"You are very welcome. I'm always glad to see you, Fyodor Alexeyitch," he said, mixing up his Christian name and his father's. "Delighted, delighted!"

He had never been so polite before, and Laptev saw that he knew of his offer; he did not like that either. He was sitting now in the drawing-room, and the room impressed him strangely, with its poor, common decorations, its wretched pictures, and though there were arm-chairs in it, and a huge lamp with a shade over it, it still looked like an uninhabited place, a huge barn, and it was obvious that no one could feel at home in such a room, except a man like the doctor. The next room, almost twice as large, was called the reception-room, and in it there were only rows of chairs, as though for a dancing class. And while Laptev was sitting in the drawing-room talking to the doctor about his sister, he began to be tortured by a suspicion. Had not Yulia Sergeyevna been to his sister Nina's, and then brought him here to tell him that she would accept him? Oh, how awful it was! But the most awful thing of all was that his soul was capable of such a suspicion. And he imagined how the father and the daughter had spent the evening, and perhaps the night before, in prolonged consultation, perhaps dispute, and at last had come to the conclusion that Yulia had acted thoughtlessly in refusing a rich man. The words that parents use in such cases kept ringing in his ears:

"It is true you don't love him, but think what good you could do!"

The doctor was going out to see patients. Laptev would have gone with him, but Yulia Sergeyevna said:

"I beg you to stay."

She was distressed and dispirited, and told herself now that to refuse an honourable, good man who loved her, simply because he was not attractive, especially when marrying him would make it possible for her to change her mode of life, her cheerless, monotonous, idle life in which youth was passing with no prospect of anything better in the future -- to refuse him under such circumstances was madness, caprice and folly, and that God might even punish her for it.

The father went out. When the sound of his steps had died away, she suddenly stood up before Laptev and said resolutely, turning horribly white as she did so:

"I thought for a long time yesterday, Alexey Fyodorovitch. . . . I accept your offer."

He bent down and kissed her hand. She kissed him awkwardly on the head with cold lips.

He felt that in this love scene the chief thing -- her love -- was lacking, and that there was a great deal that was not wanted; and he longed to cry out, to run away, to go back to Moscow at once. But she was close to him, and she seemed to him so lovely, and he was suddenly overcome by passion. He reflected that it was too late for deliberation now; he embraced her passionately, and muttered some words, calling her *thou;* he kissed her on the neck, and then on the cheek, on the head. . . .

She walked away to the window, dismayed by these demonstrations, and both of them were already regretting what they had said and both were asking themselves in confusion:

"Why has this happened?"

"If only you knew how miserable I am!" she said, wringing her hands.

"What is it?" he said, going up to her, wringing his hands too. "My dear, for God's sake, tell me -- what is it? Only tell the truth, I entreat you -- nothing but the truth!"

"Don't pay any attention to it," she said, and forced herself to smile. "I promise you I'll be a faithful, devoted wife. . . . Come this evening."

Sitting afterwards with his sister and reading aloud an historical novel, he recalled it all and felt wounded that his splendid, pure, rich feeling was met with such a shallow response. He was not loved, but his offer had been accepted -- in all probability because he was rich: that is, what was thought most of in him was what he valued least of all in himself. It was quite possible that Yulia, who was so pure and believed in God, had not once thought of his money; but she did not love him -- did not love him, and evidently she had interested motives, vague, perhaps, and not fully thought out -- still, it was so. The doctor's house with its common furniture was repulsive to him, and he looked upon the doctor himself as a wretched, greasy miser, a sort of operatic Gaspard from "Les Cloches de Corneville." The very name "Yulia" had a vulgar sound. He imagined how he and his Yulia would stand at their wedding, in reality complete strangers to one another, without a trace of feeling on her side, just as though their marriage had been made by a professional matchmaker; and the only consolation left him now, as commonplace as the marriage itself, was the reflection that he was not the first, and would not be the last; that thousands of people were married like that; and that with time, when Yulia came to know him better, she would perhaps grow fond of him.

"Romeo and Juliet!" he said, as he shut the novel, and he laughed. "I am Romeo, Nina. You may congratulate me. I made an offer to Yulia Byelavin to-day."

Nina Fyodorovna thought he was joking, but when she believed it, she began to cry; she was not pleased at the news.

"Well, I congratulate you," she said. "But why is it so sudden?"

"No, it's not sudden. It's been going on since March, only you don't notice anything. . . . I fell in love with her last March when I made her acquaintance here, in your rooms."

"I thought you would marry someone in our Moscow set," said Nina Fyodorovna after a pause. "Girls in our set are simpler. But what matters, Alyosha, is that you should be happy -- that matters most. My Grigory Nikolaitch did not love me, and there's no concealing it; you can see what our life is. Of course any woman may love you for your goodness and your brains, but, you see, Yulitchka is a girl of good family from a high-class boarding-school; goodness and brains are not enough for her. She is young, and, you, Alyosha, are not so young, and are not good-looking."

To soften the last words, she stroked his head and said:

"You're not good-looking, but you're a dear."

She was so agitated that a faint flush came into her cheeks, and she began discussing eagerly whether it would be the proper thing for her to bless Alyosha with the ikon at the wedding. She was, she reasoned, his elder sister, and took the place of his mother; and she kept trying to convince her dejected brother that the wedding must be celebrated in proper style, with pomp and gaiety, so that no one could find fault with it.

Then he began going to the Byelavins' as an accepted suitor, three or four times a day; and now he never had time to take Sasha's place and read aloud the historical novel. Yulia used to receive him in her two rooms, which were at a distance from the drawing-room and her father's study, and he liked them very much. The walls in them were dark; in the corner stood a case of ikons; and there was a smell of good scent and of the oil in the holy lamp. Her rooms were at the furthest end of the house; her bedstead and dressing-table were shut off by a screen. The doors of the bookcase were covered on the inside with a green curtain, and there were rugs on the floor, so that her footsteps were noiseless -- and from this he concluded that she was of a reserved character, and that she liked a quiet, peaceful, secluded life. In her own home she was treated as though she were not quite grown up. She had no money of her own, and sometimes when they were out for walks together, she was overcome with confusion at not having a farthing. Her father allowed her very little for dress and books, hardly ten pounds a year. And, indeed, the doctor himself had not much money in spite of his good practice. He played cards every night at the club, and always lost. Moreover, he bought mortgaged houses through a building society, and let them. The tenants were irregular in paying the rent, but he was convinced that such speculations were profitable. He had mortgaged his own house in which he and his daughter were living, and with the money so raised had bought a piece of waste ground, and had already begun to build on it a large two-storey house, meaning to mortgage it, too, as soon as it was finished.

Laptev now lived in a sort of cloud, feeling as though he were not himself, but his double, and did many things which he would never have brought himself to do before. He went three or four times to the club with the doctor, had supper with him, and offered him money for house-building. He even visited Panaurov at his other establishment. It somehow happened that Panaurov invited him to dinner, and without thinking, Laptev accepted. He was received by a lady of five-and-thirty. She was tall and thin, with hair touched with grey, and black eyebrows, apparently not Russian. There were white patches of powder on her face. She gave him a honeyed smile and pressed his hand jerkily, so that the bracelets on her white hands tinkled. It seemed to Laptev that she smiled like that because she wanted to conceal from herself and from others that she was unhappy. He also saw two little girls, aged five and three, who had a marked likeness to Sasha. For dinner they had milk-soup, cold veal, and chocolate. It was insipid and not good; but the table was splendid, with gold forks, bottles of Soyer, and cayenne pepper, an extraordinary bizarre cruet-stand, and a gold pepper-pot.

It was only as he was finishing the milk-soup that Laptev realised how very inappropriate it was for him to be dining there. The lady was embarrassed, and kept smiling, showing her teeth. Panaurov expounded didactically what being in love was, and what it was due to.

"We have in it an example of the action of electricity," he said in French, addressing the lady. "Every man has in his skin microscopic glands which contain currents of electricity. If you meet with a person whose currents are parallel with your own, then you get love."

When Laptev went home and his sister asked him where he had been he felt awkward, and made no answer.

He felt himself in a false position right up to the time of the wedding. His love grew more intense every day, and Yulia seemed to him a poetic and exalted creature; but, all the same, there was no mutual love, and the truth was that he was buying her and she was selling herself. Sometimes, thinking things over, he fell into despair and asked himself: should he run away? He did not sleep for nights together, and kept thinking how he should meet in Moscow the lady whom he had called in his letters "a certain person," and what attitude his father and his brother, difficult people, would take towards his marriage and towards Yulia. He was afraid that his father would say something rude to Yulia at their first meeting. And something strange had happened of late to his brother Fyodor. In his long letters he had taken to writing of the importance of health, of the effect of illness on the mental condition, of the meaning of religion, but not a word about Moscow or business. These letters irritated Laptev, and he thought his brother's character was changing for the worse.

The wedding was in September. The ceremony took place at the Church of St. Peter and St. Paul, after mass, and the same day the young couple set off for Moscow. When Laptev and his wife, in a black dress with a long train, already looking not a girl but a married woman, said good-bye to Nina Fyodorovna, the invalid's face worked, but there was no tear in her dry eyes. She said:

"If -- which God forbid -- I should die, take care of my little girls."

"Oh, I promise!" answered Yulia Sergeyevna, and her lips and eyelids began quivering too.

"I shall come to see you in October," said Laptev, much moved. "You must get better, my darling."

They travelled in a special compartment. Both felt depressed and uncomfortable. She sat in the corner without taking off her hat, and made a show of dozing, and he lay on the seat opposite, and he was disturbed by various thoughts -- of his father, of " a certain person," whether Yulia would like her Moscow flat. And looking at his wife, who did not love him, he wondered dejectedly "why this had happened."

V

The Laptevs had a wholesale business in Moscow, dealing in fancy goods: fringe, tape, trimmings, crochet cotton, buttons, and so on. The gross receipts reached two millions a year; what the net profit was, no one knew but the old father. The sons and the clerks estimated the profits at approximately three hundred thousand, and said that it would have been a hundred thousand more if the old man had not "been too free-handed" -- that is, had not allowed credit indiscriminately. In the last ten years alone the bad debts had mounted up to the sum of a million; and when the subject was referred to, the senior clerk would wink slyly and deliver himself of sentences the meaning of which was not clear to everyone:

"The psychological sequences of the age."

Their chief commercial operations were conducted in the town market in a building which was called the warehouse. The entrance to the warehouse was in the yard, where it was always dark, and smelt of matting and where the dray-horses were always stamping their hoofs on the asphalt. A very humble-looking door, studded with iron, led from the yard into a room with walls discoloured by damp and scrawled over with charcoal, lighted up by a narrow window covered by an iron grating. Then on the left was another room larger and cleaner with an iron stove and a couple of chairs, though it, too, had a prison window: this was the office, and from it a narrow stone staircase led up to the second storey, where the principal room was. This was rather a large room, but owing to the perpetual darkness, the low-pitched ceiling, the piles of boxes and bales, and the numbers of men that kept flitting to and fro in it, it made as unpleasant an impression on a newcomer as the others. In the offices on the top storey the goods lay in bales, in bundles and in cardboard boxes on the shelves; there was no order nor neatness in the arrangement of it, and if crimson threads, tassels, ends of fringe, had not peeped out here and there from holes in the paper parcels, no one could have guessed what was being bought and sold here. And looking at these crumpled paper parcels and boxes, no one would have believed that a million was being made out of such trash, and that fifty men were employed every day in this warehouse, not counting the buyers.

When at midday, on the day after his arrival at Moscow, Laptev went into the warehouse, the workmen packing the goods were hammering so loudly that in the outer room and the office no one heard him come in. A postman he knew was coming down the stairs with a bundle of letters in his hand; he was wincing at the noise, and he did not notice Laptev either. The first person to meet him upstairs was his brother Fyodor Fyodorovitch, who was so like him that they passed for twins. This resemblance always reminded Laptev of his own personal appearance, and now, seeing before him a short, red-faced man with rather thin hair, with narrow plebeian hips, looking so uninteresting and so unintellectual, he asked himself: "Can I really look like that?"

"How glad I am to see you!" said Fyodor, kissing his brother and pressing his hand warmly. "I have been impatiently looking forward to seeing you every day, my dear fellow. When you wrote that you were getting married, I was tormented with curiosity, and I've missed you, too, brother. Only fancy, it's six months since we saw each other. Well? How goes it? Nina's very bad? Awfully bad?"

"Awfully bad."

"It's in God's hands," sighed Fyodor. "Well, what of your wife? She's a beauty, no doubt? I love her already. Of course, she is my little sister now. We'll make much of her between us."

Laptev saw the broad, bent back -- so familiar to him -- of his father, Fyodor Stepanovitch. The old man was sitting on a stool near the counter, talking to a customer.

"Father, God has sent us joy!" cried Fyodor. "Brother has come!"

Fyodor Stepanovitch was a tall man of exceptionally powerful build, so that, in spite of his wrinkles and eighty years, he still looked a hale and vigorous man. He spoke in a deep, rich, sonorous voice, that resounded from his broad chest as from a barrel. He wore no beard, but a short-clipped military moustache, and smoked cigars. As he was always too hot, he used all the year round to wear a canvas coat at home and at the warehouse. He had lately had an operation for cataract. His sight was bad, and he did nothing in the business but talk to the customers and have tea and jam with them.

Laptev bent down and kissed his head and then his lips.

"It's a good long time since we saw you, honoured sir," said the old man -- "a good long time. Well, am I to congratulate you on entering the state of holy matrimony? Very well, then; I congratulate you."

And he put his lips out to be kissed. Laptev bent down and kissed him.

"Well, have you brought your young lady?" the old man asked, and without waiting for an answer, he said, addressing the customer: " 'Herewith I beg to inform you, father, that I'm going to marry such and such a young lady.' Yes. But as for asking for his father's counsel or blessing, that's not in the rules nowadays. Now they go their own way. When I married I was over forty, but I went on my knees to my father and asked his advice. Nowadays we've none of that."

The old man was delighted to see his son, but thought it unseemly to show his affection or make any display of his joy. His voice and his manner of saying "your young lady" brought back to Laptev the depression he had always felt in the warehouse. Here every trifling detail reminded him of the past, when he used to be flogged and put on Lenten fare; he knew that even now boys were thrashed and punched in the face till their noses bled, and that when those boys grew up they would beat others. And before he had been five minutes in the warehouse, he always felt as though he were being scolded or punched in the face.

Fyodor slapped the customer on the shoulder and said to his brother:

"Here, Alyosha, I must introduce our Tambov benefactor, Grigory Timofeitch. He might serve as an example for the young men of the day; he's passed his fiftieth birthday, and he has tiny children."

The clerks laughed, and the customer, a lean old man with a pale face, laughed too.

"Nature above the normal capacity," observed the head-clerk, who was standing at the counter close by. "It always comes out when it's there."

The head-clerk -- a tall man of fifty, in spectacles, with a dark beard, and a pencil behind his ear -- usually expressed his ideas vaguely in roundabout hints, while his sly smile betrayed that he attached particular significance to his words. He liked to obscure his utterances with bookish words, which he understood in his own way, and many such words he used in a wrong sense. For instance, the word "except." When he had expressed some opinion positively and did not want to be contradicted, he would stretch out his hand and pronounce:

"Except!"

And what was most astonishing, the customers and the other clerks understood him perfectly. His name was Ivan Vassilitch Potchatkin, and he came from Kashira. Now, congratulating Laptev, he expressed himself as follows:

"It's the reward of valour, for the female heart is a strong opponent."

Another important person in the warehouse was a clerk called Makeitchev -- a stout, solid, fair man with whiskers and a perfectly bald head. He went up to Laptev and congratulated him respectfully in a low voice:

"I have the honour, sir. . . The Lord has heard your parent's prayer. Thank God."

Then the other clerks began coming up to congratulate him on his marriage. They were all fashionably dressed, and looked like perfectly well-bred, educated men. Since between every two words they put in a "sir," their congratulations -- something like "Best wishes, sir, for happiness, sir," uttered very rapidly in a low voice -- sounded rather like the hiss of a whip in the air -- "Shshsh-s s s s s!" Laptev was soon bored and longing to go home, but it was awkward to go away. He was obliged to stay at least two hours at the warehouse to keep up appearances. He walked away from the counter and began asking Makeitchev whether things had gone well while he was away, and whether anything new had turned up, and the clerk answered him respectfully, avoiding his eyes. A boy with a cropped head, wearing a grey blouse, handed Laptev a glass of tea without a saucer; not long afterwards another boy, passing by, stumbled over a box, and almost fell down, and Makeitchev's face looked suddenly spiteful and ferocious like a wild beast's, and he shouted at him:

"Keep on your feet!"

The clerks were pleased that their young master was married and had come back at last; they looked at him with curiosity and friendly feeling, and each one thought it his duty to say something agreeable when he passed him. But Laptev was convinced that it was not genuine, and that they were only flattering him because they were afraid of him. He never could forget how fifteen years before, a clerk, who was mentally deranged, had run out into the street with nothing on but his shirt and shaking his fists at the windows, shouted that he had been ill-treated; and how, when the poor fellow had recovered, the clerks had jeered at him for long afterwards, reminding him how he had called his employers "planters" instead of "exploiters." Altogether the employees at Laptevs' had a very poor time of it, and this fact was a subject of conversation for the whole market. The worst of it was that the old man, Fyodor Stepanovitch, maintained something of an Asiatic despotism in his attitude to them. Thus, no one knew what wages were paid to the old man's favourites, Potchatkin and Makeitchev. They received no more than three thousand a year, together with bonuses, but he made out that he paid then seven. The bonuses were given to all the clerks every year, but privately, so that the man who got little was bound from vanity to say he had got more. Not one boy knew when he would be promoted to be a clerk; not one of the men knew whether his employer was satisfied with him or not. Nothing was directly forbidden, and so the clerks never knew what was allowed, and what was not. They were not forbidden to marry, but they did not marry for fear of displeasing their employer and losing their place. They were allowed to have friends and pay visits, but the gates were shut at nine o'clock, and every morning the old man scanned them all suspiciously, and tried to detect any smell of vodka about them:

"Now then, breathe," he would say.

Every clerk was obliged to go to early service, and to stand in church in such a position that the old man could see them all. The fasts were strictly observed. On great occasions, such as the birthday of their employer or of any member of his family, the clerks had to subscribe and present a cake from Fley's, or an album. The clerks lived three or four in a room in the lower storey, and in the lodges of the house in Pyatnitsky Street, and at dinner ate from a common bowl, though there was a plate set before each of them. If one of the family came into the room while they were at dinner, they all stood up.

Laptev was conscious that only, perhaps, those among them who had been corrupted by the old man's training could seriously regard him as their benefactor; the others must have looked on him as an enemy and a "planter." Now, after six months' absence, he saw no change for the better; there was indeed something new which boded nothing good. His brother Fyodor, who had always been quiet, thoughtful, and extremely refined, was now running about the warehouse with a pencil behind his ear making a show of being very busy and businesslike, slapping customers on the shoulder and shouting "Friends!" to the clerks. Apparently he had taken up a new role, and Alexey did not recognise him in the part.

The old man's voice boomed unceasingly. Having nothing to do, he was laying down the law to a customer, telling him how he should order his life and his business, always holding himself up as an example. That boastfulness, that aggressive tone of authority, Laptev had heard ten, fifteen, twenty years ago. The old man adored himself; from what he said it always appeared that he had made his wife and all her relations happy, that he had been munificent to his children, and a benefactor to his clerks and employés, and that everyone in the street and all his acquaintances remembered him in their prayers. Whatever he did was always right, and if things went wrong with people it was because they did not take his advice; without his advice nothing could succeed. In church he stood in the foremost place, and even made observations to the priests, if in his opinion they were not conducting the service properly, and believed that this was pleasing God because God loved him.

At two o'clock everyone in the warehouse was hard at work, except the old man, who still went on booming in his deep voice. To avoid standing idle, Laptev took some trimmings from a workgirl and let her go; then listened to a customer, a merchant from Vologda, and told a clerk to attend to him.

"T. V. A.!" resounded on all sides (prices were denoted by letters in the warehouse and goods by numbers). "R. I. T.!" As he went away, Laptev said good-bye to no one but Fyodor.

"I shall come to Pyatnitsky Street with my wife to-morrow," he said; "but I warn you, if father says a single rude thing to her, I shall not stay there another minute."

"You're the same as ever," sighed Fyodor. "Marriage has not changed you. You must be patient with the old man. So till eleven o'clock, then. We shall expect you impatiently. Come directly after mass, then."

"I don't go to mass."

"That does not matter. The great thing is not to be later than eleven, so you may be in time to pray to God and to lunch with us. Give my greetings to my little sister and kiss her hand for me. I have a presentiment that I shall like her," Fyodor added with perfect sincerity. "I envy you, brother!" he shouted after him as Alexey went downstairs.

"And why does he shrink into himself in that shy way as though he fancied he was naked?" thought Laptev, as he walked along Nikolsky Street, trying to understand the change that had come over his brother. "And his language is new, too: 'Brother, dear brother, God has sent us joy; to pray to God' -- just like Iudushka in Shtchedrin."

VI

At eleven o'clock the next day, which was Sunday, he was driving with his wife along Pyatnitsky Street in a light, one-horse carriage. He was afraid of his father's doing something outrageous, and was already ill at ease. After two nights in her husband's house Yulia Sergeyevna considered her marriage a mistake and a calamity, and if she had had to live with her husband in any other town but Moscow, it seemed to her that she could not have endured the horror of it. Moscow entertained her -- she was delighted with the streets, the churches; and if it had been possible to drive about Moscow in those splendid sledges with expensive horses, to drive the whole day from morning till night, and with the swift motion to feel the cold autumn air blowing upon her, she would perhaps not have felt herself so unhappy.

Near a white, lately stuccoed two-storey house the coachman pulled up his horse, and began to turn to the right. They were expected, and near the gate stood two policemen and the porter in a new full-skirted coat, high boots, and goloshes. The whole space, from the middle of the street to the gates and all over the yard from the porch, was strewn with fresh sand. The porter took off his hat, the policemen saluted. Near the entrance Fyodor met them with a very serious face.

"Very glad to make your acquaintance, little sister," he said, kissing Yulia's hand. "You're very welcome."

He led her upstairs on his arm, and then along a corridor through a crowd of men and women. The anteroom was crowded too, and smelt of incense.

"I will introduce you to our father directly," whispered Fyodor in the midst of a solemn, deathly silence. "A venerable old man, *pater-familias.*"

In the big drawing-room, by a table prepared for service, Fyodor Stepanovitch stood, evidently waiting for them, and with him the priest in a calotte, and a deacon. The old man shook hands with Yulia without saying a word. Everyone was silent. Yulia was overcome with confusion.

The priest and the deacon began putting on their vestments. A censer was brought in, giving off sparks and fumes of incense and charcoal. The candles were lighted. The clerks walked into the drawing-room on tiptoe and stood in two rows along the wall. There was perfect stillness, no one even coughed.

"The blessing of God," began the deacon. The service was read with great solemnity; nothing was left out and two canticles were sung -- to sweetest Jesus and the most Holy Mother of God. The singers sang very slowly, holding up the music before them. Laptev noticed how confused his wife was. While they were singing the canticles, and the singers in different keys brought out "Lord have mercy on us," he kept expecting in nervous suspense that the old man would make some remark such as, "You don't know how to cross yourself," and he felt vexed. Why this crowd, and why this ceremony with priests and choristers? It was too bourgeois. But when she, like the old man, put her head under the gospel and afterwards several times dropped upon her knees, he realised that she liked it all, and was reassured.

At the end of the service, during "Many, many years," the priest gave the old man and Alexey the cross to kiss, but when Yulia went up, he put his hand over the cross, and showed he wanted to speak. Signs were made to the singers to stop.

"The prophet Samuel," began the priest, "went to Bethlehem at the bidding of the Lord, and there the elders of the town with fear and trembling asked him: 'Comest thou peaceably?' And the prophet answered: 'Peaceably: I am come to sacrifice unto the Lord: sanctify yourselves and come with me to the sacrifice.' Even so, Yulia, servant of God, shall we ask of thee, Dost thou come bringing peace into this house?"

Yulia flushed with emotion. As he finished, the priest gave her the cross to kiss, and said in quite a different tone of voice:

"Now Fyodor Fyodorovitch must be married; it's high time."

The choir began singing once more, people began moving, and the room was noisy again. The old man, much touched, with his eyes full of tears, kissed Yulia three times, made the sign of the cross over her face, and said:

"This is your home. I'm an old man and need nothing."

The clerks congratulated her and said something, but the choir was singing so loud that nothing else could be heard. Then they had lunch and drank champagne. She sat beside the old father, and he talked to her, saying that families ought not to be parted but live together in one house; that separation and disunion led to permanent rupture.

"I've made money and the children only do the spending of it," he said. "Now, you live with me and save money. It's time for an old man like me to rest."

Yulia had all the time a vision of Fyodor flitting about so like her husband, but shyer and more restless; he fussed about her and often kissed her hand.

"We are plain people, little sister," he said, and patches of red came into his face as he spoke. "We live simply in Russian style, like Christians, little sister."

As they went home, Laptev felt greatly relieved that everything had gone off so well, and that nothing outrageous had happened as he had expected. He said to his wife:

"You're surprised that such a stalwart, broad-shouldered father should have such stunted, narrow-chested sons as Fyodor and me. Yes; but it's easy to explain! My father married my mother when he was forty-five, and she was only seventeen. She turned pale and trembled in his presence. Nina was born first -- born of a comparatively healthy mother, and so she was finer and sturdier than we were. Fyodor and I were begotten and born after mother had been worn out by terror. I can remember my father correcting me -- or, to speak plainly, beating me -- before I was five years old. He used to thrash me with a birch, pull my ears, hit me on the head, and every morning when I woke up my first thought was whether he would beat me that day. Play and childish mischief was forbidden us. We had to go to morning service and to early mass. When we met priests or monks we had to kiss their hands; at home we had to sing hymns. Here you are religious and love all that, but I'm afraid of religion, and when I pass a church I remember my childhood, and am overcome with horror. I was taken to the warehouse as soon as I was eight years old. I worked like a working boy, and it was bad for my health, for I used to be beaten there every day. Afterwards when I went to the high school, I used to go to school till dinner-time, and after dinner I had to sit in that warehouse till evening; and things went on like that till I was twenty-two, till I got to know Yartsev, and he persuaded me to leave my father's house. That Yartsev did a great deal for me. I tell you what," said Laptev, and he laughed with pleasure: "let us go and pay Yartsev a visit at once. He's a very fine fellow! How touched he will be!"

VII

On a Saturday in November Anton Rubinstein was conducting in a symphony concert. It was very hot and crowded. Laptev stood behind the columns, while his wife and Kostya Kotchevoy were sitting in the third or fourth row some distance in front. At the very beginning of an interval a "certain person," Polina Nikolaevna Razsudin, quite unexpectedly passed by him. He had often since his marriage thought with trepidation of a possible meeting with her. When now she looked at him openly and directly, he realised that he had all this time shirked having things out with her, or writing her two or three friendly lines, as though he had been hiding from her; he felt ashamed and flushed crimson. She pressed his hand tightly and impulsively and asked:

"Have you seen Yartsev?"

And without waiting for an answer she went striding on impetuously as though someone were pushing her on from behind.

She was very thin and plain, with a long nose; her face always looked tired, and exhausted, and it seemed as though it were an effort to her to keep her eyes open, and not to fall down. She had fine, dark eyes, and an intelligent, kind, sincere expression, but her movements were awkward and abrupt. It was hard to talk to her, because she could not talk or listen quietly. Loving her was not easy. Sometimes when she was alone with

Laptev she would go on laughing for a long time, hiding her face in her hands, and would declare that love was not the chief thing in life for her, and would be as whimsical as a girl of seventeen; and before kissing her he would have to put out all the candles. She was thirty. She was married to a schoolmaster, but had not lived with her husband for years. She earned her living by giving music lessons and playing in quartettes.

During the ninth symphony she passed again as though by accident, but the crowd of men standing like a thick wall behind the columns prevented her going further, and she remained beside him. Laptev saw that she was wearing the same little velvet blouse she had worn at concerts last year and the year before. Her gloves were new, and her fan, too, was new, but it was a common one. She was fond of fine clothes, but she did not know how to dress, and grudged spending money on it. She dressed so badly and untidily that when she was going to her lessons striding hurriedly down the street, she might easily have been taken for a young monk.

The public applauded and shouted encore.

"You'll spend the evening with me," said Polina Nikolaevna, going up to Laptev and looking at him severely. "When this is over we'll go and have tea. Do you hear? I insist on it. You owe me a great deal, and haven't the moral right to refuse me such a trifle."

"Very well; let us go," Laptev assented.

Endless calls followed the conclusion of the concert. The audience got up from their seats and went out very slowly, and Laptev could not go away without telling his wife. He had to stand at the door and wait.

"I'm dying for some tea," Polina Nikolaevna said plaintively. "My very soul is parched."

"You can get something to drink here," said Laptev. "Let's go to the buffet."

"Oh, I've no money to fling away on waiters. I'm not a shopkeeper."

He offered her his arm; she refused, in a long, wearisome sentence which he had heard many times, to the effect that she did not class herself with the feebler fair sex, and did not depend on the services of gentlemen.

As she talked to him she kept looking about at the audience and greeting acquaintances; they were her fellow-students at the higher courses and at the conservatorium, and her pupils. She gripped their hands abruptly, as though she were tugging at them. But then she began twitching her shoulders, and trembling as though she were in a fever, and at last said softly, looking at Laptev with horror:

"Who is it you've married? Where were your eyes, you mad fellow? What did you see in that stupid, insignificant girl? Why, I loved you for your mind, for your soul, but that china doll wants nothing but your money!"

"Let us drop that, Polina," he said in a voice of supplication. "All that you can say to me about my marriage I've said to myself many times already. Don't cause me unnecessary pain."

Yulia Sergeyevna made her appearance, wearing a black dress with a big diamond brooch, which her father-in-law had sent her after the service. She was followed by her suite -- Kotchevoy, two doctors of their acquaintance, an officer, and a stout young man in student's uniform, called Kish.

"You go on with Kostya," Laptev said to his wife. "I'm coming later."

Yulia nodded and went on. Polina Nikolaevna gazed after her, quivering all over and twitching nervously, and in her eyes there was a look of repulsion, hatred, and pain.

Laptev was afraid to go home with her, foreseeing an unpleasant discussion, cutting words, and tears, and he suggested that they should go and have tea at a restaurant. But she said:

"No, no. I want to go home. Don't dare to talk to me of restaurants."

She did not like being in a restaurant, because the atmosphere of restaurants seemed to her poisoned by tobacco smoke and the breath of men. Against all men she did not know she cherished a strange prejudice, regarding them all as immoral rakes, capable of attacking her at any moment. Besides, the music played at restaurants jarred on her nerves and gave her a headache.

Coming out of the Hall of Nobility, they took a sledge in Ostozhenka and drove to Savelovsky Lane, where she lodged. All the way Laptev thought about her. It was true that he owed her a great deal. He had made her acquaintance at the flat of his friend Yartsev, to whom she was giving lessons in harmony. Her love for him was deep and perfectly disinterested, and her relations with him did not alter her habits; she went on giving her lessons and wearing herself out with work as before. Through her he came to understand and love music, which he had scarcely cared for till then.

"Half my kingdom for a cup of tea!" she pronounced in a hollow voice, covering her mouth with her muff that she might not catch cold. "I've given five lessons, confound them! My pupils are as stupid as posts; I nearly died of exasperation. I don't know how long this slavery can go on. I'm worn out. As soon as I can scrape together three hundred roubles, I shall throw it all up and go to the Crimea, to lie on the beach and drink in ozone. How I love the sea -- oh, how I love the sea!"

"You'll never go," said Laptev. "To begin with, you'll never save the money; and, besides, you'd grudge spending it. Forgive me, I repeat again: surely it's quite as humiliating to collect the money by farthings from idle people who have music lessons to while away their time, as to borrow it from your friends."

"I haven't any friends," she said irritably. "And please don't talk nonsense. The working class to which I belong has one privilege: the consciousness of being incorruptible -- the right to refuse to be indebted to wretched little shopkeepers, and to treat them with scorn. No, indeed, you don't buy me! I'm not a Yulitchka! Laptev did not attempt to pay the driver, knowing that it would call forth a perfect torrent of words, such as he had often heard before. She paid herself.

She had a little furnished room in the flat of a solitary lady who provided her meals. Her big Becker piano was for the time at Yartsev's in Great Nikitsky Street, and she went there every day to play on it. In her room there were armchairs in loose covers, a bed with a white summer quilt, and flowers belonging to the landlady; there were oleographs on the walls, and there was nothing that would have suggested that there was a woman, and a woman of university education, living in it. There was no toilet table; there were no books; there was not even a writing-table. It was evident that she went to bed as soon as she got home, and went out as soon as she got up in the morning.

The cook brought in the samovar. Polina Nikolaevna made tea, and, still shivering -- the room was cold -- began abusing the singers who had sung in the ninth symphony. She was so tired she could hardly keep her eyes open. She drank one glass of tea, then a second, and then a third.

"And so you are married," she said. "But don't be uneasy; I'm not going to pine away. I shall be able to tear you out of my heart. Only it's annoying and bitter to me that you are just as contemptible as everyone else; that what you want in a woman is not brains or intellect, but simply a body, good looks, and youth. . . . Youth!" she pronounced through her nose, as though mimicking someone, and she laughed. "Youth! You must have purity,*reinheit! reinheit!*" she laughed, throwing herself back in her chair. "*Reinheit!*"

When she left off laughing her eyes were wet with tears.

"You're happy, at any rate?" she asked.

"No."

"Does she love you?"

Laptev, agitated, and feeling miserable, stood up and began walking about the room.

"No," he repeated. "If you want to know, Polina, I'm very unhappy. There's no help for it; I've done the stupid thing, and there's no correcting it now. I must look at it philosophically. She married me without love, stupidly, perhaps with mercenary motives, but without understanding, and now she evidently sees her mistake and is miserable. I see it. At night we sleep together, but by day she is afraid to be left alone with me for five minutes, and tries to find distraction, society. With me she feels ashamed and frightened."

"And yet she takes money from you?"

"That's stupid, Polina!" cried Laptev. "She takes money from me because it makes absolutely no difference to her whether she has it or not. She is an honest, pure girl. She married me simply because she wanted to get away from her father, that's all."

"And are you sure she would have married you if you had not been rich?" asked Polina.

"I'm not sure of anything," said Laptev dejectedly. "Not of anything. I don't understand anything. For God's sake, Polina, don't let us talk about it."

"Do you love her?"

"Desperately."

A silence followed. She drank a fourth glass, while he paced up and down, thinking that by now his wife was probably having supper at the doctors' club.

"But is it possible to love without knowing why?" asked Polina, shrugging her shoulders. "No; it's the promptings of animal passion! You are poisoned, intoxicated by that beautiful body, that *reinheit!* Go away from me; you are unclean! Go to her!"

She brandished her hand at him, then took up his hat and hurled it at him. He put on his fur coat without speaking and went out, but she ran after him into the passage, clutched his arm above the elbow, and broke into sobs.

"Hush, Polina! Don't!" he said, and could not unclasp her fingers. "Calm yourself, I entreat you."

She shut her eyes and turned pale, and her long nose became an unpleasant waxy colour like a corpse's, and Laptev still could not unclasp her fingers. She had fainted. He lifted her up carefully, laid her on her bed, and sat by her for ten minutes till she came to herself. Her hands were cold, her pulse was weak and uneven.

"Go home," she said, opening her eyes. "Go away, or I shall begin howling again. I must take myself in hand."

When he came out, instead of going to the doctors' club where his friends were expecting him, he went home. All the way home he was asking himself reproachfully why he had not settled down to married life with that woman who loved him so much, and was in reality his wife and friend. She was the one human being who was devoted to him; and, besides, would it not have been a grateful and worthy task to give happiness, peace, and a home to that proud, clever, overworked creature? Was it for him, he asked himself, to lay claim to youth and beauty, to that happiness which could not be, and which, as though in punishment or mockery, had kept him for the last three months in a state of gloom and oppression. The honeymoon was long over, and he still, absurd to say, did not know what sort of person his wife was. To her school friends and her father she wrote long letters of five sheets, and was never at a loss for something to say to them, but to him she never spoke except about the weather or to tell him that dinner was ready, or that it was supper-time. When at night she said her lengthy prayers and then kissed her crosses and ikons, he thought, watching her with hatred, "Here she's praying. What's she praying about? What about?" In his thoughts he showered insults on himself and her, telling himself that when he got into bed and took her into his arms, he was taking what he had paid for; but it was horrible. If only it had been a healthy, reckless, sinful woman; but here he had youth, piety, meekness, the pure eyes of innocence. . . . While they were engaged her piety had touched him; now the conventional definiteness of her views and convictions seemed to him a barrier, behind which the real truth could not be seen. Already everything in his married life was agonising. When his wife, sitting beside him in the theatre, sighed or laughed spontaneously, it was bitter to him that she enjoyed herself alone and would not share her delight with him. And it was remarkable that she was friendly with all his friends, and they all knew what she was like already, while he knew nothing about her, and only moped and was dumbly jealous.

When he got home Laptev put on his dressing-gown and slippers, and sat down in his study to read a novel. His wife was not at home. But within half an hour there was a ring at the hall door, and he heard the muffled footsteps of Pyotr running to open it. It was Yulia. She walked into the study in her fur coat, her cheeks rosy with the frost,

"There's a great fire in Pryesnya," she said breathlessly. "There's a tremendous glow. I'm going to see it with Konstantin Ivanovitch."

"Well, do, dear!"

The sight of her health, her freshness, and the childish horror in her eyes, reassured Laptev. He read for another half-hour and went to bed.

Next day Polina Nikolaevna sent to the warehouse two books she had borrowed from him, all his letters and his photographs; with them was a note consisting of one word -- *"basta."*

VIII

Towards the end of October Nina Fyodorovna had unmistakable symptoms of a relapse. There was a change in her face, and she grew rapidly thinner. In spite of acute pain she still imagined that she was getting better, and got up and dressed every morning as though she were well, and then lay on her bed, fully dressed, for the rest of the day. And towards the end she became very talkative. She would lie on her back and talk in a low voice, speaking with an effort and breathing painfully. She died suddenly under the following circumstances.

It was a clear moonlight evening. In the street people were tobogganing in the fresh snow, and their clamour floated in at the window. Nina Fyodorovna was lying on her back in bed, and Sasha, who had no one to take turns with her now, was sitting beside her half asleep.

"I don't remember his father's name," Nina Fyodorovna was saying softly, "but his name was Ivan Kotchevoy -- a poor clerk. He was a sad drunkard, the Kingdom of Heaven be his! He used to come to us, and every month we used to give him a pound of sugar and two ounces of tea. And money, too, sometimes, of course. Yes. . . . And then, this is what happened. Our Kotchevoy began drinking heavily and died, consumed by vodka. He left a little son, a boy of seven. Poor little orphan! . . . We took him and hid him in the clerk's quarters, and he lived there for a whole year, without father's knowing. And when father did see him, he only waved his hand and said nothing. When Kostya, the little orphan, was nine years old -- by that time I was engaged to be married -- I took him round to all the day schools. I went from one to the other, and no one would take him. And he cried. . . . 'What are you crying for, little silly?' I said. I took him to Razgulyay to the second school, where -- God bless them for it! -- they took him, and the boy began going every day on foot from Pyatnitsky Street to Razgulyay Street and back again. . . . Alyosha paid for him. . . . By God's grace the boy got on, was good at his lessons, and turned out well. . . . He's a lawyer now in Moscow, a friend of Alyosha's, and so good in science. Yes, we had compassion on a fellow-creature and took him into our house, and now I daresay, he remembers us in his prayers. . . Yes. . . ."

Nina Fyodorovna spoke more and more slowly with long pauses, then after a brief silence she suddenly raised herself and sat up.

"There's something the matter with me . . . something seems wrong," she said. "Lord have mercy on me! Oh, I can't breathe!

Sasha knew that her mother would soon die; seeing now how suddenly her face looked drawn, she guessed that it was the end, and she was frightened.

"Mother, you mustn't!" she began sobbing. "You mustn't."

"Run to the kitchen; let them go for father. I am very ill indeed."

Sasha ran through all the rooms calling, but there were none of the servants in the house, and the only person she found was Lida asleep on a chest in the dining-room with her clothes on and without a pillow. Sasha ran into the yard just as she was without her goloshes, and then into the street. On a bench at the gate her nurse was sitting watching the tobogganing. From beyond the river, where the tobogganing slope was, came the strains of a military band.

"Nurse, mother's dying!" sobbed Sasha. "You must go for father! . . ."

The nurse went upstairs, and, glancing at the sick woman, thrust a lighted wax candle into her hand. Sasha rushed about in terror and besought someone to go for her father, then she put on a coat and a kerchief, and ran into the street. From the servants she knew already that her father had another wife and two children with whom he lived in Bazarny Street. She ran out of the gate and turned to the left, crying, and frightened of unknown people. She soon began to sink into the snow and grew numb with cold.

She met an empty sledge, but she did not take it: perhaps, she thought, the man would drive her out of town, rob her, and throw her into the cemetery (the servants had talked of such a case at tea). She went on and on, sobbing and panting with exhaustion. When she got into Bazarny Street, she inquired where M. Panaurov lived. An unknown woman spent a long time directing her, and seeing that she did not understand, took her by the hand and led her to a house of one storey that stood back from the street. The door stood open. Sasha ran through the entry, along the corridor, and found herself at last in a warm, lighted room where her father was sitting by the samovar with a lady and two children. But by now she was unable to utter a word, and could only sob. Panaurov understood.

"Mother's worse?" he asked. "Tell me, child: is mother worse?"

He was alarmed and sent for a sledge.

When they got home, Nina Fyodorovna was sitting propped up with pillows, with a candle in her hand. Her face looked dark and her eyes were closed. Crowding in the doorway stood the nurse, the cook, the housemaid, a peasant called Prokofy and a few persons of the humbler class, who were complete strangers. The nurse was giving them orders in a whisper, and they did not understand. Inside the room at the window stood Lida, with a pale and sleepy face, gazing severely at her mother.

Panaurov took the candle out of Nina Fyodorovna's hand, and, frowning contemptuously, flung it on the chest of drawers.

"This is awful!" he said, and his shoulders quivered. "Nina, you must lie down," he said affectionately. "Lie down, dear."

She looked at him, but did not know him. They laid her down on her back.

When the priest and the doctor, Sergey Borisovitch, arrived, the servants crossed themselves devoutly and prayed for her.

"What a sad business!" said the doctor thoughtfully, coming out into the drawing-room. "Why, she was still young -- not yet forty."

They heard the loud sobbing of the little girls. Panaurov, with a pale face and moist eyes, went up to the doctor and said in a faint, weak voice:

"Do me a favour, my dear fellow. Send a telegram to Moscow. I'm not equal to it."

The doctor fetched the ink and wrote the following telegram to his daughter:

"Madame Panaurov died at eight o'clock this evening. Tell your husband: a mortgaged house for sale in Dvoryansky Street, nine thousand cash. Auction on twelfth. Advise him not miss opportunity."

IX

Laptev lived in one of the turnings out of Little Dmitrovka. Besides the big house facing the street, he rented also a two-storey lodge in the yard at the back of his friend Kotchevoy, a lawyer's assistant whom all the Laptevs called Kostya, because he had grown up under their eyes. Facing this lodge stood another, also of two storeys, inhabited by a French family consisting of a husband and wife and five daughters.

There was a frost of twenty degrees. The windows were frozen over. Waking up in the morning, Kostya, with an anxious face, took twenty drops of a medicine; then, taking two dumb-bells out of the bookcase, he did gymnastic exercises. He was tall and thin, with big reddish moustaches; but what was most noticeable in his appearance was the length of his legs.

Pyotr, a middle-aged peasant in a reefer jacket and cotton breeches tucked into his high boots, brought in the samovar and made the tea.

"It's very nice weather now, Konstantin Ivanovitch," he said.

"It is, but I tell you what, brother, it's a pity we can't get on, you and I, without such exclamations."

Pyotr sighed from politeness.

"What are the little girls doing?" asked Kotchevoy.

"The priest has not come. Alexey Fyodorovitch is giving them their lesson himself."

Kostya found a spot in the window that was not covered with frost, and began looking through a field-glass at the windows of the house where the French family lived.

"There's no seeing," he said.

Meanwhile Alexey Fyodorovitch was giving Sasha and Lida a scripture lesson below. For the last six weeks they had been living in Moscow, and were installed with their governess in the lower storey of the lodge. And three times a week a teacher from a school in the town, and a priest, came to give them lessons. Sasha was going through the New Testament and Lida was going through the Old. The time before Lida had been set the story up to Abraham to learn by heart.

"And so Adam and Eve had two sons," said Laptev. "Very good. But what were they called? Try to remember them!"

Lida, still with the same severe face, gazed dumbly at the table. She moved her lips, but without speaking; and the elder girl, Sasha, looked into her face, frowning.

"You know it very well, only you mustn't be nervous," said Laptev. "Come, what were Adam's sons called?"

"Abel and Canel," Lida whispered.

"Cain and Abel," Laptev corrected her.

A big tear rolled down Lida's cheek and dropped on the book. Sasha looked down and turned red, and she, too, was on the point of tears. Laptev felt a lump in his throat, and was so sorry for them he could not speak. He got up from the table and lighted a cigarette. At that moment Kotchevoy came down the stairs with a paper in his hand. The little girls stood up, and without looking at him, made curtsies.

"For God's sake, Kostya, give them their lessons," said Laptev, turning to him. "I'm afraid I shall cry, too, and I have to go to the warehouse before dinner."

"All right."

Alexey Fyodorovitch went away. Kostya, with a very serious face, sat down to the table and drew the Scripture history towards him.

"Well," he said; "where have you got to?"

"She knows about the Flood," said Sasha.

"The Flood? All right. Let's peg in at the Flood. Fire away about the Flood." Kostya skimmed through a brief description of the Flood in the book, and said: "I must remark that there really never was a flood such as is described here. And there was no such person as Noah. Some thousands of years before the birth of Christ, there was an extraordinary inundation of the earth, and that's not only mentioned in the Jewish Bible, but in the books of other ancient peoples: the Greeks, the Chaldeans, the Hindoos. But whatever the inundation may have been, it couldn't have covered the whole earth. It may have flooded the plains, but the mountains must have remained. You can read this book, of course, but don't put too much faith in it."

Tears trickled down Lida's face again. She turned away and suddenly burst into such loud sobs, that Kostya started and jumped up from his seat in great confusion.

"I want to go home," she said, "to papa and to nurse."

Sasha cried too. Kostya went upstairs to his own room, and spoke on the telephone to Yulia Sergeyevna.

"My dear soul," he said, "the little girls are crying again; there's no doing anything with them."

Yulia Sergeyevna ran across from the big house in her indoor dress, with only a knitted shawl over her shoulders, and chilled through by the frost, began comforting the children.

"Do believe me, do believe me," she said in an imploring voice, hugging first one and then the other. "Your papa's coming to-day; he has sent a telegram. You're grieving for mother, and I grieve too. My heart's torn, but what can we do? We must bow to God's will!"

When they left off crying, she wrapped them up and took them out for a drive. They stopped near the Iverskoy chapel, put up candles at the shrine, and, kneeling down, prayed. On the way back they went in Filippov's, and had cakes sprinkled with poppy-seeds.

The Laptevs had dinner between two and three. Pyotr handed the dishes. This Pyotr waited on the family, and by day ran to the post, to the warehouse, to the law courts for Kostya; he spent his evenings making cigarettes, ran to open the door at night, and before five o'clock in the morning was up lighting the stoves, and no one knew where he slept. He was very fond of opening seltzer-water bottles and did it easily, without a bang and without spilling a drop.

"With God's blessing," said Kostya, drinking off a glass of vodka before the soup.

At first Yulia Sergeyevna did not like Kostya; his bass voice, his phrases such as "Landed him one on the beak," "filth," "produce the samovar," etc., his habit of clinking glasses and making sentimental speeches, seemed to her trivial. But as she got to know him better, she began to feel very much at home with him. He was open with her; he liked talking to her in a low voice in the evening, and even gave her novels of his own composition to read, though these had been kept a secret even from such friends as Laptev and Yartsev. She read these novels and praised them, so that she might not disappoint him, and he was delighted because he hoped sooner or later to become a distinguished author.

In his novels he described nothing but country-house life, though he had only seen the country on rare occasions when visiting friends at a summer villa, and had only been in a real country-house once in his life, when he had been to Volokolamsk on law business. He avoided any love interest as though he were ashamed of it; he put in frequent descriptions of nature, and in them was fond of using such expressions as, "the capricious lines of the mountains, the miraculous forms of the clouds, the harmony of mysterious rhythms. . . ." His novels had never been published, and this he attributed to the censorship.

He liked the duties of a lawyer, but yet he considered that his most important pursuit was not the law but these novels. He believed that he had a subtle, æsthetic temperament, and he always had leanings towards art. He neither sang nor played on any musical instrument, and was absolutely without an ear for music, but he attended all the symphony and philharmonic concerts, got up concerts for charitable objects, and made the acquaintance of singers. . . .

They used to talk at dinner.

"It's a strange thing," said Laptev, "my Fyodor took my breath away again! He said we must find out the date of the centenary of our firm, so as to try and get raised to noble rank; and he said it quite seriously. What can be the matter with him? I confess I begin to feel worried about him."

They talked of Fyodor, and of its being the fashion nowadays to adopt some pose or other. Fyodor, for instance, tried to appear like a plain merchant, though he had ceased to be one; and when the teacher came from the school, of which old Laptev was the patron, to ask Fyodor for his salary, the latter changed his voice and deportment, and behaved with the teacher as though he were someone in authority.

There was nothing to be done; after dinner they went into the study. They talked about the decadents, about "The Maid of Orleans," and Kostya delivered a regular monologue; he fancied that he was very successful in imitating Ermolova. Then they sat down and played whist. The little girls had not gone back to the lodge but were sitting together in one arm-chair, with pale and mournful faces, and were listening to every noise in the street, wondering whether it was their father coming. In the evening when it was dark and the candles were lighted, they felt deeply dejected. The talk over the whist, the footsteps of Pyotr, the crackling in the fireplace, jarred on their nerves, and they did not like to look at the fire. In the evenings they did not want to cry, but they felt strange, and there was a load on their hearts. They could not understand how people could talk and laugh when their mother was dead.

"What did you see through the field-glasses today?" Yulia Sergeyevna asked Kostya.

"Nothing to-day, but yesterday I saw the old Frenchman having his bath."

At seven o'clock Yulia and Kostya went to the Little Theatre. Laptev was left with the little girls.

"It's time your father was here," he said, looking at his watch. "The train must be late."

The children sat in their arm-chair dumb and huddling together like animals when they are cold, while he walked about the room looking impatiently at his watch. It was quiet in the house. But just before nine o'clock someone rang at the bell. Pyotr went to open the door.

Hearing a familiar voice, the children shrieked, burst into sobs, and ran into the hall. Panaurov was wearing a sumptuous coat of antelope skin, and his head and moustaches were white with hoar frost. "In a minute, in a minute," he muttered, while Sasha and Lida, sobbing and laughing, kissed his cold hands, his hat, his antelope coat. With the languor of a handsome man spoilt by too much love, he fondled the children without haste, then went into the study and said, rubbing his hands:

"I've not come to stay long, my friends. I'm going to Petersburg to-morrow. They've promised to transfer me to another town."

He was staying at the Dresden Hotel.

X

A friend who was often at the Laptevs' was Ivan Gavrilitch Yartsev. He was a strong, healthy man with black hair and a clever, pleasant face. He was considered to be handsome, but of late he had begun to grow stout, and that rather spoilt his face and figure; another thing that spoilt him was that he wore his hair cut so close that the skin showed through.

At the University his tall figure and physical strength had won him the nickname of "the pounder" among the students. He had taken his degree with the Laptev brothers in the faculty of philology -- then he went in for science and now had the degree of *magister* in chemistry. But he had never given a lecture or even been a demonstrator. He taught physics and natural history in the modern school, and in two girls' high schools. He was enthusiastic over his pupils, especially the girls, and used to maintain that a remarkable generation was growing up. At home he spent his time studying sociology and Russian history, as well as chemistry, and he sometimes published brief notes in the newspapers and magazines, signing them "Y." When he talked of some botanical or zoological subject, he spoke like an historian; when he was discussing some historical question, he approached it as a man of science.

Kish, nicknamed "the eternal student," was also like one of the family at the Laptevs'. He had been for three years studying medicine. Then he took up mathematics, and spent two years over each year's course. His father, a provincial druggist, used to send him forty roubles a month, to which his mother, without his father's knowledge, added another ten. And this sum was not only sufficient for his board and lodging, but even for such luxuries as an overcoat lined with Polish beaver, gloves, scent, and photographs (he often had photographs taken of himself and used to distribute them among his friends). He was neat and demure, slightly bald, with golden side-whiskers, and he had the air of a man nearly always ready to oblige. He was always busy looking after other people's affairs. At one time he would be rushing about with a subscription list; at another time he would be freezing in the early morning at a ticket office to buy tickets for ladies of his acquaintance, or at somebody's request would be ordering a wreath or a bouquet. People simply said of him: "Kish will go, Kish will do it, Kish will buy it." He was usually unsuccessful in carrying out his commissions. Reproaches were showered upon him, people frequently forgot to pay him for the things he bought, but he simply sighed in hard cases and never protested. He was never particularly delighted nor disappointed; his stories were always long and boring; and his jokes invariably provoked laughter just because they were not funny. Thus, one day, for instance, intending to make a joke, he said to Pyotr: "Pyotr, you're not a sturgeon;" and this aroused a general laugh, and he, too, laughed for a long time, much pleased at having made such a successful jest. Whenever one of the professors was buried, he walked in front with the mutes.

Yartsev and Kish usually came in the evening to tea. If the Laptevs were not going to the theatre or a concert, the evening tea lingered on till supper. One evening in February the following conversation took place:

"A work of art is only significant and valuable when there are some serious social problems contained in its central idea," said Kostya, looking wrathfully at Yartsev. "If there is in the work a protest against serfdom, or the author takes up arms against the vulgarity of aristocratic society, the work is significant and valuable. The novels that are taken up with 'Ach!' and 'Och!' and 'she loved him, while he ceased to love her,' I tell you, are worthless, and damn them all, I say!"

"I agree with you, Konstantin Ivanovitch," said Yulia Sergeyevna. "One describes a love scene; another, a betrayal; and the third, meeting again after separation. Are there no other subjects? Why, there are many people sick, unhappy, harassed by poverty, to whom reading all that must be distasteful."

It was disagreeable to Laptev to hear his wife, not yet twenty-two, speaking so seriously and coldly about love. He understood why this was so.

"If poetry does not solve questions that seem so important," said Yartsev, "you should turn to works on technical subjects, criminal law, or finance, read scientific pamphlets. What need is there to discuss in 'Romeo and Juliet,' liberty of speech, or the disinfecting of prisons, instead of love, when you can find all that in special articles and textbooks?"

"That's pushing it to the extreme," Kostya interrupted. "We are not talking of giants like Shakespeare or Goethe; we are talking of the hundreds of talented mediocre writers, who would be infinitely more valuable if they would let love alone, and would employ themselves in spreading knowledge and humane ideas among the masses."

Kish, lisping and speaking a little through his nose, began telling the story of a novel he had lately been reading. He spoke circumstantially and without haste. Three minutes passed, then five, then ten, and no one could make out what he was talking about, and his face grew more and more indifferent, and his eyes more and more blank.

"Kish, do be quick over it," Yulia Sergeyevna could not resist saying; "it's really agonizing!"

"Shut up, Kish!" Kostya shouted to him.

They all laughed, and Kish with them.

Fyodor came in. Flushing red in patches, he greeted them all in a nervous flurry, and led his brother away into the study. Of late he had taken to avoiding the company of more than one person at once.

"Let the young people laugh, while we speak from the heart in here," he said, settling himself in a deep arm-chair at a distance from the lamp. "It's a long time, my dear brother, since we've seen each other. How long is it since you were at the warehouse? I think it must be a week."

"Yes, there's nothing for me to do there. And I must confess that the old man wearies me."

"Of course, they could get on at the warehouse without you and me, but one must have some occupation. 'In the sweat of thy brow thou shalt eat bread,' as it is written. God loves work."

Pyotr brought in a glass of tea on a tray. Fyodor drank it without sugar, and asked for more. He drank a great deal of tea, and could get through as many as ten glasses in the evening.

"I tell you what, brother," he said, getting up and going to his brother. "Laying aside philosophic subtleties, you must get elected on to the town council, and little by little we will get you on to the local Board, and then to be an alderman. And as time goes on -- you are a clever man and well-educated -- you will be noticed in Petersburg and asked to go there -- active men on the provincial assemblies and town councils are all the fashion there now -- and before you are fifty you'll be a privy councillor, and have a ribbon across your shoulders."

Laptev made no answer; he knew that all this -- being a privy councillor and having a ribbon over his shoulder -- was what Fyodor desired for himself, and he did not know what to say.

The brothers sat still and said nothing. Fyodor opened his watch and for a long, long time gazed into it with strained attention, as though he wanted to detect the motion of the hand, and the expression of his face struck Laptev as strange.

They were summoned to supper. Laptev went into the dining-room, while Fyodor remained in the study. The argument was over and Yartsev was speaking in the tones of a professor giving a lecture:

"Owing to differences of climate, of energy, of tastes, of age, equality among men is physically impossible. But civilised man can make this inequality innocuous, as he has already done with bogs and bears. A learned man succeeded in making a cat, a mouse, a falcon, a sparrow, all eat out of one plate; and education, one must hope, will do the same thing with men. Life continually progresses, civilisation makes enormous advances before our eyes, and obviously a time will come when we shall think, for instance, the present condition of the factory population as absurd as we now do the state of serfdom, in which girls were exchanged for dogs."

"That won't be for a long while, a very long while," said Kostya, with a laugh, "not till Rothschild thinks his cellars full of gold absurd, and till then the workers may bend their backs and die of hunger. No; that's not it. We mustn't wait for it; we must struggle for it. Do you suppose because the cat eats out of the same saucer as the mouse -- do you suppose that she is influenced by a sense of conscious intelligence? Not a bit of it! She's made to do it by force."

"Fyodor and I are rich; our father's a capitalist, a millionaire. You will have to struggle with us," said Laptev, rubbing his forehead with his hand. "Struggle with me is an idea I cannot grasp. I am rich, but what has money given me so far? What has this power given me? In what way am I happier than you? My childhood was slavery, and money did not save me from the birch. When Nina was ill and died, my money did not help her. If people don't care for me, I can't make them like me if I spend a hundred million."

"But you can do a great deal of good," said Kish.

"Good, indeed! You spoke to me yesterday of a mathematical man who is looking for a job. Believe me, I can do as little for him as you can. I can give money, but that's not what he wants -- I asked a well-known musician to help a poor violinist, and this is what he answered: 'You apply to me just because you are not a musician yourself.' In the same way I say to you that you apply for help to me so confidently because you've never been in the position of a rich man."

"Why you bring in the comparison with a well-known musician I don't understand!" said Yulia Sergeyevna, and she flushed crimson. "What has the well-known musician to do with it!"

Her face was quivering with hatred, and she dropped her eyes to conceal the feeling. And not only her husband, but all the men sitting at the table, knew what the look in her face meant.

"What has the well-known musician got to do with it?" she said slowly. "Why, nothing's easier than helping someone poor."

Silence followed. Pyotr handed the woodcock, but they all refused it, and ate nothing but salad. Laptev did not remember what he had said, but it was clear to him that it was not his words that were hateful, but the fact of his meddling in the conversation at all.

After supper he went into his study; intently, with a beating heart, expecting further humiliation, he listened to what was going on in the hall. An argument had sprung up there again. Then Yartsev sat down to the piano and played a sentimental song. He was a man of varied accomplishments; he could play and sing, and even perform conjuring tricks.

"You may please yourselves, my friends, but I'm not going to stay at home," said Yulia. "We must go somewhere."

They decided to drive out of town, and sent Kish to the merchant's club to order a three-horse sledge. They did not ask Laptev to go with them because he did not usually join these expeditions, and because his brother was sitting with him; but he took it to mean that his society bored them, and that he was not wanted in their light-hearted youthful company. And his vexation, his bitter feeling, was so intense that he almost shed tears. He was positively glad that he was treated so ungraciously, that he was scorned, that he was a stupid, dull husband, a money-bag; and it seemed to him, that he would have been even more glad if his wife were to deceive him that night with his best friend, and were afterwards to acknowledge it, looking at him with hatred. . . . He was jealous on her account of their student friends, of actors, of singers, of Yartsev, even of casual acquaintances; and now he had a passionate longing for her really to be unfaithful to him. He longed to find her in another man's arms, and to be rid of this nightmare forever. Fyodor was drinking tea, gulping it noisily. But he, too, got up to go.

"Our old father must have got cataract," he said, as he put on his fur coat. "His sight has become very poor."

Laptev put on his coat, too, and went out. After seeing his brother part of the way home, he took a sledge and drove to Yar's.

"And this is family happiness!" he said, jeering at himself. "This is love!"

His teeth were chattering, and he did not know if it were jealousy or something else. He walked about near the tables; listened to a comic singer in the hall. He had not a single phrase ready if he should meet his own party; and he felt sure beforehand that if he met his wife, he would only smile pitifully and not cleverly, and that everyone would understand what feeling had induced him to come here. He was bewildered by the electric light, the loud music, the smell of powder, and the fact that the ladies he met looked at him. He stood at the doors trying to see and to hear what was going on in the private rooms, and it seemed to him that he was somehow playing a mean, contemptible part on a level with the comic singers and those ladies. Then he went to Strelna, but he found none of his circle there, either; and only when on the way home he was again driving up to Yar's, a three-horse sledge noisily overtook him. The driver was drunk and shouting, and he could hear Yartsev laughing: "Ha, ha, ha!"

Laptev returned home between three and four. Yulia Sergeyevna was in bed. Noticing that she was not asleep, he went up to her and said sharply:

"I understand your repulsion, your hatred, but you might spare me before other people; you might conceal your feelings."

She got up and sat on the bed with her legs dangling. Her eyes looked big and black in the lamplight.

"I beg your pardon," she said.

He could not utter a single word from excitement and the trembling of his whole body; he stood facing her and was dumb. She trembled, too, and sat with the air of a criminal waiting for explanations.

"How I suffer!" he said at last, and he clutched his head. "I'm in hell, and I'm out of my mind."

"And do you suppose it's easy for me?" she asked, with a quiver in her voice. "God alone knows what I go through."

"You've been my wife for six months, but you haven't a spark of love for me in your heart. There's no hope, not one ray of light! Why did you marry me?" Laptev went on with despair. "Why? What demon thrust you into my arms? What did you hope for? What did you want?"

She looked at him with terror, as though she were afraid he would kill her.

"Did I attract you? Did you like me?" he went on, gasping for breath. "No. Then what? What? Tell me what?" he cried. "Oh, the cursed money! The cursed money!"

"I swear to God, no!" she cried, and she crossed herself. She seemed to shrink under the insult, and for the first time he heard her crying. "I swear to God, no!" she repeated. "I didn't think about your money; I didn't want it. I simply thought I should do wrong if I refused you. I was afraid of spoiling your life and mine. And now I am suffering for my mistake. I'm suffering unbearably!"

She sobbed bitterly, and he saw that she was hurt; and not knowing what to say, dropped down on the carpet before her.

"That's enough; that's enough," he muttered. "I insulted you because I love you madly." He suddenly kissed her foot and passionately hugged it. "If only a spark of love," he muttered. "Come, lie to me; tell me a lie! Don't say it's a mistake! . . ."

But she went on crying, and he felt that she was only enduring his caresses as an inevitable consequence of her mistake. And the foot he had kissed she drew under her like a bird. He felt sorry for her.

She got into bed and covered her head over; he undressed and got into bed, too. In the morning they both felt confused and did not know what to talk about, and he even fancied she walked unsteadily on the foot he had kissed.

Before dinner Panaurov came to say good-bye. Yulia had an irresistible desire to go to her own home; it would be nice, she thought, to go away and have a rest from married life, from the embarrassment and the continual consciousness that she had done wrong. It was decided at dinner that she should set off with Panaurov, and stay with her father for two or three weeks until she was tired of it.

XI

She travelled with Panaurov in a reserved compartment; he had on his head an astrachan cap of peculiar shape.

"Yes, Petersburg did not satisfy me," he said, drawling, with a sigh. "They promise much, but nothing definite. Yes, my dear girl. I have been a Justice of the Peace, a member of the local Board, chairman of the Board of

Magistrates, and finally councillor of the provincial administration. I think I have served my country and have earned the right to receive attention; but -- would you believe it? -- I can never succeed in wringing from the authorities a post in another town. . . .

Panaurov closed his eyes and shook his head.

"They don't recognise me," he went on, as though dropping asleep. "Of course I'm not an administrator of genius, but, on the other hand, I'm a decent, honest man, and nowadays even that's something rare. I regret to say I have not been always quite straightforward with women, but in my relations with the Russian government I've always been a gentleman. But enough of that," he said, opening his eyes; "let us talk of you. What put it into your head to visit your papa so suddenly?"

"Well. . . . I had a little misunderstanding with my husband," said Yulia, looking at his cap.

"Yes. What a queer fellow he is! All the Laptevs are queer. Your husband's all right -- he's nothing out of the way, but his brother Fyodor is a perfect fool."

Panaurov sighed and asked seriously:

"And have you a lover yet?"

Yulia looked at him in amazement and laughed.

"Goodness knows what you're talking about."

It was past ten o'clock when they got out at a big station and had supper. When the train went on again Panaurov took off his greatcoat and his cap, and sat down beside Yulia.

"You are very charming, I must tell you," he began. "Excuse me for the eating-house comparison, but you remind me of fresh salted cucumber; it still smells of the hotbed, so to speak, and yet has a smack of the salt and a scent of fennel about it. As time goes on you will make a magnificent woman, a wonderful, exquisite woman. If this trip of ours had happened five years ago," he sighed, "I should have felt it my duty to join the ranks of your adorers, but now, alas, I'm a veteran on the retired list."

He smiled mournfully, but at the same time graciously, and put his arm round her waist.

"You must be mad!" she said; she flushed crimson and was so frightened that her hands and feet turned cold.

"Leave off, Grigory Nikolaevitch!"

"What are you afraid of, dear?" he asked softly. "What is there dreadful about it? It's simply that you're not used to it."

If a woman protested he always interpreted it as a sign that he had made an impression on her and attracted her. Holding Yulia round the waist, he kissed her firmly on the cheek, then on the lips, in the full conviction that he was giving her intense gratification. Yulia recovered from her alarm and confusion, and began laughing. He kissed her once more and said, as he put on his ridiculous cap:

"That is all that the old veteran can give you. A Turkish Pasha, a kind-hearted old fellow, was presented by someone -- or inherited, I fancy it was -- a whole harem. When his beautiful young wives drew up in a row before him, he walked round them, kissed each one of them, and said: 'That is all that I am equal to giving you.' And that's just what I say, too."

All this struck her as stupid and extraordinary, and amused her. She felt mischievous. Standing up on the seat and humming, she got a box of sweets from the shelf, and throwing him a piece of chocolate, shouted:

"Catch!"

He caught it. With a loud laugh she threw him another sweet, then a third, and he kept catching them and putting them into his mouth, looking at her with imploring eyes; and it seemed to her that in his face, his features, his expression, there was a great deal that was feminine and childlike. And when, out of breath, she sat down on the seat and looked at him, laughing, he tapped her cheek with two fingers, and said as though he were vexed:

"Naughty girl!"

"Take it," she said, giving him the box. "I don't care for sweet things."

He ate up the sweets -- everyone of them, and locked the empty box in his trunk; he liked boxes with pictures on them.

"That's mischief enough, though," he said. "It's time for the veteran to go bye-bye."

He took out of his hold-all a Bokhara dressing-gown and a pillow, lay down, and covered himself with the dressing-gown.

"Good-night, darling!" he said softly, and sighed as though his whole body ached.

And soon a snore was heard. Without the slightest feeling of constraint, she, too, lay down and went to sleep.

When next morning she drove through her native town from the station homewards, the streets seemed to her empty and deserted. The snow looked grey, and the houses small, as though someone had squashed them. She was met by a funeral procession: the dead body was carried in an open coffin with banners.

"Meeting a funeral, they say, is lucky," she thought.

There were white bills pasted in the windows of the house where Nina Fyodorovna used to live.

With a sinking at her heart she drove into her own courtyard and rang at the door. It was opened by a servant she did not know -- a plump, sleepy-looking girl wearing a warm wadded jacket. As she went upstairs Yulia remembered how Laptev had declared his love there, but now the staircase was unscrubbed, covered with foot-marks. Upstairs in the cold passage patients were waiting in their out-door coats. And for some reason her heart beat violently, and she was so excited she could scarcely walk.

The doctor, who had grown even stouter, was sitting with a brick-red face and dishevelled hair, drinking tea. Seeing his daughter, he was greatly delighted, and even lachrymose. She thought that she was the only joy in this old man's life, and much moved, she embraced him warmly, and told him she would stay a long time -- till Easter. After taking off her things in her own room, she went back to the dining-room to have tea with him. He was pacing up and down with his hands in his pockets, humming, "Ru-ru-ru"; this meant that he was dissatisfied with something.

"You have a gay time of it in Moscow," he said. "I am very glad for your sake. . . . I'm an old man and I need nothing. I shall soon give up the ghost and set you all free. And the wonder is that my hide is so tough, that I'm alive still! It's amazing!"

He said that he was a tough old ass that everyone rode on. They had thrust on him the care of Nina Fyodorovna, the worry of her children, and of her burial; and that coxcomb Panaurov would not trouble himself about it, and had even borrowed a hundred roubles from him and had never paid it back.

"Take me to Moscow and put me in a madhouse," said the doctor. "I'm mad; I'm a simple child, as I still put faith in truth and justice."

Then he found fault with her husband for his short-sightedness in not buying houses that were being sold so cheaply. And now it seemed to Yulia that she was not the one joy in this old man's life. While he was seeing his patients, and afterwards going his rounds, she walked through all the rooms, not knowing what to do or what to think about. She had already grown strange to her own town and her own home. She felt no inclination to go into the streets or see her friends; and at the thought of her old friends and her life as a girl, she felt no sadness nor regret for the past.

In the evening she dressed a little more smartly and went to the evening service. But there were only poor people in the church, and her splendid fur coat and hat made no impression. And it seemed to her that there was some change in the church as well as in herself. In old days she had loved it when they read the prayers for the day at evening service, and the choir sang anthems such as "I will open my lips." She liked moving slowly in the crowd to the priest who stood in the middle of the church, and then to feel the holy oil on her forehead; now she only waited for the service to be over. And now, going out of the church, she was only afraid that beggars would ask for alms; it was such a bore to have to stop and feel for her pockets; besides, she had no coppers in her pocket now -- nothing but roubles.

She went to bed early, and was a long time in going to sleep. She kept dreaming of portraits of some sort, and of the funeral procession she had met that morning. The open coffin with the dead body was carried into the yard, and brought to a standstill at the door; then the coffin was swung backwards and forwards on a sheet, and dashed violently against the door. Yulia woke and jumped up in alarm. There really was a bang at the door, and the wire of the bell rustled against the wall, though no ring was to be heard.

The doctor coughed. Then she heard the servant go downstairs, and then come back.

"Madam!" she said, and knocked at the door. "Madam!"

"What is it?" said Yulia.

"A telegram for you!"

Yulia went out to her with a candle. Behind the servant stood the doctor, in his night-clothes and greatcoat, and he, too, had a candle in his hand. "Our bell is broken," he said, yawning sleepily. "It ought to have been mended long ago."

Yulia broke open the telegram and read:

"We drink to your health. -- YARTSEV, KOTCHEVOY."

"Ah, what idiots!" she said, and burst out laughing; and her heart felt light and gay.

Going back into her room, she quietly washed and dressed, then she spent a long time in packing her things, until it was daylight, and at midday she set off for Moscow.

XII

In Holy Week the Laptevs went to an exhibition of pictures in the school of painting. The whole family went together in the Moscow fashion, the little girls, the governess, Kostya, and all.

Laptev knew the names of all the well-known painters, and never missed an exhibition. He used sometimes to paint little landscape paintings when he was in the country in the summer, and he fancied he had a good deal of taste, and that if he had studied he might have made a good painter. When he was abroad he sometimes used to go to curio shops, examining the antiques with the air of a connoisseur and giving his opinion on them. When he bought any article he gave just what the shopkeeper liked to ask for it and his purchase remained afterwards in a box in the coach-house till it disappeared altogether. Or going into a print shop, he would slowly and attentively examine the engravings and the bronzes, making various remarks on them, and would buy a common frame or a box of wretched prints. At home he had pictures always of large dimensions but of inferior quality; the best among them were badly hung. It had happened to him more than once to pay large sums for things which had afterwards turned out to be forgeries of the grossest kind. And it was remarkable that, though as a rule timid in the affairs of life, he was exceedingly bold and self-confident at a picture exhibition. Why?

Yulia Sergeyevna looked at the pictures as her husband did, through her open fist or an opera-glass, and was surprised that the people in the pictures were like live people, and the trees like real trees. But she did not understand art, and it seemed to her that many pictures in the exhibition were alike, and she imagined that the whole object in painting was that the figures and objects should stand out as though they were real, when you looked at the picture through your open fist.

"That forest is Shiskin's," her husband explained to her. "He always paints the same thing. . . . But notice snow's never such a lilac colour as that. . . . And that boy's left arm is shorter than his right."

When they were all tired and Laptev had gone to look for Kostya, that they might go home, Yulia stopped indifferently before a small landscape. In the foreground was a stream, over it a little wooden bridge; on the further side a path that disappeared in the dark grass; a field on the right; a copse; near it a camp fire -- no doubt of watchers by night; and in the distance there was a glow of the evening sunset.

Yulia imagined walking herself along the little bridge, and then along the little path further and further, while all round was stillness, the drowsy landrails calling and the fire flickering in the distance. And for some reason she suddenly began to feel that she had seen those very clouds that stretched across the red part of the sky, and that copse, and that field before, many times before. She felt lonely, and longed to walk on and on along the path; and there, in the glow of sunset was the calm reflection of something unearthly, eternal.

"How finely that's painted!" she said, surprised that the picture had suddenly become intelligible to her.

"Look, Alyosha! Do you see how peaceful it is?"

She began trying to explain why she liked the landscape so much, but neither Kostya nor her husband understood her. She kept looking at the picture with a mournful smile, and the fact that the others saw nothing special in it troubled her. Then she began walking through the rooms and looking at the pictures again. She tried to understand them and no longer thought that a great many of them were alike. When, on returning home, for the first time she looked attentively at the big picture that hung over the piano in the drawing-room, she felt a dislike for it, and said:

"What an idea to have pictures like that!"

And after that the gilt cornices, the Venetian looking-glasses with flowers on them, the pictures of the same sort as the one that hung over the piano, and also her husband's and Kostya's reflections upon art, aroused in her a feeling of dreariness and vexation, even of hatred.

Life went on its ordinary course from day to day with no promise of anything special. The theatrical season was over, the warm days had come. There was a long spell of glorious weather. One morning the Laptevs attended the district court to hear Kostya, who had been appointed by the court to defend someone. They were late in starting, and reached the court after the examination of the witnesses had begun. A soldier in the reserve was accused of theft and housebreaking. There were a great number of witnesses, washerwomen; they all testified that the accused was often in the house of their employer -- a woman who kept a laundry. At the Feast of theExaltation of the Cross he came late in the evening and began asking for money; he wanted a pick-me-up, as he had been drinking, but no one gave him anything. Then he went away, but an hour afterwards he came back, and brought with him some beer and a soft gingerbread cake for the little girl. They drank and sang songs almost till daybreak, and when in the morning they looked about, the lock of the door leading up into the attic was broken, and of the linen three men's shirts, a petticoat, and two sheets were missing. Kostya asked each witness sarcastically whether she had not drunk the beer the accused had brought. Evidently he was insinuating that the washerwomen had stolen the linen themselves. He delivered his speech without the slightest nervousness, looking angrily at the jury.

He explained what robbery with housebreaking meant, and the difference between that and simple theft. He spoke very circumstantially and convincingly, displaying an unusual talent for speaking at length and in a serious tone about what had been know to everyone long before. And it was difficult to make out exactly what he was aiming at. From his long speech the foreman of the jury could only have deduced "that it was housebreaking but not robbery, as the washerwomen had sold the linen for drink themselves; or, if there had been robbery, there had not been housebreaking." But obviously, he said just what was wanted, as his speech moved the jury and the audience, and was very much liked. When they gave a verdict of acquittal, Yulia nodded to Kostya, and afterwards pressed his hand warmly.

In May the Laptevs moved to a country villa at Sokolniki. By that time Yulia was expecting a baby.

XIII

More than a year had passed. Yulia and Yartsev were lying on the grass at Sokolniki not far from the embankment of the Yaroslav railway; a little distance away Kotchevoy was lying with hands under his head, looking at the sky. All three had been for a walk, and were waiting for the six o'clock train to pass to go home to tea.

"Mothers see something extraordinary in their children, that is ordained by nature," said Yulia. "A mother will stand for hours together by the baby's cot looking at its little ears and eyes and nose, and fascinated by them. If anyone else kisses her baby the poor thing imagines that it gives him immense pleasure. And a mother talks of nothing but her baby. I know that weakness in mothers, and I keep watch over myself, but my Olga really is exceptional. How she looks at me when I'm nursing her! How she laughs! She's only eight months old, but, upon my word, I've never seen such intelligent eyes in a child of three."

"Tell me, by the way," asked Yartsev: "which do you love most -- your husband or your baby?"

Yulia shrugged her shoulders.

"I don't know," she said. "I never was so very fond of my husband, and Olga is in reality my first love. You know that I did not marry Alexey for love. In old days I was foolish and miserable, and thought that I had ruined my life and his, and now I see that love is not necessary -- that it is all nonsense."

"But if it is not love, what feeling is it that binds you to your husband? Why do you go on living with him?"

"I don't know. . . . I suppose it must be habit. I respect him, I miss him when he's away for long, but that's -- not love. He is a clever, honest man, and that's enough to make me happy. He is very kind and good-hearted. . . ."

"Alyosha's intelligent, Alyosha's good," said Kostya, raising his head lazily; "but, my dear girl, to find out that he is intelligent, good, and interesting, you have to eat a hundredweight of salt with him. . . . And what's the use of his goodness and intelligence? He can fork out money as much as you want, but when character is needed to resist insolence or aggressiveness, he is faint-hearted and overcome with nervousness. People like your amiable Alyosha are splendid people, but they are no use at all for fighting. In fact, they are no use for anything."

At last the train came in sight. Coils of perfectly pink smoke from the funnels floated over the copse, and two windows in the last compartment flashed so brilliantly in the sun, that it hurt their eyes to look at it.

"Tea-time!" said Yulia Sergeyevna, getting up.

She had grown somewhat stouter of late, and her movements were already a little matronly, a little indolent.

"It's bad to be without love though," said Yartsev, walking behind her. "We talk and read of nothing else but love, but we do very little loving ourselves, and that's really bad."

"All that's nonsense, Ivan Gavrilitch," said Yulia. "That's not what gives happiness."

They had tea in the little garden, where mignonette, stocks, and tobacco plants were in flower, and spikes of early gladiolus were just opening. Yartsev and Kotchevoy could see from Yulia's face that she was passing through a happy period of inward peace and serenity, that she wanted nothing but what she had, and they, too, had a feeling of peace and comfort in their hearts. Whatever was said sounded apt and clever; the pines were lovely -- the fragrance of them was exquisite as it had never been before; and the cream was very nice; and Sasha was a good, intelligent child.

After tea Yartsev sang songs, accompanying himself on the piano, while Yulia and Kotchevoy sat listening in silence, though Yulia got up from time to time, and went softly indoors, to take a look at the baby and at Lida, who had been in bed for the last two days feverish and eating nothing.

"My friend, my tender friend," sang Yartsev. "No, my friends, I'll be hanged if I understand why you are all so against love!" he said, flinging back his head. "If I weren't busy for fifteen hours of the twenty-four, I should certainly fall in love."

Supper was served on the verandah; it was warm and still, but Yulia wrapped herself in a shawl and complained of the damp. When it got dark, she seemed not quite herself; she kept shivering and begging her visitors to stay a little longer. She regaled them with wine, and after supper ordered brandy to keep them from going. She didn't want to be left alone with the children and the servants.

"We summer visitors are getting up a performance for the children," she said. "We have got everything -- a stage and actors; we are only at a loss for a play. Two dozen plays of different sorts have been sent us, but there isn't one that is suitable. Now, you are fond of the theatre, and are so good at history," she said, addressing Yartsev. "Write an historical play for us."

"Well, I might."

The men drank up all the brandy, and prepared to go.

It was past ten, and for summer-villa people that was late.

"How dark it is! One can't see a bit," said Yulia, as she went with them to the gate. "I don't know how you'll find your way. But, isn't it cold?"

She wrapped herself up more closely and walked back to the porch.

"I suppose my Alexey's playing cards somewhere," she called to them. "Good-night!"

After the lighted rooms nothing could be seen. Yartsev and Kostya groped their way like blind men to the railway embankment and crossed it.

"One can't see a thing," said Kostya in his bass voice, standing still and gazing at the sky. "And the stars, the stars, they are like new three-penny-bits. Gavrilitch!"

"Ah?" Yartsev responded somewhere in the darkness.

"I say, one can't see a thing. Where are you?"

Yartsev went up to him whistling, and took his arm.

"Hi, there, you summer visitors!" Kostya shouted at the top of his voice. "We've caught a socialist."

When he was exhilarated he was always very rowdy, shouting, wrangling with policemen and cabdrivers, singing, and laughing violently.

"Nature be damned," he shouted.

"Come, come," said Yartsev, trying to pacify him. "You mustn't. Please don't."

Soon the friends grew accustomed to the darkness, and were able to distinguish the outlines of the tall pines and telegraph posts. From time to time the sound of whistles reached them from the station and the telegraph wires hummed plaintively. From the copse itself there came no sound, and there was a feeling of pride, strength, and mystery in its silence, and on the right it seemed that the tops of the pines were almost touching the sky. The friends found their path and walked along it. There it was quite dark, and it was only from the long strip of sky dotted with stars, and from the firmly trodden earth under their feet, that they could tell they were walking along a path. They walked along side by side in silence, and it seemed to both of them that people were coming to meet them. Their tipsy exhilaration passed off. The fancy came into Yartsev's mind that perhaps that copse was haunted by the spirits of the Muscovite Tsars, boyars, and patriarchs, and he was on the point of telling Kostya about it, but he checked himself.

When they reached the town gate there was a faint light of dawn in the sky. Still in silence, Yartsev and Kotchevoy walked along the wooden pavement, by the cheap summer cottages, eating-houses, timber-stacks. Under the arch of interlacing branches, the damp air was fragrant of lime-trees, and then a broad, long street opened before them, and on it not a soul, not a light. . . . When they reached the Red Pond, it was daylight.

"Moscow -- it's a town that will have to suffer a great deal more," said Yartsev, looking at the Alexyevsky Monastery

"What put that into your head?"

"I don't know. I love Moscow."

Both Yartsev and Kostya had been born in Moscow, and adored the town, and felt for some reason antagonistic to every other town. Both were convinced that Moscow was a remarkable town, and Russia a remarkable country. In the Crimea, in the Caucasus, and abroad, they felt dull, uncomfortable, and ill at ease, and they thought their grey Moscow weather very pleasant and healthy. And when the rain lashed at the window-panes and it got dark early, and when the walls of the churches and houses looked a drab, dismal colour, days when one doesn't know what to put on when one is going out -- such days excited them agreeably.

At last near the station they took a cab.

"It really would be nice to write an historical play," said Yartsev, "but not about the Lyapunovs or the Godunovs, but of the times of Yaroslav or of Monomach. . . . I hate all historical plays except the monologue of Pimen. When you have to do with some historical authority or even read a textbook of Russian history, you feel that everyone in Russia is exceptionally talented, gifted, and interesting; but when I see an historical play at the theatre, Russian life begins to seem stupid, morbid, and not original."

Near Dmitrovka the friends separated, and Yartsev went on to his lodging in Nikitsky Street. He sat half dozing, swaying from side to side, and pondering on the play. He suddenly imagined a terrible din, a clanging noise, and shouts in some unknown language, that might have been Kalmuck, and a village wrapped in flames, and forests near covered with hoarfrost and soft pink in the glow of the fire, visible for miles around, and so clearly that every little fir-tree could be distinguished, and savage men darting about the village on horseback and on foot, and as red as the glow in the sky.

"The Polovtsy," thought Yartsev.

One of them, a terrible old man with a bloodstained face all scorched from the fire, binds to his saddle a young girl with a white Russian face, and the girl looks sorrowful, understanding. Yartsev flung back his head and woke up.

"My friend, my tender friend . . ." he hummed.

As he paid the cabman and went up his stairs, he could not shake off his dreaminess; he saw the flames catching the village, and the forest beginning to crackle and smoke. A huge, wild bear frantic with terror rushed through the village. . . . And the girl tied to the saddle was still looking.

When at last he went into his room it was broad daylight. Two candles were burning by some open music on the piano. On the sofa lay Polina Razsudin wearing a black dress and a sash, with a newspaper in her hand, fast asleep. She must have been playing late, waiting for Yartsev to come home, and, tired of waiting, fell asleep.

"Hullo, she's worn out," he thought.

Carefully taking the newspaper out of her hands, he covered her with a rug. He put out the candles and went into his bedroom. As he got into bed, he still thought of his historical play, and the tune of "My friend, my tender friend" was still ringing in his head. . . .

Two days later Laptev looked in upon him for a moment to tell him that Lida was ill with diphtheria, and that Yulia Sergeyevna and her baby had caught it from her, and five days later came the news that Lida and Yulia were recovering, but the baby was dead, and that the Laptevs had left their villa at Sokolniki and had hastened back to Moscow.

XIV

It had become distasteful to Laptev to be long at home. His wife was constantly away in the lodge declaring that she had to look after the little girls, but he knew that she did not go to the lodge to give them lessons but to cry in Kostya's room. The ninth day came, then the twentieth, and then the fortieth, and still he had to go to the cemetery to listen to the requiem, and then to wear himself out for a whole day and night thinking of nothing but that unhappy baby, and trying to comfort his wife with all sorts of commonplace expressions. He went rarely to the warehouse now, and spent most of his time in charitable work, seizing upon every pretext requiring his attention, and he was glad when he had for some trivial reason to be out for the whole day. He had been intending of late to go abroad, to study night-refuges, and that idea attracted him now.

It was an autumn day. Yulia had just gone to the lodge to cry, while Laptev lay on a sofa in the study thinking where he could go. Just at that moment Pyotr announced Polina Razsudin. Laptev was delighted; he leapt up and went to meet the unexpected visitor, who had been his closest friend, though he had almost begun to forget her. She had not changed in the least since that evening when he had seen her for the last time, and was just the same as ever.

"Polina," he said, holding out both hands to her. "What ages! If you only knew how glad I am to see you! Do come in!"

Polina greeted him, jerked him by the hand, and without taking off her coat and hat, went into the study and sat down.

"I've come to you for one minute," she said. "I haven't time to talk of any nonsense. Sit down and listen. Whether you are glad to see me or not is absolutely nothing to me, for I don't care a straw for the gracious attentions of you lords of creation. I've only come to you because I've been to five other places already to-day, and everywhere I was met with a refusal, and it's a matter that can't be put off. Listen," she went on, looking into his face. "Five students of my acquaintance, stupid, unintelligent people, but certainly poor, have neglected to pay their fees, and are being excluded from the university. Your wealth makes it your duty to go straight to the university and pay for them."

"With pleasure, Polina."

"Here are their names," she said, giving him a list. "Go this minute; you'll have plenty of time to enjoy your domestic happiness afterwards."

At that moment a rustle was heard through the door that led into the drawing-room; probably the dog was scratching itself. Polina turned crimson and jumped up.

"Your Dulcinea's eavesdropping," she said. "That's horrid!"

Laptev was offended at this insult to Yulia.

"She's not here; she's in the lodge," he said. "And don't speak of her like that. Our child is dead, and she is in great distress."

"You can console her," Polina scoffed, sitting down again; "she'll have another dozen. You don't need much sense to bring children into the world."

Laptev remembered that he had heard this, or something very like it, many times in old days, and it brought back a whiff of the romance of the past, of solitary freedom, of his bachelor life, when he was young and thought he could do anything he chose, when he had neither love for his wife nor memory of his baby.

"Let us go together," he said, stretching.

When they reached the university Polina waited at the gate, while Laptev went into the office; he came back soon afterwards and handed Polina five receipts.

"Where are you going now?" he asked.

"To Yartsev's."

"I'll come with you."

"But you'll prevent him from writing."

"No, I assure you I won't," he said, and looked at her imploringly.

She had on a black hat trimmed with crape, as though she were in mourning, and a short, shabby coat, the pockets of which stuck out. Her nose looked longer than it used to be, and her face looked bloodless in spite of the cold. Laptev liked walking with her, doing what she told him, and listening to her grumbling. He walked along thinking about her, what inward strength there must be in this woman, since, though she was so ugly, so angular, so restless, though she did not know how to dress, and always had untidy hair, and was always somehow out of harmony, she was yet so fascinating.

They went into Yartsev's flat by the back way through the kitchen, where they were met by the cook, a clean little old woman with grey curls; she was overcome with embarrassment, and with a honeyed smile which made her little face look like a pie, said:

"Please walk in."

Yartsev was not at home. Polina sat down to the piano, and beginning upon a tedious, difficult exercise, told Laptev not to hinder her. And without distracting her attention by conversation, he sat on one side and began turning over the pages of a "The Messenger of Europe." After practising for two hours -- it was the task she set herself every day -- she ate something in the kitchen and went out to her lessons. Laptev read the continuation of a story, then sat for a long time without reading and without being bored, glad to think that he was too late for dinner at home.

"Ha, ha, ha!" came Yartsev's laugh, and he walked in with ruddy cheeks, looking strong and healthy, wearing a new coat with bright buttons. "Ha, ha, ha!"

The friends dined together. Then Laptev lay on the sofa while Yartsev sat near and lighted a cigar. It got dark.

"I must be getting old," said Laptev. "Ever since my sister Nina died, I've taken to constantly thinking of death."

They began talking of death, of the immortality of the soul, of how nice it would be to rise again and fly off somewhere to Mars, to be always idle and happy, and, above all, to think in a new special way, not as on earth.

"One doesn't want to die," said Yartsev softly. "No sort of philosophy can reconcile me to death, and I look on it simply as annihilation. One wants to live."

"You love life, Gavrilitch?"

"Yes, I love it."

"Do you know, I can never understand myself about that. I'm always in a gloomy mood or else indifferent. I'm timid, without self-confidence; I have a cowardly conscience; I never can adapt myself to life, or become its master. Some people talk nonsense or cheat, and even so enjoy life, while I consciously do good, and feel nothing but uneasiness or complete indifference. I explain all that, Gavrilitch, by my being a slave, the grandson of a serf. Before we plebeians fight our way into the true path, many of our sort will perish on the way."

"That's all quite right, my dear fellow," said Yartsev, and he sighed. "That only proves once again how rich and varied Russian life is. Ah, how rich it is! Do you know, I feel more convinced every day that we are on the eve of the greatest triumph, and I should like to live to take part in it. Whether you like to believe it or not, to my thinking a remarkable generation is growing up. It gives me great enjoyment to teach the children, especially the girls. They are wonderful children!"

Yartsev went to the piano and struck a chord.

"I'm a chemist, I think in chemical terms, and I shall die a chemist," he went on. "But I am greedy, and I am afraid of dying unsatisfied; and chemistry is not enough for me, and I seize upon Russian history, history of art, the science of teaching music. . . . Your wife asked me in the summer to write an historical play, and now I'm longing to write and write. I feel as though I could sit for three days and three nights without moving, writing all the time. I am worn out with ideas -- my brain's crowded with them, and I feel as though there were a pulse throbbing in my head. I don't in the least want to become anything special, to create something great. I simply want to live, to dream, to hope, to be in the midst of everything. . . . Life is short, my dear fellow, and one must make the most of everything."

After this friendly talk, which was not over till midnight, Laptev took to coming to see Yartsev almost every day. He felt drawn to him. As a rule he came towards evening, lay down on the sofa, and waited patiently for Yartsev to come in, without feeling in the least bored. When Yartsev came back from his work, he had dinner, and sat down to work; but Laptev would ask him a questions a conversation would spring up, and there was no more thought of work and at midnight the friends parted very well pleased with one another.

But this did not last long. Arriving one day at Yartsev's, Laptev found no one there but Polina, who was sitting at the piano practising her exercises. She looked at him with a cold, almost hostile expression, and asked without shaking hands:

"Tell me, please: how much longer is this going on?"

"This? What?" asked Laptev, not understanding.

"You come here every day and hinder Yartsev from working. Yartsev is not a tradesman; he is a scientific man, and every moment of his life is precious. You ought to understand and to have some little delicacy! "

"If you think that I hinder him," said Laptev, mildly, disconcerted, "I will give up my visits."

"Quite right, too. You had better go, or he may be home in a minute and find you here."

The tone in which this was said, and the indifference in Polina's eyes, completely disconcerted him. She had absolutely no sort of feeling for him now, except the desire that he should go as soon as possible -- and what a contrast it was to her old love for him! He went out without shaking hands with her, and he fancied she would call out to him, bring him back, but he heard the scales again, and as he slowly went down the stairs he realised that he had become a stranger to her now.

Three days later Yartsev came to spend the evening with him.

"I have news," he said, laughing. "Polina Nikolaevna has moved into my rooms altogether." He was a little confused, and went on in a low voice: "Well, we are not in love with each other, of course, but I suppose that . . . that doesn't matter. I am glad I can give her a refuge and peace and quiet, and make it possible for her not to work if she's ill. She fancies that her coming to live with me will make things more orderly, and that under her influence I shall become a great scientist. That's what she fancies. And let her fancy it. In the South they have a saying: 'Fancy makes the fool a rich man.' Ha, ha, ha!"

Laptev said nothing. Yartsev walked up and down the study, looking at the pictures he had seen so many times before, and said with a sigh:

"Yes, my dear fellow, I am three years older than you are, and it's too late for me to think of real love, and in reality a woman like Polina Nikolaevna is a godsend to me, and, of course, I shall get on capitally with her till we're both old people; but, goodness knows why, one still regrets something, one still longs for something, and I still feel as though I am lying in the Vale of Daghestan and dreaming of a ball. In short, man's never satisfied with what he has."

He went into the drawing-room and began singing as though nothing had happened, and Laptev sat in his study with his eyes shut, and tried to understand why Polina had gone to live with Yartsev. And then he felt sad that there were no lasting, permanent attachments. And he felt vexed that Polina Nikolaevna had gone to live with Yartsev, and vexed with himself that his feeling for his wife was not what it had been.

XV

Laptev sat reading and swaying to and fro in a rocking-chair; Yulia was in the study, and she, too, was reading. It seemed there was nothing to talk about; they had both been silent all day. From time to time he looked at her from over his book and thought: "Whether one marries from passionate love, or without love at all, doesn't it come to the same thing?" And the time when he used to be jealous, troubled, distressed, seemed to him far away. He had succeeded in going abroad, and now he was resting after the journey and looking forward to another visit in the spring to England, which he had very much liked.

And Yulia Sergeyevna had grown used to her sorrow, and had left off going to the lodge to cry. That winter she had given up driving out shopping, had given up the theatres and concerts, and had stayed at home. She never cared for big rooms, and always sat in her husband's study or in her own room, where she had shrines of ikons that had come to her on her marriage, and where there hung on the wall the landscape that had pleased her so much at the exhibition. She spent hardly any money on herself, and was almost as frugal now as she had been in her father's house.

The winter passed cheerlessly. Card-playing was the rule everywhere in Moscow, and if any other recreation was attempted, such as singing, reading, drawing, the result was even more tedious. And since there were few talented people in Moscow, and the same singers and reciters performed at every entertainment, even the enjoyment of art gradually palled and became for many people a tiresome and monotonous social duty.

Moreover, the Laptevs never had a day without something vexatious happening. Old Laptev's eyesight was failing; he no longer went to the warehouse, and the oculist told them that he would soon be blind. Fyodor had for some reason given up going to the warehouse and spent his time sitting at home writing something. Panaurov had got a post in another town, and had been promoted an actual civil councillor, and was now staying at the Dresden. He came to the Laptevs' almost every day to ask for money. Kish had finished his studies at last, and while waiting for Laptev to find him a job, used to spend whole days at a time with them, telling them long, tedious stories. All this was irritating and exhausting, and made daily life unpleasant.

Pyotr came into the study, and announced an unknown lady. On the card he brought in was the name "Josephina Iosefovna Milan."

Yulia Sergeyevna got up languidly and went out limping slightly, as her foot had gone to sleep. In the doorway appeared a pale, thin lady with dark eyebrows, dressed altogether in black. She clasped her hands on her bosom and said supplicatingly

"M. Laptev, save my children!"

The jingle of her bracelets sounded familiar to him, and he knew the face with patches of powder on it; he recognised her as the lady with whom he had once so inappropriately dined before his marriage. It was Panaurov's second wife.

"Save my children," she repeated, and her face suddenly quivered and looked old and pitiful. "You alone can save us, and I have spent my last penny coming to Moscow to see you! My children are starving!"

She made a motion as though she were going to fall on her knees. Laptev was alarmed, and clutched her by the arm.

"Sit down, sit down . . ." he muttered, making her sit down. "I beg you to be seated."

"We have no money to buy bread," she said. "Grigory Nikolaevitch is going away to a new post, but he will not take the children and me with him, and the money which you so generously send us he spends only on himself. What are we to do? What? My poor, unhappy children!"

"Calm yourself, I beg. I will give orders that that money shall be made payable to you."

She began sobbing, and then grew calmer, and he noticed that the tears had made little pathways through the powder on her cheeks, and that she was growing a moustache.

"You are infinitely generous, M. Laptev. But be our guardian angel, our good fairy, persuade Grigory Nikolaevitch not to abandon me, but to take me with him. You know I love him -- I love him insanely; he's the comfort of my life."

Laptev gave her a hundred roubles, and promised to talk to Panaurov, and saw her out to the hall in trepidation the whole time, for fear she should break into sobs or fall on her knees.

After her, Kish made his appearance. Then Kostya came in with his photographic apparatus. Of late he had been attracted by photography and took photographs of everyone in the house several times a day. This new pursuit caused him many disappointments, and he had actually grown thinner.

Before evening tea Fyodor arrived. Sitting in a corner in the study, he opened a book and stared for a long time at a page, obviously not reading. Then he spent a long time drinking tea; his face turned red. In his presence Laptev felt a load on his heart; even his silence was irksome to him.

"Russia may be congratulated on the appearance of a new author," said Fyodor. "Joking apart, though, brother, I have turned out a little article -- the firstfruits of my pen, so to say -- and I've brought it to show you. Read it, dear boy, and tell me your opinion -- but sincerely."

He took a manuscript out of his pocket and gave it to his brother. The article was called "The Russian Soul"; it was written tediously, in the colourless style in which people with no talent, but full of secret vanity, usually write. The leading idea of it was that the intellectual man has the right to disbelieve in the supernatural, but it is his duty to conceal his lack of faith, that he may not be a stumbling-block and shake the faith of others. Without faith there is no idealism, and idealism is destined to save Europe and guide humanity into the true path.

"But you don't say what Europe has to be saved from," said Laptev.

"That's intelligible of itself."

"Nothing is intelligible," said Laptev, and he walked about the room in agitation. "It's not intelligible to me why you wrote it. But that's your business."

"I want to publish it in pamphlet form."

"That's your affair."

They were silent for a minute. Fyodor sighed and said:

"It's an immense regret to me, dear brother, that we think differently. Oh, Alyosha, Alyosha, my darling brother! You and I are true Russians, true believers, men of broad nature; all of these German and Jewish crochets are not for us. You and I are not wretched upstarts, you know, but representatives of a distinguished merchant family."

"What do you mean by a distinguished family?" said Laptev, restraining his irritation. "A distinguished family! The landowners beat our grandfather and every low little government clerk punched him in the face. Our grandfather thrashed our father, and our father thrashed us. What has your distinguished family done for us? What sort of nerves, what sort of blood, have we inherited? For nearly three years you've been arguing like an ignorant deacon, and talking all sorts of nonsense, and now you've written -- this slavish drivel here! While I, while I! Look at me. . . . No elasticity, no boldness, no strength of will; I tremble over every step I take as though I should be flogged for it. I am timid before nonentities, idiots, brutes, who are immeasurably my inferiors mentally and morally; I am afraid of porters, doorkeepers, policemen, gendarmes. I am afraid of everyone, because I was born of a mother who was terrified, and because from a child I was beaten and frightened! . . . You and I will do well to have no children. Oh, God, grant that this distinguished merchant family may die with us!"

Yulia Sergeyevna came into the study and sat down at the table.

"Are you arguing about something here?" she asked. "Am I interrupting?"

"No, little sister," answered Fyodor. "Our discussion was of principles. Here, you are abusing the family," he added, turning to his brother. "That family has created a business worth a million, though. That stands for something, anyway!"

"A great distinction -- a business worth a million! A man with no particular brains, without abilities, by chance becomes a trader, and then when he has grown rich he goes on trading from day to day, with no sort of system, with no aim, without having any particular greed for money. He trades mechanically, and money comes to him of itself, without his going to meet it. He sits all his life at his work, likes it only because he can domineer over his clerks and get the better of his customers. He's a churchwarden because he can domineer over the choristers and keep them under his thumb; he's the patron of a school because he likes to feel the teacher is his subordinate and enjoys lording it over him. The merchant does not love trading, he loves dominating, and your warehouse is not so much a commercial establishment as a torture chamber! And for a business like yours, you want clerks who have been deprived of individual character and personal life -- and you make them such by forcing them in childhood to lick the dust for a crust of bread, and you've trained them from childhood to believe that you are their benefactors. No fear of your taking a university man into your warehouse!"

"University men are not suitable for our business."

"That's not true," cried Laptev. "It's a lie!"

"Excuse me, it seems to me you spit into the well from which you drink yourself," said Fyodor, and he got up. "Our business is hateful to you, yet you make use of the income from it."

"Aha! We've spoken our minds," said Laptev, and he laughed, looking angrily at his brother. "Yes, if I didn't belong to your distinguished family -- if I had an ounce of will and courage, I should long ago have flung away that income, and have gone to work for my living. But in your warehouse you've destroyed all character in me from a child! I'm your product."

Fyodor looked at the clock and began hurriedly saying good-bye. He kissed Yulia's hand and went out, but instead of going into the hall, walked into the drawing-room, then into the bedroom.

"I've forgotten how the rooms go," he said in extreme confusion. "It's a strange house. Isn't it a strange house!"

He seemed utterly overcome as he put on his coat, and there was a look of pain on his face. Laptev felt no more anger; he was frightened, and at the same time felt sorry for Fyodor, and the warm, true love for his brother, which seemed to have died down in his heart during those three years, awoke, and he felt an intense desire to express that love.

"Come to dinner with us to-morrow, Fyodor," he said, and stroked him on the shoulder. "Will you come?"

"Yes, yes; but give me some water."

Laptev ran himself to the dining-room to take the first thing he could get from the sideboard. This was a tall beer-jug. He poured water into it and brought it to his brother. Fyodor began drinking, but bit a piece out of the jug; they heard a crunch, and then sobs. The water ran over his fur coat and his jacket, and Laptev, who had never seen men cry, stood in confusion and dismay, not knowing what to do. He looked on helplessly while Yulia and the servant took off Fyodor's coat and helped him back again into the room, and went with him, feeling guilty.

Yulia made Fyodor lie down on the sofa and knelt beside him.

"It's nothing," she said, trying to comfort him. "It's your nerves. . . ."

"I'm so miserable, my dear!" he said. "I am so unhappy, unhappy . . . but all the time I've been hiding it, I've been hiding it!"

He put his arm round her neck and whispered in her ear:

"Every night I see my sister Nina. She comes and sits in the chair near my bed. . . ."

When, an hour later, he put on his fur coat in the hall, he was smiling again and ashamed to face the servant. Laptev went with him to Pyatnitsky Street.

"Come and have dinner with us to-morrow," he said on the way, holding him by the arm, "and at Easter we'll go abroad together. You absolutely must have a change, or you'll be getting quite morbid."

When he got home Laptev found his wife in a state of great nervous agitation. The scene with Fyodor had upset her, and she could not recover her composure. She wasn't crying but kept tossing on the bed, clutching with cold fingers at the quilt, at the pillows, at her husband's hands. Her eyes looked big and frightened.

"Don't go away from me, don't go away," she said to her husband. "Tell me, Alyosha, why have I left off saying my prayers? What has become of my faith? Oh, why did you talk of religion before me? You've shaken my faith, you and your friends. I never pray now."

He put compresses on her forehead, chafed her hands, gave her tea to drink, while she huddled up to him in terror. . . ."

Towards morning she was worn out and fell asleep, while Laptev sat beside her and held her hand. So that he could get no sleep. The whole day afterwards he felt shattered and dull, and wandered listlessly about the rooms without a thought in his head.

XVI

The doctor said that Fyodor's mind was affected. Laptev did not know what to do in his father's house, while the dark warehouse in which neither his father nor Fyodor ever appeared now seemed to him like a sepulchre.

When his wife told him that he absolutely must go every day to the warehouse and also to his father's, he either said nothing, or began talking irritably of his childhood, saying that it was beyond his power to forgive his father for his past, that the warehouse and the house in Pyatnitsky Street were hateful to him, and so on.

One Sunday morning Yulia went herself to Pyatnitsky Street. She found old Fyodor Stepanovitch in the same big drawing-room in which the service had been held on her first arrival. Wearing slippers, and without a cravat, he was sitting motionless in his arm-chair, blinking with his sightless eyes.

"It's I -- your daughter-in-law," she said, going up to him. "I've come to see how you are."

He began breathing heavily with excitement.

Touched by his affliction and his loneliness, she kissed his hand; and he passed his hand over her face and head, and having satisfied himself that it was she, made the sign of the cross over her.

"Thank you, thank you," he said. "You know I've lost my eyes and can see nothing. . . . I can dimly see the window and the fire, but people and things I cannot see at all. Yes, I'm going blind, and Fyodor has fallen ill, and without the master's eye things are in a bad way now. If there is any irregularity there's no one to look into it; and folks soon get spoiled. And why is it Fyodor has fallen ill? Did he catch cold? Here I have never ailed in my life and never taken medicine. I never saw anything of doctors."

And, as he always did, the old man began boasting. Meanwhile the servants hurriedly laid the table and brought in lunch and bottles of wine.

Ten bottles were put on the table; one of them was in the shape of the Eiffel Tower. There was a whole dish of hot pies smelling of jam, rice, and fish.

"I beg my dear guest to have lunch," said the old man.

She took him by the arm, led him to the table, and poured him out a glass of vodka.

"I will come to you again to-morrow," she said, "and I'll bring your grandchildren, Sasha and Lida. They will be sorry for you, and fondle you."

"There's no need. Don't bring them. They are illegitimate."

"Why are they illegitimate? Why, their father and mother were married."

"Without my permission. I do not bless them, and I don't want to know them. Let them be."

"You speak strangely, Fyodor Stepanovitch," said Yulia, with a sigh.

"It is written in the Gospel: children must fear and honour their parents."

"Nothing of the sort. The Gospel tells us that we must forgive even our enemies."

"One can't forgive in our business. If you were to forgive everyone, you would come to ruin in three years."

"But to forgive, to say a kind, friendly word to anyone, even a sinner, is something far above business, far above wealth."

Yulia longed to soften the old man, to awaken a feeling of compassion in him, to move him to repentance; but he only listened condescendingly to all she said, as a grown-up person listens to a child.

"Fyodor Stepanovitch," said Yulia resolutely, "you are an old man, and God soon will call you to Himself. He won't ask you how you managed your business, and whether you were successful in it, but whether you were gracious to people; or whether you were harsh to those who were weaker than you, such as your servants, your clerks."

"I was always the benefactor of those that served me; they ought to remember me in their prayers forever," said the old man, with conviction, but touched by Yulia's tone of sincerity, and anxious to give her pleasure, he said: "Very well; bring my grandchildren to-morrow. I will tell them to buy me some little presents for them."

The old man was slovenly in his dress, and there was cigar ash on his breast and on his knees; apparently no one cleaned his boots, or brushed his clothes. The rice in the pies was half cooked, the tablecloth smelt of soap, the servants tramped noisily about the room. And the old man and the whole house had a neglected look, and Yulia, who felt this, was ashamed of herself and of her husband.

"I will be sure to come and see you to-morrow," she said.

She walked through the rooms, and gave orders for the old man's bedroom to be set to rights, and the lamp to be lighted under the ikons in it. Fyodor, sitting in his own room, was looking at an open book without reading it. Yulia talked to him and told the servants to tidy his room, too; then she went downstairs to the clerks. In the middle of the room where the clerks used to dine, there was an unpainted wooden post to support the ceiling and to prevent its coming down. The ceilings in the basement were low, the walls covered with cheap paper, and there was a smell of charcoal fumes and cooking. As it was a holiday, all the clerks were at home, sitting on their bedsteads waiting for dinner. When Yulia went in they jumped up, and answered her questions timidly, looking up at her from under their brows like convicts.

"Good heavens! What a horrid room you have!" she said, throwing up her hands. "Aren't you crowded here?"

"Crowded, but not aggrieved," said Makeitchev. "We are greatly indebted to you, and will offer up our prayers for you to our Heavenly Father."

"The congruity of life with the conceit of the personality," said Potchatkin.

And noticing that Yulia did not understand Potchatkin, Makeitchev hastened to explain:

"We are humble people and must live according to our position."

She inspected the boys' quarters, and then the kitchen, made acquaintance with the housekeeper, and was thoroughly dissatisfied.

When she got home she said to her husband:

"We ought to move into your father's house and settle there for good as soon as possible. And you will go every day to the warehouse."

Then they both sat side by side in the study without speaking. His heart was heavy, and he did not want to move into Pyatnitsky Street or to go into the warehouse; but he guessed what his wife was thinking, and could not oppose her. He stroked her cheek and said:

"I feel as though our life is already over, and that a grey half-life is beginning for us. When I knew that my brother Fyodor was hopelessly ill, I shed tears; we spent our childhood and youth together, when I loved him with my whole soul. And now this catastrophe has come, and it seems, too, as though, losing him, I am finally cut away from my past. And when you said just now that we must move into the house in Pyatnitsky Street, to that prison, it began to seem to me that there was no future for me either."

He got up and walked to the window.

"However that may be, one has to give up all thoughts of happiness," he said, looking out into the street. "There is none. I never have had any, and I suppose it doesn't exist at all. I was happy once in my life, though, when I sat at night under your parasol. Do you remember how you left your parasol at Nina's?" he asked, turning to his wife. "I was in love with you then, and I remember I spent all night sitting under your parasol, and was perfectly blissful."

Near the book-case in the study stood a mahogany chest with bronze fittings where Laptev kept various useless things, including the parasol. He took it out and handed it to his wife.

"Here it is."

Yulia looked for a minute at the parasol, recognised it, and smiled mournfully.

"I remember," she said. "When you proposed to me you held it in your hand." And seeing that he was preparing to go out, she said: "Please come back early if you can. I am dull without you.

And then she went into her own room, and gazed for a long time at the parasol.

XVII

In spite of the complexity of the business and the immense turnover, there were no bookkeepers in the warehouse, and it was impossible to make anything out of the books kept by the cashier in the office. Every day the warehouse was visited by agents, German and English, with whom the clerks talked politics and religion. A man of noble birth, ruined by drink, an ailing, pitiable creature, used to come to translate the foreign correspondence in the office; the clerks used to call him a midge, and put salt in his tea. And altogether the whole concern struck Laptev as a very queer business.

He went to the warehouse every day and tried to establish a new order of things; he forbade them to thrash the boys and to jeer at the buyers, and was violently angry when the clerks gleefully despatched to the provinces worthless shop-soiled goods as though they were new and fashionable. Now he was the chief person in the warehouse, but still, as before, he did not know how large his fortune was, whether his business was doing well, how much the senior clerks were paid, and so on. Potchatkin and Makeitchev looked upon him as young and inexperienced, concealed a great deal from him, and whispered mysteriously every evening with his blind old father.

It somehow happened at the beginning of June that Laptev went into the Bubnovsky restaurant with Potchatkin to talk business with him over lunch. Potchatkin had been with the Laptevs a long while, and had entered their service at eight years old. He seemed to belong to them -- they trusted him fully; and when on leaving the warehouse he gathered up all the takings from the till and thrust them into his pocket, it never aroused the slightest suspicion. He was the head man in the business and in the house, and also in the church, where he performed the duties of churchwarden in place of his old master. He was nicknamed Malyuta Skuratov on account of his cruel treatment of the boys and clerks under him.

When they went into the restaurant he nodded to a waiter and said:

"Bring us, my lad, half a bodkin and twenty-four unsavouries."

After a brief pause the waiter brought on a tray half a bottle of vodka and some plates of various kinds of savouries.

"Look here, my good fellow," said Potchatkin. "Give us a plateful of the source of all slander and evil-speaking, with mashed potatoes."

The waiter did not understand; he was puzzled, and would have said something, but Potchatkin looked at him sternly and said:

"Except."

The waiter thought intently, then went to consult with his colleagues, and in the end guessing what was meant, brought a plateful of tongue. When they had drunk a couple of glasses and had had lunch, Laptev asked:

"Tell me, Ivan Vassilitch, is it true that our business has been dropping off for the last year?"

"Not a bit of it."

"Tell me frankly and honestly what income we have been making and are making, and what our profits are. We can't go on in the dark. We had a balancing of the accounts at the warehouse lately, but, excuse me, I don't believe in it; you think fit to conceal something from me and only tell the truth to my father. You have been used to being diplomatic from your childhood, and now you can't get on without it. And what's the use of it? So I beg you to be open. What is our position?"

"It all depends upon the fluctuation of credit," Potchatkin answered after a moment's pause.

"What do you understand by the fluctuation of credit?"

Potchatkin began explaining, but Laptev could make nothing of it, and sent for Makeitchev. The latter promptly made his appearance, had some lunch after saying grace, and in his sedate, mellow baritone began saying first of all that the clerks were in duty bound to pray night and day for their benefactors.

"By all means, only allow me not to consider myself your benefactor," said Laptev.

"Every man ought to remember what he is, and to be conscious of his station. By the grace of God you are a father and benefactor to us, and we are your slaves."

"I am sick of all that!" said Laptev, getting angry. "Please be a benefactor to me now. Please explain the position of our business. Give up looking upon me as a boy, or to-morrow I shall close the business. My father is blind, my brother is in the asylum, my nieces are only children. I hate the business; I should be glad to go away, but there's no one to take my place, as you know. For goodness' sake, drop your diplomacy!"

They went to the warehouse to go into the accounts; then they went on with them at home in the evening, the old father himself assisting. Initiating his son into his commercial secrets, the old man spoke as though he were engaged, not in trade, but in sorcery. It appeared that the profits of the business were increasing approximately ten per cent. per annum, and that the Laptevs' fortune, reckoning only money and paper securities, amounted to six million roubles.

When at one o'clock at night, after balancing the accounts, Laptev went out into the open air, he was still under the spell of those figures. It was a still, sultry, moonlight night. The white walls of the houses beyond the river, the heavy barred gates, the stillness and the black shadows, combined to give the impression of a fortress, and nothing was wanting to complete the picture but a sentinel with a gun. Laptev went into the garden and sat down on a seat near the fence, which divided them from the neighbour's yard, where there was a garden, too. The bird-cherry was in bloom. Laptev remembered that the tree had been just as gnarled and just as big when he was a child, and had not changed at all since then. Every corner of the garden and of the yard recalled the far-away past. And in his childhood, too, just as now, the whole yard bathed in moonlight could be seen through the sparse trees, the shadows had been mysterious and forbidding, a black dog had lain in the middle of the yard, and the clerks' windows had stood wide open. And all these were cheerless memories.

The other side of the fence, in the neighbour's yard, there was a sound of light steps.

"My sweet, my precious . . ." said a man's voice so near the fence that Laptev could hear the man's breathing.

Now they were kissing. Laptev was convinced that the millions and the business which was so distasteful to him were ruining his life, and would make him a complete slave. He imagined how, little by little, he would grow accustomed to his position; would, little by little, enter into the part of the head of a great firm; would begin to grow dull and old, die in the end, as the average man usually does die, in a decrepit, soured old age, making everyone about him miserable and depressed. But what hindered him from giving up those millions and that business, and leaving that yard and garden which had been hateful to him from his childhood?

The whispering and kisses the other side of the fence disturbed him. He moved into the middle of the yard, and, unbuttoning his shirt over his chest, looked at the moon, and it seemed to him that he would order the gate to be unlocked, and would go out and never come back again. His heart ached sweetly with the foretaste of freedom; he laughed joyously, and pictured how exquisite, poetical, and even holy, life might be. . . .

But he still stood and did not go away, and kept asking himself: "What keeps me here?" And he felt angry with himself and with the black dog, which still lay stretched on the stone yard, instead of running off to the open country, to the woods, where it would have been free and happy. It was clear that that dog and he were prevented from leaving the yard by the same thing; the habit of bondage, of servitude. . . .

At midday next morning he went to see his wife, and that he might not be dull, asked Yartsev to go with him. Yulia Sergeyevna was staying in a summer villa at Butovo, and he had not been to see her for five days. When they reached the station the friends got into a carriage, and all the way there Yartsev was singing and in raptures over the exquisite weather. The villa was in a great park not far from the station. At the beginning of an avenue, about twenty paces from the gates, Yulia Sergeyevna was sitting under a broad, spreading poplar, waiting for her guests. She had on a light, elegant dress of a pale cream colour trimmed with lace, and in her hand she had the old familiar parasol. Yartsev greeted her and went on to the villa from which came the sound of Sasha's and Lida's voices, while Laptev sat down beside her to talk of business matters.

"Why is it you haven't been for so long?" she said, keeping his hand in hers. "I have been sitting here for days watching for you to come. I miss you so when you are away!"

She stood up and passed her hand over his hair, and scanned his face, his shoulders, his hat, with interest.

"You know I love you," she said, and flushed crimson. "You are precious to me. Here you've come. I see you, and I'm so happy I can't tell you. Well, let us talk. Tell me something."

She had told him she loved him, and he could only feel as though he had been married to her for ten years, and that he was hungry for his lunch. She had put her arm round his neck, tickling his cheek with the silk of her dress; he cautiously removed her hand, stood up, and without uttering a single word, walked to the villa. The little girls ran to meet him.

"How they have grown!" he thought. "And what changes in these three years. . . . But one may have to live another thirteen years, another thirty years. . . . What is there in store for us in the future? If we live, we shall see."

He embraced Sasha and Lida, who hung upon his neck, and said:

"Grandpapa sends his love. . . . Uncle Fyodor is dying. Uncle Kostya has sent a letter from America and sends you his love in it. He's bored at the exhibition and will soon be back. And Uncle Alyosha is hungry."

Then he sat on the verandah and saw his wife walking slowly along the avenue towards the house. She was deep in thought; there was a mournful, charming expression in her face, and her eyes were bright with tears. She was not now the slender, fragile, pale-faced girl she used to be; she was a mature, beautiful, vigorous woman. And Laptev saw the enthusiasm with which Yartsev looked at her when he met her, and the way her new, lovely expression was reflected in his face, which looked mournful and ecstatic too. One would have thought that he was seeing her for the first time in his life. And while they were at lunch on the verandah, Yartsev smiled with a sort of joyous shyness, and kept gazing at Yulia and at her beautiful neck. Laptev could not help watching them while he thought that he had perhaps another thirteen, another thirty years of life before him. . . . And what would he have to live through in that time? What is in store for us in the future?

And he thought:

"Let us live, and we shall see."

THE HELPMATE

"I've asked you not to tidy my table," said Nikolay Yevgrafitch. "There's no finding anything when you've tidied up. Where's the telegram? Where have you thrown it? Be so good as to look for it. It's from Kazan, dated yesterday."

The maid -- a pale, very slim girl with an indifferent expression -- found several telegrams in the basket under the table, and handed them to the doctor without a word; but all these were telegrams from patients. Then they looked in the drawing-room, and in Olga Dmitrievna's room.

It was past midnight. Nikolay Yevgrafitch knew his wife would not be home very soon, not till five o'clock at least. He did not trust her, and when she was long away he could not sleep, was worried, and at the same time he despised his wife, and her bed, and her looking-glass, and her boxes of sweets, and the hyacinths, and the lilies of the valley which were sent her every day by someone or other, and which diffused the sickly fragrance of a florist's shop all over the house. On such nights he became petty, ill-humoured, irritable, and he fancied now that it was very necessary for him to have the telegram he had received the day before from his brother, though it contained nothing but Christmas greetings.

On the table of his wife's room under the box of stationery he found a telegram, and glanced at it casually. It was addressed to his wife, care of his mother-in-law, from Monte Carlo, and signed Michel. . . . The doctor did not understand one word of it, as it was in some foreign language, apparently English.

"Who is this Michel? Why Monte Carlo? Why directed care of her mother?"

During the seven years of his married life he had grown used to being suspicious, guessing, catching at clues, and it had several times occurred to him, that his exercise at home had qualified him to become an excellent detective. Going into his study and beginning to reflect, he recalled at once how he had been with his wife in Petersburg a year and a half ago, and had lunched with an old school-fellow, a civil engineer, and how that engineer had introduced to him and his wife a young man of two or three and twenty, called Mihail Ivanovitch, with rather a curious short surname -- Riss. Two months later the doctor had seen the young man's photograph in his wife's album, with an inscription in French: "In remembrance of the present and in hope of the future." Later on he had met the young man himself at his mother-in-law's. And that was at the time when his wife had taken to being very often absent and coming home at four or five o'clock in the morning, and was constantly asking him to get her a passport for abroad, which he kept refusing to do; and a continual feud went on in the house which made him feel ashamed to face the servants.

Six months before, his colleagues had decided that he was going into consumption, and advised him to throw up everything and go to the Crimea. When she heard of this, Olga Dmitrievna affected to be very much alarmed; she began to be affectionate to her husband, and kept assuring him that it would be cold and dull in the Crimea, and that he had much better go to Nice, and that she would go with him, and there would nurse him, look after him, take care of him.

Now, he understood why his wife was so particularly anxious to go to Nice: her Michel lived at Monte Carlo.

He took an English dictionary, and translating the words, and guessing their meaning, by degrees he put together the following sentence: "I drink to the health of my beloved darling, and kiss her little foot a thousand times, and am impatiently expecting her arrival." He pictured the pitiable, ludicrous part he would play if he had agreed to go to Nice with his wife. He felt so mortified that he almost shed tears and began pacing to and fro through all the rooms of the flat in great agitation. His pride, his plebeian fastidiousness, was revolted. Clenching his fists and scowling with disgust, he wondered how he, the son of a village priest, brought up in a clerical school, a plain, straightforward man, a surgeon by profession -- how could he have let himself be enslaved, have sunk into such shameful bondage to this weak, worthless, mercenary, low creature.

" 'Little foot'!" he muttered to himself, crumpling up the telegram; " 'little foot'!"

Of the time when he fell in love and proposed to her, and the seven years that he had been living with her, all that remained in his memory was her long, fragrant hair, a mass of soft lace, and her little feet, which certainly were very small, beautiful feet; and even now it seemed as though he still had from those old embraces the feeling of lace and silk upon his hands and face -- and nothing more. Nothing more -- that is, not counting hysterics, shrieks, reproaches, threats, and lies -- brazen, treacherous lies. He remembered how in his father's house in the village a bird would sometimes chance to fly in from the open air into the house and would struggle desperately against the window-panes and upset things; so this woman from a class utterly alien to him had flown into his life and made complete havoc of it. The best years of his life had been spent as though in hell, his hopes for happiness shattered and turned into a mockery, his health gone, his rooms as vulgar in their atmosphere as a cocotte's, and of the ten thousand he earned every year he could never save ten roubles to send his old mother in the village, and his debts were already about fifteen thousand. It seemed that if a band of brigands had been living in his rooms his life would not have been so hopelessly, so irremediably ruined as by the presence of this woman.

He began coughing and gasping for breath. He ought to have gone to bed and got warm, but he could not. He kept walking about the rooms, or sat down to the table, nervously fidgeting with a pencil and scribbling mechanically on a paper.

"Trying a pen. . . . A little foot."

By five o'clock he grew weaker and threw all the blame on himself. It seemed to him now that if Olga Dmitrievna had married someone else who might have had a good influence over her -- who knows? -- she might after all have become a good, straightforward woman. He was a poor psychologist, and knew nothing of the female heart; besides, he was churlish, uninteresting. . . .

"I haven't long to live now," he thought. "I am a dead man, and ought not to stand in the way of the living. It would be strange and stupid to insist upon one's rights now. I'll have it out with her; let her go to the man she loves. . . . I'll give her a divorce. I'll take the blame on myself."

Olga Dmitrievna came in at last, and she walked into the study and sank into a chair just as she was in her white cloak, hat, and overboots.

"The nasty, fat boy," she said with a sob, breathing hard. "It's really dishonest; it's disgusting." She stamped. "I can't put up with it; I can't, I can't!"

"What's the matter?" asked Nikolay Yevgrafitch, going up to her.

"That student, Azarbekov, was seeing me home, and he lost my bag, and there was fifteen roubles in it. I borrowed it from mamma."

She was crying in a most genuine way, like a little girl, and not only her handkerchief, but even her gloves, were wet with tears.

"It can't be helped!" said the doctor. "If he's lost it, he's lost it, and it's no good worrying over it. Calm yourself; I want to talk to you."

"I am not a millionaire to lose money like that. He says he'll pay it back, but I don't believe him; he's poor . . ."

Her husband begged her to calm herself and to listen to him, but she kept on talking of the student and of the fifteen roubles she had lost.

"Ach! I'll give you twenty-five roubles to-morrow if you'll only hold your tongue!" he said irritably.

"I must take off my things!" she said, crying. "I can't talk seriously in my fur coat! How strange you are!"

He helped her off with her coat and overboots, detecting as he did so the smell of the white wine she liked to drink with oysters (in spite of her etherealness she ate and drank a great deal). She went into her room and came back soon after, having changed her things and powdered her face, though her eyes still showed traces of tears. She sat down, retreating into her light, lacy dressing-gown, and in the mass of billowy pink her husband could see nothing but her hair, which she had let down, and her little foot wearing a slipper.

"What do you want to talk about?" she asked, swinging herself in a rocking-chair.

"I happened to see this;" and he handed her the telegram.

She read it and shrugged her shoulders.

"Well?" she said, rocking herself faster. "That's the usual New Year's greeting and nothing else. There are no secrets in it."

"You are reckoning on my not knowing English. No, I don't know it; but I have a dictionary. That telegram is from Riss; he drinks to the health of his beloved and sends you a thousand kisses. But let us leave that," the doctor went on hurriedly. "I don't in the least want to reproach you or make a scene. We've had scenes and reproaches enough; it's time to make an end of them. . . . This is what I want to say to you: you are free, and can live as you like."

There was a silence. She began crying quietly.

"I set you free from the necessity of lying and keeping up pretences," Nikolay Yevgrafitch continued. "If you love that young man, love him; if you want to go abroad to him, go. You are young, healthy, and I am a wreck, and haven't long to live. In short . . . you understand me."

He was agitated and could not go on. Olga Dmitrievna, crying and speaking in a voice of self-pity, acknowledged that she loved Riss, and used to drive out of town with him and see him in his rooms, and now she really did long to go abroad.

"You see, I hide nothing from you," she added, with a sigh. "My whole soul lies open before you. And I beg you again, be generous, get me a passport."

"I repeat, you are free."

She moved to another seat nearer him to look at the expression of his face. She did not believe him and wanted now to understand his secret meaning. She never did believe anyone, and however generous were their intentions, she always suspected some petty or ignoble motive or selfish object in them. And when she looked searchingly into his face, it seemed to him that there was a gleam of green light in her eyes as in a cat's.

"When shall I get the passport?" she asked softly.

He suddenly had an impulse to say "Never"; but he restrained himself and said:

"When you like."

"I shall only go for a month."

"You'll go to Riss for good. I'll get you a divorce, take the blame on myself, and Riss can marry you."

"But I don't want a divorce!" Olga Dmitrievna retorted quickly, with an astonished face. "I am not asking you for a divorce! Get me a passport, that's all."

"But why don't you want the divorce?" asked the doctor, beginning to feel irritated. "You are a strange woman. How strange you are! If you are fond of him in earnest and he loves you too, in your position you can do nothing better than get married. Can you really hesitate between marriage and adultery?"

"I understand you," she said, walking away from him, and a spiteful, vindictive expression came into her face. "I understand you perfectly. You are sick of me, and you simply want to get rid of me, to force this divorce on me. Thank you very much; I am not such a fool as you think. I won't accept the divorce and I won't leave you -- I won't, I won't! To begin with, I don't want to lose my position in society," she continued quickly, as though afraid of being prevented from speaking. "Secondly, I am twenty-seven and Riss is only twenty-three; he'll be tired of me in a year and throw me over. And what's more, if you care to know, I'm not certain that my feeling will last long . . . so there! I'm not going to leave you."

"Then I'll turn you out of the house!" shouted Nikolay Yevgrafitch, stamping. "I shall turn you out, you vile, loathsome woman!"

"We shall see!" she said, and went out.

It was broad daylight outside, but the doctor still sat at the table moving the pencil over the paper and writing mechanically.

"My dear Sir. . . . Little foot."

Or he walked about and stopped in the drawing-room before a photograph taken seven years ago, soon after his marriage, and looked at it for a long time. It was a family group: his father-in-law, his mother-in-law, his wife Olga Dmitrievna when she was twenty, and himself in the rôle of a happy young husband. His father-in-law, a clean-shaven, dropsical privy councillor, crafty and avaricious; his mother-in-law, a stout lady with small predatory features like a weasel, who loved her daughter to distraction and helped her in everything; if her daughter were strangling someone, the mother would not have protested, but would only have screened her with her skirts. Olga Dmitrievna, too, had small predatory-looking features, but more expressive and bolder than her mother's; she was not a weasel, but a beast on a bigger scale! And Nikolay Yevgrafitch himself in the photograph looked such a guileless soul, such a kindly, good fellow, so open and simple-hearted; his whole face was relaxed in the naïve, good-natured smile of a divinity student, and he had had the simplicity to believe that that company of beasts of prey into which destiny had chanced to thrust him would give him romance and happiness and all he had dreamed of when as a student he used to sing the song "Youth is wasted, life is nought, when the heart is cold and loveless."

And once more he asked himself in perplexity how he, the son of a village priest, with his democratic bringing up -- a plain, blunt, straightforward man -- could have so helplessly surrendered to the power of this worthless, false, vulgar, petty creature, whose nature was so utterly alien to him.

When at eleven o'clock he put on his coat to go to the hospital the servant came into his study.

"What is it?" he asked.

"The mistress has got up and asks you for the twenty-five roubles you promised her yesterday."

WHITEBROW

A hungry she-wolf got up to go hunting. Her cubs, all three of them, were sound asleep, huddled in a heap and keeping each other warm. She licked them and went off.

It was already March, a month of spring, but at night the trees snapped with the cold, as they do in December, and one could hardly put one's tongue out without its being nipped. The wolf-mother was in delicate health and nervous; she started at the slightest sound, and kept hoping that no one would hurt the little ones at home while she was away. The smell of the tracks of men and horses, logs, piles of faggots, and the dark road with horse-dung on it frightened her; it seemed to her that men were standing behind the trees in the darkness, and that dogs were howling somewhere beyond the forest.

She was no longer young and her scent had grown feebler, so that it sometimes happened that she took the track of a fox for that of a dog, and even at times lost her way, a thing that had never been in her youth. Owing to the weakness of her health she no longer hunted calves and big sheep as she had in old days, and kept her distance now from mares with colts; she fed on nothing but carrion; fresh meat she tasted very rarely, only in the spring when she would come upon a hare and take away her young, or make her way into a peasant's stall where there were lambs.

Some three miles from her lair there stood a winter hut on the posting road. There lived the keeper Ignat, an old man of seventy, who was always coughing and talking to himself; at night he was usually asleep, and by day he wandered about the forest with a single-barrelled gun, whistling to the hares. He must have worked among machinery in early days, for before he stood still he always shouted to himself: "Stop the machine!" and before going on: "Full speed!" He had a huge black dog of indeterminate breed, called Arapka. When it ran too far ahead he used to shout to it: "Reverse action!" Sometimes he used to sing, and as he did so staggered violently, and often fell down (the wolf thought the wind blew him over), and shouted: "Run off the rails!"

The wolf remembered that, in the summer and autumn, a ram and two ewes were pasturing near the winter hut, and when she had run by not so long ago she fancied that she had heard bleating in the stall. And now, as she got near the place, she reflected that it was already March, and, by that time, there would certainly be lambs in the stall. She was tormented by hunger, she thought with what greediness she would eat a lamb, and these thoughts made her teeth snap, and her eyes glitter in the darkness like two sparks of light.

Ignat's hut, his barn, cattle-stall, and well were surrounded by high snowdrifts. All was still. Arapka was, most likely, asleep in the barn.

The wolf clambered over a snowdrift on to the stall, and began scratching away the thatched roof with her paws and her nose. The straw was rotten and decaying, so that the wolf almost fell through; all at once a smell of warm steam, of manure, and of sheep's milk floated straight to her nostrils. Down below, a lamb, feeling the cold, bleated softly. Leaping through the hole, the wolf fell with her four paws and chest on something soft and warm, probably a sheep, and at the same moment, something in the stall suddenly began whining, barking, and going off into a shrill little yap; the sheep huddled against the wall, and the wolf, frightened, snatched the first thing her teeth fastened on, and dashed away. . . .

She ran at her utmost speed, while Arapka, who by now had scented the wolf, howled furiously, the frightened hens cackled, and Ignat, coming out into the porch, shouted: "Full speed! Blow the whistle!"

And he whistled like a steam-engine, and then shouted: "Ho-ho-ho-ho!" and all this noise was repeated by the forest echo. When, little by little, it all died away, the wolf somewhat recovered herself, and began to notice that the prey she held in her teeth and dragged along the snow was heavier and, as it were, harder than lambs usually were at that season; and it smelt somehow different, and uttered strange sounds. . . . The wolf stopped and laid her burden on the snow, to rest and begin eating it, then all at once she leapt back in disgust. It was not a lamb, but a black puppy, with a big head and long legs, of a large breed, with a white patch on his brow, like Arapka's. Judging from his manners he was a simple, ignorant, yard-dog. He licked his crushed and wounded back, and, as though nothing was the matter, wagged his tail and barked at the wolf. She growled like a dog, and ran away from him. He ran after her. She looked round and snapped her teeth. He stopped in perplexity, and, probably deciding that she was playing with him, craned his head in the direction he had come from, and went off into a shrill, gleeful bark, as though inviting his mother Arapka to play with him and the wolf.

It was already getting light, and when the wolf reached her home in the thick aspen wood, each aspen tree could be seen distinctly, and the woodcocks were already awake, and the beautiful male birds often flew up, disturbed by the incautious gambols and barking of the puppy.

"Why does he run after me?" thought the wolf with annoyance. "I suppose he wants me to eat him."

She lived with her cubs in a shallow hole; three years before, a tall old pine tree had been torn up by the roots in a violent storm, and the hole had been formed by it. Now there were dead leaves and moss at the bottom, and around it lay bones and bullocks' horns, with which the little ones played. They were by now awake, and all three of them, very much alike, were standing in a row at the edge of their hole, looking at their returning mother, and wagging their tails. Seeing them, the puppy stopped a little way off, and stared at them for a very long time; seeing that they, too, were looking very attentively at him, he began barking angrily, as at strangers.

By now it was daylight and the sun had risen, the snow sparkled all around, but still the puppy stood a little way off and barked. The cubs sucked their mother, pressing her thin belly with their paws, while she gnawed a horse's bone, dry and white; she was tormented by hunger, her head ached from the dog's barking, and she felt inclined to fall on the uninvited guest and tear him to pieces.

At last the puppy was hoarse and exhausted; seeing they were not afraid of him, and not even attending to him, he began somewhat timidly approaching the cubs, alternately squatting down and bounding a few steps forward. Now, by daylight, it was easy to have a good look at him. . . . His white forehead was big, and on it was a hump such as is only seen on very stupid dogs; he had little, blue, dingy-looking eyes, and the expression of his whole face was extremely stupid. When he reached the cubs he stretched out his broad paws, laid his head upon them, and began:

"Mnya, myna . . . nga--nga--nga . . . !"

The cubs did not understand what he meant, but they wagged their tails. Then the puppy gave one of the cubs a smack on its big head with his paw. The cub, too, gave him a smack on the head. The puppy stood sideways to him, and looked at him askance, wagging his tail, then dashed off, and ran round several times on the frozen snow. The cubs ran after him, he fell on his back and kicked up his legs, and all three of them fell upon him, squealing with delight, and began biting him, not to hurt but in play. The crows sat on the high pine tree, and looked down on their struggle, and were much troubled by it. They grew noisy and merry. The sun was hot, as though it were spring; and the woodcocks, continually flitting through the pine tree that had been blown down by the storm, looked as though made of emerald in the brilliant sunshine.

As a rule, wolf-mothers train their children to hunt by giving them prey to play with; and now watching the cubs chasing the puppy over the frozen snow and struggling with him, the mother thought:

"Let them learn."

When they had played long enough, the cubs went into the hole and lay down to sleep. The puppy howled a little from hunger, then he, too, stretched out in the sunshine. And when they woke up they began playing again.

All day long, and in the evening, the wolf-mother was thinking how the lamb had bleated in the cattle-shed the night before, and how it had smelt of sheep's milk, and she kept snapping her teeth from hunger, and never left off greedily gnawing the old bone, pretending to herself that it was the lamb. The cubs sucked their mother, and the puppy, who was hungry, ran round them and sniffed at the snow.

"I'll eat him . . . " the mother-wolf decided.

She went up to him, and he licked her nose and yapped at her, thinking that she wanted to play with him. In the past she had eaten dogs, but the dog smelt very doggy, and in the delicate state of her health she could not endure the smell; she felt disgusted and walked away. . . .

Towards night it grew cold. The puppy felt depressed and went home.

When the wolf-cubs were fast asleep, their mother went out hunting again. As on the previous night she was alarmed at every sound, and she was frightened by the stumps, the logs, the dark juniper bushes, which stood out singly, and in the distance were like human beings. She ran on the ice-covered snow, keeping away from the road. . . . All at once she caught a glimpse of something dark, far away on the road. She strained her eyes and ears: yes, something really was walking on in front, she could even hear the regular thud of footsteps. Surely not a badger? Cautiously holding her breath, and keeping always to one side, she overtook the dark patch, looked round, and recognised it. It was the puppy with the white brow, going with a slow, lingering step homewards.

"If only he doesn't hinder me again," thought the wolf, and ran quickly on ahead.

But the homestead was by now near. Again she clambered on to the cattle-shed by the snowdrift. The gap she had made yesterday had been already mended with straw, and two new rafters stretched across the roof. The wolf began rapidly working with her legs and nose, looking round to see whether the puppy were coming, but the smell of the warm steam and manure had hardly reached her nose before she heard a gleeful burst of barking behind her. It was the puppy. He leapt up to the wolf on the roof, then into the hole, and, feeling himself at home in the warmth, recognising his sheep, he barked louder than ever. . . . Arapka woke up in the barn, and, scenting a wolf, howled, the hens began cackling, and by the time Ignat appeared in the porch with his single-barrelled gun the frightened wolf was already far away.

"Fuite!" whistled Ignat. "Fuite! Full steam ahead!"

He pulled the trigger -- the gun missed fire; he pulled the trigger again -- again it missed fire; he tried a third time -- and a great blaze of flame flew out of the barrel and there was a deafening boom, boom. It kicked him violently on the shoulder, and, taking his gun in one hand and his axe in the other, he went to see what the noise was about.

A little later he went back to the hut.

"What was it?" a pilgrim, who was staying the night at the hut and had been awakened by the noise, asked in a husky voice.

"It's all right," answered Ignat. "Nothing of consequence. Our Whitebrow has taken to sleeping with the sheep in the warm. Only he hasn't the sense to go in at the door, but always tries to wriggle in by the roof. The other night he tore a hole in the roof and went off on the spree, the rascal, and now he has come back and scratched away the roof again."

"Stupid dog."

"Yes, there is a spring snapped in his brain. I do detest fools," sighed Ignat, clambering on to the stove. "Come, man of God, it's early yet to get up. Let us sleep full steam! . . ."

In the morning he called Whitebrow, smacked him hard about the ears, and then showing him a stick, kept repeating to him:

"Go in at the door! Go in at the door! Go in at the door!"

"ANNA ON THE NECK"

I

After the wedding they had not even light refreshments; the happy pair simply drank a glass of champagne, changed into their travelling things, and drove to the station. Instead of a gay wedding ball and supper, instead of music and dancing, they went on a journey to pray at a shrine a hundred and fifty miles away. Many people commended this, saying that Modest Alexeitch was a man high up in the service and no longer young, and that a noisy wedding might not have seemed quite suitable; and music is apt to sound dreary when a government official of fifty-two marries a girl who is only just eighteen. People said, too, that Modest Alexeitch, being a man of principle, had arranged this visit to the monastery expressly in order to make his young bride realize that even in marriage he put religion and morality above everything.

The happy pair were seen off at the station. The crowd of relations and colleagues in the service stood, with glasses in their hands, waiting for the train to start to shout "Hurrah!" and the bride's father, Pyotr Leontyitch, wearing a top-hat and the uniform of a teacher, already drunk and very pale, kept craning towards the window, glass in hand and saying in an imploring voice:

"Anyuta! Anya, Anya! one word!"

Anna bent out of the window to him, and he whispered something to her, enveloping her in a stale smell of alcohol, blew into her ear -- she could make out nothing -- and made the sign of the cross over her face, her bosom, and her hands; meanwhile he was breathing in gasps and tears were shining in his eyes. And the schoolboys, Anna's brothers, Petya and Andrusha, pulled at his coat from behind, whispering in confusion:

"Father, hush! . . . Father, that's enough. . . ."

When the train started, Anna saw her father run a little way after the train, staggering and spilling his wine, and what a kind, guilty, pitiful face he had:

"Hurra--ah!" he shouted.

The happy pair were left alone. Modest Alexeitch looked about the compartment, arranged their things on the shelves, and sat down, smiling, opposite his young wife. He was an official of medium height, rather stout and puffy, who looked exceedingly well nourished, with long whiskers and no moustache. His clean-shaven, round, sharply defined chin looked like the heel of a foot. The most characteristic point in his face was the absence of moustache, the bare, freshly shaven place, which gradually passed into the fat cheeks, quivering like jelly. His deportment was dignified, his movements were deliberate, his manner was soft.

"I cannot help remembering now one circumstance," he said, smiling. "When, five years ago, Kosorotov received the order of St. Anna of the second grade, and went to thank His Excellency, His Excellency expressed himself as follows: 'So now you have three Annas: one in your buttonhole and two on your neck.' And it must be explained that at that time Kosorotov's wife, a quarrelsome and frivolous person, had just returned to him, and that her name was Anna. I trust that when I receive the Anna of the second grade His Excellency will not have occasion to say the same thing to me."

He smiled with his little eyes. And she, too, smiled, troubled at the thought that at any moment this man might kiss her with his thick damp lips, and that she had no right to prevent his doing so. The soft movements of his fat person frightened her; she felt both fear and disgust. He got up, without haste took off the order from his neck, took off his coat and waistcoat, and put on his dressing-gown.

"That's better," he said, sitting down beside Anna.

Anna remembered what agony the wedding had been, when it had seemed to her that the priest, and the guests, and everyone in church had been looking at her sorrowfully and asking why, why was she, such a sweet, nice girl, marrying such an elderly, uninteresting gentleman. Only that morning she was delighted that everything had been satisfactorily arranged, but at the time of the wedding, and now in the railway carriage, she felt cheated, guilty, and ridiculous. Here she had married a rich man and yet she had no money, her wedding-dress had been bought on credit, and when her father and brothers had been saying good-bye, she could see from their faces that they had not a farthing. Would they have any supper that day? And tomorrow? And for some reason it seemed to her that her father and the boys were sitting tonight hungry without her, and feeling the same misery as they had the day after their mother's funeral.

"Oh, how unhappy I am!" she thought. "Why am I so unhappy?"

With the awkwardness of a man with settled habits, unaccustomed to deal with women, Modest Alexeitch touched her on the waist and patted her on the shoulder, while she went on thinking about money, about her mother and her mother's death. When her mother died, her father, Pyotr Leontyitch, a teacher of drawing and writing in the high school, had taken to drink, impoverishment had followed, the boys had not had boots or goloshes, their father had been hauled up before the magistrate, the warrant officer had come and made an inventory of the furniture. . . . What a disgrace! Anna had had to look after her drunken father, darn her brothers' stockings, go to market, and when she was complimented on her youth, her beauty, and her elegant manners, it seemed to her that everyone was looking at her cheap hat and the holes in her boots that were inked over. And at night there had been tears and a haunting dread that her father would soon, very soon, be dismissed from the school for his weakness, and that he would not survive it, but would die, too, like their mother. But ladies of their acquaintance had taken the matter in hand and looked about for a good match for Anna. This Modest Alexevitch, who was neither young nor good-looking but had money, was soon found. He had a hundred thousand in the bank and the family estate, which he had let on lease. He was a man of principle and stood well with His Excellency; it would be nothing to him, so they told Anna, to get a note from His Excellency to the directors of the high school, or even to the Education Commissioner, to prevent Pyotr Leontyitch from being dismissed.

While she was recalling these details, she suddenly heard strains of music which floated in at the window, together with the sound of voices. The train was stopping at a station. In the crowd beyond the platform an accordion and a cheap squeaky fiddle were being briskly played, and the sound of a military band came from beyond the villas and the tall birches and poplars that lay bathed in the moonlight; there must have been a dance in the place. Summer visitors and townspeople, who used to come out here by train in fine weather for a breath of fresh air, were parading up and down on the platform. Among them was the wealthy owner of all the summer villas -- a tall, stout, dark man called Artynov. He had prominent eyes and looked like an Armenian. He wore a strange costume; his shirt was unbuttoned, showing his chest; he wore high boots with spurs, and a black cloak hung from his shoulders and dragged on the ground like a train. Two boar-hounds followed him with their sharp noses to the ground.

Tears were still shining in Anna's eyes, but she was not thinking now of her mother, nor of money, nor of her marriage; but shaking hands with schoolboys and officers she knew, she laughed gaily and said quickly:

"How do you do? How are you?"

She went out on to the platform between the carriages into the moonlight, and stood so that they could all see her in her new splendid dress and hat.

"Why are we stopping here?" she asked.

"This is a junction. They are waiting for the mail train to pass."

Seeing that Artynov was looking at her, she screwed up her eyes coquettishly and began talking aloud in French; and because her voice sounded so pleasant, and because she heard music and the moon was reflected in the pond, and because Artynov, the notorious Don Juan and spoiled child of fortune, was looking at her eagerly and with curiosity, and because everyone was in good spirits -- she suddenly felt joyful, and when the train started and the officers of her acquaintance saluted her, she was humming the polka the strains of which reached her from the military band playing beyond the trees; and she returned to her compartment feeling as though it had been proved to her at the station that she would certainly be happy in spite of everything.

The happy pair spent two days at the monastery, then went back to town. They lived in a rent-free flat. When Modest Alexevitch had gone to the office, Anna played the piano, or shed tears of depression, or lay down on a couch and read novels or looked through fashion papers. At dinner Modest Alexevitch ate a great deal and talked about politics, about appointments, transfers, and promotions in the service, about the necessity of hard work, and said that, family life not being a pleasure but a duty, if you took care of the kopecks the roubles would take care of themselves, and that he put religion and morality before everything else in the world. And holding his knife in his fist as though it were a sword, he would say:

"Everyone ought to have his duties!"

And Anna listened to him, was frightened, and could not eat, and she usually got up from the table hungry. After dinner her husband lay down for a nap and snored loudly, while Anna went to see her own people. Her father and the boys looked at her in a peculiar way, as though just before she came in they had been blaming her for having married for money a tedious, wearisome man she did not love; her rustling skirts, her bracelets, and her general air of a married lady, offended them and made them uncomfortable. In her presence they felt a little embarrassed and did not know what to talk to her about; but yet they still loved her as before, and were not used to having dinner without her. She sat down with them to cabbage soup, porridge, and fried potatoes, smelling of mutton dripping. Pyotr Leontyitch filled his glass from the decanter with a trembling hand and drank it off hurriedly, greedily, with repulsion, then poured out a second glass and then a third. Petya and Andrusha, thin, pale boys with big eyes, would take the decanter and say desperately:

"You mustn't, father. . . . Enough, father. . . ."

And Anna, too, was troubled and entreated him to drink no more; and he would suddenly fly into a rage and beat the table with his fists:

"I won't allow anyone to dictate to me!" he would shout. "Wretched boys! wretched girl! I'll turn you all out!"

But there was a note of weakness, of good-nature in his voice, and no one was afraid of him. After dinner he usually dressed in his best. Pale, with a cut on his chin from shaving, craning his thin neck, he would stand for half an hour before the glass, prinking, combing his hair, twisting his black moustache, sprinkling himself with scent, tying his cravat in a bow; then he would put on his gloves and his top-hat, and go off to give his private lessons. Or if it was a holiday he would stay at home and paint, or play the harmonium, which wheezed and growled; he would try to wrest from it pure harmonious sounds and would sing to it; or would storm at the boys:

"Wretches! Good-for-nothing boys! You have spoiled the instrument!"

In the evening Anna's husband played cards with his colleagues, who lived under the same roof in the government quarters. The wives of these gentlemen would come in -- ugly, tastelessly dressed women, as coarse as cooks -- and gossip would begin in the flat as tasteless and unattractive as the ladies themselves. Sometimes Modest Alexevitch would take Anna to the theatre. In the intervals he would never let her stir a step from his side, but walked about arm in arm with her through the corridors and the foyer. When he bowed to someone, he immediately whispered to Anna: "A civil councillor . . . visits at His Excellency's"; or, "A man of means . . . has a house of his own." When they passed the buffet Anna had a great longing for something sweet; she was fond of chocolate and apple cakes, but she had no money, and she did not like to ask her husband. He would take a pear, pinch it with his fingers, and ask uncertainly:

"How much?"

"Twenty-five kopecks!"

"I say!" he would reply, and put it down; but as it was awkward to leave the buffet without buying anything, he would order some seltzer-water and drink the whole bottle himself, and tears would come into his eyes. And Anna hated him at such times.

And suddenly flushing crimson, he would say to her rapidly:

"Bow to that old lady!"

"But I don't know her."

"No matter. That's the wife of the director of the local treasury! Bow, I tell you," he would grumble insistently. "Your head won't drop off."

Anna bowed and her head certainly did not drop off, but it was agonizing. She did everything her husband wanted her to, and was furious with herself for having let him deceive her like the veriest idiot. She had only married him for his money, and yet she had less money now than before her marriage. In old days her father would sometimes give her twenty kopecks, but now she had not a farthing.

To take money by stealth or ask for it, she could not; she was afraid of her husband, she trembled before him. She felt as though she had been afraid of him for years. In her childhood the director of the high school had always seemed the most impressive and terrifying force in the world, sweeping down like a thunderstorm or a steam-engine ready to crush her; another similar force of which the whole family talked, and of which they were for some reason afraid, was His Excellency; then there were a dozen others, less formidable, and among them the teachers at the high school, with shaven upper lips, stern, implacable; and now finally, there was Modest Alexeitch, a man of principle, who even resembled the director in the face. And in Anna's imagination all these forces blended together into one, and, in the form of a terrible, huge white bear, menaced the weak and erring such as her father. And she was afraid to say anything in opposition to her husband, and gave a forced smile, and tried to make a show of pleasure when she was coarsely caressed and defiled by embraces that excited her terror. Only once Pyotr Leontyitch had the temerity to ask for a loan of fifty roubles in order to pay some very irksome debt, but what an agony it had been!

"Very good; I'll give it to you," said Modest Alexeitch after a moment's thought; "but I warn you I won't help you again till you give up drinking. Such a failing is disgraceful in a man in the government service! I must remind you of the well-known fact that many capable people have been ruined by that passion, though they might possibly, with temperance, have risen in time to a very high

And long-winded phrases followed: "inasmuch as . . .," "following upon which proposition . . . ," in view of the aforesaid contention . . ."; and Pyotr Leontyitch was in agonies of humiliation and felt an intense craving for alcohol.

And when the boys came to visit Anna, generally in broken boots and threadbare trousers, they, too, had to listen to sermons.

"Every man ought to have his duties!" Modest Alexeitch would say to them.

And he did not give them money. But he did give Anna bracelets, rings, and brooches, saying that these things would come in useful for a rainy day. And he often unlocked her drawer and made an inspection to see whether they were all safe.

II

Meanwhile winter came on. Long before Christmas there was an announcement in the local papers that the usual winter ball would take place on the twenty-ninth of December in the Hall of Nobility. Every evening after cards Modest Alexeitch was excitedly whispering with his colleagues' wives and glancing at Anna, and then paced up and down the room for a long while, thinking. At last, late one evening, he stood still, facing Anna, and said:

"You ought to get yourself a ball dress. Do you understand? Only please consult Marya Grigoryevna and Natalya Kuzminishna."

And he gave her a hundred roubles. She took the money, but she did not consult anyone when she ordered the ball dress; she spoke to no one but her father, and tried to imagine how her mother would have dressed for a ball. Her mother had always dressed in the latest fashion and had always taken trouble over Anna, dressing her elegantly like a doll, and had taught her to speak French and dance the mazurka superbly (she had been a governess for five years before her marriage). Like her mother, Anna could make a new dress out of an old one, clean gloves with benzine, hire jewels; and, like her mother, she knew how to screw up her eyes, lisp, assume graceful attitudes, fly into raptures when necessary, and throw a mournful and enigmatic look into her eyes. And from her father she had inherited the dark colour of her hair and eyes, her highly-strung nerves, and the habit of always making herself look her best.

When, half an hour before setting off for the ball, Modest Alexeitch went into her room without his coat on, to put his order round his neck before her pier-glass, dazzled by her beauty and the splendour of her fresh, ethereal dress, he combed his whiskers complacently and said:

"So that's what my wife can look like . . . so that's what you can look like! Anyuta!" he went on, dropping into a tone of solemnity, "I have made your fortune, and now I beg you to do something for mine. I beg you to get introduced to the wife of His Excellency! For God's sake, do! Through her I may get the post of senior reporting clerk!"

They went to the ball. They reached the Hall of Nobility, the entrance with the hall porter. They came to the vestibule with the hat-stands, the fur coats; footmen scurrying about, and ladies with low necks putting up their fans to screen themselves from the draughts. There was a smell of gas and of soldiers. When Anna, walking upstairs on her husband's arm, heard the music and saw herself full length in the looking-glass in the full glow of the lights, there was a rush of joy in her heart, and she felt the same presentiment of happiness as in the moonlight at the station. She walked in proudly, confidently, for the first time feeling herself not a girl but a lady, and unconsciously imitating her mother in her walk and in her manner. And for the first time in her life she felt rich and free. Even her husband's presence did not oppress her, for as she crossed the threshold of the hall she had guessed instinctively that the proximity of an old husband did not detract from her in the least, but, on the contrary, gave her that shade of piquant mystery that is so attractive to men. The orchestra was already playing and the dances had begun. After their flat Anna was overwhelmed by the lights, the bright colours, the music, the noise, and looking round the room, thought, "Oh, how lovely!" She at once distinguished in the crowd all her acquaintances, everyone she had met before at parties or on picnics -- all the officers, the teachers, the lawyers, the officials, the landowners, His Excellency, Artynov, and the ladies of the highest standing, dressed up and very *décollettées,* handsome and ugly, who had already taken up their positions in the stalls and pavilions of the charity bazaar, to begin selling things for the benefit of the poor. A huge officer in epaulettes -- she had been introduced to him in Staro-Kievsky Street when she was a schoolgirl, but now she could not remember his name -- seemed to spring from out of the ground, begging her for a waltz, and she flew away from her husband, feeling as though she were floating away in a sailing-boat in a violent storm, while her husband was left far away on the shore. She danced passionately, with fervour, a waltz, then a polka and a quadrille, being snatched by one partner as soon as she was left by another, dizzy with music and the noise, mixing Russian with French, lisping, laughing, and with no thought of her husband or anything else. She excited great admiration among the men -- that was evident, and indeed it could not have been otherwise; she was breathless with excitement, felt thirsty, and convulsively clutched her fan. Pyotr Leontyitch, her father, in a crumpled dress-coat that smelt of benzine, came up to her, offering her a plate of pink ice.

"You are enchanting this evening," he said, looking at her rapturously, "and I have never so much regretted that you were in such a hurry to get married. . . . What was it for? I know you did it for our sake, but . . ." With a shaking hand he drew out a roll of notes and said: "I got the money for my lessons today, and can pay your husband what I owe him."

She put the plate back into his hand, and was pounced upon by someone and borne off to a distance. She caught a glimpse over her partner's shoulder of her father gliding over the floor, putting his arm round a lady and whirling down the ball-room with her.

"How sweet he is when he is sober!" she thought.

She danced the mazurka with the same huge officer; he moved gravely, as heavily as a dead carcase in a uniform, twitched his shoulders and his chest, stamped his feet very languidly -- he felt fearfully disinclined to dance. She fluttered round him, provoking him by her beauty, her bare neck; her eyes glowed defiantly, her movements were passionate, while he became more and more indifferent, and held out his hands to her as graciously as a king.

"Bravo, bravo!" said people watching them.

But little by little the huge officer, too, broke out; he grew lively, excited, and, overcome by her fascination, was carried away and danced lightly, youthfully, while she merely moved her shoulders and looked slyly at him as though she were now the queen and he were her slave; and at that moment it seemed to her that the whole room was looking at them, and that everybody was thrilled and envied them. The huge officer had hardly had time to thank her for the dance, when the crowd suddenly parted and the men drew themselves up in a strange way, with their hands at their sides.

His Excellency, with two stars on his dress-coat, was walking up to her. Yes, His Excellency was walking straight towards her, for he was staring directly at her with a sugary smile, while he licked his lips as he always did when he saw a pretty woman.

"Delighted, delighted . . ." he began. "I shall order your husband to be clapped in a lock-up for keeping such a treasure hidden from us till now. I've come to you with a message from my wife," he went on, offering her his arm. "You must help us. . . . M-m-yes. . . . We ought to give you the prize for beauty as they do in America. . . . M-m-yes. . . . The Americans. . . . My wife is expecting you impatiently."

He led her to a stall and presented her to a middle-aged lady, the lower part of whose face was disproportionately large, so that she looked as though she were holding a big stone in her mouth.

"You must help us," she said through her nose in a sing-song voice. "All the pretty women are working for our charity bazaar, and you are the only one enjoying yourself. Why won't you help us?"

She went away, and Anna took her place by the cups and the silver samovar. She was soon doing a lively trade. Anna asked no less than a rouble for a cup of tea, and made the huge officer drink three cups. Artynov, the rich man with prominent eyes, who suffered from asthma, came up, too; he was not dressed in the strange costume in which Anna had seen him in the summer at the station, but wore a dress-coat like everyone else. Keeping his eyes fixed on Anna, he drank a glass of champagne and paid a hundred roubles for it, then drank some tea and gave another hundred -- all this without saying a word, as he was short of breath through asthma. . . . Anna invited purchasers and got money out of them, firmly convinced by now that her smiles and glances could not fail to afford these people great pleasure. She realized now that she was created exclusively for this noisy, brilliant, laughing life, with its music, its dancers, its adorers, and her old terror of a force that was sweeping down upon her and menacing to crush her seemed to her ridiculous: she was afraid of no one now, and only regretted that her mother could not be there to rejoice at her success.

Pyotr Leontyitch, pale by now but still steady on his legs, came up to the stall and asked for a glass of brandy. Anna turned crimson, expecting him to say something inappropriate (she was already ashamed of having such a poor and ordinary father); but he emptied his glass, took ten roubles out of his roll of notes, flung it down, and walked away with dignity without uttering a word. A little later she saw him dancing in the grand chain, and by now he was staggering and kept shouting something, to the great confusion of his partner; and Anna remembered how at the ball three years before he had staggered and shouted in the same way, and it had ended in the police-sergeant's taking him home to bed, and next day the director had threatened to dismiss him from his post. How inappropriate that memory was!

When the samovars were put out in the stalls and the exhausted ladies handed over their takings to the middle-aged lady with the stone in her mouth, Artynov took Anna on his arm to the hall where supper was served to all who had assisted at the bazaar. There were some twenty people at supper, not more, but it was very noisy. His Excellency proposed a toast:

"In this magnificent dining-room it will be appropriate to drink to the success of the cheap dining-rooms, which are the object of today's bazaar."

The brigadier-general proposed the toast: "To the power by which even the artillery is vanquished," and all the company clinked glasses with the ladies. It was very, very gay.

When Anna was escorted home it was daylight and the cooks were going to market. Joyful, intoxicated, full of new sensations, exhausted, she undressed, dropped into bed, and at once fell asleep. . . .

It was past one in the afternoon when the servant waked her and announced that M. Artynov had called. She dressed quickly and went down into the drawing-room. Soon after Artynov, His Excellency called to thank her for her assistance in the bazaar. With a sugary smile, chewing his lips, he kissed her hand, and asking her permission to come again, took his leave, while she remained standing in the middle of the drawing-room, amazed, enchanted, unable to believe that this change in her life, this marvellous change, had taken place so quickly; and at that moment Modest Alexeitch walked in . . . and he, too, stood before her now with the same ingratiating, sugary, cringingly respectful expression which she was accustomed to see on his face in the presence of the great and powerful; and with rapture, with indignation, with contempt, convinced that no harm would come to her from it, she said, articulating distinctly each word:

"Be off, you blockhead!"

From this time forward Anna never had one day free, as she was always taking part in picnics, expeditions, performances. She returned home every day after midnight, and went to bed on the floor in the drawing-room, and afterwards used to tell everyone, touchingly, how she slept under flowers. She needed a very great deal of money, but she was no longer afraid of Modest Alexeitch, and spent his money as though it were her own; and she did not ask, did not demand it, simply sent him in the bills. "Give bearer two hundred roubles," or "Pay one hundred roubles at once."

At Easter Modest Alexeitch received the Anna of the second grade. When he went to offer his thanks, His Excellency put aside the paper he was reading and settled himself more comfortably in his chair.

"So now you have three Annas," he said, scrutinizing his white hands and pink nails -- "one on your buttonhole and two on your neck."

Modest Alexeitch put two fingers to his lips as a precaution against laughing too loud and said:

"Now I have only to look forward to the arrival of a little Vladimir. I make bold to beg your Excellency to stand godfather."

He was alluding to Vladimir of the fourth grade, and was already imagining how he would tell everywhere the story of this pun, so happy in its readiness and audacity, and he wanted to say something equally happy, but His Excellency was buried again in his newspaper, and merely gave him a nod.

And Anna went on driving about with three horses, going out hunting with Artynov, playing in one-act dramas, going out to supper, and was more and more rarely with her own family; they dined now alone. Pyotr Leontyitch was drinking more heavily than ever; there was no money, and the harmonium had been sold long ago for debt. The boys did not let him go out alone in the street now, but looked after him for fear he might fall down; and whenever they met Anna driving in Staro-Kievsky Street with a pair of horses and Artynov on the box instead of a coachman, Pyotr Leontyitch took off his top-hat, and was about to shout to her, but Petya and Andrusha took him by the arm, and said imploringly:

"You mustn't, father. Hush, father!"

THE MURDER

I

The evening service was being celebrated at Progonnaya Station. Before the great ikon, painted in glaring colours on a background of gold, stood the crowd of railway servants with their wives and children, and also of the timbermen and sawyers who worked close to the railway line. All stood in silence, fascinated by the glare of the lights and the howling of the snow-storm which was aimlessly disporting itself outside, regardless of the fact that it was the Eve of the Annunciation. The old priest from Vedenyapino conducted the service; the sacristan and Matvey Terehov were singing.

Matvey's face was beaming with delight; he sang stretching out his neck as though he wanted to soar upwards. He sang tenor and chanted the "Praises" too in a tenor voice with honied sweetness and persuasiveness. When he sang "Archangel Voices" he waved his arms like a conductor, and trying to second the sacristan's hollow bass with his tenor, achieved something extremely complex, and from his face it could be seen that he was experiencing great pleasure.

At last the service was over, and they all quietly dispersed, and it was dark and empty again, and there followed that hush which is only known in stations that stand solitary in the open country or in the forest when the wind howls and nothing else is heard and when all the emptiness around, all the dreariness of life slowly ebbing away is felt.

Matvey lived not far from the station at his cousin's tavern. But he did not want to go home. He sat down at the refreshment bar and began talking to the waiter in a low voice.

"We had our own choir in the tile factory. And I must tell you that though we were only workmen, our singing was first-rate, splendid. We were often invited to the town, and when the Deputy Bishop, Father Ivan, took the service at Trinity Church, the bishop's singers sang in the right choir and we in the left. Only they complained in the town that we kept the singing on too long: 'the factory choir drag it out,' they used to say. It is true we began St. Andrey's prayers and the Praises between six and seven, and it was past eleven when we finished, so that it was sometimes after midnight when we got home to the factory. It was good," sighed Matvey. "Very good it was, indeed, Sergey Nikanoritch! But here in my father's house it is anything but joyful. The nearest church is four miles away; with my weak health I can't get so far; there are no singers there. And there is no peace or quiet in our family; day in day out, there is an uproar, scolding, uncleanliness; we all eat out of one bowl like peasants; and there are beetles in the cabbage soup. . . . God has not given me health, else I would have gone away long ago, Sergey Nikanoritch."

Matvey Terehov was a middle-aged man about forty-five, but he had a look of ill-health; his face was wrinkled and his lank, scanty beard was quite grey, and that made him seem many years older. He spoke in a weak voice, circumspectly, and held his chest when he coughed, while his eyes assumed the uneasy and anxious look one sees in very apprehensive people. He never said definitely what was wrong with him, but he was fond of describing at length how once at the factory he had lifted a heavy box and had ruptured himself, and how this had led to "the gripes," and had forced him to give up his work in the tile factory and come back to his native place; but he could not explain what he meant by "the gripes."

"I must own I am not fond of my cousin," he went on, pouring himself out some tea. "He is my elder; it is a sin to censure him, and I fear the Lord, but I cannot bear it in patience. He is a haughty, surly, abusive man; he is the torment of his relations and workmen, and constantly out of humour. Last Sunday I asked him in an amiable way, 'Brother, let us go to Pahomovo for the Mass!' but he said 'I am not going; the priest there is a gambler;' and he would not come here to-day because, he said, the priest from Vedenyapino smokes and drinks vodka. He doesn't like the clergy! He reads Mass himself and the Hours and the Vespers, while his sister acts as sacristan; he says, 'Let us pray unto the Lord'! and she, in a thin little voice like a turkey-hen, 'Lord, have mercy upon us! . . .' It's a sin, that's what it is. Every day I say to him, 'Think what you are doing, brother! Repent, brother!' and he takes no notice."

Sergey Nikanoritch, the waiter, poured out five glasses of tea and carried them on a tray to the waiting-room. He had scarcely gone in when there was a shout:

"Is that the way to serve it, pig's face? You don't know how to wait!"

It was the voice of the station-master. There was a timid mutter, then again a harsh and angry shout:

"Get along!"

The waiter came back greatly crestfallen.

"There was a time when I gave satisfaction to counts and princes," he said in a low voice; "but now I don't know how to serve tea. . . . He called me names before the priest and the ladies!"

The waiter, Sergey Nikanoritch, had once had money of his own, and had kept a buffet at a first-class station, which was a junction, in the principal town of a province. There he had worn a swallow-tail coat and a gold chain. But things had gone ill with him; he had squandered all his own money over expensive fittings and service; he had been robbed by his staff, and getting gradually into difficulties, had moved to another station less bustling. Here his wife had left him, taking with her all the silver, and he moved to a third station of a still lower class, where no hot dishes were served. Then to a fourth. Frequently changing his situation and sinking lower and lower, he had at last come to Progonnaya, and here he used to sell nothing but tea and cheap vodka, and for lunch hard-boiled eggs and dry sausages, which smelt of tar, and which he himself sarcastically said were only fit for the orchestra. He was bald all over the top of his head, and had prominent blue eyes and thick bushy whiskers, which he often combed out, looking into the little looking-glass. Memories of the past haunted him continually; he could never get used to sausage "only fit for the orchestra," to the rudeness of the station-master, and to the peasants who used to haggle over the prices, and in his opinion it was as unseemly to haggle over prices in a refreshment room as in a chemist's shop. He was ashamed of his poverty and degradation, and that shame was now the leading interest of his life.

"Spring is late this year," said Matvey, listening. "It's a good job; I don't like spring. In spring it is very muddy, Sergey Nikanoritch. In books they write: Spring, the birds sing, the sun is setting, but what is there pleasant in that? A bird is a bird, and nothing more. I am fond of good company, of listening to folks, of talking of religion or singing something agreeable in chorus; but as for nightingales and flowers -- bless them, I say!"

He began again about the tile factory, about the choir, but Sergey Nikanoritch could not get over his mortification, and kept shrugging his shoulders and muttering. Matvey said good-bye and went home.

There was no frost, and the snow was already melting on the roofs, though it was still falling in big flakes; they were whirling rapidly round and round in the air and chasing one another in white clouds along the railway line. And the oak forest on both sides of the line, in the dim light of the moon which was hidden somewhere high up in the clouds, resounded with a prolonged sullen murmur. When a violent storm shakes the trees, how terrible they are! Matvey walked along the causeway beside the line, covering his face and his hands, while the wind beat on his back. All at once a little nag, plastered all over with snow, came into sight; a sledge scraped along the bare stones of the causeway, and a peasant, white all over, too, with his head muffled up, cracked his whip. Matvey looked round after him, but at once, as though it had been a vision, there was neither sledge nor peasant to be seen, and he hastened his steps, suddenly scared, though he did not know why.

Here was the crossing and the dark little house where the signalman lived. The barrier was raised, and by it perfect mountains had drifted and clouds of snow were whirling round like witches on broomsticks. At that point the line was crossed by an old highroad, which was still called "the track." On the right, not far from the crossing, by the roadside stood Terehov's tavern, which had been a posting inn. Here there was always a light twinkling at night.

When Matvey reached home there was a strong smell of incense in all the rooms and even in the entry. His cousin Yakov Ivanitch was still reading the evening service. In the prayer-room where this was going on, in the corner opposite the door, there stood a shrine of old-fashioned ancestral ikons in gilt settings, and both walls to right and to left were decorated with ikons of ancient and modern fashion, in shrines and without them. On the table, which was draped to the floor, stood an ikon of the Annunciation, and close by a cyprus-wood cross and the censer; wax candles were burning. Beside the table was a reading desk. As he passed by the prayer-room, Matvey stopped and glanced in at the door. Yakov Ivanitch was reading at the desk at that moment, his sister Aglaia, a tall lean old woman in a dark-blue dress and white kerchief, was praying with him. Yakov Ivanitch's daughter Dashutka, an ugly freckled girl of eighteen, was there, too, barefoot as usual, and wearing the dress in which she had at nightfall taken water to the cattle.

"Glory to Thee Who hast shown us the light!" Yakov Ivanitch boomed out in a chant, bowing low.

Aglaia propped her chin on her hand and chanted in a thin, shrill, drawling voice. And upstairs, above the ceiling, there was the sound of vague voices which seemed menacing or ominous of evil. No one had lived on the storey above since a fire there a long time ago. The windows were boarded up, and empty bottles lay about on the floor between the beams. Now the wind was banging and droning, and it seemed as though someone were running and stumbling over the beams.

Half of the lower storey was used as a tavern, while Terehov's family lived in the other half, so that when drunken visitors were noisy in the tavern every word they said could be heard in the rooms. Matvey lived in a room next to the kitchen, with a big stove, in which, in old days, when this had been a posting inn, bread had been baked every day. Dashutka, who had no room of her own, lived in the same room behind the stove. A cricket chirped there always at night and mice ran in and out.

Matvey lighted a candle and began reading a book which he had borrowed from the station policeman. While he was sitting over it the service ended, and they all went to bed. Dashutka lay down, too. She began snoring at once, but soon woke up and said, yawning:

"You shouldn't burn a candle for nothing, Uncle Matvey."

"It's my candle," answered Matvey; "I bought it with my own money."

Dashutka turned over a little and fell asleep again. Matvey sat up a good time longer -- he was not sleepy -- and when he had finished the last page he took a pencil out of a box and wrote on the book:

"I, Matvey Terehov, have read this book, and think it the very best of all the books I have read, for which I express my gratitude to the non-commissioned officer of the Police Department of Railways, Kuzma Nikolaev Zhukov, as the possessor of this priceless book."

He considered it an obligation of politeness to make such inscriptions in other people's books.

II

On Annunciation Day, after the mail train had been sent off, Matvey was sitting in the refreshment bar, talking and drinking tea with lemon in it.

The waiter and Zhukov the policeman were listening to him.

"I was, I must tell you," Matvey was saying, "inclined to religion from my earliest childhood. I was only twelve years old when I used to read the epistle in church, and my parents were greatly delighted, and every summer I used to go on a pilgrimage with my dear mother. Sometimes other lads would be singing songs and catching crayfish, while I would be all the time with my mother. My elders commended me, and, indeed, I was pleased myself that I was of such good behaviour. And when my mother sent me with her blessing to the factory, I used between working hours to sing tenor there in our choir, and nothing gave me greater pleasure. I needn't say, I drank no vodka, I smoked no tobacco, and lived in chastity; but we all know such a mode of life is displeasing to the enemy of mankind, and he, the unclean spirit, once tried to ruin me and began to darken my mind, just as now with my cousin. First of all, I took a vow to fast every Monday and not to eat meat any day, and as time went on all sorts of fancies came over me. For the first week of Lent down to Saturday the holy fathers have ordained a diet of dry food, but it is no sin for the weak or those who work hard even to drink tea, yet not a crumb passed into my mouth till the Sunday, and afterwards all through Lent I did not allow myself a drop of oil, and on Wednesdays and Fridays I did not touch a morsel at all. It was the same in the lesser fasts. Sometimes in St. Peter's fast our factory lads would have fish soup, while I would sit a little apart from them and suck a dry crust. Different people have different powers, of course, but I can say of myself I did not find fast days hard, and, indeed, the greater the zeal the easier it seems. You are only hungry on the first days of the fast, and then you get used to it; it goes on getting easier, and by the end of a week you don't mind it at all, and there is a numb feeling in your legs as though you were not on earth, but in the clouds. And, besides that, I laid all sorts of penances on myself; I used to get up in the night and pray, bowing down to the ground, used to drag heavy stones from place to place, used to go out barefoot in the snow, and I even wore chains, too. Only, as time went on, you know, I was confessing one day to the priest and suddenly this reflection occurred to me: why, this priest, I thought, is married, he eats meat and smokes tobacco -- how can he confess me, and what power has he to absolve my sins if he is more sinful that I? I even scruple to eat Lenten oil, while he eats sturgeon, I dare say. I went to another priest, and he, as ill luck would have it, was a fat fleshy man, in a silk cassock; he rustled like a lady, and he smelt of tobacco too. I went to fast and confess in the monastery, and my heart was not at ease even there; I kept fancying the monks were not living according to their rules. And after that I could not find a service to my mind: in one place they read the service too fast, in another they sang the wrong prayer, in a third the sacristan stammered. Sometimes, the Lord forgive me a sinner, I would stand in church and my heart would throb with anger. How could one pray, feeling like that? And I fancied that the people in the church did not cross themselves properly, did not listen properly; wherever I looked it seemed to me that they were all drunkards, that they broke the fast, smoked, lived loose lives and played cards. I was the only one who lived according to the commandments. The wily spirit did not slumber; it got worse as it went on. I gave up singing in the choir and I did not go to church at all; since my notion was that I was a righteous man and that the church did not suit me owing to its imperfections -- that is, indeed, like a fallen angel, I was puffed up in my pride beyond all belief. After this I began attempting to make a church for myself. I hired from a deaf woman a tiny little room, a long way out of town near the cemetery, and made a prayer-room like my cousin's, only I had big church candlesticks, too, and a real censer. In this prayer-room of mine I kept the rules of holy Mount Athos -- that is, every day my matins began at midnight without fail, and on the eve of the chief of the twelve great holy daysmy midnight service lasted ten hours and sometimes even twelve. Monks are allowed by rule to sit during the singing of the Psalter and the reading of the Bible, but I wanted to be better than the monks, and so I used to stand all through. I used to read and sing slowly, with tears and sighing, lifting up my hands, and I used to go straight from prayer to work without sleeping; and, indeed, I was always praying at my work, too. Well, it got all over the town 'Matvey is a saint; Matvey heals the sick and senseless.' I never had healed anyone, of course, but we all know wherever any heresy or false doctrine springs up there's no keeping the female sex away. They are just like flies on the honey. Old maids and females of all sorts came trailing to me, bowing down to my feet, kissing my hands and crying out I was a saint and all the rest of it, and one even saw a halo round my head. It was too crowded in the prayer-room. I took a bigger room, and then we had a regular tower of Babel. The devil got hold of me completely and screened the light from my eyes with his unclean hoofs. We all behaved as though we were frantic. I read, while the old maids and other females sang, and then after standing on their legs for twenty-four hours or longer without eating or drinking, suddenly a trembling would come over them as though they were in a fever; after that, one would begin screaming and then another -- it was horrible! I, too, would shiver all over like a Jew in a frying-pan, I don't know myself why, and our legs began to prance about. It's a strange thing, indeed: you don't want to, but you prance about and waggle your arms; and after that, screaming and shrieking, we all danced and ran after one another -- ran till we dropped; and in that way, in wild frenzy, I fell into fornication."

The policeman laughed, but, noticing that no one else was laughing, became serious and said:

"That's Molokanism. I have heard they are all like that in the Caucasus."

"But I was not killed by a thunderbolt," Matvey went on, crossing himself before the ikon and moving his lips. "My dead mother must have been praying for me in the other world. When everyone in the town looked upon me as a saint, and even the ladies and gentlemen of good family used to come to me in secret for consolation, I happened to go into our landlord, Osip Varlamitch, to ask forgiveness -- it was the Day of Forgiveness -- and he fastened the door with the hook, and we were left alone face to face. And he began to reprove me, and I must tell you Osip Varlamitch was a man of brains, though without education, and everyone respected and feared him, for he was a man of stern, God-fearing life and worked hard. He had been the mayor of the town, and a warden of the church for twenty years maybe, and had done a great deal of good; he had covered all the New Moscow Road with gravel, had painted the church, and had decorated the columns to look like malachite. Well, he fastened the door, and -- 'I have been wanting to get at you for a long time, you rascal, . . . ' he said. 'You think you are a saint,' he said. 'No you are not a saint, but a backslider from God, a heretic and an evildoer! . . .' And he went on and on. . . . I can't tell you how he said it, so eloquently and cleverly, as though it were all written down, and so touchingly. He talked for two hours. His words penetrated my soul; my eyes were opened. I listened, listened and -- burst into sobs! 'Be an ordinary man,' he said, 'eat and drink, dress and pray like everyone else. All that is above the ordinary is of the devil. Your chains,' he said, 'are of the devil; your fasting is of the devil; your prayer-room is of the devil. It is all pride,' he said. Next day, on Monday in Holy Week, it pleased God I should fall ill. I ruptured myself and was taken to the hospital. I was terribly worried, and wept bitterly and trembled. I thought there was a straight road before me from the hospital to hell, and I almost died. I was in misery on a bed of sickness for six months, and when I was discharged the first thing I did I confessed, and took the sacrament in the regular way and became a man again. Osip Varlamitch saw me off home and exhorted me: 'Remember, Matvey, that anything above the ordinary is of the devil.' And now I eat and drink like everyone else and pray like everyone else. . . . If it happens now that the priest smells of tobacco or vodka I don't venture to blame him, because the priest, too, of course, is an ordinary man. But as soon as I am told that in the town or in the village a saint has set up who does not eat for weeks, and makes rules of his own, I know whose work it is. So that is how I carried on in the past, gentlemen. Now, like Osip Varlamitch, I am continually exhorting my cousins and reproaching them, but I am a voice crying in the wilderness. God has not vouchsafed me the gift."

Matvey's story evidently made no impression whatever. Sergey Nikanoritch said nothing, but began clearing the refreshments off the counter, while the policeman began talking of how rich Matvey's cousin was.

"He must have thirty thousand at least," he said.

Zhukov the policeman, a sturdy, well-fed, red-haired man with a full face (his cheeks quivered when he walked), usually sat lolling and crossing his legs when not in the presence of his superiors. As he talked he swayed to and fro and whistled carelessly, while his face had a self-satisfied replete air, as though he had just had dinner. He was making money, and he always talked of it with the air of a connoisseur. He undertook jobs as an agent, and when anyone wanted to sell an estate, a horse or a carriage, they applied to him.

"Yes, it will be thirty thousand, I dare say," Sergey Nikanoritch assented. "Your grandfather had an immense fortune," he said, addressing Matvey. "Immense it was; all left to your father and your uncle. Your father died as a young man and your uncle got hold of it all, and afterwards, of course, Yakov Ivanitch. While you were going pilgrimages with your mama and singing tenor in the factory, they didn't let the grass grow under their feet."

"Fifteen thousand comes to your share," said the policeman swaying from side to side. "The tavern belongs to you in common, so the capital is in common. Yes. If I were in your place I should have taken it into court long ago. I would have taken it into court for one thing, and while the case was going on I'd have knocked his face to a jelly."

Yakov Ivanitch was disliked because, when anyone believes differently from others, it upsets even people who are indifferent to religion. The policeman disliked him also because he, too, sold horses and carriages.

"You don't care about going to law with your cousin because you have plenty of money of your own," said the waiter to Matvey, looking at him with envy. "It is all very well for anyone who has means, but here I shall die in this position, I suppose. . . ."

Matvey began declaring that he hadn't any money at all, but Sergey Nikanoritch was not listening. Memories of the past and of the insults which he endured every day came showering upon him. His bald head began to perspire; he flushed and blinked.

"A cursed life!" he said with vexation, and he banged the sausage on the floor.

III

The story ran that the tavern had been built in the time of Alexander I, by a widow who had settled here with her son; her name was Avdotya Terehov. The dark roofed-in courtyard and the gates always kept locked excited, especially on moonlight nights, a feeling of depression and unaccountable uneasiness in people who drove by with posting-horses, as though sorcerers or robbers were living in it; and the driver always looked back after he passed, and whipped up his horses. Travellers did not care to put up here, as the people of the house were always unfriendly and charged heavily. The yard was muddy even in summer; huge fat pigs used to lie there in the mud, and the horses in which the Terehovs dealt wandered about untethered, and often it happened that they ran out of the yard and dashed along the road like mad creatures, terrifying the pilgrim women. At that time there was a great deal of traffic on the road; long trains of loaded waggons trailed by, and all sorts of adventures happened, such as, for instance, that thirty years ago some waggoners got up a quarrel with a passing merchant and killed him, and a slanting cross is standing to this day half a mile from the tavern; posting-chaises with bells and the heavy *dormeuses* of country gentlemen drove by; and herds of homed cattle passed bellowing and stirring up clouds of dust.

When the railway came there was at first at this place only a platform, which was called simply a halt; ten years afterwards the present station, Progonnaya, was built. The traffic on the old posting-road almost ceased, and only local landowners and peasants drove along it now, but the working people walked there in crowds in spring and autumn. The posting-inn was transformed into a restaurant; the upper storey was destroyed by fire, the roof had grown yellow with rust, the roof over the yard had fallen by degrees, but huge fat pigs, pink and revolting, still wallowed in the mud in the yard. As before, the horses sometimes ran away and, lashing their tails dashed madly along the road. In the tavern they sold tea, hay oats and flour, as well as vodka and beer, to be drunk on the premises and also to be taken away; they sold spirituous liquors warily, for they had never taken out a licence.

The Terehovs had always been distinguished by their piety, so much so that they had even been given the nickname of the "Godlies." But perhaps because they lived apart like bears, avoided people and thought out all their ideas for themselves, they were given to dreams and to doubts and to changes of faith and almost each generation had a peculiar faith of its own. The grandmother Avdotya, who had built the inn, was an Old Believer; her son and both her grandsons (the fathers of Matvey and Yakov) went to the Orthodox church, entertained the clergy, and worshipped before the new ikons as devoutly as they had done before the old. The son in old age refused to eat meat and imposed upon himself the rule of silence, considering all conversation as sin; it was the peculiarity of the grandsons that they interpreted the Scripture not simply, but sought in it a hidden meaning, declaring that every sacred word must contain a mystery.

Avdotya's great-grandson Matvey had struggled from early childhood with all sorts of dreams and fancies and had been almost ruined by it; the other great-grandson, Yakov Ivanitch, was orthodox, but after his wife's death he gave up going to church and prayed at home. Following his example, his sister Aglaia had turned, too; she did not go to church herself, and did not let Dashutka go. Of Aglaia it was told that in her youth she used to attend the Flagellant meetings in Vedenyapino, and that she was still a Flagellant in secret, and that was why she wore a white kerchief.

Yakov Ivanitch was ten years older than Matvey -- he was a very handsome tall old man with a big grey beard almost to his waist, and bushy eyebrows which gave his face a stern, even ill-natured expression. He wore a long jerkin of good cloth or a black sheepskin coat, and altogether tried to be clean and neat in dress; he wore goloshes even in dry weather. He did not go to church, because, to his thinking, the services were not properly celebrated and because the priests drank wine at unlawful times and smoked tobacco. Every day he read and sang the service at home with Aglaia. At Vedenyapino they left out the "Praises" at early matins, and had no evening service even on great holidays, but he used to read through at home everything that was laid down forevery day, without hurrying or leaving out a single line, and even in his spare time read aloud the Lives of the Saints. And in everyday life he adhered strictly to the rules of the church; thus, if wine were allowed on some day in Lent "for the sake of the vigil," then he never failed to drink wine, even if he were not inclined.

He read, sang, burned incense and fasted, not for the sake of receiving blessings of some sort from God, but for the sake of good order. Man cannot live without religion, and religion ought to be expressed from year to year and from day to day in a certain order, so that every morning and every evening a man might turn to God with exactly those words and thoughts that were befitting that special day and hour. One must live, and, therefore, also pray as is pleasing to God, and so every day one must read and sing what is pleasing to God--that is, what is laid down in the rule of the church. Thus the first chapter of St. John must only be read on Easter Day, and "It is most meet" must not be sung from Easter to Ascension, and so on. The consciousness of this order and its importance afforded Yakov Ivanitch great gratification during his religious exercises. When he was forced to break this order by some necessity -- to drive to town or to the bank, for instance his conscience was uneasy and he fit miserable.

When his cousin Matvey had returned unexpectedly from the factory and settled in the tavern as though it were his home, he had from the very first day disturbed his settled order. He refused to pray with them, had meals and drank tea at wrong times, got up late, drank milk on Wednesdays and Fridays on the pretext of weak health; almost every day he went into the prayer-room while they were at prayers and cried: "Think what you are doing, brother! Repent, brother!" These words threw Yakov into a fury, while Aglaia could not refrain from beginning to scold; or at night Matvey would steal into the prayer-room and say softly: "Cousin, your prayer is not pleasing to God. For it is written, First be reconciled with thy brother and then offer thy gift. You lend money at usury, you deal in vodka -- repent!"

In Matvey's words Yakov saw nothing but the usual evasions of empty-headed and careless people who talk of loving your neighbour, of being reconciled with your brother, and so on, simply to avoid praying, fasting and reading holy books, and who talk contemptuously of profit and interest simply because they don't like working. Of course, to be poor, save nothing, and put by nothing was a great deal easier than being rich.

But yet he was troubled and could not pray as before. As soon as he went into the prayer-room and opened the book he began to be afraid his cousin would come in and hinder him; and, in fact, Matvey did soon appear and cry in a trembling voice: "Think what you are doing, brother! Repent, brother!" Aglaia stormed and Yakov, too, flew into a passion and shouted: "Go out of my house!" while Matvey answered him: "The house belongs to both of us."

Yakov would begin singing and reading again, but he could not regain his calm, and unconsciously fell to dreaming over his book. Though he regarded his cousin's words as nonsense, yet for some reason it had of late haunted his memory that it is hard for a rich man to enter the kingdom of heaven, that the year before last he had made a very good bargain over buying a stolen horse, that one day when his wife was alive a drunkard had died of vodka in his tavern. . . .

He slept badly at nights now and woke easily, and he could hear that Matvey, too, was awake, and continually sighing and pining for his tile factory. And while Yakov turned over from one side to another at night he thought of the stolen horse and the drunken man, and what was said in the gospels about the camel.

It looked as though his dreaminess were coming over him again. And as ill-luck would have it, although it was the end of March, every day it kept snowing, and the forest roared as though it were winter, and there was no believing that spring would ever come. The weather disposed one to depression, and to quarrelling and to hatred and in the night, when the wind droned over the ceiling, it seemed as though someone were living overhead in the empty storey; little by little the broodings settled like a burden on his mind, his head burned and he could not sleep.

IV

On the morning of the Monday before Good Friday, Matvey heard from his room Dashutka say to Aglaia:

"Uncle Matvey said, the other day, that there is no need to fast."

Matvey remembered the whole conversation he had had the evening before with Dashutka, and he felt hurt all at once.

"Girl, don't do wrong!" he said in a moaning voice, like a sick man. "You can't do without fasting; our Lord Himself fasted forty days. I only explained that fasting does a bad man no good."

"You should just listen to the factory hands; they can teach you goodness," Aglaia said sarcastically as she washed the floor (she usually washed the floors on working days and was always angry with everyone when she did it). "We know how they keep the fasts in the factory. You had better ask that uncle of yours -- ask him about his 'Darling,' how he used to guzzle milk on fast days with her, the viper. He teaches others; he forgets about his viper. But ask him who was it he left his money with -- who was it?"

Matvey had carefully concealed from everyone, as though it were a foul sore, that during that period of his life when old women and unmarried girls had danced and run about with him at their prayers he had formed a connection with a working woman and had had a child by her. When he went home he had given this woman all he had saved at the factory, and had borrowed from his landlord for his journey, and now he had only a few roubles which he spent on tea and candles. The "Darling" had informed him later on that the child was dead, and asked him in a letter what she should do with the money. This letter was brought from the station by the labourer. Aglaia intercepted it and read it, and had reproached Matvey with his "Darling" every day since.

"Just fancy, nine hundred roubles," Aglaia went on. "You gave nine hundred roubles to a viper, no relation, a factory jade, blast you!" She had flown into a passion by now and was shouting shrilly: "Can't you speak? I could tear you to pieces, wretched creature! Nine hundred roubles as though it were a farthing You might have left it to Dashutka -- she is a relation, not a stranger -- or else have it sent to Byelev for Marya's poor orphans. And your viper did not choke, may she be thrice accursed, the she-devil! May she never look upon the light of day!"

Yakov Ivanitch called to her: it was time to begin the "Hours." She washed, put on a white kerchief, and by now quiet and meek, went into the prayer-room to the brother she loved. When she spoke to Matvey or served peasants in the tavern with tea she was a gaunt, keen-eyed, ill-humoured old woman; in the prayer-room her face was serene and softened, she looked younger altogether, she curtsied affectedly, and even pursed up her lips.

Yakov Ivanitch began reading the service softly and dolefully, as he always did in Lent. After he had read a little he stopped to listen to the stillness that reigned through the house, and then went on reading again, with a feeling of gratification; he folded his hands in supplication, rolled his eyes, shook his head, sighed. But all at once there was the sound of voices. The policeman and Sergey Nikanoritch had come to see Matvey. Yakov Ivanitch was embarrassed at reading aloud and singing when there were strangers in the house, and now, hearing voices, he began reading in a whisper and slowly. He could hear in the prayer-room the waiter say:

"The Tatar at Shtchepovo is selling his business for fifteen hundred. He'll take five hundred down and an I.O.U. for the rest. And so, Matvey Vassilitch, be so kind as to lend me that five hundred roubles. I will pay you two per cent a month."

"What money have I got?" cried Matvey, amazed. "I have no money!"

"Two per cent a month will be a godsend to you," the policeman explained. "While lying by, your money is simply eaten by the moth, and that's all that you get from it."

Afterwards the visitors went out and a silence followed. But Yakov Ivanitch had hardly begun reading and singing again when a voice was heard outside the door:

"Brother, let me have a horse to drive to Vedenyapino."

It was Matvey. And Yakov was troubled again. "Which can you go with?" he asked after a moment's thought. "The man has gone with the sorrel to take the pig, and I am going with the little stallion to Shuteykino as soon as I have finished."

"Brother, why is it you can dispose of the horses and not I?" Matvey asked with irritation.

"Because I am not taking them for pleasure, but for work."

"Our property is in common, so the horses are in common, too, and you ought to understand that, brother."

A silence followed. Yakov did not go on praying, but waited for Matvey to go away from the door.

"Brother," said Matvey, "I am a sick man. I don't want possession -- let them go; you have them, but give me a small share to keep me in my illness. Give it me and I'll go away."

Yakov did not speak. He longed to be rid of Matvey, but he could not give him money, since all the money was in the business; besides, there had never been a case of the family dividing in the whole history of the Terehovs. Division means ruin.

Yakov said nothing, but still waited for Matvey to go away, and kept looking at his sister, afraid that she would interfere, and that there would be a storm of abuse again, as there had been in the morning. When at last Matvey did go Yakov went on reading, but now he had no pleasure in it. There was a heaviness in his head and a darkness before his eyes from continually bowing down to the ground, and he was weary of the sound of his soft dejected voice. When such a depression of spirit came over him at night, he put it down to not being able to sleep; by day it frightened him, and he began to feel as though devils were sitting on his head and shoulders.

Finishing the service after a fashion, dissatisfied and ill-humoured, he set off for Shuteykino. In the previous autumn a gang of navvies had dug a boundary ditch near Progonnaya, and had run up a bill at the tavern for eighteen roubles, and now he had to find their foreman in Shuteykino and get the money from him. The road had been spoilt by the thaw and the snowstorm; it was of a dark colour and full of holes, and in parts it had given way altogether. The snow had sunk away at the sides below the road, so that he had to drive, as it were, upon a narrow causeway, and it was very difficult to turn off it when he met anything. The sky had been overcast ever since the morning and a damp wind was blowing. . . .

A long train of sledges met him; peasant women were carting bricks. Yakov had to turn off the road. His horse sank into the snow up to its belly; the sledge lurched over to the right, and to avoid falling out he bent over to the left, and sat so all the time the sledges moved slowly by him. Through the wind he heard the creaking of the sledge poles and the breathing of the gaunt horses, and the women saying about him, "There's Godly coming," while one, gazing with compassion at his horse, said quickly:

"It looks as though the snow will be lying till Yegory's Day! They are worn out with it!"

Yakov sat uncomfortably huddled up, screwing up his eyes on account of the wind, while horses and red bricks kept passing before him. And perhaps because he was uncomfortable and his side ached, he felt all at once annoyed, and the business he was going about seemed to him unimportant, and he reflected that he might send the labourer next day to Shuteykino. Again, as in the previous sleepless night, he thought of the saying about the camel, and then memories of all sorts crept into his mind; of the peasant who had sold him the stolen horse, of the drunken man, of the peasant women who had brought their samovars to him to pawn. Of course, every merchant tries to get as much as he can, but Yakov felt depressed that he was in trade; he longed to get somewhere far away from this routine, and he felt dreary at the thought that he would have to read the evening service that day. The wind blew straight into his face and soughed in his collar; and it seemed as though it were whispering to him all these thoughts, bringing them from the broad white plain. . . . Looking at that plain, familiar to him from childhood, Yakov remembered that he had had just this same trouble and these same thoughts in his young days when dreams and imaginings had come upon him and his faith had wavered.

He felt miserable at being alone in the open country; he turned back and drove slowly after the sledges, and the women laughed and said:

"Godly has turned back."

At home nothing had been cooked and the samovar was not heated on account of the fast, and this made the day seem very long. Yakov Ivanitch had long ago taken the horse to the stable, dispatched the flour to the station, and twice taken up the Psalms to read, and yet the evening was still far off. Aglaia has already washed all the floors, and, having nothing to do, was tidying up her chest, the lid of which was pasted over on the inside with labels off bottles. Matvey, hungry and melancholy, sat reading, or went up to the Dutch stove and slowly scrutinized the tiles which reminded him of the factory. Dashutka was asleep; then, waking up, she went to take water to the cattle. When she was getting water from the well the cord broke and the pail fell in. The labourer began looking for a boathook to get the pail out, and Dashutka, barefooted, with legs as red as a goose's, followed him about in the muddy snow, repeating: "It's too far!" She meant to say that the well was too deep for the hook to reach the bottom, but the labourer did not understand her, and evidently she bothered him, so that he suddenly turned around and abused her in unseemly language. Yakov Ivanitch, coming out that moment into the yard, heard Dashutka answer the labourer in a long rapid stream of choice abuse, which she could only have learned from drunken peasants in the tavern.

"What are you saying, shameless girl!" he cried to her, and he was positively aghast. "What language!"

And she looked at her father in perplexity, dully, not understanding why she should not use those words. He would have admonished her, but she struck him as so savage and benighted; and for the first time he realized that she had no religion. And all this life in the forest, in the snow, with drunken peasants, with coarse oaths, seemed to him as savage and benighted as this girl, and instead of giving her a lecture he only waved his hand and went back into the room.

At that moment the policeman and Sergey Nikanoritch came in again to see Matvey. Yakov Ivanitch thought that these people, too, had no religion, and that that did not trouble them in the least; and human life began to seem to him as strange, senseless and unenlightened as a dog's. Bareheaded he walked about the yard, then he went out on to the road, clenching his fists. Snow was falling in big flakes at the time. His beard was blown about in the wind. He kept shaking his head, as though there were something weighing upon his head and shoulders, as though devils were sitting on them; and it seemed to him that it was not himself walking about, but some wild beast, a huge terrible beast, and that if he were to cry out his voice would be a roar that would sound all over the forest and the plain, and would frighten everyone. . . .

V

When he went back into the house the policeman was no longer there. but the waiter was sitting with Matvey, counting something on the reckoning beads. He was in the habit of coming often, almost every day, to the tavern; in old days he had come to see Yakov Ivanitch, now he came to see Matvey. He was continually reckoning on the beads, while his face perspired and looked strained, or he would ask for money or, stroking his whiskers, would describe how he had once been in a first-class station and used to prepare champagne-punch for officers, and at grand dinners served the sturgeon-soup with his own hands. Nothing in this world interested him but refreshment bars, and he could only talk about things to eat, about wines and the paraphernalia of the dinner-table. On one occasion, handing a cup of tea to a young woman who was nursing her baby and wishing to say something agreeable to her, he expressed himself in this way:

"The mother's breast is the baby's refreshment bar."

Reckoning with the beads in Matvey's room, he asked for money; said he could not go on living at Progonnaya, and several times repeated in a tone of voice that sounded as though he were just going to cry:

"Where am I to go? Where am I to go now? Tell me that, please."

Then Matvey went into the kitchen and began peeling some boiled potatoes which he had probably put away from the day before. It was quiet, and it seemed to Yakov Ivanitch that the waiter was gone. It was past the time for evening service; he called Aglaia, and, thinking there was no one else in the house sang out aloud without embarrassment. He sang and read, but was inwardly pronouncing other words, "Lord, forgive me! Lord, save me!" and, one after another, without ceasing, he made low bows to the ground as though he wanted to exhaust himself, and he kept shaking his head, so that Aglaia looked at him with wonder. He was afraid Matvey would come in, and was certain that he would come in, and felt an anger against him which he could overcome neither by prayer nor by continually bowing down to the ground.

Matvey opened the door very softly and went into the prayer-room.

"It's a sin, such a sin!" he said reproachfully, and heaved a sigh. "Repent! Think what you are doing, brother!"

Yakov Ivanitch, clenching his fists and not looking at him for fear of striking him, went quickly out of the room. Feeling himself a huge terrible wild beast, just as he had done before on the road, he crossed the passage into the grey, dirty room, reeking with smoke and fog, in which the peasants usually drank tea, and there he spent a long time walking from one corner to the other, treading heavily, so that the crockery jingled on the shelves and the tables shook. It was clear to him now that he was himself dissatisfied with his religion, ant could not pray as he used to do. He must repent, he must think things over, reconsider, live and pray in some other way. But how pray? And perhaps all this was a temptation of the devil, and nothing of this was necessary? . . . How was it to be? What was he to do? Who could guide him? What helplessness! He stopped and, clutching at his head, began to think, but Matvey's being near him prevented him from reflecting calmly. And he went rapidly into the room.

Matvey was sitting in the kitchen before a bowl of potato, eating. Close by, near the stove, Aglaia and Dashutka were sitting facing one another, spinning yarn. Between the stove and the table at which Matvey was sitting was stretched an ironing-board; on it stood a cold iron.

"Sister," Matvey asked, "let me have a little oil!"

"Who eats oil on a day like this?" asked Aglaia.

"I am not a monk, sister, but a layman. And in my weak health I may take not only oil but milk."

"Yes, at the factory you may have anything."

Aglaia took a bottle of Lenten oil from the shelf and banged it angrily down before Matvey, with a malignant smile evidently pleased that he was such a sinner.

"But I tell you, you can't eat oil!" shouted Yakov.

Aglaia and Dashutka started, but Matvey poured the oil into the bowl and went on eating as though he had not heard.

"I tell you, you can't eat oil!" Yakov shouted still more loudly; he turned red all over, snatched up the bowl, lifted it higher that his head, and dashed it with all his force to the ground, so that it flew into fragments. "Don't dare to speak!" he cried in a furious voice, though Matvey had not said a word. "Don't dare!" he repeated, and struck his fist on the table.

Matvey turned pale and got up.

"Brother!" he said, still munching -- "brother, think what you are about!"

"Out of my house this minute!" shouted Yakov; he loathed Matvey's wrinkled face, and his voice, and the crumbs on his moustache, and the fact that he was munching. "Out, I tell you!"

"Brother, calm yourself! The pride of hell has confounded you!"

"Hold your tongue!" (Yakov stamped.) "Go away, you devil!"

"If you care to know," Matvey went on in a loud voice, as he, too, began to get angry, "you are a backslider from God and a heretic. The accursed spirits have hidden the true light from you; your prayer is not acceptable to God. Repent before it is too late! The deathbed of the sinner is terrible! Repent, brother!"

Yakov seized him by the shoulders and dragged him away from the table, while he turned whiter than ever, and frightened and bewildered, began muttering, "What is it? What's the matter?" and, struggling and making efforts to free himself from Yakov's hands, he accidentally caught hold of his shirt near the neck and tore the collar; and it seemed to Aglaia that he was trying to beat Yakov. She uttered a shriek, snatched up the bottle of Lenten oil and with all her force brought it down straight on the skull of the cousin she hated. Matvey reeled, and in one instant his face became calm and indifferent. Yakov, breathing heavily, excited, and feeling pleasure at the gurgle the bottle had made, like a living thing, when it had struck the head, kept him from falling and several times (he remembered this very distinctly) motioned Aglaia towards the iron with his finger; and only when the blood began trickling through his hands and he heard Dashutka's loud wail, and when the ironing-board fell with a crash, and Matvey rolled heavily on it, Yakov left off feeling anger and understood what had happened.

"Let him rot, the factory buck!" Aglaia brought out with repulsion, still keeping the iron in her hand. The white bloodstained kerchief slipped on to her shoulders and her grey hair fell in disorder. "He's got what he deserved!"

Everything was terrible. Dashutka sat on the floor near the stove with the yarn in her hands, sobbing, and continually bowing down, uttering at each bow a gasping sound. But nothing was so terrible to Yakov as the potato in the blood, on which he was afraid of stepping. and there was something else terrible which weighed upon him like a bad dream and seemed the worst danger, though he could not take it in for the first minute. This was the waiter, Sergey Nikanoritch, who was standing in the doorway with the reckoning beads in his hands, very pale, looking with horror at what was happening in the kitchen. Only when he turned and went quickly into the passage and from there outside, Yakov grasped who it was and followed him.

Wiping his hands on the snow as he went, he reflected. The idea flashed through his mind that their labourer had gone away long before and had asked leave to stay the night at home in the village; the day before they had killed a pig, and there were huge bloodstains in the snow and on the sledge, and even one side of the top of the well was splattered with blood, so that it could not have seemed suspicious even if the whole of Yakov's family had been stained with blood. To conceal the murder would be agonizing, but for the policeman, who would whistle and smile ironically, to come from the station, for the peasants to arrive and bind Yakov's and Aglaia's hands, and take them solemnly to the district courthouse and from there to the town, while everyone on the way would point at them and say mirthfully, "They are taking the Godlies!" -- this seemed to Yakov more agonizing than anything, and he longed to lengthen out the time somehow, so as to endure this shame not now, but later, in the future.

"I can lend you a thousand roubles, . . ." he said, overtaking Sergey Nikanoritch. "If you tell anyone, it will do no good. . . . There's no bringing the man back, anyway;" and with difficulty keeping up with the waiter, who did not look round, but tried to walk away faster than ever, he went on: "I can give you fifteen hundred. . . ."

He stopped because he was out of breath, while Sergey Nikanoritch walked on as quickly as ever, probably afraid that he would be killed, too. Only after passing the railway crossing and going half the way from the crossing to the station, he furtively looked round and walked more slowly. Lights, red and green, were already gleaming in the station and along the line; the wind had fallen, but flakes of snow were still coming down and the road had turned white again. But just at the station Sergey Nikanoritch stopped, thought a minute, and turned resolutely back. It was growing dark.

"Oblige me with the fifteen hundred, Yakov Ivanitch," he said, trembling all over. "I agree."

VI

Yakov Ivanitch's money was in the bank of the town and was invested in second mortgages; he only kept a little at home, Just what was wanted for necessary expenses. Going into the kitchen he felt for the matchbox, and while the sulphur was burning with a blue light he had time to make out the figure of Matvey, which was still lying on the floor near the table, but now it was covered with a white sheet, and nothing could be seen but his boots. A cricket was chirruping. Aglaia and Dashutka were not in the room, they were both sitting behind the counter in the tea-room, spinning yarn in silence. Yakov Ivanitch crossed to his own room with a little lamp in his hand, and pulled from under the bed a little box in which he kept his money. This time there were in it four hundred and twenty one-rouble notes and silver to the amount of thirty-five roubles; the notes had an unpleasant heavy smell. Putting the money together in his cap, Yakov Ivanitch went out into the yard and then out of the gate. He walked, looking from side to side, but there was no sign of the waiter.

"Hi!" cried Yakov.

A dark figure stepped out from the barrier at the railway crossing and came irresolutely towards him.

"Why do you keep walking about?" said Yakov with vexation, as he recognized the waiter. "Here you are; there is a little less than five hundred. . . . I've no more in the house."

"Very well; . . . very grateful to you," muttered Sergey Nikanoritch, taking the money greedily and stuffing it into his pockets. He was trembling all over, and that was perceptible in spite of the darkness. "Don't worry yourself, Yakov Ivanitch. . . . What should I chatter for: I came and went away, that's all I've had to do with it. As the saying is, I know nothing and I can tell nothing . . ." And at once he added with a sigh "Cursed life!"

For a minute they stood in silence, without looking at each other.

"So it all came from a trifle, goodness knows how, . . ." said the waiter, trembling. "I was sitting counting to myself when all at once a noise. . . . I looked through the door, and just on account of Lenten oil you. . . . Where is he now?"

"Lying there in the kitchen."

"You ought to take him somewhere. . . . Why put it off?"

Yakov accompanied him to the station without a word, then went home again and harnessed the horse to take Matvey to Limarovo. He had decided to take him to the forest of Limarovo, and to leave him there on the road, and then he would tell everyone that Matvey had gone off to Vedenyapino and had not come back, and then everyone would think that he had been killed by someone on the road. He knew there was no deceiving anyone by this, but to move, to do something, to be active, was not as agonizing as to sit still and wait. He called Dashutka, and with her carried Matvey out. Aglaia stayed behind to clean up the kitchen.

When Yakov and Dashutka turned back they were detained at the railway crossing by the barrier being let down. A long goods train was passing, dragged by two engines, breathing heavily, and flinging puffs of crimson fire out of their funnels.

The foremost engine uttered a piercing whistle at the crossing in sight of the station.

"It's whistling, . . ." said Dashutka.

The train had passed at last, and the signalman lifted the barrier without haste.

"Is that you, Yakov Ivanitch? I didn't know you, so you'll be rich."

And then when they had reached home they had to go to bed.

Aglaia and Dashutka made themselves a bed in the tea-room and lay down side by side, while Yakov stretched himself on the counter. They neither said their prayers nor lighted the ikon lamp before lying down to sleep. All three lay awake till morning, but did not utter a single word, and it seemed to them that all night someone was walking about in the empty storey overhead.

Two days later a police inspector and the examining magistrate came from the town and made a search, first in Matvey's room and then in the whole tavern. They questioned Yakov first of all, and he testified that on the Monday Matvey had gone to Vedenyapino to confess, and that he must have been killed by the sawyers who were working on the line.

And when the examining magistrate had asked him how it had happened that Matvey was found on the road, while his cap had turned up at home -- surely he had not gone to Vedenyapino without his cap? -- and why they had not found a single drop of blood beside him in the snow on the road, though his head was smashed in and his face and chest were black with blood, Yakov was confused, lost his head and answered:

"I cannot tell."

And just what Yakov had so feared happened: the policeman came, the district police officer smoked in the prayer-room and Aglaia fell upon him with abuse and was rude to the police inspector; and afterwards when Yakov and Aglaia were led out to the yard, the peasants crowded at the gates and said, "They are taking the Godlies!" and it seemed that they were all glad.

At the inquiry the policeman stated positively that Yakov and Aglaia had killed Matvey in order not to share with him, and that Matvey had money of his own, and that if it was not found at the search evidently Yakov and Aglaia had got hold of it. And Dashutka was questioned. She said that Uncle Matvey and Aunt Aglaia quarrelled and almost fought every day over money, and that Uncle Matvey was rich, so much so that he had given someone -- "his Darling" -- nine hundred roubles.

Dashutka was left alone in the tavern. No one came now to drink tea or vodka, and she divided her time between cleaning up the rooms, drinking mead and eating rolls; but a few days later they questioned the signalman at the railway crossing, and he said that late on Monday evening he had seen Yakov and Dashutka driving from Limarovo. Dashutka, too, was arrested, taken to the town and put in prison. It soon became known, from what Aglaia said, that Sergey Nikanoritch had been present at the murder. A search was made in his room, and money was found in an unusual place, in his snowboots under the stove, and the money was all in small change, three hundred one-rouble notes. He swore he had made this money himself, and that he hadn't been in the tavern for a year, but witnesses testified that he was poor and had been in great want of money of late, and that he used to go every day to the tavern to borrow from Matvey; and the policeman described how on the day of the murder he had himself gone twice to the tavern with the waiter to help him to borrow. It was recalled at this juncture that on Monday evening Sergey Nikanoritch had not been there to meet the passenger train, but had gone off somewhere. And he, too, was arrested and taken to the town.

The trial took place eleven months later.

Yakov Ivanitch looked much older and much thinner, and spoke in a low voice like a sick man. He felt weak, pitiful, lower in stature that anyone else, and it seemed as though his soul, too, like his body, had grown older and wasted, from the pangs of his conscience and from the dreams and imaginings which never left him all the while he was in prison. When it came out that he did not go to church the president of the court asked him:

"Are you a dissenter?"

"I can't tell," he answered.

He had no religion at all now; he knew nothing and understood nothing; and his old belief was hateful to him now, and seemed to him darkness and folly. Aglaia was not in the least subdued, and she still went on abusing the dead man, blaming him for all their misfortunes. Sergey Nikanoritch had grown a beard instead of whiskers. At the trial he was red and perspiring, and was evidently ashamed of his grey prison coat and of sitting on the same bench with humble peasants. He defended himself awkwardly, and, trying to prove that he had not been to the tavern for a whole year, got into an altercation with every witness, and the spectators laughed at him. Dashutka had grown fat in prison. At the trial she did not understand the questions put to her, and only said that when they killed Uncle Matvey she was dreadfully frightened, but afterwards she did not mind.

All four were found guilty of murder with mercenary motives. Yakov Ivanitch was sentenced to penal servitude for twenty years; Aglaia for thirteen and a half; Sergey Nikanoritch to ten; Dashutka to six.

VII

Late one evening a foreign steamer stopped in the roads of Dué in Sahalin and asked for coal. The captain was asked to wait till morning, but he did not want to wait over an hour, saying that if the weather changed for the worse in the night there would be a risk of his having to go off without coal. In the Gulf of Tartary the weather is liable to violent changes in the course of half an hour, and then the shores of Sahalin are dangerous. And already it had turned fresh, and there was a considerable sea running.

A gang of convicts were sent to the mine from the Voevodsky prison, the grimmest and most forbidding of all the prisons in Sahalin. The coal had to be loaded upon barges, and then they had to be towed by a steam-cutter alongside the steamer which was anchored more than a quarter of a mile from the coast, and then the unloading and reloading had to begin -- an exhausting task when the barge kept rocking against the steamer and the men could scarcely keep on their legs for sea-sickness. The convicts, only just roused from their sleep, still drowsy, went along the shore, stumbling in the darkness and clanking their fetters. On the left, scarcely visible, was a tall, steep, extremely gloomy-looking cliff, while on the right there was a thick impenetrable mist, in which the sea moaned with a prolonged monotonous sound, "Ah!. . . ah!. . . ah!. . . ah! . . ." And it was only when the overseer was lighting his pipe, casting as he did so a passing ray of light on the escort with a gun and on the coarse faces of two or three of the nearest convicts, or when he went with his lantern close to the water that the white crests of the foremost waves could be discerned.

One of this gang was Yakov Ivanitch, nicknamed among the convicts the "Brush," on account of his long beard. No one had addressed him by his name or his father's name for a long time now; they called him simplyYashka.

He was here in disgrace, as, three months after coming to Siberia, feeling an intense irresistible longing for home, he had succumbed to temptation and run away; he had soon been caught, had been sentenced to penal servitude for life and given forty lashes. Then he was punished by flogging twice again for losing his prison clothes, though on each occasion they were stolen from him. The longing for home had begun from the very time he had been brought to Odessa, and the convict train had stopped in the night at Progonnaya; and Yakov, pressing to the window, had tried to see his own home, and could see nothing in the darkness. He had no one with whom to talk of home. His sister Aglaia had been sent right across Siberia, and he did not know where she was now. Dashutka was in Sahalin, but she had been sent to live with some ex-convict in a far away settlement; there was no news of her except that once a settler who had come to the Voevodsky Prison told Yakov that Dashutka had three children. Sergey Nikanoritch was serving as a footman at a government official's at Dué, but he could not reckon on ever seeing him, as he was ashamed of being acquainted with convicts of the peasant class.

The gang reached the mine, and the men took their places on the quay. It was said there would not be any loading, as the weather kept getting worse and the steamer was meaning to set off. They could see three lights. One of them was moving: that was the steam-cutter going to the steamer, and it seemed to be coming back to tell them whether the work was to be done or not. Shivering with the autumn cold and the damp sea mist, wrapping himself in his short torn coat, Yakov Ivanitch looked intently without blinking in the direction in which lay his home. Ever since he had lived in prison together with men banished here from all ends of the earth -- with Russians, Ukrainians, Tatars, Georgians, Chinese, Gypsies, Jews -- and ever since he had listened to their talk and watched their sufferings, he had begun to turn again to God, and it seemed to him at last that he had learned the true faith for which all his family, from his grandmother Avdotya down, had so thirsted, which they had sought so long and which they had never found. He knew it all now and understood where God was, and how He was to be served, and the only thing he could not understand was why men's destinies were so diverse, why this simple faith which other men receive from God for nothing and together with their lives, had cost him such a price that his arms and legs trembled like a drunken man's from all the horrors and agonies which as far as he could see would go on without a break to the day of his death. He looked with strained eyes into the darkness, and it seemed to him that through the thousand miles of that mist he could see home, could see his native province, his district, Progonnaya, could see the darkness, the savagery, the heartlessness, and the dull, sullen, animal indifference of the men he had left there. His eyes were dimmed with tears; but still he gazed into the distance where the pale lights of the steamer faintly gleamed, and his heart ached with yearning for home, and he longed to live, to go back home to tell them there of his new faith and to save from ruin if only one man, and to live without suffering if only for one day.

The cutter arrived, and the overseer announced in a loud voice that there would be no loading.

"Back!" he commanded. "Steady!"

They could hear the hoisting of the anchor chain on the steamer. A strong piercing wind was blowing by now; somewhere on the steep cliff overhead the trees were creaking. Most likely a storm was coming.

ARIADNE

On the deck of a steamer sailing from Odessa to Sevastopol, a rather good-looking gentleman, with a little round beard, came up to me to smoke, and said:

"Notice those Germans sitting near the shelter? Whenever Germans or Englishmen get together, they talk about the crops, the price of wool, or their personal affairs. But for some reason or other when we Russians get together we never discuss anything but women and abstract subjects -- but especially women."

This gentleman's face was familiar to me already. We had returned from abroad the evening before in the same train, and at Volotchisk when the luggage was being examined by the Customs, I saw him standing with a lady, his travelling companion, before a perfect mountain of trunks and baskets filled with ladies' clothes, and I noticed how embarrassed and downcast he was when he had to pay duty on some piece of silk frippery, and his companion protested and threatened to make a complaint. Afterwards, on the way to Odessa, I saw him carrying little pies and oranges to the ladies' compartment.

It was rather damp; the vessel swayed a little, and the ladies had retired to their cabins.

The gentleman with the little round beard sat down beside me and continued:

"Yes, when Russians come together they discuss nothing but abstract subjects and women. We are so intellectual, so solemn, that we utter nothing but truths and can discuss only questions of a lofty order. The Russian actor does not know how to be funny; he acts with profundity even in a farce. We're just the same: when we have got to talk of trifles we treat them only from an exalted point of view. It comes from a lack of boldness, sincerity, and simplicity. We talk so often about women, I fancy, because we are dissatisfied. We take too ideal a view of women, and make demands out of all proportion with what reality can give us; we get something utterly different from what we want, and the result is dissatisfaction, shattered hopes, and inward suffering, and if anyone is suffering, he's bound to talk of it. It does not bore you to go on with this conversation?

"No, not in the least."

"In that case, allow me to introduce myself," said my companion, rising from his seat a little:

"Ivan Ilyitch Shamohin, a Moscow landowner of a sort. . . . You I know very well."

He sat down and went on, looking at me with a genuine and friendly expression:

"A mediocre philosopher, like Max Nordau, would explain these incessant conversations about women as a form of erotic madness, or would put it down to our having been slave-owners and so on; I take quite a different view of it. I repeat, we are dissatisfied because we are idealists. We want the creatures who bear us and our children to be superior to us and to everything in the world. When we are young we adore and poeticize those with whom we are in love: love and happiness with us are synonyms. Among us in Russia marriage without love is despised, sensuality is ridiculed and inspires repulsion, and the greatest success is enjoyed by those tales and novels in which women are beautiful, poetical, and exalted; and if the Russian has been for years in ecstasies over Raphael's Madonna, or is eager for the emancipation of women, I assure you there is no affectation about it. But the trouble is that when we have been married or been intimate with a woman for some two or three years, we begin to feel deceived and disillusioned: we pair off with others, and again -- disappointment, again -- repulsion, and in the long run we become convinced that women are lying, trivial, fussy, unfair, undeveloped, cruel -- in fact, far from being superior, are immeasurably inferior to us men. And in our dissatisfaction and disappointment there is nothing left for us but to grumble and talk about what we've been so cruelly deceived in."

While Shamohin was talking I noticed that the Russian language and our Russian surroundings gave him great pleasure. This was probably because he had been very homesick abroad. Though he praised the Russians and ascribed to them a rare idealism, he did not disparage foreigners, and that I put down to his credit. It could be seen, too, that there was some uneasiness in his soul, that he wanted to talk more of himself than of women, and that I was in for a long story in the nature of a confession. And when we had asked for a bottle of wine and had each of us drunk a glass, this was how he did in fact begin:

"I remember in a novel of Weltmann's someone says, 'So that's the story!' and someone else answers, 'No, that's not the story -- that's only the introduction to the story.' In the same way what I've said so far is only the introduction; what I really want to tell you is my own love story. Excuse me, I must ask you again; it won't bore you to listen?"

I told him it would not, and he went on:

The scene of my story is laid in the Moscow province in one of its northern districts. The scenery there, I must tell you, is exquisite. Our homestead is on the high bank of a rapid stream, where the water chatters noisily day and night: imagine a big old garden, neat flower-beds, beehives, a kitchen-garden, and below it a river with leafy willows, which, when there is a heavy dew on them, have a lustreless look as though they had turned grey; and on the other side a meadow, and beyond the meadow on the upland a terrible, dark pine forest. In that forest delicious, reddish agarics grow in endless profusion, and elks still live in its deepest recesses. When I am nailed up in my coffin I believe I shall still dream of those early mornings, you know, when the sun hurts your eyes: or the wonderful spring evenings when the nightingales and the landrails call in the garden and beyond the garden, and sounds of the harmonica float across from the village, while they play the piano indoors and the stream babbles . . . when there is such music, in fact, that one wants at the same time to cry and to sing aloud.

We have not much arable land, but our pasture makes up for it, and with the forest yields about two thousand roubles a year. I am the only son of my father; we are both modest persons, and with my father's pension that sum was amply sufficient for us.

The first three years after finishing at the university I spent in the country, looking after the estate and constantly expecting to be elected on some local assembly; but what was most important, I was violently in love with an extraordinarily beautiful and fascinating girl. She was the sister of our neighbour, Kotlovitch, a ruined landowner who had on his estate pine-apples, marvellous peaches, lightning conductors, a fountain in the courtyard, and at the same time not a farthing in his pocket. He did nothing and knew how to do nothing. He was as flabby as though he had been made of boiled turnip; he used to doctor the peasants by homeopathy and was interested in spiritualism. He was, however, a man of great delicacy and mildness, and by no means a fool, but I have no fondness for these gentlemen who converse with spirits and cure peasant women by magnetism. In the first place, the ideas of people who are not intellectually free are always in a muddle, and it's extremely difficult to talk to them; and, secondly, they usually love no one, and have nothing to do with women, and their mysticism has an unpleasant effect on sensitive people. I did not care for his appearance either. He was tall, stout, white-skinned, with a little head, little shining eyes, and chubby white fingers. He did not shake hands, but kneaded one's hands in his. And he was always apologising. If he asked for anything it was "Excuse me"; if he gave you anything it was "Excuse me" too.

As for his sister, she was a character out of a different opera. I must explain that I had not been acquainted with the Kotlovitches in my childhood and early youth, for my father had been a professor at N., and we had for many years lived away. When I did make their acquaintance the girl was twenty-two, had left school long before, and had spent two or three years in Moscow with a wealthy aunt who brought her out into society. When I was introduced and first had to talk to her, what struck me most of all was her rare and beautiful name -- Ariadne. It suited her so wonderfully! She was a brunette, very thin, very slender, supple, elegant, and extremely graceful, with refined and exceedingly noble features. Her eyes were shining, too, but her brother's shone with a cold sweetness, mawkish as sugar-candy, while hers had the glow of youth, proud and beautiful. She conquered me on the first day of our acquaintance, and indeed it was inevitable. My first impression was so overwhelming that to this day I cannot get rid of my illusions; I am still tempted to imagine that nature had some grand, marvellous design when she created that girl.

Ariadne's voice, her walk, her hat, even her footprints on the sandy bank where she used to angle for gudgeon, filled me with delight and a passionate hunger for life. I judged of her spiritual being from her lovely face and lovely figure, and every word, every smile of Ariadne's bewitched me, conquered me and forced me to believe in the loftiness of her soul. She was friendly, ready to talk, gay and simple in her manners. She had a poetic belief in God, made poetic reflections about death, and there was such a wealth of varying shades in her spiritual organisation that even her faults seemed in her to carry with them peculiar, charming qualities. Suppose she wanted a new horse and had no money -- what did that matter? Something might be sold or pawned, or if the steward swore that nothing could possibly be sold or pawned, the iron roofs might be torn off the lodges and taken to the factory, or at the very busiest time the farm-horses might be driven to the market and sold there for next to nothing. These unbridled desires reduced the whole household to despair at times, but she expressed them with such refinement that everything was forgiven her; all things were permitted her as to a goddess or to Cæsar's wife. My love was pathetic and was soon noticed by everyone -- my father, the neighbours, and the peasants -- and they all sympathised with me. When I stood the workmen vodka, they would bow and say: "May the Kotlovitch young lady be your bride, please God!"

And Ariadne herself knew that I loved her. She would often ride over on horseback or drive in the char-à-banc to see us, and would spend whole days with me and my father. She made great friends with the old man, and he even taught her to bicycle, which was his favourite amusement.

I remember helping her to get on the bicycle one evening, and she looked so lovely that I felt as though I were burning my hands when I touched her. I shuddered with rapture, and when the two of them, my old father and she, both looking so handsome and elegant, bicycled side by side along the main road, a black horse ridden by the steward dashed aside on meeting them, and it seemed to me that it dashed aside because it too was overcome by her beauty. My love, my worship, touched Ariadne and softened her; she had a passionate longing to be captivated like me and to respond with the same love. It was so poetical!

But she was incapable of really loving as I did, for she was cold and already somewhat corrupted. There was a demon in her, whispering to her day and night that she was enchanting, adorable; and, having no definite idea for what object she was created, or for what purpose life had been given her, she never pictured herself in the future except as very wealthy and distinguished, she had visions of balls, races, liveries, of sumptuous drawing-rooms, of a salon of her own, and of a perfect swarm of counts, princes, ambassadors, celebrated painters and artists, all of them adoring her and in ecstasies over her beauty and her dresses. . . .

This thirst for personal success, and this continual concentration of the mind in one direction, makes people cold, and Ariadne was cold -- to me, to nature, and to music. Meanwhile time was passing, and still there were no ambassadors on the scene. Ariadne went on living with her brother, the spiritualist: things went from bad to worse, so that she had nothing to buy hats and dresses with, and had to resort to all sorts of tricks and dodges to conceal her poverty.

As luck would have it, a certain Prince Maktuev, a wealthy man but an utterly insignificant person, had paid his addresses to her when she was living at her aunt's in Moscow. She had refused him, point-blank. But now she was fretted by the worm of repentance that she had refused him; just as a peasant pouts with repulsion at a mug of kvass with cockroaches in it but yet drinks it, so she frowned disdainfully at the recollection of the prince, and yet she would say to me: "Say what you like, there is something inexplicable, fascinating, in a title. . . ."

She dreamed of a title, of a brilliant position, and at the same time she did not want to let me go. However one may dream of ambassadors one's heart is not a stone, and one has wistful feelings for one's youth. Ariadne tried to fall in love, made a show of being in love, and even swore that she loved me. But I am a highly strung and sensitive man; when I am loved I feel it even at a distance, without vows and assurances; at once I felt as it were a coldness in the air, and when she talked to me of love, it seemed to me as though I were listening to the singing of a metal nightingale. Ariadne was herself aware that she was lacking in something. She was vexed and more than once I saw her cry. Another time -- can you imagine it? -- all of a sudden she embraced me and kissed me. It happened in the evening on the river-bank, and I saw by her eyes that she did not love me, but was embracing me from curiosity, to test herself and to see what came of it. And I felt dreadful. I took her hands and said to her in despair: "These caresses without love cause me suffering!"

"What a queer fellow you are!" she said with annoyance, and walked away.

Another year or two might have passed, and in all probability I should have married her, and so my story would have ended, but fate was pleased to arrange our romance differently. It happened that a new personage appeared on our horizon. Ariadne's brother had a visit from an old university friend called Mihail Ivanitch Lubkov, a charming man of whom coachmen and footmen used to say: "An entertaining gentleman." He was a man of medium height, lean and bald, with a face like a good-natured bourgeois, not interesting, but pale and presentable, with a stiff, well-kept moustache, with a neck like gooseskin, and a big Adam's apple. He used to wear pince-nez on a wide black ribbon, lisped, and could not pronounce either *r* or *l*. He was always in good spirits, everything amused him.

He had made an exceedingly foolish marriage at twenty, and had acquired two houses in Moscow as part of his wife's dowry. He began doing them up and building a bath-house, and was completely ruined. Now his wife and four children lodged in Oriental Buildings in great poverty, and he had to support them -- and this amused him. He was thirty-six and his wife was by now forty-two, and that, too, amused him. His mother, a conceited, sulky personage, with aristocratic pretensions, despised his wife and lived apart with a perfect menagerie of cats and dogs, and he had to allow her seventy-five roubles a month also; he was, too, a man of taste, liked lunching at the Slavyansky Bazaar and dining at the Hermitage; he needed a great deal of money, but his uncle only allowed him two thousand roubles a year, which was not enough, and for days together he would run about Moscow with his tongue out, as the saying is, looking for someone to borrow from -- and this, too, amused him. He had come to Kotlovitch to find in the lap of nature, as he said, a rest from family life. At dinner, at supper, and on our walks, he talked about his wife, about his mother, about his creditors, about the bailiffs, and laughed at them; he laughed at himself and assured us that, thanks to his talent for borrowing, he had made a great number of agreeable acquaintances. He laughed without ceasing and we laughed too. Moreover, in his company we spent our time differently. I was more inclined to quiet, so to say idyllic pleasures; I liked fishing, evening walks, gathering mushrooms; Lubkov preferred picnics, fireworks, hunting. He used to get up picnics three times a week, and Ariadne, with an earnest and inspired face, used to write a list of oysters, champagne, sweets, and used to send me into Moscow to get them, without inquiring, of course, whether I had money. And at the picnics there were toasts and laughter, and again mirthful descriptions of how old his wife was, what fat lap-dogs his mother had, and what charming people his creditors were.

Lubkov was fond of nature, but he regarded it as something long familiar and at the same time, in reality, infinitely beneath himself and created for his pleasure. He would sometimes stand still before some magnificent landscape and say: "It would be nice to have tea here."

One day, seeing Ariadne walking in the distance with a parasol, he nodded towards her and said:

"She's thin, and that's what I like; I don't like fat women."

This made me wince. I asked him not to speak like that about women before me. He looked at me in surprise and said:

"What is there amiss in my liking thin women and not caring for fat ones?"

I made no answer. Afterwards, being in very good spirits and a trifle elevated, he said:

"I've noticed Ariadne Grigoryevna likes you. I can't understand why you don't go in and win."

His words made me feel uncomfortable, and with some embarrassment I told him how I looked at love and women.

"I don't know," he sighed; "to my thinking, a woman's a woman and a man's a man. Ariadne Grigoryevna may be poetical and exalted, as you say, but it doesn't follow that she must be superior to the laws of nature. You see for yourself that she has reached the age when she must have a husband or a lover. I respect women as much as you do, but I don't think certain relations exclude poetry. Poetry's one thing and love is another. It's just the same as it is in farming. The beauty of nature is one thing and the income from your forests or fields is quite another."

When Ariadne and I were fishing, Lubkov would lie on the sand close by and make fun of me, or lecture me on the conduct of life.

"I wonder, my dear sir, how you can live without a love affair," he would say. "You are young, handsome, interesting -- in fact, you're a man not to be sniffed at, yet you live like a monk. Och! I can't stand these fellows who are old at twenty-eight! I'm nearly ten years older than you are, and yet which of us is the younger? Ariadne Grigoryevna, which?"

"You, of course," Ariadne answered him.

And when he was bored with our silence and the attention with which we stared at our floats he went home, and she said, looking at me angrily:

"You're really not a man, but a mush, God forgive me! A man ought to be able to be carried away by his feelings, he ought to be able to be mad, to make mistakes, to suffer! A woman will forgive you audacity and insolence, but she will never forgive your reasonableness!"

She was angry in earnest, and went on:

"To succeed, a man must be resolute and bold. Lubkov is not so handsome as you are, but he is more interesting. He will always succeed with women because he's not like you; he's a man. . . ."

And there was actually a note of exasperation in her voice.

One day at supper she began saying, not addressing me, that if she were a man she would not stagnate in the country, but would travel, would spend the winter somewhere aboard -- in Italy, for instance. Oh, Italy! At this point my father unconsciously poured oil on the flames; he began telling us at length about Italy, how splendid it was there, the exquisite scenery, the museums. Ariadne suddenly conceived a burning desire to go to Italy. She positively brought her fist down on the table and her eyes flashed as she said: "I must go!"

After that came conversations every day about Italy: how splendid it would be in Italy -- ah, Italy! -- oh, Italy! And when Ariadne looked at me over her shoulder, from her cold and obstinate expression I saw that in her dreams she had already conquered Italy with all its salons, celebrated foreigners and tourists, and there was no holding her back now. I advised her to wait a little, to put off her tour for a year or two, but she frowned disdainfully and said:

"You're as prudent as an old woman!"

Lubkov was in favour of the tour. He said it could be done very cheaply, and he, too, would go to Italy and have a rest there from family life.

I behaved, I confess, as naïvely as a schoolboy.

Not from jealousy, but from a foreboding of something terrible and extraordinary, I tried as far as possible not to leave them alone together, and they made fun of me. For instance, when I went in they would pretend they had just been kissing one another, and so on. But lo and behold, one fine morning, her plump, white-skinned brother, the spiritualist, made his appearance and expressed his desire to speak to me alone.

He was a man without will; in spite of his education and his delicacy he could never resist reading another person's letter, if it lay before him on the table. And now he admitted that he had by chance read a letter of Lubkov's to Ariadne.

"From that letter I learned that she is very shortly going abroad. My dear fellow, I am very much upset! Explain it to me for goodness' sake. I can make nothing of it!"

As he said this he breathed hard, breathing straight in my face and smelling of boiled beef.

"Excuse me for revealing the secret of this letter to you, but you are Ariadne's friend, she respects you. Perhaps you know something of it. She wants to go away, but with whom? Mr. Lubkov is proposing to go with her. Excuse me, but this is very strange of Mr. Lubkov; he is a married man, he has children, and yet he is making a declaration of love; he is writing to Ariadne 'darling.' Excuse me, but it is so strange!"

I turned cold all over; my hands and feet went numb and I felt an ache in my chest, as if a three-cornered stone had been driven into it. Kotlovitch sank helplessly into an easy-chair, and his hands fell limply at his sides.

"What can I do?" I inquired.

"Persuade her. . . . Impress her mind. . . . Just consider, what is Lubkov to her? Is he a match for her? Oh, good God! How awful it is, how awful it is!" he went on, clutching his head. "She has had such splendid offers -- Prince Maktuev and . . . and others. The prince adores her, and only last Wednesday week his late grandfather, Ilarion, declared positively that Ariadne would be his wife -- positively! His grandfather Ilarion is dead, but he is a wonderfully intelligent person; we call up his spirit every day."

After this conversation I lay awake all night and thought of shooting myself. In the morning I wrote five letters and tore them all up. Then I sobbed in the barn. Then I took a sum of money from my father and set off for the Caucasus without saying good-bye.

Of course, a woman's a woman and a man's a man, but can all that be as simple in our day as it was before the Flood, and can it be that I, a cultivated man endowed with a complex spiritual organisation, ought to explain the intense attraction I feel towards a woman simply by the fact that her bodily formation is different from mine? Oh, how awful that would be! I want to believe that in his struggle with nature the genius of man has struggled with physical love too, as with an enemy, and that, if he has not conquered it, he has at least succeeded in tangling it in a net-work of illusions of brotherhood and love; and for me, at any rate, it is no longer a simple instinct of my animal nature as with a dog or a toad, but is real love, and every embrace is spiritualised by a pure impulse of the heart and respect for the woman. In reality, a disgust for the animal instinct has been trained for ages in hundreds of generations; it is inherited by me in my blood and forms part of my nature, and if I poetize love, is not that as natural and inevitable in our day as my ears' not being able to move and my not being covered with fur? I fancy that's how the majority of civilised people look at it, so that the absence of the moral, poetical element in love is treated in these days as a phenomenon, as a sign of atavism; they say it is a symptom of degeneracy, of many forms of insanity. It is true that, in poetizing love, we assume in those we love qualities that are lacking in them, and that is a source of continual mistakes and continual miseries for us. But to my thinking it is better, even so; that is, it is better to suffer than to find complacency on the basis of woman being woman and man being man.

In Tiflis I received a letter from my father. He wrote that Ariadne Grigoryevna had on such a day gone abroad, intending to spend the whole winter away. A month later I returned home. It was by now autumn. Every week Ariadne sent my father extremely interesting letters on scented paper, written in an excellent literary style. It is my opinion that every woman can be a writer. Ariadne described in great detail how it had not been easy for her to make it up with her aunt and induce the latter to give her a thousand roubles for the journey, and what a long time she had spent in Moscow trying to find an old lady, a distant relation, in order to persuade her to go with her. Such a profusion of detail suggested fiction, and I realised, of course, that she had no chaperon with her.

Soon afterwards I, too, had a letter from her, also scented and literary. She wrote that she had missed me, missed my beautiful, intelligent, loving eyes. She reproached me affectionately for wasting my youth, for stagnating in the country when I might, like her, be living in paradise under the palms, breathing the fragrance of the orange-trees. And she signed herself "Your forsaken Ariadne." Two days later came another letter in the same style, signed "Your forgotten Ariadne." My mind was confused. I loved her passionately, I dreamed of her every night, and then this "your forsaken," "your forgotten" -- what did it mean? What was it for? And then the dreariness of the country, the long evenings, the disquieting thoughts of Lubkov. . . . The uncertainty tortured me, and poisoned my days and nights; it became unendurable. I could not bear it and went abroad.

Ariadne summoned me to Abbazzia. I arrived there on a bright warm day after rain; the rain-drops were still hanging on the trees and glistening on the huge, barrack-like dépendance where Ariadne and Lubkov were living.

They were not at home. I went into the park; wandered about the avenues, then sat down. An Austrian General, with his hands behind him, walked past me, with red stripes on his trousers such as our generals wear. A baby was wheeled by in a perambulator and the wheels squeaked on the damp sand. A decrepit old man with jaundice passed, then a crowd of Englishwomen, a Catholic priest, then the Austrian General again.

A military band, only just arrived from Fiume, with glittering brass instruments, sauntered by to the bandstand -- they began playing.

Have you ever been at Abbazzia? It's a filthy little Slav town with only one street, which stinks, and in which one can't walk after rain without goloshes. I had read so much and always with such intense feeling about this earthly paradise that when afterwards, holding up my trousers, I cautiously crossed the narrow street, and in my ennui bought some hard pears from an old peasant woman who, recognising me as a Russian, said: "Tcheeteery" for "tchetyry" (four) -- "davadtsat" for "dvadtsat" (twenty), and when I wondered in perplexity where to go and what to do here, and when I inevitably met Russians as disappointed as I was, I began to feel vexed and ashamed. There is a calm bay there full of steamers and boats with coloured sails. From there I could see Fiume and the distant islands covered with lilac mist, and it would have been picturesque if the view over the bay had not been hemmed in by the hotels and their dépendances -- buildings in an absurd, trivial style of architecture, with which the whole of that green shore has been covered by greedy money grubbers, so that for the most part you see nothing in this little paradise but windows, terraces, and little squares with tables and waiters black coats. There is a park such as you find now in every watering-place abroad. And the dark, motionless, silent foliage of the palms, and the bright yellow sand in the avenue, and the bright green seats, and the glitter of the braying military horns -- all this sickened me in ten minutes! And yet one is obliged for some reason to spend ten days, ten weeks, there!

Having been dragged reluctantly from one of these watering-places to another, I have been more and more struck by the inconvenient and niggardly life led by the wealthy and well-fed, the dulness and feebleness of their imagination, the lack of boldness in their tastes and desires. And how much happier are those tourists, old and young, who, not having the money to stay in hotels, live where they can, admire the view of the sea from the tops of the mountains, lying on the green grass, walk instead of riding, see the forests and villages at close quarters, observe the customs of the country, listen to its songs, fall in love with its women. . . .

While I was sitting in the park, it began to get dark, and in the twilight my Ariadne appeared, elegant and dressed like a princess; after her walked Lubkov, wearing a new loose-fitting suit, bought probably in Vienna.

"Why are you cross with me?" he was saying. "What have I done to you?"

Seeing me, she uttered a cry of joy, and probably, if we had not been in the park, would have thrown herself on my neck. She pressed my hands warmly and laughed; and I laughed too and almost cried with emotion. Questions followed, of the village, of my father, whether I had seen her brother, and so on. She insisted on my looking her straight in the face, and asked if I remembered the gudgeon, our little quarrels, the picnics. . . .

"How nice it all was really!" she sighed. "But we're not having a slow time here either. We have a great many acquaintances, my dear, my best of friends! To-morrow I will introduce you to a Russian family here, but please buy yourself another hat." She scrutinised me and frowned. "Abbazzia is not the country," she said; "here one must be *comme il faut.*"

Then we went to the restaurant. Ariadne was laughing and mischievous all the time; she kept calling me "dear," "good," "clever," and seemed as though she could not believe her eyes that I was with her. We sat on till eleven o'clock, and parted very well satisfied both with the supper and with each other.

Next day Ariadne presented me to the Russian family as: "The son of a distinguished professor whose estate is next to ours."

She talked to this family about nothing but estates and crops, and kept appealing to me. She wanted to appear to be a very wealthy landowner, and did, in fact, succeed in doing so. Her manner was superb like that of a real aristocrat, which indeed she was by birth.

"But what a person my aunt is!" she said suddenly, looking at me with a smile. "We had a slight tiff, and she has bolted off to Meran. What do you say to that?"

Afterwards when we were walking in the park I asked her:

"What aunt were you talking of just now? What aunt is that?"

"That was a saving lie," laughed Ariadne. "They must not know I'm without a chaperon."

After a moment's silence she came closer to me and said:

"My dear, my dear, do be friends with Lubkov. He is so unhappy! His wife and mother are simply awful."

She used the formal mode of address in speaking to Lubkov, and when she was going up to bed she said good-night to him exactly as she did to me, and their rooms were on different floors. All this made me hope that it was all nonsense, and that there was no sort of love affair between them, and I felt at ease when I met him. And when one day he asked me for the loan of three hundred roubles, I gave it to him with the greatest pleasure.

Every day we spent in enjoying ourselves and in nothing but enjoying ourselves; we strolled in the park, we ate, we drank. Every day there were conversations with the Russian family. By degrees I got used to the fact that if I went into the park I should be sure to meet the old man with jaundice, the Catholic priest, and the Austrian General, who always carried a pack of little cards, and wherever it was possible sat down and played patience, nervously twitching his shoulders. And the band played the same thing over and over again.

At home in the country I used to feel ashamed to meet the peasants when I was fishing or on a picnic party on a working day; here too I was ashamed at the sight of the footmen, the coachmen, and the workmen who met us. It always seemed to me they were looking at me and thinking: "Why are you doing nothing?" And I was conscious of this feeling of shame every day from morning to night. It was a strange, unpleasant, monotonous time; it was only varied by Lubkov's borrowing from me now a hundred, now fifty guldens, and being suddenly revived by the money as a morphia-maniac is by morphia, beginning to laugh loudly at his wife, at himself, at his creditors.

At last it began to be rainy and cold. We went to Italy, and I telegraphed to my father begging him for mercy's sake to send me eight hundred roubles to Rome. We stayed in Venice, in Bologna, in Florence, and in every town invariably put up at an expensive hotel, where we were charged separately for lights, and for service, and for heating, and for bread at lunch, and for the right of having dinner by ourselves. We ate enormously. In the morning they gave us *café complet;* at one o'clock lunch: meat, fish, some sort of omelette, cheese, fruits, and wine. At six o'clock dinner of eight courses with long intervals, during which we drank beer and wine. At nine o'clock tea. At midnight Ariadne would declare she was hungry, and ask for ham and boiled eggs. We would eat to keep her company.

In the intervals between meals we used to rush about the museums and exhibitions in continual anxiety for fear we should be late for dinner or lunch. I was bored at the sight of the pictures; I longed to be at home to rest; I was exhausted, looked about for a chair and hypocritically repeated after other people: "How exquisite, what atmosphere!" Like overfed boa constrictors, we noticed only the most glaring objects. The shop windows hypnotised us; we went into ecstasies over imitation brooches and bought a mass of useless trumpery.

The same thing happened in Rome, where it rained and there was a cold wind. After a heavy lunch we went to look at St. Peter's, and thanks to our replete condition and perhaps the bad weather, it made no sort of impression on us, and detecting in each other an indifference to art, we almost quarrelled.

The money came from my father. I went to get it, I remember, in the morning. Lubkov went with me.

"The present cannot be full and happy when one has a past," said he. "I have heavy burdens left on me by the past. However, if only I get the money, it's no great matter, but if not, I'm in a fix. Would you believe it, I have only eight francs left, yet I must send my wife a hundred and my mother another. And we must live here too. Ariadne's like a child; she won't enter into the position, and flings away money like a duchess. Why did she buy a watch yesterday? And, tell me, what object is there in our going on playing at being good children? Why, our hiding our relations from the servants and our friends costs us from ten to fifteen francs a day, as I have to have a separate room. What's the object of it?"

I felt as though a sharp stone had been turned round in my chest. There was no uncertainty now; it was all clear to me. I turned cold all over, and at once made a resolution to give up seeing them, to run away from them, to go home at once. . . .

"To get on terms with a woman is easy enough," Lubkov went on. "You have only to undress her; but afterwards what a bore it is, what a silly business!"

When I counted over the money I received he said:

"If you don't lend me a thousand francs, I am faced with complete ruin. Your money is the only resource left to me."

I gave him the money, and he at once revived and began laughing about his uncle, a queer fish, who could never keep his address secret from his wife. When I reached the hotel I packed and paid my bill. I had still to say good-bye to Ariadne.

I knocked at the door.

"Entrez!"

In her room was the usual morning disorder: tea-things on the table, an unfinished roll, an eggshell; a strong overpowering reek of scent. The bed had not been made, and it was evident that two had slept in it.

Ariadne herself had only just got out of bed and was now with her hair down in a flannel dressing-jacket.

I said good-morning to her, and then sat in silence for a minute while she tried to put her hair tidy, and then I asked her, trembling all over:

"Why . . . why . . . did you send for me here?"

Evidently she guessed what I was thinking; she took me by the hand and said:

"I want you to be here, you are so pure."

I felt ashamed of my emotion, of my trembling. And I was afraid I might begin sobbing, too! I went out without saying another word, and within an hour I was sitting in the train. All the journey, for some reason, I imagined Ariadne with child, and she seemed disgusting to me, and all the women I saw in the trains and at the stations looked to me, for some reason, as if they too were with child, and they too seemed disgusting and pitiable. I was in the position of a greedy, passionate miser who should suddenly discover that all his gold coins were false. The pure, gracious images which my imagination, warmed by love, had cherished for so long, my plans, my hopes, my memories, my ideas of love and of woman -- all now were jeering and putting out their tongues at me. "Ariadne," I kept asking with horror, "that young, intellectual, extraordinarily beautiful girl, the daughter of a senator, carrying on an intrigue with such an ordinary, uninteresting vulgarian? But why should she not love Lubkov?" I answered myself. "In what is he inferior to me? Oh, let her love anyone she likes, but why lie to me? But why is she bound to be open with me?" And so I went on over and over again till I was stupefied.

It was cold in the train; I was travelling first class, but even so there were three on a side, there were no double windows, the outer door opened straight into the compartment, and I felt as though I were in the stocks, cramped, abandoned, pitiful, and my legs were fearfully numb, and at the same time I kept recalling how fascinating she had been that morning in her dressing-jacket and with her hair down, and I was suddenly overcome by such acute jealousy that I leapt up in anguish, so that my neighbours stared at me in wonder and positive alarm.

At home I found deep snow and twenty degrees of frost. I'm fond of the winter; I'm fond of it because at that time, even in the hardest frosts, it's particularly snug at home. It's pleasant to put on one's fur jacket and felt overboots on a clear frosty day, to do something in the garden or in the yard, or to read in a well warmed room, to sit in my father's study before the open fire, to wash in my country bath-house. . . . Only if there is no mother in the house, no sister and no children, it is somehow dreary on winter evenings, and they seem extraordinarily long and quiet. And the warmer and snugger it is, the more acutely is this lack felt. In the winter when I came back from abroad, the evenings were endlessly long, I was intensely depressed, so depressed that I could not even read; in the daytime I was coming and going, clearing away the snow in the garden or feeding the chickens and the calves, but in the evening it was all up with me.

I had never cared for visitors before, but now I was glad of them, for I knew there was sure to be talk of Ariadne. Kotlovitch, the spiritualist, used often to come to talk about his sister, and sometimes he brought with him his friend Prince Maktuev, who was as much in love with Ariadne as I was. To sit in Ariadne's room, to finger the keys of her piano, to look at her music was a necessity for the prince -- he could not live without it; and the spirit of his grandfather Ilarion was still predicting that sooner or later she would be his wife. The prince usually stayed a long time with us, from lunch to midnight, saying nothing all the time; in silence he would drink two or three bottles of beer, and from time to time, to show that he too was taking part in the conversation, he would laugh an abrupt, melancholy, foolish laugh. Before going home he would always take me aside and ask me in an undertone: "When did you see Ariadne Grigoryevna last? Was she quite well? I suppose she's not tired of being out there?"

Spring came on. There was the harrowing to do and then the sowing of spring corn and clover. I was sad, but there was the feeling of spring. One longed to accept the inevitable. Working in the fields and listening to the larks, I asked myself: "Couldn't I have done with this question of personal happiness once and for all? Couldn't I lay aside my fancy and marry a simple peasant girl?"

Suddenly when we were at our very busiest, I got a letter with the Italian stamp, and the clover and the beehives and the calves and the peasant girl all floated away like smoke. This time Ariadne wrote that she was profoundly, infinitely unhappy. She reproached me for not holding out a helping hand to her, for looking down upon her from the heights of my virtue and deserting her at the moment of danger. All this was written in a large, nervous handwriting with blots and smudges, and it was evident that she wrote in haste and distress. In conclusion she besought me to come and save her. Again my anchor was hauled up and I was carried away. Ariadne was in Rome. I arrived late in the evening, and when she saw me, she sobbed and threw herself on my neck. She had not changed at all that winter, and was just as young and charming. We had supper together and afterwards drove about Rome until dawn, and all the time she kept telling me about her doings. I asked where Lubkov was.

"Don't remind me of that creature!" she cried. "He is loathsome and disgusting to me!"

"But I thought you loved him," I said.

"Never," she said. "At first he struck me as original and aroused my pity, that was all. He is insolent and takes a woman by storm. And that's attractive. But we won't talk about him. That is a melancholy page in my life. He has gone to Russia to get money. Serve him right! I told him not to dare to come back."

She was living then, not at an hotel, but in a private lodging of two rooms which she had decorated in her own taste, frigidly and luxuriously.

After Lubkov had gone away she had borrowed from her acquaintances about five thousand francs, and my arrival certainly was the one salvation for her.

I had reckoned on taking her back to the country, but I did not succeed in that. She was homesick for her native place, but her recollections of the poverty she had been through there, of privations, of the rusty roof on her brother's house, roused a shudder of disgust, and when I suggested going home to her, she squeezed my hands convulsively and said:

"No, no, I shall die of boredom there!"

Then my love entered upon its final phase.

"Be the darling that you used to be; love me a little," said Ariadne, bending over to me. "You're sulky and prudent, you're afraid to yield to impulse, and keep thinking of consequences, and that's dull. Come, I beg you, I beseech you, be nice to me! . . . My pure one, my holy one, my dear one, I love you so!"

I became her lover. For a month anyway I was like a madman, conscious of nothing but rapture. To hold in one's arms a young and lovely body, with bliss to feel her warmth every time one waked up from sleep, and to remember that she was there -- she, my Ariadne! -- oh, it was not easy to get used to that! But yet I did get used to it, and by degrees became capable of reflecting on my new position. First of all, I realised, as before, that Ariadne did not love me. But she wanted to be really in love, she was afraid of solitude, and, above all, I was healthy, young, vigorous; she was sensual, like all cold people, as a rule -- and we both made a show of being united by a passionate, mutual love. Afterwards I realised something else, too.

We stayed in Rome, in Naples, in Florence; we went to Paris, but there we thought it cold and went back to Italy. We introduced ourselves everywhere as husband and wife, wealthy landowners. People readily made our acquaintance and Ariadne had great social success everywhere. As she took lessons in painting, she was called an artist, and only imagine, that quite suited her, though she had not the slightest trace of talent.

She would sleep every day till two or three o'clock; she had her coffee and lunch in bed. At dinner she would eat soup, lobster, fish, meat, asparagus, game, and after she had gone to bed I used to bring up something, for instance roast beef, and she would eat it with a melancholy, careworn expression, and if she waked in the night she would eat apples and oranges.

The chief, so to say fundamental, characteristic of the woman was an amazing duplicity. She was continually deceitful every minute, apparently apart from any necessity, as it were by instinct, by an impulse such as makes the sparrow chirrup and the cockroach waggle its antennæ. She was deceitful with me, with the footman, with the porter, with the tradesmen in the shops, with her acquaintances; not one conversation, not one meeting, took place without affectation and pretence. A man had only to come into our room -- whoever it might be, a waiter, or a baron -- for her eyes, her expression, her voice to change, even the contour of her figure was transformed. At the very first glance at her then, you would have said there were no more wealthy and fashionable people in Italy than we. She never met an artist or a musician without telling him all sorts of lies about his remarkable talent.

"You have such a talent!" she would say, in honeyed cadences, "I'm really afraid of you. I think you must see right through people."

And all this simply in order to please, to be successful, to be fascinating! She waked up every morning with the one thought of "pleasing"! It was the aim and object of her life. If I had told her that in such a house, in such a street, there lived a man who was not attracted by her, it would have caused her real suffering. She wanted every day to enchant, to captivate, to drive men crazy. The fact that I was in her power and reduced to a complete nonentity before her charms gave her the same sort of satisfaction that visitors used to feel in tournaments. My subjection was not enough, and at nights, stretched out like a tigress, uncovered -- she was always too hot -- she would read the letters sent her by Lubkov; he besought her to return to Russia, vowing if she did not he would rob or murder someone to get the money to come to her. She hated him, but his passionate, slavish letters excited her. She had an extraordinary opinion of her own charms; she imagined that if somewhere, in some great assembly, men could have seen how beautifully she was made and the colour of her skin, she would have vanquished all Italy, the whole world. Her talk of her figure, of her skin, offended me, and observing this, she would, when she was angry, to vex me, say all sorts of vulgar things, taunting me. One day when we were at the summer villa of a lady of our acquaintance, and she lost her temper, she even went so far as to say: "If you don't leave off boring me with your sermons, I'll undress this minute and lie naked here on these flowers."

Often looking at her asleep, or eating, or trying to assume a naïve expression, I wondered why that extraordinary beauty, grace, and intelligence had been given her by God. Could it simply be for lolling in bed, eating and lying, lying endlessly? And was she intelligent really? She was afraid of three candles in a row, of the number thirteen, was terrified of spells and bad dreams. She argued about free love and freedom in general like a bigoted old woman, declared that Boleslav Markevitch was a better writer than Turgenev. But she was diabolically cunning and sharp, and knew how to seem a highly educated, advanced person in company.

Even at a good-humoured moment, she could always insult a servant or kill an insect without a pang; she liked bull-fights, liked to read about murders, and was angry when prisoners were acquitted.

For the life Ariadne and I were leading, we had to have a great deal of money. My poor father sent me his pension, all the little sums he received, borrowed for me wherever he could, and when one day he answered me: "Non habeo," I sent him a desperate telegram in which I besought him to mortgage the estate. A little later I begged him to get money somehow on a second mortgage. He did this too without a murmur and sent me every farthing. Ariadne despised the practical side of life; all this was no concern of hers, and when flinging away thousands of francs to satisfy her mad desires I groaned like an old tree, she would be singing "Addio bella Napoli" with a light heart.

Little by little I grew cold to her and began to be ashamed of our tie. I am not fond of pregnancy and confinements, but now I sometimes dreamed of a child who would have been at least a formal justification of our life. That I might not be completely disgusted with myself, I began reading and visiting museums and galleries, gave up drinking and took to eating very little. If one keeps oneself well in hand from morning to night, one's heart seems lighter. I began to bore Ariadne too. The people with whom she won her triumphs were, by the way, all of the middling sort; as before, there were no ambassadors, there was no salon, the money did not run to it, and this mortified her and made her sob, and she announced to me at last that perhaps she would not be against our returning to Russia.

And here we are on our way. For the last few months she has been zealously corresponding with her brother; she evidently has some secret projects, but what they are -- God knows! I am sick of trying to fathom her underhand schemes! But we're going, not to the country, but to Yalta and afterwards to the Caucasus. She can only exist now at watering-places, and if you knew how I hate all these watering-places, how suffocated and ashamed I am in them. If I could be in the country now! If I could only be working now, earning my bread by the sweat of my brow, atoning for my follies. I am conscious of a superabundance of energy and I believe that if I were to put that energy to work I could redeem my estate in five years. But now, as you see, there is a complication. Here we're not abroad, but in mother Russia; we shall have to think of lawful wedlock. Of course, all attraction is over; there is no trace left of my old love, but, however that may be, I am bound in honour to marry her.

Shamohin, excited by his story, went below with me and we continued talking about women. It was late. It appeared that he and I were in the same cabin.

"So far it is only in the village that woman has not fallen behind man," said Shamohin. "There she thinks and feels just as man does, and struggles with nature in the name of culture as zealously as he. In the towns the woman of the bourgeois or intellectual class has long since fallen behind, and is returning to her primitive condition. She is half a human beast already, and, thanks to her, a great deal of what had been won by human genius has been lost again; the woman gradually disappears and in her place is the primitive female. This dropping-back on the part of the educated woman is a real danger to culture; in her retrogressive movement she tries to drag man after her and prevents him from moving forward. That is incontestable."

I asked: "Why generalise? Why judge of all women from Ariadne alone? The very struggle of women for education and sexual equality, which I look upon as a struggle for justice, precludes any hypothesis of a retrograde movement."

But Shamohin scarcely listened to me and he smiled distrustfully. He was a passionate, convinced misogynist, and it was impossible to alter his convictions.

"Oh, nonsense!" he interrupted. "When once a woman sees in me, not a man, not an equal, but a male, and her one anxiety all her life is to attract me -- that is, to take possession of me -- how can one talk of their rights? Oh, don't you believe them; they are very, very cunning! We men make a great stir about their emancipation, but they don't care about their emancipation at all, they only pretend to care about it; they are horribly cunning things, horribly cunning!"

I began to feel sleepy and weary of discussion. I turned over with my face to the wall.

"Yes," I heard as I fell asleep -- "yes, and it's our education that's at fault, sir. In our towns, the whole education and bringing up of women in its essence tends to develop her into the human beast -- that is, to make her attractive to the male and able to vanquish him. Yes, indeed" -- Shamohiri sighed -- "little girls ought to be taught and brought up with boys, so that they might be always together. A woman ought to be trained so that she may be able, like a man, to recognise when she's wrong, or she always thinks she's in the right. Instil into a little girl from her cradle that a man is not first of all a cavalier or a possible lover, but her neighbour, her equal in everything. Train her to think logically, to generalise, and do not assure her that her brain weighs less than a man's and that therefore she can be indifferent to the sciences, to the arts, to the tasks of culture in general. The apprentice to the shoemaker or the house painter has a brain of smaller size than the grown-up man too, yet he works, suffers, takes his part in the general struggle for existence. We must give up our attitude to the physiological aspect, too -- to pregnancy and childbirth, seeing that in the first place women don't have babies every month; secondly, not all women have babies; and, thirdly, a normal countrywoman works in the fields up to the day of her confinement and it does her no harm. Then there ought to be absolute equality in everyday life. If a man gives a lady his chair or picks up the handkerchief she has dropped, let her repay him in the same way. I have no objection if a girl of good family helps me to put on my coat or hands me a glass of water --"

I heard no more, for I fell asleep.

Next morning when we were approaching Sevastopol, it was damp, unpleasant weather; the ship rocked. Shamohin sat on deck with me, brooding and silent. When the bell rang for tea, men with their coat-collars turned up and ladies with pale, sleepy faces began going below; a young and very beautiful lady, the one who had been so angry with the Customs officers at Volotchisk, stopped before Shamohin and said with the expression of a naughty, fretful child:

"Jean, your birdie's been sea-sick."

Afterwards when I was at Yalta I saw the same beautiful lady dashing about on horseback with a couple of officers hardly able to keep up with her. And one morning I saw her in an overall and a Phrygian cap, sketching on the sea-front with a great crowd admiring her a little way off. I too was introduced to her. She pressed my hand with great warmth, and looking at me ecstatically, thanked me in honeyed cadences for the pleasure I had given her by my writings.

"Don't you believe her," Shamohin whispered to me, "she has never read a word of them."

When I was walking on the sea-front in the early evening Shamohin met me with his arms full of big parcels of fruits and dainties.

"Prince Maktuev is here!" he said joyfully. "He came yesterday with her brother, the spiritualist! Now I understand what she was writing to him about! Oh, Lord!" he went on, gazing up to heaven, and pressing his parcels to his bosom. "If she hits it off with the prince, it means freedom, then I can go back to the country with my father!"

And he ran on.

"I begin to believe in spirits," he called to me, looking back. "The spirit of grandfather Ilarion seems to have prophesied the truth! Oh, if only it is so!"

The day after this meeting I left Yalta and how Shamohin's story ended I don't know.

5593842R00327

Printed in Great Britain
by Amazon.co.uk, Ltd.,
Marston Gate.